The Best of JACK LONDON

CASTLE

ISBN 0-89009-818-2

Manufactured in the United States of America.

84 85 86 87 3 2 1 0 9 8 7 6 5 4 3 2 1

TABLE OF CONTENTS

INTRODUCTION

I would rather be ashes than dust!
I would rather
that my spark should burn out in a brilliant blaze
than it should be stifled by dryrot.
I would rather be a superb meteor,
every atom of me in magnificent glow,
than a sleepy and permanent plant.
The proper function of man is to live, not to exist.
I shall not waste my days in trying to prolong them.
I shall use my time.

Jack London 1876-1916

Many anthologies of Jack London have been produced but, in my opinion, this is by far the best. It is a magic journey through the far reaches of human endeavor and world-wide adventure with something new and exciting at every turn of the page. That you might have the ultimate experience in reading this most read of all American writers, the publisher has brought London's work to you in its most dramatic form: reproducing his novels and stories in facsimilie of the original turn-of-the-century magazines, just as they first appeared in print.

Four of the five novels in this collection, *The Call of the Wild, White Fang, The Sea-Wolf* and *Martin Eden* are considered by most critics to have earned ''classic'' status. *Before Adam* is universally acclaimed as a classic of its genre. The short stories in this volume have been carefully selected to give you an enticing sample of the two hundred that flowed from London's fertile and imaginative mind.

The Call of the Wild has been read and re-read by millions since its publication in 1903. Though it is one of the most popular books of all time in children's literature, it is certainly one of the finest philosophical studies of atavism ever written–a human allegory of Buck's life and death struggle to adapt to a new, frightening and extremely hostile environment.

Buck is taken from his pampered life on Judge Miller's estate, where he had basked in an environment full of love, through a series of experiences in the Klondike where exploitation, cruelty and hatred reverts him to a wild beast. Carl Sandburg caught the essence of the story when he wrote, ''*The Call of the Wild* is the greatest dog story ever written and is at the same time a study of one of the most curious and profound motives that plays hide and seek in the human soul.''

White Fang never achieved the acclaim it deserved since it has always been overshadowed by *The Call of the Wild*. Even Jack London was unable to surpass his own masterpiece and yet, according to him, it is superior in many ways to his first attempt to use a dog as the protagonist in a novel.

Jack wrote to his publishers that he had decided to compose a ''complete antithesis and companion book.'' He stated in his letter, ''I'm going to reverse the process. Instead of devolution or decivilization of a dog I'm going to give the evolution, the civilization of a dog–development of domesticity, faithfulness, love, morality, and all the amenities and virtues.''

White Fang leaves the wilderness of the frozen Northland and becomes civilized because his new environment is enclosed in love and care. It is a study of the controlling and modifying influence of love and tenderness as he learns the real spirit of true humanity.

Jack once said, ''But I am an evolutionist, therefore a broad optimist, hence my love for the human (in the slime though he may be) comes from my knowing him as he is and seeing the divine possibilities ahead of him. That's the whole motive of my *White Fang*. Every atom of life is plastic. The finest specimens now in existence were once all pulpy infants capable of being moulded this way or that. Let the presence be one way and we have atavism–the reversion to the wild; the other the domestication, civilization. I feel that I can never lay enough stress upon the marvelous power and influence of environment."

By using canine protagonists London could speak out boldly for the causes he espoused. In *The Call of the Wild* he revealed how Buck was taught to steal and rob without it bothering his conscience and to kill without pity for his victim. Had he written the same story about a working man in the same situation it would never have been published. After all, Buck was only a dog. However, Buck was, in reality, a poor working man who was forced into similar situations by a social system of exploitation and in which his children were raised in a hostile environment which could only lead to futility and despair.

The Sea-Wolf was an immediate success. To some the book was cruel, brutal and revolting. But most critics saw it as a rollicking sea-story that surpassed Melville and Dana with a rarity and genius that was like a breath of fresh air in American literature.

Irving Stone pointed out in *Sailor on Horseback*, "Jack had taken the scholar's revolution of the nineteenth century, dramatized it, made it thrilling and intelligible to the great mass of people who had never even heard of evolution, biology, or scientific materialism."

Many critics call *The Sea-Wolf* London's most powerful work. Ambrose Bierce stated, "The hewing out and setting up of such a figure (Wolf Larsen) is enough for a man to do in a lifetime." Carl Sandburg stated, "*The Sea-Wolf* bore down on me for all my brain-traffic would bear."

The underlying motive is an attempt to prove that Nietzsche's superman cannot exist in modern life; that anti-social persons in a complex society must cooperate or be defeated. An interest in the humanity of his crew and people in general would have been the answer to all of Wolf Larsen's troubles. Larsen is sensitive, intelligent, powerful and rebellious of society. He can quote Browning's poetry and passages from the Bible with ease but is unable to empathize with those who can't equal his own abilities. He is a rampant individualist and has everything except the ability to fit into the social customs for which he has utter contempt. He needs no one and uses others to gain his own ends. The result is catastrophe, senseless violence and self-destruction. Once again London is using his story as a vehicle for the denunciation of social injustices.

This underlying motive seldom varies in the writings of Jack London. Jack said of his motive in *The Sea-Wolf,* "The superman is anti-social in his tendencies and in these days of our complex society and sociology he cannot be successful in his hostile aloofness. The plea is for cooperation. The strength of the strong should be the strength of the group."

Actually Humphrey van Weyden is the true hero of *The Sea-Wolf* as he evolves from the effete snobbery of the middle upperclass into dynamic manhood as he learns the value of hard physical labor and proves his ability to cope with adversity and the hostile sea-environment into which he is thrust.

Martin Eden is essentially an attempt to succeed in the denunciation of individualism which he failed to do in *The Sea-Wolf.* Eden becomes a civilized and socialized Wolf Larsen. In a letter to Rev. Charles Brown, Jack said, "Martin Eden lived for himself, fought for himself, and if you please, died for himself. He fought for entrance into the bourgeois circles where he expected to find refinement, culture, high-living and high-thinking. He won his way into these circles and was appalled by the colossal, unlovely mediocrity of the bourgeoise. He fought for a woman whom he loved and had idealized. He found that love had tricked him and failed him, and that he had loved his idealization more than the woman herself. These were the things he had found life worth living in order to fight for. When they failed him, being a consistent individualist, being unaware of the collective human need, there remained nothing for which to live and fight. And so he died."

Martin Eden is one of the most powerful contributions to American literature. Had the book never been written there would have been no books by Irving Stone and dozens like him who found the courage to struggle for acceptance in the world of literature after reading *Martin Eden*. Nearly all of the first part of the book relates the actual experiences of Jack's own desperate struggle to become a writer. However, you must remember that the book is fiction. Since some of it is autobiographical, too many biographers have accepted it as an actual autobiography. No matter what your goal in life may be, you will find the courage to succeed in this classic of endeavor by Jack London.

Before Adam is a study of biological evolution. It is a personal tale of Big Tooth, a child of the Tree People, who had learned to live among the terrors of early man. When Big Tooth is deserted by his parents he is adopted by the Cave People. It is a world of fear and sudden death. It is only with cunning and sheer bravado that they are able to survive. Their human enemies are feared more than the wild animals. Big Tooth finds himself caught between the cannibalistic savagery of Red Eye and the mysterious People of the Smoke in the North.

The story is set before Adam, before fire, before the wearing of clothes, before the use of weapons and when man could only utter sounds because there was no language. The plot is ingenious, simple and dramatic. Jack used the Arboreal state, the Semi-Terrestial missing link stage, and the Upper Paleolithic stage as represented by the Fire People in this story of primordial man.

Prof. Loren Eiseley, formerly of the University of Pennsylvania, said of *Before Adam*, "What, I ask myself, is its remaining significance–this old book of my childhood which I fondle so affectionately and which long ago unconsciously set me on the path of my profession." Again Dr. Eiseley said, "Fifty-five years have passed since *Before Adam* was written. Within that time many men have tried their hand at picturing the lives of our remote ancestors. Most have confined themselves to those later folk whom London calls the Fire People. In all this long half-century, though our knowledge of human evolution has increased tremendously, it is my belief that no writer has since produced so moving and vivid a picture of man's primordial past as has Jack London."

In his article, "Jack London: a Writer for All Seasons" Donald Pizer writes, "Jack London is a true 'folk writer': the archetypal 'kosmos' envisioned by Walt Whitman–the poet-seer embraced as lovingly by the people, particularly the common folk, as he has embraced them. He has achieved a popularity so widespread and so long-standing that he is evidently a permanent legend in the American heritage. Other writers have become house hold words in the American common culture ... *e.g.*, Horatio Alger, Zane Grey, O. Henry ... but in combining sustained popular appeal with serious literary merit and heroic personal stature, London is comparable to only one other figure in our literature–Mark Twain–and even that great writer did not excite the American yearnings for romantic adventure as profoundly as London. Moreover, the range of thematic interests far exceeds Twain's. He produced more than fifty books on subjects as various as agronomy, architecture, astral projection, boating, ecology, gold-hunting, hoboing, loving, penal reform, prize-fighting, socialism and welfare."

Earle Labor writes, "Despite his immense and long-standing popular reputation, and despite his great esteem abroad, London has been until recently considered a minor force in American literature by his country's academic critics. A dramatic change has taken place since the mid-60's when three major works–*Letters From Jack London,* edited by King Hendricks and Irving Shepard; *Jack London and the Klondike,* by eminent scholar Franklin Walker; and *Jack London: A Bibliography,* compiled by Hensley Woodbridge and others appeared.

"More recently, the publication of such journals as the *Jack London Newsletter,* Jack London *Echoes* and Jack London *Update*, along with special issues of such respected scholarly journals as *Modern Fiction Studies, Western American Literature* and the *Pacific Historian* have provided an important forum for London scholars.

"Prestigious university presses such as Wisconsin, North Carolina, Stanford, Utah State and Washington have also begun to publish books on London. The critical pendulum is now clearly swinging in London's favor." Again Labor says, "How much has really been made of Jack's incredible versatility? Who can compare with him? I can't think of anyone. Aside from the question of his literary greatness, there can be little doubt about Jack London's extraordinary versatility as a writer. No other writer in American literature manifests such an astonishing range of tone and subject matter. No other writer has written so well on so many different topics. Truly he was a writer for all seasons.''

Numberless critics agree that Jack's own life is an even greater story than the ones he wrote. It is nearly impossible to fully understand his work without a thorough knowledge of the man himself and of the time in which he lived. Most London biographers have not made the attempt. The information is readily available, however, since most of the thousands of original works by him reside in the vaults of Huntington Library in Pasadena, California. Another valuable source of original material can be found at Utah State University in Logan, Utah and a wealth of secondary and primary research material is available at the Jack London Research Center located in the Jack London Bookstore in Glen Ellen, California.

On January 12, 1876 the San Francisco newspapers announced the birth of John Griffith Chaney at 615 Third Street in that city. His mother, Flora, and his father, William H. Chaney, had dissolved their marriage before his birth. When he was eight months old his mother married Jack London and the boy was known as Johnny London until he decided, fifteen years later, that he wanted to be called Jack. The family lived in San Francisco for about three years until Jack and his stepsister Eliza nearly died from diphtheria. On the advice of their doctor the Londons moved to Oakland where Jack's father operated a truck garden and later a small grocery store in West Oakland. The store venture failed and they moved to Alameda. On Johnny's seventh birthday they loaded their meager possessions in an old wagon and moved to a small farm near what is now Pacifica. After a fairly successful period here John bought a small ranch in Livermore Valley. Flora's ineptness and the unstable financial problems of the period ultimately resulted in bankruptcy. Once more the old wagon was piled high and Oakland was home again.

During the days in Livermore, Johnny discovered the world of books and, though he didn't know it at the time, his future career was born. Actually, the reading of Ouida's *Signa* was to Jack what *Martin Eden* was to Irving Stone. It was a challenge to excel regardless of the price one had to pay. Fame could be achieved even if faced with the obstacles of poverty or the worst of hardships. This book was the basis for his lifetime belief in the necessity and ability to adapt to any problems that life threw his way and the theme of overcoming environmental conditions became a strong motif in most of his later literary output.

London's formative years were spent in near poverty. His father barely eked out a living. From the age of ten Jack found himself the major breadwinner for the family–a little ''work-beast'' as he later recalled. He worked on paper routes from four in the morning before school and again in the evening. In any spare time he set pins in bowling alleys, swabbed decks on waterfront boats, mowed lawns, worked on ice wagons, beat carpets and did any other menial task that would buy a few groceries.

After graduation from Cole Grammar School he took a ten-cents-an-hour job stuffing pickles into jars at Hickmott's Cannery. He had heard many complaints about how the working class was exploited but now it became stark reality. The added value of putting the pickles in those little jars was divided between owner and employee but the men who did the job received very little of the profit, the owner receiving the lion's share. Young Jack London soon decided that society was badly put together and he never changed his opinion. The problem was where could a working man find even a slim hope of bettering his condition? Ten cents an hour was the wage. Take it or leave it.

The men who raided the oyster beds in the lower end of San Francisco Bay made more in a night than he made in a month. Hearing that French Frank wanted to sell his *Razzle Dazzle* for $300.00, Jack rushed to Alameda and borrowed the money from Aunt Jennie, the black lady who had taken him in as a baby to nurse. She did her best to disuade him by a vivid description of life in the penitentiary if he were to be arrested. Jack told her that life in San Quentin was far better than that of a work-beast who slaved for a pittance.

The waterfront was a continuous round of drinking and brawling, but to a young lad it was high adventure. Jack learned to out-drink, out-sail and out-fight the toughest of them all. He soon realized, however, that this kind of living could only lead to prison or death and when Charley LeGrant offered him a job with the California Fish Patrol he left the oyster pirates and put on a badge. Now he could still have as much fun and excitement on the waters of the Bay without the danger of being on the wrong side of the law. Since his job would be in Benicia to keep the Greek and Chinese fisherman honest, he would be spared the embarrassment of arresting his former cronies.

Discovering that the men of the Fish Patrol were worse roisterers than the oyster pirates, he resigned and, at the age of seventeen, signed on as an able-bodied seaman for a seven month sealing venture to the Bering Sea on the *Sophia Sutherland*. Not only did this trip give him material for future books but it changed him from a rowdy hoodlum into a man with a new purpose. It was a new Jack London who came through the Golden Gate on the *Sophie*, as he called her. He had no trouble finding work but it was the same old seven-days-a-week from dark to dark and the pay was still ten cents an hour.

Deciding to learn a trade, Jack left the jute mill and started a career in electricity with the Oakland, San Leandro and Haywards Railway. Once more he was exploited to the hilt, and when he discovered that he had been hired as a coal shoveler to replace *two* men and thus save the company fifty dollars a month he quit in disgust and went tramping across the United States and back across Canada. Everywhere he went the conditions were the same. Exploitation, dismal pay and long hours were the lot of the working class everywhere.

On the road Jack learned another lesson about society. Jails were used by the rich to keep the poor in hand. While walking down the streets enroute to Niagara Falls he was arrested for being a tramp and, without even being allowed to plead guilty or not guilty, was sentenced to thirty days in the Erie County Penitentiary. This was no city or county jail—it was one of the toughest penitentiaries in the country. For an eighteen year old boy it was one long horrible nightmare. While meditating in his cell he decided that he would go home and get an education. As Jack put it, "I returned to California with the firm intention of developing my brain. This meant school education, so I entered the Oakland High School. To pay my way I worked as a janitor. My sister helped me, too, and I was not above mowing somebody's lawn or taking up and beating carpets when I had half a day to spare. I was working to get away from work, and I buckled down to it with a grim realization of the paradox. No trade for me, was my decision and no criminality. I decided that would be almost as disastrous as to be a laborer. Brains paid, not brawn, and I resolved never again to offer my muscles for sale in the brawn market. Brain, and brain only, would I sell."

After completing one year of High School he decided that his progress was too slow so he spent the summer studying for the University exams. He said of this period, "For weeks I crammed until simultaneous quadratic equations and chemical formulas oozed from my ears." He emerged from his tiny bedroom in August and passed the entrance examinations for the University of California. However, his dreams were broken again when his father became ill and he had to leave the University after the first semester to earn a living for the family. After a stint of slave labor in the Belmont Academy laundry he was once more hunting work when the school year ended. Again he had endured ugly exploitation. The Academy had installed the most modern equipment which only required a four man crew so, as usual, the owner employed two men to do the job of four. Writing and studying on his time off was impossible. Working long, strenuous hours he was too tired to even read the local newspapers. It was hopeless–there was no escape!

On July 14, 1897 the *Excelsior* landed in San Francisco with the first word of the gold strike in the Yukon. The world and Jack London caught gold fever overnight. On July 25th the *Umatilla* sailed north and Jack was aboard. Nearly a year was spent in getting to the Yukon, finding a claim and living in a deep-freeze called a cabin with the hope of finding a fortune in gold with the Spring thaw. Fate dealt him another cruel blow when Dr. Harvey ordered him to return to California or die of the scurvey which he had contracted. He returned nearly penniless but with a renewed determination. During the long winter nights of the Klondike he had found himself. He had decided on a writing career. He well knew that to become a successful writer would be nearly impossible but that was what he would be. He still remembered Ouida's *Signa* and the memory of that book would work the miracle.

While Jack was in the Klondike John London had died, so Jack was now the breadwinner for his mother, himself and his nephew, "Little Johnny" Miller. But, even with this heavy responsibility, he was confident that he could earn a living as a writer. As you read *Martin Eden* you will discover his extraordinary struggle for success.

Without guidance he studied everything he could find in the Oakland Public Library on literature. Late into the night he wrote. Behind him was the vision of the pit, the abyss, the human cesspool, the shambles and the charnel houses of civilization. Ahead was the brilliant hope of success as a writer. He was willing to pay the price. He studied poetry, drama, and every type of literature. He wrote Kipling's material in long hand, by the hour, to improve his own writing style and devoured everything available on philosophy and psychology to establish his own systematic beliefs in these fields. He practically lived with the dictionary in one hand to always have just the right word for description and the Bible in the other to improve his style.

In 1899 the *Overland Monthly* published eight of London's short stories and in January, 1900 the prestigious *Century Magazine* opened the 20th Century with *"An Odyssey of the North."*

Bessie May Maddern and Jack London were married on April 7th, 1900, the day his first book was published by Houghton Mifflin & Co. The marriage was ill-fated but his literary future was secure. His two daughters, Joan and Bess, were born of the first marriage. Having separated from Bessie in July of 1903, Jack courted and won the heart of his second wife, Charmian. They were married in Chicago in 1905 and were lovers until Jack's stroke, heart attack and death at the early age of forty on November 22, 1916.

A giant in numerous ways, Jack London lived at least three full lives in his short lifetime. During the period from 1898 to 1916 he lectured extensively; wrote well over fifty books (much of his unpublished material has now been published so the number stands at fifty-eight with more to come); 200 short stories, many of which are included in book collections; several plays, poems, jokes, etc. and hundreds of articles for newspapers and magazines; went to London to research material for *The People of the Abyss*; covered the Russo-Japanese War as a reporter for the Hearst newspapers; built *The Snark* and sailed her on a two-and-a-half year cruise to Guadalcanal; drove four horses over thirteen hundred miles from California to Oregon and back researching his *The Valley of the Moon;* sailed from Baltimore around the Horn to Seattle for the setting of his *The Mutiny of the Elsinore;* reported and photographed the Mexican Revolution for *Collier's* magazine; spent three-fourths of his last two years in Hawaii and built a fabulous scientific ranch of over 1400 acres.

In this collection you will have an opportunity to read dozens of the works of Jack London. It is our sincere hope that they will provide you with many hours of exciting adventure and an impetus to read the rest of his works. As you read more of his work you will realize how much American literature owes to this robust youngster who exploded into the 20th Century with stories of savage, lusty realism that dealt a crushing blow to the romantic idealism which had been in vogue for far too long. As his nephew, Irving Shepard stated so succinctly, "If his untempered enthusiasm seemed to lead him astray and to excesses it was only the natural consequences of an exuberant, unfettered imagination and a boundless lust for life."

Russ Kingman
June, 1984

1
Before Adam

BEFORE ADAM

By JACK LONDON

Author of "The Call of the Wild," "The Sea Wolf," etc.

EDITOR'S NOTE.—One might expect daring of Jack London, an author who has been gold-miner, sailor, frontiersman, adventurer; whose writing can no more be trite or commonplace than can the narrative of his own life history. But no fictionist ever dreamed of daring to attempt what Jack London has done here—to plunge into the gray mist that shrouds the beginnings of our race; to paint in vivid colors a picture of that alleged and disputed ancestor of ours; to outline his brutal life, his loves, his hates, his first efforts toward human reasoning power; to do all this with such wonderful vividness that the skeptic is convinced by the plain truth of it. Such a story is "Before Adam"—strange, powerful, often grotesque, yet never revolting, and new. There has been no precedent for it. It carries the reader beyond all soundings into an hitherto unimagined experience. Believe in the Darwinian theory or not, as you will; thrust aside as absurd the author's claim to a superdeveloped racial memory; yet the fascination of the tale will get its grip on you and perforce you will grant our claim—that as a daring feat of imagination it is unsurpassed—that Jack London has achieved the literary sensation of the year.

"These are our ancestors, and their history is our history. Remember that as surely as we one day swung down out of the trees and walked upright, just as surely, on a far earlier day, did we crawl up out of the sea and achieve our first adventure on land."

CHAPTER I

PICTURES! Pictures! Pictures! Often, before I learned, did I wonder whence came the multitudes of pictures that thronged my dreams; for they were pictures the like of which I had never seen in real wake-a-day life. They tormented my childhood, making of my dreams a procession of nightmares and a little later convincing me that I was different from my kind, a creature unnatural and accursed.

In my days only did I attain any measure of happiness. My nights marked the reign of fear—and such fear! I make bold to state that no man of all the men who walk the earth with me ever suffers fear of like kind and degree. For my fear is the fear of long ago, the fear that was rampant in the Younger World, and in the youth of the Younger World; in short, the fear that reigned supreme in that period known as the Mid-Pleistocene.

What do I mean? I see explanation is necessary before I can tell you of the substance of my dreams. Otherwise, little could you know of the meaning of the things I know so well. As I write this, all the beings and happenings of that other world rise up before me in vast phantasmagoria, and I know that to you they would be rimeless and reasonless.

What to you the friendship of Lop-Ear, the warm lure of the Swift One, the lust and the atavism of Red-Eye? A screaming incoherence and no more. And a screaming incoherence, likewise, the doings of the Fire People and the Tree People, and the gibbering councils of the horde. For you know not the peace of the cool caves in the cliffs, the circus of the drinking-places at the end of the day. You have never felt the bite of the morning wind in the tree-tops, nor is the taste of young bark sweet in your mouth.

It would be better, I dare say, for you to make your approach, as I made mine, through my childhood. As a boy I was very like other boys—in my waking hours. It was in my sleep that I was different. As a rule, my dreams were stuffed with fear—and with a fear so strange and alien that it had no ponderable quality. No fear that I experienced in my waking life resembled the fear that possessed me in my sleep. It was of a quality and kind that transcended all my experiences.

For instance, I was a city child, to whom the country was an unexplored domain. Yet I never dreamed of cities; nor did a house ever occur in any of my dreams. Nor, for that matter, did any human being ever break through the wall of my sleep. I, who had seen trees only in parks and illustrated books, wandered in my sleep through interminable forests. And further, these dream trees were not a mere blur on my vision. They were sharp and distinct. I was on terms of practised intimacy with them. I saw every branch and twig; I saw and knew every different leaf.

Well do I remember the first time in my waking life that I saw an oak tree. As I looked at the leaves and branches and gnarls, it came to me with distressing vividness that I had seen that same kind of tree many and countless times in my sleep. So I was not surprised, still later on in my life, to recognize instantly, the first time I saw them, trees such as the spruce, the yew, the birch, and the laurel. I had seen them all before, and was seeing them even then, every night, in my sleep.

This, as you have already discerned, violates the first law of dreaming, namely, that in one's dreams one sees only what he has seen in his waking life, or combinations of the things he has seen in his waking life. But all my dreams violated this law. In my dreams I never saw *anything* of which I had knowledge in my waking life. My dream life and my waking life were lives apart, with not one thing in common save myself. I was the connecting link that somehow lived both lives.

Early in my childhood I learned that nuts came from the grocer, berries from the fruit man; but before ever that knowledge was mine, in my dreams I picked nuts from trees, or gathered them and ate them from the ground underneath trees, and in the same way I ate berries from vines and bushes. This was beyond any experience of mine.

I shall never forget the first time I saw blueberries served on the table. I had never seen blueberries before, and yet, at the sight of them, there leaped up in my mind memories of dreams wherein I had wandered through swampy land eating my fill of them. My mother set before me a dish of the berries. I filled my spoon, but before I raised it to my mouth I knew just how they would taste. Nor was I disappointed. It was the same tang that I had tasted a thousand times in my sleep.

Snakes? Long before I had heard of the existence of snakes, I was tormented by them in my sleep. They lurked for me in the forest glades; leaped up, striking, under my feet; squirmed off through the dry grass or across naked patches of rock; or pursued me into the tree-tops, encircling the trunks with their great shining bodies, driving me higher and higher, or farther and farther out on swaying and crackling branches, the ground a dizzy distance beneath me. Snakes!—with their forked tongues, their beady eyes and glittering scales, their hissing and their rattling—did I not already know them far too well on that day of my first circus when I saw the snake-charmer lift them up? They were old friends of mine, enemies rather, that peopled my nights with fear.

When I was five years old I went to my first circus. I came home from it sick—but not from peanuts and pink lemonade. Let me tell you. As we entered the animal-tent, a hoarse roaring shook the air. I tore my hand loose from my father's and dashed wildly back through the entrance. I collided with people, fell down; and all the time I was screaming with terror. My father caught me and soothed me. He pointed to the crowd of people, all careless of the roaring, and cheered me with assurances of safety.

Nevertheless, it was in fear and trembling, and with much encouragement on his part, that I at last approached the lion's cage. Ah, I knew him on the instant. The beast! The terrible one! And on my inner vision flashed the memories of my dreams—the midday sun shining on tall grass, the wild bull grazing quietly, the sudden parting of the grass before the swift rush of the tawny one, his leap to the bull's back, the crashing and the bellowing, and the crunch crunch of bones; or again, the cool quiet of the water-hole, the wild horse up to his knees and drinking softly, and then the tawny one—always the tawny one!—the leap, the screaming and the splashing of the horse, and the crunch crunch of bones; and yet again, the somber twilight and the sad silence of the end of day, and then the great full-throated roar, sudden, like a trump of doom, and swift upon it the insane shrieking and chattering among the trees, and I, too, am trembling with fear and am one of the many shrieking and chattering.

At the sight of him, helpless, within the bars of his cage, I became enraged. I gritted my teeth at him, danced up and down, screaming an incoherent mockery and making antic faces. He responded, rushing against the bars and roaring back at me his impotent wrath. Ah, he knew me, too, and the sounds I made were the sounds of old time and intelligible to him.

My parents were frightened. "The child is ill," said my mother. "He is hysterical," said my father. I never told them, and they never knew. Already had I developed reticence concerning this duality of mine, this semi-disassociation of personality, as I think I am justified in calling it.

I saw the snake-charmer, and no more of the circus did I see that night. I was taken home, nervous and overwrought, sick with the invasion of my real life by that other life of my dreams.

I have mentioned my reticence. Only once did I confide the strangeness of it all to another. He was a boy—my chum; and we were eight years old. From my dreams I reconstructed for him pictures of that vanished world in which I do believe I once lived. I told him of the terrors of that early time, of Lop-Ear and the pranks we played, of the gibbering councils, and of the Fire People and their squatting-places.

He laughed at me, and jeered, and told me tales of ghosts and of the dead that walk at night. But mostly did he laugh at my feeble fancy. I told him more, and he laughed the harder. I swore in all earnestness that these things were so, and he began to look upon me queerly. Also, he gave amazing garblings of my tales to our playmates, until all began to look upon me queerly.

It was a bitter experience, but I learned my lesson. I was different from my kind. I was abnormal with something they could not understand, the telling of which would cause only misunderstanding. When the stories of ghosts and goblins went around, I kept quiet. I smiled grimly to myself. I thought of my nights of fear, and knew that mine were the real things—real as life itself, not attenuated vapors and surmised shadows.

CHAPTER II

I HAVE said that in my dreams I never saw a human being. Of this fact I became aware very early, and felt poignantly the lack of my own kind. As a very little child, even, I had a feeling, in the midst of the horror of my dreaming, that if I could find but one man, only one human being, I should be saved from my dreaming, I should be surrounded no more by haunting terrors. This thought obsessed me every night of my life for years—if only I could find that one man and be saved!

I must iterate that I had this thought in the midst of my dreaming, and I take it as an evidence of the merging of my two personalities, as evidence of a point of contact between the two disassociated parts of me. My dream personality lived in the long ago, before ever man, as we know him, came to be; and my other and wake-a-day personality projected itself, to the extent of the knowledge of man's existence, into the substance of my dreams.

Perhaps the psychologists of the book will find fault with my way of using the phrase "disassociation of personality." I know their use of it, yet am compelled to use it in my own way in default of a better phrase. I take shelter behind the inadequacy of the English language. And now to the explanation of my use, or misuse, of the phrase.

It was not till I was a young man, at college, that I got any clue to the significance of my dreams, and to the cause of them. Up to that time they had been meaningless and without apparent causation. But at college I came upon evolution and psychology, and learned the explanation of various strange mental states and experiences. For instance, there was the falling-through-space dream—the commonest dream experience, one practically known, by first-hand experience, to all men.

This, my professor told me, was a racial memory. It dated back to our remote ancestors who lived in trees. With them, being tree-dwellers, the liability of falling was an ever-present menace. Many lost their lives that way; all of them experienced terrible falls, saving themselves by clutching branches as they fell toward the ground.

Now a terrible fall, averted in such fashion, was productive of shock. Such shock was productive of molecular changes in the cerebral cells. These molecular changes were transmitted to the cerebral cells of progeny, became, in short, racial memories. Thus, when you and I, asleep or dozing off to sleep, fall through space and awake to sickening consciousness just before we strike, we are merely remembering what happened to our arboreal ancestors, and what has been stamped by cerebral changes into the hereditary constitution of the race.

There is nothing strange in this, any more than there is anything strange in an instinct. An instinct is merely a habit that is stamped into the stuff of our heredity, that is all. It will be noted, in passing, that in this falling dream which is so familiar to you and me and all of us, we never strike bottom. To dream that would be destruction. Those of our arboreal ancestors who struck bottom died forthwith. True, the shock of their fall was communicated to the cerebral cells, but they died immediately, before they could have progeny. You and I are descended from those who did not strike bottom; that is why we never strike bottom in our dreams.

We never have this sense of falling when we are wide awake. Our wake-a-day personality has no experience of it. Then—and here the argument is irresistible—it must be another and distinct personality that falls when we are asleep, and that has had experience of such falling—that has, in short, a memory of past-day race experiences just as our wake-a-day personality has a memory of our wake-a-day experiences.

It was at this stage in my reasoning that I began to see the light. And quickly it burst upon me with dazzling brightness, illuminating and explaining all that had been weird and uncanny and unnaturally impossible in my dream experiences. In my sleep it was not my wake-a-day personality that took charge of me; it was another and distinct personality, possessing a totally different fund of experiences, and, to the point of my dreaming, possessing memories of those totally different experiences.

What was this personality? When had it itself lived a wake-a-day life on this planet in order to collect this fund of strange experiences? These were questions that my dreams themselves answered. He lived in the long ago, when the world was young, in that period which we call the Mid-Pleistocene. He fell from the trees, but did not strike bottom. He gibbered with fear at the roaring of the lions. He was pursued by beasts of prey, struck at by deadly snakes. He chattered with his kind in council, and he received rough usage at the hands of the Fire People in the day that he fled before them. This other-self of mine is an ancestor, a progenitor of my progenitors in the early line of my race, himself the progeny of a line that long before his time developed fingers and toes and climbed up into the trees.

But, I hear you objecting, why is it that these racial memories are not ours as well, seeing that we have a vague other-personality that falls through space while we sleep?

And I may answer with another question: Why is a two-headed calf? And my own answer to this is that it is a freak. And so I answer your question. I have this other-personality and these complete racial memories because I am a freak.

But let me be more explicit. The commonest race memory we have is the falling-through-space dream. This other-personality is very vague. About the only memory it has is that of falling. But many of us have sharper, more distinct other-personalities. Many of us have the flying dream, the pursuing monster dream, color dreams, suffocation dreams, and the reptile and vermin dreams. In short, while this other-personality is vestigial in all of us, in some of us it is almost obliterated, while in others of us it is more pronounced.

In myself, the degree of possession of the other-personality is enormous. My other-personality is almost equal in power to my own. And in this matter I am, as I said, a freak—a freak of heredity.

And now, before I take up my tale, I want to anticipate the doubting Thomases of psychology, who are prone to scoff, and who would otherwise surely say that the coherence of my dreams is due to overstudy and the subconscious projection of my knowledge of evolution into my dreams. In the first place, I have never been a zealous student. I graduated last of my class. I cared more for athletics, and—there is no reason why I should not confess it—more for billiards.

Further, I had no knowledge of evolution until I was at college, whereas in my childhood and youth I had already lived in my dreams all the details of that other, long-ago life. I will say, however, that these details were mixed and incoherent until I came to know the science of evolution. Evolution was the key. It gave the explanation, gave sanity to the pranks of this atavistic brain of mine that, modern and normal, harked back to a past so remote as to be contemporaneous with the raw beginnings of mankind.

For in this past I know of, man, as we today know him, did not exist. It was in the period of his becoming that I must have lived and had my being.

CHAPTER III

THE commonest dream of my early childhood was something like this: It seemed that I was very small and that I lay curled up in a sort of nest of twigs and boughs. Sometimes I was lying on my back. In this position it seemed that I spent many hours, watching the play of sunlight on the foliage overhead and the stirring of the leaves by the wind. Often the nest itself moved back and forth when the wind was strong.

But always, while so lying in the nest, I was mastered by a feeling as of tremendous space beneath me. I never saw it, I never peered over the edge of the nest to see; but I *knew* and feared the space that lurked just beneath me and that ever threatened me like a maw of some all-devouring monster.

This dream, in which I was quiescent and which was more like a condition than an experience of action, I dreamed very often in my early childhood. But suddenly there would rush into the very midst of it strange forms and ferocious happenings, the thunder and crashing of storm, or unfamiliar landscapes such as in my wake-a-day life I had never seen. The result was confusion and nightmare. I could comprehend nothing of it. There was no logic of sequence.

You see, I did not dream consecutively. One moment I was a wee babe of the Younger World lying in my tree nest; the next moment I was a grown man of the Younger World locked in combat with the hideous Red-Eye; and the next moment I was creeping carefully down to the water-hole in the heat of the day. Events, years apart in their occurrence in the Younger World, occurred with me within the space of several minutes, or seconds.

It was all a jumble, but this jumble I shall not inflict upon you. It was not until I was a young man and had dreamed many thousands of times, that everything straightened out and became clear and plain. Then it was that I got the clue of time, and was able to piece together events and actions in their proper order. Thus was I able to reconstruct the vanished Younger World as it was at the time I lived in it—or at the time my other-self lived in it. The distinction does not matter; for I, too, the modern man, have gone back and lived that early life in the company of my other-self.

For your convenience, since this is to be no sociological screed, I shall frame together the different events into a comprehensive story. For there is a certain thread of continuity and happening that runs through all the dreams. There is my friendship with Lop-Ear, for instance. Also, there are the enmity of Red-Eye and the love of the Swift One. Taking it all in all, a fairly coherent and interesting story, I am sure you will agree.

I do not remember much of my mother. Possibly the earliest recollection I have of her—and certainly the sharpest—is the following: It seemed I was lying on the ground. I was somewhat older than during the nest days, but still helpless. I rolled about in the dry leaves, playing with them and making crooning, rasping noises in my throat. The sun shone warmly, and I was happy and comfortable. I was in a little open space. Around me, on all sides, were bushes and fern-like growths, and overhead and all about were the trunks and branches of forest trees.

Suddenly I heard a sound. I sat upright and listened. I made no movement. The little noises died down in my throat, and I sat as one petrified. The sound came closer. It was like the grunt of a pig. Then I began to hear the noises caused by the moving of a body through the brush. Next I saw the ferns agitated by the passage of a body. Then the ferns parted, and I saw gleaming eyes, a long snout, and white tusks.

It was a wild boar. He peered at me curiously. He grunted once or twice and shifted his weight from one fore leg to the other, at the same time moving his head from side to side and swaying the ferns. Still I sat as one petrified, my eyes unblinking as I stared at him, fear eating at my heart.

It seemed that this movelessness and silence on my part was what was expected of me. I was not to cry out in the face of fear. It was a dictate of instinct. And so I sat there and waited for I knew not what. The boar thrust the ferns aside and stepped into the open. The curiosity went out of his eyes, and they gleamed cruelly. He tossed his head at me threateningly and advanced a step. This he did again, and yet again.

Then I screamed . . . or shrieked—I cannot describe it, but it was a shrill and terrible cry. And it seems that it, too, at this stage of the proceedings, was the thing expected of me. From not far away came an answering cry. My sounds seemed momentarily to disconcert the boar, and while he halted and shifted his weight with indecision, an apparition burst upon us.

She was like a large orang-utan, my mother, or like a chimpanzee, and yet, in sharp and definite ways, quite different. She was heavier of build than they, and had less hair. Her arms were not so long, and her legs were stouter. She wore no clothes—only her natural hair. And I can tell you she was a fury when she was excited.

And like a fury she dashed upon the scene. She was gritting her teeth, making frightful grimaces, snarling, uttering sharp and continuous cries that sounded like "Kh-ah! kh-ah!" So sudden and formidable was her appearance that the boar involuntarily bunched himself together on the defensive and bristled as she swerved toward him. Then she swerved toward me. She had quite taken the breath out of him. I knew just what to do in that moment of time she had gained. I leaped to meet her, catching her about the waist, and holding on hand and foot—yes, by my feet; I could hold on by them as readily as by my hands. I could feel in my tense grip the pull of the hair as her skin and her muscles moved beneath with her efforts.

As I say, I leaped to meet her, and on the instant she leaped straight up into the air, catching an overhanging branch with her hands. The next instant, with clashing tusks, the boar drove past underneath. He had recovered from his surprise and sprung forward, emitting a squeal that was almost a trumpeting. At any rate it was a call, for it was followed by the rushing of bodies through the ferns and brush from all directions.

From every side wild hogs dashed into the open space—a score of them. But my mother swung over the top of a thick limb, a dozen feet from the ground, and I still holding on to her, we perched there in safety. She was very excited. She chattered and screamed, and scolded down at the bristling, tooth-gnashing circle that had gathered beneath. I, too, trembling, peered down at the angry beasts and did my best to imitate my mother's cries.

From the distance came similar cries, only pitched deeper, into a sort of roaring bass. These grew momentarily louder, and soon I saw him approaching, my father—at least, by all the evidence of the times, I am driven to conclude that he was my father.

He was not an extremely prepossessing father, as fathers go. He seemed half man and half ape, and yet not ape, and not yet man. I fail to describe him. There is nothing like him to-day on the earth, under the earth, nor in the earth. He was a large man in his day, and he must have weighed all of a hundred and thirty pounds. His face was broad and flat, and the eyebrows overhung the eyes. The eyes themselves were small, deep-set, and close together. He had practically no nose at all. It was squat and broad, apparently without any bridge, while the nostrils were like two holes in the face, opening outward instead of down.

The forehead slanted back from the eyes, and the hair began right at the eyes and ran up over the head. The head itself was preposterously small and was supported on an equally preposterous, thick, short neck.

There was an elemental economy about his body—as there was about all our bodies. The chest was deep, it is true, cavernously deep; but there were no full-swelling muscles, no wide-spreading shoulders, no clean-limbed straightness, no generous symmetry of outline. It represented strength, that body of my father's, strength without beauty; ferocious, primordial strength, made to clutch and gripe and rend and destroy.

His hips were thin; and the legs, lean and hairy, were crooked and stringy-muscled. In fact, they were more like arms than legs. They were twisted and gnarly, and with scarcely the semblance of the full, meaty calf such as graces your leg and mine. I remember that he could not walk on the flat of his foot. This was because it was prehensile, more like a hand than a foot. The great toe, instead of being in line with the other toes, opposed them like a thumb, and this was what enabled him to get a grip.

But his appearance was no more unusual than the manner of his coming there to my mother and me as we perched above the angry wild pigs. He came through the trees, leaping from limb to limb and from tree to tree; and he came swiftly. I can see him now, in my wake-a-day life, as I write this, swinging along through the trees, a four-handed, hairy creature, howling with rage, pausing now and again to beat his chest with his clenched fist, leaping ten- and fifteen-foot gaps, catching a branch with one hand and swinging on across another gap to catch with his other hand and go on, never hesitating, never at a loss as to how to proceed on his arboreal way.

And as I watched him I felt in my own being, in my very muscles themselves, the surge and thrill of desire to go leaping from bough to bough; and I felt also the guarantee of the latent power in that being and in those muscles of mine. And why not? Little boys watch their fathers swing axes and fell trees, and feel in themselves that some day they, too, will swing axes and fell trees. And so with me. The life that was in me was constituted to do what my father did, and it whispered to me secretly and ambitiously of aerial paths and forest flights.

At last my father joined us. He was extremely angry. I remember the outthrust of his protruding underlip as he glared down at the wild pigs. He snarled somewhat like a dog, and I remember that his eye-teeth were large, like fangs, and that they impressed me tremendously.

His conduct served only the more to infuriate the pigs. He broke off twigs and small branches and flung them down upon our enemies. He even hung by one hand, tantalizingly just beyond reach, and mocked them as they gnashed their tusks with impotent rage. Not content with this, he broke off a stout branch, and, holding on with one hand and one foot, jabbed the infuriated beasts in the sides and whacked them across their noses. Needless to state, my mother and I enjoyed the sport.

But one tires of all good things, and in the end, my father, chuckling maliciously the while, led the way across the trees. Now it was that my ambitions ebbed away, and I became timid, holding tightly to my mother as she climbed and swung through the forest. I remember when the branch broke with her weight. She had made a wild leap, and with the snap of the wood I was overwhelmed with a sickening consciousness of falling through space, the pair of us. The forest and the sunshine on the rustling leaves vanished from my eyes. I had a fading glimpse of my father abruptly arresting his progress to look, and then all was blackness.

The next moment I was awake, in my sheeted bed, sweating, trembling, nauseated. The window was up, and a cool air was blowing through the room. The night-lamp was burning calmly. And because of this I take it that the wild pigs did not get us, that we never fetched bottom; else my other-self would not be here now, a thousand centuries after, to remember the event.

CHAPTER IV

THERE is one puzzling thing about these prehistoric memories of mine. It is the vagueness of the time element. I do not always know the order of events; nor can I tell, between some events, whether one, two, or four or five years have elapsed. I can only roughly tell the passage of time by judging the changes in the appearance and pursuits of my fellows.

Also, I can apply the logic of events to the various happenings. For instance, there is no doubt whatever that my mother and I were treed by the wild pigs and fled and fell in the days before I made the acquaintance of Lop-Ear, who became what I may call my boyhood chum. And it is just as certain that between these two periods I must have left my mother.

I have no other memory of my father than the one I have given. Never, in the years that followed, did he reappear. And from my knowledge of the times, the only explanation possible is that he perished shortly after the adventure with the wild pigs. That it must have been an untimely end, there is no doubt. He was in full vigor, and only sudden and violent death could have taken him off. But I know not the manner of his going—whether he was drowned in the river, or was swallowed by a snake, or went into the stomach of old Saber Tooth, the tiger, is beyond my knowledge.

For know that I remember only the things I saw myself, with my own eyes, in those prehistoric days. If my mother knew my father's end, she never told me. For that matter I doubt if she had a vocabulary adequate to convey such information. Perhaps, all told, the Folk in that day had a vocabulary of thirty or forty sounds.

I call them *sounds*, rather than *words*, because sounds they were primarily. They had no fixed values, to be altered by adjectives and adverbs. These latter were tools of speech not yet invented. Instead of qualifying nouns or verbs by the use of adjectives and adverbs, we qualified sounds by intonation, by changes in quantity and pitch, by retarding and by accelerating. The length of time employed in the utterance of a particular sound shaded its meaning.

We had no conjugation. One judged the tense by the context. We talked only concrete things because we thought only concrete things. Also, we depended largely on pantomime. The simplest abstraction was practically beyond our thinking; and when one did happen to think an abstraction, he was hard put to communicate it to his fellows. There were no sounds for it. He was pressing beyond the limits of his vocabulary. If he invented sounds for it, his fellows did not understand the sounds. Then it was that he fell back on pantomime, illustrating the thought wherever possible and at the same time repeating the new sound over and over again.

Thus language grew. By the few sounds we possessed we were enabled to think a short distance beyond those sounds; then came the need for new sounds wherewith to express the new thought. Sometimes, however, we thought too long a distance in advance of our sounds, and managed to achieve abstractions (dim ones, I grant), which we failed utterly to make known to other folk. After all, language did not grow fast in that day.

Oh, believe me, we were amazingly simple. But we could do a lot that is not done today. We could twitch our ears, prick them up and flatten them down at will. And we could scratch between our shoulders with ease. We could throw stones with our feet. I have done it many a time. And, for that matter, I could keep my knees straight, bend forward from the hips, and touch, not the tips of my fingers, but the points of my elbows, to the ground. And as for bird-nesting—well, I only wish the twentieth-century boy could see us. But we made no collections of eggs. We ate them.

I remember—but I outrun my story. First let me tell of Lop-Ear and our friendship. Very early in my life, I separated from my mother. Possibly this was because, after the death of my father, she took to herself a second husband. I have few recollections of him, and they are not of the best. He was a light fellow. There was no solidity to him. He was too voluble. His infernal chattering worries me even now as I think of it. His mind was too inconsequential to permit him to possess purpose. Monkeys in their cages always remind me of him. He was monkeyish. That is the best description I can give of him.

He hated me from the first. And I quickly learned to be afraid of him and his malicious pranks. Whenever he came in sight I crept close to my mother and clung to her. But I was growing older all the time, and it was inevitable that I should from time to time stray from her, and stray farther and farther. And these were the opportunities that the Chatterer waited for. (I may as well explain that we bore no names in those days. For the sake of convenience I have myself given names to the various Folk I was more closely in contact with, and the "Chatterer" is the most fitting description I can find for that precious stepfather of mine. As for me, I have named myself "Big-Tooth." My eye-teeth were pronouncedly large.)

But to return to the Chatterer. He persistently terrorized me. He was always pinching me and cuffing me, and on occasion he was not above biting me. Often my mother interfered, and the way she made his fur fly was a joy to see. But the result of all this was a beautiful and unending family quarrel, in which I was the bone of contention.

No, my home life was not happy. I smile to myself as I write the phrase. Home life! Home! I had no home in the modern sense of the term. My home was an association, not a habitation. I lived in my mother's care, not in a house. And my mother lived anywhere, so long as when night came she was above the ground.

My mother was old-fashioned. She still clung to her trees. It is true, the more progressive members of our horde lived in the caves above the river. But my mother was suspicious and unprogressive. The trees were good enough for her. Of course, we had one particular tree in which we usually roosted, though we often roosted in other trees when nightfall caught us. In a convenient fork was a sort of rude platform of twigs and branches and vines. It was more like a huge bird-nest than anything else, though it was a thousand times cruder in the weaving than any bird-nest. But it had one feature that I have never seen attached to any bird-nest, namely, a roof.

Oh, not a roof such as modern man makes! Nor a roof such as is made by the lowest aborigines of to-day. It was infinitely more clumsy than the clumsiest handiwork of man—of man as we know him. It was put together in a casual, helter-skelter sort of way. Above the fork of the tree whereon we rested was a pile of dead branches and brush. Four or five adjacent forks held what I may term the various ridge-poles. These were merely stout sticks an inch or so in diameter. On them rested the brush and branches which seemed to have been tossed on almost aimlessly. There was no attempt at thatching. And I must confess that the roof leaked miserably in a heavy rain.

But the Chatterer. He made home life a burden for both my mother and me—and by home life I mean, not the leaky nest in the tree, but the group-life of the three of us. He was most malicious in his persecution of me. That was the one purpose to which he held steadfastly for longer than five minutes. Also, as time went by, my mother was less eager in her defense of me. I think, what of the continuous rows raised by the Chatterer, that I must have become a nuisance to her. At any rate, the situation went from bad to worse so rapidly that I should soon, of my own volition, have left home. But the satisfaction of performing so independent an act was denied me. Before I was ready to go, I was thrown out. And I mean this literally.

The opportunity came to the Chatterer one day when I was alone in the nest. My mother and the Chatterer had gone away together toward the blueberry swamp. He must have planned the whole thing, for I heard him returning alone through the forest, roaring with self-induced rage as he came. Like all the men of our horde, when they were angry, or were trying to make themselves angry, he stopped now and again to hammer on his chest with his fist.

I realized the helplessness of my situation, and crouched trembling in the nest. The Chatterer came directly to the tree—I remember it was an oak-tree—and began to climb up. And he never ceased for a moment from his infernal row. As I have said, our language was extremely meager, and he must have strained it by the variety of ways in which he informed me of his undying hatred of me and of his intention there and then to have it out with me.

As he climbed to the fork, I fled out the great horizontal limb. He followed me, and out I went, farther and farther. At last I was out among the small twigs and leaves. The Chatterer was ever a coward, and greater always than any anger he worked up was his caution. He was afraid to follow me out among the leaves and twigs. For that matter, his greater weight would have crashed him through the foliage before he could have got to me.

But it was not necessary for him to reach me, and well he knew it, the scoundrel! With a malevolent expression on his face, his beady eyes gleaming with cruel intelligence, he began teetering. Teetering!—and with me out on the very edge of the bough, clutching at the twigs that broke continually with my weight. Twenty feet beneath me was the earth.

Wildly and more wildly he teetered, grinning at me his gloating hatred. Then came the end. All four holds broke at the same time, and I fell, back downward, looking up at him, my hands and feet still clutching the broken twigs. Luckily, there were no wild pigs under me, and my fall was broken by the tough and springy bushes.

Usually, my falls destroy my dreams, the nervous shock being sufficient to bridge the thousand centuries in an instant and hurl me wide awake into my bed, where, perchance, I lie sweating and trembling and hear the cuckoo clock calling the hour in the hall. But this dream of my leaving home I have had many times, and never yet have I been awakened by it. Always do I crash, shrieking, down through the brush and fetch up with a bump on the ground.

Scratched and bruised and whimpering, I lay where I had fallen. Peering up through the bushes, I could see the Chatterer. He had set up a demoniacal chant of joy and was keeping time to it with his teetering. I quickly hushed my whimpering. I was no longer in the safety of the trees, and I knew the danger I ran of bringing upon myself the hunting animals by too audible an expression of my grief.

I remember, as my sobs died down, that I became interested in watching the strange light-effects produced by partially opening and closing my tear-wet eyelids. Then I began to investigate, and found that I was not so very badly damaged by my fall. I had lost some hair and hide, here and there; the sharp and jagged end of a broken branch had thrust fully an inch into my forearm; and my right hip, which had borne the brunt of my contact with the ground, was aching intolerably. But these, after all, were only petty hurts. No bones were broken, and in those days the flesh of man had finer healing qualities than it has to-day. Yet it was a severe fall, for I limped with my injured hip for fully a week afterward.

Next, as I lay in the bushes, there came upon me a feeling of desolation, a consciousness that I was homeless. I made up my mind never to return to my mother and the Chatterer. I would go far away through the terrible forest, and find some tree for myself in which to roost. As for food, I knew where to find it. For the last year at least I had not been beholden to my mother for food. All she had furnished me was protection and guidance.

I crawled softly out through the bushes. Once I looked back and saw the Chatterer still chanting and teetering. It was not a pleasant sight. I knew pretty well how to be cautious, and I was exceedingly careful on this my first journey in the world.

I gave no thought as to where I was going. I had but one purpose, and that was to go away beyond the reach of the Chatterer. I climbed into the trees and wandered on among them for hours, passing from tree to tree and never touching the ground. But I did not go in any particular direction, nor did I travel steadily. It was my nature, as it was the nature of all my folk, to be inconsequential. Besides, I was a mere child, and I stopped a great deal to play by the way.

The events that befell me on my leaving home are very vague in my mind. My dreams do not cover them. Much has my other-self forgotten, and particularly of this very period. Nor have I been able to frame up the various dreams so as to bridge the gap between my leaving the home-tree and my arrival at the caves.

I remember that several times I came to open spaces. These I crossed in great trepidation, descending to the ground and running at the top of my speed. I remember that there were days of rain and days of sunshine, so that I must have wandered alone for quite a time. I especially dream of my misery in the rain, and of my sufferings from hunger and how I appeased it. One very strong impression is of hunting little lizards on the rocky top of an open knoll. They ran under the rocks, and most of them escaped; but occasionally I turned over a stone and caught one. I was frightened away from this knoll by snakes. They did not pursue me. They were merely basking on flat rocks in the sun. But such was my inherited fear of them that I fled as fast as if they had been after me.

Then I gnawed bitter bark from young trees. I remember vaguely eating many green nuts, with soft shells and milky kernels. And I remember most distinctly suffering from a stomach-ache. It may have been caused by the green nuts, and maybe by the lizards. I do not know. But I do know that I was fortunate in not being devoured during the several hours I was knotted up on the ground with the colic.

CHAPTER V

My vision of the scene came abruptly, as I emerged from the forest. I found myself on the edge of a large, clear space. On one side of this space rose high bluffs. On the other side was the river. The earth bank ran steeply down to the water, but here and there, in several places, where at some time slides of earth had occurred, there were runways. These were the drinking-places of the Folk that lived in the caves.

And this was the main abiding-place of the Folk that I had chanced upon. This was, I may say, by stretching the word, the village. My mother and the Chatterer and I, and a few other simple bodies, were what might be termed suburban residents. We were part of the horde, though we lived a distance away from it. It was only a short distance, though it had taken me, what of my wandering, all of a week to arrive. Had I come directly, I could have covered the trip in an hour.

From the edge of the forest I saw the caves in the bluff, the open space, and the runways to the drinking-places. And in the open space I saw many of the Folk. I had been straying, alone and a child, for a week. During that time I had seen not one of my kind. I had lived in terror and desolation. And now, at the sight of my kind, I was overcome with gladness, and ran wildly toward them.

Then it was that a strange thing happened. Some one of the Folk saw me and uttered a warning cry. On the instant, crying out with fear and panic, the Folk fled away. Leaping and scrambling over the rocks, they plunged into the mouths of the caves and disappeared . . . all but one, a little baby, that had been dropped in the excitement close to the base of the bluff. He was wailing dolefully. His mother dashed out; he sprang to meet her and held on tightly as she scrambled back into the cave.

I was all alone. The populous open space had of a sudden become deserted. I sat down forlornly and whimpered. I could not understand. Why had the Folk run away from me? In later time, when I came to know their ways, I was to learn. When they saw me dashing out of the forest at top speed they had concluded that I was being pursued by some hunting animal. By my unceremonious approach I had stampeded them.

As I sat and watched the cave-mouths I became aware that the Folk were watching me. Soon they were thrusting their heads out. A little later they were calling back and forth to one another. In the hurry and confusion it had happened that all had not gained their own caves. Some of the young ones had sought refuge in other caves. The mothers did not call for them by name, because, as I said, names were an invention we had not yet made. They merely uttered querulous, anxious cries, which were recognized by the young ones. Thus, had my mother been there calling to me, I should have recognized her voice among the voices of a thousand mothers, and in the same way would she have recognized mine among a thousand.

This calling back and forth continued for some time, but the Folk were too cautious to come out of their caves and descend to the ground. Finally one did come. He was destined to play a large part in my life, and for that matter he already played a large part in the lives of all the members of the horde. He it was whom I shall call Red-Eye in the pages of this history—so called because of his inflamed eyes, the lids being always red, and, by the peculiar effect they produced, seeming to advertise the terrible savagery of him. The color of his soul was red.

He was a monster in all ways. Physically he was a giant. He must have weighed a hundred and seventy pounds. He was the largest one of our kind I ever saw. Nor did I ever see one of the Fire People so large as he, nor one of the Tree People. Sometimes, when in the newspapers I happen upon descriptions of our modern bruisers and prizefighters, I wonder what chance the best of them would have had against him.

I am afraid not much of a chance. With one grip of his iron fingers and a pull, he could have plucked a muscle, say a biceps, by the roots, clear out of their bodies. A backhanded, loose blow of his fist would have smashed their skulls like egg-shells. With a sweep of his wicked feet (or hind-hands) he could have disemboweled them. A twist would have broken their necks, and I know that with a single crunch of his jaws he could have pierced, at the same moment, the great vein of the throat in front and the spinal marrow at the back.

He could spring twenty feet horizontally from a sitting position. He was abominably hairy. It was a matter of pride with us to be not very hairy. But he was covered with hair all over, on the inside of the arms as well as on the outside, and even the ears. The only places on him where the hair did not grow were the soles of his hands and feet and beneath his eyes. He was frightfully ugly, his ferocious, grinning mouth and huge, down-hanging underlip being but in harmony with his terrible eyes.

This was Red-Eye. And right gingerly he crept out of his cave and descended to the ground. Ignoring me, he proceeded to reconnoiter. He bent forward from the hips as he walked; and so far forward did he bend, and so long were his arms, that with every step he touched the knuckles of his hands to the ground on either side of him. He was awkward in the semi-erect position of walking that he assumed, and he really touched his knuckles to the ground in order to balance himself. But, oh, I tell you he could run on all fours! Now this was something at which we were particularly awkward. Furthermore, it was a rare individual among us who balanced himself with his knuckles when walking. Such an individual was an atavism, and Red-Eye was an even greater atavism.

That is what he was—an atavism. We were in the process of changing our tree-life to life on the ground. For many generations we had been going through this change, and our bodies and carriage had likewise changed. But Red-Eye had reverted to the more primitive tree-dwelling type. Perforce, because he was born in our horde he stayed with us; but in actuality he was an atavism and his place was elsewhere.

Very circumspect and very alert, he moved here and there about the open place, peering through the vistas among the trees and trying to catch a glimpse of the hunting animal that all suspected had pursued me. And while he did this, taking no notice of me, the Folk crowded at the cave-mouths and watched.

BEFORE ADAM

By JACK LONDON

Author of "The Call of the Wild," "The Sea Wolf," etc.

CHAPTER V (*Continued*)

AT last Red-Eye decided that there was no danger lurking about. He was returning from the head of the runway, from where he had taken a peep down at the drinking-place. His course brought him near, but still he did not notice me. He proceeded casually on his way until abreast of me, and then, without warning and with incredible swiftness, he smote me a buffet on the head. I was knocked backward fully a dozen feet before I fetched up against the ground, and I remember, even as the stunning blow was struck, hearing the wild uproar of clucking and shrieking laughter that arose from the caves. It was a great joke—at least in that day; and right heartily the Folk appreciated it.

Thus was I received into the horde. Red-Eye paid no further attention to me, and I was at liberty to whimper and sob to my heart's content. Several of the women gathered curiously about me, and I recognized them. I had encountered them the preceding year when my mother had taken me to the hazel-nut cañons.

But they quickly left me alone, being replaced by a dozen curious and teasing youngsters. These formed a circle around me, pointing their fingers, making faces, and poking and pinching me. I was frightened, and for a time I endured them; then anger got the best of me and I sprang tooth and nail upon the most audacious one of them—none other than Lop-Ear himself. I have so named him because he could prick up only one of his ears. The other always hung limp and without movement. Some accident had injured the muscles and deprived him of the use of it.

He closed with me, and we went at it for all the world like a couple of small boys fighting. We scratched and bit, pulled hair, clinched, and threw each other down. I remember I succeeded in getting on him what in my college days I learned was called a half-Nelson. This hold gave me the decided advantage. But I did not enjoy it long. He twisted up one leg, and with the foot (or hind-hand) made so savage an onslaught upon my abdomen as to threaten to disembowel me. I had to release him in order to save myself, and then we went at it again.

Lop-Ear was a year older than I, but I was several times angrier than he, and in the end he took to his heels. I chased him across the open and down a runway to the river. But he was better acquainted with the locality and ran along the edge of the water and up another runway. He cut diagonally across the open space and dashed into a wide-mouthed cave.

Before I knew it, I had plunged after him into the darkness. The next moment I was badly frightened. I had never been in a cave before. I began to whimper and cry out. Lop-Ear chattered mockingly at me, and, springing upon me unseen, tumbled me over. He did not risk a second encounter, however, and took himself off. I was between him and the entrance, and he did not pass me; yet he seemed to have gone away. I listened, but could get no clue as to where he was. This puzzled me, and when I regained the outside I sat down to watch.

He did not come out of the entrance, of that I was certain; yet at the end of several minutes he chuckled at my elbow. Again I ran after him, and again he ran into the cave; but this time I stopped at the mouth. I dropped back a short distance and watched. He did not come out; yet, as before, he chuckled at my elbow, and was chased by me a third time into the cave.

This performance was repeated several times. Then I followed him into the cave, where I searched vainly for him. I was curious. I could not understand how he eluded me. Always he went into the cave, never did he come out of it, yet always did he arrive there at my elbow and mock me. Thus did our fight transform itself into a game of hide and seek.

All afternoon, with occasional intervals, we kept it up, and a playful, friendly spirit arose between us. In the end, he did not run away from me, and we sat together with our arms around each other. A little later he disclosed the mystery of the wide-mouthed cave. Holding me by the hand, he led me inside. It connected by a narrow crevice with another cave, and it was through this that we regained the open air.

We were now good friends. When the other young ones gathered around to tease, he joined with me in attacking them; and so viciously did we behave that before long I was let alone. Lop-Ear made me acquainted with the village. There was little that he could tell me of conditions and customs—he had not the necessary vocabulary; but by observing his actions I learned much, and also he showed me places and things.

He took me up the open space, between the caves and the river, into the forest beyond, where, in a grassy place among the trees, we made a meal of stringy-rooted carrots.

As twilight came on, the open space was deserted. The Folk were seeking the safety of the caves. Lop-Ear led the way to bed. High up the bluff we climbed, higher than all the other caves, to a tiny crevice that could not be seen from the ground. Into this Lop-Ear squeezed. I followed with difficulty, so narrow was the entrance, and found myself in a small rock chamber. It was very low—not more than a couple of feet in height, and possibly three feet by four in width and length. Here, cuddled together in each other's arms, we slept out the night.

CHAPTER VI

WHILE the more courageous of the youngsters played in and out of the large-mouthed caves, I early learned that such caves were unoccupied. No one slept in them at night. Only the crevice-mouthed caves were used, the narrower the mouth the better. This was from fear of the preying animals that made life a burden to us in those days and nights.

The first morning, after my night's sleep with Lop-Ear, I learned the advantage of the narrow-mouthed caves. It was just daylight when old Saber-Tooth, the tiger, walked into the open space. Two of the Folk were already up. They made a rush to escape. Whether they were panic-stricken, or whether he was too close on their heels for them to attempt to scramble up the bluff to the crevices, I do not know; but at any rate they dashed into the wide-mouthed cave wherein Lop-Ear and I had played the afternoon before.

What happened inside there was no way of telling, but it is fair to conclude that the two Folk slipped through the connecting crevice into the other cave. This crevice was too small to allow for the passage of Saber-Tooth, and he came out the way he had gone in, unsatisfied and angry. It was evident that his night's hunting had been unsuccessful and that he had expected to make a meal off of us. He caught sight of the two Folk at the other cave-mouth and sprang for them. Of course, they darted through the passageway into the first cave. He emerged angrier than ever and snarling.

Pandemonium broke loose among the rest of us. All up and down the great bluff, we crowded the crevices and outside ledges, and we were all chattering and shrieking in a thousand keys. And we were all making faces—snarling faces; this was an instinct with us. We were as angry as Saber-Tooth, though our anger was allied with fear. I remember that I shrieked and made faces with the best of them. Not only did they set the example, but I felt the urge from within me to do the same things they were doing. My hair was bristling, and I was convulsed with a fierce, unreasoning rage.

For some time old Saber-Tooth continued dashing in and out of first the one cave and then the other. But the two Folk merely slipped back and forth through the connecting crevice and eluded him. In the meantime the rest of us up the bluff had proceeded to action. Every time he appeared outside we pelted him with rocks. At first we merely dropped them on him, but we soon began to whiz them down with the added force of our muscles.

This bombardment drew Saber-Tooth's attention to us and made him angrier than ever. He abandoned his pursuit of the two Folk and sprang up the bluff toward the rest of us, clawing at the crumbling rock and snarling as he clawed his upward way. At this awful sight, the last one of us sought refuge inside our caves. I know this, because I peeped out and saw the whole bluffside deserted, save for Saber-Tooth, who had lost his footing and was sliding and falling down.

I called out the cry of encouragement, and again the bluff was covered by the screaming horde and the stones were falling faster than ever. Saber-Tooth was frantic with rage. Time and again he assaulted the bluff. Once he even gained the first crevice entrances before he fell back, but was unable to force his way inside. With each upward rush he made, waves of fear surged over us. At first, at such times, most of us dashed inside; but some remained outside to hammer him with stones, and soon all of us remained outside and kept up the fusillade.

Never was so masterly a creature so completely baffled. It hurt his pride terribly, thus to be outwitted by the small and tender Folk. He stood on the ground and looked up at us, snarling, lashing his tail, snapping at the stones that fell near to him. Once I whizzed down a stone, and just at the right moment he looked up. It caught him full on the end of his nose, and he went straight up in the air, all four feet of him, roaring and caterwauling, what of the hurt and surprise.

He was beaten and he knew it. Recovering his dignity, he stalked out solemnly from under the rain of stones. He stopped in the middle of the open space and looked wistfully and hungrily back at us. He hated to forego the meal — we were just so much meat, cornered but inaccessible. This sight of him started us to laughing. We laughed derisively and uproariously, all of us. Now animals do not like mockery. To be laughed at makes them angry. And in such fashion our laughter affected Saber-Tooth. He turned with a roar and charged the bluff again. This was what we wanted. The fight had become a game, and we took huge delight in pelting him.

But his attack did not last long. He quickly recovered his common sense, and, besides, our missiles were shrewd to hurt. Vividly do I recollect the vision of one bulging eye of his, swollen almost shut by a stone we had thrown. And vividly do I retain the picture of him as he stood on the edge of the forest whither he had finally retreated. He was looking back at us, his writhing lips lifted clear of the very roots of his huge fangs, his hair bristling, and his tail lashing. He gave one last snarl and slid from view among the trees.

And then such a chattering as went up. We swarmed out of our holes, examining the marks his claws had made on the crumbling rock of the bluff, all of us talking at once. One of the two Folk who had been caught in the double cave was part-grown, half child and half youth. They had come out proudly from their refuge, and we surrounded them in an admiring crowd. Then the young fellow's mother broke through and fell upon him in a tremendous rage, boxing his ears, pulling his hair, and shrieking like a demon. She was a strapping big woman, very hairy, and the thrashing she gave him was a delight to the horde. We roared with laughter, holding on to one another or rolling on the ground in our glee.

In spite of the reign of fear under which we lived, the Folk were always great laughers. We had the sense of humor. Our merriment was Gargantuan. It was never restrained. There was nothing half-way about it. When a thing was funny we were convulsed with appreciation of it, and the simplest, crudest things were funny to us. Oh, we were great laughers, I can tell you.

The way we had treated Saber-Tooth was the way we treated all animals that invaded the village. We kept our runways and drinking-places to ourselves by making life miserable for the animals that trespassed or strayed upon our immediate territory. Even the fiercest hunting animals we so bedeviled that they learned to leave our places alone. We were not fighters like them; we were cunning and cowardly, and it was because of our cunning and cowardice, and our inordinate capacity for fear, that we survived in that frightfully hostile environment of the Younger World.

Lop-Ear, I figure, was a year older than I. What his past history was he had no way of telling me, but as I never saw anything of his mother I believed him to be an orphan. After all, fathers did not count in our horde. Marriage was as yet in a rude state, and couples had a way of quarreling and separating. Modern man, what of his divorce institution, does the same thing legally. But we had no laws. Custom was all we went by, and our custom in this particular matter was rather promiscuous.

Nevertheless, as this narrative will show later on, we betrayed glimmering adumbrations of the monogamy that was later to give power to, and make mighty, such tribes as embraced it. Furthermore, even at the time I was born, there were several faithful couples that lived in the trees in the neighborhood of my mother. Living in the thick of the horde did not conduce to monogamy. It was for this reason, undoubtedly, that the faithful couples went away and lived by themselves. Through many years these couples stayed together, though when the man or woman died or was eaten, the survivor invariably found a new mate.

There was one thing that greatly puzzled me during the first days of my residence in the horde. There was a nameless and incommunicable fear that rested upon all. At first it appeared to be connected wholly with direction. The horde feared the northeast. It lived in perpetual apprehension of that quarter of the compass. And every individual gazed more frequently and with greater alarm in that direction than in any other.

When Lop-Ear and I went toward the northeast to eat the stringy-rooted carrots that at that season were at their best, he became unusually timid. He was content to eat the leavings, the big tough carrots and the little ropy ones, rather than venture a short distance farther on to where the carrots were as yet untouched. When I so ventured, he scolded me and quarreled with me. He gave me to understand that in that direction was some horrible danger, but just what the horrible danger was his paucity of language would not permit him to say.

Many a good meal I got in this fashion, while he scolded and chattered vainly at me. I could not understand. I kept very alert, but I could see no danger. I calculated always the distance between myself and the nearest tree, and knew that to that haven of refuge I could outfoot the Tawny One, or old Saber-Tooth, did one or the other suddenly appear.

One late afternoon, in the village, a great uproar arose. The horde was animated with a single idea, and it was an idea of fear. The bluffside swarmed with the Folk, all gazing and pointing into the northeast. I did not know what it was, but I scrambled all the way up to the safety of my own high little cave before ever I turned around to see.

And then, across the river, away into the northeast, I saw for the first time the mystery of smoke. It was the biggest animal I had ever seen. I thought it was a monster snake, up-ended, rearing its head high among the trees and swaying back and forth. And yet, somehow, I seemed to gather from the conduct of the Folk that the smoke itself was not the danger. They appeared to fear it as the token of something else. What this something else was I could not guess. Nor could they tell me. Yet I was soon to know, and I was to know it as a thing more terrible than the Tawny One, than old Saber-Tooth, than the snakes themselves, which had seemed to me the most terrible things possible.

CHAPTER VII

Broken-Tooth was another youngster who lived by himself. His mother lived in the caves, but two more children had come after him and he had been thrust out to shift for himself. We had witnessed the performance during the several preceding days, and it had given us no little glee. Broken-Tooth did not want to go, and every time his mother left the cave he sneaked back into it. When she returned and found him there her rages were delightful. Half the horde made a practise of watching for these moments. First, from within the cave, would come her scolding and shrieking. Then we could hear sounds of the thrashing and the yelling of Broken-Tooth. About this time the two younger children joined in. And finally, like the eruption of a miniature volcano, Broken-Tooth would come flying out.

At the end of several days his final ejection was accomplished. He wailed his grief, unheeded, from the center of the open space, for at least half an hour, and then came to live with Lop-Ear and me. Our cave was small, but with squeezing there was room for three. I have no recollection of Broken-Tooth spending more than one night with us, so the accident must have happened right away.

It came in the middle of the day. In the morning we had eaten our fill of carrots, and then, made heedless by play, we had ventured on to the big trees just beyond. I cannot understand how Lop-Ear got over his habitual caution, but it must have been the play. We were having a great time playing tree tag. And such tag! We leaped ten- or fifteen-foot gaps as a matter of course. And a twenty- or twenty-five-foot deliberate drop clear down to the ground was nothing to us. In fact, I am almost afraid to say the great distances we dropped. As we grew older and heavier we found we had to be more cautious in dropping, but at that age our bodies were all strings and springs and we could do anything.

Broken-Tooth displayed remarkable agility in the game. He was "It" less frequently than any of us, and in the course of the game he discovered one difficult "slip" that neither Lop-Ear nor I was able to accomplish. To be truthful, we were afraid to attempt it.

When we were "It," Broken-Tooth always ran out to the end of a lofty branch in a certain tree. From the end of the branch to the ground it must have been seventy feet, and nothing intervened to break a fall. But about twenty feet lower down, and fully fifteen feet out from the line of the perpendicular, was the thick branch of another tree.

As we ran out the limb, Broken-Tooth, facing us, would begin teetering. This naturally impeded our progress; but there was more in the teetering than that. He teetered with his back to the jump he was to make. Just as we nearly reached him he would let go. The branch was like a spring-board. It threw him far out, backward, and as he fell he turned around sidewise in the air so as to face the other branch into which he was falling. This branch bent far down under the impact, and sometimes there was an ominous crackling; but it never broke, and out of the leaves was always to be seen the face of Broken-Tooth grinning triumphantly up at us.

I was "It" the last time Broken-Tooth tried this. He had gained the end of the branch and begun his teetering, and I was creeping out after him, when suddenly there came a low warning cry from Lop-Ear. I looked down and saw him in the main fork of the tree crouching close against the trunk. Instinctively I crouched down upon the thick limb. Broken-Tooth stopped teetering, but the branch would not stop, and his body continued bobbing up and down with the rustling leaves.

I heard the crackle of a dry twig, and looking down saw my first Fire-Man. He was creeping stealthily along on the ground and peering up into the tree. At first I thought he was a wild animal, because he wore around his waist and over his shoulders a ragged piece of bearskin. And then I saw his hands and feet, and more clearly his features. He was very much like my kind, except that he was less hairy and that his feet were less like hands than ours.

It came to me instantly, as I looked at him. This was the terror of the northeast, of which the mystery of smoke was a token. Yet I was puzzled. Certainly he was nothing of which to be afraid. Red-Eye or any of our strong men would have been more than a match for him. He was old, too, wizened with age, and the hair on his face was gray. Also he limped badly with one leg. There was no doubt at all that we could outrun him and outclimb him. He could never catch us, that was certain.

But he carried something in his hand that I had never seen before. It was a bow and arrow. But at that time a bow and arrow had no meaning for me. How was I to know that death lurked in that bent piece of wood? But Lop-Ear knew. He had evidently seen the Fire People before and knew something of their ways. The Fire-Man peered up at him and circled around the tree. And around the main trunk above the fork Lop-Ear circled too, keeping always the trunk between himself and the Fire-Man.

The latter abruptly reversed his circling. Lop-Ear, caught unawares, also hastily reversed, but did not win the protection of the trunk until after the Fire-Man had twanged the bow. I saw the arrow leap up, miss Lop-Ear, glance against a limb, and fall back to the ground. I danced up and down on my lofty perch with delight. It was a game!

The Fire-Man was throwing things at Lop-Ear as we sometimes threw things at one another.

The game continued a little longer, but Lop-Ear did not expose himself a second time. Then the Fire-Man gave it up. I leaned far out over my horizontal limb and chattered down at him. I wanted to play. I wanted to have him try to hit me with the thing. He saw me, but ignored me, turning his attention to Broken-Tooth, who was still teetering slightly and involuntarily on the end of the branch.

The first arrow leaped upward. Broken-Tooth yelled with fright and pain. It had reached its mark. This put a new complexion on the matter. I no longer cared to play, but crouched trembling close to my limb. A second arrow and a third soared up, missing Broken-Tooth, rustling the leaves as they passed through, arching in their flight, and returning to earth.

The Fire-Man stretched his bow again. He shifted his position, walking away several steps, then shifted it a second time. The bowstring twanged, the arrow leaped upward, and Broken-Tooth, uttering a terrible scream, fell off the branch. I saw him as he went down, turning over and over, all arms and legs it seemed, the shaft of the arrow projecting from his chest and appearing and disappearing with each revolution of his body.

Sheer down, screaming, seventy feet he fell, smashing to the earth with an audible thud and crunch, his body rebounding slightly and settling down again. Still he lived, for he moved and squirmed, clawing with his hands and feet. I remember the Fire-Man running forward with a stone and hammering him on the head . . . and then I remember no more.

Always, during my childhood, at this stage of the dream, did I wake up screaming with fright—to find, often, my mother or my nurse, anxious and startled, by my bedside, passing soothing hands through my hair and telling me that she was there and that there was nothing to fear.

My next dream, in the order of succession of events, begins always with the flight of Lop-Ear and myself through the forest. The Fire-Man and Broken-Tooth and the tree of the tragedy are gone. Lop-Ear and I, in a cautious panic, are fleeing through the trees. In my right leg is a burning pain; and from the flesh, protruding head and shaft from either side, is an arrow of the Fire-Man. Not only did the pull and strain of it pain me severely, but it bothered my movements and made it impossible for me to keep up with Lop-Ear.

At last I gave up, crouching in the secure fork of a tree. Lop-Ear went right on. I called to him—most plaintively, I remember—and he stopped and looked back. Then he returned to me, climbing into the fork and examining the arrow. He tried to pull it out, but one way the flesh resisted the barbed head, and the other way it resisted the feathered shaft. Also it hurt grievously, and I stopped him.

For some time we crouched there, Lop-Ear nervous and anxious to be gone, perpetually and apprehensively peering this way and that, and myself whimpering softly and sobbing. Lop-Ear was plainly in a funk, and yet his conduct in remaining by me, in spite of his fear, I take as a foreshadowing of the altruism and comradeship that have helped make man the mightiest of the animals.

Once again Lop-Ear tried to drag the arrow through the flesh, and I angrily stopped him. Then he bent down and began gnawing the shaft of the arrow with his teeth. As he did so he held it firmly in both hands so that it would not play about in the wound, and at the same time I held on to him. I often meditate upon this scene—the two of us, half-grown cubs, in the childhood of the race, the one mastering his fear, beating down his selfish impulse of flight, in order to stand by and succor the other. And there rises before me all that was there foreshadowed: I see visions of Damon and Pythias, of life-saving crews and Red Cross nurses, of martyrs and leaders of forlorn hopes, of Father Damien, and of the Christ Himself, and of all the men of earth, mighty of stature, whose strength may trace back to the elemental loins of Lop-Ear and Big-Tooth and other dim denizens of the Younger World.

When Lop-Ear had chewed off the head of the arrow, the shaft was withdrawn easily enough. I started to go on, but this time it was he that stopped me. My leg was bleeding profusely. Some of the smaller veins had doubtless been ruptured. Running out to the end of a branch, Lop-Ear gathered a handful of green leaves. These he stuffed into the wound. They accomplished the purpose, for the bleeding soon stopped. Then we went on together, back to the safety of the caves.

CHAPTER VIII

WELL do I remember that first winter after I left home. I have long dreams of sitting shivering in the cold. Lop-Ear and I sit close together, with our arms and legs about each other, blue-faced and with chattering teeth. It got particularly crisp along toward morning. In those chill early hours we slept little, huddling together in numb misery and waiting for the sunrise in order to get warm.

When we went outside there was a crackle of frost under foot. One morning we discovered ice on the surface of the quiet water in the eddy where was the drinking-place, and there was a great howdy-do about it. Old Marrow-Bone was the oldest member of the horde, and he had never seen anything like it before. I remember the worried, plaintive look that came into his eyes as he examined the ice. (This plaintive look always came into our eyes when we did not understand a thing, or when we felt the prod of some vague and inexpressible desire.) Red-Eye, too, when he investigated the ice, looked bleak and plaintive, and stared across the river into the northeast, as though in some way he connected the Fire People with this latest happening.

But we found ice only on that one morning, and that was the coldest winter we experienced. I have no memory of other winters when it was so cold. I have often thought that that cold winter was a forerunner of the countless others to come, as the ice sheet from farther north crept down over the face of the land. But we never saw that ice sheet. Many generations must have passed away before the descendants of the horde migrated south, or remained and adapted themselves to the changed conditions.

Life was hit or miss and happy go lucky with us. Little was ever planned, and less was executed. We were illogical, and inconsequential. We had no steadfastness of purpose, and it was here that the Fire People were ahead of us. They possessed all these qualities which we possessed in such small measure. Occasionally, however, especially in the realm of the emotions, we were capable of long-cherished purpose. The faithfulness of the monogamic couples I have referred to may be explained as a matter of habit; but my long desire for the Swift One cannot be so explained, any more than can the undying enmity between me and Red-Eye.

But it is our inconsequentiality and stupidity that especially distress me when I look back upon that life in the long ago. Once I found a broken gourd which happened to lie right side up and which had been filled with the rain. The water was sweet, and I drank it. I even took the gourd down to the stream and filled it with more water, some of which I drank and some of which I poured over Lop-Ear. And then I threw the gourd away. It never entered my head to fill the gourd with water and carry it into my cave. Yet often I was thirsty at night, especially after eating wild onions and water-cress, and no one ever dared leave the caves at night for a drink.

Another time I found a dry gourd, inside of which the seeds rattled. I had great fun with it for a while. But it was a plaything, nothing more. And yet it was not long after this that the using of gourds for storing water became the general practise of the horde. But I was not the inventor. The honor was due to old Marrow-Bone, and it is fair to assume that it was the necessity of his great age that brought about the innovation.

At any rate, the first member of the horde to use gourds was Marrow-Bone. He kept a supply of drinking-water in the cave that belonged to his son, the Hairless One, who permitted his father to occupy a corner of it. We used to see Marrow-Bone filling his gourd at the drinking-place and carrying it carefully up to his cave. Imitation was strong in the Folk, and first one and then another and another procured a gourd and used it in similar fashion, until it was a general practise with all of us so to store water.

Sometimes old Marrow-Bone had sick spells and was unable to leave the cave. Then the Hairless One filled the gourd for him. A little later the Hairless One deputed the task to Long-Lip, his son. And after that, even when Marrow-Bone was well again, Long-Lip continued carrying water for him. By and by, except on unusual occasions, the men never carried any water at all, leaving the task to the women and larger children. Lop-Ear and I were independent. We carried water only for ourselves, and we often mocked the young water-carriers when they were called away from play to fill the gourds.

The one big invention of the horde, during the time I lived with it, was the use of gourds. At first we stored only water in the gourds—in imitation of old Marrow-Bone. But one day some one of the women—I do not know which one—filled a gourd with blackberries and carried it to her cave. In no time all the women were carrying berries and nuts and roots in the gourds. The idea, once started, had to go on. Another stage in the evolution of the carrying receptacle was due to the women. Without doubt, some woman's gourd was too small, or else she had forgotten her gourd; be that as it may, she bent two great leaves together, pinning the seams with twigs, and carried home a bigger quantity of berries than could have been contained in the largest gourd.

So far we got, and no farther, in the transportation of supplies during the years I lived with the Folk. It never entered anybody's head to weave a basket out of willow-withes. Sometimes the men and women tied tough vines about the bundles of ferns and branches that they carried to the caves to sleep upon. Possibly in ten or twenty generations we might have worked up to the weaving of baskets. And in this connection, one thing is sure: if once we had woven withes into baskets, the next and inevitable step would have been the weaving of cloth. Clothes would have followed, and with covering our nakedness would have come modesty.

Progress was slow with us. The adults played through life, much in the same way that children play, and we played as none of the other animals. What little we learned was usually in the course of play, and was due to our curiosity and keenness of appreciation. We were just getting started, and we could not go far in a single generation. We were without weapons, without fire, and in the raw beginnings of speech. The device of writing lay so far in the future that I am appalled when I think of it.

Even I was once on the verge of a great discovery. To show you how fortuitous was development in those days let me state that had it not been for the gluttony of Lop-Ear I might have brought about the domestication of the dog. And this was something that the Fire People who lived to the northeast had not yet achieved. They were without dogs; this I knew from observation. But let me tell you how Lop-Ear's gluttony possibly set back our social development many generations.

Well, to the west of our caves was a great swamp; but to the south lay a stretch of low, rocky hills. These were little frequented for two reasons. First of all, there was no food there of the kind we ate; and next, those rocky hills were filled with the lairs of carnivorous beasts.

But Lop-Ear and I strayed over to the hills one day. We should not have strayed had we not been teasing a tiger. Please do not laugh. It was old Saber-Tooth himself. We were perfectly safe. We chanced upon him in the forest, early in the morning, and from the safety of the branches overhead we chattered down at him our dislike and hatred. And from branch to branch, and from tree to tree, we followed overhead, making an infernal row and warning all the forest-dwellers that old Saber-Tooth was coming.

We spoiled his hunting for him anyway. And we made him good and angry. He snarled at us and lashed his tail, and sometimes he paused and stared up at us quietly for a long time, as if debating in his mind some way by which he could get hold of us. But we only laughed and pelted him with twigs and the ends of branches.

This tiger-baiting was common sport among the Folk. Sometimes half the horde would follow from overhead a tiger or a lion that had ventured out in the daytime. It was our revenge; for more than one member of the horde, caught unexpectedly, had gone the way of the tiger's belly or the lion's. Also by such ordeals of helplessness and shame we taught the hunting animals to some extent to keep out of our territory. And then it was funny. It was a great game.

And so Lop-Ear and I had chased Saber-Tooth across three miles of forest. Toward the last he put his tail between his legs and fled from our gibing like a beaten cur. We did our best to keep up with him; but when we reached the edge of the forest he was no more than a streak in the distance.

I don't know what prompted us, unless it was curiosity; but after playing around a while, Lop-Ear and I ventured across the open ground to the edge of the rocky hills. We did not go far. Possibly at no time were we more than a hundred yards from the trees. Coming around a sharp corner of rock (we went very carefully, because we did not know what we might encounter), we came upon three puppies playing in the sun.

They did not see us, and we watched them for some time. They were wild dogs. In the rock wall was a horizontal fissure—evidently the lair where their mother had left them, and where they would have remained had they been obedient. But the growing life, which in Lop-Ear and me had impelled us to venture away from the forest, had driven the puppies out of the cave to frolic. I know how their mother would have punished them had she caught them.

But it was Lop-Ear and I who caught them. He looked at me, and then we made a dash for them. The puppies knew no place to run except into the lair, and we headed them off. One rushed between my legs. I squatted and grabbed him. He sank his little teeth into my arm, and I dropped him in the suddenness of the hurt and surprise. The next moment he had scurried inside.

Lop-Ear, struggling with the second puppy, scowled at me and intimated by a variety of sounds the different kinds of a fool and a bungler that I was. This made me ashamed and spurred me to valor. I grabbed the remaining puppy by the tail. He got his teeth into me once, and then I got him by the neck. Lop-Ear and I sat down and held the puppies up, and looked at them and laughed.

They were snarling and yelping and crying. Lop-Ear started suddenly. He thought he had heard something. We looked at each other in fear, realizing the danger of our position. The one thing that made animals raging demons was tampering with their young. And these puppies that raised such a racket belonged to the wild dogs. Well we knew them, running in packs, the terror of the grass-eating animals. We had watched them following the herds of cattle and bison and dragging down the calves, the aged, and the sick. We had been chased by them ourselves more than once. I had seen one of the Folk, a woman, run down by them and caught just as she reached the shelter of the woods. Had she not been tired out by the run, she might have made it into a tree. She tried, and slipped, and fell back. They made short work of her.

We did not stare at each other longer than a moment. Keeping tight hold of our prizes, we ran for the woods. Once in the security of a tall tree, we held up the puppies and laughed again. You see, we had to have our laugh out, no matter what happened.

And then began one of the hardest tasks I ever attempted. We started to carry the puppies to our cave. Our hands could not be used for climbing; most of the time they were occupied with holding our squirming captives. Once we tried to walk on the ground, but were treed by a miserable hyena, who followed along underneath. He was a wise hyena.

Lop-Ear got an idea. He remembered how we tied up bundles of leaves to carry home for beds. Breaking off some tough vines, he tied his puppy's legs together, and then, with another piece of vine passed around his neck, slung the puppy on his back. This left him with hands and feet free to climb. He was jubilant, and did not wait for me to finish tying my puppy's legs, but started on. There was one difficulty, however. The puppy wouldn't stay slung on Lop-Ear's back. It swung around to the side and then on in front. Its teeth were not tied, and the next thing it did was to sink them into Lop-Ear's soft and unprotected stomach. He let out a scream, nearly fell, and clutched a branch violently with both hands to save himself. The vine around his neck broke, and the puppy, its four legs tied, dropped to the ground. The hyena proceeded to dine.

Lop-Ear was disgusted and angry. He abused the hyena, and then went off alone through the trees. I had no reason for carrying the puppy to the cave except that I *wanted* to; and I stayed by my task. I made the work a great deal easier by elaborating on Lop-Ear's idea. Not only did I tie the puppy's legs, but I thrust a stick through his jaws and tied them together securely.

At last I got the puppy home. I imagine I had more pertinacity than the average Folk, or else I should not have succeeded. They laughed at me when they saw me lugging the puppy up to my high little cave, but I did not mind. Success crowned my efforts, and there was the puppy. He was a plaything such as none of the Folk possessed. He learned rapidly. When I played with him and he bit me, I boxed his ears, and then he did not try again to bite for a long time.

I was quite taken up with him. He was something new, and it was a characteristic of the Folk to like new things. When I saw that he refused fruits and vegetables, I caught birds for him, and squirrels and young rabbits. (We Folk were meat-eaters as well as vegetarians, and we were adept at catching small game.) The puppy ate the meat and thrived. As well as I can estimate, I must have had him over a week. And then, coming back to the cave one day with a nest full of young-hatched pheasants, I found that Lop-Ear had killed the puppy and was just beginning to eat him. I sprang for Lop-Ear—the cave was small—and we went at it tooth and nail.

And thus, in a fight, ended one of the earliest attempts to domesticate the dog. We pulled hair out in handfuls, and scratched and bit and gouged. Then we sulked and made up. After that we ate the puppy. Raw? Yes. We had not yet discovered fire. Our evolution into cooking animals lay in the tight-rolled scroll of the future.

CHAPTER IX

RED-EYE was an atavism. He was the great discordant element in our horde. He was more primitive than any of us. He did not belong with us, yet we were still so primitive ourselves that we were incapable of a cooperative effort strong enough to kill him or cast him out. Rude as was our social organization, he was, nevertheless, too rude to live in it. He tended always to destroy the horde by his unsocial acts. He was really a reversion to an earlier type, and his place was with the Tree People rather than with us who were in the process of becoming men.

He was a monster of cruelty, which is saying a great deal in that day. He beat his wives—not that he ever had more than one wife at a time, but he was married many times. It was impossible for any woman to live with him, and yet they did, out of compulsion. There was no gainsaying him.

Often do I have visions of the quiet hour before the twilight. From drinking-place and carrot-patch and berry-swamp the Folk are trooping into the open space before the caves. They dare linger no later than this, for the dreadful darkness is approaching, in which the world is given over to the carnage of the hunting animals, while the forerunners of man hide tremblingly in their holes.

There yet remain to us a few minutes before we climb to our caves. We are tired from the play of the day, and the sounds we make are subdued. Even the cubs, still greedy for fun and antics, play with restraint. The wind from the sea has died down, and the shadows are lengthening with the last of the sun's descent. And then, suddenly, from Red-Eye's cave breaks a wild screaming and the sound of blows. He is beating his wife.

At first an awed silence comes upon us. But as the blows and screams continue we break out into an insane gibbering of helpless rage. It is plain that the men resent Red-Eye's actions, but they are afraid of him. The blows cease, and a low groaning dies away, while we chatter among ourselves and the sad twilight creeps upon us.

We, to whom most happenings were jokes, never laughed during Red-Eye's wife-beatings. We knew too well the tragedy of them. On more than one morning, at the base of the cliff, did we find the body of his latest wife. He had tossed her there, after she had died, from his cave-mouth. He never buried his dead. The task of carrying away the bodies, which else would have polluted our abiding-place, he left to the horde.

Not only did Red-Eye murder his wives, but he also murdered in order to get them. When he wanted a new wife and selected another man's, he promptly killed that man. Two of these murders I saw myself. The whole horde knew, but could do nothing. We had not yet developed any government, to speak of, inside the horde. We had certain customs and visited our wrath upon the unlucky ones who violated those customs. Thus, for example, the individual who defiled a drinking-place would be attacked by every onlooker, while one who deliberately gave a false alarm was the recipient of much rough usage at our hands. But Red-Eye walked roughshod over all our customs, and we so feared him that we were incapable of the collective action necessary to punish him.

It was during the sixth winter in our cave that Lop-Ear and I discovered that we were really growing up. From the first it had been a squeeze to get in through the entrance crevice. This had had its advantages, however. It had prevented the larger folk from taking our cave away from us.

At first we dug the crumbling rocks away with our fingers until our nails got sore, when I accidentally stumbled upon the idea of using a piece of wood on the rock. This worked well. Also it worked woe. One morning, early, we had scratched out of the wall quite a heap of fragments. I gave the heap a shove over the lip of the entrance. The next moment there came up from below a howl of rage. There was no need to look. We knew the voice only too well. The rubbish had descended upon Red-Eye. We crouched down in the cave in consternation. A minute later he was at the entrance, peering in at us with his inflamed eyes and raging like a demon.

BEFORE ADAM

By JACK LONDON

Author of "The Call of the Wild," "The Sea Wolf," etc.

CHAPTER IX (*Continued*)

BUT he was too large. He could not get in to us. Suddenly he went away. This was suspicious. By all we knew of Folk nature he should have remained and had out his rage. I crept to the entrance and peeped down. I could see him just beginning to mount the bluff again. In one hand he carried a long stick. Before I could divine his plan, he was back at the entrance and savagely jabbing the stick in at us.

His thrusts were prodigious, capable of disemboweling us. We shrank back against the side walls, where we were almost out of range. But by industrious poking he got us now and again—cruel, scraping jabs with the end of the stick, which raked off the hide and hair. When we screamed with the hurt, he roared his satisfaction and jabbed the harder.

I began to grow angry. I had a temper of my own in those days, and considerable courage, too, albeit it was largely the courage of the cornered rat. I caught hold of the stick with my hands, but such was Red-Eye's strength that he jerked me into the crevice. He reached for me with his long arm, and his nails tore my flesh as I leaped back from the clutch and gained the comparative safety of the side wall.

He began poking again, and caught me a painful blow on the shoulder. Beyond shivering with fright and yelling when he was hit, Lop-Ear did nothing. I looked for a stick with which to jab back, but found only the end of a branch, an inch through and a foot long. I threw this at Red-Eye. It did no damage, though he howled with a sudden increase of rage at my daring to strike back. He began jabbing furiously. I found a fragment of rock and threw it at him, striking him on the chest.

This emboldened me, and, besides, I was now as angry as he, and had lost all fear. I ripped a fragment of rock from the wall. The piece must have weighed two or three pounds. With all my strength I slammed it full into Red-Eye's face. It nearly finished him. He staggered backward, dropping his stick, and almost fell off the cliff.

He was a ferocious sight. His face was covered with blood, and he was snarling and gnashing his fangs like a wild boar. He wiped the blood from his eyes, caught sight of me, and roared with fury. His stick was gone, so he began ripping out chunks of crumbling rock and throwing them in at me. This supplied me with ammunition. I gave him as good as he sent, and better; for he presented a good target, while he caught only glimpses of me as I snuggled against the side wall.

Suddenly he disappeared again. From the lip of the cave I saw him descending. All the horde had gathered outside and in awed silence was looking on. As he descended, the more timid ones scurried for their caves. I could see old Marrow-Bone tottering along as fast as he could. Red-Eye sprang out from the wall and finished the last twenty feet through the air. He landed alongside a mother who was just beginning the ascent. She screamed with fear, and the two-year-old child that was clinging to her released its grip and rolled at Red-Eye's feet. Both he and the mother reached for it, and he got it. The next moment the frail little body had whirled through the air and shattered against the wall. The mother ran to it, caught it up in her arms, and crouched over it, crying.

Red-Eye started over to pick up the stick. Old Marrow-Bone had tottered into his way. Red-Eye's great hand shot out and clutched the old man by the back of the neck. I looked to see his neck broken. His body went limp as he surrendered himself to his fate. Red-Eye hesitated a moment, and Marrow-Bone, shivering terribly, bowed his head and covered his face with his crossed arms. Then Red-Eye slammed him face downward to the ground. Old Marrow-Bone did not struggle. He lay there crying with the fear of death. I saw the Hairless One, out in the open space, beating his chest and bristling, but afraid to come forward. And then, in obedience to some whim of his erratic spirit, Red-Eye let the old man alone, and, passing on, recovered the stick.

He returned to the wall and began to climb up. Lop-Ear, who was shivering and peeping alongside of me, scrambled back into the cave. It was plain that Red-Eye was bent upon murder. I was desperate and angry, and fairly cool. Running back and forth along the neighboring ledges, I gathered a heap of rocks at the cave entrance. Red-Eye was now several yards beneath me, concealed for the moment by an outjut of the cliff. As he climbed, his head came into view, and I banged a rock down. It missed, striking the wall and shattering; but the flying dust and grit filled his eyes and he drew back out of view.

A chuckling and chattering arose from the horde that played the part of audience. At last there was one of the Folk who dared to face Red-Eye. As their approval and acclamation arose on the air, Red-Eye snarled down at them, and on the instant they were subdued to silence. Encouraged by this evidence of his power, he again thrust his head into view, and, by scowling and snarling and gnashing his fangs, tried to intimidate me. He scowled horribly, contracting the scalp strongly over the brows and bringing the hair down from the top of the head until each hair stood separate and pointed straight forward.

The sight chilled me, but I mastered my fear, and, with a stone poised in my hand, threatened him back. He still tried to advance. I drove the stone down at him and made a sheer miss. The next shot was a success. The stone struck him on the neck. He slipped back out of sight, but as he disappeared I could see him clawing for a grip on the wall with one hand, and with the other clutching at his throat. The stick fell clattering to the ground.

I could not see him any more, though I could hear him choking and strangling and coughing. The audience kept a deathlike silence. I crouched on the lip of the entrance and waited. The strangling and coughing died down, and I could hear him now and again clearing his throat. A little later he began to climb down. He went very quietly, pausing every moment or so to stretch his neck or to feel it with his hand.

At the sight of him descending, the whole horde, with wild screams and yells, stampeded for the woods. Old Marrow-Bone, hobbling and tottering, followed behind. Red-Eye took no notice of the flight. When he reached the ground he skirted the base of the bluff and climbed up and into his own cave. He did not once look around.

I stared at Lop-Ear and he stared back. We understood each other. Immediately, and with great caution and quietness, we began climbing up the cliff. When we reached the top we looked back. The abiding-place was deserted. Red-Eye remained in his cave, and the horde had disappeared in the depths of the forest.

We turned and ran. We dashed across the open spaces and down the slopes, unmindful of possible snakes in the grass, until we reached the woods. Up into the trees we went, and on and on, swinging our arboreal flight until we had put miles between us and the caves. And then, and not till then, in the security of a great fork, we paused, looked at each other, and began to laugh. We held on to each other, arms and legs, our eyes streaming tears, our sides aching, and laughed and laughed and laughed.

CHAPTER X

After we had out our laugh, Lop-Ear and I curved back in our flight and got breakfast in the blueberry swamp. It was the same swamp to which I had made my first journeys in the world, years before, accompanied by my mother. I had seen little of her in the intervening time. Usually, when she visited the horde at the caves, I was away in the forest. I had once or twice caught glimpses of the Chatterer in the open space, and had had the pleasure of making faces at him and angering him from the mouth of my cave. Beyond such amenities I had left my family severely alone. I was not much interested in it, and anyway I was doing very well by myself.

After eating our fill of berries, with two nestfuls of partly hatched quail eggs for dessert, Lop-Ear and I wandered circumspectly into the woods toward the river. Here was where stood my old home tree, out of which I had been thrown by the Chatterer. It was still occupied. There had been increase in the family. Clinging tight to my mother was a little baby. Also, there was a girl, partly grown, who cautiously regarded us from one of the lower branches. She was evidently my half-sister.

My mother recognized me, but she warned me away when I started to climb into the tree. Lop-Ear, who was more cautious by far than I, beat a retreat, nor could I persuade him to return. Later in the day, however, my sister came down to the ground, and there and in neighboring trees we romped and played all afternoon. And then came trouble. She was my sister, but that did not prevent her from treating me abominably, for she had inherited all the viciousness of the Chatterer. She turned upon me suddenly, in a petty rage, and scratched me, tore my hair, and sank her sharp little teeth deep into my forearm. I lost my temper. I did not injure her, but gave her what was undoubtedly the soundest spanking she had received up to that time.

How she yelled and squalled! The Chatterer, who had been away all day and who was only then returning, heard the noise and rushed for the spot. My mother also rushed, but he got there first. Lop-Ear and I did not wait his coming. We were off and away, and the Chatterer gave us the chase of our lives through the trees.

After the chase was over, and Lop-Ear and I had had out another laugh, we discovered that twilight was falling. Here was night with all its terrors upon us, and to return to the caves was out of the question. Red-Eye made that impossible. We took refuge in a tree that stood apart from others, and high up in a fork we passed the night. It was a miserable night. For the first few hours it rained heavily, then it turned cold, and a chill wind blew upon us. Soaked through, with shivering bodies and chattering teeth, we huddled in each other's arms. We missed the snug, dry cave that so quickly warmed with the heat of our bodies.

Morning found us wretched and resolved. We would not spend another such night. Remembering the tree shelters of our elders, we set to work to make one for ourselves. We built the framework of a rough nest, and on higher forks overhead even got in several ridge-poles for the roof. Then the sun came out, and under its benign influence we forgot the hardships of the night and went off in search of breakfast. After that—to show the inconsequentiality of life in those days—we fell to playing. It must have taken us all of a month, working intermittently, to make our tree house; and then, when it was completed, we never used it again.

But I run ahead of my story. When we fell to playing, after breakfast on the second day away from the caves, Lop-Ear led me a chase through the trees and down to the river. We came out upon it where a large slough entered from the blueberry swamp. It was wide at the mouth, and was practically without a current. In the dead water, just inside its mouth, lay a tangled mass of tree trunks. Some of these, what of the wear and tear of freshets and of being stranded long summers on sand bars, were seasoned and dry and without branches. They floated high in the water, and bobbed up and down or rolled over when we put our weight upon them.

Here and there between the trunks were

water cracks, and through them we could see schools of small fish, like minnows, darting back and forth. Lop-Ear and I became fishermen at once. Lying flat on the logs, keeping perfectly quiet, waiting till the minnows came close, we made swift passes with our hands. Our prizes we ate on the spot, wriggling and moist. We did not notice the lack of salt.

The mouth of the slough became our favorite playground. Here we spent many hours every day, catching fish and playing on the logs, and here, one day, we learned our first lessons in navigation. The log on which Lop-Ear was lying got adrift. He was curled up on his side, asleep. A light fan of air slowly drifted the log away from the shore, and when I noticed his predicament the distance was already too great for him to leap.

At first the episode seemed merely funny to me. But when one of the vagrant impulses of fear, common in that age of perpetual insecurity, moved within me, I was struck with my own loneliness. I was made suddenly aware of Lop-Ear's remoteness out there on that alien element a few feet away. I called a loud warning cry. He awoke frightened, and shifted his weight rashly on the log. It turned over, sousing him under. Three times again it ducked him as he tried to climb out upon it. Then he succeeded, crouching upon it and chattering with fear.

There was nothing either of us could do. We were already too far removed from the lower life forms to have the instinct for swimming, and we had not yet become sufficiently manlike to undertake it as the working out of a problem. I roamed disconsolately up and down the bank, keeping as close to Lop-Ear in his involuntary travels as I could, while he wailed and cried till it was a wonder that he did not bring down upon us every kind of hunting animal.

The hours passed. The sun climbed overhead and began its descent to the west. The light wind died down and left Lop-Ear on his log floating around a hundred feet away. And then, somehow, I know not how, Lop-Ear made the great discovery. He began paddling with his hands. At first his progress was slow and erratic. Then he straightened out and began laboriously to paddle nearer and nearer. I could not understand. I sat down and watched and waited until he gained the shore.

But he had learned something, which was more than I had done. Later in the afternoon he deliberately launched out from shore on the log. Still later he persuaded me to join him, and I, too, learned the trick of paddling. For the next few days we could not tear ourselves away from the slough. So absorbed were we in our new game that we almost neglected to eat. We even roosted in a near-by tree at night. And we forgot that Red-Eye existed.

We were always trying new logs, and we learned that the smaller the log the faster we could make it go. Also, we learned that the smaller the log the more liable it was to roll over and give us a ducking. Still another thing about small logs we learned. One day we paddled our individual logs alongside each other. And then, quite by accident, in the course of play, we discovered that when each, with one hand and foot, held on to the other's log, the logs were steadied and did not turn over. Lying side by side in this position, our outside hands and feet were left free for paddling. Our final discovery was that this arrangement enabled us to use still smaller logs and thereby gain greater speed. And there our discoveries ended. We had invented the most primitive catamaran, and we did not have sense enough to know it. It never entered our heads to lash the logs together with tough vines or stringy roots. We were content to hold the logs together with our hands and feet.

It was not until we had got over our first enthusiasm for navigation and had begun to return to our tree house to sleep at night, that we found the Swift One. I saw her first, gathering young acorns from the branches of a large oak near our tree. She was very timid. At first she kept perfectly still; but when she saw that she was discovered, she dropped to the ground and dashed wildly away. We caught occasional glimpses of her from day to day, and came to look for her when we traveled back and forth between our tree and the mouth of the slough.

And then, one day, she did not run away. She waited our coming, and made soft peace sounds. We could not get very near, however. When we approached too close, she darted suddenly away, and from a safe distance uttered the soft sounds again. This continued for some days. It took a long while to get acquainted with her, but finally it was accomplished and she joined us sometimes in our play.

I liked her from the first. She was of most pleasing appearance. She was very mild. Her eyes were the mildest I had ever seen. In this she was quite unlike the rest of the girls and women of the Folk, who were born viragos. She never made harsh, angry cries, and it seemed to be her nature to flee away from trouble rather than to remain and fight.

The mildness I have mentioned seemed to emanate from her whole being. Her eyes were larger than those of most of her kind, and they were not so deep set, while the lashes were longer and more regular. Nor was her nose so thick and squat. It had quite a bridge, and the nostrils opened downward. Her incisors were not large, nor was her upper lip long and down-hanging, nor her lower lip protruding. She was not very hairy, except on the outsides of the arms and legs and across the shoulders; and though she was thin-hipped, her calves were not twisted and gnarly.

Looking back upon her from the twentieth century through the medium of my dreams, it has always occurred to me that possibly she may have been related to the Fire People. Her father or mother might well have come from that higher stock. While such things were not common, still they did occur, and I have seen the proof of them with my own eyes, even to the extent of members of the horde turning renegade and going to live with the Tree People.

All of which is neither here nor there. The Swift One was radically different from any of the females of the horde, and I had a liking for her from the first. Her mildness and gentleness attracted me. She was never rough, and she never fought. She always ran away, and right here may be noted the significance of her name. She was a better climber than Lop-Ear or I. When we played tag we could never catch her except by accident, while she could catch us at will. She was remarkably swift in all her movements, and she had a genius for judging distances that was equaled only by her daring. Excessively timid in all other matters, she was without fear when it came to climbing or running through the trees, and Lop-Ear and I were awkward and lumbering and cowardly in comparison.

She was an orphan. We never saw her with any one, and there was no telling how long she had lived alone in the world. She must have learned early in her helpless childhood that safety lay only in flight. She was very wise and very discreet. It became a sort of game with Lop-Ear and me to try to find where she lived. It was certain that she had a tree shelter somewhere, and not very far away; but trail her as we would, we could never find it. She was willing enough to join with us at play in the daytime, but the secret of her abiding-place she guarded jealously.

CHAPTER XI

It must be remembered that the description I have just given of the Swift One is not the description that would have been given by Big-Tooth, my other self of my dreams, my prehistoric ancestor. It is by the medium of my dreams that I, the modern man, look through the eyes of Big-Tooth and see.

And so it is with much that I narrate of the events of that far-off time. There is a duality about my impressions that is too confusing to inflict upon my readers. I shall merely pause here in my narrative to indicate this duality, this perplexing mixing of personality. It is I, the modern, who look back across the centuries and weigh and analyze the emotions and motives of Big-Tooth, my other self. He did not bother to weigh and analyze. He was simplicity itself. He just lived events, without ever pondering why he lived them in his particular and often erratic way.

As I, my real self, grew older, I entered more and more into the substance of my dreams. Even in the midst of a dream one may be aware that he is dreaming, and if it be bad, may comfort himself with the thought that it is only a dream. This is a common experience with all of us. And so it was that I, the modern, often entered into my dreaming, and in the consequent strange dual personality was both actor and spectator. And right often have I, the modern, been perturbed and vexed by the foolishness, illogicality, obtuseness, and general all-around stupendous stupidity of myself, the primitive.

And one thing more before I end this digression. Have you ever dreamed that you dreamed? Dogs dream, horses dream, all animals dream. In Big-Tooth's day the half-men dreamed, and when the dreams were bad they howled in their sleep. Now I, the modern, have lain down with Big-Tooth and dreamed his dreams.

This is getting almost beyond the grip of the intellect, I know; but I do know that I have done this thing. And let me tell you that the flying and crawling dreams of Big-Tooth were as vivid to him as the falling-through-space dream is to you.

For Big-Tooth also had an other-self, and when he slept that other-self dreamed back into the past, back to the winged reptiles and the clash and the onset of dragons, and beyond that to the scurrying, rodent-like life of the tiny mammals, and, far remoter still, to the shore slime of the primeval sea. I cannot, I dare not, say more. It is all too vague and complicated and awful. I can only hint at those vast and terrific vistas through which I have peered hazily at the progression of life, not upward from the ape to man, but upward from the worm.

And now to return to my tale. I, Big-Tooth, knew not the Swift One as a creature of finer facial and bodily symmetry, with long-lashed eyes and a bridge to her nose and down-opening nostrils that made toward beauty. I knew her only as the mild-eyed young female who made soft sounds and did not fight. I liked to play with her, I knew not why, to seek food in her company, and to go bird-nesting with her. And I must confess she taught me things about tree-climbing. She was very wise, very strong, and no clinging skirts impeded her movements.

It was about this time that there was a slight defection on the part of Lop-Ear. He got into the habit of wandering off in the direction of the tree where my mother lived. He had taken a liking to my vicious sister, and the Chatterer had come to tolerate him. Also there were several other young people, progeny of the monogamic couples that lived in the neighborhood, and Lop-Ear played with them.

I could never get the Swift One to join with these young people. Whenever I visited them she dropped behind and disappeared. I remember once making a strong effort to persuade her. But she cast backward, anxious glances, then retreated, calling to me from a tree. So it was that I did not make a practise of accompanying Lop-Ear when he went to visit his new friends. I preferred the comradeship of the Swift One. Undoubtedly, had nothing happened, we should have soon mated, for our liking was mutual; but the something did happen.

One morning, the Swift One not having put in an appearance, Lop-Ear and I were down at the mouth of the slough playing on the logs. We had scarcely got out on the water when we were startled by a roar of rage. It was Red-Eye. He was crouching on the edge of the timber-jam and glowering his hatred at us. We were badly frightened, for here was no narrow-mouthed cave for refuge. But the twenty feet of water that intervened gave us temporary safety, and we plucked up courage.

Red-Eye stood up erect and began beating his hairy chest with his fist. Our two logs were side by side, and we sat on them and laughed at him. At first our laughter was half-hearted, tinged with fear, but as we became convinced of his impotence we waxed uproarious. He raged and raged at us, and ground his teeth in helpless fury. And in our fancied security we mocked and mocked him. We were ever short-sighted, we Folk.

Red-Eye abruptly ceased his breast-beating and tooth-grinding, and ran across the timber-jam to the shore. And just as abruptly our merriment gave way to consternation. It was not Red-Eye's way to forego revenge so easily. We waited in fear and trembling for whatever was to happen. It never struck us to paddle away. He came back with great leaps across the jam, one huge hand filled with round, water-washed pebbles. I am glad that he was unable to find larger missiles, say stones weighing two or three pounds, for we were no more than a score of feet away, and he surely would have killed us.

As it was, we were in no small danger. Zip! A tiny pebble whirred past with almost the force of a bullet. Lop-Ear and I began paddling frantically. Whiz-zip-bang! Lop-Ear screamed with sudden anguish. The pebble had struck him between the shoulders. Then I got one and yelled. The only thing that saved us was the exhausting of Red-Eye's ammunition. He dashed back to the gravel-bed for more, while Lop-Ear and I paddled away.

Gradually we drew out of range, though Red-Eye continued making trips for more ammunition, and the pebbles continued to whiz about us. Out in the center of the slough there was a slight current, and in our excitement we failed to notice that it was drifting us into the river. We paddled, and Red-Eye kept as close as he could to us by following along the shore. Then he discovered larger rocks. Such ammunition increased his range. One fragment, fully five pounds in weight, crashed on the log alongside of me, and such was its impact that it drove a score of splinters, like fiery needles, into my leg. Had it struck me it would have killed me.

And then the river current caught us. So wildly were we paddling that Red-Eye was the first to notice it, and our first warning was his yell of triumph. Where the edge of the current struck the slough water was a series of eddies or small whirlpools. These caught our clumsy logs and whirled them end for end, back and forth and around. We quit paddling and devoted our whole energy to holding the logs together alongside each other. In the meanwhile Red-Eye continued to bombard us, the rock fragments falling about us, splashing water on us, and menacing our lives. At the same time he gloated over us wildly and vociferously.

It happened that there was a sharp turn in the river at the point where the slough entered, and the whole main current of the river was deflected to the other bank. And toward that bank, which was the northern, we drifted rapidly, at the same time going down-stream. This quickly took us out of range of Red-Eye, and the last we saw of him, he was far out on a point of land, jumping up and down and chanting a pæan of victory.

Beyond holding the two logs together, Lop-Ear and I did nothing. We were resigned to our fate, and we remained resigned until we aroused to the fact that we were drifting along not a hundred feet from the north shore. We began to paddle for it. Here the main force of the current was flung back toward the south shore, and the result of our paddling was that we crossed the current where it was swiftest and narrowest. Before we were aware, we were out of it and in a quiet eddy.

Our logs drifted slowly and at last grounded gently on the bank. Lop-Ear and I crept ashore. The logs drifted on out of the eddy and swept away down the stream. We looked at each other, but we did not laugh. We were in a strange land, and it did not enter our minds that we could return to our own shore in the same manner that we had come.

We had learned how to cross a river, though we did not know it. And this was something that no one else of the Folk had ever done. We were the first of the Folk to set foot on the north bank of the river, and for that matter I believe the last. That they would have made the crossing in the time to come is undoubted; but the migration of the Fire People, and the consequent migration of the survivors of the Folk, set back our evolution for centuries.

Indeed, there is no telling how disastrous was the outcome of the Fire People's migration. Personally, I am prone to believe that it brought about the destruction of the Folk; that we, a branch of lower life budding toward the human, were nipped short off and perished down by the roaring surf where the river entered the sea. Of course, in such an eventuality I remain to be accounted for; but I outrun my story, and such accounting will be made before I am done.

CHAPTER XII

I HAVE no idea how long Lop-Ear and I wandered in the land north of the river. We were like mariners wrecked on a desert isle, so far as concerned the likelihood of our getting home again. We turned our backs upon the river and for weeks and months adventured in that wilderness where there were no Folk. It is very difficult for me to reconstruct our journeying, and impossible to do it from day to day. Most of it is hazy and indistinct, though here and there I have vivid recollections of things that happened.

Especially do I remember the hunger we endured on the mountains between Long Lake and Far Lake, and the calf we caught sleeping in the thicket. Also there are the Tree People who dwelt in the forest between Long Lake and the mountains. It was they who chased us into the mountains and compelled us to travel on to Far Lake.

First, after we left the river, we worked toward the west till we came to a small stream that flowed through marsh-lands. Here we turned away toward the north, skirting the marshes, and after several days arriving at what I have called Long Lake. We spent some time around its upper end, where we found food in plenty; and then, one day, in the forest, we ran foul of the Tree People. These creatures were ferocious apes, nothing more. And yet they were not so different from us. They were more hairy, it is true; their legs were a trifle more twisted and gnarly, their eyes a bit smaller, their necks a bit thicker and shorter, and their nostrils slightly more like orifices in a sunken surface; but they had no hair on their faces and on the palms of their hands and the soles of their feet, and they made sounds similar to ours, with somewhat similar meanings. After all, the Tree People and the Folk were not so unlike.

I found him first, a little withered, dried-up old fellow, wrinkle-faced and bleary-eyed and tottery. He was legitimate prey. In our world there was no sympathy between the kinds, and he was not our kind. He was a Tree-Man, and he was very old. He was sitting at the foot of a tree—evidently his tree, for we could see the tattered nest in the branches, in which he slept at night.

I pointed him out to Lop-Ear, and we made a rush for him. He started to climb, but was too slow. I caught him by the leg and dragged him back. Then we had fun. We pinched him, pulled his hair, tweaked his ears, and poked twigs into him, and all the while we laughed with streaming eyes. His futile anger was most absurd. He was a comical sight, striving to fan into flame the cold ashes of his youth, to resurrect his strength, dead and gone with the years—making woful faces in place of the ferocious ones he intended, grinding his worn teeth together, beating his meager chest with feeble fists.

Also he had a cough, and he gasped and hacked and spluttered prodigiously. Every time he tried to climb the tree we pulled him back, until at last he surrendered to his weakness and did no more than sit and weep. And Lop-Ear and I sat with him, our arms around each other, and laughed at his wretchedness.

From weeping he went to whining, and from whining to wailing, until at last he achieved a scream. This alarmed us, but the more we tried to make him cease, the louder he screamed. And then, from not far away in the forest, came a "Goëk! Goëk!" to our ears. To this there were answering cries, several of them, and from very far off we could hear a big, bass "Goëk! Goëk! Goëk!" Also the "Whoo-whoo!" call was rising in the forest all around us.

Then came the chase. It seemed it never would end. They raced us through the trees, the whole tribe of them, and nearly caught us. We were forced to take to the ground, and here we had the advantage, for they were truly the Tree People, and though they outclimbed us, we outfooted them on the ground. We broke away toward the north, the tribe howling on our track. Across the open spaces we gained, and in the brush they caught up with us, and more than once it was nip and tuck. As the chase continued, we realized that we were not their kind either, and that the bonds between us were anything but sympathetic.

They pursued us for hours. The forest seemed interminable. We kept to the glades as much as possible, but they always ended in more thick forest. Sometimes we thought we had escaped, and sat down to rest; but always, before we could recover our breath, we would hear the hateful "Whoo-whoo!" cries and the terrible "Goëk! Goëk! Goëk!" This latter sometimes terminated in a savage "Ha ha ha ha haaaaa!!!"

In this fashion were we hunted through the forest by the exasperated Tree People. At last, by mid-afternoon, the slopes began rising higher and higher and the trees were becoming smaller. Then we came out on the grassy flanks of the mountains. Here was where we could make time, and here the Tree People gave up and returned toward their forest.

The mountains were bleak and inhospitable, and three times that afternoon we tried to regain the woods. But the Tree People were lying in wait, and they drove us back. Lop-Ear and I slept that night in a dwarf tree, no larger than a bush. Here was no security, and we would have been easy prey for any hunting animal that chanced along.

In the morning, what of our new-gained respect for the Tree People, we faced into the mountains. That we had no definite plan, nor even idea, I am confident. We were merely driven on by the danger we had escaped. Of our wanderings through the mountains I have only misty memories. We were in that bleak region many days, and we suffered much, especially from fear; it was all so new and strange. Also we suffered from the cold and later from hunger.

It was a desolate land of rocks and foaming streams and clattering cataracts. We climbed and descended mighty cañons and gorges; and ever, from every view-point, there spread out before us, in all directions, range upon range, the unceasing mountains. We slept at night in holes and crevices, and on one cold night we perched on top of a slender pinnacle of rock that was almost like a tree.

And then, at last, one hot midday, dizzy with hunger, we gained the divide. From this high backbone of earth, to the north, across the diminishing, down-falling ranges, we caught a glimpse of a far lake. The sun shone upon it, and about it were open, level grass-lands, while to the eastward we saw the dark line of a wide-stretching forest.

We were two days in gaining the lake, and we were weak with hunger; but on its shore, sleeping snugly in a thicket, we found a part-grown calf. It gave us much trouble, for we knew no other way to kill than with our hands. When we had gorged our fill, we carried the remainder of the meat to the eastward forest and hid it in a tree. We never returned to that tree, for the shore of the stream that drained Far Lake was packed thick with salmon that had come up from the sea to spawn.

Westward from the lake stretched the grass-lands, and here were multitudes of bison and wild cattle. Also were there many packs of wild dogs, and as there were no trees it was not a safe place for us. We followed north along the stream for days. Then, for what reason I do not know, we abruptly left the stream and swung to the east, and then to the southeast, through a great forest. I shall not bore you with our journey. I but indicate it to show how we finally arrived at the Fire People's country.

We came out upon the river, but we did not know it for our river. We had been lost so long that we had come to accept the condition of being lost as habitual. As I look back, I see clearly how our lives and destinies are shaped by the merest chance. We did not know it was our river—there was no way of telling; and if we had not crossed it we would most probably never have returned to the horde; and I, the modern, a thousand centuries later, would never have been born.

And yet Lop-Ear and I wanted greatly to return. We had experienced homesickness on our journey, the yearning for our own kind and land; and often had I had recollections of the Swift One, the young female who made soft sounds, whom it was good to be with, and who lived by herself nobody knew where. My recollections of her were accompanied by sensations of hunger, and these I felt when I was not hungry and when I had just eaten.

But to come back to the river. Food was plentiful, principally berries and succulent roots, and on the river bank we played and lingered for days. And then the idea came to Lop-Ear. It was a visible process, the coming of the idea. I saw it. The expression in his eyes became plaintive and querulous, and he was greatly perturbed. Then his eyes went muddy, as if he had lost his grip on the inchoate thought. This was followed by the plaintive, querulous expression as the idea persisted and he clutched it anew. He looked at me and at the river and the far shore. He tried to speak, but had no sounds with which to express the idea. The result was a gibberish that made me laugh. This angered him, and he grabbed me suddenly and threw me on my back. Of course we fought, and in the end I chased him up a tree, where he secured a long branch and poked me every time I tried to get at him.

And the idea had gone glimmering. I did not know, and he had forgotten. But the next morning it awoke in him again. Perhaps it was the homing instinct in him asserting itself that made the idea persist. At any rate it was there, and clearer than before. He led me down to the water, where a log had grounded in an eddy. I thought he was minded to play, as we had played in the mouth of the slough. Nor did I change my mind as I watched him tow up a second log from farther down the shore.

It was not until we were on the logs, side by side and holding them together, and had paddled out into the current, that I learned his intention. He paused to point at the far shore, and resumed his paddling, at the same time uttering loud and encouraging cries. I understood, and we paddled energetically. The swift current caught us, flung us toward the south shore, but before we could make a landing, flung us back toward the north bank.

Here arose dissension. Seeing the north shore so near, I began to paddle for it. Lop-Ear tried to paddle for the southern. The logs swung around in circles, and we got nowhere, and all the time the forest was flashing past as we drifted down the stream. We could not fight. We knew better than to let go the grips of hands and feet that held the logs together. But we chattered and abused each other with our tongues until the current flung us toward the south bank again. That was now the nearest goal, and together and amicably we paddled for it. We landed in an eddy. That night we discovered the Fire People.

BEFORE ADAM

By JACK LONDON

Author of "The Call of the Wild," "The Sea Wolf," etc.

CHAPTER XIII

WHAT must have been a band of wandering hunters went into camp not far from the tree in which Lop-Ear and I had elected to roost for the night. The voices of these Fire People at first alarmed us, but later, when darkness had come, we were attracted by the fire. We crept cautiously and silently from tree to tree till we got a good view of the scene.

In an open space among the trees, near to the river, the fire was burning. About it were half a dozen Fire-Men. Lop-Ear clutched me suddenly, and I could feel him tremble. I looked more closely, and saw the wizened little old hunter who had shot Broken-Tooth out of the tree long before. When he got up and walked about, throwing fresh wood upon the fire, I saw that he still limped with his crippled leg. He seemed more dried up and wizened than ever, and the hair on his face was quite gray.

The other hunters were young men. I noted, lying near them on the ground, their bows and arrows, and I knew the weapons for what they were. The Fire-Men wore animal skins around their waists and across their shoulders. Their arms and legs, however, were bare, and they wore no foot-gear. As I have said before, they were not quite so hairy as we of the Folk. They did not have large heads, and between them and the Folk there was very little difference in the degree of the slant of the head back from the eyes.

They were less stooped than we, less springy in their movements. Their backbones and hips and knee-joints seemed more rigid. Their arms were not so long as ours either, and I did not notice that they ever balanced themselves, when they walked, by touching the ground on either side with their hands. Also, their muscles were more rounded and symmetrical than ours, and their faces were more pleasing. Their nose-orifices opened downward; likewise the bridges of their noses were more developed, and did not look so squat nor crushed as ours. Their lips were less flabby and pendent, and their eyeteeth did not look so much like fangs. However, they were quite as thin-hipped as we, and did not weigh much more. Take it all in all, they were less different from us than were we from the Tree People. Certainly, all three kinds were related, and not so remotely related at that.

The fire around which they were gathered was very attractive. Lop-Ear and I sat for hours watching the flames and smoke. It was most fascinating when fresh fuel was thrown on and showers of sparks went flying upward. I wanted to go closer and look at the fire, but there was no way. We were crouching in the forks of a tree on the edge of the open space, and we did not dare run the risk of being discovered.

The Fire-Men squatted around the fire and slept with their heads bowed forward on their knees. They did not sleep soundly. Their ears twitched in their sleep, and they were restless. Every little while one or another got up and threw more wood upon the fire. About the circle of light in the forest, in the darkness beyond, roamed hunting animals. Lop-Ear and I could tell them by their sounds. There were wild dogs and a hyena, and for a time there was a great yelping and snarling that awakened on the instant the whole circle of sleeping Fire-Men.

Once a lion and a lioness stood beneath our tree and gazed out with bristling hair and blinking eyes. The lion licked his chops and was nervous with eagerness, as if he wanted to go forward and make a meal. But the lioness was more cautious. It was she that discovered us, and the pair stood and looked up at us, silently, with twitching, scenting nostrils. Then they growled, looked once again at the fire, and turned away into the forest.

For a much longer time Lop-Ear and I remained and watched. Now and again we could hear the crashing of heavy bodies in the thickets and underbrush, and from the darkness of the other side, across the circle, we could see eyes gleaming in the firelight. In the distance we heard a lion roar, and from far off came the scream of some stricken animal, splashing and floundering in a drinking-place. Also from the river came a great grunting of rhinoceroses.

In the morning, after having had our sleep, we crept down to the fire. It was still smoldering, but the Fire-Men were gone. We made a circle through the forest to make sure, and then we ran to the fire. I wanted to see what it was like, and between thumb and finger I picked up a glowing coal. My cry of pain and fear, as I dropped it, stampeded Lop-Ear into the trees, and his flight frightened me after him.

The next time we came back more cautiously, and we avoided the glowing coals. We fell to imitating the Fire-Men. We squatted down by the fire, and, with heads bent forward on our knees, made believe to sleep. Then we mimicked their speech, talking to each other in their fashion and making a great gibberish. I remembered seeing the wizened old hunter poke the fire with a stick. I poked the fire with a stick, turning up masses of live coals and clouds of white ashes. This was great sport, and soon we were coated white with the ashes.

It was inevitable that we should imitate the Fire-Men in replenishing the fire. We tried at first with small pieces of wood. It was a success. The wood flamed up and crackled, and we danced and gibbered with delight. Then we began to throw on larger pieces of wood. We put on more and more, until we had a mighty fire. We dashed excitedly back and forth, dragging dead limbs and branches from out the forest. The flames soared higher and higher, and the smoke-column outtowered the trees. There was a tremendous snapping and crackling and roaring. It was the most monumental work we had ever effected with our hands, and we were proud of it. We, too, were Fire-Men, we thought, as we danced there, white gnomes in the conflagration.

The dried grass and underbrush caught fire, but we did not notice it. Suddenly a great tree on the edge of the open space burst into flames. We looked at it with startled eyes. The heat of it drove us back. Another tree caught, and another, and then half a dozen. We were frightened. The monster had broken loose. We crouched down in fear, while the fire ate around the circle and hemmed us in. Into Lop-Ear's eyes came the plaintive look that always accompanied incomprehension, and I know that in my eyes must have been the same look. We huddled down, with our arms around each other, until the heat began to reach us and the odor of burning hair was in our nostrils. Then we made a dash of it, and fled away westward through the forest, looking back and laughing as we ran.

By the middle of the day we came to a neck of land, made, as we afterward discovered, by a great curve of the river that almost completed a circle. Right across the neck lay bunched several low and partly wooded hills. Over these we climbed, looking backward at the forest, which had become a sea of flame that swept eastward before a rising wind. We continued to the west, following the river bank, and before we knew it we were in the midst of the abiding-place of the Fire People.

This abiding-place was a splendid strategic selection. It was a peninsula, protected on three sides by the curving river. On only one side was it accessible by land. This was the narrow neck of the peninsula, and here the several low hills were a natural obstacle. Practically isolated from the rest of the world, the Fire People must have here lived and prospered for a long time. In fact, I think it was their prosperity that was responsible for the subsequent migration that worked such calamity upon the Folk. The Fire People must have increased in numbers until they pressed uncomfortably against the bounds of their habitat. They were expanding, and in the course of their expanding they drove the Folk before them and settled down themselves in the caves and occupied the territory that we had occupied.

But Lop-Ear and I little dreamed of all this when we found ourselves in the Fire People's stronghold. We had but one idea, and that was to get away, though we could not forbear humoring our curiosity by peeping out upon the village. For the first time we saw the women and children of the Fire People. The latter ran for the most part naked, though the former wore skins of wild animals.

The Fire People, like ourselves, lived in caves. In the open space that sloped from the caves down to the river burned many small fires. But whether or not the Fire People cooked their food, I do not know. Lop-Ear and I did not see them cook. Yet it is my opinion that they surely must have performed some sort of rude cookery. Like us, they carried water in gourds from the river. There was much coming and going, and loud cries made by the women and children. The latter played about and cut up antics quite in the same way as did the children of the Folk, whom they more nearly resembled than did the grown Fire People resemble the grown Folk.

Lop-Ear and I did not linger long. We saw some of the part-grown boys shooting with bow and arrow, and we sneaked back into the thicker forest and made our way to the river. And there we found a catamaran, a real catamaran, one evidently made by some Fire-Man. The two logs were small and straight, and were lashed together by means of tough roots and crosspieces of wood.

This time the idea occurred simultaneously to us. We were trying to escape out of the Fire People's territory. What better way than by crossing the river on these logs? We climbed on board and shoved off. A sudden something gripped the catamaran and flung it down-stream violently against the bank. The abrupt stoppage almost whipped us off into the water. The catamaran was tied to a tree by a rope of twisted roots. This we untied before shoving off again.

By the time we had paddled well out into the current, we had drifted so far down-stream that we were in full view of the Fire People's abiding-place. So occupied were we with our paddling, our eyes fixed upon the other bank, that we knew nothing of this until aroused by a yell from the shore. We looked around. There were the Fire People, many of them, looking at us and pointing at us, and more were crawling out of the caves. We sat up to watch, and forgot all about paddling. There was a great hullabaloo on the shore. Some of the Fire-Men discharged their bows at us, and a few of the arrows fell near us, but the range was too great.

It was a great day for Lop-Ear and me. To the east the conflagration we had started was filling half the sky with smoke. And here we were, perfectly safe in the middle of the river that encircled the Fire People's stronghold. We sat and laughed at them as we dashed by, swinging south, and southeast to east, and even to northeast, and then east again, southeast and south and on around to the west, a great double curve where the river nearly tied a knot in itself.

As we swept on to the west, the Fire People far behind, a familiar scene flashed upon our eyes. It was the great drinking-place where we had wandered once or twice to watch the circus of the animals when they came down to drink. Beyond it, we knew, was the carrot-patch, and beyond that the caves and the abiding-place of the horde. We began to paddle for the bank that slid swiftly past, and before we knew it we were down upon the drinking-places. There were the women and children, the water-carriers, a number of them, filling their gourds. At sight of us they stampeded madly up the runways, leaving behind them a trail of gourds they had dropped.

We landed, and of course we neglected to tie up the catamaran, which floated off down the river. Right cautiously we crept up a runway. The Folk had all disappeared into their holes, though here and there we could see a face peering out at us. There was no sign of Red-Eye. We were home again. And that night we slept in our own little cave high up on the cliff, though first we had to evict a couple of pugnacious youngsters who had taken possession.

CHAPTER XIV

THE months came and went. The drama and tragedy of the future were yet to come upon the stage, and in the meantime we pounded nuts and lived. It was a good year, I remember, for nuts. We used to fill gourds with nuts and carry them to the pounding-places. We placed them in depressions in the rock, and, with a piece of rock in our hands, we cracked them, and ate them as we cracked.

It was the fall of the year when Lop-Ear and I returned from our long adventure journey, and the winter that followed was mild. I made frequent trips to the neighborhood of my old home-tree, and frequently I searched the whole territory that lay between the blueberry-swamp and the mouth of the slough where Lop-Ear and I had learned navigation, but no clue could I get to the Swift One. She had disappeared. And I wanted her. But all my search was vain.

Life was not monotonous at the caves, however. There was Red-Eye to be considered. Lop-Ear and I never knew a moment's peace except when we were in our own little cave. In spite of the enlargement of the entrance we had made, it was still a tight squeeze for us to get in. And though from time to time we continued to enlarge the entrance, it was still too small for Red-Eye's monstrous body. But he never stormed our cave again. He had learned the lesson well, and he carried on his neck a bulging lump to show where I had hit him with the rock. This lump never went away, and it was prominent enough to be seen at a distance. I often took great delight in looking at that evidence of my handiwork, and sometimes, when I was myself assuredly safe, the sight of it caused me to laugh.

While the other Folk would not have come to our rescue had Red-Eye proceeded to tear Lop-Ear and me to pieces before their eyes, nevertheless they sympathized with us. Possibly it was not sympathy but the expression of their hatred for Red-Eye; at any rate they always warned us of his approach. Whether in the forest, at the drinking-places, or in the open space before the caves, they were always quick to warn us. Thus we had the advantage of many eyes in our feud with Red-Eye, the atavism.

Once he nearly got me. It was early in the morning, and the Folk were not yet up. The surprise was complete. I was cut off from the way up the cliff to my cave. Before I knew it I had dashed into the double cave—the cave where Lop-Ear had first eluded me long years before, and where old Saber-Tooth had come to discomfiture when he pursued the two Folk. By the time I had got through the connecting passage between the two caves, I discovered that Red-Eye was not following me. The next moment he charged into the cave from the outside. I slipped back through the passage, and he charged out and around and in upon me again. I merely repeated my performance of slipping through the passage.

He kept me there half a day before he gave up. After that, when Lop-Ear and I were reasonably sure of gaining the double cave, we did not retreat up the cliff to our own when Red-Eye came upon the scene. All we did was to keep an eye on him and see that he did not cut across our line of retreat.

It was during this winter that Red-Eye killed his latest wife with abuse and repeated beatings. I have called him an atavism, but in this he was worse than an atavism, for the males of the lower animals do not maltreat and murder their mates. In this I take it that Red-Eye, in spite of his tremendous atavistic tendencies, foreshadowed the coming of man, for it is the males of the human species only that murder their mates.

As was to be expected, with the doing away of one wife Red-Eye proceeded to get another. He decided upon the Singing One. She was the granddaughter of old Marrow-Bone, and the daughter of the Hairless One. She was a young thing, greatly given to singing at the mouth of her cave in the twilight, and she had but recently mated with Crooked-Leg. He was a quiet individual, molesting no one and not given to bickering with his fellows. He was no fighter anyway. He was small and lean, and not so active on his legs as the rest of us.

Red-Eye never committed a more outrageous deed. It was in the quiet at the end of the day, when we began to congregate in the open space before climbing into our caves. Suddenly the Singing One dashed up a runway from a drinking-place, pursued by Red-Eye. She ran to her husband. Poor little Crooked-Leg was terribly scared. But he was a hero. He knew that death was upon him, yet he did not run away. He stood up, and chattered, bristling, showing his teeth.

Red-Eye roared with rage. It was an offense to him that any of the Folk should dare to withstand him. His hand shot out and clutched Crooked-Leg by the neck. The latter sank his teeth into Red-Eye's arm; but the next moment, with a broken neck, Crooked-Leg was floundering and squirming on the ground. The Singing One screeched and gibbered. Red-Eye seized her by the hair of her head and dragged her toward his cave. He handled her roughly when the climb began, and he dragged and hauled her up into the cave.

We were very angry, insanely, vociferously angry. Beating our chests, bristling, and gnashing our teeth, we gathered together in our rage. We felt the prod of gregarious instinct, the drawing together as though for united action, the impulse toward cooperation. In dim ways this need for united action was impressed upon us. But there was no way to achieve it because there was no way to express it. We did not turn to, all of us, and destroy Red-Eye, because we lacked a vocabulary. We were vaguely thinking thoughts for which there were no thought-symbols. These thought-symbols were yet to be slowly and painfully invented.

We tried to freight sound with the vague thoughts that flitted like shadows through our consciousness. The Hairless One began to chatter loudly. By his noises he expressed anger against Red-Eye and desire to hurt him. Thus far he got, and thus far we understood. But when he tried to express the cooperative impulse that stirred within him, his noises became gibberish. Then Big-Face, with brow bristling and hands pounding his chest, began to chatter. One after another of us joined in the orgy of rage, until even old Marrow-Bone was mumbling and spluttering with his cracked voice and withered lips. Some one seized a stick and began pounding a log. In a moment he had struck a rhythm. Unconsciously our yells and exclamations yielded to this rhythm. It had a soothing effect upon us; and before we knew it, our rage forgotten, we were in the full swing of a hee-hee council.

These hee-hee councils splendidly illustrate the inconsequentiality of the Folk. Here were we, drawn together by mutual rage and the impulse toward cooperation, led off into forgetfulness by the establishment of a rude rhythm. We were sociable and gregarious, and these singing and laughing councils satisfied us. In some ways the hee-hee council was an adumbration of the councils of primitive man, and of the great national assemblies and international conventions of latter-day man. But we Folk of the Younger World lacked speech, and whenever we were so drawn together we precipitated Babel, out of which arose a unanimity of rhythm that contained within itself the essentials of art yet to come. It was art nascent.

There was nothing long-continued about these rhythms that we struck. A rhythm was soon lost, and pandemonium reigned until we could find the rhythm again or start a new one. Sometimes half a dozen rhythms would be swinging simultaneously, each one backed by a group that strove ardently to drown out the others.

In the quiet intervals each chattered, cut up, hooted, screeched, and danced, himself sufficient unto himself, filled with his own ideas and volitions to the exclusion of all others, a veritable center of the universe, divorced for the time being from any unanimity with the other universe centers leaping and yelling around him. Then would come the rhythm—a clapping of hands; the beating of a stick upon a log; a repeated leaping in some particular manner; or the chanting of one that uttered, explosively and regularly, with inflection that rose and fell, "A-bang, a-bang! A-bang, a-bang!" One after another of the self-centered Folk would yield to the suggestion, and soon all would be dancing or chanting in chorus. "Ha-ah, ha-ah, ha-ah-ha!" was one of our favorite choruses, and another was, "Eh-wah, eh-wah, eh-wah-hah!"

And so, with mad antics, leaping, reeling, and overbalancing, we danced and sang in the somber twilight of the primeval world, inducing forgetfulness, achieving unanimity, and working ourselves up into sensuous frenzy. And so it was that our rage against Red-Eye was soothed away by art, and we screamed the wild choruses of the hee-hee council until the night warned us of its terrors and we crept away to our holes in the rocks, calling softly to one another, while the stars came out and darkness settled down.

We were afraid only of the dark. We had no germs of religion, no conceptions of an unseen world. We knew only the real world, and the things we feared were the real things, the concrete dangers, the flesh-and-blood animals that preyed. It was they that made us afraid of the dark, for darkness was the time of the hunting animals. It was then that they came out of their lairs and pounced upon us from the dark wherein they lurked invisible.

Possibly it was out of this fear of the real denizens of the dark that the fear of the unreal denizens was later to develop and to culminate in a whole, mighty unseen world. As imagination grew it is likely that the fear of death increased until the Folk that were to come projected this fear into the dark and peopled the dark with spirits. I think the Fire People had already begun to be afraid of the dark in this fashion; but the reasons we Folk had for breaking up our hee-hee councils and fleeing to our holes were old Saber-Tooth, the lions and the jackals, the wild dogs and the wolves, and all the other hungry, meat-eating breeds.

CHAPTER XV

Lop-Ear got married. It was the second winter after our adventure journey, and it was most unexpected. He gave me no warning. The first I knew was one twilight when I climbed the cliff to our cave. I squeezed into the entrance and there I stopped. There was no room for me. Lop-Ear and his mate were in possession, and she was none other than my sister, the daughter of my stepfather, the Chatterer.

I tried to force my way in. There was space only for two, and that space was already occupied. Also, they had me at a disadvantage, and what of the scratching and hair-pulling I received, I was glad to retreat. I slept that night, and for many nights, in the connecting passage of the double cave. From my experience it seemed reasonably safe. As the two Folk had dodged old Saber-Tooth, and as I had dodged Red-Eye, so it seemed to me that I could dodge the hunting animals by going back and forth between the two caves.

I had forgotten the wild dogs. They were small enough to go through any passage that I could squeeze through. One night they nosed me out. Had they entered both caves at the same time they would have got me. As it was, followed by some of them through the passage, I dashed out at the mouth of the other cave. Outside were the rest of the wild dogs. They leaped for me, as I sprang for the cliff wall and began to climb. One of them, a lean and hungry brute, caught me in mid-leap. His teeth sank into my thigh-muscles, and he nearly dragged me back. He held on, but I made no effort to dislodge him, devoting my whole energy to climbing out of reach of the rest of the brutes.

Not until I was safe from them did I turn my attention to that live agony on my thigh. And then, a dozen feet above the snapping pack that leaped and scrambled against the wall and fell back, I got the dog by the throat and slowly throttled him. I was a long time doing it. He clawed and ripped my hair and hide with his hind paws, and ever he jerked and lunged with his weight to drag me from the wall.

At last his teeth opened and released my torn flesh. I carried his body up the cliff with me, and perched out the night in the entrance of my old cave, wherein were Lop-Ear and my sister. But first I had to endure a storm of abuse from the aroused horde for being the cause of the disturbance. I had my revenge. From time to time, as the noise of the pack below eased down, I dropped a rock and started it up again. Whereupon, from all around, the abuse of the exasperated Folk began afresh. In the morning I shared the dog with Lop-Ear and his wife, and for several days the three of us were neither vegetarians nor fruitarians.

Lop-Ear's marriage was not a happy one, and the consolation about it is that it did not last very long. Neither he nor I was happy during that period. I was lonely. I suffered the inconvenience of being cast out of my safe little cave, and somehow I did not make it up with any other of the young males. I suppose my long-continued chumming with Lop-Ear had become a habit.

I might have married, it is true; and most likely I should have done so, had it not been for the dearth of females in the horde. This dearth, it is fair to assume, was caused by the exorbitance of Red-Eye, and it illustrates the menace he was to the existence of the horde. Then there was the Swift One, whom I had not forgotten.

At any rate, during the period of Lop-Ear's marriage I knocked about from pillar to post, in danger every night that I slept, and never comfortable. One of the Folk died, and his widow was taken into the cave of another one of the Folk. I took possession of the abandoned cave, but it was wide-mouthed, and after Red-Eye nearly trapped me in it one day, I returned to sleeping in the passage of the double cave. During the summer, however, I used to stay away from the abiding-place for weeks, sleeping in a tree-shelter I made near the mouth of the slough.

I have said that Lop-Ear was not happy. My sister was the daughter of the Chatterer, and she made Lop-Ear's life miserable for him. In no cave was there so much squabbling and bickering. If Red-Eye was a Bluebeard, Lop-Ear was henpecked; and I imagine that Red-Eye was too shrewd ever to covet Lop-Ear's wife.

Fortunately for Lop-Ear, she died. An unusual thing happened that summer. Late, almost at the end of it, a second crop of the stringy-rooted carrots sprang up. These unexpected second-crop roots were young and juicy and tender, and for some time the carrot-patch was the favorite feeding-place of the horde. One morning, early, several score of us were there making our breakfast. On one side of me was the Hairless One. Beyond him were his father and his son, old Marrow-Bone and Long-Lip. On the other side of me were Lop-Ear and my sister, she being next to me.

There was no warning. On the sudden, both the Hairless One and my sister sprang and screamed. At the same instant I heard the thud of the arrows that transfixed them. The next instant they were down on the ground, floundering and gasping, and the rest of us were stampeding for the trees. An arrow drove past me and entered the ground, its feathered shaft vibrating and oscillating from the impact of its arrested flight. I remember clearly how I swerved as I ran, to go past it, and that I gave it a needlessly wide berth. I must have shied at it as a horse shies at an object it fears.

Lop-Ear took a smashing fall as he ran beside me. An arrow had driven through the calf of his leg and tripped him. He tried to run, but was tripped and thrown by it a second time. He sat up, crouching, trembling with fear, and called to me pleadingly. I dashed back. He showed me the arrow. I caught hold of it to pull it out, as he had once done for me, but the consequent hurt made him seize my hand and stop me. A flying arrow passed between us. Another struck a rock, splintered, and fell to the ground. This was too much. I pulled, suddenly, with all my might. Lop-Ear screamed as the arrow came out, and struck at me angrily. But the next moment we were in full flight again.

I looked back. Old Marrow-Bone, deserted and far behind, was tottering silently along in his handicapped race with death. Sometimes he almost fell, and once he did fall; but no more arrows were coming. He scrambled weakly to his feet. Age burdened him heavily, but he did not want to die. The three Fire-Men, who were now running forward from their forest ambush, could easily have got him, but they did not try. Perhaps he was too old and tough. But they did want the Hairless One and my sister, for as I looked back from the trees I could see the Fire-Men beating in their heads with rocks. One of the Fire-Men was the wizened old hunter who limped.

We went on through the trees toward the caves—an excited and disorderly mob that drove before it to their holes all the small life of the forest, and that set the blue jays screaming impudently. Now that there was no immediate danger, Long-Lip waited for his grandfather, Marrow-Bone; and with the gap of a generation between them, the old fellow and the youth brought up our rear.

And so it was that Lop-Ear became a bachelor once more. That night I slept with him in the old cave, and our old life of chumming began again. The loss of his mate seemed to cause him no grief. At least he showed no signs of it, nor of need for her. It was the wound in his leg that seemed to bother him, and it was all of a week before he got back again to his old spryness.

Marrow-Bone was the only old member in the horde. Sometimes, on looking back upon him, when the vision of him is most clear, I note a striking resemblance between him and the father of my father's gardener. The gardener's father was very old, very wrinkled, and withered; and when he peered through his tiny, bleary eyes and mumbled with his toothless gums, he looked and acted for all the world like old Marrow-Bone. This resemblance used to frighten me as a child. I always ran when I saw the old man tottering along on his two canes. Old Marrow-Bone even had a bit of sparse and straggly white beard that seemed identical with the whiskers of the old man.

As I have said, Marrow-Bone was the only old member of the horde. He was an exception. The Folk never lived to old age. Middle age was fairly rare. They died as my father had died, as Broken-Tooth had died, as my sister and the Hairless One had just died—abruptly and brutally, in the full possession of their faculties, in the full swing and rush of life. Natural death? To die violently was the natural way of dying in those days.

I never knew of a case of death from old age among the Folk. Even Marrow-Bone did not die that way, and he was the only one in my generation who had the chance. A bad crippling, any serious accidental or temporary impairment of the faculties, meant swift death. As a rule, these deaths were not witnessed. Members of the horde simply dropped out of sight. They left the caves in the morning, and they never came back. They disappeared—into the ravenous maws of the hunting creatures.

This inroad of the Fire People on the carrot-patch was the beginning of the end, though we did not know it. The hunters of the Fire People began to appear more frequently as the time went by. They came in twos and threes, creeping silently through the forest, with their flying arrows able to annihilate distance and bring down prey from the top of the loftiest tree without themselves climbing into it. The bow and arrow was like an enormous extension of their leaping and striking muscles, so that virtually they could leap and kill at a hundred feet and more. This made them far more terrible than Saber-Tooth himself. And then they were very wise. They had speech that enabled them to reason more effectively than we, and in addition they understood cooperation.

We Folk came to be very circumspect when we were in the forest. We were more alert and vigilant, and timid. No longer were the trees a protection to be relied upon. No longer could we perch on a branch and laugh down at our carnivorous enemies on the ground. The Fire People were carnivorous, with claws and fangs a hundred feet long, the most terrible of all the hunting animals that ranged the primeval world.

One morning, before the Folk had dispersed to the forest, there was a panic among the water-carriers and those who had gone down to the river to drink. The whole horde fled to the caves. It was our habit, at such times, to flee first and investigate afterward. We waited in the mouths of our caves and watched. After some time a Fire-Man stepped cautiously into the open space. It was the little wizened old hunter. He stood for a long time and watched us, looking our caves and the cliff wall up and down. He descended one of the runways to a drinking-place, returning a few minutes later by another runway. Again he stood and watched us carefully for a long time. Then he turned on his heel and limped into the forest, leaving us calling querulously and plaintively to one another from the cave-mouths.

CHAPTER XVI

I FOUND her down in the old neighborhood near the blueberry-swamp, where my mother lived and where Lop-Ear and I had built our first tree-shelter. It was unexpected. As I came under the tree I heard the familiar soft sound and looked up. There she was, the Swift One, sitting on a limb and swinging her legs back and forth as she looked at me.

I stood still for some time. The sight of her had made me very happy. And then an unrest and a pain began to creep in on this happiness. I started to climb the tree after her, and she retreated slowly out the limb. Just as I reached for her, she sprang through the air and landed in the branches of the next tree. From amid the rustling leaves she peeped out at me and made soft sounds. I leaped straight for her, and after an exciting chase the situation was duplicated, for there she was, making soft sounds and peeping out from the leaves of a third tree.

It was borne in upon me that somehow it was not the same now as in the old days before Lop-Ear and I had gone on our adventure journey. I wanted her, and I knew that I wanted her. And she knew it too. That was why she would not let me come near her. I forgot that she was truly the Swift One, and that in the art of climbing she had been my teacher. I pursued her from tree to tree, and ever she eluded me, peeping back at me with kindly eyes, making soft sounds, and dancing and leaping and teetering before me just out of reach. The more she eluded me, the more I wanted to catch her, and the lengthening shadows of the afternoon bore witness to the futility of my effort.

As I pursued her, or sometimes rested in an adjoining tree and watched her, I noticed the change in her. She was larger, heavier, more grown up. Her lines were rounder, her muscles fuller, and there was about her that indefinite something of maturity that was new to her and that incited me on. Four years she had been gone—four years at the very least, and the change in her was marked.

Where she went, why she went, and what happened to her during that time, I do not know. There was no way for her to tell me, any more than there was a way for Lop-Ear and me to tell the Folk what we had seen when we were away. The chance is that, like us, she had gone off on an adventure journey, and by herself. On the other hand, it is possible that Red-Eye may have been the cause of her going. From subsequent events I am led to believe that she must have traveled far to the south, across a range of mountains and down to the banks of a strange river, away from any of her kind. Many Tree People lived down there, and I think it must have been they who finally drove her back to the horde and to me. My reasons for this I shall explain later.

The shadows grew longer, and I pursued more ardently than ever, and still I could not catch her. She made believe that she was trying desperately to escape me, and all the time she managed to keep just beyond reach. I forgot everything—time, the oncoming of night, and my meat-eating enemies. I was insane with love of her, and with anger, too, because she would not let me come up with her. It was strange how this anger against her seemed to be part of my desire for her.

As I have said, I forgot everything. In racing across an open space I ran full tilt upon a colony of snakes. They did not deter me. I was mad. They struck at me, but I ducked and dodged and ran on. Then there was a python that ordinarily would have sent me screeching to a tree-top. He did run me into a tree; but the Swift One was going out of sight, and I sprang back to the ground and went on. It was a close shave. Then there was my old enemy, the hyena. From my conduct he was sure something was going to happen, and he followed me for an hour. Once we exasperated a band of wild pigs, and they took after us. The Swift One dared a wide leap between trees that was too much for me. I had to take to the ground. There were the pigs. I didn't care. I struck the earth within a yard of the nearest one. They flanked me as I ran, and chased me into two different trees out of the line of my pursuit of the Swift One. I ventured the ground again, doubled back, and crossed a wide open space with the whole band grunting, bristling, and tusk-gnashing at my heels.

If I had tripped or stumbled in that open space, there would have been no chance for me. But I didn't. And I didn't care whether I did or not. I was in such mood that I would have faced old Saber-Tooth himself, or a score of arrow-shooting Fire People. Such was the madness of love with me. With the Swift One it was different. She was very wise. She did not take any real risks; and I remember, on looking back across the centuries to that wild love-chase, that when the pigs delayed me she did not run away very fast, but waited, rather, for me to take up the pursuit again. Also, she directed her retreat before me, going always in the direction she wanted to go.

At last came the dark. She led me around the mossy shoulder of a cañon wall that outjutted among the trees. After that we penetrated a dense mass of underbrush that scraped and ripped me in passing. But she never ruffled a hair. She knew the way. In the midst of the thicket was a large oak. I was very close to her when she climbed it; and in the forks, in the nest-shelter I had sought so long and vainly, I caught her.

The hyena had taken our trail again, and he now sat down on the ground and made hungry noises. But we did not mind, and we laughed at him when he snarled and went away through the thicket. It was the springtime, and the night noises were many and varied. As was the custom at that time of the year, there was much fighting among the animals. From the nest we could hear the squealing and neighing of wild horses, the trumpeting of elephants, and the roaring of lions. But the moon came out, and the air was warm, and we laughed and were unafraid.

I remember, next morning, that we came upon two ruffled cock-birds that fought so ardently that I went right up to them and caught them by their necks. Thus did the Swift One and I get our wedding breakfast.

BEFORE ADAM

By JACK LONDON

Author of "The Call of the Wild," "The Sea Wolf," etc.

CHAPTER XVI *(Continued)*

THERE is no telling how long we might have lived in the Swift One's tree-shelter. But one day, while we were away, the tree was struck by lightning. Great limbs were riven, and the nest was demolished. I started to rebuild, but the Swift One would have nothing to do with it. She was greatly afraid of lightning, and I could not persuade her back into the tree. So it came about that, our honeymoon over, we went to the caves to live. As Lop-Ear had evicted me from the cave when he got married, I now evicted him; and the Swift One and I settled down in it, while he slept at night in the connecting passage of the double cave.

And with our coming to live with the horde came trouble. Red-Eye had had I don't know how many wives since the Singing One, who had gone the way of her predecessors. At that time he had a little, soft, spiritless thing that whimpered and wept all the time, whether he beat her or not; and her passing was a question of very little time. Even before she died, Red-Eye set his eyes on the Swift One; and immediately afterward, the persecution of the Swift One began.

Well for her that she was the Swift One, that she had that amazing aptitude for swift flight through the trees. She needed all her wisdom and daring in order to keep out of the clutches of Red-Eye.

To make the situation worse, she fell ill. It must have been a touch of the malaria from which we sometimes suffered; but whatever it was, it made her dull and heavy. She did not have the accustomed spring to her muscles, and was indeed in poor shape for flight when Red-Eye cornered her near the lair of the wild dogs several miles south of the caves. In her normal condition, she would have circled around him, beaten him in the straightaway, and gained the protection of our small-mouthed cave. But this time she could not circle him. She was too dull and slow. Each time he headed her off, until she gave over the attempt and devoted her energies wholly to keeping out of his clutches.

Had she not been sick it would have been child's play for her to elude him; but as it was, it required all her caution and cunning. It was to her advantage that she could travel on thinner branches than he, and make wider leaps. Also, she was an unerring judge of distance, and she had an instinct for knowing the strength of twigs, branches, and rotten limbs.

It was an interminable chase. Round and round and back and forth for long stretches through the forest they dashed. There was great excitement among the other Folk. They set up a wild chattering, which was loudest when Red-Eye was at a distance, and which quieted when the chase led him near. They were impotent onlookers. The females screeched and gibbered, and the males beat their chests in helpless rage. Big-Face was especially angry, and he did not hush his racket so much as the others did.

As for me, I played no brave part. I know I was anything but a hero. But of what use would it have been for me to encounter Red-Eye? He was the mighty monster, the primitive brute, and there was no hope for me in a conflict of strength. He would have killed me, torn me limb from limb, and the situation would have remained unchanged. He would have caught the Swift One before she could gain the cave. As it was, I could only look on in helpless fury, and dodge out of the way and cease my raging when he came too near.

The hours passed. It was late afternoon. And still the chase went on. Red-Eye was bent upon exhausting the Swift One. After a long time she began to tire and could no longer maintain her headlong flight. Then it was that she began going far out on the thinnest branches, where he could not follow. Thus she might have got a breathing-spell, but Red-Eye was fiendish. Unable to follow her, he dislodged her by shaking her off. With all his strength and weight, he would shake the branch back and forth until he snapped her off as one would snap a fly from a whip-lash. The first time, she saved herself by falling into branches lower down. Another time, though they did not save her from striking the ground, they broke her fall. Still another time, so fiercely did he snap her from the branch that she was flung clear across a gap into another tree. It was remarkable, the way she gripped and saved herself. Only when driven to it did she seek the temporary safety of the thin branches. But she was so tired that she could not otherwise avoid him, and time after time she was compelled to take to them.

Still the chase went on, and still the Folk screeched, beat their chests, and gnashed their teeth. Then came the end. It was almost twilight. Trembling, panting, struggling for breath, the Swift One clung pitiably to a high, thin branch. It was thirty feet from the ground, and nothing intervened. Red-Eye swung back and forth on the same branch farther down. It became a pendulum, swinging wider and wider with every lunge. Then he reversed suddenly, just before the downward swing was completed. The Swift One's grips were torn loose, and, screaming, she was hurled toward the ground.

But she righted herself in mid-air and descended feet first. Ordinarily, the spring in her legs would have eased the shock of impact with the ground. But she was exhausted. She could not exercise this spring. Her legs gave under her, having only partly met the shock, and she crashed over on her side. This, as it turned out, did not injure her, but it did knock the breath from her lungs. She lay helpless and struggling for air.

Red-Eye rushed upon her and seized her. With his gnarly fingers twisted into the hair of her head, he stood up and roared in triumph and defiance at the awed Folk that watched from the trees. Then it was that I went mad. Caution was thrown to the winds; forgotten was the will of my flesh to live. Even as Red-Eye roared, from behind I dashed upon him. So unexpected was my charge that I knocked him off his feet. I twined my arms and legs around him and strove to hold him down. This would have been impossible to accomplish had he not held tightly with one hand to the Swift One's hair.

Encouraged by my conduct, Big-Face became a sudden ally. He charged in, sank his teeth in Red-Eye's arm, and ripped and tore at his face. This was the time for the rest of the Folk to have joined in. It was the chance to do for Red-Eye for all time. But they remained afraid in the trees.

It was inevitable that Red-Eye should win in the struggle against the two of us. The reason he did not finish us off immediately was that the Swift One clogged his movements. She had regained her breath and was beginning to resist. He would not release his clutch on her hair, and this handicapped him. He got a grip on my arm. It was the beginning of the end for me. He began to draw me toward him into a position where he could sink his teeth into my throat. His mouth was open, and he was grinning. And yet, though he had just begun to exert his strength, in that moment he wrenched my shoulder so that I suffered from it for the remainder of my life.

And in that moment something happened. There was no warning. A great body smashed down upon the four of us locked together. We were driven violently apart and rolled over and over, and in the suddenness of surprise we released our holds on one another. At the moment of the shock Big-Face screamed terribly. I did not know what had happened, though I smelled tiger and caught a glimpse of striped fur as I sprang for a tree.

It was old Saber-Tooth. Aroused in his lair by the noise we had made, he had crept upon us unnoticed. The Swift One gained the next tree to mine, and I immediately joined her. I put my arms around her and held her close to me while she whimpered and cried softly. From the ground came a snarling and crunching of bones. It was Saber-Tooth making his supper off what had been Big-Face. From beyond, with inflamed rims and eyes, Red-Eye peered down. Here was a monster mightier than he. The Swift One and I turned and went away quietly through the trees toward the cave, while the Folk gathered overhead and showered down abuse and twigs and branches upon their ancient enemy. He lashed his tail and snarled, but went on eating.

And in such fashion were we saved. It was an accident, the sheerest accident. Else would I have died, there in Red-Eye's clutch, and there would have been no bridging of a thousand centuries down to a progeny that reads newspapers and rides on electric cars—aye, and that writes narratives of bygone happenings even as this is written.

CHAPTER XVII

It was in the early fall of the following year that it happened. After his failure to get the Swift One, Red-Eye had taken another wife; and, strange to relate, she was still alive. Stranger still, they had a baby several months old—Red-Eye's first child. His previous wives had never lived long enough to bear him children. The year had gone well for all of us. The weather had been exceptionally mild and food plentiful. I remember especially the turnips of that year. The nut-crop was also very heavy, and the wild plums were larger and sweeter than usual.

In short, it was a golden year. And then it happened. It was in the early morning, and we were surprised in our caves. In the chill gray light we awoke from sleep, most of us to encounter death. The Swift One and I were aroused by a pandemonium of screeching and gibbering. Our cave was the highest of all on the cliff, and we crept to the mouth and peered down. The open space was filled with the Fire People. Their cries and yells were added to the clamor, but they had order and plan, while we Folk had none. Each one of us fought and acted for himself, and no one of us knew the extent of the calamity that was befalling us.

By the time we got to stone-throwing, the Fire People had massed thick at the base of the cliff. Our first volley must have mashed some heads, for when they swerved back from the cliff three of their number were left upon the ground. These were struggling and floundering, and one was trying to crawl away. But we fixed them. By this time we males were roaring with rage, and we rained rocks upon the three men that were down. Several of the Fire-Men returned to drag them into safety, but our rocks drove the rescuers back.

The Fire People became enraged. Also they became cautious. In spite of their angry yells, they kept at a distance and sent flights of arrows against us. This put an end to the rock-throwing. By the time half a dozen of us had been killed and a score injured, the rest of us retreated inside our caves. While the Swift One remained well within the cave, trembling with fear and making low wailing sounds because I would not come in, I crouched at the entrance and watched. I was not out of range, but the distance was great enough to spoil effective shooting, and the Fire People did not waste many arrows on me. And I was curious. I wanted to see.

The fighting had now become intermittent. It was a sort of deadlock. We were in the caves, and the question with the Fire People was how to get us out. They did not dare come in after us, and in general we would not expose ourselves to their arrows. Occasionally, when one of them drew in close to the base of the cliff, one or another of the Folk would smash a rock down. In return, he would be transfixed by half a dozen arrows. This ruse worked well for some time, but finally the Folk no longer were inveigled into showing themselves. The deadlock was complete.

Behind the Fire People I could see the little wizened old hunter directing it all. They obeyed him, and went here and there at his commands. Some of them went into the forest and returned with loads of dry wood, leaves, and grass. All the Fire People drew in closer. While most of them stood by with bows and arrows, ready to shoot any of the Folk that exposed themselves, several of the Fire-Men heaped the dry grass and wood at the mouths of the lower tier of caves. Out of these heaps they conjured the monster we feared—*FIRE.* At first wisps of smoke arose and curled up the cliff. Then I could see the red-tongued flames darting in and out through the wood like tiny snakes.

The smoke grew thicker and thicker, at times shrouding the whole face of the cliff. But I was high up and it did not bother me much, though it stung my eyes, and I rubbed them with my knuckles.

Old Marrow-Bone was the first to be smoked out. A light fan of air drifted the smoke away at the time so that I saw clearly. He broke out through the smoke, stepping on a burning coal and screaming with the sudden hurt of it, and essayed to climb up the cliff. The arrows showered about him. He came to a pause on a ledge, clutching a knob of rock for support, gasping and sneezing and shaking his head. He swayed back and forth. The feathered ends of a dozen arrows were sticking out of him. He was an old man, but he did not want to die. He swayed wider and wider, his knees giving under him, and as he swayed he wailed most plaintively. His hand released its grip and he lurched outward to the fall. His old bones must have been sadly broken. He groaned and strove feebly to rise, but a Fire-Man rushed in upon him and brained him with a club.

And as it happened with Marrow-Bone, so it happened with many of the Folk. Unable to endure the smoke-suffocation, they rushed out to fall beneath the arrows. Some of the women and children remained in the caves to strangle, but the majority met death outside.

When the Fire-Men had in this fashion cleared the first tier of caves, they began making arrangements to duplicate the operation on the second tier. It was while they were climbing up with their grass and wood that Red Eye, followed by his wife with the baby holding to her tightly, made a successful flight up the cliff. The Fire-Men must have concluded that in the interval between the smoking-out operations we would remain in our caves; so that they were unprepared, and their arrows did not begin to fly till Red-Eye and his wife were well up the wall. When he reached the top, he turned about and glared down at them, roaring and beating his chest. They arched their arrows at him, and though he was untouched he fled on.

I watched a third tier smoked out, and a fourth. A few of the Folk escaped up the cliff, but most of them were shot off the face of it as they strove to climb. I remember Long-Lip. He got as far as my ledge, crying piteously, an arrow clear through his chest, the feathered shaft sticking out behind, the bone head sticking out before, shot through the back as he climbed. He sank down on my ledge, bleeding profusely at the mouth.

It was about this time that the upper tiers seemed to empty themselves spontaneously. Nearly all the Folk not yet smoked out stampeded up the cliff at the same time. This was the saving of many. The Fire People could not shoot arrows fast enough. They filled the air with them, and scores of the stricken Folk came tumbling down; but still there were a few who reached the top and got away.

The impulse of flight was now stronger in me than curiosity. The arrows had ceased flying. The last of the Folk seemed gone, though there may have been a few still hiding in the upper caves. The Swift One and I started to make a scramble for the cliff-top. At sight of us a great cry went up from the Fire People. This was not caused by me, but by the Swift One. They were chattering excitedly and pointing her out to one another. They did not try to shoot her. Not an arrow was discharged. They began calling softly and coaxingly. I stopped and looked down. She was afraid, and whimpered and urged me on. So we went up over the top and plunged into the trees.

This event has often caused me to wonder and speculate. If she were really of their kind, she must have been lost from them at a time when she was too young to remember, else she would not have been afraid of them. On the other hand, it may well have been that though she was of their kind, she had never been lost from them; that she had been born in the wild forest far from their haunts, her father maybe a renegade Fire-Man, her mother perhaps one of my own kind, one of the Folk. But who shall say? These things are beyond me, and the Swift One knew no more about them than I did.

We lived through a day of terror. Most of the survivors fled toward the blueberry-swamp and took refuge in the forest in that neighborhood. And all day hunting parties of the Fire People ranged the forest, killing us wherever they found us. It must have been a deliberately executed plan. Increasing beyond the limits of their own territory, they had decided on making a conquest of ours. Sorry the conquest! We had no chance against them. It was slaughter, indiscriminate slaughter, for they were merciless, killing old and young, effectively ridding the land of our presence.

It was like the end of the world to us. We fled to the trees as a last refuge, only to be surrounded and killed, family by family. Inevitably, we saw much of this during that day, and, besides, I wanted to see. The Swift One and I never remained long in one tree, and so escaped being surrounded. But there seemed no place to go. The Fire-Men were everywhere, bent on their task of extermination. Every way we turned we encountered them.

I did not see what became of my mother, but I did see the Chatterer shot down out of the old home-tree. And I am afraid that at the sight I did a bit of joyous teetering. Before I leave this portion of my narrative, I must tell of Red-Eye. He was caught with his wife in a tree down by the blueberry-swamp. The Swift One and I stopped long enough in our flight to see. The Fire-Men were too intent upon their work to notice us, and, furthermore, we were well screened by the thicket in which we crouched.

Fully a score of the hunters were under the tree, discharging arrows into it. They always picked up their arrows when they fell back to earth. I could not see Red-Eye, but I could hear him howling from somewhere in the tree. After a short interval his howling grew muffled. He must have crawled into a hollow in the trunk. But his wife did not win this shelter. An arrow brought her to the ground. Evidently she was severely hurt, for she made no effort to get away. She crouched in a sheltering way over her baby (which clung tightly to her), and made pleading signs and sounds to the Fire-Men. They gathered about her and laughed at her —even as Lop-Ear and I had laughed at the old Tree-Man. And even as we had poked him with twigs and sticks, so did the Fire-Men with Red-Eye's wife. They poked her with the ends of their bows, and prodded her in the ribs. But she was poor fun. She would not fight. Nor, for that matter, would she get angry. She continued to crouch over her baby and to plead. One of the Fire-Men stepped close to her. In his hand was a club. She saw and understood, but she made only the pleading sounds until the blow fell.

Red-Eye, in the hollow of the trunk, was safe from their arrows. They stood together and debated for a while; then one of them climbed into the tree. What happened up there I could not tell, but I heard him yell and saw the excitement of those that remained beneath. After several minutes his body crashed down to the ground. He did not move. They looked at him and raised his head, but it fell back limply when they let go. Red-Eye had accounted for himself.

They were very angry. There was an opening into the trunk close to the ground. They gathered wood and grass and built a fire. The Swift One and I, our arms around each other, waited and watched in the thicket. Sometimes they threw upon the fire green branches with many leaves, whereupon the smoke became very thick.

We saw them suddenly swerve back from the tree. They were not quick enough. Red-Eye's flying body landed in the midst of them. He was in a frightful rage, smashing about with his long arms right and left. He pulled the face off one of them, literally pulled it off with those gnarly fingers of his and those tremendous muscles. He bit another through the neck. The Fire-Men fell back with wild, fierce yells, then rushed upon him. He managed to get hold of a club and began crushing heads like egg-shells. He was too much for them, and they were compelled to fall back again. This was his chance, and he turned his back upon them and ran for it, still howling wrathfully. A few arrows sped after him, but he plunged into a thicket and was gone.

The Swift One and I crept quietly away, only to run foul of another party of Fire-Men. They chased us into the blueberry-swamp, but we knew the tree-paths across the farther morasses where they could not follow on the ground, and so we escaped. We came out on the other side into a narrow strip of forest that separated the blueberry-swamp from the great swamp that extended westward. Here we met Lop-Ear. How he had escaped I cannot imagine, unless he had not slept the preceding night at the caves.

Here, in the strip of forest, we might have built tree-shelters and settled down; but the Fire People were performing their work of extermination thoroughly. In the afternoon, Hair-Face and his wife fled out from among the trees to the east, passed us, and were gone. They fled silently and swiftly, with alarm in their faces. In the direction from which they had come we heard the cries and yells of the hunters, and the screeching of some one of the Folk. The Fire People had found their way across the swamp.

The Swift One, Lop-Ear, and I followed on the heels of Hair-Face and his wife. When we came to the edge of the great swamp, we stopped. We did not know its paths. It was outside our territory, and it had always been avoided by the Folk. None had ever gone into it—at least, to return. For us it held the mysterious terror of the unknown. As I say, we stopped at the edge of it. We were afraid. The cries of the Fire-Men were drawing nearer. We looked at one another. Hair-Face ran out on the quaking morass and gained the firmer footing of a grass-hummock a dozen yards away. His wife did not follow. She tried to, but shrank back from the treacherous surface and cowered down.

The Swift One did not wait for me, nor did she pause till she had passed beyond Hair-Face a hundred yards and gained a much larger hummock. By the time Lop-Ear and I had caught up with her, the Fire-Men appeared among the trees. Hair-Face's wife, driven by them into panic, dashed after us. But she ran blindly, without caution, and broke through the crust. We turned and watched, and saw them shoot her with arrows as she sank down in the mud. The arrows began falling about us. Hair-Face had now joined us, and the four of us plunged on, we knew not whither, deeper and deeper into the swamp.

CHAPTER XVIII

Of our wanderings in the great swamp I have no clear knowledge. When I strive to remember, I have a riot of unrelated impressions and a loss of time-value. I have no idea of how long we were in that vast everglade, but it must have been for weeks. My memories of what occurred invariably take the form of nightmare. For untold ages, oppressed by protean fear, I am aware of wandering, endlessly wandering, through a dank and soggy wilderness, where poisonous snakes struck at us, and animals roared around us, and the mud quaked under us and sucked at our heels.

Countless times we were turned from our course by streams and lakes and slimy seas. Then there were storms and risings of the water over great areas of the low-lying lands; and there were periods of hunger and misery when we were kept prisoners in the trees for days and days by these transient floods.

Very strong upon me is one picture. Large trees are about us, and from their branches hang gray filaments of moss, while great creepers, like monstrous serpents, curl around the trunks and writhe in tangles through the air. And all about is the mud, soft mud, that bubbles forth gases, and that heaves and sighs with internal agitations. And in the midst of all this are a dozen of us. We are lean and wretched, and our bones show through our tight-stretched skins. We do not sing and chatter and laugh. We play no pranks. For once our volatile and exuberant spirits are hopelessly subdued. We make plaintive, querulous noises, look at one another, and cluster close together.

This event is without connection with the other events in the swamp. How we ever managed to cross it I do not know, but at last we came out where a low range of hills ran down to the bank of the river. It was our river, emerging like ourselves from the great swamp. On the south bank, where the river had broken its way through the hills, we found many sandstone caves. Beyond, toward the west, the ocean boomed on the bar that lay across the river's mouth. And here, in the caves, we settled down in our abiding-place by the sea.

There were not many of us. From time to time, as the days went by, more of the Folk appeared. They dragged themselves from the swamp singly, and in twos and threes, more dead than alive, until at last there were thirty of us. Then no more came from the swamp, and Red-Eye was not among us. It was noticeable that no children had survived the frightful journey.

I shall not tell in detail of the years we lived by the sea. It was not a happy abiding-place. The air was raw and chill, and we suffered continually from coughing and colds. We could not survive in such an environment. True, we had children; but they had little hold on life and died early, while we died faster than new ones were born. Our number steadily diminished.

Besides, the radical change in our diet was not good for us. We got few vegetables and fruits, and became fish-eaters. There were mussels and abalones and clams and rock-oysters and great ocean crabs that were thrown upon the beaches in stormy weather. Also, we found several kinds of seaweed that were good to eat. But the change in diet caused us stomach troubles, and none of us ever waxed fat. We were all lean and dyspeptic-looking. It was in getting the big abalones that Lop-Ear was lost. One of them closed upon his fingers at low tide, and then the flood-tide came in and drowned him. We found his body the next day, and it was a lesson to us. Not another one of us was ever caught in the closing shell of an abalone.

And then, one day, the Fire People appeared again. They had come down the river, not on a catamaran, but in a rude dugout. There were three of them that paddled in it, and one of them was the little wizened old hunter. They landed on our beach, and he limped across the sand and examined our caves.

They went away in a few minutes, but the Swift One was badly scared. We were all frightened, but none of us to the extent that she was. She whimpered and cried and was restless all that night. In the morning, by sharp cries, gestures, and example. she started me on our second long flight. There were eight of the Folk (all that was left of the horde) that remained behind in the caves. There was no hope for them. Without doubt, even if the Fire People did not return, they must soon have perished. It was a bad climate down there by the sea. The Folk were not constituted for the coast-dwelling life.

We traveled south, for days skirting the great swamp, but never venturing into it. Once we broke back to the westward, crossing a range of mountains and coming down to the coast. But it was no place for us. There were no trees—only bleak headlands, a thundering surf, and strong winds that seemed never to cease from blowing. We turned back across the mountains, traveling east and south, until we neared the great swamp again.

Soon we gained its southern extremity, and we continued our course south and east. It was a pleasant land. The air was warm, and we were again in the forest. Later on we crossed a low-lying range of hills and found ourselves in an even better forest country. The farther we penetrated from the coast the warmer we found it, and we went on and on until we came to a large river that seemed familiar to the Swift One. It was where she must have come during the four years' absence from the horde. This river we crossed on logs, landing on the other side at the base of a large bluff. High up on the bluff we found our new home—a cave most difficult of access and quite hidden from any eye beneath.

There is little more of my tale to tell. Here the Swift One and I lived and reared our family. And here my memories end. We never made another migration. I never dream beyond our high, inaccessible cave. And here must have been born the child that inherited the stuff of my dreams, that had molded into its being all the impressions of my life—or of the life of Big-Tooth, rather, who is my other-self, and not my real self, but who is so real to me that often I am unable to tell in what age I am living.

I often wonder about this line of descent. I, the modern, am incontestably a man; yet I, Big-Tooth, the primitive, am not a man. Somewhere, and by straight line of descent, these two parties to my dual personality were connected. Were the Folk, before their destruction, in the process of becoming men? And did I and mine carry through this process? On the other hand, may not some descendant of mine have gone in to the Fire People and become one of them? I do not know. There is no way of learning. One thing only is certain, and that is that Big-Tooth did stamp into the cerebral constitution of one of his progeny all the impressions of his life, and stamped them in so indelibly that the hosts of intervening generations have failed to obliterate them.

There is one other thing of which I must speak before I close. It is a dream that I dream often. In point of time the real event must have occurred during the period of my living in the high, inaccessible cave. I remember that I wandered far in the forest toward the east. There I came upon a tribe of Tree People. I crouched in a thicket and watched them at play. They were holding a laughing council, jumping up and down and screeching rude choruses.

Suddenly they hushed their noise and ceased their capering. They shrank down in fear, and quested anxiously about with their eyes for a way of retreat. Then Red-Eye walked in among them. They cowered away from him. All were frightened. But he made no attempt to hurt them. He was one of them. At his heels, on stringy bended legs, supporting herself with knuckles to the ground on either side, walked an old female of the Tree People, his latest wife. He sat down in the midst of the circle. I can see him now, as I write this, scowling, his eyes inflamed, as he peers about him at the circle of the Tree People. He had found his place.

THE END

2
A Relic of the Pliocene

I WASH MY HANDS of him at the start. I cannot father his tales, nor will I be responsible for them. I make these preliminary reservations, observe, as a guard upon my own integrity. I possess a certain definite position in a small way, also a wife; and for the good name of the community which honors my existence with its approval, and for the sake of her posterity and mine, I cannot take the chances I once did, nor foster probabilities with the careless improvidence of youth. So, I repeat, I wash my hands of him, this Nimrod, this mighty hunter, this homely, blue-eyed, freckle-faced Thomas Stevens.

Having been honest to myself, and to whatever prospective olive branches my wife may be pleased to tender me, I can now afford to be generous. I shall not criticise the tales told me by Thomas Stevens, and, further, I shall withhold my judgment. If it be asked why, I can only add that judgment I have none. Long have I pondered, weighed and balanced, but never have my conclusions been twice the same—forsooth! because Thomas Stevens is a greater man than I. If he have told truths, well and good; if untruths, still well and good. For who can prove? or who disprove? I eliminate myself from the proposition, while those of little faith may do as I have done—go find the said Thomas Stevens and discuss to his face the various matters, which, if fortune serve, I shall relate. As to where he may be found? The directions are simple: anywhere between 53 north latitude and the Pole, on the one hand; and, on the other, the likeliest hunting grounds which lie between the east coast of Siberia and furthermost Labrador. That he is there, somewhere, within that clearly defined territory, I pledge the word of an honorable man whose expectations entail straight speaking and right living.

Thomas Stevens may have toyed prodigiously with truth, but when we first met (it were well to mark this point), he wandered into my camp when I thought myself a thousand miles beyond the outermost post of civilization. At the sight of his human face, the first in weary months, I could have sprung forward and folded him in my arms (and I am not by any means a demonstrative man); but to him his visit seemed the most casual thing under the sun. He just strolled into the light of my camp, passed the time of day after the custom of men on beaten trails, threw my snowshoes the one way and a couple of dogs the other, and so made room for himself by the fire. Said he'd just dropped in to borrow a pinch of soda and to see if I had any decent tobacco. He plucked forth an ancient pipe, loaded it with painstaking care, and. without as much as by your leave, whacked half the tobacco of my pouch into his. Yes, the stuff was fairly good. He sighed with the contentment of the just, and literally absorbed the smoke from

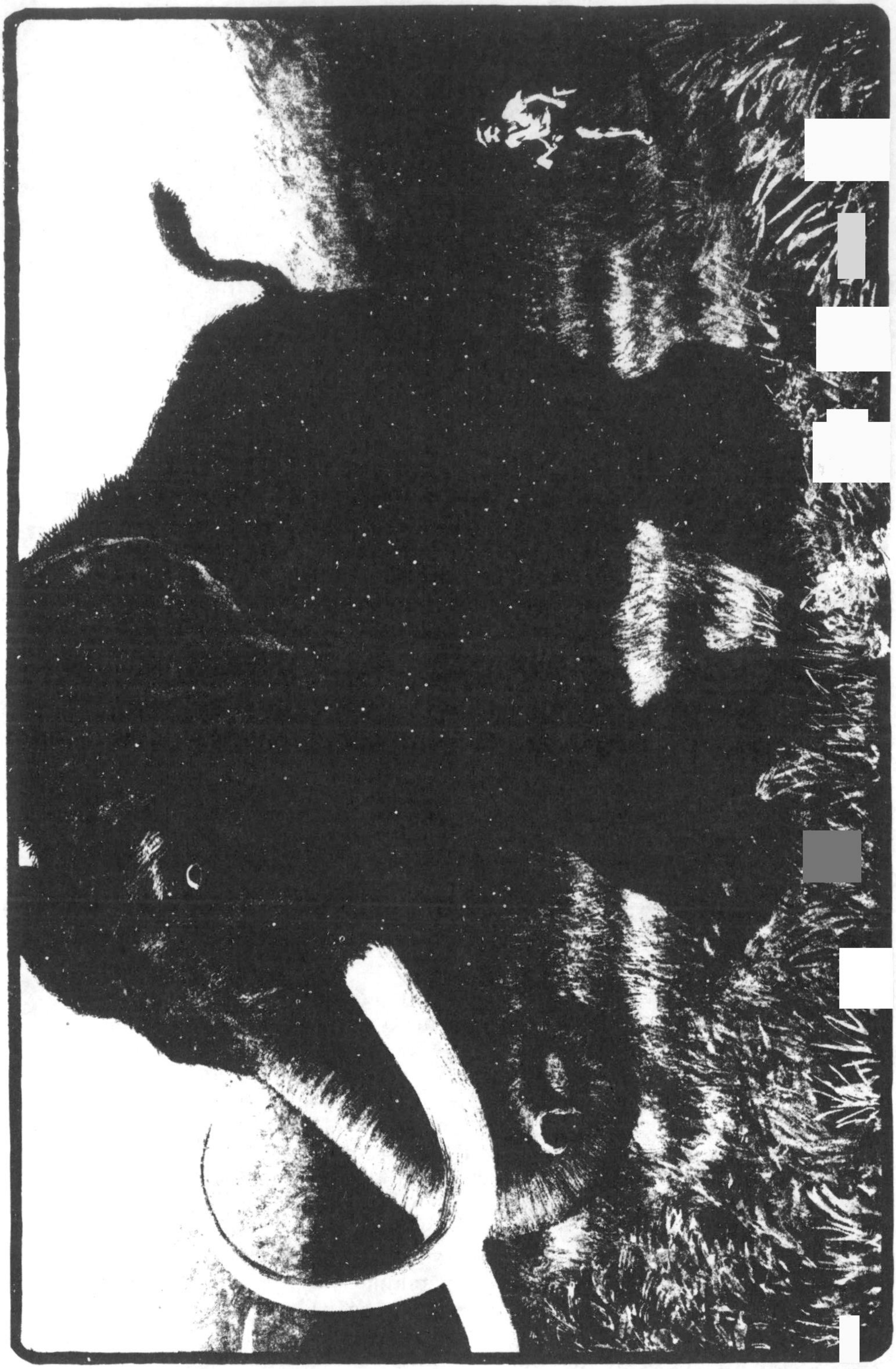

the crisping yellow flakes, and it did my smoker's heart good to behold him.

Hunter? Trapper? Prospector? He shrugged his shoulders No; just sort of knocking round a bit. Had come up from the Great Slave some time since, and was thinking of trapsing over into the Yukon country. The Factor of Koshim had spoken about the discoveries on the Klondike, and he was of a mind to run over for a peep. I noticed that he spoke of the Klondike in the archaic vernacular, calling it the Reindeer River—a conceited custom which the Old Timers employ against the *che-cha-quas* and all tenderfeet in general. But he did it so naïvely and as such a matter of course, that there was no sting, and I forgave him. He also had it in view, he said, before he crossed the divide into the Yukon, to make a little run up Fort o' Good Hope way.

Now Fort o' Good Hope is a far journey to the north, over and beyond the Circle, in a place where the feet of few men have trod; and when a nondescript ragamuffin comes in out of the night, from nowhere in particular, to sit by one's fire and discourse on such in terms of "trapsing" and "a little run," it is fair time to rouse up and shake off the dream. Wherefore I looked about me; saw the fly, and, underneath, the pine boughs spread for the sleeping furs; saw the grub sacks, the camera, the frosty breaths of the dogs circling on the edge of the light; and, above, a great streamer of the aurora bridging the zenith from southeast to northwest I shivered. There is a magic in the Northland night which steals in on one like fevers from malarial marshes. You are clutched and downed before you are aware. Then I looked to the snowshoes, lying prone and crossed where he had flung them. Also I had an eye to my tobacco pouch. Half, at least, of its goodly store had vamosed. That settled it. Fancy had not tricked me after all.

Crazed with suffering, I thought, looking steadfastly at the man. One of those wild stampeders, strayed far from his bearings and wandering like a lost soul through great vastnesses and unknown deeps. Oh, well, let his moods slip on, until, mayhap, he gathers his tangled wits together. Who knows?—the mere sound of a fellow creature's voice may bring all straight again.

So I led him on in talk, and soon I marvelled, for he talked of game and the ways thereof. He had killed the Siberian wolf of westernmost Alaska, and the chamois in the secret Rockies. He averred he knew the haunts where the last buffalo still roamed; that he had hung on the flanks of the caribou when they ran by the hundred thousand, and slept in the Great Barrens on the musk-ox's winter trail.

And I shifted my judgment accordingly (the first revision, but by no account the last), and deemed him a monumental effigy of truth. Why it was I know not, but the spirit moved me to repeat a tale told to me by a man who had dwelt in the land too long to know better. It was of the great bear which hugs the steep slopes of St. Elias, never descending to the levels of the gentler inclines. Now God so constituted this creature for its hillside habitat that the legs of one side are all of a foot longer than those of the other. This is mighty convenient, as will be readily admitted. So I hunted this rare beast in my own name, told it in the first person, present tense, painted the requisite locale, gave it the necessary garnishings and touches of verisimilitude, and looked to see the man stunned by the recital.

Not he. Had he doubted, I could have forgiven him. Had he objected, denying the dangers of such a hunt by virtue of the animal's inability to turn about and go the other way—had he done this, I say, I could have taken him by the hand for the true sportsman that he was. Not he. He sniffed, looked on me, and sniffed again; then gave my tobacco due praise, thrust one foot into my lap, and bade me examine the gear. It was a *mucluc* of the Innuit pattern, sewed together with sinew threads, and devoid of beads or furbelows. But it was the skin itself that was remarkable. In that it was all of half an inch thick it reminded me of walrus-hide; but there the resemblance ceased, for no walrus ever bore so marvellous a growth of hair. On the side and ankles this hair was well-nigh worn away, what of friction with underbrush and snow, but around the top and down the more sheltered back it was coarse, dirty-black, and very thick. I parted it with difficulty and looked beneath for the fine fur which is common with northern animals, but found it in this case to be absent. This, however, was compensated for by the length. Indeed, the tufts which had survived wear and tear measured all of seven or eight inches.

I looked up into the man's face, and he pulled his foot down and asked, "Find hide like that on your St. Elias bear?"

I shook my head. "Nor on any other creature of land or sea," I answered candidly. The thickness of it, and the length of the hair, puzzled me.

"That," he said, and said without the slightest hint of impressiveness, "that came from a mammoth."

"Nonsense!" I exclaimed, for I could not forbear the protest of my unbelief. "The mammoth, my dear sir, long ago vanished from the earth. We know it once existed by the fossil remains which we have unearthed, and by a frozen carcass which the Siberian sun saw fit to melt from out the bosom of a glacier; but we also know that no living specimen exists. Our explorers—"

At this word he broke in impatiently. "Your explorers? Pish! A weakly breed. Let us hear no more of them. But tell me, O man, what you may know of the mammoth and his ways."

Beyond contradiction, this was leading to a yarn; so I baited my hook by ransacking my memory for whatever data I possessed on the subject in hand. To begin with, I emphasized that the animal was prehistoric, and marshalled all my facts in support of this. I mentioned the Siberian sand bars which abounded with ancient mammoth bones; spoke of the large quantities of fossil ivory purchased from the Innuits by the Alaska Commercial Company; and acknowledged having myself mined six and eight-foot tusks from the pay gravel of the Klondike creeks. "All fossils," I concluded, "found in the midst of débris deposited through countless ages."

"I remember when I was a kid," Thomas Stevens sniffed (he had a most confounded way of sniffing), "that I saw a petrified watermelon. Hence, though mistaken people sometimes delude themselves into thinking that they are really raising or eating them, there is no such thing as extant watermelons?"

"But the question of food," I objected, ignoring his point, which was puerile and without bearing. "The soil must bring forth vegetable life in lavish abundance to support such monstrous creations. Nowhere in the North is the soil so prolific. Ergo, the mammoth cannot exist."

"I pardon your ignorance concerning many matters of this Northland, for you are a young man and have travelled little; but, at the same time, I am inclined to agree with you on one thing. The mammoth no longer exists. How do I know? I killed the last one with my own right arm."

Thus spake Nimrod, the Mighty Hunter. I threw a stick of firewood at the dogs and bade them quit their unholy howling, and waited. Undoubtedly this liar of singular felicity would open his mouth and requite me for my St. Elias bear.

"It was this way," he at last began, after the appropriate silence had intervened. "I was in camp one day—"

"Where?" I interrupted.

He waved his hand vaguely in the direction of the northeast, where stretched a terra incognita into which vastness few men have strayed and fewer emerged. "I was in camp one day with Klooch. Klooch was as handsome a little *kamooks* as ever whined betwixt the traces or shoved nose into a camp kettle. Her father was a full-blood Malemute from Russian Pastilik on Bering Sea, and I bred her, and with understanding, out of a clean-legged bitch of the Hudson Bay stock. I tell you, O man, she was a corker combination. And now, on this day I have in mind, she was brought to pup through a pure wild wolf of the woods—gray, and long of limb, with big lungs and no end of staying powers. Say! Was there ever the like? It was a new breed of dog I had started, and I could look forward to big things.

"As I have said, she was brought neatly to pup, and safely delivered. I was squatting on my hams over the litter—seven sturdy, blind little beggars—when from behind came a bray of trumpets and crash of brass. There was a rush, like the wind-squall which kicks the heels of the rain, and I was midway to my feet when knocked flat on my face. At the same instant I heard Klooch sigh, very much as a man does when you've planted your fist in his belly. You can stake your sack I lay quiet, but I twisted my head around and saw a huge bulk swaying above me. Then the blue sky flashed into view and I got to my feet. A hairy mountain of flesh was just disappearing in the underbrush on the edge of the open. I caught a rear-end glimpse, with a stiff tail, as big in girth as my body, standing out straight behind. The next second only a tremendous hole remained in the thicket, though I could still hear the sounds as of a tornado dying quickly away, underbrush ripping and tearing and trees snapping and crashing.

"I cast about for my rifle. It had been lying on the ground with the muzzle against a log; but now the stock was smashed, the barrel out of line and the working-gear in a thousand bits. Then I looked for the slut, and—and what do you suppose?"

I shook my head.

"May my soul burn in a thousand hells if there was anything left of her! Klooch, the seven sturdy, blind little beggars—gone, all gone. Where she had stretched was a slimy, bloody depression in the soft dirt, all of a yard in diameter, and around the edges a few scattered hairs."

I measured three feet on the snow, threw about it a circle, and glanced at Nimrod.

"The beast was thirty long and twenty high," he answered, "and its tusks scaled over six times three feet. I couldn't believe, myself, at the time, for all that it had just happened. But if my senses had played me, there was the broken gun and the hole in the brush. And there was—or, rather, there was not—Klooch and the pups. O man, it makes me hot all over now when I think of it. Klooch! Another Eve! The mother of a new race! And a rampaging, ranting, old bull mammoth, like a second flood wiping them, root and branch, off the face of the earth! Do you wonder that the blood-soaked dirt cried out to high God? Or that I grabbed the hand-axe and took the trail?"

"The hand-axe?" I exclaimed, startled out of myself by the picture. "The hand-axe, and a big bull mammoth, thirty feet long, twenty feet—"

Nimrod joined me in my merriment, chuckling gleefully. "Wouldn't it kill you?" he cried. "Wasn't it a beaver's dream? Many's the time I've laughed about it since, but at the time it was no laughing matter, I was that danged mad, what of the gun and Klooch. Think of it, O man! A brand-new, unclassified, uncopyrighted breed, and wiped out before ever it opened its eyes or took out its intention papers! Well, so be it. Life's full of disappointments, and rightly so. Meat is best after a famine, and a bed soft after a hard trail.

"As I was saying, I took out after the beast with the hand-axe, and hung to its heels down the valley; but when he circled back toward the head I was left winded at the lower end. Speaking of grub, I might as well stop long enough to explain a couple of points. Up thereabouts, in the midst of the mountains, is an almighty curious formation. There are no end of little valleys, each like the other much as peas in a pod, and all neatly tucked away with straight rocky walls rising on all sides. And at the lower ends are always small openings where the drainage or glaciers must have broken out. The only way in is through these mouths, and they are all small, and some smaller than others. As to grub—you've slushed around on the rain-soaked islands of the Alaskan coast down Sitka-way, most likely, seeing as you're a traveller. And you know how stuff grows there—big, and juicy, and jungly. Well, that's the way it was with those valleys. Thick, rich soil, with ferns and grasses and such things in patches higher than your head. Rain three days out of four during the summer months; and food in them for a thousand mammoths, to say nothing of small game tor man.

"But to get back. Down at the lower end of the valley I got winded and gave over. I began to speculate, for when my wind left me my dander got hotter and hotter, and I knew I'd never know peace of mind till I dined on roasted mammoth-foot. And I knew, also, that that stood for *skookum mamook pukapuk*—excuse Chinook, I mean there was a big fight coming. Now the mouth of my valley was very narrow, and the walls steep. High up on one side was one of those big pivot rocks, or balancing rocks as some call them, weighing all of a couple of hundred tons. Just the thing. I hit back for camp, keeping an eye open so the bull couldn't slip past, and got my ammunition. It wasn't worth anything with the rifle smashed; so I opened the shells, planted the powder under the rock, and touched it off with slow fuse. Wasn't much of a charge, but the old bowlder tilted up lazily and dropped down into place, with just space enough to let the creek drain nicely. Now I had him."

"But how did you have him?" I queried. "Who ever heard of a man killing a mammoth with a hand-axe? And, for that matter, with anything else?"

"O man, have I not told you I was mad?" Nimrod replied, with a slight manifestation of sensitiveness. "Mad clean through, what of Klooch and the gun? Also, was I not a hunter? And was this not new and most unusual game? A hand-axe? Pish! I did not need it. Listen, and you shall hear of a hunt, such as might have happened in the youth of the world when caveman rounded up the kill with hand-axe of stone. Such would have served me as well. Now is it not a fact that man can outwalk the dog or horse? That he can wear them out with the intelligence of his endurance?"

I nodded.

"Well?"

The light broke in on me, and I bade him continue.

"My valley was perhaps five miles around. The mouth was closed. There was no way to get out. A timid beast was that bull mammoth, and I had him at my mercy. I got on his heels again, hollered like a fiend, pelted him with cobbles, and raced him around the valley three times before I knocked off for supper. Don't you see? A race-course! A man and a mammoth! A hippodrome, with sun, moon, and stars to referee!

"It took me two months to do it, but I did it. And that's no beaver dream. Round and round I ran him, me travelling on the inner circle, eating jerked meat and salmon berries on the run, and snatching winks of sleep between. Of course, he'd get desperate at times and turn. Then I'd head for soft ground where the creek spread out, and lay anathema upon him and his ancestry, and dare him to come on. But he was too wise to bog in a mud puddle. Once he pinned me in against the walls, and I crawled back into a deep crevice and waited. Whenever he felt for me with his trunk I'd belt him with the hand-axe till he pulled out, shrieking fit to split my ear drums, he was that mad. He knew he had me and didn't have me, and it near drove him wild. But he was no man's fool. He knew he was safe as long as I stayed in the crevice, and he made up his mind to keep me there. And he was dead right, only he hadn't figured on the commissary. There was neither grub nor water around that spot, so on the face of it he couldn't keep up the siege. He'd stand before the opening for hours, keeping an eye on me and flapping mosquitoes away with his big blanket ears. Then the thirst'd come on him, and he'd ramp round and roar till the earth shook, calling me every name he could lay tongue to. This was to frighten me, of course; and when he thought I was sufficiently impressed, he'd back away softly and try to make a sneak for the creek. Sometimes I'd let him get almost there—only a couple of hundred yards away it was—when out I'd pop and back he'd come, lumbering along like the old landslide he was. After I'd done this a few times, and he'd figured it out, he changed his tactics. Grasped the time element, you see. Without a word of warning, away he'd go, tearing for the water like mad, scheming to get there and back before I ran away. Finally, after cursing me most horrible, he raised the siege and deliberately stalked off to the water hole.

"That was the only time he penned me—three days of it—but after that the hippodrome never stopped. Round, and round, and round, like a six days' go-as-I-please, for he never pleased. My clothes went in rags and tatters, but I never stopped to mend, till at last I ran naked as a son of earth, with nothing but the old hand-axe in one hand and a cobble in the other. In fact, I never stopped, save for peeps of sleep in the crannies and ledges of the cliffs. As for the bull, he got perceptibly thinner and thinner—must have lost several tons at least—and as nervous as a schoolmarm on the wrong side of matrimony. When I'd come up with him and yell, or lam him with a rock at long range, he'd jump like a skittish colt and tremble all over. Then he'd pull out on the run, tail and trunk waving stiff, head over one shoulder and wicked eyes blazing, and the way he'd swear at me was something dreadful. A most immoral beast he was, a murderer and a blasphemer.

"But toward the end he quit all this, and fell to whimpering and crying like a baby. His spirit broke and he became a quivering jelly-mountain of misery. He'd get attacks of palpitation of the heart, and stagger around like a drunken man, and fall down and bark his shins. And then he'd cry, but always on the run. O man, the gods themselves would have wept with him, and you yourself or any other man. It was pitiful, and there was so much of it, but I only hardened my heart and hit up the pace. At last I wore him clean out, and he lay down, broken-winded, broken-hearted, hungry and thirsty. When I found he wouldn't budge, I hamstrung him, and spent the better part of the day wading into him with the hand-axe, he a sniffling and sobbing till I worked in far enough to shut him off. Thirty feet long he was, and twenty high, and a man could sling a hammock between his tusks and sleep comfortably. Barring the fact that I had run most of the juices out of him, he was fair eating, and his four feet, alone, roasted whole, would have lasted a man a twelvemonth. I spent the winter there myself."

"And where is this valley?" I asked.

He waved his hand in the direction of the northeast, and said, "Your tobacco is very good. I carry a fair share of it in my pouch, but I shall carry the recollection of it until I die. In token of my appreciation, and in return for the moccasins on your own feet, I will present to you these *muclucs*. They commemorate Klooch and the seven blind little beggars. They are also souvenirs of an unparalleled event in history, namely, the destruction of the oldest breed of animal on earth, and the youngest. And their chief virtue lies in that they will never wear out."

Having effected the exchange, he knocked the ashes from his pipe, gripped my hand good-night, and wandered off through the snow. Concerning this tale, for which I have already disclaimed responsibility, I would recommend those of little faith to make a visit to the Smithsonian Institute. If they bring the requisite credentials and do not come in vacation time, they will undoubtedly gain an audience with Professor Dolvidson. The *muclucs* are in his possession, and he will verify, not the manner in which they were obtained, but the material of which they are composed. When he states that they are made from the skin of the mammoth, the scientific world accepts his verdict. What more would you have?

THE END

3
Trust

TRUST

BY JACK LONDON

Author of "The Call of the Wild," "The Sea Wolf," etc.

ALL lines had been cast off, and the *Seattle No. 4* was pulling slowly out from the shore. Her decks were piled high with freight and baggage, and swarmed with a heterogeneous company of Indians, dogs, and dog-mushers, prospectors, traders, and homeward-bound gold-seekers. A goodly portion of Dawson lined up on the bank, saying good-by. As the gang-plank came in and the steamer nosed into the stream, the clamor of farewell became deafening. Also, in that eleventh moment, everybody began to remember final farewell messages and to shout them back and forth across the widening stretch of water. Louis Bondell, curling his yellow mustache with one hand and languidly waving the other hand to his friends on shore, suddenly remembered something and sprang to the rail.

"Oh, Fred!" he bawled. "Oh, Fred!"

The "Fred" desired thrust a strapping pair of shoulders through the forefront of the crowd on the bank and tried to catch Louis Bondell's message, who grew red in the face with vain vociferation. Still the water widened between steamboat and shore.

"Hey, you, Captain Scott!" he yelled at the pilot-house. "Stop the boat!"

The gongs clanged, and the big stern wheel reversed, then stopped. All hands on steamboat and on bank took advantage of this respite to exchange final, new, and imperative farewells. More futile than ever was Louis Bondell's effort to make himself heard. The *Seattle No. 4* lost way and drifted down-stream, and Captain Scott had to go ahead with her and reverse a second time. His head disappeared inside the pilot-house, coming into view a moment later behind a big megaphone.

Now Captain Scott had a remarkable voice, and the "Shut up!" he launched at the crowd on deck and on shore could have been heard at the top of Moosehide Mountain and as far as Klondike City. This official remonstrance from the pilot-house spread a film of silence over the tumult.

"Now, what do you want to say?" Captain Scott demanded.

"Tell Fred Churchill—he 's on the bank there—tell him to go to Macdonald. It 's in his safe—a small gripsack of mine. Tell him to get it and bring it out when he comes."

In the silence Captain Scott bellowed the message ashore through the megaphone:

"You, Fred Churchill, go to Macdonald—in his safe—small gripsack—belongs to Louis Bondell—important! Bring it out when you come! Got it?"

Churchill waved his hand in token that he had got it. In truth, had Macdonald, half a mile away, opened his window, he 'd have got it, too. The tumult of farewell rose again, the gongs clanged, and the *Seattle No. 4* went ahead, swung out into the stream, turned on her heel, and headed down the Yukon, Bondell and Churchill waving farewell and mutual affection to the last.

That was in mid-summer. In the fall of the year, the *W. H. Willis* started up the Yukon with two hundred homeward-bound pilgrims on board. Among them was Churchill. In his state-room, in the middle of a clothes-bag, was Louis Bondell's grip. It was a small, stout leather affair, and its weight of forty pounds always made Churchill nervous when he wandered too far from it. The man in the adjoining state-room had a treasure of gold-dust hidden similarly in a clothes-

Drawn by Oliver Kemp. Half-tone plate engraved by H. C. Merrill

"AFTER THAT, CHURCHILL FOUGHT ON ALONE"

bag, and the pair of them ultimately arranged to stand watch and watch. While one went down to eat, the other kept an eye on the two state-room doors. When Churchill wanted to take a hand at whist, the other man mounted guard, and when the other man wanted to relax his soul, Churchill read four-months'-old newspapers on a camp-stool between the two doors.

There were signs of an early winter, and the question that was discussed from dawn till dark, and far into the dark, was whether they would get out before the freeze-up or be compelled to abandon the steamboat and tramp out over the ice. There were irritating delays. Twice the engines broke down and had to be tinkered up, and each time there were snow flurries to warn them of the imminence of winter. Nine times the *W. H. Willis* essayed to ascend the Five-Finger Rapids with her impaired machinery, and when she succeeded, she was four days behind her very liberal schedule. The question that then arose was whether or not the steamboat *Flora* would wait for her above the Box Cañon. The stretch of water between the head of the Box Cañon and the foot of the White Horse Rapids was unnavigable for steamboats, and passengers were trans-shipped at that point, walking around the rapids from one steamboat to the other. There were no telephones in the country, hence no way of informing the waiting *Flora* that the *Willis* was four days late, but coming.

When the *W. H. Willis* pulled into White Horse, it was learned that the *Flora* had waited three days over the limit, and had departed only a few hours before. Also, it was learned that she would tie up at Tagish Post till nine o'clock, Sunday morning. It was then four o'clock, Saturday afternoon. The pilgrims called a meeting. On board was a large Peterborough canoe, consigned to the police post at the head of Lake Bennett. They agreed to be responsible for it and to deliver it. Next, they called for volunteers. Two men were needed to make a race for the *Flora*. A score of men volunteered on the instant. Among them was Churchill, such being his nature that he volunteered before he thought of Bondell's gripsack. When this thought came to him, he began to hope that he would not be selected; but a man who had made a name as captain of a college foot-ball eleven, as a president of an athletic club, as a dog-musher and a stampeder in the Yukon, and, moreover, who possessed such shoulders as he, had no right to avoid the honor. It was thrust upon him and upon a gigantic German, Nick Antonsen.

While a crowd of the pilgrims, the canoe on their shoulders, started on a trot over the portage, Churchill ran to his state-room. He turned the contents of the clothes-bag on the floor and caught up the grip, with the intention of intrusting it to the man next door. Then the thought smote him that it was not his grip, and that he had no right to let it out of his own possession. So he dashed ashore with it and ran up the portage, changing it often from one hand to the other, and wondering if it really did not weigh more than forty pounds.

It was half-past four in the afternoon when the two men started. The current of the Thirty Mile River was so strong that rarely could they use the paddles. It was out on one bank with a tow-line over the shoulders, stumbling over the rocks, forcing a way through the underbrush, slipping at times and falling into the water, wading often up to the knees and waist; and then, when an insurmountable bluff was encountered, it was into the canoe, out paddles, and a wild and losing dash across the current to the other bank, in paddles, over the side, and out towline again. It was exhausting work. Antonsen toiled like the giant he was, uncomplaining, persistent, but driven to his utmost by the powerful body and indomitable brain of Churchill. They never paused for rest. It was go, go, and keep on going. A crisp wind blew down the river, freezing their hands and making it imperative, from time to time, to beat the blood back into the numb fingers.

As night came on they were compelled to trust to luck. They fell repeatedly on the untraveled banks and tore their clothing to shreds in the underbrush they could not see. Both men were badly scratched and bleeding. A dozen times, in their wild dashes from bank to bank, they struck snags and were capsized. The first time this happened, Churchill dived and groped in three feet of water for the gripsack. He lost half an hour in recovering it, and after that it was carried securely lashed to the canoe. As long as the canoe floated it was safe. Antonsen jeered at the grip, and toward morning began to curse it; but Churchill vouchsafed no explanations.

Their delays and mischances were endless. On one swift bend, around which poured a healthy young rapid, they lost two hours, making a score of attempts and capsizing twice. At this point, on both banks, were precipitous bluffs, rising out of deep water, and along which they could neither tow nor pole, while they could not gain with the paddles against the current. At each attempt they strained to the utmost with the paddles, and each time, with hearts nigh to bursting from the effort, they were played out and swept back. They succeeded finally by an accident. In the swiftest current, near the end of another failure, a freak of the current sheered the canoe out of Churchill's control and flung it against the bluff. Churchill made a blind leap at the bluff and landed in a crevice. Holding on with one hand, he held the swamped canoe with the other till Antonsen dragged himself out of the water. Then they pulled the canoe out and rested. A fresh start at this crucial point took them by. They landed on the bank above, and plunged immediately ashore and into the brush with the tow-line.

Daylight found them far below Tagish Post. At nine o'clock Sunday morning they could hear the *Flora* whistling her departure. And when, at ten o'clock, they dragged themselves in to the Post, they could just barely see the *Flora's* smoke far to the southward. It was a pair of worn-out tatterdemalions that Captain Jones of the Mounted Police welcomed and fed, and he afterward averred that they possessed two of the most tremendous appetites he had ever observed. They lay down and slept in their wet rags by the stove. At the end of two hours Churchill got up, carried Bondell's grip, which he had used for a pillow, down to the canoe, kicked Antonsen awake, and started in pursuit of the *Flora*.

"There 's no telling what might happen—machinery break down, or something," was his reply to Captain Jones's expostulations. "I 'm going to catch that steamer and send her back for the boys."

Tagish Lake was white with a fall gale that blew in their teeth. Big, swinging seas rushed upon the canoe, compelling one man to bail and leaving one man to paddle. Headway could not be made. They ran along the shallow shore and went overboard, one man ahead on the tow-line, the other shoving on the canoe. They fought the gale up to their waists in the icy water, often up to their necks, often over their heads, and buried by the big, crested waves. There was no rest, never a moment's pause from the cheerless, heart-breaking battle. That night, at the head of Tagish Lake, in the thick of a driving snow-squall, they overhauled the *Flora*. Antonsen fell on board, lay where he had fallen, and snored. Churchill looked like a wild man. His clothes barely clung to him. His face was iced up and swollen from the protracted effort of twenty-four hours, while his hands were so swollen that he could not close the fingers. As for his feet, it was an agony to stand upon them.

The captain of the *Flora* was loath to go back to White Horse. Churchill was persistent and imperative; the captain was stubborn. He pointed out finally that nothing was to be gained by going back, because the only ocean steamer at Dyea, the *Athenian,* was to sail on Tuesday morning, and that he could not make the back trip to White Horse and bring up the stranded pilgrims in time to make the connection.

"What time does the *Athenian* sail?" Churchill demanded.

"Seven o'clock, Tuesday morning."

"All right," Churchill said, at the same time kicking a tattoo on the ribs of the snoring Antonsen. "You go back to White Horse. We 'll go ahead and hold the *Athenian.*"

Antonsen, stupid with sleep, not yet clothed in his waking mind, was bundled into the canoe, and did not realize what had happened till he was drenched with the icy spray of a big sea, and heard Churchill snarling at him through the darkness:

"Paddle, can't you! Do you want to be swamped?"

Daylight found them at Caribou Crossing, the wind dying down, and Antonsen too far gone to dip a paddle. Churchill grounded the canoe on a quiet beach, where they slept. He took the precaution of twisting his arm under the weight of his head. Every few minutes the pain of the pent circulation aroused him, whereupon he would look at his watch and twist the other arm under his head. At the end of two hours he fought with Antonsen to rouse him. Then they started. Lake Bennett, thirty miles in length, was like a mill-pond; but, half-way across, a gale from the south smote them and turned the water white. Hour after hour they repeated the struggle on Tagish, over the side, pulling and shoving on the canoe, up to their waists and necks, and over their heads in the icy water; toward the last the good-natured giant played completely out. Churchill drove him mercilessly; but when he pitched forward and bade fair to drown in three feet of water, the other dragged him into the canoe. After that, Churchill fought on alone, arriving at the police post at the head of Bennett in the early afternoon. He tried to help Antonsen out of the canoe, but failed. He listened to the exhausted man's heavy breathing, and envied him when he thought of what he himself had yet to undergo. Antonsen could lie there and sleep; but he, behind time, must go on over mighty Chilcat and down to the sea. The real struggle lay before him, and he almost regretted the strength that resided in his frame because of the torment it could inflict upon that frame.

Churchill pulled the canoe up on the beach, seized Bondell's grip, and started on a limping dog-trot for the police post.

"There 's a canoe down there, consigned to you from Dawson," he hurled at the officer who answered his knock. "And there 's a man in it pretty near dead. Nothing serious; only played out. Take care of him. I 've got to rush. Good-by. Want to catch the *Athenian.*"

A mile portage connected Lake Bennett and Lake Linderman, and his last words he flung back after him as he resumed the trot. It was a very painful trot, but he clenched his teeth and kept on, forgetting his pain most of the time in the fervent heat with which he regarded the gripsack. It was a severe handicap. He swung it from one hand to the other, and back again. He tucked it under his arm. He threw one hand over the opposite shoulder, and the bag bumped and pounded on his back as he ran along. He could scarcely hold it in his bruised and swollen fingers, and several times he dropped it. Once, in changing from one hand to the other, it escaped his clutch and fell in front of him, tripped him up, and threw him violently to the ground.

At the far end of the portage he bought an old set of pack-straps for a dollar, and in them he swung the grip. Also, he chartered a launch to run him the six miles to the upper end of Lake Linderman, where he arrived at four in the afternoon. The *Athenian* was to sail from Dyea next morning at seven. Dyea was twenty-eight miles away, and between towered Chilcat. He sat down to adjust his foot-gear for the long climb, and woke up. He had dozed the instant he sat down, though he had not slept thirty seconds. He was afraid his next doze might be longer, so he finished fixing his foot-gear standing up. Even then he was overpowered for a fleeting moment. He experienced the flash of unconsciousness; becoming aware of it, in mid-air, as his relaxed body was sinking to the ground, and as he caught himself together, stiffened his muscles with a spasmodic wrench, and escaped the fall. The sudden jerk back to consciousness left him sick and trembling. He beat his head with the heel of his hand, knocking wakefulness into the numb brain.

Jack Burns's pack-train was starting back light for Crater Lake, and Churchill was invited to a mule. Burns wanted to put the gripsack on another animal, but Churchill held on to it, carrying it on his saddle-pommel. But he dozed, and the grip persisted in dropping off the pommel, one side or the other, each time wakening him with a sickening start. Then, in the early darkness, Churchill's mule brushed him against a projecting branch that laid his cheek open. To cap it, the mule blundered off the trail and fell, throwing rider and gripsack out upon the rocks. After that, Churchill walked, or stumbled, rather, over the apology for a trail, leading the mule. Stray and awful odors, drifting from each side the trail, told of the horses that had died in the rush for gold. But he did not mind. He was too sleepy. By the time Long Lake was reached, however, he had recovered from his sleepiness; and at Deep Lake he resigned the gripsack to Burns. But thereafter, by the light of the dim stars, he kept his eyes on Burns. There were not going to be any accidents with that bag.

At Crater Lake the pack-train went into camp, and Churchill, slinging the grip on his back, started the steep climb for the summit. For the first time, on that precipitous wall, he realized how tired he was. He crept and crawled like a crab, burdened by the weight of his limbs. A distinct and painful effort of will was required each time he lifted a foot. An hallucination came to him that he was shod with lead, like a deep-sea diver, and it was all he could do to resist the desire to reach down and feel the lead. As for Bondell's gripsack, it was inconceivable that forty pounds could weigh so much. It pressed him down like a mountain, and he looked back with unbelief to the year before, when he had climbed that same pass with a hundred and fifty pounds on his back. If those loads had weighed a hundred and fifty pounds, then Bondell's grip weighed five hundred.

The first rise of the divide from Crater Lake was across a small glacier. Here was a well-defined trail. But above the glacier, which was also above timber-line, was naught but a chaos of naked rock and enormous boulders. There was no way of seeing the trail in the darkness, and he blundered on, paying thrice the ordinary exertion for all that he accomplished. He won the summit in the thick of howling wind and driving snow, providentially stumbling upon a small, deserted tent, into which he crawled. There he found and bolted some ancient fried potatoes and half a dozen raw eggs.

When the snow ceased and the wind eased down, he began the almost impossible descent. There was no trail, and he stumbled and blundered, often finding himself, at the last moment, on the edge of rocky walls and steep slopes the depth of which he had no way of judging. Part way down, the stars clouded over again, and in the consequent obscurity he slipped and rolled and slid for a hundred feet, landing bruised and bleeding on the bottom of a large, shallow hole. From all about him arose the stench of dead horses. The hole was handy to the trail, and the packers had made a practice of tumbling into it their broken and dying animals. The stench overpowered him, making him deathly sick, and as in a nightmare he scrambled out. Half-way up, he recollected Bondell's gripsack. It had fallen into the hole with him; the pack-strap had evidently broken, and he had forgotten it. Back he went into the pestilential charnel-pit, where he crawled around on hands and knees and vainly groped for half an hour. Altogether he encountered and counted seventeen dead horses (and one horse still alive that he shot with his revolver), before he found Bondell's grip. Looking back upon a life that had not been without valor and achievement, he unhesitatingly declared to himself that this return after the grip was the most heroic act he had ever performed. So heroic was it that he was twice on the verge of fainting before he crawled out of the hole.

By this time he had descended to the Scales, the steep pitch of Chilcat was past, and the way became easier. Not that it was an easy way, however, in the best of places; but it became a really possible trail, along which he could have made good time if he had not been worn out, if he had had light with which to pick his steps, and if it had not been for Bondell's gripsack. To him, in his exhausted condition, it was the last straw. Having barely strength to carry himself along, the additional weight of the grip was sufficient to throw him nearly every time he tripped or stumbled. And when he escaped tripping, branches reached out in the darkness, hooked the grip between his shoulders, and held him back.

His mind was made up that if he missed the *Athenian* it would be the fault of the gripsack. In fact, only two things remained in his consciousness—Bondell's grip and the steamer. He knew only those two things, and they became identified, in a way, with some stern mission upon which he had journeyed and toiled for centuries. He walked and struggled on as in a dream. As part of the dream was his arrival at Sheep Camp. He stumbled into a saloon, slid his shoulders out of the straps, and started to deposit the grip at his feet. But it slipped from his fingers and struck the floor with a heavy thud that was not unnoticed by two men who were just leaving. Churchill drank a glass of whisky, told the barkeeper to call him in ten minutes, and sat down, his feet on the grip, his head on his knees.

So badly did his misused body stiffen, that when he was called it required another ten minutes and a second glass of whisky to unbend his joints and limber up the muscles.

"Hey! not that way!" the barkeeper shouted, and then went after him and started him through the darkness toward Canyon City. Some little husk of inner consciousness told Churchill that the direction was right, and, still as in a dream, he took the cañon trail. He did not know what warned him, but, after what seemed several centuries of traveling, he sensed danger and drew his revolver. Still in the dream, he saw two men step out and heard them halt him. His revolver went off four times, and he saw the flashes and heard the explosions of their revolvers. Also, he was aware that he had been hit in the thigh. He saw one man go down, and, as the other came for him, he smashed him a straight blow with the heavy revolver full in the face. Then he turned and ran. He came from the dream shortly afterward, to find himself plunging down the trail at a limping lope. His first thought was for the gripsack. It was still on his back. He was convinced that what had happened was a dream till he felt for his revolver and found it gone. Next he became aware of a sharp stinging of his thigh, and, after investigating, he found his hand warm with blood. It was a superficial wound, but it was incontestable. He became wider awake, and kept up the lumbering run to Canyon City.

He found a man, with a team of horses and a wagon, who got out of bed and harnessed up for twenty dollars. Churchill crawled in on the wagon-bed and slept, the gripsack still on his back. It was a rough ride, over water-washed boulders down the Dyea Valley; but he roused only when the wagon hit the highest places. Any altitude of his body above the wagon-bed of less than a foot did not faze him. The last mile was smooth going, and he slept soundly.

He came to in the gray dawn, the driver shaking him savagely and howling into his ear that the *Athenian* was gone. Churchill looked blankly at the deserted harbor.

"There 's a smoke over at Skaguay," the man said.

Churchill's eyes were too swollen to see that far, but he said: "It 's she. Get me a boat."

The driver was obliging, and found a skiff and a man to row it for ten dollars, payment in advance. Churchill paid, and was helped into the skiff. It was beyond him to get in by himself. It was six miles to Skaguay, and he had a blissful thought of sleeping those six miles. But the man did not know how to row, and Churchill took the oars and toiled for a few more centuries. He never knew six longer and more excruciating miles. A snappy little breeze blew up the inlet and held him back. He had a gone feeling at the pit of the stomach, and suffered from faintness and numbness. At his command, the man took the bailer and threw salt water into his face.

The *Athenian's* anchor was up-and-down when they came alongside, and Churchill was at the end of his last remnant of strength.

"Stop her! Stop her!" he shouted hoarsely. "Important message! Stop her!"

Then he dropped his chin on his chest and slept. When half a dozen men started to carry him up the gang-plank, he awoke, reached for the grip, and clung to it like a drowning man.

On deck he became a center of horror and curiosity. The clothing in which he had left White Horse was represented by a few rags, and he was as frayed as his clothing. He had traveled for fifty-five hours at the top notch of endurance. He had slept six hours in that time, and he was twenty pounds lighter than when he started. Face and hands and body were scratched and bruised, and he could scarcely see. He tried to stand up, but failed, sprawling out on the deck, hanging on to the gripsack, and delivering his message.

"Now, put me to bed," he finished; "I 'll eat when I wake up."

They did him honor, carrying him down in his rags and dirt and depositing him and Bondell's grip in the bridal chamber, which was the biggest and most luxurious state-room in the ship. Twice he slept the clock around, and he had bathed and shaved and eaten and was leaning over the rail smoking a cigar when the two hundred pilgrims from White Horse came alongside.

By the time the *Athenian* arrived in Seattle, Churchill had fully recuperated, and he went ashore with Bondell's grip in his hand. He felt proud of that grip. To him it stood for achievement and integrity and trust. "I 've delivered the goods," was the way he expressed these various high terms to himself. It was early in the evening, and he went straight to Bondell's home. Louis Bondell was glad to see him, shaking hands with both hands at the same time and dragging him into the house.

"Oh, thanks, old man; it was good of you to bring it out," Bondell said when he received the gripsack.

He tossed it carelessly upon a couch, and Churchill noted with an appreciative eye the rebound of its weight from the springs. Bondell was volleying him with questions.

"How did you make out? How 're the boys? What became of Bill Smithers? Is Del Bishop still with Pierce? Did he sell my dogs? How did Sulphur Bottom show up? You 're looking fine. What steamer did you come out on?"

To all of which Churchill gave answer, till half an hour had gone by and the first lull in the conversation had arrived.

"Had n't you better take a look at it?" he suggested, nodding his head at the gripsack.

"Oh, it 's all right," Bondell answered. "Did Mitchell's dump turn out as much as he expected?"

"I think you 'd better look at it," Churchill insisted. "When I deliver a thing, I want to be satisfied that it 's all right. There 's always the chance that somebody might have got into it when I was asleep, or something."

"It 's nothing important, old man," Bondell answered, with a laugh.

"Nothing important," Churchill echoed in a faint, small voice. Then he spoke with decision: "Louis, what 's in that bag? I want to know."

Louis looked at him curiously, then left the room and returned with a bunch of keys. He inserted his hand and drew out a heavy 44 Colt's revolver. Next came out a few boxes of ammunition for the revolver and several boxes of Winchester cartridges.

Churchill took the gripsack and looked into it. Then he turned it upside down and shook it gently.

"The gun 's all rusted," Bondell said. "Must have been out in the rain."

"Yes," Churchill answered. "Too bad it got wet. I guess I was a bit careless."

He got up and went outside. Ten minutes later Louis Bondell went out and found him on the steps, sitting down, elbows on knees and chin on hands, gazing steadfastly out into the darkness.

4
Thanksgiving on Slav Creek

THANKSGIVING ON Slav Creek

By Jack London

Illustrated by E. W. Deming

SHE woke up with a start. Her husband was speaking in a low voice, insistently.

"Come," he added. "Get up. Get up, Nella. Quick. Get up."

"But I don't want to get up," she objected, striving vainly to lapse back into the comfortable drowse.

"But I say you must. And don't make any noise, but come along. Hurry! Oh, do hurry! Our fortune's made if you will only hurry!"

Nella Tichborne was now wide awake, what with the suppressed excitement in his whispers, and she thrust her feet out with a shiver upon the cold cabin floor.

"What is it?" she asked, petulantly. "What is it?"

"'Ssh!" he sibilated. "Don't make a noise. Mum's the word. Dress at once."

"But what is it?"

"Be quiet, if you love me, and dress."

"Now, George, I won't move an inch until you tell me." She capped the ultimatum by sitting back on the edge of the bunk.

The man groaned. "Oh, the time, the precious time, you're losing! Didn't I tell you our fortune was made? Do hurry! It's a tip. Nobody knows. A secret. There's a stampede on. 'Ssh! Put on warm clothes. It's the coldest yet. The frost is sixty-five below. I'm going to call Ikeesh. She would like to be in on it, I know. And oh, Nella—"

"Yes?"

"Do be quick."

He stepped across to the other end of the cabin where a blanket partitioned the room into two, and called Ikeesh. The Indian woman was already awake. Her husband was up on his Bonanza claim, though this was her cabin, in which she was entertaining George Tichborne and Nella.

"What um matter, Tichborne?" she asked. "Um Nella sick?"

"No, no. Stampede. Rich creek. Plenty gold. Hurry up and dress."

"What um time?"

"Twelve o'clock. Midnight. Don't make any noise."

Five minutes later the cabin door opened and they passed out.

"'Ssh!" he cautioned.

"Oh, George! Have you got the frying-pan?"

"Yes."

"And the gold-pan? And the axe?"

"Yes, yes, Nella. And did you remember the baking-powder?"

They crunched rapidly through the snow, down the hill into sleeping Dawson. Light stampeding packs were on their backs, containing a fur robe each, and the barest necessaries for a camp in the polar frost. But Dawson was not sleeping, after all. Cabin windows were flashing into light, and ever and anon the mumble of voices drifted to them through the darkness. The dogs were beginning to howl and the doors to slam. By the time they reached the Barracks the whole town was aroar behind them. Here the trail dropped abruptly over the bank and crossed the packed ice of the Yukon to the farther shore.

George Tichborne swore softly and to himself; but aloud: "It's leaked out somehow, and everybody's in it. Sure to be a big stampede now. But hurry up; they're all behind us, and we'll make it yet!"

"George!" A frightened wail punctured the still air and died away as Nella slipped on the icy footing and shot down the twenty-foot embankment into the pit of darkness beneath.

"Nella! Nella! Where are you?" He was falling over the great ice-blocks and groping his way to her as best he could. "Are you hurt? Where are you?"

"All right! Coming!" she answered, cheerily. "Only the snow's all down my back and melting. Brrr!"

Hardly were the trio reunited when two black forms plumped into their midst from above. These were followed by others, some arriving decorously, but the majority scorning conventional locomotion and peregrinating along on every other portion of their anatomies but their feet. They also had stampeding packs on their backs and a great haste in their hearts.

"Where's the trail?" the cry went up. And thereat all fell to seeking for the path across the river.

At last George Tichborne found it, and, with Nella and Ikeesh, led the way. But in the darkness they lost it repeatedly, slipping, stumbling, and falling over the wildly piled ice. Finally, in desperation, he lighted a candle, and as there was not a breath of wind, the way was easier. Nella looked back at th fifty stampeders behind and laughed half hysterically. Her husband gritted his teet and plunged savagely on.

"At least we're at the head of the bunch the very first," he whispered to her, as the swung south on the smoother trail which ra along under the shadow of the bluffs.

But just then a flaming ribbon rose athwar the sky, spilling pulsating fire over the fac of the night. The trail ahead lighted up, an as far as they could see it was cumbered wit shadowy forms, all toiling in the one direc tion. And now those behind began to pas them, one by one, straining mightily with th endeavor.

"Oh, Nella! Hurry!" He seized he hand and strove to drag her along. "It's th one chance we've been waiting for so long Think of it if we fail!"

"Oh! Oh!" She gasped and tottered "We will never make it! No, never!"

There was a sharp pain in her side, and sh was dizzy with the unwonted speed. Ikees grunted encouragement and took her othe hand. But none the less the vague form from the rear continued steadily to overtak and pass them.

Hours which were as centuries passed. Th night seemed without end to Nella. Gradual ly her consciousness seemed to leave her, he whole soul narrowing down to the one me chanical function of walking. Ever lifting ever falling, and ever lifting anon, her limb seemed to have become great pendulums o time. And before and behind glimmered tw eternities, and between the two eternities ever lifting, ever falling, she pulsed in vas rhythmical movement. She was no longe Nella Tichborne, a woman, but a rhythm— that was all, a rhythm. Sometimes the voice of Ikeesh and her husband came to her faint ly; but in her semi-conscious condition sh really did not hear. To-morrow there woul be no record of the sounds; for a rhythm i not receptive to sound. The stars paled an dimmed, but she did not heed; the aurora borealis shrouded its fires, and the darknes which is of the dawn fell upon the earth but she did not know.

But ere the darkness fell, Ikeesh drew u to Tichborne and pointed to the loom of th mountains above the west shore of the river.

"Um Swede Creek?" she asked, laconical ly, pointing whither the trail led.

"No," he replied. "Slav Creek."

"EVEN THE MAN AND THE INDIAN WOMAN GREW WEARY."
Drawn by E. W. DEMING.

"Um no Slav Creek. Slav Creek—" She turned and pointed into the darkness five degrees to the south. "Um Slav Creek."

He came suddenly to a stop. Nella persisted in walking on, heedless of his outcries, till he ran after her and forced her to stop. She was obedient, but as a rhythm she no longer existed. The two eternities, which it was her task to hold apart, had rushed together, and she was not. So she wandered off to the old home down in the States, and sat under the great trees, and joyed in the warm sunshine—the old home, the old mortgaged home, which had driven them poleward after the yellow gold! The old home which it was their one aim to redeem! But she forgot all this, and laughed, and babbled, and poured the sunshine back and forth from hand to hand. How warm it was! Was there ever the like?

Tichborne conferred with Ikeesh. She so stolidly reiterated that Slav Creek lay farther to the south that he believed.

"Somebody went astray in the dark," he exulted, "and the rest followed his trail like sheep. Come on! Come on! We'll be in at the finish yet, and ahead of no end of those that passed us!"

He cut across a five-mile flat into the southwest, and two hours later, with gray dawn creeping over the landscape, entered the wood-hidden mouth of Slav Creek. The fresh signs of the stampede were so many and so various that he knew Ikeesh had spoken true, though he feared that the mistake had occurred too late in the night to have led enough on the wild-goose chase up Swede Creek.

"Oh, Nella," he called to his wife, stumbling blindly at his heels, "it's all right. We are sure to get a claim. Day has come. Look about you. This is Slav Creek, and behold, the day is Thanksgiving day!"

She turned a blank face upon him. "Yes, the mortgage shall be lifted, principal and interest, I promise you—George and I both promise you. Even now, to-morrow, do we go north to lift the mortgage."

Tichborne glanced helplessly at Ikeesh.

"Um much tired," she commented, dryly. "But um be all right bime-by. Bime-by make camp, um be all right."

They hastened on for five miles more, when they came to the first white-blazed trees and fresh-planted stakes of the newly located claims. Hour after hour they travelled up the frozen bed of the creek, and still, stake to stake, the claims stretched in an unbroken line. Even the man and the Indian woman grew weary and panted. Ikeesh kept a jealous eye on Nella's face, and now and again, when it turned white, rubbed with snow the tip of the nose and the stretched skin of the cheek-bones. They passed many men—the successful ones—rolled in their furs by the side of the trail, or cooking and warming themselves over crackling fires of dry spruce. At eleven o'clock the sun rose in the south-east; but though there was no warmth in its rays, it gave a cheerier aspect to things.

"How much farther do the stakes run?" Tichborne asked of a man limping down the trail.

"I staked 179," the man answered, stopping to pound the aching muscles of his legs. "But there were about ten more behind me; so I guess they've run it up to 189."

"And this is 107," Tichborne calculated aloud. "Five-hundred-foot claims—ten to the mile—about eight miles yet, eh?"

"Reckon you've 'bout hit it on the head," the other assured him. "But you'd better hurry. Half the stampede went wrong up Swede Creek—that's the next one to this—but they're onto themselves now, and crossing the divide and tapping Slav Creek in the hundred-and-eighties.

"But they're having a terrible time," he shouted back as he went on his way. "I met the first one that succeeded in crossing over. He said the trail was lined with people teetotally played out, and that he knew himself of five frozen to death on the divide."

Frozen to death! The phrase served to rouse Nella from her maze of memory visions. Her glimmering senses came back to her, and she opened her eyes with a start. The interminable night was gone — spent where or how she could not say—and day broke upon her with a blinding flash. She looked about. Everything was strange and unreal. Both her companions were limping pitifully, and she was aware of a great dull pain in her own limbs. Her husband turned his head, and she saw his face and beard a mass of bristling ice. Ikeesh's mouth was likewise matted with frost, and her brows and lashes long and white. And Nella felt the weight on her own lashes, and the difficulty of drawing them apart from each other whenever she closed her eyes. The doubly excessive demand of the toil and the frost had burned up all the fuel of her body, and she felt cold and faint with hunger. This latter she found worse than the agony of the overused muscles; for a quivering nausea came upon her, and her knees trembled and knocked together with weakness.

Occasionally Tichborne made excursions to one side or the other in search of the claim-stakes, which were not always posted in the creek-bed. At such times Nella dropped down to rest, but Ikeesh dragged her afoot again, and shook her, and struck her harsh blows upon her body. For Ikeesh knew the way of the cold, and that a five-minute rest without fire meant death. So Nella had lapses and cruel awakenings till the whole thing seemed a hideous nightmare. Sometimes the trees became gibbering shades, and Slav Creek turned to an Inferno, with her husband as Virgil, and leading her from circle to circle of the damned. But at other times, when she was dimly conscious, the memory of the old home was strong upon her, and the mortgage nerved her on.

A long, long time afterward—ages afterward, it seemed—she heard George cry aloud joyfully, and looking at him as though from a great distance, she saw him slashing the bark from a standing tree, and writing on the white surface with a lead-pencil. *At last!* She sank down into the snow, but Ikeesh struck her a stinging blow across the mouth. Nella came back angrily to her feet, but Ikeesh pushed her away and set her to work gathering dry wood.

Again came a long lapse, during which she toiled mechanically and unknowing; and when she next found herself she was in the furs by a big fire, and Ikeesh was stirring a batter of flour and water and boiling coffee. To her surprise, Nella felt much better after the rest, and was able to look about her. George ran up with a gold-pan of gravel which he had got from the creek bottom through an air-hole, and warmed his hands by the fire. When he had panned it out he brought the prospect over to her. The streak of black sand on the bottom was specked with yellow grains of glistening gold, and there were several small nuggets besides. He leaped up and down and about like a boy, for all his weary body.

"We've struck it at last, Nella!" he cried. "The home is safe! If that is a surface indication, what must it be on bed-rock?"

"Tell you what—"

They turned their heads, startled. A man had crawled up to the fire unobserved in their excitement.

"Tell you what," he glowed, "it's the richest creek in Alaska and the Northwest.

"GEORGE RAN UP WITH A GOLD PAN OF GOLD."
Drawn by E. W. Deming.

Sure!" He sat down uninvited, and tried to unfasten his ice-bound moccasins. "Say, I broke through the ice up here a piece and wet my feet. I kind of think they're freezing."

Ikeesh stopped from her cooking, and Tichborne lending a hand, they cut off the new-comer's moccasins and socks and rubbed his white feet till the glow of life returned.

"Tell you what," the sufferer went on, unconcernedly, while they worked over him, "judging from indications, you people are located on the richest run of the creek. Sure! But I got in on it; you betcher life I did! Got lost on Swede Creek, too, and hit across the divide. Say! No end of frozen men on that trail. But I got in on it, tell you what!"

"A true Thanksgiving, Nella."

George Tichborne passed her a tin plate of flapjacks swimming in bacon grease and a great mug of piping black coffee. She seized his hand impulsively and pressed it, and her eyes grew luminously soft....

"Tell you what—" she heard the new-comer begin; but a vision of the old home, warm in the sunshine, came into her eyes, and she dropped off to sleep without hearing "what."

5
Housekeeping in the Klondike

HOUSEKEEPING IN THE KLONDIKE

BY JACK LONDON

ILLUSTRATED BY E. W. DEMING

HOUSEKEEPING in the Klondike—that's bad! And by *men*—worse. Reverse the proposition, if you will, yet you will fail to mitigate, even by a hair's-breadth, the woe of it. It is bad, unutterably bad, for a man to keep house, and it is equally bad to keep house in the Klondike. That's the sum and substance of it. Of course men will be men, and especially is this true of the kind who wander off to the frozen rim of the world. The glitter of gold is in their eyes, they are borne along by uplifting ambition, and in their hearts is a great disdain for everything in the culinary department save "grub." "Just so long as it's grub," they say, coming in off trail, gaunt and ravenous, "grub, and piping

"SARCASTIC COMMENTS ON THE WAY YOU FRY THE BACON."
Drawn by E. W. DEMING.

hot." Nor do they manifest the slightest regard for the genesis of the same; they prefer to begin at "revelations."

Yes, it would seem a pleasant task to cook for such men; but just let them lie around cabin to rest up for a week, and see with what celerity they grow high-stomached and make sarcastic comments on the way you fry the bacon or boil the coffee. And behold how each will spring his own strange and marvellous theory as to how sour-dough bread should be mixed and baked. Each has his own recipe (formulated, mark you, from personal experience only), and to him it is an idol of brass, like unto no other man's, and he'll fight for it—ay,. down to the last wee pinch of soda—and if need be, die for it. If you should happen to catch him on trail, completely exhausted, you may blacken his character, his flag, and his ancestral tree with impunity; but breathe the slightest whisper against his sour-dough bread, and he will turn upon and rend you.

From this it may be gathered what an unstable thing sour dough is. Never was coquette so fickle. You cannot depend upon it. Still, it is the simplest thing in the world. Make a batter and place it near the stove (that it may not freeze) till it ferments or sours. Then mix the dough with it, and sweeten with soda to taste—of course replenishing the batter for next time. There it is. Was there ever anything simpler? But, oh, the tribulations of the cook! It is never twice the same. If the batter could only be placed away in an equable temperature, all well and good. If one's comrades did not interfere, much vexation of spirit might be avoided. But this cannot be; for Tom fires up the stove till the cabin is become like the hot-room of a Turkish bath; Dick forgets all about the fire till the place is a refrigerator; then along comes Harry and shoves the sour-dough bucket right against the stove to make way for the drying of his mittens. Now heat is a most potent factor in accelerating the fermentation of flour and water, and hence the unfortunate cook is constantly in disgrace with Tom, Dick, and Harry. Last week his bread was yellow from a plethora of soda; this week it is sour from a prudent lack of the same; and next week—ah, who can tell save the god of the fire-box?

Some cooks aver they have so cultivated their olfactory organs that they can tell to the fraction of a degree just how sour the batter is. Nevertheless they have never been known to bake two batches of bread which were at all alike. But this fact casts not the slightest shadow upon the infallibility of their theory. One and all, they take advantage of circumstances, and meanly crawl out by laying the blame upon the soda, which was dampened "the time the canoe overturned," or upon the flour, which they got in trade from "that half-breed fellow with the dogs."

The pride of the Klondike cook in his bread is something which passes understanding. The highest commendatory degree which can be passed upon a man in that country, and the one which distinguishes him from the tenderfoot, is that of being a "sour-dough boy." Never was a college graduate prouder of his "sheepskin" than the old-timer of this appellation. There is a certain distinction about it, from which the new-comer is invidiously excluded. A tenderfoot with his baking-powder is an inferior creature, a freshman; but a "sour-dough boy" is a man of stability, a post-graduate in that art of arts—bread-making.

Next to bread a Klondike cook strives to achieve distinction by his doughnuts. This may appear frivolous at first glance, and at second, considering the materials with which he works, an impossible feat. But doughnuts are all-important to the man who goes on trail for a journey of any length. Bread freezes easily, and there is less grease and sugar, and hence less heat in it, than in doughnuts. The latter do not solidify except at extremely low temperatures, and they are very handy to carry in the pockets of a Mackinaw jacket and munch as one travels along. They are made much after the manner of their brethren in warmer climes, with the exception that they are cooked in bacon grease—the more grease, the better they are. Sugar is the cook's chief stumbling-block; if it is very scarce, why, add more grease. The men never mind—on trail. In the cabin?—well, that's another matter; besides, bread is good enough for them then.

The cold, the silence, and the darkness somehow seem to be considered the chief woes of the Klondiker. But this is all wrong. There is one woe which overshadows all others —the lack of sugar. Every party which goes north signifies a manly intention to do without sugar, and after it gets there bemoans itself upon its lack of foresight. Man can endure hardship and horror with equanimity,

"OH, THE TRIBULATIONS OF THE COOK!"
Drawn by E. W. DEMING.

but take from him his sugar, and he raises his lamentations to the stars. And the worst of it is that it all falls back upon the long-suffering cook. Naturally, coffee, and mush, and dried fruit, and rice, eaten without sugar, do not taste exactly as they should. A certain appeal to the palate is missing. Then the cook is blamed for his vile concoctions. Yet, if he be a man of wisdom, he may judiciously escape the major part of this injustice. When he places a pot of mush upon the table, let him see to it that it is accompanied by a pot of stewed dried apples or peaches. This propinquity will suggest the combination to the men, and the flatness of the one will be neutralized by the sharpness of the other. In the distress of a sugar famine, if he be a cook of parts, he will boil rice and fruit together in one pot; and if he cook a dish of rice and prunes properly, of a verity he will cheer up the most melancholy member of the party, and extract from him great gratitude.

Such a cook must indeed be a man of resources. Should his comrades cry out that vinegar be placed upon the beans, and there is no vinegar, he must know how to make it out of water, dried apples, and brown paper. He obtains the last from the bacon-wrappings, and it is usually saturated with grease. But that does not matter. He will early learn that in a land of low temperatures it is impossible for bacon grease to spoil anything. It is to the white man what blubber and seal oil are to the Eskimo. Soul-winning gravies may be made from it by the addition of water and browned flour over the fire. Some cooks base far-reaching fame solely upon their gravy, and their names come to be on the lips of men wherever they forgather at the feast. When the candles give out, the cook fills a sardine-can with bacon grease, manufactures a wick out of the

"'SWAPPING' FOR CHILLI-PEPPERS."
Drawn by E. W. DEMING.

carpenter's sail-twine, and behold! the slush-lamp stands complete. It goes by another and less complimentary name in the vernacular, and, next to sour-dough bread, is responsible for more men's souls than any other single cause of degeneracy in the Klondike.

The ideal cook should also possess a Semitic incline to his soul. Initiative in his art is not the only requisite; he must keep an eye upon the variety of his larder. He must "swap" grub with the gentile understandingly; and woe unto him should the balance of trade be against him. His comrades will thrust it into his teeth every time the bacon is done over the turn, and they will even rouse him from his sleep to remind him of it. For instance, previous to the men going out for a trip on trail, he cooks several gallons of beans in the company of numerous chunks of salt pork and much bacon grease. This mess he then moulds into blocks of convenient size and places on the roof, where it freezes into bricks in a couple of hours. Thus the men, after a weary day's travel, have but to chop off chunks with an axe and thaw out in the frying-pan. Now the chances preponderate against more than one party in ten having chilli-peppers in their outfits. But the cook, supposing him to be fitted for his position, will ferret out that one party, discover some particular shortage in its grub-supply of which he has plenty, and swop the same for chilli-peppers. These in turn he will incorporate in the mess aforementioned, and behold a dish which even the hungry arctic gods may envy. Variety in the grub is as welcome to the men as nuggets. When, after eating dried peaches for months, the cook trades a few cupfuls of the same for apricots, the future at once takes on a more roseate hue. Even a change in the brand of bacon will revivify blasted faith in the country.

fire, then proceeds to dress. After that the centre of his orbit is the front of the stove, the diameter the length of his arms. Even then his comrades are continually encroaching upon his domain, and he is at constant warfare to prevent territorial grabs.

If the men are working hard on the claim, the cook is also expected to find his own wood and water. The former he chops up and sleds into camp, the latter he brings home in a sack—unless he is unusually diligent, in which case he has a ton or so of water piled up before the door. Whenever he is not cooking, he is thawing out ice, and betweenwhiles running out and hoisting on the windlass for his comrades in the shaft.

FEEDING THE DOGS.
Drawn by E. W. Deming.

It is no sinecure, being cook in the Klondike. Often he must do his work in a cabin measuring ten by twelve on the inside, and occupied by three other men besides himself. When it is considered that these men eat, sleep, lounge, smoke, play cards, and entertain visitors there, and also in that small space house the bulk of their possessions, the size of the cook's orbit may be readily computed. In the morning he sits up in bed, reaches out and strikes the

The care of the dogs also devolves upon him, and he carries his life and a long club in his hand every time he feeds them.

But there is one thing the cook does not have to do, nor any man in the Klondike — and that is, make another man's bed. In fact, the beds are never made except when the blankets become unfolded, or when the pine needles have all fallen off the boughs which form the mattress. When the cabin has a dirt floor and the men do their carpenter-work inside, the cook never sweeps it. It is much warmer to let the chips and shavings remain. Whenever he kindles a fire he uses a couple of handfuls of the floor. However, when the deposit becomes so deep that his head is knocking against the roof, he seizes a shovel and removes a foot or so of it.

Nor does he have any windows to wash; but if the carpenter is busy he must make his own windows. This is simple. He saws a hole out of the side of the cabin, inserts a home-made sash, and for panes falls back upon the treasured writing-tablet. A sheet of this paper, rubbed thoroughly with bacon grease, becomes transparent, sheds water when it thaws, and keeps the cold out and the heat in. In cold weather the ice will form upon the inside of it to the thickness of sometimes two or three inches. When the bulb of the mercurial thermometer has frozen solid, the cook turns to his window, and by the thickness of the icy coating infallibly gauges the outer cold within a couple of degrees.

A certain knowledge of astronomy is required of the Klondike cook, for another task of his is to keep track of the time. Before going to bed he wanders outside and studies the heavens. Having located the Pole Star by means of the Great Bear, he inserts two slender wands in the snow, a couple of yards apart and in line with the North Star. The next day, when the sun on the southern horizon casts the shadows of the wands to the northward and in line, he knows it to be twelve o'clock, noon, and sets his watch and those of his partners accordingly. As stray dogs are constantly knocking his wands out of line with the North Star, it becomes his habit to verify them regularly every night, and thus another burden is laid upon him.

But, after all, while the woes of the man who keeps house and cooks food in the northland are innumerable, there is one redeeming feature in his lot which does not fall to the women housewives of other lands. When things come to a pass with his feminine prototype, she throws her apron over her head and has a good cry. Not so with him, being a man and a Klondiker. He merely cooks a little more atrociously, raises a storm of grumbling, and resigns. After that he takes up his free out-door life again, and exerts himself mightily in making life miserable for the unlucky comrade who takes his place in the management of the household destinies.

6
The Call of the Wild

THE CALL OF THE WILD

"Old longings nomadic leap,
Chafing at custom's chain;
Again from its brumal sleep
Wakens the ferine strain."

Buck did not read the newspapers, or he would have known that trouble was brewing, not alone for himself but for every tidewater dog, strong of muscle and with warm, long hair, from Puget Sound to San Diego. Because men, groping in the Arctic darkness, had found a yellow metal, and because steamship and transportation companies were booming the find, thousands of men were rushing into the Northland. These men wanted dogs, and the dogs they wanted were heavy dogs, strong of muscle and with warm, long hair.

Buck lived at a big house in the sun-kissed Santa Clara Valley; Judge Miller's place, it was called. It stood back from the road, half-hidden among the trees, through which glimpses could be caught of the great cool veranda that ran around its four sides. The house was approached by graveled driveways which wound about through wide-spreading lawns and under the interlacing boughs of tall poplars. At the rear things were on even a more spacious scale than at the front. There were great stables, where a dozen grooms and boys held forth, rows of vine-clad servants' cottages, an endless and orderly array of outhouses, long grape arbors, green pastures, orchards and berry patches. Then there was the pumping plant for the artesian well, and the big cement tank where Judge Miller's boys took their morning plunge and kept cool in the hot afternoons.

And over this great demesne Buck ruled. Here he was born, and here he had lived the four years of his life. It was true, there were other dogs. There could not but be other dogs on so vast a place, but they did not count. They came and went, resided in the populous kennels, or lived obscurely in the recesses of the house after the fashion of Toots, the Japanese pug, or Ysabel, the Mexican hairless—strange creatures that rarely put nose out of doors or set foot to ground. On the other hand, there were the fox terriers, a score of them at least, who yelped fearful promises at Toots and Ysabel looking out of the windows and protected by a legion of housemaids armed with brooms and mops.

But Buck was neither house-dog nor kennel-dog. The whole realm was his. He plunged into the swimming tank or went hunting with the Judge's sons; he escorted Mollie and Alice, the Judge's daughters, on long twilight or early morning rambles; on wintry nights he lay at the Judge's feet before the roaring library fire; he carried the Judge's grandsons on his back or rolled them in the grass, and guarded their footsteps through wild adventures down to the fountain in the stable yard, and even beyond, where the paddocks were and the berry patches. Among the terriers he stalked imperiously, and Toots and Ysabel he utterly ignored, for he was King, king over all creeping, crawling, flying things of

Judge Miller's place, humans included.

His father, Elmo, a huge St. Bernard, had been the Judge's inseparable companion, and Buck bade fair to follow in the way of his father. He was not so large—he weighed only one hundred and forty pounds—for his mother, Shep, had been a Scotch shepherd dog. Nevertheless, one hundred and forty pounds, to which was added the dignity that comes of good living and universal respect, enabled him to carry himself in right royal fashion. During the four years since his puppyhood he had lived the life of a sated aristocrat; he had a fine pride in himself, was even a trifle egotistical, just as country gentlemen sometimes become because of their insular situation. But he had saved himself by not becoming a mere pampered house-dog. Hunting and kindred outdoor delights had kept down the fat and hardened his muscles; and like the cold-tubbing races, the love of water had been to him a tonic and a health-preserver.

And this was the manner of dog Buck was in the fall of 1897, when the Klondike Rush sprang up and dragged men from all the world into the frozen North. But Buck did not read the newspapers, and he did not know that Manuel, one of the gardener's helpers, was an undesirable acquaintance. Manuel had one besetting sin. He loved to play Chinese lottery. Also, in his gambling, he had one besetting weakness: faith in a system, and this made his damnation certain. For to play a system requires money, whereas the wages of a gardener's helper do not lap over the needs of a wife and numerous progeny.

The Judge was at a meeting of the Raisin Growers' Association and the boys were busy organizing an athletic club on the memorable night of Manuel's treachery. No one saw him and Buck go off through the orchard on what Buck imagined was merely a stroll. And with the exception of a solitary man, no one saw them arrive at the little flag station known as College Park. This man talked with Manuel, and money chinked between them.

"You might wrap up the goods before you deliver 'm," the stranger said gruffly, and Manuel doubled a piece of stout rope arck's neck under the collar.

"Twist it, an' you'll choke' m plentee," said Manuel, and the stranger grunted a ready affirmative.

Buck had accepted the rope with quiet dignity. To be sure, it was an unwonted performance, but he had learned to trust in men he knew and to give them credit for a wisdom that outreached his own. But when the ends of the rope were placed in the stranger's hands he growled menacingly. He merely intimated his displeasure, in his pride believing that to intimate was to command. But to his surprise the rope tightened around his neck, shutting off his breath. In quick rage he sprang at the man, who met him half-way, grappled him close by the throat, and with a deft twist threw him over on his back. Then the rope tightened mercilessly, while Buck struggled in a fury, his tongue lolling out of his mouth and his great chest panting futilely. Never in all his life had he been so vilely treated, and never in all his life had he been so angry. But his strength ebbed, his eyes glazed, and he knew nothing when the train was flagged and the two men threw him into the baggage car.

The next he knew he was dimly aware that his tongue was hurting and that he was being jolted along in some kind of a conveyance. The hoarse shriek of a locomotive, whistling a crossing, told him where he was. He had traveled too often with the Judge not to know the sensation of riding in a baggage car. He opened his eyes, and into them came the unbridled anger of a kidnaped king. The man sprang for his throat, but Buck was too quick for him. His jaws closed on the hand, nor did they relax till his senses were choked out of him once more.

"Yep; has fits," the man said, hiding his mangled hand from the baggageman, whc had been attracted by the sounds of struggle. "I'm takin' 'm up for the boss to 'Frisco. A crack dog-doctor there thinks he can cure 'em."

Concerning that night's ride the man spoke most eloquently for himself in a little shed back of a saloon on the San Francisco water front.

"All I get is fifty for it," he grumbled. "An' I wouldn't do it over for a thousand, cold cash."

His hand was wrapped in a bloody handkerchief, and the right trouser-leg was ripped from knee to ankle.

"How much did the other mug get?" the saloonkeeper demanded.

"A hundred," was the reply. "Wouldn't

take a sou less, so help me."

"That makes a hundred and fifty," the saloonkeeper calculated; "and he's worth it, or I'm a squarehead."

The kidnaper undid the bloody wrappings and looked at his lacerated hand. "If I don't get the hydrophoby——"

"It'll be because you was born to hang," laughed the saloonkeeper. "Here, lend me a hand before you pull your freight," he added.

Dazed, suffering intolerable pain from throat and tongue, with the life half throttled out of him, Buck attempted to face his tormentors. But he was thrown down and choked repeatedly, till they succeeded in filing the heavy brass collar from off his neck. Then the rope was removed and he was flung into a cagelike crate. There he lay for the remainder of the weary night, nursing his wrath and wounded pride. He could not understand what it all meant. What did they want with him, these strange men? Why were they keeping him pent up in this narrow crate? He did not know why, but he felt oppressed by the vague sense of impending calamity. Several times during the night he sprang to his feet when the shed-door rattled open, expecting to see the Judge, or the boys at least. But each time it was the bulging face of the saloonkeeper that peered in at him by the sickly light of a tallow candle. And each time the joyful bark that trembled in Buck's throat was twisted into a savage growl.

But the saloonkeeper let him alone, and in the morning four men entered and picked up the crate. More tormentors, Buck decided, for they were evil-looking creatures, ragged and and he stormed and raged at them through the bars. They only laughed and poked sticks at him, which he promptly assailed with his teeth till he realized that that was what they wanted. Whereupon he lay down sullenly and allowed the crate to be lifted into a wagon. Then he, and the crate in which he was imprisoned, began a passage through many hands. Clerks in the express office took charge of him; he was carted about in another wagon; a truck carried him, with an assortment of boxes and parcels, upon a ferry steamer; he was trucked off the steamer into a great railway depot; and finally he was deposited in an express car.

For two days and nights this express car was dragged along at the tail of shrieking locomotives. And for two days and nights Buck neither ate nor drank. In his anger he had met the first advances of the express messengers with growls, and they had retaliated by teasing him. When he flung himself against the bars, quivering and frothing, they laughed at him and taunted him. They growled and barked like detestable dogs, mewed, and flapped their arms and crowed. It was all very silly, he knew, but therefore the more outrage to his dignity, and his anger waxed and waxed. He did not mind the hunger so much, but the lack of water caused him severe suffering and fanned his wrath to fever-pitch. For that matter, high-strung and finely sensitive, the ill-treatment had flung him into a fever, which was fed by the inflammation of his parched and swollen throat and tongue.

He was glad for one thing; the rope was off his neck. That had given them an unfair advantage; but now that it was off he would show them. They should never get another rope around his neck. Upon that he was resolved. For two days and nights he neither ate nor drank, and during those two days and nights of torment he accumulated a fund of wrath that boded ill for whomever first fell foul of him. His eyes

PERRAULT

turned bloodshot; he became metamorphosed into a raging fiend. So changed was he that the Judge himself would not have recognized him; while the express messengers breathed with relief when they bundled him off the train at Seattle.

Four men gingerly carried the crate from the wagon into a small, high-walled back yard. A stout man with a red sweater that sagged generously at the neck came out and signed the book for the driver. That was the man, Buck divined, the next tormentor, and he hurled himself savagely against the bars. The man smiled grimly, and brought a hatchet and a club.

"You ain't going to take him out now?" the driver asked.

"Sure," the man replied, driving the hatchet into the crate.

There was an instantaneous scattering of the four men who had carried it in, and from safe perches on the wall they prepared to watch the performance.

Buck rushed at the splintering wood, sinking his teeth into it, surging and wrestling with it. Wherever the hatchet fell on the outside he was there on the inside, snarling and growling, as furiously anxious to get out as the man in the red sweater was calmly intent on getting him out.

FRANÇOIS

"Now, you red-eyed devil," he said, when he had made an opening sufficient for the passage of Buck's body. At the same time he dropped the hatchet and shifted the club to his right hand.

And Buck was truly a red-eyed devil as he drew himself together for the spring, hair bristling, mouth foaming, and a mad glitter in his bloodshot eyes. Straight at the man he launched his one hundred and forty pounds of fury, surcharged with the pent passion of two days and nights. In midair, just as his jaws were about to close on the man, he received a shock that checked his body and brought his teeth together with an agonizing clip. He whirled over, fetching the ground on his back and side; he had never been struck by a club in his life and did not understand. With a snarl that was part bark and more scream, he was on his feet and launched into the air again. And again the shock came and he was brought crushingly to the ground. This time he knew it was the club, but his madness knew no caution. A dozen times he charged, and as often the club broke the charge and smashed him down.

Following upon a particularly fierce blow he crawled to his feet, too dazed to rush. He staggered limply about, the blood flowing from nose and mouth and ears, his beautiful coat sprayed and flecked with bloody slaver. Then the man advanced and deliberately dealt him a frightful blow on the nose. All the pain he had endured was nothing compared with the exquisite agony of this. With a roar that was almost lionlike in its ferocity he again hurled himself at the man. But the man, shifting the club from right to left, coolly caught him by the under jaw, at the same time wrenching downward and backward. Buck described a complete circle in the air, and half of another, then crashed to the ground on his head and chest.

For the last time he rushed. The man struck the shrewd blow he had purposely withheld for so long, and Buck crumpled up and went down, knocked utterly senseless.

"He's no slouch at dog-breakin', that's wot I say," one of the men on the wall cried enthusiastically.

"'Druther break cayuses any day, and twice on Sundays" was the reply of the driver as he climbed on to the wagon and started the horses.

Buck's senses came back to him, but not his strength. He lay where he had fallen, and from there he watched the man in the red sweater.

" 'Answers to the name of Buck,' " the man soliloquized, quoting from the saloonkeeper's letter, which had announced the consignment of the crate and contents. "Well, Buck, my boy," he went on in a genial voice, "we've had our little ruction, and the best thing we can do is to let it go at that. You've learned your place, and I know mine. Be a good dog and all'll go well and the goose hang high. Be a bad dog and I'll whale the stuffin' outer yer. Understand?"

As he spoke he fearlessly patted the head he had so mercilessly pounded, and though Buck's hair involuntarily bristled at the touch he endured it without protest. When the man brought him water he drank eagerly, and later bolted a generous meal of raw meat, chunk by chunk, from the man's hand.

He was beaten (he knew that); but he was not broken. He saw, once for all, that he stood no chance against a man with a club. He had learned the lesson, and in all his after life he never forgot it. That club was a revelation. It was his introduction to the reign of primitive law, and he met the introduction half-way. The facts of life took on a fiercer aspect; and though he faced that aspect uncowed, he faced it with all the latent cunning of his nature aroused. As the days went by other dogs came, in crates and at the ends of ropes, some docilely and some raging and roaring as he had come; and one and all, he watched them pass under the dominion of the man in the red sweater. Again and again, as he looked at each brutal performance, the lesson was driven home to Buck: a man with a club was a lawgiver, a master to be obeyed, though not necessarily conciliated. Of this last Buck was never guilty, though he did see beaten dogs that fawned upon the man and wagged their tails and licked his hand. Also, he saw one dog that would neither be conciliated nor obey finally killed in the struggle for mastery.

Now and again men came, strangers, who talked excitedly, wheedlingly, and in all kinds of fashions to the man in the red sweater. And at such times that money passed between them the strangers took one or more of the dogs away with them. Buck wondered where they went, for they never came back; but the fear of the future was strong upon him, and he was glad, each time, when he was not selected.

Yet his time came, in the end, in the form of a little weazened man who spat broken English and many strange and uncouth exclamations which Buck could not understand.

"Sacrédam!" he cried, when his eyes lbuck. "Dat one dam bully dog! Eh? How moch?"

"Three hundred, and a present at that," was the prompt reply of the man in the red sweater. "And seein' it's government money, you ain't got no kick coming, eh, Perrault?"

Perrault grinned. Considering that the price of dogs had been boomed skyward by the unwonted demand, it was not an unfair sum for so fine an animal. The Canadian Government would be no loser, nor would its dispatches travel the slower.

Perrault knew dogs, and when he looked at Buck he knew that he was one in a thousand— "One in ten t'ousand," he commented mentally.

Buck saw money pass between them, and was not surprised when Curly, a good-natured Newfoundland, and he were led away by the little weazened man. That was the last he saw of the man in the red sweater, and as Curly and he looked at receding Seattle from the deck of the Narwhal, it was the last he saw of the warm Southland. Curly and he were taken below by Perrault and turned over to a black-faced giant called François. Perrault was a French-Canadian, and swarthy; but François was a French-Canadian half-breed, and twice as swarthy. They were a new kind of men to Buck (of which he was destined to see many more), and though he developed no affection for them, he none the less grew honestly to respect them. He speedily learned that Perrault and François were fair men, calm and impartial in administering justice, and too wise in the ways of dogs to be ever fooled by dogs.

In the 'tween decks of the Narwhal, Buck and Curly joined two other dogs. One of them was a big, snow white fellow from Spitzbergen who had been brought away by a whaling captain, and who had later accompanied a Geological Survey into the Barrens. He was friendly, in a treacherous sort of way, smiling into one's face the while he meditated some underhand trick; as, for instance, when he stole from Buck's food at the first meal. As Buck sprang to punish him the lash of François' whip sang through the air, reaching the culprit first; and nothing remained to Buck but to recover the bone.

That was fair of François, he decided, and the half-breed began his rise in Buck's estimation.

The other dog made no advances nor received any; also, he did not attempt to steal from the newcomers. He was a gloomy, morose fellow, and he showed Curly plainly that all he desired was to be left alone, and further, that there would be trouble if he were not left alone. Dave, he was called, and he ate and slept or yawned between times, and took interest in nothing, not even when the Narwhal crossed Queen Charlotte Sound and rolled and pitched and bucked like a thing possessed. When Buck and Curly grew excited, half wild with fear, he raised his head as though annoyed, favored them with an incurious glance, yawned, and went to sleep again.

Day and night the ship throbbed to the tireless pulse of the propeller, and though one day was very like another it was apparent to Buck that the weather was steadily growing colder. At last, one morning the propeller was quiet and the Narwhal was pervaded with an atmosphere of excitement. He felt it, as did the other dogs, and knew that a change was at hand. François leashed them and brought them on deck. At the first step upon the cold surface Buck's feet sank into a white mushy something very like mud. He sprang back with a snort. More of this white stuff was falling through the air. He shook himself, but more of it fell upon him. He sniffed it curiously, then licked some up on his tongue. It bit like fire, and the next instant was gone. This puzzled him. He tried it again with the same result. The onlookers laughed uproariously, and he felt ashamed, he knew not why. It was his first snow.

Buck's first day on the Dyea beach was like a nightmare. Every hour was filled with shock and surprise. He had been suddenly jerked from the heart of civilization and flung into the heart of things primordial. No lazy, sun-kissed life was this, with nothing to do but loaf and be bored. Here was neither peace, nor rest, nor a moment's safety. All was confusion and action, and every moment life and limb were in peril. There was imperative need to be constantly alert, for these dogs and men were not town dogs and men. They were savages, all of them, who knew no law but the law of club and fang.

He had never seen dogs fight as these wolfish creatures fought, and his first experience taught him an unforgetable lesson. It is true, it was a vicarious experience, else he would not have lived to profit by it. Curly was the victim. They were camped near the log store, where she in her friendly way made advances to a husky-dog the size of a full-grown wolf, though not half so large as she. There was no warning, only a leap in like a flash, a metallic clip of teeth, a leap out equally swift, and Curly's face was ripped open from eye to jaw.

It was the wolf manner of fighting, to strike and leap away; but there was more to it than this. Thirty or forty huskies ran to the spot and surrounded the combatants in an intent and silent circle. Buck did not comprehend that silent intentness, nor the eager way with which they were licking their chops. Curly rushed her antagonist, who struck again and leaped aside. He met her next rush with his chest, in a peculiar fashion that tumbled her off her feet. She never regained them. This was for what the onlooking huskies had waited. They closed in upon her, snarling and yelping, and she was buried beneath the bristling mass of bodies.

So sudden was it and so unexpected that Buck was taken aback. He saw Spitz run out his scarlet tongue in a way he had of laughing; and he saw François, swinging an ax, spring into the mess of dogs. Three men with clubs were helping him to scatter them. It did not take long. Two minutes from the time Curly went down the last of her assailants were clubbed off. But she lay there limp and lifeless in the bloody, trampled snow, almost torn to pieces, the swarthy half-breed standing over her and cursing horribly. The scene often came back to Buck to trouble him in his sleep. So that was the way. No fair play. Once down, that was the end of you. Well, he would see to it that he never went down. Spitz ran out his tongue and laughed again, and from that moment Buck hated him with a bitter and deathless hatred.

Before he had recovered from the shock

caused by the tragic passing of Curly he received another shock. François fastened on him an arrangement of straps and buckles. It was a harness, such as he had seen the grooms put on the horses at home. And as he had seen horses work, so he was set to work, hauling François on a sled to the forest that fringed the valley, and returning with a load of firewood. Though his dignity was sorely hurt by thus being made a draft animal, he was too wise to rebel. He buckled down with a will and did his best, though it was all new and strange. François was stern, demanding instant obedience, and by virtue of his whip receiving instant obedience; while Dave, who was an experienced wheeler, nipped Buck's hindquarters whenever he was in error. Spitz was the leader, likewise experienced, and though he could not always get at Buck, he growled sharp reproof now and again, or cunningly threw his weight in the traces to jerk Buck into the way he should go. Buck learned easily, and under the combined tuition of his two mates and François made remarkable progress. Ere they returned to camp he knew enough to stop at "ho!" to go ahead at "mush!" to swing wide on the bends, and to keep clear of the wheeler when the loaded sled shot down-hill at their heels.

"T'ree vair' good dogs," François told Perrault. "Dat Buck, heem pool lak h—l. I tich heem queek as anyt'ing."

By afternoon, Perrault, who was in a hurry to be on the trail with his dispatches, returned with two more dogs. "Billee" and "Jo," he called them, two brothers, and true huskies both. Sons of the one mother though they were, they were as different as day and night. Billee's one fault was his excessive good nature, whereas Jo was the very opposite, sour and introspective, with a perpetual snarl and a malignant eye. Buck received them in comradely fashion; Dave ignored them; while Spitz proceeded to thrash first one and then the other. Billee wagged his tail appeasingly, turned to run when he saw that appeasement was of no avail, and cried (still appeasingly) when Spitz's sharp teeth scored his flank. But no matter how Spitz circled, Jo whirled around on his heels to face him, mane bristling, ears laid back, lips writhing and snarling, jaws clipping together as fast as he could snap, and eyes diabolically gleaming—the incarnation of belligerent fear. So terrible was his appearance that Spitz was forced to forego disciplining him; but to cover his own discomfiture he turned upon the inoffensive and wailing Billee and drove him to the confines of the camp.

By evening Perrault secured another dog, an old husky, long and lean and gaunt, with a battle-scarred face and a single eye which flashed a warning of prowess that commanded respect. He was called Sol-leks, which means the Angry One. Like Dave, he asked nothing, gave nothing, expected nothing, and when he marched slowly and deliberately into their midst even Spitz left him alone. He had one peculiarity which Buck was unlucky enough to discover. He did not like to be approached on his blind side. Of this offense Buck was unwittingly guilty, and the first knowledge he had of his indiscretion was when Sol-leks whirled upon him and slashed his shoulder to the bone for three inches up and down. Forever after Buck avoided his blind side, and to the last of their comradeship had no more trouble. His only apparent ambition, like Dave's, was to be left alone; though, as Buck was afterward to learn, each of them possessed one other and far more vital ambition.

That night Buck faced the great problem of sleeping. The tent, illumined by a candle, glowed warmly in the midst of the white plain; and when he, as a matter of course, entered it, both Perrault and François bombarded him with curses and cooking utensils, till he recovered from his consternation and fled ignominiously into the outer cold. A chill wind was blowing that nipped him sharply and bit with especial venom into his wounded shoulder. He lay down on the snow and attempted to sleep, but the frost soon drove him shivering to his feet. Miserable and disconsolate, he wandered about among the many tents, only to find that one place was as cold as another. Here and there savage dogs rushed upon him, but he bristled his neck-hair and snarled (for he was learning fast) and they let him go his way unmolested.

Finally an idea came to him. He would return and see how his own team-mates were making out. To his astonishment they had disappeared. Again he wandered about through the great camp, looking for them, and again he returned. Were they in

Straight at the man he launched

the tent? No, that could not be, else he would not have been driven out. Then where could they possibly be? With drooping tail and shivering body, very forlorn indeed, he aimlessly circled the tent. Suddenly the snow gave way beneath his forelegs and he sank down. Something wriggled under his feet. He sprang back, bristling and snarling, fearful of the unseen and unknown. But a friendly little yelp reassured him, and he went back to investigate. A whiff of warm air ascended to his nostrils, and there, curled up under the snow in a snug ball, lay Billee. He whined placatingly, squirmed and wriggled to show his good will and intentions, and even ventured, as a bribe for peace, to lick Buck's face with his warm, wet tongue.

Another lesson. So that was the way they did it, eh? Buck confidently selected a spot, and with much fuss and waste effort proceeded to dig a hole for himself. In a trice the heat from his body filled the confined space and he was asleep. The day had been long and arduous, and he slept soundly and comfortably, though he growled and barked and wrestled with bad dreams.

Nor did he open his eyes till roused by the noises of the waking camp. At first he did not know where he was. It had snowed during the night and he was completely buried. The snow-walls pressed him on every side, and a great surge of fear swept through him—the fear of the wild thing for the trap, a token that he was harking back through his own life to the lives of his forebears; for he was a civilized dog, an unduly civilized dog, and of his own experience knew no trap and so could not of himself fear it. The muscles of his whole body contracted spasmodically and instinctively, the hair on his neck and shoulders stood on end, and with a ferocious snarl he bounded straight up into the blinding day, the snow flying about him in a flashing cloud. Ere he landed on his feet he saw the white camp spread out before him and knew where he was, and remembered all that had passed from the time he went for a stroll with Manuel to the hole he had dug for himself the night before.

A shout from François hailed his appearance. "Wot I say?" the dog-driver cried to Perrault. "Dat Buck for sure learn queek as anyt'ing."

Perrault nodded gravely. As courier for the Canadian Government, bearing important dispatches, he was anxious to secure the best dogs, and he was particularly gladdened by the possession of Buck.

Three more huskies were added to the team inside of an hour, making a total of nine, and before another quarter of an hour had passed they were in harness and swinging up the trail toward the Dyea Cañon. Buck was glad to be gone, and though the work was hard he found he did not particularly despise it. He was surprised at the eagerness which animated the whole team and which was communicated to him; but still more surprising was the change wrought in Dave and Sol-leks. They were new dogs, utterly transformed by the harness. All passiveness and unconcern had dropped from them. They were alert and active, anxious that the work should go well, and fiercely irritable with whatever, by delay or confusion, retarded that work. The toil of the traces seemed the supreme expression of their being, and all that they lived for and the only thing in which they took delight.

Dave was wheeler or sled dog, pulling in front of him was Buck, then came Sol-leks; the rest of the team was strung out ahead, single file, to the leader, which position was filled by Spitz.

Buck had been purposely placed between Dave and Sol-leks so that he might receive instruction. Apt scholar that he was, they were equally apt teachers, never allowing him to linger long in error and enforcing their teaching with their sharp teeth. Dave was fair, and very wise. He never nipped Buck without cause, and he never failed to nip him when he stood in need of it. As François' whip backed him up, Buck found it to be cheaper to mend his ways than to retaliate. Once, during a brief halt, when he got tangled in the traces and delayed the start, both Dave and Sol-leks flew at him and administered a sound trouncing. The resulting tangle was even worse, but Buck took good care to keep the traces clear thereafter. And ere the day was done, so well had he mastered his work his mates about ceased nagging him. François' whip snapped less frequently, and Perrault even honored Buck by lifting up his feet and carefully examining them.

It was a hard day's run, up the Cañon, through Sheep Camp, past the Scales and the timber-line, across glaciers and snowdrifts hundreds of feet deep, and over the great Chilkoot Divide which stands between the salt water and the fresh and guards forbiddingly the sad and lonely North. They made good time down the chain of lakes which fill the craters of extinct volcanoes, and late that night pulled into the huge camp at the head of Lake Bennett, where thousands of gold-seekers were building boats against the break-up of the ice in the spring. Buck made his hole in the snow and slept the sleep of the exhausted just, but all too early was routed out in the cold darkness and harnessed with his mates to the sled.

That day the trail was packed and they made forty miles; but the next day, and for many days to follow, they broke their own trail, worked harder, and made poorer time. As a rule, Perrault traveled ahead of the team, packing the snow with webbed shoes to make it easier for them. François, guiding the sled at the gee-pole, sometimes exchanged places with him, but not often. Perrault was in a hurry, and he prided himself on his knowledge of ice, a knowledge indispensable, for the fall ice was very thin, and where there was swift water there was no ice at all.

Day after day, for days unending, Buck toiled in the traces. Always they broke camp in the dark, and the first gray of dawn found them hitting the trail with fresh miles reeled off behind them. And always they pitched camp after dark, eating their bit of fish and crawling to sleep into the snow. Buck was ravenous. The pound and a half of sun-dried salmon, which was his ration for each day, seemed to go nowhere. He never had enough, and suffered from perpetual hunger yearnings. Yet the other dogs, because they weighed less and were born to the life, received a pound only of the fish, and managed to keep in good condition.

He swiftly lost the fastidiousness which had characterized his old life. A dainty eater, he found that his mates, finishing first, robbed him of his unfinished ration. There was no defending it. While he was fighting off two or three it was disappearing down the throats of the others. To remedy this he ate as fast as they; and, so greatly did hunger compel him, he was not above taking what did not belong to him. He watched and learned. When he saw Pike, one of the new dogs, a clever malingerer and thief, slyly steal a slice of bacon when Perrault's back was turned, he duplicated the performance the following day, getting away with the whole chunk. A great uproar was raised, but he was unsuspected, while Dub, an awkward blunderer who was always getting caught, was punished for Buck's misdeed.

This first theft marked Buck as fit to survive in the hostile Northland environment. It marked his adaptability, his capacity to adjust himself to changing conditions, the lack of which would have meant swift and terrible death. It marked, further, the decay or going to pieces of his moral nature, a vain thing and a handicap in the ruthless struggle for existence. It was all well enough in the Southland, under the law of love and fellowship, to respect private property and personal feelings; but in the Northland, under the law of club and fang, whoso took such things into account was a fool, and in so far as he observed them he would fail to prosper.

Not that Buck reasoned it out. He was fit, that was all, and unconsciously he accommodated himself to the new mode of life. All his days, no matter what the odds, he had never run from a fight. But the club of the man in the red sweater had beaten into him a more fundamental and primitive code. Civilized, he could have died for a moral consideration, say the defense of Judge Miller's riding-whip; but the completeness of his decivilization was now evidenced by his ability to flee from the defense of a moral consideration and so save his hide. He did not steal for joy of it, but because of the clamor of his stomach. He did not rob openly, but stole secretly and cunningly, out of respect for club and fang. In short, the things he did were done because it was easier to do them than not to do them.

His development (or retrogression) was rapid. His muscles became hard as iron, and he grew callous to ordinary pain. He achieved an internal as well as external economy. He could eat anything, no matter how loathsome or indigestible; and, once eaten, the juices of his stomach extracted the last least particle of nutriment, and his blood carried it to the farthest reaches of his body, building it into the toughest and stoutest of tissues. Sight and scent became remarkably keen, while his hearing developed such acuteness that in his sleep he heard the faintest sound and knew whether it heralded peace or peril. He learned to bite the ice out with his teeth when it collected between his toes; and when he was thirsty and there was a thick scum of ice over the water-hole, he would break it by rearing and striking it with stiff forelegs. His most conspicuous trait was an ability to scent the wind and forecast it a night in advance. No matter how breathless the air when he dug his nest by tree or bank, the wind that later blew inevitably found him to leeward, sheltered and snug.

And not only did he learn by experience, but instincts long dead became alive again. The domesticated generations fell from him. In vague ways he remembered back to the youth of the breed, to the time the wild-dogs ranged in packs through the primeval forest and killed their meat as they ran it down. It was no task for him to learn to fight with cut and slash and the quick wolf-snap. In this manner had fought forgotten ancestors. They quickened the old life within him, and the old tricks which they had stamped into the heredity of the breed were his tricks. They came to him without effort or discovery, as though they had been his always. And when, on the still, cold nights, he pointed his nose at a star and howled long and wolflike, it was his ancestors, dead and dust, pointing nose at star and howling down through the centuries and through him. And his cadences were their cadences, the cadences which voiced their woe and what to them was the meaning of the stillness, and the cold, and dark.

Thus, as token of what a puppet thing life is, the ancient song surged through him and he came into his own again, and he came because men had found a yellow metal in the North, and because Manuel was a gardener's helper whose wages did not lap over the needs of his wife and the divers small copies of himself which he had managed to accumulate.

The dominant primordial beast was strong in Buck, and under the fierce conditions of trail life it grew and grew. Yet it was a secret growth. His new-born cunning gave him poise and control. He was too busy adjusting himself to the new life to feel at ease, and not only did he not pick fights, but he avoided them whenever possible. A certain deliberateness characterized his attitude. He was not prone to rashness and precipitate action; and in the bitter hatred between him and Spitz he betrayed no impatience, shunned all offensive acts.

On the other hand, possibly because he divined in Buck a dangerous rival, Spitz never lost an opportunity of showing his teeth. He even went out of his way to bully Buck, striving constantly to start the fight which could end only in the death of one or the other. Early in the trip this might have taken place had it not been for an unwonted accident. At the end of this day they made a bleak and miserable camp on the shore of Lake Le Barge. Driving snow, a wind that cut like a white-hot knife, and darkness had forced them to grope for a camping-place. They could hardly have fared worse. At their backs rose a perpendicular wall of rock, and Perrault and François were compelled to make their fire and spread their sleeping-robes on the ice of the lake itself. The tent they had discarded at Dyea in order to travel light. A few sticks of driftwood furnished them with a fire that thawed down through the ice and left them to eat supper in the dark.

Close in under the sheltering rock Buck made his nest. So snug and warm was it that he was loth to leave it when François distributed the fish which he had first thawed over the fire. But when Buck finished his ration and returned he found his nest occupied. A warning snarl told him that the trespasser was Spitz. Till now Buck had avoided trouble with his enemy, but this was too much. The beast in him roared. He sprang upon Spitz with a fury which surprised them both, and Spitz particularly, for his whole experience with Buck had gone to teach him that his rival was an unusually timid dog who managed to hold his own only because of his great weight and size.

François was surprised, too, when they shot out in a tangle from the disrupted nest and he divined the cause of the trouble. "A-a-ah!" he cried to Buck. "Gif it to heem, by Gar! Gif it to heem, the dirty t'eef!"

Buck was nothing loth. He was crying with sheer rage and eagerness as he circled back and forth for a chance to spring in. Spitz was no less eager and no less cautious, as he likewise circled back and forth for the advantage. But it was then that the unexpected happened, the thing which projected their struggle for supremacy far into the future, past many a weary mile of trail and toil.

An oath from Perrault, the resounding impact of a club upon a bony frame, and a shrill yelp of pain heralded the breaking forth of pandemonium. The camp was suddenly discovered to be alive with skulking furry forms — starving huskies, four or five score of them, who had scented the camp from some Indian village. They had crept in while Buck and Spitz were fighting, and when the two men sprang among them with stout clubs they showed their teeth and fought back. They were crazed by the smell of the food. Perrault found one with head buried in the grub box. His his club landed mightily on the gaunt ribs, and the grub-box was capsized on the ground. On the instant a score of the famished brutes were scrambling for the bread and bacon. The clubs fell upon them unheeded. They yelped and howled under the rain of blows, but struggled none the less madly till the last crumb had been devoured.

In the mean time the astonished team-dogs had burst out of their nests only to be set upon by the fierce invaders. Never had Buck seen such dogs. It seemed as though their bones would burst through their skins. They were mere skeletons, draped loosely in draggled hides, with blazing eyes and slavered fangs. But the hunger-madness made them terrifying, irresistible. There was no opposing them. The team-dogs were swept back against the cliff at the first onset. Buck was beset by three huskies, and in a trice his head and shoulders were ripped and slashed. The din was frightful. Billee was crying as usual. Dave and Sol-leks, dripping blood from a score of wounds, were fighting bravely side by side. Joe was snapping like a demon. Once his teeth closed on the foreleg of a husky, and he crunched down through the bone. Pike, the malingerer, leaped upon the crippled animal, breaking its neck with a quick flash of teeth and a jerk. Buck got a frothing adversary by the throat, and was sprayed with blood when his teeth sank through the jugular. The warm taste of it in his mouth goaded him to greater fierceness. He flung himself upon another, and at the same time felt teeth sink into his own throat. It was Spitz, treacherously attacking from the side.

Perrault and François, having cleared out their part of the camp, hurried to save their sled-dogs. The wild wave of famished beasts rolled back before them, and Buck shook himself free. But it was only for a moment. The two men were compelled to run back to save the grub; upon which the huskies returned from the attack on the team. Billee, terrified into bravery, sprang through the savage circle and fled away over the ice. Pike and Dub followed on his heels, with the rest of the team behind. As Buck drew himself together to spring after them, out of the tail of his eye he saw Spitz rush upon him with the evident intention of overthrowing him. Once off his feet and under that mass of huskies there was no hope for him. But he braced himself to the shock of Spitz' charge, then joined the flight out on the lake.

Later, the nine team-dogs gathered together and sought shelter in the forest. Though unpursued, they were in a sorry plight. There was not one who was not wounded in four or five places, while some were wounded grievously. Dub was badly injured in a hindleg; Dolly, the last husky added to the team at Dyea had a badly torn throat; Jo had lost an eye; while Billee, the good-natured, with an ear chewed and rent to ribbons, cried and whimpered throughout the night. At daybreak they limped warily back to camp, to find the marauders gone and the two men in bad tempers. Fully half their grub supply was gone. the huskies had chewed through the sled-lashings and canvas coverings. In fact, nothing, no matter how remotely edible, had escaped them. They had eaten a pair of Perrault's moose-hide moccasins, chunks out of the leather traces, and even two feet of lash from the end of François' whip.He broke from a mournful contemplation of it to look over his wounded dogs.

"Ah, my frien's," he said softly, "mebbe it mek you mad dog, dose many bites. Mebbe all mad dog, sacrédam! Wot you t'ink, eh, Perrault?"

The courier shook his head dubiously. He could ill afford to have madness break out among his dogs, with four hundred miles of trail still between him and Dawson. Two hours of cursing and exertion got the harnesses into shape, and the wound-stiffened team was under way, struggling

The time had come. It was to the death

painfully over the hardest part of the trail they had yet encountered, and for that matter, the hardest between them and Dawson.

The Thirty-Mile River was wide open. Its wild water defied the frost, and it was in the eddies only and in the quiet places that the ice held at all. Six days of exhausting toil were required to cover those thirty terrible miles. And terrible they were, for every foot of them was accomplished at the risk of life to dog and man. A dozen times Perrault, nosing the way, broke through the ice-bridges, and was saved only by the long pole he carried, which he so held that it fell each time across the hole made by his body. But a cold snap was on, the thermometer registered fifty below zero, and each time he broke through he was compelled for very life to build a fire and dry his garments.

Nothing daunted him. It was because nothing daunted him that he had been chosen for Government courier. He took all manner of risks, resolutely thrusting his little weazened face into the frost and struggling on from dim dawn to dark. He skirted the frowning shores on rim-ice that

DRAWN BY CHARLES LIVINGSTON BULL

With the Aurora Borealis flaming coldly overhead

bent and crackled under foot and upon which they dared not halt. Once the sled broke through with Dave and Buck, and they were half-frozen and all but drowned by the time they were dragged out. The usual fire was necessary to save them. They were coated solidly with ice, and the two men kept them on the run around the fire, sweating and thawing, so close that they were singed by the flames.

At another time Spitz went through, dragging the whole team after him up to Buck, who strained backward with all his strength, his forepaws on the slippery edge and the ice quivering and snapping all around. But behind him was Dave, likewise straining backward, and behind the sled was François, pulling till his tendons cracked.

Again the rim-ice broke away before and behind, and there was no escape except up the cliff. Perrault scaled it by a miracle, while François prayed for just that miracle; and with every thong and sled-lashing and the last bit of harness rove into a long rope, the dogs were hoisted, one by one, to the cliff crest. François came up last, after the sled and load.Then came the search for a place to descend; a descent was made ultimately by the aid of the rope, and night found them back on the river with a quarter of a mile to the day's credit.

By the time they made the Hootalinqua and good ice Buck was played out. The rest of the dogs were in like condition, but Perrault, to make up lost time, pushed them late and early. The first day they covered thirty-five miles to the Big Salmon; the next day thirty-five more to the Little Salmon; the third day forty miles, which brought them well up toward the Five Fingers.

Buck's feet were not so compact and hard as the feet of the huskies. His had softened during the many generations since the day his last wild ancestor was tamed by a cave-dweller or river-man. All day long he limped in agony, and camp once made lay down like a dead dog. Hungry as he was, he would not move to receive his ration of fish, which François had to bring to him. Also, the dog-driver rubbed Buck's feet for half an hour each night after supper, and sacrificed the tops of his own moccasins to make four moccasins for Buck. This was a great relief, and Buck caused even the weazened face of Perrault to twist itself into a grin, one morning, when François forgot the moccasins and Buck lay on his back, his four feet waving appealingly in the air, and refused to budge without them. Later, his feet grew hardened to the trail, and the worn-out footgear was thrown away.

At the Pelly, one morning, as they were harnessing up, Dolly, who had never been conspicuous for anything, went suddenly mad. She announced her condition by a long, heart-breaking wolf-howl that sent every dog bristling with fear, then sprang straight for Buck. He had never seen a dog go mad, nor did he have any reason to fear madness; yet he knew that here was horror, and fled from it in panic. Straightaway he raced, with Dolly, panting and frothing, one leap behind; nor could she gain on him, so great was his terror, nor could he leave her, so great was her madness. He plunged through the wooded breast of the island, flew down to the lower end, crossed a back-channel filled with rough ice to another island, gained a third island, curved back to the main river, and in desperation started to cross it. And all the time, though he did not look, he could hear her snarling just one leap behind. François called to him a quarter of a mile away and he doubled back, still one leap ahead, gasping painfully for air and putting all his faith in François. The dog-driver held the ax poised in his hand, and as Buck shot past him the ax crashed down upon mad Dolly's head.

Buck staggered over against the sled, exhausted, sobbing for breath, helpless. This was Spitz' opportunity. He sprang upon Buck, and twice his teeth sank into his unresisting foe and ripped and tore the flesh to the bone. Then François' lash descended, and Buck had the satisfaction of watching Spitz receive the worst whipping as yet administered to any of the team.

"One devil, dat Spitz," remarked Perrault. "Some day heem keel dat Buck."

"Dat Buck two devils," was François' rejoinder. "All de tam I watch dat Buck. I know for sure. Lissen! Some day heem get mad lak hell an' then heem chew dat Spitz all up an' spit heem out on de snow. Sure. I know."

From then on it was war between them. Spitz, as lead-dog and acknowledged master of the team, felt his supremacy threatened by this strange Southland dog. And strange Buck was to him, for of the many Southland dogs he had known not one had shown up worthily in camp and on trail. They were all too soft, dying under the toil, the frost and starvation. Buck was the exception. He alone endured and prospered, matching the husky in strength, savagery and cunning. Then he was a masterful dog, and what made him dangerous was the fact that the club of the man in the red sweater had knocked all blind pluck and rashness out of his desire for mastery. He was preëminently cunning, and could bide his time with a patience that was nothing less than primitive.

It was inevitable that the clash for leadership should come. Buck wanted it. He wanted it because it was his nature, because he had been gripped tight by that nameless, incomprehensible pride of the trail and trace; that pride which holds dogs in the toil to the last gasp, which lures them to die joyfully in the harness and breaks their hearts if they are cut out of the harness. This was the pride of Dave as wheel-dog, of Sol-leks as he pulled with all his strength; the pride that laid hold of them at break of camp, transforming them from sour and sullen brutes into straining, eager, ambitious creatures; the pride that spurred them on all day and dropped them at pitch of camp at night, letting them fall back into gloomy unrest and discontent. This was the pride that bore up Spitz and made him thrash the sled-dog who blundered and shirked in the traces or hid away at harness-up time in the morning. Likewise, it was this pride that made him fear Buck as a possible lead dog — . . . And this was Buck's pride, too.

Buck openly threatened the other's leadership. He came between him and the shirks he should have punished. And he did it deliberately. One night there was a heavy snowfall, and in the morning Pike, the malingerer, did not appear. He was securely hidden in his nest under a foot of snow. François called him and sought him in vain. Spitz was wild with wrath. He raged through the camp, smelling and digging in every likely place, snarling so frightfully that Pike heard and shivered in his hiding-place.

But when he was at last unearthed, and Spitz flew at him to punish him, Buck flew, with equal rage, in between. So unexpected was it, and so shrewdly managed, that Spitz was hurled backward and off his feet. Pike, who had been trembling abjectly, took heart at this open mutiny, and sprang upon his overthrown leader. Buck, to whom fair play was a forgotten code, likewise sprang upon Spitz. But François, chuckling at the incident, though unswerving in the administration of justice, brought his lash down upon Buck with all his might. This failed to drive Buck from his prostrate rival, and the butt of the whip was brought into play. Half-stunned by the blow, Buck was knocked backward and the lash laid upon him again and again, while Spitz soundly punished the many times offending Pike.

In the days that followed, as Dawson grew closer and closer, Buck still continued to interfere between Spitz and the culprits, but he did it craftily, when François was not in sight. With the covert mutiny of Buck a general insubordination sprang up and increased. Dave and Sol-leks were unaffected, but the rest of the team went from bad to worse. Things no longer went right. There was continual bickering and jangling. Trouble was always afoot, and at the bottom of it was Buck. He kept François busy, for the dog-driver was in constant apprehension of the life-and-death struggle between the two which he knew must come, sooner or later; and on more than one night the sounds of quarreling and strife among the other dogs turned him out of his sleeping-robe fearful that Buck and Spitz were at it.

But the opportunity did not present itself, and they pulled into Dawson one dreary afternoon with the great fight still to come. Here were many men and countless dogs, and Buck found them all at work. It seemed the ordained order of things that dogs should work. All day they swung up and down the main street in long teams, and in the night their jingling bells still went by. They hauled cabin-logs and firewood, freighted to the mines, and did all manner of work that horses did in the Santa Clara Valley. Here and there Buck met Southland dogs, but in the main they were the wild-wolf husky breed. Every night regularly, at nine, at twelve, at three, they lifted a nocturnal song, a weird and eerie chant, in which it was Buck's delight to join.

With the aurora borealis flaming coldly overhead, or the stars leaping in the frost-dance, and the land numb and frozen under its pall of snow, this song of the huskies might have been the defiance of life, only it was pitched in minor key, with long-drawn wailings and half-sobs, and was more the pleading of life, the articulate travail of existence. It was an old song, old as the breed itself — one of the first songs of the Younger World in a day when songs were sad. It was invested with the woe of unnumbered generations, this plaint by which Buck was so strangely stirred. When he moaned and sobbed it was with the pain of living that was of old the pain of his wild fathers, and the fear and mystery of the cold and dark that were to them fear and mystery. And that he should be stirred by it marked the completeness with which he harked back through the ages of fire and roof to the raw beginnings of life in the howling ages.

Seven days from the time they pulled into Dawson they dropped down the steep bank by the Barracks to the Yukon Trail, and pulled for Dyea and Salt Water. Perrault was carrying dispatches if anything more urgent than those he had brought in; also, the travel-pride had gripped him, and he purposed to make the record trip of the year. Several things favored him in this. The week's rest had recuperated the dogs and put them in thorough trim. The trail they had broken into the country was packed hard by later journeyers. And further, the police had arranged in two or three places deposits of grub for dog and man, and he was traveling light.

They made Sixty Mile, which is a fifty-mile run, on the first day; and the second day saw them booming up the Yukon well on their way to Pelly. But such spledid running was achieved not without great trouble and vexation on the part of François. The insidious revolt led by Buck had destroyed the solidarity of the team. It no longer was as one dog leaping in the traces. The encouragement Buck gave the rebels led them into all kinds of petty misdemeanors. No more was Spitz a leader greatly to be feared. The old awe departed, and they grew equal to challenging his authority. Pike robbed him of half a fish one night and gulped it down under the protection of Buck. Another night Dub and Joe fought Spitz and made him forego the punishment they deserved. And even Billee, the good-natured, was less good-natured, and whined not half so placatingly as in former days. Buck never came near Spitz without snarling and bristling menacingly. In fact, his conduct approached that of a bully, and he was given to swaggering up and down before Spitz' very nose.

The breaking down of discipline likewise affected the dogs in their relations with one another. They quarreled and bickered more than ever among themselves, till at times the camp was a howling bedlam. Dave and Sol-leks alone were unaltered, though they were made irritable by the unending squabbling. François swore strange, barbarous oaths, and stamped the snow in futile rage, and tore his hair. His lash was always singing among the dogs, but it was of small avail. Directly his back was turned they were at it again. He backed up Spitz with his whip, while Buck backed up the remainder of the team. François knew he was behind all the trouble, and Buck knew he knew; but Buck was too clever ever again to be caught red-handed. He worked faithfully in the harness, for the toil had become a delight to him; yet it was a greater delight slyly to precipitate a fight amongst his mates and tangle the traces.

At the mouth of the Tahkeena, one night after supper, Dub turned up a snowshoe rabbit, blundered it, and missed. In a second the whole team was in full cry. A hundred yards away was a camp of the Northwest Police, with fifty dogs, huskies all, who joined the chase. The rabbit sped down the river, turned off into a small creek, up the frozen bed of which it held steadily. It ran lightly on the surface of the snow, while the dogs ploughed through by main strength. Buck led the pack, sixty strong, around bend after bend, but he could not gain. He laid down low to the race, whining eagerly, his splendid body flashing forward, leap by leap, in the wan, white moonlight. And leap by leap, like some pale frost-wraith, the snowshoe rabbit flashed on ahead.

All that stirring of old instincts which at stated periods drives men out from the sounding cities to forest and plain to kill things by chemically-propelled leaden pellets — the bloodlust, the joy to kill — all this was Buck's, infinitely more intimate. He was ranging at the head of the pack, running the wild thing down, the living meat, to kill with his own teeth and wash his muzzle to the eyes in warm blood.

There is an ecstasy that marks the summit of life and beyond which life cannot rise. And, such is the paradox of living, this ecstasy comes when one is most alive, and it comes as a complete forgetfulness that one is alive. This ecstasy, this forgetfulness of living, comes to the artist, caught up and out of himself in a sheet of flame; it comes to the soldier, war-mad on a stricken field and refusing quarter; and it came to Buck, leading the pack, sounding the old wolf-cry, straining after the food that was alive and that fled swiftly before him through the moonlight. He was sounding the deeps of his nature, and of the parts of his nature, that were deeper than he, going back into the womb of Time. He was mastered by the sheer surging of life, the tidal-wave of being, the perfect joy of each separate muscle, joint and sinew, in that it was everything that was not death, that it was aglow and rampant, expressing itself in movement, flying exultantly under the stars and over the face of dead matter that did not move.

But Spitz, cold and calculating even in his supreme moods, left the pack and cut across a narrow neck of land where the creek made a long bend around. Buck did not know of this, and as he rounded the bend, the frost-wraith of a rabbit still flitting before him, he saw another and larger frost-wraith leap from the overhanging bank into the immediate path of the rabbit. It was Spitz. The rabbit could not turn and as the white teeth broke its back in midair it shrieked as loudly as a stricken man may shriek. At sound of this, the cry of Life plunging down from life's apex in the grip of Death, the full pack at Buck's heels raised a hell's chorus of delight.

Buck did not cry out. He did not check himself, but drove in upon Spitz, shoulder to shoulder, so hard that he missed the throat. They rolled over and over in the powdery snow. Spitz gained his feet almost as though he had not been overthrown, slashing Buck down the shoulder and leaping clear. Twice his teeth clipped together like the steel jaws of a trap, as he backed away for better footing, with lean and lifting lips that writhed and snarled.

In a flash Buck knew it. The time had come. It was to the death. As they circled about, snarling, ears laid back, keenly watchful for the advantage, the scene came to Buck with a sense of familiarity. He seemed to remember it all — the white woods, and earth, and moonlight, and the thrill of battle. Over the whiteness and silence brooded a ghostly calm. There was not the faintest whisper of air. Nothing moved, not a leaf quivered, the visible breaths of the dogs rising slowly and lingering in the frosty air. They had made short work of the snowshoe rabbit, these dogs that were ill-tamed wolves; and they were now drawn up in an expectant circle. They, too, were silent, their eyes only gleaming and their breaths drifting slowly upward. To Buck it was nothing new or strange, this scene of old time. It was as though it had always been, the wonted way of things.

Spitz was a practiced fighter. From Spitzbergen through the Arctic, and across Canada and the Barrens, he had held his own with all manner of dogs and achieved to mastery over them. Bitter rage was his, but never blind rage. In his passion to rend and destroy he never forgot that his enemy was in like passion to rend and destroy. He never rushed till he was prepared to receive a rush; never attacked till he had first defended that attack.

In vain Buck strove to sink his teeth in the neck of the big white dog. Wherever his fangs struck for the softer flesh they were countered by the fangs of Spitz. Fang clashed on fang, and lips were cut and bleeding, but Buck could not penetrate his enemy's guard. Then he warmed up and enveloped Spitz in a whirlwind of rushes. Time and time again he tried for the snow-white throat where life bubbled near to the surface, and each time and every time Spitz slashed him and got away. Then Buck took to rushing, as though for the throat, when, suddenly drawing back his head and curving in from the side, he would drive his shoulder at the shoulder of Spitz, as a ram by which to overthrow him. But instead, each time Buck's shoulder was slashed down as Spitz leaped lightly away.

Spitz was untouched, while Buck was streaming with blood and panting hard. The fight was growing desperate. And all the while the silent and wolfish circle waited to finish off whichever dog went down. As Buck grew winded, Spitz took to rushing, and he kept him staggering for footing. Once Buck went over, and the whole circle of sixty dogs started up; but he recovered himself, almost in midair, and the circle sank down again and waited.

But Buck possessed a quality that made for greatness: imagination. He fought by instinct, but he could fight by head as well. He rushed as though attempting the old shoulder-trick, but at the last instant swept low to the snow and in. His teeth closed on Spitz' left foreleg. There was a crunch of breaking bone, and the white dog faced him on three legs. Thrice he tried to knock him over, then repeated the trick and broke the right foreleg. Despite the pain and helplessness, Spitz struggled madly to keep up. He saw the silent circle with gleaming eyes, lolling tongues and silvery breaths drifting upward, closing in upon him as he had seen similar circles close in upon beaten antagonists in the past. Only this time he was the one who was beaten.

There was no hope for him. Buck was inexorable. Mercy was a thing reserved for gentler climes. He maneuvered for the final rush. The circle had tightened till he could feel the breaths of the huskies on his flanks. He could see them, beyond Spitz and to either side, half-crouching for the spring, their eyes fixed upon him. A pause seemed to fall. Every animal was motionless as though turned to stone. Only Spitz quivered and bristled as he staggered back and forth, snarling with horrible menace, as though to frighten off impending death. Then Buck sprang in and out, but while he was in shoulder had at last squarely met shoulder. The dark circle became a dot on the moon-flooded snow as Spitz disappeared from view. Buck stood and looked on, the successful champion, the dominant primordial beast who had made his kill and found it good.

"Eh? Wot I say? I spik true w'en I say dat Buck two devils."

This was François' speech next morning when he discovered Spitz missing and Buck covered with wounds. He drew him to the fire and by its light pointed them out.

"Dat Spitz fight lak hell," said Perrault as he surveyed the gaping rips and cuts.

"An' dat Buck fight lak two hells," was François' answer. "An' now we make good time. No more Spitz, no more trouble sure."

While Perrault packed the camp outfit and loaded the sled, the dog-driver proceeded to harness the dogs. Buck trotted up to the place Spitz would have occupied as leader; but François, not noticing him, brought Sol-leks to the coveted position. In his judgment, Sol-leks was the best lead-dog left. Buck sprang upon Sol-leks in a fury, driving him back and standing in his place.

"Eh? Eh?" François cried, slapping his thighs gleefully. "Look at dat Buck. Heem keel dat Spitz; heem t'ink to take de job."

"Go 'way! Chook!" he cried; but Buck refused to budge.

He took Buck by the scruff of the neck, and though he growled threateningly dragged him to one side and replaced Sol-leks. The old dog did not like it, and showed plainly that he was afraid of Buck. François was obdurate, but when he turned his back Buck again displaced Sol-leks, who was not at all unwilling to go.

François was angry. "Now, by Gar! I feex you!" he cried, coming back with a heavy club in his hand.

Buck remembered the man in the red sweater and retreated slowly; nor did he attempt to charge in when Sol-leks was once more brought forward. But he circled just beyond the range of the club, snarling with bitterness and rage; and while he circled he watched the club so as to dodge it if thrown by François.

The driver went about his work, and he called to Buck when he was ready to put him in his old place in front of Dave. Buck retreated two or three steps. François followed him up, whereupon he again retreated. After some time of this François threw down the club, thinking that Buck feared a thrashing. But Buck was in open revolt. He wanted, not to escape a clubbing, but to have the leadership. It was his by right. He had earned it, and he would not be content with less.

Perrault took a hand. Between them they ran him about for the better part of an hour. They threw clubs at him. He dodged. They cursed him, and his fathers and mothers before him, and all his seed to come after him down to the remotest generation, and every hair on his body and drop of blood in his veins; and he answered curse with snarl and kept out of their reach. He did not try to run away, but retreated around and around the camp, advertising plainly that when his desire was met he would come in and be good.

François sat down and scratched his head. Perrault looked at his watch and swore. Time was flying and they should have been on the trail an hour gone. François scratched his head again. He shook it and grinned sheepishly at the courier, who shrugged his shoulders in sign that they were beaten. Then François went up to where Sol-leks stood and called to Buck. Buck laughed, as dogs laugh, yet kept his distance. François unfastened Sol-leks' traces and put him back in his old place. The team stood harnessed to the sled in an unbroken line, ready for the trail. There was no place for Buck save at the front. Once more François called and once more Buck laughed and kept away.

"T'row down de club," Perrault commanded.

François complied; whereupon Buck trotted in, laughing triumphantly, and swung around into position at the head of the team, his traces were fastened, the sled broken out, and with both men running they dashed out on to the river trail. Highly as the dog-driver had forevalued Buck, with his two devils, he found, while the day was yet young, that he had undervalued. At a bound, Buck took up the duties of leadership; and where judgment was required, and quick thinking and quick acting, he showed himself the superior even of Spitz, of whom François had never seen an equal.

But it was in giving the law and making his mates live up to it that Buck excelled. Dave and Sol-leks did not mind the change in leadership. It was none of their business. Their business was to toil, and toil mightily, in the traces. So long as that was not interfered with they did not care what happened. Billee, the good-natured, could lead for all they cared, so long as he kept order. They rest of the team, however, had grown unruly during the last days of Spitz, and their surprise was great now that Buck proceeded to lick them into shape.

Pike, who pulled at Buck's heels, and who never put an ounce more of his weight against the breastband than what he was compelled, was swiftly and repeatedly shaken for loafing; and ere the first day was done he was pulling more than ever before in his life. The first night in camp, Jo, the sour one, was punished roundly — a thing that Spitz had never succeeded in doing. Buck simply smothered him by virtue of superior weight, and cut him up till he began to whine for mercy.

The general tone of the team picked up

DRAWN BY CHARLES LIVINGSTON BULL

And leap by leap, like some pale frost-wraith,

immediately. The team recovered its old-time solidarity, and once more the dogs leaped as one dog in the traces. At the Rink Rapids two native huskies, Teek and Koona, were added; and the celerity with which Buck broke them in took away François' breath.

"Nevaire such a dog as dat Buck!" he cried. "Nevaire! Heem worth one t'ousan' dollair. Eh? Wot you say, Perrault?"

And Perrault nodded. He was ahead of the record then, and gaining day by day. The trail was in excellent condition, well-packed and hard, and there was no new-fallen snow with which to contend. It was not too cold. The temperature dropped to fifty below zero and remained there the whole trip. The men rode and ran by turn, and the dogs were kept on the jump.

The Thirty-Mile River was comparatively coated with ice, and they covered in one day going out what had taken them ten days coming in. In one run they made a sixty-mile dash from the foot of Lake Le Barge to the White Horse Rapids. Across Marsh, Tagish and Bennett (seventy miles of lakes) they flew so fast that the man whose turn it was to run towed behind the sled at the end of a rope. And on the last night of the second week they topped White Pass and dropped down the sea-slope with the lights of Skaguay and of the shipping at their feet.

It was a record run. Each day for fourteen days they had averaged forty miles. For three days Perrault and François threw chests up and down the main street of Skaguay and were deluged with invitations to drink, while the team was the constant centre of a worshipful crowd of dog-busters and mushers. Then three or four Western bad men aspired to clean out the town, were riddled like pepper-boxes for their pains, and public interest turned to other idols. Next came official orders. François called Buck to him and cursed him through excess of affection, threw his arms around him, wept over him. And that was the last of François and Perrault. Like other men, they passed out of Buck's life for good.

A Scotch half-breed took charge of Buck and his mates, and in company with a dozen other dog-teams he started back over the weary trail to Dawson. It was no light running now, nor record time, but heavy toil each day, with a heavy load behind; for this was the mail-train, carrying

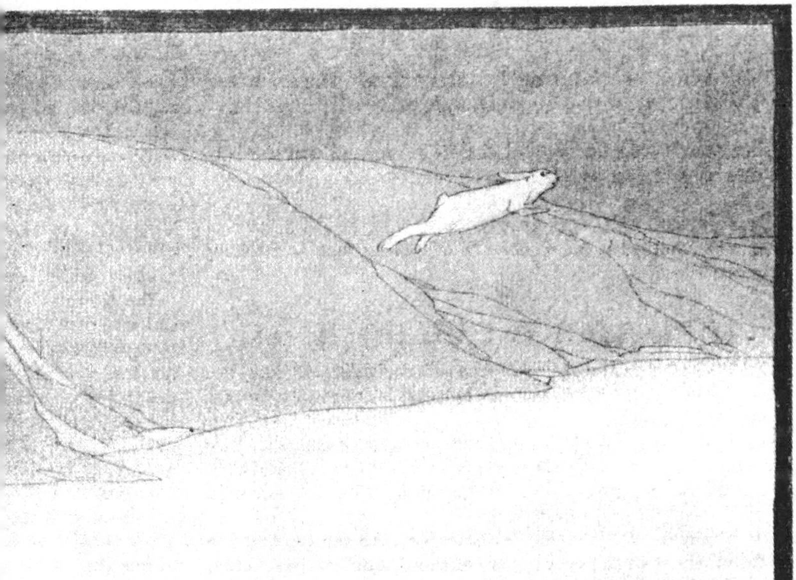

the snowshoe rabbit flashed on ahead

word from the world to the men who sought gold under the shadow of the Pole.

Buck did not like it, but he bore up well to the work, taking pride in it after the manner of Dave and Sol-leks, and seeing that his mates, whether they prided in it or not, did their fair share. It was a monotonous life, operating with machine-like regularity. One day was very like another. At a certain time each morning the cooks turned out, fires were built, and breakfast was eaten. Then, while some broke camp, others harnessed the dogs, and they were under way an hour or so before the darker darkness fell which gave warning of dawn. At night camp was made. Some pitched the flies, others cut firewood and pine boughs for the beds, and still others carried water or ice for the cooks. Also, the dogs were fed. To them, this was the one feature of the day, though it was good to loaf around, after the fish was eaten, for an hour or so with the other dogs, of which there were five score and odd.

There were fierce fighters among them, but three battles with the fiercest brought Buck to mastery, so that when he bristled and showed his teeth they got out of his way.

Best of all, perhaps, he loved to lie near the fire, hindlegs crouched under him, forelegs stretched out in front, head raised, and eyes blinking dreamily at the flames. Sometimes he thought of Judge Miller's big house in the sun-kissed Santa Clara Valley, and of the cement swimming tank, and Ysabel, the Mexican hairless, and Toots, the Japanese pug; but oftener he remembered the man in the red sweater, the death of Curly, the great fight with Spitz, and the good things he had eaten or would like to eat. He was not homesick. The Sunland was very dim and distant, and though he remembered, such memories had no power over him. Far more potent were the memories of his heredity that gave things he had never seen before a seeming familiarity; the instincts (which were but the memories of his ancestors become habits), which had lapsed in later days, and still later, in him, quickened and become alive again.

Sometimes, as he crouched there, blinking dreamily at the flames, it seemed that the flames were of another fire, and that as he crouched by this other fire he saw another and different man from the half-breed cook before him. This other man was shorter of leg and longer of arm, with muscles that were stringy and knotty rather than rounded and swelling. The hair of this man was long and matted, and his head slanted back under it from the eyes. He uttered strange sounds, and seemed very much afraid of the darkness, into which he peered continually, clutching in his hand, which hung midway between knee and foot, a stick with a heavy stone made fast to the end. He was all but naked; a ragged and fire-scorched skin hung part way down his back. He did not stand erect, but with trunk inclined forward from the hips, on legs that bended at the knees. About his body there was a peculiar springiness, or resiliency, almost catlike, and a quick alertness as of one who lived in perpetual fear of things seen and unseen.

At other times this hairy man squatted by the fire with head between his legs and slept. On such occasions his elbows were on his knees, his hands clasped above his head as though to shed rain by the hairy arms. And beyond that fire, in the circling darkness, Buck could see many gleaming coals, two by two, always two by two, which he knew for the eyes of great beasts of prey. He could hear the crashing of their bodies through the undergrowth, and the noises they made in the night; and dreaming there by the Yukon bank, with lazy eyes blinking at the fire, these sounds and sights of another world would make the hair to rise along his back and stand on end across his shoulders and up his neck, till he whimpered low and suppressedly, or growled softly, and the half-breed cook shouted at him:

"Hey! You Buck! Wake up!"

Whereupon the other world would vanish and the real world come into his eyes, and he would get up and yawn and stretch as though he had been asleep.

It was a hard trip, with the mail behind them, and the heavy work wore them down. They were short of weight and in poor condition when they made Dawson, and should have had a ten days' or a week's rest, at least. But in two days' time they dropped down the Yukon bank from the Barracks, loaded with letters for the Outside. The dogs were tired, the drivers grumbling, and to make matters worse, it snowed every day. This meant a soft trail, greater friction on the runners, and heavier pulling for the dogs; yet the drivers were fair through it all, and did their best for the welfare of the animals.

Each night the dogs were attended to first. They ate before the drivers ate, and no man sought his sleeping-robe till he had seen to the feet of the dogs he drove. Still, their strength went down. Since the beginning of the winter they had traveled eighteen hundred miles, dragging sleds the whole weary distance, and eighteen hundred miles will tell upon life of the toughest. Buck stood it, keeping his mates up to their work and maintaining discipline, though he, too, was very tired. Billee cried and whimpered regularly in his sleep each night. Jo was sourer than ever, and Sol-leks was unapproachable, blind side or other side.

The Scotch half-breed

But it was Dave who suffered most of all. Something had gone wrong with him. He became more morose and irritable, and when camp was pitched at once made his nest, where his driver fed him. Once out of the harness and down, he did not get on his feet again till harness-up time in the morning.

Sometimes, in the traces, when jerked by a sudden stoppage of the sled, or by straining to start it, he would cry out with pain. The driver examined him, but could find nothing. All the drivers became interested in his case. They talked it over at meal-time, and over their last pipes before going to bed, and one night they held a consultation. He was brought from his nest to the fire and was pressed and prodded till he cried out many times. Something was wrong inside, but they could locate no broken bones, could not make it out.

By the time Cassiar Bar was reached he was so weak that he was falling repeatedly in the traces. The Scotch half-breed called a halt and took him out of the team, making the next dog, Sol-leks, fast to the sled. His intention was to rest Dave, letting him run free behind the sled. Sick as he was, Dave resented being taken out, grunting and growling while the traces were unfastened, and whimpering broken-heartedly when he saw Sol-leks in the position he had held and served so long. For the pride of trace and trail was his, and, sick unto death, he could not bear that another dog should do his work.

When the sled started he floundered in the soft snow alongside the beaten trail, attacking Sol-leks with his teeth, rushing against him and trying to thrust him off into the soft snow on the other side, striving to leap inside his traces and get between him and the sled, and all the while whining and yelping and crying with grief and pain. The half-breed tried to drive him away with the whip, but he paid no heed to the stinging lash, and the man had not the heart to strike harder. Dave refused to run quietly on the trail behind the sled, where the going was easy, but continued to flounder alongside in the soft snow, where the going was most difficult, till exhausted. Then he fell, and lay where he fell, howling lugubriously as the long train of sleds churned by.

With the last remnant of his strength he managed to stagger along behind till the train made another stop, when he floundered past the sleds to his own, where he stood alongside Sol-leks. His driver lingered a moment to get a light for his pipe from the man behind. Then he returned and started his dogs. They swung out on the trail with remarkable lack of exertion, turned their heads uneasily, and stopped in surprise. The driver was surprised, too. The sled had not moved. He called his comrades to witness the sight. Dave had bitten through both of Sol-leks traces, and was standing directly in front of the sled in his proper place.

He pleaded with his eyes to remain there. The driver was perplexed. His comrades talked of how a dog could break its heart through being denied the work that killed it, and recalled instances they had known where dogs, too old for the toil, or injured, had died because they were cut out of the traces. Also, they held it a mercy, since Dave was to die anyway, that he should die in the traces, heart-easy and content. So he was harnessed in again, and proudly he pulled as of old, though more than once he cried out involuntarily from the bite of his inward hurt. Several times he fell down and was dragged in the traces, and once the sled ran upon him so that he limped thereafter in one of his hindlegs.

But he held out till camp was reached, when his driver made a place for him by the fire. Morning found him too weak to travel. At harness-up time he tried to crawl to his driver. By convulsive efforts he got on his feet, staggered, and fell. Then he wormed his way forward slowly toward where the harnesses were being put on his mates. He would advance and drag up his body with a sort of hitching movement, when he would push out his forelegs and hitch ahead again for a few more inches. His strength left him, and the last his mates saw of him he lay gasping in the snow and yearning toward them. But they could hear him mournfully howling till they passed out of sight behind a belt of river timber.

Here the train was halted. The Scotch half-breed slowly retraced his steps to the camp they had left. The men ceased talking. A revolver-shot rang out. The half-breed came back hurriedly. The whips snapped, the bells tinkled merrily, the sleds churned along the trail; but Buck knew, and every dog knew, what had taken place behind the river trees.

Thirty days from the time it left Dawson the Salt Water Mail, with Buck and his mates at the fore, arrived at Skaguay. They were in a wretched state, worn out and worn down. Buck's one hundred and forty pounds had dwindled to one hundred and fifteen. The rest of his mates, though lighter dogs, had relatively lost more weight than he. Pike, the malingerer, who in his lifetime of deceit had often successfully feigned a hurt leg, was now limping in earnest; and Dub was suffering from a wrenched shoulder-blade.

They were all terribly footsore. No spring or rebound was left in them. Their feet fell heavily on the trail, jarring their bodies and doubling the fatigue of a day's travel. There was nothing the matter with them except that they were dead tired. It was not the dead-tiredness that comes through brief and excessive effort, from which recovery is the matter of hours; but it was the dead-tiredness that comes through the slow and prolonged drainage of months of toil. There was no power of recuperation left, no reserve strength to call upon. It had been all used, the last least bit of it. Every muscle, every fibre, every cell was tired, dead tired. And there was reason for it. In less than five months they had traveled two thousand five hundred miles, during the

She persisted in

last eighteen hundred of which they had had but five days' rest. When they arrived at Skaguay they were apparently on their last legs. They could barely keep the traces taut, and on the down-grades just managed to keep out of the way of the sleds.

"Mush on, poor sore-feets," the driver encouraged them as they tottered down the main street of Skaguay. "Dis is de las'. Den we get one long res'. Eh? For sure. One bully long res'."

The drivers confidently expected a long stop-over. Themselves, they had covered twelve hundred miles with two days' rest, and in the nature of reason and common justice they deserved an interval of loafing. But so many were the men who had rushed into the Klondike, and so many were the sweethearts, wives and kin that had not rushed in, that the congested mail was taking on Alpine proportions. Also, there were official orders. Fresh batches of Hudson Bay dogs were to take the places of those worthless for the trail. The worthless ones were to be got rid of, and, since dogs count for little against dollars, they were to be sold.

Three days passed, by which time Buck and his mates found how really tired and weak they were. Then, on the morning of the fourth day two men from the States came along and bought them, harness and all, for a song. The men addressed each other as "Hal" and "Charles." Charles was a middle-aged, lightish-colored man, with weak and watery eyes and a mustache that twisted fiercely and vigorously up, giving the lie to the limply-drooping lip it concealed. Hal was a youngster of nineteen or twenty, with a big Colt's revolver and a hunting-knife strapped about him on a belt that fairly bristled with cartridges. This belt was the most salient thing about him. Both men were manifestly out of place, and why such as they should adventure the North is part of the mystery of things that passes understanding.

Buck heard the chaffering, saw the money pass between them and the Government agent, and knew that the Scotch half-breed and the mail-train drivers were passing out of his life on the heels of Perrault and François and the others who had gone before. When driven with his mates to the new owners' camp, Buck saw a slipshod and slovenly affair, tent half-stretched, dishes unwashed, everything in disorder. Also, he saw a woman. "Mercedes," the men called her. She was Charles' wife and Hal's sister—a nice family party.

Buck watched them apprehensively as they proceeded to take down the tent and load the sled. There was a great deal of effort about their manner, but no businesslike method. The tent was rolled into an awkward bundle three times as large as it should have been. The tin dishes were packed away unwashed. Mercedes continually fluttered in the way of her men and kept up an unbroken chattering of remonstrance and advice. When they put a clothes-sack on the front of the sled she suggested it should go on the back; and when they had put in on the back and covered it over with a couple of other bundles, she discovered overlooked articles which could abide nowhere else but in it, and they unloaded again.

Three men from a neighboring tent came out and looked on, grinning and winking at one another.

"You've got a right smart load as it is," said one of them, "and it's not me should tell you your business, but I wouldn't tote that tent along if I was you."

riding on the sled

"Undreamed of!" cried Mercedes, throwing up her hands in dainty dismay. "However in the world could I manage without a tent?"

"It's springtime, and you won't get any more cold weather," the man replied.

She shook her head decidedly, and Charles and Hal put the last odds and ends on top of the mountainous load.

"Think it'll ride?" one of the men asked.

"Why shouldn't it?" Charles demanded rather shortly.

"Oh, that's all right, that's all right," the man hastened meekly to say. "I was just a-wonderin', that is all. It seemed a mite top-heavy."

Charles turned his back and drew the lashings down as well as he could, which was not in the least well.

"An' of course the dogs can hike along all day with that contraption behind them," affirmed a second of the men.

"Certainly," said Hal with freezing politeness, taking hold of the gee-pole with one hand and swinging his whip from the other. "Mush!" he shouted. "Mush on, there!"

The dogs sprang against the breast-bands, strained hard for a few moments, then relaxed. They were unable to move the sled.

"The lazy brutes, I'll show them!" he cried, preparing to lash out at them with the whip.

But Mercedes interfered, crying, "Oh, Hal, you mustn't," as she caught hold of the whip and wrenched it from him. "The poor dears! Now you must promise you won't be harsh with them for the rest of the trip, or I won't go a step."

"Precious lot you know about dogs," her brother sneered; "and I wish you'd leave me alone. They're lazy, I tell you, and you've got to whip them to get anything out of them. That's their way. You ask any one. Ask one of those men."

Mercedes looked at them imploringly, untold repugnance, at sight of pain, written in her pretty face.

"They're weak as water, if you want to know," came the reply from one of the men. "Plum tuckered out, that's what's the matter. They need a rest."

"Rest be blanked," said Hal with his beardless lips; and Mercedes said "Oh!" in pain and sorrow.

But she was a clannish creature, and rushed at once to the defense of her brother. "Never mind that man," she said pointedly. "You're driving our dogs, and you do what you think best with them."

Again Hal's whip fell upon the dogs. They threw themselves against the breast-bands, dug their feet into the packed snow, got down low to it, and put forth all their strength. The sled held as though it were an anchor. After two efforts they stood still, panting. The whip was whistling savagely, when once more Mercedes interfered. She dropped on her knees before Buck, with tears in her eyes, and put her arms around his neck.

"You poor, poor dears," she cried sympathetically, "why don't you pull hard, then you wouldn't be whipped?" Buck did not like her, but he was feeling too miserable to resist her, taking it as part of the day's miserable work.

One of the onlookers, who had been clenching his teeth to suppress hot speech, now spoke up, saying:

"It's not that I care a whoop what becomes of you, but for the dogs' sakes I just want to tell you you can help them a mighty lot by breaking out that sled. The runners are froze fast. Throw your weight against the gee-pole, right and left, and break it out."

A third time the attempt was made, but this time, following the advice, Hal broke out the runners which had been frozen to the snow. The overloaded and unwieldly sled forged ahead, Buck and his mates struggling frantically under the rain of blows. A hundred yards ahead the path turned and sloped steeply into the main street. It would have required an experienced man to keep the top-heavy sled upright, and Hal was not such a man. As they swung on the turn the sled went over, spilling half its load through the loose lashings. The dogs never stopped. The lightened sled bounded on its side behind them. They were angry because of the ill-treatment they had received and the unjust load. Buck was raging. He broke into a run, the team following his lead. Hal cried "Whoa! Whoa!" but they gave no heed. He tripped and was pulled off his feet. The capsized sled ground over him, and the dogs dashed on up the street, adding to the gayety of Skaguay as they scattered the remainder of the outfit along its chief thoroughfare.

Kind-hearted citizens caught the dogs

and gathered up the scattered belongings. Also, they gave advice. Half the load and twice the dogs if they ever expected to reach Dawson, was what was said. Hal and his sister and brother-in-law listened unwillingly, pitched tent, and overhauled the outfit. Canned goods were turned out that made men laugh, for canned goods on the Long Trail are a thing to dream about."Blankets for a hotel," quoth one of the men, who laughed and helped. "Half as many is too much; get rid of them. Throw away that tent. And all those dishes; who's going to wash them, anyway? Do you think you're traveling on a Pullman?"

And so it went, the inexorable elimination of the superfluous. Mercedes cried when her clothes-bags were dumped on the ground and article after article was thrown out. She cried in general, and she cried in particular over each discarded thing. She clasped hands about knees, rocking back and forth broken-heartedly. She averred she would not go an inch, not for a dozen Charleses. She appealed to everybody and to everything, finally wiping her eyes and proceeding to cast out even articles of apparel that were imperative necessities. And in her zeal, when she had finished with her own, she attacked the belongings of her men and went through them like a tornado.

This accomplished, the outfit, though cut in half, was still a formidable bulk. Charles and Hal went out in the evening and bought six outside dogs. These, added to the six of the original team and Teek and Koona, the huskies obtained at the Rink Rapids on the record trip, brought the team up to fourteen. But the outside dogs, though practically broken in since their landing, did not amount to much. Three were short-haired pointers, one was a Newfoundland, and the other two were mongrels of indeterminate breed. They did not seem to know anything, these newcomers. Buck and his comrades looked upon them with disgust, and though he speedily taught them their places and what not to do, he could not teach them what to do. They did not take kindly to trace and trail. With the exception of the two mongrels, they were bewildered and spirit-broken by the strange, savage environment in which they found themselves and by the ill-treatment they had received. The two mongrels were without spirit at all; bones were the only things breakable about them.

With the newcomers hopeless and forlorn, and the old team worn out by twenty-five hundred miles of continuous trail, the outlook was anything but bright. The two men, however, were quite cheerful. And they were proud, too. They were doing the thing in style, with fourteen dogs. They had seen other sleds depart over the Pass for Dawson, or come in from Dawson, but never had they seen a sled with so many as fourteen dogs. In the nature of Arctic travel there was a reason why fourteen dogs should not drag one sled, and that was that one sled could not carry the food for fourteen dogs. But Charles and Hal did not know this. They had worked the trip out with a pencil — so much to a dog, so many dogs, so many days, Q.E.D. Mercedes looked over their shoulders and nodded comprehensively; it was all so very simple.

Late next morning Buck led the long team up the street. There was nothing lively about it: no snap or go in him and his fellows. They were starting dead weary. Four times he had covered the distance between Salt Water and Dawson, and the knowledge that, jaded and tired, he was facing the same trail once more made him bitter. His heart was not in the work; nor was the heart of any dog. The outsiders were timid, the insiders without confidence in their masters.

Buck felt vaguely that there was no depending upon these two men and the woman. They did not know how to do anything, and as the days went by it became apparent that they could not learn. They were slack in all things, without order or discipline. It took them half the night to pitch a slovenly camp, and half the morning to break that camp and get the sled loaded in such fashion that for the rest of the day they were occupied in stopping and rearranging the load. Some days they did not make ten miles. On other days they were unable to get started at all. And on no day did they succeed in making more than half the distance used by the men as a basis in their dog-food computation.

It was inevitable that they should go short on dog-food. But they hastened it by overfeeding, bringing the day nearer when underfeeding would commence. The outside dogs, whose digestions had not been trained by chronic famine to make the most on little, had voracious appetites. And when, in addition to this, the worn-out huskies pulled weakly, Hal decided that the orthodox ration was too small. He doubled it. And to cap it all, when Mercedes, with tears in her pretty eyes and a quaver in her throat, could not cajole him into giving the dogs still more, she stole from the fish-sacks and fed them slyly. But it was not food that Buck and the huskies needed; it was rest. And though they were making poor time, the heavy load they dragged sapped their strength severely.

Then came the underfeeding. Hal awoke one day to the fact that his dog-food was half gone and the distance only quarter covered; further, that for love or money no additional dog-food was to be obtained. So he cut down even the orthodox ration and tried to increase the day's travel. His sister and brother-in-law seconded him, but they were frustrated by their heavy outfit and their own incompetence. It was a simple matter to give the dogs less food; but it was impossible to make the dogs travel faster, while their own inability to get under way earlier in the morning prevented them from traveling longer hours. Not only did they not know how to work dogs, but they did not know how to work themselves.

The first to go was Dub. Poor blundering thief that he was, always getting caught and punished, he had none the less been a faithful worker. His wrenched shoulder-blade, untreated and unrested, went from bad to worse, till finally Hal shot him with the big Colt's revolver. It is a saying of the country that an outside dog starves to death on the ration of the husky, so the six outside dogs under Buck could do no less than die on half the ration of the husky. The Newfoundland went first, followed by the three short-haired pointers, the two mongrels hanging on more grittily to life, but going in the end.

By this time all the amenities and gentlenesses of the Southland had fallen away from the three people. Shorn of its glamor and romance, Arctic travel became to them a reality too harsh for their manhood and womanhood. Mercedes ceased weeping over the dogs, being too occupied with weeping over herself and with quarreling with her husband and brother. To quarrel was the one thing they were never too weary to do. Their irritability arose out of their misery, increased with it, doubled upon it, outdistanced it. The wonderful patience of the trail which comes to men who toil hard and suffer sore and remain sweet of speech and kindly did not come to these two men and the woman. They had no inkling of such a patience. They were stiff and in pain; their muscles ached, their bones ached, their very hearts ached; and because of this they became sharp of speech, and hard words were first on their lips in the morning and last at night.

Charles and Hal wrangled whenever Mercedes gave them a chance. It was the cherished belief of each that he did more than his share of the work, and neither forbore to speak this belief at every opportunity. Sometimes Mercedes sided with her husband, sometimes with her brother. The result was a beautiful and unending family quarrel. Starting from a dispute as to which should chop a few sticks for the fire (a dispute which concerned only Charles and Hal), presently would be lugged in the rest of the family — fathers, mothers, uncles, cousins, people thousands of miles away and some of them dead. That Hal's views on art, or the sort of society plays his mother's brother wrote, should have anything to do with the chopping of a few sticks of firewood, passes comprehension; nevertheless the quarrel was as likely to tend in that direction as in the direction of Charles' political prejudices. And that Charles' sister's talebearing tongue should be relevant to the building of a Yukon fire was apparent only to Mercedes, who disburdened herself of copious opinions upon that topic, and incidentally upon a few other traits unpleasantly peculiar to her husband's family. In the mean time the fire remained unbuilt, the camp half-pitched, and the dogs unfed.

Mercedes nursed a special grievance — the grievance of sex. She was pretty and soft, and had been chivalrously treated all her days. But the present treatment by her husband and brother was everything save chivalrous. It was her custom to be helpless. They complained. Upon which impeachment of what to her was her most essential sex-prerogative she made their lives unendurable. She no longer considered the dogs, and because she was sore and tired she persisted in riding on the sled. She was pretty and soft, but she weighed one hundred and twenty pounds — a lusty last straw to a load dragged by

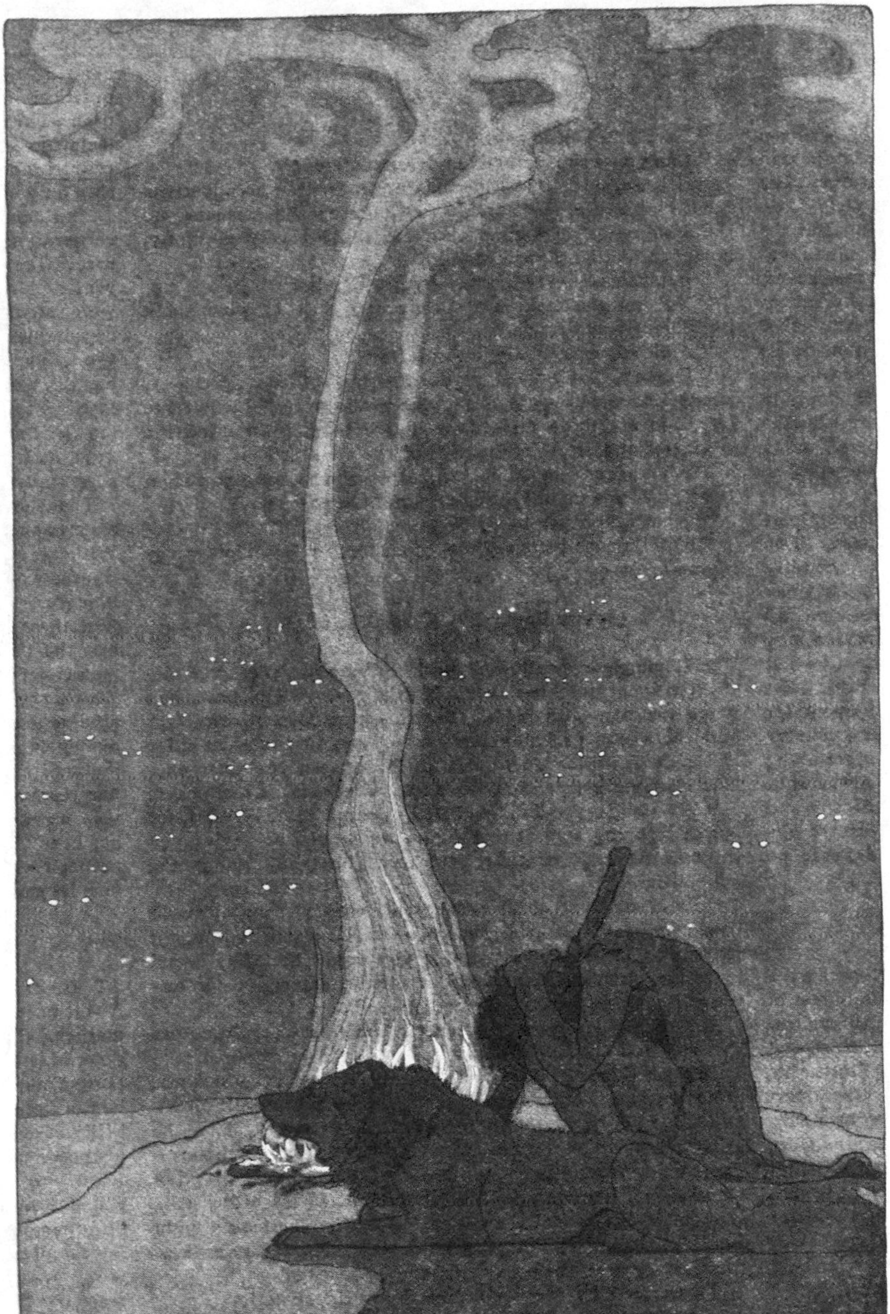

And beyond that fire, in the circling darkness, Buck could see many gleaming coals, two by two

weak and starving animals. She rode for days, till they fell in the traces and the sled stood still. Charles and Hal begged her to get off and walk, pleaded with her, entreated, the while she wept and importuned Heaven with a recital of their brutality.

On one occasion they took her off the sled by main strength. They never did it again. She let her legs go limp like a spoiled child, and sat down on the trail. They went on their way, but she did not move. After they had traveled three miles they unloaded the sled, came back for her, and by main strength put her on the sled again.

In the excess of their own misery they were callous to the suffering of their animals. Hal's theory, which he practiced on others, was that one must get hardened. He had started out preaching it to his sister and brother-in-law. Failing there, he hammered it into the dogs with a club. At the Five Fingers the dog-food gave out, and a toothless old squaw offered to trade them a few pounds of frozen horsehide for the Colt's revolver that kept the big hunting-knife company at Hal's hip. A poor substitute for food was this hide, just as it had been stripped from the starved horses of the cattlemen six months back. In its frozen state it was more like strips of galvanized iron, and when a dog wrestled it into his stomach it thawed into thin and innutritious leathery strings and into a mass of short hair, irritating and indigestible.

And through it all Buck staggered along at the head of the team as in a nightmare. He pulled when he could; when he could no longer pull he fell down and remained down till blows from whip or club drove him to his feet again. All the stiffness and gloss had gone out of his beautiful furry coat. The hair hung down, limp and draggled, or matted with dried blood where Hal's club had bruised him. His muscles had wasted away to knotty strings, and the flesh-pads had disappeared, so that each rib and every bone in his frame was outlined cleanly through the loose hide wrinkled in folds of emptiness. It was heartbreaking, only Buck's heart was unbreakable. The man in the red sweater had proved that.

As it was with Buck, so was it with his mates. They were perambulating skeletons. There were seven altogether, including him. In their very great misery they had become insensible to the bite of the lash or the bruise of the club. The pain of the beating was dull and distant, just as the things their eyes saw and their ears heard seemed dull and distant. They were not half living or quarter living. They were simply so many bags of bones in which sparks of life fluttered faintly. When a halt was made they dropped down in the traces like dead dogs, and the spark dimmed and paled and seemed to go out. And when the club or whip fell upon them the spark fluttered feebly up and they tottered on.

There came a day when Billee, the good-natured, fell and could not rise. Hal had traded off his revolver, so he took the ax and knocked Billee on the head as he lay in the traces, then cut the carcass out of the harness and dragged it to one side. Buck saw, and his mates saw, and they knew that this thing was very close to them. On the next day Koona went, and but five of them remained — Jo, too far gone to be malignant; Pike, crippled and limping, only half conscious and not conscious enough longer to malinger; Sol-leks, the one-eyed, still faithful to the toil of trace and trail, and mournful in that he had so little strength with which to pull; Teek, who had not traveled so far that winter and who was now beaten more than the others because he was fresher; and Buck, still at the head of the team, but no longer enforcing discipline or striving to enforce it, blind with weakness, and keeping the trail by the loom of it and by the dim feel of his feet.

It was beautiful spring weather, but neither dogs nor humans were aware of it. Each day the sun rose earlier and set later. It was dawn by three in the morning, and twilight lingered till nine at night. The whole long day was a blaze of sunshine. The ghostly winter silence had given way to the great spring murmur of awakening life. This murmur arose from all the land, fraught with the joy of living. It came from the things that lived and moved again, things which had been as dead and which had not moved during the long months of frost. The sap was rising in the pines. The willows and aspens were bursting out in young buds. Shrubs and vines were putting on fresh garbs of green. Crickets sang in the nights, and in the days all manner of creeping, crawling things rustled forth into the sun. Partridges and woodpeckers were booming and knocking in the forest. Squirrels were chattering, birds singing, and overhead honked the wild-fowl driving up from the south in cunning wedges that split the air. From every hillslope came the trickle of running water, the music of unseen fountains. All things were thawing, bending, snapping. The Yukon was straining to break loose the ice that bound it down. It ate away from beneath; the sun ate from above. Air-holes formed, fissures sprang and spread apart, while thin sections of ice fell through bodily into the river. And amid all this bursting, rending, throbbing of awakening life, under the blazing sun and through the soft, sighing breezes, like wayfarers to death staggered the two men, the woman, and the huskies.

With the dogs falling, Mercedes weeping and riding, Hal swearing innocuously, and Charles' eyes wistfully watering, they staggered into John Thornton's camp at the mouth of White River. When they halted the dogs dropped down as though they had all been struck dead. Mercedes dried her eyes and looked at John Thornton. Charles sat down on a log to rest. He sat down very slowly and painstakingly what of his great stiffness. Hal did the talking. John Thornton was whittling the last touches on an ax-handle he had made from a stick of birch. He listened, gave monosyllabic replies, and, when it was asked, terse advice. He knew the breed, and he gave his advice in the certainty that it would not be followed.

"They told us up above that the bottom

DRAWN BY PHILIP R. GOODWIN

"You Poor Devil," said John Thornton, and Buck licked his hand

was dropping out of the trail and that the best thing for us to do was to lay over," Hal said in response to Thornton's warning to take no more chances on the rotten ice. "They told us we couldn't make White River, and here we are." This last with a sneering ring of triumph in it.

"And they told you true," John Thornton answered. "The bottom's likely to drop out at any moment. Only fools, with the blind luck of fools, could have made it. I tell you straight, I wouldn't risk my carcass on that ice for all the gold in Alaska."

"That's because you're not a fool, I suppose," said Hal. "All the same we'll go on to Dawson." He uncoiled his whip. "Get up there, Buck! Hi! Get up there! Mush on!"

Thornton went on whittling. It was idle, he knew, to get between a fool and his folly; while two or three fools more or less would not alter the scheme of things.

But the team did not get up at the command. It had long since passed into the stage where blows were required to rouse it. The whip flashed out, here and there, on its merciless errands. John Thornton compressed his lips. Sol-leks was the first to crawl to his feet. Teek followed. Jo came next, yelping with pain. Pike made painful efforts. Twice he fell over when half up, and on the third attempt managed to rise. Buck made no effort. He lay quietly where he had fallen. The lash bit into him again and again, but he neither whined nor struggled. Several times Thornton started, as though to speak, but changed his mind. A moisture came into his eyes, and, as the whipping continued, he arose and walked irresolutely up and down.

This was the first time Buck had failed, in itself a sufficient reason to drive Hal into a rage. He exchanged the whip for the customary club. Buck refused to move under the rain of heavier blows which now fell upon him. Like his mates he was barely able to get up, but, unlike them, he had made up his mind not to get up. He had a vague feeling of impending doom. This had been strong upon him when he pulled in to the bank, and it had not departed from him. What of the thin and rotten ice he had felt under his feet all day, it seemed that he sensed disaster close at hand, out there ahead on the ice where his master was trying to drive him. He refused to stir. So greatly had he suffered, and so far gone was he, that the blows did not hurt much. And as they continued to fall upon him the spark of life within flickered and went down. It was nearly out. He felt strangely numb. As though from a great distance he was aware that he was being beaten. The last sensations of pain left him. He no longer felt anything, though very faintly he could hear the impact of the club upon his body. But it was no longer his body, it seemed so far away.

And then, suddenly, without warning, uttering a cry that was inarticulate and more like the cry of an animal, John Thornton sprang upon the man who wielded the club. Hal was hurled backward as though struck by a falling tree. Mercedes screamed. Charles looked on wistfully, wiped his watery eyes, but did not get up because of his stiffness.

John Thornton stood over Buck, struggling to control himself, too convulsed with rage to speak.

"If you strike that dog again I'll kill you," he at last managed to say in a choking voice.

"It's my dog," Hal replied, wiping the blood from his mouth as he came back. "Get out of my way or I'll fix you. I'm going to Dawson."

Thornton stood between him and Buck, and evinced no intention of getting out of the way. Hal drew his long hunting-knife. Mercedes screamed, cried, laughed, and manifested the chaotic abandonment of hysteria. Thornton rapped Hal's knuckles with the ax-handle, knocking the knife to the ground. He rapped his knuckles again as he tried to pick it up. Then he stooped, picked it up himself, and with two strokes cut Buck's traces.

Hal had no fight left in him. Besides, his hands were full with his sister, or his arms, rather; while Buck was too near dead to be of further use in hauling the sled. A few minutes later they pulled out from the bank and down the river. Buck heard them go and raised his head to see. Pike was leading, Sol-leks was at the wheel, and between were Jo and Teek. They were limping and staggering. Mercedes was riding the loaded sled. Hal guided at the gee-pole, and Charles stumbled along in the rear.

As Buck watched them Thornton knelt beside him and with rough, kindly hands searched for broken bones. By the time his search had disclosed nothing more than many bruises and a state of terrible starvation the sled was a quarter of a mile away. Dog and man watched it crawling over the ice. Suddenly they saw its back end drop down, as into a rut, and the gee-pole, with Hal clinging to it, jerk into the air. Mercedes' scream came to their ears. They saw Charles turn and make one step to run back, and then a whole section of ice give way and dogs and humans disappear. A yawning hole was all that was to be seen. The bottom had dropped out of the trail.

John Thornton and Buck looked at each other.

DRAWN BY CHARLES LIVINGSTON BULL

He loved to run down dry water-courses

"You poor devil," said John Thornton, and Buck licked his hand.

"Old longings nomadic leap,
Chafing at custom's chain;
Again from its brumal sleep
Wakens the ferine strain."

When John Thornton froze his feet in the previous December his partners had made him comfortable and left him to get well, going on themselves up the river to get out a raft of saw-logs for Dawson. He was still limping slightly at the time he rescued Buck, but with the continued warm weather even the slight limp left him. And here, lying by the river bank through the long spring days, watching the running water, listening lazily to the songs of birds and the hum of Nature, Buck slowly won back his strength.

A rest comes very well after one has traveled three thousand miles, and it must be confessed that Buck waxed lazy as his wounds healed, his muscles swelled out, and the flesh came back to cover his bones. For that matter, they were all loafing — Buck, John Thornton, and Skeet and Nig — waiting for the raft to come that was to carry them down to Dawson. Skeet was a little Irish setter who early made friends with Buck, who, in a dying condition, was unable to resent her first advances. She had the doctor-trait, which some dogs possess, and as a ,mother-cat washes her kittens so she washed and cleansed Buck's wounds. Regularly, each morning after he had finished his breakfast, she performed her self-appointed task, till he came to look for her ministrations as much as he did for Thornton's. Nig, equally friendly though less demonstrative, was a huge black dog, half bloodhound and half deerhound, with eyes that laughed and a boundless good nature.

To Buck's surprise these dogs manifested no jealousy toward him. They seemed to share the kindliness and largeness of John Thornton. As Buck grew stronger they enticed him into all sorts of ridiculous games, in which Thornton himself could not forbear to join; and in this fashion Buck romped through his convalescence and into a new existence. Love, genuine passionate love, was his for the first time. This he had never experienced at Judge Miller's down in the sun-kissed Santa Clara Valley. With the Judge's sons, hunting and tramping, it had been a working partnership; with the Judge's grandsons, a sort of pompous guardianship; and with the Judge himself, a stately and dignified friendship. But love that was feverish and burning, that was adoration, that was madness, it had taken John Thornton to arouse.

This man had saved his life, which was something; but, further, he was the ideal master. Other men saw to the welfare of their dogs from a sense of duty and business expediency; he saw to the welfare of his as if they were his own children, because he could not help it. And he saw further. He never forgot a kindly greeting or a cheering word, and to sit down for a long talk with them ("gas," he called it) was as much his delight as theirs. He had a way of taking Buck's head roughly between his hands, and, resting his own head upon Buck's, of shaking him back and forth, the while calling him ill names that to Buck were love-names. Buck knew no greater joy than that rough embrace and the sound of murmured oaths, and at each jerk back and forth it seemed that his heart would be shaken out of his body so great was its ecstasy. And, when released, he sprang to his feet, his mouth laughing, his eyes eloquent, his throat vibrant with unuttered sound, and in that fashion remained without movement, John Thornton would exclaim: "Gad! you can all but speak!"

Buck had a trick of love-expression that was akin to hurt. He would often seize Thornton's hand in his mouth and close so fiercely that the flesh bore the impress of his teeth for some time afterward. And as Buck understood the oaths to be love-words so the man understood this feigned bite for a caress.

For the most part, however, Buck's love was expressed in adoration. Though he went wild with happiness when Thornton touched him or spoke to him, he did not seek these tokens. Unlike Skeet, who was wont to shove her nose under Thornton's hand and nudge and nudge till petted, or Nig, who would stalk up and rest his great head on Thornton's knee, Buck was content to adore at a distance. He would lie by the hour, eager, alert, at Thornton's feet, looking up into his face, dwelling upon it, studying it, following with keenest interest each fleeting expression, every movement or change of feature. Or, as chance might have it, he would lie farther away, to the side or rear, watching the outlines of the man and the occasional movements of his body. And often, such was the communion in which they lived, the strength of Buck's gaze would draw Thornton's head around and he would return the gaze, without speech, his heart shining out of his eyes as Buck's heart shone out.

For a long time after his rescue Buck did not like Thornton to get out of his sight. From the moment he left the tent to when he entered it again Buck would follow at his heels. His transient masters since he had come into the Northland had bred in him a fear that no master could be permanent. He was afraid that Thornton would pass out of his life as Perrault and François and the Scotch half-breed had passed out. Even in the night, in his dreams, he was haunted by this fear. At such times he would shake off sleep and creep through the chill to the flap of the tent, where he would stand and listen to the sound of his master's breathing.

But in spite of this great love he bore John Thornton, which seemed to bespeak the soft, civilizing influence, the strain of the primitives, which the Northland had aroused in him, remained alive and active. Faithfulness and devotion, things born of fire and roof, were his; yet he retained his wildness and wiliness. He was a thing of the wild, come in from the wild to sit by John Thornton's fire, rather than a dog of the soft Southland stamped with the marks of generations of civilization. Because of his very great love he could not steal from this man, but from any other man, in any other camp, he did not hesitate an instant; while the cunning with which he stole enabled him to escape detection.

His face and body were scored by the teeth of many dogs, and he fought as fiercely as ever and more shrewdly. Skeet and Nig were too good-natured for quarreling, besides, they belonged to John Thornton; but the strange dog, no matter what the breed or valor, swiftly acknowledged Buck's supremacy or found himself struggling for life with a terrible antagonist. And Buck was merciless. He had learned well the law of club and fang, and he never forewent an advantage or drew back from a foe he had started on the way to death. He had learned from Spitz, and from the chief fighting dogs of the police and mail, and knew there was no middle course. He must master or be mastered; while to show mercy was a weakness. Mercy did not exist in the primordial life. It was misunderstood for fear, and such misunderstandings made for death. Kill or be killed, eat or be eaten, was the law; and this mandate, down out of the depths of Time, he obeyed.

He was older than the days he had seen and the breaths he had drawn. He linked the Past with the Present, and the Eternity behind him throbbed through him in a mighty rhythm to which he swayed as the tides and seasons swayed. He sat by John Thornton's fire, a broad-breasted dog, white-fanged and long-furred, but behind him were the shades of all dogs, half-wolves and wild wolves, urgent and prompting, tasting the savor of the meat he ate, thirsting for the water he drank, scenting the wind with him, listening with him and telling him the sounds made by the wild life in the forest, dictating his moods, directing his actions, lying down to sleep with him when he lay down and dreaming with him and beyond him and becoming themselves the stuff of his dreams.

So peremptorily did these shades beckon him that each day mankind and the claims of mankind slipped farther from him. Deep in the forest a call was sounding, and as often as he heard this call, mysteriously thrilling and luring, he felt compelled to turn his back upon the fire and the beaten earth around it, and to plunge into the forest, and on and on, he knew not where or why, nor did he wonder where or why; the call sounded imperiously, deep in the forest. But as often as he gained the soft, unbroken earth and the green shade, the love for John Thornton drew him back to the fire again.

DRAWN BY CHARLES LIVINGSTON BULL

Behind him were the shades of all dogs, half wolves and wild wolves

John Thornton's partners, Hans and Pete, arrived on the long-expected raft, which, sold to the saw-mill at Dawson, equipped them for a journey into the East after a fabled lost mine, the history of which was as old as the history of the country. Many men had sought it; few had found it; and more than a few there were who had never returned from the quest. This lost mine was steeped in tragedy and shrouded in mystery. No one knew of the first man. The oldest tradition stopped before it got back to him. From the beginning there had been an ancient and ramshackle cabin. Dying men had sworn to it and to the mine, the site of which it marked, clinching their testimony with nuggets that were unlike any known grade of gold in the Northland.

But no living man had looted this treasure-house, and the dead were dead; wherefore John Thornton, and Pete and Hans, with Buck and half a dozen other dogs, faced into the East on an unknown trail to achieve where men and dogs as good as themselves had failed. They sledded seventy miles up the Yukon, swung to the left into the Stewart River, passed the Mayo and the McQuestion, and held on until the Stewart itself became a streamlet, threading the upstanding peaks which marked the backbone of the continent.

John Thornton asked little of man or nature. He was unafraid of the wild. With a handful of salt and a rifle he could plunge into the wilderness and fare wherever he pleased and as long as he pleased. Being in no haste, Indian fashion, he hunted his dinner in the course of the day's travel; and if he failed to find it, like the Indian, he kept on traveling, secure in the knowledge that sooner or later he should come to it. So, on this great journey into the East, straight meat was the bill-of-fare, ammunition and tools principally made up the load on the sled, and the time-card was drawn upon the limitless future.

To Buck it was boundless delight, this hunting, fishing and indefinite wandering through strange places. For weeks at a time they would hold on steadily, day after day; and for weeks on end they would camp, here and there, the dogs loafing and the men burning holes through frozen muck and gravel and washing countless pans of dirt by the heat of the fire. Sometimes they went hungry, sometimes they feasted riotously, all according to the abundance of game and the fortune of hunting. Summer arrived and dogs and men packed on their backs, rafted across blue mountain lakes, and descended or ascended unknown rivers in slender boats whip-sawed from the standing forest.

The months came and went, and back and forth they twisted through the uncharted vastness where no men were and yet where men had been if the Lost Cabin were true. And through another winter they wandered on the obliterated trails of men who had gone before. Once they came upon a path blazed through the forest, an ancient path, and the Lost Cabin seemed very near. But the path began nowhere and ended nowhere, and it remained to them a mystery, as the man who made it and the reason he made it remained a mystery.

Spring came on once more, and at the end of all their wandering they found, not the Lost Cabin, but a shallow placer in a broad valley where the gold showed like yellow butter across the bottom of the washing-pan. They sought no further. Each day they worked earned them thousands of dollars in clean dust and nuggets, and they worked every day. The gold was sacked in moose-hide bags, fifty pounds to the bag, and piled like so much firewood outside the spruce-bough lodge. Like giants they toiled, days flashing on the heels of days like dreams, as they heaped the treasure up.

There was nothing for the dogs to do save the hauling in of meat now and again that Thornton killed, and Buck spent long hours musing by the fire. The vision of the short-legged hairy man came to him more frequently, now that there was little work to be done; and often, blinking by the fire, Buck wandered with him in that other world which he remembered.

The salient thing of this other world seemed fear. When he watched the hairy man sleeping by the fire, head between his knees and hands clasped above, Buck saw that he slept restlessly, with many starts and awakenings, at which times he would peer fearfully into the darkness and fling more wood on the fire. Did they walk by a beach of a sea, where the hairy man gathered shellfish and ate them as he gathered, it was with eyes that roved everywhere for hidden danger and with legs prepared to run like the wind at its first appearance. Through the forest they crept noiselessly, Buck at the hairy man's heels; and they were alert and vigilant, the pair of them, ears twitching and moving, and nostrils quivering, for the man heard and smelled as keenly as Buck. The hairy man could spring up into the trees and travel ahead as fast as on the ground, swinging by the arms from limb to limb, sometimes a dozen feet apart, letting go and catching, never falling, never missing his grip. In fact, he seemed as much at home among the trees as on the ground; and Buck had memories of nights of vigil spent beneath trees wherein the hairy man roosted, holding on tightly as he slept.

And closely akin to the visions of the hairy man was the call still sounding in the depths of the forest. It filled him with a great unrest and strange desires. It caused him to feel a vague-sweet gladness, and he was aware of wild yearnings and stirrings for he knew not what. Sometimes he pursued the call into the forest, looking for it as though it were a tangible thing, barking softly or defiantly, as the mood might dictate. He would thrust his nose into the cool wood-moss, or into the black soil where long grasses grew, and snort with joy at the fat earth-smells; or he would crouch for hours, as if in concealment, behind fungus-covered trunks of fallen trees, wide-eyed and wide-eared to all that moved and sounded about him. It might be, lying thus, that he hoped to surprise this call he could not understand. But he did not know why he did these various things. He was impelled to do them, and did not reason about them at all.

Irresistible impulses seized him. He would be lying in camp, dozing lazily in the heat of the day, when suddenly his head would lift and his ears cock up, intent and listening, and he would spring to his feet and dash away, and on and on for hours, through the forest aisles and across the open spaces where the grassy mounds bunched. He loved to run down dry watercourses, and to creep and spy upon the birdlife in the woods. For a day at a time he would lie in the underbrush where he could watch the partridges drumming. But especially he loved to run in the dim twilight of the summer midnights, listening to the subdued and sleepy murmurs of the forest, reading signs and sounds as man may read a book, and seeking for the mysterious something that called, called, waking or sleeping, at all times, for him to come.

One night he sprang from sleep with a start — eager eyed, nostrils quivering and scenting, his mane bristling in recurrent waves. From the forest came the call (or one note of it, for the call was many-noted), distinct and definite as never before — a long-drawn howl, like, yet unlike, any noise made by husky-dog. And he knew it, in the old familiar way, as a sound heard before. He sprang through the sleeping camp and in swift silence dashed through the woods. As he drew closer to the cry he went more slowly, with caution in every movement, till he came to an open place among the trees, and looking out saw, erect on haunches, with nose pointed to the sky, a long, lean, timber wolf.

He had made no noise, yet it ceased from its howling and tried to sense his presence. Buck stalked into the open, half-crouching, body gathered compactly together, tail straight and stiff, feet falling with unwonted care. Every movement advertised commingled threatening and overtures of friendliness. It was the menacing truce that marks the meeting of wild beasts that prey. But the wolf fled at sight of him. He followed with wild leapings, in a frenzy to overtake. He ran him into a blind channel in the bed of the creek where a timber-jam barred the way. The wolf whirled about, pivoting on his hindlegs after the fashion of Jo and of all cornered husky-dogs, snarling and bristling, clipping his teeth together in a continuous and rapid succession of snaps.

Buck did not attack, but circled him about and hedged him in with friendly advances. The wolf was suspicious and afraid; for Buck made three of him in weight, while his head barely reached Buck's shoulder. Watching his chance he darted away, and the chase was resumed. Time and again he was cornered and the thing repeated, though he was in poor condition, or Buck could not so easily have overtaken him. He would run till Buck's head was even with his flank, when he would whirl around at bay, only to dash away again at the first opportunity.

But in the end Buck's pertinacity was rewarded; for the wolf, finding that no

In this angle he came to bay

harm was intended, finally sniffed noses with him. They became friendly, and played about in the nervous, half-coy way with which fierce beasts belie their fierceness. After some time of this the wolf started off at an easy lope in a manner that plainly showed he was going somewhere. He made it clear to Buck that he was to come, and they ran side by side through the sombre twilight, straight up the creek-bed, into the gorge from which it issued, and across the bleak divide where it took its rise.

On the opposite slope of the water-shed they came down into a level country where were great stretches of forest and many streams, and through these great stretches they ran steadily, hour after hour, the sun rising higher and the day growing warmer. Buck was wildly glad. He knew he was at last answering the call, running by the side of his wood-brother toward the place from where the call surely came. Old memories were coming upon him fast, and he was stirring to them as of old he stirred to the realities of which they were the shadows. He had done this thing before, somewhere in that other and dimly remembered world, and he was doing it again, now, running free in the open, the unpacked earth underfoot, the wide sky overhead.

They stopped by a running stream to drink, and, stopping, Buck remembered John Thornton. He sat down. The wolf started on toward the place from where the call surely came, then returned to him, sniffing noses and making actions as though to encourage him. But Buck turned about and started slowly on the back track. For the better part of an hour the wild brother ran by his side, whining softly. Then he sat down, pointed his nose upward, and howled. It was a mournful howl, and as Buck held steadily on his way he heard it grow faint and fainter until it was lost in the distance.

John Thornton was eating dinner when Buck dashed into camp and sprang upon him in a frenzy of affection, overturning him, scrambling upon him, licking his face, biting his hand — "playing the general Tom-fool," as John Thornton characterized it, the while he shook Buck back and forth and cursed him lovingly.

For two days and nights Buck never left camp, never let Thornton out of his sight. He followed him about at his work, watched him while he ate, saw him into his blankets at night and out of them in the morning. But after two days the call in the forest began to sound more imperiously than ever. Buck's restlessness came back on him, and he was haunted by recollections of the wild brother and the smiling land beyond the divide and the run side by side through the wide forest-stretches. Once again he took to wandering in the woods, but the wild brother came no more; and though he listened through long vigils the mournful howl was never raised.

He began to sleep out at night, staying away from camp for days at a time; and once he crossed the divide at the head of the creek and went down into the land of timber and streams. There he wandered for a week, seeking vainly for fresh sign of the wild brother, killing his meat as he traveled and traveling with the long, easy lope that seems never to tire. He fished for salmon in a broad stream that emptied somewhere into the sea, and by this stream he killed a large black bear, blinded by the mosquitoes while likewise fishing, and raging through the forest helpless and terrible. Even so, it was a hard fight, and it aroused the last latent remnants of Buck's ferocity. And two days later, when he returned to his kill and found a dozen wolverines quarreling over the spoil, he scattered them like chaff; and those that fled left two behind who would quarrel no more.

The blood-longing became stronger than ever before. He was a killer, a thing that preyed, living on the things that lived, unaided, alone, by virtue of his own strength and prowess, surviving triumphantly in a hostile environment where only the strong survived. Because of all this he became possessed of great pride in himself, which communicated itself like a contagion to his physical being. It advertised itself in all his movements, was apparent in the play of every muscle, spoke plainly as speech in the way he carried himself, and made his glorious furry coat if anything more glorious. But for the stray brown on his muzzle and above his eyes, and for the slash of white hair that ran midmost down his chest, he might well have been mistaken for a gigantic wolf, larger than the largest of the breed. From his St. Bernard father he had inherited size and weight, but it was his shepherd mother who had given shape to that size and weight. His muzzle was the long wolf-muzzle, save that it was larger than the muzzle of any wolf; and his head, somewhat broader, was the wolf-head on a massive scale.

His cunning was wolf cunning and wild cunning; his intelligence, shepherd intelligence and St. Bernard intelligence; and all this, plus an experience gained in the fiercest of schools, made him as formidable a creature as any that roamed the wild. A carnivorous animal, living on a straight meat diet, he was in full flower, at the high tide of his life, over-spilling with vigor and virility. When Thornton passed a caressing hand along his back a snapping and crackling followed the hand, each hair discharging its pent electricity at the contact. Every part, brain and body, nerve, tissue and fibre, was keyed to the most exquisite pitch; and between all the parts there was a perfect equilibrium or adjustment. To sights and sounds and events which required action he responded with lightning- like rapidity. Quickly as a husky dog could leap to defend from attack or to attack, he could leap twice as quickly. He saw movement, or heard sound, and responded in less time than another dog required to compass the mere seeing or hearing. He perceived and determined and responded in the same instant. In point of fact, the three actions of perceiving, determining and responding were sequential; but so infinitesimal were the intervals of time between them that they appeared simultaneous. His muscles were surcharged with vitality, and snapped into play sharply, like steel springs. Life streamed through him in splendid flood, glad and rampant, until it seemed that it would burst him asunder in sheer ecstasy and pour forth generously over the world.

"Never was there such a dog," said John Thornton, one day, as the partners watched Buck marching out of camp.

"When he was made the mould was broke," said Pete.

"Py jingo! I t'ink so mineself," Hans affirmed.

They saw him marching out of the camp, but they did not see the instant and terrible transformation which took place as soon as he was within the secrecy of the forest. He no longer marched. At once he became a thing of the wild, stealing along softly, cat-footed, a passing shadow that appeared and disappeared among the shadows. He knew how to take advantage of every cover, to crawl on his belly like a snake, and like a snake to leap and strike. He could take a ptarmigan from its nest, kill a rabbit as it slept, and snap in midair the little chipmunks fleeing a second too late for the trees. Fish, in open pools, were not too quick; nor were beaver, mending their dams, too wary. He killed to eat, not from wantonness; but he preferred to eat what he killed himself. So a lurking humor ran through his deeds, and it was his delight to steal upon the squirrels, and, when he all but had them, to let them go, chattering in mortal fear, to the treetops.

As the fall of the year came on the moose appeared in greater abundance, moving slowly down to meet the winter in the lower and less rigorous valleys. Buck had already dragged down a stray part-grown calf; but he wished strongly for larger and more formidable quarry, and he came upon it one day on the divide at the head of the creek. A band of twenty moose had crossed over from the land of streams and timber, and chief among them was a great bull. He was in a savage temper, and standing over six feet from the ground was as formidable an antagonist as even Buck could desire. Back and forth the bull tossed his great palmated antlers, branching to fourteen points and embracing seven feet within the tips. His small eyes burned with a vicious and bitter light, while he roared with fury at sight of Buck.

From the bull's side, just forward of the flank, protruded a feathered arrow-end, which accounted for his savageness. Guided by that instinct which came from the old hunting days of the primordial world, Buck proceeded to cut the bull out from the herd. It was no slight task. He would bark and dance about in front of the bull, just out of reach of the great antlers and of the terrible splay hoofs which could have stamped his life out with a single blow. Unable to turn his back on the fanged danger and go on, the bull would be driven into paroxysms of rage. At such moments he charged Buck, who retreated craftily, luring him on by a simulated inability to escaped. But when he was thus separated from his fellows, two or three of the younger bulls would charge back upon Buck and enable the wounded bull to rejoin the herd.

There is a patience of the wild — dogged, tireless, persistent as life itself — that holds motionless for endless hours the spider in its web, the snake in its coils, the panther in its ambuscade; this patience belongs peculiarly to life when it hunts its living food; and it belonged to Buck as he clung to the flank of the herd, retarding its march, irritating the young bulls, worrying the cows with their half-grown calves, and driving the wounded bull mad with helpless rage. For half a day this continued. Buck multiplied himself, attacking from all sides, enveloping the herd in a whirlwind of menace, cutting out his victim as fast as it could rejoin its mates, wearing out the patience of creatures preyed upon, which is a lesser patience than that of creatures preying.

As the day wore along and the sun dropped to its bed in the Northwest (the darkness had come back and the fall nights were six hours long), the young bulls retraced their steps more and more reluctantly to the aid of their beset leader. The down-coming winter was harrying them on to the lower levels, and it seemed they could never shake off this tireless creature that held them back. Besides, it

He followed with wild leapings

was not the life of the herd or of the young bulls that was threatened. The life only of one member was demanded, which was a remoter interest than their lives, and in the end they were content to pay the toll.

As twilight fell, the old bull stood with lowered head watching his mates — the cows he had known, the calves he had fathered, the bulls he had mastered — as they shambled on at a rapid pace through the fading light. He could not follow, for before his nose leaped the merciless fanged terror that would not let him go. Three hundredweight more than half a ton he weighed, he had lived a long, strong life full of fight and struggle, and at the end he faced death at the teeth of a creature whose head did not reach beyond his great knuckled knees.

From then on, night and day, Buck never left his prey, never gave it a moment's rest, never permitted it to browse the leaves of trees or the shoots of young birch and willow. Nor did he give the wounded bull opportunity to slake his burning thirst in the slender, trickling streams they crossed. Often, in desperation, he burst into long stretches of flight. At such times Buck did not attempt to stay him, but loped easily at his heels, satisfied with the way the game was played, lying down when the moose stood still, attacking him fiercely when he strove to eat or drink.

The great head drooped more and more under its tree of horns, and the shambling trot grew weak and weaker. He took to standing for long periods, with nose to the ground and dejected ears dropped limply; and Buck found more time in which to get water for himself and in which to rest. At such moments, panting with red-lolling tongue and with eyes fixed upon the big bull, it appeared to Buck that a change was coming over the face of things. He could feel a new stir in the land. As the moose were coming into the land other kinds of life were coming in. Forest and stream and air seemed palpitant with their presence. The news of it was borne in upon him, not by sight, or sound, or smell, but by some other and subtler sense. He heard nothing, saw nothing, yet knew that the land was somehow different, that through it strange things were afoot and ranging; and he resolved to investigate after he had finished the business in hand.

At last, at the end of the fourth day, he pulled the great moose down. For a day and a night he remained by the kill, eating and sleeping turn and turn about. Then, rested, refreshed and storng, he turned his face toward camp and John Thornton. He broke into the long easy lope, and went on, hour after hour, never at loss for the tangled way, heading straight home through strange country with a certitude of direction that put man and his magnetic needle to shame.

As he held on he became more and more conscious of the new stir in the land. There was life abroad in it different from the life which had been there throughout the summer. No longer was this fact borne in upon him in same subtle, mysterious way. The birds talked of it, the squirrels chattered about it, the very breeze whispered of it. Several times he stopped and drew in the fresh morning air in great sniffs, reading a message which made him leap on with greater speed. He was oppressed by a sense of calamity happening, if it were not calamity already happened; and as he crossed the last water-shed and dropped down into the valley toward camp he proceeded with greater caution.

Three miles away he came upon a fresh trail that sent his neck-hair rippling and bristling. It led straight toward camp and John Thornton. Buck hurried on, swiftly and stealthily, every nerve straining and tense, alert to the multitudinous details which told a story all but the end. His nose gave him a varying description of the passage of the life on the heels of which he was traveling. He remarked the pregnant silence of the forest. The bird-life had flitted. The squirrels were in hiding. One only he saw — a sleek, gray fellow, flattened against a gray, dead limb so that he seemed a part of it, a woody excrescence upon the wood itself.

As Buck slid along with the obscurity of a gliding shadow his nose was jerked suddenly to the side as though a positive force had gripped and pulled it. He followed the new scent into a thicket and found Nig. He was lying on his side, dead where he had dragged himself, an arrow protruding, head and feathers, from either side of his body.

A hundred yards farther on Buck came upon one of the sled-dogs Thornton had bought in Dawson. This dog was thrashing about in a death-struggle, directly on the trail, and Buck passed around him without stopping. From the camp came the faint sound of many voices, rising and falling in a sing-song chant. Bellying forward to the edge of the clearing he found Hans, lying on his face, feathered with arrows like a porcupine. At the same instant Buck peered out where the spruce-bough lodge had been and saw what made his hair leap straight up on his neck and shoulders. A gust of overpowering rage swept over him. He did not know that he growled, but he growled aloud with a terrible ferocity. For the last time in his life he allowed passion to usurp cunning and reason, and it was because of his great love for John Thornton that he lost his head.

The Yeehats were dancing about the wreckage of the spruce-bough lodge when they heard a fearful roaring, and saw rushing upon them an animal the like of which they had never seen before. It was Buck, a live hurricane of fury, hurling himself upon them in a frenzy to destroy. He sprang at the foremost man (it was the chief of the Yeehats), ripping the throat wide open till the rent jugular spouted a fountain of blood. He did not pause to worry the victim, but ripped in passing, with the next bound tearing wide the throat of a second man. There was no withstanding him. He plunged about in their very midst, tearing, rending, destroying, in constant and terrific motion which defied the arrows they discharged at him. In fact, so inconceivably rapid were his movements, and so closely were the Indians tangled together, that they shot one another with the arrows; and one young hunter hurling a spear at Buck in midair drove it through the chest of another hunter with such force that the point broke through the skin of the back and stood out beyond. Then a panic seized the Yeehats, and they fled in terror to the woods, proclaiming as they fled the advent of the Evil Spirit.

And truly Buck was the Fiend incarnate, raging at their heels and dragging them down like deer as they raced through the trees. It was a fateful day for the Yeehats. They scattered far and wide over the country, and it was not till a week later that the last of the survivors gathered together in a lower valley and counted their losses. As for Buck, wearying of the pursuit, he returned to the desolated camp. He found Pete where he had been killed in his blankets in the first moment of surprise. Thornton's desperate struggle was fresh-written on the earth, and Buck scented every detail of it down to the edge of a deep pool. By the edge, head and forefeet in the water, lay Skeet, faithful to the last. The pool itself, muddy and discolored from the sluice-boxes, effectually hid what it contained, and it contained John Thornton; for Buck followed his trace into the water, from which no trace led away.

All day Buck brooded by the pool or roamed restlessly about the camp. Death, as a cessation of movement, as a passing out and away from the lives of the living, he knew, and he knew John Thornton was dead. It left a great void in him, somewhat akin to hunger, but a void which ached and ached and which meat could not fill. At times when he paused to contemplate the carcasses of the Yeehats he forgot the pain of it; and at such times he was aware of a great pride in himself, a pride greater than any he had yet experienced. He had killed man, the noblest game of all, and he had killed in the face of the law of club and fang. He sniffed the bodies curiously. They had died so easily. It was harder to kill a husky-dog than them. They were no match at all — were it not for their arrows and spears and clubs. Thenceforward he would be unafraid of them except when they bore in their hands their arrows, spears and clubs.

Night came on, and a full moon rose high over the trees into the sky, lighting the land till it lay bathed in ghostly day. And with the coming of the night, brooding and mourning by the pool, Buck became alive to a stirring of the new life in the forest other than that which the Yeehats had made. He stood up, listening and scenting. From far away drifted a faint, sharp yelp, followed by a chorus of similar sharp yelps. As the moments passed the yelps grew closer and louder. Again Buck knew them as things heard in that other world which persisted in his memory. He walked to the centre of the open space and listened. It was the call, the many-noted call, sounding more luringly and compellingly than ever before. And as never before he was ready to obey. John Thornton was dead. The last tie was broken. Man and the

DRAWN BY CHARLES LIVINGSTON BULL

The great head drooped more and more under its tree of horns

claims of man no longer bound him.

Hunting their living meat as the Yeehats were hunting it on the flanks of the migrating moose, the wolf-pack had at last crossed over from the land of streams and timber and invaded Buck's valley. Into the clearing where the moonlight streamed they poured in a silvery flood. And in the centre of the clearing stood Buck, motionless as a statue, waiting their coming. They were awed, so still and large he stood, and a moment's pause fell, till the boldest one leaped straight for him. Like a flash Buck struck, breaking the neck. Then he stood, without movement, as before, the stricken wolf rolling in agony behind him. Three others tried it in sharp succession; and one after the other they drew back, streaming blood from slashed throats or shoulders.

This was sufficient to fling the whole pack forward, pell mell, crowded together, blocked and confused by its eagerness to pull down the prey. Buck's marvelous quickness and agility stood him in a good stead. Pivoting on his hindlegs, and snapping and gashing, he was everywhere at once, presenting a front which was apparently unbroken, so swiftly did he whirl and guard from side to side. But to prevent them from getting behind him he was forced back, down past the pool and into the creek-bed, till he brought up against a high gravel bank. He worked along to a right-angle in the bank which the men had made in the course of mining, and in this angle he came to bay, protected on three sides and with nothing to do but face the front.

And so well did he face it that at the end of half an hour the wolves drew back discomfited. The tongues of all were out and lolling, the white fangs showing cruelly white in the moonlight. Some were lying down with heads raised and ears pricked forward; others stood on their feet, watching him; and still others were lapping water from the pool. One wolf, long and lean and gray, advanced cautiously, in a friendly manner, and Buck recognized the wild brother with whom he had run for a night and a day. He was whining softly, and, as Buck whined, they touched noses.

Then an old wolf, gaunt and battle-scarred, came forward. Buck writhed his lips into the preliminary of a snarl, but sniffed noses with him. Whereupon the old wolf sat down, pointed nose at the moon, and broke out the long wolf-howl. The others sat down and howled. And now the call came to Buck in unmistakable accents. He, too, sat down and howled. This over, he came out of his angle and the pack crowded around him, sniffing in half-friendly, half-savage manner. The leaders lifted the yelp of the pack and sprang away into the woods. The wolves swung in behind, yelping in chorus. And Buck ran with them, side by side with the wild brother, yelping as he ran.

And here may well end the story of Buck. The years were not many when the Yeehats noted a change in the breed of timber-wolves; for some were seen with splashes of brown on head and muzzle and with a rift of white centering down the chest. But more remarkable than this, the Yeehats tell of a Ghost-Dog that runs at the head of the pack. They are afraid of this Ghost-Dog, for it has cunning greater than they, stealing from their camps in fierce winters, robbing their traps, slaying their dogs, and defying their bravest hunters.

Nay, the tale grows worse. Hunters there are who fail to return to the camp, and hunters there have been whom their tribesmen found with throats slashed cruelly open and with wolf-prints about them in the snow greater than the prints of any wolf. Each fall when the Yeehats follow the movement of the moose there is a certain valley which they never enter.

In the summers there is one visitor, however, to that valley, of which the Yeehats do not know. It is a great, gloriously-coated wolf, like, and yet unlike, all other wolves. He crosses alone from the smiling timberland and comes down into an open space among the trees. Here a yellow stream flows from rotted moose-hide sacks and sinks into the ground, with long grasses growing through it and vegetable mould overrunning it and hiding its yellow from the sun; and here he muses for a time, howling once, long and mournfully, ere he departs.

But he is not always alone. When the long winter nights come on and the wolves follow their meat into the lower valleys, he may be seen running at the head of the pack through the pale moonlight or glimmering borealis, leaping gigantic above his fellows, his great throat a-bellow as he sings a song of the Younger World which is the song of the pack.

7
Brown Wolf

Everybody's Magazine

AUGUST, 1906.

BROWN WOLF

By JACK LONDON

Author of "The Call of the Wild," "The Sea Wolf," etc.

Illustrations by Philip R. Goodwin

SHE had delayed because of the dew-wet grass, in order to put on her rubbers, and when she emerged from the house found her waiting husband absorbed in the wonder of a bursting almond-bud. She sent a questing glance across the tall grass and in and out among the orchard trees.

"Where's Wolf?" she asked.

"He was here a moment ago." Walt Irvine drew himself away with a jerk from the metaphysics and poetry of the organic miracle of blossom, and surveyed the landscape. "He was running a rabbit the last I saw of him."

"Wolf! Wolf! Here, Wolf!" she called, as they left the clearing and took the trail that led down through the waxen-belled manzanita jungle to the country road.

Irvine thrust between his lips the little finger of each hand and lent to her efforts a shrill whistling.

She covered her ears hastily, and made a wry grimace.

"My! for a poet, delicately attuned and all the rest of it, you can make unlovely noises. My ear-drums are pierced. You outwhistle——"

"Orpheus."

"I was about to say a street arab," she concluded severely.

"Poesy does not prevent one from being practical—at least it doesn't prevent *me*. Mine is no futility of genius that can't sell gems to the magazines."

He assumed a mock extravagance, and went on:

"I am no attic singer, no ballroom warbler. And why? Because I am practical. Mine is no squalor of song that cannot transmute itself, with proper exchange value, into a flower-crowned cottage, a sweet mountain meadow, a grove of redwoods, an orchard of thirty-seven trees, one long row of blackberries, and two short rows of strawberries, to say nothing of a quarter of a mile of gurgling brook. I am a beauty merchant, a trader in song, and I pursue utility, dear Madge. I sing a song, and, thanks to the magazine editors, I transmute my song into a waft of the west wind sighing through our redwoods, into a murmur of waters over mossy stones that sings back to me another song than the one I sang and yet the same song wonderfully —er—transmuted."

"Oh, that all your song transmutations were as successful!" she laughed.

"Name one that wasn't."

"Those two beautiful sonnets that you transmuted into the cow that was accounted the worst milker in the township."

"She was beautiful—" he began.

"But she didn't give milk," Madge interrupted.

"But she *was* beautiful, now, wasn't she?" he insisted.

"And here's where beauty and utility fall out," was her reply. "And there's the Wolf!"

From the thicket-covered hillside came a crashing of underbrush, and then, forty feet above them, on the edge of the sheer wall of rock, appeared a wolf's head and shoulders. His braced fore paws dislodged a pebble, and with sharp-pricked ears and peering gaze he watched the fall of the pebble till it struck at their feet. Then he transferred his gaze and with open mouth laughed down at them.

"You Wolf, you!" and "You blessed Wolf!" the man and woman called out to him.

The ears flattened back and down at the sound, and the head seemed to snuggle under the caress of an invisible hand.

They watched him scramble backward into the thicket, then proceeded on their way. Several minutes later, rounding a turn in the trail, where the descent was less precipitous, he joined them in the midst of a miniature avalanche of pebbles and loose soil. He was not demonstrative. A pat and a rub around the ears from the man, and a more prolonged caressing from the woman, and he was away down the trail in front of them, gliding effortlessly over the ground in true wolf fashion.

WITH OPEN MOUTH LAUGHED DOWN AT THEM.

In build and coat and brush he was a huge timber-wolf; but the lie was given to his wolfhood by his color and marking. There the dog unmistakably advertised itself. No wolf was ever colored like him. He was brown, deep brown, red brown, an orgy of browns. Back and shoulders were a warm brown that paled on the sides and underneath to a yellow that was dingy because of the brown that lingered in it. The white of the throat and paws and the spots over the eyes were dirty because of the persistent and ineradicable brown, while the eyes themselves were twin topazes, golden and brown.

The man and woman loved the dog very much; perhaps this was because it had been such a task to win his love. It had been no easy matter, when he first drifted in mysteriously out of nowhere to their little mountain cottage. Footsore and famished, he had killed a rabbit under their very noses and under their very windows, and then crawled away and slept by the spring at the foot of the blackberry bushes. When Walt Irvine went down to inspect the intruder, he was snarled at for his pains, and Madge likewise was snarled at when she went down to present, as a peace-offering, a large pan of bread and milk.

A most unsociable dog he proved to be, resenting all their advances, refusing to let them lay hands on him, menacing them with bared fangs and bristling hair. Nevertheless, he remained, sleeping and resting by the spring, and eating the food they gave him after they had set it down at a safe distance and retreated. His wretched physical condition explained why he lingered; and when he had recuperated, after several days' sojourn, he disappeared.

And this would have been the end of him so far as Irvine and his wife were concerned, had not Irvine at that particular time been called away into the northern part of the State. Riding along on the train, near to the line between California and Oregon, he chanced to look out of the window and saw his unsociable guest sliding along the wagon road, brown and wolfish, tired yet tireless, dust-covered and soiled with two hundred miles of travel.

Now, Irvine was a man of impulse, a poet. He got off the train at the next station, bought a piece of meat at a butcher shop, and captured the vagrant on the outskirts of the town. The return trip was made in the baggage-car, and so Wolf came a second time to the mountain cottage. Here he was tied up for a week and made love to by the man and woman. But it was very circumspect love-making. Remote and alien as a traveler from another planet, he snarled down their soft-spoken love-words. He never barked. In all the time they had him he was never known to bark.

To win him became a problem. Irvine liked problems. He had a metal plate made on which was stamped: "RETURN TO WALT IRVINE, GLEN ELLEN, SONOMA COUNTY, CALIFORNIA." This was riveted to a collar and strapped about the dog's neck. Then he was turned loose, and promptly he disappeared. A day later came a telegram from Mendocino County. In twenty hours he had made over a hundred miles to the north, and was still going when captured.

He came back by Wells-Fargo Express, was tied up three days, and was loosed on the fourth and lost. This time he gained southern Oregon before he was caught and returned. Always, as soon as he received his liberty, he fled away, and always he fled north. He was possessed of an obsession that drove him north. The homing instinct, Irvine called it, after he had expended the selling price of a sonnet in getting the animal back from northern Oregon.

Another time the brown wanderer succeeded in traversing half the length of California, all of Oregon, and most of Washington before he was picked up and returned collect. A remarkable thing was the speed with which he traveled. Fed up and rested, as soon as he was loosed he devoted all his energy to getting over the ground. On the first day's run he was known to cover as high as a hundred and fifty miles, and after that he would average a hundred miles a day until caught. He always arrived back lean and hungry and savage, and always departed fresh and vigorous, cleaving his way northward in response to some prompting of his being that no one could understand.

But at last, after a futile year of flight, he accepted the inevitable and elected to remain at the cottage where first he had killed the rabbit and slept by the spring. Even after that, a long time elapsed before the man and woman succeeded in patting him. It was a great victory, for they alone were allowed to put hands on him. He was fastidiously exclusive, and no guest at the cottage ever succeeded in making up to him. A low growl greeted a stranger's approach; if he had the hardihood to come nearer, the lips lifted, the naked fangs appeared, and the growl became a snarl—a snarl so terrible and malignant that it awed the stoutest of them, as it likewise awed the farmers' dogs, that knew ordinary dog-snarling but had never heard wolf-snarling before.

A SNARL SO TERRIBLE AND MALIGNANT THAT IT AWED THE STOUTEST OF THEM.

He was without antecedents. His history began with Walt and Madge. He had come up from the south, but never a clue did they get of the owner from whom he had evidently fled. Mrs. Johnson, their nearest neighbor and the one who supplied them with milk, proclaimed him a Klondike dog. Her brother was burrowing for frozen pay-streaks in that far country, and so she constituted herself an authority on the subject.

But they did not dispute her. There were the tips of Wolf's ears, obviously so severely frozen at some time that they would never quite heal again. Besides, he looked like the photographs of the Alaskan dogs they saw published in magazines and newspapers. They often speculated over his past, and tried to conjure up (from what they had read and heard) what his Northland life had been. That the Northland still drew him they knew; for at night they sometimes heard him crying softly; and when the north wind blew and the bite of frost was in the air, a great restlessness would come upon him and he would lift a mournful lament which they knew to be the long wolf-howl. Yet he never barked. No provocation was great enough to draw from him that canine cry.

Long discussion they had, during the time of winning him, as to whose dog he was. Each claimed him, and each proclaimed loudly any expression of affection made by him. But the man had the best of it at first, chiefly because he was a man. It was patent that Wolf had had no experience with women. He did not understand women. Madge's skirts were something he never quite accepted. The rustle of them was enough to set him a-bristle with suspicion, and on a windy day she could not approach him at all.

On the other hand, it was Madge who fed him; also it was she who ruled the kitchen, and it was by her favor, and her favor alone, that he was permitted to come within that sacred precinct. It was because of these things that she bade fair to overcome the handicap of her garments. Then it was that Walt put forth special effort, making it a practise to have Wolf lie at his feet while he wrote, and, between petting and talking, losing much time from his work. Walt won in the end, and his victory was most probably due to the fact that he was a man, though Madge averred that they would have had another quarter of a mile of gurgling brook, and at least two west winds sighing through their redwoods, had Walt properly devoted his energies to song-transmutation and left Wolf alone to exercise a natural taste and an unbiased judgment.

"It's about time I heard from those triolets," Walt said, after a silence of five minutes, during which they had swung steadily down the trail. "There'll be a check at the post-office, I know, and we'll transmute it into beautiful buckwheat flour, a gallon of maple syrup, and a new pair of rubbers for you."

"And into beautiful milk from Mrs. Johnson's beautiful cow," Madge added. "To-morrow's the first of the month, you know."

Walt scowled unconsciously, then his face brightened and he clapped his hand to his breast pocket.

"Never mind. I have here a nice beautiful new cow, the best milker in California."

"When did you write it?" she demanded eagerly. Then, reproachfully, "And you never showed it to me."

"I saved it to read to you on the way to the post-office, in a spot remarkably like this one," he answered, indicating with a wave of his hand a dry log on which to sit.

A tiny stream flowed out of a dense fern-brake, slipped down a mossy-lipped stone, and ran across the path at their feet. From the valley arose the mellow song of meadow-larks, while about them, in and out, through sunshine and shadow, fluttered great yellow butterflies.

Up from below came another sound that broke in upon Walt reading softly from his manuscript. It was a crunching of heavy feet, punctuated now and again by the clattering of a displaced stone. As Walt finished and looked to his wife for approval, a man came into view around the turn of the trail. He was bareheaded and sweaty. With a handkerchief in one hand he mopped his face, while in the other hand he carried a new hat and a wilted starched collar which he had removed from his neck. He was a well-built man, and his muscles seemed on the point of bursting out of the painfully new and ready-made black clothes he wore.

"Warm day," Walt greeted him. Walt believed in country democracy, and never missed an opportunity to practise it.

The man paused and nodded.

"I guess I ain't used much to the warm," he vouchsafed half-apologetically. "I'm more accustomed to zero weather."

"You don't find any of that in this country," Walt laughed.

"Should say not," the man answered. "An' I ain't here a-lookin' for it, neither. I'm tryin' to find my sister. Mebbe you know where she lives. Her name's Johnson, Mrs. William Johnson."

"You're not her Klondike brother," Madge cried, her eyes bright with interest, "about whom we've heard so much?"

"Yes'm, that's me," he answered modestly. "My name's Miller, Skiff Miller. I just thought I'd s'prise her."

"You are on the right track, then. Only you've come by the foot-path." Madge stood up to direct him, pointing up the canyon a quarter of a mile. "You see that blasted redwood? Take the little trail turning off to the right. It's the short cut to her house. You can't miss it."

"Yes'm, thank you, ma'am," he said.

He made tentative efforts to go, but seemed awkwardly rooted to the spot. He was gazing at her with an open admiration of which he was quite unconscious, and which was drowning, along with him, in the rising sea of embarrassment in which he floundered.

"We'd like to hear you tell about the Klondike," Madge said. "Mayn't we come over some day while you are at your sister's? Or, better yet, won't you come over and have dinner with us?"

"Yes'm; thank you, ma'am," he mumbled mechanically. Then he caught himself up and added, "I ain't stoppin' long. I got to be pullin' north again. I go out on to-night's train. You see, I've got a mail contract with the Government."

When Madge had said that it was too bad, he made another futile effort to go. But he could not take his eyes from her face. He forgot his embarrassment in his admiration, and it was her turn to flush and feel uncomfortable.

It was at this juncture, when Walt had just decided it was time for him to be saying something to relieve the strain, that Wolf, who had been away nosing through the brush, trotted wolf-like into view.

Skiff Miller's abstraction disappeared. The

HE WOULD LIFT A MOURNFUL LAMENT WHICH THEY KNEW
TO BE THE LONG WOLF-HOWL.

pretty woman before him passed out of his field of vision. He had eyes only for the dog, and a great wonder came into his face.

"Well, I'll be durned!" he enunciated slowly and solemnly.

He sat down ponderingly on the log, leaving Madge standing. At the sound of his voice, Wolf's ears had flattened down, and his mouth had opened in a laugh. He trotted slowly up to the stranger and first smelled his hands, then licked them with his tongue.

Skiff Miller patted the dog's head, and

WOLF SPRANG AFTER HIM AND STROVE GENTLY TO MAKE HIM PAUSE.

slowly and solemnly repeated, "Well, I'll be durned!"

"Excuse me, ma'am," he said the next moment; "I was just s'prised some, that was all."

"We're surprised too," she answered lightly. "We never saw Wolf make up to a stranger before."

"Is that what you call him—Wolf?" the man asked.

Madge nodded. "But I can't understand his friendliness toward you—unless it's because you're from the Klondike. He's a Klondike dog, you know."

"Yes'm," Miller said absently. He lifted one of Wolf's fore legs and examined the footpads, pressing them and denting them with his thumb. "Kind of soft," he remarked. "He ain't been on trail for a long time."

"I say," Walt broke in, "it is remarkable the way he lets you handle him."

Skiff Miller arose, no longer awkward with admiration of Madge, and in a sharp, businesslike manner asked, "How long have you had him?"

But just then the dog, squirming and rubbing against the newcomer's legs, opened his mouth and barked. It was an explosive bark, brief and joyous, but a bark.

"That's a new one on me," Skiff Miller remarked.

Walt and Madge stared at each other. The miracle had happened. Wolf had barked.

"It's the first time he ever barked," Madge said.

"First time I ever heard him, too," Miller volunteered.

Madge smiled at him. The man was evidently a humorist.

"Of course," she said, "since you have only seen him for five minutes."

Skiff Miller looked at her sharply, seeking in her face the guile her words had led him to suspect.

"I thought you understood," he said slowly. "I thought you tumbled to it from his makin' up to me. He's my dog. His name ain't Wolf. It's Brown."

"Oh, Walt!" was Madge's instinctive cry to her husband.

Walt was on the defensive at once.

"How do you know he's your dog?" he demanded.

"Because he is," was the reply.

"Mere assertion," Walt said sharply.

In his slow and pondering way Skiff Miller looked at him, then asked, with a nod of his head toward Madge:

"How d'you know she's your wife? You just say, 'Because she is,' and I'll say it's mere assertion. The dog's mine. I bred 'm an' raised 'm, an' I guess I ought to know. Look here, I'll prove it to you."

Skiff Miller turned to the dog. "Brown!" His voice rang out sharply, and at the sound the dog's ears flattened down as to a caress. "Gee!" The dog made a swinging turn to the right. "Now mush on!" And the dog ceased his swing abruptly and started straight ahead, halting obediently at command.

"I can do it with whistles," Skiff Miller said proudly. "He was my lead dog."

"But you are not going to take him away with you?" Madge asked tremulously.

The man nodded.

"Back into that awful Klondike world of suffering?"

He nodded and added, "Oh, it ain't so bad as all that. Look at me. Pretty healthy specimen, ain't I?"

"But the dog! The terrible hardship, the heart-breaking toil, the starvation, the frost! Oh, I've read about it and I know."

"I nearly ate him once, over on Little Fish River," Miller volunteered grimly. "Gettin' a moose that day was all that saved 'm."

"I'd have died first!" Madge cried.

"Things is different down here," Miller explained. "You don't have to eat dogs. You think differently just about the time you're all in. You've never been all in, so you don't know anything about it."

"That's the very point," she argued warmly. "Dogs are not eaten in California. Why not leave him here? He is happy. He'll never want for food—you know that. He'll never suffer from cold and hardship. Here all is softness and gentleness. Neither the human nor nature is savage. He will never know a whip-lash again. And as for the weather—why, it never snows here."

"But it's all-fired hot in summer, beggin' your pardon," Skiff Miller laughed.

"But you do not answer," Madge continued passionately. "What have you to offer him in that Northland life?"

"Grub, when I've got it, and that's most of the time," came the answer.

"And the rest of the time?"

"No grub."

"And the work?"

"Yes, plenty of work," Miller blurted out impatiently. "Work without end, an' famine, an' frost, an' all the rest of the miseries—that's what he'll get when he comes with me. But he likes it. He is used to it. He knows that life. He was born to it an' brought up to it. An' you don't know anything about it. You don't know what you're talking about. That's where the dog belongs, and that's where he'll be happiest."

"The dog doesn't go," Walt announced in a determined voice. "So there is no need of further discussion."

"What's that?" Skiff Miller demanded, his brows lowering and an obstinate flush of blood reddening his forehead.

"I said the dog doesn't go, and that settles it. I don't believe he's your dog. You may have seen him sometime. You may even sometime have driven him for his owner. But his obeying the ordinary driving-commands of the Alaskan trail is no demonstration that he is yours. Any dog in Alaska would obey you as he obeyed. Besides, he is undoubtedly a valuable dog, as dogs go in Alaska, and that is sufficient explanation of your desire to get possession of him. Anyway, you've got to prove property."

Skiff Miller, cool and collected, the obstinate flush a trifle deeper on his forehead, his huge muscles bulging under the black cloth of his coat, carefully looked the poet up and down as though measuring the strength of his slenderness.

The Klondiker's face took on a contemptuous expression as he said finally, "I reckon there's nothing in sight to prevent me takin' the dog right here an' now."

Walt's face reddened, and the striking-muscles of his arms and shoulders seemed to stiffen and grow tense. His wife fluttered apprehensively into the breach.

"Maybe Mr. Miller is right," she said. "I am afraid that he is. Wolf does seem to know him, and certainly he answers to the name of 'Brown.' He made friends with him instantly, and you know that's something he never did with anybody before. Besides, look at the way he barked. He was just bursting with joy. Joy over what? Without doubt at finding Mr. Miller."

Walt's striking-muscles relaxed, and his

shoulders seemed to droop with hopelessness.

"I guess you're right, Madge," he said. "Wolf isn't Wolf, but Brown, and he must belong to Mr. Miller."

"Perhaps Mr. Miller will sell him," she suggested. "We can buy him."

Skiff Miller shook his head, no longer belligerent, but kindly, quick to be generous in response to generousness.

"I had five dogs," he said, casting about for the easiest way to temper his refusal. "He was the leader. They was the crack team of Alaska. Nothin' could touch 'em. In 1898 I refused five thousand dollars for the bunch. Dogs was high then, anyway; but that wasn't what made the fancy price. It was the team itself. Brown was the best in the team. That winter I refused twelve hundred for 'm. I didn't sell 'm then, an' I ain't a-sellin' 'm now. Besides, I think a mighty lot of that dog. I've been lookin' for 'm for three years. It made me fair sick when I found he'd been stole—not the value of him, but the—well, I liked 'm like hell, that's all, beggin' your pardon. I couldn't believe my eyes when I seen 'm just now. I thought I was dreamin'. It was too good to be true. Why, I was his wet-nurse. I put 'm to bed snug every night. His mother died, an' I brought 'm up on condensed milk at two dollars a can when I couldn't afford it in my own coffee. He never knew any mother but me. He used to suck my finger regular, the darn little cuss—that finger right there!"

And Skiff Miller, too overwrought for speech, held up a forefinger for them to see.

"That very finger," he managed to articulate, as though somehow it clinched the proof of ownership and the bond of affection.

He was still gazing at his extended finger, when Madge began to speak.

"But the dog," she said. "You haven't considered the dog."

Skiff Miller looked puzzled.

"Have you thought about him?" she asked.

"Don't know what you're drivin' at," was the response.

"Maybe the dog has some choice in the matter," Madge went on. "Maybe he has his likes and desires. You have not considered him. You give him no choice. It has never entered your mind that possibly he might prefer California to Alaska. You consider only what you like. You do with him as you would with a sack of potatoes or a bale of hay."

This was a new way of looking at it, and Miller was visibly impressed as he debated it in his mind. Madge took advantage of his indecision.

"If you really love him, what would be happiness to him would be your happiness also," she urged.

Skiff Miller continued to debate with himself, and Madge stole a glance of exultation to her husband, who looked back warm approval.

"What do you think?" the Klondiker suddenly demanded.

It was her turn to be puzzled. "What do you mean?" she asked.

"D'ye think he'd sooner stay in California?"

She nodded her head with positiveness. "I am sure of it."

Skiff Miller again debated with himself, though this time aloud, at the same time running his gaze in a judicial way over the mooted animal.

"He was a good worker. He's done a heap of work for me. He never loafed on me, an' he was a joe-dandy at hammerin' a raw team into shape. He's got a head on him. He can do everything but talk. He knows what you say to him. Look at 'm now. He knows we're talkin' about him."

The dog was lying at Skiff Miller's feet, head close down on paws, ears erect and listening, and eyes that were quick and eager to follow the sound of speech as it fell from the lips of first one and then the other.

"An' there's a lot of work in 'm yet. He's good for years to come. An' I do like him. I do like him!"

Once or twice after that Skiff Miller opened his mouth and closed it again without speaking. Finally he said:

"I'll tell you what I'll do. Your remarks, ma'am, has some weight in them. The dog's worked hard, and maybe he's earned a soft berth an' has got a right to choose. Anyway, we'll leave it up to him. Whatever he says goes. You people stay right here settin' down. I'll say good-by and walk of casual like. If he wants to stay he can stay If he wants to come with me, let 'm come. I won't call 'm to come and don't you call 'm to come back."

He looked with sudden suspicion at Madge, and added, "Only you must play fair. No persuadin' after my back is turned."

"We'll play fair," Madge began, but Skif Miller broke in on her assurances.

STRUGGLING WITH ALL HIS BODY TO EXPRESS THE THOUGHT THAT WAS IN HIM.

"I know the ways of women," he announced. "Their hearts is soft. When their hearts is touched they're likely to stack the cards, look at the bottom of the deck, and lie like the devil—beggin' your pardon, ma'am. I'm only discoursin' about women in general."

"I don't know how to thank you," Madge quavered.

"I don't see as you've got any call to thank me," he replied. "Brown ain't decided yet. Now, you won't mind if I go away slow? It's no more'n fair, seein' I'll be out of sight inside a hundred yards."

Madge agreed, and added, "And I promise you faithfully that we won't do anything to influence him."

"Well, then, I might as well be gettin' along," Skiff Miller said in the ordinary tones of one departing.

At this change in his voice Wolf lifted his head quickly, and still more quickly got to his feet when the man and woman shook hands. He sprang up on his hind legs, resting his fore paws on her hip, and at the same time licking Skiff Miller's hand. When the latter shook hands with Walt, Wolf repeated his act, resting his weight on Walt and licking both men's hands.

"It ain't no picnic, I can tell you that," were the Klondiker's last words, as he turned and went slowly up the trail.

For the distance of twenty feet Wolf watched him go, himself all eagerness and expectancy, as though waiting for the man to turn and retrace his steps. Then, with a quick, low whine, Wolf sprang after him, overtook him, caught his hand between his teeth with reluctant tenderness, and strove gently to make him pause.

Failing in this, Wolf raced back to where Walt Irvine sat, catching his coat-sleeve in his teeth and trying vainly to drag him after the retreating man.

Wolf's perturbation began to wax. He desired ubiquity. He wanted to be in two places at the same time, with the old master and the new, and steadily the distance between them was increasing. He sprang about excitedly, making short, nervous leaps and twists, now toward one, now toward the other, in painful indecision, not knowing his own mind, desiring both and unable to choose, uttering quick, sharp whines, and beginning to pant.

He sat down abruptly on his haunches, thrusting his nose upward, the mouth opening and closing with jerking movements, each time opening wider. These jerking movements were in unison with the recurrent spasms that attacked the throat, each spasm severer and more intense than the preceding one. And in accord with jerks and spasms the larynx began to vibrate, at first silently, accompanied by the rush of air expelled from the lungs, then sounding a low, deep note, the lowest in the register of the human ear. All this was the nervous and muscular preliminary to howling.

But just as the howl was on the verge of bursting from the full throat, the wide-opened mouth was closed, the paroxysms ceased, and he looked long and steadily at the retreating man. Suddenly Wolf turned his head and over his shoulder just as steadily regarded Walt. The appeal was unanswered. Not a word nor a sign did the dog receive, no suggestion and no clue as to what his conduct should be.

A glance ahead to where the old master was nearing the curve of the trail excited him again. He sprang to his feet with a whine, and then, struck by a new idea, turned his attention to Madge. Hitherto he had ignored her, but now, both masters failing him, she alone was left. He went over to her and snuggled his head in her lap, nudging her arm with his nose—an old trick of his when begging for favors. He backed away from her and began writhing and twisting playfully, curveting and prancing, half rearing and striking his fore paws to the earth, struggling with all his body, from the wheedling eyes and flattening ears to the wagging tail, to express the thought that was in him and that was denied him utterance.

This, too, he soon abandoned. He was depressed by the coldness of these humans who had never been cold before. No response could he draw from them, no help could he get. They did not consider him. They were as dead.

He turned and silently gazed after the old master. Skiff Miller was rounding the curve. In a moment he would be gone from view. Yet he never turned his head, plodding straight onward, slowly and methodically, as though possessed of no interest in what was occurring behind his back.

And in this fashion he went out of view. Wolf waited for him to reappear. He waited a long moment, silently, quietly, without movement, as though turned to stone—withal stone quick with eagerness and desire. He barked once, and waited. Then he turned and trotted back to Walt Irvine. He sniffed his hand and dropped down heavily at his feet, watching the trail where it curved emptily from view.

The tiny stream slipping down the mossy-lipped stone seemed suddenly to increase the volume of its gurgling noise. Save for the meadow-larks, there was no other sound. The great yellow butterflies drifted silently through the sunshine and lost themselves in the drowsy shadows. Madge gazed triumphantly at her husband.

A few minutes later Wolf got upon his feet. Decision and deliberation marked his movements. He did not glance at the man and woman. His eyes were fixed up the trail. He had made up his mind. They knew it. And they knew, so far as they were concerned, that the ordeal had just begun.

He broke into a trot, and Madge's lips pursed, forming an avenue for the caressing sound that it was the will of her to send forth. But the caressing sound was not made. She was impelled to look at her husband, and she saw the sternness with which he watched her. The pursed lips relaxed, and she sighed inaudibly.

Wolf's trot broke into a run. Wider and wider were the leaps he made. Not once did he turn his head, his wolf's brush standing out straight behind him, his speed not once lessened. He cut sharply across the curve of the trail and was gone.

8

The Son of the Wolf

THE SON OF THE WOLF

By JACK LONDON

MAN rarely places a proper valuation upon his womankind, at least not until deprived of them. He has no conception of the subtle atmosphere exhaled by the sex feminine, so long as he bathes in it; but let it be withdrawn, and an ever-growing void begins to manifest itself in his existence, and he becomes hungry, in a vague sort of way, for a something so indefinite that he cannot characterize it. If his comrades have no more experience than himself, they will shake their heads dubiously and dose him with strong physic. But the hunger will continue and become stronger; he will lose interest in the things of his every-day life and wax morbid; and one day, when the emptiness has become unbearable, a revelation will dawn upon him.

In the Yukon country, when this comes to pass, the man usually provisions a poling-boat, if it is summer, and if winter, harnesses his dogs, and heads for the Southland. A few months later, supposing him to be possessed of a faith in the country, he returns with a wife to share with him in that faith, and incidentally in his hardships. This but serves to show the innate selfishness of man. It also brings us to the trouble of "Scruff" Mackenzie, which occurred in the old days, before the country was stampeded and staked by a tidal-wave of *che-cha-quas*. and when the Klondike's only claim to notice was its salmon fisheries.

"Scruff" Mackenzie bore the ear-marks of a frontier birth and a frontier life. His face was stamped with twenty-five years of incessant struggle with Nature in her wildest moods,—the last two, the wildest and hardest of all, having been spent in groping for the gold which lies in the shadow of the Arctic Circle. When the yearning sickness came upon him, he was not surprised, for he was a practical man and had seen other men thus stricken. But he showed no sign of his malady, save that he worked harder. All summer he fought mosquitoes and washed the sure-thing bars of the Stuart River for a double grub-stake. Then he floated a raft of house-logs down the Yukon to Forty Mile, and put together as comfortable a cabin as any the camp could boast of. In fact, it showed such cozy promise that many men elected to be his partner and to come and live with him. But he crushed their aspirations with rough speech, peculiar for its strength and brevity, and bought a double supply of grub from the trading-post.

As has been noted, "Scruff" Mackenzie was a practical man. If he wanted a thing he usually got it, but in doing so, went no farther out of his way than was necessary. Though a son of toil and hardship, he was averse to a journey of six hundred miles on the ice, a second of two thousand miles on the ocean, and still a third thousand miles or so to his last stamping-grounds,—all in the mere quest of a wife. Life was too short. So he rounded up his dogs, lashed a curious freight to his sled, and faced across the divide whose westward slopes were drained by the head-reaches of the Tanana.

He was a sturdy traveler, and his wolf-dogs could work harder and travel farther on less grub than any other team in the Yukon. Three weeks later he strode into a hunting-camp of the Upper Tanana Sticks. They marveled at his temerity; for they had a bad name and had been known to kill white men for as trifling a thing as a sharp ax or a broken rifle. But he went among them single-handed, his bearing being a delicious composite of humility, familiarity, *sang-froid*, and insolence. It required a deft hand and deep knowledge of the barbaric mind effectually to handle such diverse weapons; but he was a past-master in the art, knowing when to conciliate and when to threaten with Jove-like wrath.

He first made obeisance to the Chief Thling-Tinneh, presenting him with a couple of pounds of black tea and tobacco, and thereby winning his most cordial regard. Then he mingled with the men and maidens, and that night gave a *pot-lach*. The snow was beaten down in the form of an oblong, perhaps a hundred feet in length and quarter as many across. Down the center a long fire was built, while either side was carpeted with spruce boughs. The lodges were forsaken, and the fivescore or so members of the tribe gave tongue to their folk-chants in honor of their guest.

"Scruff" Mackenzie's two years had taught him the not many hundred words of their vocabulary, and he had likewise conquered their deep gutturals, their Japanese idioms, constructions, and honorific and agglutinative particles. So he made oration after their manner, satisfying their instinctive poetry-love with crude flights of eloquence and metaphorical contortions. After Thling-Tinneh and the Shaman had responded in kind, he made trifling presents to the menfolk, joined in their singing, and proved an expert in their fifty-two-stick gambling game.

And they smoked his tobacco and were pleased. But among the younger men there was a defiant attitude, a spirit of braggadocio, easily understood by the raw insinuations of the toothless squaws and the giggling of the maidens. They had known few white men, "Sons of the Wolf," but from those few they had learned strange lessons.

Nor had "Scruff" Mackenzie, for all his seeming carelessness, failed to note these phenomena. In truth, rolled in his sleeping-furs, he thought it all over, thought seriously, and emptied many pipes in mapping out a campaign. One maiden only had caught his fancy,—none other than Zarinska, daughter to the chief. In features, form, and poise, answering more nearly to the white man's type of beauty, she was almost an anomaly among her tribal sisters. He would possess her, make her his wife, and name her—ah, he would name her Gertrude! Having thus decided, he rolled over on his side and dropped off to sleep, a true son of his all-conquering race, a Samson among the Philistines.

It was slow work and a stiff game; but "Scruff" Mackenzie maneuvered cunningly, with an unconcern which served to puzzle the Sticks. He took great care to impress the men that he was a sure shot and a mighty hunter, and the camp rang with his plaudits when he brought down a moose at six hundred yards. Of a night he visited in Chief Thling-Tinneh's lodge of moose and cariboo skins, talking big and dispensing tobacco with a lavish hand. Nor did he fail to likewise honor the Shaman; for he realized the medicine-man's influence with his people, and was anxious to make of him an ally. But that worthy was high and mighty, refused to be propitiated, and was unerringly marked down as a prospective enemy.

Though no opening presented for an interview with Zarinska, Mackenzie stole many a glance to her, giving fair warning of his intent. And well she knew, yet coquettishly surrounded herself with a ring of women whenever the men were away and he had a chance. But he was in no hurry; besides, he knew she could not help but think of him, and a few days of such thought would only better his suit.

At last, one night, when he deemed the time to be ripe, he abruptly left the chief's smoky dwelling and hastened to a neighboring lodge. As usual, she sat with squaws and maidens about her, all engaged in sewing moccasins and beadwork. They laughed at his entrance, and badinage, which linked Zarinska to him, ran high. But one after the other they were unceremoniously bundled into the outer snow, whence they hurried to spread the tale through all the camp.

His cause was well pleaded, in her tongue, for she did not know his, and at the end of two hours he rose to go.

"So Zarinska will come to the White Man's lodge? Good! I go now to have talk with thy father, for he may not be so minded. And I will give him many tokens; but he must not ask too much. If he say no? Good! Zarinska shall yet come to the White Man's lodge."

He had already lifted the skin flap to depart, when a low exclamation brought him back to the girl's side. She brought herself to her knees on the bearskin mat, her face aglow with true Eve-light, and shyly unbuckled his heavy belt. He looked down, perplexed, suspicious, his ears alert for the slightest sound without. But her next move disarmed his doubt, and he smiled with pleasure. She took from her sewing-bag a moosehide sheath, brave with bright beadwork, fantastically designed. She drew his great hunting-knife,

"The Bear has spoken"

gazed reverently along the keen edge, half tempted to try it with her thumb, and shot it into place in its new home. Then she slipped the sheath along the belt to its customary resting-place, just above the hip.

For all the world, it was like a scene of olden time,— a lady and her knight. Mackenzie drew her up full height and swept her red lips with his moustache,—the, to her, foreign caress of the Wolf. It was a meeting of the stone age and the steel; but she was none the less a woman, as her crimson cheeks and the luminous softness of her eyes attested.

There was a thrill of excitement in the air as "Scruff" Mackenzie, a bulky bundle under his arm, threw open the flap of Thling-Tinneh's tent. Children were running about in the open, dragging dry wood to the scene of the *potlach*, a babble of women's voices was growing in intensity, the young men were consulting in sullen groups, while from the Shaman's lodge rose the eerie sounds of an incantation.

The chief was alone with his blear-eyed wife, but a glance sufficed to tell Mackenzie that the news was already old. So he plunged at once into the business, shifting the beaded sheath prominently to the fore as advertisement of the betrothal.

"O Thling-Tinneh, mighty chief of the Sticks and the land of the Tanana, ruler of the salmon and the bear, the moose and the cariboo! The White Man is before thee with a great purpose. Many moons has his lodge been empty, and he is lonely. And his heart has eaten itself in silence, and grown hungry for a woman to sit beside him in his lodge, to meet him from the hunt with warm fire and good food. He has heard strange things, the patter of baby moccasins and the sound of children's voices. And one night a vision came upon him, and he beheld the Raven, who is thy father, the great Raven, who is the father of all the Sticks. And the Raven spake to the lonely White Man, saying: 'Bind thou thy moccasins upon thee, and gird thy snow-shoes on, and lash thy sled with food for many sleeps and fine tokens for the Chief Thling-Tinneh. For thou shalt turn thy face to where the midspring sun is wont to sink below the land and journey to this great chief's hunting-grounds. There thou shalt make big presents, and Thling-Tinneh, who is my son, shall become to thee as a father. In his lodge there is a maiden into whom I breathed the breath of life for thee. This maiden shalt thou take to wife.'

"O Chief, thus spake the great Raven; thus do I lay many presents at thy feet; thus am I come to take thy daughter!"

The old man drew his furs about him with crude consciousness of royalty, but delayed reply while a youngster crept in, delivered a quick message to appear before the council, and was gone.

"O White Man, whom we have named Moose-Killer, also known as the Wolf, and the Son of the Wolf! We know thou comest of a mighty race; we are proud to have thee our *potlach*-guest; but the king-salmon does not mate with the dog-salmon, nor the Raven with the Wolf."

"Not so!" cried Mackenzie. "The daughters of the Raven have I met in the camps of the Wolf,—the squaw of Mortimer, the squaw of Tregidgo, the squaw of Barnaby, who came two ice-runs back, and I have heard of other squaws, though my eyes beheld them not."

"Son, your words are true; but it were evil mating, like the water with the sand, like the snow-flake with the sun. But met you one Mason and his squaw? No? He came ten ice-runs ago,—the first of all the Wolves. And with him there was a mighty man, straight as a willow-shoot, and tall; strong as the bald-faced grizzly, with a heart like the full summer moon; his ——"

"Oh!" interrupted Mackenzie, recognizing the well-known Northland figure,—"Malemute Kid!"

"The same,—a mighty man. But saw you aught of the squaw? She was full sister to Zarinska."

"Nay, Chief; but I have heard. Mason —far, far to the north, a spruce-tree, heavy with years, crushed out his life beneath. But his love was great, and he had much gold. With this, and her boy, she journeyed countless sleeps toward the winter's noonday sun, and there she yet lives,—no biting frost, no snow, no summer's midnight sun, no winter's noonday night."

A second messenger interrupted with imperative summons from the council. As

Mackenzie threw him into the snow, he caught a glimpse of the swaying forms before the council-fire, heard the deep basses of the men in rhythmic chant, and knew the Shaman was fanning the anger of his people. Time pressed. He turned upon the chief.

"Come! I wish thy child. And now, see! Here are tobacco, tea, many cups of sugar, warm blankets, handkerchiefs, both good and large; and here, a true rifle, with many bullets and much powder."

"Nay," replied the old man, struggling against the great wealth spread before him. "Even now are my people come together. They will not have this marriage."

"But thou art chief."

"Yet do my young men rage because the Wolves have taken their maidens so that they may not marry."

"Listen, O Thling-Tinneh! Ere the night has passed into the day, the Wolf shall face his dogs to the Mountains of the East and fare forth to the Country of the Yukon. And Zarinska shall break trail for his dogs."

"And ere the night has gained its middle, my young men may fling to the dogs the flesh of the Wolf, and his bones be scattered in the snow till the springtime lay them bare."

It was threat and counter-threat. Mackenzie's bronzed face flushed darkly. He raised his voice. The old squaw, who till now had sat an impassive spectator, made to creep by him for the door. The song of the men broke suddenly and there was a hubbub of many voices as he whirled the old woman roughly to her couch of skins.

"Again I cry — listen, O Thling-Tinneh! The Wolf dies with teeth fast-locked, and with him there shall sleep ten of thy strongest men, — men who are needed, for the hunting is but begun, and the fishing is not many moons away. And again, of what profit should I die? I know the custom of thy people; thy share of my wealth shall be very small. Grant me thy child, and it shall all be thine. And yet again, my brothers will come, and they are many, and their maws are never filled; and the daughters of the Raven shall bear children in the lodges of the Wolf. My people are greater than thy people. It is destiny. Grant, and all this wealth is thine."

Moccasins were crunching the snow without. Mackenzie threw his rifle to cock, and loosened the twin Colts in his belt.

"Grant, O Chief!'

"And yet will my people say no."

"Grant, and the wealth is thine. Then shall I deal with thy people after."

"The Wolf will have it so. I will take his tokens,— but I would warn him."

Mackenzie passed over the goods, taking care to clog the rifle's ejector, and capping the bargain with a kaleidoscopic silk kerchief. The Shaman and half a dozen young braves entered, but he shouldered boldly among them and passed out.

"Pack!" was his laconic greeting to Zarinska as he passed her lodge and hurried to harness his dogs. A few minutes later he swept into the council at the head of the team, the woman by his side. He took his place at the upper end of the oblong, by the side of the chief. To his left, a step to the rear, he stationed Zarinska,— her proper place. Besides, the time was ripe for mischief, and there was need to guard his back.

On either side, the men crouched to the fire, their voices lifted in a folk-chant out of the forgotten past. Full of strange, halting cadences and haunting recurrences, it was not beautiful. "Fearful" may inadequately express it. At the lower end, under the eye of the Shaman, danced half a score of women. Stern were his reproofs to those who did not wholly abandon themselves to the ecstasy of the rite. Half hidden in their heavy masses of raven hair, all dishevelled and falling to their waists, they slowly swayed to and fro, their forms rippling to an ever-changing rhythm.

It was a weird scene; an anachronism. To the south, the nineteenth century was reeling off the few years of its last decade; here flourished man primeval, a shade removed from the prehistoric cave-dweller, a forgotten fragment of the Elder World. The tawny wolf-dogs sat between their skin-clad masters or fought for room, the firelight cast backward from their red eyes and dripping fangs. The woods, in ghostly shroud, slept on unheeding. The White Silence, for the moment driven to the rimming forest, seemed ever crushing inward; the stars danced with great leaps, as is their wont in the time of the Great Cold; while the Spirits of the Pole trailed their robes of glory athwart the heavens.

"Scruff" Mackenzie dimly realized the wild grandeur of the setting as his eyes ranged down the fur-fringed sides in quest of missing faces. They rested for a moment on a new-born babe, suckling at its mother's naked breast. It was forty below,—seventy and odd degrees of frost. He thought of the tender women of his own race and smiled grimly. Yet from the loins of some such tender woman had he sprung with a kingly inheritance,—an inheritance which gave to him and his dominance over the land and sea, over the animals and the peoples of all the zones. Single-handed against fivescore, girt by the Arctic winter, far from his own, he felt the prompting of his heritage, the desire to possess, the wild danger-love, the thrill of battle, the power to conquer or to die.

The singing and the dancing ceased, and the Shaman flared up in rude eloquence. Through the sinuosities of their vast mythology, he worked cunningly upon the credulity of his people. The case was strong. Opposing the creative principles as embodied in the Crow and the Raven, he stigmatized Mackenzie as the Wolf, the fighting and the destructive principle. Not only was the combat of these forces spiritual, but men fought, each to his totem. They were the children of Jelchs, the Raven, the Promethean fire-bringer; Mackenzie was the child of the Wolf, or in other words, the Devil. For them to bring a truce to this perpetual warfare, to marry their daughters to the arch-enemy, were treason and blasphemy of the highest order. No phrase was harsh nor figure vile enough in branding Mackenzie as a sneaking interloper and emissary of Satan. There was a subdued, savage roar in the deep chests of his listeners as he took the swing of his peroration.

"Aye, my brothers, Jelchs is all-powerful! Did he not bring heaven-born fire that we might be warm? Did he not draw the sun, moon, and stars, from their holes that we might see? Did he not teach us that we might fight the Spirits of Famine and of Frost? But now Jelchs is angry with his children, and they are grown to a handful, and he will not help. For they have forgotten him, and done evil things, and trod bad trails, and taken his enemies into their lodges to sit by their fires. And the Raven is sorrowful at the wickedness of his children; but when they shall rise up and show they have come back, he will come out of the darkness to aid them. O brothers! the Fire-Bringer has whispered messages to thy Shaman; the same shall ye hear. Let the young men take the young women to their lodges; let them fly at the throat of the Wolf; let them be undying in their enmity! Then shall their women become fruitful and they shall multiply into a mighty people! And the Raven shall lead great tribes of their fathers and their fathers' fathers from out of the North; and they shall beat back the Wolves till they are as last year's campfires; and they shall again come to rule over all the land! 'T is the message of Jelchs, the Raven."

This foreshadowing of the Messiah's coming brought a hoarse howl from the Sticks as they leaped to their feet. Mackenzie slipped the thumbs of his mittens and waited. There was a clamor for the "Fox," not to be stilled till one of the young men stepped forward to speak.

"Brothers! The Shaman has spoken wisely. The Wolves have taken our women, and our men are childless. We are grown to a handful. The Wolves have taken our warm furs and given for them evil spirits which dwell in bottles, and clothes which come not from the beaver or the lynx, but are made from the grass. And they are not warm, and our men die of strange sicknesses. I, the Fox, have taken no woman to wife; and why? Twice have the maidens which pleased me gone to the camps of the Wolf. Even now have I laid by skins of the beaver, of the moose, of the cariboo, that I might win favor in the eyes of Thling-Tinneh, that I might marry Zarinska, his daughter. Even now are her snow-shoes bound to her feet, ready to break trail for the dogs of the Wolf. Nor do I speak for myself alone. As I have done, so has the Bear. He, too, had fain been the father of her children, and many skins has he cured thereto. I speak for all the young men who know not wives. The Wolves are ever hungry. Always do they take the choice meat at the killing. To the Ravens are left the leavings.

"There is Gugkla," he cried, brutally pointing out one of the women, who was a cripple. "Her legs are bent like the ribs of a birch canoe. She cannot gather wood nor carry the meat of the hunters. Did the Wolves choose her?"

"Ai! ai!" vociferated his tribesmen.

"There is Moyri, whose eyes are crossed by the Evil Spirit. Even the babes are affrighted when they gaze upon her, and it is said the bald-face gives her the trail. Was she chosen?"

Again the cruel applause rang out.

"And there sits Pischet. She does not hearken to my words. Never has she heard the cry of the chit-chat, the voice of her husband, the babble of her child. She lives in the White Silence. Cared the Wolves aught for her? No! Theirs is the choice of the kill; ours is the leavings.

"Brothers, it shall not be! No more shall the Wolves slink among our camp-fires. The time is come."

A great streamer of fire, the aurora borealis, purple, green, and yellow, shot across the zenith, bridging horizon to horizon. With head thrown back and arms extended, he swayed to his climax.

"Behold! The spirits of our fathers have arisen and great deeds are afoot this night!"

He stepped back, and another young man somewhat diffidently came forward, pushed on by his comrades. He towered a full head above them, his broad chest defiantly bared to the frost. He swung tentatively from one foot to the other. Words halted upon his tongue, and he was ill at ease. His face was horrible to look upon, for it had at one time been half torn away by some terrific blow. At last he struck his breast with his clenched fist, drawing sound as from a drum, and his voice rumbled forth as does the surf from an ocean cavern.

"I am the Bear,—the Silver-Tip and the Son of the Silver-Tip! When my voice was yet as a girl's, I slew the lynx, the moose, and the cariboo; when it whistled like the wolverines from under a cache, I crossed the Mountains of the South and slew three of the White Rivers; when it became as the roar of the Chinook, I met the bald-faced grizzly, but gave no trail."

At this he paused, his hand significantly sweeping across his hideous scars.

"I am not as the Fox. My tongue is frozen like the river. I cannot make great talk. My words are few. The Fox says great deeds are afoot this night. Good! Talk flows from his tongue like the freshets of the spring, but he is chary of deeds. This night shall I do battle with the Wolf. I shall slay him, and Zarinska shall sit by my fire. The Bear has spoken."

Though pandemonium raged about him, "Scruff" Mackenzie held his ground. Aware how useless was the rifle at close quarters, he slipped both holsters to the fore, ready for action, and drew his mittens till his hands were barely shielded by the elbow gauntlets. He knew there was no hope in attack *en masse*, but true to his boast, was prepared to die with teeth fast-locked. But the Bear restrained his comrades, beating back the more impetuous with his terrible fist. As the tumult began to die away, Mackenzie shot a glance in the direction of Zarinska. It was a superb picture. She was leaning forward on her snow-shoes, lips apart and nostrils quivering, like a tigress about to spring. Her great black eyes were fixed upon her tribesmen, in fear and in defiance. So extreme the tension, she had forgotten to breathe. With one hand pressed spasmodically against her breast and the other as tightly gripped about the dog-whip, she was as turned to stone. Even as he looked, relief came to her. Her muscles loosened; with a heavy sigh she settled back, giving him a look of more than love—of worship.

Thling-Tinneh was trying to speak, but his people drowned his voice. Then Mackenzie strode forward. The Fox opened his mouth to a piercing yell, but so savagely did Mackenzie whirl upon him that he shrank back, his larynx all a-gurgle with suppressed sound. His discomfiture was greeted with roars of laughter, and served to soothe his fellows to a listening mood.

"Brothers! The White Man, whom ye have chosen to call the Wolf, came among you with fair words. He was not like the Innuit; he spoke not lies. He came as a friend, as one who would be a brother. But your men have had their say, and the time for soft words is past. First, I will tell you that the Shaman has an evil tongue and is a false prophet, that the messages he spake are not those of the Fire-Bringer. His ears are locked to the voice of the Raven, and out of his own head he weaves cunning fancies, and he has made fools of you. He has no power. When the dogs were killed and eaten, and your stomachs were heavy with untanned hide and strips of moccasins; when the old men died, and the old women died, and the babes at the dry dugs of the mothers died; when the land was dark, and ye perished as do the salmon in the fall; aye, when the famine was upon you, did the Shaman bring reward to your hunters? did the Shaman put meat in your bellies? Again I say, the Shaman is without power. Thus I spit upon his face!"

Though taken aback by the sacrilege, there was no uproar. Some of the women were even frightened, but among the men there was an uplifting, as though in preparation or anticipation of the miracle. All eyes were turned upon the two central figures. The priest realized the crucial moment, felt his power tottering, opened his mouth in denunciation, but fled backward before the truculent advance, upraised fist, and flashing eyes, of Mackenzie. He sneered and resumed.

"Was I stricken dead? Did the lightning burn me? Did the stars fall from the sky and crush me? Pish! I have done with the dog. Now will I tell you of my people, who are the mightiest of all the peoples, who rule in all the lands. At first we hunt as I hunt, alone. After that we hunt in packs; and at last, like the cariboo-run, we sweep across all the land. Those whom we take into our lodges live; those who will not come die. Zarinska is a comely maiden, full and strong, fit to become the mother of Wolves. Though I die, such shall she become; for my brothers are many, and they will follow the scent of my dogs. Listen to the Law of the Wolf: *Whoso taketh the life of one Wolf, the forfeit shall ten of his people pay.* In many lands has the price been paid; in many lands shall it yet be paid.

"Now will I deal with the Fox and the Bear. It seems they have cast eyes upon the maiden. So? Behold, I have bought her! Thling-Tinneh leans upon the rifle; the goods of purchase are by his fire. Yet will I be fair to the young men. To the Fox, whose tongue is dry with many words, will I give of tobacco five long plugs. Thus will his mouth be wetted that he may make much noise in the council. But to the Bear, of whom I am well proud, will I give of blankets two; of flour, twenty cups; of tobacco, double that of the Fox; and if he fare with me over the Mountains of the East, then will I give him a rifle, mate to Thling-Tinneh's. If not? Good! The Wolf is weary of speech. Yet once again will he say the Law: *Whoso taketh the life of one Wolf, the forfeit shall ten of his people pay.*"

Mackenzie smiled as he stepped back to his old position, but at heart he was full of trouble. The night was yet dark. The girl came to his side, and he listened closely as she told of the Bear's battle-tricks with the knife.

The decision was for war. In a trice, scores of moccasins were widening the space of beaten snow by the fire. There was much chatter about the seeming defeat of the Shaman; some averred he had but withheld his power, while others conned past events and agreed with the Wolf. The Bear came to the center of the battle-ground, a long naked hunting-knife of Russian make in his hand. The Fox called attention to Mackenzie's revolvers; so he stripped his belt, buckling it about Zarinska, into whose hands he also intrusted his rifle. She shook her head that she could not shoot,—small chance had a woman to handle such precious things.

"Then, if danger come by my back, cry aloud, 'My husband!' No; thus, 'My husband!'"

He laughed as she repeated it, pinched her cheek, and re-entered the circle. Not only in reach and stature had the Bear the advantage of him, but his blade was longer by a good two inches. "Scruff" Mackenzie had looked into the eyes of men before, and he knew it was a man who stood against him; yet he quickened to the glint of light on the steel, to the dominant pulse of his race.

Time and again he was forced to the edge of the fire or the deep snow, and time and again, with the foot tactics of the pugilist, he worked back to the center. Not a voice was lifted in encouragement, while his antagonist was heartened with applause, suggestions, and warnings. But his teeth only shut the tighter as the knives clashed together, and he thrust or eluded with a coolness born of conscious strength. At first he felt compassion for his enemy; but this fled before the primal instinct of life, which in turn gave way to the lust of slaughter. The ten thousand years of culture fell from him, and he was a cave-dweller, doing battle for his female.

Twice he pricked the Bear, getting away unscathed; but the third time caught, and to save himself, free hands closed on fighting hands, and they came together. Then did he realize the tremendous strength of his opponent. His muscles were knotted in painful lumps, and cords and tendons threatened to snap with the strain; yet nearer and nearer came the Russian steel. He tried to break away, but only weakened himself. The fur-clad circle closed in, certain of and anxious to see the final stroke. But with wrestler's trick, swinging partly to the side, he struck at his adversary with his head. Involuntarily the Bear leaned back, disturbing his center of gravity. Simultaneous with this, Mackenzie tripped properly and threw his whole weight forward, hurling him clear through the circle into the deep snow. The Bear floundered out and came back full tilt.

"O my husband!" Zarinska's voice rang out, vibrant with danger.

To the twang of a bow-string, Mackenzie swept low to the ground, and a bone-barbed arrow passed over him into the breast of the Bear, whose momentum carried him over his crouching foe. The next instant Mackenzie was up and about. The Bear lay motionless, but across the fire was the Shaman, drawing a second arrow.

Mackenzie's knife leaped short in the air. He caught the heavy blade by the point. There was a flash of light as it spanned the fire. Then the Shaman, the hilt alone appearing without his throat, swayed a moment and pitched forward into the glowing embers.

Click! click!—the Fox had possessed himself of Thling-Tinneh's rifle and was vainly trying to throw a shell into place. But he dropped it at the sound of Mackenzie's laughter.

"So the Fox has not learned the way of the plaything? He is yet a woman. Come! Bring it, that I may show thee!"

The Fox hesitated.

"Come, I say!"

He slouched forward like a beaten cur.

"Thus, and thus; so the thing is done." A shell flew into place and the trigger was at cock as Mackenzie brought it to shoulder.

"The Fox has said great deeds were afoot this night, and he spoke true. There have been great deeds, yet least among them were those of the Fox. Is he still intent to take Zarinska to his lodge? Is he minded to tread the trail already broken by the Shaman and the Bear? No? Good!"

Mackenzie turned contemptuously and drew his knife from the priest's throat.

"Are any of the young men so minded? If so, the Wolf will take them by two and three till none are left. No? Good! Thling-Tinneh, I now give thee this rifle a second time. If, in the days to come, thou shouldst journey to the Country of the Yukon, know thou that there shall always be a place and much food by the fire of the Wolf. The night is now passing into the day. I go, but I may come again. And for the last time, remember the Law of the Wolf!"

He was supernatural in their sight as he rejoined Zarinska. She took her place at the head of the team, and the dogs swung into motion. A few moments later they were swallowed up by the ghostly forest. Till now Mackenzie had waited; he slipped into his snow-shoes to follow.

"Has the Wolf forgotten the five long plugs?"

Mackenzie turned upon the Fox angrily; then the humor of it struck him.

"I will give thee one short plug."

"As the Wolf sees fit," meekly responded the Fox, stretching out his hand.

9
In the Forests of the North

PEARSON'S MAGAZINE

IN THE FORESTS OF THE NORTH.

By Jack London.

A weary journey beyond the last scrub timber and straggling copses, into the heart of the Barrens, where the niggard North is supposed to deny the Earth, are to be found great sweeps of forest and stretches of smiling land. But this the world is just beginning to know. The world's explorers have known it, from time to time, but hitherto they have never returned to tell the world.

The Barrens—well, they are the Barrens, the bad lands of the Arctic, the deserts of the Circle, the bleak and bitter home of the musk-ox and the lean plains-wolf. So Avery Van Brunt found them, treeless and cheerless, sparsely clothed with moss and lichens, and altogether uninviting. At least so he found them till he penetrated to the white blank spaces on the map, and came upon undreamed-of rich spruce forests and unrecorded Esquimo tribes. It had been his intention (and his bid for fame) to break up these white blank spaces, and diversify them with the black markings of mountain chains, sinks and basins, and sinuous river-courses; and it was with added delight that he came to speculate upon the possibilities of timber-belts and native villages.

Avery Van Brunt, or, in full distinction, Professor A. Van Brunt of the Geological Survey, was second in command of the expedition, and first in command of the sub-expedition which he had led on a side tour of some half a thousand miles up one of the branches of the Thelon, and which he was now leading into one of its unrecorded villages. At his back plodded eight men, two of them French-Canadian *voyageurs*, and the remainder strapping Crees from Manitoba-way. He, alone, was full-blooded Saxon, and his blood was pounding fiercely through his veins to the traditions of his race.

The village emptied itself, and a motley crowd trooped out to meet him, men in the forefront, with bows and spears clutched menacingly, and women and children faltering timidly in the rear. Van Brunt lifted his right arm and made the universal peace sign, a sign which all peoples know, and the villagers answered in peace. But to his chagrin, a skin-clad man ran forward and thrust out his hand with a familiar "Hello." He was a bearded man, with cheeks and brow bronzed to copper brown, and in him Van Brunt knew his kind.

"Who are you?" he asked, gripping the extended hand. "Andrée?"

"Who's Andrée?" the man asked back.

Van Brunt looked at him more sharply. "By George, you've been here some time."

"Five years," the man answered, a dim flicker of pride in his eyes. "But come on, let's talk."

"Let them camp alongside of me," he answered Van Brunt's glance at his party. "Old Tantlatch will take care of them. Come on."

He swung off in a long stride, Van Brunt following at his heels through the village. In irregular fashion, wherever the ground favored, the lodges of moosehide were pitched. Van Brunt ran his practised eye over them and calculated.

"Two hundred, not counting the young ones," he summed up.

The man nodded. "Pretty close to it. But here's where I live, out of the thick of it, you know, more privacy and all that. Sit down. I'll eat with you when your men get something cooked up. I've forgotten what tea tastes like. . . . Five years and never a taste or smell. . . . Any tobacco? . . . A-h, thanks, and a pipe? Good. Now for a fire-stick, and we'll see if the weed has lost its cunning."

He drew in the first mouthful of smoke and blew it out through his pursed lips slowly and caressingly. He sighed happily, with immeasurable content.

Van Brunt nodded sympathetically. "Five years, you say?"

"Five years." The man sighed again. "And you, I presume, wish to know about it, being naturally curious, and this a sufficiently strange situation, and all that. But it's not much. I came in from Edmonton after musk-ox, and like Pike and the rest of them, had my mischances, only I lost my party and outfit. Starvation, hardship, the regular tale, you know, sole survivor, and all that, till I crawled into Tantlatch's here on hand and knee. Five years on February last. I crossed the Great Slave early in May ——."

"And you are . . . Fairfax?" Van Brunt interjected.

The man nodded.

"Let me see . . . John, I think it is, John Fairfax."

"How did you know?" Fairfax queried lazily, half-absorbed in curling smoke-spirals upward in the quiet air.

"The papers were full of it at the time. Prevanche——"

"Prevanche!" Fairfax sat up, suddenly alert. "He was lost in the Smoke Mountains."

"Yes, but he pulled through and came out."

Fairfax settled back again and resumed his smoke-spirals. "I am glad to hear it. Prevanche was a bully fellow if he *did* have ideas about head-straps, the beggar. And he pulled through? Well, I'm glad."

Five years. . . . The phrase drifted recurrently through Van Brunt's thought, and somehow the face of Emily Southwaithe seemed to rise up and take form before him. Five years. . . . Van Brunt pulled out his watch. It was an hour past midnight. The northward clouds flushed bloodily, and rays of sombre-red shot southward, firing the gloomy woods with a lurid radiance. The air was in breathless calm, not a needle quivered. Far off somewhere a child was crying, and from the depths of the forest, like a silver thread, rose a woman's voice in mournful chant: "O-o-o-o-o-o-a-haa-ha-a-ha-aa-a-a, O-o-o-o-o-o-a-ha-a-ha-a."

Van Brunt shivered and rubbed the backs of his hands briskly.

"And they gave me up for dead?" his companion asked slowly.

"Well, you never came back, so your friends——"

"Promptly forgot." Fairfax laughed harshly, defiantly.

"Why didn't you come out?"

"Partly disinclination, I suppose, and partly because of circumstances over which I had no control. You see, Tantlatch here was down with a broken leg when I made his acquaintance, a nasty fracture, and I set it for him and got him into shape. I stayed some time, getting my strength back. I was the first white man he had seen, and of course I seemed very wise and showed his people no end of things. Coached them up in military tactics, among other things, so that they conquered the four other tribal villages, which you have not yet seen, and came to rule the land. And they naturally grew to think a good deal of me, so much so that when I was ready to go they wouldn't hear of it. Were most hospitable, in fact. Put a couple of guards over me, and watched me day and night. And then Tantlatch offered me inducements, so to say, and as it didn't matter much one way or the other, I reconciled myself to remaining."

"I knew your brother at Freiburg. I am Van Brunt."

Fairfax reached forward impulsively and shook his hand. "You were Billy's friend, eh? Poor Billy! He spoke of you often."

"Rum meeting place, though," he added, casting a glance over the landscape, and listening for a moment to the woman's mournful notes. "Her man was clawed by a bear, and she's taking it hard."

"Beastly life!" Van Brunt grimaced his disgust. "I suppose, after five years of it civilization will be sweet?

Fairfax's face took on a stolid expression. "Oh, I don't know. At least they're honest folk, and live according to their lights. And then they are amazingly simple. No complexity about them, no thousand and one subtle ramifications to every single emotion they experience. They love, fear, hate, are angered or made happy in common, ordinary, and unmistakable terms. It may be a beastly life, but at least it is easy to live. No mistakes, no misunderstandings. It has its charm, after civilization's fitful fever. Comprehend? No, it's a pretty good life," he said, after a pause; "good enough for me, and I intend to stay with it."

Van Brunt lowered his head in a musing manner, and an imperceptible smile played on his mouth. Fairfax also was taking it hard, he thought, just because Emily Southwaithe had been mistakenly clawed by a bear. And not a bad sort of a bear, either, was Carlton Southwaithe.

"But you are coming along with me," Van Brunt said deliberately.

"No, I'm not."

"Yes, you are."

"Life's too easy here, I tell you." Fairfax spoke with decision. "I understand everything, and I am understood. Summer and winter alternate like the sun flashing through the palings of a fence, the seasons are a blur of light and shade, and time slips by, and life slips by, and then . . . a wailing in the forest, and the dark. Listen!"

He held up his hand, and the silver thread of the woman's sorrow rose through the silence. Fairfax joined in softly.

"O-o-o-o-o-o-a-haa-ha-a-ha-aa-a-a, O-o-o-o-o-o-a-ha-a-ha-a," he sang. "Can't you hear it? Can't you see it? The women mourning,—the funeral chant,—my hair white-locked,—my skins wrapped in rude splendor about me,—my hunting spear by my side? And who shall say it is not well?"

Van Brunt looked at him coolly. "Fairfax, you are a damned fool. Five years of this is enough to knock any man, and you are in an unhealthy, morbid condition. Further, Carlton Southwaithe is dead."

Van Brunt filled his pipe and lighted it, the while watching slyly and with almost professional interest. Fairfax's eyes flashed on the instant, his fists clenched, he half rose up, then his muscles relaxed, and he seemed to brood. Michael, the cook, signalled that the meal was ready, but Van Brunt motioned back to delay. The silence hung heavy, and he fell to analyzing the forest scents, the odors of mould and rotting vegetation, the resiny smells of pine cones and needles, the aromatic savors of many

"Keen bent the bow and drew back the arrow to its head. Twice he did so, calmly and for certainty, and then drove the bone-barbed missile straight home."

camp-smokes. Twice Fairfax looked up, but said nothing, and then:

"And . . . Emily . . . ?"

"Three years a widow; still a widow."

Another long silence broken by Fairfax finally. "I guess you're right, Van Brunt. I'll go along."

"I knew you would." Van Brunt laid his hand on Fairfax's shoulder. "Of course, one cannot know, but I imagine, for one in her position, she has had offers——"

"When do you start?" Fairfax interrupted.

"After the men have had some sleep. Which reminds me, Michael is getting angry, so come and eat."

After supper, when the Crees and *voyageurs* had rolled into their blankets, snoring, the two men lingered by the dying fire. There was much to talk about, wars and politics and explorations, the doings of men and the happening of things, mutual friends, marriages, deaths—five years of history for which Fairfax clamored.

"So the Spanish fleet was bottled up in Santiago," Vant Brunt was saying, when a young woman stepped lightly before him and stood by Fairfax's side. She looked swiftly into his face, then turned a troubled gaze upon Van Brunt.

"Chief Tantlatch's daughter, sort of princess," Fairfax explained with an honest flush. "One of the inducements, in short, to make me stay. Thom, this is Van Brunt, friend of mine."

Van Brunt held out his hand, but the woman maintained a rigid repose quite in keeping with her general appearance. Not a line of her face softened. She looked him straight in the eyes, her own piercing, questioning, searching.

"Precious lot she understands," Fairfax laughed. "Her first introduction, you know. But as you were saying, with the Spanish fleet bottled up in Santiago——"

Thom crouched down by her husband's side, motionless as a bronze statue, only her eyes flashing from face to face in ceaseless search. And Avery Van Brunt, as he talked on and on, felt a nervousness under the dumb gaze. In the midst of his most graphic battle-descriptions he would become suddenly conscious of the black eyes burning into him, and would stumble and flounder till he could catch the gait and go again. Fairfax, hands clasped round knees, pipe out, absorbed, spurred him on, and repictured the world he thought he had forgotten.

One hour passed, and two, and Fairfax rose reluctantly to his feet. "And Cronje was cornered, eh? Well, just wait a moment till I run over to Tantlatch. He'll be expecting you, and I'll arrange for you to see him after breakfast. That will be all right, won't it?"

He went off between the pines, and Van Brunt found himself staring into Thom's warm eyes.

He laughed and stood up. Her insistent stare disconcerted him. A dog was prowling among the grub-sacks. He would drive it away and place them in safety against Fairfax's return. But Thom stretched out a detaining hand and stood up facing him.

"You?" she said, in the arctic tongue which differs little from Greenland to Point Barrow. "You?"

And the swift expression of her face demanded all for which "you" stood, his reason for existence, his presence there, his relation to her husband—everything.

"Brother," he answered in the same tongue, with a sweeping gesture to the south. "Brothers we be, your man and I."

She shook her head. "It is not good that you be here."

"After one sleep I go."

"And my man?" she demanded with tremulous eagerness.

Van Brunt shrugged his shoulders. He was aware of a certain secret shame, of an impersonal sort of shame, and an anger against Fairfax. And he felt the warm blood in his face as he regarded the young savage. She was just a woman. That was all, a woman. The whole sordid story over again, over and over again, as old as Eve and young as the last new love-light.

"My man! My man! My man!" she was reiterating vehemently, her face passionately dark, and the ruthless tenderness of the Eternal Woman, the Mate-Woman, looking out at him from her eyes.

"Thom," he said gravely, in English,

"you were born in the Northland forest, and you have eaten fish and meat, and fought with frost and famine, and lived simply all the days of your life. And there are many things, indeed, not simple, which you do not know and cannot come to understand. You do not know what it is to long for the flesh-pots afar, you cannot understand what it is to yearn for a fair woman's face. And the woman is fair, Thom, the woman is nobly fair. You have been woman to this man, and you have been your all, but your all is very little, very simple. Too little and too simple, and he is an alien man. Fairfax you have never known, you can never know. It is so ordained."

Though she did not understand, she had listened with intense attention, as though life hung on his speech. But she caught at her husband's name, and cried out in Esquimo:

"Yes! Yes! Fairfax! My man!"

"Poor little fool, how could he be your man?"

But she could not understand his English tongue, and deemed that she was being trifled with. The dumb, insensate anger of the Mate-Woman flamed in her face, and it almost seemed to the man as though she crouched panther-like for the spring.

He cursed softly to himself, and watched the fire fade from her face and the soft luminous glow of the appealing woman spring up, of the appealing woman who foregoes strength and panoplies herself wisely in her weakness.

"He is my man," she said gently. "Never have I known other. It cannot be that I should ever know other. Nor can it be that he should go from me."

"Who has said he shall go from thee?" he demanded sharply, half in exasperation, half in impotence.

"It is for thee to say he shall not go from me," she answered softly, a half-sob in her throat.

Van Brunt kicked the embers of the fire savagely and sat down.

"It is for thee to say. He is my man. Before all women he is my man. Thou art big, thou art strong, and behold, I am very weak. See, I am at thy feet. It is for thee to deal with me. It is for thee."

"Get up!" He jerked her roughly erect and stood up himself. "Thou art a woman. Wherefore the dirt is no place for thee, nor the feet of any man."

"He is my man."

"Then Jesus forgive all men!" Van Brunt cried out passionately.

"He is my man," she repeated monotonously, beseechingly.

"He is my brother," he answered.

"My father is Chief Tantlatch. He is a power over five villages. I will see that the five villages be searched for thy choice of all maidens, that thou mayest stay here, by thy brother, and dwell in comfort."

"After one sleep I go."

"And my man?"

"Thy man comes now. Behold!"

From among the gloomy spruces came the light carolling of Fairfax's voice.

As the day is quenched by a sea of fog, so his song smote the light out of her face. "It is the tongue of his own people," she said; "the tongue of his own people."

She turned, with the free movement of a lithe young animal, and made off into the forest.

"It's all fixed," Fairfax called as he came up. "His regal highness will receive you after breakfast."

"Have you told him?" Van Brunt asked.

"No. Nor shall I tell him till we're ready to pull out."

Van Brunt looked with moody affection over the sleeping forms of his men.

"I shall be glad when we are a hundred leagues upon our way," he said.

Thom raised the skin-flap of her father's lodge. Two men sat with him, and the three looked at her with swift interest. But her face betokened nothing as she entered and took seat quietly, without speech. Tantlatch drummed with his knuckles on a spear-haft across his knees, and gazed idly along the path of a sun-ray which pierced a lacing-hole and flung a glittering track across the murky atmosphere of the lodge. To his right, at his shoulder, crouched Chugungatte, the shaman. Both were old men, and the weariness of many years brooded in their eyes. But opposite them sat Keen, a young man and chief favorite in the tribe. He was quick and alert of movement, and his black eyes flashed from face to face in ceaseless scrutiny and challenge.

Silence reigned in the place. Now and again camp noises penetrated, and from the distance, faint and far, like the shadows of voices, came the wrangling of boys in thin, shrill tones. Tantlatch glanced apathetically at his daughter:

"And thy man, how is it with him and thee?"

"He sings strange songs," Thom made answer, "and there is a new look on his face, a new light in his eyes, and with the Newcomer he sits by the fire, and they talk and talk, and the talk is without end. There be something calling him from afar, and he seems to sit and listen, and to answer, singing, in his own people's tongue."

"But she caught at her husband's name, and cried out in Esquimo: 'Yes! Yes! Fairfax! My man!'"

Keen leaned forward, and Thom held speech till her father nodded for her to proceed.

"It be known to thee, O Tantlatch, that the wild goose and the swan and the little ringed duck be born here in the low-lying lands. It be known that they go away before the face of the frost to unknown places. And it be known, likewise, that always do they return when the sun is in the land and the waterways are free. Always do they return to where they were born, that new life may go forth. The land calls to them, and they come. And now there is another land that calls, and it is calling to my man; the land where he was born, and he hath it in mind to answer the call. Yet is he my man. Before all women is he my man."

"Is it well, Tantlatch? Is it well?" Chugungatte demanded with the hint of menace in his voice.

"Ay, it is well!" Keen cried boldly. "The land calls to its children, and all lands call their children home again. As the wild goose and the swan and the little ringed duck are called, so is called this Stranger Man who has lingered with us and who now must go. Also there be the call of kind. The goose mates with the goose, nor does the swan mate with the little ringed duck. It is not well that the swan should mate with the little ringed duck. Nor is it well that Stranger Men should mate with the women of our villages. Wherefore I say the man should go, to his own kind, in his own land."

"He is my own man," Thom answered; "and he is a great man."

"Ay, he is a great man." Chugungatte lifted his head with a faint recrudescence of youthful vigor. "He is a great man, and he put strength in thy arm, O Tantlatch, and gave thee power, and made thy name to be feared in the land, to be feared and to be respected. He is very wise, and there be much profit in his wisdom. And there be questions yet to arise, and needs upon his wisdom yet to come, and we cannot bear to let him go. It is not well that we should let him go."

Tantlatch continued to drum on the spear-haft, and gave no sign that he had heard. Thom studied his face in vain, and Chugungatte seemed to shrink together and droop down as the weight of years descended upon him again.

"No man makes my kill." Keen smote his breast a valorous blow. "I make my own kill. I am glad to live when I make my own kill. When I creep through the snow upon the great moose, I am glad. And when I draw the bow, so, with my full strength, and drive the arrow fierce and swift and to the heart, I am glad. And the meat of no man's kill tastes as sweet as the meat of my kill. I am glad to live, glad in my own cunning and strength, glad that I am a doer of things, a doer of things for myself. And so I say it is well this Stranger Man should go. His wisdom does not make us wise. We do not live when he does our living for us. We grow fat and like women, and we are afraid to work, and we forget how to do things for ourselves. Let the man go, O Tantlatch, that we may be men! I am Keen, a man, and I make my own kill!"

Tantlatch turned a gaze upon him in which seemed the vacancy of eternity. Keen waited the decision expectantly; but the lips did not move, and the old chief turned toward his daughter.

"That which be given cannot be taken away," she burst forth. "I was but a girl when this Stranger Man, who is my man, came among us. And I knew not men, or the ways of men, and my heart was in the play of girls, when thou, Tantlatch, thou and none other, didst call me to thee and press me into the arms of the Stranger Man. Thou and none other, Tantlatch, and as thou didst give me to the man, so didst thou give the man to me. He is my man. In my arms has he slept, and from my arms he cannot be taken."

"It were well, O Tantlatch," Keen followed quickly, with a significant glance at Thom; "it were well to remember that that which be given cannot be taken away."

Chugungatte straightened up. "Out of thy youth, Keen, come the words of thy mouth. As for ourselves, O Tantlatch, we be old men and we understand. We, too, have looked into the eyes of women and felt our blood go hot with strange desires. But the years have chilled us, and we have learned the wisdom of the council, the shrewdness of the cool head and hand, and we know that the warm heart be over-warm and prone to rashness. We know that Keen found favor in thy eyes. We know that Thom was promised him in the old days when she was yet a child. And we know that the new days came, and the Stranger Man, and that out of our wisdom and desire for welfare was Thom lost to Keen and the promise broken."

The old shaman paused and looked directly at the young man.

"And be it known that I, Chugungatte, did advise that the promise be broken."

"Nor have I taken other woman to my bed," Keen broke in. "And I have builded my own fire, and cooked my own food, and ground my teeth in my loneliness."

Chugungatte waved his hand that he had not finished. "I am an old man, and I speak from understanding. It be good to be strong and grasp for power. It be better to forego power that good come out of it. In the old days I sat at thy shoulder, Tantlatch, and my voice was heard over all in the council, and my advice taken in affairs of moment. And I was strong and held power. Under Tantlatch, I was the greatest man. Then came the Stranger Man, and I saw that he was cunning and wise and great. And in that he was wiser and greater than I, it was plain that greater profit should arise from him than me. And I had thy ear, Tantlatch, and thou didst listen to my words, and the Stranger Man was given power and place, and thy daughter, Thom. And the tribe prospered under the new laws in the new days, and so shall it continue to prosper with the Stranger Man in our midst. We be old men, we two, O Tantlatch, thou and I, and this be an affair of head, not heart. Hear my words, Tantlatch! Hear my words! The man remains!"

There was a long silence. The old chief pondered with the massive certitude of Fate, and Chugungatte seemed to wrap himself in the mists of a great antiquity. Keen looked with yearning upon the woman, and she, unnoting, held her eyes steadfastly upon her father's face. The wolf-dog shoved the tent-flap aside, and plucking courage at the quiet, wormed forward on his belly. He sniffed curiously at Thom's listless hand, cocked ears challengingly at Chugungatte, and hunched down upon his haunches before Tantlatch. The spear rattled to the ground, and the dog, with a frightened yell, sprang sideways, snapping in mid-air, and on the second leap cleared the entrance.

Tantlatch looked from face to face, pondering each one long and carefully. Then he raised his head, with rude royalty, and gave judgment in cold and even tones: "The man remains. Let the hunters be called together. Send a runner to the next village with word to bring on the fighting men. I shall not see the Newcomer. Do thou, Chugungatte, have talk with him. Tell him he may go at once, if he would go in peace. And if fight there be, kill, kill, kill, to the last man, but let my word go forth that no harm befall our man, the man whom my daughter hath wedded. It is well."

Chugungatte rose and tottered out, Thom followed; but as Keen stooped to the entrance the voice of Tantlatch stopped him.

"Keen, it were well to harken to my word. The man remains. Let no harm befall him."

Because of Fairfax's instructions in the art of war, the tribesmen did not hurl themselves forward boldly and with clamor. Instead, there was great restraint and self-control, and they were content to advance silently, creeping and crawling from shelter to shelter. By the river bank, and partly protected by a narrow open space, crouched the Crees and *voyageurs*. Their eyes could see nothing, and only in vague ways did their ears hear, but they felt the thrill of life which ran through the forest, the indistinct, indefinable movement of an advancing host.

"Damn them," Fairfax muttered. "They've never faced powder, but I taught them the trick."

Avery Van Brunt laughed, knocked the ashes out of his pipe, and put it carefully away with the pouch, and loosened the hunting-knife in its sheath at his hip.

"Wait," he said. "We'll wither the face of the charge and break their hearts."

"They'll rush scattered if they remember my teaching."

"Let them. Magazine rifles were made to pump. We'll—good! First blood! Extra tobacco, Loon!"

Loon, a Cree, had spotted an exposed shoulder, and with a stinging bullet apprised its owner of his discovery.

"If we can tease them into breaking forward," Fairfax muttered, "if we can only tease them into breaking forward."

Van Brunt saw a head peer from behind a distant tree, and with a quick shot sent the man sprawling to the ground in a death-struggle. Michael potted a third, and Fairfax and the rest took a hand, firing at every exposure and into each clump of agitated brush. In crossing one little swale out of cover, five of the tribesmen remained on their faces, and to the left, where the covering was sparse, a dozen men were struck. But they took the punishment with sullen

"The old chief pondered with the massive certitude of Fate."

steadiness, coming on cautiously, deliberately, without haste, and without lagging.

Ten minutes later, when they were quite close, all movement was suspended, the advance ceased abruptly, and the quietness that followed was portentous, threatening. Only could be seen the green and gold of the woods and undergrowth, shivering and trembling to the first faint puffs of the day-wind. The wan white morning sun mottled the earth with long shadows and streaks of light. A wounded man lifted head and crawled painfully out of the swale, Michael following him with his rifle, but forbearing to shoot. A whistle ran along the invisible line from left to right, and a flight of arrows arched through the air.

"Get ready," Van Brunt commanded, a new metallic note in his voice. "Now!"

They broke cover simultaneously. The forest heaved into sudden life. A great yell went up, and the rifles barked back sharp defiance. Tribesmen knew their deaths in mid-leap, and as they fell their brothers surged over them in a roaring, irresistible wave. In the forefront of the rush, hair flying and arms swinging free, flashing past the tree-trunks and leaping the obstructing logs, came Thom. Fairfax sighted on her and almost pulled trigger ere he knew her.

"The woman! Don't shoot!" he cried. "See! She is unarmed!"

The Crees never heard, nor Michael and his brother *voyageur*, nor Van Brunt, who was keeping one shell continuously in the air. But Thom bore straight on, unharmed, at the heels of a skin-clad hunter who had veered in before her from the side. Fairfax emptied his magazine into the men to right and left of her, and swung his rifle to meet the big hunter. But the man, seeming to recognize him, swerved suddenly aside and plunged his spear into the body of Michael. On the moment, Thom had one arm passed around her husband's neck, and twisting half about, with voice and gesture was splitting the mass of charging warriors. A score of men hurled past on either side, and Fairfax, for a brief instant's space, stood looking upon her and her bronze beauty, thrilling, exulting, stirred to unknown deeps, visioning strange things, dreaming, immortally dreaming. Snatches and scraps of Old World philosophies and New World ethics floated through his mind, and things wonderfully concrete and woefully incongruous —hunting scenes, stretches of sombre forest, vastnesses of silent snow, the glittering of ball-room lights, great galleries and lecture halls, a fleeting shimmer of glistening test tubes, long rows of book-lined shelves, the throb of machinery, and the roar of traffic, a fragment of forgotten song, faces of dear women and old chums, a lonely watercourse amid upstanding peaks, a shattered boat on a pebbly strand, quiet, moonlit fields, fat vales, the smell of hay. . . .

A hunter, struck between the eyes with a rifle-ball, pitched forward lifeless, and with the momentum of his charge slid along the ground. Fairfax came back to himself. His comrades, those that lived, had been swept far back among the trees beyond. He could hear the fierce "Hia! Hia!" of the hunters as they closed in and cut and thrust with their weapons of bone and ivory. The cries of the stricken men smote him like blows. He knew the fight was over, the cause was lost, but all his race-traditions and race-royalty impelled him into the welter that he might die at least with his kind.

"My man! My man!" Thom cried. "Thou art safe!"

He tried to struggle on, but her dead weight clogged his steps.

"There is no need! They are dead, and life be good!"

She held him close till he tripped and stumbled, tripped again, and fell backward to the ground. His head struck a jutting root, and he was half-stunned and could struggle but feebly. In the fall she had heard the feathered swish of an arrow darting past, and she covered his body with hers, as with a shield, her arms holding him tightly, her face pressed to his.

Then it was that Keen rose up from a tangled thicket a score of feet away. He looked about him with care. The fight had swept on, and the cry of the last man was dying away. There was no one to see. He fitted an arrow to the string and glanced at the man and woman. Between her breast and arm the flesh of the man's side showed white. Keen bent the bow and drew back the arrow to its head. Twice he did so, calmly and for certainty, and then drove the bone-barbed missile straight home to the white flesh gleaming yet more white in the dark-armed, dark-breasted embrace.

10
The Wisdom of the Trail

THE WISDOM OF THE TRAIL

By JACK LONDON

SITKA CHARLEY had achieved the impossible. Other Indians might have known as much of the wisdom of the trail as did he; but he alone knew the white man's wisdom, the honor of the trail, and the law. Yet these things had not come to him in a day. The aboriginal mind is slow to generalize, and many facts, repeated often, are required to compass an understanding. Sitka Charley, from boyhood, had been thrown continually with white men, and as a man he had elected to cast his fortunes with them, expatriating himself, once and for all, from his own people. Even then, respecting, almost venerating, their power, and pondering over it, he had yet to divine its secret essence—the honor and the law. And it was only by the cumulative evidence of the years that he had finally come to understand. Being an alien, when he did know, he knew it better than the white man himself; being an Indian, he had achieved the impossible.

And of these things had been bred a certain contempt for his own people; a contempt which he made it a habit to conceal, but which now burst forth in a polyglot whirlwind of curses upon the heads of Kah-Chucte and Gowhee. They cringed before him like a pair of snarling wolf-dogs, too cowardly to spring, too wolfish to cover their fangs. They were not handsome creatures; neither was Sitka Charley. All three were frightful-looking. There was no flesh to their faces; their cheek-bones were massed with hideous scabs which had cracked and frozen alternately under the intense frost, while their eyes burned luridly with the light which alone is born of desperation and hunger. Men so situated, beyond the pale of the honor and the law, are not to be trusted. Sitka Charley knew this; and this was why he had forced them to abandon their rifles with the rest of the camp outfit ten days before. His rifle and Captain Effingwell's were the only ones that remained.

"Come, get a fire started!" he commanded, drawing out the precious matchbox with its attendant strips of dry birch-bark.

The two Indians fell sullenly to the task of gathering dead branches and underwood. They were weak, and paused often, catching themselves, in the act of stooping, with giddy motions, or staggering to the center of operations with their knees shaking like castanets. After each trip they rested for a moment, as though sick and deadly weary. At times their eyes took on the patient stoicism of dumb suffering; and again, the *ego* seemed almost bursting forth with its wild cry, "I, I, I want to exist!"—the one dominant note of the whole living universe.

A light breath of air blew from the south, nipping the exposed portions of their bodies and driving the frost, in needles of fire, through fur and flesh to the very bones. So, when the fire had grown lusty and thawed a damp circle in the snow about it, Sitka Charley forced his reluctant comrades to lend a hand in pitching a fly. It was a primitive affair—merely a blanket, stretched parallel with the fire and to windward of it, at an angle of perhaps forty-five degrees. This shut out the chill wind and threw the heat backward and down upon those who were to huddle in its shelter. Then a layer of green spruce-boughs was spread, that their bodies might not come in contact with the snow. When this task was completed, Kah-Chucte and Gowhee proceeded to take care of their feet. Their ice-bound moccasins were sadly worn by much travel, and the sharp ice of the river jams had cut them to rags. Their Siwash-socks were in similar condition, and when these had been thawed and removed, the dead-white tips of the toes, in the various stages of mortification, told their simple tale of the trail.

Leaving the two to the drying of their foot-gear, Sitka Charley turned back over the course he had come. He, too, had a mighty longing to sit by the fire and tend his complaining flesh, but the honor and the law forbade. He toiled painfully over the frozen field, each step a protest, every muscle in revolt. Several times, where the open water between the jams had recently crusted, he was forced to miserably accelerate his movements as the fragile footing swayed and threatened beneath him. In such places, to stop was to break through; to break through was to die—to die quickly and easily. But it was not his desire to endure no more, so he hastened.

His deepening anxiety vanished as two Indians dragged into view round a bend in the river. They staggered and panted like men under heavy burdens; yet the packs on their backs were a matter of but few pounds. He questioned them eagerly, and their replies seemed to relieve him. He hurried on. Next came two white men, supporting a woman between them. They also behaved as though drunken, and their limbs shook with weakness. But the woman leaned lightly upon them, choosing to carry herself forward with her own strength. At sight of her, a flash of joy cast its fleeting light upon Sitka Charley's face. He cherished a very great regard for Mrs. Effingwell. He had seen many white women, but this was the first to travel the trail with him. When Captain Effingwell had proposed the hazardous undertaking and made him an offer for his services, he had shaken his head gravely; for it was an unknown journey through the dismal vastnesses of the Northland, and he knew it to be of the kind that tries to the uttermost the souls of men. But when he learned that the captain's wife was to accompany them, he had refused flatly to have anything further to do with it. Had it been a woman of his own race he would have harbored no objections; but these women of the Southland—no, no, they were too soft, too tender for such enterprises. The idea was not to be entertained for an instant.

Sitka Charley did not know this kind of woman. Five minutes before, he did not even dream of taking charge of the expedition; but when she came to him with her wonderful smile and her straight clean English, and talked to the point, without pleading or persuading, he had incontinently yielded. Had there been a softness and appeal in the eyes, a tremble to the voice, a taking advantage of sex, he would have stiffened to steel; instead, her clear-searching eyes and clear-ringing voice, her utter frankness and assertion of equality, had robbed him of his reason. He felt, then, that this was a new breed of woman; and ere they had been trail-mates for many days, he knew why the sons of such women mastered the land and the sea, and why the sons of his own womankind could not prevail against them. *Tender and soft!*—day after day he watched her, muscle-weary, exhausted, indomitable, and the words beat upon his brain in a perennial refrain. *Tender and soft!* He knew her feet had been born to easy paths in sunny lands, strangers to the moccasined pain of the North, unkissed by the chill lips of the frost, and he watched and marveled at them twinkling ever through the weary day.

She had always a smile and a word of cheer, from which not even the meanest packer was excluded. As the way grew darker she seemed to stiffen and gather greater strength, and when Kah-Chucte and Gowhee, who had bragged that they knew every landmark of the way as a child did the skin-bales of the teepee, acknowledged that they knew not where they were, it was she who raised a forgiving voice amid the curses of the men. She had sung to them that night, till they felt the weariness fall from them and were ready to face the future with fresh hope. And when the food failed and each scant stint was measured jealously, she it was who rebelled against the machinations of her husband and Sitka Charley, and demanded and received a share neither greater nor less than that of the others.

Sitka Charley was proud to know this woman. A new richness, a greater breadth had come into his life with her presence. Hitherto he had been his own mentor, had turned to right or left at no man's beck; he had molded himself according to his own dictates, nourished his manhood regardless of all save his own opinion. For the first time he had felt a call from without for the best that was in him. Just a glance of appreciation from the clear-searching eyes, a word of thanks from the clear-ringing voice, just a slight wreathing of the lips in that wonderful smile, and he felt his reward to be greater than he deserved. It was a new stimulant to his manhood; for the first time he thrilled with a conscious pride in his wisdom of the trail; and between the twain they ever lifted the sinking hearts of their comrades.

The faces of the two men and the woman brightened as they saw him, for after all he was the staff they leaned upon. But Sitka Charley, rigid as was his wont, concealing pain and pleasure impartially, asked them the welfare of the rest, told the distance to the fire, and continued on the back-trip. Next he met a single Indian, unburdened, limping, lips compressed and eyes set with the pain of a foot in which the quick fought a losing battle with the dead. All possible care had been taken of him; but in the last extremity the weak and unfortunate must perish, and Sitka Charley deemed his days to be few. The man could not keep up for long; so he gave him rough cheering words. After that came two more Indians, to whom he had allotted the task of helping along Joe, the third white man of the party. They had deserted him. Sitka Charley saw at a glance the lurking spring in their bodies, and knew they had at last cast off his mastery. So he was not taken unawares when he ordered them back in quest of their abandoned charge, and saw the gleam of the hunting-knives as they drew them from the sheaths. A pitiful spectacle, three weak men lifting their puny strength in the face of the mighty vastness! But the two recoiled under the fierce rifle-blows of the one, and returned like beaten dogs to the leash. Two hours later, with Joe reeling between them and Sitka Charley bringing up the rear, they came to the fire where the remainder of the expedition crouched in the shelter of the fly.

"A few words, my comrades, before we sleep," Sitka Charley said, after they had devoured their slim rations of unleavened bread. He was speaking to the Indians, in their own tongue, having already given the import to the whites. "A few words, my comrades, for your own good, that perchance ye may yet live. I shall give ye the law; on his own head be the death of him that breaks it! We have passed the Hills of Silence, and we now travel the head-reaches of the Stuart. It may be one sleep, it may be several, it may be many sleeps; but in time we shall come among the Men of the Yukon, who have much grub. It were well that we look to the law. To-day, Kah-Chucte and Gowhee, whom I commanded to break trail, forgot they were men and, like frightened children, ran away. True, they forgot; so let us forget. But hereafter let them remember. If it should happen that they do not ——" He touched his rifle carelessly, grimly. "To-morrow they shall carry the flour and see that the white man Joe lies not down by the trail. The cups of flour are counted; should so much as an ounce be wanting at nightfall—— Dost understand? To-day there were others that forgot. Moose-Head and Three-Salmon left the white man Joe to lie in the snow. Let them forget no more. With the light of day shall they go forth and break trail. Ye have heard the law. Look well, lest ye break it!"

Sitka Charley found it beyond him to keep the line close up. From Moose-Head and Three-Salmon, who broke trail in advance, to Kah-Chucte, Gowhee and Joe, it straggled out over a mile. Each staggered, fell, or rested, as he saw fit. The line of march was a progression through a series of irregular halts. Each drew upon the last remnant of his strength and stumbled onward till it was expended; but in some miraculous way there was always another last remnant. Each time a man fell, it was with the firm belief that he would rise no more; yet he did rise, and again, and again. The flesh yielded, the will conquered; but each triumph was a tragedy. The Indian with the frozen foot, no longer erect, crawled forward on hand and knee. He rarely rested, for he knew the penalty exacted by the frost. Even Mrs. Effingwell's lips were at last set, and her eyes seeing, saw not. Often she stopped, pressing a mittened hand to her heart, gasping and dizzy.

Joe, the white man, had passed beyond the stage of suffering. He no longer begged to be let alone—prayed to die; but was soothed and content under the anodyne of delirium. Kah-Chucte and Gowhee dragged him on roughly, venting upon him many a savage glance or blow. To them it seemed the acme of injustice. Their hearts were bitter with hate, heavy with fear. Why should they cumber their strength with his weakness? To do so, meant death; to not do so—and they remembered the law of Sitka Charley and the rifle.

Joe, the white man, fell with greater frequency as the daylight waned; and so hard was he to raise that they dropped farther and farther behind. Sometimes all three pitched into the snow, so weak were they. Yet on their backs was life and strength and warmth. Within the flour-sacks were all the potentialities of existence. They could not but think of this, and it was not strange, that which followed. They had fallen by the side of a great timber-jam where a thousand cords of firewood awaited the match. Near by was an air-hole through the ice. Kah-Chucte looked on the wood and the water, as did Gowhee; then they looked at each other. Never a word was spoken. Gowhee struck a fire. Kah-Chucte filled a tin-cup with water and heated it. Joe babbled of things in another land, in a tongue they did not understand. They mixed flour with the warm water till it was a thin paste, and of this they drank many cups. They did not offer any to Joe; but he did not mind. He did not mind anything, not even his moccasins, which scorched and smoked among the coals.

A crystal mist of snow fell about them, softly, caressingly, wrapping them in clinging robes. And their feet would have yet trod many trails had not destiny brushed the clouds aside and cleared the air. Nay, ten minutes' delay would have been salvation. Sitka Charley, looking back, saw the pillared smoke of their fire, and guessed. And he looked ahead at those who were faithful, and at Mrs. Effingwell.

"So, my good comrades, ye have again forgotten that ye were men? Good, very good; there will be fewer bellies to feed." Sitka Charley re-tied the flour as he spoke, strapping the pack to that on his own back. He kicked Joe till the pain broke through the poor devil's bliss and brought him to his feet, doddering like a dead man. Then he shoved him out onto the trail and started him on his way. The two Indians attempted to slip off.

"Hold, Gowhee! And thou, too, Kah-Chucte! Has the flour given such strength to thy legs that they may outrun the swift-winged lead? Think not to cheat the law. Be men for the last time, and be content that ye die full-stomached. Come, step up, back to the timber, shoulder to shoulder!"

The two men obeyed, quietly, without fear; for it is the future which presses upon the man, not the present.

"Thou, Gowhee, hast a wife and children and a deerskin lodge in the Chippewyan. What is thy will in the matter?"

"Give thou her of the goods which are mine by the word of the Captain—the blankets, the beads, the tobacco, the box which makes strange sounds after the manner of the white man. Say that I died on the trail, but say not how."

"And thou, Kah-Chucte, who hast nor wife nor child?"

"Mine is a sister, the wife of the factor at Koshim. He beats her, and she is not happy. Give thou her the goods which are mine by the contract, and tell her that it were well she go back to her own people. Shouldst thou meet the man, and be so minded, it were a good deed that he should die. He beats her, and she is afraid."

"Are ye content to die by the law?"

"We are!"

"Then, good-by, my comrades! May ye sit by the well-filled pot, in warm lodges, ere the day is done!"

As he spoke, he raised his rifle, and many echoes broke the silence. Hardly had they died away, when other rifles spoke in the distance. Sitka Charley started. There had been more than one, yet there was but one other gun in the party. He gave one fleeting glance at the men who lay so quietly, smiled viciously at the wisdom of the trail, and hurried on to meet the Men of the Yukon.

11
The Law of Life

THE LAW OF LIFE.

By Jack London.

OLD Koskoosh listened greedily. Though his sight had long since faded, his hearing was still acute, and the slightest sound penetrated to the glimmering intelligence which yet abode behind the withered forehead, but which no longer gazed forth upon the things of the world. Ah! that was Sit-cum-to-ha, shrilly anathematizing the dogs as she cuffed and beat them into the harnesses. Sit-cum-to-ha was his daughter's daughter, but she was too busy to waste a thought upon her broken grandfather, sitting alone there in the snow, forlorn and helpless. Camp must be broken. The long trail waited while the short day refused to linger. Life called her, and the duties of life, not death. And he was very close to death now.

The thought made the old man panicky for the moment, and he stretched forth a palsied hand which wandered tremblingly over the small heap of dry wood beside him. Reassured that it was indeed there, his hand returned to the shelter of his mangy furs, and he again fell to listening. The sulky crackling of half-frozen hides told him that the chief's moose-skin lodge had been struck, and even then was being rammed and jammed into portable compass. The chief was his son, stalwart and strong, head man of the tribesmen, and a mighty hunter. As the women toiled with the camp luggage, his voice rose, chiding them for their slowness. Old Koskoosh strained his ears. It was the last time he would hear that voice. There went Geehow's lodge! And Tusken's! Seven, eight, nine; only the Shaman's could be still standing. There! They were at work upon it now He could hear the Shaman grunt as he piled it on the sled. A child whimpered, and a woman soothed it with soft, crooning gutturals. Little Koo-tee, the old man thought, a fretful child, and not over strong. It would die soon, perhaps, and they would burn a hole through the frozen tundra and pile rocks above to keep the wolverines away. Well, what did it matter? A few years at best, and as many an empty belly as a full one. And in the end, Death waited, ever-hungry and hungriest of them all.

What was that? Oh, the men lashing the sleds and drawing tight the thongs. He listened, who would listen no more. The whip-lashes snarled and bit among the dogs. Hear them whine! How they hated the work and the trail! They were off! Sled after sled churned slowly away into the silence. They were gone. They had passed out of his life, and he faced the last bitter hour alone. No. The snow crunched beneath a moccasin; a man stood beside him; upon his head a hand rested gently. His son was good to do this thing. He remembered other old men whose sons had not waited after the tribe. But his son had. He wandered away into the past, till the young man's voice brought him back.

"Is it well with you?" he asked.

And the old man answered, "It is well."

"There be wood beside you," the younger man continued, "and the fire burns bright. The morning is gray, and the cold has broken. It will snow presently. Even now is it snowing."

"Ay, even now is it snowing."

"The tribesmen hurry. Their bales are heavy, and their bellies flat with lack of feasting. The trail is long and they travel fast. I go now. It is well?"

"It is well. I am as a last year's leaf, clinging lightly to the stem. The first breath that blows, and I fall. My voice is become like an old woman's. My eyes no longer show me the way of my feet, and my feet are heavy, and I am tired. It is well."

He bowed his head in content till the last noise of the complaining snow had died away, and he knew his son was beyond recall. Then his hand crept out in haste to the wood. It alone stood betwixt him and the eternity which yawned in upon him. At last the measure of his life was a handful of fagots. One by one they would go to feed the fire, and just so, step by step, death would creep upon him. When the last stick had surrendered up its heat, the frost would begin to gather strength. First his feet would yield, then his hands; and the numbness would travel, slowly, from the extremities to the body. His head would fall forward upon his knees, and he would rest. It was easy. All men must die.

He did not complain. It was the way of life, and it was just. He had been born close to the earth, close to the earth had he lived, and the law thereof was not new to him. It was the law of all flesh. Nature was not kindly to the flesh. She had no concern for that concrete thing called the individual. Her interest lay in the species, the race. This was the deepest abstraction old Koskoosh's barbaric mind was capable of, but he grasped it firmly. He saw it exemplified in all life. The rise of the sap, the bursting greenness of the willow bud, the fall of the yellow leaf—in this alone was told the whole history. But one task did nature set the individual. Did he not perform it, he died. Did he perform it, it was all the same, he died. Nature did not care; there were plenty who were obedient, and it was only the obedience in this matter, not the obedient, which lived and lived always. The tribe of Koskoosh was very old. The old men he had known when a boy, had known old men before them. Therefore it was true that the tribe lived, that it stood for the obedience of all its members, way down into the forgotten past, whose very resting places were unremembered. They did not count; they were episodes. They had passed away like clouds from a summer sky. He also was an episode, and would pass away. Nature did not care. To life she set one task, gave one law. To perpetuate was the task of life, its law was death. A maiden was a good creature to look upon, full-breasted and strong, with spring to her step and light in her eyes. But her task was yet before her. The light in her eyes brightened, her step quickened, she was now bold with the young men, now timid, and she gave them of her own unrest. And ever she grew fairer and yet fairer to look upon, till some hunter, able no longer to withhold himself, took her to his lodge to cook and toil for him and to become the mother of his children. And with the coming of her offspring her looks left her. Her limbs dragged and shuffled, her eyes dimmed and bleared, and only the little children found joy against the withered cheek of the old squaw by the fire. Her task was done. But a little while, on the first pinch of famine or the first long trail, and she would be left, even as he had been left, in the snow, with a little pile of wood. Such was the law.

He placed a stick carefully upon the fire and resumed his meditations. It was the same everywhere, with all things. The mosquitos vanished with the first frost. The little tree-squirrel crawled away to die. When age settled upon the rabbit it became slow and heavy, and could no longer outfoot its enemies. Even the big bald-face grew clumsy and blind and quarrelsome, in the end to be dragged down by a handful of yelping huskies. He remembered how he had abandoned his own father on an upper reach of the Klondike one winter, the winter before the missionary came with his talk-books and his box of medicines. Many a time had Koskoosh smacked his lips over the recollection of that box, though now his mouth refused to moisten. The "painkiller" had been especially good. But the missionary was a bother after all, for he brought no meat into the camp, and he ate heartily, and the hunters grumbled. But he chilled his lungs on the divide by the Mayo, and the dogs afterwards nosed the stones away and fought over his bones.

Koskoosh placed another stick on the fire and harked back deeper into the past. There was the time of the Great Famine, when the old men crouched empty-bellied to the fire, and from their lips fell dim traditions of the ancient day when the Yukon ran wide open for three winters, and then lay frozen for three summers. He had lost his mother in that famine. In the summer the salmon run had failed, and the tribe looked forward to the winter and the coming of the caribou. Then the winter came, but with it there were no caribou. Never had the like been known, not even in the lives of the old men. But the caribou did not come, and it was the seventh year, and the rabbits had not replenished, and the dogs were naught but bundles of bones. And through the long darkness the children wailed and died, and the women, and the old men ; and not one in ten of the tribe lived to meet the sun when it came back in the spring. That *was* a famine!

But he had seen times of plenty, too, when the meat spoiled on their hands, and the dogs were fat and worthless with over-eating—times when they let the game go unkilled, and the women were fertile, and the lodges were cluttered with sprawling men-children and women-children. Then it was the men became high-stomached, and revived ancient quarrels, and crossed the divides to the south to kill the Pellys, and to the west that they might sit by the dead fires of the Tananas. He remembered, when a boy, during a time of plenty, when he saw a moose pulled down by the wolves. Zing-ha lay with him in the snow and watched—Zing-ha, who later became the craftiest of hunters, and who, in the end, fell through an air-hole on the Yukon. They found him, a month afterward, just as he had crawled half-way out and frozen stiff to the ice.

But the moose. Zing-ha and he had gone out that day to play at hunting after the manner of their fathers. On the bed of the creek they struck the fresh track of a moose, and with it the tracks of many wolves. "An old one," Zing-ha, who was quicker at reading the sign, said—"an old one who cannot keep up with the herd. The wolves have cut him out from his brothers, and they will never leave him." And it was so. It was their way. By day and by night, never resting, snarling on his heels, snapping at his nose, they would stay by him to the end. How Zing-ha and he felt the blood-lust quicken! The finish would be a sight to see!

Eager-footed, they took the trail, and even he, Koskoosh, slow of sight and an unversed tracker, could have followed it blind, it was so wide. Hot were they on the heels of the chase, reading the grim tragedy, fresh-written, at every step. Now they came to where the moose had made a stand. Thrice the length of a grown man's body, in every direction, had the snow been stamped about and uptossed. In the midst were the deep impressions of the splay-hoofed game, and all about, everywhere, were the lighter foot-marks of the wolves. Some, while their brothers harried the kill, had lain to one side and rested. The full-stretched impress of their bodies in the snow was as perfect as though made the moment before. One wolf had been caught in a wild lunge of the maddened victim and trampled to death. A few bones, well picked, bore witness.

Again, they ceased the uplift of their

snowshoes at a second stand. Here the great animal had fought desperately. Twice had he been dragged down, as the snow attested, and twice had he shaken his assailants clear and gained footing once more. He had done his task long since, but none the less was life dear to him. Zing-ha said it was a strange thing, a moose once down to get free again; but this one certainly had. The Shaman would see signs and wonders in this when they told him.

And yet again, they came to where the moose had made to mount the bank and gain the timber. But his foes had laid on from behind, till he reared and fell back upon them, crushing two deep into the snow. It was plain the kill was at hand, for their brothers had left them untouched. Two more stands were hurried past, brief in time-length and very close together. The trail was red now, and the clean stride of the great beast had grown short and slovenly. Then they heard the first sounds of the battle—not the full-throated chorus of the chase, but the short, snappy bark which spoke of close quarters and teeth to flesh. Crawling up the wind, Zing-ha bellied it through the snow, and with him crept he, Koskoosh, who was to be chief of the tribesmen in the years to come. Together they shoved aside the under branches of a young spruce and peered forth. It was the end they saw.

The picture, like all of youth's impressions, was still strong with him, and his dim eyes watched the end played out as vividly as in that far-off time. Koskoosh marveled at this, for in the days which followed, when he was a leader of men and a head of councilors, he had done great deeds and made his name a curse in the mouths of the Pellys, to say naught of the strange white man he had killed, knife to knife, in open fight.

For long he pondered on the days of his youth, till the fire died down and the frost bit deeper. He replenished it with two sticks this time, and gauged his grip on life by what remained. If Sit-cum-to-ha had only remembered her grandfather, and gathered a larger armful, his hours would have been longer. It would have been easy. But she was ever a careless child, and honored not her ancestors from the time the Beaver, son of the son of Zing-ha, first cast eyes upon her. Well, what mattered it? Had he not done likewise in his own quick youth? For a while he listened to the silence. Perhaps the heart of his son might soften, and he would come back with the dogs to take his old father on with the tribe to where the caribou ran thick and the fat hung heavy upon them.

He strained his ears, his restless brain for the moment stilled. Not a stir, nothing. He alone took breath in the midst of the great silence. It was very lonely, Hark! What was that? A chill passed over his body. The familiar, long-drawn howl broke the void, and it was close at hand. Then on his darkened eyes was projected the vision of the moose—the old bull moose—the torn flanks and bloody sides, the riddled mane, and the great branching horns, down low and tossing to the last. He saw the flashing forms of gray, the gleaming eyes, the lolling tongues, the slavered fangs. And he saw the inexorable circle close in till it became a dark point in the midst of the stamped snow.

A cold muzzle thrust against his cheek, and at its touch his soul leaped back to the present. His hand shot into the fire and dragged out a burning faggot. Overcome for the nonce by his hereditary fear of man, the brute retreated, raising a prolonged call to his brothers; and greedily they answered, till a ring of crouching, jaw-slobbered gray was stretched round about. The old man listened to the drawing in of this circle. He waved his brand wildly, and sniffs turned to snarls; but the panting brutes refused to scatter. Now one wormed his chest forward, dragging his haunches after, now a second, now a third; but never a one drew back. Why should he cling to life? he asked, and dropped the blazing stick into the snow. It sizzled and went out. The circle grunted uneasily, but held its own. Again he saw the last stand of the old bull moose, and Koskoosh dropped his head wearily upon his knees. What did it matter after all? Was it not the law of life?

12
The White Silence

THE WHITE SILENCE

ANOTHER STORY OF MALEMUTE KID

By JACK LONDON

"CARMEN won't last more than a couple of days." Mason spat out a chunk of ice and surveyed the poor animal ruefully, then put her foot in his mouth and proceeded to bite out the ice which clustered cruelly between the toes.

"I never saw a dog with a highfalutin name that ever was worth a rap," he said, as he concluded his task and shoved her aside. "They just fade away and die under the responsibility. Did ye ever see one go wrong with a sensible name like Cassiar, Siwash, or Husky? No, sir! Take a look at Shookum here, he 's——"

Snap! The lean brute flashed up, the white teeth just missing Mason's throat.

"Ye will, will ye?" A shrewd clout behind the ear with the butt of the dog-whip stretched the animal in the snow, quivering softly, a yellow slaver dripping from its fangs.

"As I was saying, just look at Shookum, here—he 's got the spirit. Bet ye he eats Carmen before the week's out."

"I 'll bank another proposition against that," replied Malemute Kid, reversing the frozen bread placed before the fire to thaw. "We 'll eat Shookum before the trip is over. What d' ye say, Ruth?"

The Indian woman settled the coffee with a piece of ice, glanced from Malemute Kid to her husband, then at the dogs, but vouchsafed no reply. It was such a palpable truism that none was necessary. Two hundred miles of unbroken trail in prospect, with a scant six days' grub for themselves and none for the dogs, could admit no other alternative. The two men and the woman grouped about the fire and began their meager meal. The dogs lay in their harnesses, for it was a mid-day halt, and watched each mouthful enviously.

"No more lunches after to-day," said Malemute Kid. "And we 've got to keep a close eye on the dogs,—they 're getting vicious. They 'd just as soon pull a fellow down as not, if they get a chance."

"And I was president of an Epworth once, and taught in the Sunday-school." Having irrelevantly delivered himself of this, Mason fell into a dreamy contemplation of his steaming moccasins, but was aroused by Ruth filling his cup. "Thank God, we 've got slathers of tea! I 've seen it growing, down in Tennessee. What would n't I give for a hot corn pone just now! Never mind, Ruth; you won't starve much longer, nor wear moccasins either."

The woman threw off her gloom at this, and in her eyes welled up a great love for her white lord,—the first white man she had ever seen,—the first man whom she had known to treat a woman as something better than a mere animal or beast of burden.

"Yes, Ruth," continued her husband, having recourse to the macaronic jargon in which it was alone possible for them to understand each other, and which it is impossible to reproduce; "wait till we clean up and pull for the Outside. We 'll take the White Man's canoe and go to the Salt Water. Yes, bad water, rough water,—great mountains dance up and down all the time. And so big, so far, so far away,—you travel ten sleep, twenty sleep, forty sleep," (he graphically enumerated the days on his fingers,) "all the time water, bad water. Then you come to great village, plenty people, just the same mosquitoes next summer. Wigwams oh, so high,—ten, twenty pines. Hi-yu skookum!"

He paused impotently, cast an appealing glance at Malemute Kid, then laboriously placed the twenty pines, end on end, by sign language. Malemute Kid smiled with cheery cynicism; but Ruth's eyes were wide with wonder, and with pleasure; for she half believed he was joking, and such condescensions pleased her poor woman's heart.

"And then you step into a—a box, and pouf! up you go." He tossed his empty cup in the air by way of illustration, and as he deftly caught it, cried: "And biff! down you come. Oh, great medicine-men!

You go Fort Yukon, I go Arctic City,—twenty-five sleep,—big string, all the time. —I catch him string,—I say, 'Hello Ruth! How are ye?'—and you say, 'Is that my good husband?'—and I say 'Yes,' —and you say, 'No can bake good bread, no more soda,'—then I say, 'Look in cache, under flour; good-by.' You look and catch plenty soda. All the time you Fort Yukon, me Arctic City. Hi-yi medicine-man!"

Ruth smiled so ingenuously at the fairy story, that both men burst into laughter. A row among the dogs cut short the wonders of the Outside, and by the time the snarling combatants were separated, she had lashed the sleds and all was ready for the trail.

"Mush! Baldy! Hi! Mush on!" Mason worked his whip smartly, and as the dogs whined low in the traces, broke out the sled with the gee-pole. Ruth followed with the second team, leaving Malemute Kid, who had helped her start, to bring up the rear. Strong man, noble brute that he was, capable of felling an ox at a blow, he could not bear to beat the poor animals, but humored them as a dog-driver rarely does,—nay, almost wept with them in their misery.

"Come, mush on there, you poor sore-footed brutes," he murmured, after several ineffectual attempts to start the load. But his patience was at last rewarded, and though whimpering with pain, they hastened to join their fellows.

No more conversation; the toil of the trail will not permit such extravagance. And of all deadening labors, that of the Northland trail is the worst. Happy is the man who can weather a day's travel at the price of silence, and that on a beaten track.

And of all heart-breaking labors, that of breaking trail is the worst. At every step the great webbed shoe sinks till the snow is level with the knee. Then up, straight up, the deviation of a fraction of an inch being a certain precursor of disaster, the snow-shoe must be lifted till the surface is cleared; then forward, down, and the other foot is raised perpendicularly for the matter of half a yard. He who tries this for the first time, if haply he avoids bringing his shoes in dangerous propinquity and measures not his length on the treacherous footing, will give up exhausted at the end of a hundred yards; he who can keep out of the way of the dogs for a whole day may well crawl into his sleeping-bag with a clear conscience, and a pride which passeth all understanding; and he who travels twenty sleeps on the Long Trail is a man whom the gods may envy.

The afternoon wore on, and with the awe, born of the White Silence, the voiceless travelers bent to their work. Nature has many tricks wherewith she convinces man of his finity,—the ceaseless flow of the tides, the fury of the storm, the shock of the earthquake, the long roll of heaven's artillery,—but the most tremendous, the most stupefying of all, is the passive phase of the White Silence. All movement ceases, the sky clears, the heavens are as brass; the slightest whisper seems sacrilege, and man becomes timid, affrighted at the sound of his own voice. Sole speck of life journeying across the ghostly wastes of a dead world, he trembles at his audacity, realizes that his is a maggot's life, nothing more. Strange thoughts arise unsummoned, and the mystery of all things strives for utterance. And the fear of death, of God, of the universe, comes over him,—the hope of the Resurrection and the Life, the yearning for immortality, the vain striving of the imprisoned essence,—it is then, if ever, man walks alone with God.

So wore the day away. The river took a great bend, and Mason headed his team for the cut-off across the narrow neck of land. But the dogs balked at the high bank. Again and again, though Ruth and Malemute Kid were shoving on the sled, they slipped back. Then came the concerted effort. The miserable creatures, weak from hunger, exerted their last strength. Up—up—the sled poised on the top of the bank; but the leader swung the string of dogs behind him to the right, fouling Mason's snow-shoes. The result was grievous. Mason was whipped off his feet; one of the dogs fell in the traces; and the sled toppled back, dragging everything to the bottom again.

Slash! the whip fell among the dogs

cruelly, especially upon the one which had fallen.

"Don't, Mason," entreated Malemute Kid; "the poor devil's on its last legs. Wait and we'll put my team on."

Mason deliberately withheld the whip till the last word had fallen, then out flashed the long lash, completely curling about the offending creature's body. Carmen,—for it was Carmen,—cowered in the snow, cried piteously, then rolled over on her side.

It was a tragic moment, a pitiful incident of the trail,—a dying dog, two comrades in anger. Ruth glanced solicitously from man to man. But Malemute Kid restrained himself, though there was a world of reproach in his eyes, and bending over the dog, cut the traces. No word was spoken. The teams were double-spanned and the difficulty overcome; the sleds were under way again, the dying dog dragging herself along in the rear. As long as an animal can travel, it is not shot, and this last chance is accorded it,—the crawling into camp, if it can, in the hope of a moose being killed.

Already penitent for his angry action, but too stubborn to make amends, Mason toiled on at the head of the cavalcade, little dreaming that danger hovered in the air. The timber clustered thick in the sheltered bottom, and through this they threaded their way. Fifty feet or more from the trail towered a lofty pine. For generations it had stood there, and for generations destiny had had this one end in view,—perhaps the same had been decreed of Mason.

He stooped to fasten the loosened thong of his moccasin. The sleds came to a halt and the dogs lay down in the snow without a whimper. The stillness was weird; not a breath rustled the frost-encrusted forest; the cold and silence of outer space had chilled the heart and smote the trembling lips of nature. A sigh pulsed through the air,—they did not seem to actually hear it, but rather felt it, like the premonition of movement in a motionless void. Then the great tree, burdened with its weight of years and snow, played its last part in the tragedy of life. He heard the warning crash and attempted to spring up, but almost erect, caught the blow squarely on the shoulder.

The sudden danger, the quick death,—how often had Malemute Kid faced it! The pine needles were still quivering as he gave his commands and sprang into action. Nor did the Indian girl faint or raise her voice in idle wailing, as would many of her white sisters. At his order, she threw her weight on the end of a quickly extemporized handspike, easing the pressure and listening to her husband's groans, while Malemute Kid attacked the tree with his ax. The steel rang merrily as it bit into the frozen trunk, each stroke being accompanied by a forced, audible respiration, the "Huh!" "Huh!" of the woodsman.

At last the Kid laid the pitiable thing that was once a man in the snow. But worse than his comrade's pain, was the dumb anguish in the woman's face, the blended look of hopeful, hopeless query. Little was said; those of the Northland are early taught the futility of words and the inestimable value of deeds. With the temperature at sixty-five below zero, a man cannot lie many minutes in the snow and live. So the sled-lashings were cut, and the sufferer, rolled in furs, laid on a couch of boughs. Before him roared a fire, built of the very wood which wrought the mishap. Behind and partially over him was stretched the primitive fly,—a piece of canvas, which caught the radiating heat and threw it back and down upon him,—a trick which men may know who study physics at the fount.

And men who have shared their bed with death know when the call is sounded. Mason was terribly crushed. The most cursory examination revealed it. His right arm, leg, and back, were broken; his limbs were paralyzed from the hips; and the likelihood of internal injuries was large. An occasional moan was his only sign of life.

No hope; nothing to be done. The pitiless night crept slowly by,—Ruth's portion, the despairing stoicism of her race, and Malemute Kid adding new lines to his face of bronze. In fact, Mason suffered least of all, for he spent his time in Eastern Tennessee, in the Great Smoky Mountains, living over the scenes of his childhood. And most pathetic was the melody of his long-forgotten Southern vernacular, as he raved of swimming-holes and coon-hunts and watermelon raids. It was as Greek to Ruth, but the Kid understood and felt,—felt as only one can feel who has been shut out for years from all that civilization means.

Morning brought consciousness to the stricken man, and Malemute Kid bent closer to catch his whispers.

"You remember when we foregathered on the Tanana, four years come next ice-run? I did n't care so much for her then. It was more like she was pretty, and there was a smack of excitement about it, I think. But d' ye know, I 've come to think a heap of her. She 's been a good wife to me, always at my shoulder in the pinch. And when it comes to trading, you know there is n't her equal. D' ye recollect the time she shot the Moosehorn Rapids to pull you and me off that rock, the bullets whipping the water like hailstones?—and the time of the famine at Nuklukyeto?—or when she raced the ice-run to bring the news? Yes, she 's been a good wife to me, better 'n that other one. Did n't know I 'd been there? Never told you, eh? Well, I tried it once, down in the States. That 's why I 'm here. Been raised together, too. I came away to give her a chance for divorce. She got it.

"But that 's got nothing to do with Ruth. I had thought of cleaning up and pulling for the Outside next year,—her and I,—but it 's too late. Don't send her back to her people, Kid. It 's beastly hard for a woman to go back. Think of it!—nearly four years on our bacon and beans and flour and dried fruit, and then to go back to her fish and cariboo. It 's not good for her to have tried our ways, to come to know they 're better 'n her people's, and then return to them. Take care of her, Kid,—why don't you,—but no, you always fought shy of them,—and you never told me why you came to this country. Be kind to her, and send her back to the States as soon as you can. But fix it so as she can come back,—liable to get homesick, you know.

"And the youngster—it 's drawn us closer, Kid. I only hope it is a boy. Think of it!—flesh of my flesh, Kid. He must n't stop in this country. And if it 's a girl, why she can't. Sell my furs; they 'll fetch at least five thousand, and I 've got as much more with the company. And handle my interests with yours. I think that bench claim will show up. See that he gets a good schooling; and Kid, above all, don't let him come back. This country was not made for white men.

"I 'm a gone man, Kid. Three or four sleeps at the best. You 've got to go on. You must go on! Remember, it 's my wife, it 's my boy,—O God! I hope it 's a boy! You can't stay by me,—and I charge you, a dying man, that you pull on."

"Give me three days," pleaded Malemute Kid. "You may change for the better; something may turn up."

"No."

"Just three days."

"You must pull on."

"Two days."

"It 's my wife and my boy, Kid. You would not ask it."

"One day."

"No, no! I charge—"

"Only one day. We can shave it through on the grub, and I might knock over a moose."

"No,—all right; one day, but not a minute more. And Kid, don't—don't leave me to face it alone. Do as you would ask of me. Just a shot, one pull on the trigger. You understand. Think of it! Think of it! Flesh of my flesh, and I 'll never live to see him!

"Send Ruth here. I want to say good-by and tell her that she must think of the boy and not wait till I 'm dead. She might refuse to go with you if I did n't. Good-by, old man; good-by.

"Kid! I say—a—sink a hole above the pup, next to the slide. I panned out forty cents on my shovel there.

"And Kid," he stooped lower to catch the last faint words, the dying man's surrender of his pride. "I 'm sorry—for—you know—Carmen."

Leaving the girl crying softly over her man, Malemute Kid slipped into his parka and snow-shoes, tucked his rifle under his arm, and crept away into the forest. He was no tyro in the stern sorrows of the Northland, but never had he faced so stiff a problem as this. In the abstract, it was a plain, mathematical proposition,—three possible lives as against one doomed one. But now he hesitated. For five years, shoulder to shoulder, on the rivers and trails, in the camps and mines, facing death by field and flood and famine, had they knitted the bonds of their comradeship. So close was the tie, that he had often been conscious of a vague jealousy of Ruth, from the first time she had come between. And now the severance must be hastened by his own hand.

Though he prayed for a moose, just one moose, all game seemed to have deserted the land, and nightfall found the exhausted man crawling into camp, light-handed, heavy-hearted. An uproar from the dogs and shrill cries from Ruth hastened him.

Bursting into the camp, he saw the girl in the midst of the snarling pack, laying about her with an ax. The dogs had broken the iron rule of their masters and were rushing the grub. He joined the issue with his rifle reversed, and the hoary game of natural selection was played with all the ruthlessness of its primeval environment. Rifle and ax went up and down, hit or missed with monotonous regularity; lithe bodies flashed, with wild eyes and dripping fangs; and man and beast fought for supremacy to the bitterest conclusion. Then the beaten brutes crept to the edge of the firelight, licking their wounds, voicing their misery to the stars.

The whole stock of dried salmon had been devoured, and perhaps five pounds of flour remained to tide them over two hundred miles of wilderness. Ruth returned to her husband, while Malemute Kid cut up the warm body of one of the dogs, the skull of which had been crushed by the ax. Every portion was carefully put away, save the hide and offal, cast to his fellows of the moment before.

Morning brought fresh trouble. The animals were turning on each other. Carmen, who still clung to her slender thread of life, was downed by the pack. The lash fell among them unheeded. They cringed and cried under the blows, but refused to scatter till the last wretched bit had disappeared,—bones, hide, hair, everything.

Malemute Kid went about his work, listening to Mason, who was back in Tennessee, delivering tangled discourses and wild exhortations to his brethren of other days.

Taking advantage of neighboring pines, he worked rapidly, and Ruth watched him make a cache similar to those sometimes used by hunters to preserve their meat from the wolverines and dogs. One after the other, he bent the tops of two small pines toward each other and nearly to the ground, making them fast with thongs of moose-hide. Then he beat the dogs into submission and harnessed them to two of the sleds, loading the same with everything but the furs which enveloped Mason. These he wrapped and lashed tightly about him, fastening either end of the robes to the bent pines. A single stroke of his hunting-knife would release them and send the body high in the air.

Ruth had received her husband's last wishes and made no struggle. Poor girl, she had learned the lesson of obedience well. From a child, she had bowed and seen all women bow to the lords of creation, and it did not seem in the nature of things for woman to resist. The Kid permitted her one outburst of grief, as she kissed her husband,—her own people had no such custom,—then led her to the foremost sled and helped her into her snowshoes. Blindly, instinctively, she took the gee-pole and whip, and "mushed" the dogs out on the trail. Then he returned to Mason, who had fallen into a coma; and long after she was out of sight, he crouched by the fire, waiting, hoping, praying for his comrade to die.

It is not pleasant to be alone with painful thoughts in the White Silence. The silence of gloom is merciful, shrouding one as with protection and breathing a thousand intangible sympathies; but the bright White Silence, clear and cold, under steely skies, is pitiless.

An hour passed,—two hours,—but the man would not die. At high noon, the sun, without raising its rim above the southern horizon, threw a suggestion of fire athwart the heavens, then quickly drew it back. Malemute Kid roused and dragged himself to his comrade's side. He cast one glance about him. The White Silence seemed to sneer, and a great fear came upon him. There was a sharp report; Mason swung into his aerial sepulcher; and Malemute Kid, sole speck of life, lashed the dogs into a wild gallop as he fled across the snow.

13
White Fang

THE
OUTING
MAGAZINE

WHITE FANG

BY JACK LONDON

ILLUSTRATED BY FRANK E. SCHOONOVER

PART I—THE WILD

CHAPTER I

THE TRAIL OF THE MEAT

DARK spruce forest frowned on either side the frozen waterway. The trees had been stripped by a recent wind of their white covering of frost, and they seemed to lean toward each other, black and ominous, in the fading light. A vast silence reigned over the land. The land itself was a desolation, lifeless, without movement, so lone and cold that the spirit of it was not even that of sadness. There was a hint in it of laughter, but of a laughter more terrible than any sadness—a laughter that was mirthless as the smile of the sphinx, a laughter cold as the frost and partaking of the grimness of infallibility. It was the masterful and incommunicable wisdom of eternity laughing at the futility of life and the effort of life. It was the Wild, the savage, frozen-hearted Northland Wild.

But there *was* life, abroad in the land and defiant. Down the frozen waterway toiled a string of wolfish dogs. Their bristly fur was rimed with frost. Their breath froze in the air as it left their mouths, spouting forth in spumes of vapor that settled upon the hair of their bodies and formed into crystals of frost. Leather harness was on the dogs, and leather traces attached them to a sled which dragged along behind. The sled was without runners. It was made of stout birch-bark, and its full surface rested on the snow. The front end of the sled was turned up, like a scroll, in order to force down and under the bore of soft snow that surged like a wave before it. On the sled, securely lashed, was a long and narrow oblong box. There were other things on the sled—blankets, an axe, and a coffee-pot and frying-pan; but prominent, occupying most of the space, was the long and narrow oblong box.

In advance of the dogs, on wide snowshoes, toiled a man. At the rear of the sled toiled a second man. On the sled, in the box, lay a third man, whose toil was over—a man whom the Wild had conquered and beaten down until he would never move nor struggle again. It is not the way of the Wild to like movement. Life is an offense to it, for life is movement; and the Wild aims always to destroy movement. It freezes the water to prevent it running to the sea; it drives the sap out of the trees till they are frozen to their mighty hearts; and most ferociously and terribly of all does the Wild harry and crush into submission man—man, who is the most restless of life, ever in revolt against the dictum that all movement must in the end come to the cessation of movement.

But at front and rear, unawed and indomitable, toiled the two men who were not yet dead. Their bodies were covered with fur and soft-tanned leather. Eyelashes and cheeks and lips were so coated with the crystals from their frozen breath that their faces were not discernible. This gave them the seeming of ghostly masques, undertakers in a spectral world at the funeral of some ghost. But under it all they were men, penetrating the land of desolation and mockery and silence, puny adventurers bent on colossal adventure, pitting themselves against the might of a world as remote and alien and pulseless as the abysses of space.

They traveled on without speech, saving their breath for the work of their bodies. On every side was the silence, pressing upon them with a tangible presence. It affected their minds as the many atmospheres of deep water affect the body of the diver. It crushed them with the weight of unending vastness and unalterable decree. It crushed them into the remotest recesses of their own minds, pressing out of them, like juices from the grape, all the false ardors and exaltations and undue self-values of the human soul, until they perceived themselves finite and small, specks and motes, moving with weak cunning and little wisdom amidst the play and interplay of the great blind elements and forces.

An hour went by, and a second hour. The pale light of the short, sunless day was beginning to fade, when a faint, far cry arose on the still air. It soared upward with a swift rush, till it reached its topmost note, where it persisted, palpitant and tense, and then slowly died away. It might have been a lost soul wailing, had it not been invested with a certain sad fierceness and hungry eagerness. The front man turned his head until his eyes met the eyes of the man behind. And then, across the narrow, oblong box, each nodded to the other.

A second cry arose, piercing the silence with needle-like shrillness. Both men located the sound. It was to the rear, somewhere in the snowy expanse they had just traversed. A third and answering cry arose, also to the rear and to the left of the second cry.

"They're after us, Bill," said the man at the front.

His voice sounded hoarse and unreal, and he had spoken with apparent effort.

"Meat is scarce," answered his comrade. "I ain't seen a rabbit sign for days."

Thereafter they spoke no more, though their ears were keen for the hunting-cries that continued to rise behind them.

At the fall of darkness they swung the dogs into a cluster of spruce trees on the edge of the waterway and made a camp. The coffin, at the side of the fire, served for seat and table. The wolf-dogs, clustered on the far side of the fire, snarled and bickered among themselves, but evinced no inclination to stray off into the darkness.

"Seems to me, Henry, they're stayin' remarkable close to camp," Bill commented.

Henry, squatting over the fire and settling the pot of coffee with a piece of ice, nodded. Nor did he speak till he had taken his seat on the coffin and begun to eat.

"They know where their hides is safe," he said. "They'd sooner eat grub than be grub. They're pretty wise, them dogs."

Bill shook his head. "Oh, I don't know."

His comrade looked at him curiously. "First time I ever heard you say anything about their not bein' wise."

"Henry," said the other, munching with deliberation the beans he was eating, "did you happen to notice the way them dogs kicked up when I was a-feedin' 'em?"

"They did cut up more 'n usual," Henry acknowledged.

"How many dogs 've we got, Henry?"

"Six."

"Well, Henry, . . . " Bill stopped for a moment, in order that his words might gain greater significance. "As I was sayin', Henry, we've got six dogs. I took six fish out of the bag. I gave one fish to each dog, an', Henry, I was one fish short."

"You counted wrong."

"We've got six dogs," the other reiterated dispassionately. "I took out six fish. One Ear didn't get no fish. I come back to the bag afterward an' got 'm his fish."

"We've only got six dogs," Henry said.

"Henry," Bill went on. "I won't say they was all dogs, but there was seven of 'em that got fish."

Henry stopped eating to glance across the fire and count the dogs.

"There's only six now," he said.

"I saw the other one run off across the snow," Bill announced with cool positiveness. "I saw seven."

Henry looked at him commiseratingly, and said, "I'll be almighty glad when this trip's over."

"What d'ye mean by that?" Bill demanded.

"I mean that this load of ourn is gettin' on your nerves, an' that you're beginnin' to see things."

"I thought of that," Bill answered gravely. "An' so, when I saw it run off across the snow, I looked in the snow an' saw its tracks. Then I counted the dogs an' there was still six of 'em. The tracks is there in the snow now. D'ye want to look at 'em? I'll show 'em to you."

Henry did not reply, but munched on in silence, until, the meal finished, he topped it with a final cup of coffee. He wiped his mouth with the back of his hand and said:

"Then you're thinkin' as it was——"

A long, wailing cry, fiercely sad, from somewhere in the darkness, had interrupted him. He stopped to listen to it, then he finished his sentence with a wave of his hand toward the sound of the cry, "—one of 'em?"

Bill nodded. "I'd a blame sight sooner think that than anything else. You noticed yourself the row the dogs made."

Cry after cry, and answering cries, were turning the silence into a bedlam. From every side the cries arose, and the dogs betrayed their fear by huddling together and so close to the fire that their hair was scorched by the heat. Bill threw on more wood, before lighting his pipe.

"I'm thinkin' you're down in the mouth some," Henry said.

"Henry, . . . " He sucked meditatively at his pipe for some time before he went on. "Henry, I was a-thinkin' what a blame sight luckier he is than you an' me'll ever be."

He indicated the third person by a downward thrust of the thumb to the box on which they sat.

"You an' me, Henry, when we die we'll be lucky if we get enough stones over our carcasses to keep the dogs off of us."

"But we ain't got people an' money an' all the rest, like him," Henry rejoined. "Long-distance funerals is somethin' you an' me can't exactly afford."

"What gets me, Henry, is what a chap like this, that's a lord or something in his own country, and that's never had to bother about grub nor blankets, why he comes a-buttin' round the God-forsaken ends of the earth—that's what I can't exactly see."

"He might have lived to a ripe old age if he'd stayed to home," Henry agreed.

Bill opened his mouth to speak, but changed his mind. Instead, he pointed toward the wall of darkness that pressed about them from every side. There was no suggestion of form in the utter blackness; only could be seen a pair of eyes gleaming like live coals. Henry indicated with his head a second pair, and a third. A circle of the gleaming eyes had drawn about their camp. Now and again a pair of eyes moved, or disappeared to appear again a moment later.

The unrest of the dogs had been increasing, and they stampeded, in a surge of sudden fear, to the near side of the fire, cringing and crawling about the legs of the men. In the scramble, one of the dogs had been overturned on the edge of the fire, and it had yelped with pain and fright as the smell of its singed coat possessed the air. The commotion caused the circle of eyes to shift restlessly for a moment and even to withdraw a bit, but it settled down again as the dogs became quiet.

"Henry, it's a blame misfortune to be out of ammunition."

Bill had finished his pipe and was helping his companion spread the bed of fur and blanket upon the spruce boughs which he had laid over the snow before supper. Henry grunted, and began unlacing his moccasins.

"How many cartridges did you say you had left?" he asked.

"Three," came the answer. "An' I wisht 'twas three hundred. Then I'd show 'em what for, damn 'em!"

He shook his fist angrily at the gleaming eyes, and began securely to prop his moccasins before the fire.

"An' I wisht this cold snap 'd break," he went on. "It's ben fifty below for two weeks now. An' I wisht I'd never started on this trip, Henry. I don't like the looks of it. It don't feel right, somehow. An' while I'm wishin', I wisht the trip was over an' done with, an' you an' me a-sittin' by the fire in Fort McGurry just about now an' playin' cribbage—that's what I wisht."

Henry grunted and crawled into bed. As he dozed off he was aroused by his comrade's voice.

"Say, Henry, that other one that come in an' got a fish—why didn't the dogs pitch into it? That's what's botherin' me."

"You're botherin' too much, Bill," came the sleepy response. "You was never like this before. You jes' shut up, now, an' go to sleep, an' you'll be all hunkydory in the mornin'. Your stomach's sour, that's what's botherin' you."

The men slept, breathing heavily, side by side, under the one covering. The fire died down, and the gleaming eyes drew closer the circle they had flung about the camp. The dogs clustered together in fear, now and again snarling menacingly as a pair of eyes drew close. Once, their uproar became so loud that Bill woke up. He got out of bed carefully, so as not to disturb the sleep of his comrade, and threw more wood on the fire. As it began to flame up, the circle of eyes drew farther back. He glanced casually at the huddling dogs. He rubbed his eyes and looked at them more sharply. Then he crawled back into the blankets.

"Henry," he said. "Oh, Henry."

Henry groaned as he passed from sleep to waking, and demanded, "What's wrong now?"

"Nothin'," came the answer; "only there's seven of 'em again. I just counted."

Henry acknowledged receipt of the information with a grunt that slid into a snore as he drifted back into sleep.

In the morning it was Henry who awoke first and routed his companion out of bed. Daylight was yet three hours away, though it was already six o'clock; and in the darkness Henry went about preparing breakfast, while Bill rolled the blankets and made the sled ready for lashing.

"Say, Henry," he asked suddenly, "how many dogs did you say we had?"

"Six."

"Wrong," Bill proclaimed triumphantly.

"Seven again?" Henry queried.

"No, five; one's gone."

"The hell!" Henry cried in wrath, leaving the cooking to come and count the dogs.

"You're 'right, Bill," he concluded. "Fatty's gone."

"An' he went like greased-lightnin' once he got started. Couldn't 've seen 'm for smoke."

"No chance at all," Henry concluded. "They jes' swallowed 'm alive. I bet he was yelpin' as he went down their throats, damn 'em!"

"He always was a fool dog," said Bill.

"But no fool dog ought to be fool enough to go off an' commit suicide that way." He looked over the remainder of the team with a speculative eye that summed up instantly the salient traits of each animal. "I bet none of the others would do it."

"Couldn't drive 'em away from the fire with a club," Bill agreed. "I always did think there was somethin' wrong with Fatty, anyway."

And this was the epitaph of a dead dog on the Northland trail—less scant than the epitaph of many another dog, of many a man.

CHAPTER II

THE SHE-WOLF

Breakfast eaten and the slim camp-outfit lashed to the sled, the men turned their backs on the cheery fire and launched out into the darkness. At once began to rise the cries that were fiercely sad—cries that called through the darkness and cold to one another and answered back. Conversation ceased. Daylight came at nine o'clock. At midday the sky to the south warmed to rose-color, and marked where the bulge of the earth intervened between the meridian sun and the Northern world. But the rose-color swiftly faded. The gray light of day that remained lasted until three o'clock, when it, too, faded, and the pall of the arctic night descended upon the lone and silent land.

As darkness came on, the hunting cries to right and left and rear drew closer—so close that more than once they sent surges of fear through the toiling dogs, throwing them into short-lived panics.

At the conclusion of one such panic, when he and Henry had got the dogs back in the traces, Bill said:

"I wisht they'd strike game somewheres, an' go away an' leave us alone."

"They do get on the nerves horrible," Henry sympathized.

They spoke no more until camp was made.

Henry was bending over and adding ice to the bubbling pot of beans when he was startled by the sound of a blow, an exclamation from Bill, and a sharp, snarling cry of pain from among the dogs. He straightened up in time to see a dim form disappearing across the snow into the shelter of the dark. Then he saw Bill, standing amid the dogs, half triumphant, half crestfallen, in one hand a stout club, in the other the tail and part of the body of a sun-cured salmon.

"It got half of it," he announced; "but I got a whack at it jes' the same. D'ye hear it squeal?"

"What 'd it look like?" Henry asked.

"Couldn't see. But it had four legs an' a mouth an' hair an' looked like any dog."

"Must be a tame wolf, I reckon."

"It's damned tame, whatever it is, comin' in here at feedin' time an' gettin' its whack of fish."

That night, when supper was finished and they sat on the oblong box and pulled at their pipes, the circle of gleaming eyes drew in even closer than before.

"I wisht they'd spring up a bunch of moose or something, an' go away an' leave us alone," Bill said.

Henry grunted with an intonation that was not all sympathy, and for a quarter of an hour they sat on in silence, Henry staring at the fire and Bill at the circle of eyes that burned in the darkness just beyond the fire-light.

"I wisht we was pullin' into McGurry right now," he began again.

"Shut up your wishin' an' your croakin'," Henry burst out angrily. "Your stomach's sour. That's what's ailin' you. Swallow a spoonful of sody, an' you'll sweeten up wonderful an' be more pleasant company."

In the morning Henry was aroused by fervid blasphemy that proceeded from the mouth of Bill. Henry propped himself up on an elbow and looked to see his comrade standing among the dogs beside the replenished fire, his arms raised in objuration, his face distorted with passion.

"Hello!" Henry called. "What's up now?"

"Frog's gone," came the answer.

"No!"

"I tell you yes."

Henry leaped out of the blankets and to the dogs. He counted them with care and then joined his partner in cursing the powers of the Wild that had robbed them of another dog.

"Frog was the strongest dog of the bunch," Bill pronounced finally.

"An' he was no fool dog neither," Henry added.

And so was recorded the second epitaph in two days.

A gloomy breakfast was eaten, and the four remaining dogs were harnessed to the sled. The day was a repetition of the days that had gone before. The men toiled without speech across the face of the frozen world. The silence was unbroken save by the cries of their pursuers, that, unseen, hung upon their rear. With the coming of night in the mid-afternoon the cries sounded closer, as the pursuers drew in according to their custom; and the dogs grew excited and frightened, and were guilty of panics that tangled the traces and further depressed the two men.

"There, that 'll fix you fool critters," Bill said with satisfaction that night, standing erect at completion of his task.

Henry left his cooking to come and see. Not only had his partner tied the dogs up, but he had tied them, after the Indian fashion, with sticks. About the neck of each dog he had fastened a leather thong.

To this, and so close to the neck that the dog could not get his teeth to it, he had tied a stout stick four or five feet in length. The other end of the stick, in turn, was made fast to a stake in the ground by means of a leather thong. The dog was unable to gnaw through the leather at his own end of the stick. The stick prevented him from getting at the leather that fastened the other end.

Henry nodded his head approvingly.

"It's the only contraption that 'll ever hold One Ear," he said. "He can gnaw through leather as clean as a knife an' jes' about half as quick. They all 'll be here in the mornin' hunkydory."

"You jes' bet they will," Bill affirmed. "If one of 'em turns up missin' I'll go without my coffee."

"They jes' know we ain't loaded to kill," Henry remarked at bedtime, indicating the gleaming circle that hemmed them in. "If we could put a couple of shots into 'em they'd be more respectful. They come closer every night. Get the fire-light out of your eyes an' look hard—there! Did you see that one?"

For some time the two men amused themselves with watching the movement of vague forms on the edge of the fire-light. By looking closely and steadily at where a pair of eyes burned in the darkness, the form of the animal would slowly take shape. They could even see these forms move at times.

A sound among the dogs attracted the men's attention. One Ear was uttering quick, eager whines, lunging at the length of his stick toward the darkness, and desisting now and again in order to make frantic attacks on the stick with his teeth.

"Look at that, Bill," Henry whispered.

Full into the fire-light, with a stealthy, sidelong movement, glided a dog-like animal. It moved with commingled mistrust and daring, cautiously observing the men, its attention fixed on the dogs. One Ear strained the full length of the stick toward the intruder and whined with eagerness.

"That fool One Ear don't seem scairt much," Bill said in a low tone.

"It's a she-wolf," Henry whispered back, "an' that accounts for Fatty an' Frog. She's the decoy for the pack. She draws out the dog an' then all the rest pitches in an' eats 'm up."

The fire crackled. A log fell apart with a loud, spluttering noise. At the sound of it the strange animal leaped back into the darkness.

"Henry, I'm a-thinkin'," Bill announced.

"Thinkin' what?"

"I'm a-thinkin' that was the one I lambasted with the club."

"Ain't the slightest doubt in the world," was Henry's response.

"An' right here I want to remark," Bill went on, "that that animal's familiarity with camp fires is suspicious an' immoral."

"It knows for certain more 'n a self-respectin' wolf ought to know," Henry agreed. "A wolf that knows enough to come in with the dogs at feedin' time has had experiences."

"Ol' Villan had a dog once that run away with the wolves," Bill cogitated aloud. "I ought to know. I shot it out of the pack in a moose pasture over on Little Stick. An' Ol' Villan cried like a baby. Hadn't seen it for three years, he said. Ben with the wolves all that time."

"I reckon you've called the turn, Bill. That wolf's a dog, an' it's eaten fish many's the time from the hand of man."

"An' if I get a chance at it, that wolf that's a dog 'll be jes' meat," Bill declared. "We can't afford to lose no more animals."

"But you've only got three cartridges," Henry objected.

"I'll wait for a dead sure shot," was the reply.

In the morning Henry renewed the fire and cooked breakfast to the accompaniment of his partner's snoring.

"You was sleepin' jes' too comfortable for anything," Henry told him as he routed him out for breakfast. "I hadn't the heart to rouse you."

Bill began sleepily to eat. He noticed that his cup was empty, and started to reach for the pot. But the pot was beyond arm's length and beside Henry.

"Say, Henry," he chided gently; "ain't you forgot somethin'?"

Henry looked about with great carefulness and shook his head. Bill held up the empty cup.

"You don't get no coffee," Henry announced.

"Ain't run out?" Bill asked anxiously.

"Nope."

"Ain't thinkin' it 'll hurt my digestion?"

"Nope."

A flush of angry blood pervaded Bill's face.

"Then it's jes' warm an' anxious I am to be hearin' you explain yourself," he said.

"Spanker's gone," Henry answered.

Without haste, with the air of one resigned to misfortune, Bill turned his head and from where he sat counted the dogs.

"How'd it happen?" he asked apathetically.

Henry shrugged his shoulders. "Don't know. Unless One Ear gnawed 'm loose. He couldn't 'a' done it himself, that's sure."

"The darned cuss." Bill spoke gravely and slowly, with no hint of the anger that was raging within. "Jes' because he couldn't chew himself loose, he chews Spanker loose."

"Well, Spanker's troubles is over anyway; I guess he's digested by this time an' cavortin' over the landscape in the bellies of twenty different wolves," was Henry's epitaph on this, the latest lost dog. "Have some coffee, Bill?"

But Bill shook his head.

"Go on," Henry pleaded, elevating the pot.

Bill shoved his cup aside. "I'll be ding-dong-danged if I do. I said I wouldn't if ary dog turned up missin', an' I won't."

"It's darn good coffee," Henry said enticingly.

But Bill was stubborn, and he ate a dry breakfast, washed down with mumbled curses at One Ear for the trick he had played.

"I'll tie 'em up out of reach of each other to-night," Bill said, as they took the trail.

They had traveled little more than a hundred yards, when Henry, who was in front, bent down and picked up something with which his snowshoe had collided. It was dark, and he could not see it, but he recognized it by the touch. He flung it back, so that it struck the sled and bounced along until it fetched up on Bill's snowshoes.

"Mebbe you'll need that in your business," Henry said.

Bill uttered an exclamation. It was all that was left of Spanker—the stick with which he had been tied.

"They ate 'm hide an' all," Bill announced. "The stick's as clean as a whistle. They've ate the leather offen both ends. They're damn hungry, Henry, an' they'll have you an' me guessin' before this trip's over."

Henry laughed defiantly. "I ain't been trailed this way by wolves before, but I've gone through a whole lot worse an' kept my health. Takes more 'n a handful of them pesky critters to do for yours truly, Bill, my son."

"I don't know, I don't know," Bill muttered ominously.

"Well, you'll know all right when we pull into McGurry."

"I ain't feelin' special enthusiastic," Bill persisted.

"You're off color, that's what's the matter with you," Henry dogmatized. "What you need is quinine, an' I'm goin' to dose you up stiff as soon as we make McGurry."

Bill grunted his disagreement with the diagnosis, and lapsed into silence. The day was like all the days. Light came at nine o'clock. At twelve o'clock the southern horizon was warmed by the unseen sun; and then began the cold gray of afternoon that would merge, three hours later, into night.

It was just after the sun's futile effort to appear that Bill slipped the rifle from under the sled lashings and said:

"You keep right on, Henry. I'm goin' to see what I can see."

"You'd better stick by the sled," his partner protested. "You've only got three cartridges, an' there's no tellin' what might happen."

"Who's croakin' now?" Bill demanded triumphantly.

Henry made no reply, and plodded on alone, though often he cast anxious glances back into the gray solitude where his partner had disappeared. An hour later, taking advantage of the cut-offs around which the sled had to go, Bill arrived.

"They're scattered an' rangin' along wide," he said; "keepin' up with us an' lookin' for game at the same time. You see, they're sure of us, only they know they've got to wait to get us. In the meantime they're willin' to pick up anything eatable that comes handy."

"You mean they *think* they're sure of us," Henry objected pointedly.

But Bill ignored him. "I seen some of them. They're pretty thin. They ain't had a bite in weeks, I reckon, outside of

Fatty an' Frog an' Spanker; an' there's so many of 'em that that didn't go far. They're remarkable thin. Their ribs is like washboards, an' their stomachs is right up against their backbones. They're pretty desperate, I can tell you. They'll be goin' mad, yet, an' then watch out."

A few minutes later Henry, who was now traveling behind the sled, emitted a low, warning whistle. Bill turned and looked, then quietly stopped the dogs. To the rear, from around the last bend and plainly into view, on the very trail they had just covered, trotted a furry, slinking form. Its nose was to the trail, and it trotted with a peculiar sliding effortless gait. When they halted, it halted, throwing up its head and regarding them steadily with nostrils that twitched as it caught and studied the scent of them.

"It's the she-wolf," Bill whispered.

The dogs had lain down in the snow, and he walked past them to join his partner at the sled. Together they watched the strange animal that had pursued them for days and that had already accomplished the destruction of half their dog-team.

After a searching scrutiny the animal trotted forward a few steps. This it repeated several times, till it was a short hundred yards away. It paused, head up, close by a clump of spruce trees, and with sight and scent studied the outfit of the watching men. It looked at them in a strangely wistful way, after the manner of a dog; but in its wistfulness there was none of the dog affection. It was a wistfulness bred of hunger, as cruel as its own fangs, as merciless as the frost itself.

It was large for a wolf, its gaunt frame advertising the lines of an animal that was among the largest of its kind.

"Stands pretty close to two feet an' a half at the shoulders," Henry commented. "An' I'll bet it ain't far from five feet long."

"Kind of strange color for a wolf," was Bill's criticism. "I never seen a red wolf before. Looks almost cinnamon to me."

The animal was certainly not cinnamon-colored. Its coat was the true wolf coat. The dominant color was gray, and yet there was to it a faint, reddish hue—a hue that was baffling, that appeared and disappeared, that was more like an illusion of the vision, now gray, distinctly gray, and again giving hints and glints of a vague redness of color not classifiable in terms of ordinary experience.

"Looks for all the world like a big, husky sled-dog," Bill said. "I wouldn't be s'prised to see it wag its tail.

"Hello, you husky!" he called. "Come here, you, Whatever-your-name-is!"

"Ain't a bit scairt of you," Henry laughed.

Bill waved his hand at it threateningly and shouted loudly; but the animal betrayed no fear. The only change in it that they could notice was an accession of alertness. It still regarded them with the merciless wistfulness of hunger. They were meat, and it was hungry; and it would like to go in and eat them if it dared.

"Look here, Henry," Bill said, unconsciously lowering his voice to a whisper because of what he meditated. "We've got three cartridges. But it's a dead shot. Couldn't miss it. It's got away with three of our dogs, an' we oughter put a stop to it. What d'ye say?"

Henry nodded his consent. Bill cautiously slipped the gun from under the sled lashing. The gun was on the way to his shoulder, but it never got there. For in that instant the she-wolf leaped sidewise from the trail into the clump of spruce trees and disappeared.

The two men looked at each other. Henry whistled long and comprehendingly.

"I might have knowed it," Bill chided himself aloud, as he replaced the gun. "Of course a wolf that knows enough to come in with the dogs at feedin' time, 'd know all about shooting-irons. I tell you right now, Henry, that critter's the cause of all our trouble. We'd have six dogs at the present time, 'stead of three, if it wasn't for her. An' I tell you right now, Henry, I'm goin' to get her. She's too smart to be shot in the open. But I'm goin' to lay for her. I'll bushwhack her as sure as my name is Bill."

"You needn't stray off too far in doin' it," his partner admonished. "If that pack ever starts to jump you, them three cartridges 'd be wuth no more 'n three whoops in hell. Them animals is damn hungry, an' once they start in they'll sure get you, Bill."

They camped early that night. Three dogs could not drag the sled so fast nor for so long hours as could six, and they were showing unmistakable signs of playing out. And the men went early to bed, Bill first seeing to it that the dogs were tied out of gnawing reach of one another.

But the wolves were growing bolder, and the men were roused more than once from their sleep. So near did the wolves approach that the dogs became frantic with terror, and it was necessary to replenish the fire from time to time in order to keep the adventurous marauders at safer distance.

"I've hearn sailors talk of sharks followin' a ship," Bill remarked, as he crawled back into the blankets after one such replenishing of the fire. "Well, them wolves is land sharks. They know their business better 'n we do, an' they ain't a-holdin' our trail this way for their health. They're goin' to get us. They're sure goin' to get us, Henry."

"They've half got you a'ready, a-talkin' like that," Henry retorted sharply. "A man's half licked when he says he is. An' you're half eaten from the way you're goin' on about it."

"They've got away with better men than you an' me," Bill answered.

"Oh, shet up your croakin'. You make me all-fired tired."

Henry rolled over angrily on his side, but was surprised that Bill made no similar display of temper. This was not Bill's way, for he was easily angered by sharp words. Henry thought long over it before he went to sleep, and as his eyelids fluttered down and he dozed off, the thought in his mind was: "There's no mistakin' it, Bill's almighty blue. I'll have to cheer him up to-morrow."

CHAPTER III

THE HUNGER CRY

The day began auspiciously. They had lost no dogs during the night, and they swung out upon the trail and into the silence, the darkness and the cold, with spirits that were fairly light. Bill seemed to have forgotten his forebodings of the previous night, and even waxed facetious with the dogs when, at midday, they overturned the sled on a bad piece of trail.

It was an awkward mix-up. The sled was upside down and jammed between a tree trunk and a huge rock, and they were forced to unharness the dogs in order to straighten out the tangle. The two men were bent over the sled and trying to right it, when Henry observed One Ear sidling away.

"Here, you, One Ear!" he cried, straightening up and turning around on the dog.

But One Ear broke into a run across the snow, his traces trailing behind him. And there, out in the snow of their back track, was the she-wolf waiting for him. As he neared her, he became suddenly cautious. He slowed down to an alert and mincing walk and then stopped. He regarded her carefully and dubiously, yet desirefully. She seemed to smile at him, showing her teeth in an ingratiating rather than a menacing way. She moved toward him a few steps, playfully, and then halted. One Ear drew near to her, still alert and cautious, his tail and ears in the air, his head held high.

He tried to sniff noses with her, but she retreated playfully and coyly. Every advance on his part was accompanied by a corresponding retreat on her part. Step by step she was luring him away from the security of his human companionship. Once, as though a warning had in vague ways filtered through his intelligence, he turned his head and looked back at the overturned sled, at his team mates and at the two men who were calling to him.

But whatever idea was forming in his mind was dissipated by the she-wolf, who advanced upon him, sniffed noses with him for a fleeting instant and then resumed her coy retreat before his renewed advances.

In the meantime Bill had bethought himself of the rifle. But it was jammed beneath the overturned sled, and by the time Henry had helped him to right the load, One Ear and the she-wolf were too close together and the distance too great to risk a shot.

Too late One Ear learned his mistake. Before they saw the cause the two men saw him turn and start to run back toward them. Then, approaching at right angles to the trail and cutting off his retreat, they saw a dozen wolves, lean and gray, bounding across the snow. On the instant, the she wolf's coyness and playfulness disappeared. With a snarl she sprang upon One Ear. He thrust her off with his shoulder, and, his retreat cut off and still intent on regaining the sled, he altered his course in an attempt to circle around to it. More wolves were appearing every moment and joining in the chase. The she-wolf was one leap behind One Ear and holding her own.

"Where are you goin'?" Henry suddenly demanded, laying his hand on his partner's arm.

Bill shook it off. "I won't stand it," he said. "They ain't a-goin' to get any more of our dogs if I can help it."

Gun in hand, he plunged into the underbrush that lined the side of the trail. His intention was apparent enough. Taking the sled as the center of the circle that One Ear was making, Bill planned to tap that circle at a point in advance of the pursuit. With his rifle, in the broad daylight, it might be possible for him to awe the wolves and save the dog.

"Say, Bill!" Henry called after him. "Be careful! Don't take no chances!"

Henry sat down on the sled and watched. There was nothing else for him to do. Bill had already gone from sight; but now and again, appearing and disappearing amongst the underbrush and the scattered clumps of spruce, could be seen One Ear. Henry judged his case to be hopeless. The dog was thoroughly alive to its danger, but it was running on the outer circle, while the wolf-pack was running on the inner and shorter circle. It was vain to think of One Ear so outdistancing his pursuers as to be able to cut across their circle in advance of them and to regain the sled.

The different lines were rapidly approaching a point. Somewhere out there in the snow, screened from the sight by trees and thickets, Henry knew that the wolf-pack, One Ear and Bill were coming together. All too quickly, far more quickly than he had expected, it happened. He heard a shot, then two shots in rapid succession, and he knew that Bill's ammunition was gone. Then he heard a great outcry of snarls and yelps. He recognized One Ear's yell of pain and terror, and he heard a wolf-cry that bespoke a stricken animal. And that was all. The snarls ceased The yelping died away. Silence settled down again over the lonely land.

He sat for a long while upon the sled. There was no need for him to go and see what had happened. He knew it as though it had taken place before his eyes. Once he roused with a start and hastily got the axe out from underneath the lashings. But for some time longer he sat and brooded, the two remaining dogs crouching and trembling at his feet.

At last he arose in a weary manner, as though all the resilience had gone out of his body, and proceeded to fasten the dogs to the sled. He passed a rope over his shoulder, a man-trace, and pulled with the dogs. He did not go far. At the first hint of darkness he hastened to make a camp, and he saw to it that he had a generous supply of firewood. He fed the dogs, cooked and ate his supper, and made his bed close to the fire.

But he was not destined to enjoy that bed. Before his eyes closed the wolves had drawn too near for safety. It no longer required an effort of the vision to see them. They were all about him and the fire, in a narrow circle, and he could see them plainly in the firelight, lying down, sitting up, crawling forward on their bellies, or slinking back and forth. They even slept. Here and there he could see one curled up in the snow like a dog, taking the sleep that was now denied himself.

He kept the fire brightly blazing, for he knew that it alone intervened between the flesh of his body and their hungry fangs. His two dogs stayed close by him, one on either side, leaning against him for protection, crying and whimpering, and at times snarling desperately when a wolf approached a little closer than usual. At such moments, when his dogs snarled, the whole circle would be agitated, the wolves coming to their feet and pressing tentatively forward, a chorus of snarls and eager yelps rising about him. Then the circle would lie down again, and here and there a wolf would resume its broken nap.

But this circle had a continuous tendency to draw in upon him. Bit by bit—an inch at a time, with here a wolf bellying forward, and there a wolf bellying forward, the circle would narrow until the brutes were almost within springing distance.

Then he would seize brands from the fire and hurl them into the pack. A hasty drawing back always resulted, accompanied by angry yelps and frightened snarls when a well-aimed brand struck and scorched a too-daring animal.

Morning found the man haggard and worn, wide-eyed from want of sleep. He cooked breakfast in the darkness, and at nine o'clock, when, with the coming of daylight, the wolf-pack drew back, he set about the task he had planned through the long hours of the night. Chopping down young saplings, he made them cross-bars of a scaffold by lashing them high up to the trunks of standing trees. Using the sled lashing for a heaving rope, and with the aid of the dogs, he hoisted the coffin to the top of the scaffold.

"They got Bill, an' they may get me, but they'll sure never get you, young man," he said, addressing the dead body in its tree-sepulcher.

Then he took the trail, the lightened sled bounding along behind the willing dogs; for they, too, knew that safety lay only in the gaining of Fort McGurry. The wolves were now more open in their pursuit, trotting sedately behind and ranging along on either side, their red tongues lolling out, their lean sides showing the undulating ribs with every movement. They were very lean, mere skin-bags stretched over bony frames, with strings for muscles—so lean that Henry found it in his mind to marvel that they still kept their feet and did not collapse forthright in the snow.

He did not dare travel until dark. At midday, not only did the sun warm the southern horizon, but it even thrust its upper rim, pale and golden, above the sky line. He received it as a sign. The days were growing longer. The sun was returning. But scarcely had the cheer of its light departed than he went into camp. There were still several hours of gray daylight and somber twilight, and he utilized them in chopping an enormous supply of firewood.

With night came horror. Not only were the starving wolves growing bolder, but lack of sleep was telling upon Henry. He dozed despite himself, crouching by the fire, the blankets about his shoulders, the axe between his knees, and on either side a dog pressing close against him. He awoke once and saw in front of him, not a dozen feet away, a big gray wolf, one of the largest of the pack. And even as he looked the brute deliberately stretched himself after the manner of a lazy dog, yawning full in his face and looking upon him with a possessive eye, as if, in truth, he were merely a delayed meal that was soon to be eaten.

This certitude was shown by the whole pack. Fully a score he could count, staring hungrily at him or calmly sleeping in the snow. They reminded him of children gathered about a spread table and awaiting permission to begin to eat! And he was the food they were to eat! He wondered how and when the meal would begin.

As he piled wood on the fire he discovered an appreciation of his own body which he had never felt before. He watched his moving muscles and was interested in the cunning mechanism of his fingers. By the light of the fire he crooked his fingers slowly and repeatedly, now one at a time, now all together, spreading them wide or making quick, gripping movements. He studied the nail-formation, and prodded the finger-tips, now sharply, and again softly, gauging the while the nerve-sensations produced. It fascinated him, and he grew suddenly fond of this subtle flesh of his that worked so beautifully and smoothly and delicately. Then he would cast a glance of fear at the wolf-circle drawn expectantly about him, and like a blow the realization would strike him that this wonderful body of his, this living flesh, was no more than so much meat, a quest of ravenous animals, to be torn and slashed by their hungry fangs, to be sustenance to them as the moose and the rabbit had often been sustenance to him.

He came out of a doze that was half nightmare, to see the red-hued she-wolf before him. She was not more than half a dozen feet away, sitting in the snow and wistfully regarding him. The two dogs were whimpering and snarling at his feet, but she took no notice of them. She was looking at the man, and for some time he returned her look. There was nothing threatening about her. She looked at him merely with a great wistfulness, but he knew it to be the wistfulness of an equally great hunger. He was the food, and the sight of him excited in her the gustatory sensations. Her mouth opened, the saliva drooled forth, and she licked her chops with the pleasure of anticipation.

A spasm of fear went through him. He reached hastily for a brand to throw at her. But even as he reached, and before his fingers had closed on the missile, she sprang back into safety; and he knew that she was used to having things thrown at her. She had snarled as she sprang away, baring her white fangs to their roots, all her wistfulness vanishing, being replaced by a carnivorous malignity that made him shudder. He glanced at the hand that held the brand, noticing the cunning delicacy of the fingers that gripped it, how they adjusted themselves to all the inequalities of the surface, curling over and under and about the rough wood, and in the same instant he seemed to see a vision of those same sensitive and delicate fingers being crushed and torn by the white teeth of the she-wolf. Never had he been so fond of this body of his as now when his tenure of it was so precarious.

All night, with burning brands, he fought off the hungry pack. When he dozed, despite himself, the whimpering and snarling of the dogs aroused him. Morning came, but for the first time the light of day failed to scatter the wolves. The man waited in vain for them to go. They remained in a circle about his fire, displaying an arrogance of possession that shook his courage born of the morning light.

He made one desperate attempt to pull out on the trail. But the moment he left the protection of the fire the boldest wolf leaped for him, but leaped short. He saved himself by springing back, the jaws snapping together a scant six inches from his thigh. The rest of the pack was now up and surging upon him, and a throwing of firebrands right and left was necessary to drive them back to a respectful distance.

Even in the daylight he did not dare leave the fire to chop fresh wood. Twenty feet away towered a huge dead spruce. He spent half the day extending his camp fire to the tree.

The night was a repetition of the night before, save that the need for sleep was becoming overpowering. The snarling of his dogs was losing its efficacy. Besides, they were snarling all the time, and his benumbed and drowsy senses no longer took note of changing pitch and intensity. He awoke with a start. The she-wolf was less than a yard from him. Mechanically, at short range, without letting go of it, he thrust a brand full into her open and snarling mouth. She sprang away, yelling with pain, and while he took delight in the smell of burning flesh and hair, he watched her shaking her head and growling wrathfully a score of feet away.

But this time, before he dozed again, he tied a burning pine-knot to his right hand. His eyes were closed but a few minutes when the burn of the flame on his flesh awakened him. For several hours he adhered to this programme. Every time he was thus awakened he drove back the wolves with flying brands, replenishing the fire, and rearranged the pine-knot on his hand. All worked well, but there came a time when he fastened the pine-knot insecurely. As his eyes closed it fell away from his hand.

He dreamed. It seemed to him that he was in Fort McGurry. It was warm and comfortable, and he was playing cribbage with the Factor. Also, it seemed to him that the fort was besieged by wolves. They were howling at the very gates, and sometimes he and the Factor paused from the game to listen and laugh at the futile efforts of the wolves to get in. And then, so strange was the dream, there was a crash. The door was burst open. He could see the wolves flooding into the big living-room of the fort. They were leaping straight for him and the Factor. With the bursting open of the door, the noise of their howling had increased tremendously. This howling now bothered him. His dream was merging into something else—he knew not what; but through it all, following him, persisted the howling.

And then he awoke to find the howling real. There was a great snarling and yelping. The wolves were rushing him. They were all about him and upon him. The teeth of one had closed upon his arm. Instinctively he leaped into the fire, and as he leaped he felt the sharp slash of teeth that tore through the flesh of his leg. Then began a fire fight. His stout mittens temporarily protected his hands, and he scooped live coals into the air in all directions until the camp fire took on the semblance of a volcano.

But it could not last long. His face was blistering in the heat, his eyebrows and lashes were singed off, and the heat was becoming unbearable to his feet. With a flaming brand in each hand, he sprang to the edge of the fire. The wolves had been driven back. On every side, wherever the live coals had fallen, the snow was sizzling, and every little while a retiring wolf, with wild leap and snarl, announced that one such live coal had been stepped upon.

Flinging his brands at the nearest of his enemies, the man thrust his smoldering mittens into the snow and stamped about to cool his feet. His two dogs were missing, and he well knew that they had served as a course in the protracted meal which had begun days before with Fatty, the last course of which would likely be himself in the days to follow.

"You ain't got me yet!" he cried, savagely shaking his fist at the hungry beasts.

He set to work to carry out a new idea that had come to him. He extended the fire into a large circle. Inside this circle he crouched, his sleeping outfit under him as a protection against the melting snow. When he had thus disappeared within his shelter of flame, the whole pack came curiously to the rim of the fire to see what had become of him. Hitherto they had been denied access to the fire, and they now settled down in a close-drawn circle, like so many dogs, blinking and yawning and stretching their lean bodies in the unaccustomed warmth. Then the she-wolf sat down, pointed her nose at a star, and began to howl. One by one the wolves joined her, till the whole pack, on haunches, with noses pointed skyward, was howling its hunger-cry.

Dawn came, and daylight. The fire was burning low. The fuel had run out, and there was need to get more. The man attempted to step out of his circle of flame, but the wolves surged to meet him. Burning brands made them spring aside, but they no longer sprang back. In vain he strove to drive them back. As he gave up and stumbled inside his circle a wolf leaped for him, missed, and landed with all four feet in the coals. It cried out with terror, at the same time snarling, and scrambled back to cool its paws in the snow.

The man sat down on his blankets in a crouching position. His body leaned forward from the hips. His shoulders, relaxed and drooping, and his head on his knees, advertised that he had given up the struggle. Now and again he raised his head to note the dying down of the fire. The circle of flame and coals was breaking into segments with openings in between. These openings grew in size, the segments diminished.

"I guess you can come an' get me any time," he mumbled. "Anyway, I'm goin' to sleep."

Once he wakened, and in an opening in the circle, directly in front of him, he saw the she-wolf gazing at him.

Again he awakened, a little later, though it seemed hours to him. A mysterious change had taken place—so mysterious a change that he was shocked wider awake. Something had happened. He could not understand at first. Then he discovered it. The wolves were gone. Remained only the trampled snow to show how closely they had pressed him. Sleep was welling up and gripping him again, his head was sinking down upon his knees, when he roused with a sudden start.

There were cries of men, the churn of sleds, the creaking of harnesses, and the eager whimpering of straining dogs. Four sleds pulled in from the river bed to the camp among the trees. Half a dozen men were about the man who crouched in the center of the dying fire. They were shaking and prodding him into consciousness. He looked at them like a drunken man and maundered in strange, sleepy speech:

"Red she-wolf—come in with the dogs at feedin' time—first she ate the dog food —then she ate the dogs—an' after that she ate Bill——"

"Where's Lord Alfred?" one of the men bellowed in his ear, shaking him roughly.

He shook his head slowly. "No, she didn't eat him—he's roostin' in a tree at the last camp."

"Dead?" the man shouted.

"An' in a box," Henry answered. He jerked his shoulder petulantly away from the grip of his questioner. "Say, you lemme alone—I'm jes' plumb tuckered out —Goo'-night, everybody."

His eyes fluttered and went shut. His chin fell forward on his chest. And even as they eased him down upon the blankets his snores were rising on the frosty air.

But there was another sound. Far and faint it was, in the remote distance—the cry of the hungry wolf-pack as it took the trail of other meat than the man it had just missed.

WHITE FANG

BY JACK LONDON

ILLUSTRATED BY FRANK E. SCHOONOVER

PART II—BORN OF THE WILD

CHAPTER I

THE BATTLE OF THE FANGS

IT was the she-wolf who had first caught the sound of men's voices and the whining of the sled-dogs; and it was the she-wolf who was first to spring away from the cornered man in his circle of dying flame. The pack had been loath to forego the kill it had hunted down, and it lingered for several minutes, making sure of the sounds, and then it, too, sprang away on the trail made by the she-wolf.

Running at the forefront of the pack was a large gray wolf—one of its several leaders. It was he who directed the pack's course on the heels of the she-wolf. It was he who snarled warningly at the younger members of the pack or slashed at them with his fangs when they ambitiously tried to pass him. And it was he who increased the pace when he sighted the she-wolf, now trotting slowly across the snow.

She dropped in alongside by him, as though it were her appointed position, and took the pace of the pack. He did not snarl at her, nor show his teeth, when any leap of hers chanced to put her in advance of him. On the contrary, he seemed kindly disposed toward her—too kindly to suit her, for he was prone to run near to her, and when he ran too near it was she who snarled and showed her teeth. Nor was she above slashing his shoulder sharply on occasion. At such times he betrayed no anger. He merely sprang to the side and ran stiffly ahead for several awkward leaps, in carriage and conduct resembling an abashed country swain.

This was his one trouble in the running of the pack; but she had other troubles. On her other side ran a gaunt old wolf, grizzled and marked with the scars of many battles. He ran always on her right side. The fact that he had but one eye, and that the left eye, might account for this. He, also, was addicted to crowding her, to veering toward her till his scarred muzzle touched her body, or shoulder, or neck. As with the running mate on the left, she repelled these attentions with her teeth; but when both bestowed their attentions at the same time she was roughly jostled, being compelled, with quick snaps to either side, to drive both lovers away and at the same time to maintain her forward leap with the pack and see the way of her feet before her. At such times her running mates flashed their teeth and growled threateningly across at each other. They might have fought, but even wooing and its rivalry waited upon the more pressing hunger-need of the pack.

After each repulse, when the old wolf sheered abruptly away from the sharp-toothed object of his desire, he shouldered against a young three-year-old that ran on his blind right side. This young wolf had attained his full size; and, considering the weak and famished condition of the pack, he possessed more than the average vigor and spirit. Nevertheless, he ran with his head even with the shoulder of his one-eyed elder. When he ventured to run abreast of the older wolf (which was seldom), a snarl and a snap sent him back even with the shoulder again. Sometimes, however, he dropped cautiously and slowly behind and edged in between the old leader and the she-wolf. This was doubly resented, even triply resented.

When she snarled her displeasure, the old leader would whirl on the three-year-old. Sometimes she whirled with him. And sometimes the young leader on the left whirled, too.

At such times, confronted by three sets of savage teeth, the young wolf stopped precipitately, throwing himself back on his haunches, with fore legs stiff, mouth menacing, and mane bristling. This confusion in the front of the moving pack always caused confusion in the rear. The wolves behind collided with the young wolf and expressed their displeasure by administering sharp nips on his hind legs and flanks. He was laying up trouble for himself, for lack of food and short tempers went together; but with the boundless faith of youth he persisted in repeating the maneuver every little while, though it never succeeded in gaining anything for him but discomfiture.

Had there been food, love-making and fighting would have gone on apace, and the pack formation would have been broken up. But the situation of the pack was desperate. It was lean with long-standing hunger. It ran below its ordinary speed. At the rear limped the weak members, the very young and the very old. At the front were the strongest. Yet all were more like skeletons than full-bodied wolves. Nevertheless, with the exception of the ones that limped, the movements of the animals were effortless and tireless. Their stringy muscles seemed founts of inexhaustible energy. Behind every steel-like contraction of a muscle lay another steel-like contraction, and another and another, apparently without end.

They ran many miles that day. They ran through the night. And the next day found them still running. They were running over the surface of a world frozen and dead. No life stirred. They alone moved through the vast inertness. They alone were alive, and they sought for other things that were alive in order that they might devour them and continue to live.

They crossed low divides and ranged a dozen small streams in a lower-lying country before their quest was rewarded. Then they came upon moose. It was a big bull they first found. Here was meat and life, and it was guarded by no mysterious fires nor flying missiles of flame. Splay hoofs and palmated antlers they knew, and they flung their customary patience and caution to the wind. It was a brief fight and fierce. The big bull was beset on every side. He ripped them open or split their skulls with shrewdly driven blows of his great hoofs. He crushed them and broke them on his large horns. He stamped them into the snow under him in the wallowing struggle. But he was foredoomed, and he went down with the she-wolf tearing savagely at his throat, and with other teeth fixed everywhere upon him, devouring him alive, before ever his last struggle ceased or his last damage had been wrought.

There was food in plenty. The bull weighed over eight hundred pounds—fully twenty pounds of meat per mouth for the forty-odd wolves of the pack. But if they could fast prodigiously they could feed prodigiously, and soon a few scattered bones were all that remained of the splendid live brute that had faced the pack a few hours before.

There was now much resting and sleeping. With full stomachs, bickering and quarreling began among the younger males, and this continued through the few days that followed before the breaking-up of the pack. The famine was over. The wolves were now in the country of game, and though they still hunted in pack, they hunted more cautiously, cutting out heavy cows or crippled old bulls from the small moose-herds they ran across.

There came a day, in this land of plenty, when the wolf-pack split in half and went in different directions. The she-wolf, the young leader on her left, and the one-eyed elder on her right, led their half of the pack down to the Mackenzie River and across into the lake country to the east. Each day this remnant of the pack dwindled. Two by two, male and female, the wolves were deserting. Occasionally a solitary male was driven out by the sharp teeth of his rivals. In the end there remained only four: the she-wolf, the young leader, the one-eyed one, and the ambitious three-year-old.

The she-wolf had by now developed a ferocious temper. Her three suitors all bore the marks of her teeth. Yet they never replied in kind, never defended themselves against her. They turned their shoulders to her most savage slashes, and with wagging tails and mincing steps strove to placate her wrath. But if they were all mildness toward her, they were all fierceness toward one another. The three-year-old grew too ambitious in his fierceness. He caught the one-eyed elder on his blind side and ripped his ear into ribbons. Though the grizzled old fellow could see only on one side, against the youth and vigor of the other he brought into play the wisdom of long years of experience. His lost eye and his scarred muzzle bore evidence to the nature of his experience. He had survived too many battles to be in doubt for a moment about what to do.

The battle began fairly, but it did not end fairly. There was no telling what the outcome would have been, for the third wolf joined the elder, and together, old leader and young leader, they attacked the ambitious three-year-old and proceeded to destroy him. He was beset on either side by the merciless fangs of his erstwhile comrades. Forgotten were the days they had hunted together, the game they had pulled down, the famine they had suffered. That business was a thing of the past. The business of love was at hand—ever a sterner and crueler business than that of food-getting.

And in the meanwhile the she-wolf, the cause of it all, sat down contentedly on her haunches and watched. She was even pleased. This was her day—and it came not often—when manes bristled, and fang smote fang or ripped and tore the yielding flesh, all for the possession of her.

And in the business of love the three-year-old, who had made this his first adventure upon it, yielded up his life. On either side of his body stood his two rivals. They were gazing at the she-wolf, who sat smiling in the snow. But the elder leader was wise, very wise, in love even as in battle. The younger leader turned his head to lick a wound on his shoulder. The curve of his neck was turned toward his rival. With his one eye the elder saw the opportunity. He darted in low and closed with his fangs. It was a long, ripping slash, and deep as well. His teeth, in passing, burst the wall of the great vein of the throat. Then he leaped clear.

The young leader snarled terribly, but his snarl broke midmost into a tickling cough. Bleeding and coughing, already stricken, he sprang at the elder and fought while life faded from him, his legs going weak beneath him, the light of day dulling on his eyes, his blows and springs falling shorter and shorter.

And all the while the she-wolf sat on her haunches and smiled. She was made glad in vague ways by the battle, for this was the love-making of the Wild, the sex-tragedy of the natural world that was tragedy only to those that died. To those that survived it was not tragedy, but realization and achievement.

When the young leader lay in the snow and moved no more, One Eye stalked over to the she-wolf. His carriage was one of mingled triumph and caution. He was plainly expectant of a rebuff, and he was just as plainly surprised when her teeth did not flash out at him in anger. For the first time she met him with a kindly manner. She sniffed noses with him, and even condescended to leap about and frisk and play with him in quite puppyish fashion. And he, for all his gray years and sage experience, behaved quite as puppyishly and even a little more foolishly.

Forgotten already were the vanquished rivals and the love tale red-written on the snow. Forgotten, save once, when old One Eye stopped for a moment to lick his stiffening wounds. Then it was that his lips half writhed into a snarl, and the hair of his neck and shoulders involuntarily bristled, while he half-crouched for a spring, his claws spasmodically clutching into the snow surface for firmer footing. But it was all forgotten the next moment as he sprang after the she-wolf, who was coyly leading him a chase through the woods.

After that they ran side by side, like good friends who have come to an understanding. The days passed by, and they kept together, hunting their meat and killing and eating it in common. After a time the she-wolf began to grow restless. She seemed to be searching for something that she could not find. The hollows under fallen trees seemed to attract her, and she spent much time nosing about among the larger snow-piled crevices in the rocks and in the caves of overhanging banks. Old One Eye was not interested at all, but he followed her good-naturedly in her quest,

Drawing by Frank E. Schoonover.

"In the full glare of the afternoon light, crouching in the entrance of the cave, the cubs saw the lynx mother."

and when her investigations in particular places were unusually protracted he would lie down and wait until she was ready to go on.

They did not remain in one place, but traveled across country until they regained the Mackenzie River, down which they slowly went, leaving it often to hunt game along the small streams that entered it, but always returning to it again. Sometimes they chanced upon other wolves, usually in pairs; but there was no friendliness of intercourse displayed on either side, no gladness at meeting, no desire to return to the pack formation. Several times they encountered solitary wolves. These were always males, and they were pressingly insistent on joining with One Eye and his mate. This he resented, and when she stood shoulder to shoulder with him, bristling and showing her teeth, the aspiring solitary ones would back off, turn tail, and continue on their lonely way.

One moonlight night, running through the quiet forest, One Eye suddenly halted. His muzzle went up, his tail stiffened, and his nostrils dilated as he scented the air. One foot also he held up, after the manner of a dog. He was not satisfied, and he continued to smell the air, striving to understand the message borne upon it to him. One careless sniff had satisfied his mate, and she trotted on to reassure him. Though he followed her, he was still dubious, and he could not forbear an occasional halt in order more carefully to study the warning.

She crept out cautiously on the edge of a large open space in the midst of the trees. For some time she stood alone. Then One Eye, creeping and crawling, every sense on the alert, every hair radiating infinite suspicion, joined her. They stood side by side, watching and listening and smelling.

To their ears came the sounds of dogs wrangling and scuffling, the guttural cries of men, the sharper voices of scolding women, and once the shrill and plaintive cry of a child. With the exception of the huge bulks of the skin lodges, little could be seen save the flames of the fire, broken by the movements of intervening bodies, and the smoke rising slowly on the quiet air. But to their nostrils came the myriad smells of an Indian camp, carrying a story that was largely incomprehensible to One Eye, but every detail of which the she-wolf knew.

She was strangely stirred, and sniffed and sniffed with an increasing delight. But old One Eye was doubtful. He betrayed his apprehension, and started tentatively to go. She turned and touched his neck with her muzzle in a reassuring way, then regarded the camp again. A new wistfulness was in her face, but it was not the wistfulness of hunger. She was thrilling to a desire that urged her to go forward, to be in closer to that fire, to be squabbling with the dogs and to be avoiding and dodging the stumbling feet of men.

One Eye moved impatiently beside her; her unrest came back upon her, and she knew again her pressing need to find the thing for which she searched. She turned and trotted back into the forest, to the great relief of One Eye, who trotted a little to the fore until they were well within the shelter of the trees.

As they slid along, noiseless as shadows, in the moonlight, they came upon a runway. Both noses went down to the footprints in the snow. These footprints were very fresh. One Eye ran ahead cautiously, his mate at his heels. The broad pads of their feet were spread wide and in contact with the snow were like velvet. One Eye caught sight of a dim movement of white in the midst of the white. His sliding gait had been deceptively swift, but it was as nothing to the speed at which he now ran. Before him was bounding the faint patch of white he had discovered.

They were running along a narrow alley flanked on either side by a growth of young spruce. Through the trees the mouth of the alley could be seen, opening out on a moonlit glade. Old One Eye was rapidly overhauling the fleeing shape of white. Bound by bound he gained. Now he was upon it. One leap more and his teeth would be sinking into it. But that leap was never made. High in the air, and straight up, soared the shape of white, now a struggling snowshoe rabbit that leaped and bounded, executing a fantastic dance there above him in the air and never once returning to earth.

One Eye sprang back with a snort of sudden fright, then shrank down to the snow and crouched, snarling threats at this thing of fear he did not understand. But the she-wolf coolly thrust past him. She poised for a moment, then sprang for the dancing rabbit. She, too, soared high, but not so high as the quarry, and her teeth clipped emptily together with a metallic snap. She made another leap, and another.

Her mate had slowly relaxed from his crouch and was watching her. He now evinced displeasure at her repeated failures, and himself made a mighty spring upward. His teeth closed upon the rabbit, and he bore it back to earth with him. But at the same time there was a suspicious crackling movement beside him, and his astonished eye saw a young spruce sapling bending down above him to strike him. His jaws let go their grip, and he leaped backward to escape this strange danger, his lips drawn back from his fangs, his throat snarling, every hair bristling with rage and fright. And in that moment the sapling reared its slender length upright and the rabbit soared dancing in the air again.

The she-wolf was angry. She sank her fangs into her mate's shoulder in reproof; and he, frightened, unaware of what constituted this new onslaught, struck back ferociously and in still greater fright, ripping down the side of the she-wolf's muzzle. For him to resent such reproof was equally unexpected to her, and she sprang upon him in snarling indignation. Then he discovered his mistake and tried to placate her. But she proceeded to punish him roundly, until he gave over all attempts at placation, and whirled in a circle, his head away from her, his shoulders receiving the punishment of her teeth.

In the meantime the rabbit danced above them in the air. The she-wolf sat down in the snow, and old One Eye, now more in fear of his mate than of the mysterious sapling, again sprang for the rabbit. As he sank back with it between his teeth, he kept his eye on the sapling. As before, it followed him back to earth. He crouched down under the impending blow, his hair bristling, but his teeth still keeping tight hold of the rabbit. But the blow did not fall. The sapling remained bent above him. When he moved it moved, and he growled at it through his clenched jaws; when he remained still, it remained still, and he concluded it was safer to continue remaining still. Yet the warm blood of the rabbit tasted good in his mouth.

It was his mate who relieved him from the quandary in which he found himself. She took the rabbit from him, and while the sapling swayed and teetered threateningly above her she calmly gnawed off the rabbit's head. At once the sapling shot up, and after that gave no more trouble, remaining in the decorous and perpendicular position in which nature had intended it to grow. Then between them the she-wolf and One Eye devoured the game which the mysterious sapling had caught for them.

There were other runways and alleys where rabbits were hanging in the air, and the wolf pair prospected them all, the she-wolf leading the way, old One Eye following and observant, learning the method of robbing snares—a knowledge destined to stand him in good stead in the days to come.

CHAPTER II

THE LAIR

For two days the she-wolf and One Eye hung about the Indian camp. He was worried and apprehensive, yet the camp lured his mate and she was loath to depart. But when, one morning, the air was rent with the report of a rifle close at hand, and a bullet smashed against a tree trunk several inches from One Eye's head, they hesitated no more, but went off on a long, swinging lope that put quick miles between them and the danger.

They did not go far—a couple of days' journey. The she-wolf's need to find the thing for which she searched had now become imperative. She was getting very heavy and could run but slowly. Once, in the pursuit of a rabbit, which she ordinarily would have caught with ease, she gave over and lay down and rested. One Eye came to her; but when he touched her neck gently with his muzzle she snapped at him with such quick fierceness that he tumbled over backward and cut a ridiculous figure in his effort to escape her teeth. Her temper was now shorter than ever; but he had become more patient than ever and more solicitous.

And then she found the thing for which she sought. It was a few miles up a small stream that in the summer time flowed into the Mackenzie, but that then was frozen over and frozen down to its rocky bottom—a dead stream of solid white from source to mouth. The she-wolf was trotting wearily along, her mate well in advance, when she came upon the overhanging high clay bank. She turned aside and trotted over to it. The wear and tear of spring storms and melting snows had underwashed the bank, and in one place had made a small cave out of a narrow fissure.

She paused at the mouth of the cave and looked the wall over carefully. Then, on one side and the other, she ran along the base of the wall to where its abrupt bulk merged from the softer-lined landscape. Returning to the cave, she entered its narrow mouth. For a short three feet she was compelled to crouch, then the walls widened and rose higher in a little round chamber nearly six feet in diameter. The roof barely cleared her head. It was dry and cozy. She inspected it with painstaking care, while One Eye, who had returned, stood in the entrance and patiently watched her. She dropped her head, with her nose to the ground and directed toward a point near to her closely bunched feet, and around this point she circled several times; then, with a tired sigh that was almost a grunt, she curled her body in, relaxed her legs, and dropped down, her head toward the entrance. One Eye, with pointed, interested ears, laughed at her, and beyond, outlined against the white light, she could see the brush of his tail waving good-naturedly. Her own ears, with a snuggling movement, laid their sharp points backward and down against the head for a moment, while her mouth opened and her tongue lolled peaceably out, and in this way she expressed that she was pleased and satisfied.

One Eye was hungry. Though he lay down in the entrance and slept, his sleep was fitful. He kept awaking and cocking his ears at the bright world without, where the April sun was blazing across the snow. When he dozed, upon his ears would steal the faint whispers of hidden trickles of running water, and he would rouse and listen intently. The sun had come back, and all the awakening Northland world was calling to him. Life was stirring. The feel of spring was in the air, the feel of growing life under the snow, of sap ascending in the trees, of buds bursting the shackles of the frost.

He cast anxious glances at his mate, but she showed no desire to get up. He looked ouside, and half a dozen snow-birds fluttered across his field of vision. He started to get up, then looked back at his mate again and settled down and dozed. A shrill and minute singing stole upon his hearing. Once, and twice, he sleepily brushed his nose with his paw. Then he woke up. There, buzzing in the air at the tip of his nose, was a lone mosquito. It was a full-grown mosquito, one that had lain frozen in a dry log all winter and that had now been thawed out by the sun. He could resist the call of the world no longer. Besides, he was hungry.

He crawled over to his mate and tried to persuade her to get up. But she only snarled at him, and he walked out alone into the bright sunshine to find the snow surface soft under foot, and the traveling difficult. He went up the frozen bed of the stream, where the snow, shaded by the trees, was yet hard and crystalline. He was gone eight hours, and he came back through the darkness hungrier than when he had started. He had found game, but he had not caught it. He had broken through the melting snow-crust and wallowed, while the snowshoe rabbits had skimmed along on top lightly as ever.

He paused at the mouth of the cave with a sudden shock of suspicion. Faint, strange sounds came from within. They were sounds not made by his mate, and yet they were remotely familiar. He bellied cautiously inside and was met by a warning snarl from the she-wolf. This he received without perturbation, though he obeyed it by keeping his distance; but he remained interested in the other sounds—faint, muffled sobbings and slubberings.

His mate warned him irritably away, and he curled up and slept in the entrance. When morning came and a dim light pervaded the lair, he again sought after the source of the remotely familiar sounds. There was a new note in his mate's warning snarl. It was a jealous note, and he was very careful in keeping a respectful distance. Nevertheless, he made out, sheltering between her legs against the length of her body, five strange little bundles of life, very feeble, very helpless, making tiny whimpering noises, with eyes that did not open to the light. He was surprised. It was not the first time in his long and successful life that this thing had happened. It had happened many times, yet each time it was as fresh a surprise as ever to him.

His mate looked at him anxiously. Every little while she emitted a low growl, and at times, when it seemed to her he approached too near, the growl shot up in her throat to a sharp snarl. Of her own experience she had no memory of the thing happening; but in her instinct, which was the experience of all the mothers of wolves, there lurked a memory of fathers that had eaten their new-born and helpless progeny. It manifested itself as a fear strong within her, that made her prevent One Eye from more closely inspecting the cubs he had fathered.

But there was no danger. Old One Eye was feeling the urge of an impulse, that was, in turn, an instinct that had come down to him from all the fathers of wolves. He did not question it, nor puzzle over it. It was there, in the fiber of his being; and it was the most natural thing in the world that he should obey it by turning his back on his new-born family and by trotting out and away on the meat trail whereby he lived.

Five or six miles from the lair the stream divided, its forks going off among the mountains at a right angle. Here, leading up the left fork, he came upon a fresh track. He smelled it and found it so recent that he crouched swiftly and looked in the direction in which it disappeared. Then he turned deliberately and took the right fork. The footprint was much larger than the one his own feet made, and he knew that in the wake of such a trail there was little meat for him.

Half a mile up the right fork, his quick ears caught the sound of gnawing teeth. He stalked the quarry and found it to be a porcupine, standing upright against a tree and trying his teeth on the bark. One Eye approached carefully, but hopelessly. He knew the breed, though he had never met it so far north before; and never in his long life had porcupine served him for a meal. But he had long since learned that there was such a thing as Chance, or Opportunity, and he continued to draw near. There was never any telling what might happen, for with live things events were somehow always happening differently.

The porcupine rolled itself into a ball, radiating long sharp needles in all directions that defied attack. In his youth One Eye had once sniffed too near a similar apparently inert ball of quills, and had the tail flick out suddenly in his face. One quill he had carried away in his muzzle, where it had remained for weeks, a rankling flame, until it finally worked out. So he lay down, in a comfortable crouching position, his nose fully a foot away and out of the line of the tail. Thus he waited, keeping perfectly quiet. There was no telling. Something might happen. The porcupine might unroll. There might be opportunity for a deft and ripping thrust of paw into the tender, unguarded belly.

But at the end of half an hour he arose, growled wrathfully at the motionless ball and trotted on. He had waited too often and futilely in the past for porcupines to unroll, to waste any more time. He continued up the right fork. The day wore along, and nothing rewarded his hunt.

The urge of his awakened instinct of fatherhood was strong upon him. He must find meat. In the afternoon he blundered upon a ptarmigan. He came out of a thicket and found himself face to face with the slow-witted bird. It was sitting on a log, not a foot beyond the end of his nose. Each saw the other. The bird made a startled rise, but he struck it with his paw and smashed it down to earth, then pounced upon it and caught it in his teeth as it scuttled across the snow trying to rise in the air again. As his teeth crunched through the tender flesh and fragile bones, he began naturally to eat. Then he remembered, and, turning on the back-track, started for home, carrying the ptarmigan in his mouth.

A mile above the forks, running velvet-footed as was his custom, a gliding shadow that cautiously prospected each new vista of the trail, he came upon later imprints of the large tracks he had discovered in the early morning. As the track led his way, he followed, prepared to meet the maker of it at every turn of the stream.

He slid his head around a corner of rock, where began an unusually large bend in the stream, and his quick eyes made out something that sent him crouching swiftly down. It was the maker of the track, a large female lynx. She was crouching, as he had crouched once that day, in front of her the tight-rolled ball of quills. If he had been a gliding shadow before, he now became the ghost of such a shadow, as he crept and circled around and came up well to leeward of the silent, motionless pair.

He lay down in the snow, depositing the ptarmigan beside him, and with eyes peering through the needles of a low-growing spruce he watched the play of life before him—the waiting lynx and the waiting porcupine, each intent on life; and, such was the curiousness of the game, the way of life for one lay in the eating of the other, and the way of life for the other lay in being not eaten. While old One Eye, the wolf, crouching in the covert, played his part too, in the game, waiting for some strange freak of Chance that might help him on the meat trail which was his way of life.

Half an hour passed, an hour; and nothing happened. The ball of quills might have been a stone for all it moved; the lynx might have been frozen to marble; and old One Eye might have been dead. Yet all three animals were keyed to a tenseness of living that was almost painful, and scarcely ever would it come to them to be more alive than they were then in their seeming petrifaction.

One Eye moved slightly and peered forth with increased eagerness. Something was happening. The porcupine had at last decided that its enemy had gone away. Slowly, cautiously, it was unrolling its ball of impregnable armor. It was agitated by no tremor of anticipation. Slowly, slowly, the bristling ball straightened out and lengthened. One Eye, watching, felt a sudden moistness in his mouth and a drooling of saliva, involuntary, excited by the living meat that was spreading itself like a repast before him.

Not quite entirely had the porcupine unrolled when it discovered its enemy. In that instant the lynx struck. The blow was like a flash of light. The paw, with rigid claws curving like talons, shot under the tender belly and came back with a swift ripping movement. Had the porcupine been entirely unrolled, or had it not discovered its enemy a fraction of a second before the blow was struck, the paw would have escaped unscathed, but a side-flick of the tail sank sharp quills into it as it was withdrawn.

Everything had happened at once—the blow, the counter blow, the squeal of agony from the porcupine, the big cat's squall of sudden hurt and astonishment. One Eye half arose in his excitement, his ears up, his tail straight out and quivering behind him. The lynx's bad temper got the best of her. She sprang savagely at the thing that had hurt her. But the porcupine, squealing and grunting, with disrupted anatomy trying feebly to roll up into its ball protection, flicked out its tail again, and again the big cat squalled with hurt and astonishment. Then she fell to backing away and sneezing, her nose bristling with quills like a monstrous pin-cushion. She brushed her nose with her paws, trying to dislodge the fiery darts, thrust it into the snow, and rubbed it against twigs and branches, and all the time leaped about, ahead, sidewise, up and down, in a frenzy of pain and fright.

She sneezed continually, and her stub of a tail was doing its best toward lashing about by giving quick, violent jerks. She quit her antics, and quieted down for a long minute. One Eye watched. And even he could not repress a start and an involuntary bristling of hair along his back, when she suddenly leaped, without warning, straight up in the air, at the same time emitting a long and most terrible squall. Then she sprang away, up the trail, squalling with every leap she made.

It was not until her racket had faded away in the distance and died out that One Eye ventured forth. He walked as delicately as though all the snow were carpeted with porcupine quills, erect and ready to pierce the soft pads of his feet. The porcupine met his approach with a furious squealing and a clashing of its long teeth. It had managed to roll up in a ball again, but it was not quite the old compact ball; its muscles were too much torn for that. It had been ripped almost in half, and was still bleeding profusely.

One Eye scooped out mouthfuls of the blood-soaked snow, and chewed and tasted and swallowed. This served as a relish, and his hunger increased mightily; but he was too old in the world to forget his caution. He waited. He lay down and waited, while the porcupine grated its teeth and uttered grunts and sobs and occasional sharp little squeals. In a little while One Eye noticed that the quills were drooping and that a great quivering had set up. The quivering came to an end suddenly. There was a final defiant clash of the long teeth. Then all the quills drooped quite down, and the body relaxed and moved no more.

With a nervous, shrinking paw One Eye stretched out the porcupine to its full length and turned it over on its back. Nothing had happened. It was surely dead. He studied it intently for a moment, then took a careful grip with his teeth and started off down the stream, partly carrying, partly dragging the porcupine, with head turned to the side so as to avoid stepping on the prickly mass. He recollected something, dropped the burden, and trotted back to where he had left the ptarmigan. He did not hesitate a moment. He knew clearly what was to be done, and this he did by promptly eating the ptarmigan. Then he returned and took up his burden.

When he dragged the result of his day's hunt into the cave, the she-wolf inspected it, turned her muzzle to him, and lightly licked him on the neck. But the next instant she was warning him away from the cubs with a snarl that was less harsh than usual and that was more apologetic than menacing. Her instinctive fear of the father of her progeny was toning down. He was behaving as a wolf-father should, and manifesting no unholy desire to devour the young lives she had brought into the world.

CHAPTER III

THE GRAY CUB

He was different from his brothers and sisters. Their hair already betrayed the reddish hue inherited from their mother, the she-wolf; while he alone, in this particular, took after his father. He was the one little gray cub of the litter. He had bred true to the straight wolf-stock—in fact, he had bred true to old One Eye himself in physical respects, with but a single exception, and that was that he had two eyes to his father's one.

The gray cub's eyes had not been open long, yet already he could see with steady clearness. And while his eyes were still closed, he had felt, tasted and smelled. He knew his two brothers and his two sisters very well. He had begun to romp with them in a feeble, awkward way, and even to squabble, his little throat vibrating with a queer rasping noise (the forerunner of the growl) as he worked himself into a passion. And long before his eyes had opened he had learned, by touch, taste and smell, to know his mother—a fount of warmth and liquid food and tenderness. She possessed a gentle, caressing tongue that soothed him when it passed over his soft little body, and that impelled him to snuggle close against her and to doze off to sleep.

Most of the first month of his life had been passed thus in sleeping; but now he could see quite well, and he stayed awake for longer periods of time, and he was coming to learn his world quite well. His world was gloomy; but he did not know that, for he knew no other world. It was dim-lighted; but his eyes had never had to adjust themselves to any other light. His world was very small. Its limits were the walls of the lair; but as he had no knowledge of the wide world outside, he was never oppressed by the narrow confines of his existence.

But he had early discovered that one wall of his world was different from the rest. This was the mouth of the cave and the source of light. He had discovered that it was different from the other walls long before he had any thoughts of his own, any conscious volitions. It had been an irresistible attraction before ever his eyes opened and looked upon it. The light from it had beat upon his sealed lids, and the eyes and the optic nerves had pulsated to little, spark-like flashes, warm-colored and strangely pleasing. The life of his body, and of every fiber of his body, the life that was the very substance of his body and that was apart from his own personal life, had yearned toward this light and urged his body toward it in the same way that the cunning chemistry of a plant urges it toward the sun.

Always, in the beginning, before his conscious life dawned, he had crawled toward the mouth of the cave. And in this his brothers and sisters were one with him. Never, in that period, did any of them crawl toward the dark corners of the back wall. The light drew them as if they were plants; the chemistry of the life that composed them demanded the light as a necessity of being; and their little puppet bodies crawled blindly and chemically, like the tendrils of a vine. Later on, when each developed individuality and became personally conscious of impulsions and desires, the attraction of the light increased. They were always crawling and sprawling toward it, and being driven back from it by their mother.

It was in this way that the gray cub learned other attributes of his mother than the soft, soothing tongue. In his insistent crawling toward the light, he discovered in her a nose that with a sharp nudge administered rebuke, and later a paw that crushed him down or rolled him over and over with swift, calculating stroke. Thus he learned hurt; and on top of it he learned to avoid hurt, first, by not incurring the risk of it; and second, when he had incurred the risk, by dodging and by retreating. These were conscious actions, and were the results of his first generalizations upon the world. Before that he had recoiled automatically from hurt, as he had crawled automatically toward the light. After that he recoiled from hurt because he *knew* that it was hurt.

He was a fierce little cub. So were his brothers and sisters. It was to be expected. He was a carnivorous animal. He came of a breed of meat-killers and meat-eaters. His father and mother lived wholly upon meat. The milk he had sucked with his first flickering life was milk transformed directly from meat, and now, at a month old, when his eyes had been open for but a week, he was beginning himself to eat meat—meat half digested by the she-wolf, and disgorged for the five growing cubs that already made too great demand upon her breast.

But he was, further, the fiercest of the litter. He could make a louder rasping growl than any of them. His tiny rages were much more terrible than theirs. It was he that first learned the trick of rolling a fellow-cub over with a cunning paw-stroke. And it was he that first gripped another cub by the ear and pulled and tugged and growled through jaws tight-clenched. And certainly it was he that caused the mother the most trouble in keeping her litter from the mouth of the cave.

The fascination of the light for the gray cub increased from day to day. He was perpetually departing on yard-long adventures toward the cave's entrance, and as perpetually being driven back. Only he did not know it for an entrance. He did not know anything about entrances—passages whereby one goes from one place to another place. He did not know any other place, much less of a way to get there. So to him the entrance of the cave was a wall—a wall of light. As the sun was to the outside dweller, this wall was to him the sun of his world. It attracted him as a candle attracts a moth. He was always striving to attain it. The life that was so swiftly expanding within him urged him continually toward the wall of light. The life that was within him knew that it was the one way out, the way he was predestined to tread. But he himself did not know anything about it. He did not know there was any outside at all.

There was one strange thing about this wall of light. His father (he had already come to recognize his father as the one other dweller in the world, a creature like his mother, who slept near the light and was a bringer of meat)—his father had a way of walking right into the white, far wall and disappearing. The gray cub could not understand this. Though never permitted by his mother to approach that wall, he had approached the other walls, and encountered hard obstruction on the end of his tender nose. This hurt. And after several such adventures he left the walls alone. Without thinking about it, he accepted this disappearing into the wall as a peculiarity of his father, as milk and half-digested meat were peculiarities of his mother.

In fact, the gray cub was not given to thinking—at least, to the kind of thinking customary of men. His brain worked in dim ways. Yet his conclusions were as sharp and distinct as those achieved by men. He had a method of accepting things, without questioning the why and wherefore. In reality, this was the act of classification. He was never disturbed over *why* a thing happened. *How* it happened was sufficient for him. Thus, when he had bumped his nose on the back wall a few times, he accepted that he could not disappear into walls. In the same way he accepted that his father could disappear into walls. But he was not in the least disturbed by desire to find out the reason for the difference between his father and himself. Logic and physics were no part of his mental make-up.

Like most creatures of the Wild, he early experienced famine. There came a time when not only did the meat-supply cease, but the milk no longer came from his mother's breast. At first, the cubs whimpered and cried, but for the most part they slept. It was not long before they were reduced to a coma of hunger. There were no more spats and squabbles, no more tiny rages nor attempts at growling; while the adventures toward the far, white wall ceased altogether. The cubs slept, while the life that was in them flickered and died down.

One Eye was desperate. He ranged far and wide, and slept but little in the lair that had now become cheerless and miserable. The she-wolf, too, left her litter and went out in search of meat. In the first days after the birth of the cubs One Eye had journeyed several times back to the Indian camp and robbed the rabbit snares; but, with the melting of the snow and the opening of the streams, the Indian camp had moved away, and that source of supply was closed to him.

When the gray cub came back to life and again took interest in the far white wall, he found that the population of his world had been reduced. Only one sister remained to him. The rest were gone. As he grew stronger, he found himself compelled to play alone, for the sister no longer lifted her head nor moved about. His little body rounded out with the meat he now ate; but the food had come too late for her. She slept continuously, a tiny skeleton flung round with skin in which the flame flickered lower and lower and at last went out.

Then there came a time when the gray cub no longer saw his father appearing and disappearing in the wall nor lying down asleep in the entrance. This had happened at the end of a second and less severe famine. The she-wolf knew why One Eye never came back, but there was no way by which she could tell what she had seen to the gray cub. Hunting herself for meat, up the left fork of the stream where lived the lynx, she had followed a day-old trail of One Eye. And she had found him, or what remained of him, at the end of the trail. There were many signs of the battle that had been fought, and of the lynx's withdrawal to her lair after having won the victory. Before she went away, the she-wolf had found this lair, but the signs told her that the lynx was inside, and she had not dared to venture in.

After that the she-wolf in her hunting avoided the left fork. For she knew that in the lynx's lair was a litter of kittens, and she knew the lynx for a fierce, bad-tempered creature and a terrible fighter. It was all very well for half a dozen wolves to drive a lynx, spitting and bristling, up a tree; but it was quite a different matter for a lone wolf to encounter a lynx—especially when the lynx was known to have a litter of hungry kittens at her back.

But the Wild is the Wild, and motherhood is motherhood, at all times fiercely protective whether in the Wild or out of it; and the time was to come when the she-wolf, for her gray cub's sake, would venture the left fork, and the lair in the rocks, and the lynx's wrath.

CHAPTER IV

THE WALL OF THE WORLD

By the time his mother began leaving the cave on hunting expeditions, the cub had learned well the law that forbade his approaching the entrance. Not only had this law been forcibly and many times impressed on him by his mother's nose and paw, but in him the instinct of fear was developing. Never, in his brief cave life, had he encountered anything of which to be afraid. Yet fear was in him. It had come down to him from a remote ancestry through a thousand thousand lives. It was a heritage he had received directly from One Eye and the she-wolf; but to them, in turn, it had been passed down through all the generations of wolves that had gone before. Fear!—that legacy of the Wild, which no animal may escape nor exchange for pottage.

So the gray cub knew fear, though he knew not the stuff of which fear was made. Possibly he accepted it as one of the restrictions of life. For he had already learned that there were such restrictions. Hunger he had known; and when he could not appease his hunger he had felt restriction. The hard obstruction of the cave wall, the sharp nudge of his mother's nose, the smashing stroke of her paw, the hunger unappeased of several famines, had borne in upon him that all was not freedom in the world, that to life there were limitations and restraints. These limitations and restraints were laws. To be obedient to them was to escape hurt and make for happiness.

He did not reason the question out in this man fashion. He merely classified the things that hurt and the things that did not hurt. And after such classification he avoided the things that hurt, the restrictions and restraints, in order to enjoy the satisfactions and the remunerations of life.

Thus it was that in obedience to the law laid down by his mother, and in obedience to the law of that unknown and nameless thing, fear, he kept away from the mouth of the cave. It remained to him a white wall of light. When his mother was absent, he slept most of the time; while during the intervals that he was awake he kept very quiet, suppressing the whimpering cries that tickled in his throat and strove for noise.

Once, lying awake, he heard a strange sound in the white wall. He did not know that it was a wolverine, standing outside, all a-tremble with its own daring, and cautiously scenting out the contents of the cave. The cub knew only that the sniff was strange, a something unclassified, therefore unknown and terrible—for the unknown was one of the chief elements that went into the making of fear.

The hair bristled up on the gray cub's back, but it bristled silently. How was he to know that this thing that sniffed was a thing at which to bristle? It was not born of any knowledge of his, yet it was the visible expression of the fear that was in him, and for which, in his own life, there was no accounting. But fear was accompanied by another instinct—that of concealment. The cub was in a frenzy of terror, yet he lay without movement or sound, frozen, petrified into immobility, to all appearance dead. His mother, coming home, growled as she smelt the wolverine's track, and bounded into the cave and licked and nozzled him with undue vehemence of affection. And the cub felt that somehow he had escaped a great hurt.

But there were other forces at work in the cub, the greatest of which was growth. Instinct and law demanded of him obedience. But growth demanded disobedience. His mother and fear impelled him to keep away from the white wall. Growth is life, and life is forever destined to make for light. So there was no damming up the tide of life that was rising within him—rising with every mouthful of meat he swallowed, with every breath he drew. In the end, one day, fear and obedience were swept away by the rush of life, and the cub straddled and sprawled toward the entrance.

Unlike any other wall with which he had had experience, this wall seemed to recede from him as he approached. No hard surface collided with the tender little nose he thrust out tentatively before him. The substance of the wall seemed as permeable and yielding as light. And as condition, in his eyes, had the seeming of form, so he entered into what had been wall to him and bathed in the substance that composed it.

It was bewildering. He was sprawling through solidity. And ever the light grew brighter. Fear urged him to go back, but growth drove him on. Suddenly he found himself at the mouth of the cave. The wall, inside which he had thought himself, as suddenly leaped back before him to an immeasurable distance. The light had become painfully bright. He was dazzled by it. Likewise he was made dizzy by this abrupt and tremendous extension of space. Automatically, his eyes were adjusting themselves to the brightness, focusing themselves to meet the increased distance of objects. At first, the wall had leaped beyond his vision. He now saw it again; but it had taken upon itself a remarkable remoteness. Also, its appearance had changed. It was now a variegated wall, composed of the trees that fringed the stream, the opposing mountain that towered above the trees, and the sky that out-towered the mountain.

A great fear came upon him. This was more of the terrible unknown. He crouched down on the lip of the cave and gazed out on the world. He was very much afraid. Because it was unknown, it was hostile to him. Therefore the hair stood up on end along his back, and his lips wrinkled weakly in an attempt at a ferocious and intimidating snarl. Out of his puniness and fright he challenged and menaced the whole wide world.

Nothing happened.. He continued to gaze, and in his interest he forgot to snarl. Also, he forgot to be afraid. For the time fear had been routed by growth, while growth had assumed the guise of curiosity. He began to notice near objects—an open portion of the stream that flashed in the sun, the blasted pine tree that stood at the base of the slope, and the slope itself, that ran right up to him and ceased two feet beneath the lip of the cave on which he crouched.

Now the gray cub had lived all his days on a level floor. He had never experienced the hurt of a fall. He did not know what a fall was. So he stepped boldly out upon the air. His hind legs still rested on the cave lip, so he fell forward head downward. The earth struck him a harsh blow on the nose that made him yelp. Then he began rolling down the slope, over and over. He was in a panic of terror. The unknown had caught him at last. It had gripped savagely hold of him and was about to wreak upon him some terrific hurt. Growth was now routed by fear, and he ki-yi'd like any frightened puppy.

The unknown bore him on he knew not to what frightful hurt, and he yelped and ki-yi'd unceasingly. This was a different proposition from crouching in frozen fear while the unknown lurked just alongside. Now the unknown had caught tight hold of him. Silence would do no good. Besides, it was not fear, but terror, that convulsed him.

But the slope grew more gradual, and its base was grass-covered. Here the cub lost momentum. When at last he came to a stop, he gave one last agonized yelp and then a long, whimpering wail. Also, and quite as a matter of course, as though in his life he had already made a thousand toilets, he proceeded to lick away the dry clay that soiled him.

After that he sat up and gazed about him, as might the first man of the earth who landed upon Mars. The cub had broken through the wall of the world, the unknown had let go its hold of him, and here he was without hurt. But the first man on Mars would have experienced less unfamiliarity than did he. Without any antecedent knowledge, without any warning whatever that such existed, he found himself an explorer in a totally new world.

Now that the terrible unknown had let go of him, he forgot that the unknown had any terrors. He was aware only of curiosity in all the things about him. He inspected the grass beneath him, the moss-berry plant just beyond, and the dead trunk of the blasted pine that stood on the edge of an open space among the trees. A squirrel, running around the base of the trunk, came full upon him, and gave him a great fright. He cowered down and snarled. But the squirrel was as badly scared. It ran up the tree, and from a point of safety chattered back savagely.

This helped the cub's courage, and though the woodpecker he next encountered gave him a start, he proceeded confidently on his way. Such was his confidence, that when a moose bird impudently hopped up to him he reached out at it with a playful paw. The result was a sharp peck on the end of his nose that made him cower down and ki-yi. The noise he made was too much for the moose bird, who promptly sought safety in flight.

But the cub was learning. His misty little mind had already made an unconscious classification. There were live things and things not alive. Also, he must watch out for the live things. The things not alive remained always in one place; but the live things moved about and there was no telling what they might do. The thing to expect of them was the unexpected, and for this he must be prepared.

He traveled very clumsily. He ran into sticks and things. A twig that he thought a long way off would the next instant hit him on the nose or rake along his ribs. There were inequalities of surface. Sometimes he overstepped and stubbed his nose. Quite as often he understepped and stubbed his feet. Then there were the pebbles and stones that turned under him when he trod upon them; and from them he came to know that the things not alive were not all in the same state of stable equilibrium as was his cave; also, that small things not alive were more liable than large things to fall down or turn over.

But with every mishap he was learning. The longer he walked the better he walked. He was adjusting himself. He was learning to calculate his own muscular movements, to know his physical limitations, to measure distances between objects and between objects and himself.

His was the luck of the beginner. Born to be a hunter of meat (though he did not know it), he blundered upon meat just outside his own cave-door on his first foray into the world. It was by sheer blundering that he chanced upon the shrewdly hidden ptarmigan nest. He fell into it. He had essayed to walk along the trunk of a fallen pine. The rotten bark gave way under his feet, and with a despairing yelp he pitched down the rounded descent, smashed through the leafage and stalks of a small bush, and in the heart of the bush, on the ground, fetched up in the midst of seven ptarmigan chicks.

They made noises, and at first he was frightened at them. Then he perceived that they were very little, and he became bolder. They moved. He placed his paw on one, and its movements were accelerated. This was a source of enjoyment to him. He smelled it. He picked it up in his mouth. It struggled and tickled his tongue. At the same time he was made aware of a sensation of hunger. His jaws closed together. There was a crunching of fragile bones, and warm blood ran in his mouth. The taste of it was good. This was meat, the same as his mother gave him, only it was alive between his teeth, and therefore better. So he ate the ptarmigan. Nor did he stop till he had devoured the whole brood. Then he licked his chops in quite the same way his mother did, and began to crawl out of the bush.

He encountered a feathered whirlwind. He was confused and blinded by the rush of it and the beat of angry wings. He hid his head between his paws and yelped. The blows increased. The mother ptarmigan was in a fury. Then he became angry. He rose up, snarling, striking out with his paws. He sank his tiny teeth into one of the wings and pulled and tugged sturdily. The ptarmigan struggled against him, showering blows upon him with her free wing. It was his first battle. He was elated. He forgot all about the unknown. He no longer was afraid of anything. He was fighting, tearing at a live thing that was striking at him. Also, this live thing was meat. The lust to kill was on him. He had just destroyed little live things. He would now destroy a big live thing. He was too busy and happy to know that he was happy. He was thrilling and exulting in ways new to him and greater to him than any he had known before.

He held on to the wing and growled between his tight-clenched teeth. The ptarmigan dragged him out of the bush. When she turned and tried to drag him back into the bush's shelter, he pulled her away from it and on into the open. And all the time she was making outcry and striking with her wing, while feathers were flying like a snowfall. The pitch to which he was aroused was tremendous. All the fighting blood of his breed was up in him and surging through him. This was living, though he did not know it. He was realizing his own meaning in the world; he was doing that for which he was made—killing meat and battling to kill it. He was justifying his existence, than which life can do no greater; for life achieves its summit when it does to the uttermost that which it was equipped to do.

After a time the ptarmigan ceased her struggling. He still held her by the wing, and they lay on the ground and looked at each other. He tried to growl threateningly, ferociously. She pecked on his nose, which by now, what of previous adventures, was sore. He winced but held on. She pecked him again and again. From wincing he went to whimpering. He tried to back away from her, oblivious of the fact that by his hold on her he dragged her after him. A rain of pecks fell on his ill-used nose. The flood of fight ebbed down in him, and, releasing his prey, he turned tail and scampered off across the open in inglorious retreat.

He lay down to rest on the other side of the open, near the edge of the bushes, his tongue lolling out, his chest heaving and panting, his nose still hurting him and causing him to continue his whimper. But as he lay there, suddenly there came to him a feeling as of something terrible impending. The unknown with all its terrors rushed upon him, and he shrank back instinctively into the shelter of the bush. As he did so a draught of air fanned him, and a large, winged body swept ominously and silently past. A hawk, driving down out of the blue, had barely missed him.

While he lay in the bush, recovering from this fright and peering fearfully out, the mother ptarmigan, on the other side of the open space, fluttered out of the ravaged nest. It was because of her loss that she paid no attention to the winged bolt of the sky. But the cub saw, and it was a warning and a lesson to him—the swift downward swoop of the hawk, the short skim of its body just above the ground, the strike of its talons in the body of the ptarmigan, the ptarmigan's squawk of agony and fright, and the hawk's rush upward into the blue, carrying the ptarmigan away with it.

It was a long time before the cub left his shelter. He had learned much. Live things were meat. They were good to eat. Also, live things, when they were large enough, could give hurt. It was better to eat small live things like ptarmigan chicks, and to let alone large live things like ptarmigan hens. Nevertheless he felt a little prick of ambition, a sneaking desire to have another battle with that ptarmigan hen—only the hawk had carried her away. Maybe there were other ptarmigan hens. He would go and see.

He came down a shelving bank to the stream. He had never seen water before. The footing looked good. There were no inequalities of surface. He stepped boldly out on it, and went down, crying with fear, into the embrace of the unknown. It was cold, and he gasped, breathing quickly. The water rushed into his lungs instead of the air that had always accompanied his act of breathing. The suffocation he experienced was like the pang of death. To him it signified death. He had no conscious knowledge of death, but like every animal of the Wild, he possessed the instinct of death. To him it stood as the greatest of hurts. It was the very essence of the unknown; it was the sum of the terrors of the unknown, the one culminating and unthinkable catastrophe that could happen to him, about which he knew nothing and about which he feared everything.

He came to the surface, and the sweet air rushed into his open mouth. He did not go down again. Quite as though it had been a long-established custom of his, he struck out with all his legs and began to swim. The near bank was a yard away; but he had come up with his back to it, and the first thing his eyes rested upon was the opposite bank, toward which he immediately began to swim. The stream was a small one, but in the pool it widened out to a score of feet.

Midway in the passage the current picked up the cub and swept him downstream. He was caught in the miniature rapid at the bottom of the pool. Here was little chance for swimming. The quiet water had become suddenly angry. Sometimes he was under, sometimes on top. At all times he was in violent motion, now being turned over or around, and again being smashed against a rock. And with every rock he struck he yelped. His progress was a series of yelps, from which might have been adduced the number of rocks he encountered.

Below the rapid was a second pool, and here, captured by the eddy, he was gently borne to the bank and as gently deposited on a bed of gravel. He crawled frantically clear of the water and lay down. He had learned some more about the world. Water was not alive. Yet it moved. Also, it looked as solid as the earth, but was without any solidity at all. His conclusion was that things were not always what they appeared to be. The cub's fear of the unknown was an inherited distrust, and it had now been strengthened by experience. Thenceforth, in the nature of things, he would possess an abiding distrust of appearances. He would have to learn the reality of a thing before he could put his faith into it.

One other adventure was destined for him that day. He had recollected that there was such a thing in the world as his mother. And then there came to him a feeling that he wanted her more than all the rest of the things in the world. Not only was his body tired with the adventures he had undergone, but his little brain was equally tired. In all the days he had lived it had not worked so hard as on this one day. Furthermore, he was sleepy. So he started out to look for the cave and his mother, feeling at the same time an overwhelming rush of loneliness and helplessness.

He was sprawling along between some bushes, when he heard a sharp intimidating cry. There was a flash of yellow before his eyes. He saw a weasel leaping swiftly away from him. It was a small live thing, and he had no fear. Then, before him, at his feet, he saw an extremely small live thing, only several inches long, a young weasel, that, like himself, had disobediently gone out adventuring. It tried to retreat before him. He turned it over with his paw. It made a queer, grating noise. The next moment the flash of yellow reappeared before his eyes. He heard again the intimidating cry, and at the same instant received a severe blow on the side of the neck and felt the sharp teeth of the mother weasel cut into his flesh.

While he yelped and ki-yi'd and scrambled backward, he saw the mother weasel leap upon her young one and disappear with it into the neighboring thicket. The cut of her teeth in his neck still hurt, but his feelings were hurt more grievously, and he sat down and weakly whimpered. This mother weasel was so small and so savage! He was yet to learn that for size and weight the weasel was the most ferocious, vindictive and terrible of all the killers of the Wild. But a portion of this knowledge was quickly to be his.

He was still whimpering when the mother weasel reappeared. She did not rush him, now that her young one was safe. She approached more cautiously, and the cub had full opportunity to observe her lean, snake-like body, and her head, erect, eager and snake-like itself. Her sharp, menacing cry sent the hair bristling along his back, and he snarled warningly at her. She came closer and closer. There was a leap, swifter than his unpracticed sight, and the lean, yellow body disappeared for a moment out of the field of vision. The next moment she was at his throat, her teeth buried in his hair and flesh.

At first he snarled and tried to fight; but he was very young, and this was only his first day in the world, and his snarl became a whimper, his fight a struggle to escape. The weasel never relaxed her hold. She hung on, striving to press down with her teeth to the great vein where his life-blood bubbled. The weasel was a drinker of blood, and it was ever her preference to drink from the throat of life itself.

The gray cub would have died, and there would have been no story to write about him, had not the she-wolf come bounding through the bushes. The weasel let go the cub and flashed at the she-wolf's throat, missing, but getting a hold on the jaw instead. The she-wolf flirted her head like the snap of a whip, breaking the weasel's hold and flinging it high in the air. And, still in the air, the she-wolf's jaws closed on the lean, yellow body, and the weasel knew death between the crunching teeth.

The cub experienced another access of affection on the part of his mother. Her joy at finding him seemed greater even than his joy at being found. She nozzled him and caressed him and licked the cuts made in him by the weasel's teeth. Then, between them, mother and cub, they ate the blood-drinker, and after that went back to the cave and slept.

CHAPTER V

THE LAW OF MEAT

The cub's development was rapid. He rested for two days, and then ventured forth from the cave again. It was on this adventure that he found the young weasel whose mother he had helped eat, and he saw to it that the young weasel went the way of its mother. But on this trip he did not get lost. When he grew tired he found his way back to the cave and slept. And every day thereafter found him out and ranging a wider area.

He began to get an accurate measurement of his strength and his weakness, and to know when to be bold and when to be cautious. He found it expedient to be cautious all the time, except for the rare moments when, assured of his own intrepidity, he abandoned himself to petty rages and lusts.

He was always a little demon of fury when he chanced upon a stray ptarmigan. Never did he fail to respond savagely to the chatter of the squirrel he had first met on the blasted pine, while the sight of a moose bird almost invariably put him into the wildest of rages; for he never forgot the peck on the nose he had received from the first of that ilk he encountered.

But there were times when even a moose bird failed to affect him, and those were times when he felt himself to be in danger from some other prowling meat-hunter. He never forgot the hawk, and its moving shadow always sent him crouching into the nearest thicket. He no longer sprawled and straddled, and already he was developing the gait of his mother, slinking and furtive, apparently without exertion, yet sliding along with a swiftness that was as deceptive as it was imperceptible.

In the matter of meat, his luck had been all in the beginning. The seven ptarmigan chicks and the baby weasel represented the sum of his killings. His desire to kill strengthened with the days, and he cherished hungry ambitions for the squirrel that chattered so volubly and always informed all wild creatures that the wolf-cub was approaching. But as birds flew in the air, squirrels could climb trees, and the cub could only try to crawl unobserved upon the squirrel when it was on the ground.

The cub entertained a great respect for his mother. She could get meat, and she never failed to bring him his share. Further, she was unafraid of things. It did not occur to him that this fearlessness was founded upon experience and knowledge. Its effect on him was that of an impression of power. His mother represented power; and as he grew older he felt this power in the sharper admonishment of her paw; while the reproving nudge of her nose gave place to the slash of her fangs. For this, likewise, he respected his mother. She compelled obedience from him, and the older he grew the shorter grew her temper.

Famine came again, and the cub with clearer consciousness knew once more the bite of hunger. The she-wolf ran herself thin in the quest for meat. She rarely slept any more in the cave, spending most of her time on the meat trail and spending it vainly. This famine was not a long one, but it was severe while it lasted. The cub found no more milk in his mother's breast, nor did he get one mouthful of meat for himself.

Before, he had hunted in play, for the sheer joyousness of it; now he hunted in deadly earnestness, and found nothing. Yet the failure of it accelerated his development. He studied the habits of the squirrel with greater carefulness, and strove with greater craft to steal upon it and surprise it. He studied the wood-mice and tried to dig them out of their burrows; and he learned much about the ways of moose birds and woodpeckers. And there came a day when the hawk's shadow did not drive him crouching into the bushes. He had grown stronger, and wiser, and more confident. Also, he was desperate. So he sat on his haunches, conspicuously, in an open space, and challenged the hawk down out of the sky. For he knew that there, floating in the blue above him, was meat, the meat his stomach yearned after so insistently. But the hawk refused to come down and give battle, and the cub crawled away into a thicket and whimpered his disappointment and hunger.

The famine broke. The she-wolf brought home meat. It was strange meat, different from any she had ever brought before. It was a lynx kitten, partly grown, like the cub, but not so large. And it was all for him. His mother had satisfied her hunger elsewhere; though he did not know that it was the rest of the lynx litter that had gone to satisfy her. Nor did he know the desperateness of her deed. He knew only that the velvet-furred kitten was meat, and he ate and waxed happier with every mouthful.

A full stomach conduces to inaction, and the cub lay in the cave, sleeping against his mother's side. He was aroused by her snarling. Never had he heard her snarl so terribly. Possibly in her whole life it was the most terrible snarl she ever gave. There was reason for it, and none knew it better than she. A lynx's lair is not despoiled with impunity. In the full glare of the afternoon light, crouching in the entrance of the cave, the cub saw the lynx mother. The hair rippled up all along his back at the sight. Here was fear, and it did not require his instinct to tell him of it. And if sight alone were not sufficient the cry of rage the intruder gave, beginning with a snarl and rushing abruptly upward into a hoarse screech, was convincing enough in itself.

The cub felt the prod of the life that was in him, and stood up and snarled valiantly by his mother's side. But she thrust him ignominiously away and behind her. Because of the low-roofed entrance the lynx could not leap in, and when she made a crawling rush of it the she-wolf sprang upon her and pinned her down. The cub saw little of the battle. There was a tremendous snarling and spitting and screeching. The two animals threshed about, the lynx ripping and tearing with her claws and using her teeth as well, while the she-wolf used her teeth alone.

Once, the cub sprang in and sank his teeth into the hind leg of the lynx. He clung on, growling savagely. Though he did not know it, by the weight of his body he clogged the action of the leg and thereby saved his mother much damage. A change in the battle crushed him under both their bodies and wrenched loose his hold. The next moment the two mothers separated, and, before they rushed together again, the lynx lashed out at the cub with a huge fore paw that ripped his shoulder open to the bone and sent him hurtling sidewise against the wall. Then was added to the uproar the cub's shrill yelp of pain and fright. But the fight lasted so long that he had time to cry himself out and to experience a second burst of courage; and the end of the battle found him again clinging to a hind leg and furiously growling between his teeth.

The lynx was dead. But the she-wolf was very weak and sick. At first she caressed the cub and licked his wounded shoulder; but the blood she had lost had taken with it her strength, and for all of a day and a night she lay by her dead foe's side, without movement, scarcely breathing. For a week she never left the cave, except for water, and then her movements were slow and painful. At the end of that time the lynx was devoured, while the she-wolf's wounds had healed sufficiently to permit her to take the meat trail again.

The cub's shoulder was stiff and sore, and for some time he limped from the terrible slash he had received. But the world now seemed changed. He went about in it with greater confidence, with a feeling of prowess that had not been his in the days before the battle with the lynx. He had looked upon life in a more ferocious aspect; he had fought; he had buried his teeth in the flesh of a foe; and he had survived. And because of all this he carried himself more boldly, with a touch of defiance that was new in him. He was no longer afraid of minor things, and much of his timidity had vanished, though the unknown never ceased to press upon him with its mysteries and terrors, intangible and ever-menacing.

He began to accompany his mother on the meat trail, and he saw much of the killing of meat and began to play his part in it. And in his own dim way he learned the law of meat. There were two kinds of life—his own kind and the other kind. His own kind included his mother and himself. The other kind included all live things that moved. But the other kind was divided. One portion was what his own kind killed and ate. This portion was composed of the non-killers and the small killers. The other portion killed and ate his own kind, or was killed and eaten by his own kind. And out of this classification arose the law. The aim of life was meat. Life itself was meat. Life lived on life. There were the eaters and the eaten. The law was: EAT OR BE EATEN. He did not formulate the law in clear, set terms and moralize about it. He did not even think the law; he merely lived the law without thinking about it at all.

He saw the law operating around him on every side. He had eaten the ptarmigan chicks. The hawk had eaten the ptarmigan mother. The hawk would also have eaten him. Later, when he had grown more formidable, he wanted to eat the hawk. He had eaten the lynx kitten. The lynx mother would have eaten him had she not herself been killed and eaten. And so it went. The law was being lived about him by all live things, and he himself was part and parcel of the law. He was a killer. His only food was meat, live meat, that ran away swiftly before him, or flew into the air, or climbed trees, or hid in the ground, or faced him and fought with him, or turned the tables and ran after him.

Had the cub thought in man-fashion, he might have epitomized life as a voracious appetite, and the world as a place wherein ranged a multitude of appetites, pursuing and being pursued, hunting and being hunted, eating and being eaten, all in blindness and confusion, with violence and disorder, a chaos of gluttony and slaughter, ruled over by chance, merciless, endless.

But the cub did not think in man-fashion. He did not look at things with wide vision. He was single-purposed, and entertained but one thought or desire at a time. Besides the law of meat there were a myriad other and lesser laws for him to learn and obey. The world was filled with surprise. The stir of the life that was in him, the play of his muscles, was an unending happiness. To run down meat was to experience thrills and elations. His rages and battles were pleasures. Terror itself, and the mystery of the unknown, lent to his living.

And there were easements and satisfactions. To have a full stomach, to doze lazily in the sunshine—such things were remuneration in full for his ardors and toils; while his ardors and toils were in themselves self-remunerative. They were expressions of life, and life is always happy when it is expressing itself. So the cub had no quarrel with his hostile environment. He was very much alive, very happy and very proud of himself.

WHITE FANG

BY JACK LONDON

ILLUSTRATED BY FRANK E. SCHOONOVER

PART III.—THE GODS OF THE WILD

CHAPTER I

THE MAKERS OF FIRE

THE cub came upon it suddenly. It was his own fault. He had been careless. He had left the cave and run down to the stream to drink. It might have been that he took no notice because he was heavy with sleep. (He had been out all night on the meat-trail, and had but just then awakened.) And his carelessness might have been due to the familiarity of the trail to the pool. He had traveled it often, and nothing had ever happened on it.

He went down past the blasted pine, crossed the open space and trotted in amongst the trees. Then, at the same instant, he saw and smelt. Before him, sitting silently on their haunches, were five live things, the like of which he had never seen before. It was his first glimpse of mankind. But at the sight of him the five men did not spring to their feet, nor show their teeth, nor snarl. They did not move, but sat there, silent and ominous.

Nor did the cub move. Every instinct of his nature would have impelled him to dash wildly away, had there not suddenly and for the first time arisen in him another and counter instinct. A great awe descended upon him. He was beaten down to movelessness by an overwhelming sense of his own weakness and littleness. Here was mastery and power, something far and away beyond him.

The cub had never seen man, yet the instinct concerning man was his. In dim ways he recognized in man the animal that had fought itself to primacy over the other animals of the wild. Not alone out of his own eyes, but out of the eyes of all his ancestors was the cub now looking upon man—out of eyes that had circled in the darkness around countless winter camp fires, that had peered from safe distances and from the hearts of thickets at the strange, two-legged animal that was lord over living things. The spell of the cub's heritage was upon him—the fear and the respect born of the centuries of struggle and the accumulated experience of the generations. The heritage was too compelling for a wolf that was only a cub. Had he been full grown he would have run away. As it was, he cowered down in a paralysis of fear, already half proffering the submission that his kind had proffered from the first time a wolf came in to sit by man's fire and be made warm.

One of the Indians arose and walked over to him and stooped above him. The cub cowered closer to the ground. It was the unknown, objectified at last, in concrete flesh and blood, bending over him and reaching down to seize hold of him. His hair bristled involuntarily; his lips writhed back and his little fangs were bared. The hand, poised like doom above him, hesitated, and the man spoke laughing, "*Wabam wabisca ip pit tah.*" ("Look! The white fangs!")

The other Indians laughed loudly, and urged the man on to pick up the cub. As the hand descended closer and closer, there raged within the cub a battle of the instincts. He experienced two great impulsions—to yield and to fight. The resulting action was a compromise. He did both. He yielded till the hand almost touched him. Then he fought, his teeth flashing in a snap that sank them into the hand.

The next moment he received a clout alongside the head that knocked him over on his side. Then all fight fled out of him. His puppyhood and the instinct of submission took charge of him. He sat up on his haunches and ki-yi'd. But the man whose hand he had bitten was angry. The cub received a clout on the other side of his head. Whereupon he sat up and ki-yi'd louder than ever.

The four Indians laughed more loudly, while even the man who had been bitten began to laugh. They surrounded the cub and laughed at him, while he wailed out his terror and his hurt. In the midst of it he heard something. The Indians heard it, too. But the cub knew what it was, and with a last, long wail that had in it more of triumph than grief, he ceased his noise and waited for the coming of his mother, of his ferocious and indomitable mother, who fought and killed all things and was never afraid. She was snarling as she ran. She had heard the cry of her cub and was dashing to save him.

She bounded in amongst them, her anxious and militant motherhood making her anything but a pretty sight. But to the cub the spectacle of her protective rage was pleasing. He uttered a glad little cry and bounded to meet her, while the man-animals went back hastily several steps. The she-wolf stood over against her cub, facing the men, with bristling hair, a snarl rumbling deep in her throat. Her face was distorted and malignant with menace, even the bridge of the nose wrinkling from tip to eyes, so prodigious was her snarl.

Then it was that a cry went up from one of the men. "Kiche!" was what he uttered. It was an exclamation of surprise. The cub felt his mother wilting at the sound.

"Kiche!" the man cried again, this time with sharpness and authority.

And then the cub saw his mother, the she-wolf, the fearless one, crouching down till her belly touched the ground, whimpering, wagging her tail, making peace signs. The cub could not understand. He was appalled. The awe of man rushed over him again. His instinct had been true. His mother verified it. She, too, rendered submission to the man-animals.

The man who had spoken came over to her. He put his hand upon her head, and she only crouched closer. She did not snap, nor threaten to snap. The other men came up and surrounded her, and felt her and pawed her, which actions she made no attempt to resent. They were greatly excited, and made many noises with their mouths. These noises were not indications of danger, the cub decided, as he crouched near his mother, still bristling from time to time, but doing his best to submit.

"It is not strange," an Indian was saying. "Her father was a wolf. It is true, her mother was a dog; but did not my brother tie her out in the woods all of three nights in the mating season? Therefore was the father of Kiche a wolf."

"It is a year, Gray Beaver, since she ran away," spoke a second Indian.

"It is not strange, Salmon Tongue," Gray Beaver answered. "It was the time of the famine, and there was no meat for the dogs."

"She has lived with the wolves," said a third Indian.

"So it would seem, Three Eagles," Gray Beaver answered, laying his hand on the cub; "and this be the sign of it."

The cub snarled a little at the touch of the hand, and the hand flew back to administer a clout. Whereupon the cub covered his fangs and sank down submissively, while the hand, returning, rubbed behind his ears and up and down his back.

"This be the sign of it," Gray Beaver went on. "It is plain that his mother is Kiche. But his father was a wolf. Wherefore is there in him little dog and much wolf. His fangs be white, and White Fang shall be his name. I have spoken. He is my dog. For was not Kiche my brother's dog? And is not my brother dead?"

The cub, who had thus received a name in the world, lay and watched. For a time the man-animals continued to make their mouth-noises. Then Gray Beaver took a knife from a sheath that hung around his neck, and went into the thicket and cut a stick. White Fang watched him. He notched the stick at each end and in the notches fastened strings of rawhide. One string he tied around the throat of Kiche. Then he led her to a small pine, around which he tied the other string.

White Fang followed and lay down beside her. Salmon Tongue's hand reached out to him and rolled him over on his back. Kiche looked on anxiously. White Fang felt fear mounting in him again. He could not quite suppress a snarl, but he made no offer to snap. The hand, with fingers crooked and spread apart, rubbed his stomach in a playful way and rolled him from side to side. It was ridiculous and ungainly, lying there on his back with legs sprawling in the air. Besides, it was a position of such utter helplessness that White Fang's whole nature revolted against it. He could do nothing to defend himself. If this man-animal intended harm, White Fang knew that he could not escape it. How could he spring away with his four legs in the air above him? Yet submission made him master his fear, and he only growled softly. This growl he could not suppress; nor did the man-animal resent it by giving him a blow on the head. And furthermore, such was the strangeness of it, White Fang experienced an unaccountable sensation of pleasure as the hand rubbed back and forth. When he was rolled on his side he ceased the growl; when the fingers pressed and prodded at the base of his ears the pleasurable sensation increased; and when, with a final rub and scratch, the man left him alone and went away, all fear had died out of White Fang. He was to know fear many times in his dealings with man; yet it was a token of the fearless companionship with man that was ultimately to be his.

After a time White Fang heard strange noises approaching. He was quick in his classification, for he knew them at once for man-animal noises. A few minutes later the remainder of the tribe, strung out as it was on the march, trailed in. There were more men and many women and children, forty souls of them, and all heavily burdened with camp equipage and outfit. Also, there were many dogs; and these, with the exception of the part-grown puppies, were likewise burdened with camp outfit. On their backs, in bags that fastened tightly around underneath, the dogs carried from twenty to thirty pounds of weight.

White Fang had never seen dogs before, but at sight of them he felt that they were his own kind, only somehow different. But they displayed little difference from the wolf when they discovered the cub and his mother. There was a rush. White Fang bristled and snarled and snapped in the face of the open-mouthed, oncoming wave of dogs, and went down and under them, feeling the sharp slash of teeth in his body, himself biting and tearing at the legs and bellies above him. There was a great uproar. He could hear the snarl of Kiche as she fought for him; and he could hear the cries of the man-animals, the sound of clubs striking upon bodies, and the yelps of pain from the dogs so struck.

Only a few seconds elapsed before he was on his feet again. He could now see the man-animals driving back the dogs with clubs and stones, defending him, saving him from the savage teeth of his kind that somehow was not his kind. And though there was no reason in his brain for a clear conception of so abstract a thing as justice, nevertheless, in his own way, he felt the justice of the man-animals, and he knew them for what they were, makers of law and executors of law. Also, he appreciated the power with which they administered the law. Unlike any animals he had ever encountered, they did not bite nor claw. They enforced their live strength with the power of dead things. Dead things did their bidding. Thus, sticks and stones, directed by these strange creatures, leaped through the air like living things, inflicting grievous hurts upon the dogs.

To his mind this was power unusual, power inconceivable and beyond the natural, power that was godlike. White Fang, in the very nature of him, could never know anything about gods; at the best he could know only things that were beyond knowing; but the wonder and awe that he had of these man-animals in ways resembled what would be the wonder and awe of man at sight of some celestial creature, on a mountain top, hurling thunderbolts from either hand at an astonished world.

The last dog had been driven back. The hubbub died down. And White Fang licked his hurts and meditated upon this, his first taste of pack cruelty, and his introduction to the pack. He had never dreamed that his own kind consisted of more than One Eye, his mother and himself. They had constituted a kind apart, and here, abruptly, he had discovered many more creatures apparently of his own kind. And there was a sub-conscious re-

Drawing by Frank E. Schoonover.

"White Fang's free nature flashed forth again, and he sank his teeth into the moccasined foot."

sentment that these, his kind, at first sight had pitched upon him and tried to destroy him. In the same way he resented his mother being tied with a stick, even though it was done by the superior man-animals. It savored of the trap, of bondage. Yet of the trap and of bondage he knew nothing. Freedom to roam and run and lie down at will had been his heritage; and here it was being infringed upon. His mother's movements were restricted to the length of a stick, and by the length of that same stick was he restricted, for he had not yet got beyond the need of his mother's side.

He did not like it. Nor did he like it when the man-animals arose and went on with their march; for a tiny man-animal took the other end of the stick and led Kiche captive behind him, and behind Kiche followed White Fang, greatly perturbed and worried by this new adventure he had entered upon.

They went down the valley of the stream, far beyond White Fang's widest ranging, until they came to the end of the valley, where the stream ran into the Mackenzie River. Here, where canoes were cached on poles high in the air and where stood fish racks for the drying of fish, camp was made; and White Fang looked on with wondering eyes. The superiority of these man-animals increased with every moment. There was their mastery over all these sharp-fanged dogs. It breathed of power. But greater than that, to the wolf-cub, was their mastery over things not alive; their capacity to communicate motion to unmoving things; their capacity to change the very face of the world.

It was this last that especially affected him. The elevation of frames of poles caught his eye; yet this in itself was not so remarkable, being done by the same creatures that flung sticks and stones to great distances. But when the frames of poles were made into tepees by being covered with cloth and skins, White Fang was astounded. It was the colossal bulk of them that impressed him. They arose around him on every side like some monstrous, quick-growing form of life. They occupied nearly the whole circumference of his field of vision. He was afraid of them. They loomed ominously above him; and when the breeze stirred them into huge movements he cowered down in fear, keeping his eyes warily upon them, and prepared to spring away if they attempted to precipitate themselves upon him.

But in a short while his fear of the tepees passed away. He saw the women and children passing in and out of them without harm, and he saw the dogs trying often to get into them and being driven away with sharp words and flying stones. After a time, he left Kiche's side and crawled cautiously toward the wall of the nearest tepee. It was the curiosity of growth that urged him on—the necessity of learning and living and doing that brings experience. The last few inches to the wall of the tepee were crawled with painful slowness and precaution. The day's events had prepared him for the unknown to manifest itself in most stupendous and unthinkable ways. At last his nose touched the canvas. He waited. Nothing happened. Then he smelled the strange fabric, saturated with the man-smell. He closed on the canvas with his teeth and gave a gentle tug. Nothing happened, though the adjacent portions of the tepee moved. He tugged harder. There was a greater movement. It was delightful. He tugged still harder and repeatedly until the whole tepee was in motion. Then the sharp cry of a squaw inside sent him scampering back to Kiche. But after that he was afraid no more of the looming bulks of the tepees.

A moment later he was straying away again from his mother. Her stick was tied to a peg in the ground and she could not follow him. A part-grown puppy, somewhat larger and older than he, came toward him slowly, with ostentatious and belligerent importance. The puppy's name, as White Fang was afterward to hear him called, was Lip-lip. He had had experience in puppy fights and was already something of a bully.

Lip-lip was White Fang's own kind, and, being only a puppy, did not seem dangerous; so White Fang prepared to meet him in friendly spirit. But when the stranger's walk became stiff-legged and his lips lifted clear of his teeth, White Fang stiffened too, and answered with lifted lips. They half circled about each other tentatively, snarling and bristling. This lasted several minutes, and White Fang was beginning to enjoy it, as a sort of game. But suddenly, with remarkable swiftness, Lip-lip leaped in, delivered a slashing snap, and leaped away again. The snap had taken effect on the shoulder that had been hurt by the lynx and that was still sore deep down near the bone. The surprise and hurt of it brought a yelp out of White Fang; but the next moment, in a rush of anger, he was upon Lip-lip and snapping viciously.

But Lip-lip had lived his life in camp and had fought many puppy fights. Three times, four times, and half a dozen times his sharp little teeth scored on the newcomer, until White Fang, yelping shamelessly, fled to the protection of his mother. It was the first of the many fights he was to have with Lip-lip, for they were enemies from the start, born so, with natures destined perpetually to clash.

Kiche licked White Fang soothingly with her tongue, and tried to prevail upon him to remain with her. But his curiosity was rampant, and several minutes later he was venturing forth on a new quest. He came upon one of the man-animals, Gray Beaver, who was squatting on his hams and doing something with sticks and dry moss spread before him on the ground. White Fang came near to him and watched. Gray Beaver made mouth-noises which White Fang interpreted as not hostile, so he came still nearer.

Women and children were carrying more sticks and branches to Gray Beaver. It was evidently an affair of moment. White Fang came in until he touched Gray Beaver's knee, so curious was he and already forgetful that this was a terrible man-animal. Suddenly he saw a strange thing like mist beginning to arise from the sticks and moss beneath Gray Beaver's hands. Then, amongst the sticks themselves, appeared a live thing, twisting and turning, of a color like the color of the sun in the sky. White Fang knew nothing about fire. It drew him as the light in the mouth of the cave had drawn him in his early puppyhood. He crawled the several steps toward the flame. He heard Gray Beaver chuckle above him, and he knew the sound was not hostile. Then his nose touched the flame, and at the same instant his little tongue went out to it.

For a moment he was paralyzed. The unknown, lurking in the midst of the sticks and moss, was savagely clutching him by the nose. He scrambled backward, bursting out in an astonished explosion of ki-yi's. At the sound, Kiche leaped snarling to the end of her stick, and there raged terribly because she could not come to his aid. But Gray Beaver laughed loudly, and slapped his thighs, and told the happening to all the rest of the camp, till everybody was laughing uproariously. But White Fang sat on his haunches and ki-yi'd and ki-yi'd, a forlorn and pitiable little figure in the midst of the man-animals.

It was the worst hurt he had ever known. Both nose and tongue had been scorched by the live thing, sun-colored, that had grown up under Gray Beaver's hands. He cried and cried interminably, and every fresh wail was greeted by bursts of laughter on the part of the man-animals. He tried to soothe his nose with his tongue, but the tongue was burnt, too, and the two hurts coming together produced greater hurt; whereupon he cried more hopelessly and helplessly than ever.

And then shame came to him. He knew laughter and the meaning of it. It is not given us to know how some animals know laughter and know when they are being laughed at; but it was this same way that White Fang knew it. And he felt shame that the man-animals should be laughing at him. He turned and fled away, not from the hurt of the fire, but from the laughter that sank even deeper and hurt in the spirit of him. And he fled to Kiche, raging at the end of her stick like an animal gone mad—to Kiche, the one creature in the world who was not laughing at him.

Twilight drew down and night came on, and White Fang lay by his mother's side. His nose and tongue still hurt, but he was perplexed by a greater trouble. He was homesick. He felt a vacancy in him, a need for the hush and quietude of the stream and the cave in the cliff. Life had become too populous. There were so many of the man-animals, men, women and children, all making noises and irritations. And there were the dogs, ever squabbling and bickering, bursting into uproars and creating confusions. The restful loneliness of the only life he had known was gone. Here the very air was palpitant with life. It hummed and buzzed unceasingly. Continually changing its intensity and abruptly variant in pitch, it impinged on his nerves and senses, made him nervous and restless and worried him with a perpetual imminence of happening.

He watched the man-animals coming and going and moving about the camp. In fashion distantly resembling the way men look upon the gods they create, so looked White Fang upon the man-animals before him. They were superior creatures, of a verity gods. To his dim comprehension they were as much wonder-workers as gods are to men. They were creatures of mastery, possessing all manner of unknown and impossible potencies, overlords of the alive and the not alive — making obey that which moved, imparting movement to that which did not move, and making life, sun-colored and biting life, to grow out of dead moss and wood. They were fire-makers! They were gods!

CHAPTER II

THE BONDAGE

The days were thronged with experience for White Fang. During the time that Kiche was tied by the stick, he ran about over all the camp, inquiring, investigating, learning. He quickly came to know much of the ways of the man-animals, but familiarity did not breed contempt. The more he came to know them, the more they vindicated their superiority, the more they displayed their mysterious powers, the greater loomed their god-likeness.

To man has been given the grief, often, of seeing his gods overthrown and his altars crumbling; but to the wolf and the wild dog that have come in to crouch at man's feet this grief has never come. Unlike man, whose gods are of the unseen and the over-guessed, vapors and mists of fancy eluding the garmenture of reality, wandering wraiths of desired goodness and power, intangible out-croppings of self into the realm of spirit—unlike man, the wolf and the wild dog that have come in to the fire find their gods in the living flesh, solid to the touch, occupying earth-space and requiring time for the accomplishment of their ends and their existence. No effort of faith is necessary to believe in such a god; no effort of will can possibly induce disbelief in such a god. There is no getting away from it. There it stands, on its two hind legs, club in hand, immensely potential, passionate and wrathful and loving, god and mystery and power all wrapped up and around by flesh that bleeds when it is torn and that is good to eat like any flesh.

And so it was with White Fang. The man-animals were gods unmistakable and unescapable. As his mother, Kiche, had rendered her allegiance to them at the first cry of her name, so he was beginning to render his allegiance. He gave them the trail as a privilege indubitably theirs. When they walked, he got out of their way. When they called, he came. When they threatened, he cowered down. When they commanded him to go, he went away hurriedly For behind any wish of theirs was power to enforce that wish, power that hurt, power that expressed itself in clouts and clubs, in flying stones and stinging lashes of whips.

He belonged to them as all dogs belonged to them. His actions were theirs to command. His body was theirs to maul, to stamp upon, to tolerate. Such was the lesson that was quickly borne in upon him. It came hard, going as it did counter to much that was strong and dominant in his own nature; and, while he disliked it in the learning of it, unknown to himself he was learning to like it. It was a placing of his destiny in another's hands, a shifting of the responsibilities of existence. This in itself was compensation, for it is always easier to lean upon another than to stand alone.

But it did not all happen in a day, this giving over of himself, body and soul, to the man-animals. He could not immediately forego his wild heritage and his memories of the wild. There were days when he crept to the edge of the forest and stood and listened to something calling him far and away. And always he returned, restless and uncomfortable, to whimper softly and wistfully at Kiche's side and to lick her face with eager, questioning tongue.

White Fang learned rapidly the ways of the camp. He knew the injustice and greediness of the older dogs when meat or fish was thrown out to be eaten. He came to know that men were more just, children more cruel, and women more kindly and more likely to toss him a bit of meat or bone. And after two or three painful adventures with the mothers of part-grown puppies, he came into the knowledge that it was always good policy to let such mothers alone, to keep away from them as far as possible, and to avoid them when he saw them coming.

But the bane of his life was Lip-lip. Larger, older and stronger, Lip-lip had selected White Fang for his special object of persecution. White Fang fought willingly enough, but he was outclassed. His enemy was too big. Lip-lip became a nightmare to him. Whenever he ventured away from his mother, the bully was sure to appear, trailing at his heels, snarling at him, picking upon him, and watchful of an opportunity, when no man-animal was near, to spring upon him and force a fight. As Lip-lip invariably won, he enjoyed it hugely. It became his chief delight in life, as it became White Fang's chief torment.

But the effect upon White Fang was not to cow him. Though he suffered most of the damage and was always defeated, his spirit remained unsubdued. Yet a bad effect was produced. He became malignant and morose. His temper had been savage by birth, but it became more savage under this unending persecution. The genial, playful, puppyish side of him found little expression. He never played and gamboled about with the other puppies of the camp. Lip-lip would not permit it. The moment White Fang appeared near them Lip-lip was upon him, bullying and hectoring him, or fighting with him until he had driven him away.

The effect of all this was to rob White Fang of much of his puppyhood and to make him in his comportment older than his age. Denied the outlet, through play, of his energies, he recoiled upon himself and developed his mental processes. He became cunning; he had idle time in which to devote himself to thoughts of trickery. Prevented from obtaining his share of meat and fish when a general feed was given to the camp dogs, he became a clever thief. He had to forage for himself, and he foraged well, though he was ofttimes a plague to the squaws in consequence. He learned to sneak about camp, to be crafty, to know what was going on everywhere, to see and to hear everything and to reason accordingly, and successfully to devise ways and means of avoiding his implacable persecutor. It was early in the days of his persecution that he played his first really big crafty game and got therefrom his first taste of revenge. As Kiche, when with the wolves, had lured out to destruction dogs from the camps of men, so White Fang, in manner somewhat similar, lured Lip-lip into Kiche's avenging jaws. Retreating before Lip-lip, White Fang made an indirect flight that led in and out and around the various tepees of the camp. He was a good runner, swifter than any puppy of his size, and swifter than Lip-lip. But he did not run his best in this chase. He barely held his own, one leap ahead of his pursuer.

Lip-lip, excited by the chase and by the persistent nearness of his victim, forgot caution and locality. When he remembered locality, it was too late. Dashing at top speed around a tepee, he ran full tilt into Kiche lying at the end of her stick. He gave one yelp of consternation, and then her punishing jaws closed upon him. She was tied, but he could not get away from her easily. She rolled him off his legs so that he could not run, while she repeatedly ripped and slashed him with her fangs.

When at last he succeeded in rolling clear of her, he crawled to his feet, badly disheveled, hurt both in body and in spirit. His hair was standing out all over him in tufts where her teeth had mauled. He stood where he had arisen, opened his mouth, and broke out the long, heart-broken puppy wail. But even this he was not allowed to complete. In the middle of it White Fang, rushing in, sank his teeth into Lip-lip's hind leg. There was no fight left in Lip-lip, and he ran away shamelessly, his victim hot on his heels and worrying him all the way back to his own tepee. Here the squaws came to his aid, and White Fang, transformed into a raging demon, was finally driven off only by a fusillade of stones.

Came the day when Gray Beaver, deciding that the liability of her running away was past, released Kiche. White Fang was delighted with his mother's freedom. He accompanied her joyfully about the camp; and, so long as he remained close by her side, Lip-lip kept a respectful distance. White Fang even bristled up to him and walked stiff-legged, but Lip-lip ignored the challenge. He was no fool himself, and whatever vengeance he desired to wreak could wait until he caught White Fang alone.

Later on that day, Kiche and White Fang strayed into the edge of the woods next to the camp. He had led his mother there, step by step, and now, when she stopped, he tried to inveigle her farther. The stream, the lair and the quiet woods were calling to him, and he wanted her to come. He ran on a few steps, stopped, and looked back. She had not moved. He whined pleadingly, and scurried playfully in and out of the underbrush. He ran back to her, licked her face, and ran on again. And still she did not move. He stopped and regarded her, all of an intentness and eagerness, physically expressed, that slowly faded out of him as she turned her head and gazed back at the camp.

There was something calling to him out there in the open. His mother heard it, too. But she heard also that other and louder call, the call of the fire and of man—the call which has been given alone of all animals to the wolf to answer, to the wolf and the wild dog, who are brothers.

Kiche turned and slowly trotted back toward camp. Stronger than the physical restraint of the stick was the clutch of the camp upon her. Unseen and occultly, the gods still gripped with their power and would not let her go. White Fang sat down in the shadow of a birch and whimpered softly. There was a strong smell of pine, and subtle wood fragrances filled the air, reminding him of his old life of freedom before the days of his bondage. But he was still only a part-grown puppy, and stronger than the call either of man or of the Wild, was the call of his mother. All the hours of his short life he had depended upon her. The time was yet to come for independence. So he arose and trotted forlornly back to camp, pausing once, and twice, to sit down and whimper and to listen to the call that still sounded in the depths of the forest.

In the Wild the time of a mother with her young is short; but under the dominion of man it is sometimes even shorter. Thus it was with White Fang. Gray Beaver was in the debt of Three Eagles. Three Eagles was going away on a trip up the Mackenzie to the Great Slave Lake. A strip of scarlet cloth, a bearskin, twenty cartridges and Kiche went to pay the debt. White Fang saw his mother taken aboard Three Eagles' canoe, and tried to follow her. A blow from Three Eagles knocked him backward to the land. The canoe shoved off. He sprang into the water and swam after it, deaf to the sharp cries of Gray Beaver to return. Even a man-animal, a god, White Fang ignored, such was the terror he was in of losing his mother.

But gods are accustomed to being obeyed, and Gray Beaver wrathfully launched a canoe in pursuit. When he overtook White Fang, he reached down and by the nape of the neck lifted him clear of the water. He did not deposit him at once in the bottom of the canoe. Holding him suspended with one hand, with the other hand he proceeded to give him a beating. And it *was* a beating. His hand was heavy. Every blow was shrewd to hurt; and he delivered a multitude of blows.

Impelled by the blows that rained upon him, now from this side, now from that, White Fang swung back and forth like an erratic and jerky pendulum. Varying were the emotions that surged through him. At first he had known surprise. Then came a momentary fear, when he yelped several times to the impact of the hand. But this was quickly followed by anger. His free nature asserted itself, and he showed his teeth and snarled fearlessly in the face of the wrathful god. This but served to make the god more wrathful. The blows came faster, heavier, more shrewd to hurt.

Gray Beaver continued to beat, White Fang continued to snarl. But this could not last forever. One or the other must give over, and that one was White Fang. Fear surged through him again. For the first time he was being really man-handled. The occasional blows of sticks and stones he had previously experienced were as caresses compared with this. He broke down and began to cry and yelp. For a time each blow brought a yelp from him; but fear passed into terror, until finally his yelps were voiced in unbroken succession, unconnected with the rhythm of the punishment. At last Gray Beaver withheld his hand. White Fang, hanging limply, continued to cry. This seemed to satisfy his master, who flung him down roughly in the bottom of the canoe. In the meantime the canoe had drifted down the stream. Gray Beaver picked up the paddle. White Fang was in his way. He spurned him savagely with his foot. In that moment White Fang's free nature flashed forth again, and he sank his teeth into the moccasined foot.

The beating that had gone before was as nothing compared with the beating he now received. Gray Beaver's wrath was terrible; likewise was White Fang's fright. Not only the hand, but the hard wooden paddle was used upon him; and he was bruised and sore in all his small body when he was again flung down in the canoe. Again, and this time with purpose, did Gray Beaver kick him. White Fang did not repeat his attack on the foot. He had learned another lesson of his bondage. Never, no matter what the circumstance, must he dare to bite the god who was lord and master over him; the body of the lord and master was sacred, not to be defiled by the teeth of such as he. That was evidently the crime of crimes, the one offense there was no condoning nor overlooking.

When the canoe touched the shore, White Fang lay whimpering and motionless, waiting the will of Gray Beaver. It was Gray Beaver's will that he should go ashore, for ashore he was flung, striking heavily on his side and hurting his bruises afresh. He crawled tremblingly to his feet and stood whimpering. Lip-lip, who had watched the whole proceeding from the bank, now rushed upon him, knocking him over and sinking his teeth into him. White Fang was too helpless to defend himself, and it would have gone hard with him had not Gray Beaver's foot shot out, lifting Lip-lip into the air with its violence so that he smashed down to earth a dozen feet away. This was the man-animal's justice; and even then, in his own pitiable plight, White Fang experienced a little grateful thrill. At Gray Beaver's heels he limped obediently through the village to the tepee. And so it came that White Fang learned that the right to punish was something the gods reserved for themselves and denied to the lesser creatures under them.

That night, when all was still, White Fang remembered his mother and sorrowed for her. He sorrowed too loudly and woke up Gray Beaver, who beat him. After that he mourned gently when the gods were around. But sometimes, straying off to the edge of the woods by himself, he gave rein to his grief, and cried it out with loud whimperings and wailings.

It was during this period that he might have hearkened to the memories of the lair and the stream and run back to the Wild. But the memory of his mother held him. As the hunting man-animals went out and came back, so she would come back to the village some time. So he remained in his bondage, waiting for her.

But it was not altogether an unhappy bondage. There was much to interest him. Something was always happening. There was no end to the strange things these gods did, and he was always curious to see. Besides, he was learning how to get along with Gray Beaver. Obedience—rigid, undeviating obedience, was what was exacted of him; and in return he escaped beatings and his existence was tolerated.

Nay, Gray Beaver himself sometimes tossed him a piece of meat, and defended him against the other dogs in the eating of it. And such a piece of meat was of value. It was worth more, in some strange way, than a dozen pieces of meat from the hand of a squaw. Gray Beaver never petted nor caressed. Perhaps it was the weight of his hand, perhaps his justice, perhaps the sheer power of him, and perhaps it was all these things that influenced White Fang; for a certain tie of attachment was forming between him and his surly lord.

Insidiously and by remote ways, as well as by the power of stick and stone and clout of hand, were the shackles of White Fang's bondage being riveted upon him. The qualities in his kind that in the beginning made it possible for them to come in to the fires of men were qualities capable of development. They were developing in him, and the camp life, replete with misery as it was, was secretly endearing itself to him all the time. But White Fang was unaware of it. He knew only grief for the loss of Kiche, hope for her return and a hungry yearning for the free life that had been his.

CHAPTER III

THE OUTCAST

Lip-lip continued so to darken his days that White Fang became wickeder and more ferocious than it was his natural right to be. Savageness was a part of his make-up, but the savageness thus developed exceeded his make-up. He acquired a reputation for wickedness amongst the man-animals themselves. Wherever there was trouble and uproar in camp, fighting and squabbling or the outcry of a squaw over a bit of stolen meat, they were sure to find White Fang mixed up in it and usually at the bottom of it. They did not bother to look after the causes of his conduct. They saw only the effects, and the effects were bad. He was a sneak and a thief, a mischief-maker, a fomenter of trouble; and irate squaws told him to his face, the while he eyed them alert and ready to dodge any quick-flung missile, that he was a wolf and worthless and bound to come to an evil end.

He found himself an outcast in the midst of the populous camp. All the young dogs followed Lip-lip's lead. There was a difference between White Fang and them. Perhaps they sensed his wild-wood breed, and instinctively felt for him the enmity that the domestic dog feels for the wolf. But be that as it may, they joined with Lip-lip in the persecution. And, once declared against him, they found good reason to continue declared against him. One and all, from time to time, they felt his teeth; and to his credit, he gave more than he received. Many of them he could whip in single fight; but single fight was denied him. The beginning of such a fight was a signal for all the young dogs in camp to come running and pitch upon him.

Out of this pack persecution he learned two important things: how to take care of himself in a mass-fight against him; and how, on a single dog, to inflict the greatest amount of damage in the briefest space of time. To keep one's feet in the midst of the hostile mass meant life, and this he learned well. He became cat-like in his ability to stay on his feet. Even grown dogs might hurtle him backward or sideways with the impact of their heavy bodies, and backward or sideways he would go, in the air or sliding on the ground, but always with his legs under him and his feet downward to the mother earth.

When dogs fight there are usually preliminaries to the actual combat—snarlings and bristlings and stiff-legged struttings. But White Fang learned to omit these preliminaries. Delay meant the coming against him of all the young dogs. He must do his work quickly and get away. So he learned to give no warning of his intention. He rushed in and snapped and slashed on the instant, without notice, before his foe could prepare to meet him. Thus he learned how to inflict quick and severe damage. Also he learned the value of surprise. A dog taken off its guard, its shoulder slashed open or its ear ripped in ribbons before it knew what was happening, was a dog half whipped.

Furthermore, it was remarkably easy to overthrow a dog taken by surprise; while a dog, thus overthrown, invariably exposed for a moment the soft under side of its neck—the vulnerable point at which to strike for its life. White Fang knew this point. It was a knowledge bequeathed to him directly from the hunting generations of wolves. So it was that White Fang's method, when he took the offensive, was: first, to find a young dog alone; second, to surprise it and knock it off its feet; and, third, to drive in with his teeth at the soft throat.

Being but partly grown, his jaws had not yet become large enough nor strong enough to make his throat-attack deadly; but many a young dog went around camp with a lacerated throat in token of White Fang's intention. And one day, catching one of his enemies alone on the edge of the woods, he managed, by repeatedly overthrowing him and attacking the throat, to cut the great vein and let out the life. There was a great row that night. He had been observed, the news had been carried to the dead dog's master, the squaws remembered all the instances of stolen meat, and Gray Beaver was beset by many angry voices. But he resolutely held the door of his tepee, inside which he had placed the culprit, and refused to permit the vengeance for which his tribespeople clamored.

White Fang became hated by man and dog. During this period of his development he never knew a moment's security. The tooth of every dog was against him, the hand of every man. He was greeted with snarls by his kind, with curses and stones by his gods. He lived tensely. He was always keyed up, alert for attack, wary of being attacked, with an eye for sudden and unexpected missiles, prepared to act precipitately and coolly, to leap in with a flash of teeth, or to leap away with a menacing snarl.

As for snarling, he could snarl more terribly than any dog, young or old, in camp. The intent of the snarl is to warn or frighten, and judgment is required to know when it should be used. White Fang knew how to make it and when to make it. Into his snarl he incorporated all that was vicious, malignant and horrible. With nose serrulated by continuous spasms, hair bristling in recurrent waves, tongue whipping out like a red snake and whipping back again, ears flattened down, eyes gleaming hatred, lips wrinkled back, and fangs exposed and dripping, he could compel a pause on the part of almost any assailant. A temporary pause, when taken off his guard, gave him the vital moment in which to think and determine his action. But often a pause so gained lengthened out until it evolved into a complete cessation from the attack. And before more than one of the grown dogs, White Fang's snarl enabled him to beat an honorable retreat.

An outcast himself from the pack of the part-grown dogs, his sanguinary methods and remarkable efficiency made the pack pay for its persecution of him. Not permitted himself to run with the pack, the curious state of affairs obtained that no member of the pack could run outside the pack. White Fang would not permit it. What of his bushwhacking and waylaying tactics, the young dogs were afraid to run by themselves. With the exception of Lip-lip, they were compelled to hunch together for mutual protection against the terrible enemy they had made. A puppy alone by the river bank meant a puppy dead or a puppy that aroused the camp with its shrill pain and terror as it fled back from the wolf-cub that had waylaid it.

But White Fang's reprisals did not cease, even when the young dogs had learned thoroughly that they must stay together. He attacked them when he caught them alone, and they attacked him when they were bunched. The sight of him was sufficient to start them rushing after him, at which times his swiftness usually carried him into safety. But woe the dog that outran his fellows in such pursuit! White Fang had learned to turn suddenly upon the pursuer that was ahead of the pack and thoroughly to rip him up before the pack could arrive. This occurred with great frequency, for, once in full cry, the dogs were prone to forget themselves in the excitement of the chase, while White Fang never forgot himself. Stealing backward glances as he ran, he was always ready to whirl around and down the over-zealous pursuer that outran his fellows.

Young dogs are bound to play, and out of the exigencies of the situation they realized their play in this mimic warfare. Thus it was that the hunt of White Fang became their chief game--a deadly game, withal, and at all times a serious game. He, on the other hand, being the fastest-footed, was unafraid to venture anywhere. During the period that he waited vainly for his mother to come back, he led the pack many a wild chase through the adjacent woods. But the pack invariably lost him. Its noise and outcry warned him of its presence, while he ran alone, velvet-footed, silently, a moving shadow among the trees, after the manner of his father and mother before him. Further, he was more directly connected with the Wild than they; and he knew more of its secrets and stratagems. A favorite trick of his was to lose his trail in running water and then lie quietly in a near-by thicket while their baffled cries arose around him.

Hated by his kind and by mankind, indomitable, perpetually warred upon and himself waging perpetual war, his development was rapid and one-sided. This was no soil for kindliness and affection to blossom in. Of such things he had not the faintest glimmering. The code he learned was to obey the strong and to oppress the weak. Gray Beaver was a god, and strong. Therefore, White Fang obeyed him. But the dog younger or smaller than himself was weak, a thing to be destroyed. His development was in the direction of power. In order to face the constant danger of hurt and even of destruction, his predatory and protective faculties were unduly developed. He became quicker of movement than the other dogs, swifter of foot, craftier, deadlier, more lithe, more lean with iron-like muscle and sinew, more enduring, more cruel, more ferocious and more intelligent. He had to become all these things, else he would not have held his own nor survived the hostile environment in which he found himself.

CHAPTER IV

THE TRAIL OF THE GODS

In the fall of the year, when the days were shortening and the bite of the frost was coming into the air, White Fang got his chance for liberty. For several days there had been a great hubbub in the village. The summer camp was being dismantled, and the tribe, bag and baggage, was preparing to go off to the fall hunting. White Fang watched it all with eager eyes, and when the tepees began to come down and the canoes were loading at the bank, he understood. Already the canoes were departing, and some had disappeared down the river.

Quite deliberately he determined to stay behind. He waited his opportunity to slink out of camp to the woods. Here, in the running stream where ice was beginning to form, he hid his trail. Then he crawled into the heart of a dense thicket and waited. The time passed by, and he slept intermittently for hours. Then he was aroused by Gray Beaver's voice calling him by name. There were other voices. White Fang could hear Gray Beaver's squaw taking part in the search, and Mit-sah, who was Gray Beaver's son.

White Fang trembled with fear, and though the impulse came to crawl out of his hiding-place, he resisted it. After a time the voices died away, and some time after that he crept out to enjoy the success of his undertaking. Darkness was coming on, and for a while he played about among the trees, pleasuring in his freedom. Then, and quite suddenly, he became aware of loneliness. He sat down to consider, listening to the silence of the forest and perturbed by it. That nothing moved nor sounded seemed ominous. He felt the lurking of danger, unseen and unguessed. He was suspicious of the looming bulks of the trees and of the dark shadows that might conceal all manner of perilous things.

Then it was cold. Here was no warm side of a tepee against which to snuggle. The frost was in his feet, and he kept lifting first one fore-foot and then the other. He curved his bushy tail around to cover them, and at the same time he saw a vision. There was nothing strange about it. Upon his inward sight was impressed a succession of memory pictures. He saw the camp again, the tepees, and the blaze of the fires. He heard the shrill voices of the women, the gruff basses of the men, and the snarling of the dogs. He was hungry, and he remembered pieces of meat and fish that had been thrown him. Here was no meat, nothing but a threatening and inedible silence.

His bondage had softened him. Irresponsibility had weakened him. He had forgotten how to shift for himself. The night yawned about him. His senses, accustomed to the hum and bustle of the camp, used to the continuous impact of sights and sounds, were now left idle. There was nothing to do, nothing to see nor hear. They strained to catch some interruption of the silence and immobility of nature. They were appalled by inaction and by the feel of something terrible impending.

He gave a great start of fright. A colossal and formless something was rushing across the field of his vision. It was a tree shadow flung by the moon, from whose face the clouds had been brushed away. Reassured, he whimpered softly; then he suppressed the whimper for fear that it might attract the attention of the lurking dangers.

A tree, contracting in the cool of the night, made a loud noise. It was directly above him. He yelped in his fright. A panic seized him and he ran madly toward the village. He knew an overpowering desire for the protection and companionship of man. In his nostrils was the smell of the camp smoke. In his ears the camp sounds and cries were ringing loud. He passed out of the forest and into the moonlit open where were no shadows nor darknesses. But no village greeted his eyes. He had forgotten. The village had gone away.

His wild flight ceased abruptly. There was no place to which to flee. He slunk forlornly through the deserted camp, smelling the rubbish heaps and the discarded rags and tags of the gods. He would have been glad for the rattle of stones about him flung by an angry squaw, glad for the hand of Gray Beaver descending upon him in wrath; while he would have welcomed with delight Lip-lip and the whole snarling, cowardly pack.

He came to where Gray Beaver's tepee

had stood. In the center of the space it had occupied he sat down. He pointed his nose at the moon. His throat was afflicted by rigid spasms, his mouth opened, and in a heart-broken cry bubbled up his loneliness and fear, his grief for Kiche, all his past sorrows and miseries as well as his apprehension of sufferings and dangers to come. It was the long wolf-howl, full-throated and mournful, the first howl he had ever uttered.

The coming of daylight dispelled his fears, but increased his loneliness. The naked earth, which so shortly before had been so populous, thrust his loneliness more forcibly upon him. It did not take him long to make up his mind. He plunged into the forest and followed the river bank down the stream. All day he ran. He did not rest. He seemed made to run on forever. His iron-like body ignored fatigue. And even after fatigue came, his heritage of endurance braced him to endless endeavor and enabled him to drive his complaining body onward.

Where the river swung in against precipitous bluffs, he climbed the high mountains behind. Rivers and streams that entered the main river he forded or swam. Often he took to the rim-ice that was beginning to form, and more than once he crashed through and struggled for life in the icy current. Always he was on the lookout for the trail of the gods where it might leave the river and proceed inland.

White Fang was intelligent beyond the average of his kind; yet his mental vision was not wide enough to embrace the other bank of the Mackenzie. What if the trail of the gods led out on that side? It never entered his head. Later on, when he had traveled more and grown older and wiser and come to know more of trails and rivers, it might be that he could grasp and apprehend such a possibility. But that mental power was yet in the future. Just now he ran blindly, his own bank of the Mackenzie alone entering into his calculations.

All night he ran, blundering in the darkness into mishaps and obstacles that delayed but did not daunt. By the middle of the second day he had been running continuously for thirty hours, and the iron of his flesh was giving out. It was the endurance of his mind that kept him going. He had not eaten in forty hours and he was weak with hunger. The repeated drenchings in the icy water had likewise had their effect on him. His handsome coat was draggled. The broad pads of his feet were bruised and bleeding. He had begun to limp, and this limp increased with the hours. To make it worse, the light of the sky was obscured and snow began to fall—a raw, moist, melting, clinging snow, slippery under foot, that hid from him the landscape he traversed, and that covered over the inequalities of the ground so that the way of his feet was more difficult and painful.

Gray Beaver had intended camping that night on the far bank of the Mackenzie, for it was in that direction that the hunting lay. But on the near bank, shortly before dark, a moose, coming down to drink, had been espied by Kloo-kooch, who was Gray Beaver's squaw. Now, had not the moose come down to drink, had not Mit-sah been steering out of the course because of the snow, had not Kloo-kooch sighted the moose, and had not Gray Beaver killed it with a lucky shot from his rifle, all subsequent things would have happened differently. Gray Beaver would not have camped on the near side of the Mackenzie, and White Fang would have passed by and gone on, either to die or to find his way to his wild brothers and become one of them, a wolf to the end of his days.

Night had fallen. The snow was flying more thickly, and White Fang, whimpering softly to himself as he stumbled and limped along, came upon a fresh trail in the snow. So fresh was it that he knew it immediately for what it was. Whining with eagerness, he followed back from the river bank and in among the trees. The camp sounds came to his ears. He saw the blaze of the fire, Kloo-kooch cooking, and Gray Beaver squatting on his hams and mumbling a chunk of raw tallow. There was fresh meat in camp!

White Fang expected a beating. He crouched and bristled a little at the thought of it. Then he went forward again. He feared and disliked the beating he knew to be waiting for him. But he knew, further, that the comfort of the fire would be his, the protection of the gods, the companionship of the dogs—the last a companionship of enmity, but none the less a companionship and satisfying to his gregarious needs.

He came cringing and crawling into the firelight. Gray Beaver saw him and stopped munching the tallow. White Fang crawled slowly, cringing and groveling in the abjectness of his abasement and submission. He crawled straight toward Gray Beaver, every inch of his progress becoming slower and more painful. At last he lay at the master's feet, into whose possession he now surrendered himself, voluntarily, body and soul. Of his own choice, he came in to sit by man's fire and to be ruled by him. White Fang trembled, waiting for the punishment to fall upon him. There was a movement of the hand above him. He cringed involuntarily under the expected blow. It did not fall. He stole a glance upward. Gray Beaver was breaking the lump of tallow in half! Gray Beaver was offering him one piece of the tallow! Very gently and somewhat suspiciously, he first smelled the tallow and then proceeded to eat it. Gray Beaver ordered meat to be brought to him, and guarded him from the other dogs while he ate. After that, grateful and content, White Fang lay at Gray Beaver's feet, gazing at the fire that warmed him, blinking and dozing, secure in the knowledge that the morrow would find him, not wandering forlorn through bleak forest stretches, but in the camp of the man-animals, with the gods to whom he had given himself and upon whom he was now dependent.

CHAPTER V

THE COVENANT

When December was well along, Gray Beaver went on a journey up the Mackenzie. Mit-sah and Kloo-kooch went with him. One sled he drove himself, drawn by dogs he had traded for or borrowed. A second and smaller sled was driven by Mit-sah, and to this was harnessed a team of puppies. It was more of a toy affair than anything else, yet it was the delight of Mit-sah, who felt that he was beginning to do a man's work in the world. Also, he was learning to drive dogs and to train dogs; while the puppies themselves were being broken in to the harness. Furthermore, the sled was of some service, for it carried nearly two hundred pounds of outfit and food.

White Fang had seen the camp dogs toiling in the harness, so that he did not resent over-much the first placing of the harness upon himself. About his neck was put a moss-stuffed collar, which was connected by two pulling-traces to a strap that passed around his chest and over his back. It was to this that was fastened the long rope by which he pulled at the sled.

There were seven puppies in the team. The others had been born earlier in the year and were nine and ten months old, while White Fang was only eight months old. Each dog was fastened to the sled by a single rope. No two ropes were of the same length, while the difference in length between any two ropes was at least that of a dog's body. Every rope was brought to a ring at the front end of the sled. The sled itself was without runners, being a birch-bark toboggan, with up-turned forward end to keep it from plowing under the snow. This construction enabled the weight of the sled and load to be distributed over the largest snow surface; for the snow was crystal powder and very soft. Observing the same principle of widest distribution of weight, the dogs, at the ends of their ropes, radiated fan-fashion from the nose of the sled, so that no dog trod in another's footsteps.

There was, furthermore, another virtue in the fan formation. The ropes of varying length prevented the dogs attacking from the rear those that ran in front of them. For a dog to attack another, it would have to turn upon one at a shorter rope, in which case it would find itself face to face with the dog attacked, and also it would find itself facing the whip of the driver. But the most peculiar virtue of all lay in the fact that the dog that strove to attack one in front of him must pull the sled faster, and the faster the sled traveled the faster could the dog attacked run away. Thus the dog behind could never catch up with the one in front. The faster he ran the faster ran the one he was after, and the faster ran all the dogs. Incidentally the sled went faster, and thus, by cunning indirection, did man increase his mastery over the beasts.

Mit-sah resembled his father, much of whose gray wisdom he possessed. In the past he had observed Lip-lip's persecution of White Fang; but at that time Lip-lip was another man's dog, and Mit-sah had never dared more than to shy an occasional stone at him. But now Lip-lip was his dog, and he proceeded to wreak his vengeance on him by putting him at the end of the longest rope. This made Lip-lip the leader, and was apparently an honor; but in reality it took away from him all honor, and instead of being bully and master of the pack he now found himself hated and persecuted by the pack.

Because he ran at the end of the longest rope, the dogs had always the view of him running away before them. All that they saw of him was his bushy tail and fleeing hind legs—a view far less ferocious and intimidating than his bristling mane and gleaming fangs. Also, dogs being so constituted in their mental ways, the sight of him running away gave desire to run after him and a feeling that he ran away from them.

The moment the sled started, the team took after Lip-lip in a chase that extended throughout the day. At first he had been prone to turn upon his pursuers, jealous of his dignity and wrathful; but at such times Mit-sah would throw the stinging lash of the thirty-foot cariboo-gut whip into his face and compel him to turn tail and run on. Lip-lip might face the pack, but he could not face that whip, and all that was left him to do was to keep his long rope taut and his flanks ahead of the teeth of his mates.

But a still greater cunning lurked in the recesses of the Indian mind. To give point to unending pursuit of the leader, Mit-sah favored him over the other dogs. These favors aroused in them jealousy and hatred. In their presence Mit-sah would give him meat and would give it to him only. This was maddening to them. They would rage around just outside the throwing distance of the whip, while Lip-lip devoured the meat and Mit-sah protected him. And when there was no meat to give, Mit-sah would keep the team at a distance and make believe to give meat to Lip-lip.

White Fang took kindly to the work. He had traveled a greater distance than the other dogs in the yielding of himself to the rule of the gods, and he had learned more thoroughly the futility of opposing their will. In addition, the persecution he had suffered from the pack had made the pack less to him in the scheme of things, and man more. He had not learned to be dependent on his kind for companionship. Besides, Kiche was well-nigh forgotten; and the chief outlet of expression that remained to him was in the allegiance he tendered the gods he had accepted as masters. So he worked hard, learned discipline and was obedient. Faithfulness and willingness characterized his toil. These are essential traits of the wolf and the wild dog when they have become domesticated, and these traits White Fang possessed in unusual measure.

A companionship did exist between White Fang and the other dogs, but it was one of warfare and enmity. He had never learned to play with them. He knew only how to fight, and fight with them he did, returning to them a hundred-fold the snaps and slashes they had given him in the days when Lip-lip was leader of the pack. But Lip-lip was no longer leader—except when he fled away before his mates at the end of his rope, the sled bounding along behind. In camp he kept close to Mit-sah or Gray Beaver or Kloo-kooch. He did not dare venture away from the gods, for now the fangs of all dogs were against him, and he tasted to the dregs the persecution that had been White Fang's.

With the overthrow of Lip-lip, White Fang could have become leader of the pack. But he was too morose and solitary for that. He merely thrashed his team-mates. Otherwise he ignored them. They got out of his way when he came along; nor did the boldest of them ever dare to rob him of his meat. On the contrary, they devoured their own meat hurriedly, for fear that he would take it away from them. White Fang knew the law well: *to oppress the weak and obey the strong.* He ate his share of meat as rapidly as he could. And then woe the dog that had not yet finished! A snarl and a flash of fangs, and that dog would wail his indignation to the uncomforting stars while White Fang finished his portion for him.

Every little while, however, one dog or another would flame up in revolt and be promptly subdued. Thus White Fang was kept in training. He was jealous of the isolation in which he kept himself in the midst of the pack, and he fought often to maintain it. But such fights were of brief duration. He was too quick for the others. They were slashed open and bleeding before they knew what had happened, were whipped almost before they had begun to fight.

As rigid as the sled discipline of the gods was the discipline maintained by White Fang amongst his fellows. He never allowed them any latitude. He compelled them to an unremitting respect for him. They might do as they pleased amongst themselves. That was no concern of his. But it *was* his concern that they leave him alone in his isolation, get out of his way when he elected to walk among them, and at all times acknowledge his mastery over them. A hint of stiff-leggedness on their part, a lifted lip or a bristle of hair, and he would be upon them, merciless and cruel, swiftly convincing them of the error of their way.

He was a monstrous tyrant. His mastery was rigid as steel. He oppressed the weak with a vengeance. Not for nothing had he been exposed to the pitiless struggle for life in the days of his cubhood, when his mother and he, alone and unaided, held their own and survived in the ferocious environment of the Wild. And not for nothing had he learned to walk softly when superior strength went by. He oppressed the weak, but he respected the strong. And in the course of the long journey with Gray Beaver he walked softly indeed amongst the full-grown dogs in the camps of the strange man-animals they encountered.

The months passed by. Still continued the journey of Gray Beaver. White Fang's strength was developed by the long hours on trail and the steady toil at the sled; and it would have seemed that his mental development was well-nigh complete. He had come to know quite thoroughly the world in which he lived. His outlook was bleak and materialistic. The world as he saw it was a fierce and brutal world, a world without warmth, a world in which caresses and affection and the bright sweetnesses of the spirit did not exist.

He had no affection for Gray Beaver. True, he was a god, but a most savage god. White Fang was glad to acknowledge his lordship, but it was a lordship based upon superior intelligence and brute strength. There was something in the fiber of White Fang's being that made this lordship a thing to be desired, else he would not have come back from the Wild when he did to tender his allegiance. There were deeps in his nature which had never been sounded. A kind word, a caressing touch of the hand, on the part of Gray Beaver, might have sounded these deeps; but Gray Beaver did not caress nor speak kind words. It was not his way. His primacy was savage, and savagely he ruled, administering justice with a club, punishing transgression with the pain of a blow, and rewarding merit, not by kindness, but by withholding a blow.

So White Fang knew nothing of the heaven a man's hand might contain for him. Besides, he did not like the hands of the man-animals. He was suspicious of them. It was true that they sometimes gave meat, but more often they gave hurt. Hands were things to keep away from. They hurled stones, wielded sticks and clubs and whips, administered slaps and clouts, and, when they touched him, were cunning to hurt with pinch and twist and wrench. In strange villages he had encountered the hands of the children and learned that they were cruel to hurt. Also, he had once nearly had an eye poked out by a toddling papoose. From these experiences he became suspicious of all children. He could not tolerate them. When they came near with their ominous hands, he got up and walked away.

It was in a village at the Great Slave Lake that, in the course of resenting the evil of the hands of the man-animals, he came to modify the law that he had learned from Gray Beaver: namely, that the unpardonable crime was to bite one of the gods. In this village, after the custom of all dogs in all villages, White Fang went foraging for food. A boy was chopping frozen moose-meat with an axe, and the chips were flying in the snow. White Fang, sidling by in quest of meat, stopped and began to eat the chips. He observed the boy lay down the axe and take up a stout club. White Fang sprang clear, just in time to escape the descending blow. The boy pursued him, and he, a stranger in the village, fled between two tepees to find himself cornered against a high earth bank.

There was no escape for White Fang. The only way out was between the two tepees, and this the boy guarded. Holding his club prepared to strike, he drew in on his cornered quarry. White Fang was furious. He faced the boy, bristling and snarling, his sense of justice outraged. He knew the law of forage. All the wastage of meat, such as the frozen chips, belonged to the dog that found it. He had done no wrong, broken no law, yet here was this boy preparing to give him a beating. White Fang scarcely knew what happened. He did it in a surge of rage. And he did it so quickly that the boy did not know either. All the boy knew was that he had in some unaccountable way been overturned into the snow, and that his club hand had been ripped wide open by White Fang's teeth.

But White Fang knew that he had broken the law of the gods. He had driven his teeth into the sacred flesh of one of them, and could expect nothing but a most terrible punishment. He fled away to Gray Beaver, behind whose protecting legs he crouched when the bitten boy and the boy's family came, demanding vengeance. But they went away with vengeance unsatisfied. Gray Beaver defended White Fang. So did Mit-sah and Kloo-kooch. White Fang, listening to the wordy war and watching the angry gestures, knew that his act was justified. And so it came that he learned there were gods and gods. There were his gods, and there were other gods, and between them there was a difference. Justice or injustice, it was all the same, he must take all things from the hands of his own gods. But he was not compelled to take injustice from the other gods. It was his privilege to resent it with his teeth. And this also was a law of the gods.

Before the day was out White Fang was to learn more about this law. Mit-sah, alone, gathering firewood in the forest, encountered the boy that had been bitten. With him were other boys. Hot words passed. Then all the boys attacked Mit-sah. It was going hard with him. Blows were raining upon him from all sides. White Fang looked on at first. This was an affair of the gods, and no concern of his.

Then he realized that this was Mit-sah, one of his own particular gods, who was being maltreated. It was no reasoned impulse that made White Fang do what he then did. A mad rush of anger sent him leaping in amongst the combatants. Five minutes later the landscape was covered with fleeing boys, many of whom dripped blood upon the snow in token that White Fang's teeth had not been idle. When Mit-sah told his story in camp, Gray Beaver ordered meat to be given to White Fang. He ordered much meat to be given, and White Fang, gorged and sleepy by the fire, knew that the law had received its verification.

It was in line with these experiences that White Fang came to learn the law of property and the duty of the defense of property. From the protection of his god's body to the protection of his god's possessions was a step, and this step he made. What was his god's was to be defended against all the world—even to the extent of biting other gods. Not only was such an act sacrilegious in its nature, but it was fraught with peril. The gods were all-powerful, and a dog was no match against them; yet White Fang learned to face them, fiercely belligerent and unafraid. Duty rose above fear, and thieving gods learned to leave Gray Beaver's property alone.

One thing, in this connection, White Fang quickly learned, and that was that a thieving god was usually a cowardly god and prone to run away at the sounding of the alarm. Also, he learned that but brief time elapsed between his sounding of the alarm and Gray Beaver coming to his aid. He came to know that it was not fear of him that drove the thief away, but fear of Gray Beaver. White Fang did not give the alarm by barking. He never barked. His method was to drive straight at the intruder, and to sink his teeth in if he could. Because he was morose and solitary, having nothing to do with the other dogs, he was unusually fitted to guard his master's property; and in this he was encouraged and trained by Gray Beaver. One result of this was to make White Fang more ferocious and indomitable, and more solitary.

The months went by, binding stronger and stronger the covenant between dog and man. This was the ancient covenant that the first wolf that came in from the Wild entered into with man. And, like all succeeding wolves and wild dogs that had done likewise, White Fang worked the covenant out for himself. The terms were simple. For the possession of a flesh-and-blood god, he exchanged his own liberty. Food and fire, protection and companionship, were some of the things he received from the god. In return, he guarded the god's property, defended his body, worked for him and obeyed him.

The possession of a god implies service. White Fang's was a service of duty and awe, but not of love. He did not know what love was. He had no experience of love. Kiche was a remote memory. Besides, not only had he abandoned the Wild and his kind when he gave himself up to man, but the terms of the covenant were such that if he ever met Kiche again he would not desert his god to go with her. His allegiance to man seemed somehow a law of his being greater than the love of liberty, of kind and kin.

CHAPTER VI

THE FAMINE

The spring of the year was at hand when Gray Beaver finished his long journey. It was April, and White Fang was a year old when he pulled into the home village and was loosed from the harness by Mit-sah. Though a long way from his full growth, White Fang, next to Lip-lip, was the largest yearling in the village. Both from his father, the wolf, and from Kiche, he had inherited stature and strength, and already he was measuring up alongside the full-grown dogs. But he had not yet grown compact. His body was slender and rangy, and his strength more stringy than massive. His coat was the true wolf gray, and to all appearances he was true wolf himself. The quarter strain of dog he had inherited from Kiche had left no mark on him physically, though it played its part in his mental make-up.

He wandered through the village, recognizing with staid satisfaction the various gods he had known before the long journey. Then there were the dogs, puppies growing up like himself and grown dogs that did not look so large and formidable as the memory pictures he retained of them. Also, he stood less in fear of them than formerly, stalking among them with a certain careless ease that was as new to him as it was enjoyable.

There was Baseek, a grizzled old fellow that in his younger days had but to uncover his fangs to send White Fang cringing and crouching to the right-about. From him White Fang had learned much of his own insignificance; and from him he was now to learn much of the change and development that had taken place in himself. While Baseek had been growing weaker with age, White Fang had been growing stronger with youth.

It was at the cutting up of a moose, fresh killed, that White Fang learned of the changed relations in which he stood to the dog world. He had got for himself a hoof and part of the shin-bone, to which quite a bit of meat was attached. Withdrawn from the immediate scramble of the other dogs—in fact, out of sight behind a thicket—he was devouring his prize, when Baseek rushed in upon him. Before he knew what he was doing, he had slashed the intruder twice and sprung clear. Baseek was surprised by the other's temerity and swiftness of attack. He stood gazing stupidly across at White Fang, the raw, red shin-bone between them.

Baseek was old, and already he had come to know the increasing valor of the dogs it had been his wont to bully. Bitter experiences these, which, perforce, he swallowed, calling upon all his wisdom to cope with them. In the old days, he would have sprung upon White Fang in a fury of righteous wrath. But now his waning powers would not permit such a course. He bristled fiercely and looked ominously across the shin-bone at White Fang. And White Fang, resurrecting quite a deal of the old awe, seemed to wilt and to shrink in upon himself and grow small, as he cast about in his mind for a way to beat a retreat not too inglorious.

And right here Baseek erred. Had he contented himself with looking fierce and ominous all would have been well. White Fang, on the verge of retreat, would have retreated, leaving the meat to him. But Baseek did not wait. He considered the victory already his and stepped forward to the meat. As he bent his head carelessly to smell it White Fang bristled slightly. Even then it was not too late for Baseek to retrieve the situation. Had he merely stood over the meat, head up and glowering, White Fang would ultimately have slunk away. But the fresh meat was strong in Baseek's nostrils, and greed urged him to take a bite of it.

This was too much for White Fang. Fresh upon his months of mastery over his own team-mates, it was beyond his self-control to stand idly by while another devoured the meat that belonged to him. He struck, after his custom, without warning. With the first slash, Baseek's right ear was ripped into ribbons. He was astounded at the suddenness of it. But more things, and most grievous ones, were happening with equal suddenness. He was knocked off his feet. His throat was bitten. While he was struggling to his feet the young dog sank teeth twice into his shoulder. The swiftness of it was bewildering. He made a futile rush at White Fang, clipping the empty air with an outraged snap. The next moment his nose was laid open and he was staggering backward away from the meat.

The situation was now reversed. White Fang stood over the shin-bone, bristling and menacing, while Baseek stood a little way off, preparing to retreat. He dared not risk a fight with this young lightning-flash, and again he knew, and more bitterly, the enfeeblement of oncoming age. His attempt to maintain his dignity was heroic. Calmly turning his back upon young dog and shin-bone, as though both were beneath his notice and unworthy of consideration, he stalked grandly away. Nor until well out of sight did he stop to lick his bleeding wounds.

The effect on White Fang was to give him a greater faith in himself, and a greater pride. He walked less softly among the grown dogs; his attitude toward them was less compromising. Not that he went out of his way looking for trouble. Far from it. But upon his way he demanded consideration. He stood upon his right to go his way unmolested and to give trail to no dog. He had to be taken into account, that was all. He was no longer to be disregarded and ignored, as was the lot of puppies and as continued to be the lot of the puppies that were his team-mates. They got out of the way, gave trail to the grown dogs, and gave up meat to them under compulsion. But White Fang, uncompanionable, solitary, morose, scarcely looking to right or left, redoubtable, forbidding of aspect, remote and alien, was accepted as an equal by his puzzled elders. They quickly learned to leave him alone, neither venturing hostile acts nor making overtures of friendliness. If they left him alone, he left them alone—a state of affairs that they found, after a few encounters, to be pre-eminently desirable.

In midsummer White Fang had an experience. Trotting along in his silent way to investigate a new tepee which had been erected on the edge of the village while he was away with the hunters after moose, he came full upon Kiche. He paused and looked at her. He remembered her vaguely, but he *remembered* her, and that was more than could be said for her. She lifted her lip at him in the old snarl of menace, and his memory became clear. His forgotten cubhood, all that was associated with that familiar snarl, rushed back to him. Before he had known the gods, she had been to him the center-pin of the universe. The old familiar feelings of that time came back upon him, surged up within him. He bounded toward her joyously, and she met him with shrewd fangs that laid his cheek open to the bone. He did not understand. He backed away, bewildered and puzzled.

But it was not Kiche's fault. A wolf-mother was not made to remember her cubs of a year or so before. So she did not remember White Fang. He was a strange animal, an intruder; and her present litter of puppies gave her the right to resent such intrusion.

One of the puppies sprawled up to White Fang. They were half-brothers, only they did not know it. White Fang sniffed the puppy curiously, whereupon Kiche rushed upon him, gashing his face a second time. He backed farther away. All the old memories and associations died down again and passed into the grave from which they had been resurrected. He looked at Kiche licking her puppy and stopping now and then to snarl at him. She was without value to him. He had learned to get along without her. Her meaning was forgotten. There was no place for her in his scheme of things, as there was no place for him in hers.

He was still standing, stupid and bewildered, the memories forgotten, wondering what it was all about, when Kiche attacked him a third time, intent on driving him away altogether from the vicinity. And White Fang allowed himself to be driven away. This was a female of his kind, and it was a law of his kind that the males must not fight the females. He did not know anything about this law, for it was no generalization of the mind, not a something acquired by experience in the world. He knew it as a secret prompting, as an urge of instinct—of the same instinct that made him howl at the moon and stars of nights and that made him fear death and the unknown.

The months went by. White Fang grew stronger, heavier and more compact, while his character was developing along the lines laid down by his heredity and his environment. His heredity was a life-stuff that may be likened to clay. It possessed many possibilities, was capable of being molded into many different forms. Environment served to model the clay, to give it a particular form. Thus, had White Fang never come in to the fires of man, the Wild would have molded him into a true wolf. But the gods had given him a different environment, and he was molded into a dog that was rather wolfish, but that was a dog and not a wolf.

And so, according to the clay of his nature and the pressure of his surroundings, his character was being molded into a certain particular shape. There was no escaping it. He was becoming more morose, more uncompanionable, more solitary, more ferocious; while the dogs were learning more and more that it was better to be at peace with him than at war, and Gray Beaver was coming to prize him more greatly with the passage of each day.

White Fang, seeming to sum up strength in all his qualities, nevertheless suffered from one besetting weakness. He could not stand being laughed at. The laughter of men was a hateful thing. They might laugh among themselves about anything they pleased except himself, and he did not mind. But the moment laughter was turned upon him he would fly into a most terrible rage. Grave, dignified, somber, a laugh made him frantic to ridiculousness. It so outraged him and upset him that for hours he would behave like a demon. And woe to the dog that at such times ran foul of him. He knew the law too well to take it out on Gray Beaver; behind Gray Beaver were a club and god-head. But behind the dogs there was nothing but space, and into this space they fled when White Fang came on the scene made mad by laughter.

In the third year of his life there came a great famine to the Mackenzie Indians. In the summer the fish failed. In the winter the cariboo forsook their accustomed track. Moose were scarce, the rabbits almost disappeared, hunting and preying animals perished. Denied their usual food supply, weakened by hunger, they fell upon and devoured one another. Only the strong survived. White Fang's gods were also hunting animals. The old and the weak of them died of hunger. There was wailing in the village, where the women and children went without in order that what little they had might go into the bellies of the lean and hollow-eyed hunters who trod the forest in the vain pursuit of meat.

To such extremity were the gods driven that they ate the soft-tanned leather of their moccasins and mittens, while the dogs ate the harnesses off their backs and the very whip-lashes. Also, the dogs ate one another, and also the gods ate the dogs. The weakest and the more worthless were eaten first. The dogs that still lived looked on and understood. A few of the boldest and wisest forsook the fires of the gods, which had now become a shambles, and fled into the forest, where, in the end, they starved to death or were eaten by wolves.

In this time of misery White Fang, too, stole away into the woods. He was better fitted for the life than the other dogs, for he had the training of his cubhood to guide him. Especially adept did he become in stalking small living things. He would lie concealed for hours, following every movement of a cautious tree-squirrel, waiting, with a patience as huge as the hunger he suffered from, until the squirrel ventured out upon the ground. Even then White Fang was not premature. He waited until he was sure of striking before the squirrel could gain a tree refuge. Then, and not until then, would he flash from his hiding place, a gray projectile, incredibly swift, never failing its mark—the fleeing squirrel that fled not fast enough.

Successful as he was with squirrels, there was one difficulty that prevented him from living and growing fat on them. There were not enough squirrels. So he was driven to hunt still smaller things. So acute did his hunger become at times that he was not above rooting out wood-mice from their burrows in the ground. Nor did he scorn to do battle with a weasel as hungry as himself and many times more ferocious.

In the worst pinches of the famine he stole back to the fires of the gods. But he did not go in to the fires. He lurked in the forest, avoiding discovery and robbing the snares at the rare intervals when game was caught. He even robbed Gray Beaver's snare of a rabbit at a time when Gray Beaver staggered and tottered through the forest, sitting down often to rest, what of weakness and of shortness of breath.

One day White Fang encountered a young wolf, gaunt and scrawny, loose-jointed with famine. Had he not been hungry himself, White Fang might have gone with him and eventually found his way into the pack amongst his wild brethren. As it was, he ran the young wolf down and killed and ate him.

Fortune seemed to favor him. Always, when hardest pressed for food, he found something to kill. Again, when he was weak, it was his luck that none of the larger preying animals chanced upon him. Thus, he was strong from the two days' eating a lynx had afforded him when the hungry wolf pack ran full tilt upon him. It was a long, cruel chase, but he was better nourished than they and in the end outran them. And not only did he outrun them, but, circling widely back on his track, he gathered in one of his exhausted pursuers.

After that he left that part of the country and journeyed over to the valley wherein he had been born. Here, in the old lair, he encountered Kiche. Up to her old tricks, she, too, had fled the inhospitable fires of the gods and gone back to her old refuge to give birth to her young. Of this litter but one remained alive when White Fang came upon the scene, and this one was not destined to live long. Young life had little chance in such a famine.

Kiche's greeting of her grown son was anything but affectionate. But White Fang did not mind. He had outgrown his mother. So he turned tail philosophically and trotted on up the stream. At the forks he took the turning to the left, where he found the lair of the lynx with whom his mother and he had fought long before. Here, in the abandoned lair, he settled down and rested for a day.

During the early summer, in the last days of the famine, he met Lip-lip, who had likewise taken to the woods, where he had eked out a miserable existence. White Fang came upon him unexpectedly. Trotting in opposite directions along the base of a high bluff, they rounded a corner of rock and found themselves face to face. They paused with instant alarm, and looked at each other suspiciously.

White Fang was in splendid condition. His hunting had been good, and for a week he had eaten his fill. He was even gorged from his latest kill. But in the moment he looked at Lip-lip his hair rose on end all along his back. It was an involuntary bristling on his part, the physical state that in the past had always accompanied the mental state produced in him by Lip-lip's bullying and persecution. As in the past he had bristled and snarled at sight of Lip-lip, so now, and automatically, he bristled and snarled. He did not waste any time. The thing was done thoroughly and with dispatch. Lip-lip essayed to back away, but White Fang struck him hard, shoulder to shoulder. Lip-lip was overthrown and rolled upon his back. White Fang's teeth drove into the scrawny throat. There was a death-struggle, during which White Fang walked around, stiff-legged and observant. Then he resumed his course and trotted on along the base of the bluff.

One day, not long after, he came to the edge of the forest, where a narrow stretch of open land sloped down to the Mackenzie. He had been over this ground before, when it was bare, but now a village occupied it. Still hidden amongst the trees, he paused to study the situation. Sights and sounds and scents were familiar to him. It was the old village changed to a new place. But sights and sounds and smells were different from those he had last had when he fled away from it. There was no whimpering nor wailing. Contented sounds saluted his ear, and when he heard the angry voice of a woman he knew it to be the anger that proceeds from a full stomach. And there was a smell in the air of fish. There was food. The famine was gone. He came out boldly from the forest and trotted into camp straight to Gray Beaver's tepee. Gray Beaver was not there; but Kloo-kooch welcomed him with glad cries and the whole of a fresh-caught fish, and he lay down to wait Gray Beaver's coming.

WHITE FANG

BY JACK LONDON

ILLUSTRATED BY FRANK E. SCHOONOVER

PART IV.—THE SUPERIOR GODS

CHAPTER I

THE ENEMY OF HIS KIND

HAD there been in White Fang's nature any possibility, no matter how remote, of his ever coming to fraternize with his kind, such possibility was irretrievably destroyed when he was made leader of the sled-team. For now the dogs hated him—hated him for the extra meat bestowed upon him by Mit-sah; hated him for all the real and fancied favors he received; hated him for that he fled always at the head of the team, his waving brush of a tail and his perpetually retreating hind-quarters forever maddening their eyes.

And White Fang just as bitterly hated them back. Being sled leader was anything but gratifying to him. To be compelled to run away before the yelling pack, every dog of which, for three years, he had thrashed and mastered, was almost more than he could endure. But endure it he must, or perish, and the life that was in him had no desire to perish. The moment Mit-sah gave his order for the start, that moment the whole team, with eager, savage cries, sprang forward at White Fang.

There was no defense for him. If he turned upon them, Mit-sah would throw the stinging lash of the whip into his face. Only remained to him to run away. He could not encounter that howling horde with his tail and hind-quarters. These were scarcely fit weapons with which to meet the many merciless fangs. So run away he did, violating his own nature and pride with every leap he made, and leaping all day long.

One cannot violate the promptings of one's nature without having that nature recoil upon itself. Such a recoil is like that of a hair, made to grow out from the body, turning unnaturally upon the direction of its growth and growing into the body—a rankling, festering thing of hurt. And so with White Fang. Every urge of his being impelled him to spring upon the pack that cried at his heels, but it was the will of the gods that this should not be; and behind the will, to enforce it, was the whip of cariboo-gut with its biting thirty-foot lash. So White Fang could only eat his heart in bitterness and develop a hatred and malice commensurate with the ferocity and indomitability of his nature.

If ever a creature was the enemy of its kind, White Fang was that creature. He asked no quarter, gave none. He was continually marred and scarred by the teeth of the pack, and as continually he left his own marks upon the pack. Unlike most leaders, who, when camp was made and the dogs were unhitched, huddled near to the gods for protection, White Fang disdained such protection. He walked boldly about the camp, inflicting punishment in the night for what he had suffered in the day. In the time before he was made leader of the team, the pack had learned to get out of his way. But now it was different. Excited by the day-long pursuit of him, swayed subconsciously by the insistent iteration on their brains of the sight of him fleeing away, mastered by the feeling of mastery enjoyed all day, the dogs could not bring themselves to give way to him. When he appeared amongst them there was always a squabble. His progress was marked by snarl and snap and growl. The very atmosphere he breathed was surcharged with hatred and malice, and this but served to increase the hatred and malice within him.

When Mit-sah cried out his command for the team to stop, White Fang obeyed. At first this caused trouble for the other dogs. All of them would spring upon the hated leader only to find the tables turned. Behind him would be Mit-sah, the great whip stinging in his hand. So the dogs came to understand that when the team stopped by order, White Fang was to be let alone. But when White Fang stopped without orders, then it was allowed them to spring upon him and destroy him if they could. After several experiences, White Fang never stopped without orders. He learned quickly. It was in the nature of things that he must learn quickly, if he were to survive the unusually severe conditions under which life was vouchsafed him.

But the dogs could never learn the lesson to leave him alone in camp. Each day, pursuing him and crying defiance at him, the lesson of the previous night was erased, and that night would have to be learned over again, to be as immediately forgotten. Besides, there was a greater consistence in their dislike of him. They sensed between themselves and him a difference of kind—cause sufficient in itself for hostility. Like him, they were domesticated wolves. But they had been domesticated for generations. Much of the Wild had been lost, so that to them the Wild was the unknown, the terrible, the ever-menacing and ever-warring. But to him, in appearance and action and impulse, still clung the Wild. He symbolized it, was its personification; so that when they showed their teeth to him they were defending themselves against the powers of destruction that lurked in the shadows of the forest and in the dark beyond the camp fire.

But there was one lesson the dogs did learn, and that was to keep together. White Fang was too terrible for any of them to face single-handed. They met him with the mass-formation, otherwise he would have killed them, one by one, in a night. As it was, he never had a chance to kill them. He might roll a dog off its feet, but the pack would be upon him before he could follow up and deliver the deadly throat-stroke. At the first hint of conflict the whole team drew together and faced him. The dogs had quarrels among themselves, but these were forgotten when trouble was brewing with White Fang.

On the other hand, try as they would, they could not kill White Fang. He was too quick for them, too formidable, too wise. He avoided tight places, and always backed out when they bade fair to surround him. While as for getting him off his feet, there was no dog among them capable of doing the trick. His feet clung to the earth with the same tenacity that he clung to life. For that matter, life and footing were synonymous in this unending warfare with the pack, and none knew it better than White Fang.

So he became the enemy of his kind, domesticated wolves that they were, softened by the fires of man, weakened in the sheltering shadow of man's strength. White Fang was bitter and implacable. The clay of him was so molded. He declared a vendetta against all dogs. And so terribly did he live this vendetta that Gray Beaver, fierce savage himself, could not but marvel at White Fang's ferocity. Never, he swore, had there been the like of this animal; and the Indians in strange villages swore likewise when they considered the tale of his killings amongst their dogs.

When White Fang was nearly five years old, Gray Beaver took him on another great journey, and long remembered was the havoc he worked amongst the dogs of the many villages along the Mackenzie, across the Rockies, and down the Porcupine to the Yukon. He reveled in the vengeance he wreaked upon his kind. They were ordinary, unsuspecting dogs. They were not prepared for his swiftness and directness, for his attack without warning. They did not know him for what he was, a lightning-flash of slaughter. They bristled up to him, stiff-legged and challenging, while he, wasting no time on elaborate preliminaries, snapping into action like a steel spring, was at their throats and destroying them before they knew what was happening and while they were yet in the throes of surprise.

He became an adept at fighting. He economized. He never wasted his strength, never tussled. He was in too quickly for that, and, if he missed, was out again too quickly. The dislike of the wolf for close quarters was his to an unusual degree. He could not endure a prolonged contact with another body. It smacked of danger. It made him frantic. He must be away, free, on his own legs, touching no living thing. It was the Wild still clinging to him, asserting itself through him. This feeling had been accentuated by the Ishmaelite life he had led from his puppyhood. Danger lurked in contacts. It was the trap, ever the trap, the fear of it lurking deep in the life of him, woven into the fiber of him.

In consequence the strange dogs he encountered had no chance against him. He eluded their fangs. He got them, or got away, himself untouched in either event. In the natural course of things there were exceptions to this. There were times when several dogs, pitching onto him, punished him before he could get away; and there were times when a single dog scored deeply on him. But these were accidents. In the main, so efficient a fighter had he become, he went his way unscathed.

Another advantage he possessed was that of correctly judging time and distance. Not that he did this consciously, however. He did not calculate such things. It was all automatic. His eyes saw correctly, and the nerves carried the vision correctly to his brain. The parts of him were better adjusted than those of the average dog. They worked together more smoothly and steadily. His was a better, far better, nervous, mental, and muscular co-ordination. When his eyes conveyed to his brain the moving image of an action, his brain, without conscious effort, knew the space that limited that action and the time required for its completion. Thus, he could avoid the leap of another dog, or the drive of its fangs, and at the same moment could seize the infinitesimal fraction of time in which to deliver his own attack. Body and brain, his was a more perfected mechanism. Not that he was to be praised for it. Nature had been more generous to him than to the average animal, that was all.

It was in the summer that White Fang arrived at Fort Yukon. Gray Beaver had crossed the great water-shed between the Mackenzie and the Yukon in the late winter, and spent the spring in hunting among the western outlying spurs of the Rockies. Then, after the break-up of the ice on the Porcupine, he had built a canoe and paddled down that stream to where it effected its junction with the Yukon just under the Arctic Circle. Here stood the old Hudson's Bay Company fort; and here were many Indians, much food, and unprecedented excitement. It was the summer of 1898, and thousands of gold-hunters were going up the Yukon to Dawson and the Klondike. Still hundreds of miles from their goal, nevertheless many of them had been on the way for a year, and the least any of them had traveled to get that far was five thousand miles, while some had come from the other side of the world.

Here Gray Beaver stopped. A whisper of the gold-rush had reached his ears, and he had come with several bales of furs, and another of gut-sewn mittens and moccasins. He would not have ventured so long a trip had he not expected generous profits. But what he had expected was nothing to what he realized. His wildest dream had not exceeded a hundred per cent. profit; he made a thousand per cent. And like a true Indian, he settled down to trade carefully and slowly, even if it took all summer and the rest of the winter to dispose of his goods.

It was at Fort Yukon that White Fang saw his first white men. As compared with the Indians he had known, they were to him another race of beings, a race of superior gods. They impressed him as possessing superior power, and it is on power that godhead rests. White Fang did not reason it out, did not in his mind make the sharp generalization that the white gods were more powerful. It was a feeling, nothing more, and yet none the less potent. As in his puppyhood, the looming bulks of the tepees, man-reared, had affected him as manifestations of power, so was he affected now by the houses and the huge fort, all of massive logs. Here was power. These white gods were strong. They possessed greater mastery over matter than the gods he had known, most powerful among which was Gray Beaver. And yet Gray Beaver was as a child-god among these white-skinned ones.

To be sure, White Fang only felt these things. He was not conscious of them. Yet it is upon feeling, more often than thinking, that animals act; and every act White Fang now performed was based upon the feeling that the white men were the superior gods. In the first place, he was very suspicious of them. There was no telling what unknown terrors were theirs, what unknown hurts they could administer. He was curious to observe them, fearful of being noticed by them. For the first few hours he was content with slinking around and watching them from a safe distance. Then he saw that no harm befell the dogs that were near to them, and he came in closer.

In turn, he was an object of great curiosity to them. His wolfish appearance caught their eyes at once, and they pointed him out to one another. This act of pointing put White Fang on his guard, and when they tried to approach him he showed his teeth and backed away. Not one succeeded in laying a hand on him, and it was well that they did not.

White Fang soon learned that very few of these gods—not more than a dozen—lived at this place. Every two or three days a steamer (another and colossal manifestation of power) came in to the bank and stopped for several hours. The white men came from off these steamers and went away on them again. There seemed untold numbers of these white men. In the first day or so he saw more of them than he had seen Indians in all his life; and as the days went by they continued to come up the river, stop, and then go on up the river and out of sight.

But if the white gods were all-powerful, their dogs did not amount to much. This White Fang quickly discovered by mixing with those that came ashore with their masters. They were of irregular shapes and sizes. Some were short-legged—too short; others were long-legged—too long. They had hair instead of fur, and a few had very little hair at that. And none of them knew how to fight.

As an enemy of his kind, it was in White Fang's province to fight with them. This he did, and he quickly achieved for them a mighty contempt. They were soft and helpless, made much noise, and floundered around clumsily, trying to accomplish by main strength what he accomplished by dexterity and cunning. They rushed bellowing at him. He sprang to the side. They did not know what had become of him; and in that moment he struck them on the shoulder, rolling them off their feet and delivering his stroke at the throat.

Sometimes this stroke was successful, and a stricken dog rolled in the dirt, to be pounced upon and torn to pieces by the pack of Indian dogs that waited. White Fang was wise. He had long since learned that the gods were made angry when their dogs were killed. The white men were no exception to this. So he was content, when he had overthrown and slashed wide the throat of one of their dogs, to drop back and let the pack go in and do the cruel finishing work. It was then that the white men rushed in, visiting their wrath heavily on the pack, while White Fang went free. He would stand off at a little distance and look on, while stones, clubs, axes, and all sorts of weapons fell upon his fellows. White Fang was very wise.

But his fellows grew wise, in their own way; and in this White Fang grew wise with them. They learned that it was when a steamer first tied to the bank that they had their fun. After the first two or three strange dogs had been downed and destroyed, the white men hustled their own animals back on board and wreaked savage vengeance on the offenders. One white man, having seen his dog, a setter, torn to pieces before his eyes, drew a revolver. He fired rapidly, six times, and six of the pack lay dead or dying—another manifestation of power that sank deep into White Fang's consciousness.

White Fang enjoyed it all. He did not love his kind, and he was shrewd enough to escape hurt himself. At first, the killing of the white men's dogs had been a diversion. After a time it became his occupation. There was no work for him to do. Gray Beaver was busy trading and getting wealthy. So White Fang hung around the landing with the disreputable gang of Indian dogs, waiting for steamers. With the arrival of a steamer the fun began. After a few minutes, by the time the white men had got over their surprise, the gang scattered. The fun was over until the next steamer should arrive.

But it can scarcely be said that White Fang was a member of the gang. He did not mingle with it, but remained aloof, always himself, and was even feared by it.

It is true he worked with it. He picked the quarrel with the strange dog while the gang waited. And when he had overthrown the strange dog the gang went in to finish it. But it is equally true that he then withdrew, leaving the gang to receive the punishment of the outraged gods.

It did not require much exertion to pick these quarrels. All he had to do, when the strange dogs came ashore, was to show himself. When they saw him they rushed for him. It was their instinct. He was the Wild—the unknown, the terrible, the ever-menacing, the thing that prowled in the darkness around the fires of the primeval world when they, cowering close to the fires, were reshaping their instincts, learning to fear the Wild out of which they had come, and which they had deserted and betrayed. Generation by generation, down all the generations, had this fear of the Wild been stamped into their natures. For centuries the Wild had stood for terror and destruction. And during all this time free license had been theirs, from their masters, to kill the things of the Wild. In doing this they had protected both themselves and the gods whose companionship they shared.

And so, fresh from the soft southern world, these dogs, trotting down the gangplank and out upon the Yukon shore, had but to see White Fang to experience the irresistible impulse to rush upon him and destroy him. They might be town-reared dogs, but the instinctive fear of the Wild was theirs just the same. Not alone with their own eyes did they see the wolfish creature in the clear light of day, standing before them. They saw him with the eyes of their ancestors, and by their inherited memory they knew White Fang for the wolf, and they remembered the ancient feud.

All of which served to make White Fang's days enjoyable. If the sight of him drove these strange dogs upon him, so much the better for him, so much the worse for them. They looked upon him as legitimate prey, and as legitimate prey he looked upon them.

Not for nothing had he first seen the light of day in a lonely lair and fought his first fights with the ptarmigan, the weasel and the lynx. And not for nothing had his puppyhood been made bitter by the persecution of Lip-lip and the whole puppy pack. It might have been otherwise, and he would then have been otherwise. Had Lip-lip not existed he would have passed his puppyhood with the other puppies and grown up more dog-like and with more liking for dogs. Had Gray Beaver possessed the plummet of affection and love, he might have sounded the deeps of White Fang's nature and brought up to the surface all manner of kindly qualities. But these things had not been so. The clay of White Fang had been molded until he became what he was, morose and lonely, unloving and ferocious, the enemy of all his kind.

CHAPTER II

THE MAD GOD

A small number of white men lived in Fort Yukon. Tnese men had been long in the country. They called themselves Sour-doughs, and took great pride in so classifying themselves. For other men, new in the land, they felt nothing but disdain. The men who came ashore from the steamers were new-comers. They were known as *chechaquos*, and they always wilted at the application of the name. They made their bread with baking-powder. This was the invidious distinction between them and the Sour-doughs, who, forsooth, made their bread from sour-dough because they had no baking-powder.

All of which is neither here nor there. The men in the fort disdained the new-comers, and enjoyed seeing them come to grief. Especially did they enjoy the havoc worked amongst the new-comers' dogs by White Fang and his disreputable gang. When a steamer arrived, the men of the fort made it a point always to come down to the bank and see the fun. They looked forward to it with as much anticipation as did the Indian dogs, while they were not slow to appreciate the savage and crafty part played by White Fang.

But there was one man amongst them who particularly enjoyed the sport. He would come running at the first sound of a steamboat's whistle; and when the last fight was over and White Fang and the pack had scattered, he would return slowly to the fort, his face heavy with regret. Sometimes, when a soft southland dog went down, shrieking its death-cry under the fangs of the pack, this man would be unable to contain himself, and would leap into the air and cry out with delight. And always he had a sharp and covetous eye for White Fang.

This man was called "Beauty" by the other men of the fort. No one knew his first name, and in general he was known in the country as Beauty Smith. But he was anything save a beauty. To antithesis was due his naming. He was pre-eminently unbeautiful. Nature had been niggardly with him. He was a small man to begin with; and upon his meager frame was deposited an even more strikingly meager head. Its apex might be likened to a point. In fact, in his boyhood, before he had been named Beauty by his fellows, he had been called "Pinhead."

Backward, from the apex, his head slanted down to his neck; and forward, it slanted uncompromisingly to meet a low and remarkably wide forehead. Beginning here, as though regretting her parsimony, Nature had spread his features with a lavish hand. His eyes were large, and between them was the distance of two eyes. His face, in relation to the rest of him, was prodigious. In order to discover the necessary area, Nature had given him an enormous prognathous jaw. It was wide and heavy, and protruded outward and down until it seemed to rest on his chest. Possibly this appearance was due to the weariness of the slender neck, unable properly to support so great a burden.

This jaw gave the impression of ferocious determination. But something lacked. Perhaps it was from excess. Perhaps the jaw was too large. At any rate, it was a lie. Beauty Smith was known far and wide as the weakest of weak-kneed and sniveling cowards. To complete his description, his teeth were large and yellow, while the two eye-teeth, larger than their fellows, showed under his lean lips like fangs. His eyes were yellow and muddy, as though Nature had run short on pigments and squeezed together the dregs of all her tubes. It was the same with his hair, sparse and irregular of growth, muddy-yellow and dirty-yellow, rising on his head and sprouting out of his face in unexpected tufts and bunches, in appearance like clumped and wind-blown grain.

In short, Beauty Smith was a monstrosity, and the blame of it lay elsewhere. He was not responsible. The clay of him had been so molded in the making. He did the cooking for the other men in the fort, the dish-washing and the drudgery. They did not despise him. Rather did they tolerate him in a broad human way, as one tolerates any creature evilly treated in the making. Also they feared him. His cowardly rages made them dread a shot in the back or poison in their coffee. But somebody had to do the cooking, and whatever else his shortcomings, Beauty Smith could cook.

This was the man that looked at White Fang, delighted in his ferocious prowess, and desired to possess him. He made overtures to White Fang from the first. White Fang began by ignoring him. Later on, when the overtures became more insistent, White Fang bristled and bared his teeth and backed away. He did not like the man. The feel of him was bad. He sensed the evil in him, and feared the extended hand and the attempts at soft-spoken speech. Because of all this he hated the man.

With the simpler creatures, good and bad are things simply understood. The good stands for all things that bring easement and satisfaction and surcease from pain. Therefore, the good is liked. The bad stands for all things that are fraught with discomfort, menace and hurt, and is hated accordingly. White Fang's feel of Beauty Smith was bad. From the man's distorted body and twisted mind, in occult ways, like mists rising from malarial marshes, came emanations of the unhealth within. Not by reasoning, not by the five senses alone, but by other and remoter and uncharted senses, came the feeling to White Fang that the man was ominous with evil, pregnant with hurtfulness, and therefore a thing bad, and wisely to be hated.

White Fang was in Gray Beaver's camp when Beauty Smith first visited it. At the faint sound of his distant feet, before he came in sight, White Fang knew who was coming and began to bristle. He had been lying down in an abandon of comfort, but he arose quickly, and, as the man arrived, slid away in true wolf fashion to the edge of the camp. He did not know what they said, but he could see the man and Gray

Beaver talking together. Once the man pointed at him, and White Fang snarled back as though the hand were just descending upon him instead of being, as it was, fifty feet away. The man laughed at this; and White Fang slunk away to the sheltering woods, his head turned to observe as he glided softly over the ground.

Gray Beaver refused to sell the dog. He had grown rich with his trading and stood in need of nothing. Besides, White Fang was a valuable animal, the strongest sled-dog he had ever owned, and the best leader. Furthermore, there was no dog like him on the Mackenzie nor the Yukon. He could fight. He killed other dogs as easily as men killed mosquitoes. (Beauty Smith's eyes lighted up at this, and he licked his thin lips with an eager tongue.) No, White Fang was not for sale at any price.

But Beauty Smith knew the ways of Indians. He visited Gray Beaver's camp often, and hidden under his coat was always a black bottle or so. One of the potencies of whiskey is the breeding of thirst. Gray Beaver got the thirst. His fevered membranes and burnt stomach began to clamor for more and more of the scorching fluid; while his brain, thrust all awry by the unwonted stimulant, permitted him to go any length to obtain it. The money he had received for his furs and mittens and moccasins began to go. It went faster and faster, and the shorter his money-sack grew the shorter grew his temper.

In the end his money and goods and temper were all gone. Nothing remained to him but his thirst, a prodigious possession in itself that grew more prodigious with every sober breath he drew. Then it was that Beauty Smith had talk with him again about the sale of White Fang; but this time the price offered was in bottles, not dollars, and Gray Beaver's ears were more eager to hear.

"You ketch um dog you take um all right," was his last word.

The bottles were delivered, but after two days, "You ketch um dog," were Beauty Smith's words to Gray Beaver.

White Fang slunk into camp one evening and dropped down with a sigh of content. The dreaded white god was not there. For days his manifestations of desire to lay hands on him had been growing more insistent, and during that time White Fang had been compelled to avoid the camp. He did not know what evil was threatened by those insistent hands. He knew only that they did threaten evil of some sort, and that it was best for him to keep out of their reach.

But scarcely had he lain down when Gray Beaver staggered over to him and tied a leather thong around his neck. He sat down beside White Fang, holding the end of the thong in his hand. In the other hand he held a bottle, which, from time to time, was inverted above his head to the accompaniment of gurgling noises.

An hour of this passed, when the vibrations of feet in contact with the ground foreran the one who approached. White Fang heard it first, and he was bristling with recognition while Gray Beaver still nodded stupidly. White Fang tried to draw the thong softly out of his master's hand; but the relaxed fingers closed tightly and Gray Beaver roused himself.

Beauty Smith strode into camp and stood over White Fang. He snarled softly up at the thing of fear, watching keenly the deportment of the hands. One hand extended outward and began to descend upon his head. His soft snarl grew tense and harsh. The hand continued slowly to descend, while he crouched beneath it, eyeing it malignantly, his snarl growing shorter and shorter as, with quickening breath, it approached its culmination. Suddenly he snapped, striking with his fangs like a snake. The hand was jerked back, and the teeth came together emptily with a sharp click. Beauty Smith was frightened and angry. Gray Beaver clouted White Fang alongside the head, so that he cowered down close to the earth in respectful obedience.

White Fang's suspicious eyes followed every movement. He saw Beauty Smith go away and return with a stout club. Then the end of the thong was given over to him by Gray Beaver. Beauty Smith started to walk away. The thong grew taut. White Fang resisted it. Gray Beaver clouted him right and left to make him get up and follow. He obeyed, but with a rush, hurling himself upon the stranger who was dragging him away. Beauty Smith did not jump away. He had been waiting for this. He swung the club smartly, stopping the rush midway and smashing White Fang down upon the ground. Gray Beaver laughed and nodded approval. Beauty Smith tightened the thong again, and White Fang crawled limply and dizzily to his feet.

He did not rush a second time. One smash from the club was sufficient to convince him that the white god knew how to handle it, and he was too wise to fight the inevitable. So he followed morosely at Beauty Smith's heels, his tail between his legs, yet snarling softly under his breath. But Beauty Smith kept a wary eye on him, and the club was held always ready to strike.

At the fort Beauty Smith left him securely tied and went in to bed. White Fang waited an hour. Then he applied his teeth to the thong and in the space of ten seconds was free. He had wasted no time with his teeth. There had been no useless gnawing. The thong was cut across, diagonally, almost as clean as though done by a knife. White Fang looked up at the fort, at the same time bristling and growling. Then he turned and trotted back to Gray Beaver's camp. He owed no allegiance to this strange and terrible god. He had given himself to Gray Beaver, and to Gray Beaver he considered he still belonged.

But what had occurred before was repeated—with a difference. Gray Beaver again made him fast with a thong, and in the morning turned him over to Beauty Smith. And here was where the difference came in. Beauty Smith gave him a beating. Tied securely, White Fang could only rage futilely and endure the punishment. Club and whip were both used upon him, and he experienced the worst beating he had ever received in his life. Even the big beating given him in his puppyhood by Gray Beaver was mild compared with this.

Beauty Smith enjoyed the task. He delighted in it. He gloated over his victim, and his eyes flamed dully as he swung the whip or club and listened to White Fang's cries of pain and to his helpless bellows and snarls. For Beauty Smith was cruel in the way that cowards are cruel. Cringing and sniveling himself before the blows or angry speech of a man, he revenged himself, in turn, upon creatures weaker than he. All life likes power, and Beauty Smith was no exception. Denied the expression of power amongst his own kind, he fell back upon the lesser creatures and there vindicated the life that was in him. But Beauty Smith had not created himself, and no blame was to be attached to him. He had come into the world with a twisted body and a brute intelligence. This had constituted the clay of him, and it had not been kindly molded by the world.

White Fang knew why he was being beaten. When Gray Beaver tied the thong around his neck and passed the end of the thong into Beauty Smith's keeping, White Fang knew that it was his god's will for him to go with Beauty Smith. And when Beauty Smith left him tied outside the fort, he knew that it was Beauty Smith's will that he should remain there. Therefore, he had disobeyed the will of both the gods and earned the consequent punishment. He had seen dogs change owners in the past, and he had seen the runaways beaten as he was being beaten. He was wise, and yet in the nature of him there were forces greater than wisdom. One of these was fidelity. He did not love Gray Beaver; yet, even in the face of his will and his anger, he was faithful to him. He could not help it. This faithfulness was a quality of the clay that composed him. It was the quality that was peculiarly the possession of his kind; the quality that set apart his species from all other species; the quality that had enabled the wolf and the wild dog to come in from the open and be the companions of man.

After the beating, White Fang was dragged back to the fort. But this time Beauty Smith left him tied with a stick. One does not give up a god easily, and so with White Fang. Gray Beaver was his own particular god, and, in spite of Gray Beaver's will, White Fang still clung to him and would not give him up. Gray Beaver had betrayed and forsaken him, but that had no effect upon him. Not for nothing had he surrendered himself body and soul to Gray Beaver There had been no reservation on White Fang's part, and the bond was not to be broken easily.

So, in the night, when the men in the fort were asleep, White Fang applied his teeth to the stick that held him. The wood was seasoned and dry, and it was tied so closely to his neck that he could scarcely get his teeth to it. It was only by the severest muscular exertion and neck-arching that he succeeded in getting the wood between his teeth, and barely between his teeth at that; and it was only by the exercise of an immense patience, extending through many hours, that he succeeded in gnawing through the stick. This was something that dogs were not supposed to do. It was unprecedented. But White Fang did it, trotting away from the fort in the early morning with the end of the stick hanging to his neck.

He was wise. But had he been merely wise he would not have gone back to Gray Beaver who had already twice betrayed him. But there was his faithfulness, and he went back to be betrayed yet a third time. Again he yielded to the tying of a thong around his neck by Gray Beaver, and again Beauty Smith came to claim him. And this time he was beaten even more severely than before.

Gray Beaver looked on stolidly while the white man wielded the whip. He gave no protection. It was no longer his dog. When the beating was over White Fang was sick. A soft southland dog would have died under it, but not he. His school of life had been sterner, and he was himself of sterner stuff. He had too great vitality. His clutch on life was too strong. But he was very sick. At first he was unable to drag himself along, and Beauty Smith had to wait half an hour on him. And then, blind and reeling, he followed at Beauty Smith's heels back to the fort.

But now he was tied with a chain that defied his teeth, and he strove in vain, by lunging, to draw the staple from the timber into which it was driven. After a few days, sober and bankrupt, Gray Beaver departed up the Porcupine on his long journey to the Mackenzie. White Fang remained on the Yukon, the property of a man more than half mad and all brute. But what is a dog to know in its consciousness of madness? To White Fang Beauty Smith was a veritable, if terrible, god. He was a mad god at best, but White Fang knew nothing of madness; he knew only that he must submit to the will of this new master, obey his every whim and fancy.

CHAPTER III

THE REIGN OF HATE

Under the tutelage of the mad god, White Fang became a fiend. He was kept chained in a pen at the rear of the fort, and here Beauty Smith teased and irritated and drove him wild with petty torments. The man early discovered White Fang's susceptibility to laughter, and made it a point, after painfully tricking him, to laugh at him. This laughter was uproarious and scornful, and at the same time the god pointed his finger derisively at White Fang. At such times reason fled from White Fang, and in his transports of rage he was even more mad than Beauty Smith.

Formerly, White Fang had been merely the enemy of his kind, withal a ferocious enemy. He now became the enemy of all things, and more ferocious than ever. To such an extent was he tormented, that he hated blindly and without the faintest spark of reason. He hated the chain that bound him, the men who peered in at him through the slats of the pen, the dogs that accompanied the men and that snarled malignantly at him in his helplessness. He hated the very wood of the pen that confined him. And first, last and most of all, he hated Beauty Smith.

But Beauty Smith had a purpose in all that he did to White Fang. One day a number of men gathered about the pen. Beauty Smith entered, club in hand, and took the chain from off White Fang's neck. When his master had gone out, White Fang turned loose and tore around the pen, trying to get at the men outside. He was magnificently terrible. Fully five feet in length, and standing two and one half feet at the shoulder, he far outweighed a wolf of corresponding size. From his mother he had inherited the heavier proportions of the dog, so that he weighed, without any fat and without an ounce of superfluous flesh, over ninety pounds. It was all muscle, bone and sinew—fighting flesh in the finest condition. The door of the pen was being opened again. White Fang paused. Something unusual was happening. He waited. The door was opened wider. Then a huge dog was thrust inside, and the door was slammed shut behind him. White Fang had never seen such a dog (it was a mastiff); but the size and fierce aspect of the intruder did not deter him. Here was something, not wood nor iron, upon which to wreak his hate. He leaped in with a flash of fangs that ripped down the side of the mastiff's neck. The mastiff shook his head, growled hoarsely, and plunged at White Fang. But White Fang was here, there, and everywhere, always evading and eluding, and always leaping in and slashing with his fangs, and leaping out again in time to escape punishment.

The men outside shouted and applauded while Beauty Smith, in an ecstasy of delight, gloated over the ripping and mangling performed by White Fang. There was no hope for the mastiff from the first. He was too ponderous and slow. In the end, while Beauty Smith beat White Fang back with a club, the mastiff was dragged out by its owner. Then there was a payment of bets, and money clinked in Beauty Smith's hand.

White Fang came to look forward eagerly to the gathering of the men around his pen. It meant a fight; and this was the only way that was now vouchsafed him of expressing the life that was in him. Tormented, incited to hate, he was kept a prisoner so that there was no way of satisfying that hate except at the times his master saw fit to pit another dog against him. Beauty Smith had estimated his powers well, for he was invariably the victor. One day three dogs were turned in upon him in succession. Another day a full-grown wolf, fresh caught from the Wild, was shoved in through the door of the pen. And on still another day two dogs were set against him at the same time. This was his severest fight, and though in the end he killed them both he was himself half killed in doing it.

In the fall of the year, when the first snows were falling and mush-ice was running in the river, Beauty Smith took passage for himself and White Fang on a steamboat bound up the Yukon to Dawson. White Fang had now achieved a reputation in the land. As the "Fighting Wolf," he was known far and wide, and the cage in which he was kept on the steamboat's deck was usually surrounded by curious men. He raged and snarled at them, or lay quietly and studied them with cold hatred. Why should he not hate them? He never asked himself the question. He knew only hate and lost himself in the passion of it. Life had become a hell to him. He had not been made for the close confinement wild beasts endure at the hands of men. And yet it was in precisely this way that he was treated. Men stared at him, poked sticks between the bars to make him snarl, and then laughed at him.

They were his environment, these men, and they were molding the clay of him into a more ferocious thing than had been intended by Nature. Nevertheless, Nature had given him plasticity. Where many another animal would have died or had its spirit broken, he adjusted himself and lived, and at no expense of the spirit. Possibly Beauty Smith, arch-fiend and tormentor, was capable of breaking White Fang's spirit, but as yet there were no signs of his succeeding.

If Beauty Smith had in him a devil, White Fang had another; and the two of them raged against each other unceasingly. In the days before, White Fang had had the wisdom to cower down and submit to a man with a club in his hand; but this wisdom now left him. The mere sight of Beauty Smith was sufficient to send him into transports of fury. And when they came to close quarters, and he had been beaten back by the club, he went on growling and snarling and showing his fangs. The last growl could never be extracted from him. No matter how terribly he was beaten, he had always another growl, and when Beauty Smith gave up and withdrew, the defiant growl followed after him, or White Fang sprang at the bars of the cage bellowing his hatred.

When the steamboat arrived at Dawson, White Fang went ashore. But he still lived a public life, in a cage, surrounded by curious men. He was exhibited as "The Fighting Wolf," and men paid fifty cents in gold-dust to see him. He was given no rest. Did he lie down to sleep, he was stirred up by a sharp stick—so that the audience might get its money's worth. In order to make the exhibition interesting, he was kept in a rage most of the time. But worse than all this was the atmosphere in which he lived. He was regarded as the most fearful of wild beasts, and this was borne in to him through the bars of the cage. Every word, every cautious action on the part of the men, impressed upon him his own terrible ferocity. It was so much added fuel to the flame of his fierceness. There could be but one result, and that was that his ferocity fed upon itself and increased. It was another instance of the plasticity of his clay, of his capacity for being molded by the pressure of environment.

In addition to being exhibited, he was a professional fighting animal. At irregular intervals, whenever a fight could be arranged, he was taken out of his cage and led off into the woods a few miles from town. Usually this occurred at night, so as to avoid interference from the mounted police of the Territory. After a few hours of waiting, when daylight had come, the audience and the dog with which he was to fight arrived. In this manner it came about that he fought all sizes and breeds of dogs. It was a savage land, the men were savage, and the fights were usually to the death.

Since White Fang continued to fight, it is obvious that it was the other dogs that died. He never knew defeat. His early training, when he fought with Lip-lip and the whole puppy-pack, stood him in good stead. There was the tenacity with which he clung to the earth. No dog could make him lose his footing. This was the favorite trick of the wolf breeds—to rush in upon him, either directly or with an unexpected swerve, in the hope of striking his shoulder and overthrowing him. Mackenzie hounds, Eskimo and Labrador dogs, huskies and Malemutes—all tried it on him, and all failed. He was never known to lose his footing. Men told this to one another, and looked each time to see it happen; but White Fang always disappointed them.

Then there was his lightning quickness. It gave him a tremendous advantage over his antagonists. No matter what their fighting experience, they had never encountered a dog that moved so swiftly as he. Also to be reckoned with was the immediateness of his attack. The average dog was accustomed to the preliminaries of snarling and bristling and growling, and the average dog was knocked off his feet and finished before he had begun to fight or recovered from his surprise. So often did this happen, that it became the custom to hold White Fang until the other dog went through his preliminaries, was good and ready, and even made the first attack.

But greatest of all the advantages in White Fang's favor was his experience. He knew more about fighting than did any of the dogs that faced him. He had fought more fights, knew how to meet more tricks and methods, and had more tricks himself, while his own method was scarcely to be improved upon.

As the time went by, he had fewer and fewer fights. Men despaired of matching him with an equal, and Beauty Smith was compelled to pit wolves against him. These were trapped by the Indians for the purpose, and a fight between White Fang and a wolf was always sure to draw a crowd. Once, a full-grown female lynx was secured, and this time White Fang fought for his life. Her quickness matched his; her ferocity equaled his; while he fought with his fangs alone, and she fought with her sharp-clawed feet as well.

But after the lynx all fighting ceased for White Fang. There were no more animals with which to fight—at least, there was none considered worthy of fighting with him. So he remained on exhibition until spring, when one Tim Keenan, a faro-dealer, arrived in the land. With him came the first bulldog that had ever entered the Klondike. That this dog and White Fang should come together was inevitable, and for a week the anticipated fight was the mainspring of conversation in certain quarters of the town.

CHAPTER IV

THE CLINGING DEATH

Beauty Smith slipped the chain from his neck and stepped back.

For once White Fang did not make an immediate attack. He stood still, ears pricked forward, alert and curious, surveying the strange animal that faced him. He had never seen such a dog before. Tim Keenan shoved the bulldog forward with a muttered, "Go to it." The animal waddled toward the center of the circle, short and squat and ungainly. He came to a stop and blinked across at White Fang.

There were cries from the crowd of, "Go to him, Cherokee! Sick 'm, Cherokee! Eat 'm up!"

But Cherokee did not seem anxious to fight. He turned his head and blinked at the men who shouted, at the same time wagging his stump of a tail good-naturedly. He was not afraid, but merely lazy. Besides, it did not seem to him that it was intended he should fight with the dog he saw before him. He was not used to fighting with that kind of dog, and he was waiting for them to bring on the real dog.

Tim Keenan stepped in and bent over Cherokee, fondling him on both sides of the shoulders with hands that rubbed against the grain of the hair and that made slight, pushing-forward movements. These were so many suggestions. Also, their effect was irritating, for Cherokee began to growl, very softly, deep down in his throat. There was a correspondence in rhythm between the growls and the movements of the man's hands. The growl rose in the throat with the culmination of each forward-pushing movement, and ebbed down, to start up afresh with the beginning of the next movement. The end of each movement was the accent of the rhythm, the movement ending abruptly and the growling rising with a jerk.

This was not without its effect on White Fang. The hair began to rise on his neck and across the shoulders. Tim Keenan gave a final shove forward and stepped back again. As the impetus that carried Cherokee forward died down, he continued to go forward of his own volition, in a swift, bow-legged run. Then White Fang struck. A cry of startled admiration went up. He had covered the distance and gone in more like a cat than a dog; and with the same cat-like swiftness he had slashed with his fangs and leaped clear.

The bulldog was bleeding back of one ear from a rip in his thick neck. He gave no sign, did not even snarl, but turned and followed after White Fang. The display on both sides, the quickness of the one and the steadiness of the other, had excited the partisan spirit of the crowd, and the men were making new bets and increasing original bets. Again, and yet again, White Fang sprang in, slashed, and got away untouched; and still his strange foe followed after him, without too great haste, not slowly, but deliberately and determinedly, in a business-like sort of way. There was purpose in his method—something for him to do that he was intent upon doing and from which nothing could distract him.

His whole demeanor, every action, was stamped with this purpose. It puzzled White Fang. Never had he seen such a dog. It had no hair protection. It was soft, and bled easily. There was no thick mat of fur to baffle White Fang's teeth, as they were often baffled by dogs of his own breed. Each time that his teeth struck they sank easily into the yielding flesh, while the animal did not seem able to defend itself. Another disconcerting thing was that it made no outcry, such as he had been accustomed to with the other dogs he had fought. Beyond a growl or a grunt, the dog took its punishment silently. And never did it flag in its pursuit of him.

Not that Cherokee was slow. He could turn and whirl swiftly enough, but White Fang was never there. Cherokee was puzzled, too. He had never fought before with a dog with which he could not close. The desire to close had always been mutual. But here was a dog that kept at a distance, dancing and dodging here and there and all about. And when it did get its teeth into him it did not hold on, but let go instantly and darted away again.

But White Fang could not get at the soft under side of the throat. The bulldog stood too short, while its massive jaws were an added protection. White Fang darted in and out unscathed, while Cherokee's wounds increased. Both sides of his neck and head were ripped and slashed. He bled freely, but showed no signs of being disconcerted. He continued his plodding pursuit, though once, for the moment baffled, he came to a full stop and blinked at the men who looked on, at the same time wagging his stump of a tail as an expression of his willingness to fight.

In that moment White Fang was in upon him and out, in passing ripping his trimmed remnant of an ear. With a slight manifestation of anger, Cherokee took up the pursuit again, running on the inside of the circle White Fang was making, and striving to fasten his deadly grip on White Fang's throat. The bulldog missed by a hair's-breadth, and cries of praise went up as White Fang doubled suddenly out of danger in the opposite direction.

The time went by. White Fang still danced on, dodging and doubling, leaping

Painting by Frank E. Schoonover.

"After the break-up of the ice on the Porcupine he . . . paddled down that stream to where it effected its junction with the Yukon."

in and out, and ever inflicting damage. And still the bulldog, with grim certitude, toiled after him. Sooner or later he would accomplish his purpose, get the grip that would win the battle. In the meantime he accepted all the punishment the other could deal him. His tufts of ears had become tassels, his neck and shoulders were slashed in a score of places, and his very lips were cut and bleeding—all from those lightning snaps that were beyond his foreseeing and guarding.

Time and again White Fang had attempted to knock Cherokee off his feet; but the difference in their height was too great. Cherokee was too squat, too close to the ground. White Fang tried the trick once too often. The chance came in one of his quick doublings and counter-circlings. He caught Cherokee with head turned away as he whirled more slowly. His shoulder was exposed. White Fang drove in upon it; but his own shoulder was high above, while he struck with such force that his momentum carried him on across over the other's body. For the first time in his fighting history, men saw White Fang lose his footing. His body turned a half-somersault in the air, and he would have landed on his back had he not twisted, cat-like, still in the air, in the effort to bring his feet to the earth. As it was, he struck heavily on his side. The next instant he was on his feet, but in that instant Cherokee's teeth closed on his throat.

It was not a good grip, being too low down toward the chest; but Cherokee held on. White Fang sprang to his feet and tore wildly around, trying to shake off the bulldog's body. It made him frantic, this clinging, dragging weight. It bound his movements, restricted his freedom. It was like the trap, and all his instinct resented it and revolted against it. It was a mad revolt. For several minutes he was to all intents insane. The basic life that was in him took charge of him. The will of his body to exist surged over him. He was dominated by this mere flesh-love of life. All intelligence was gone. It was as though he had no brain. His reason was unseated by the blind yearning of the flesh to exist and move, at all hazards to move, to continue to move, for movement was the expression of its existence.

Round and round he went, whirling and turning and reversing, trying to shake off the fifty-pound weight that dragged at his throat. The bulldog did little but keep his grip. Sometimes, and rarely, he managed to get his feet to the earth and for a moment to brace himself against White Fang. But the next moment his footing would be lost and he would be dragging around in the whirl of one of White Fang's mad gyrations. Cherokee identified himself with his instinct. He knew that he was doing the right thing by holding on, and there came to him certain blissful thrills of satisfaction. At such moments he even closed his eyes and allowed his body to be hurled hither and thither, willy-nilly, careless of any hurt that might thereby come to it. That did not count. The grip was the thing, and the grip he kept.

White Fang ceased only when he had tired himself out. He could do nothing, and he could not understand. Never, in all his fighting, had this thing happened. The dogs he had fought with did not fight that way. With them it was snap and slash and get away, snap and slash and get away. He lay partly on his side, panting for breath. Cherokee, still holding his grip, urged against him, trying to get him over entirely on his side. White Fang resisted, and he could feel the jaws shifting their grip, slightly relaxing and coming together again in a chewing movement. Each shift brought the grip closer in to his throat. The bulldog's method was to hold what he had, and when opportunity favored to work in for more. Opportunity favored when White Fang remained quiet. When White Fang struggled, Cherokee was content merely to hold on.

The bulging back of Cherokee's neck was the only portion of his body that White Fang's teeth could reach. He got hold toward the base, where the neck comes out from the shoulders; but he did not know the chewing method of fighting, nor were his jaws adapted to it. He spasmodically ripped and tore with his fangs for a space. Then a change in their position diverted him. The bulldog had managed to roll him over on his back, and, still hanging to his throat, was on top of him. Like a cat, White Fang bowed his hind-quarters in, and, with the feet digging into his enemy's abdomen above him, he began to claw with long tearing strokes. Cherokee might well have been disemboweled had he not quickly pivoted on his grip and got his body off of White Fang's and at right angles to it.

There was no escaping that grip. It was like Fate itself, and as inexorable. Slowly it shifted up along the jugular. All that saved White Fang from death was the loose skin of his neck and the thick fur that covered it. This served to form a large roll in Cherokee's mouth, the fur of which well nigh defied his teeth. But bit by bit, whenever the chance offered, he was getting more of the loose skin and fur in his mouth. The result was that he was slowly throttling White Fang. The latter's breath was drawn with greater and greater difficulty as the moments went by.

It began to look as though the battle were over. The backers of Cherokee waxed jubilant and offered ridiculous odds. White Fang's backers were correspondingly depressed and refused bets of ten to one and twenty to one, though one man was rash enough to close a wager of fifty to one. This man was Beauty Smith. He took a step into the ring and pointed his finger at White Fang. Then he began to laugh derisively and scornfully. This produced the desired effect. White Fang went wild with rage. He called up his reserves of strength and gained his feet. As he struggled around the ring, the fifty pounds of his foe ever dragging on his throat, his anger passed on into panic. The basic life of him dominated him again, and his intelligence fled before the will of his flesh to live. Round and round and back again, stumbling and falling and rising, even uprearing at times on his hind-legs and lifting his foe clear of the earth, he struggled vainly to shake off the clinging death.

At last he fell, toppling backward, exhausted; and the bulldog promptly shifted his grip, getting in closer, mangling more and more of the fur-folded flesh, throttling White Fang more severely than ever. Shouts of applause went up for the victor, and there were many cries of "Cherokee!" "Cherokee!" To this Cherokee responded by vigorous wagging of the stump of his tail. But the clamor of approval did not distract him. There was no sympathetic relation between his tail and his massive jaws. The one might wag, but the others held their terrible grip on White Fang's throat.

It was at this time that a diversion came to the spectators. There was a jingle of bells. Dog-mushers' cries were heard. Everybody, save Beauty Smith, looked apprehensive, the fear of the police strong upon them. But they saw, up the trail and not down, two men running with sled and dogs. They were evidently coming down the creek from some prospecting trip. At sight of the crowd they stopped their dogs and came over and joined it, curious to see the cause of the excitement. The dog-musher wore a moustache, but the other, a taller and younger man, was smooth-shaven, his skin rosy from the pounding of his blood and the running in the frosty air.

White Fang had practically ceased struggling. Now and again he resisted spasmodically and to no purpose. He could get little air, and that little grew less and less under the merciless grip that ever tightened. In spite of his armor of fur, the great vein of his throat would have long since been torn open, had not the first grip of the bulldog been so low down as to be practically on the chest. It had taken Cherokee a long time to shift that grip upward, and this had also tended further to clog his jaws with fur and skin-fold.

In the meantime, the abysmal brute in Beauty Smith had been rising up into his brain and mastering the small bit of sanity that he possessed at best. When he saw White Fang's eyes beginning to glaze, he knew beyond doubt that the fight was lost. Then he broke loose. He sprang upon White Fang and began savagely to kick him. There were hisses from the crowd and cries of protest, but that was all. While this went on, and Beauty Smith continued to kick White Fang, there was a commotion in the crowd. The tall young newcomer was forcing his way through, shouldering men right and left without ceremony or gentleness. When he broke through into the ring, Beauty Smith was just in the act of delivering another kick. All his weight was on one foot, and he was in a state of unstable equilibrium. At that moment the newcomer's fist landed a smashing blow full in his face. Beauty Smith's remaining leg left the ground, and his whole body seemed to lift into the air as he turned over backward and struck the snow. The newcomer turned upon the crowd.

"You cowards!" he cried. "You beasts!"

He was in a rage himself—a sane rage. His gray eyes seemed metallic and steel-like as they flashed upon the crowd. Beauty Smith regained his feet and came toward him, sniffling and cowardly. The newcomer did not understand. He did not know how abject a coward the other was, and thought he was coming back intent on fighting. So, with a "You beast!" he smashed Beauty Smith over backward with a second blow in the face. Beauty Smith decided that the snow was the safest place for him, and lay where he had fallen, making no effort to get up.

"Come on, Matt, lend a hand," the newcomer called to the dog-musher, who had followed him into the ring.

Both men bent over the dogs. Matt took hold of White Fang, ready to pull when Cherokee's jaws should be loosened. This the younger man endeavored to accomplish by clutching the bulldog's jaws in his hands and trying to spread them. It was a vain undertaking. As he pulled and tugged and wrenched, he kept exclaiming with every expulsion of breath, "Beasts!"

The crowd began to grow unruly, and some of the men were protesting against the spoiling of the sport; but they were silenced when the newcomer lifted his head from his work for a moment and glared at them.

"You damn beasts!" he finally exploded, and went back to his task.

"It's no use, Mr. Scott, you can't break 'm apart that way," Matt said at last.

The pair paused and surveyed the locked dogs.

"Ain't bleedin' much," Matt announced. "Ain't got all the way in yet."

"But he's liable to any moment," Scott answered. "There, did you see that! He shifted his grip in a bit."

The younger man's excitement and apprehension for White Fang was growing. He struck Cherokee about the head, savagely, again and again. But that did not loosen the jaws. Cherokee wagged the stump of his tail in advertisement that he understood the meaning of the blows, but that he knew he was himself in the right and only doing his duty by keeping his grip.

"Won't some of you help?" Scott cried desperately at the crowd.

But no help was offered. Instead, the crowd began sarcastically to cheer him on and showered him with facetious advice.

"You'll have to get a pry," Matt counseled.

The other reached into the holster at his hip, drew his revolver, and tried to thrust its muzzle between the bulldog's jaws. He shoved, and shoved hard, till the grating of the steel against the locked teeth could be distinctly heard. Both men were on their knees, bending over the dogs. Tim Keenan strode into the ring. He paused beside Scott and touched him on the shoulder, saying ominously:

"Don't break them teeth, stranger."

"Then I'll break his neck," Scott retorted, continuing his shoving and wedging with the revolver muzzle.

"I said don't break them teeth," the faro-dealer repeated more ominously than before.

But if it was a bluff he intended, it did not work. Scott never desisted from his efforts, though he looked up coolly and asked:

"Your dog?"

The faro-dealer grunted.

"Then get in here and break this grip."

"Well, stranger," the other drawled irritatingly, "I don't mind telling you that's something I ain't worked out for myself. I don't know how to turn the trick."

"Then get out of the way," was the reply, "and don't bother me. I'm busy."

Tim Keenan continued standing over him, but Scott took no further notice of his presence. He had managed to get the muzzle in between the jaws on one side, and was trying to get it out between the jaws on the other side. This accomplished, he pried gently and carefully, loosening the jaws a bit at a time, while Matt, a bit at a time, extricated White Fang's mangled neck.

"Stand by to receive your dog," was Scott's peremptory order to Cherokee's owner.

The faro-dealer stooped down obediently and got a firm hold on Cherokee.

"Now!" Scott warned, giving the final pry.

The dogs were drawn apart, the bulldog struggling vigorously.

"Take him away," Scott commanded, and Tim Keenan dragged Cherokee back into the crowd.

White Fang made several ineffectual efforts to get up. Once he gained his feet, but his legs were too weak to sustain him, and he slowly wilted and sank back into the snow. His eyes were half closed, and the surface of them was glassy. His jaws were apart, and through them the tongue protruded, draggled and limp. To all appearances he looked like a dog that had been strangled to death. Matt examined him.

"Just about all in," he announced; "but he's breathin' all right."

Beauty Smith had regained his feet and come over to look at White Fang.

"Matt, how much is a good sled-dog worth?" Scott asked.

The dog-musher, still on his knees and stooping over White Fang, calculated for a moment.

"Three hundred dollars," he answered.

"And how much for one that's all chewed up like this one?" Scott asked, nudging White Fang with his foot.

"Half of that," was the dog-musher's judgment.

Scott turned upon Beauty Smith.

"Did you hear, Mr. Beast? I'm going to take your dog from you, and I'm going to give you a hundred and fifty for him."

He opened his pocketbook and counted out the bills.

Beauty Smith put his hands behind his back, refusing to touch the proffered money.

"I ain't a-sellin'," he said.

"Oh, yes you are," the other assured him. "Because I'm buying. Here's your money. The dog's mine."

Beauty Smith, his hands still behind him, began to back away.

Scott sprang toward him, drawing his fist back to strike. Beauty Smith cowered down in anticipation of the blow.

"I've got my rights," he whimpered.

"You've forfeited your rights to own that dog," was the rejoinder. "Are you going to take the money? or do I have to hit you again?"

"All right," Beauty Smith spoke up with the alacrity of fear. "But I take the money under protest," he added. "The dog's a mint. I ain't a-goin' to be robbed. A man's got his rights."

"Correct," Scott answered, passing the money over to him. "A man's got his rights. But you're not a man. You're a beast."

"Wait till I get back to Dawson," Beauty Smith threatened. "I'll have the law on you."

"If you open your mouth when you get back to Dawson, I'll have you run out of town. Understand?"

Beauty Smith replied with a grunt.

"Understand?" the other thundered with abrupt fierceness.

"Yes," Beauty Smith grunted, shrinking away.

"Yes what?"

"Yes, sir," Beauty Smith snarled.

"Look out! He'll bite!" some one shouted, and a guffaw of laughter went up.

Scott turned his back on him, and returned to help the dog-musher, who was working over White Fang.

Some of the men were already departing; others stood in groups, looking on and talking. Tim Keenan joined one of the groups.

"Who's that mug?" he asked.

"Weedon Scott," some one answered.

"And who in hell is Weedon Scott?" the faro-dealer demanded.

"Oh, one of them crack-a-jack minin' experts. He's in with all the big bugs. If you want to keep out of trouble you'll steer clear of him, that's my talk. He's all hunky with the officials. The Gold Commissioner's a special pal of his."

"I thought he must be somebody," was the faro-dealer's comment. "That's why I kept my hands offen him at the start."

WHITE FANG

BY JACK LONDON

CHAPTER V

THE INDOMITABLE

"IT'S hopeless," Weedon Scott confessed.

He sat on the step of his cabin and stared at the dog-musher, who responded with a shrug that was equally hopeless.

Together they looked at White Fang, at the end of his stretched chain, bristling, snarling, ferocious, straining to get at the sled-dogs. Having received sundry lessons from Matt, said lessons being imparted by means of a club, the sled-dogs had learned to leave White Fang alone; and even then they were lying down at a distance, apparently oblivious of his existence.

"It's a wolf, and there's no taming it," Weedon Scott announced.

"Oh, I don't know about that," Matt objected. "Might be a lot of dog in 'm, for all you can tell. But there's one thing I know sure, an' that there's no gettin' away from."

The dog-musher paused and nodded his head confidentially at Moosehide Mountain.

"Well, don't be a miser with what you know," Scott said sharply, after waiting a suitable length of time. "Spit it out. What is it?"

The dog-musher indicated White Fang with a backward thrust of his thumb.

"Wolf or dog, it's all the same—he's ben tamed a'ready."

"No!"

"I tell you yes, an' broke to harness. Look close there. D'ye see them marks across the chest?"

"You're right, Matt. He was a sled-dog before Beauty Smith got hold of him."

"An' there's not much reason against his bein' a sled-dog again."

"What d'ye think?" Scott queried eagerly. Then the hope died down as he added, shaking his head, "We've had him two weeks now, and if anything, he's wilder than ever at the present moment."

"Give 'm a chance," Matt counseled. "Turn 'm loose for a spell."

The other looked at him incredulously

"Yes," Matt went on, "I know you've tried to, but you didn't take a club."

"You try it then."

The dog-musher secured a club and went over to the chained animal. White Fang watched the club after the manner of a caged lion watching the whip of its trainer.

"See 'm keep his eye on that club," Matt said. "That's a good sign. He's no fool. Don't dast tackle me so long as I got that club handy. He's not clean crazy, sure."

As the man's hand approached his neck, White Fang bristled and snarled and crouched down. But while he eyed the approaching hand, he at the same time contrived to keep track of the club in the other hand, suspended threateningly above him. Matt unsnapped the chain from the collar and stepped back.

White Fang could scarcely realize that he was free. Many months had gone by since he passed into the possession of Beauty Smith, and in all that period he had never known a moment of freedom except at the times he had been loosed to fight with other dogs. Immediately after such fights he had always been imprisoned again.

He did not know what to make of it. Perhaps some new deviltry of the gods was about to be perpetrated on him. He walked slowly and cautiously, prepared to be assailed at any moment. He did not know what to do, it was all so unprecedented. He took the precaution to sheer off from the two watching gods, and walked carefully to the corner of the cabin. Nothing happened. He was plainly perplexed, and he came back again, pausing a dozen feet away and regarding the two men intently

"Won't he run away?" his new owner asked.

Matt shrugged his shoulders. "Got to take a gamble. Only way to find out is to find out."

"Poor devil," Scott murmured pityingly. "What he needs is some show of human kindness," he added, turning and going into the cabin.

He came out with a piece of meat, which he tossed to White Fang. He sprang away from it, and from a distance studied it suspiciously.

"Hi-yu! Major!" Matt shouted warningly, but too late.

Major had made a spring for the meat. At the instant his jaws closed on it White Fang struck him. He was overthrown. Matt rushed in, but quicker than he was White Fang. Major staggered to his feet, but the blood spouting from his throat reddened the snow in a widening path.

"It's too bad, but it served him right," Scott said hastily.

But Matt's foot had already started on its way to kick White Fang. There was a leap, a flash of teeth, a sharp exclamation. White Fang, snarling fiercely, scrambled backward for several yards, while Matt stooped and investigated his leg.

"He got me all right," he announced, pointing to the torn trousers and underclothes, and the growing stain of red.

"I told you it was hopeless, Matt," Scott said in a discouraged voice. "I've thought about it off and on, while not wanting to think of it. But we've come to it now. It's the only thing to do."

As he talked, with reluctant movements he drew his revolver, threw open the cylinder, and assured himself of its contents.

"Look here, Mr. Scott," Matt objected; "that dog's ben through hell. You can't expect 'm to come out a white an' shinin' angel. Give 'm time."

"Look at Major," the other rejoined.

The dog-musher surveyed the stricken dog. He had sunk down on the snow in the circle of his blood, and was plainly in the last gasp.

"Served 'm right. You said so yourself, Mr. Scott. He tried to take White Fang's meat, an' he's dead-O. That was to be expected. I wouldn't give two whoops in hell for a dog that wouldn't fight for his own meat."

"But look at yourself, Matt. It's all right about the dogs, but we must draw the line somewhere."

"Served me right," Matt argued stubbornly. "What 'd I want to kick 'm for? You said yourself that he'd done right. Then I had no right to kick 'm."

"It would be a mercy to kill him," Scott insisted. "He's untamable."

"Now look here, Mr. Scott, give the poor devil a fightin' chance. He ain't had no chance yet. He's just come through hell, an' this is the first time he's ben loose. Give 'm a fair chance, an' if he don't deliver the goods, I'll kill 'm myself. There!"

"God knows I don't want to kill him or have him killed," Scott answered, putting away the revolver. "We'll let him run loose and see what kindness can do for him. And here's a try at it."

He walked over to White Fang and began talking to him gently and soothingly.

"Better have a club handy," Matt warned.

Scott shook his head and went on trying to win White Fang's confidence.

White Fang was suspicious. Something was impending. He had killed this god's dog, bitten his companion god, and what else was to be expected than some terrible punishment? But in the face of it he was indomitable. He bristled and showed his teeth, his eyes vigilant, his whole body wary and prepared for anything. The god had no club, so he suffered him to approach quite near. The god's hand had come out and was descending upon his head. White Fang shrank together and grew tense as he crouched under it. Here was danger, some treachery or something. He knew the hands of the gods, their proved mastery, their cunning to hurt. Besides, there was his old antipathy to being touched. He snarled more menacingly, crouched still lower, and still the hand descended. He did not want to bite the hand, and he endured the peril of it until his instinct surged up in him, mastering him with its insatiable yearning for life.

Weedon Scott had believed that he was

quick enough to avoid any snap or slash. But he had yet to learn the remarkable quickness of White Fang, who struck with the certainty and swiftness of a coiled snake.

Scott cried out sharply with surprise, catching his torn hand and holding it tightly in his other hand. Matt uttered a great oath and sprang to his side. White Fang crouched down and backed away, bristling, showing his fangs, his eyes malignant with menace. Now he could expect a beating as fearful as any he had received from Beauty Smith.

"Here! What are you doing?" Scott cried suddenly.

Matt had dashed into the cabin and come out with a rifle.

"Nothin'," he said slowly, with a careless calmness that was assumed, "only goin' to keep that promise I made. I reckon it's up to me to kill 'm as I said I'd do."

"No, you don't!"

"Yes, I do. Watch me."

As Matt had pleaded for White Fang when he had been bitten, it was now Weedon Scott's turn to plead.

"You said to give him a chance. Well, give it to him. We've only just started, and we can't quit at the beginning. It served me right, this time. And—look at him!"

White Fang, near the corner of the cabin and forty feet away, was snarling with blood-curdling viciousness, not at Scott, but at the dog-musher.

"Well I'll be everlastin'ly gosh-swoggled!" was the dog-musher's expression of astonishment.

"Look at the intelligence of him," Scott went on hastily. "He knows the meaning of firearms as well as you do. He's got intelligence, and we've got to give that intelligence a chance. Put up the gun."

"All right, I'm willin'," Matt agreed, leaning the rifle against the wood-pile.

"But will you look at that!" he exclaimed the next moment.

White Fang had quieted down and ceased snarling.

"This is worth investigatin'. Watch."

Matt reached for the rifle, and at the same moment White Fang snarled. He stepped away from the rifle, and White Fang's lifted lips descended, covering his teeth.

"Now, just for fun."

Matt took the rifle and began slowly to raise it to his shoulder. White Fang's snarling began with the movement, and increased as the movement approached its culmination. But the moment before the rifle came to a level on him, he leaped sidewise behind the corner of the cabin. Matt stood staring along the sights at the empty space of snow which had been occupied by White Fang.

The dog-musher put the rifle down solemnly, then turned and looked at his employer.

"I agree with you, Mr. Scott. That dog's too intelligent to kill."

CHAPTER VI

THE LOVE-MASTER

As White Fang watched Weedon Scott approach, he bristled and snarled to advertise that he would not submit to punishment. Twenty-four hours had passed since he had slashed open the hand that was now bandaged and held up by a sling to keep the blood out of it. In the past White Fang had experienced delayed punishments, and he apprehended that such a one was about to befall him. How could it be otherwise? He had committed what was to him sacrilege, sunk his fangs into the holy flesh of a god, and of a white-skinned superior god at that. In the nature of things, and of intercourse with gods, something terrible awaited him.

The god sat down several feet away. White Fang could see nothing dangerous in that. When the gods administered punishment they stood on their legs. Besides, this god had no club, no whip, no firearm. And furthermore he himself was free. No chain nor stick bound him. He could escape into safety while the god was scrambling to his feet. In the meantime he would wait and see.

The god remained quiet, made no movement; and White Fang's snarl slowly dwindled to a growl that ebbed down in his throat and ceased. Then the god spoke, and at the first sound of his voice the hair rose on White Fang's neck and the growl rushed up in his throat. But the god made no hostile movement, and went on calmly talking. For a time White

Fang growled in unison with him, a correspondence of rhythm being established between growl and voice. But the god talked on interminably. He talked to White Fang as White Fang had never been talked to before. He talked softly and soothingly, with a gentleness that somehow, somewhere, touched White Fang. In spite of himself and all the pricking warnings of his instinct, White Fang began to have confidence in this god. He had a feeling of security that was belied by all his experience with men.

After a long time the god got up and went into the cabin. White Fang scanned him apprehensively when he came out. He had neither whip nor club nor weapon. Nor was his uninjured hand behind his back hiding something. He sat down as before, in the same spot, several feet away. He held out a small piece of meat. White Fang pricked his ears and investigated it suspiciously, managing to look at the same time both at the meat and the god, alert for any overt act, his body tense and ready to spring away at the first sign of hostility.

Still the punishment delayed. The god merely held near to his nose a piece of meat. And about the meat there seemed nothing wrong. Still White Fang suspected; and though the meat was proffered to him with short inviting thrusts of the hand, he refused to touch it. The gods were all-wise, and there was no telling what masterful treachery lurked behind that apparently harmless piece of meat. In past experience, especially in dealing with squaws, meat and punishment had often been disastrously related.

In the end, the god tossed the meat on the snow at White Fang's feet. He smelled the meat carefully. But he did not look at it. While he smelled it he kept his eyes on the god. Nothing happened. He took the meat into his mouth and swallowed it. Still nothing happened. The god was actually offering him another piece of meat. Again he refused to take it from the hand, and again it was tossed to him. This was repeated a number of times. But there came a time when the god refused to toss it. He kept it in his hand and steadfastly proffered it.

The meat was good meat, and White Fang was hungry. Bit by bit, infinitely cautious, he approached the hand. At last the time came that he decided to eat the meat from the hand. He never took his eyes from the god, thrusting his head forward with ears flattened back and hair involuntarily rising and cresting on his neck. Also a low growl rumbled in his throat as warning that he was not to be trifled with. He ate the meat, and nothing happened. Piece by piece he ate all the meat, and nothing happened. Still the punishment delayed.

He licked his chops and waited. The god went on talking. In his voice was kindness—something of which White Fang had no experience whatever. And within him it aroused feelings which he had likewise never experienced before. He was aware of a certain strange satisfaction, as though some need were being gratified, as though some void in his being were being filled. Then again came the prod of his instinct and the warning of past experience. The gods were ever crafty, and they had unguessed ways of attaining their ends.

Ah, he had thought so! There it came now, the god's hand, cunning to hurt, thrusting out at him, descending upon his head. But the god went on talking. His voice was soft and soothing. In spite of the menacing hand, the voice inspired confidence. And in spite of the assuring voice, the hand inspired distrust. White Fang was torn by conflicting feelings, impulses. It seemed he would fly to pieces, so terrible was the control he was exerting, holding together by an unwonted indecision the counter-forces that struggled within him for mastery.

He compromised. He snarled and bristled and flattened his ears. But he neither snapped nor sprang away. The hand descended. Nearer and nearer it came. It touched the ends of his upstanding hair. He shrank down under it. It followed down after him, pressing more closely against him. Shrinking, almost shivering, he still managed to hold himself together. It was a torment, this hand that touched him and violated his instinct. He could not forget in a day all the evil that had been wrought him at the hands of men. But it was the will of the god, and he strove to submit.

The hand lifted and descended again in a patting caressing movement. This continued, but every time the hand lifted. the hair lifted under it. And every time the hand descended, the ears flattened down and a cavernous growl surged in his throat. White Fang growled and growled with insistent warning. By this means he announced that he was prepared to retaliate for any hurt he might receive. There was no telling when the god's ulterior motive might be disclosed. At any moment that soft, confidence-inspiring voice might break forth in a roar of wrath, that gentle and caressing hand transform itself into a vise-like grip to hold him helpless and administer punishment.

But the god talked on softly, and ever the hand rose and fell with non-hostile pats. White Fang experienced dual feelings. It was distasteful to his instinct. It restrained him, opposed the will of him toward personal liberty. And yet it was not physically painful. On the contrary, it was even pleasant, in a physical way. The patting movement slowly and carefully changed to a rubbing of the ears about their bases, and the physical pleasure even increased a little. Yet he continued to fear, and he stood on guard, expectant of unguessed evil, alternately suffering and enjoying as one feeling or the other came uppermost and swayed him.

"Well, I'll be gosh-swoggled!"

So spoke Matt, coming out of the cabin, his sleeves rolled up, a pan of dirty dish-water in his hands, arrested in the act of emptying the pan by the sight of Weedon Scott patting White Fang.

At the instant his voice broke the silence, White Fang leaped back, snarling savagely at him.

Matt regarded his employer with grieved disapproval.

"If you don't mind my expressin' my feelin's, Mr. Scott, I'll make free to say you're seventeen kinds of a damn fool an' all of 'em different, an' then some."

Weedon Scott smiled with a superior air, gained his feet, and walked over to White Fang. He talked soothingly to him, but not for long, then slowly put out his hand, rested it on White Fang's head, and resumed the interrupted patting. White Fang endured it, keeping his eyes fixed suspiciously, not upon the man that petted him, but upon the man that stood in the doorway.

"You may be a number one, tip-top minin' expert, all right all right," the dog-musher delivered himself oracularly, "but you missed the chance of your life when you was a boy an' didn't run off an' join a circus."

White Fang snarled at the sound of his voice, but this time did not leap away from under the hand that was caressing his head and the back of his neck with long, soothing strokes.

It was the beginning of the end for White Fang—the ending of the old life and the reign of hate. A new and incomprehensibly fairer life was dawning. It required much thinking and endless patience on the part of Weedon Scott to accomplish this. And on the part of White Fang it required nothing less than a revolution. He had to ignore the urges and promptings of instinct and reason, defy experience, give the lie to life itself.

Life, as he had known it, not only had had no place in it for much that he now did; but all the currents had gone counter to those to which he now abandoned himself. In short, when all things were considered, he had to achieve an orientation far vaster than the one he had achieved at the time he came voluntarily in from the Wild and accepted Gray Beaver as his lord. At that time he was a mere puppy, soft from the making, without form, ready for the thumb of circumstance to begin its work upon him. But now it was different. The thumb of circumstance had done its work only too well. By it he had been formed and hardened into the Fighting Wolf, fierce and implacable, unloving and unlovable. To accomplish the change was like a reflux of being, and this when the plasticity of youth was no longer his; when the fiber of him had become tough and knotty; when the warp and the woof of him had made of him an adamantine texture, harsh and unyielding; when the face of his spirit had become iron, and all his instincts and axioms had crystallized into set rules, cautions, dislikes, and desires.

Yet again, in this new orientation, it was the thumb of circumstance that pressed and prodded him, softening that which had become hard and remolding it into fairer form. Weedon Scott was in truth this thumb. He had gone to the roots of White Fang's nature, and with kindness touched to life potencies that had languished and well nigh perished. One such potency was *love*. It took the place of *like*, which latter had been the highest feeling that thrilled him in his intercourse with the gods.

But this love did not come in a day. It began with *like* and out of it slowly developed. White Fang did not run away, though he was allowed to remain loose, because he liked this new god. This was certainly better than the life he had lived in the cage of Beauty Smith, and it was necessary that he should have some god. The lordship of man was a need of his nature. The seal of his dependence on man had been set upon him in that early day when he turned his back on the Wild and crawled to Gray Beaver's feet to receive the expected beating. This seal had been stamped upon him again, and ineradicably, on his second return from the Wild, when the long famine was over and there was fish once more in the village of Gray Beaver.

And so because he needed a god, and because he preferred Weedon Scott to Beauty Smith, White Fang remained. In acknowledgment of fealty, he proceeded to take upon himself the guardianship of his master's property. He prowled about the cabin while the sled-dogs slept, and the first night visitor to the cabin fought him off with a club until Weedon Scott came to the rescue. But White Fang soon learned to differentiate between thieves and honest men, to appraise the true value of step and carriage. The man who traveled, loud-stepping, the direct line to the cabin door, he let alone—though he watched him vigilantly until the door opened and he received the indorsement of the master. But the man who went softly, by circuitous ways, peering with caution, seeking after secresy—that was the man who received no suspension of judgment from White Fang, and who went away abruptly, hurriedly, and without dignity.

Weedon Scott had set himself the task of redeeming White Fang—or rather, of redeeming mankind from the wrong it had done White Fang. It was a matter of principle and conscience. He felt that the ill done White Fang was a debt incurred by man and that it must be paid. So he went out of his way to be especially kind to the Fighting Wolf. Each day he made it a point to caress and pet White Fang, and to do it at length.

At first suspicious and hostile, White Fang grew to like this petting. But there was one thing that he never outgrew—his growling. Growl he would, from the moment the petting began until it ended. But it was a growl with a new note in it. A stranger could not hear this note, and to such a stranger the growling of White Fang was an exhibition of primordial savagery, nerve-racking and blood-curdling. But White Fang's throat had become harsh-fibered from the making of ferocious sounds through the many years since his first little rasp of anger in the lair of his cubhood, and he could not soften the sounds of that throat now to express the gentleness he felt. Nevertheless, Weedon Scott's ear and sympathy were fine enough to catch the new note all but drowned in the fierceness—the note that was the faintest hint of a croon of content and that none but he could hear.

As the days went by, the evolution of *like* into *love* was accelerated. White Fang himself began to grow aware of it, though in his consciousness he knew not what love was. It manifested itself to him as a void in his being—a hungry, aching, yearning void that clamored to be filled. It was a pain and an unrest; and it received easement only by the touch of the new god's presence. At such times love was a joy to him, a wild, keen-thrilling satisfaction. But when away from his god, the pain and the unrest returned; the void in him sprang up and pressed against him with its emptiness, and the hunger gnawed and gnawed unceasingly.

White Fang was in the process of finding himself. In spite of the maturity of his years and of the savage rigidity of the mold that had formed him, his nature was undergoing an expansion. There was a bourgeoning within him of strange feelings and unwonted impulses. His old code of conduct was changing. In the past he had liked comfort and surcease from pain, disliked discomfort and pain, and he had adjusted his actions accordingly. But now it was different. Because of this new feeling within him, he ofttimes elected discomfort and pain for the sake of his god. Thus, in the early morning, instead of roaming and foraging, or lying in a sheltered nook, he would wait for hours on the cheerless cabin-stoop for a sight of the god's face. At night, when the god returned home, White Fang would leave the warm sleeping place he had burrowed in the snow in order to receive the friendly snap of fingers and the word of greeting. Meat, even meat itself, he would forego to be with his god, to receive a caress from him or to accompany him down into the town.

Like had been replaced by *love*. And love was the plummet dropped down into the deeps of him where like had never gone. And responsive out of his deeps had come the new thing—love. That which was given unto him did he return. This was a god indeed, a love-god, a warm and radiant god, in whose light White Fang's nature expanded as a flower expands under the sun.

But White Fang was not demonstrative. He was too old, too firmly molded, to become adept at expressing himself in new ways. He was too self-possessed, too strongly poised in his own isolation. Too long had he cultivated reticence, aloofness and moroseness. He had never barked in his life, and he could not now learn to bark a welcome when his god approached. He was never in the way, never extravagant nor foolish in the expression of his love. He never ran to meet his god. He waited at a distance; but he always waited, was always there. His love partook of the nature of worship—dumb, inarticulate, a silent adoration. Only by the steady regard of his eyes did he express his love, and by the unceasing following with his eyes of his god's every movement. Also, at times, when his god looked at him and spoke to him, he betrayed an awkward self-consciousness, caused by the struggle of his love to express itself and his physical inability to express it.

He learned to adjust himself in many ways to his new mode of life. It was borne in upon him that he must let his master's dogs alone. Yet his dominant nature asserted itself, and he had first to thrash them into an acknowledgment of his superiority and leadership. This accomplished, he had little trouble with them. They gave trail to him when he came and went or walked among them, and when he sserted his will they obeyed.

In the same way, he came to tolerate Matt—as a possession of his master. His master rarely fed him. Matt did that, it was his business; yet White Fang divined that it was his master's food he ate and that it was his master who thus fed him vicariously. Matt it was who tried to put him into the harness and make him haul sled with the other dogs. But Matt failed. It was not until Weedon Scott put the harness on White Fang and worked him, that he understood. He took it as his master's will that Matt should drive him and work him just as he drove and worked his master's other dogs.

Different from the Mackenzie toboggans were the Klondike sleds with runners under them. And different was the method of driving the dogs. There was no fan formation of the team. The dogs worked in single file, one behind another, hauling on double traces. And here, in the Klondike, the leader was indeed the leader. The wisest as well as strongest dog was the leader, and the team obeyed him and feared him. That White Fang should quickly gain this post was inevitable. He could not be satisfied with less, as Matt learned after much inconvenience and trouble. White Fang picked out the post for himself, and Matt backed his judgment with strong language after the experiment had been tried. But, though he worked in the sled in the day, White Fang did not forego the guarding of his master's property in the night. Thus he was on duty all the time, ever vigilant and faithful, the most valuable of all the dogs.

"Makin' free to spit out what's in me," Matt said, one day, "I beg to state that you was a wise guy all right when you paid the price you did for that dog. You clean swindled Beauty Smith on top of pushin' his face in with your fist."

A recrudescence of anger glinted in Weedon Scott's gray eyes, and he muttered savagely, "The beast!"

In the late spring a great trouble came to White Fang. Without warning, the love-master disappeared. There had been warning, but White Fang was unversed in such things and did not understand the packing of a grip. He remembered afterward that this packing had preceded the master's disappearance; but at the time he suspected nothing. That night he waited for the master to return. At midnight the chill wind that blew drove him to shelter at the rear of the cabin. There he drowsed, only half asleep, his ears keyed for the first sound of the familiar step. But, at two in the morning, his anxiety drove him out to the cold front stoop, where he crouched and waited.

But no master came. In the morning the door opened and Matt stepped outside. White Fang gazed at him wistfully. There was no common speech by which he might learn what he wanted to know. The days came and went, but never the master. White Fang, who had never known sickness in his life, became sick. He became very sick, so sick that Matt was finally compelled to bring him inside the cabin. Also, in writing to his employer, Matt devoted a postscript to White Fang.

Weedon Scott, reading the letter down in Circle City, came upon the following:

"That dam wolf won't work. Won't eat. Ain't got no spunk left. All the dogs is licking him. Wants to know what has become of you, and I don't know how to tell him. Mebbe he is going to die."

It was as Matt had said. White Fang had ceased eating, lost heart, and allowed every dog of the team to thrash him. In the cabin he lay on the floor near the stove, without interest in food, in Matt, or in life. Matt might talk gently to him or swear at him, it was all the same; he never did more than turn his dull eyes upon the man, then drop his head back to its customary position on his fore-paws.

And then, one night, Matt, reading to himself with moving lips and mumbled sounds, was startled by a low whine from White Fang. He had got upon his feet, his ears cocked toward the door, and he was listening intently. A moment later, Matt heard a footstep. The door opened and Weedon Scott stepped in. The two men shook hands. Then Scott looked around the room.

"Where's the wolf?" he asked.

Then he discovered him, standing where he had been lying, near to the stove. He had not rushed forward after the manner of other dogs. He stood, watching and waiting.

"Holy smoke!" Matt exclaimed. "Look at 'm wag his tail!"

Weedon Scott strode half across the room toward him, at the same time calling him. White Fang came to him, not with a great bound, yet quickly. He was awkward from self-consciousness, but as he drew near, his eyes took on a strange expression. Something, an incommunicable vastness of feeling, rose up into his eyes as a light and shone forth.

"He never looked at me that way all the time you was gone," Matt commented.

Weedon Scott did not hear. He was squatting down on his heels, face to face with White Fang and petting him—rubbing at the roots of the ears, making long caressing strokes down the neck to the shoulders, tapping the spine gently with the balls of his fingers. And White Fang was growling responsively, the crooning note of the growl more pronounced than ever.

But that was not all. What of his joy, the great love in him, ever surging and struggling to express itself, succeeded in finding a new mode of expression. He suddenly thrust his head forward and nudged his way in between the master's arm and body. And here, confined, hidden from view all except his ears, no longer growling, he continued to nudge and snuggle.

The two men looked at each other. Scott's eyes were shining.

"Gosh!" said Matt in an awe-stricken voice.

A moment later, when he had recovered himself, he said, "I always insisted that wolf was a dog. Look at 'm!"

With the return of the love-master, White Fang's recovery was rapid. Two nights and a day he spent in the cabin. Then he sallied forth. The sled-dogs had forgotten his prowess. They remembered only the latest, which was his weakness and sickness. At the sight of him as he came out of the cabin they sprang upon him.

"Talk about your rough-houses," Matt murmured gleefully, standing in the doorway and looking on. "Give 'm hell, you wolf! Give 'm hell—an' then some."

White Fang did not need the encouragement. The return of the love-master was enough. Life was flowing through him again, splendid and indomitable. He fought from sheer joy, finding in it an expression of much that he felt and that otherwise was without speech. There could be but one ending. The team dispersed in ignominious defeat, and it was not until after dark that the dogs came sneaking back, one by one, by meekness and humility signifying their fealty to White Fang.

Having learned to snuggle, White Fang was guilty of it often. It was the final word. He could not go beyond it. The one thing of which he had always been particularly jealous was his head. He had always disliked to have it touched. It was the Wild in him, the fear of hurt and of the trap, that had given rise to the panicky impulses to avoid contacts. It was the mandate of his instinct that that head must be free. And now, with the love-master, his snuggling was the deliberate act of putting himself into a position of hopeless helplessness. It was an expression of perfect confidence, of absolute self-surrender, as though he said: "I put myself into thy hands. Work thou thy will with me."

One night, not long after the return, Scott and Matt sat at a game of cribbage, preliminary to going to bed. "Fifteen-two, fifteen-four, an' a pair makes six," Matt was pegging up, when there was an outcry and sound of snarling without. They looked at each other as they started to rise to their feet.

"The wolf's nailed somebody," Matt said.

A wild scream of fear and anguish hastened them.

"Bring a light!" Scott shouted, as he sprang outside.

Matt followed with the lamp, and by its light they saw a man lying on his back in the snow. His arms were folded, one above the other, across his face and throat. Thus he was trying to shield himself from White Fang's teeth. And there was need for it. White Fang was in a rage, wickedly making his attack on the most vulnerable spot. From shoulder to wrist of the crossed arms, the coat-sleeve, blue flannel shirt and undershirt were ripped in rags, while the arms themselves were terribly slashed and streaming blood.

All this the two men saw in the first instant. The next instant Weedon Scott had White Fang by the throat and was dragging him clear. White Fang struggled and snarled, but made no attempt to bite, while he quickly quieted down at a sharp word from the master.

Matt helped the man to his feet. As he arose he lowered his crossed arms, exposing the bestial face of Beauty Smith. The dog-musher let go of him precipitately, with action similar to that of a man who has picked up live fire. Beauty Smith blinked in the lamplight and looked about him. He caught sight of White Fang and terror rushed into his face.

At the same moment Matt noticed two objects lying in the snow. He held the lamp close to them, indicating them with his toe for his employer's benefit—a steel dog-chain and a stout club.

Weedon Scott saw and nodded. Not a word was spoken. The dog-musher laid his hand on Beauty Smith's shoulder and faced him to the right about. No word needed to be spoken. Beauty Smith started.

In the meantime the love-master was patting White Fang and talking to him.

"Tried to steal you, eh? And you wouldn't have it! Well, well, he made a mistake, didn't he?"

"Must 'a' thought he had hold of seventeen devils," the dog-musher sniggered.

White Fang, still wrought up and bristling, growled and growled, the hair slowly lying down, the crooning note remote and dim, but growing in his throat.

WHITE FANG

BY JACK LONDON

PART V.—THE TAME

CHAPTER I

THE LONG TRAIL

IT was in the air. White Fang sensed the coming calamity, even before there was tangible evidence of it. In vague ways it was borne in upon him that a change was impending. He knew not how nor why, yet he got his feel of the oncoming event from the gods themselves. In ways subtler than they knew, they betrayed their intentions to the wolf-dog that haunted the cabin stoop, and that, though he never came inside the cabin, knew what went on inside their brains.

"Listen to that, will you!" the dog-musher exclaimed at supper one night.

Weedon Scott listened. Through the door came a low, anxious whine, like a sobbing under the breath that has just grown audible. Then came the long sniff, as White Fang reassured himself that his god was still inside and had not yet taken himself off in mysterious and solitary flight.

"I do believe that wolf's onto you," the dog-musher said.

Weedon Scott looked across at his companion with eyes that almost pleaded, though this was given the lie by his words.

"What the devil can I do with a wolf in California?" he demanded.

"That's what I say," Matt answered. "What the devil can you do with a wolf in California?"

But this did not satisfy Weedon Scott The other seemed to be judging him in a non-committal sort of way.

"White man's dogs would have no show against him," Scott went on. "He'd kill them on sight. If he didn't bankrupt me with damage suits, the authorities would take him away from me and electrocute him."

"He's a downright murderer, I know," was the dog-musher's comment.

Weedon Scott looked at him suspiciously.

"It would never do," he said decisively.

"It would never do," Matt concurred. "Why, you'd have to hire a man 'specially to take care of 'm."

The other's suspicion was allayed. He nodded cheerfully. In the silence that followed, the low, half-sobbing whine was heard at the door and then the long, questing sniff.

"There's no denyin' he thinks a hell of a lot of you," Matt said.

The other glared at him in sudden wrath. "Damn it all, man! I know my own mind and what's best!"

"I'm agreein' with you, only——"

"Only what?" Scott snapped out.

"Only—" the dog-musher began softly, then changed his mind and betrayed a rising anger of his own. "Well, you needn't get so all-fired het-up about it. Judgin' by your actions one 'd think you didn't know your own mind."

Weedon Scott debated with himself for a while, and then said more gently, "You are right, Matt. I don't know my own mind, and that's what's the trouble."

"Why, it would be rank ridiculousness for me to take that dog along," he broke out after another pause.

"I'm agreein' with you," was Matt's answer and again his employer was not quite satisfied with him.

"But how in the name of the great Sardanapalus he knows you're goin' is what gets me," the dog-musher continued innocently.

"It's beyond me, Matt," Scott answered, with a mournful shake of the head.

Then came the day when, through the open cabin door, White Fang saw the fatal grip on the floor and the love-master packing things into it. Also, there were comings and goings, and the erstwhile placid atmosphere of the cabin was vexed with strange perturbations and unrest. Here was indubitable evidence. White Fang had already sensed it. He now reasoned it. His god was preparing for another flight. And since he had not taken him with him before, so, now, he could look to be left behind.

That night he lifted the long wolf howl. As he had howled in his puppy days, when he fled back from the Wild to the village to find it vanished, and naught but a rubbish-heap to mark the site of Gray Beaver's tepee, so now he pointed his muzzle to the cold stars and told to them his woe.

Inside the cabin the two men had just gone to bed.

"He's gone off his feed again," Matt remarked from his bunk.

There was a grunt from Weedon Scott's bunk, and a stir of blankets.

"From the way he cut up the other time you went away, I wouldn't wonder this time but what he died."

The blankets in the other bunk stirred irritably.

"Oh, shut up!" Scott cried out through the darkness. "You nag worse than a woman."

"I'm agreein' with you," the dog-musher answered, and Weedon Scott was not quite sure whether or not the other had snickered.

The next day White Fang's anxiety and restlessness were even more pronounced. He dogged his master's heels whenever he left the cabin, and haunted the front stoop when he remained inside. Through the open door he could catch glimpses of the luggage on the floor. The grip had been joined by two large canvas bags and a box. Matt was rolling the master's blankets and fur robe inside a small tarpaulin. White Fang whined as he watched the operation.

Later on, two Indians arrived. He watched them closely as they shouldered the luggage and were led off down the hill by Matt, who carried the bedding and the grip. But White Fang did not follow them. The master was still in the cabin. After a time, Matt returned. The master came to the door and called White Fang inside.

"You poor devil," he said gently, rubbing White Fang's ears and tapping his spine. "I'm hitting the long trail, old man, where you cannot follow. Now give me a growl—the last, good, good-by growl."

But White Fang refused to growl. Instead, and after a wistful, searching look, he snuggled in, burrowing his head out of sight between the master's arm and body.

"There she blows!" Matt cried. From the Yukon arose the hoarse bellowing of a river steamboat. "You've got to cut it short. Be sure and lock the front door. I'll go out the back. Get a move on!"

The two doors slammed at the same moment, and Weedon Scott waited for Matt to come around to the front. From inside the door came a low whining and sobbing. Then there were long, deep-drawn sniffs.

"You must take good care of him, Matt," Scott said, as they started down the hill. "Write and let me know how he gets along."

"Sure," the dog-musher answered. "But listen to that, will you!"

Both men stopped. White Fang was howling as dogs howl when their masters lie dead. He was voicing an utter woe, his cry bursting upward in great, heart-breaking rushes, dying down into quavering misery, and bursting upward again with rush upon rush of grief.

The *Aurora* was the first steamboat of the year for the Outside, and her decks were jammed with prosperous adventurers and broken gold-seekers, all equally as mad to get to the Outside as they had been originally to get to the Inside. Near the gangplank, Scott was shaking hands with Matt, who was preparing to go ashore. But Matt's hand went limp in the other's grasp as his gaze shot past and remained fixed on something behind him. Scott turned to see. Sitting on the deck several feet away and watching wistfully was White Fang.

The dog-musher swore softly, in awe-stricken accents. Scott could only look in wonder.

"Did you lock the front door?" Matt demanded.

The other nodded, and asked, "How about the back?"

"You just bet I did," was the fervent reply.

White Fang flattened his ears ingratiatingly, but remained where he was, making no attempt to approach.

"I'll have to take 'm ashore with me."

Matt made a couple of steps toward White Fang, but the latter slid away from him. The dog-musher made a rush of it, and White Fang dodged between the legs of a group of men. Ducking, turning, doubling, he slid about the deck, eluding the other's efforts to capture him.

But when the love-master spoke, White Fang came to him with prompt obedience.

"Won't come to the hand that's fed 'm all these months," the dog-musher muttered resentfully. "And you—you ain't never fed 'm after them first days of gettin' acquainted. I'm blamed if I can see how he works it out that you're the boss."

Scott, who had been patting White Fang, suddenly bent closer and pointed out fresh-made cuts on his muzzle, and a gash between the eyes.

Matt bent over and passed his hand along White Fang's belly.

"We plumb forgot the window. He's all cut an' gouged underneath. Must 'a' butted clean through it, b'gosh!"

But Weedon Scott was not listening. He was thinking rapidly. The *Aurora's* whistle hooted a final announcement of departure. Men were scurrying down the gangplank to the shore. Matt loosened the bandana from his own neck and started to put it around White Fang's. Scott grasped the dog-musher's hand.

"Good-by, Matt, old man. About the wolf—you needn't write. You see, I've ——"

"What!" the dog-musher exploded. "You don't mean to say——"

"The very thing I mean. Here's your bandana. *I'll* write to *you* about him."

Matt paused half way down the gangplank.

"He'll never stand the climate," he shouted back, "unless you clip 'm in warm weather!"

The gangplank was hauled in and the *Aurora* swung out from the bank. Weedon Scott waved a last good-by. Then he turned and bent over White Fang, standing by his side.

"Now growl, damn you, growl," he said, as he patted the responsive head and rubbed the flattening ears.

CHAPTER II

THE SOUTHLAND

White Fang landed from the steamer in San Francisco. He was appalled. Deep in him, below any reasoning process or act of consciousness, he had associated power with godhead. And never had the white men seemed such marvelous gods as now, when he trod the slimy pavement of San Francisco. The log-cabins he had known were replaced by towering buildings. The streets were crowded with perils—wagons, carts, automobiles; great, straining horses pulling huge trucks; and monstrous cable and electric cars hooting and clanging through the midst, screeching their insistent menace after the manner of the lynxes he had known in the northern woods.

All this was the manifestation of power. Through it all, behind it all, was man, governing and controlling, expressing himself, as of old, by his mastery over matter. It was colossal, stunning. White Fang was awed. Fear sat upon him. As in his cubhood he had been made to feel his smallness and puniness on the day he first came in from the Wild to the village of Gray Beaver, so now, in his full-grown stature and pride of strength, he was made to feel small and puny. And there were so many gods! He was made dizzy by the swarming of them. The thunder of the streets smote upon his ears. He was bewildered by the tremendous and endless rush and movement of things. As never before, he felt his dependence on the love-master, close at whose heels he followed, no matter what happened never losing sight of him.

But White Fang was to have no more than a nightmare vision of the city—an experience that was like a bad dream, unreal and terrible, that haunted him for long after in his dreams. He was put into a baggage-car by his master, chained in a corner in the midst of heaped trunks and valises. Here a squat and brawny god held sway, with much noise, hurling trunks and boxes about, dragging them in through the door and tossing them into the piles, or flinging them out of the door, smashing and crashing, to other gods who awaited them.

And here, in this inferno of luggage, was White Fang deserted by the master. Or at least White Fang thought he was deserted, until he smelled out the master's canvas clothes-bags alongside of him and proceeded to mount guard over them.

"'Bout time you come," growled the god of the car, an hour later, when Weedon Scott appeared at the door. "That dog of yourn won't let me lay a finger on your stuff."

White Fang emerged from the car. He was astonished. The nightmare city was gone. The car had been to him no more than a room in a house, and when he had entered it the city had been all around him. In the interval the city had disappeared. The roar of it no longer dinned upon his ears. Before him was smiling country, streaming with sunshine, lazy with quietude. But he had little time to marvel at the transformation. He accepted it as he accepted all the unaccountable doings and manifestations of the gods. It was their way.

There was a carriage waiting. A man and a woman approached the master. The woman's arms went out and clutched the master around the neck—a hostile act! The next moment Weedon Scott had torn loose from the embrace and closed with White Fang, who had become a snarling, raging demon.

"It's all right, mother," Scott was saying as he kept tight hold of White Fang and placated him. "He thought you were going to injure me, and he wouldn't stand for it. It's all right. It's all right. He'll learn soon enough."

"And in the meantime I may be permitted to love my son when his dog is not around," she laughed, though she was pale and weak from the fright.

She looked at White Fang, who snarled and bristled and glared malevolently.

"He'll have to learn, and he shall, without postponement," Scott said.

He spoke softly to White Fang until he had quieted him, then his voice became firm.

"Down, sir! Down with you!"

This had been one of the things taught him by the master, and White Fang obeyed, though he lay down reluctantly and sullenly.

"Now, mother."

Scott opened his arms to her, but kept his eyes on White Fang.

"Down!" he warned. "Down!"

White Fang, bristling silently, half-crouching as he rose, sank back and watched the hostile act repeated. But no harm came of it, nor of the embrace from the strange man-god that followed. Then the clothes-bags were taken into the carriage, the strange gods and the love-master followed, and White Fang pursued, now running vigilantly behind, now bristling up to the running horses and warning them that he was there to see that no harm befell the god they dragged so swiftly across the earth.

At the end of fifteen minutes the carriage swung in through a stone gateway and on between a double row of arched and interlacing walnut trees. On either side stretched lawns, their broad sweep broken, here and there, by great, sturdy-limbed oaks. In the near distance, in contrast with the young green of the tended grass, sunburnt hay-fields showed tan and gold; while beyond were the tawny hills and upland pastures. From the head of the lawn, on the first soft swell from the valley-level, looked down the deep-porched, many-windowed house.

Little opportunity was given White Fang to see all this. Hardly had the carriage entered the grounds, when he was set upon by a sheep-dog, bright-eyed, sharp-muzzled, righteously indignant and angry. It was between him and the master, cutting him off. White Fang snarled no warning, but his hair bristled as he made his silent and deadly rush. This rush was never completed. He halted with awkward abruptness, with stiff fore legs bracing himself against his momentum, almost sitting down on his haunches, so desirous was he of avoiding contact with the dog he was in the act of attacking. It was a female, and the law of his kind thrust a barrier between. For him to attack her would require nothing less than a violation of his instinct.

But with the sheep-dog it was otherwise. Being a female, she possessed no such instinct. On the other hand, being a sheep-dog, her instinctive fear of the Wild, and especially of the wolf, was unusually keen. White Fang was to her a wolf, the hereditary marauder who had preyed upon her flocks from the time sheep were first herded and guarded by some dim ancestor of hers. And so, as he abandoned his rush at her and braced himself to avoid the contact, she sprang upon him. He snarled involuntarily as he felt her teeth in his shoulder, but beyond this made no effort to hurt her. He backed away, stiff-legged with self-consciousness, and tried to go around her. He dodged this way and that, and curved and turned, but to no purpose. She remained always between him and the way he wanted to go.

"Here, Collie!" called the strange man in the carriage.

Weedon Scott laughed.

"Never mind, father. It is good discipline. White Fang will have to learn many things, and it's just as well that he begins now. He'll adjust himself all right."

The carriage drove on, and still Collie blocked White Fang's way. He tried to outrun her by leaving the drive and circling across the lawn; but she ran on the inner and smaller circle, and was always there, facing him with her two rows of gleaming teeth. Back he circled, across the drive to the other lawn, and again she headed him off.

The carriage was bearing the master away. White Fang caught glimpses of it disappearing amongst the trees. The situation was desperate. He essayed another circle. She followed, running swiftly. And then, suddenly, he turned upon her. It was his old fighting trick. Shoulder to shoulder, he struck her squarely. Not only was she overthrown; so fast had she been running that she rolled along, now on her back, now on her side, as she struggled to stop, clawing gravel with her feet and crying shrilly her hurt pride and indignation.

White Fang did not wait. The way was clear, and that was all he had wanted. She took after him, never ceasing her outcry. It was the straightaway now, and when it came to real running, White Fang could teach her things. She ran frantically, hysterically, straining to the utmost, advertising the effort she was making with every leap; and all the time White Fang slid smoothly away from her, silently, without effort, gliding like a ghost over the ground.

As he rounded the house to the *porte-cochère*, he came upon the carriage. It had stopped, and the master was alighting. At this moment, still running at top speed, White Fang became suddenly aware of an attack from the side. It was a deer-hound rushing upon him. White Fang tried to face it. But he was going too fast, and the hound was too close. It struck him on the side; and such was his forward momentum and the unexpectedness of it, White Fang was hurled to the ground and rolled clear over. He came out of the tangle a spectacle of malignancy, ears flattened back, lips writhing, nose wrinkling, his teeth clipping together as the fangs barely missed the hound's soft throat.

The master was running up, but was too far away; and it was Collie that saved the hound's life. Before White Fang could spring in and deliver the fatal stroke, and just as he was in the act of springing in, Collie arrived. She had been out-maneuvered and out-run, to say nothing of her having been unceremoniously tumbled in the gravel, and her arrival was like that of a tornado—made up of offended dignity, justifiable wrath, and instinctive hatred for this marauder from the Wild She struck White Fang at right angles in the midst of his spring, and again he was knocked off his feet and rolled over.

The next moment the master arrived, and with one hand held White Fang, while the father called off the dogs.

"I say, this is a pretty warm reception for a poor lone wolf from the Arctic," the master said, while White Fang calmed down under his caressing hand. "In all his life he's only been known once to go off his feet, and here he's been rolled twice in thirty seconds."

The carriage had driven away, and other strange gods had appeared from out the house. Some of these stood respectfully at a distance; but two of them, women, perpetrated the hostile act of clutching the master around the neck. White Fang, however, was beginning to tolerate this act. No harm seemed to come of it, while the noises the gods made were certainly not threatening. These gods also made overtures to White Fang, but he warned them off with a snarl, and the master did likewise with word of mouth. At such times White Fang leaned in close against the master's legs and received reassuring pats on the head.

The hound, under the command, "Dick! Lie down, sir!" had gone up the steps and lain down to one side on the porch, still growling and keeping a sullen watch on the intruder. Collie had been taken in charge by one of the woman-gods, who held arms around her neck and petted and caressed her; but Collie was very much perplexed and worried, whining and restless, outraged by the permitted presence of this wolf and confident that the gods were making a mistake.

All the gods started up the steps to enter the house. White Fang followed closely at the master's heels. Dick, on the porch, growled, and White Fang, on the steps, bristled and growled back.

"Take Collie inside and leave the two of them to fight it out," suggested Scott's father. "After that they'll be friends."

"Then White Fang, to show his friendship, will have to be chief mourner at the funeral," laughed the master.

The elder Scott looked incredulously, first at White Fang, then at Dick, and finally at his son.

"You mean that——"

Weedon nodded his head. "I mean just that. You'd have a dead Dick inside of one minute—two minutes at the farthest."

He turned to White Fang. "Come on, you wolf. It's you that 'll have to come inside."

White Fang walked stiff-legged up the steps and across the porch, with tail rigidly erect, keeping his eyes on Dick to guard against a flank attack, and at the same time prepared for whatever fierce manifestation of the unknown that might pounce out upon him from the interior of the house. But no thing of fear pounced out, and when he had gained the inside he scouted carefully around, looking for it and finding it not. Then he lay down with a contented grunt at the master's feet, observing all that went on, ever ready to spring to his feet and fight for life with the terrors he felt must lurk under the trap-roof of the dwelling.

CHAPTER III

THE GOD'S DOMAIN

Not only was White Fang adaptable by nature, but he had traveled much, and knew the meaning and necessity of adjustment. Here, in Sierra Vista, which was the name of Judge Scott's place, White Fang quickly began to make himself at home. He had no further serious trouble with the dogs. They knew more about the ways of the Southland gods than did he, and in their eyes he had qualified when he accompanied the gods inside the house. Wolf that he was, and unprecedented as it was, the gods had sanctioned his presence, and they, the dogs of the gods, could only recognize this sanction.

Dick, perforce, had to go through a few stiff formalities at first, after which he calmly accepted White Fang as an addition to the premises. Had Dick had his way, they would have been good friends; but Whit Fang was averse to friendship. All he asked of other dogs was to be left alone. His whole life he had kept aloof from his kind, and he still desired to keep aloof. Dick's overtures bothered him, so he snarled Dick away. In the North he had learned the lesson that he must let the master's dogs alone, and he did not forget that lesson now. But he insisted on his own privacy and self-seclusion, and so thoroughly ignored Dick that that good-natured creature finally gave him up and scarcely took as much interest in him as in the hitching-post near the stables.

Not so with Collie. While she accepted him because it was the mandate of the gods, that was no reason that she should leave him in peace. Woven into her being was the memory of countless crimes he and his had perpetrated against her ancestry. Not in a day nor a generation were the ravaged sheep-folds to be forgotten. All this was a spur to her, pricking her to retaliation. She could not fly in the face of the gods who permitted him, but that did not prevent her from making life miserable for him in petty ways. A feud, ages old, was between them, and she, for one, would see to it that he was reminded.

So Collie took advantage of her sex to pick upon White Fang and maltreat him. His instinct would not permit him to attack her, while her persistence would not permit him to ignore her. When she rushed at him he turned his fur-protected shoulder to her sharp teeth and walked away stiff-legged and stately. When she forced him too hard, he was compelled to go about in a circle, his shoulder presented to her, his head turned from her, and on his face and in his eyes a patient and bored expression. Sometimes, however, a nip on his hind-quarters hastened his retreat and made it anything but stately. But as a rule he managed to maintain a dignity that was almost solemnity. He ignored her existence whenever it was possible, and made it a point to keep out of her way. When he saw or heard her coming, he got up and walked off.

There was much in other matters for White Fang to learn. Life in the Northland was simplicity itself when compared with the complicated affairs of Sierra Vista. First of all, he had to learn the family of the master. In a way he was prepared to do this. As Mit-sah and Kloo-kooch had belonged to Gray Beaver, sharing his food, his fire, and his blankets, so now, at Sierra Vista, belonged to the love-master all the denizens of the house.

But in this matter there was a difference, and many differences. Sierra Vista was a far vaster affair than the tepee of Gray Beaver. There were many persons to be considered. There was Judge Scott, and there was his wife. There were the master's two sisters, Beth and Mary. There was his wife, Alice, and then there were his children, Weedon and Maud, toddlers of four and six. There was no way for anybody to tell him about all these people, and of blood ties and relationship he knew nothing whatever, and never would be capable of knowing. Yet he quickly worked it out that all of them belonged to the master. Then, by observation, whenever opportunity offered, by study of action, speech, and the very intonations of the voice, he slowly learned the intimacy and the degree of favor they enjoyed with the master. And by this ascertained standard, White Fang treated them accordingly. What was of value to the master he valued; what was dear to the master was to be cherished by White Fang and guarded carefully.

Thus it was with the two children. All his life he had disliked children. He hated and feared their hands. The lessons were not tender that he had learned of their tyranny and cruelty in the days of the Indian villages. When Weedon and Maud had first approached him, he growled warningly and looked malignant. A cuff from the master and a sharp word had then compelled him to permit their caresses, though he growled and growled under their tiny hands, and in the growl there was no crooning note. Later, he observed that the boy and girl were of great value in the master's eyes. Then it was that no cuff nor sharp word was necessary before they could pat him.

Yet White Fang was never effusively affectionate. He yielded to the master's children with an ill but honest grace, and endured their fooling as one would endure a painful operation. When he could no longer endure, he would get up and stalk determinedly away from them. But after a time, he grew even to like the children. Still he was not demonstrative. He would not go up to them. On the other hand, instead of walking away at sight of them, he waited for them to come to him. And still later, it was noticed that a pleased light came into his eyes when he saw them approaching, and that he looked after them with an appearance of curious regret when they left him for other amusements.

All this was a matter of development, and took time. Next in his regard, after the children, was Judge Scott. There were two reasons, possibly, for this. First, he was evidently a valuable possession of the master's, and next, he was undemonstrative. White Fang liked to lie at his feet on the wide porch when he read the newspaper, from time to time favoring White Fang with a look or a word—untroublesome tokens that he recognized White Fang's presence and existence. But this was only when the master was not around. When the master appeared, all the other beings ceased to exist so far as White Fang was concerned.

White Fang allowed all the members of the family to pet him and make much of him; but he never gave to them what he gave to the master. No caress of theirs could put the love-croon into his throat, and, try as they would, they could never persuade him into snuggling against them. This expression of abandon and surrender, of absolute trust, he reserved for the master alone. In fact, he never regarded the members of the family in any other light than possessions of the love-master.

Also, White Fang had early come to differentiate between the family and the servants of the household. The latter were afraid of him, while he merely refrained from attacking them. This because he considered that they were likewise possessions of the master. Between White Fang and them existed a neutrality and no more. They cooked for the master and washed the dishes and did other things just as Matt had done up in the Klondike. They were, in short, appurtenances of the household.

Outside the household there was even more for White Fang to learn. The master's domain was wide and complex, yet it had its metes and bounds. The land itself ceased at the county road. Outside was the common domain of all gods—the roads and streets. Then inside other fences were the particular domains of other gods. A myriad laws governed all these things and determined conduct; yet he did not know the speech of the gods, nor was there any way for him to learn save by experience. He obeyed his natural impulses until they ran him counter to some law. When this had been done a few times he learned the law and after that observed it.

But most potent in his education was the cuff of the master's hand, the censure of the master's voice. Because of White Fang's very great love, a cuff from the master hurt him far more than any beating Gray Beaver or Beauty Smith had ever given him. They had hurt only the flesh of him; beneath the flesh the spirit had still raged, splendid and invincible. But with the master the cuff was always too light to hurt the flesh. Yet it went deeper. It was an expression of the master's disapproval, and White Fang's spirit wilted under it.

In point of fact, the cuff was rarely administered. The master's voice was sufficient. By it White Fang knew whether he did right or not. By it he trimmed his conduct and adjusted his actions. It was the compass by which he steered and learned to chart the manners of a new land and life.

In the Northland, the only domesticated animal was the dog. All other animals lived in the Wild, and were, when not too formidable, lawful spoil for any dog. All his days White Fang had foraged among the live things for food. It did not enter his head that in the Southland it was otherwise. But this he was to learn early in his residence in Santa Clara Valley. Sauntering around the corner of the house in the early morning, he came upon a chicken that had escaped from the chicken-yard. White Fang's natural impulse was to eat it. A couple of bounds, a flash of teeth and a frightened squawk, and he had scooped in the adventurous fowl. It was farm-bred and fat and tender; and White Fang licked his chops and decided that such fare was good.

Later in the day, he chanced upon another stray chicken near the stables. One of the grooms ran to the rescue. He did not know White Fang's breed, so for weapon he took a light buggy-whip. At the first cut of the whip, White Fang left the chicken for the man. A club might have stopped White Fang, but not a whip. Silently, without flinching, he took a second cut in his forward rush, and as he leaped for the throat the groom cried out, "My God!" and staggered backward. He dropped the whip and shielded his throat with his arms. In consequence, his fore-arm was ripped open to the bone.

The man was badly frightened. It was not so much White Fang's ferocity as it was his silence that unnerved the groom. Still protecting his throat and face with his torn and bleeding arm, he tried to retreat to the barn. And it would have gone hard with him had not Collie appeared on the scene. As she had saved Dick's life, she now saved the groom's. She rushed upon White Fang in frenzied wrath. She had been right. She had known better than the blundering gods. All her suspicions were justified. Here was the ancient marauder up to his old tricks again.

The groom escaped into the stables, and White Fang backed away before Collie's wicked teeth, or presented his shoulder to them and circled round and round. But Collie did not give over, as was her wont, after a decent interval of chastisement. On the contrary, she grew more excited and angry every moment, until, in the end, White Fang flung dignity to the winds and frankly fled away from her across the fields.

"He'll learn to leave chickens alone," the master said. "But I can't give him the lesson until I catch him in the act."

Two nights later came the act, but on a more generous scale than the master had anticipated. White Fang had observed closely the chicken-yards and the habits of the chickens. In the night time, after they had gone to roost, he climbed to the top of a pile of newly hauled lumber. From there he gained the roof of a chicken-house, passed over the ridgepole and dropped to the ground inside. A moment later he was inside the house, and the slaughter began.

In the morning, when the master came out on to the porch, fifty white Leghorn hens, laid out in a row by the groom, greeted his eyes. He whistled to himself softly, first with surprise, and then, at the end, with admiration. His eyes were likewise greeted by White Fang, but about the latter there were no signs of shame nor guilt. He carried himself with pride, as though, forsooth, he had achieved a deed praiseworthy and meritorious. There was about him no consciousness of sin. The master's lips tightened as he faced the disagreeable task. Then he talked harshly to the unwitting culprit, and in his voice there was nothing but godlike wrath. Also, he held White Fang's nose down to the slain hens, and at the same time cuffed him again. It was against the law, and he had learned it. Then the master took him into the chicken-yards. White Fang's natural impulse, when he saw the live food fluttering about him and under his very nose, was to spring upon it. He obeyed the impulse, but was checked by the master's voice. They continued in the yards for half an hour. Time and again the impulse surged over White Fang, and each time, as he yielded to it, he was checked by the master's voice. Thus it was he learned the law, and ere he left the domain of the chickens, he had learned to ignore their existence.

"You can never cure a chicken-killer." Judge Scott shook his head sadly at luncheon table, when his son narrated the lesson he had given White Fang. "Once they've got the habit and the taste of blood . . ." Again he shook his head sadly.

But Weedon Scott did not agree with his father.

"I'll tell you what I'll do," he challenged finally. "I'll lock White Fang in with the chickens all afternoon."

"But think of the chickens," objected the Judge.

"And furthermore," the son went on, "for every chicken he kills I'll pay you one dollar gold coin of the realm."

"But you should penalize father, too," interposed Beth.

Her sister seconded her, and a chorus of approval arose around the table. Judge Scott nodded his head in agreement.

"All right." Weedon Scott pondered for a moment. "And if, at the end of the afternoon, White Fang hasn't harmed a chicken, for every ten minutes of the time he has spent in the yard, you will have to say to him, gravely and with deliberation, just as if you were sitting on the bench and solemnly passing judgment, 'White Fang, you are smarter than I thought.'"

From hidden points of vantage the family watched the performance. But it was a fizzle. Locked in the yard and there deserted by the master, White Fang lay down and went to sleep. Once he got up and walked over to the trough for a drink of water. The chickens he calmly ignored. So far as he was concerned they did not exist. At four o'clock he executed a running jump, gained the roof of the chicken-house and leaped to the ground outside, whence he sauntered gravely to the house. He had learned the law. And on the porch, before the delighted family, Judge Scott, face to face with White Fang, said slowly and solemnly, sixteen times, "White Fang, you are smarter than I thought."

But it was the multiplicity of laws that befuddled White Fang and often brought him into disgrace. He had to learn that he must not touch the chickens that belonged to other gods. Then there were cats, and rabbits, and turkeys; all these he must let alone. In fact, when he had but partly learned the law, his impression was that he must leave all live things alone. Out in the back pasture, a quail could flutter up under his nose unharmed. All tense and trembling with eagerness and desire, he mastered his instinct and stood still. He was obeying the will of the gods.

And then, one day, again out in the back pasture, he saw Dick start a jack rabbit and run it. The master himself was looking on and did not interfere. Nay, he encouraged White Fang to join in the chase. And thus he learned that there was no taboo on jack rabbits. In the end he worked out the complete law. Between him and all domestic animals there must be no hostilities. If not amity, at least neutrality must obtain. But the other animals, the squirrels, and quail, and cottontails, were creatures of the Wild who had never yielded allegiance to man. They were the lawful prey of any dog. It was only the tame that the gods protected, and between the tame deadly strife was not permitted. The gods held the power of life and death over their subjects, and the gods were jealous of their power.

Life was complex in the Santa Clara Valley after the simplicities of the Northland. And the chief thing demanded by these intricacies of civilization was control, restraint—a poise of self that was as delicate as the fluttering of gossamer wings and at the same time as rigid as steel. Life had a thousand faces, and White Fang found he must meet them all—thus, when he went to town, in to San José, running behind the carriage or loafing about the streets when the carriage stopped. Life flowed past him, deep and wide and varied, continually impinging upon his senses, demanding of him instant and endless adjustments and correspondences, and compelling him, almost always, to suppress his natural impulses.

There were butcher-shops where meat hung within reach. This meat he must not touch. There were cats at the houses the master visited that must be let alone. And there were dogs everywhere that snarled at him and that he must not attack. And then, on the crowded sidewalks there were persons innumerable whose attention he attracted. They would stop and look at him, point him out to one another, examine him, talk to him, and, worst of all, pat him. And these perilous contacts from all these strange hands he must endure. Yet this endurance he achieved. Furthermore he got over being awkward and self-conscious. In a lofty way he received the attentions of the multitudes of strange gods. With condescension he accepted their condescension. On the other hand, there was something about him that prevented great familiarity. They patted him on the head and passed on, contented and pleased with their own daring.

But it was not all easy for White Fang. Running behind the carriage in the outskirts of San José, he encountered certain small boys who made a practice of flinging stones at him. Yet he knew that it was not permitted him to pursue and drag them down. Here he was compelled to violate his instinct of self-preservation, and violate it he did, for he was becoming tame and qualifying himself for civilization.

Nevertheless, White Fang was not quite satisfied with the arrangement. He had no abstract ideas about justice and fair play. But there is a certain sense of equity that resides in life, and it was this sense in him that resented the unfairness of his being permitted no defense against the stone-throwers. He forgot that in the covenant entered into between him and the gods they were pledged to care for him and defend him. But one day the master sprang from the carriage, whip in hand, and gave the stone-throwers a thrashing. After that they threw stones no more, and White Fang understood and was satisfied.

One other experience of similar nature was his. On the way to town, hanging around the saloon at the cross-roads, were three dogs that made a practice of rushing out upon him when he went by. Knowing his deadly method of fighting, the master had never ceased impressing upon White Fang the law that he must not fight. As a result, having learned the lesson well, White Fang was hard put whenever he passed the cross-roads saloon. After the first rush, each time, his snarl kept the three dogs at a distance, but they trailed along behind, yelping and bickering and insulting him. This endured for some time. The men at the saloon even urged the dogs on to attack White Fang. One day they openly sicked the dogs on him. The master stopped the carriage.

"Go to it," he said to White Fang.

But White Fang could not believe. He looked at the master, and he looked at the dogs. Then he looked back eagerly and questioningly at the master.

The master nodded his head. "Go to them, old fellow. Eat them up."

White Fang no longer hesitated. He turned and leaped silently among his enemies. All three faced him. There was a great snarling and growling, a clashing of teeth and a flurry of bodies. The dust of the road arose in a cloud and screened the battle. But at the end of several minutes two dogs were struggling in the dirt and the third was in full flight. He leaped a ditch, went through a rail fence, and fled across a field. White Fang followed, sliding over the ground in wolf fashion and with wolf speed, swiftly and without noise, and in the center of the field he dragged down and slew the dog.

With this triple killing, his main troubles with dogs ceased. The word went up and down the valley, and men saw to it that their dogs did not molest the Fighting Wolf.

CHAPTER IV

THE CALL OF KIND

The months came and went. There was plenty of food and no work in the Southland, and White Fang lived fat and prosperous and happy. Not alone was he in the geographical Southland, for he was in the Southland of life. Human kindness was like a sun shining upon him, and he flourished like a flower planted in good soil.

And yet he remained somehow different from other dogs. He knew the law even better than did the dogs that had known no other life, and he observed the law more punctiliously; but still there was about him a suggestion of lurking ferocity, as though the Wild still lingered in him and the wolf in him merely slept.

He never chummed with other dogs. Lonely he had lived, so far as his kind was concerned, and lonely he would continue to live. In his puppyhood, under the persecution of Lip-lip and the puppy pack, and in his fighting days with Beauty Smith, he had acquired a fixed aversion f r dogs. The natural course of his life had been diverted, and, recoiling from his kind, he had clung to the human.

Besides, all Southland dogs looked upon him with suspicion. He aroused in them their instinctive fear of the Wild, and they greeted him always with snarl and growl and belligerent hatred. He, on the other hand, learned that it was not necessary to use his teeth upon them. His naked fangs and writhing lips were uniformly efficacious, rarely failing to send a bellowing onrushing dog back on its haunches.

But there was one trial in White Fang's life—Collie. She never gave him a moment's peace. She was not so amenable to the law as he. She defied all efforts of the master to make her become friends with White Fang. Ever in his ears was sounding her sharp and nervous snarl. She had never forgiven him the chicken-killing episode, and persistently held to the belief that his intentions were bad. She found him guilty before the act, and treated him accordingly. She became a pest to him, like a policeman following him around the stable and the grounds, and, if he even so much as glanced curiously at a pigeon or chicken, bursting into an outcry of indignation and wrath. His favorite way of ignoring her was to lie down, with his head on his fore-paws, and pretend sleep. This always dumbfounded and silenced her.

With the exception of Collie, all things went well with White Fang. He had learned control and poise, and he knew the law. He achieved a staidness, and calmness, and philosophic tolerance. He no longer lived in a hostile environment. Danger and hurt and death did not lurk everywhere about him. In time, the unknown, as a thing of terror and menace ever impending, faded away. Life was soft and easy. It flowed along smoothly, and neither fear nor foe lurked by the way.

He missed the snow without being aware of it. "An unduly long summer," would have been his thought had he thought about it; as it was, he merely missed the snow in a vague, sub-conscious way. In the same fashion, especially in the heat of summer when he suffered from the sun, he experienced faint longings for the Northland. Their only effect upon him, however, was to make him uneasy and restless, without his knowing what was the matter.

White Fang had never been very demonstrative. Beyond his snuggling and the throwing of a crooning note into his love-growl, he had no way of expressing his love. Yet it was given to him to discover a third way. He had always been susceptible to the laughter of the gods. Laughter had affected him with madness, made him frantic with rage. But he did not have it in him to be angry with the love-master, and when that god elected to laugh at him in a good-natured, bantering way, he was nonplused. He could feel the pricking and stinging of the old anger as it strove to rise up in him, but it strove against love. He could not be angry; yet he had to do something. At first he was dignified, and the master laughed the harder Then he tried to be more dignified, and the master laughed harder than before. In the end, the master laughed him out of his dignity. His jaws slightly parted, his lips lifted a little, and a quizzical expression that was more love than humor came into his eyes. He had learned to laugh.

Likewise he learned to romp with the master, to be tumbled down and rolled over, and be the victim of innumerable rough tricks. In return he feigned anger, bristling and growling ferociously, and clipping his teeth together in snaps that had all the seeming of deadly intention. But he never forgot himself. Those snaps were always delivered on the empty air. At the end of such a romp, when blow and cuff and snap and snarl were fast and furious, they would break off suddenly and stand several feet apart, glaring at each other. And then, just as suddenly, like the sun rising on a stormy sea, they would begin to laugh. This would always culminate with the master's arms going around White Fang's neck and shoulders while the latter crooned and growled his love-song.

But nobody else ever romped with White Fang. He did not permit it. He stood on his dignity, and when they attempted it, his warning snarl and bristling mane were anything but playful. That he allowed the master these liberties was no reason that he should be a common dog, loving here and loving there, everybody's property for a romp and good time. He loved with single heart and refused to cheapen himself or his love.

The master went out on horseback a great deal, and to accompany him was one of White Fang's chief duties in life. In the Northland he had evidenced his fealty by toiling in the harness; but there were no sleds in the Southland, nor did dogs pack burdens on their backs. So he rendered fealty in the new way, by running with the master's horse. The longest day never played White Fang out. His was the gait of the wolf, smooth, tireless and effortless, and at the end of fifty miles he would come in jauntily ahead of the horse.

It was in connection with the riding that White Fang achieved one other mode of expression—remarkable in that he did it but twice in all his life. The first time occurred when the master was trying to teach a spirited thoroughbred the method of opening and closing gates without the rider's dismounting. Time and again and many times he ranged the horse up to the gate in the effort to close it, and each time the horse became frightened and backed and plunged away. It grew more nervous and excited every moment. When it reared, the master put the spurs to it and made it drop its fore legs back to earth, whereupon it would begin kicking with its hind legs. White Fang watched the performance with increasing anxiety until he could contain himself no longer, when he sprang in front of the horse and barked savagely and warningly.

Though he often tried to bark thereafter, and the master encouraged him, he succeeded only once, and then it was not in the master's presence. A scamper across the pasture, a jack rabbit rising suddenly under the horse's feet, a violent sheer, a stumble, a fall to earth, and a broken leg for the master, was the cause of it. White Fang sprang in a rage at the throat of the offending horse, but was checked by the master's voice.

"Home! Go home!" the master commanded, when he ascertained his injury.

White Fang was disinclined to desert him. The master thought of writing a note, but searched his pockets vainly for pencil and paper. Again he commanded White Fang to go home.

The latter regarded him wistfully, started away, then returned and whined softly. The master talked to him gently but seriously, and he cocked his ears and listened with painful intentness.

"That's all right, old fellow, you just run along home," ran the talk. "Go on home and tell them what's happened to me. Home with you, you wolf. Get along home!"

White Fang knew the meaning of "home," and though he did not understand the remainder of the master's language he knew it was his will that he should go home. He turned and trotted reluctantly away. Then he stopped, undecided, and looked back over his shoulder.

"Go home!" came the sharp command, and this time he obeyed.

The family was on the porch, taking the cool of the afternoon, when White Fang arrived. He came in among them, panting, covered with dust.

"Weedon's back," Weedon's mother announced.

The children welcomed White Fang with glad cries and ran to meet him. He avoided them and passed down the porch, but they cornered him against a rocking-chair and the railing. He growled and tried to push by them. Their mother looked apprehensively in their direction.

"I confess, he makes me nervous around the children," she said. "I have a dread that he will turn upon them unexpectedly some day."

Growling savagely, White Fang sprang out of the corner, overturning the boy and the girl. The mother called them to her and comforted them, telling them not to bother White Fang.

"A wolf is a wolf," commented Judge Scott. "There is no trusting one."

"But he is not all wolf," interposed Beth, standing for her brother in his absence.

"You have only Weedon's opinion for that," rejoined the judge. "He merely surmises that there is some strain of dog in White Fang; but, as he will tell you himself, he knows nothing about it. As for his appearance——"

He did not finish the sentence. White Fang stood before him, growling fiercely.

"Go away! Lie down, sir!" Judge Scott commanded.

White Fang turned to the love-master's wife. She screamed with fright as he seized her dress in his teeth and dragged on it till the frail fabric tore away. By this time he had become the center of interest. He had ceased from his growling and stood, head up, looking into their faces. His throat worked spasmodically, but made no sound, while he struggled with all his body, convulsed with the effort to rid himself of the incommunicable something that strained for utterance.

"I hope he is not going mad," said Weedon's mother. "I told Weedon that I was afraid the warm climate would not agree with an Arctic animal."

"He's trying to speak, I do believe," Beth announced.

At that moment speech came to White Fang, rushing up in a great burst of barking.

"Something has happened to Weedon," his wife said decisively.

They were all on their feet now, and White Fang ran down the steps, looking back for them to follow. For the second and last time in his life he had barked and made himself understood.

After this event, he found a warmer place in the hearts of the Sierra Vista people, and even the groom whose arm he had slashed admitted that he was a wise dog even if he was a wolf. Judge Scott still held to the same opinion, and proved it to everybody's dissatisfaction by measurements and descriptions taken from the encyclopedia and various works on natural history.

The days came and went, streaming their unbroken sunshine over the Santa Clara Valley. But as they grew shorter and White Fang's second winter in the Southland came on, he made a strange discovery. Collie's teeth were no longer sharp. There was a playfulness about her nips and a gentleness that prevented them from really hurting him. He forgot that she had made life a burden to him, and when she disported herself around him he responded solemnly, striving to be playful and becoming no more than ridiculous.

One day she led him off on a long chase through the back pasture and into the woods. It was the afternoon that the master was to ride, and White Fang knew it. The horse stood saddled and waiting at the door. White Fang hesitated. But there was that in him deeper than all the law he had learned, than the customs that had molded him, than his love for the master, than the very will to live of himself; and when, in the moment of his indecision, Collie nipped him and scampered off, he turned and followed after. The master rode alone that day; and in the woods, side by side, White Fang ran with Collie, as his mother, Kiche, and old One Eye had run long years before in the silent Northland forest.

CHAPTER V

THE SLEEPING WOLF

It was about this time that the newspapers were full of the daring escape of a convict from San Quentin prison. He was a ferocious man. He had been ill made in the making. He had not been born right, and he had not been helped any by the molding he had received at the hands of society. The hands of society are harsh, and this man was a striking sample of its handiwork. He was a beast—a human beast, it is true, but nevertheless so terrible a beast that he can best be characterized as carnivorous.

In San Quentin prison he had proved incorrigible. Punishment failed to break his spirit. He could die dumb mad and fighting to the last, but he could not live and be beaten. The more fiercely he fought, the more harshly society handled him, and the only effect of harshness was to make him fiercer. Strait-jackets, starvation, and beatings and clubbings were the wrong treatment for Jim Hall; but it was the treatment he received. It was the treatment he had received from the time he was a little pulpy boy in a San Francisco slum—soft clay in the hands of society and ready to be formed into something.

It was during Jim Hall's third term in prison that he encountered a guard that was almost as great a beast as he. The guard treated him unfairly, lied about him to the warden, lost him his credits, persecuted him. The difference between them was that the guard carried a bunch of keys and a revolver. Jim Hall had only his naked hands and his teeth. But he sprang upon the guard one day and used his teeth on the other's throat just like any jungle animal.

After this Jim Hall went to live in the incorrigible cell. He lived there three years. The cell was of iron, the floor, the walls, the roof. He never left this cell. He never saw the sky nor the sunshine. Day was a twilight and night was a black silence. He was in an iron tomb, buried alive. He saw no human face, spoke to no human thing. When his food was shoved in to him he growled like a wild animal. He hated all things. For days and nights he bellowed his rage at the universe. For weeks and months he never made a sound, in the black silence eating his very soul. He was a man and a monstrosity, as fearful a thing of fear as ever gibbered in the visions of a maddened brain.

And then, one night, he escaped. The warden said it was impossible, but nevertheless the cell was empty, and half in, half out of it lay the body of a dead guard. Two other dead guards marked his trail through the prison to the outer walls, and he had killed with his hands to avoid noise.

He was armed with the weapons of the slain guards—a live arsenal that fled through the hills pursued by the organized might of society. A heavy price of gold was upon his head. Avaricious farmers hunted him with shotguns. His blood might pay off a mortgage or send a son to college. Public-spirited citizens took down their rifles and went out after him. A pack of blood-hounds followed the way of his bleeding feet. And the sleuth hounds of the law, the paid fighting animals of society, with telephone, and telegraph, and special train, clung to his trail night and day.

Sometimes they came upon him, and men faced him like heroes or stampeded through barb-wire fences to the delight of the commonwealth reading the account at the breakfast table. It was after such encounters that the dead and wounded were carted back to the towns, and their places filled by men eager for the man-hunt.

And then Jim Hall disappeared. The blood-hounds vainly quested on the lost trail. Inoffensive ranchers in remote valleys were held up by armed men and compelled to identify themselves, while the remains of Jim Hall were discovered on a dozen mountain sides by greedy claimants for blood-money.

In the meantime the newspapers were read at Sierra Vista, not so much with interest as with anxiety. The women were afraid. Judge Scott pooh-poohed and laughed, but not with reason, for it was in his last days on the bench that Jim Hall had stood before him and received sentence. And in open courtroom, before all men, Jim Hall had proclaimed that the day would come when he would wreak vengeance on the judge that sentenced him.

For once Jim Hall was right. He was innocent of the crime for which he was sentenced. It was a case, in the parlance of thieves and police, of "railroading." Jim Hall was being "railroaded" to prison for a crime he had not committed. Because of the two prior convictions against him, Judge Scott imposed upon him a sentence of fifty years.

Judge Scott did not know all things, and he did not know that he was a party to a police conspiracy, that the evidence was hatched and perjured, that Jim Hall was guiltless of the crime charged. And Jim Hall, on the other hand, did not know that Judge Scott was merely ignorant. Jim Hall believed that the judge knew all about it and was hand in glove with the police in the perpetration of the monstrous injustice. So it was, when the doom of fifty years of living death was uttered by Judge Scott, that Jim Hall, hating all things in the society that misused him, rose up and raged in the courtroom until dragged down by half a dozen of his blue-coated enemies. To him, Judge Scott was the keystone in the arch of injustice, and upon Judge Scott he emptied the vials of his wrath and hurled the threats of his revenge yet to come. Then Jim Hall went to his living death . . . and escaped.

Of all this White Fang knew nothing. But between him and Alice, the master's wife, there existed a secret. Each night, after Sierra Vista had gone to bed, she arose and let in White Fang to sleep in the big hall. Now White Fang was not a house-dog, nor was he permitted to sleep in the house; so each morning, early, she slipped down and let him out before the family was awake.

On one such night, while all the house slept, White Fang awoke and lay very quietly. And very quietly he smelled the air and read the message it bore of a strange god's presence. And to his ears came sounds of the strange god's movements. White Fang burst into no furious outcry. It was not his way. The strange god walked softly, but more softly walked White Fang, for he had no clothes to rub against the flesh of his body. He followed silently. In the Wild he had hunted live meat that was infinitely timid, and he knew the advantage of surprise.

The strange god paused at the foot of the great staircase and listened, and White Fang was as dead, so without movement was he as he watched and waited. Up that staircase the way led to the love-master and to the love-master's dearest possessions. White Fang bristled, but waited. The strange god's foot lifted. He was beginning the ascent.

Then it was that White Fang struck. He gave no warning, with no snarl anticipated his own action. Into the air he lifted his body in the spring that landed him on the strange god's back. White Fang clung with his fore paws to the man's shoulders, at the same time burying his fangs into the back of the man's neck. He clung on for a moment, long enough to drag the god over backward. Together they crashed to the floor. White Fang leaped clear, and, as the man struggled to rise, was in again with his slashing fangs.

Sierra Vista awoke in alarm. The noise from down stairs was as that of a score of battling fiends. There were revolver shots. A man's voice screamed once in horror and anguish. There was a great snarling and growling, and over all arose a smashing and crashing of furniture and glass.

But almost as quickly as it had arisen, the commotion died away. The struggle had not lasted more than three minutes. The frightened household clustered at the top of the stairway. From below, as from out an abyss of blackness, came up a gurgling sound, as of air bubbling through water. Sometimes this gurgle became sibilant, almost a whistle. But this, too, quickly died down and ceased. Then naught came up out of the blackness save a heavy panting of some creature struggling sorely for air.

Weedon Scott pressed a button, and the staircase and downstairs hall were flooded with light. Then he and Judge Scott, revolvers in hand, cautiously descended. There was no need for this caution. White Fang had done his work. In the midst of the wreckage of overthrown and smashed furniture, partly on his side, his face hidden by an arm, lay a man. Weedon Scott bent over, removed the arm, and turned the man's face upward. A gaping throat explained the manner of his death.

"Jim Hall," said Judge Scott, and father and son looked significantly at each other.

Then they turned to White Fang. He, too, was lying on his side. His eyes were closed, but the lids slightly lifted in an effort to look at them as they bent over him, and the tail was perceptibly agitated in a vain effort to wag. Weedon Scott patted him, and his throat rumbled an acknowledging growl. But it was a weak growl at best, and it quickly ceased. His eyelids drooped and went shut, and his whole body seemed to relax and flatten out upon the floor.

"He's all in, poor devil," muttered the master.

"We'll see about that," asserted the judge, as he started for the telephone.

"Frankly, he has one chance in a thousand," announced the surgeon, after he had worked an hour and a half on White Fang.

Dawn was breaking through the windows and dimming the electric lights. With the exception of the children, the whole family was gathered about the surgeon to hear his verdict.

"One broken hind leg," he went on. "Three broken ribs, one at least of which has pierced the lungs. He has lost nearly all the blood in his body. There is a large likelihood of internal injuries. He must have been jumped upon. To say nothing of three bullet holes clear through him. One chance in a thousand is really optimistic. He hasn't a chance in ten thousand."

"But he mustn't lose any chance that might be of help to him," Judge Scott exclaimed. "Never mind expense. Put him under the X-ray—anything. Weedon, telegraph at once to San Francisco for Doctor Nichols. No reflection on you, doctor, you understand; but he must have the advantage of every chance."

The surgeon smiled indulgently. "Of course I understand. He deserves all that can be done for him. He must be nursed as you would nurse a human being, a sick child. And don't forget what I told you about temperature. I'll be back at ten o'clock again."

White Fang received the nursing. Judge Scott's suggestion of a trained nurse was indignantly clamored down by the girls, who themselves undertook the task. And White Fang won out on the one chance in ten thousand denied him by the surgeon.

The latter was not to be censured for his misjudgment. All his life he had tended and operated on the soft humans of civilization, who lived sheltered lives and had descended out of many sheltered generations. Compared with White Fang, they were frail and flabby, and clutched life without any strength in their grip. White Fang had come straight from the Wild, where the weak perish early and shelter is vouchsafed to none. In neither his father nor his mother was there any weakness, nor in the generations before them. A constitution of iron and the vitality of the Wild were White Fang's inheritance, and he clung to life, the whole of him and every part of him, in spirit and in flesh, with the tenacity that of old belonged to all creatures.

Bound down a prisoner, denied even movement by the plaster casts and bandages, White Fang lingered out the weeks. He slept long hours and dreamed much, and through his mind passed an unending pageant of Northland visions. All the ghosts of the past arose and were with him. Once again he lived in the lair with Kiche, crept trembling to the knees of Gray Beaver to tender his allegiance, ran for his life before Lip-lip and all the howling bedlam of the puppy pack.

He ran again through the silence, hunting his living food through the months of famine; and again he ran at the head of the team, the gut-whips of Mit-sah and Gray Beaver snapping behind, their voices crying "Raa! Raa!" when they came to a narrow passage and the team closed together like a fan to go through. He lived again all his days with Beauty Smith and the fights he had fought. At such times he whimpered and snarled in his sleep, and they that looked on said that his dreams were bad.

But there was one particular nightmare from which he suffered — the clanking, clanging monsters of electric cars that were to him colossal screaming lynxes. He would lie in a screen of bushes, watching for a squirrel to venture far enough out on the ground from its tree refuge. Then, when he sprang out upon it, it would transform itself into an electric car, menacing and terrible, towering over him like a mountain, screaming and clanging and spitting fire at him. It was the same when he challenged the hawk down out of the sky. Down out of the blue it would rush, as it dropped upon him changing itself into the ubiquitous electric car. Or again, he would be in the pen of Beauty Smith. Outside the pen men would be gathering, and he knew that a fight was on. He watched the door for his antagonist to enter. The door would open, and thrust in upon him would come the awful electric car. A thousand times this occurred, and each time the terror it inspired was as vivid and great as ever.

Then came the day when the last bandage and the last plaster cast were taken off. It was a gala day. All Sierra Vista was gathered around. The master rubbed his ears, and he crooned his love-growl. The master's wife called him the "Blessed Wolf," which name was taken up with acclaim, and all the women called him the Blessed Wolf.

He tried to rise to his feet, and after several attempts fell down from weakness. He had lain so long that his muscles had lost their cunning, and all the strength had gone out of them. He felt a little shame because of his weakness, as though, forsooth, he were failing the gods in the service he owed them. Because of this he made heroic efforts to arise, and at last he stood on his four legs, tottering and swaying back and forth.

"The Blessed Wolf!" chorused the women.

Judge Scott surveyed them triumphantly. "Out of your own mouths be it," he said. "Just as I contended right along. No mere dog could have done what he did. He's a wolf."

"A Blessed Wolf," amended the judge's wife.

"Yes, Blessed Wolf," agreed the judge. "And henceforth that shall be my name for him."

"He'll have to learn to walk again," said the surgeon; "so he might as well start in right now. It won't hurt him. Take him outside."

And outside he went, like a king, with all Sierra Vista about him and tending on him. He was very weak, and when he reached the lawn he lay down and rested for a while.

Then the procession started on, little spurts of strength coming into White Fang's muscles as he used them and the blood began to surge through them. The stables were reached, and there in the doorway lay Collie, a half dozen pudgy puppies playing about her in the sun.

White Fang looked on with a wondering eye. Collie snarled warningly at him, and he was careful to keep his distance. The master with his toe helped one sprawling puppy toward him. He bristled suspiciously, but the master warned him that all was well. Collie, clasped in the arms of one of the women, watched him jealously and with a snarl warned him that all was not well.

The puppy sprawled in front of him. He cocked his ears and watched it curiously. Then their noses touched, and he felt the warm little tongue of the puppy on his jowl. White Fang's tongue went out, he knew not why, and he licked the puppy's face.

Hand-clapping and pleased cries from the gods greeted the performance. He was surprised, and looked at them in a puzzled way. Then his weakness asserted itself, and he lay down, his ears cocked, his head on one side, as he watched the puppy. The other puppies came sprawling toward him, to Collie's great disgust; and he gravely permitted them to clamber and tumble over him. At first, amid the applause of the gods, he betrayed a trifle of his old self-consciousness and awkwardness. This passed away as the puppies' antics and mauling continued, and he lay with half-shut, patient eyes, drowsing in the sun.

THE END

14
Diable — a Dog

DIABLE—A DOG

BY

Jack London

THE dog was a devil. This was recognized throughout the northland. "Hell's Spawn" he was called by many men, but his master, Black Leclère, chose for him the shameful name, "Diable." Now Black Leclère was also a devil, and the twain were well matched. The first they met, Diable was a puppy, lean and hungry and with bitter eyes; and they met with snap and snarl and wicked looks, for Leclère's upper lip had a wolfish way of lifting and showing the cruel white teeth. And it lifted then and his eyes glinted viciously as he reached for Diable and dragged him out from the squirming litter. It was certain that they divined each other, for on the instant Diable had buried his puppy fangs in Leclère's hand and Leclère, with thumb and finger, was coolly choking his young life out of him.

"Sacrédam!" the Frenchman said softly, flirting the quick blood from his bitten hand and gazing down on the little puppy choking and gasping in the snow.

Leclère turned to John Hamlin, storekeeper of the Sixty Mile Post. "Dat fo' w'at Ah lak heem. 'Ow moch, eh, you, m'sieu'? 'Ow moch? Ah buy heem, now."

And because he hated him with an exceeding bitter hate, Leclère bought Diable. And for five years the twain adventured across the northland, from St. Michael's and the Yukon Delta to the head-reaches of the Pelly and even so far as the Peace River, Athabasca and the Great Slave. And they acquired a reputation for uncompromising wickedness the like of which never before had attached itself to man and dog.

Diable's father was a great gray timber-wolf. But the mother of Diable, as he dimly remembered her, was a snarling, bickering husky, full-fronted and heavy-chested, with a malign eye, a cat-like grip on life, and a genius for trickery and evil. There was neither faith nor trust in her. Much of evil and much of strength were there in these, Diable's progenitors, and, bone and flesh of their bone and flesh, he had inherited it all. And then came Black Leclère, to lay his heavy hand on the bit of pulsating puppy-life, to press and prod and mold it till it became a big, bristling beast, acute in knavery, overspilling with hate, sinister, malignant, diabolical. With a proper master the puppy might have made a fairly ordinary, efficient sled-dog. He never got the chance. Leclère but confirmed him in his congenital iniquity.

The history of Leclère and the dog is a history of war—of five cruel, relentless years, of which their first meeting is fit summary. To begin with, it was Leclère's fault, for he hated with understanding and intelligence, while the long-legged, ungainly puppy hated only blindly, instinctively, without reason or method. At first there were no refinements of cruelty (these were to come later), but simple beatings and crude brutalities. In one of these,

Diable had an ear injured. He never regained control of the riven muscles, and ever after the ear drooped limply down to keep keen the memory of his tormentor. And he never forgot.

His puppyhood was a period of foolish rebellion. He was always worsted, but he fought back because it was his nature to fight back. And he was unconquerable. Yelping shrilly from the pain of lash and club, he none the less always contrived to throw in the defiant snarl, the bitter, vindictive menace of his soul, which fetched without fail more blows and beatings. But his was his mother's tenacious grip on life. Nothing could kill him. He flourished under misfortune, grew fat with famine, and out of his terrible struggle for life developed a preternatural intelligence. His was the stealth and cunning of his mother, the fierceness and valor of his wolf sire.

Possibly it was because of his father that he never wailed. His puppy yelps passed with his lanky legs, so that he became grim and taciturn, quick to strike, slow to warn. He answered curse with snarl and blow with snap, grinning the while his implacable hatred; but never again, under the extremest agony, did Leclère bring from him the cry of fear or pain. This unconquerableness only fanned Leclère's wrath and stirred him to greater deviltries. Did Leclère give Diable half a fish and to his mates whole ones, Diable went forth to rob other dogs of their fish. Also he robbed caches and expressed himself in a thousand rogueries till he became a terror to all dogs and the masters of dogs. Did Leclère beat Diable and fondle Babette—Babette, who was not half the worker he was—why, Diable threw her down in the snow and broke her hind leg in his heavy jaws, so that Leclère was forced to shoot her. Likewise, in bloody battles Diable mastered all his team-mates, set them the law of trail and forage, and made them live to the law he set.

In five years he heard but one kind word, received but one soft stroke of a hand, and then he did not know what manner of things they were. He leaped like the untamed thing he was, and his jaws were together in a flash. It was the missionary at Sunrise, a newcomer in the country, who spoke the kind word and gave the soft stroke of the hand. And for six months after, he wrote no letters home to the States, and the surgeon at McQuestion traveled two hundred miles on the ice to save him from blood-poisoning.

Men and dogs looked askance at Diable when he drifted into their camps and posts, and they greeted him with feet threateningly lifted for the kick, or with bristling manes and bared fangs. Once a man did kick Diable, and Diable, with quick wolf-snap, closed his jaws like a steel trap on the man's leg and crunched down to the bone. Whereat the man was determined to have his life, only Black Leclère, with ominous eyes and naked hunting-knife, stepped in between. The killing of Diable —ah, sacrédam! *that* was a pleasure Leclère reserved for himself. Some day it would happen, or else—bah! who was to know? Anyway, the problem would be solved.

For they had become problems to each other, this man and beast, or rather, they had become a problem, the pair of them. The very breath each drew was a challenge and a menace to the other. Their hate bound them together as love could never bind. Leclère was bent on the coming of the day when Diable should wilt in spirit and cringe and whimper at his feet. And Diable—Leclère knew what was in Diable's mind, and more than once had read it in his eyes. And so clearly had he read that when the dog was at his back he made it a point to glance often over his shoulder.

Men marveled when Leclère refused large money for the dog. "Some day you'll kill him and be out his price," said John Hamlin, once, when Diable lay panting in the snow where Leclère had kicked him and no one knew whether his ribs were broken and no one dared look to see.

"Dat," said Leclère dryly, "dat is my biz'ness, m'sieu'."

And the men marveled that Diable did not run away. They did not understand. But Leclère understood. He was a man who had lived much in the open, beyond the sound of human tongue, and he had learned the voices of wind and storm, the sigh of night, the whisper of dawn, the clash of day. In a dim way he could hear the green things growing, the running of the sap, the bursting of the bud. And he knew the subtle speech of the things that moved, of the rabbit in the snare, the moody raven beating the air with hollow wing, the baldface shuffling under the moon, the wolf like a gray shadow gliding betwixt the twilight and the dark. And to him Diable spoke clear and direct. Full well he understood why Diable did not run away, and he looked more often over his shoulder.

When in anger, Diable was not nice to look upon, and more than once had he leaped for Leclère's throat, to be stretched quivering and senseless in the snow by the butt of the ever-ready dog-whip. And so Diable learned to bide his time. When he reached his full strength and prime of youth, he thought the time had come. He was broad-chested, powerfully muscled, of far more than ordinary size, and his neck from head to shoulders was a mass of bristling hair—to all appearances a full-blooded wolf. Leclère was lying asleep in his furs when Diable deemed the time to be ripe. He crept upon him stealthily, head low to earth and lone ear laid back, with a feline softness of tread to which even Leclère's delicate tympanum could not responsively vibrate. The dog breathed gently, very gently, and not till he was close at hand did he raise his head. He paused for a moment and looked at the bronzed bull-throat, naked and knotty and swelling to a deep and steady pulse. The slaver dripped down his fangs and slid off his tongue at the sight, and in that moment he remembered his drooping ear, his uncounted blows and wrongs, and without a sound sprang on the sleeping man.

Leclère awoke to the pang of the fangs in his throat, and, perfect animal that he was, he awoke clear-headed and with full comprehension. He closed on the hound's windpipe with both his hands and rolled out of his furs to get his weight uppermost. But the thousands of Diable's ancestors had clung at the throats of unnumbered moose and caribou and dragged them down, and the wisdom of those ancestors was his. When Leclère's weight came on top of him, he drove his hind legs upward and in and clawed down chest and abdomen, ripping and tearing through skin and muscle. And when he felt the man's body wince above him and lift, he worried and shook at the man's throat. His team-mates closed around in a snarling, slavering circle, and Diable, with failing breath and fading sense, knew that their jaws were hungry for him. But that did not matter—it was the man, the man above him, and he ripped and clawed and shook and worried to the last ounce of his strength. But Leclère choked him with both his hands till Diable's chest heaved and writhed for the air denied, and his eyes glazed and his jaws slowly loosened and his tongue protruded black and swollen.

"Eh? Bon, you devil!" Leclère gurgled, mouth and throat clogged with his own blood, as he shoved the dizzy dog from him.

And then Leclère cursed the other dogs off as they fell upon Diable. They drew back into a wider circle, squatting alertly on their haunches and licking their chops, each individual hair on every neck bristling and erect.

Diable recovered quickly, and at sound of Leclère's voice, tottered to his feet and swayed weakly back and forth.

"A-h-ah! You beeg devil!" Leclère spluttered. "Ah fix you. Ah fix you plentee, by Gar!"

Diable, the air biting into his exhausted lungs like wine, flashed full into the man's face, his jaws missing and coming together with a metallic clip. They rolled over and over on the snow, Leclère striking madly with his fists. Then they separated, face to face, and circled back and forth before each other for an opening. Leclère could have drawn his knife. His rifle was at his feet. But the beast in him was up and raging. He would do the thing with his hands—and his teeth. The dog sprang in, but Leclère knocked him over with a blow of his fist, fell upon him, and buried his teeth to the bone in the dog's shoulder.

It was a primordial setting and a primordial scene, such as might have been in the savage youth of the world. An open space in a dark forest, a ring of grinning wolf-dogs, and in the center two beasts, locked in combat, snapping and snarling, raging madly about, panting, sobbing, cursing, straining, wild with passion, blind with lust, in a fury of murder, ripping, tearing and clawing in elemental brutishness.

But Leclère caught the dog behind the

ear with a blow from his fist, knocking him over and for an instant stunning him. Then Leclère leaped upon him with his feet, and sprang up and down, striving to grind him into the earth. Both Diable's hind legs were broken ere Leclère ceased that he might catch breath.

"A-a-ah! A-a-ah!" he screamed, incapable of articulate speech, shaking his fist through sheer impotence of throat and larynx.

But Diable was indomitable. He lay there in a hideous, helpless welter, his lip feebly lifting and writhing to the snarl he had not the strength to utter. Leclère kicked him, and the tired jaws closed on the ankle but could not break the skin.

Then Leclère picked up the whip and proceeded almost to cut him to pieces, at each stroke of the lash crying: "Dis taim Ah break you! Eh? By Gar, Ah break you!"

In the end, exhausted, fainting from loss of blood, he crumpled up and fell by his victim, and, when the wolf-dogs closed in to take their vengeance, with his last consciousness dragged his body on top of Diable to shield him from their fangs.

Drawn by E. Hering.

"FLIRTING THE QUICK BLOOD FROM HIS BITTEN HAND."

This occurred not far from Sunrise, and the missionary, opening the door to Leclère a few hours later, was surprised to note the absence of Diable from the team. Nor did his surprise lessen when Leclère threw back the robes from the sled, gathered Diable into his arms, and staggered across the threshold. It happened that the surgeon of McQuestion was up on a gossip, and between them they proceeded to repair Leclère.

"Merci, non," said he. "Do you fix firs' de dog. To die? Non. Eet is not good. Becos' heem Ah mus' yet break. Dat fo' w'at he mus' not die."

The surgeon called it a marvel, the missionary a miracle, that Leclère lived through at all; but so weakened was he that in the spring the fever got him and he went on his back again. The dog had been in even worse plight, but his grip on life prevailed, and the bones of his hind legs knitted and his internal organs righted themselves during the several weeks he lay strapped to the floor. And by the time Leclère, finally convalescent, sallow and shaky, took the sun by the cabin door, Diable had reasserted his supremacy and brought not only his own team-mates but the missionary's dogs into subjection.

He moved never a muscle nor twitched a hair when for the first time Leclère tottered out on the missionary's arm and sank down slowly and with infinite caution on the three-legged stool.

"Bon!" he said. "Bon! De good sun!" And he stretched out his wasted hands and washed them in the warmth.

Then his gaze fell on the dog, and the old light blazed back in his eyes. He touched the missionary lightly on the arm. "Mon père, dat is one beeg devil, dat Diable. You will bring me one pistol, so dat Ah drink the sun in peace."

And thenceforth, for many days, he sat in the sun before the cabin door. He never dozed, and the pistol lay always across his knees. The dog had a way, the first thing each day, of looking for the weapon in its wonted place. At sight of it he would lift his lip faintly in token that he understood, and Leclère would lift his own lip in an answering grin. One day the missionary took note of the trick. "Bless me!" he said. "I really believe the brute comprehends."

Leclère laughed softly. "Look you, mon père. Dat w'at Ah now spik, to dat does he lissen."

As if in confirmation, Diable just perceptibly wriggled his lone ear up to catch the sound.

"Ah say 'keel'——"

Diable growled deep down in his throat, the hair bristled along his neck, and every muscle went tense and expectant.

"Ah lift de gun, so, like dat——" And suiting action to word, he sighted the pistol at the dog.

Diable, with a single leap sidewise, landed around the corner of the cabin out of sight.

"Bless me!" the missionary remarked. "Bless me!" he repeated at intervals, unconscious of his paucity of expression.

Leclère grinned proudly.

"But why does he not run away?"

The Frenchman's shoulders went up in a racial shrug which means all things from total ignorance to infinite understanding.

"Then why do you not kill him?"

Again the shoulders went up.

"Mon père," he said, after a pause, "de taim is not yet. He is one beeg devil. Some taim Ah break heem, so, an' so, all to leetle bits. Heh? Some taim. Bon!"

A day came when Leclère gathered his dogs together and floated down in a bateau to Forty Mile and on to the Porcupine, where he took a commission from the P. C. Company and went exploring for the better part of a year. After that he poled up the Koyokuk to deserted Arctic City, and later came drifting back, from camp to camp, along the Yukon. And during the long months Diable was well lessoned. He learned many tortures—the torture of hunger, the torture of thirst, the torture of fire, and, worst of all, the torture of music.

Like the rest of his kind, he did not enjoy music. It gave him exquisite anguish, racking him nerve by nerve and ripping apart every fiber of his being. It made him howl, long and wolf-like, as when the wolves bay the stars on frosty nights. He could not help howling. It was his one weakness in the contest with Leclère, and it was his shame. Leclère, on the other hand, passionately loved music—as passionately as he loved strong drink. And when his soul clamored for expression, it usually uttered itself in one or both of the two ways. And when he had drunk, not too much but just enough for the perfect poise of exaltation, his brain alilt with unsung song and the devil in him aroused and rampant, his soul found its supreme utterance in the bearding of Diable.

"Now we will haf a leetle museek," he would say. "Eh? W'at you t'ink, Diable?"

It was only an old and battered harmonica, tenderly treasured and patiently repaired; but it was the best that money could buy, and out of its silver reeds he drew weird, vagrant airs which men had never heard before. Then the dog, dumb of throat, with teeth tight-clenched, would back away, inch by inch, to the farthest cabin corner. And Leclère, playing, playing, a stout club tucked handily under his arm, followed the animal up, inch by inch, step by step, till there was no further retreat.

At first Diable would crowd himself into the smallest possible space, groveling close to the floor; but as the music came nearer and nearer he was forced to uprear, his back jammed into the logs, his fore legs

Drawn by E. Hering.

"'A LEETLE FAVOR. . . . FIRS' YOU HANG HEEM, AN' DEN YOU HANG ME.'"

fanning the air as though to beat off the rippling waves of sound. He still kept his teeth together, but severe muscular contractions attacked his body, strange twitchings and jerkings, till he was all aquiver and writhing in silent torment. As he lost control, his jaws spasmodically wrenched apart and deep, throaty vibrations issued forth, too low in the register of sound for human ear to catch. And then, as he stood reared with nostrils distended, eyes dilated, slaver dripping, hair bristling in helpless rage, arose the long wolf-howl. It came with a slurring rush upward, swelling to a great heartbreaking burst of sound and dying away in sadly cadenced woe—then the next rush upward, octave upon octave; the bursting heart; and the infinite sorrow and misery, fainting, fading, falling, and dying slowly away.

It was fit for hell. And Leclère, with fiendish ken, seemed to divine each particular nerve and heartstring and, with long wails and tremblings and sobbing minors, to make it yield up its last least shred of grief. It was frightful, and for twenty-four hours after, the dog was nervous and unstrung, starting at common sounds, tripping over his own shadow, but withal, vicious and masterful with his team-mates. Nor did he show signs of a breaking spirit. Rather did he grow more grim and taciturn, biding his time with an inscrutable patience which began to puzzle and weigh upon Leclère. The dog would lie in the firelight, motionless, for hours, gazing straight before him at Leclère and hating him with his bitter eyes.

Often the man felt that he had bucked up against the very essence of life—the unconquerable essence that swept the hawk down out of the sky like a feathered thunderbolt, that drove the great gray goose across the zones, that hurled the spawning salmon through two thousand miles of boiling Yukon flood. At such times he felt impelled to express his own unconquerable essence; and with strong drink, wild music and Diable, he indulged in vast orgies, wherein he pitted his puny strength in the face of things and challenged all that was, and had been, and was yet to be. "Dere is somet'ing dere," he affirmed, when the rhythmed vagaries of his mind touched the secret chords of the dog's being and brought forth the long, lugubrious howl. "Ah pool eet out wid bot' my han's, so, an' so. Ha! Ha! Eet is fonee! Eet is ver' fonee! De mans swear, de leetle bird go peep-peep, Diable heem go yow-yow—an' eet is all de ver' same t'ing."

Father Gautier, a worthy priest, once reproved him with instances of concrete perdition. He never reproved him again.

"Eet may be so, mon père," he made answer. "An' Ah t'ink Ah go troo hell a-snappin', lak de hemlock troo de fire. Eh, mon père?"

But all bad things come to an end as well as good, and so with Black Leclère. On the summer low-water, in a poling-boat, he left McDougall for Sunrise. He left McDougall in company with Timothy Brown, and arrived at Sunrise by himself. Further, it was known that they had quarreled just previous to pulling out; for the "Lizzie," a wheezy ten-ton sternwheeler, twenty-four hours behind, beat Leclère in by three days. And when he did get in, it was with a clean-drilled bullet-hole through his shoulder-muscle and a tale of ambush and murder.

A strike had been made at Sunrise, and things had changed considerably. With the infusion of several hundred gold-seekers, a deal of whisky, and half a dozen equipped gamblers, the missionary had seen the page of his years of labor with the Indians wiped clean. When the squaws became preoccupied with cooking beans and keeping the fire going for the wifeless miners, and the bucks with swapping their warm furs for black bottles and broken timepieces, he took to his bed, said "Bless me!" several times, and departed to his final accounting in a rough-hewn oblong box. Whereupon the gamblers moved their roulette and faro tables into the mission-house, and the click of chips and clink of glasses went up from dawn till dark and to dawn again.

Now Timothy Brown was well beloved among these adventurers of the north. The one thing against him was his quick temper and ready fist—a little thing, for which his kind heart and forgiving hand more than atoned. On the other hand, there was nothing to atone for Black Leclère. He was "black," as more than one remembered deed bore witness, while he was as well hated as the other was beloved. So the men of Sunrise put a dressing on his shoulder and haled him before Judge Lynch.

It was a simple affair. He had quarreled with Timothy Brown at McDougall. With Timothy Brown he had left McDougall. Without Timothy Brown he had arrived at Sunrise. Considered in the light of his evilness, the unanimous conclusion was that he had killed Timothy Brown. On the other hand, Leclère acknowledged their facts, but challenged their conclusion and gave his own explanation. Twenty miles out of Sunrise he and Timothy Brown were poling the boat along the rocky shore. From that shore two rifle-shots rang out. Timothy Brown pitched out of the boat and went down bubbling red, and that was the last of Timothy Brown. He, Leclère, pitched into the bottom of the boat with a stinging shoulder. He lay very quietly, peeping at the shore. After a time two Indians stuck up their heads and came out to the water's edge, carrying between them a birch-bark canoe. As they launched it, Leclère let fly. He potted one, who went over the side after the manner of Timothy Brown. The other dropped into the bottom of the canoe, and then canoe and poling-boat went down the stream in a drifting battle. Only they hung up on a split current, and the canoe passed on one side of an island, the poling-boat on the other. That was the last of the canoe, and he came on into Sunrise. Yes, from the way the Indian in the canoe jumped, he was sure he had potted him. That was all.

This explanation was not deemed adequate. They gave him ten hours' grace while the "Lizzie" steamed down to investigate. Ten hours later she came wheezing back to Sunrise. There had been nothing to investigate. No evidence had been found to back up his statements. They told him to make his will, for he possessed a fifty-thousand-dollar Sunrise claim and they were a law-abiding as well as a law-giving breed.

Leclère shrugged his shoulders. "Bot one t'ing," he said; "a leetle, w'at you call, favor—a leetle favor, dat is eet. I gif my feefty t'ousan' dollair to de church. I gif my husky-dog, Diable, to de devil. De leetle favor? Firs' you hang heem, an' den you hang me. Eet is good, eh?"

Good it was, they agreed, that Hell's Spawn should break trail for his master across the last divide, and the court was adjourned down to the river-bank, where a big spruce-tree stood by itself. Slackwater Charley put a hangman's knot in the end of a hauling-line, and the noose was slipped over Leclère's head and pulled tight around his neck. His hands were tied behind his back, and he was assisted to the top of a cracker-box. Then the running end of the line was passed over an overhanging branch, drawn taut, and made fast. To kick the box out from under would leave him dancing on the air.

"Now for the dog," said Webster Shaw, sometime mining engineer. "You'll have to rope him, Slackwater."

Leclère grinned. Slackwater took a chew of tobacco, rove a running noose, and proceeded leisurely to coil a few turns in his hand. He paused once or twice to brush particularly offensive mosquitoes from off his face. Everybody was brushing mosquitoes, except Leclère, about whose head a small cloud was distinctly visible. Even Diable, lying full-stretched on the ground, with his fore paws rubbed the pests away from eyes and mouth.

But while Slackwater waited for Diable to lift his head, a faint call came down the quiet air and a man was seen waving his arms and running across the flat from Sunrise. It was the storekeeper.

"C–call 'er off, boys," he panted, as he came in among them. "Little Sandy and Bernadotte's jes' got in," he explained with returning breath. "Landed down below an' come up by the short cut. Got the Beaver with 'm. Picked 'm up in his canoe, stuck in a back channel, with a couple of bullet-holes in 'm. Other buck was Klok-Kutz, the one that knocked spots out of his squaw and dusted."

"Eh? W'at Ah say? Eh?" Leclère cried exultantly. "Dat de one fo' sure! Ah know. Ah spik true."

"The thing to do is to teach these damned Siwashes a little manners," spoke Webster Shaw. "They're getting fat and sassy, and we'll have to bring them down a peg. Round in all the bucks and string up the Beaver for an object-lesson. That's the program. Come on and let's see what he's got to say for himself."

"Heh, m'sieu'!" Leclère called, as

the crowd began to melt away through the twilight in the direction of Sunrise, "Ah lak ver' moch to see de fon."

"Oh, we'll turn you loose when we come back," Webster Shaw shouted over his shoulder. "In the mean time, meditate on your sins and the ways of Providence. It will do you good, so be grateful."

As is the way with men who are accustomed to great hazards, whose nerves are healthy and trained to patience, so Leclère settled himself down to the long wait—which is to say that he reconciled his mind to it. There was no settling for the body, for the taut rope forced him to stand rigidly erect. The least relaxation of the leg-muscles pressed the rough-fibered noose into his neck, while the upright position caused him much pain in his wounded shoulder. He projected his under lip and expelled his breath upward along his face to blow the mosquitoes away from his eyes. But the situation had its compensation. To be snatched from the maw of death was well worth a little bodily suffering, only it was unfortunate that he should miss the hanging of the Beaver.

And so he mused, till his eyes chanced to fall upon Diable, head between fore paws and stretched on the ground asleep. And then Leclère ceased to muse. He studied the animal closely, striving to sense if the sleep were real or feigned. The dog's sides were heaving regularly, but Leclère felt that the breath came and went a shade too quickly; also he felt there was a vigilance or an alertness to every hair which belied unshackling sleep. He would have given his Sunrise claim to be assured that the dog was not awake, and once, when one of his joints cracked, he looked quickly and guiltily at Diable to see if he roused.

He did not rouse then, but a few minutes later he got up slowly and lazily, stretched, and looked carefully about him.

"Sacrédam!" said Leclère under his breath.

Assured that no one was in sight or hearing, Diable sat down, curled his upper lip almost into a smile, looked up at Leclère, and licked his chops.

"Ah see my feenish," the man said, and laughed sardonically aloud.

Diable came nearer, the useless ear wobbling, the good ear cocked forward with devilish comprehension. He thrust his head on one side, quizzically, and advanced with mincing, playful steps. He rubbed his body gently against the box till it shook and shook again. Leclère teetered carefully to maintain his equilibrium.

"Diable," he said calmly, "look out. Ah keel you."

Diable snarled at the word and shook the box with greater force. Then he upreared and with his fore paws threw his weight against it higher up. Leclère kicked out with one foot, but the rope bit into his neck and checked so abruptly as nearly to overbalance him.

"Hi! Ya! Chook! Mush-on!" he screamed.

Diable retreated for twenty feet or so, with a fiendish levity in his bearing which Leclère could not mistake. He remembered the dog's often breaking the scum of ice on the water-hole by lifting up and throwing his weight upon it; and remembering, he understood what he now had in mind. Diable faced about and paused. He showed his white teeth in a grin, which Leclère answered; and then hurled his body through the air straight for the box.

Fifteen minutes later, Slackwater Charley and Webster Shaw, returning, caught a glimpse of a ghostly pendulum swinging back and forth in the dim light. As they hurriedly drew in closer, they made out the man's inert body, and a live thing that clung to it, and shook and worried, and gave to it the swaying motion.

"Hi! Ya! Chook! you Spawn of Hell!" yelled Webster Shaw.

Diable glared at him, and snarled threateningly, without loosing his jaws.

Slackwater Charley got out his revolver, but his hand was shaking as with a chill and he fumbled.

"Here, you take it," he said, passing the weapon over.

Webster Shaw laughed shortly, drew a sight between the gleaming eyes, and pressed the trigger. Diable's body twitched with the shock, thrashed the ground spasmodically a moment, and went suddenly limp. But his teeth still held fast-locked.

15

Love of Life

LOVE OF LIFE

BY

JACK LONDON

AUTHOR OF "THE GOD OF HIS FATHERS," "THE CALL OF THE WILD," ETC.

ILLUSTRATED BY E. L. BLUMENSCHEIN

"This out of all will remain —
They have lived and have tossed:
So much of the game will be gain,
Though the gold of the dice has been lost."

THEY limped painfully down the bank, and once the foremost of the two men staggered among the rough-strewn rocks. They were tired and weak, and their faces had the drawn expression of patience which comes of hardship long endured. They were heavily burdened with blanket packs which were strapped to their shoulders. Head-straps, passing across the forehead, helped support these packs. Each man carried a rifle. They walked in a stooped posture, the shoulders well forward, the head still farther forward, the eyes bent upon the ground.

"I wish we had just about two of them cartridges that's layin' in that cache of ourn," said the second man.

His voice was utterly and drearily expressionless. He spoke without enthusiasm; but the first man, limping into the milky stream that foamed over the rocks, vouchsafed no reply.

The other man followed at his heels. They did not remove their foot-gear, though the water was icy cold — so cold that their ankles ached and their feet went numb. In places the water dashed against their knees, and both men staggered for footing.

The man who followed slipped on a smooth boulder, nearly fell, but recovered himself with a violent effort, at the same time uttering a sharp exclamation of pain. He seemed faint and dizzy, and put out his free hand while he reeled, as though seeking support against the air. When he had steadied himself he stepped forward, but reeled again and nearly fell. Then he stood still and looked at the other man, who had never turned his head.

"HE CRIED LOUDLY TO THE PITILESS DESOLATION THAT RINGED HIM AROUND"

The man stood still for fully a minute, as though debating with himself. Then he called out:

"I say, Bill, I've sprained my ankle."

Bill staggered on through the milky water. He did not look around. The man watched him go, and though his face was expressionless as ever, his eyes were like the eyes of a wounded deer.

The other man limped up the farther bank and continued straight on without looking back. The man in the stream watched him. His lips trembled a little, so that the rough thatch of brown hair which covered them was visibly agitated. His tongue even strayed out to moisten them.

"Bill!" he cried out.

It was the pleading cry of a strong man in distress, but Bill's head did not turn. The man watched him go, limping grotesquely and lurching forward with stammering gait up the slow slope toward the soft sky-line of the low-lying hill. He watched him go till he passed over the crest and disappeared. Then he turned his gaze and slowly took in the circle of the world that remained to him now that Bill was gone.

Near the horizon the sun was smoldering dimly, almost obscured by formless mists and vapors, which gave an impression of mass and density without outline or tangibility. The man pulled out his watch, the while resting his weight on one leg. It was four o'clock, and as the season was near the last of July or first of August — he did not know the precise date within a week or two — he knew that the sun roughly marked the northwest. He looked to the south and knew that somewhere beyond those bleak hills lay the Great Bear Lake; also, he knew that in that direction the Arctic Circle cut its forbidding way across the Canadian Barrens. This stream in which he stood was a feeder to the Coppermine River, which in turn flowed north and emptied into Coronation Gulf and the Arctic Ocean. He had never been there, but he had seen it, once, on a Hudson Bay Company chart.

Again his gaze completed the circle of the world about him. It was not a heartening spectacle. Everywhere was soft sky-line. The hills were all low-lying. There were no trees, no shrubs, no grasses — naught but a tremendous and terrible desolation that sent fear swiftly dawning into his eyes

"Bill!" he whispered, once and twice; "Bill!"

He cowered in the midst of the milky water, as though the vastness were pressing in upon him with overwhelming force, brutally crushing him with its complacent awfulness. He began to shake as with an ague-fit, till the gun fell from his hand with a splash. This served to rouse him. He fought with his fear and pulled himself together, groping in the water and recovering the weapon. He hitched his pack farther over on his left shoulder, so as to take a portion of its weight from off the injured ankle. Then he proceeded, slowly and carefully, wincing with pain, to the bank.

He did not stop With a desperation that was madness, unmindful of the pain, he hurried up the slope to the crest of the hill over which his comrade had disappeared — more grotesque and comical by far than that limping, jerking comrade. But at the crest he saw a shallow valley, empty of life. He fought with his fear again, overcame it, hitched the pack still farther over on his left shoulder, and lurched on down the slope.

The bottom of the valley was soggy with water, which the thick moss held, sponge-like, close to the surface. This water squirted out from under his feet at every step, and each time he lifted a foot the action culminated in a sucking sound as the wet moss reluctantly released its grip. He picked his way from muskeg to muskeg, and followed the other man's footsteps along and across the rocky ledges which thrust like islets through the sea of moss.

Though alone he was not lost. Farther on he knew he would come to where dead spruce and fir, very small and weazened, bordered the shore of a little lake, the *titchin-nichilie* — in the tongue of the country, the "land of little sticks." And into that lake flowed a small stream, the water of which was not milky. There was rush-grass on that stream — this he remembered well — but no timber, and he would follow it till its first trickle ceased at a divide. He would cross this divide to the first trickle of another stream, flowing to the west, which he would follow until it emptied into the River Dease, and here he would find a cache under an upturned canoe and piled over with many rocks. And in this cache would be ammunition for his empty gun, fish-hooks and lines, a small net — all the utilities for

"YET THE LIFE THAT WAS IN HIM DROVE HIM ON"

the killing and snaring of food. Also, he would find flour — not much — a piece of bacon and some beans.

Bill would be waiting for him there, and they would paddle away south down the Dease to the Great Bear Lake. And south across the lake they would go, ever south, till they gained the Mackenzie. And south, still south, they would go, while the winter raced vainly after them, and the ice formed in the eddies, and the days grew chill and crisp, south to some warm Hudson Bay Company post, where timber grew tall and generous and there was grub without end.

These were the thoughts of the man as he strove onward. But hard as he strove with his body, he strove equally hard with his mind, trying to think that Bill had not deserted him, that Bill would surely wait for him at the cache. He was compelled to think this thought, or else there would not be any use to strive, and he would have lain down and died. And as the dim ball of the sun sank slowly into the northwest he covered every inch, and many times, of his and Bill's flight south before the downcoming winter. And he conned the grub of the cache and the grub of the Hudson Bay Company post over and over again. He had not eaten for two days; for a far longer time he had not had all he wanted to eat. Often he stooped and picked pale muskeg berries, put them into his mouth and chewed and swallowed them. A muskeg berry is a bit of seed inclosed in a bit of water. In the mouth the water melts away and the seed chews sharp and bitter. The man knew there was no nourishment in the berries, but he chewed them patiently with a hope greater than knowledge and defying experience.

At nine o'clock he stubbed his toe on a rocky ledge, and from sheer weariness and weakness staggered and fell. He lay for some time, without movement, on his side. Then he slipped out of the pack-straps and clumsily dragged himself into a sitting posture. It was not yet dark, and in the lingering twilight he groped about among the rocks for shreds of dry moss. When he had gathered a heap he built a fire — a smoldering, smudgy fire — and put a tin pot of water on to boil.

He unwrapped his pack and the first thing he did was to count his matches. There were sixty-seven. He counted them three times to make sure. He divided them into several portions, wrapping them in oil paper, disposing of one bunch in his empty tobacco pouch, of another bunch in the inside band of his battered hat, of a third bunch under his shirt on the chest. This accomplished, a panic came upon him and he unwrapped them all and counted them again. There were still sixty-seven.

He dried his wet foot-gear by the fire. The moccasins were in soggy shreds. The blanket socks were worn through in places and his feet were raw and bleeding. His ankle was throbbing and he gave it an examination. It had swollen to the size of his knee. He tore a long strip from one of his two blankets and bound the ankle tightly. He tore other strips and bound them about his feet to serve for both moccasins and socks. Then he drank the pot of water, steaming hot, wound his watch, and crawled between his blankets.

He slept like a dead man. The brief darkness around midnight came and went. The sun arose in the northeast — at least the day dawned in that quarter, for the sun was hidden by gray clouds.

At six o'clock he awoke, quietly lying on his back. He gazed straight up into the gray sky and knew that he was hungry. As he rolled over on his elbow he was startled by a loud snort, and saw a bull caribou regarding him with alert curiosity. The animal was not more than fifty feet away, and instantly into the man's mind leaped the vision and the savor of a caribou steak sizzling and frying over a fire. Mechanically he reached for the empty gun, drew a bead, and pulled the trigger. The bull snorted and leaped away, his hoofs rattling and clattering as he fled across the ledges.

The man cursed and flung the empty gun from him. He groaned aloud as he started to drag himself to his feet. It was a slow and arduous task. His joints were like rusty hinges. They worked harshly in their sockets, with much friction, and each bending or unbending was accomplished only through a sheer exertion of will. When he finally gained his feet another minute or so was consumed in straightening up, so that he could stand erect as a man should stand.

He crawled up a small knoll and surveyed the prospect. There were no trees, no bushes, nothing but a gray sea of moss scarcely diversified by gray rocks, gray-colored lakelets, and gray streamlets. The sky was gray. There was no sun or hint of sun. He had no idea of north, and he had forgotten the way he had come to this spot the night before. But he was not lost. He knew that. Soon he would come to the land of the little sticks. He felt that it lay off to the left somewhere, not far — possibly just over the next low hill.

He went back to put his pack into shape for traveling. He assured himself of the existence of his three separate parcels of matches, though he did not stop to count them. But he did linger, debating, over a squat moose-hide sack. It was not large. He could hide it under his two hands. He knew that it weighed fifteen pounds — as much as all the rest of the pack — and it worried him. He finally set it to one side and proceeded to roll the pack. He paused to gaze at the squat moose-hide sack. He picked it up hastily with a defiant glance about him, as though the desolation were trying to rob him of it; and when he rose to his feet to stagger on into the day, it was included in the pack on his back.

He bore away to the left, stopping now and again to eat muskeg berries. His ankle had stiffened, his limp was more pronounced, but the pain of it was as nothing compared with the pain of his stomach. The hunger pangs were sharp. They gnawed and gnawed until he could not keep his mind steady on the course he must pursue to gain the land of little sticks. The muskeg berries did not allay this gnawing, while they made his tongue and the roof of his mouth sore with their irritating bite.

He came upon a valley where rock ptarmigan rose on whirring wings from the ledges and muskegs. Ker — ker — ker was the cry they made. He threw stones at them but could not hit them. He placed his pack on the ground and stalked them as a cat stalks a sparrow. The sharp rocks cut through his pants' legs till his knees left a trail of blood; but the hurt was lost in the hurt of his hunger. He squirmed over the wet moss, saturating his clothes and chilling his body; but he was not aware of it, so great was his fever for food. And always the ptarmigan rose, whirring, before him, till their ker — ker — ker became a mock to him, and he cursed them and cried aloud at them with their own cry.

Once he crawled upon one that must have been asleep. He did not see it till it shot up in his face from its rocky nook. He made a clutch as startled as was the rise of the ptarmigan, and there remained in his hand three tail-feathers. As he watched its flight he hated it, as though it had done him some terrible wrong. Then he returned and shouldered his pack.

As the day wore along he came into valleys or swales where game was more plentiful. A band of caribou passed by, twenty and odd animals, tantalizingly within rifle range. He felt a wild desire to run after them, a certitude that he could run them down. A black fox came toward him, carrying a ptarmigan in his mouth. The man shouted. It was a fearful cry, but the fox leaping away in fright did not drop the ptarmigan.

Late in the afternoon he followed a stream, milky with lime, which ran through sparse patches of rush-grass. Grasping these rushes firmly near the root, he pulled up what resembled a young onion-sprout no larger than a shingle-nail. It was tender and his teeth sank into it with a crunch that promised deliciously of food. But its fibers were tough. It was composed of stringy filaments saturated with water, like the berries, and devoid of nourishment. But he threw off his pack and went into the rush-grass on hands and knees, crunching and munching, like some bovine creature.

He was very weary and often wished to rest — to lie down and sleep; but he was continually driven on — not so much by his desire to gain the land of little sticks as by his hunger. He searched little ponds for frogs and dug up the earth with his nails for worms, though he knew in spite that neither frogs nor worms existed so far north.

He looked into every pool of water vainly, until, as the long twilight came on, he discovered a solitary fish, the size of a minnow, in such a pool. He plunged his arm in up to the shoulder, but it eluded him. He reached for it with both hands and stirred up the milky mud at the bottom. In his excitement he fell in, wetting himself to the waist. Then the water was too muddy to admit of his seeing the fish and he was compelled to wait until the sediment had settled.

The pursuit was renewed, till the water was again muddied. But he could not wait. He unstrapped the tin bucket and began to bale the pool. He baled wildly at first, splashing himself and flinging the water so short a distance that it ran back into the pool. He worked more carefully, striving

"HIS MIRTH WAS HOARSE AND GHASTLY, LIKE A RAVEN'S CROAK, AND THE SICK WOLF JOINED HIM, HOWLING LUGUBRIOUSLY"

to be cool, though his heart was pounding against his chest and his hands were trembling. At the end of half an hour the pool was nearly dry. Not a cupful of water remained. And there was no fish. He found a hidden crevice among the stones through which it had escaped to the adjoining and larger pool — a pool which he could not empty in a night and a day. Had he known of the crevice, he could have closed it with a rock at the beginning and the fish would have been his.

Thus he thought, and crumpled up and sank down upon the wet earth. At first he cried softly to himself, then he cried loudly to the pitiless desolation that ringed him around; and for a long time after he was shaken by great dry sobs.

He built a fire and warmed himself by drinking quarts of hot water, and made camp on a rocky ledge in the same fashion he had the night before. The last thing he did was to see that his matches were dry and to wind his watch. The blankets were wet and clammy. His ankle pulsed with pain. But he knew only that he was hungry, and through his restless sleep he dreamed of feasts and banquets and of food served and spread in all imaginable ways.

He awoke chilled and sick. There was no sun. The gray of earth and sky had become deeper, more profound. A raw wind was blowing, and the first flurries of snow were whitening the hilltops. The air about him thickened and grew white while he made a fire and boiled more water. It was wet snow, half rain, and the flakes were large and soggy. At first they melted as soon as they came in contact with the earth, but ever more fell, covering the ground, putting out the fire, spoiling his supply of moss-fuel.

This was the signal for him to strap on his pack and stumble onward he knew not where. He was not concerned with the land of little sticks, nor with Bill and the cache under the upturned canoe by the River Dease. He was mastered by the verb, "to eat." He was hunger-mad. He took no heed of the course he pursued, so long as that course led him through the swale bottoms. He felt his way through the wet snow to the watery muskeg berries, and went by feel as he pulled up the rush-grass by the roots. But it was tasteless stuff and did not satisfy. He found a weed that tasted sour and he ate all he could find of it, which was not much, for it was a creeping growth, easily hidden under the several inches of snow.

He had no fire that night nor hot water, and crawled under his blanket to sleep the broken hunger-sleep. The snow turned into a cold rain. He awakened many times to feel it falling on his upturned face. Day came — a gray day and no sun. It had ceased raining. The keenness of his hunger had departed. Sensibility, so far as concerned the yearning for food, had been exhausted. There was a dull, heavy ache in his stomach, but it did not bother him so much. He was more rational, and once more he was chiefly interested in the land of little sticks and the cache by the River Dease.

He ripped the remnant of one of his blankets into strips and bound his bleeding feet. Also, he recinched the injured ankle and prepared himself for a day of travel. When he came to his pack he paused long over the squat moose-hide sack, but in the end it went with him.

The snow had melted under the rain and only the hilltops showed white. The sun came out and he succeeded in locating the points of the compass, though he knew now that he was lost. Perhaps, in his previous days' wanderings, he had edged away too far to the left. He now bore off to the right to counteract the possible deviation from his true course.

Though the hunger pangs were no longer so exquisite, he realized that he was weak. He was compelled to pause for frequent rests when he attacked the muskeg berries and rush-grass patches. His tongue felt dry and large, as though covered with a fine hairy growth, and it tasted bitter in his mouth. His heart gave him a great deal of trouble. When he had traveled a few minutes it would begin a remorseless thump, thump, thump, and then leap up and away in a painful flutter of beats that choked him and made him go faint and dizzy.

In the middle of the day he found two minnows in a large pool. It was impossible to bale it, but he was calmer now and managed to catch them in his tin bucket. They were no longer than his little finger, but he was not particularly hungry. The dull ache in his stomach had been growing duller and fainter. It seemed almost that his stomach was dozing. He ate the fish raw, masticating with painstaking care, for the eating was

"SLOWLY, WHILE THE WOLF STRUGGLED FEEBLY AND THE HAND CLUTCHED FEEBLY, THE OTHER HAND CREPT ACROSS TO A GRIP"

an act of pure reason. While he had no desire to eat he knew that he must eat to live.

In the evening he caught three more minnows, eating two and saving the third for breakfast. The sun had dried stray shreds of moss, and he was able to warm himself with hot water. He had not covered more than ten miles that day, and the next day, traveling whenever his heart permitted him, he covered no more than five miles. But his stomach did not give him the slightest uneasiness. It had gone to sleep. He was in a strange country, too, and the caribou were growing more plentiful, also the wolves. Often their yelps drifted across the desolation, and once he saw three of them slinking away before his path.

Another night, and in the morning, being more rational, he untied the leather string that fastened the squat moose-hide sack. From its open mouth poured a yellow stream of coarse gold-dust and nuggets. He roughly divided the gold in halves, caching one half on a prominent ledge, wrapped in a piece of blanket, and returning the other half to the sack. He also began to use strips of the one remaining blanket for his feet. He still clung to his gun, for there were cartridges in that cache by the River Dease.

This was a day of fog, and this day hunger awoke in him again. He was very weak and was afflicted with a giddiness which at times blinded him. It was no uncommon thing now for him to stumble and fall; and stumbling once, he fell squarely into a ptarmigan nest. There were four newly hatched chicks a day old — little specks of pulsating life no more than a mouthful; and he ate them ravenously, thrusting them alive into his mouth and crunching them like egg-shells between his teeth. The mother ptarmigan beat about him with great outcry. He used his gun as a club with which to knock her over, but she dodged out of reach. He threw stones at her and with one chance shot broke a wing. Then she fluttered away, running, trailing the broken wing, with him in pursuit.

The little chicks had no more than whetted his appetite. He hopped and bobbed clumsily along on his injured ankle, throwing stones and screaming hoarsely at times; at other times hopping and bobbing silently along, picking himself up grimly and patiently when he fell, or rubbing his eyes with his hand when the giddiness threatened to overpower him.

The chase led him across swampy ground in the bottom of the valley, and he came upon footprints in the soggy moss. They were not his own — he could see that. They must be Bill's. But he could not stop, for the mother ptarmigan was running on. He would catch her first, then he would return and investigate.

He exhausted the mother ptarmigan; but he exhausted himself. She lay panting on her side. He lay panting on his side, a dozen feet away, unable to crawl to her. And as he recovered she recovered, fluttering out of reach as his hungry hand went out to her. The chase was resumed. Night settled down and she escaped. He stumbled from weakness and pitched head-foremost on his face, cutting his cheek, his pack upon his back. He did not move for a long while; then he rolled over on his side, wound his watch, and lay there until morning.

Another day of fog. Half of his last blanket had gone into foot-wrappings. He failed to pick up Bill's trail. It did not matter. His hunger was driving him too compellingly — only — only he wondered if Bill, too, were lost. By midday the irk of his pack became too oppressive. Again he divided the gold, this time merely spilling half of it on the ground. In the afternoon he threw the rest of it away, there remaining to him only the half-blanket, the tin bucket, and the rifle.

An hallucination began to trouble him. He felt confident that one cartridge remained to him. It was in the chamber of the rifle and he had overlooked it. On the other hand, he knew all the time that the chamber was empty. But the hallucination persisted. He fought it off for hours, then threw his rifle open and was confronted with emptiness. The disappointment was as bitter as though he had really expected to find the cartridge.

He plodded on for half an hour, when the hallucination arose again. Again he fought it and still it persisted, till for very relief he opened his rifle to unconvince himself. At times his mind wandered farther afield, and he plodded on, a mere automaton, strange conceits and whimsicalities gnawing at his brain like worms. But these excursions out of the real were of brief duration, for ever the pangs of the hunger-bite called him back. He was jerked back abruptly once from such an excursion by a sight that caused him nearly to faint. He reeled and swayed, doddering like a drunken man to keep from falling. Before him stood a horse. A horse! He could not believe his eyes. A thick mist was in them, intershot with sparkling points of light. He rubbed his eyes savagely to clear his vision, and beheld not a horse but a great brown bear. The animal was studying him with bellicose curiosity.

The man had brought his gun half way to his shoulder before he realized. He lowered it and drew his hunting-knife from its beaded sheath at his hip. Before him was meat and life. He ran his thumb along the edge of his knife. It was sharp. The point was sharp. He would fling himself upon the bear and kill it. But his heart began its warning thump, thump, thump. Then followed the wild upward leap and tattoo of flutters, the pressing as of an iron band about his forehead, the creeping of the dizziness into his brain.

His desperate courage was evicted by a great surge of fear. In his weakness, what if the animal attacked him! He drew himself up to his most imposing stature, gripping the knife and staring hard at the bear. The bear advanced clumsily a couple of steps, reared up and gave vent to a tentative growl. If the man ran he would run after him; but the man did not run. He was animated now with the courage of fear. He, too, growled, savagely, terribly, voicing the fear that is to life germane and that lies twisted about life's deepest roots.

The bear edged away to one side, growling menacingly, himself appalled by this mysterious creature that appeared upright and unafraid. But the man did not move. He stood like a statue till the danger was past, when he yielded to a fit of trembling and sank down into the wet moss.

He pulled himself together and went on, afraid now in a new way. It was not the fear that he should die passively from lack of food, but that he should be destroyed violently before starvation had exhausted the last particle of the endeavor in him that made toward surviving. There were the wolves. Back and forth across the desolation drifted their howls, weaving the very air into a fabric of menace that was so tangible that he found himself, arms in the air, pressing it back from him as it might be the walls of a wind-blown tent.

Now and again the wolves in packs of two and three crossed his path. But they sheered clear of him. They were not in sufficient numbers, and besides they were hunting the caribou which did not battle, while this strange creature that walked erect might scratch and bite.

In the late afternoon he came upon scattered bones where the wolves had made a kill. The débris had been a caribou calf an hour before, squawking and running and very much alive. He contemplated the bones, clean-picked and polished, pink with the cell-life in them which had not yet died. Could it possibly be that he might be that ere the day was done! Such was life, eh? A vain and fleeting thing. It was only life that pained. There was no hurt in death. To die was to sleep. It meant cessation, rest. Then why was he not content to die?

But he did not moralize long. He was squatting in the moss, a bone in his mouth, sucking at the shreds of life that still dyed it faintly pink. The sweet meaty taste, thin and elusive almost as a memory, maddened him. He closed his jaws on the bones and crunched. Sometimes it was the bone that broke, sometimes his teeth. Then he crushed the bones between rocks, pounded them to a pulp and swallowed them. He pounded his fingers, too, in his haste, and yet found a moment in which to feel surprise at the fact that his fingers did not hurt much when caught under the descending rock.

Came frightful days of snow and rain. He did not know when he made camp, when he broke camp. He traveled in the night as much as in the day. He rested wherever he fell, crawled on whenever the dying life in him flickered up and burned less dimly. He as a man no longer strove. It was the life in him, unwilling to die, that drove him on. He did not suffer. His nerves had become blunted, numb, while his mind was filled with weird visions and delicious dreams.

But ever he sucked and chewed on the crushed bones of the caribou calf, the least remnants of which he had gathered up and carried with him. He crossed no more hills or divides, but automatically followed a large stream which flowed through a wide and shallow valley. He did not see this stream or this valley. He saw nothing save visions. Soul and body walked or crawled side by side, yet apart, so slender was the thread that bound them.

He awoke in his right mind, lying on his back on a rocky ledge. The sun was shining bright and warm. Afar off he heard the squawking of caribou calves. He was aware of vague memories of rain and wind and snow, but whether he had been beaten by the storm for two days or two weeks he did not know.

For some time he lay without movement, the genial sunshine pouring upon him and saturating his miserable body with its warmth. A fine day, he thought. Perhaps he could manage to locate himself. By a painful effort he rolled over on his side. Below him flowed a wide and sluggish river. Its unfamiliarity puzzled him. Slowly he followed it with his eyes, winding in wide sweeps among the bleak bare hills, bleaker and barer and lower-lying than any hills he had yet encountered. Slowly, deliberately, without excitement or more than the most casual interest, he followed the course of the strange stream toward the sky-line and saw it emptying into a bright and shining sea. He was still unexcited. Most unusual, he thought, a vision or a mirage — more likely a vision, a trick of his disordered mind. He was confirmed in this by sight of a ship lying at anchor in the midst of the shining sea. He closed his eyes for a while, then opened them. Strange how the vision persisted! Yet not strange. He knew there were no seas or ships in the heart of the barren lands, just as he had known there was no cartridge in the empty rifle.

He heard a snuffle behind him — a half-choking gasp or cough. Very slowly, because of his exceeding weakness and stiffness, he rolled over on his other side. He could see nothing near at hand, but he waited patiently. Again came the snuffle and cough, and outlined between two jagged rocks not a score of feet away he made out the gray head of a wolf. The sharp ears were not pricked so sharply as he had seen them on other wolves; the eyes were bleared and blood-shot, the head seemed to droop limply and forlornly. The animal blinked continually in the sunshine. It seemed sick. As he looked it snuffled and coughed again.

This, at least, was real, he thought, and turned on the other side so that he might see the reality of the world which had been veiled from him before by the vision. But the sea still shone in the distance and the ship's spars were plainly discernible. Was it reality after all? He closed his eyes for a long while and thought, and then it came to him. He had been making north by east, away from the Dease Divide and into the Coppermine Valley. This wide and sluggish river was the Coppermine. That shining sea was the Arctic Ocean. That ship was a whaler, strayed east, far east, from the mouth of the Mackenzie, and it was lying at anchor in Coronation Gulf. He remembered the Hudson Bay Company chart he had seen long ago, and it was all clear and reasonable to him.

He sat up and turned his attention to immediate affairs. He had worn through the blanket-wrappings, and his feet were like shapeless lumps of raw meat. His last blanket was gone. Rifle and knife were both missing. He had lost his hat somewhere, with the bunch of matches in the band, but the matches against his chest were safe and dry inside the tobacco pouch and oil-paper. He looked at his watch. It marked eleven o'clock and was still running. Evidently he had kept it wound.

He was calm and collected. Though extremely weak he had no sensation of pain. He was not hungry. The thought of food was not even pleasant to him, and whatever he did was done by his reason alone. He ripped off his pants' legs to the knees and bound them about his feet. Somehow he had succeeded in retaining the tin bucket. He would have some hot water before he began what he foresaw was to be a terrible journey to the ship.

His movements were slow. He shook as with a palsy. When he started to collect dry moss he found he could not rise to his feet. He tried again and again, then contented himself with crawling about on hands and knees. Once he crawled near to the sick wolf. The animal dragged itself reluctantly out of his way, licking its chops with a tongue which seemed hardly to have the strength to curl. The man noticed that the tongue was not the customary healthful red. It was a yellowish brown and seemed coated with a rough and half-dry mucus.

After he had drunk a quart of hot water the man found he was able to stand, and even to walk as well as a dying man might be supposed to walk. Every minute or so he was compelled to rest. His steps were feeble and uncertain, just as the wolf's that trailed him were feeble and uncertain; and that night, when the shining sea was blotted out by blackness, he knew he was nearer to it by no more than four miles.

Throughout the night he heard the cough of the sick wolf, and now and then the squawking of the caribou calves. There was life all around him, but it was strong life, very much alive and well, and he knew the sick wolf clung to the sick man's trail in the hope that the man would die first. In the morning, on opening his eyes, he beheld it regarding him with a wistful and hungry stare. It stood crouched, with tail between its legs, like a miserable and woe-begone dog. It shivered in the chill morning wind, and grinned dispiritedly when the man spoke to it in a voice which achieved no more than a hoarse whisper.

The sun rose brightly, and all morning the man tottered and fell toward the ship on the shining sea. The weather was perfect. It was the brief Indian Summer of the high latitudes. It might last a week. To-morrow or next day it might be gone.

In the afternoon the man came upon a trail. It was of another man, who did not walk, but who dragged himself on all fours. The man thought it might be Bill, but he thought in a dull, uninterested way. He had no curiosity. In fact sensation and emotion had left him. He was no longer susceptible to pain. Stomach and nerves had gone to sleep. Yet the life that was in him drove him on. He was very weary, but it refused to die. It was because it refused to die that he still ate muskeg berries and minnows, drank his hot water, and kept a wary eye on the sick wolf.

He followed the trail of the other man who dragged himself along, and soon came to the end of it — a few fresh-picked bones where the soggy moss was marked by the foot-pads of many wolves. He saw a squat moose-hide sack, mate to his own, which had been torn by sharp teeth. He picked it up, though its weight was almost too much for his feeble fingers. Bill had carried it to the last. Ha! ha! He would have the laugh on Bill. He would survive and carry it to the ship in the shining sea. His mirth was hoarse and ghastly, like a raven's croak, and the sick wolf joined him, howling lugubriously. The man ceased suddenly. How could he have the laugh on Bill if that were Bill; if those bones, so pinky-white and clean, were Bill!

He turned away. Well, Bill had deserted him; but he would not take the gold, nor would he suck Bill's bones. Bill would have, though, had it been the other way around, he mused as he staggered on.

He came to a pool of water. Stooping over in quest of minnows, he jerked his head back as though he had been stung. He had caught sight of his reflected face. So horrible was it that sensibility awoke long enough to be shocked. There were three minnows in the pool, which was too large to drain; and after several ineffectual attempts to catch them in the tin bucket he forbore. He was afraid, because of his great weakness, that he might fall in and drown. It was for this reason that he did not trust himself to the river astride one of the many drift-logs which lined its sand-spits.

That day he decreased the distance between him and the ship by three miles; the next day by two — for he was crawling now as Bill had crawled; and the end of the fifth day found the ship still seven miles away and him unable to make even a mile a day. Still the Indian summer held on, and he continued to crawl and faint, turn and turn about; and ever the sick wolf coughed and wheezed at his heels. His knees had become raw meat like his feet, and though he padded them with the shirt from his back it was a red track he left behind him on the moss and stones. Once glancing back he saw the wolf licking hungrily his bleeding trail, and he saw sharply what his own end might be — unless — unless he could get the wolf. Then began as grim a tragedy of existence as was ever played — a sick man that crawled, a sick wolf that limped, two creatures dragging their dying carcasses across the desolation and hunting each other's lives.

Had it been a well wolf, it would not have mattered so much to the man; but the thought of going to feed the maw of that loathsome and all but dead thing was repugnant to him. He was finicky. His mind had begun to wander again, and to be perplexed by hallucinations, while his lucid intervals grew rarer and shorter.

He was awakened once from a faint by a wheeze close in his ear. The wolf leaped lamely back, losing its footing and falling in its weakness. It was ludicrous, but he was not amused. Nor was he even afraid. He was too far gone for that. But his mind was for the moment clear, and he lay and considered. The ship was no more than four miles away. He could see it quite distinctly when he rubbed the mists out of his eyes, and he could see the white sail of a small boat cutting the water of the shining sea. But he could never crawl those four miles. He knew that, and was very calm in the knowledge. He knew that he could not crawl half a mile. And yet he wanted to live. It was unreasonable that he should die after all he had undergone. Fate asked too much of him. And, dying, he declined to die. It was stark madness, perhaps, but in the very grip of Death he defied Death and refused to die.

He closed his eyes and composed himself with infinite precaution. He steeled himself to keep above the suffocating languor that lapped like a rising tide through all the wells of his being. It was very like a sea, this deadly languor, that rose and rose and drowned his consciousness bit by bit. Sometimes he was all but submerged, swimming through oblivion with a faltering stroke; and again, by some strange alchemy of soul, he would find another shred of will and strike out more strongly.

Without movement he lay on his back, and he could hear slowly drawing near and nearer the wheezing intake and output of the sick wolf's breath. It drew closer, ever closer, through an infinitude of time, and he did not move. It was at his ear. The harsh dry tongue grated like sandpaper against his cheek. His hands shot out — or at least he willed them to shoot out. The fingers were curved like talons, but they closed on empty air. Swiftness and certitude require strength, and the man had not this strength.

The patience of the wolf was terrible. The man's patience was no less terrible. For half a day he lay motionless, fighting off unconsciousness and waiting for the thing that was to feed upon him and upon which he wished to feed. Sometimes the languid sea rose over him and he dreamed long dreams; but ever through it all, waking and dreaming, he waited for the wheezing breath and the harsh caress of the tongue.

He did not hear the breath, and he slipped slowly from some dream to the feel of the tongue along his hand. He waited. The fangs pressed softly; the pressure increased; the wolf was exerting its last strength in an effort to sink teeth in the food for which it had waited so long. But the man had waited long, and the lacerated hand closed on the jaw. Slowly, while the wolf struggled feebly and the hand clutched feebly, the other hand crept across to a grip. Five minutes later the whole weight of the man's body was on top of the wolf. The hands had not sufficient strength to choke the animal, but the face of the man was pressed close to the throat of the wolf and the mouth was full of hair. At the end of half an hour the man was aware of a warm trickle in his throat. It was not pleasant. It was like molten lead being forced into his stomach, but it was forced by his will alone. Later the man rolled over on his back and slept.

There were some members of a scientific expedition on the whaleship *Bedford*. From the deck they remarked a strange object on the shore. It was moving down the beach toward the water. They were unable to classify it, and, being scientific men, they climbed into the whaleboat alongside and went ashore to see. And they saw something that was alive but that could hardly be called a man. It was blind, unconscious. It squirmed along the ground like some monstrous worm. Most of its efforts were ineffectual, but it was persistent, and it writhed and twisted and went ahead perhaps a score of feet an hour.

Three weeks afterward the man lay in a bunk on the whaleship *Bedford*, and with tears streaming down his wasted cheeks told who he was and what he had undergone. He also babbled incoherently of his mother, of sunny Southern California, and a home among the orange groves and flowers.

The days were not many after that when he sat at table with the scientific men and ship's officers. He gloated over the spectacle of so much food, watching it anxiously as it went into the mouths of others. With the disappearance of each mouthful an expression of deep regret came into his eyes. He was quite sane, yet he hated those men at meal-time because they ate so much food. He was haunted by a fear that it would not last. He inquired of the cook, the cabin-boy, the captain, concerning the food stores. They reassured him countless times; but he could not believe them, and pried cunningly about the lazarette to see with his own eyes.

It was noticed that the man was getting fat. He grew stouter with each day. The scientific men shook their heads and theorized. They limited the man at his meals, but still his girth increased and his body swelled prodigiously under his shirt.

The sailors grinned. They knew. And when the scientific men set a watch on the man, they knew too. They saw him slouch for'ard after breakfast, and like a mendicant, with outstretched palm, accost a sailor. The sailor grinned and passed him a fragment of sea biscuit. He clutched it avariciously, looked at it as a miser looks at gold, and thrust it into his shirt bosom. Similar were the donations from other grinning sailors.

The scientific men were discreet. They left him alone. But they privily examined his bunk. It was lined with hardtack; the mattress was stuffed with hardtack; every nook and cranny was filled with hardtack. Yet he was sane. He was taking precautions against another possible famine—that was all. He would recover from it, the scientific men said; and he did, ere the *Bedford's* anchor rumbled down in San Francisco Bay.

16
The Sea Wolf

THE SEA-WOLF

BY JACK LONDON

Author of "The Call of the Wild," "The God of his Fathers," etc.

I SCARCELY know where to begin, though I sometimes facetiously place the cause of it all to Charley Furuseth's credit. He kept a summer cottage in Mill Valley, under the shadow of Mount Tamalpais, and never occupied it except when he loafed through the winter months and read Nietzsche and Schopenhauer to rest his brain. When summer came on, he elected to sweat out a hot and dusty existence in the city and to toil incessantly. Had it not been my custom to run up to see him every Saturday afternoon and to stop over till Monday morning, this particular January Monday morning would not have found me afloat on San Francisco Bay.

Not but that I was afloat in a safe craft, for the *Martinez* was a new ferry-steamer, making her fourth or fifth trip on the run between Sausalito and San Francisco. The danger lay in the heavy fog which blanketed the bay, and of which, as a landsman, I had little apprehension. In fact, I remember the placid exaltation with which I took up my position on the forward upper deck, directly beneath the pilot-house, and allowed the mystery of the fog to lay hold of my imagination. A fresh breeze was blowing, and for a time I was alone in the moist obscurity; yet not alone, for I was dimly conscious of the presence of the pilot, and of what I took to be the captain, in the glass house above my head.

I remember thinking how comfortable it was, this division of labor which made it unnecessary for me to study fogs, winds, tides, and navigation in order to visit my friend who lived across an arm of the sea. It was good that men should be specialists, I mused. The peculiar knowledge of the pilot and captain sufficed for many thousands of people who knew no more of the sea and navigation than I knew. On the other hand, instead of having to devote my energy to the learning of a multitude of things, I concentrated it upon a few particular things, such as, for instance, the analysis of Poe's place in American literature, an essay of mine, by the way, in the current "Atlantic." Coming aboard, as I passed through the cabin, I had noticed with greedy eyes a stout gentleman reading the "Atlantic," which was open at my very essay. And there it was again, the division of labor, the special knowledge of the pilot and captain which permitted the stout gentleman to read my special knowledge on Poe while they carried him safely from Sausalito to San Francisco.

A red-faced man, slamming the cabin door behind him and stumping out on the deck, interrupted my reflections, though I made a mental note of the topic for use in a projected essay which I had thought of calling "The Necessity for Freedom: A Plea for the Artist." The red-faced man shot a glance up at the pilot-house, gazed around at the fog, stumped across the deck and back (he evidently had artificial legs), and stood still by my side, legs wide apart and with an expression of keen enjoyment on his face. I was not wrong when I decided that his days had been spent on the sea.

"It 's nasty weather like this here that turns heads gray before their time," he said, with a nod toward the pilot-house.

"I had not thought there was any particular strain," I answered. "It seems as simple as a-b-c. They know the direction by compass, the distance, and the speed. I should not call it anything more than mathematical certainty."

"Strain!" he snorted. "Simple as a-b-c! Mathematical certainty!" He seemed to brace himself up and lean backward against the air as he stared at me. "How about this here tide that 's rushin' out through the Golden Gate?" he demanded, or bellowed, rather. "How fast is she ebbin'? What 's the drift, eh? Listen to that, will you! A bell-buoy, and we 're atop of it! See 'em alterin' the course!"

From out of the fog came the mournful tolling of a bell, and I could see the pilot turning the wheel with great rapidity. The bell, which had seemed straight ahead, was now sounding from the side. Our own whistle was blowing hoarsely, and from time to time the sound of other whistles came to us from out of the fog.

"That 's a ferry-boat of some sort," the newcomer said, indicating a whistle off to the right. "And there! D' ye hear that? Blown by mouth. Some scow schooner, most likely. Better watch out, Mr. Schooner-man. Ah, I thought so."

The unseen ferry-boat was blowing blast after blast, and the mouth-blown horn was tooting in terror-stricken fashion.

"And now they 're payin' their respects to each other and tryin' to get clear," the red-faced man went on, as the hurried whistling ceased.

His face was shining, his eyes flashing with excitement, as he translated into articulate language the speech of the horns and sirens. "That 's a steam-siren a-goin' it over there to the left. And you hear that fellow with a frog in his throat—a steam-schooner, as near as I can judge, crawlin' in from the Heads against the tide."

A shrill little whistle, piping as if gone mad, came from directly ahead and from very near at hand. Gongs sounded on the *Martinez*. Our paddle-wheels stopped, their pulsing beat died away, and then they started again. The shrill little whistle, like the chirping of a cricket amid the cries of great beasts, shot through the fog from more to the side and swiftly grew faint and fainter. I looked to my companion for enlightenment.

"One of them daredevil launches," he said. "I almost wish we 'd sunk him, the little rip! They 're the cause of more trouble. And what good are they? Any jackass gets aboard one and thinks he can run it, blowin' his whistle to beat the band and tellin' the rest of the world to look out for him because he 's comin' and can't look out for himself. Because he 's comin'! And you 've got to look out, too. Right of way! Common decency! They don't know the meanin' of it!"

I felt quite amused at his unwarranted choler, and while he stumped moodily up and down I fell to dwelling upon the romance of the fog. And romantic it certainly was—the fog, like the gray shadow of infinite mystery, brooding over the whirling speck of earth; and men, mere motes of light and sparkle, cursed with an insane relish for work, riding their steeds of wood and steel through the heart of the mystery, groping their way blindly through the unseen, and clamoring and clanging in confident speech the while their hearts are heavy with incertitude and fear.

The voice of my companion brought me back to myself with a laugh. I, too, had been groping and floundering, the while I thought I rode clear-eyed through the mystery.

"Hello! Somebody comin' our way," he was saying. "And d' ye hear that? He 's comin' fast. Walkin' right along. Guess he don't hear us yet. Wind 's in wrong direction."

The fresh breeze was blowing right down upon us, and I could hear the whistle plainly, off to one side and a little ahead.

"Ferry-boat?" I asked.

He nodded, then added: "Or he would n't be keepin' up such a clip." He gave a short chuckle. "They 're gettin' anxious up there."

I glanced up. The captain had thrust his head and shoulders out of the pilot-house and was staring intently into the fog, as though by sheer force of will he could penetrate it. His face was anxious, as was the face of my companion, who had stumped over to the rail and was gazing with a like intentness in the direction of the invisible danger.

Then everything happened, and with inconceivable rapidity. The fog seemed to break away as though split by a wedge, and the bow of a steamboat emerged, trailing fog-wreaths on each side like seaweed on the snout of Leviathan. I could see the pilot-house and a white-bearded man leaning partly out of it, on his elbows. He was clad in a blue uniform, and I remember noting how trim and quiet he was. His quietness, under the circumstances, was terrible. He accepted Destiny, marched hand in hand with it, and coolly

Drawn by W. J. Aylward.

"'AHOY! TAKE ME ASHORE! A THOUSAND DOLLARS IF YOU TAKE ME ASHORE!'"

measured the stroke. As he leaned there, he ran a calm and speculative eye over us, as though to determine the precise point of the collision, and took no notice whatever when our pilot, white with rage, shouted, "Now you 've done it!"

"Grab hold of something and hang on!" the red-faced man said to me. All his bluster had gone, and he seemed to have caught the contagion of preternatural calm. "And listen to the women scream," he said grimly, almost bitterly, I thought, as though he had been through the experience before.

The vessels came together before I could follow his advice. We must have been struck squarely amidships, for I saw nothing, the strange steamboat having passed beyond my line of vision. The *Martinez* heeled over sharply, and there was a crashing and rending of timber. I was thrown flat on the wet deck, and before I could scramble to my feet I heard the screams of the women. This it was, I am certain,—the most indescribable of blood-curdling sounds,—that threw me into a panic. I remembered the life-preservers stored in the cabin, but was met at the door and swept backward by a wild rush of men and women. What happened in the next few minutes I do not recollect, though I have a clear remembrance of pulling down life-preservers from the overhead racks while the red-faced man fastened them about the bodies of an hysterical group of women. This memory is as distinct and sharp as that of any picture I have seen. It is a picture, and I can see it now—the jagged edges of the hole in the side of the cabin, through which the gray fog swirled and eddied; the empty upholstered seats, littered with all the evidences of sudden flight, such as packages, hand-satchels, umbrellas, and wraps; the stout gentleman who had been reading my essay, incased in cork and canvas, the magazine still in his hand, and asking me with monotonous insistence if I thought there was any danger; the red-faced man stumping gallantly around on his artificial legs and buckling life-preservers on all comers; and, finally, the screaming bedlam of women.

This it was, the screaming of the women, that most tried my nerves. It must have tried, too, the nerves of the red-faced man, for I have another picture which will never fade from my mind. The stout gentleman is stuffing the magazine into his overcoat pocket and looking on curiously. A tangled mass of women, with drawn, white faces and open mouths, is shrieking like a chorus of lost souls; and the red-faced man, his face now purplish with wrath, and with arms extended overhead, as in the act of hurling thunderbolts, is shouting, "Shut up! Oh, shut up!"

I remember the scene impelled me to sudden laughter, and in the next instant I realized that I was becoming hysterical myself; for these were women, of my own kind, like my mother and sisters, with the fear of death upon them and unwilling to die. And I remember that the sounds they made reminded me of the squealing of pigs under the knife of the butcher, and I was struck with horror at the vividness of the analogy. These women, capable of the most sublime emotions, of the tenderest sympathies, were open-mouthed and screaming. They wanted to live; they were helpless, like rats in a trap, and they screamed.

The horror of it drove me out on deck. I was feeling sick and squeamish, and sat down on a bench. In a hazy way I saw and heard men rushing and shouting as they strove to lower the boats. It was just as I had read descriptions of such scenes in books. The tackles jammed. Nothing worked. One boat lowered away with the plugs out, filled with women and children and then with water, and capsized. Another boat had been lowered by one end and still hung in the tackle by the other end where it had been abandoned. Nothing was to be seen of the strange steamboat which had caused the disaster, though I heard men saying that she would undoubtedly send boats to our assistance.

I descended to the lower deck. The *Martinez* was sinking fast, for the water was very near. Numbers of the passengers were leaping overboard. Others, in the water, were clamoring to be taken aboard again. No one heeded them. A cry arose that we were sinking. I was seized by the consequent panic, and went over the side in a surge of bodies. How I went over I do not know, though I did know, and instantly, why those in the water were so desirous of getting back on the steamer. The water was cold—so cold that it was painful. The pang, as I plunged into it, was as quick and sharp as that of fire. It bit to the marrow. It was like the grip of death. I gasped with the anguish and shock of it, filling my lungs before the life-preserver popped me to the surface. The taste of the salt was strong in my mouth, and I was strangling with the acrid stuff in my throat and lungs.

But it was the cold that was most distressing. I felt that I could survive but a few minutes. People were struggling and floundering in the water about me. I could hear them crying out to one another. And I heard, also, the sound of oars. Evidently the strange steamboat had lowered its boats. As the time went by I marveled that I was still alive. I had no sensation whatever in my lower limbs, while a chilling numbness was wrapping about my heart and creeping into it. Small waves, with spiteful foaming crests, continually broke over me and into my mouth, sending me off into more strangling paroxysms.

The noises grew indistinct, though I heard a final and despairing chorus of screams in the distance and knew that the *Martinez* had gone down. Later,—how much later I have no knowledge,—I came to myself with a start of fear. I was alone. I could hear no calls or cries—only the sound of the waves, made weirdly hollow and reverberant by the fog. A panic in a crowd, which partakes of a sort of community of interest, is not so terrible as a panic when one is by oneself; and such a panic I now suffered. Whither was I drifting? The red-faced man had said that the tide was ebbing through the Golden Gate. Was I, then, being carried out to sea? And the life-preserver in which I floated? Was it not liable to go to pieces at any moment? I had heard of such things being made of paper and hollow rushes, which quickly became saturated and lost all buoyancy. I could not swim a stroke, and I was alone, floating, apparently, in the midst of a gray primordial vastness. I confess that a madness seized me, that I shrieked aloud as the women had shrieked, and beat the water with my numb hands.

How long this lasted I have no conception, for a blankness intervened, of which I remember no more than one remembers of troubled and painful sleep. When I aroused, it was as after centuries of time, and I saw, almost above me and emerging from the fog, the bow of a vessel and three triangular sails, each shrewdly lapping the other and filled with wind. Where the bow cut the water there was a great foaming and gurgling, and I seemed directly in its path. I tried to cry out, but was too exhausted. The bow plunged down, just missing me and sending a swash of water clear over my head. Then the long black side of the vessel began slipping past, so near that I could have touched it with my hands. I tried to reach it, in a mad resolve to claw into the wood with my nails; but my arms were heavy and lifeless. Again I strove to call out, but made no sound.

The stern of the vessel shot by, dropping, as it did so, into a hollow between the waves; and I caught a glimpse of a man standing at a wheel, and of another man who seemed to be doing little else than smoke a cigar. I saw the smoke issuing from his lips as he slowly turned his head and glanced out over the water in my direction. It was a careless, unpremeditated glance, one of those haphazard things men do when they have no immediate call to do anything in particular, but act because they are alive and must do something.

But life and death were in that glance. I could see the vessel being swallowed up in the fog; I saw the back of the man at the wheel, and the head of the other man turning, slowly turning, as his gaze struck the water and casually lifted along it toward me. His face wore an absent expression, as of deep thought, and I became afraid that if his eyes did light upon me he would nevertheless not see me. But his eyes did light upon me, and looked squarely into mine; and he did see me, for he sprang to the wheel, thrusting the other man aside, and whirled it round and round, hand over hand, at the same time shouting orders of some sort. The vessel seemed to go off at a tangent to its former course and to leap almost instantly from view into the fog.

I felt myself slipping into unconsciousness, and tried with all the power of my will to fight above the suffocating blankness and darkness that was rising around me. A little later I heard the stroke of oars, growing nearer and nearer, and the calls of a man. When he was very near I heard him crying, in vexed fashion: "Why in —— don't you sing out?"

This meant me, I thought, and then the blankness and darkness rose over me.

II

I SEEMED swinging in a mighty rhythm through orbit vastness. Sparkling points of light spluttered and shot past me. They were stars, I knew, and flaring comets, that peopled my flight among the suns. As I reached the limit of my swing and prepared to rush back on the counter-swing, a great gong struck, and thundered and reverberated through abysmal space. For an immeasurable period, quiescent, lapped in the rippling of placid centuries, I enjoyed and pondered my tremendous flight.

But a change came over the face of the dream, for a dream I told myself it must be. My rhythm grew shorter and shorter. I was jerked from swing to counter-swing with irritating haste. I could scarcely catch my breath, so fiercely was I impelled through the heavens. The gong thundered more frequently and more furiously. I grew to await it with a nameless dread. Then it seemed as though I were being dragged over rasping sands, white and hot in the sun. This gave place to a sense of intolerable anguish. My skin was scorching in the torment of fire. The gong clanged and knelled. The sparkling points of light flashed past me in an interminable stream, as though the whole sidereal system were dropping into the void. I gasped, caught my breath painfully, and opened my eyes. Two men were kneeling beside me, working over me. My mighty rhythm was the lift and forward plunge of a ship on the sea. The terrific gong was a frying-pan, hanging on the wall, that rattled and clattered with each leap of the ship. The rasping, scorching sands were a man's hard hands chafing my naked chest. I squirmed under the pain of it and half lifted my head. My chest was raw and red, and I could see tiny blood-globules starting through the torn and inflamed cuticle.

"That 'll do, Yonson," one of the men said. "Carn't yer see you 've bloomin' well rubbed all the gent's skin orf?"

The man addressed as Yonson, a man of the heavy Scandinavian type, ceased chafing me and arose awkwardly to his feet. The man who had spoken to him was clearly a Cockney, with the clean lines and weakly pretty, almost effeminate, face of the man who has absorbed the sound of Bow Bells with his mother's milk. A draggled muslin cap on his head, and a dirty gunny-sack about his slim hips, proclaimed him cook of the decidedly dirty ship's galley in which I found myself.

"An' 'ow yer feelin' now, sir?" he asked, with the subservient smirk which comes only of generations of tip-seeking ancestors.

For reply, I twisted weakly into a sitting posture, and was helped by Yonson to my feet. The rattle and bang of the frying-pan was grating horribly on my nerves. I could not collect my thoughts. Clutching the woodwork of the galley for support,—and I confess the grease with which it was scummed put my teeth on edge,—I reached across a hot cooking-range to the offending utensil, unhooked it, and wedged it securely into the coal-box.

The cook grinned at my exhibition of nerves, and thrust into my hand a steaming mug with an "'Ere, this 'll do yer good."

It was a nauseous mess,—ship's coffee,—but the heat of it was revivifying. Between gulps of the molten stuff I glanced down at my raw and bleeding chest and turned to the Scandinavian.

"Thank you, Mr. Yonson," I said; "but don't you think your measures were rather heroic?"

It was because he understood the reproof of my action, rather than of my words, that he held up his palm for inspection. It was remarkably calloused. I passed my hand over the horny projections, and my teeth went on edge once more from the horrible rasping sensation produced.

"My name is Johnson, not Yonson," he said in very good, though slow, English, with no more than a shade of accent to it.

There was mild protest in his pale-blue eyes, and, withal, a timid frankness and manliness that quite won me to him.

"Thank you, Mr. Johnson," I corrected, and reached out my hand for his.

He hesitated, awkward and bashful, shifted his weight from one leg to the other, then blunderingly gripped my hand in a hearty shake.

"Have you any dry clothes I may put on?" I asked the cook.

"Yes, sir," he answered, with cheerful

alacrity. "I 'll run down an' tyke a look over my kit, if you 've no objections, sir, to wearin' my things."

He dived out of the galley door, or glided, rather, with a swiftness and smoothness of gait that struck me as being not so much cat-like as oily. In fact, this oiliness, or greasiness, as I was later to learn, was probably the most salient expression of his personality.

"And where am I?" I asked Johnson, whom I took, and rightly, to be one of the sailors. "What vessel is this? And where is she bound?"

"Off the Farralones, heading about sou'-west," he answered slowly and methodically, as though groping for his best English, and rigidly observing the order of my queries. "The schooner *Ghost*; bound seal-hunting to Japan."

"And who is the captain? I must see him as soon as I am dressed."

Johnson looked puzzled and embarrassed. He hesitated while he groped in his vocabulary and framed a complete answer. "The cap'n is Wolf Larsen, or so men call him. I never heard his other name. But you better speak soft with him. He is mad this morning. The mate—"

But he did not finish. The cook had glided in.

"Better sling yer 'ook out of 'ere, Yonson," he said. "The Old Man 'll be wantin' yer on deck, an' this ayn't no d'y to fall foul of 'im."

Johnson turned obediently to the door, at the same time, over the cook's shoulder, favoring me with an amazingly solemn and portentous wink, as though to emphasize his interrupted remark and the need for me to be soft-spoken with the captain.

Hanging over the cook's arm was a loose and crumpled array of evil-looking and sour-smelling garments.

"They was put aw'y wet, sir," he vouchsafed explanation. "But you 'll 'ave to make them do while I dry yours out by the fire."

Clinging to the woodwork, staggering with the roll of the ship, and aided by the cook, I managed to slip into a rough woolen undershirt. On the instant my flesh was creeping and crawling from the harsh contact. He noticed my involuntary twitching and grimacing, and smirked:

"I only 'ope yer don't ever 'ave to get used to such as that in this life, 'cos you 've got a bloomin' soft skin, that you 'ave, more like a lydy's than any I know of. I was bloomin' well sure you was a gentleman as soon as I set eyes on yer."

I had taken a dislike to him at the first, and as he helped to dress me this dislike increased. There was something repulsive about his touch. I shrank from his hand; my flesh revolted. And between this and the smells arising from various pots boiling and bubbling on the galley fire, I was in haste to get out into the fresh air. Further, there was the need of seeing the captain about what arrangements could be made for getting me ashore.

A cheap cotton shirt, with frayed collar and a bosom discolored with what I took to be ancient blood-stains, was put on me amidst a running and apologetic fire of comment. A pair of workman's brogans incased my feet, and for trousers I was furnished with a pair of pale-blue, washed-out overalls, one leg of which was fully ten inches shorter than the other. The abbreviated leg looked as though the devil had there clutched for the Cockney's soul and missed the shadow for the substance.

"And whom have I to thank for this kindness?" I asked, when I stood completely arrayed, a tiny boy's cap on my head, and for coat a dirty, striped cotton jacket which ended at the small of my back, and the sleeves of which reached just below my elbows.

The cook drew himself up in smugly humble fashion, a deprecating smirk on his face. Out of my experience with stewards on the Atlantic liners at the end of the voyage, I could have sworn he was waiting for his tip. From my fuller knowledge of the creature I now know that the posture was unconscious. An hereditary servility, no doubt, was responsible.

"Mugridge, sir," he fawned, his effeminate features running into a greasy smile. "Thomas Mugridge, sir, an' at yer service."

"All right, Thomas," I said. "I shall not forget you—when my clothes are dry."

A soft light suffused his face, and his eyes glistened, as though somewhere in the deeps of his being his ancestors had quickened and stirred with dim memories of tips received in former lives.

"Thank you, sir," he said very gratefully and very humbly indeed.

Precisely in the way that the door slid back, he slid aside, and I stepped out on deck. I was still weak from my prolonged immersion. A puff of wind caught me, and I staggered across the moving deck to a corner of the cabin, to which I clung for support. The schooner, heeled over far out from the perpendicular, was bowing and plunging into the long Pacific roll. If she were heading southwest, as Johnson had said, the wind, then, I calculated, was blowing nearly from the south. The fog was gone, and in its place the sun sparkled crisply on the surface of the water. I turned to the east, where I knew California must lie, but could see nothing save low-lying fog-banks—the same fog, doubtless, that had brought about the disaster to the *Martinez* and placed me in my present situation. To the north, not far away, a group of naked rocks thrust above the sea, on one of which I could distinguish a lighthouse. In the southwest, and almost in our course, I saw the pyramidal loom of some vessel's sails.

Having completed my survey of the horizon, I turned to my more immediate surroundings. My first thought was that a man who had come through a collision and rubbed shoulders with death merited more attention than I received. Beyond a sailor at the wheel, who stared curiously across the top of the cabin, I attracted no notice whatever.

Everybody seemed interested in what was going on amidships. There, on a hatch, a large man was lying on his back. He was fully clothed, though his shirt was ripped open in front. Nothing was to be seen of his chest, however, for it was covered with a mass of black hair, in appearance like the furry coat of a dog. His face and neck were hidden beneath a black beard, intershot with gray, which would have been stiff and bushy had it not been limp and draggled and dripping with water. His eyes were closed, and he was apparently unconscious; but his mouth was wide open, his breast heaving as though from suffocation as he labored noisily for breath. A sailor, from time to time and quite methodically, as a matter of routine, dropped a canvas bucket into the ocean at the end of a rope, hauled it in hand under hand, and sluiced its contents over the prostrate man.

Pacing back and forth the length of the hatchway, and savagely chewing the end of a cigar, was the man whose casual glance had rescued me from the sea. His height was probably five feet ten inches, or ten and a half; but my first impression or feel of the man was not of this, but of his strength. And yet, while he was of massive build, with broad shoulders and deep chest, I could not characterize his strength as massive. It was what might be termed a sinewy, knotty strength, of the kind we ascribe to lean and wiry men, but which, in him, because of his heavy build, partook more of the enlarged gorilla order. Not that in appearance he seemed in the least gorilla-like. What I am striving to express is this strength itself, more as a thing apart from his physical semblance. It was a strength we are wont to associate with things primitive, with wild animals and the creatures we imagine our tree-dwelling prototypes to have been—a strength savage, ferocious, alive in itself, the essence of life in that it is the potency of motion, the elemental stuff itself out of which the many forms of life have been molded.

Such was the impression of strength I gathered from this man who paced up and down. He was firmly planted on his legs; his feet struck the deck squarely and with surety: every movement of a muscle, from the heave of the shoulders to the tightening of the lips about the cigar, was decisive and seemed to come out of a strength that was excessive and overwhelming. In fact, though this strength pervaded every action of his, it seemed but the advertisement of a greater strength that lurked within, that lay dormant and no more than stirred from time to time, but which might arouse at any moment, terrible and compelling, like the rage of a lion or the wrath of a storm.

The cook stuck his head out of the galley door and grinned encouragingly at me, at the same time jerking his thumb in the direction of the man who paced up and down by the hatchway. Thus I was given to understand that he was the captain, the "Old Man," in the cook's vernacular, the person whom I must interview and put to the trouble of somehow getting me ashore. I had half started forward, to get over with what I was certain would be a stormy quarter of an hour, when a more violent suffocating paroxysm seized the unfortunate person who was lying on his back. He writhed about convulsively. The chin, with the damp black beard, pointed higher in the air as the back muscles stiffened and the chest swelled in an unconscious and instinctive effort to get more air.

The captain, or Wolf Larsen, as men called him, ceased pacing, and gazed down at the dying man. So fierce had this final struggle become that the sailor paused in the act of flinging more water over him, and stared curiously, the canvas bucket partly tilted and dripping its contents to the deck. The dying man beat a tattoo on the hatch with his heels, straightened out his legs, stiffened in one great, tense effort, and rolled his head from side to side. Then the muscles relaxed, the head stopped rolling, and a sigh, as of profound relief, floated upward from his lips. The jaw dropped, the upper lip lifted, and two rows of tobacco-discolored teeth appeared. It seemed as though his features had frozen into a diabolical grin at the world he had left and outwitted.

Then a most surprising thing occurred. The captain broke loose upon the dead man like a thunderclap. Oaths rolled from his lips in a continuous stream. And they were not namby-pamby oaths, or mere expressions of indecency. Each word was a blasphemy, and there were many words. They crisped and crackled like electric sparks. I had never heard anything like it in my life, nor could I have conceived it possible. With a turn for literary expression myself, and a penchant for forcible figures and phrases, I appreciated as no other listener, I dare say, the peculiar vividness and strength and absolute blasphemy of his metaphors. The cause of it all, as near as I could make out, was that the man, who was mate, had gone on a debauch before leaving San Francisco, and then had the poor taste to die at the beginning of the voyage and leave Wolf Larsen short-handed.

It should be unnecessary to state, at least to my friends, that I was shocked. Oaths and vile language of any sort had always been unutterably repellent to me. I felt a wilting sensation, a sinking at the heart, and, I might just as well say, a giddiness. To me death had always been invested with solemnity and dignity. It had been peaceful in its occurrence, sacred in its ceremonial. But death in its more sordid and terrible aspects was a thing with which I had been unacquainted till now. As I say, while I appreciated the power of the terrific denunciation that swept out of Wolf Larsen's mouth, I was inexpressibly shocked. But the dead man continued to grin unconcernedly with a sardonic humor, a cynical mockery and defiance. He was master of the situation.

III

WOLF LARSEN ceased swearing as suddenly as he had begun. He relighted his cigar and glanced around. His eyes chanced upon the cook.

"Well, Cooky?" he began, with a suaveness that was cold and of the temper of steel.

"Yes, sir," the cook eagerly interpolated, with appeasing and apologetic servility.

"Don't you think you 've stretched that neck of yours just about enough? It 's unhealthy, you know. The mate 's gone, so I can't afford to lose you, too. You must be very, very careful of your health, Cooky. Understand?"

His last word, in striking contrast with the smoothness of his previous utterance, snapped like the lash of a whip. The cook quailed under it.

"Yes, sir," was the meek reply, as the offending head disappeared into the galley.

At this rebuke the rest of the crew became uninterested and fell to work at one task or another. A number of men, however, who were lounging about a companionway between the galley and the hatch, and who did not seem to be sailors, continued talking in low tones with one another. These, I afterward learned, were the hunters, the men who shot the seals, and a very superior breed to common sailor-folk.

"Johansen!" Wolf Larsen called out. A sailor stepped forward obediently. "Get your palm and needle and sew the beggar up. You 'll find some old canvas in the sail-locker. Make it do."

"What 'll I put on his feet, sir?" the man asked, after the customary "Aye, aye, sir."

"We 'll see to that," Wolf Larsen answered, and elevated his voice in a call of "Cooky!"

Thomas Mugridge popped out of his galley like a jack-in-the-box.

"Go below and fill a sack with coal."

"Any of you fellows got a Bible or

prayer-book?" was the captain's next demand, this time of the hunters lounging about the companionway.

They shook their heads, and some one made a jocular remark which I did not catch, but which raised a general laugh.

Wolf Larsen made the same demand of the sailors. Bibles and prayer-books seemed scarce articles, but one of the men volunteered to pursue the quest among the watch below, returning in a minute with the information that "they ain't none."

The captain shrugged his shoulders. "Then we 'll drop him over without any palavering, unless our clerical-looking castaway has the burial service at sea by heart."

By this time he had swung fully around and was facing me.

"You 're a preacher, are n't you?" he asked.

The hunters—there were six of them—to a man turned and regarded me. I was painfully aware of my likeness to a scarecrow. A laugh went up at my appearance—a laugh that was not lessened or softened by the dead man stretched and grinning on the deck before us; a laugh that was as rough and harsh and frank as the sea itself; that arose out of coarse feelings and blunted sensibilities, from natures that knew neither courtesy nor gentleness.

Wolf Larsen did not laugh, though his gray eyes lighted with a slight glint of amusement; and in that moment, having stepped forward quite close to him, I received my first impression of the man himself—of the man as apart from his body and from the torrent of blasphemy I had heard. The face, with large features and strong lines, of the square order, yet well filled out, was apparently massive at first sight; but again, as with the body, the massiveness seemed to vanish and a conviction to grow of a tremendous and excessive mental or spiritual strength that lay behind, sleeping, in the deeps of his being. The jaw, the chin, the brow rising to a goodly height and swelling heavily above the eyes—these, while strong in themselves, unusually strong, seemed to speak an immense vigor or virility of spirit that lay behind and beyond and out of sight. There was no sounding such a spirit, no measuring, no determining of metes and bounds, or neatly classifying in some pigeonhole with others of similar type.

The eyes—and it was my destiny to know them well—were large and handsome, wide apart, as the true artist's are wide, sheltering under a heavy brow and arched over by thick black eyebrows. The eyes themselves were of that baffling protean gray which is never twice the same; which runs through many shades and colorings like intershot silk in sunshine; which is gray, dark and light, and greenish gray, and sometimes of the clear azure of the deep sea. They were eyes that masked the soul with a thousand guises, and that sometimes opened, at rare moments, and allowed it to rush up as though it were about to fare forth nakedly into the world on some wonderful adventure—eyes that could brood with the hopeless somberness of leaden skies; that could snap and crackle points of fire like those that sparkle from a whirling sword; that could grow chill as an arctic landscape, and yet again, that could warm and soften and be all adance with love-lights, intense and masculine, luring and compelling, which at the same time fascinate and dominate women till they surrender in a gladness of joy and of relief and sacrifice.

But to return. I told him that, unhappily for the burial service, I was not a preacher, when he sharply demanded:

"What do you do for a living?"

I confess I had never had such a question asked me before, nor had I ever canvassed it. I was quite taken aback, and, before I could find myself, had sillily stammered: "I am a gentleman."

His lip curled in a swift sneer.

"I have worked, I do work," I cried impetuously, as though he were my judge and I required vindication, and at the same time very much aware of my arrant idiocy in discussing the subject at all.

"For your living?"

There was something so imperative and masterful about him that I was quite beside myself—"rattled," as Furuseth would have termed it, like a quaking child before a stern schoolmaster.

"Who feeds you?" was his next question.

"I have an income," I answered stoutly, and could have bitten my tongue the next instant. "All of which, you will pardon my observing, has nothing whatsoever to do with what I wish to see you about."

But he disregarded my protest.

"Who earned it? Eh? I thought so. Your father. You stand on dead men's legs. You 've never had any of your own. You could n't walk alone between two sunrises and hustle the meat for your belly for three meals. Let me see your hand."

His tremendous, dormant strength must have stirred swiftly and accurately, or I must have slept a moment, for before I knew it he had stepped two paces forward, gripped my right hand in his, and held it up for inspection. I tried to withdraw it, but his fingers tightened, without visible effort, till I thought mine would be crushed. It is hard to maintain one's dignity under such circumstances. I could not squirm or struggle like a school-boy. Nor could I attack such a creature, who had but to twist my arm to break it. Nothing remained but to stand still and accept the indignity. I had time to notice that the pockets of the dead man had been emptied on the deck and that his body and his grin had been wrapped from view in canvas, the folds of which the sailor Johansen was sewing together with coarse white twine, shoving the needle through with a leather contrivance fitted on the palm of his hand.

Wolf Larsen dropped my hand with a flirt of disdain.

"Dead men's hands have kept it soft. Good for little else than dish-washing and scullion-work."

"I wish to be put ashore," I said firmly, for I now had myself in control. "I shall pay you whatever you judge your delay and trouble to be worth."

He looked at me curiously. Mockery shone in his eyes.

"I have a counter-proposition to make, and for the good of your soul. My mate 's gone, and there 'll be a lot of promotion. A sailor comes aft to take mate's place, cabin-boy goes for'ard to take sailor's place, and you take the cabin-boy's place, sign the articles for the cruise, twenty dollars per month and found. Now, what do you say? And mind you, it 's for your own soul's sake. It will be the making of you. You might learn in time to stand on your own legs and perhaps to toddle along a bit."

But I took no notice. The sails of the vessel I had seen off to the southwest had grown larger and plainer. They were of the same rig as the *Ghost's*, though the hull itself, I could see, was smaller. She was a pretty sight, leaping and flying toward us, and evidently bound to pass at close range. The wind had been momentarily increasing, and the sun, after a few angry gleams, had disappeared. The sea had turned a dull leaden gray and grown rougher, and was now tossing foaming whitecaps to the sky. We were traveling faster and heeled farther over. Once, in a gust, the rail dipped under the sea, and the decks on that side were for the moment awash with water that made a couple of the hunters hastily lift their feet.

"That vessel will soon be passing us," I said, after a moment's pause. "As she is going in the opposite direction, she is very probably bound for San Francisco."

"Very probably," was Wolf Larsen's answer, as he turned partly away from me and cried out, "Cooky! Oh, Cooky!"

The Cockney popped out of the galley.

"Where 's that boy? Tell him I want him."

"Yes, sir," and Thomas Mugridge fled swiftly aft and disappeared down another companionway near the wheel. A moment later he emerged, a heavy-set young fellow of eighteen or nineteen, with a glowering, villainous countenance, trailing at his heels.

"'Ere 'e is, sir," the cook said.

But Wolf Larsen ignored that worthy, turning at once to the cabin-boy.

"What 's your name, boy?"

"George Leach, sir," came the sullen answer, and the boy's bearing showed clearly that he divined the reason for which he had been summoned.

"Not an Irish name," the captain snapped sharply. "O'Toole or McCarthy would suit your mug a —— sight better.

"But let that go," he continued. "You may have very good reasons for forgetting your name, and I 'll like you none the worse for it as long as you toe the mark. Telegraph Hill, of course, is your port of entry. It sticks out all over your mug. Tough as they make them and twice as nasty. I know the kind. Well, you can make up your mind to have it taken out of you on this craft. Understand? Who shipped you, anyway?"

"McCready & Swanson."

"Sir!" Wolf Larsen thundered.

"McCready & Swanson, sir," the boy corrected, his eyes burning with a bitter light.

"Who got the advance money?"

"They did, sir."

"I thought as much. And devilish glad you were to let them have it. Could n't make yourself scarce too quick, with several gentlemen you may have heard of looking for you."

The boy metamorphosed into a savage on the instant. His body bunched together as though for a spring, and his face became as an infuriated beast's as he snarled, "It 's a—"

"A what?" Wolf Larsen asked, a peculiar softness in his voice, as though he were overwhelmingly curious to hear the unspoken word.

The boy hesitated, then mastered his temper. "Nothin', sir. I take it back."

"And you have shown me I was right." This with a gratified smile. "How old are you?"

"Just turned sixteen, sir."

"A lie. You 'll never see eighteen again. Big for your age at that, with muscles like a horse. Pack up your kit and go for'ard into the fo'c's'le. You 're a boat-puller now. You 're promoted; see?"

Without waiting for the boy's acceptance, the captain turned to the sailor who had just finished the gruesome task of sewing up the body. "Johansen, do you know anything about navigation?"

"No, sir."

"Well, never mind; you 're mate just the same. Get your traps aft into the mate's berth."

"Aye, aye, sir," was the cheery response, as Johansen started forward.

In the meantime the erstwhile cabin-boy had not moved.

"What are you waiting for?" Wolf Larsen demanded.

"I did n't sign for boat-puller, sir," was the reply. "I signed for cabin-boy. An' I don't want no boat-pullin' in mine."

"Pack up and go for'ard."

This time Wolf Larsen's command was thrillingly imperative. The boy glowered sullenly, but refused to move.

Then came another vague stirring of Wolf Larsen's tremendous strength. It was utterly unexpected, and it was over and done with between the ticks of two seconds. He had sprung fully six feet across the deck and driven his fist into the other's stomach. At the same moment, as though I had been struck myself, I felt a sickening shock in the pit of my stomach. I instance this to show the sensitiveness of my nervous organization at the time and how unused I was to spectacles of brutality. The cabin-boy—and he weighed one hundred and sixty-five at the very least—crumpled up. His body wrapped limply about the fist like a wet rag about a stick. He lifted into the air, described a short curve, and struck the deck on his head and shoulders, where he lay and writhed about in agony.

"Well?" Larsen asked of me. "Have you made up your mind?"

I had glanced occasionally at the approaching schooner, and it was now almost abreast of us and not more than a couple of hundred yards away. It was a very trim and neat little craft. I could see a large black number on one of its sails, and I had seen pictures of pilot-boats.

"What vessel is that?" I asked.

"The pilot-boat *Lady Mine*," Wolf Larsen answered grimly. "Got rid of her pilots and running into San Francisco. She 'll be there in five or six hours with this wind."

"Will you please signal it, then, so that I may be put ashore?"

"Sorry, but I 've lost the signal-book overboard," he remarked, and the group of hunters grinned.

I debated a moment, looking him squarely in the eyes. I had seen the frightful treatment of the cabin-boy, and knew that I should very probably receive the same, if not worse. As I say, I debated with myself, and then I did what I consider the bravest act of my life. I ran to the side, waving my arms and shouting:

"*Lady Mine*, ahoy! Take me ashore! A thousand dollars if you take me ashore!"

I waited, watching two men who stood by the wheel, one of them steering. The other was lifting a megaphone to his lips. I did not turn my head, though I expected every moment a killing blow from the human brute behind me. At last, after what seemed centuries, unable longer to stand the strain, I looked around. He had not moved. He was standing in the same position, swaying easily to the roll of the ship and lighting a fresh cigar.

"What is the matter? Anything wrong?"

This was the cry from the *Lady Mine*.

"Yes!" I shouted at the top of my

lungs. "Life or death! One thousand dollars if you take me ashore!"

"Too much 'Frisco tanglefoot for the health of my crew!" Wolf Larsen shouted after. "This one"—indicating me with his thumb—"fancies sea-serpents and monkeys just now."

The man on the *Lady Mine* laughed back through the megaphone. The pilot-boat plunged past.

"Give him —— for me!" came a final cry, and the two men waved their arms in farewell.

I leaned despairingly over the rail, watching the trim little schooner swiftly increasing the bleak sweep of ocean between us. And she would probably be in San Francisco in five or six hours! My head seemed bursting. There was an ache in my throat as though my heart were up in it. A curling wave struck the side and splashed salt spray on my lips. The wind puffed strongly, and the *Ghost* heeled far over, burying her lee rail. I could hear the water rushing down upon the deck.

When I turned around, a moment later, I saw the cabin-boy staggering to his feet. His face was ghastly white, twitching with suppressed pain. He looked very sick.

"Well, Leach, are you going for'ard?" Wolf Larsen asked.

"Yes, sir," came the answer of a spirit cowed.

"And you?" I was asked.

"I 'll give you a thousand—" I began, but was interrupted.

"Stow that! Are you going to take up your duties as cabin-boy? Or do I have to take you in hand?"

What was I to do? To be brutally beaten, to be killed perhaps, would not help my case. I looked steadily into the cruel gray eyes. They might have been granite for all the light and warmth of a human soul they contained. One may see the soul stir in some men's eyes, but his were bleak and cold and gray as the sea itself.

"Well?"

"Yes," I said.

"Say 'Yes, sir.'"

"Yes, sir," I corrected.

"What is your name?"

"Van Weyden, sir."

"First name?"

"Humphrey, sir—Humphrey Van Weyden."

"Age?"

"Thirty-five, sir."

"That 'll do. Go to the cook and learn your duties."

And thus it was that I passed into a state of involuntary servitude to Wolf Larsen. He was stronger than I, that was all. But it was very unreal at the time. It is no less unreal now that I look back upon it. It will always be to me as a monstrous, inconceivable thing, a horrible nightmare.

"Hold on; don't go yet."

I stopped obediently in my walk toward the galley.

"Johansen, call all hands. Now that we 've everything cleaned up, we 'll have the funeral and get the decks cleared of useless lumber."

While Johansen was summoning the watch below, a couple of sailors, under the captain's direction, laid the canvas-swathed corpse upon a hatch-cover. On each side the deck, against the rail, and bottoms up, were lashed a number of small boats. Several men picked up the hatch-cover with its ghastly freight, carried it to the lee side, and rested it on the boats, the feet pointing overboard. To the feet was attached the sack of coal which the cook had fetched.

I had always conceived a burial at sea to be a very solemn and awe-inspiring event, but I was quickly disillusioned, by this burial at any rate. One of the hunters, a little dark-eyed man whom his mates called "Smoke," was telling stories, liberally intersprinkled with oaths and obscenities; and every minute or so the group of hunters gave mouth to a laughter that sounded to me like a chorus of wolves. The sailors trooped noisily aft, some of the watch below rubbing the sleep from their eyes, and talked in low tones together. There was an ominous and worried expression on their faces. It was evident that they did not like the outlook of a voyage under such a captain and begun so inauspiciously. From time to time they stole glances at Wolf Larsen, and I could see that they were apprehensive of the man.

He stepped up to the hatch cover, and all caps came off. I ran my eyes over them—twenty men all told, twenty-two, including the man at the wheel and myself. I was pardonably curious in my survey, for it appeared my fate to be pent up with them on this miniature floating world for I knew not how many weeks or months. The sailors, in the main, were English and Scandinavian, and their faces seemed of the heavy, stolid order. The hunters, on the other hand, had stronger and more diversified faces, with hard lines and the marks of the free play of passions. Strange to say, and I noted it at once, Wolf Larsen's features showed no such evil stamp. There seemed nothing vicious in them. True, there were lines, but they were the lines of decision and firmness. It seemed, rather, a frank and open countenance, which frankness or openness was enhanced by the fact that he was smooth-shaven. I could hardly believe, until the next incident occurred, that it was the face of a man who could behave as he had behaved to the cabin-boy.

At this moment, as he opened his mouth to speak, puff after puff struck the schooner and pressed her side under. The wind shrieked a wild song through the rigging. Some of the hunters glanced anxiously aloft. The whole lee rail, where the dead man lay, was buried in the sea, and as the schooner lifted and righted, the water swept across the deck, wetting us above our shoe-tops. A shower of rain drove down upon us, each drop stinging like a hailstone. As it passed, Wolf Larsen began to speak, the bareheaded men swaying in unison to the heave and lunge of the deck.

"I only remember one part of the service," he said, "and that is, 'And the body shall be cast into the sea.' So cast it in."

He ceased speaking. The men holding the hatch-cover seemed perplexed, puzzled no doubt by the briefness of the ceremony. He burst upon them in a fury.

"Lift up that end there! What the —— 's the matter with you?"

They elevated the end of the hatch-cover with pitiful haste, and, like a dog flung overside, the dead man slid feet first into the sea. The coal at his feet dragged him down. He was gone.

"Johansen," Wolf Larsen said briskly to the new mate, "keep all hands on deck now they 're here. Get in the topsails and outer jibs. We 're in for a sou'easter. Reef the jib and the mainsail, too, while you 're about it."

In a moment the decks were in commotion, Johansen bellowing orders and the men pulling or letting go ropes of various sorts—all naturally confusing to a landsman such as myself. But it was the heartlessness of it that especially struck me. The dead man was an episode that was past, an incident that was dropped, in a canvas covering with a sack of coal, while the ship sped along and her work went on. Nobody had been affected. The hunters were laughing at a fresh story of Smoke's; the men pulling and hauling, and two of them climbing aloft; Wolf Larsen was studying the clouding sky to windward; and the dead man, buried sordidly, and sinking down, down—

Then it was that the cruelty of the sea, its relentlessness and awfulness, rushed upon me. Life had become cheap and tawdry, a beastly and inarticulate thing, a soulless stirring of the ooze and slime. I held on to the weather rail, close by the shrouds, and gazed out across the desolate foaming waves to the low-lying fog-banks that hid San Francisco and the California coast. Rain-squalls were driving in between, and I could scarcely see the fog. And this strange vessel, with its terrible men, pressed under by wind and sea and ever leaping up and out, as for very life, was heading away into the southwest, into the great and lonely Pacific expanse.

Drawn by William J. Aylward.

"LOUIS DROPPED INTO THE GALLEY FOR A 'YARN'"

THE SEA-WOLF

BY JACK LONDON

Author of "The Call of the Wild," "The God of his Fathers," etc.

IN the opening chapters of "The Sea-Wolf," the narrator of the tale, Humphrey Van Weyden, a literary critic and man of leisure, in crossing San Francisco Bay in a ferry-boat, is wrecked in the fog. He is carried out to sea, and picked up by the sealing-schooner *Ghost*, outward bound. The captain, "Wolf" Larsen, refuses to put him ashore or to permit him to be taken off by a pilot-boat, and, being short-handed by the death of his mate, forces upon Van Weyden the duties of cabin-boy.—EDITOR.

IV

WHAT happened to me next on the sealing-schooner *Ghost*, as I strove to fit into my new environment, are matters of humiliation and pain. The cook, who was called "the doctor" by the crew, "Tommy" by the hunters, and "Cooky" by Wolf Larsen, was a changed personage. The difference worked in my status brought about a corresponding difference in treatment from him. Servile and fawning as he had been before, he was now as domineering and bellicose.

He absurdly insisted upon my addressing him as Mr. Mugridge, and his behavior and carriage were insufferable as he showed me my duties. Besides my work in the cabin, with its four small state-rooms, I was supposed to be his assistant in the galley, and my colossal ignorance concerning such things as peeling potatoes or washing greasy pots was a source of unending and sarcastic wonder to him. This was part of the attitude he chose to adopt toward me; and I confess, before the day was done, that I hated him with more lively feelings than I had ever hated any one in my life before.

This first day was made more difficult for me from the fact that the *Ghost*, under close reefs (terms such as these I did not learn till later), was plunging through what Mr. Mugridge called an "'owlin' sou'-easter." At half-past five, under his directions, I set the table in the cabin, with rough-weather trays in place, and then carried the tea and cooked food down from the galley.

"Look sharp or you 'll get doused," was Mr. Mugridge's parting injunction as I left the galley with a big tea-pot in one hand and in the hollow of the other arm several loaves of fresh-baked bread. One of the hunters, a tall, loose-jointed chap named Henderson, was going aft at the time from the steerage (the name the hunters facetiously gave their amidships sleeping-quarters) to the cabin. Wolf Larsen was on the poop, smoking his everlasting cigar.

"'Ere she comes! Sling yer 'ook!" the cook cried.

I stopped, for I did not know what was coming, and saw the galley door slide shut with a bang. Then I saw Henderson leaping like a madman for the main rigging, up which he shot, on the inside, till he was many feet higher than my head. Also, I saw a great wave, curling and foaming, poised far above the rail. I was directly under it. My mind did not work quickly, everything was so new and strange. I grasped that I was in danger, but that was all. I stood still, in trepidation. Then Wolf Larsen shouted from the poop:

"Grab hold something, you—you Hump!"

But it was too late. I sprang toward the rigging, to which I might have clung, and was met by the descending wall of water. What happened after that was very confusing. I was beneath the water, suffocating and drowning. My feet were out from under me, and I was turning over and over and being swept along I knew not where. Several times I collided against hard objects, once striking my right knee a terrible blow. Then the flood seemed suddenly to subside, and I was breathing the good air again. I had been swept against the galley and around the steerage companionway from the weather side into the lee scuppers. The pain from my hurt knee was agonizing. I could not put my weight on it, or at least I thought I could not put my weight on it; and I felt sure the leg was broken. But the cook was after me, shouting through the lee galley door:

"'Ere, you! Don't tyke all night about it! Where 's the pot? Lost overboard? Serve you bloody well right if yer neck was broke!"

I managed to struggle to my feet. The great tea-pot was still in my hand. I limped to the galley and handed it to him. But he was consuming with indignation, real or feigned.

"Gawd blime me if you ayn't a slob. Wot 're you good for, anyw'y, I 'd like to know. Eh? Wot 're you good for, anyw'y? Cawn't even carry a bit of tea aft without losin' it. Now I 'll 'ave to boil some more.

"An' wot 're you snifflin' about?" he burst out at me with renewed rage. "'Cos you 've 'urt yer pore little leg, pore little mama's darlin'!"

I was not sniffling, though my face might well have been drawn and twitching from the pain. But I called up all my resolution, set my teeth, and hobbled back and forth from galley to cabin, and cabin to galley, without further mishap. Two things I had acquired by my accident: an injured kneecap that went undressed and from which I suffered for weary months, and the name of "Hump," which Wolf Larsen had called me from the poop. Thereafter, fore and aft, I was known by no other name, until the term became a part of my thought processes and I identified it with myself, thought of myself as Hump, as though Hump were I and had always been I.

It was no easy task waiting on the cabin table, where sat Wolf Larsen, Johansen, and the six hunters. The cabin was small, to begin with, and to move around, as I was compelled to, was not made easier by the schooner's violent pitching and wallowing. But what struck me most forcibly was the total lack of sympathy on the part of the men whom I served. I could feel my knee through my clothes swelling up to the size of an apple, and I was sick and faint from the pain of it. I could catch glimpses of my face, white and ghastly, distorted with pain, in the cabin mirror. All the men must have seen my condition, but not one spoke or took notice of me, till I was almost grateful to Wolf Larsen later on (I was washing the dishes) when he said:

"Don't let a little thing like that bother you. You 'll get used to such things in time. It may cripple you some, but, all the same, you 'll be learning to walk. That 's what you call a paradox, is n't it?" he added.

He seemed pleased when I nodded my head with the customary "Yes, sir."

"I suppose you know a bit about literary things? Eh? Good. I 'll have some talks with you sometime."

And then, taking no further account of me, he turned his back and went up on deck.

That night, when I had finished an endless amount of work, I was sent to sleep in the steerage, where I made up a spare bunk. I was glad to get out of the detestable presence of the cook and to be off my feet. To my surprise, my clothes had dried on me, and there seemed no indications of catching cold either from the last soaking or from the prolonged soaking after the foundering of the *Martinez*. Under ordinary circumstances, after all that I had undergone I should have been a fit subject for a funeral.

But my knee was bothering me terribly. As well as I could make out, the kneecap seemed turned up on edge in the midst of the swelling. As I sat in my bunk examining it (the six hunters were all in the steerage, smoking, and talking in loud voices), Henderson took a passing glance at it.

"Looks nasty," he commented. "Tie a rag around it, and it 'll be all right."

That was all. And on the land I should have been lying on the broad of my back, with a surgeon attending me, and with strict injunctions to do nothing but rest. But I must do these men justice. Callous as they were to my suffering, they were equally callous to their own when anything befell them. And this was due, I believe, first to habit and second to the fact that they were less sensitively organized. I really believe that a finely organized, high-strung man would suffer twice or thrice as much as they from a like injury.

Tired as I was, exhausted in fact, I was prevented from sleeping by the pain in my knee. It was all I could do to keep from groaning aloud. At home I should undoubtedly have given vent to my anguish, but this new and elemental environment seemed to call for a savage repression. Like the savage, the attitude of these men was stoical in great things, childish in little things. I remember, later in the voyage, seeing Kerfoot, another of the hunters, lose a finger by having it smashed to a jelly; and he did not even murmur or change the expression on his face. Yet I have seen the same man, time and again, fly into the most outrageous passion over a trifle.

He was doing it now, vociferating, bellowing, waving his arms, and cursing like a fiend, and all because of a disagreement with another hunter as to whether a seal-pup knew instinctively how to swim. He held that it did; that it could swim the moment it was born. The other hunter, Latimer, a lean, Yankee-looking fellow, with shrewd, narrow-slitted eyes, held otherwise; held that the seal-pup was born on the land for no other reason than that it could not swim; that its mother was compelled to teach it to swim, as birds were compelled to teach their nestlings how to fly.

For the most part, the remaining four hunters leaned on the table or lay in their bunks and left the discussion to the two antagonists. But they were supremely interested, for every little while they ardently took sides, and sometimes all were talking at once, till their voices surged back and forth in waves of sound like mimic thunder-rolls in the confined space. Childish and immaterial as the topic was, the quality of their reasoning was still more childish and immaterial. In truth, there was very little reasoning or none at all. Their method was one of assertion, assumption, and denunciation. They proved that a seal-pup could swim or not swim at birth by stating the proposition very bellicosely and then following it up with an attack on the opposing man's judgment, common sense, nationality, or past history. Rebuttal was similar in all respects. I have related this in order to show the mental caliber of the men with whom I was thrown in contact. Intellectually they were children, inhabiting the physical bodies of men.

And they smoked, incessantly smoked, using a coarse, cheap, and offensive-smelling tobacco. The air was thick and murky with the smoke of it; and this, combined with the violent movement of the ship as she struggled through the storm, would surely have made me seasick had I been a victim to that malady. As it was, it made me quite squeamish, though this nausea might have been due to the pain of my leg and my exhaustion.

As I lay there thinking, I naturally dwelt upon myself and my situation. It was unparalleled, undreamed-of, that I, Humphrey Van Weyden, a scholar and a dilettante, if you please, in things artistic and literary, should be lying here on a Bering Sea seal-hunting schooner. Cabin-boy! I had never done any hard manual labor, or scullion labor, in my life. I had lived a placid, uneventful, sedentary existence all my days—the life of a scholar and a recluse on an assured and comfortable income. Violent life and athletic sports had never appealed to me. I had always been a bookworm; so my sisters and father had called me during my childhood. I had gone camping but once in my life, and then I left the party almost at its start and returned to the comforts and conveniences of a roof. And here I was, with dreary and endless vistas before me of table-setting, potato-peeling, and dish-washing. And I was not strong. The doctors had always said that I had a remarkable constitution, but I had never developed it or my body through exercise. My muscles were small and soft, like a woman's, or so the doctors had said time and again in the course of their attempts to persuade me to go in for physical-culture fads. But I had preferred to use my head rather than my body; and here I was, in no fit condition for the rough life in prospect.

These are merely a few of the things that went through my mind, and are related for the sake of vindicating in advance the weak and helpless rôle I was destined to play. But I thought also of my mother and sisters, and pictured their grief. I was among the missing dead of the *Martinez* disaster, an unrecovered body. I could see the head-lines in the papers, the fellows at the University Club and the Bibelot shaking their heads and saying, "Poor chap!" And I could see Charley Furuseth, as I had said good-by to him that morning, lounging in a dressing-gown on the be-pillowed window-couch and delivering himself of oracular and pessimistic epigrams.

And all the while, rolling, plunging, climbing the moving mountains and falling and wallowing in the foaming valleys, the schooner *Ghost* was fighting her way farther and farther into the heart of the Pacific—and I was on her. I could hear the wind above. It came to my ears as a muffled roar. Now and again feet stamped overhead. An endless creaking was going on all about me, the woodwork and the fittings groaning and squeaking and complaining in a thousand keys. The hunters were still arguing and roaring like some semi-human, amphibious breed. The air was filled with oaths and indecent expressions. I could see their faces, flushed and angry, the brutality distorted and emphasized by the sickly yellow of the sea-lamps, which rocked back and forth with the ship. Through the dim smoke-haze the bunks looked like the sleeping-dens of animals in a menagerie. Oilskins and sea-boots were hanging from the walls, and here and there rifles and shot-guns rested securely in the racks. It was a sea-fitting for the bucaneers and pirates of bygone years. My imagination ran riot, and still I could not sleep. And it was a long, long night, weary and dreary and long.

V

BUT my first night in the hunters' steerage was also my last. Next day Johansen, the new mate, was routed from the cabin by Wolf Larsen and sent into the steerage to sleep thereafter, while I took possession of the tiny cabin state-room, which, on the first day of the voyage, had already had two occupants. The reason for this change was quickly learned by the hunters and became the cause of a deal of grumbling on their part. It seemed that Johansen, in his sleep, lived over each night the events of the day. His incessant talking and shouting and bellowing of orders had been too much for Wolf Larsen, who accordingly foisted the nuisance upon his hunters.

After a sleepless night, I arose, weak and in agony, to hobble through my second day on the *Ghost*. Thomas Mugridge routed me out at half-past five, much in the fashion that Bill Sykes must have routed out his dog. But Mr. Mugridge's brutality to me was paid back in kind and with interest. The unnecessary noise he made (I had lain wide-eyed the whole night) must have awakened one of the hunters; for a heavy shoe whizzed through the semi-darkness, and Mr. Mugridge, with a sharp howl of pain, humbly begged everybody's pardon. Later on, in the galley, I noticed that his ear was bruised and swollen. It never went entirely back to its normal shape, and was called a "cauliflower ear" by the sailors.

The day was filled with miserable variety. I had taken my dried clothes down from the galley the night before, and the first thing I did was to exchange the cook's garments for them. I looked for my purse. In addition to some small change (and I have a good memory for such things), it had contained one hundred and eighty-five dollars in gold and paper. The purse I found, but its contents, with the exception of the small silver, had been abstracted. I spoke to the cook about it, when I went on deck to take up my duties in the galley; and though I had looked forward to a surly answer, I had not expected the belligerent harangue that I received.

"Look 'ere, 'Ump," he began, a malicious light in his eyes and a snarl in his throat, "d' ye want yer nose punched? If yer think I 'm a thief, just keep it to yerself, or you 'll find 'ow bloody well mistyken you are. Strike me blind if this ayn't gratitude for yer! 'Ere yer come, a pore mis'rable specimen of 'uman scum, an' I tykes yer into my galley an' treats yer 'andsome, an' this is wot I get for it. Nex' time yer can go to 'ell, say I, an' I 've a good mind to give yer what-for, anyw'y."

So saying, he put up his fists and started for me. To my eternal shame be it, I cowered away from the blow and ran out the galley door. What else was I to do? Force, nothing but force, obtained on this brute-ship. Moral suasion was a thing unknown. Picture it to yourself: a man of ordinary stature, slender of build and with weak, undeveloped muscles, who has lived a peaceful, placid life, and is unused to violence of any sort—what could such a man possibly do? There was no more reason that I should stand and face these human beasts than that I should stand and face an infuriated bull.

So I thought it out at the time, feeling the need for vindication, and desiring to be at peace with my conscience. But this vindication did not satisfy. Nor to this day can I permit my manhood to look back upon those events and feel entirely exonerated. The situation was something that really exceeded rational formulas for conduct, and demanded more than the cold conclusions of reason. When viewed in the light of formal logic, there is not one thing of which to be ashamed, but, nevertheless, a shame rises within me at the recollection, and in the pride of my manhood I feel that my manhood has in unaccountable ways been smirched and sullied.

All of which is neither here nor there. The speed with which I ran from the galley caused excruciating pain in my knee, and I sank down helplessly at the break of the poop. But the Cockney had not pursued me.

"Look at 'im run! Look at 'im run!" I could hear him crying. "An' with a gyme leg at that! Come on back, you pore little mama's darlin'! I won't 'it yer; no, I won't."

I came back and went on with my work, and here the episode ended for the time, though further developments were yet to take place. I set the breakfast-table in the cabin, and at seven o'clock waited on the hunters and officers. The storm had evidently broken during the night, though a huge sea was still running and a stiff wind blowing. Sail had been made in the early watches, so that the *Ghost* was racing along under everything except the two topsails and the flying jib. These three sails, I gathered from the conversation, were to be set immediately after breakfast. I learned, also, that Wolf Larsen was anxious to make the most of the storm, which was driving him to the southwest, into that portion of the sea where he expected to pick up with the northeast trades. It was before this steady wind that he hoped to make the major portion of the run to Japan, curving south into the tropics and north again as he approached the coast of Asia.

After breakfast I had another unenviable experience. When I had finished washing the dishes, I cleaned the cabin stove and carried the ashes up on deck to empty them. Wolf Larsen and Henderson were standing near the wheel, deep in conversation. The sailor Johnson was steering. As I started toward the weather side, I saw him make a sudden motion with his head, which I mistook for a token of recognition and good morning. In reality he was attempting to warn me to throw my ashes over the lee side. Unconscious of my blunder, I passed by Wolf Larsen and the hunter, and flung the ashes over the side to windward. The wind drove them back, and not only over me, but over Henderson and Wolf Larsen. The next instant the latter kicked me violently, as a cur is kicked. I had not realized there could be so much pain in a kick. I reeled away from him and leaned against the cabin in a half-fainting condition. Everything was swimming before my eyes, and I turned sick. The nausea overpowered me, and I managed to crawl to the side in time to save the deck. But Wolf Larsen did not follow me up. Brushing the ashes from his clothes, he had resumed his conversation with Henderson. Johansen, who had seen the affair from the break of the poop, sent a couple of sailors aft to clean up the mess.

Later in the morning I received a surprise of a totally different sort. Following the cook's instructions, I had gone into Wolf Larsen's state-room to put it to rights and make the bed. Against the wall, near the head of the bunk, was a rack filled with books. I glanced over them, noting with astonishment such names as Shakspere, Tennyson, Poe, and De Quincey. There were scientific works, too, among which were represented men such as Tyndall, Proctor, and Darwin, and I remarked Bulfinch's "Age of Fable," Shaw's "History of English and American Literature," and Johnson's "Natural History" in two large volumes. Then there were a number of grammars, such as Metcalf and Reed & Kellogg; and I smiled as I saw a copy of "The Dean's English."

I could not reconcile these books with the man from what I had seen of him, and I wondered if he could possibly read them. But when I came to make the bed, I found, between the blankets, dropped apparently as he had sunk off to sleep, a complete

Browning. It was open at "In a Balcony," and I noticed here and there passages underlined in pencil. Further, letting drop the volume during a lurch of the ship, a sheet of paper fell out. It was scrawled over with geometrical diagrams and calculations of some sort.

It was patent that this terrible man was no ignorant clod, such as one would inevitably suppose him to be from his exhibitions of brutality. At once he became an enigma. One side or the other of his nature was perfectly comprehensible, but both sides together were bewildering. I had already remarked that his language was excellent, marred with an occasional slight inaccuracy. Of course, in common speech with the sailors and hunters, it sometimes fairly bristled with errors, which was due to the vernacular itself; but in the few words he had held with me it had been clear and correct.

This glimpse I had caught of his other side must have emboldened me, for I resolved to speak to him about the money I had lost.

"I have been robbed," I said to him a little later, when I found him pacing up and down the poop alone.

"Sir," he corrected, not harshly, but sternly.

"I have been robbed, sir," I amended.

"How did it happen?" he asked.

Then I told him the whole circumstance: how my clothes had been left to dry in the galley, and how, later, I was nearly beaten by the cook when I mentioned the matter.

He smiled at my recital.

"Pickings," he concluded; "Cooky's pickings. And don't you think your miserable life worth the price? Besides, consider it a lesson. You 'll learn in time how to take care of your money for yourself. I suppose, up to now, your lawyer has done it for you, or your business agent."

I could feel the quiet sneer through his words, but demanded, "How can I get it back again?"

"That 's your lookout. You have n't any lawyer or business agent now, so you 'll have to depend on yourself. When you get a dollar, hang on to it. A man who leaves his money lying around the way you did deserves to lose it. Besides, you have sinned. You have no right to put temptation in the way of your fellow-creatures. You tempted Cooky, and he fell. You have placed his immortal soul in jeopardy. By the way, do you believe in the immortal soul?"

His lids lifted lazily as he asked the question, and it seemed that the deeps were opening to me and that I was gazing into his soul. But it was an illusion. Far as it might have seemed, no man has ever seen very far into Wolf Larsen's soul, or seen it at all; of this I am convinced. It was a very lonely soul, I was to learn, that never unmasked, though at rare moments it played at doing so.

"I read immortality in your eyes," I answered, dropping the "sir"—an experiment, for I thought the intimacy of the conversation warranted it.

He took no notice. "By that, I take it, you see something that is alive, but that necessarily does not have to live forever."

"I read more than that," I continued boldly.

"Then you read consciousness. You read the consciousness of life that it is alive; but still no further away, no endlessness of life."

How clearly he thought, and how well he expressed what he thought! From regarding me curiously, he turned his head and glanced out over the leaden sea to windward. A bleakness came into his eyes, and the lines of his mouth grew severe and harsh. He was evidently in a pessimistic mood.

"Then, to what end?" he demanded abruptly, turning back to me. "If I am immortal, why?"

I halted. How could I explain my idealism to this man? How could I put into speech a something felt, a something like the strains of music heard in sleep, a something that convinced, yet transcended utterance?

"What do you believe, then?" I countered.

"I believe that life is a mess," he answered promptly. "It is like yeast, a ferment, a thing that moves, and may move for a minute, an hour, a year, or a hundred years, but that in the end will cease to move. The big eat the little that they may continue to move; the strong eat the weak that they may retain their strength. The lucky eat the most and move the longest, that is all. What do you make of those things?"

He swept his arm in an impatient gesture toward a number of the sailors who were working on some kind of rope-stuff amidships.

"They move. So does the jellyfish move. They move in order to eat in order that they may keep moving. There you have it. They live for their belly's sake, and the belly is for their sake. It 's a circle; you get nowhere. Neither do they. In the end they come to a standstill. They move no more. They are dead."

"They have dreams," I interrupted; "radiant, flashing dreams—"

"Of grub," he concluded sententiously.

"And of more—"

"Grub. Of a larger appetite and more luck in satisfying it." His voice sounded harsh. There was no levity in it. "For, look you, they dream of making lucky voyages which will bring them more money, of becoming the masters of ships, of finding fortunes—in short, of being in a better position for preying on their fellows, of having all night in, good grub, and somebody else to do the dirty work. You and I are just like them. There is no difference, except that we have eaten more and better. I am eating them now, and you, too. But in the past you have eaten more than I have. You have slept in soft beds, and worn fine clothes, and eaten good meals. Who made those beds, and those clothes, and those meals? Not you. You never made anything in your own sweat. You live on an income which your father earned. You are like a frigate-bird swooping down upon the boobies and robbing them of the fish they have caught. You are one with a crowd of men who have made what they call a government, who are masters of all the other men, and who eat the food the other men get and would like to eat themselves. You wear the warm clothes. They made the clothes, but they shiver in rags and ask you, or the lawyer or business agent who handles your money, for a job."

"But that is beside the matter," I cried.

"Not at all." He was speaking rapidly now, and his eyes were flashing. "It is piggishness, and it is life. Of what use or sense is an immortality of piggishness? What is the end? What is it all about? You have made no food, yet the food you have eaten or wasted might have saved the lives of a score of wretches who made the food, but did not eat it. What immortal end did you serve? Or did they? Consider yourself and me. What does your boasted immortality amount to when your life runs foul of mine? You would like to go back to the land, which is a favorable place for your kind of piggishness. It is a whim of mine to keep you aboard this ship, where my piggishness flourishes. And keep you I will. I may make or break you. You may die to-day, this week, or next month. I could kill you now, with a blow of my fist, for you are a miserable weakling. But if we are immortal, what is the reason for this? To be piggish as you and I have been all our lives does not seem to be just the thing for immortals to be doing. Again, what 's it all about? Why have I kept you here?"

"Because you are stronger," I managed to blurt out.

"But why stronger?" he went on at once with his perpetual queries. "Because I am a bigger bit of the ferment than you. Don't you see? Don't you see?"

"But the hopelessness of it," I protested.

"I agree with you," he answered. "Then why move at all, since moving is living? Without moving and being part of the yeast there would be no hopelessness. But —and there it is—we want to live and move, though we have no reason to, because it happens that it is the nature of life to live and move, to want to live and move. If it were not for this, life would be dead. It is because of this life that is in you that you dream of your immortality. The life that is in you is alive and wants to go on being alive forever. Bah! An eternity of piggishness!"

He abruptly turned on his heel and started forward. He stopped at the break of the poop and called me to him.

"By the way, how much was it that Cooky got away with?" he asked.

"One hundred and eighty-five dollars, sir," I answered.

He nodded his head. A moment later, as I started down the companion-stairs to lay the table for dinner, I heard him loudly cursing some man amidships.

VI

By the following morning the storm had blown itself quite out, and the *Ghost* was rolling slightly on a calm sea without a breath of wind. Occasional light airs were felt, however, and Wolf Larsen patrolled the poop constantly, his eyes ever searching the sea to the northeast, from which direction the great trade-wind must blow.

The men are all on deck and busy preparing their various boats for the season's hunting. There are seven boats aboard, the captain's dinghy and the six which the hunters will use. Three, a hunter, a boat-puller, and a boat-steerer, compose a boat's crew. On board the schooner the boat-pullers and -steerers are the crew. The hunters, too, are supposed to be in command of the watches, subject always to the orders of Wolf Larsen.

All this, and more, I have learned. The *Ghost* is considered the fastest schooner in both the San Francisco and Victoria fleets. In fact, she was once a private yacht, and was built for speed. Her lines and fittings, though I know nothing about such things, speak for themselves. Johnson was telling me about her in a short chat I had with him during yesterday's second dog-watch. He spoke most enthusiastically, with the love for a fine craft such as some men feel for horses. He is greatly disgusted with the outlook, and I am given to understand that Wolf Larsen bears a very unsavory reputation among the sealing-captains. It was the *Ghost* herself that lured Johnson into signing for the voyage, but he is already beginning to repent.

As he told me, the *Ghost* is an eighty-ton schooner of a remarkably fine model. Her beam, or width, is twenty-three feet, and her length a little over ninety feet. A lead keel of fabulous but unknown weight makes her very stable, while she carries an immense spread of canvas. From the deck to the truck of the maintopmast is something over a hundred feet, while the foremast with its topmast is eight or ten feet shorter. I am giving these details so that the size of this little floating world which holds twenty-two men may be appreciated. It is a very little world, a mote, a speck, and I marvel that men should dare to venture the sea on a contrivance so small and fragile.

Wolf Larsen has also a reputation for reckless carrying on of sail. I overheard Henderson and another of the hunters, Standish, a Californian, talking about it. Two years ago he dismasted the *Ghost* in a gale in Bering Sea, whereupon the present masts were put in, which are stronger and heavier in every way. He is said to have remarked, when he put them in, that he preferred turning her over to losing the sticks.

Every man aboard, with the exception of Johansen, who is rather overcome by his promotion, seems to have an excuse for having sailed on the *Ghost*. Half the men forward are deep-water sailors, and their excuse is that they did not know anything about her or her captain. And those who do know whisper that the hunters, while excellent shots, were so notorious for their quarrelsome and rascally proclivities that they could not sign on any decent schooner.

I have made the acquaintance of another one of the crew. Louis he is called, a rotund and jovial-faced Nova Scotia Irishman, and a very sociable fellow, prone to talk as long as he can find a listener. In the afternoon, while the cook was below asleep and I was peeling the everlasting potatoes, Louis dropped into the galley for a "yarn." His excuse for being aboard was that he was drunk when he signed. He assured me again and again that it was the last thing in the world he would dream of doing in a sober moment. It seems that he has been seal-hunting regularly each season for a dozen years, and is accounted one of the two or three very best boat-steerers in both fleets.

"Ah, my boy,"—he shook his head ominously at me,—"'t is the worst schooner ye could iv selected; nor were ye drunk at the time, as was I. 'T is sealin' is the sailor's paradise—on other ships than this. The mate was the first, but, mark me words, there 'll be more dead men before the trip is done with. Hist, now, between you an' meself an' the stanchion there, this Wolf Larsen is a regular devil, an' the *Ghost* 'll be a hell-ship like she 's always be'n since he had hold iv her. Don't I know? Don't I know? Don't I remember him in Hakodate two years gone, when he had a row an' shot four iv his men? Was n't I a-layin' on the *Emma L.*, not three hundred yards away? An' there was a man the same year he killed with a blow iv his fist. Yes, sir, killed 'im dead-oh. His head must iv smashed like an egg-shell. 'T is the beast he is, this Wolf Larsen—the great big beast mentioned iv in Revelations; an' no good end will he ever come to. But I 've said nothin' to ye, mind ye; I 've whispered never a word; for old fat Louis 'll live the voyage out, if the last mother's son of yez go to the fishes.

"Wolf Larsen!" he snorted a moment later. "Listen to the word, will ye! Wolf—'t is what he is. He 's not black-hearted, like some men. 'T is no heart he has at all. Wolf, just wolf, 't is what he is. D' ye wonder he 's well named?"

"But if he is so well known for what he is," I queried, "how is it that he can get men to ship with him?"

"An' how is it ye can get men to do annything on God's earth an' sea?" Louis demanded with Celtic fire. "How d' ye find me aboard if 't was n't that I was drunk as a pig when I put me name down? There 's them that can't sail with better men, like the hunters, an' them that don't know, like the poor devils of wind-jammers for'ard there. But they 'll come to it, they 'll come to it, an' be sorry the day they was born. I could weep for the poor creatures, did I but forget poor old fat Louis and the troubles before him. But 't is not a whisper I 've dropped; mind ye, not a whisper.

"Them hunters is the wicked boys," he broke forth again, for he suffered from a constitutional plethora of speech. "But wait till they get to cuttin' up iv jinks an' rowin' round. He 's the boy 'll fix 'em. 'T is him that 'll put the fear of God in their rotten black hearts. Look at that hunter iv mine, Horner. 'Jock' Horner they call him, so quiet-like an' easy-goin'; soft-spoken as a girl, till ye 'd think butter would n't melt in the mouth iv him. Did n't he kill his boat-steerer last year? 'T was called a sad accident, but I met the boat-puller in Yokohama, an' the straight iv it was given me. An' there 's Smoke, the black little devil—did n't the Roosians have him for three years in the salt-mines of Siberia for poachin' on Copper Island, which is a Roosian preserve? Shackled he was, hand an' foot, with his mate. An' did n't they have words or a ruction of some kind? For 't was the other fellow Smoke sent up in the buckets to the top of the mine; an' a piece at a time he went up, a leg to-day, an' to-morrow an arm, the next day the head, an' so on."

"But you can't mean it!" I cried out, overcome with the horror of it.

"Mean what?" he demanded, quick as a flash. "'T is nothin' I 've said. Deef I am, an' dumb, as ye should be for the sake iv your mother; an' never once have I opened me lips but to say fine things iv them an' him, God curse his soul! an' may he rot in purgatory ten thousand years, an' then go down to the last an' deepest hell iv all!"

Johnson, the man who had chafed me raw when I first came aboard, seemed the least equivocal of the men for'ard or aft. In fact, there was nothing equivocal about him. One was struck at once by his straightforwardness and manliness, which, in turn, were tempered by a modesty which might be mistaken for timidity. But timid he was not. He seemed rather to have the courage of his convictions, the certitude of his manhood. It was this that made him protest, at the beginning of our acquaintance, against being called Yonson. And upon this and him Louis passed judgment and prophecy.

"'T is a fine chap, that squarehead Johnson we 've for'ard with us," he said. "The best sailorman in the fo'c's'le. He 's my boat-puller. But it 's to trouble he 'll come with Wolf Larsen, as the sparks fly upward. It 's meself that knows. I can see it brewin' an' comin' up like a storm in the sky. I 've talked to him like a brother, but it 's little he sees in takin' in his lights or flyin' false signals. He grumbles out when things don't go to suit him, an' there 'll be always some telltale carryin' word iv it aft to the Wolf. The Wolf is strong, an' it 's the way of a wolf to hate strength, an' strength it is he 'll see in Johnson—no knucklin' under, an' a 'Yes, sir; thank ye kindly, sir,' for a curse or a blow. Oh, she 's a-comin'! She 's a-comin'! An' God knows where I 'll get another boat-puller. What does the fool up an' say, when the Old Man calls him Yonson, but 'Me name is Johnson, sir,' an' then spells it out, letter for letter. Ye should iv seen the Old Man's face! I thought he 'd let drive at him on the spot. He did n't, but he will, an' he 'll break that squarehead's heart, or it 's little I know iv the ways iv men on the ships iv the sea."

Thomas Mugridge is becoming unendurable. I am compelled to mister him and to sir him with every speech. One reason for this is that Wolf Larsen seems to have taken a fancy to him. It is an unprecedented thing, I take it, for a captain to be chummy with the cook, but this is certainly what Wolf Larsen is doing. Two or three times he put his head into the galley and chaffed Mugridge good-naturedly, and once, this afternoon, he stood by the break of the poop and chatted with him for fully fifteen minutes. When it was over, and Mugridge was back in the galley, he became greasily radiant and went about his work humming Coster songs in a nerve-racking and discordant falsetto.

"I always get along with the officers," he remarked to me in a confidential tone. "I know the w'y, I do, to myke myself uppreci-yted. There was my last skipper —w'y, I thought nothin' of droppin' down in the cabin for a little chat an' a friendly glass. 'Mugridge,' says 'e to me, 'Mugridge,' says 'e, 'you 've missed yer vocytion.' 'An' 'ow 's that?' says I. 'Yer should 'a' been born a gentleman, an' never 'ad to work for yer livin'.' God strike me dead, 'Ump, if that ayn't wot 'e says, an' me a-sittin' there in 'is own cabin, jolly-like an' comfortable, a-smokin' 'is cigars an' drinkin' 'is rum."

This chitter-chatter drove me to distraction. I never heard a voice I hated so. His oily, insinuating tones, his greasy smile, and his monstrous self-conceit grated on my nerves till sometimes I was all in a tremble. Positively he was the most disgusting and loathsome person I have ever met. The filth of his cooking was indescribable; and as he cooked everything that was eaten aboard, I was compelled to select with great circumspection what I ate, choosing from the least dirty of his concoctions.

My hands bothered me a great deal, unused as they were to work. The nails were discolored and black, while the skin was already grained with dirt which even a scrubbing-brush could not remove. Then blisters came, in a painful and never-ending procession, and I had a great burn on my forearm, acquired by losing my balance in a roll of the ship and pitching against the galley stove. Nor was my knee any better. The swelling had not gone down, and the cap was still up on edge. Hobbling about on it from morning to night was not helping it any. What I needed was rest, if it were ever to get well.

Rest! I never before knew the meaning of the word. I had been resting all my life and did not know it. But now could I sit still for one half-hour and do nothing, not even think, it would be the most pleasurable thing in the world. But it is a revelation, on the other hand. I shall be able to appreciate the lives of the working-people hereafter. I did not dream that work was so terrible a thing. From half-past five in the morning till ten o'clock at night I am everybody's slave, with not one moment to myself except such as I can steal near the end of the second dog-watch. Let me pause for a minute to look out over the sea sparkling in the sun, or to gaze at a sailor going aloft to the gaff topsails or running out the bowsprit, and I am sure to hear the hateful voice, "'Ere, you, 'Ump! No sodgerin'! I 've got my peepers on yer."

There are signs of rampant bad temper in the steerage, and the gossip is going around that Smoke and Henderson have had a fight. Henderson seems the best of the hunters, a slow-going fellow and hard to rouse; but roused he must have been, for Smoke had a bruised and discolored eye and looked particularly vicious when he came into the cabin for supper.

A cruel thing happened just before supper, indicative of the callousness and brutishness of these men. There is one green hand in the crew, Harrison by name, a clumsy-looking country boy, mastered, I imagine, by the spirit of adventure, and making his first voyage. In the light, baffling airs, the schooner has been tacking about a great deal, at which times the sails pass from one side to the other, and a man is sent aloft to shift over the fore-gaff topsail.

In some way, when Harrison was aloft, the sheet jammed in the block through which it runs at the end of the gaff. As I understood it, there were two ways of getting it cleared—first, by lowering the foresail, which was comparatively easy and without danger; and, second, by climbing out on the peak-halyards to the end of the gaff itself, a very hazardous performance.

Johansen called out to Harrison to go out on the halyards. It was patent to everybody that the boy was afraid. And well he might be, eighty feet above the deck, to trust himself on those thin and jerking ropes. Had there been a steady breeze it would not have been so bad, but the *Ghost* was rolling emptily in a long sea, and with each roll the canvas flapped and boomed and the halyards slacked and jerked taut. They were capable of snapping a man off like a fly from a whip-lash.

Harrison heard the order and understood what was demanded of him, but hesitated. It was probably the first time in his life he had been aloft. Johansen, who had caught the contagion of Wolf Larsen's masterfulness, burst out with a volley of abuse and curses.

"That 'll do, Johansen!" Wolf Larsen said brusquely. "I 'll have you know that I do the swearing on this ship. If I need your assistance, I 'll call you in."

"Yes, sir," the mate acknowledged submissively.

In the meantime Harrison had started out on the halyards. I was looking up from the galley door, and I could see him trembling in every limb as with ague. He proceeded very slowly and cautiously, an inch at a time. Outlined against the clear blue of the sky, he had the appearance of an enormous spider crawling along the tracery of its web.

It was a slightly uphill climb, for the foresail peaked high; and the halyards, running through various blocks on the gaff and mast, gave him separate holds for hands and feet. But the trouble lay in that the wind was not strong enough or steady enough to keep the sail full. When he was half-way out, the *Ghost* took a long roll to windward and back again into the hollow between two seas. Harrison ceased his progress and held on tightly. Eighty feet beneath I could see the agonized strain of his muscles as he gripped for very life.

The sail emptied and the gaff swung amidships. The halyards slackened, and, though it all happened very quickly, I could see them sag beneath the weight of his body. Then the gaff swung to the side with an abrupt swiftness, the great sail boomed like a cannon, and the three rows of reef-points slatted against the canvas like a volley of rifles. Harrison, clinging on, made the giddy rush through the air. This rush ceased abruptly. The halyards became instantly taut. It was the snap of the whip. His clutch was broken. One hand was torn loose from its hold. The other lingered desperately for a moment, and followed. His body pitched out and down, but in some way he managed to save himself with his legs. He was hanging by them, head downward. A quick effort brought his hands up to the halyards again; but he was a long time regaining his former position, where he hung, a pitiable object.

"I 'll bet he has no appetite for supper," I heard Wolf Larsen's voice, which came to me from around the corner of the galley. "Look at his gills."

In truth Harrison was very sick, as a person is seasick; and for a long time he clung to his precarious perch without attempting to move. Johansen, however, continued violently to urge him on to the completion of his task.

"It is a shame," I heard Johnson growling in painfully slow and correct English. He was standing by the main rigging, a few feet away from me. "The boy is willing enough. He will learn if he has a chance. But this is—" He paused a while, for the word "murder" was his final judgment.

"Hist, will ye!" Louis whispered to him. "For the love iv your mother, hold your mouth!"

But Johnson, looking on, still continued his grumbling.

"Look here,"—the hunter Standish spoke to Wolf Larsen,—"that 's my boat-puller, and I don't want to lose him."

"That 's all right, Standish," was the reply. "He 's your boat-puller when you 've got him in the boat, but he 's my sailor when I have him aboard, and I 'll do what I —— well please with him."

"But that 's no reason—" Standish began in a torrent of speech.

"That 'll do; easy as she goes," Wolf Larsen counseled back. "I 've told you what 's what, and let it stop at that. The man 's mine, and I 'll make soup of him and eat it if I want to."

There was an angry gleam in the hunter's eye, but he turned on his heel and entered the steerage companionway, where he remained, looking upward. All hands were on deck now, and all eyes were aloft, where a human life was at grapples with death. The callousness of these men, to whom industrial organization gave control of the lives of other men, was appalling. I, who had lived out of the whirl of the world, had never dreamed that its work was carried on in such fashion. Life had always seemed a peculiarly sacred thing; but here it counted for nothing, was a cipher in the arithmetic of commerce. I must say, however, that the sailors themselves were sympathetic, as instance the case of Johnson; but the masters (the hunters and the captain) were heartlessly indifferent. Even the protest of Standish arose out of the fact that he did not wish to lose his boat-puller. Had it been some other hunter's boat-puller, he, like them, would have been no more than amused.

But to return to Harrison. It took Johansen, insulting and reviling the poor wretch, fully ten minutes to get him started again. A little later he made the end of the gaff, where, astride the spar itself, he had a better chance for holding on. He cleared the sheet, and was free to return, slightly downhill now, along the halyards to the mast. But he had lost his nerve. Unsafe as was his present position, he was loath to forsake it for the more unsafe position on the halyards.

He looked along the airy path he must traverse, and then down to the deck. His eyes were wide and staring, and he was trembling violently. I had never seen fear so strongly stamped upon a human face. Johansen called vainly for him to come down. At any moment he was liable to be snapped off the gaff, but he was helpless with fright. Wolf Larsen, walking up and down with Smoke and in conversation, took no more notice of him, though he cried sharply, once, to the man at the wheel:

"You 're off your course, my man! Be careful, unless you 're looking for trouble."

"Aye, aye, sir," the helmsman responded, putting a couple of spokes down.

He had been guilty of running the *Ghost* several points off her course, in order that what little wind there was should fill the foresail and hold it steady. He had striven to help the unfortunate Harrison at the risk of incurring Wolf Larsen's anger.

The time went by, and the suspense, to me, was terrible. Thomas Mugridge, on the other hand, considered it a laughable affair, and was continually bobbing his head out of the galley door to make jocose remarks. How I hated him! And how my hatred for him grew and grew, during that fearful time, to cyclopean dimensions! For the first time in my life I experienced the desire to murder—"saw red," as some of our picturesque writers phrase it. Life in general might still be sacred, but life in the particular case of Thomas Mugridge had become very profane indeed. I was frightened when I became conscious that I was seeing red, and the thought flashed through my mind: Was I, too, becoming tainted by the brutality of my environment?—I, who even in the most flagrant crimes had denied the justice and righteousness of capital punishment.

Fully half an hour went by, and then I saw Johnson and Louis in some sort of altercation. It ended with Johnson flinging off Louis's detaining arm and starting forward. He crossed the deck, sprang into the fore rigging, and began to climb. But the quick eye of Wolf Larsen caught him.

"Here, you, what are you up to?" he cried.

Johnson's ascent was arrested. He looked his captain in the eyes and replied slowly:

"I am going to get that boy down."

"You 'll get down out of that rigging, and —— lively about it! D' ye hear! Get down!"

Johnson hesitated, but the long years of obedience to the masters of ships overpowered him, and he dropped sullenly to the deck and went on forward.

At half after five I went below to set the cabin table; but I hardly knew what I did, for my eyes and brain were filled with the vision of a man, white-faced and trembling, comically, like a bug, clinging to the thrashing gaff. At six o'clock, when I served supper, going on deck to get the food from the galley, I saw Harrison, still in the same position. The conversation at the table was of other things. Nobody seemed interested in the wantonly imperiled life. But, making an extra trip to the galley a little later, I was gladdened by the sight of Harrison staggering weakly from the rigging to the forecastle scuttle. He had finally summoned the courage to descend.

Before closing this incident, I must give a scrap of conversation I had with Wolf Larsen in the cabin, while I was washing the dishes.

"You were looking squeamish this afternoon," he began. "What was the matter?"

I could see that he knew what had made me possibly as sick as Harrison, that he was trying to draw me, and I answered: "It was because of the brutal treatment of that boy."

He gave a short laugh. "Like seasickness, I suppose. Some men are subject to it, and others are not."

"Not so," I objected.

"Just so," he went on. "The earth is as full of brutality as the sea is full of motion. And some men are made sick by the one, and some by the other. That 's the only reason."

"But you who make a mock of human life, don't you place any value upon it whatever?" I demanded.

"Value? What value?" He looked at me, and though his eyes were steady and motionless, there seemed a cynical smile in them. "What kind of value? How do you measure it? Who values it?"

"I do," I made answer.

"Then what is it worth to you? Another man's life, I mean. Come, now, what is it worth?"

The value of life? How could I put a tangible value upon it? Somehow I, who have always had expression, lacked expression when with Wolf Larsen. I have since determined that a part of it was due to the man's personality, but that the greater part was due to his totally different outlook. Unlike other materialists I had met, and with whom I had something in common to start on, I had nothing in common with him. Perhaps, also, it was the elemental simplicity of his mind that baffled me. He drove so directly to the core of the matter, divesting a question always of all superfluous details, and with such an air of finality, that I seemed to find myself struggling in deep water with no footing under me. Value of life? How could I answer the question on the spur of the moment? The sacredness of life I had accepted as axiomatic. That it was intrinsically valuable was a truism I had never questioned. But when he challenged the truism I was speechless.

"We were talking about this yesterday," he said. "I held that life was a ferment, a yeasty something which devoured life that it might live, and that living was merely successful piggishness. Why, if there is anything in supply and demand, life is the cheapest thing in the world. There is only so much water, so much earth, so much air; but the life that is demanding to be born is limitless. Nature is a spendthrift. Look at the fish and their millions of eggs. For that matter, look at you and me. In our loins are the possibilities of millions of lives. Could we but find time and opportunity and utilize the last bit and every bit of the unborn life that is in us, we could become the fathers of nations and populate continents. Life? Bah! It has no value. Of cheap things it is the cheapest. Everywhere it goes begging. Nature spills it out with a lavish hand. Where there is room for one life, she sows a thousand lives, and it 's life eat life till the strongest and most piggish life is left."

"You have read Darwin," I said. "But you read him misunderstandingly when you conclude that the struggle for existence sanctions your wanton destruction of life."

He shrugged his shoulders. "You know you only mean that in relation to human life, for of the flesh and the fowl and the fish you destroy as much as I or any other man. And human life is in no wise different, though you feel it is and think that you reason why it is. Why should I be parsimonious with this life which is cheap and without value? There are more sailors than there are ships on the sea for them, more workers than there are factories or machines for them. Why, you who live on the land know that you house your poor people in the slums of cities and loose famine and pestilence upon them, and that there still remain more poor people, dying for want of a crust of bread and a bit of meat (which is life destroyed), than you know what to do with. Have you ever seen the London dockers fighting like wild beasts for a chance to work?"

He started for the companion-stairs, but turned his head for a final word. "Do you know, the only value life has is what life puts upon itself; and it is of course overestimated, since it is of necessity prejudiced in its own favor. Take that man I had aloft. He held on as if he were a precious thing, a treasure beyond diamonds or rubies. To you? No. To me? Not at all. To himself, yes. But I do not accept his estimate. He sadly overrates himself. There is plenty more life demanding to be born. Had he fallen and dripped his brains upon the deck like honey from the comb, there would have been no loss to the world. He was worth nothing to the world. The supply is too large. To himself only was he of value, and to show how fictitious even this value was, being dead, he is unconscious that he has lost himself. He alone rated himself beyond diamonds and rubies. Diamonds and rubies are gone, spread out on the deck to be washed away by a bucket of sea-water, and he does not even know that the diamonds and rubies are gone. He does not lose anything, for with the loss of himself he loses the knowledge of loss. Don't you see? And what have you to say?"

"That you are at least consistent," was all I could say, and I went on washing the dishes.

THE SEA-WOLF

BY JACK LONDON

Author of "The Call of the Wild," "The God of his Fathers," etc.

IN the opening chapters of "The Sea-Wolf," the narrator of the tale, Humphrey Van Weyden, a literary critic and man of leisure, in crossing San Francisco Bay in a ferry-boat, is wrecked in the fog. He is carried out to sea, and picked up by the sealing-schooner *Ghost*, outward bound. The captain, "Wolf" Larsen, refuses to put him ashore or to permit him to be taken off by a pilot-boat, and, being short-handed by the death of his mate, forces upon Van Weyden the duties of cabin-boy. Van Weyden is robbed and ill used by the cook, but obtains no redress from the captain, who is a curious compound of brutality and self-culture. The captain varies the monotony of life at sea by acts of cruelty to his men, and at times entertains Van Weyden with his singular views of life.—EDITOR.

VII

AT last, after three days of variable winds, we caught the northeast trades. I came on deck, after a good night's rest in spite of my poor knee, to find the *Ghost* foaming along, wing-and-wing and with every sail drawing except the jibs, with a fresh breeze astern. Oh, the wonder of the great trade-wind! All day we sailed, and all night, and the next day, and the next, day after day, the wind always astern and blowing steadily and strong. The schooner sailed herself. There was no pulling and hauling on sheets and tackles, no shifting of topsails, no work at all for the sailors to do except to steer. At night, when the sun went down, the sheets were slackened; in the morning, when they yielded up the damp of the dew and relaxed, they were pulled tight again—and that was all.

Ten knots, twelve knots, eleven knots, varying from time to time, was the speed we were making; and ever out of the northeast the brave wind blew, driving us on our course two hundred and fifty miles between the dawns. It saddened me and gladdened me, the gait with which we were leaving San Francisco behind and with which we were foaming down upon the tropics. Each day grew perceptibly warmer. In the second dog-watch the sailors came on deck, stripped, and threw buckets of water upon one another from overside. Flying-fish were beginning to be seen, and during the night the watch above scrambled over the deck in pursuit of those that fell aboard. In the morning, Thomas Mugridge being duly bribed, the galley was pleasantly areek with the odor of their frying, while dolphin meat was served fore and aft on such occasions as Johnson caught the blazing beauties from the bowsprit end.

Johnson seemed to spend all his spare time there, or aloft at the cross-trees, watching the *Ghost* cleaving the water under her press of sail. There was passion, adoration, in his eyes, and he went about in a sort of trance, gazing in ecstasy at the swelling sails, the foaming wake, and the heave and the run of her over the liquid mountains that were moving with us in stately procession.

The days and nights were all "a wonder and a wild delight," and though I had little time from my dreary work, I stole odd moments to gaze and gaze at the unending glory of what I never dreamed the world possessed. Above, the sky was stainless blue—blue as the sea itself, which, under the forefoot, was of the color and sheen of azure satin. All around the horizon were pale, fleecy clouds, never changing, never moving, like a silver setting for the flawless turquoise sky.

I do not forget one night, when I should have been asleep, of lying on the forecastle-head and gazing down at the spectral ripple of foam thrust aside by the *Ghost's* forefoot. It sounded like the gurgling of a brook over mossy stones in some quiet dell, and the crooning song of it lured me away and out of myself till I was no longer Hump the cabin-boy, or Van Weyden the man who had dreamed away thirty-five years among books. But a voice behind me, the unmistakable voice of Wolf Larsen, strong with the invincible certitude of the man and mellow with appreciation of the words he was quoting, aroused me.

"O the blazing tropic night, when the wake 's a welt of light
That holds the hot sky tame,
And the steady forefoot snores through the planet-powdered floors
Where the scared whale flukes in flame.

Her plates are scarred by the sun, dear lass,
And her ropes are taut with the dew,
For we 're booming down on the old trail, our own trail, the out trail,
We 're sagging south on the Long Trail—the trail that is always new.

"Eh, Hump? How 's it strike you?" he asked, after the due pause which words and setting demanded.

I looked into his face. It was aglow with light, as the sea itself, and the eyes were flashing in the starshine.

"It strikes me as remarkable, to say the least, that you should show enthusiasm," I answered coldly.

"Why, man, it 's living; it 's life!" he cried.

"Which is a cheap thing and without value." I flung his words at him.

He laughed, and it was the first time I had heard honest mirth in his voice.

"Ah, I cannot get you to understand, cannot drive it into your head, what a thing this life is. Of course life is valueless, except to itself. And I can tell you that my life is pretty valuable just now—to myself. It is beyond price, which you will acknowledge is a terrific overrating, but which I cannot help, for it is the life that is in me that makes the rating."

He appeared waiting for the words with which to express the thought that was in him, and finally went on:

"Do you know, I am filled with a strange uplift; I feel as if all time were echoing through me, as though all powers were mine. I know truth, divine good from evil, right from wrong. My vision is clear and far. I could almost believe in God. But"—and his voice changed, and the light went out of his face—"what is this condition in which I find myself—this joy of living, this exultation of life, this inspiration, I may well call it? It is what comes when there is nothing wrong with one's digestion, when his stomach is in trim, and his appetite has an edge, and all goes well. It is the bribe for living, the champagne of the blood, the effervescence of the ferment, that makes some men think holy thoughts, and other men to see God or to create him when they cannot see him. That is all—the drunkenness of life, the stirring and crawling of the yeast, the babbling of the life that is insane with consciousness that it is alive. And—bah! To-morrow I shall pay for it as the drunkard pays, as the miser clutching for a pot of gold pays on waking to penury. And I shall know that I must die, at sea most likely; cease crawling of myself, to be all acrawl with the corruption of the sea; to be fed upon, to yield up all the strength and movement of my muscles, that they may become strength and movement in fin and scale and the guts of fishes. Bah! And bah! again. The champagne is already flat. The sparkle and bubble have gone out, and it is a tasteless drink."

He left me as suddenly as he had come, springing to the deck with the weight and softness of a tiger. The *Ghost* plowed on her way. I noted that the gurgling forefoot was very like a snore, and as I listened to it the effect of Wolf Larsen's swift rush from sublime exultation to despair slowly left me. Then some deep-water sailor, from the waist of the ship, lifted a rich tenor voice in the "Song of the Trade-wind":

"Oh, I am the wind the seamen love—
I am steady, and strong, and true;
They follow my track by the clouds above,
O'er the fathomless tropic blue."

VIII

SOMETIMES I thought Wolf Larsen mad, or half mad at least, what with his strange moods and vagaries. At other times I took him for a great man, a genius who had never arrived. And, finally, I was convinced that he was the perfect type of the primitive man, born a thousand years or generations too late, and an anachronism in this culminating century of civilization. He was certainly an individualist of the most pronounced type. Not only that, but he was very lonely. There was no congeniality between him and the rest of the men aboard ship; his tremendous virility and mental strength walled him apart. They were more like children to him, even the hunters, and as children he treated them, descending perforce to their level and playing with them as a man plays with puppies. Or else he probed them with the cruel hand of a vivisectionist, groping about in their mental processes and examining their souls as though to see of what this soul-stuff was made.

I had seen him a score of times, at table, insulting this hunter or that with cool and level eyes and, withal, a certain air of interest, pondering their actions or replies or petty rages with a curiosity almost laughable to me who stood onlooker and who understood. Concerning his own rages, I was convinced that they were not real, that they were sometimes experiments, but that in the main they were the habits of a pose or attitude he had seen fit to take toward his fellow-men. I knew, with the possible exception of the incident of the dead mate, that I had not seen him really angry; nor did I wish ever to see him in a genuine rage, when all the force of him would be called into play.

While on the question of vagaries, I shall tell what befell Thomas Mugridge in the cabin, and at the same time complete an incident upon which I have already touched once or twice. The twelve-o'clock dinner was over, one day, and I had just finished putting the cabin in order, when Wolf Larsen and Thomas Mugridge descended the companion-stairs. Though the cook had a cubby-hole of a state-room opening off from the cabin, in the cabin itself he had never dared to linger or to be seen, and he flitted to and fro, once or twice a day, like a timid specter.

"So you know how to play Nap," Wolf Larsen was saying in a pleased sort of voice. "I might have guessed an Englishman would know. I learned it myself in English ships."

Thomas Mugridge was beside himself, a blithering imbecile, so pleased was he at chumming thus with the captain. The little airs he put on, and the painful striving to assume the easy carriage of a man born to a dignified place in life, would have been sickening had they not been ludicrous. He quite ignored my presence, though I credited him with being simply unable to see me. His pale, wishy-washy eyes were swimming like lazy summer seas, though what blissful visions they beheld were beyond my imagination.

"Get the cards, Hump," Wolf Larsen ordered, as they took seats at the table, "and bring out the cigars and the whisky you 'll find in my berth."

I returned with the articles in time to hear the Cockney hinting broadly that there was a mystery about him—that he might be a gentleman's son gone wrong or something or other; also, that he was a remittance-man, and was paid to keep away from England—"p'yed 'an'somely, sir," was the way he put it; "p'yed 'an'somely to sling my 'ook an' keep slingin' it."

I had brought the customary liquor-glasses, but Wolf Larsen frowned, shook his head, and signaled with his hands for me to bring the tumblers. These he filled two thirds full with undiluted whisky,—"a gentleman's drink," quoth Thomas Mugridge,—and they clinked their glasses to the glorious game of Nap, lighted cigars, and fell to shuffling and dealing the cards.

They played for money. They increased the amounts of the bets. They drank whisky, they drank it neat, and I fetched more. I do not know whether Wolf Larsen cheated,—a thing he was thoroughly capable of doing,—but he won steadily. The cook made repeated journeys to his bunk for money. Each time he performed the journey with greater swagger, but he never brought more than a few dollars at a time. He grew maudlin, familiar, could hardly see the cards or sit upright. As a preliminary to another journey to his bunk, he hooked Wolf Larsen's buttonhole with a greasy forefinger and vacuously proclaimed and reiterated: "I got money. I got money, I tell yer, an' I 'm a gentleman's son."

Wolf Larsen was unaffected by the drink, yet he drank glass for glass, and, if anything, his glasses were fuller. There was no change in him. He did not appear even amused at the other's antics.

In the end, with loud protestations that he could lose like a gentleman, the cook's last money was staked on the game and lost. Whereupon he leaned his head on his hands and wept. Wolf Larsen looked curiously at him, as though about to probe and vivisect him, then changed his mind, as from the foregone conclusion that there was nothing there to probe.

"Hump," he said to me, elaborately polite, "kindly take Mr. Mugridge's arm and help him up on deck. He is not feeling very well. And tell Johansen to douse him with a few buckets of salt water," he added in a lower tone, for my ear alone.

I left Mr. Mugridge on deck, in the hands of a couple of grinning sailors who had been told off for the purpose. Mr. Mugridge was sleepily spluttering that he was a gentleman's son. But as I descended the companion-stairs to clear the table I heard him shriek as the first bucket of water struck him.

Wolf Larsen was counting his winnings.

"One hundred and eighty-five dollars, even," he said aloud. "Just as I thought. The beggar came aboard without a cent."

"And what you have won is mine, sir," I said boldly.

He favored me with a quizzical smile. "Hump, I have studied some grammar in my time, and I think your tenses are tangled. 'Was mine,' you should have said, not 'is mine.'"

"It is a question, not of grammar, but of ethics," I answered.

It was possibly a minute before he spoke.

"D' ye know, Hump," he said, with a slow seriousness which had in it an indefinable strain of sadness, "that this is the first time I have heard the word 'ethics' in the mouth of a man. You and I are the only men on this ship who know its meaning."

"At one time in my life," he continued, after another pause, "I dreamed that I might some day talk with men who used such language, that I might lift myself out of the place in life in which I had been born, and hold conversations and mingle with men who talked about just such things as ethics. And this is the first time I have ever heard the word pronounced. Which is all by the way, for you are wrong. It is a question neither of grammar nor ethics, but of fact."

"I understand," I said. "The fact is that you have the money."

His face brightened. He seemed pleased at my perspicacity.

"But it 's avoiding the real question," I continued, "which is one of right."

"Ah," he remarked, with a wry pucker of his mouth, "I see you still believe in such things as right and wrong."

"But don't you—at all?" I demanded.

"Not the least bit. Might is right, and that is all there is to it. Weakness is wrong. Which is a very poor way of saying that it is good for oneself to be strong, and evil for oneself to be weak, or, better yet, it is pleasurable to be strong, because of the profits; painful to be weak, because of the penalties. Just now the possession of this money is a pleasurable thing. It is good for one to possess it. Being able to possess it, I wrong myself and the life that is in me if I give it to you and forgo the pleasure of possessing it."

"But you wrong me by withholding it," I objected.

"Not at all. One man cannot wrong another man. He can only wrong himself. As I see it, I do wrong always when I consider the interests of others. Don't you see? How can two particles of the yeast wrong each other by striving to devour each other? It is their inborn heritage to strive to devour, and to strive not to be devoured. When they depart from this they sin."

"Then you don't believe in altruism?" I asked.

He received the word as though it had a familiar ring, though he pondered it thoughtfully. "Let me see; it means something about coöperation, does n't it?"

"Well, in a way there has come to be a sort of connection," I answered, unsurprised by this time at such gaps in his vocabulary, which, like his knowledge, was the acquirement of a self-read, self-educated man whom no one had directed in his studies, and who had thought much and talked little or not at all. "An altruistic act is an act performed for the welfare of others. It is unselfish, as opposed to an act performed for self, which is selfish."

He nodded his head. "Oh, yes, I remember it now. I ran across it in Spencer."

"Spencer!" I cried. "Have you read him?"

"Not very much," was his confession. "I understood quite a good deal of 'First Principles,' but his 'Biology' took the wind out of my sails, and his 'Psychology' left me butting around in the doldrums for many a day. I honestly could not understand what he was driving at. I put it down to mental deficiency on my part, but since then I have decided that it was for want of preparation. I had no proper basis. Only Spencer and myself know how hard I hammered. But I did get something out of his 'Data of Ethics.' There 's where I ran across 'altruism,' and I remember now how it was used."

I wondered what this man could have got from such a work. Spencer I remembered enough to know that altruism was imperative to his ideal of highest conduct. Wolf Larsen evidently had sifted the great philosopher's teachings, rejecting and selecting according to his needs and desires.

"What else did you run across?" I asked.

His brows drew in slightly with the mental effort of suitably phrasing thoughts which he had never before put into speech. I felt an elation of spirit. I was groping in his soul-stuff, as he made a practice of groping in the soul-stuff of others. I was exploring virgin territory. A strange, a terribly strange region was unrolling itself before my eyes.

"In as few words as possible," he began, "Spencer puts it something like this: First, a man must act for his own benefit—to do this is to be moral and good. Next, he must act for the benefit of his children. And third, he must act for the benefit of his race."

"And the highest, finest right conduct," I interjected, "is that act which benefits at the same time the man, his children, and his race."

"I would n't stand for that," he replied. "Could n't see the necessity for it, nor the common sense. I cut out the race and the children. I would sacrifice nothing for them. It 's just so much slush and sentiment, and you must see it yourself, at least for one who does not believe in eternal life. With immortality before me, altruism would be a paying business proposition. I might elevate my soul to all kinds of altitudes. But with nothing eternal before me but death, given for a brief spell this yeasty crawling and squirming which is called life, why, it would be immoral for me to perform any act that was a sacrifice. Any sacrifice that makes me lose one crawl or squirm is foolish; and not only foolish, for it is a wrong against myself, and a wicked thing. I must not lose one crawl or squirm if I am to get the most out of the ferment. Nor will the eternal movelessness that is coming to me be made easier or harder by the sacrifices or selfishnesses of the time when I was yeasty and acrawl."

"Then you are an individualist, a materialist, and, logically, a hedonist."

"Big words," he smiled. "But what is a hedonist?"

He nodded agreement when I had given the definition.

"And you are also," I continued, "a man one could not trust in the least thing where it was possible for a selfish interest to intervene?"

"Now you 're beginning to understand," he said, brightening.

"You are a man utterly without what the world calls morals?"

"That 's it."

"A man of whom to be always afraid—"

"That 's the way to put it."

"As one is afraid of a snake, or a tiger, or a shark?"

"Now you know me," he said. "And you know me as I am generally known. Other men call me 'Wolf.'"

"You are a sort of monster," I added audaciously, "a Caliban who has pondered Setebos, and who acts as you act, in idle moments, by whim and fancy."

His brow clouded at the allusion. He did not understand, and I quickly learned that he did not know the poem.

"I 'm just reading Browning," he confessed, "and it 's pretty tough. I have n't got very far along, and as it is, I 've about lost my bearings."

Not to be tiresome, I shall say that I fetched the book from his state-room and read "Caliban" aloud. He was delighted. It was a primitive mode of reasoning and of looking at things that he understood thoroughly. He interrupted again and again with comment and criticism. When I finished, he had me read it over a second time, and a third. We fell into discussion —philosophy, science, evolution, religion. He betrayed the inaccuracies of the self-read man, and, it must be granted, the certitude and directness of the primitive mind. The very simplicity of his reasoning was its strength, and his materialism was far more compelling than the subtly complex materialism of Charley Furuseth. Not that I, a confirmed, and, as Furuseth phrased it, a temperamental, idealist, was to be compelled; but that Wolf Larsen stormed the last strongholds of my faith with a vigor that received respect while not accorded conviction.

Time passed. Supper was at hand and the table not laid. I became restless and anxious, and when Thomas Mugridge glared down the companionway, sick and angry of countenance, I prepared to go about my duties. But Wolf Larsen cried out to him:

"Cooky, you 've got to hustle to-night. I 'm busy with Hump, and you 'll do the best you can without him."

And again the unprecedented was established. That night I sat at table with the captain and the hunters, while Thomas Mugridge waited on us and washed the dishes afterward—a whim, a Caliban-mood of Wolf Larsen's, and one I foresaw would bring me trouble. In the meantime we talked and talked, much to the disgust of the hunters, who could not understand a word.

IX

THREE days of rest, three blessed days of rest, are what I had with Wolf Larsen, eating at the cabin table and doing nothing but discuss life, literature, and the universe, the while Thomas Mugridge fumed and raged and did my work as well as his own.

"Watch out for squalls, is all I can say to you," was Louis's warning, given during a spare half-hour on deck while Wolf Larsen was engaged in straightening out a row among the hunters.

"Ye can't tell what 'll be happenin'," Louis went on, in response to my query for more definite information. "The man 's as contrary as air-currents or water-currents. You can never guess the ways iv him. 'T is just as you 're thinkin' you know him an' are makin' a favorable slant along him that he whirls around, dead ahead, an' comes howlin' down upon you an' a-rippin' all iv your fine-weather sails to rags."

So I was not altogether surprised when the squall foretold by Louis smote me. We had been having a heated discussion, —upon life, of course,—and, grown overbold, I was passing stiff strictures upon Wolf Larsen and the life of Wolf Larsen. In fact, I was vivisecting him and turning over his soul-stuff as keenly and thoroughly as it was his custom to do it to others. It may be a weakness of mine that I have an incisive way of speech, but I threw all restraint to the winds and cut and slashed until the whole man of him was snarling. The dark sun-bronze of his face went black with wrath; his eyes became ablaze. There was no clearness or sanity in them—nothing but the terrific rage of a madman. It was the wolf in him that I saw, and a mad wolf at that.

He sprang for me with a half-roar, gripping my arm. I had steeled myself to brazen it out, though I was trembling inwardly; but the enormous strength of the man was too much for my fortitude. He had gripped me by the biceps with his single hand, and when that grip tightened I wilted and shrieked aloud. My feet went out from under me. I simply could not stand upright and endure the agony. The muscles refused their duty. The pain was too great. My biceps was being crushed to a pulp.

He seemed to recover himself, for a lurid gleam came into his eyes, and he relaxed his hold with a short laugh that was more like a growl. I fell to the floor, feeling very faint, while he sat down, lighted a cigar, and watched me as a cat watches a mouse. As I writhed about I could see in his eyes that curiosity I had so often noted, that wonder and perplexity, that questing, that everlasting query of his as to what it was all about.

I finally crawled to my feet and ascended the companion-stairs. Fair weather was over, and there was nothing left but to return to the galley. My left arm was numb, as though paralyzed, and days passed before I could use it, while weeks went by before the last stiffness and pain went out of it. And he had done nothing but put his hand upon my arm and squeeze. There had been no wrenching or jerking.

He had just closed his hand with a steady pressure. What he might have done I did not fully realize till next day, when he put his head into the galley, and, as a sign of renewed friendliness, asked me how my arm was getting on.

"It might have been worse," he smiled.

I was peeling potatoes. He picked one up from the pan. It was fair-sized, firm, and unpeeled. He closed his hand upon it, squeezed, and the potato squirted out between his fingers in mushy streams. The pulpy remnant he dropped back into the pan and turned away, and I had a sharp vision of how it might have fared with me had the monster put his strength upon me.

But the three days' rest was good, in spite of it all, for it had given my knee the very chance it needed. It felt much better, the swelling had materially decreased, and the cap seemed descending into its proper place. Also, the three days' rest brought the trouble I had foreseen. It was plainly Thomas Mugridge's intention to make me pay for those three days. He treated me vilely, cursed me continually, and heaped his own work upon me. He even ventured to raise his fist to me, but I was becoming animal-like myself, and I snarled in his face so terribly that it must have frightened him back. It is no pleasant picture I can conjure up of myself, Humphrey Van Weyden, in that noisome ship's galley, crouched in a corner over my task, my face raised to the face of the creature about to strike me, my lips lifted and snarling like a dog's, my eyes gleaming with fear and helplessness and the courage that comes of fear and helplessness. I do not like the picture. It reminds me too strongly of a rat in a trap. I do not care to think of it; but it was effective, for the threatened blow did not descend.

Thomas Mugridge backed away, glaring as hatefully and viciously as I glared. A pair of beasts is what we were, penned together and showing our teeth. He was a coward, afraid to strike me because I had not quailed sufficiently in advance; so he chose a new way to intimidate me. There was only one galley knife that as a knife amounted to anything. This, through many years of service and wear, had acquired a long, lean blade. It was unusually cruel-looking, and at first I had shuddered every time I used it. The cook borrowed a stone from Johansen and proceeded to sharpen the knife. He did it with great ostentation, glancing significantly at me the while. He whetted it up and down all day long. Every odd moment he could find he had the knife and stone out and was whetting away. The steel acquired a razor-edge. He tried it with the ball of his thumb or across the nail, he shaved hairs from the back of his hand, glanced along the edge with microscopic acuteness, and found, or feigned that he found, always, a slight inequality in its edge somewhere. Then he would put it on the stone again, and whet, whet, whet, till I could have laughed aloud, it was so very ludicrous.

It was also serious, for I learned that he was capable of using it, that under all his cowardice there was a courage of cowardice, like mine, that would impel him to do the very thing his whole nature protested against doing and was afraid of doing. "Cooky 's sharpening his knife for Hump," was being whispered about among the sailors, and some of them twitted him about it. This he took in good part, and was really pleased, nodding his head with direful foreknowledge and mystery, until George Leach, the erstwhile cabin-boy, ventured some rough pleasantry on the subject.

Now it happened that Leach was one of the sailors told off to douse Mugridge after his game of cards with the captain. Leach had evidently done his task with a thoroughness that Mugridge had not forgiven, for words followed, and evil names involving smirched ancestries. Mugridge menaced with the knife he was sharpening for me. Leach laughed and hurled more of his Telegraph Hill billingsgate, and before either he or I knew what had happened, his right forearm had been ripped open from elbow to wrist by a quick slash of the knife. The cook backed away, a fiendish expression on his face, the knife held before him in a position of defense. But Leach took it quite calmly, though his blood was spouting upon the deck as generously as water from a fountain.

"I 'm goin' to get you, Cooky," he said, "and I 'll get you hard. And I won't be in no hurry about it. You 'll be without that knife when I come for you."

So saying, he turned and walked quietly forward. Mugridge's face was livid with fear at what he had done and at what he might expect sooner or later from the man he had stabbed. But his demeanor toward me was more ferocious than ever. In spite of his fear at the reckoning he must expect to pay for what he had done, he could see that it had been an object-lesson to me, and he became more domineering and exultant. Also, there was a lust in him, akin to madness, which had come with sight of the blood he had drawn. He was beginning to see red in whatever direction he looked. The psychology of it is sadly tangled, and yet I could read the workings of his mind as clearly as though it were a printed book.

Several days went by, the *Ghost* still foaming down the trades, and I could swear I saw madness growing in Thomas Mugridge's eyes. And I confess that I became afraid, very much afraid. Whet, whet, whet, it went, all day long. The look in his eyes as he felt the keen edge and glared at me was positively carnivorous. I was afraid to turn my shoulder to him, and when I left the galley I went out backward—to the amusement of the sailors and hunters, who made a point of gathering in groups to witness my exit. The strain was too great. I sometimes thought my mind would give way under it—a meet thing on this ship of madmen and brutes. Every hour, every minute, of my existence was in jeopardy. I was a human soul in distress, and yet no soul, fore or aft, betrayed sufficient sympathy to come to my aid. At times I thought of throwing myself on the mercy of Wolf Larsen; but the vision of the mocking devil in his eyes that questioned life and sneered at it would come strong upon me and compel me to refrain. At other times I seriously contemplated suicide, and the whole force of my hopeful philosophy was required to keep me from going over the side in the darkness of night.

Several times Wolf Larsen tried to inveigle me into discussion, but I gave him short answers and eluded him. Finally, he commanded me to resume my seat at the cabin table for a time and let the cook do my work. Then I spoke frankly, telling him what I was enduring from Thomas Mugridge because of the three days of favoritism which had been shown me. Wolf Larsen regarded me with smiling eyes.

"So you 're afraid, eh?" he sneered.

"Yes," I said defiantly and honestly, "I am afraid."

"That 's the way with you fellows," he cried half angrily; "sentimentalizing about your immortal souls, and afraid to die. At sight of a sharp knife and a cowardly Cockney, the clinging of life to life overcomes all your fond foolishness. Why, my dear fellow, you will live forever. You are a god, and a god cannot be killed. Cooky cannot hurt you. You are sure of your resurrection. What 's there to be afraid of?

"You have eternal life before you. You are a millionaire in immortality, a millionaire whose fortune cannot be lost, whose fortune is less perishable than the stars and as lasting as space or time. It is impossible for you to diminish your principal. Immortality is a thing without beginning or end. Eternity is eternity, and though you die here and now, you will go on living somewhere else and hereafter. And it is all very beautiful, this shaking off of the flesh and soaring of the imprisoned spirit. Cooky cannot hurt you. He can only give you a boost on the path you eternally must tread.

"Or, if you do not wish to be boosted just yet, why not boost Cooky? According to your ideas, he too must be an immortal millionaire. You cannot bankrupt him. His paper will always circulate at par. You cannot diminish the length of his living by killing him, for he is without beginning or end. He 's bound to go on living, somewhere, somehow. Then boost him. Stick a knife in him and let his spirit free. As it is, it 's in a nasty prison, and you 'll do him only a kindness by breaking down the door. And who knows? It may be a very beautiful spirit that will go soaring up into the blue from that ugly carcass. Boost him along, and I 'll promote you to his place, and he 's getting forty-five dollars a month."

It was plain that I could look for no help or mercy from Wolf Larsen. Whatever was to be done I must do for myself; and out of the courage of fear I evolved the plan of fighting Thomas Mugridge with his own weapons. I borrowed a whetstone from Johansen. Louis, the boat-steerer, had already begged me for condensed milk and sugar. The lazaret, where such delicacies were stored, was situated beneath the cabin floor. Watching my chance, I stole five cans of the milk, and that night, when it was Louis's watch on deck, I traded them with him for a dirk, as lean and cruel-looking as Thomas Mugridge's vegetable-knife. It was rusty and dull, but I turned the grindstone while Louis gave it an edge. I slept more soundly than usual that night.

Next morning, after breakfast, Thomas Mugridge began his whet, whet, whet. I glanced warily at him, for I was on my knees taking the ashes from the stove. When I returned from throwing them overside, he was talking to Harrison, whose honest yokel's face was filled with fascination and wonder.

"Yes," Mugridge was saying, "an' wot does 'is worship do but give me two years in Reading. But blimey if I cared. The other mug was fixed plenty. Should 'a' seen 'im. Knife just like this." He shot a glance in my direction to see if I was taking it in, and went on with a gory narrative of his prowess.

A call from the mate interrupted him, and Harrison went aft. Mugridge sat down on the raised threshold to the galley and went on with his knife-sharpening. I put the shovel away and calmly sat down on the coal-box, facing him. He favored me with a vicious stare. Still calmly, though my heart was going pitapat, I pulled out Louis's dirk and began to whet it on the stone. I had looked for almost any sort of explosion on the Cockney's part, but, to my surprise, he did not appear aware of what I was doing. He went on whetting his knife; so did I; and for two hours we sat there, face to face, whet, whet, whet, till the news of it spread abroad, and half the ship's company was crowding the galley doors to see the sight.

Encouragement and advice were freely tendered, and Jock Horner, the quiet, soft-spoken hunter who looked as though he would not harm a mouse, advised me to leave the ribs alone and to thrust upward, at the same time giving what he called the "Spanish twist" to the blade. Leach, his bandaged arm prominently to the fore, begged me to leave a few remnants of the cook for him, and Wolf Larsen paused once or twice at the break of the poop to glance curiously at what must have been to him a stirring and crawling of the yeasty thing he knew as life.

And I make free to say that for the time being life assumed the same sordid values to me. There was nothing pretty about it, nothing divine—only two cowardly moving things that sat whetting steel upon stone, and a group of other moving things, cowardly and otherwise, that looked on. Half of them, I am sure, were anxious to see us shedding each other's blood. It would have been entertainment. And I do not think there was one who would have interfered had we closed in a death-struggle.

On the other hand, the whole thing was laughable and childish. Whet, whet, whet—Humphrey Van Weyden sharpening his knife in a ship's galley and trying its edge with his thumb. Of all situations this was the most inconceivable. I know that my own kind could not have believed it possible. I had not been called "Sissy" Van Weyden all my days without reason, and that "Sissy" Van Weyden should be capable of doing this thing was a revelation to Humphrey Van Weyden, who knew not whether to be exultant or ashamed.

But nothing happened. At the end of two hours Thomas Mugridge put away knife and stone and held out his hand.

"Wot 's the good of mykin' a 'oly show of ourselves for them mugs?" he demanded. "They don't love us, an' bloody well glad they 'd be a-seein' us cuttin' our throats. Yer not 'arf bad, 'Ump. You 've got spunk, as you Yanks s'y, an' I like yer in a w'y. So come on an' shyke."

Coward that I might be, I was less a coward than he. It was a distinct victory I had gained, and I refused to forgo any of it by shaking his detestable hand.

"All right," he said pridelessly; "tyke it or leave it. I 'll like yer none the less for it." And, to save his face, he turned fiercely upon the onlookers. "Get outer my galley door, you bloomin' swabs!"

This command was reinforced by a steaming kettle of water, and at sight of it the sailors scrambled out of the way. This was a sort of victory for Thomas Mugridge and enabled him to accept more gracefully the defeat I had given him, though, of course, he was too discreet to attempt to drive the hunters away.

"I see Cooky's finish," I heard Smoke say to Horner.

"You bet," was the reply. "Hump runs the galley from now on, and Cooky pulls in his horns."

Mugridge heard and shot a swift glance at me, but I gave no sign that the conversation had reached me. I had not thought my victory was so far-reaching and complete, but I resolved to let go nothing I had gained. As the days went by, Smoke's prophecy was verified. The Cockney became more humble and slavish to me than even to Wolf Larsen. I mistered him and sirred him no longer, washed no more greasy pots, and peeled no more potatoes. I did my own work, and my own work only, and when and in what fashion I saw fit. Also, I carried the dirk in a sheath at my hip, sailor-fashion, and maintained toward Thomas Mugridge a constant attitude which was composed of equal parts of domineering, insult, and contempt.

X

MY intimacy with Wolf Larsen increased, if by intimacy may be denoted those relations which exist between master and man, or, better yet, between king and jester. I was to him no more than a toy, and he valued me no more than a child values a toy. My function was to amuse, and so long as I amused all went well; but let him become bored, or let him have one of his black moods come upon him, and at once I was relegated from cabin table to galley, while, at the same time, I was fortunate to escape with my life and a whole body.

The loneliness of the man was slowly being borne in upon me. There was not a man aboard but hated or feared him, nor was there a man whom he did not despise. He seemed consuming with the tremendous power that was in him and that seemed never to have found adequate expression in works. He was as Lucifer would be, were that proud spirit banished to a society of soulless, Tomlinsonian ghosts.

This loneliness was bad enough in itself, but, to make it worse, he was oppressed by the primal melancholy of the race. Knowing him, I reviewed the old Scandinavian myths with clearer understanding. The white-skinned, fair-haired savages who created that terrible pantheon were of the same fiber as he. The frivolity of the laughter-loving Latins was no part of him. When he laughed it was from a humor that was nothing else than ferocious. But he laughed rarely; he was too often sad. And it was a sadness as deep-reaching as the roots of the race. It was the race heritage, the sadness which had made the race sober-minded, clean-lived, and fanatically moral.

In point of fact, the chief vent to this primal melancholy has been religion in its more agonizing forms. But the compensations of such religion were denied Wolf Larsen. His brutal materialism would not permit it. So, when his blue moods came on, nothing remained for him but to be devilish. Had he not been so terrible a man, I could sometimes have felt sorry for him, as, for instance, one morning when I went into his state-room to fill his water-bottle and came unexpectedly upon him. He did not see me. His head was buried in his hands, and his shoulders were heaving convulsively as with sobs. He seemed torn by some mighty grief. As I softly withdrew, I could hear him groaning, "God! God! God!" Not that he was calling upon God; it was a mere expletive, but it came from his soul.

At dinner he asked the hunters for a remedy for headache, and by evening, strong man that he was, he was half blind, and reeling about the cabin.

"I 've never been sick in my life, Hump," he said, as I guided him to his room. "Nor did I ever have a headache except the time my head was healing after having been laid open for six inches by a capstan-bar."

For three days this blinding headache lasted, and he suffered as wild animals suffer, as it seemed the way on ship to suffer, without plaint, without sympathy, utterly alone.

This morning, however, on entering his state-room to make the bed and put things in order, I found him well and hard at work. Table and bunk were littered with designs and calculations. On a large transparent sheet, compass and square in hand, he was copying what appeared to be a scale of some sort or other.

"Hello, Hump!" he greeted me genially. "I 'm just finishing the finishing touches. Want to see it work?"

"But what is it?" I asked.

"A labor-saving device for mariners, navigation reduced to kindergarten simplicity," he answered gaily. "From to-day a child will be able to navigate a ship. No more long-winded calculations. All you need is one star in the sky on a dirty night to know instantly where you are. Look. I place the transparent scale on this star-map, revolving the scale on the North Pole. On the scale I 've worked out the circles of altitude and the lines of bearing. All I do is put it on a star, revolve the scale till it is opposite those figures on the map underneath, and presto, there you are, the ship's precise location!"

There was a ring of triumph in his voice, and his eyes, clear blue this morning as the sea, were sparkling with light.

"You must be well up in mathematics," I said. "Where did you go to school?"

"Never saw the inside of one, worse luck," was the answer. "I had to dig it out for myself.

"And why do you think I have made this thing?" he demanded abruptly. "Dreaming to leave footprints on the sands of time?" He laughed one of his horrible mocking laughs. "Not at all. To get it patented, to make money from it, to revel in piggishness, with all night in while other men do the work. That 's my purpose. Also, I have enjoyed working it out."

"The creative joy," I murmured.

"I guess that 's what it ought to be called. Which is another way of expressing the joy of life in that it is alive, the triumph of movement over matter, of the quick over the dead, the pride of the yeast because it is yeast and crawls."

I threw up my hands with helpless disapproval of his inveterate materialism, and went about making the bed. He continued copying lines and figures upon the transparent scale. It was a task requiring the utmost nicety and precision, and I could not but admire the way he tempered his strength to the fineness and delicacy of the need.

When I had finished the bed, I caught myself looking at him in a fascinated sort of way. He was certainly a handsome man—beautiful in the masculine sense. And again, with never-failing wonder, I remarked the total lack of viciousness, or wickedness, or sinfulness, in his face. It was the face, I am convinced, of a man who did no wrong. And by this I do not wish to be misunderstood. What I mean is that it was the face of a man who either did nothing contrary to the dictates of his conscience, or who had no conscience. I incline to the latter way of accounting for it. He was a magnificent atavism, a man so purely primitive that he was of the type that came into the world before the development of the moral nature. He was not immoral, but merely unmoral.

As I have said, in the masculine sense his was a beautiful face. Smooth-shaven, every line was distinct, and it was cut as clear and sharp as a cameo; while sea and sun had tanned the naturally fair skin to a dark bronze which bespoke struggle and battle, and added to both his savagery and his beauty. The lips were full, yet possessed of the firmness, almost harshness, which is characteristic of thin lips. The set of his mouth, his chin, his jaw, was likewise firm or harsh, with all the fierceness and indomitableness of the male; the nose also. It was the nose of a being born to conquer and command. It just hinted of the eagle beak. It might have been Grecian, it might have been Roman, only it was a shade too massive for the one, a shade too delicate for the other. And while the whole face was the incarnation of fierceness and strength, the primal melancholy from which he suffered seemed to greaten the lines of mouth and eye and brow, seemed to give a largeness and completeness which otherwise the face would have lacked.

And so I caught myself standing idly and studying him. I cannot say how greatly the man had come to interest me. Who was he? What was he? How had he happened to be? All powers seemed his, all potentialities; why, then, was he no more than the obscure master of a seal-hunting schooner, with a reputation for frightful brutality among the men who hunted seals?

My curiosity burst from me in a flood of speech:

"Why is it that you have not done great things in this world? With the power that is yours you might have risen to any height. Unpossessed of conscience or moral instinct, you might have mastered the world, broken it to your hand. And yet here you are, at the top of your life, where diminishing and dying begin, living an obscure and sordid existence hunting sea-animals for the satisfaction of woman's vanity and love of decoration, reveling in a piggishness, to use your own words, which is anything and everything except splendid. Why, with all that wonderful strength, have you not done something? There was nothing to stop you, nothing that could stop you. What was wrong? Did you lack ambition? Did you fall under temptation? What was the matter? What was the matter?"

He had lifted his eyes to me at the beginning of my outburst and followed me complacently until I had done and stood before him breathless and dismayed. He waited a moment, as though seeking where to begin, and then said:

"Hump, do you know the parable of the sower who went forth to sow? If you will remember, some of the seed fell upon stony places, where there was not much earth, and forthwith they sprung up because they had no deepness of earth. And when the sun was up, they were scorched; and because they had no root they withered away. And some fell among thorns, and the thorns sprung up and choked them."

"Well?" I said.

"Well?" he queried half petulantly. "It was not well. I was one of those seeds."

He dropped his head to the scale and resumed the copying. I finished my work, and had opened the door to leave, when he spoke to me.

"Hump, if you will look on the west coast of the map of Norway you will see an indentation called Romsdal Fiord. I was born within a hundred miles of that stretch of water. But I was not born Norwegian. I am a Dane. My father and mother were Danes, and how they ever came to that bleak bight of land on the west coast I do not know. I never heard. Outside of that, there is nothing mysterious. They were poor people and unlettered. They came of generations of poor, unlettered people—peasants of the sea who sowed their sons on the waves as has been their custom since time began. There is no more to tell."

"But there is," I objected. "It is still obscure to me."

"What can I tell you," he demanded, with a recrudescence of fierceness, "of the meagerness of a child's life—of fish diet and coarse living; of going out with the boats from the time I could crawl; of my brothers, who went away one by one to the deep-sea farming and never came back; of myself, unable to read or write, cabin-boy at the mature age of ten on the coastwise, old-country ships; of the rough fare and rougher usage, where kicks and blows were bed and breakfast and took the place of speech, and fear and hatred and pain were my only soul-experiences? I do not care to remember. A madness comes up in my brain even now as I think of it. But there were coastwise skippers I would have sought and killed when a man's strength came to me, only the lines of my life were cast at the time in other places. I did return, not long ago, but unfortunately the skippers were dead, all but one, a mate in the old days, a skipper when I met him, and when I left him, a cripple who would never walk again."

"But you who read Spencer and Darwin and have never seen the inside of a school, how did you learn to read and write?" I queried.

"In the English merchant service. Cabin-boy at twelve, ship's boy at fourteen, ordinary seaman at sixteen, able seaman at seventeen and cock of the fo'c's'le; infinite ambition and infinite loneliness, receiving neither help nor sympathy, I did it all for myself—navigation, mathematics, science, literature, and what not. And of what use has it been? Master and owner of a ship at the top of my life, as you say, when I am beginning to diminish and die. Paltry, is n't it? And when the sun was up I was scorched, and because I had no root I withered away."

"But history tells of slaves who rose to the purple," I chided.

"And history tells of opportunities that came to the slaves who rose to the purple," he answered grimly. "No man makes opportunity. All the great men ever did was to know it when it came to them. The Corsican knew. I have dreamed as greatly as the Corsican. I should have known the opportunity, but it never came. The thorns sprung up and choked me. And, Hump, I can tell you that you know more about me than any living man except my own brother."

"And what is he? And where is he?"

"Master of the steamship *Macedonia*, seal-hunter," was the answer. "We will meet him most probably on the Japan coast. Men call him 'Death' Larsen."

"Death Larsen!" I involuntarily cried. "Is he like you?"

"Hardly. He is a lump of an animal without any head. He has all my—my—"

"Brutishness," I suggested.

"Yes, thank you for the word—all my brutishness; but he can scarcely read or write."

"And he has never philosophized on life," I added.

"No," Wolf Larsen answered, with an indescribable air of sadness. "And he is all the happier for leaving life alone. He is too busy living it to think about it. My mistake was in ever opening the books."

XI

THE *Ghost* has attained the southernmost point of the arc she is describing across the Pacific, and is already beginning to edge away to the west and north toward some lone island, it is rumored, where she will fill her water-casks before proceeding to the season's hunt along the coast of Japan. The hunters have experimented and practised with their rifles and shot-guns till they are satisfied, and the boat-pullers and steerers have made their sprit-sails, bound the oars and rowlocks in leather and sennit so that they will make no noise when creeping on the seals, and put their boats in apple-pie order, to use Leach's homely phrase.

His arm, by the way, has healed nicely, though the scar will remain all his life. Thomas Mugridge lives in mortal fear of him, and is afraid to venture on deck after dark. There are two or three standing quarrels in the forecastle. Louis tells me that the gossip of the sailors finds its way aft, and that two of the telltales have been badly beaten by their mates. He shakes his head dubiously over the outlook for the man Johnson, who is boat-puller in the same boat with him. Johnson has been guilty of speaking his mind too freely, and has collided two or three times with Wolf Larsen over the pronunciation of his name. Johansen he thrashed on the amidships deck the other night, since which time the mate has called him by his proper name. But of course it is out of the question that Johnson should thrash Wolf Larsen.

Louis has also given me additional information about Death Larsen, which tallies with the captain's brief description. We may expect to meet Death Larsen on the Japan coast. "And look out for squalls," is Louis's prophecy, "for they hate one another like the wolf-whelps they are." Death Larsen is in command of the only sealing-steamer in the fleet, which carries fourteen boats, where the schooners carry only six. There is wild talk of cannon aboard, and of strange raids and expeditions she may make, ranging from opium-smuggling into the States and arms-smuggling into China, to blackbirding and open piracy. Yet I cannot but believe Louis, for I have never yet caught him in a lie, while he has a cyclopedic knowledge of sealing and the men of the sealing-fleets.

As it is forward and in the galley, so it is in the steerage and aft, on this veritable hell-ship. Men fight and struggle ferociously for one another's lives. The hunters are looking for a shooting scrape at any moment between Smoke and Henderson, whose old quarrel has not healed, while Wolf Larsen says positively that he will kill the survivor of the affair if such affair comes off. He frankly states that the position he takes is based on no moral grounds, that all the hunters could kill and eat one another, so far as he is concerned, were it not that he needs them alive for the hunting. If they will only hold their hands until the season is over, he promises them a royal carnival, when all grudges can be settled and the survivors may toss the non-survivors overboard and arrange a story as to how the missing men were lost at sea. I think even the hunters are appalled at his cold-bloodedness. Wicked men though they be, they are certainly very much afraid of him.

Thomas Mugridge is cur-like in his subjection to me, while I go about in secret dread of him. His is the courage of fear, a strange thing I know well of myself, and at any moment it may master the fear and impel him to the taking of my life. My knee is much better, though it often aches for long periods, and the stiffness is gradually leaving the arm which Wolf Larsen squeezed. Otherwise I am in splendid condition, feel that I am in splendid condition. My muscles are growing harder and increasing in size. My hands, however, are a spectacle for grief. Also, I am suffering from boils, due to the diet most likely, for I was never so afflicted before.

I was amused, a couple of evenings back, by seeing Wolf Larsen reading the Bible, a copy of which, after the futile search for one at the beginning of the voyage, had been found in the dead mate's sea-chest. I wondered what Wolf Larsen could get from it, and he read aloud to me from Ecclesiastes. I could imagine he was speaking the thoughts of his own mind as he read to me, and his voice, reverberating deeply and mournfully in the confined cabin, charmed and held me. He may be uneducated, but he certainly knows how to express the significance of the written word. I can hear him now, as I shall always hear him, the primal melancholy vibrant in his voice, as he read from Ecclesiastes the passage beginning: "I gathered me also silver and gold."

"There you have it, Hump," he said, closing the book upon his finger and looking up at me. "The Preacher who was king over Israel in Jerusalem thought as I think. You call me a pessimist. Is not this pessimism of the blackest?—'all is vanity and vexation of spirit'; 'there is no profit under the sun'; 'there is one event unto all,' to the fool and the wise, the clean and the unclean, the sinner and the saint; and that event is death, and an evil thing, he says. For the Preacher loved life, and did not want to die, saying, 'For a living dog is better than a dead lion.' He preferred the vanity and vexation to the silence and unmovableness of the grave. And so I. To crawl is piggish; but to not crawl, to be as the clod and rock, is loathsome to contemplate. It is loathsome to the life that is in me, the very essence of which is movement, the power of movement, and the consciousness of the power of movement. Life itself is unsatisfaction, but to look ahead to death is greater unsatisfaction."

"You are worse off than Omar," I said. "He, at least, after the customary agonizing of youth, found content and made of his materialism a joyous thing."

"Who was Omar?" Wolf Larsen asked, and I did no more work that day, nor the next, or next.

In his random reading he had never chanced upon the "Rubáiyát," and it was to him like a great find of treasure. Much I remembered, possibly two thirds of the quatrains, and I managed to piece out the remainder without difficulty. We talked for hours over single stanzas, and I found him reading into them a wail of regret and a rebellion which for the life of me I could not discover myself. Possibly I recited with a certain joyous lilt which was my own, for—his memory was good, and at a second rendering, very often the first, he made a quatrain his own—he recited the same lines and invested them with an unrest and passionate revolt that were well-nigh convincing.

I was interested as to which quatrain he would like best, and was not surprised when he hit upon the one born of an instant's irritability and quite at variance with the Persian's complacent philosophy and genial code of life:

"What, without asking, hither hurried *Whence?*
And, without asking, *Whither* hurried hence!
Oh, many a Cup of this forbidden Wine
Must drown the memory of that insolence!"

"Great!" Wolf Larsen cried. "Great! That 's the key-note. Insolence! He could not have used a better word."

In vain I objected and denied. He deluged me, overwhelmed me with argument.

"It 's not the nature of life to be otherwise. Life, when it knows that it must cease living, will always rebel. It cannot help itself. The Preacher found life and the works of life all a vanity and vexation, an evil thing; but death, the ceasing to be able to be vain and vexed, he found an eviler thing. Through chapter after chapter he is worried by the one event that cometh to all alike. So Omar, so I, so you, even you, for you rebelled against dying when Cooky sharpened a knife for you. You were afraid to die; the life that was in you, that composes you, that is greater than you, did not want to die. You have talked of the instinct of immortality. I talk of the instinct of life, which is to live, and which, when death looms near and large, masters the instinct, so called, of immortality. It mastered it in you (you cannot deny it), because a crazy Cockney cook sharpened a knife.

"You are afraid of him now. You are afraid of me. You cannot deny it. If I catch you by the throat thus,"—his hand was about my throat, and my breath was shut off,—"and begin to press the life out of you, thus, and thus, your instinct of immortality will go glimmering, and your instinct of life, which is longing for life, will flutter up, and you will struggle to save yourself. Eh? I see the fear of death in your eyes. You beat the air with your arms. You exert all your puny strength to struggle to live. Your hand is clutching my arm; lightly it feels as a butterfly resting there. Your chest is heaving, your tongue protruding, your skin turning dark, your eyes swimming. 'To live! To live! To live!' you are crying; and you are crying to live here and now, not hereafter. You doubt your im-

Drawn by W. J. Aylward.

"THE COOK BACKED AWAY, . . . THE KNIFE HELD BEFORE HIM IN A POSITION OF DEFENSE"

mortality, eh? Ha! ha! You are not sure of it. You won't chance it. This life only you are certain is real. Ah, it is growing dark and darker. It is the darkness of death, the ceasing to be, the ceasing to feel, the ceasing to move, that is gathering about you, descending upon you, rising around you. Your eyes are becoming set. They are glazing. My voice sounds faint and far. You cannot see my face. And still you struggle in my grip. You kick with your legs. Your body draws itself up in knots like a snake's. Your chest heaves and strains. To live! To live! To live—"

I heard no more. Consciousness was blotted out by the darkness he had so graphically described, and when I came to myself I was lying on the floor, and he was smoking a cigar and regarding me thoughtfully with that old, familiar light of curiosity in his eyes.

"Well, have I convinced you?" he demanded. "Here, take a drink of this. I want to ask you some questions."

I rolled my head negatively on the floor. "Your arguments are too—er—forcible," I managed to articulate, at cost of great pain to my aching throat.

"You 'll be all right in half an hour," he assured me. "And I promise I won't use any more physical demonstrations. Get up now. You can sit on a chair."

And, toy that I was of this monster, the discussion of Omar and the Preacher was resumed. And half the night we sat up over it.

THE SEA-WOLF

BY JACK LONDON

Author of "The Call of the Wild," "The God of his Fathers," etc.

IN the early chapters of "The Sea-Wolf," the narrator of the tale, Humphrey Van Weyden, a literary critic and man of leisure, in crossing San Francisco Bay in a ferry-boat, is wrecked in the fog. He is carried out to sea, and picked up by the sealing-schooner *Ghost*, outward bound. The captain, "Wolf" Larsen, refuses to put him ashore or to permit him to be taken off by a pilot-boat, and, being short-handed by the death of his mate, forces upon Van Weyden the duties of cabin-boy. Van Weyden is robbed and ill used by Mugridge, the cook, but obtains no redress from the captain, who is a curious compound of brutality and self-culture. The captain varies the monotony of life at sea by acts of cruelty to his men, and at times entertains Van Weyden with his singular views of life. Meanwhile he plays cards with his cook, and wins from him the money that has been stolen from Van Weyden. For days he keeps the latter by him, discussing life and literature, but after tormenting him physically, sends him back to the galley, where the cook threatens his life and stabs one of the crew. For three days a blinding headache confines the Sea-Wolf to his room; after it has passed he resumes his discussions with Van Weyden, illustrating his theory of the love of life by choking his companion into insensibility.—EDITOR.

XII

THE last twenty-four hours have witnessed a carnival of brutality. From cabin to forecastle it seems to have broken out like a contagion. I scarcely know where to begin. Wolf Larsen was really the cause of it. The relations among the men, strained and made tense by feuds, quarrels, and grudges, were in a state of unstable equilibrium. Wolf Larsen disturbed the equilibrium, and evil passions flared up like flame in prairie-grass.

Thomas Mugridge was proving himself a sneak, a spy, an informer. He attempted to curry favor and reinstate himself in the good graces of the captain by carrying tales of the men forward. He it was, I know, that carried some of Johnson's hasty talk to Wolf Larsen. Johnson, it seems, had bought a suit of oilskins from the slop-chest and found them to be of greatly inferior quality. Nor was he slow in advertising the fact. The slop-chest is a sort of miniature dry-goods store which is carried by all sealing-schooners and which is stocked with articles peculiar to the needs of the sailors. Whatever a sailor purchases is taken from his subsequent earnings on the sealing-grounds; for, as it is with the hunters, so it is with the boat-pullers and steerers: in the place of wages, they receive a "lay," a rate of so much per skin for every skin captured in their particular boat.

But of Johnson's grumbling at the slop-chest I knew nothing, so that what I witnessed came with the shock of sudden surprise. I had just finished sweeping the cabin, and had been inveigled by Wolf Larsen into a discussion of Hamlet, his favorite Shaksperian character, when Johansen descended the companion-stairs, followed by Johnson. The latter's cap came off, after the custom of the sea, and he stood respectfully in the middle of the cabin, swaying heavily and uneasily to the roll of the schooner, and facing the captain.

Drawn by William J. Aylward.

"THE BOY HURLED HIS IMPRECATIONS RECKLESSLY FULL IN THE FACE OF THE CAPTAIN"

"Shut the doors and draw the slide," Wolf Larsen said to me.

I noticed an anxious light in Johnson's eyes, but mistook it for the native shyness and embarrassment of the man. The mate, Johansen, stood away several feet to the side of him, and fully three yards in front of him sat Wolf Larsen on one of the revolving cabin chairs. An appreciable pause fell after I had closed the doors and drawn the slide—a pause that must have lasted fully a minute. It was broken by Wolf Larsen.

"Yonson," he began.

"My name is Johnson, sir," the sailor boldly corrected.

"Well, Johnson, then, —— you! Can you guess why I have sent for you?"

"Yes, and no, sir," was the slow reply. "My work is done well. The mate knows that, and you know it, sir. So there cannot be any complaint."

"And is that all?" Wolf Larsen queried, his voice soft and low and purring.

"I know you have it in for me," Johnson continued with his unalterable and ponderous slowness. "You do not like me. You—you—"

"Go on," Wolf Larsen prompted. "Don't be afraid of my feelings."

"I am not afraid," the sailor retorted, a slight angry flush rising through his sunburn. "You do not like me because I am too much of a man, that is why, sir."

"You are too much of a man for ship discipline, if that is what you mean, and if you know what I mean," was Wolf Larsen's retort.

"I know English, and I know what you mean, sir," Johnson answered, his flush deepening at the slur on his knowledge of the English language.

"Johnson," Wolf Larsen said, with an air of dismissing all that had gone before as introductory to the main business in hand, "I understand you 're not quite satisfied with those oilskins."

"No, I am not. They are no good, sir."

"And you 've been shooting off your mouth about them."

"I say what I think, sir," the sailor answered courageously, not failing at the same time in ship courtesy, which demanded that "sir" be appended to each speech he made.

It was at this moment that I chanced to glance at Johansen. His big fists were clenching and unclenching, and his face was positively fiendish, so malignantly did he look at Johnson. I noticed a black discoloration, still faintly visible, under Johansen's eye, a mark of the thrashing he had received a few nights before from the sailor. For the first time I began to divine that something terrible was about to be enacted—what, I could not imagine.

"Do you know what happens to men who say what you 've said about my slop-chest and me?" Wolf Larsen was demanding.

"I know, sir," was the answer.

"What?" Wolf Larsen demanded sharply and imperatively.

"What you and the mate there are going to do to me, sir."

At this Larsen sprang from the sitting posture like a wild animal, a tiger, and like a tiger covered the intervening space in an avalanche of fury that Johnson strove vainly to fend off. He threw one arm down to protect the stomach, the other arm up to protect the head; but Wolf Larsen's fist drove midway between, on the chest, with a crushing, resounding impact. Johnson's breath, suddenly expelled, shot from his mouth, and as suddenly checked, with the forced, audible expiration of a man wielding an ax. He almost fell backward, and swayed from side to side in an effort to recover his balance.

Johnson fought bravely enough, but he was no match for Wolf Larsen, much less for Wolf Larsen and the mate. It was frightful. I had not imagined a human being could endure so much and still live and struggle on. And struggle on Johnson did. Of course there was no hope for him, not the slightest, and he knew it as well as I, but by the manhood that was in him he could not cease from fighting for that manhood.

It was too much for me to witness. I felt that I should lose my mind, and I ran up the companion-stairs to open the doors and escape on deck. But Wolf Larsen, leaving his victim for the moment, and with one of his tremendous springs, gained my side, and flung me into the far corner of the cabin.

"The phenomenon of life, Hump," he girded at me. "Stay and watch it. You may gather data on the immortality of the soul. Besides, you know, we can't hurt Johnson's soul. It 's only the fleeting form we may demolish."

It seemed centuries, possibly it was no more than ten minutes, that the beating continued. And when Johnson could no longer rise, they still continued to beat and kick him where he lay.

"Easy, Johansen; easy as she goes," Wolf Larsen finally said.

But the beast in the mate was up and rampant, and Wolf Larsen was compelled to brush him away with a back-handed sweep of the arm, gentle enough, apparently, but which hurled Johansen back like a cork, driving his head against the wall with a crash. He fell to the floor, half stunned for the moment, breathing heavily and blinking his eyes in a stupid sort of way.

"Jerk open the doors, Hump," Larsen commanded.

I obeyed, and the two brutes picked up the senseless man like a sack of rubbish and hove him clear up the companion-stairs, through the narrow doors, and out on deck. Louis, his boat-mate, gave a turn of the wheel and gazed imperturbably into the binnacle.

Not so George Leach, the erstwhile cabin-boy. Fore and aft there was nothing that could have surprised us more than his consequent behavior. He it was that came up on the poop, without orders, and dragged Johnson forward, where he set about dressing his wounds as well as he could and making him comfortable.

I had come up on deck for a breath of fresh air and to try to get some repose for my overwrought nerves. Wolf Larsen was smoking a cigar and examining the patent log which the *Ghost* usually towed astern, but which had been hauled in for some purpose. Suddenly Leach's voice came to my ears. It was tense and hoarse with an overmastering rage. I turned and saw him standing just beneath the break of the poop on the port side of the galley. His face was convulsed and white, his eyes were flashing, his clenched fists raised overhead, as the boy hurled his imprecations recklessly full in the face of the captain, who had sauntered slowly forward to the break of the poop, and leaning his elbow on the corner of the cabin, gazed down thoughtfully and curiously at the excited boy.

Leach went on, indicting Wolf Larsen as he had never been indicted before. The sailors assembled in a fearful group just outside the forecastle scuttle, and watched and listened. The hunters piled pell-mell out of the steerage, but as Leach's tirade continued I saw that there was no levity in their faces. Even they were frightened, not at the boy's terrible words, but at his terrible audacity. It did not seem possible that any living creature could thus beard Wolf Larsen to his teeth. I know for myself that I was shocked into admiration of the boy, and I saw in him the splendid invincibleness of immortality rising above the flesh and the fears of the flesh, as in the prophets of old, to condemn unrighteousness.

And such condemnation! He haled forth Wolf Larsen's soul naked to the scorn of men. He rained upon it curses from God and high heaven, and withered it with a heat of invective that savored of a medieval excommunication of the Catholic Church. He ran the gamut of denunciation, rising to heights of wrath, and from sheer exhaustion sinking to the most indecent abuse.

Everybody looked for Larsen to leap upon the boy and destroy him. But it was not his whim. His cigar went out, and he continued to gaze silently and curiously.

Leach had worked himself into an ecstasy of impotent rage.

"Pig! Pig! Pig!" he was reiterating at the top of his lungs. "Why don't you come down and kill me, you murderer? You can do it. I ain't afraid. There 's no one to stop you! Come on, you coward! Kill me! Kill me! Kill me!"

It was at this stage that Thomas Mugridge's erratic soul brought him into the scene. He had been listening at the galley door, but he now came out, ostensibly to fling some scraps over the side, but obviously to see the killing he was certain would take place. He smirked greasily up into the face of Wolf Larsen, who seemed not to see him. But the Cockney was unabashed, and turned to Leach, saying:

"Such language! Shockin'!"

Leach's rage was no longer impotent. Here at last was something ready to hand, and for the first time since the stabbing the Cockney had appeared outside the galley without his knife. The words had barely left his mouth when he was knocked down by Leach. Three times he struggled to his feet, striving to gain the galley, and each time was knocked down.

"Oh, Lord!" he cried. "'Elp! 'Elp!

Tyke 'im aw'y, carn't yer? Tyke 'im aw'y!"

The hunters laughed from sheer relief. Tragedy had dwindled, the farce had begun. The sailors now crowded boldly aft, grinning and shuffling, to watch the pommeling of the hated Cockney. And even I felt a great joy surge up within me. I confess that I delighted in this beating Leach was giving to Thomas Mugridge, though it was as terrible, almost, as the one Mugridge had caused to be given to Johnson. But the expression of Wolf Larsen's face did not change, nor did his position. For all his pragmatic certitude, it seemed as if he watched the play and movement of life in the hope of discovering something more about it. And no one interfered. Leach could have killed the Cockney, but, having evidently filled the measure of his vengeance, he drew away from his prostrate foe, who was whimpering and wailing in a puppyish sort of way, and walked forward.

But these two affairs were only the opening events of the day's program. In the afternoon Smoke and Henderson fell foul of each other, and a fusillade of shots came up from the steerage, followed by a stampede of the other four hunters for the deck. A column of thick, acrid smoke, the kind always made by black powder, was arising through the open companion-way, and down through it leaped Wolf Larsen. The sound of blows and scuffling came to our ears. Both men were wounded, and he was thrashing them both for having disobeyed his orders and crippled themselves in advance of the hunting season. In fact, they were badly wounded, and, having thrashed them, he proceeded to operate upon them in a rough surgical fashion and to dress their wounds. I served as assistant while he probed and cleansed the passages made by the bullets, and I saw the two men endure his crude surgery without anesthetics and with no more to uphold them than a stiff tumbler of whisky.

Then, in the first dog-watch, trouble came to a head in the forecastle. It took its rise out of the tittle-tattle and tale-bearing that had been the cause of Johnson's beating, and from the noise we heard, and from the sight of the bruised men next day, it was patent that half the forecastle had soundly drubbed the other half.

The second dog-watch and the day wound up with a fight between Johansen and the lean, Yankee-looking hunter, Latimer. It was caused by some remarks of Latimer's concerning the noises made by the mate in his sleep, and though Johansen was whipped, he kept the steerage awake for the rest of the night while he blissfully slumbered and fought the fight over and over again.

XIII

For three days I did my own work and Thomas Mugridge's, too, and I flatter myself that I did his work well. I know that it won Wolf Larsen's approval, while the sailors beamed with satisfaction during the brief time my régime lasted.

"The first clean bite since I come aboard," Harrison said to me at the galley door, as he returned the dinner pots and pans from the forecastle. "Somehow, Tommy's grub always tastes of grease,—stale grease,—and I reckon he ain't changed his shirt since he left 'Frisco."

"I know he has n't," I answered.

"And I 'll bet he sleeps in it," Harrison added.

"And you won't lose," I agreed. "The same shirt, and he has n't had it off once in all this time."

But three days were all Wolf Larsen allowed him in which to recover from the effects of the beating. On the fourth day, lame and sore, scarcely able to see, so closed were his eyes, he was haled from his bunk by the nape of the neck and set to his duty. He sniffled and wept, but Wolf Larsen was pitiless.

"And see that you serve no more slops," was his parting injunction. "No more grease and dirt, mind, and a clean shirt occasionally, or you 'll get a tow over the side. Understand?"

Thomas Mugridge crawled weakly across the galley floor, and a short lurch of the *Ghost* sent him staggering. In attempting to recover himself, he reached for the iron railing which surrounded the stove and kept the pots from sliding off; but he missed the railing, and his hand, with his weight behind it, landed squarely on the hot surface.

"Oh, Gawd, Gawd, wot 'ave I done?" he wailed, sitting down in the coal-box and nursing his new hurt by rocking back and forth. "W'y 'as all this come on me? It mykes me fair sick, it does, an' I try so 'ard to go through life 'armless an' 'urtin' nobody."

The tears were running down his puffed and discolored cheeks, and his face was drawn with pain. A savage expression flitted across it.

"Oh, 'ow I 'ate 'im! 'Ow I 'ate 'im!" he gritted out.

"Whom?" I asked; but the poor wretch was weeping again over his misfortunes. Less difficult it was to guess whom he hated than whom he did not hate; for I had come to see a malignant devil in him which impelled him to hate all the world. I sometimes thought that he hated even himself, so grotesquely had life dealt with him, and so monstrously. At such moments a great sympathy welled up within me, and I felt shame that I had ever joyed in his discomfiture or pain. Life had been unfair to him. It had played him a scurvy trick when it fashioned him into the thing he was, and it had played him scurvy tricks ever since. What chance had he to be anything else than what he was? And as though answering my unspoken thought, he wailed:

"I never 'ad no chance, nor 'arf a chance! 'Oo was there to send me to school, or put tommy in my 'ungry belly w'en I was a kiddy? 'Oo ever did anything for me, heh? 'Oo, I s'y?"

"Never mind, Tommy," I said, placing a soothing hand on his shoulder. "Cheer up. It 'll all come right in the end. You 've long years before you, and you can make anything you please of yourself."

"It 's a lie!" he shouted in my face, flinging off the hand. "It 's a lie, an' you know it. I 'm already myde, an' myde out of leavin's an' scraps. It 's all right for you, 'Ump. You was born a gentleman. You never knew wot it was to go 'ungry, to cry yerself asleep with a gnawin' an' gnawin', like a rat, inside yer. It carn't come right. If I was President of the United Stytes to-morrer, 'ow would it fill my belly for one time w'en I was a kiddy an' it went empty?

"'Ow could it, I s'y? I was born to sufferin' an' sorrer. I 've 'ad more cruel sufferin' than any ten men, I 'ave. I 've been in 'orspital 'arf my bleedin' life. I 've 'ad the fever in Aspinwall, in 'Avana, in New Orleans. I near died of the scurvy, an' was rotten with it six months in Barbados. Smallpox in 'Onolulu, two broken legs in Shanghai, pneumonia in Unalaska, three busted ribs an' my insides all twisted in 'Frisco. An' 'ere I am now. Look at me! Look at me! My ribs kicked loose from my back again. I 'll be coughin' blood before eyght bells. 'Ow can it be myde up to me, I arsk? 'Oo 's goin' to do it? Gawd? 'Ow Gawd must 'ave 'ated me w'en 'e signed me on for a voyage in this bloomin' world of 'is!"

This tirade against destiny went on for an hour or more, and then he buckled to his work, limping and groaning, and in his eyes a great hatred for all created things.

Several days more passed before Johnson crawled on deck and went about his work in a half-hearted way. He was still a sick man, and I more than once observed him creeping painfully aloft to a topsail or drooping wearily as he stood at the wheel. But, still worse, it seemed that his spirit was broken. He was abject before Wolf Larsen, and almost groveled to Johansen. Not so Leach. He went about the deck like a tiger-cub, glaring his hatred openly at Wolf Larsen and Johansen.

"I 'll do for you yet, you slab-footed Swede," I heard him say to Johansen one night on deck.

The mate cursed him in the darkness, and the next moment some missile struck the galley a sharp rap. There was more cursing, and a mocking laugh, and when all was quiet I stole outside and found a heavy knife embedded over an inch in the solid wood. A few minutes later the mate came fumbling about in search of it, but I returned it privily to Leach next day. He grinned when I handed it over, yet it was a grin that contained more sincere thanks than a multitude of the verbosities of speech common to the members of my own class.

Unlike any one else in the ship's company, I now found myself with no quarrels on my hands and in the good graces of all. The hunters possibly no more than tolerated me, though none of them disliked me; while Smoke and Henderson, convalescent under a deck awning and swinging day and night in their hammocks, assured me that I was better than any hospital nurse, and that they would not forget me at the end of the voyage when they were paid off. As though I stood in need of their money—I, who could have bought them out, bag and baggage, and the schooner and its equipment, a hundred times over! But upon me had devolved the task of tending their wounds and pulling them through, and I did my best by them.

Wolf Larsen underwent another bad attack of headache, which lasted two days. He must have suffered severely, for he called me in and obeyed my commands like a sick child. But nothing I could do seemed to relieve him. At my suggestion, however, he gave up smoking and drinking, though why so magnificent an animal as he should have headaches at all puzzled me.

"'T is the hand of God, I 'm tellin' you," was the way Louis saw it. "'T is a visitation for his black-hearted deeds, an' there 's more behind an' comin', or else—"

"Or else," I prompted.

"God is noddin' an' not doin' his duty, though it 's me as should n't say it."

I was mistaken when I said that I was in the good graces of all. Not only did Thomas Mugridge continue to hate me, but he had discovered a new reason for hating me. It took me no little while to puzzle it out, but I finally discovered that it was because I was more luckily born than he—"gentleman born," he put it.

"And still no more dead men," I twitted Louis, when Smoke and Henderson, side by side, in friendly conversation, took their first exercise on deck.

Louis surveyed me with his shrewd gray eyes and shook his head portentously.

"She 's a-comin', I tell you, an' it 'll be sheets an' halyards, stand by all hands, when she begins to howl. I 've had the feel iv it this long time, an' I can feel it now as plainly as I feel the riggin' iv a dark night. She 's close, she 's close."

"Who goes first?" I queried.

"Not old fat Louis, I promise you," he laughed. "For 't is in the bones iv me I know that come this time next year I 'll be gazin' in the old mother's eyes, weary with watchin' iv the sea for the five sons she gave to it."

"Wot 's 'e been s'yin' to yer?" Thomas Mugridge demanded a moment later.

"That he 's going home some day to see his mother," I answered diplomatically.

"I never 'ad none," was the Cockney's comment, as he gazed with lusterless, hopeless eyes into mine.

XIV

It dawned upon me that I had never placed a proper valuation upon womankind. For that matter, though not amative to any considerable degree, so far as I have discovered, I was never outside the atmosphere of women until now. My mother and sisters were always about me, and I was always trying to escape them, for they worried me to distraction with their solicitude for my health, and with their periodic inroads on my den, when my orderly confusion, upon which I prided myself, was turned into worse confusion and less order, though it looked neat enough to the eye. I never could find anything when they had departed. But now, alas! how welcome would have been the feel of their presence, the frou-frou and swish-swish of their skirts, which I had so cordially detested! I am sure, if I ever get home, that I shall never be irritable with them again. They may dose me and doctor me morning, noon, and night, and dust and sweep and put my den to rights every minute of the day, and I shall only lean back and survey it all and be thankful that I am possessed of a mother and some several sisters.

All of which has set me wondering. Where are the mothers of these twenty and odd men on the *Ghost?* It strikes me as unnatural and unhealthful that men should be totally separated from women and herd through the world by themselves. Coarseness and savagery are the inevitable results. These men about me should have sisters and wives and daughters; then would they be capable of softness and tenderness and sympathy. As it is, not one of them is married. In years and years not one of them has been in contact with a good woman, or within the influence, or redemption, which irresistibly radiates from such a creature. There is no balance in their lives. Their masculinity, which in itself is of the brute, has been overdeveloped. The other and spiritual side of their natures has been dwarfed—atrophied, in fact.

Rendered curious by this new direction of ideas, I talked with Johansen last night—the first superfluous words with which he has favored me since the voyage began. He left Sweden when he was eighteen, is now thirty-eight, and in all the intervening time has not been home once. He had met a townsman, a couple of years before, in some sailor boarding-house in Chile, so that he knew his mother to be still alive.

"She must be a pretty old woman now," he said, staring meditatively into the binnacle and then jerking a sharp glance at Harrison, who was steering a point off the course.

"When did you last write to her?"

He performed his mental arithmetic aloud. "Eighty-one; no—eighty-two, eh? no—eighty-three? Yes, eighty-three. Ten years ago. From some little port in Madagascar. I was trading."

"You see," he went on, as though addressing his neglected mother across half the girth of the earth, "each year I was going home. So what was the good to write? It was only a year. And each year something happened, and I did not go. But I am mate now, and when I pay off at 'Frisco, maybe with five hundred dollars, I will ship myself on a windjammer round the Horn to Liverpool, which will give me more money; and then I will pay my passage from there home. Then she will not do any more work."

"But does she work? Now? How old is she?"

"About seventy," he answered. And then, boastingly: "We work from the time we are born until we die, in my country. That 's why we live so long. I will live to a hundred."

I shall never forget this conversation. The words were the last I ever heard him utter. Perhaps they were the last he did utter, too.

Going down into the cabin to turn in, I decided that it was too stuffy to sleep below. It was a calm night. We were out of the trades, and the *Ghost* was forging ahead barely a knot an hour. So I tucked a blanket and pillow under my arm and went up on deck.

As I passed between Harrison and the binnacle, which was built into the top of the cabin, I noticed that he was this time fully three points off. Thinking that he was asleep, and wishing him to escape reprimand or worse, I spoke to him. But he was not asleep. His eyes were wide and staring. He seemed greatly perturbed, unable to reply to me.

"What 's the matter?" I asked. "Are you sick?"

He shook his head, and with a deep sigh, as of awakening, caught his breath.

"You'd better get on your course, then," I chided.

He put a few spokes over, and I watched the compass-card swing slowly to NNW and steady itself with slight oscillations.

I took a fresh hold on my bedclothes and was preparing to start on, when some movement caught my eye, and I looked astern to the rail. A sinewy hand, dripping with water, was clutching the rail. A second hand took form in the darkness beside it. I watched, fascinated. What visitant from the gloom of the deep was I to behold? Whatever it was, I knew that it was climbing aboard by the log-line. I saw a head, the hair wet and straight, shape itself, and then the unmistakable eyes and face of Wolf Larsen. His right cheek was red with blood, which flowed from some wound in the head.

He drew himself inboard with a quick effort, and rose to his feet, glancing swiftly, as he did so, at the man at the wheel, as though to assure himself of his identity and that there was nothing to fear from him. The sea-water was streaming from him.

"All right, Hump," he said in a low voice. "Where 's the mate?"

I shook my head.

"Johansen!" he called softly. "Johansen!"

"Where is he?" he demanded of Harrison.

The young fellow seemed to have recovered his composure, for he answered steadily enough:

"I don't know, sir. I saw him go for'ard a little while ago."

"So did I go for'ard; but you will observe that I did n't come back the way I went. Can you explain it?"

"You must have been overboard, sir."

"Shall I look for him in the steerage, sir?" I asked.

Wolf Larsen shook his head.

"You would n't find him, Hump. But you 'll do. Come on. Never mind your bedding. Leave it where it is."

I followed at his heels. There was nothing stirring amidships.

"Those cursed hunters!" was his comment. "Too fat and lazy to stand a four-hour watch."

But on the forecastle head we found three sailors asleep. He turned them over and looked at their faces. They composed the watch on deck, and it was the ship's custom, in good weather, to let the watch sleep, with the exception of the officer, the helmsman, and the lookout.

"Who 's lookout?" he demanded.

"Me, sir," answered Holyoak, one of the deep-water sailors, a slight tremor in his voice. "I winked off just this very minute, sir. I 'm sorry, sir. It won't happen again."

"Did you hear or see anything on deck?"

"No, sir; I—"

But Wolf Larsen had turned away with a snort of disgust, leaving the sailor rubbing his eyes with surprise at having been let off so easily.

"Softly, now," Wolf Larsen warned me in a whisper, as he doubled his body into the forecastle scuttle and prepared to descend.

I followed with a quaking heart. What was to happen I knew no more than did I know what had happened. But blood had been shed, and it was through no whim of Wolf Larsen's that he had gone over the side with his scalp laid open. Besides, Johansen was missing.

It was my first descent into the forecastle, and I shall not soon forget my impression of it, caught as I stood on my feet at the bottom of the ladder. Built directly in the eyes of the schooner, it was of the shape of a triangle, along the three sides of which stood the bunks, in double tier—twelve of them. It was no larger than a hall bedroom in Grub street, and yet twelve men were herded into it, to eat and sleep and carry on all the functions of living. My bedroom at home was not large, yet it could have contained a dozen similar forecastles, and taking into consideration the height of the ceiling, a score at least.

It smelled sour and musty, and by the dim light of the swinging sea-lamp I saw every bit of available wall-space hung deep with sea-boots, oilskins, and garments, clean and dirty, of various sorts. These swung back and forth with every roll of the vessel, giving rise to a brushing sound, as of trees against a roof or wall. Somewhere a boot thumped loudly and at irregular periods against the wall; and, though it was a mild night on the sea, there was a continual chorus of the creaking timbers and bulkheads, and of abysmal noises beneath the flooring.

The sleepers did not mind. There were eight of them,—the two watches below,—and the air was thick with the warmth and odor of their breathing, and the ear was filled with the noise of their snoring, and of their sighs and half-groans—tokens plain of the rest of the animal-man. But were they sleeping—all of them? Or had they been sleeping? This was evidently Wolf Larsen's quest—to find the men who appeared to be asleep, and who were not asleep or who had not been asleep very recently. And he went about it in a way that reminded me of a story out of Boccaccio.

He took the sea-lamp from its swinging frame and handed it to me. He began at the first bunks forward on the starboard side. In the top one lay Oofty-Oofty, a Kanaka and a splendid seaman, so named by his mates. He was asleep on his back and breathing as placidly as a woman. One arm was under his head, the other lay on top of the blankets. Wolf Larsen put thumb and forefinger to the wrist and counted the pulse. In the midst of it the Kanaka roused. He awoke as gently as he slept. There was no movement of the body whatever. Only the eyes moved. They flashed wide open, big and black, and stared unblinking into our faces. Wolf Larsen put his finger to his lips as a sign for silence, and the eyes closed again.

In the lower bunk lay Louis, grossly fat and warm and sweaty, asleep unfeignedly, and sleeping laboriously. While Wolf Larsen held his wrist he stirred uneasily, bowing his body so that for a moment it rested on shoulders and heels. His lips moved, and he gave voice to this enigmatic utterance:

"A shilling 's worth a quarter; but keep your lamps out for thruppenny bits, or the publicans 'll shove 'em on you for sixpence."

Then he rolled over on his side with a heavy, sobbing sigh, saying:

"A sixpence is a tanner, and a shilling a bob, but what a pony is I don't know."

Satisfied with the honesty of his and the Kanaka's sleep, Wolf Larsen passed on to the next two bunks on the starboard side, occupied top and bottom, as we saw in the light of the sea-lamp, by Leach and Johnson.

As Wolf Larsen bent down to the lower bunk to take Johnson's pulse, I, standing erect and holding the lamp, saw Leach's head raise stealthily as he peered over the side of his bunk to see what was going on. He must have divined Wolf Larsen's trick and the sureness of detection, for the light was at once dashed from my hand and the forecastle left in darkness. He must have leaped, also, at the same instant, straight down on Wolf Larsen.

The first sounds were those of a conflict between a bull and a wolf. I heard a great infuriated bellow go up from Wolf Larsen, and from Leach a snarling that was desperate and blood-curdling. Johnson must have joined him immediately, so that his abject and groveling conduct on deck for the last few days had been no more than planned deception.

I was so terror-stricken by this fight in the dark that I leaned against the ladder, trembling and unable to ascend. And upon me was that old sickness at the pit of the stomach, caused always by the spectacle of physical violence. In this instance I could not see, but I could hear the impact of the blows—the soft crushing sound made by flesh striking forcibly against flesh. Then there was the crashing about of the entwined bodies, the labored breathing, the short quick gasps of sudden pain.

There must have been more men in the conspiracy to murder the captain and the mate, for by the sounds I knew that Leach and Johnson had been quickly reinforced.

"Get a knife, somebody!" Leach was shouting.

"Pound him on the head! Mash his brains out!" was Johnson's cry.

But after his first bellow Wolf Larsen made no noise. He was fighting grimly and silently for very life. Down at the very first, he had been unable to gain his feet, and for all of his tremendous strength I felt that there was no hope for him.

The force with which they struggled was vividly impressed on me, for I was knocked down by their surging bodies and badly bruised. But in the confusion I managed to crawl into a lower bunk out of the way.

"All hands! We 've got him! We 've got him!" I could hear Leach crying.

"Who?" asked those who had been asleep.

"It 's the bloody mate!" was Leach's crafty answer. The words were strained from him in a smothered sort of way.

This was greeted with whoops of joy, and from then on Wolf Larsen had seven strong men on top of him, Louis, I believe, taking no part in it. The forecastle was like an angry hive of bees.

"What 's the row there?" I heard Latimer shout down the scuttle, too cautious to descend into the inferno.

"Won't somebody get a knife?" Leach pleaded in the first interval of comparative silence.

The number of the assailants was a cause of confusion. They blocked their own efforts, while Wolf Larsen, with but a single purpose, achieved his. This was to fight his way across the floor to the ladder. Though in total darkness, I followed his progress by its sound. No man less than a giant could have done what he did, once he had gained the foot of the ladder. Step by step, by the might of his arms, the whole pack of men striving to drag him back and down, he drew his body up from the floor till he stood erect. And then, step by step, hand and foot, he slowly struggled up the ladder.

The very last of all, I saw. For Latimer, having finally gone for a lantern, held it so that its light shone down the scuttle. Wolf Larsen was nearly to the top, though I could not see him. All that was visible was the mass of men fastened upon him. It squirmed about, like some huge, many-legged spider, and swayed back and forth to the regular roll of the vessel. And still, step by step, with long intervals between, the mass ascended. Once it tottered, about to fall back, but the broken hold was regained, and it still went up.

"Who is it?" Latimer cried.

"Larsen," I heard a muffled voice from within the mass.

Latimer reached down with his free hand. I saw a hand shoot up to clasp his. Latimer pulled, and the next couple of steps were made with a rush. Then Wolf Larsen's other hand reached up and clutched the edge of the scuttle. The mass swung clear of the ladder, the men still clinging to their escaping foe. They began to drop off, to be brushed off against the sharp edge of the scuttle, to be knocked off by the legs, which were now kicking powerfully. Leach was the last to go, falling sheer back from the top of the scuttle and striking on head and shoulders upon his sprawling mates. Larsen and the lantern disappeared, and we were left in darkness.

XV

THERE was a deal of cursing and groaning as the men at the bottom of the ladder crawled to their feet.

"Somebody strike a light; my thumb 's out of joint," said one of the men, Parsons, a swarthy, saturnine man, steerer in Standish's boat, in which Harrison was puller.

"You 'll find it knockin' about by the bitts," Leach said, sitting down on the edge of the bunk in which I was concealed.

There was a fumbling and a scratching of matches, and the sea-lamp flared up, dim and smoky, and in its weird light bare-legged men moved about, nursing their bruises and caring for their hurts. Oofty-Oofty laid hold of Parsons's thumb, pulling it out stoutly and snapping it back into place. I noticed at the same time that the Kanaka's knuckles were laid open clear across and to the bone. Exposing his beautiful white teeth in a grin, he explained that the wounds had come from striking Wolf Larsen in the mouth.

"So it was you, was it, you black beggar?" belligerently demanded Kelly, an Irish-American and a longshoreman making his first trip, and puller for Kerfoot.

As he made the demand he shoved his pugnacious face close to Oofty-Oofty. The Kanaka leaped backward to his bunk, to return with a leap, flourishing a long knife.

"Aw, go lay down; you make me tired," Leach interfered. He was evidently, for all of his youth and inexperience, cock of the forecastle. "G'wan, you Kelly. You leave Oofty alone. How in —— did he know it was you in the dark?"

Kelly subsided with some muttering, and the Kanaka flashed his white teeth in a grateful smile. He was a beautiful creature, almost feminine in the pleasing lines of his figure, and there was a softness and dreaminess in his large eyes which seemed to contradict his reputation for strife and action.

"How did he get away?" said Johnson.

He was sitting on the side of his bunk, the whole pose of his figure indicating utter dejection and hopelessness. He was still breathing heavily from the exertion he had made. His shirt had been ripped entirely from him in the struggle.

"Because he is the devil, as I told you before," was Leach's answer, and thereat he was on his feet and raging his disappointment with tears in his eyes.

"And not one of you to get a knife!" was his unceasing lament.

But the rest had a lively fear of consequences, and gave no heed to him.

"How 'll he know which was which?" Kelly asked, and as he went on he looked murderously about him—"unless one of us peaches."

"He 'll know as soon as ever he claps eyes on us," Parsons replied. "One look at you 'd be enough."

"Tell him the deck flopped up an' gouged yer teeth out iv yer jaw," Louis grinned. He was the only man who was not out of his bunk, and he was jubilant in that he possessed no bruises to advertise that he had had a hand in the night's work. "Just wait till he gets a glimpse iv yer mugs to-morrow—the gang iv ye," he chuckled.

"We 'll say we thought it was the mate," said one. And another: "I know what I 'll say—that I heared a row, jumped out of my bunk, got a jolly good crack on the jaw for my pains, an' sailed in myself. Could n't tell who or what it was in the dark an' just hit out."

"An' 't was me you hit, of course," Kelly seconded, his face brightening.

Leach and Johnson took no part in the discussion, and it was plain to see that their mates looked upon them as men for whom the worst was inevitable, who were beyond hope and already dead. Leach stood their fears and reproaches for some time. Then he broke out:

"You make me tired! A nice lot of gazabas you are! If you talked less with yer mouth an' did something with yer hands, he 'd 'a' be'n done with by now. Why could n't one of you, just one of you, get me a knife when I sung out? You make me sick! A-beefin' an' bellerin' round as though he 'd kill you when he gets you! You know he won't. Can't afford to. No shippin'-masters or beachcombers over here, an' he wants yer in his business, an' he wants yer bad. Who 's to pull or steer or sail ship if he loses yer? It 's me an' Johnson have to face the music. Get into yer bunks, now, and shut yer faces; I want to get some sleep."

"That 's all right, all right," Parsons spoke up. "Mebbe he won't do for us, but, mark my words, hell 'll be an ice-box to this ship from now on."

All the while I had been apprehensive. What would happen to me when these men discovered my presence? I could never fight my way out as Wolf Larsen had done. And at this moment Latimer called down the scuttle:

"Hump, the Old Man wants you."

"He ain't down here!" said Parsons.

"Yes, he is," I said, sliding out of the bunk and striving my hardest to keep my voice steady and bold.

The sailors looked at me in consternation. Fear was strong in their faces, and the devilishness which comes of fear.

"I 'm coming!" I shouted up to Latimer.

"No, you don't!" Kelly cried, stepping between me and the ladder, his right hand shaped into a veritable strangler's clutch. "You sneak! I 'll shut yer mouth!"

"Let him go!" Leach commanded.

"Not on yer life!" was the angry retort.

Leach never changed his position on the edge of the bunk. "Let him go, I say," he repeated, but this time his voice was gritty and metallic.

The Irishman wavered. I made to step by him, and he stood aside. When I had gained the ladder I turned to the circle of brutal and malignant faces peering at me through the semi-darkness. A sudden and deep sympathy welled up in me.

"I have seen and heard nothing, believe me," I said quietly.

"I tell yer, he 's all right," I could hear Leach say as I went up. "He don't like the Old Man no more nor you or me."

I found Wolf Larsen in the cabin, stripped and bloody, waiting for me. He greeted me with his whimsical smile.

"Come, get to work, doctor. The signs are favorable for an extensive practice this voyage. I don't know what the *Ghost* would have been without you, and if I could cherish such noble sentiments, I 'd tell you that her master is deeply grateful."

I knew the run of the simple medicine-chest the *Ghost* carried, and while I was heating water on the cabin stove and getting the things ready for dressing his wounds, he moved about, laughing and chatting, and examining his hurts with a calculating eye. I had never before seen him stripped, and the sight of his body quite took my breath away.

I must say that I was fascinated by the perfect lines of Wolf Larsen's figure, and by what I may term the terrible beauty of it. I had noted the men in the forecastle. Powerfully muscled though some of them were, Oofty-Oofty had been the only one whose lines were at all pleasing, while, in so far as they pleased, had they been what I should call feminine.

But Wolf Larsen was the man type, the masculine, and almost a god in his perfectness. As he moved about or raised his arms, the great muscles leapt and moved under the satiny skin. I have forgotten to say that the bronze ended with his face. His body, thanks to his Scandinavian stock, was fair as the fairest woman's. I remember his putting his hand up to feel of the wound on his head, and my watching the biceps move like a living thing under its white sheath.

He noticed me, and I became aware that I was staring at him.

"God made you well," I said.

"Did he?" he answered. "I have often thought so myself, and wondered why."

"Purpose—" I began.

"Utility," he interrupted. "This body was made for use. These muscles were made to grip and tear and destroy living things that get between me and life. Feel them," he commanded.

They were as hard as iron. And I observed, also, that his whole body had unconsciously drawn itself together, tense and alert; that muscles were softly crawling and shaping about the hips, along the back, and across the shoulders; that the arms were slightly lifted, their muscles contracting, the fingers crooking till the hands were like talons; and that even the eyes had changed expression and into them were coming watchfulness and measurement and a light none other than of battle.

"Stability, equilibrium," he said, relaxing on the instant and sinking his body back into repose. "Feet with which to clutch the ground, legs to stand on and to help withstand, while with arms and hands, teeth and nails, I struggle to kill and not to be killed. Purpose? Utility is the word."

I did not argue. I had seen the mechanism of the primitive fighting beast, and I was as strongly impressed as if I had seen the engines of a battle-ship or Atlantic liner.

I was surprised, considering the fierce struggle in the forecastle, at the superficiality of his hurts, and I pride myself that I dressed them dexterously. With the exception of two bad wounds, the rest were merely severe bruises and lacerations. The blow which he had received before going overboard had laid his scalp open several inches. This, under his direction, I cleansed and sewed together.

"By the way, Hump, as I have remarked, you are a handy man," Wolf Larsen began when my work was done. "As you know, we 're short a mate. Hereafter you shall stand watches, receive seventy-five dollars per month, and be addressed fore and aft as Mr. Van Weyden."

"I—I don't understand navigation, you know," I gasped.

"Not necessary at all."

"I really do not care to sit in the high places," I objected. "I find life precarious enough in my present humble situation. I have no experience. Mediocrity, you see, has its compensations."

He smiled as though it were all settled.

"I won't be mate on this hell-ship!" I cried defiantly.

I saw his face grow hard and the merciless glitter come into his eyes. He walked to the door of his room, saying:

"And now, Mr. Van Weyden, good night."

"Good night, Mr. Larsen," I answered weakly.

THE SEA-WOLF

BY JACK LONDON

Author of "The Call of the Wild," "The God of his Fathers," etc.

IN the early chapters of "The Sea-Wolf" the narrator of the tale, Humphrey Van Weyden, a literary critic and man of leisure, in crossing San Francisco Bay in a ferry-boat, is wrecked in the fog. He is carried out to sea, and picked up by the sealing-schooner *Ghost*, outward bound. The captain, "Wolf" Larsen, refuses to put him ashore or to permit him to be taken off by a pilot-boat, and, being short-handed by the death of his mate, forces upon Van Weyden the duties of cabin-boy. Van Weyden is robbed and ill used by Mugridge, the cook, but obtains no redress from the captain, who is a curious compound of brutality and self-culture. The captain varies the monotony of life at sea by acts of cruelty to his men, and at times entertains Van Weyden with his singular views of life. Meanwhile he plays cards with his cook, and wins from him the money that has been stolen from Van Weyden. For days he keeps the latter by him, discussing life and literature; but after tormenting him physically, sends him back to the galley, where the cook threatens his life and stabs one of the crew. For three days a blinding headache confines the Sea-Wolf to his room; after it has passed he resumes his discussions with Van Weyden, illustrating his theory of the love of life by choking his companion into insensibility. Various outbreaks of brutality occur, in which a seaman is cruelly beaten by the captain and the mate, the cook is disabled by a seaman, two of the hunters are shot in a quarrel, the mate mysteriously disappears from the schooner, and the captain is nearly killed in a fight with the crew. Van Weyden is then chosen to take the place of the lost mate.—EDITOR.

XVI

I CANNOT say that the position of mate carried with it anything more joyful than that there were no more dishes to wash. I was ignorant of the simplest duties of mate, and would have fared badly indeed had not the sailors sympathized with me. I knew nothing of the minutiæ of ropes and rigging, of the trimming and setting of sails; but the sailors took pains to put me to rights, Louis proving a specially good teacher, and I had little trouble with those under me.

With the hunters it was otherwise. Familiar in varying degree with the sea, they took me as a sort of joke. In truth, it was a joke to me that I, the veriest landsman, should be filling the office of mate; but to be taken as a joke by others was a different matter. I made no complaint, but Wolf Larsen demanded the most punctilious sea-etiquette in my case,—far more than poor Johansen had ever received,—and at the expense of several rows, threats, and much grumbling, he brought the hunters to time. I was "Mr. Van Weyden" fore and aft, and only Wolf Larsen himself ever addressed me as "Hump."

It was amusing. Perhaps the wind would haul a few points while we were at dinner, and as I left the table he would say, "Mr. Van Weyden, will you kindly put about on the port tack?" And I would go on deck, beckon Louis to me, and learn from him what was to be done. Then, a few minutes later, having digested his instructions and thoroughly mastered the manœuver, I would proceed to issue my orders. I remember an early instance of this kind, when Wolf Larsen appeared on the scene just as I had begun to give orders. He smoked his cigar and looked on quietly till the thing was done, and then paced aft by my side along the weather poop.

"Hump," he said,—"I beg pardon, Mr.

Van Weyden,—I congratulate you. I think you can now fire your father's legs back into the grave to him. You 've discovered your own, and learned to stand on them. A little rope-work, sail-making, and experience with storms and such things, and by the end of the voyage you could ship on any coasting-schooner."

It was during this period, between the death of Johansen and the arrival on the sealing-grounds, that I passed my pleasantest hours on the *Ghost*. Wolf Larsen was considerate, the sailors helped me, and I was no longer in irritating contact with Thomas Mugridge. And I make free to say, as the days went by, that I found I was taking a certain secret pride in myself. Fantastic as the situation was,—a landlubber second in command,—I was nevertheless carrying it off well; and during that brief time I was proud of myself, and I grew to love the heave and roll of the *Ghost* under my feet as she wallowed north and west through the tropic sea to the islet where we filled our water-casks.

But my happiness was not unalloyed. It was comparative, a period of less misery slipped in between a past of great miseries and a future of great miseries. For the *Ghost*, so far as the seamen were concerned, was a hell-ship of the worst description. They never had a moment's rest or peace. Wolf Larsen treasured against them the attempt on his life and the drubbing he had received in the forecastle, and morning, noon, and night, and all night as well, he devoted himself to making life unlivable for them.

He knew well the psychology of the little thing, and it was the little things by which he kept the crew worked up to the verge of madness. I have seen Harrison called from his bunk to put properly away a misplaced paint-brush, and the two watches below haled from their tired sleep to accompany him and see him do it. A little thing, truly, but when multiplied by the thousand ingenious devices of such a mind, the mental state of the men in the forecastle may be slightly comprehended.

Of course much grumbling went on, and little outbursts were continually occurring. Blows were struck, and there were always two or three men nursing injuries at the hands of the human beast who was their master. Concerted action was impossible in face of the heavy arsenal of weapons carried in the steerage and cabin. Leach and Johnson were the two particular victims of Wolf Larsen's diabolic temper, and the look of profound melancholy which had settled on Johnson's face and in his eyes made my heart bleed.

With Leach it was different. There was too much of the fighting beast in him. He seemed possessed by an insatiable fury which gave no time for grief. His lips had become distorted into a permanent snarl, which, at mere sight of Wolf Larsen, broke out in sound, horrible and menacing, and, I do believe, unconsciously. I have seen him follow Wolf Larsen about with his eyes, like an animal its keeper, the while the animal-like snarl sounded deep in his throat and vibrated forth between his teeth.

I remember once, on deck, in bright day, touching him on the shoulder as preliminary to giving an order. His back was toward me, and at the first feel of my hand he leaped upright in the air and away from me, snarling and turning his head as he leaped. He had for the moment mistaken me for the man he hated.

Both he and Johnson would have killed Wolf Larsen at the slightest opportunity, but the opportunity never came. Wolf Larsen was too wise for that, and, besides, they had no adequate weapons. With their fists alone they had no chance whatever. Time and again he fought it out with Leach, who fought back always, like a wildcat, tooth and nail and fist, until stretched exhausted or unconscious on the deck. And he was never averse to another encounter. All the devil that was in him challenged the devil in Wolf Larsen. They had but to appear on deck at the same time, when they would be at it, cursing, snarling, striking; and I have seen Leach fling himself upon Wolf Larsen without warning or provocation. Once he threw his heavy sheath-knife, missing Wolf Larsen's throat by an inch. Another time he dropped a steel marlinespike from the main-crosstree. It was a difficult cast to make on a rolling ship, but the sharp point of the spike, whistling seventy-five feet through the air, barely missed Wolf Larsen's head as he emerged from the cabin companionway, and drove its length two inches and over into the solid deck-planking. Still another time he stole into the steerage, possessed himself of a loaded shot-gun, and was making a rush for the deck with it when caught by Kerfoot and disarmed.

I often wondered why Wolf Larsen did not kill him and make an end of it. But he only laughed and seemed to enjoy it. There seemed a certain spice about it, such as men must feel who take delight in making pets of ferocious animals.

"It gives a thrill to life," he explained to me, "when life is carried in one's hand. Man is a natural gambler, and life is the biggest stake he can lay. The greater the odds, the greater the thrill. Why should I deny myself the joy of exciting Leach's soul to fever-pitch? For that matter, I do him a kindness. The greatness of sensation is mutual. He is living more royally than any man for'ard, though he does not know it. For he has what they have not—purpose, something to do and be done, an all-absorbing end to strive to attain, the desire to kill me, the hope that he may kill me. Really, Hump, he is living deep and high. I doubt that he has ever lived so swiftly and keenly before, and I honestly envy him, sometimes, when I see him raging at the summit of passion and sensibility."

"Ah, but it is cowardly, cowardly," I cried. "You have all the advantage."

"Of the two of us, you and I, who is the greater coward?" he asked seriously. "If the situation is unpleasing, you compromise with your conscience when you make yourself a party to it. If you were really great, really true to yourself, you would join forces with Leach and Johnson. But you are afraid, you are afraid. You want to live. The life that is in you cries out that it must live, no matter what the cost; so you live ignominiously, untrue to the best you dream of, sinning against your whole pitiful little code, and, if there were a hell, heading your soul straight for it. Bah! I play the braver part. I do no sin, for I am true to the promptings of the life that is in me. I am sincere with my soul at least, and that is what you are not."

There was a sting in what he said. Perhaps, after all, I was playing a cowardly part. And the more I thought about it the more it appeared that my duty to myself lay in doing what he had advised, lay in joining forces with Johnson and Leach and working for his death. Right here, I think, entered the austere conscience of my Puritan ancestry, impelling me toward lurid deeds and sanctioning even murder as right conduct. I dwelt upon the idea. It would be a most moral act to rid the world of such a monster. Humanity would be better and happier for it, life fairer and sweeter.

I pondered it long, lying sleepless in my bunk and reviewing in endless procession the facts of the situation. I talked with Johnson and Leach during the night watches when Wolf Larsen was below. But both men had lost hope, Johnson because of temperamental despondency, Leach because he had beaten himself out in the vain struggle and was exhausted. But he caught my hand in a passionate grip one night, saying:

"I think ye 're square, Mr. Van Weyden. But stay where you are an' keep yer mouth shut. Say nothin', but saw wood. We 're dead men, I know it; but, all the same, you might be able to do us a favor sometime when we need it damn bad."

It was only next day, when Wainwright Island loomed to windward, close abeam, that Wolf Larsen opened his mouth in prophecy. He had attacked Johnson, been attacked by Leach, and had just finished whipping the pair of them.

"Leach," he said, "you know I 'm going to kill you sometime or other, don't you?"

A snarl was the answer.

"And as for you, Johnson, you 'll get so tired of life before I 'm through with you that you 'll fling yourself over the side. See if you don't."

"That 's suggestion," he added, in an aside to me. "I 'll bet you a month's pay he acts upon it."

I had cherished a hope that his victims would find an opportunity to escape while filling our water-barrels, but Wolf Larsen had selected his spot well. The *Ghost* lay half a mile beyond the surf-line of a lonely beach. Here debouched a deep gorge, with precipitous, volcanic walls which no man could scale. And here, under his direct supervision,—for he went ashore himself,—Leach and Johnson filled the small casks and rolled them down to the beach. They had no chance to make a break for liberty in one of the boats.

Harrison and Kelly, however, made such an attempt. They composed the crew of one of the boats, and their task was to ply between the schooner and the shore, carrying a single cask each trip. Just before dinner, starting for the beach with an empty barrel, they altered their course and bore away to the left to round the promontory which jutted into the sea between them and liberty. Beyond its foaming base lay the pretty villages of the Japanese colonists and smiling valleys which penetrated deep into the interior. Once in the fastnesses they promised, and the two men could defy Wolf Larsen.

I had observed Henderson and Smoke loitering about the deck all morning, and I now learned why they were there. Procuring their rifles, they opened fire in a leisurely manner upon the deserters. It was a most cold-blooded exhibition of marksmanship. At first their bullets zipped harmlessly along the surface of the water on each side the boat; but, as the men continued to pull lustily, they struck closer and closer.

"Now watch me take Kelly's right oar," Smoke said, drawing a more careful aim.

I was looking through the glasses, and I saw the oar-blade shattered as he shot. Henderson duplicated his feat, selecting Harrison's right oar. The boat slued around. The two remaining oars were quickly broken. The men tried to row with the splinters, and had them shot out of their hands. Kelly ripped up a bottom-board and began paddling, but dropped it with a cry of pain as its splinters drove into his hands. Then they gave up, letting the boat drift till a second boat, sent from the shore by Wolf Larsen, took them in tow and brought them aboard.

Late that afternoon we hove up anchor and got away. Nothing was before us but the three or four months' hunting on the sealing-grounds. The outlook was black indeed, and I went about my work with a heavy heart. An almost funereal gloom seemed to have descended upon the *Ghost*. Wolf Larsen had taken to his bunk with one of his strange splitting headaches. Harrison stood listlessly at the wheel, half supporting himself by it, as though wearied by the weight of his flesh. The rest of the men were morose and silent. I came upon Kelly crouching in the lee of the forecastle scuttle, his head on his knees, his arms about his head, in an attitude of unutterable despondency.

Johnson I found lying full-length on the forecastle head, staring at the troubled churn of the forefoot, and I remembered with horror the suggestion Wolf Larsen had made. It seemed likely to bear fruit. I tried to break in on the man's morbid thoughts by calling him away; but he smiled sadly at me, and refused to obey.

Leach approached me as I returned aft.

"I want to ask a favor, Mr. Van Weyden," he said. "If it 's yer luck to ever make 'Frisco once more, will you hunt up Matt McCarthy? He 's my old man. He lives on the Hill, back of the Mayfair bakery, runnin' a cobbler's shop that everybody knows, an' you 'll have no trouble. Tell him I lived to be sorry for the trouble I brought him an' the things I done, an'—an' just tell him 'God bless him,' for me."

I nodded my head, but said:

"We 'll all win back to San Francisco, Leach, and you 'll be with me when I go to see Matt McCarthy."

"I 'd like to believe you," he answered, shaking my hand, "but I can't. Wolf Larsen 'll do for me, I know it, and all I can hope is he 'll do it quick."

And as he left me I was aware of the same desire at my heart. Since it was to be done, let it be done with despatch. The general gloom had gathered me into its folds. The worst appeared inevitable; and as I paced the deck hour after hour, I found myself afflicted with Wolf Larsen's repulsive ideas. What was it all about? Where was the grandeur of life that it should permit such wanton destruction of human souls? It was a cheap and sordid thing, after all, this life, and the sooner over the better. Over and done with! Over and done with! I, too, leaned upon the rail and gazed longingly into the sea, with the certitude that sooner or later I should be sinking down, down, through the cool green depths of its oblivion.

XVII

STRANGE to say, in spite of the general foreboding, nothing of especial moment happened on the *Ghost*. We ran on to the north and west till we raised the coast of Japan and picked up with the great seal herd. Coming from no man knew where in the illimitable Pacific, it was traveling north on its annual migration to the rookeries of Bering Sea. And north we traveled with it, ravaging and destroying, flinging the naked carcasses to the shark, and salting down the skins, so that they might later adorn the fair shoulders of the women of the cities.

It was wanton slaughter, and all for woman's sake. No man ate of the seal-meat or the oil. After a good day's killing I have seen our decks covered with hides and bodies, slippery with fat and blood, the scuppers running red; masts, ropes, and rails splattered high with the sanguinary color; and the men, like butchers plying their trade, naked and red of arm and hand, hard at work with ripping- and flensing-knives, removing the skins from the pretty sea-creatures they had killed.

It was my task to tally the pelts as they came aboard from the boats, to oversee the skinning, and afterward the cleansing of the decks and bringing things shipshape again. It was not pleasant work,—my soul and my stomach revolted at it,—and yet, in a way, this handling and directing of many men was good for me. It developed what little executive ability I possessed, and I was aware of a toughening or hardening which I was undergoing and which could not be anything but wholesome for "Sissy" Van Weyden.

One thing I was beginning to feel, and that was that I could never again be quite the same man I had been. While my hope and faith in human life still survived Wolf Larsen's destructive criticism, he had nevertheless been a cause of change in minor matters. He had opened up for me the world of the real, of which I had known virtually nothing, and from which I had always shrunk. I had learned to look more closely at life as it is lived, to recognize that there were such things as facts in the world; to emerge from the realm of mind and idea, and to place certain values on the concrete and objective phases of existence.

I saw more of Wolf Larsen than ever when we had gained the grounds; for when the weather was fair and we were in the midst of the herd, all hands were away in the boats, and left on board were only he and I, and Thomas Mugridge, who did not count. But there was no play about it. The six boats, spreading out fanwise from the schooner until the first weather boat and the last lee boat were anywhere from ten to twenty miles apart, cruised along a straight course over the sea till nightfall or bad weather drove them in. It was our duty to sail the *Ghost* well to leeward of the last lee boat, so that all the boats would have fair wind to run for us in case of squalls or threatening weather.

It is no slight matter for two men, particularly when a stiff wind has sprung up, to handle a vessel like the *Ghost*, steering, keeping lookout for the boats, and setting or taking in sail, so it devolved upon me to learn, and learn quickly. Steering I picked up easily, but running aloft to the crosstrees, and swinging my whole weight by my arms when I left the ratlines and climbed still higher, was more difficult. This, too, I learned, and quickly, for I felt somehow a wild desire to vindicate myself in Wolf Larsen's eyes, to prove my right to live in ways other than of the mind. Nay, the time came when I took joy in the run to the masthead, and in the clinging on by my legs at that precarious height while I swept the sea with the glasses in search of the boats.

I remember one beautiful day, when the boats left early and the reports of the hunters' guns grew dim and distant and died away as they scattered far and wide over the sea. There was just the faintest wind from the westward; but it breathed its last by the time we managed to get to leeward of the last lee boat. One by one —I was at the masthead and saw—the six boats disappeared over the bulge of the earth as they followed the seal into the west. We lay, scarcely rolling on the placid sea, unable to follow. Wolf Larsen was apprehensive. The barometer was down, and the sky to the east did not please him. He studied it with unceasing vigilance.

"If she comes out of there," he said, "hard and snappy, putting us to windward of the boats, it 's likely there 'll be empty bunks in steerage and fo'c's'le."

By eleven o'clock the sea had become glass. By midday, though we were well up in the northerly latitudes, the heat was sickening. There was no freshness in the air. It was sultry and oppressive, reminding me of what the old Californians term "earthquake weather." There was something ominous about it, and in intangible ways one was made to feel that the worst was about to come. Slowly the whole eastern sky filled with clouds that overtowered us like some black sierra of the infernal regions. So clearly could one see cañon, gorge, and precipice, and the shadows that lay therein, that one looked unconsciously for the white surf-line and bellowing caverns where the sea charges forever on the land. And still we rocked gently, and there was no wind.

"It 's no squall," Wolf Larsen said. "Old Mother Nature 's going to get up on her hind legs and howl for all that 's in her, and it 'll keep us jumping, Hump, to pull through with half our boats. You 'd better run up and loosen the topsails."

"But if it is going to howl, and there are only two of us?" I asked, a note of protest in my voice.

"Why, we 've got to make the best of the first of it and run down to our boats before our canvas is ripped out of us. After that I don't give a rap what happens. The sticks 'll stand it, and you and I will have to, though we 've plenty cut out for us."

Still the calm continued. We ate dinner, a hurried and anxious meal for me, with eighteen men abroad on the sea and beyond the bulge of the earth, and with that heaven-rolling mountain range of clouds moving slowly down upon us. Wolf Larsen did not seem affected, however, though I noticed, when we returned to the deck, a slight twitching of the nostrils, a perceptible quickness of movement. His face was stern, the lines of it had grown hard, and yet in his eyes—blue, clear blue this day—there was a strange brilliancy, a bright, scintillating light. It struck me that he was joyous in a ferocious sort of way; that he was glad there was an impending struggle; that he was thrilled and upborne with knowledge that one of the great moments of living, when the tide of life surges up in flood, was upon him.

Once, and unwitting that he did so or that I saw, he laughed aloud mockingly and defiantly at the advancing storm. I see him yet, standing there like a pygmy out of the "Arabian Nights" before the huge front of some malignant jinnee. He was daring destiny, and he was unafraid.

He walked to the galley.

"Cooky," I heard him say, "by the time you 've finished pots and pans you 'll be wanted on deck. Stand ready for a call."

"Hump," he said, becoming cognizant of the fascinated gaze I bent upon him, "this beats whisky, and is where your Omar misses. I think he only half lived, after all."

The western half of the sky had by now grown murky. The sun had dimmed and faded out of sight. It was two in the afternoon, and a ghostly twilight, shot through by wandering purplish lights, had descended upon us, and Wolf Larsen's face glowed in the purplish light. We lay in the midst of an unearthly quiet, while all about us were signs and omens of oncoming sound and movement. The sultry heat had become unendurable. The sweat was standing on my forehead, and I could feel it trickling down my nose. I felt as though I should faint, and reached out to the rail for support.

And then, just then, the faintest possible whisper of air passed by. It was from the east, and like a whisper it came and went. The drooping canvas was not stirred, and yet my face had felt the air and been cooled.

"Cooky," Wolf Larsen called in a low voice (Thomas Mugridge turned a pitiable, scared face), "let go that fore-boom-tackle and pass it across, and when she 's willing, let go the sheet and come in snug with the tackle. And if you make a mess of it, it will be the last you ever make. Understand?"

"Mr. Van Weyden, stand by to pass the head-sails over. Then jump for the topsails and spread them quick as God 'll let you—the quicker you do it, the easier you 'll find it. As for Cooky, if he is n't lively, bat him between the eyes."

I was aware of the compliment and pleased in that no threat had accompanied my instructions. We were lying head to northwest, and it was his intention to jibe over with the first puff.

"We 'll have the breeze on our quarter," he explained to me. "By the last guns the boats were bearing away slightly to the south'ard."

He turned and walked aft to the wheel. I went forward and took my station at the jibs. Another whisper of wind, and another, passed by. The canvas flapped lazily.

"Thank Gawd she 's not comin' all of a bunch, Mr. Van Weyden!" was the Cockney's fervent ejaculation.

And I was indeed thankful, for I had by this time learned enough to know, with all our canvas spread, what disaster in such event awaited us. The whispers of wind became puffs, the sails filled, the *Ghost* moved. Wolf Larsen put the wheel hard up to port, and we began to pay off. The wind was now dead astern, muttering and puffing stronger and stronger, and my head-sails were pounding lustily. I did not see what went on elsewhere, though I felt the sudden surge and heel of the schooner as the wind-pressures changed to the jibing of the fore- and main-sails. My hands were full with the flying jib, jib, and staysail, and by the time this part of my task was accomplished the *Ghost* was leaping into the southwest, the wind on her quarter and all her sheets to starboard. Without pausing for breath, though my heart was beating like a trip-hammer from my exertions, I sprang to the topsails, and before the wind had become too strong we had them fairly set and were coiling down. Then I went aft for orders.

Wolf Larsen nodded approval and relinquished the wheel to me. The wind strengthening steadily and the sea rising, for an hour I steered, each moment becoming more difficult. I had not the experience to steer at the gait we were going on a quartering course.

"Now take a run up with the glasses and raise some of the boats. We 've made at least ten knots, and we 're going twelve or thirteen now. The old girl knows how to walk. Might as well get some of that head-sail off of her," Larsen added, and turned to Mugridge: "Cooky, run down that flying jib and staysail, and make the downhauls good and fast."

I contented myself with the fore-crosstrees, some seventy feet above the deck. As I searched the vacant stretch of water before me, I comprehended thoroughly the need for haste if we were to recover any of our men. Indeed, as I gazed at the heavy sea through which we were running, I doubted that there was a boat afloat. It did not seem possible that so frail craft could survive such stress of wind and water.

I could not feel the full force of the wind, for we were running with it, but from my lofty perch I looked down as though outside the *Ghost* and apart from her, and saw the shape of her outlined sharply against the foaming sea as she tore along instinct with life. Sometimes she would lift and send across some great wave, burying her starboard rail from view and covering her deck to the hatches with the boiling ocean. At such moments, starting from a windward roll, I would go flying through the air with dizzying swiftness, as though I clung to the end of a huge, inverted pendulum, the arc of which, between the greater rolls, must have been seventy feet or more. Once the terror of this giddy sweep overpowered me, and for a while I clung on, hand and foot, weak and trembling, unable to search the sea for the missing boats or to behold aught of the sea but that which roared beneath and strove to overwhelm the *Ghost*.

But the thought of the men in the midst of it steadied me, and in my quest for them I forgot myself. For an hour I saw nothing but the naked, desolate sea. And then, where a vagrant shaft of sunlight struck the ocean and turned its surface to wrathful silver, I caught a small black speck thrust skyward for an instant and swallowed up. I waited patiently. Again the tiny point of black projected itself through the wrathful blaze, a couple of points off our port bow. I did not attempt to shout, but communicated the news to Wolf Larsen by waving my arm. He changed the course, and I signaled affirmation when the speck showed dead ahead.

It grew larger, and so swiftly that for the first time I fully appreciated the speed of our flight. Wolf Larsen motioned for me to come down, and when I stood beside him at the wheel he gave me instructions for heaving to.

"Expect all hell to break loose," he cautioned me, "but don't mind it. Yours is to do your own work and to have Cooky stand by the fore-sheet."

I managed to make my way forward, but there was little choice of sides, for the weather rail seemed buried as often as the lee. Having instructed Thomas Mugridge as to what he was to do, I clambered into the fore rigging a few feet. The boat was now very close, and I could make out plainly that it was lying head to wind and sea and dragging on its mast and sail, which had been thrown overboard and made to serve as a sea-anchor. The three men were bailing. Each rolling mountain whelmed them from view, and I would wait with sickening anxiety, fearing that they would never appear again. Then, and with black suddenness, the boat would shoot clear through the foaming crest, bow pointed to the sky and the whole length of her bottom showing, wet and dark, till she seemed on end. There would be a fleeting glimpse of the three men flinging water in frantic haste, when she would topple over and fall into the yawning valley, bow down and showing her full inside length to the stern upreared almost directly above the bow. Each time that she reappeared was a recurrent miracle.

The *Ghost* suddenly changed her course, keeping away, and it came to me with a shock that Wolf Larsen was giving up the rescue as impossible. Then I realized that he was preparing to heave to, and dropped to the deck to be in readiness. We were now dead before the wind, the boat far away and abreast of us. I felt an abrupt easing of the schooner, a loss for the moment of all strain and pressure coupled with a swift acceleration of speed. She was rushing around on her heel into the wind.

As she arrived at right angles to the sea, the full force of the wind, from which we had hitherto run away, caught us. I was unfortunately and ignorantly facing it. It stood up against me like a wall, filling my lungs with air which I could not expel. And as I choked and strangled, and as the *Ghost* wallowed for an instant, broadside on and rolling straight over and far into the wind, I beheld a huge sea rise far above my head. I turned aside, caught my breath, and looked again. The wave overtopped the *Ghost*, and I gazed sheer up and into it. A shaft of sunlight smote the over-curl, and I caught a glimpse of translucent, rushing green, backed by a milky smother of foam.

Then it descended, pandemonium broke loose, everything happened at once. I was struck a crushing, stunning blow, nowhere in particular and yet everywhere. My hold had been broken loose, I was under water, and the thought passed through my mind that this was the terrible thing of which I had heard, the being swept in the trough of the sea. My body struck and pounded as it was dashed helplessly along and turned over and over, and when I could hold my breath no longer I breathed the stinging salt water into my lungs. But through it all I clung to the one idea—I must get the jib backed over to windward. I had no fear of death. I had no doubt but that I should come through somehow. And as this idea of fulfilling Wolf Larsen's order persisted in my dazed consciousness, I seemed to see him standing at the wheel in the midst of the wild welter, pitting his will against the will of the storm and defying it.

I brought up violently against what I took to be the rail, breathed, and breathed the sweet air again. I tried to rise, but struck my head, and was knocked back on hands and knees. By some freak of the waters I had been swept clear under the forecastle head and into the eyes. As I scrambled out on all fours, I passed over the body of Thomas Mugridge, who lay in a groaning heap. There was no time to investigate. I must get the jib backed over.

When I emerged on deck it seemed that the end of everything had come. On all sides there was a rending and crashing of wood and steel and canvas. The *Ghost* was being wrenched and torn to fragments. The foresail and foretopsail, emptied of the wind by the manœuver, and with no one to bring in the sheet in time, were thundering into ribbons, the heavy boom thrashing and splintering from rail to rail. The air was thick with flying wreckage, detached ropes and stays were hissing and coiling like snakes, and down through it all crashed the gaff of the foresail.

The spar could not have missed me by many inches, while it spurred me to action. Perhaps the situation was not hopeless. I remembered Wolf Larsen's caution. He had expected "all hell to break loose," and here it was. And where was he? I caught sight of him toiling at the mainsheet, heaving it in and flat with his tremendous muscles, the stern of the schooner lifted high in the air, and his body outlined against a white surge of sea sweeping past. All this and more—a whole world of chaos and wreck—in possibly fifteen seconds I had seen and heard and grasped.

I did not stop to see what had become of the small boat, but sprang to the jib-sheet. The jib itself was beginning to slap, partly filling and emptying with sharp reports; but with a turn of the sheet, and the application of my whole strength each time it slapped, I slowly backed it. This I know: I did my best. Either the down-hauls had been carelessly made fast by Mugridge, or else the pins carried away, for, while I pulled till I burst open the ends of all my fingers, the flying jib and staysail filled and fluttered with the wind, split their cloths apart, and thundered into nothingness.

Still I pulled, holding what I gained each time with a double turn until the next slap gave me more. Then the sheet gave with greater ease, and Wolf Larsen was beside me, heaving in alone while I was busied taking up the slack.

"Make fast," he shouted, "and come on!"

As I followed him, I noted that, in spite of wrack and ruin, a rough order obtained. The *Ghost* was hove to. She was still in working order, and she was still working. Though the rest of her sails were gone, the jib, backed to windward, and the mainsail, hauled down flat, were themselves holding, and holding her bow to the furious sea as well.

I looked for the boat, and, while Wolf Larsen cleared the boat-tackles, saw it lift to leeward on a big sea and not a score of feet away. And, so nicely had he made his calculation, we drifted fairly down upon it, so that nothing remained to do but hook the tackles to each end and hoist it aboard. But this was not done so easily as it is written.

In the bow was Kerfoot, Oofty-Oofty in the stern, and Kelly amidships. As we drifted closer, the boat would rise on a wave while we sank in the trough, till, almost straight above me, I could see the heads of the three men craned overside and looking down. Then, the next moment, we would lift and soar upward while they sank far down beneath us. It seemed incredible that the next surge should not crush the *Ghost* down upon the tiny egg-shell.

But, at the right moment, I passed the tackle to the Kanaka, while Wolf Larsen did the same thing forward to Kerfoot. Both tackles were hooked in a trice, and the three men, deftly timing the roll, made a simultaneous leap aboard the schooner. As the *Ghost* rolled her side out of water, the boat was lifted snugly against her, and before the return roll came we had heaved it in over the side and turned it bottom up on the deck. I noticed blood spouting from Kerfoot's left hand. In some way the third finger had been crushed to a pulp. But he gave no sign of pain, and with his single right hand helped us lash the boat in its place.

"Stand by to let that jib over, you Oofty," Wolf Larsen commanded, the very second we had finished with the boat. "Kelly, come aft and slack off the main-sheet. You, Kerfoot, go for'ard and see what 's become of Cooky. Mr. Van Weyden, run aloft again, and cut away any stray stuff in your way."

And having commanded, he went aft, with his peculiar tigerish leaps, to the wheel. While I toiled up the fore-shrouds the *Ghost* slowly paid off. This time, as we went into the trough of the sea and were swept, there were no sails to carry away. And half-way to the crosstrees, and flattened against the rigging by the full force of the wind, so that it would have been impossible for me to have fallen, with the *Ghost* almost on her beam-ends and the masts parallel with the water, I looked, not down, but at right angles from the perpendicular, to the deck of the *Ghost*. But I saw not the deck, but where the deck should have been, for it was buried beneath a wild tumbling of water. Out of this water I could see the two masts rising, and that was all. The *Ghost*, for the moment, was buried beneath the sea. As she squared off more and more, escaping from the side pressure, she righted herself and broke her deck, like a whale's back, through the ocean surface.

Then we raced, and wildly, across the wild sea, the while I hung like a fly in the crosstrees and searched for the other boats. In half an hour I sighted the second one, swamped and bottom up, to which were desperately clinging Jock Horner, fat Louis, and Johnson. This time I remained aloft, and Wolf Larsen succeeded in heaving to without being swept. As before, we drifted down upon the boat. Tackles were made fast and lines flung to the men, who scrambled aboard like monkeys. The boat itself was crushed and splintered against the schooner's side as it came inboard; but the wreck was securely lashed, for it could be patched and made whole again.

Once more the *Ghost* bore away before the storm, this time so submerging herself that for some seconds I thought she would never reappear. Even the wheel, quite a deal higher than the waist, was covered and swept again and again. At such moments I felt strangely alone with God, and watching the chaos of his wrath. And then the wheel would reappear, and

Wolf Larsen's broad shoulders, his hands gripping the spokes and holding the schooner to the course of his will, himself an earth-god, dominating the storm, flinging its descending waters from him, and riding it to his own ends. And oh, the marvel of it, the marvel of it, that tiny men should live and breathe and work, and drive so frail a contrivance of wood and cloth through so tremendous an elemental strife!

As before, the *Ghost* swung out of the trough, lifting her deck again out of the sea, and dashed before the howling blast. It was now half-past five, and half an hour later, when the last of the day lost itself in a dim and furious twilight, I sighted a third boat. It was bottom up, and there was no sign of its crew. Wolf Larsen repeated his manœuver, holding off and then rounding up to windward and drifting down upon it. But this time he missed by forty feet, the boat passing astern.

"No. 4 boat!" Oofty-Oofty cried, his keen eyes reading its number in the one second when it lifted clear of the foam and upside down.

It was Henderson's boat, and with him had been lost Holyoak and Williams, another of the deep-water crowd. Lost they indubitably were; but the boat remained, and Wolf Larsen made one more reckless effort to recover it. I had come down to the deck, and I saw Horner and Kerfoot vainly protest against the attempt.

"By God, I 'll not be robbed of my boat by any storm that ever blew out of hell!" he shouted, and though we four stood with our heads together that we might hear, his voice seemed faint and far, as though removed from us an immense distance.

"Mr. Van Weyden," he cried, and I heard through the tumult as one might hear a whisper, "stand by that jib with Johnson and Oofty! The rest of you tail aft to the main-sheet! Lively now, or I 'll sail you all into kingdom come! Understand?"

And when he put the wheel hard over and the *Ghost's* bow swung off, there was nothing for the hunters to do but obey and make the best of a risky chance. How great the risk I realized when I was once more buried beneath the pounding seas and clinging for life to the pin-rail at the foot of the foremast. My fingers were torn loose, and I was swept across to the side and over the side into the sea. I could not swim, but before I could sink I was swept back again. A strong hand gripped me, and when the *Ghost* finally emerged I found that I owed my life to Johnson. I saw him looking anxiously about him, and noted that Kelly, who had come forward at the last moment, was missing.

This time, having missed the boat, and not being in the same position as in the previous instances, Wolf Larsen was compelled to resort to a different manœuver. Running off before the wind with everything to starboard, he came about and returned close-hauled on the port tack.

"Grand!" Johnson shouted in my ear, as we successfully came through the attendant deluge; and I knew he referred, not to Wolf Larsen's seamanship, but to the performance of the *Ghost* herself.

It was now so dark that there was no sign of the boat; but Wolf Larsen held back through the frightful turmoil as if guided by unerring instinct. This time, though we were continually half-buried, there was no trough in which to be swept, and we drifted squarely down upon the upturned boat, badly smashing it as it was heaved inboard.

Two hours of terrible work followed, in which all hands of us—two hunters, three sailors, Wolf Larsen, and I—reefed, first one and then the other, the jib and mainsail. Hove to under this short canvas, our decks were comparatively free of water, while the *Ghost* bobbed and ducked among the combers like a cork.

I had burst open the ends of my fingers at the very first, and during the reefing I had worked with tears of pain running down my cheeks. And when all was done, I gave up like a woman and rolled upon the deck in the agony of exhaustion.

In the meantime, Thomas Mugridge, like a drowned rat, was being dragged out from under the forecastle head, where he had cravenly ensconced himself. I saw him pulled aft to the cabin, and noted with a shock of surprise that the galley had disappeared. A clean space of deck showed where it had stood.

In the cabin I found all hands assembled, sailors as well, and while coffee was being cooked over the small stove we drank whisky and crunched hardtack. Never in my life had food been so welcome, and never had hot coffee tasted so good. So violently did the *Ghost* pitch and toss and tumble that it was impossible for even the sailors to move about without holding on, and several times, after a cry of "Now she takes it!" we were heaped upon the wall of the port cabin as though it had been the deck.

"To —— with a lookout," I heard Wolf Larsen say when we had eaten and drunk our fill. "There 's nothing can be done on deck. If anything 's going to run us down, we could n't get out of its way. Turn in, all hands, and get some sleep."

The sailors slipped forward, setting the side-lights as they went, while the two hunters remained to sleep in the cabin, it not being deemed advisable to open the slide to the steerage companionway. Wolf Larsen and I, between us, cut off Kerfoot's crushed finger and sewed up the stump. Mugridge, who, during all the time he had been compelled to cook and serve coffee and keep the fire going, had complained of internal pains, now swore that he had a broken rib or two. On examination we found that he had three. But his case was deferred to next day, principally for the reason that I did not know anything about broken ribs, and would first have to read it up.

"I don't think it was worth it," I said to Wolf Larsen, "a broken boat for Kelly's life."

"But Kelly did n't amount to much," was the reply. "Good night."

After all that had passed, suffering intolerable anguish in my finger-ends, and with three boats missing, to say nothing of the wild capers the *Ghost* was cutting, I would have thought it impossible to sleep. But my eyes must have closed the instant my head touched the pillow, and in utter exhaustion I slept throughout the night, the while the *Ghost*, lonely and undirected, fought her way through the storm.

XVIII

THE next day, while the storm was blowing itself out, Wolf Larsen and I "crammed" anatomy and surgery and set Mugridge's ribs. Then, when the storm broke, Wolf Larsen cruised back and forth over that portion of the ocean where we had encountered it, and somewhat more to the westward, while the boats were being repaired and new sails made and bent. Also, a new galley was being constructed out of odds and ends of lumber from the hold. Sealing-schooner after sealing-schooner we sighted and boarded, most of which were in search of lost boats, and most of which were carrying boats and crews that they had picked up and that did not belong to them. For the thick of the fleet had been to the westward of us, and the boats, scattered far and wide, had headed in mad flight for the nearest refuge.

Two of our boats, with men all safe, we took off the *Cisco*, and, to Wolf Larsen's huge delight and my own grief, he culled Smoke, with Nilson and Leach, from the *San Diego*. So that, at the end of five days, we found ourselves short but four men, Henderson, Holyoak, Williams, and Kelly, and were once more hunting on the flanks of the herd.

As we followed north, we began to encounter the dreaded sea-fogs. Day after day the boats were lowered and swallowed up almost before they touched the water, while we on board pumped the horn at regular intervals, and every fifteen minutes fired the bomb-gun. Boats were continually being lost and found, it being the custom for a boat to hunt, on lay, with whatever schooner picked it up, until such time as it was recovered by its own schooner. But Wolf Larsen, as was to be expected, being a boat short, took possession of the first stray one and compelled its men to hunt with the *Ghost*, not permitting them to return to their own schooner when we sighted it. I remember how he forced the hunter and his two men below, a rifle at their breasts, when their captain passed by at biscuit-toss and hailed us for information.

Thomas Mugridge, so strangely and pertinaciously clinging to life, was soon limping about again and performing his double duties of cook and cabin-boy. Johnson and Leach were bullied and beaten as much as ever, and they looked for their lives to end with the end of the hunting season; while the rest of the crew lived the lives of dogs and were worked like dogs by their pitiless master. As for Wolf Larsen and me, we got along fairly well, though I could not quite rid myself of the idea that right conduct for me lay in killing him. He fascinated me immeasurably, and I feared him immeasurably;

and yet I could not imagine him lying prone in death. There was an endurance, as of perpetual youth, about him, which rose up and forbade the picture. I could see him only as living always and dominating always, fighting and destroying, himself surviving.

One diversion of his, when we were in the midst of the herd and the sea was too rough to lower the boats, was to lower with two boat-pullers and a steerer and go out himself. He was a good shot, too, and brought many a skin aboard under what the hunters termed "impossible hunting conditions." It seemed the breath of his nostrils, this carrying his life in his hands and struggling for it against tremendous odds.

I was learning more and more seamanship, and one clear day, a thing we rarely encountered now, I had the satisfaction of running and handling the *Ghost* and picking up the boats myself. Wolf Larsen had been smitten with one of his headaches, and I stood at the wheel from morning until evening, sailing across the ocean after the last lee boat, and heaving to and picking it and the other five up without command or suggestion from him.

Gales we encountered now and again, for it was a raw and stormy region, and, in the middle of June, a typhoon most memorable to me, and most important because of the changes wrought through it upon my future. We must have been caught nearly at the center of this circular storm, and Wolf Larsen ran out of it and to the southward, first under a double-reefed jib, and finally under bare poles. Never had I imagined so great a sea. The seas previously encountered were as ripples compared with these, which ran a half-mile from crest to crest and which upreared, I am confident, above our masthead. So great was it that Wolf Larsen himself did not dare heave to, though he was being driven far to the southward and out of the seal herd.

We must have been well in the path of the transpacific steamships when the typhoon moderated, and here, to the surprise of the hunters, we found ourselves in the midst of seals—a second herd, or sort of rear-guard, they declared, and a most unusual thing. But it was "Boats over!" the *boom, boom* of guns, and pitiful slaughter through the long day.

It was at this time that I was approached by Leach. I had just finished tallying the skins of the last boat aboard when he came to my side, in the darkness, and said in a low tone:

"Can you tell me, Mr. Van Weyden, how far we are off the coast, and what the bearings of Yokohama are?"

My heart leaped with gladness, for I knew what he had in mind, and I gave him the bearings—west-northwest and five hundred miles away.

"Thank you, sir," was all he said as he slipped back into the darkness.

Next morning No. 3 boat and Johnson and Leach were missing. The water-breakers and grub-boxes from all the other boats were likewise missing, as were the beds and sea-bags of the two men. Wolf Larsen was furious. He set sail and bore away into the west-northwest, two hunters constantly at the mastheads and sweeping the sea with glasses, himself pacing the deck like an angry lion. He knew too well my sympathy for the runaways to send me aloft as lookout.

The wind was fair but fitful, and it was like looking for a needle in a haystack to raise that tiny boat out of the blue immensity. But he put the *Ghost* through her best paces, so as to get between the deserters and the land. This accomplished, he cruised back and forth across what he knew must be their course.

On the morning of the third day, shortly after eight bells, a cry that the boat was sighted came down from Smoke at the masthead. All hands lined the rail. A snappy breeze was blowing from the west, with the promise of more wind behind it; and there, to leeward, in the troubled silver of the rising sun, appeared and disappeared a black speck.

We squared away and ran for it. My heart was as lead. I felt myself turning sick in anticipation; and as I looked at the gleam of triumph in Wolf Larsen's eyes, his form swam before me, and I felt almost irresistibly impelled to fling myself upon him. So unnerved was I by the thought of impending violence to Leach and Johnson that my reason must have left me. I know that I slipped down into the steerage, in a daze, and that I was just beginning the ascent to the deck, a loaded shot-gun in my hands, when I heard the startled cry:

Drawn by W. J. Aylward.

THE DESERTERS UNDER FIRE

"There 's five men in that boat!"

I supported myself in the companion-way, weak and trembling, while the observation was being verified by the remarks of the rest of the men. Then my knees gave from under me, and I sank down, myself again, but overcome by shock at knowledge of what I had so nearly done. Also, I was very thankful as I put the gun away and slipped back on deck.

No one had remarked my absence. The boat was near enough for us to make out that it was larger than any sealing-boat and built on different lines. As we drew closer, the sail was taken in and the mast unstepped. Oars were shipped, and its occupants waited for us to heave to and take them aboard.

Smoke, who had descended to the deck and was now standing by my side, began to chuckle in a significant way. I looked at him inquiringly.

"Talk of a mess!" he giggled. "It 's a pretty one we 've got now."

"What 's wrong?" I demanded.

Again he chuckled. "Don't you see there, in the stern-sheets, on the bottom? May I never shoot a seal again if that ain't a woman!"

I looked closely, but was not sure until exclamations broke out on all sides. The boat contained four men, and its fifth occupant was certainly a woman.

We were agog with excitement, all except Wolf Larsen, who was too evidently disappointed in that it was not his own boat with the two victims of his malice.

We ran down the flying jib, hauled the jib-sheets to windward and the main-sheet flat, and came up into the wind. The oars struck the water, and with a few strokes the boat was alongside. I now caught my first fair glimpse of the woman. She was wrapped in a long ulster, for the morning was raw, and I could see nothing but her face and a mass of light-brown hair escaping from under the seaman's cap on her head. The eyes were large and brown and lustrous, the mouth sweet and sensitive, and the face itself a delicate oval, though sun and exposure to briny wind had burned the face scarlet.

She seemed to me like a being from another world. I was aware of a hungry outreaching for her, as of a starving man for bread. But then I had not seen a woman for a very long time. I know that I was lost in a great wonder, almost a stupor,—this, then, was a woman?—so that I forgot myself and my mate's duties, and took no part in helping the newcomers aboard. For when one of the sailors lifted her into Wolf Larsen's down-stretched arms, she looked up into our curious faces and smiled amusedly and sweetly, as only a woman can smile, and as I had seen no one smile for so long that I had forgotten such smiles existed.

"Mr. Van Weyden!"

Wolf Larsen's voice brought me sharply back to myself.

"Will you take the lady below and see to her comfort? Make up that spare port cabin. Put Cooky to work on it. And see what you can do for that face. It 's burned badly."

He turned brusquely away from us and began to question the new men. The boat was cast adrift, though one of them called it a "bloody shame," with Yokohama so near.

I found myself strangely afraid of this woman I was escorting aft. Also, I was awkward. It seemed to me that I was realizing for the first time what a delicate, fragile creature a woman is, and as I caught her arm to help her down the companion-stairs, I was startled by its smallness and softness. Indeed, she was a slender, delicate woman, as women go, but to me she was so ethereally slender and delicate that I was quite prepared for her arm to crumble in my grasp. All this in frankness, to show my first impression, after long deprivation, of women in general and of Maud Brewster in particular.

"No need to go to any great trouble for me," she protested, when I had seated her in Wolf Larsen's arm-chair, which I had dragged hastily from his cabin. "The men were looking for land at any moment this morning, and the vessel should be in by night, don't you think so?"

Her simple faith in the immediate future took me aback. How could I explain to her the situation, the strange man who stalked the sea like Destiny, all that it had taken me months to learn? But I answered honestly:

"If it were any other captain except ours, I should say you would be ashore in Yokohama to-morrow. But our captain is a strange man, and I beg of you to be prepared for anything—understand?—for anything."

"I—I confess I hardly do understand," she hesitated, a perturbed but not frightened expression in her eyes. "Or is it a misconception of mine that shipwrecked people are always shown every consideration? This is such a little thing, you know. We are so close to the land."

"Candidly, I do not know," I strove to reassure her. "I wished merely to prepare you for the worst, if the worst is to come. This man, this captain, is a brute, a demon, and one can never tell what will be his next fantastic act."

I was growing excited, but she interrupted me with an "Oh, I see," and her voice sounded weary. To think was patently an effort. She was clearly on the verge of physical collapse.

She asked no further questions, and I vouchsafed no remarks, devoting myself to Wolf Larsen's command, which was to make her comfortable. I bustled about in quite housewifely fashion, procuring soothing lotions for her sunburn, raiding Wolf Larsen's private stores for a bottle of port I knew to be there, and directing Thomas Mugridge in the preparation of the spare state-room.

The wind was freshening rapidly, the *Ghost* heeling over more and more, and by the time the state-room was ready she was dashing through the water at a lively clip. I had quite forgotten the existence of Leach and Johnson, when suddenly, like a thunder-clap, "Boat ho!" came down the open companionway. It was Smoke's unmistakable voice, crying from the masthead. I shot a glance at the woman, but she was leaning back in the arm-chair, her eyes closed, unutterably tired. I doubted that she had heard, and I resolved to prevent her seeing the brutality I knew would follow the capture of the deserters. She was tired. Very good. She should sleep.

There were swift commands on deck, a stamping of feet and a slapping of reef-points, as the *Ghost* shot into the wind and about on the other tack. As she filled away and heeled, the arm-chair began to slide across the cabin floor, and I sprang for it just in time to prevent the rescued woman from being spilled out.

Her eyes were too heavy to suggest more than a hint of the sleepy surprise that perplexed her as she looked up at me, and she half stumbled, half tottered as I led her to her cabin. Mugridge grinned insinuatingly in my face as I shoved him out and ordered him back to his galley work, and he won his revenge by spreading glowing reports among the hunters as to what an excellent "lydy's-myde" I was proving myself to be.

She leaned heavily against me, and I do believe that she had fallen asleep again between the arm-chair and the state-room. This I discovered when she nearly fell into the bunk during a sudden lurch of the schooner. She aroused, smiled drowsily, and was off to sleep again; and asleep I left her, under a heavy pair of sailor's blankets, her head resting on a pillow I had appropriated from Wolf Larsen's bunk.

Drawn by William J. Aylward.

"MUGRIDGE KICKED SAVAGELY"

THE SEA-WOLF

BY JACK LONDON

Author of "The Call of the Wild," "The God of his Fathers," etc.

XIX

I CAME on deck to find the *Ghost* heading up close on the port tack and cutting in to windward of a familiar spritsail close-hauled on the same tack ahead of us. All hands were on deck, for they knew that something was to happen when Leach and Johnson were dragged aboard.

It was four bells. Louis came aft to relieve the wheel. There was a dampness in the air, and I noticed he had on his oilskins.

"What are we going to have?" I asked him.

"A healthy young slip of a gale from the breath of it, sir," he answered, "with a splatter of rain just to wet our gills an' no more."

"Too bad we sighted them," I said, as the *Ghost's* bow was flung off a point by a large sea, and the boat leaped for a moment past the jibs and into our line of vision.

Louis turned a spoke of the wheel and temporized.

"They 'd never of made the land, sir, I 'm thinkin'."

"Think not?" I queried.

"No, sir. Did you feel that?" A puff had caught the schooner, and he was forced to put the wheel up rapidly to keep her out of the wind. "'T is no egg-shell 'll float on this sea an hour come. An' it 's a stroke of luck for them we 're here to pick 'em up."

Wolf Larsen strode aft from amidships, where he had been talking with the rescued men. The cat-like springiness in his tread was a little more pronounced than usual, and his eyes were bright and snappy.

"Three oilers and a fourth engineer," was his greeting. "But we 'll make sailors out of them, or boat-pullers, at any rate. Now, what of the lady?"

I knew not why, but I was aware of a twinge or pang, like the cut of a knife, when he mentioned her. I thought it a certain silly fastidiousness on my part, but it persisted in spite of me, and I merely shrugged my shoulders in answer.

Wolf Larsen pursed his lips in a long quizzical whistle.

"What 's her name, then?" he demanded.

"I don't know," I replied. "She is asleep. She was very tired. In fact, I am waiting to hear the news from you. What vessel was it?"

"Mail-steamer," he answered shortly. "The *City of Tokio*, from 'Frisco, bound for Yokohama. Disabled in that typhoon. Old tub. Opened up top and bottom like a sieve. They were adrift four days. And you don't know who or what she is, eh—maid, wife, or widow? Well, well."

He shook his head in a bantering way and regarded me with laughing eyes.

"Are you—" I began. It was on the verge of my tongue to ask if he were going to take the castaways in to Yokohama.

"Am I what?" he asked.

"What do you intend doing with Leach and Johnson?"

He shook his head.

"Really, Hump, I don't know. You see, with these additions I 've about all the crew I want."

"And they 've about all the escaping they want," I said. "Why not give them a change of treatment? Take them aboard and deal gently with them. Whatever they have done, they have been hounded into doing."

"By me?"

"By you," I answered steadily. "And I give you warning, Wolf Larsen, that I may forget the love of my own life in the desire to kill you if you go too far in maltreating those poor wretches."

"Bravo!" he cried. "You do me proud, Hump! You 've found your legs with a vengeance. You 're quite an individual. You were unfortunate in having your life cast in easy places, but you 're developing, and I like you the better for it."

His voice and expression changed. His face was serious. "Do you believe in promises?" he asked. "Are they sacred things?"

"Of course," I answered.

"Then here 's a compact," he went on, consummate actor that he was. "If I promise not to lay hands upon Leach and Johnson, will you promise, in turn, not to attempt to kill me? Oh, not that I 'm afraid of you, not that I 'm afraid of you," he hastened to add.

I could hardly believe my ears. What was coming over the man?

"Is it a go?" he asked impatiently.

"A go," I answered.

His hand went out to mine, and as I shook it heartily I could have sworn I saw the mocking devil shine up for a moment in his eyes.

We strolled across the poop to the lee side. The boat was close at hand now and in desperate plight. Johnson was steering, Leach bailing. We overhauled them about two feet to their one. Wolf Larsen motioned Louis to keep off slightly, and we dashed abreast of the boat not a score of feet to windward.

It was at this moment that Leach and Johnson looked up into the faces of their shipmates who lined the rail amidships. There was no greeting. They were as dead men in their comrades' eyes, and between them was the gulf that parts the living and the dead.

The next instant they were opposite the poop, where stood Wolf Larsen and I. We were falling in the trough, and they were rising on the surge. Johnson looked at me, and I could see that his face was worn and haggard. I waved my hand to him, and he answered the greeting, but with a wave that was hopeless and despairing. It was as if he were saying farewell. I did not see into the eyes of Leach, for he was looking at Wolf Larsen, the old and implacable snarl of hatred as strong as ever on his face.

Then they were gone astern. The spritsail filled with the wind suddenly, careening the frail, open craft till it seemed it would surely capsize.

Wolf Larsen barked a short laugh in my ear and strode away to the weather side of the poop. I expected him to give orders for the *Ghost* to heave to, but she kept on her course and he made no sign. Louis stood imperturbably at the wheel, but I noticed the grouped sailors forward turning troubled faces in our direction. Still the *Ghost* tore along till the boat dwindled to a speck, when Wolf Larsen's voice rang out in command, and we went about on the starboard tack.

Back we held, two miles and more to windward of the struggling cockle-shell, when the flying jib was run down and the schooner hove to. In all that wild waste there was no refuge for Leach and Johnson save on the *Ghost*, and they resolutely began the windward beat. At the end of an hour and a half they were nearly alongside, standing past our stern on the last leg out, aiming to fetch us on the next leg back.

"So you 've changed your mind?" I heard Wolf Larsen mutter, half to himself, half to them, as though they could hear. "You want to come aboard, eh? Well, then, just keep a-coming. Hard up with that helm!" he commanded Oofty-Oofty, the Kanaka, who had in the meantime relieved Louis at the wheel.

Command followed command. As the schooner paid off, the fore- and main-sheets were slacked away for fair wind. And before the wind we were, and leaping, when Johnson, easing his sheet at imminent peril, cut across our wake a hundred feet away. Again Wolf Larsen laughed, at the same time beckoning them with his arm to follow. It was evidently his intention to play with them—a lesson, I took it, in lieu of a beating, though a dangerous lesson, for the frail craft stood in momentary danger of being overwhelmed.

"'T is the fear of death at the hearts of them," Louis muttered in my ear as I passed forward to see to taking in the flying jib and staysail.

"Oh, he 'll heave to in a little while and pick them up," I answered cheerfully.

Louis looked at me shrewdly. "Think so?" he asked.

"Surely," I answered. "Don't you?"

"I think nothing but of my own skin, these days," was his answer. "An' 't is with wonder I 'm filled as to the workin' out of things. A pretty mess that 'Frisco whisky got me into, an' a prettier mess that woman 's got you into aft there. Ah, it 's myself that knows ye for a blitherin' fool."

"What do you mean?" I demanded; for, having sped his shaft, he was turning away.

"What do I mean?" he cried. "An' it 's you that asks me! 'T is not what I mean, but what the Wolf 'll mean. The Wolf, I said, the Wolf!"

"If trouble comes, will you stand by?" I asked impulsively, for he had voiced my own fear.

"Stand by? 'T is old fat Louis I stand by, an' trouble enough it 'll be. We 're at the beginnin' of things, I 'm tellin' ye, the bare beginnin' of things."

"I had not thought you so great a coward," I sneered.

He favored me with a contemptuous stare.

"If I raised never a hand for that poor fool,"—pointing astern to the tiny sail,—"d' ye think I 'm hungerin' for a broken head for a woman I never laid me eyes upon before this day?"

I turned scornfully away and went aft.

"Better get in those topsails, Mr. Van Weyden," Wolf Larsen said, as I came on the poop.

I felt relief, at least as far as the two men were concerned. I had scarcely opened my mouth to issue the necessary commands, when eager men were springing to halyards and downhauls, and others were racing aloft. This eagerness on their part was noted by Wolf Larsen with a grim smile.

Still we increased our lead, and when the boat had dropped astern several miles we hove to and waited. All eyes watched it coming, even Wolf Larsen's; but he was the only unperturbed man aboard. Louis, gazing fixedly, betrayed a trouble in his face he was not quite able to hide.

The boat drew closer and closer, hurling along through the seething green like a thing alive, lifting and sending and uptossing across the huge-backed breakers, or disappearing behind them only to rush into sight again and shoot skyward. It seemed impossible that it could continue to live, yet with each dizzying sweep it did achieve the impossible. A rain-squall drove past, and out of the flying wet the boat emerged, almost upon us.

"Hard up, there!" Wolf Larsen shouted, himself springing to the wheel and whirling it over.

Again the *Ghost* sprang away and raced before the wind, and for two hours Johnson and Leach pursued us. We hove to and ran away, hove to and ran away; and ever astern the struggling patch of sail tossed skyward and fell into the rushing valleys. It was a quarter of a mile away when a thick squall of rain veiled it from view. It never emerged. The wind blew the air clear again, but no patch of sail broke the troubled surface. I thought I saw, for an instant, the boat's bottom show black in a breaking crest. At the best, that was all. For Johnson and Leach the travail of existence had ceased.

The men remained grouped amidships. No one had gone below, and no one was speaking. Nor were any looks being exchanged. Each man seemed stunned—deeply contemplative, as it were, and, not quite sure, trying to realize just what had taken place. Wolf Larsen gave them little time for thought. He at once put the *Ghost* upon her course—a course which meant the seal-herd and not Yokohama harbor. But the men were no longer eager as they pulled and hauled, and I heard curses among them which left their lips smothered and as heavy and lifeless as were they. Not so was it with the hunters. Smoke the irrepressible related a story, and they descended into the steerage bellowing with laughter.

As I passed to leeward of the galley on my way aft, I was approached by the engineer we had rescued. His face was white, his lips were trembling.

"Good God! sir, what kind of a craft is this?" he cried.

"You have eyes; you have seen," I answered almost brutally, what of the pain and fear at my own heart.

"Your promise?" I said to Wolf Larsen.

"I was not thinking of taking them aboard when I made that promise," he answered. "And, anyway, you 'll agree I 've not laid my hands upon them. Far from it, far from it," he laughed a moment later.

I made no reply. I was incapable of speaking, my mind was too confused. I must have time to think, I knew. This woman, sleeping even now in the spare cabin, was a responsibility which I must consider, and the only rational thought that flickered through my mind was that I must do nothing hastily if I were to be any help to her at all.

XX

THE remainder of the day passed uneventfully. The young slip of a gale, having wetted our gills, proceeded to moderate. The fourth engineer and the three oilers, after a warm interview with Wolf Larsen, were furnished with outfits from the slop-chest, assigned places under the hunters in the various boats and watches on the vessel, and bundled forward into the forecastle. They went protestingly, but their voices were not loud. They were awed by what they had already seen of Wolf Larsen's character, while the tale of woe they speedily heard in the forecastle took the last bit of rebellion out of them.

Miss Brewster—we had learned her name from the engineer—slept on and on. At supper I requested the hunters to lower their voices, so she was not disturbed; and it was not till next morning that she made her appearance. It had been my intention to have her meals served apart, but Wolf Larsen put down his foot. Who was she that she should be too good for cabin table and cabin society? had been his demand.

But her coming to the table had something amusing in it. The hunters fell as silent as clams. Jock Horner and Smoke alone were unabashed, stealing stealthy glances at her now and again, and even taking part in the conversation. The other four men glued their eyes on their plates and chewed steadily and with thoughtful precision, their ears moving and wabbling, in time with their jaws, like the ears of so many animals.

Wolf Larsen had little to say at first, doing no more than reply when he was addressed. Not that he was abashed. Far from it. This woman was a new type to him, a different breed from any he had ever known, and he was curious. He studied her, his eyes rarely leaving her face, unless to follow the movements of her hands or shoulders. I studied her myself, and though it was I who maintained the conversation, I know that I was a bit shy, not quite self-possessed. His was the perfect poise, the supreme confidence in self which nothing could shake; and he was no more timid of a woman than he was of storm and battle.

"And when shall we arrive at Yokohama?" she asked, turning to him and looking him square in the eyes.

There it was, the question flat. The jaws stopped working, the ears ceased wabbling, and though eyes remained glued on plates, each man listened greedily for the answer.

"In four months, possibly three, if the season closes early," Wolf Larsen said.

She caught her breath and stammered: "I—I thought—I was given to understand that Yokohama was only a day's sail away. It—" Here she paused and looked about the table at the circle of unsympathetic faces staring hard at the plates. "It is not right," she concluded.

"That is a question you must settle with Mr. Van Weyden there," he replied, bowing to me with a mischievous twinkle. "Mr. Van Weyden is what you may call an authority on such things as rights. Now I, who am only a sailor, would look upon the situation somewhat differently. It may possibly be your misfortune that you have to remain with us, but it is certainly our good fortune."

He regarded her smilingly. Her eyes fell before his gaze, but she lifted them again, and defiantly, to mine. I read the unspoken question there: Was it right? But I had decided that the part I was to play must be a neutral one, so I did not answer.

"What do you think?" she demanded.

"It is unfortunate," I said, "especially if you have any engagements falling due in the course of the next several months. But, since you say that you were voyaging to Japan for your health, I can assure you that it will improve no better anywhere than aboard the *Ghost*."

I saw her eyes flash with indignation,

and this time it was I who dropped mine, while I felt my face flushing under her gaze. It was cowardly, but what else could I do?

"Mr. Van Weyden speaks with the voice of authority." Wolf Larsen laughed.

I nodded my head, and she, having recovered herself, waited expectantly.

"Not that he is much to speak of now," Wolf Larsen went on; "but he has improved wonderfully. You should have seen him when he came on board. A more scrawny, pitiful specimen of humanity one could hardly conceive. Is n't that so, Kerfoot?"

Kerfoot, thus directly addressed, was startled into dropping his knife on the floor, though he managed to grunt affirmation.

"Developed himself by peeling potatoes and washing dishes. Eh, Kerfoot?"

Again that worthy grunted.

"Look at him now. True, he is not what you would term muscular, but still he has muscles, which is more than he had when he came aboard. Also, he has legs to stand on. You would not think so to look at him, but he was quite unable to stand alone at first."

The hunters were snickering, but she looked at me with a sympathy in her eyes which more than compensated for Wolf Larsen's nastiness. In truth, it had been so long since I had received sympathy that I was softened, and I became then, and gladly, her willing slave. But I was angry with Wolf Larsen. He was challenging my manhood with his slurs, challenging the very legs he claimed to be instrumental in getting for me.

"I may have learned to stand on my own legs," I retorted. "But I have yet to stamp upon others with them."

He looked at me insolently. "Your education is only half completed, then," he said dryly, and turned to her. "We are very hospitable upon the *Ghost*. Mr. Van Weyden has discovered that. We do everything to make our guests feel at home, eh, Mr. Van Weyden?"

"Even to the peeling of potatoes and the washing of dishes," I answered, "to say nothing of wringing their necks, out of very fellowship."

"I beg of you not to receive false impressions of us from Mr. Van Weyden," he interposed with mock anxiety. "You will observe, Miss Brewster, that he carries a dirk in his belt, a—ahem—a most unusual thing for a ship's officer to do. While really very estimable, Mr. Van Weyden is sometimes—how shall I say?—er—quarrelsome, and harsh measures are necessary. He is quite reasonable and fair in his calm moments, and as he is calm now, he will not deny that only yesterday he threatened my life."

I was well-nigh choking, and my eyes were certainly fiery. He drew attention to me.

"Look at him now. He can scarcely control himself in your presence. He is not accustomed to the presence of ladies, anyway. I shall have to arm myself before I dare go on deck with him."

He shook his head sadly, murmuring, "Too bad, too bad," while the hunters burst into guffaws of laughter.

The deep sea-voices of these men, rumbling and bellowing in the confined space, produced a wild effect. The whole setting was wild, and for the first time, regarding this strange woman and realizing how incongruous she was in it, I was aware of how much a part of it I was myself. I knew these men and their mental processes, was one of them myself, living the seal-hunting life, eating the seal-hunting fare, thinking largely the seal-hunting thoughts. There was no strangeness to it, to the rough clothes, the coarse faces, the wild laughter, and the lurching cabin walls and swaying sea-lamps.

As I buttered a piece of bread my eyes chanced to rest upon my hand. The knuckles were skinned and inflamed clear across, the fingers swollen, the nails rimmed with black. I felt the mattress-like growth of beard on my neck, knew that the sleeve of my coat was ripped, that a button was missing from the throat of the blue shirt I wore. The dirk mentioned by Wolf Larsen rested in its sheath on my hip. It was very natural that it should be there—how natural I had not imagined until now, when I looked upon it with her eyes and knew how strange it and all that went with it must appear to her.

But she divined the mockery in Wolf Larsen's words, and again favored me with a sympathetic glance. But there was a look of bewilderment also in her eyes. That it was mockery made the situation more puzzling to her.

"I may be taken off by some passing vessel, perhaps," she suggested.

"There will be no passing vessels, except other sealing-schooners," Wolf Larsen made answer.

"I have no clothes, nothing," she objected. "You hardly realize, sir, that I am not a man, or that I am unaccustomed to the vagrant, careless life which you and your men seem to lead."

"The sooner you get accustomed to it the better," he said. "I 'll furnish you with cloth, needles, and thread," he added. "I hope it will not be too dreadful a hardship for you to make yourself a dress or two."

She made a wry pucker with her mouth, as though to advertise her ignorance of dressmaking. That she was frightened and bewildered, and that she was bravely striving to hide it, was quite plain to me.

"I suppose you 're like Mr. Van Weyden there, accustomed to having things done for you. Well, I think doing a few things for yourself will hardly dislocate any joints. By the way, what do you do for a living?"

She regarded him with amazement unconcealed.

"I mean no offense, believe me. People eat, therefore they must procure the wherewithal. These men here shoot seals in order to live; for the same reason I sail this schooner; and Mr. Van Weyden, for the present at any rate, earns his salty grub by assisting me. Now what do you do?"

She shrugged her shoulders.

"Do you feed yourself, or does some one else feed you?"

"I 'm afraid some one else has fed me most of my life," she laughed, trying bravely to enter into the spirit of his quizzing, though I could see a terror dawning and growing in her eyes as she watched Wolf Larsen.

"And I suppose some one else makes your bed for you?"

"I *have* made beds," she replied.

"Very often?"

She shook her head with mock ruefulness.

"Do you know what they do to poor men in the States who, like you, do not work for their living?"

"I am very ignorant," she pleaded. "What do they do to the poor men who are like me?"

"They send them to jail. The crime of not earning a living, in their case, is called vagrancy. If I were Mr. Van Weyden, who harps eternally on questions of right and wrong, I 'd ask, By what right do you live when you do nothing to deserve living?"

"But as you are not Mr. Van Weyden, I don't have to answer, do I?"

She beamed upon him through her terror-filled eyes, and the pathos of it cut me to the heart. I felt that I must in some way break in and lead the conversation into other channels.

"Have you ever earned a dollar by your own labor?" he demanded, certain of her answer, a triumphant vindictiveness in his voice.

"Yes, I have," she answered slowly, and I could have laughed aloud at his crestfallen visage. "I remember my father giving me a dollar once, when I was a little girl, for remaining absolutely quiet for five minutes."

He smiled indulgently.

"But that was long ago," she continued. "And you would scarcely demand a little girl of nine to earn her own living. At present, however," she said, after another slight pause, "I earn about eighteen hundred dollars a year."

With one accord all eyes left the plates and settled on her. A woman who earned eighteen hundred dollars a year was worth looking at. Wolf Larsen was undisguised in his admiration.

"Salary or piece-work?" he asked.

"Piece-work," she answered promptly.

"Eighteen hundred," he calculated. "That 's a hundred and fifty dollars a month. Well, Miss Brewster, there is nothing small about the *Ghost*. Consider yourself on salary during the time you remain with us."

She made no acknowledgment. She was too unused as yet to the whims of the man to accept them with equanimity.

"I forgot to inquire," he went on suavely, "as to the nature of your occupation. What commodities do you turn out? What tools and materials do you require?"

"Paper and ink," she laughed. "And, oh! also a type-writer."

"You are Maud Brewster," I said slowly and with certainty, almost as though I were charging her with a crime.

Her eyes lifted curiously to mine.

"How do you know?"

"Are n't you?" I demanded.

She acknowledged her identity with a nod. It was Wolf Larsen's turn to be puzzled. The name and its magic signified nothing to him. I was proud that it did mean something to me, and for the first time in a weary while I was convincingly conscious of a superiority over him.

"I remember writing a review of a thin little volume—" I had begun carelessly, when she interrupted me.

"You!" she cried. "You are—"

She was now staring at me in wide-eyed wonder.

I nodded my identity, in turn.

"Humphrey Van Weyden," she concluded; then added, with a sigh of relief and unaware that she had glanced that relief at Wolf Larsen, "I am so glad.

"I remember the review," she went on hastily, becoming aware of the awkwardness of her remark, "that too, too flattering review."

"Not at all," I denied valiantly. "You impeach my sober judgment and make my canons of little worth. Besides, all my brother critics were with me."

"You are very kind, I am sure," she murmured; and the very conventionality of her tones and words, with the host of associations it aroused of the old life on the other side of the world, gave me a quick thrill—rich with remembrance but stinging sharp with homesickness.

"And you are Maud Brewster," I said solemnly, gazing across at her.

"And you are Humphrey Van Weyden," she said, gazing back at me with equal solemnity and awe. "How unusual! I don't understand. We surely are not to expect some wildly romantic sea-story from your sober pen."

"No, I am not gathering material, I assure you," was my answer. "I have neither aptitude nor inclination for fiction."

"Tell me, why have you always buried yourself in California?" she next asked. "It has not been kind of you. We of the East have seen so very little of you—too little indeed of the Dean of American Letters the Second."

I bowed to, and disclaimed, the compliment.

"I nearly met you, once, in Philadelphia, some Browning affair or other—you were to lecture, you know. My train was four hours late."

And then we quite forgot where we were, leaving Wolf Larsen stranded and silent in the midst of our flood of gossip. The hunters left the table and went on deck, and still we talked. Wolf Larsen alone remained. Suddenly I became aware of him, leaning back from the table and listening curiously to our alien speech of a world he did not know.

I broke short off in the middle of a sentence. The present, with all its perils and anxieties, rushed upon me with stunning force. It smote Miss Brewster likewise, a vague and nameless terror rushing into her eyes as she regarded Wolf Larsen.

He rose to his feet and laughed awkwardly. The sound of it was metallic.

"Oh, don't mind me," he said, with a self-depreciatory wave of his hand. "I don't count. Go on, go on, I pray you."

But the gates of speech were closed, and we, too, rose from the table and laughed awkwardly.

XXI

THE chagrin Wolf Larsen felt from being ignored by Maud Brewster and me in the conversation at table had to express itself in some fashion, and it fell to Thomas Mugridge to be the victim. He had not mended his ways or his shirt, though the latter he contended he had changed. The garment itself did not bear out the assertion, nor did the accumulations of grease on stove and pot and pan attest a general cleanliness.

"I 've given you warning, Cooky," Wolf Larsen said, "and now you 've got to take your medicine."

Mugridge's face turned white under its sooty veneer, and when Wolf Larsen called for a rope and a couple of men, the miserable Cockney fled wildly out of the galley and dodged and ducked about the deck, with the grinning crew in pursuit. Few things could have been more to their liking than to give him a tow over the side, for to the forecastle he had sent messes and concoctions of the vilest order. Conditions favored the undertaking. The *Ghost* was slipping through the water at no more than three miles an hour, and the sea was fairly calm. But Mugridge had little stomach for a dip in it. Possibly he had seen men towed before. Besides, the water was frightfully cold, and his was anything but a rugged constitution.

As usual, the watches below and the hunters turned out for what promised sport. Mugridge seemed to be in rabid fear of the water, and he exhibited a nimbleness and speed we did not dream he possessed. Cornered in the right angle of the poop and galley, he sprang like a cat to the top of the cabin and ran aft. But, his pursuers forestalling him, he doubled back across the cabin, passed over the galley, and gained the deck by means of the steerage scuttle. Straight forward he raced, the boat-puller Harrison at his heels and gaining on him. But Mugridge, leaping suddenly, caught the jib-boom-lift. It happened in an instant. Holding his weight by his arms and in mid-air doubling his body at the hips, he let fly with both feet. The oncoming Harrison caught the kick squarely in the pit of the stomach, groaned involuntarily, and doubled up and backward to the deck.

Hand-clapping and roars of laughter from the hunters greeted the exploit, while Mugridge, eluding half of his pursuers at the foremast, ran aft and through the remainder like a runner on the foot-ball field. Straight aft he held to the poop, and along the poop to the stern. So great was his speed that as he curved past the corner of the cabin he slipped and fell. Nilson was standing at the wheel, and the Cockney's hurtling body struck his legs. Both went down together, but Mugridge alone arose. By some freak of pressures, his frail body had snapped the strong man's leg like a pipe-stem.

Parsons took the wheel, and the pursuit continued. Round and round the decks they went, Mugridge sick with fear, the sailors hallooing and shouting directions to one another, and the hunters bellowing encouragement and laughter. Mugridge went down on the fore-hatch, under three men; but he emerged from the mass like an eel, bleeding at the mouth, the offending shirt ripped into tatters, and sprang for the main-rigging. Up he went, clear up, beyond the ratlines, to the very masthead.

Half a dozen sailors swarmed to the crosstrees after him, where they clustered and waited while two of their number, Oofty-Oofty and Black (who was Latimer's boat-steerer), continued up the thin steel stays, lifting their bodies higher and higher by means of their arms.

It was a perilous undertaking, for, at a height of over a hundred feet from the deck, holding on by their hands, they were not in the best of positions to protect themselves from Mugridge's feet. And Mugridge kicked savagely, till the Kanaka, hanging on with one hand, seized the Cockney's foot with the other. Black duplicated the performance a moment later with the other foot. Then the three writhed together in a swaying tangle, struggling, sliding, and falling into the arms of their mates on the crosstrees.

The aërial battle was over, and Thomas Mugridge, whining and gibbering, was brought down to the deck. Wolf Larsen rove a bowline in a piece of rope and slipped it under his shoulders. Then he was carried aft and flung into the sea. Forty—fifty—sixty feet of line ran out, when Wolf Larsen cried, "Belay!" Oofty-Oofty took a turn on a bitt, the rope tautened, and the *Ghost*, lunging onward, jerked the cook to the surface.

It was a pitiful spectacle. Though he could not drown, and was nine-lived in addition, he was suffering all the agonies of half-drowning. The *Ghost* was going very slowly, and when her stern lifted on a wave and she slipped forward, she pulled the wretch to the surface and gave him a moment in which to breathe; but after each lift the stern fell, and while the bow lazily climbed the next wave the line slacked and he sank beneath.

I had forgotten the existence of Maud Brewster, and I remembered her with a start as she stepped lightly beside me. It was her first time on deck since she had come aboard. A dead silence greeted her appearance.

"What is the cause of the merriment?" she asked.

"Ask Captain Larsen," I answered composedly and coldly, though inwardly my blood was boiling at the thought that she should be witness to such brutality.

She took my advice and was turning to put it into execution when her eyes lighted on Oofty-Oofty, immediately before her, his body instinct with alertness and grace as he held the turn of the rope.

"Are you fishing?" she asked him.

He made no reply. His eyes, fixed intently on the sea astern, suddenly flashed.

"Shark, ho, sir!" he cried.

"Heave in! Lively! All hands tail on!" Wolf Larsen shouted, springing himself to the rope in advance of the quickest.

Mugridge had heard the Kanaka's warning cry and was screaming madly. I could see a black fin cutting the water and making for him with greater swiftness than he was being pulled aboard. It was an even toss whether the shark or we would get him, and it was a matter of moments. When Mugridge was directly beneath us, the stern descended the slope of a passing wave, thus giving the advantage to the shark. The fin disappeared. The belly flashed white in a swift upward rush. Almost equally swift, but not quite, was Wolf Larsen. He threw his strength into one tremendous jerk. The Cockney's body left the water, so did part of the shark's. He drew up his legs, and the man-eater seemed no more than barely to touch one foot, sinking back into the water with a splash. But at the moment of contact Thomas Mugridge cried out. Then he came in like a fresh-caught fish on a line, clearing the rail generously and striking the deck in a heap, on hands and knees, and rolling over. The right foot was missing, amputated neatly at the ankle!

I looked instantly at Maud Brewster. Her face was white, her eyes dilated with horror. She was gazing, not at Thomas Mugridge, but at Wolf Larsen. And he was aware of it, for he said, with one of his short laughs:

"Man-play, Miss Brewster. Somewhat rougher, I warrant, than what you have been used to, but still man-play. The shark was not in the reckoning. It—"

But at this juncture, Mugridge, who had lifted his head and ascertained the extent of his loss, floundered over on the deck and buried his teeth in Wolf Larsen's leg. Wolf Larsen stooped, coolly, to the Cockney, and pressed with thumb and finger at the rear of the jaws and below the ears. The jaws opened with reluctance, and Wolf Larsen stepped free.

"As I was saying," he went on, as though nothing unwonted had happened, "the shark was not in the reckoning. It was—ahem—shall we say Providence?"

She gave no sign that she had heard, though the expression of her eyes changed to one of inexpressible loathing as she started to turn away. She no more than started, for she swayed and tottered, and reached her hand weakly out to mine. I caught her in time to save her from falling, and helped her to a seat on the cabin. I thought she must faint outright, but she controlled herself.

"Will you get a tourniquet, Mr. Van Weyden?" Wolf Larsen called to me.

I hesitated. Her lips moved, and though they formed no words, she commanded me with her eyes, plainly as speech, to go to the help of the unfortunate man. "Please," she managed to whisper, and I could but obey.

By now I had developed such skill at surgery that Wolf Larsen, beyond several words of advice, left me to my task with a couple of sailors for assistants. For his task he elected a vengeance on the shark.

A heavy swivel-hook, baited with fat salt pork, was dropped overside; and by the time I had compressed the severed veins and arteries the sailors were singing and heaving in the offending monster. I did not see it myself, but my assistants, first one and then the other, deserted me for a few moments to run amidships and look at what was going on. The shark, a sixteen-footer, was hoisted up against the main-rigging. Its jaws were pried apart to their greatest extension, and a stout stake, sharpened at both ends, was so inserted that when the pries were removed the spread jaws were fixed upon it. This accomplished, the hook was cut out. The shark dropped back into the sea, helpless, yet with its full strength, doomed to lingering starvation—a living death less meet for it than for the man who devised the punishment.

THE SEA-WOLF

BY JACK LONDON

Author of "The Call of the Wild," "The God of his Fathers," etc.

XXII

I KNEW what it was as she came toward me. For ten minutes I had watched her talking earnestly with the engineer, and now, with a sign for silence, I drew her out of earshot of the helmsman. Her face was white and set; her large eyes—larger than usual, what of the purpose in them—looked penetratingly into mine. I felt rather timid and apprehensive, for she had come to search Humphrey Van Weyden's soul, and Humphrey Van Weyden had nothing of which to be particularly proud since his advent on the *Ghost.*

We walked to the break of the poop, where she turned and faced me. I glanced around to see that no one was within hearing distance.

"What is it?" I asked gently; but the expression of grim determination on her face did not relax.

"I can readily understand," she began, "that this morning's affair was largely an accident; but I have been talking with Mr. Haskins. He tells me that the day we were rescued, even while I was in the cabin, two men were drowned, deliberately drowned—murdered."

There was a query in her voice, and she faced me accusingly, as though I were guilty of the deed, or at least a party to it.

"The information is quite correct," I answered. "The two men were murdered."

"And you permitted it!" she cried.

"I was unable to prevent it, is a better way of phrasing it," I replied, still gently.

"But you tried to prevent it?" There was an emphasis on the "tried," and a pleading little note in her voice. "Oh, but you did n't!" she hurried on, divining my answer. "But why did n't you?"

I shrugged my shoulders.

"You must remember, Miss Brewster, that you are a new inhabitant of this little world, and that you do not yet understand the laws which operate within it. You bring with you certain fine conceptions of humanity, manhood, conduct, and such things; but here you will find them misconceptions. I have found it so," I added, with an involuntary sigh.

She shook her head incredulously.

"What would you advise, then?" I asked. "That I should take a knife, or a gun, or an ax, and kill this man?"

She started back.

"No, not that!"

"Then what should I do? Kill myself?"

"You speak in purely materialistic terms," she objected. "There is such a thing as moral courage, and moral courage is never without effect."

"Ah," I smiled, "you advise me to kill neither him nor myself, but to let him kill me." I held up my hand as she was about to speak. "For moral courage is a worthless asset on this little floating world. Leach, one of the men who were murdered, had moral courage to an unusual degree.

So had the other man, Johnson. Not only did it not stand them in good stead, but it destroyed them. And so with me, if I should exercise what little moral courage I may possess. You must understand, Miss Brewster, and understand clearly, that this man is a monster. He is without conscience. Nothing is sacred to him, nothing is too terrible for him to do. It was due to his whim that I was detained aboard in the first place. It is due to his whim that I am still alive. I do nothing, can do nothing, because I am a slave to this monster, as you are now a slave to him; because I desire to live, as you will desire to live; because I cannot fight and overcome him, just as you will not be able to fight and overcome him."

She waited for me to go on.

"What remains? Mine is the rôle of the weak. I remain silent and suffer ignominy as you will remain silent and suffer ignominy. And it is well. It is the best we can do if we wish to live. The battle is not always to the strong. We have not the strength with which to fight this man; we must dissimulate, and win, if win we can, by craft. If you will be advised by me, this is what you will do. I know my position is perilous, and I may say frankly that yours is even more perilous. We must stand together, without appearing to do so, in secret alliance. I shall not be able to side with you openly, and, no matter what indignities may be put upon me, you are to remain likewise silent. We must provoke no scenes with this man, or cross his will. And we must keep smiling faces and be friendly with him, no matter how repulsive it may be."

She brushed her hand across her forehead in a puzzled way, saying, "Still, I do not understand."

"You must do as I say," I interrupted authoritatively, for I saw Wolf Larsen's gaze wandering toward us from where he paced up and down with Latimer amidships. "Do as I say, and before long you will find I am right."

"What shall I do, then?" she asked, detecting the anxious glance I had shot at the object of our conversation, and impressed, I flatter myself, with the earnestness of my manner.

"Dispense with all the moral courage you can," I said briskly. "Don't arouse this man's animosity. Be quite friendly with him, talk with him, discuss literature and art with him—he is fond of such things. You will find him an interested listener and no fool. And for your own sake try to avoid witnessing, as much as you can, the brutalities of the ship. It will make it easier for you to act your part."

"I am to lie," she said in steady, rebellious tones; "by speech and action to lie."

Wolf Larsen had separated from Latimer and was coming toward us. I was desperate.

"Please, please understand me," I said hurriedly, lowering my voice. "All your experience of men and things is worthless here. You must begin over again. I know—I can see it—you have, among other ways, been used to managing people with your eyes, letting your moral courage speak out through them, as it were. You have already managed me with your eyes, commanded me with them. But don't try it on Wolf Larsen. You could as easily control a lion, while he would make a mock of you. He would—

"I have always been proud of the fact that I discovered him," I said, turning the conversation as Wolf Larsen stepped on the poop and joined us. "The editors were afraid of him, and the publishers would have none of him. But I knew, and his genius and my judgment were vindicated when he made that magnificent hit with his 'Plowman.'"

"And it was a newspaper poem," she said glibly.

"It did happen to see the light in a newspaper," I replied, "but not because the magazine editors had been denied a glimpse at it.

"We were talking of Harris," I said to Wolf Larsen.

"Oh, yes," he acknowledged. "I remember 'The Ring.' Filled with pretty sentiments and an almighty faith in human illusions. By the way, Mr. Van Weyden, you 'd better look in on Cooky. He 's complaining and restless."

Thus was I bluntly dismissed from the poop, only to find Mugridge sleeping soundly from the morphine I had given him. I made no haste to return on deck, and when I did, I was gratified to see Miss Brewster in animated conversation with Wolf Larsen. As I say, the sight gratified me. She was following my advice. And yet I was conscious of a slight shock or hurt in that she was able to do the thing I had begged her to do, and which she had notably disliked.

XXIII

BRAVE winds, blowing fair, swiftly drove the *Ghost* northward into the seal-herd. We encountered it well up to the forty-fourth parallel, in a raw and stormy sea across which the wind harried the fog-banks in eternal flight. For days at a time we could never see the sun or take an observation; then the wind would sweep the face of the ocean clean, the waves would ripple and flash, and we would learn where we were. A day of clear weather might follow, or three days or four, and then the fog would settle down upon us seemingly thicker than ever.

The hunting was perilous; yet the boats were lowered day after day, were swallowed up in the gray obscurity, and were seen no more till nightfall, and often not till long after, when they would creep in like sea-wraiths, one by one, out of the gray. Wainwright, the hunter whom Wolf Larsen had stolen with boat and men, took advantage of the veiled sea and escaped. He disappeared one morning in the encircling fog with his two men, and we never saw them again, though it was not many days before we learned that they had passed from schooner to schooner until they finally regained their own.

This was the thing I had set my mind upon doing, but the opportunity never offered. It was not in the mate's province to go out in the boats, and though I manœuvered cunningly for it, Wolf Larsen never granted me the privilege. Had he done so, I should have managed somehow to carry Miss Brewster away with me. As it was, the situation was approaching a stage which I was afraid to consider. I involuntarily shunned the thought of it, and yet the thought continually arose in my mind like a haunting specter.

I had read sea-romances in my time, wherein figured, as a matter of course, the lone woman in the midst of a ship-load of men; but I learned now that I had never comprehended the deeper significance of such a situation—the thing the writers harped upon and exploited so thoroughly. And here it was now, and I was face to face with it. That it should be as vital as possible, it required no more than that the woman should be Maud Brewster, who now charmed me in person as she had long charmed me through her work.

No one more out of environment could be imagined. She was a delicate, ethereal creature, swaying and willowy, light and graceful of movement. It never seemed to me that she walked, or, at least, walked after the ordinary manner of mortals. Hers was an extreme lithesomeness, and she moved with a certain indefinable airiness, approaching one as down might float or as a bird on noiseless wings.

She was like a bit of Dresden china, and I was continually impressed with what I may call her fragility. As at the time I caught her arm when helping her below, so at any time I was quite prepared, should stress or rough handling befall her, to see her crumble away. I have never seen body and spirit in such perfect accord. Describe her verse, as the critics have, as sublimated and spiritual, and you have described her body. It seemed to partake of her soul, to have analogous attributes, and to link it to life with the slenderest of chains. Indeed, she trod the earth lightly, and in her constitution there was little of the robust clay.

She was in striking contrast to Wolf Larsen. Each was nothing that the other was, everything that the other was not. I noted them walking the deck together one morning, and I likened them to the extreme ends of the human ladder of evolution—the one the culmination of all savagery, the other the finished product of the finest civilization. True, Wolf Larsen possessed intellect to an unusual degree, but it was directed solely to the exercise of his savage instincts and made him but the more formidable a savage. He was splendidly muscled, a heavy man, and though he strode with the certitude and directness of the physical man, there was nothing heavy about his stride. The jungle and the wilderness lurked in the lift and downput of his feet. He was cat-footed, lithe, and strong, always strong. I likened him to some great tiger, a beast of prowess and prey. He looked it, and the piercing glitter that arose at times in his eyes was the same piercing glitter I had observed in the eyes of caged leopards and other preying creatures of the wild.

But this day, as I noted them pacing up

and down, I saw that it was she who terminated the walk. They came up to where I was standing by the entrance to the companionway. Though she betrayed it by no outward sign, I felt, somehow, that she was greatly perturbed. She made some idle remark, looking at me, and laughed lightly enough, but I saw her eyes return to his, involuntarily, as though fascinated; then they fell, but not swiftly enough to veil the rush of terror that filled them.

It was in his eyes that I saw the cause of her perturbation. Ordinarily gray and cold and harsh, they were now warm and soft and golden, and all adance with tiny lights that dimmed and faded, or welled up till the full orbs were flooded with a glowing radiance. Perhaps it was to this that the golden color was due; but golden his eyes were, enticing and masterful, at the same time luring and compelling, and speaking a demand and clamor of the blood which no woman, much less Maud Brewster, could misunderstand.

Her own terror rushed upon me, and in that moment of fear, the most terrible fear a man can experience, I knew that in inexpressible ways she was dear to me. The knowledge that I loved her rushed upon me with the terror, and with both emotions gripping at my heart and causing my blood at the same time to chill and to leap riotously, I felt myself drawn by a power without me and beyond me, and found my eyes returning against my will to gaze into the eyes of Wolf Larsen. But he had recovered himself. The golden color and the dancing lights were gone. Cold and gray and glittering they were as he bowed brusquely and turned away.

"I am afraid," she whispered, with a shiver. "I am so afraid."

I, too, was afraid, and, what of my discovery of how much she meant to me, my mind was in a turmoil; but I succeeded in answering quite calmly: "All will come right, Miss Brewster. Trust me; it will come right."

She answered with a grateful little smile that sent my heart pounding, and started to descend the companion-stairs.

For a long while I remained standing where she had left me. There was imperative need to adjust myself, to consider the significance of the changed aspect of things. It had come at last: love had come when I least expected it, and under the most forbidding conditions. Of course my philosophy had always recognized the inevitableness of the love-call sooner or later; but long years of bookish silence had made me inattentive and unprepared.

And now it had come! Maud Brewster! My memory flashed back to that first thin little volume on my desk, and I saw before me, as though in the concrete, the row of thin little volumes on my library shelf. How I had welcomed each of them! Each year one had come from the press, and to me each was the advent of the year. They had voiced a kindred intellect and spirit, and as such I had received them into a camaraderie of the mind; but now their place was in my heart.

My heart? A revulsion of feeling came over me. I seemed to stand outside myself and to look at myself incredulously. Maud Brewster! Humphrey Van Weyden, the "cold-blooded fish," the "emotionless monster," the "analytical demon," of Charley Furuseth's christening, in love! And then, without rhyme or reason, all skeptical, my mind flew back to a small note in a biographical directory, and I said to myself: "She was born in Cambridge, and she is twenty-seven years old." And then I said: "Twenty-seven years old, and still free and fancy-free." But how did I know she was fancy-free? And the pang of new-born jealousy put all incredulity to flight. There was no doubt about it. I was jealous; therefore I loved. And the woman I loved was Maud Brewster.

I, Humphrey Van Weyden, was in love! And again the doubt assailed me. Not that I was afraid of it, however, or reluctant to meet it. On the contrary, idealist that I was to the most pronounced degree, my philosophy had always recognized and guerdoned love as the greatest thing in the world, the aim and the summit of being, the most exquisite pitch of joy and happiness to which life could thrill, the thing of all things to be hailed and welcomed and taken into the heart. But now that it had come I could not believe. I could not be so fortunate. It was too good, too good to be true. These lines came into my head:

"I wandered all these years among
A world of women, seeking you."

And then I had ceased seeking. It was not for me, this greatest thing in the world,

Drawn by W. J. Aylward.

"HE SAW WOLF LARSEN'S RIFLE BEARING UPON HIM"

I had decided. Furuseth was right; I was abnormal, an "emotionless monster," a strange bookish creature capable of pleasuring in sensations only of the mind. And though I had been surrounded by women all my days, my appreciation of them had been esthetic and nothing more. I had actually, at times, considered myself outside the pale, a monkish fellow denied the eternal or the passing passions I saw and understood so well in others. And now it had come! Undreamed of and unheralded, it had come. In what could have been no less than an ecstasy, I left my post at the head of the companionway and started along the deck, murmuring to myself those beautiful lines of Mrs. Browning:

"I lived with visions for my company
Instead of men and women years ago,
And found them gentle mates, nor thought to know
A sweeter music than they played to me."

But the sweeter music was playing in my ears, and I was blind and oblivious to all about me. The sharp voice of Wolf Larsen aroused me.

"What the hell are you up to?" he was demanding.

I had strayed forward where the sailors were painting, and I came to myself to find my advancing foot on the verge of overturning a paint-pot.

"Sleep-walking, sunstroke—what?" he barked.

"No; indigestion," I retorted, and continued my walk as if nothing untoward had occurred.

XXIV

AMONG the most vivid memories of my life are those of the events on the *Ghost* which occurred during the forty hours succeeding the discovery of my love for Maud Brewster. I, who had lived my life in quiet places, only to enter at the age of thirty-five upon a course of the most irrational adventure I could have imagined, never had more incident and excitement crammed into any forty hours of my experience. Nor can I quite close my ears to a small voice of pride which tells me I did not do so badly, all things considered.

To begin with, at the midday dinner Wolf Larsen informed the hunters that they were to eat thenceforth in the steerage. It was an unprecedented thing on sealing-schooners, where it is the custom for the hunters to rank unofficially as officers. He gave no reason, but his motive was obvious enough. Horner and Smoke had been displaying a gallantry toward Maud Brewster, ludicrous in itself and inoffensive to her, but to him evidently distasteful.

The announcement was received with black silence, though the other four hunters glanced significantly at the two who had been the cause of their banishment. Jock Horner, quiet as was his way, gave no sign; but the blood surged darkly across Smoke's forehead, and he half opened his mouth to speak. Wolf Larsen was watching him, waiting for him, the steely glitter in his eyes; but Smoke closed his mouth again without having said anything.

"Anything to say?" the other demanded aggressively.

It was a challenge, but Smoke refused to accept it.

"About what?" he asked so innocently that Wolf Larsen was disconcerted, while the others smiled.

"Oh, nothing," Wolf Larsen said lamely. "I just thought you might want to register a kick."

"About what?" asked the imperturbable Smoke.

Smoke's mates were now smiling broadly. His captain could have killed him, and I doubt not that blood would have flowed had not Maud Brewster been present. For that matter, it was her presence which enabled Smoke to act as he did. He was too discreet and cautious a man to incur Wolf Larsen's anger at a time when that anger could be expressed in terms stronger than words. I was in fear that a struggle might take place, but a cry from the helmsman made it easy for the situation to save itself.

"Smoke ho!" the cry came down the open companionway.

"How 's it bear?" Wolf Larsen called up.

"Dead astern, sir!"

"Maybe it 's a Russian," suggested Latimer.

His words brought anxiety into the faces of the other hunters. A Russian could mean but one thing—a cruiser. The hunters, never more than roughly aware of the position of the ship, nevertheless knew that we were close to the boundaries of the forbidden sea, while Wolf Larsen's record as a poacher was notorious. All eyes centered upon him.

"We 're dead safe," he assured them, with a laugh. "No salt-mines this time, Smoke. But I 'll tell you what—I 'll lay odds of five to one it 's the *Macedonia*."

No one accepted his offer, and he went on: "In which event I 'll lay ten to one there 's trouble breezing up."

"No, thank you," Latimer spoke up. "I don't object to losing my money, but I like to get a run for it, anyway. There never was a time when there was n't trouble when you and that brother of yours got together, and I 'll lay twenty to one on that."

A general smile followed, in which Wolf Larsen joined, and the dinner went on smoothly, thanks to me, for he treated me abominably the rest of the meal, sneering at me and patronizing me till I was all a-tremble with suppressed rage. Yet I knew I must control myself for Maud Brewster's sake, and I received my reward when her eyes caught mine for a fleeting second, and they said as distinctly as if she spoke, "Be brave, be brave!"

We left the table to go on deck, for a steamer was a welcome break in the monotony of the sea on which we floated, while the conviction that it was "Death" Larsen and the *Macedonia* added to the excitement. The stiff breeze and heavy sea which had sprung up the previous afternoon had been moderating all the morning, so that it was now possible to lower the boats for an afternoon's hunt. The hunting promised to be profitable. We had sailed since daylight across a sea barren of seals and were now running into the herd.

The smoke was still miles astern, but overhauling us rapidly, when we lowered our boats. They spread out and struck a northerly course across the ocean. Now and again we saw a sail lower, heard the reports of the shot-guns, and saw the sail go up again. The seals were thick, the wind dying away; everything favored a big catch. As we ran off to get our leeward position of the last lee boat, we found the ocean fairly carpeted with sleeping seals. They were all about us, thicker than I had ever seen them before, in twos and threes and bunches, stretched full-length on the surface, and sleeping for all the world like so many lazy young dogs.

Under the approaching smoke the hull and upper works of a steamer were growing larger and larger. It was the *Macedonia*. I read her name through the glasses as she passed by scarcely a mile to starboard. Wolf Larsen looked savagely at the vessel, while Maud Brewster was curious.

"Where is the trouble you were so sure was breezing up, Captain Larsen?" she asked gaily.

He glanced at her, a moment's amusement softening his features.

"What did you expect? That they 'd come aboard and cut our throats?"

"Something like that," she confessed. "You understand, seal-hunters are so new and strange to me that I am quite ready to expect anything."

He nodded his head.

"Quite right, quite right. Your error is that you failed to expect the worst."

"Why, what can be worse than cutting our throats?" she asked, with pretty, naïve surprise.

"Cutting our purses," he answered. "Man is so made these days that his capacity for living is determined by the money he possesses."

"'Who steals my purse steals trash,'" she quoted.

"Who steals my purse steals my right to live," was the reply, "old saws to the contrary. For he steals my bread and meat and bed, and in so doing imperils my life. There are not enough soup-kitchens and bread-lines to go around, you know, and when men have nothing in their purses they usually die, and die miserably—unless they are able to fill their purses pretty speedily."

"But I fail to see that this steamer has any designs on your purse."

"Wait and you will see," he answered grimly.

We did not have long to wait. Having passed several miles beyond our line of boats, the *Macedonia* proceeded to lower her own. We knew she carried fourteen boats to our five (we were one short through the desertion of Wainwright), and she began dropping them far to leeward of our last boat, continued dropping them athwart our course, and finished dropping them far to windward of our first weather boat. The hunting, for us, was spoiled. There were no seals behind us, and ahead of us the line of fourteen boats, like a huge broom, swept the herd before it.

Our boats hunted across the two or three miles of water between them and the point where the *Macedonia's* had been dropped, and then headed for home. The wind had fallen to a whisper, the ocean was growing calmer and calmer, and this, coupled with the presence of the great herd, made a perfect hunting-day—one of the two or three days to be encountered in the whole of a lucky season. An angry lot of men, boat-pullers and steerers as well as hunters, swarmed over our side. Each man felt that he had been robbed, and the boats were hoisted in amid curses, which, if curses had power, would have settled Death Larsen for all eternity—"Dead and damned for a dozen of eternities," commented Louis, his eyes twinkling up at me as he rested from hauling taut the lashings of his boat.

"Listen to them, and find if it is hard to discover the most vital thing in their souls," said Wolf Larsen. "Faith, and love, and high ideals? The good, the beautiful, the true?"

"Their innate sense of right has been violated," Maud Brewster said, joining the conversation.

She was standing a dozen feet away, one hand resting on the main-shrouds and her body swaying gently to the slight roll of the ship. She had not raised her voice, and yet I was struck by its clear and bell-like tone. Ah, it was sweet in my ears! I scarcely dared look at her just then, for fear of betraying myself. A small boy's cap was perched on her head, and her hair, light brown and arranged in a loose and fluffy order that caught the sun, seemed an aureole about the delicate oval of her face. She was positively bewitching, and, withal, sweetly spirituelle, if not saintly. All my old-time marvel at life returned to me at sight of this splendid incarnation of it, and Wolf Larsen's cold explanation of life and its meaning was truly ridiculous and laughable.

"A sentimentalist," he sneered, "like Mr. Van Weyden. Those men are cursing because their desires have been outraged. That is all. What desires? The desires for the good grub and soft beds ashore which a handsome pay-day brings them—the women and the drink, the gorging and the beastliness which so truly express them, the best that is in them, their highest aspirations, their ideals, if you please. The exhibition they make of their feelings is not a touching sight, yet it shows how deeply they have been touched, how deeply their purses have been touched; for to lay hands on their purses is to lay hands on their souls."

"You hardly behave as if your purse had been touched," she said smilingly.

"Then it so happens that I am behaving differently, for my purse and my soul have both been touched. At the current price of skins in the London market, and based on a fair estimate of what the afternoon's catch would have been had not the *Macedonia* hogged it, the *Ghost* has lost about fifteen hundred dollars' worth of skins."

"You speak so calmly—" she began.

"But I do not feel calm; I could kill the man who has robbed me," he interrupted. "Yes, yes, I know, and that man my brother—more sentiment! Bah!"

His face underwent a sudden change. His voice was less harsh and wholly sincere as he said:

"You must be happy, you sentimentalists, really and truly happy at dreaming and finding things good, and, because you find some of them good, feeling good yourselves. Now, tell me, you two, do you find me good?"

"You are good to look upon—in a way," I qualified.

"There are in you all powers for good," was Maud Brewster's answer.

"There you are!" he cried at her, half angrily. "Your words are empty to me. There is nothing clear and sharp and definite about the thought you have expressed. You cannot pick it up in your two hands and look at it. In point of fact, it is not a thought. It is a feeling, a sentiment, a something based upon illusion, and not a product of the intellect at all."

As he went on, his voice again grew soft, and a confiding note came into it. "Do you know, I sometimes catch myself wishing that I, too, were blind to the facts of life and knew only its fancies and illusions. They 're wrong, all wrong, of course, and contrary to reason, but in the face of them my reason tells me, wrong and most wrong, that to dream and live illusions gives greater delight. And, after all, delight is the wage for living. Without delight, living is a worthless act. To labor at living and be unpaid is worse than to be dead. He who delights the most, lives the most, and your dreams and unrealities are less disturbing to you and more gratifying than are my facts to me."

He shook his head slowly, pondering.

"I often doubt the worthwhileness of reason. Dreams must be more substantial and satisfying. Emotional delight is more filling and lasting than intellectual delight; and, besides, you pay for your moments of intellectual delight by having the blues. Emotional delight is followed by no more than jaded senses, which speedily recuperate. I envy you, I envy you." He stopped abruptly, and then on his lips formed one of his strange quizzical smiles, as he added: "It 's from my brain I envy you, take notice, and not from my heart. My reason dictates it. The envy is an intellectual product. I am like a sober man looking upon drunken men, and, greatly weary, wishing he, too, were drunk."

"Or like a wise man looking upon fools and wishing he, too, were a fool," I laughed.

"Quite so," he said. "You are a blessed, bankrupt pair of fools. You have no facts in your pocket-book."

"Yet we spend as freely as you," was Maud Brewster's contribution.

"More freely, because it costs you nothing."

"And because we draw upon eternity," she retorted.

"Whether you do or think you do, it 's the same thing. You spend what you have n't got, and in return you get greater value from spending what you have n't got than I get from spending what I have got and what I have sweated to get."

"Why don't you change the basis of your coinage, then?" she queried teasingly.

He looked at her quickly, half hopefully, and then said, all regretfully: "Too late. I 'd like to, perhaps, but I can't. My pocket-book is stuffed with the old coinage, and it 's a stubborn thing. I can never bring myself to recognize anything else as valid."

He ceased speaking, and his gaze wandered absently past her and became lost in the placid sea. The old primal melancholy was strong upon him. He was quivering to it. He had reasoned himself into a spell of the blues, and within a few hours one could look for the devil within him to be up and stirring. I remembered Charley Furuseth, and knew this man's sadness for the penalty which the materialist ever pays for his materialism.

XXV

"You 've been on deck, Mr. Van Weyden," Wolf Larsen said the following morning at the breakfast-table. "How do things look?"

"Clear enough," I answered, glancing at the sunshine which streamed down the open companionway. "Fair westerly breeze, with a promise of stiffening, if Louis predicts correctly."

He nodded his head in a pleased way. "Any signs of fog?"

"Thick banks in the north and northwest."

He nodded his head again, evincing even greater satisfaction than before.

"What of the *Macedonia?*"

"Not sighted," I answered.

I could have sworn his face fell at the intelligence, but why he should be disappointed I could not conceive.

I was soon to learn. "Smoke ho!" came the hail from on deck, and his face brightened.

"Good!" he exclaimed, and left the table at once to go on deck and into the steerage, where the hunters were taking the first breakfast of their exile.

Maud Brewster and I scarcely touched the food before us, gazing, instead, in silent anxiety at each other and listening to Wolf Larsen's voice, which easily penetrated the cabin through the intervening bulkhead. He spoke at length, and his conclusion was greeted with a wild roar of cheers. The bulkhead was too thick for us to hear what he said; but, whatever it was, it had affected the hunters strongly, for the cheering was followed by loud exclamations and shouts of joy.

From the sounds on deck I knew that the sailors had been routed out and were preparing to lower the boats. Maud Brewster accompanied me on deck, but I left her at the break of the poop, where she might watch the scene and not be in it. The sailors must have learned whatever project was on hand, and the vim and snap they put into their work attested their enthusiasm. The hunters came trooping on deck with shot-guns and ammunition-boxes, and, most unusual, their rifles. The latter were rarely taken in the boats, for a seal shot at long range with a rifle invariably sank before a boat could reach it. But each hunter this day had his rifle and a large supply of cartridges. I noticed they grinned with satisfaction whenever they looked at the *Macedonia's* smoke, which was rising higher and higher as she approached from the west.

The five boats went over the side with a rush, spread out like the ribs of a fan, and set a northerly course, as on the preceding afternoon, for us to follow. I watched for some time, curiously, but there seemed nothing extraordinary about their behavior. They lowered sails, shot seals, and hoisted sails again and continued on their way, as I had always seen them do. The *Macedonia* repeated her performance of yesterday, "hogging" the sea by dropping her line of boats in advance of ours and across our course. Fourteen boats require a considerable spread of ocean for comfortable hunting, and when she had completely lapped our line she continued steaming into the northeast, dropping more boats as she went.

"What 's up?" I asked Wolf Larsen, unable longer to keep my curiosity in check.

"Never mind what 's up," he answered gruffly. "You won't be a thousand years in finding out, and in the meantime just pray for plenty of wind.

"Oh, well, I don't mind telling you," he said the next moment. "I 'm going to give that brother of mine a taste of his own medicine. In short, I 'm going to play the hog myself, and not for one day, but for the rest of the season—if we 're in luck."

"And if we 're not?" I queried.

"Not to be considered," he laughed. "We simply must be in luck, or it 's all up with us."

He had the wheel at the time, and I went forward to my hospital in the forecastle, where lay the two crippled men, Nilson and Thomas Mugridge. Nilson was as cheerful as could be expected, for his broken leg was knitting nicely; but the Cockney was desperately melancholy, and I was aware of a great sympathy for the unfortunate creature. And the marvel of it was that still he lived and clung to life. The brutal years had reduced his meager body to splintered wreckage, and yet the spark of light within burned as brightly as ever.

"With an artificial foot,—and they make excellent ones,—you will be stumping ships' galleys to the end of time," I assured him, jovially.

But his answer was serious, nay, solemn.

"I don't know about wot you s'y, Mr. Van W'yden, but I do know I 'll never rest 'appy till I see that 'ell-'ound dead. 'E cawn't live as long as me. 'E 's got no right to live, an', as the Good Word puts it, ''E shall shorely die,' an' I s'y, 'Amen, an' d—— soon at that.'"

When I returned on deck I found Wolf Larsen steering mainly with one hand, while with the other hand he held the marine glasses and studied the situation of the boats, paying particular attention to the position of the *Macedonia*. The only change noticeable in our boats was that they had hauled close on the wind and were heading several points west of north. Still, I could not see the expediency of the manœuver, for the free sea was intercepted by the *Macedonia's* five weather boats, which, in turn, had hauled close on the wind. Thus they slowly diverged toward the west, drawing farther and farther away from the remainder of the boats in their line.

Our boats were rowing as well as sailing. Even the hunters were pulling, and with three pairs of oars in the water they rapidly overhauled what I may appropriately term the enemy.

The smoke of the *Macedonia* had dwindled to a dim blot on the northeastern horizon. Of the steamer herself nothing was to be seen. We had been loafing along till now, our sails shaking half the time and spilling the wind; and twice, for short periods, we had been hove to. But there was no more loafing. Sheets were trimmed, and Wolf Larsen proceeded to put the *Ghost* through her paces. We ran past our line of boats and bore down upon the first weather boat of the other line.

"Down that flying jib, Mr. Van Weyden," Wolf Larsen commanded. "And stand by to back over the jibs."

I ran forward, and had the downhaul of the flying jib all in and fast as we slipped by the boat a hundred feet to leeward. The three men in it gazed at us suspiciously. They had been hogging the sea, and they knew Wolf Larsen by reputation at any rate. I noted that the hunter, a huge Scandinavian sitting in the bow, held his rifle, ready to hand, across his knees. It should have been in its proper place in the rack. When they came opposite our stern, Wolf Larsen greeted them with a wave of the hand, and cried:

"Come on aboard and have a 'gam'?"

"To gam," among the sealing-schooners, is a substitute for the verbs "to visit," "to gossip." It expresses the garrulity of the sea, and is a pleasant break in the monotony of the life.

The *Ghost* swung around into the wind, and I finished my work forward in time to run aft and lend a hand with the mainsheet.

"You will please stay on deck, Miss Brewster," Wolf Larsen said, as he started forward to meet his guest. "And you, too, Mr. Van Weyden."

The boat had lowered its sail and run alongside. The hunter, golden-bearded like a sea-king, came over the rail and dropped on deck. But his hugeness could not quite overcome his apprehensiveness. Doubt and distrust showed strongly in his face. It was a transparent face, for all of its hairy shield, and advertised instant relief when he glanced from Wolf Larsen to me, noted that there was only the pair of us, and then glanced over his own two men, who had joined him. Surely he had little reason to be afraid. He towered like a Goliath above Wolf Larsen. He must have measured six feet eight or nine inches in stature, and I subsequently learned his weight—two hundred and forty pounds. And there was no fat about him; it was all bone and muscle.

A return of apprehension was apparent, when, at the top of the companionway, Wolf Larsen invited him below. But he reassured himself with a glance down at his host, a big man himself, but dwarfed by the propinquity of the giant. So all hesitancy vanished, and the pair descended into the cabin. In the meantime his two men, as was the wont of visiting sailors, had gone forward into the forecastle to do some visiting themselves.

Suddenly from the cabin came a great choking bellow, followed by all the sounds of a furious struggle. It was the leopard and the lion, and the lion made all the noise. Wolf Larsen was the leopard.

"You see the sacredness of our hospitality," I said bitterly to Maud Brewster.

She nodded her head that she heard, and I noted in her face the signs of the same sickness at sight or sound of violent struggle from which I had suffered so severely during my first weeks on the *Ghost*.

"Would n't it be better if you went forward, say by the steerage companionway, until it is over?" I suggested.

She shook her head and gazed at me pitifully. She was not frightened, but appalled, rather, at the human animality of it.

"You will understand," I took advantage of the opportunity to say, "whatever part I take in what is going on and what is to come, that I am compelled to take it—if you and I are ever to get out of this scrape with our lives. It is not nice—for me," I added.

"I understand," she said in a weak, far-away voice, and her eyes showed me that she did understand.

The sounds from below soon died away. Then Wolf Larsen came alone on deck. There was a slight flush under his bronze, but otherwise he bore no signs of the battle.

"Send those two men aft, Mr. Van Weyden," he said.

I obeyed, and a minute or two later they stood before him.

"Hoist in your boat," he said to them. "Your hunter 's decided to stay aboard awhile and does n't want it pounding alongside.

"Hoist in your boat, I said," he repeated, this time in sharper tones, as they hesitated to do his bidding.

"Who knows, you may have to sail with me for a time," he said quite softly, with a silken threat that belied the softness, as they moved slowly to comply, "and we might as well start with a friendly understanding. Lively now! Death Larsen makes you jump better than that, and you know it."

Their movements perceptibly quickened under his coaching, and as the boat swung inboard I was sent forward to let go the jibs. Wolf Larsen, at the wheel, directed the *Ghost* after the *Macedonia's* second weather boat.

Under way, and with nothing for the time being to do, I turned my attention to the situation of the boats. The *Macedonia's* third weather boat was being attacked by two of ours, the fourth by our remaining three; and the fifth, turn about, was taking a hand in the defense of its nearest mate.

The fight had opened at long distance, and the rifles were cracking steadily. A quick, snappy sea was being kicked up by the wind, a condition which prevented fine shooting; and now and again, as we drew closer, we could see the bullets zip-zipping from wave to wave.

The boat we were pursuing had squared away and was running before the wind to escape us, and, in the course of its flight, to take part in repulsing our general boat attack.

Attending to sheets and tacks now left me little time to see what was taking place, but I happened to be on the poop when Wolf Larsen ordered the two strange sailors forward and into the forecastle. They went sullenly, but they went. He next ordered Miss Brewster below, and smiled at the instant horror that leapt into her eyes.

"You 'll find nothing gruesome down there," he said. "Only an unhurt man securely made fast to the ring-bolts. Bullets are liable to come aboard, and I don't want you killed, you know."

Even as he spoke, a bullet was deflected by a brass-capped spoke of the wheel between his hands and screeched off through the air to windward.

"You see," he said to her; and then to me, "Mr. Van Weyden, will you take the wheel?"

Maud Brewster had stepped inside the companionway, so that only her head was exposed. Wolf Larsen had procured a rifle and was throwing a cartridge into the barrel. I begged her with my eyes to go below, but she smiled and said:

"We may be feeble land-creatures without legs, but we can show Captain Larsen that we are at least as brave as he."

He gave her a quick look of admiration.

"I like you a hundred per cent. better for that," he said. "Books, and brains, and bravery. You are well rounded—a blue-stocking fit to be the wife of a pirate chief. Ahem! we 'll discuss that later," he smiled, as a bullet struck solidly into the cabin wall.

I saw his eyes flash golden as he spoke, and I saw the terror mount in her own.

"We are braver," I hastened to say. "At least, speaking for myself, I know I am braver than Captain Larsen."

It was I who was now favored by a quick look. He was wondering if I was making fun of him. I put three or four spokes over to counteract a sheer toward the wind on the part of the *Ghost*, and then steadied her. Wolf Larsen was still waiting an explanation, and I pointed down to my knees.

"You will observe there," I said, "a slight trembling. It is because I am afraid, the flesh is afraid; and I am afraid in my mind because I do not wish to die. But my spirit masters the trembling flesh and the qualms of the mind. I am more than brave: I am courageous. Your flesh is not afraid. You are not afraid. On the one hand, it costs you nothing to encounter danger; on the other hand, it even gives you delight. You enjoy it. You may be unafraid, Mr. Larsen, but you must grant that the bravery is mine."

"You 're right," he acknowledged at once. "I never thought of it in that way before. But is the opposite true? If you are braver than I, am I more cowardly than you?"

We both laughed at the absurdity, and he dropped down to the deck and rested his rifle across the rail. The bullets we had received had traveled nearly a mile, but by now we had cut that distance in half. He fired three careful shots. The first struck fifty feet to windward of the boat, the second alongside; and at the third the boat-steerer let loose his steering-oar and crumpled up in the bottom of the boat.

"I guess that 'll fix them," Wolf Larsen said, rising to his feet. "I could n't afford to let the hunter have it, and there is a chance the boat-puller does n't know how to steer. In which case, the hunter cannot steer and shoot at the same time."

His reasoning was justified, for the boat rushed at once into the wind, and the hunter sprang aft to take the boat-steerer's place. There was no more shooting, though the rifles were still cracking merrily from the other boats.

The hunter had managed to get the boat before the wind again, but we ran down upon it, going at least two feet to its one. A hundred yards away I saw the boat-puller pass a rifle to the hunter. Wolf Larsen went amidships and took the coil of the throat-halyards from its pin. Then he peered over the rail with leveled rifle. Twice I saw the hunter let go the steering-oar with one hand, reach for his rifle, and hesitate. We were now alongside and foaming past.

"Here, you!" Wolf Larsen cried suddenly to the boat-puller. "Take a turn!"

At the same time he flung the coil of rope. It struck fairly, nearly knocking the man over, but he did not obey. Instead, he looked to his hunter for orders. The hunter, in turn, was in a quandary. His rifle was between his knees, but if he let go the steering-oar in order to shoot, the boat would sweep around and collide with the schooner. Also, he saw Wolf Larsen's rifle bearing upon him and knew he would be shot before he could get his rifle into play.

"Take a turn," he said quietly to the man.

The boat-puller obeyed, taking a turn around the little forward thwart and paying out the line as it jerked taut. The boat sheered out with a rush, and the hunter steadied it to a parallel course some twenty feet from the side of the *Ghost.*

"Now get that sail down and come alongside!" Wolf Larsen ordered.

He never let go his rifle, even passing down the tackles with one hand. When they were fast, bow and stern, and the two uninjured men prepared to come aboard, the hunter picked up his rifle as if to place it in a secure position.

"Drop it!" Wolf Larsen cried, and the hunter dropped it as though it were hot and had burned him.

Once aboard, the two prisoners hoisted in the boat, and under Wolf Larsen's direction carried the wounded boat-steerer down into the forecastle.

"If our five boats do as well as you and I have done, we 'll have a pretty full crew," Wolf Larsen said to me.

"The man you shot—he is—I hope?" Maud Brewster quavered.

"In the shoulder," he answered. "Nothing serious. Mr. Van Weyden will pull him around as good as ever in three or four weeks.

"But he won't pull those chaps around, from the look of it," he added, pointing at the *Macedonia's* third boat, for which I had been steering and which was now nearly abreast of us. "That 's Horner's and Smoke's work. I told them we wanted live men, not carcasses. But the joy of shooting to hit is a most compelling thing, when once you 've learned how to shoot. Have you ever experienced it, Mr. Van Weyden?"

I shook my head and regarded their work. It had indeed been bloody, for they had drawn off and joined our other three boats in the attack on the remaining two of the enemy. The deserted boat was in the trough of the sea, rolling drunkenly across each comber, its loose spritsail out at right angles to it and fluttering and flapping in the wind. The hunter and boat-puller were both lying awkwardly in the bottom, but the boat-steerer lay across the gunwale, half in and half out, his arms trailing in the water and his head rolling from side to side.

"Don't look, Miss Brewster, please don't look!" I had begged of her, and I was glad that she had minded me and been spared the sight.

"Head right into the bunch, Mr. Van Weyden," was Wolf Larsen's command.

As we drew nearer, the firing ceased, and we saw that the fight was over. The remaining two boats had been captured by our five, and the seven were grouped together, waiting to be picked up.

"Look at that!" I cried involuntarily, pointing to the northeast.

The blot of smoke which indicated the *Macedonia's* position had reappeared.

"Yes, I 've been watching it," was Wolf Larsen's calm reply. He measured the distance away to the fog-bank, and for an instant paused to feel the weight of the wind on his cheek. "We 'll make it, I think; but you can depend upon it that blessed brother of mine has twigged our little game and is just a-humping for us. Ah, look at that!"

The blot of smoke had suddenly grown larger, and it was very black.

"I 'll beat you out, though, brother mine," he chuckled. "I 'll beat you out, and I hope you no worse than that you rack your old engines into scrap."

When we hove to, a hasty though orderly confusion reigned. The boats came aboard from every side at once. As fast as the prisoners came over the rail they were marshaled forward into the forecastle by our hunters, while our sailors hoisted in the boats, dropping them anywhere upon the deck and not stopping to lash them. We were already under way, all sails set and drawing, and the sheets being slacked off for a wind abeam, as the last boat lifted clear of the water and swung in the tackles.

Drawn by W. J. Aylward.

"THEY WERE SHOOTING AT US WITH ONE OF THE SMALL CANNON"

THE SEA-WOLF

BY JACK LONDON

Author of "The Call of the Wild," "The God of his Fathers," etc.

XXVI

THERE was need for haste. The *Macedonia*, belching the blackest of smoke from her funnel, was charging down upon us from out of the northeast. Neglecting the boats that remained to her, she had altered her course so as to anticipate ours. She was not running straight for us, but ahead of us. Our courses were converging like the sides of an angle, the vertex of which was at the edge of the fog-bank. It was there, or not at all, that the *Macedonia* could hope to catch us. The hope for the *Ghost* lay in that she should pass that point before the *Macedonia* arrived at it.

Wolf Larsen was steering, his eyes glistening and snapping as they dwelt upon and leapt from detail to detail of the chase. Now he studied the sea to windward for signs of the wind slackening or freshening, now the *Macedonia*; and, again, his eyes roved over every sail, and he gave commands to slack a sheet here a trifle, to come in on one there a trifle, till he was drawing out of the *Ghost* the last bit of speed she possessed. All feuds and grudges were forgotten, and I was surprised at the alacrity with which the men who had so long endured his brutality sprang to execute his orders. Strange to say, the unfortunate Johnson came into my mind as we lifted and surged and heeled along, and I was aware of a regret that he was not alive and present; he had so loved the *Ghost* and delighted in her sailing powers.

"Better get your rifles, you fellows," Wolf Larsen called to our hunters; and the five men lined the lee rail, guns in hand, and waited.

The *Macedonia* was now but a mile away, the black smoke pouring from her funnel at a right angle, so madly she raced, pounding through the sea at a seventeen-knot gait—"'sky-hooting through the brine,'" as Wolf Larsen quoted while gazing at her. We were not making more than nine knots, but the fog-bank was very near.

A puff of smoke broke from the *Macedonia's* deck, we heard a heavy report, and a round hole took form in the stretched canvas of our mainsail. They were shooting at us with one of the small cannon which rumor had said they carried on board. Our men, clustering amidships, waved their hats and raised a derisive cheer. Again there was a puff of smoke and a loud report, this time the cannon-ball striking not more than twenty feet astern and glancing twice from sea to sea to windward before it sank.

But there was no rifle-firing, for the reason that all their hunters were out in the boats or our prisoners. When the two vessels were half a mile apart, a third shot made another hole in our mainsail. Then we entered the fog. It was about us, veiling and hiding us in its dense wet gauze.

The sudden transition was startling. The moment before we had been leaping through the sunshine, the clear sky above us, the sea breaking and rolling wide to the horizon, and a ship, vomiting smoke and fire and iron missiles, rushing madly upon us. And at once, as in an instant's leap, the sun was blotted out, there was no sky, even our mastheads were lost to view, and our horizon was such as tear-blinded eyes may see. The gray mist drove by us like a rain. Every woolen filament of our garments, every hair of our heads and faces, was jeweled with a crystal globule. The shrouds were wet with moisture; it dripped from our rigging overhead; and on the under side of our booms, drops of water took shape in long swaying lines, which were detached and flung to the deck in mimic showers at each surge of the schooner. I was aware of a pent, stifled feeling. As the sounds of the ship thrusting herself through the waves were hurled back upon us by the fog, so were one's thoughts. The mind recoiled from contemplation of a world beyond this wet veil which wrapped us around. This was the world, the universe itself, its bounds so near that one felt impelled to reach out both arms and push them back. It was impossible that the rest could be beyond these walls of gray. The rest was a dream, no more than the memory of a dream.

It was weird, strangely weird. I looked at Maud Brewster and knew that she was similarly affected. Then I looked at Wolf Larsen, but there was nothing subjective about his state of consciousness. His whole concern was with the immediate, objective present. He still held the wheel, and I felt that he was timing Time, reckoning the passage of the minutes with each forward lunge and leeward roll of the *Ghost*.

"Go for'ard and hard alee without any noise," he said to me in a low voice. "Clew up the topsails first. Set men at all the sheets. Let there be no rattling of blocks, no sound of voices. No noise, understand, no noise."

When all was ready, the word, "Hard alee," was passed forward to me from man to man; and the *Ghost* heeled about on the port tack with virtually no noise at all. And what little there was—the slapping of a few reef-points and the creaking of a sheave in a block or two—was ghostly under the hollow echoing pall in which we were swathed.

We had scarcely filled away, it seemed, when the fog thinned abruptly and we were again in the sunshine, the wide-stretching sea breaking before us to the sky-line. But the ocean was bare. No wrathful *Macedonia* broke its surface or blackened the sky with her smoke.

Wolf Larsen at once squared away and ran down along the rim of the fog-bank. His trick was obvious. He had entered the fog to windward of the steamer, and while the steamer had blindly driven on into the fog in the chance of catching him, he had come about and out of his shelter and was now running down to reënter to leeward. Successful in this, the old simile of the needle in the haystack would be mild indeed compared with his brother's chance of finding him.

He did not run long. Jibing the fore- and mainsails and setting the topsails again, we headed back into the bank. As we entered I could have sworn I saw a vague bulk emerging to windward. I looked quickly at Wolf Larsen. Already we were ourselves buried in the fog, but he nodded his head. He, too, had seen it—the *Macedonia*, guessing his manœuver and failing by a moment in anticipating it. There was no doubt that we had escaped unseen.

"He can't keep this up," Wolf Larsen said. "He 'll have to go back for the rest of his boats. Send a man to the wheel, Mr. Van Weyden, keep this course for the present, and you might as well set the watches, for we won't do any lingering to-night.

"I 'd give five hundred dollars, though," he added, "just to be aboard the *Macedonia* for five minutes, listening to my brother curse.

"And now, Mr. Van Weyden," he said to me when he had been relieved from the wheel, "we must make these newcomers welcome. Serve out plenty of whisky to the hunters and see that a few bottles slip for'ard. I 'll wager every man Jack of them is over the side to-morrow, hunting for Wolf Larsen as contentedly as ever they hunted for Death Larsen."

"But won't they escape as Wainwright did?" I asked.

He laughed shrewdly. "Not as long as our old hunters have anything to say about it. I 'm dividing amongst them a dollar a skin for all the skins shot by our new hunters. At least half of their enthusiasm to-day was due to that. Oh, no, there won't be any escaping if they have anything to say about it. And now you 'd better get for-'ard to your hospital duties. There must be a full ward waiting for you."

Wolf Larsen took the distribution of the whisky off my hands, and the bottles began to make their appearance while I worked over the fresh batch of wounded men in the forecastle. I had seen whisky drunk, such as whisky and soda by the men of the clubs, but never as these men drank it, from pannikins and mugs, and from the bottles—great brimming drinks, each one of which was in itself a debauch. But they did not stop at one or two. They drank and drank, and ever the bottles slipped forward and they drank more.

Everybody drank: the wounded drank; Oofty-Oofty, who helped me, drank. Only Louis refrained, no more than cautiously wetting his lips with the liquor, though he joined in the revels with an abandon equal to that of most of them. It was a Saturnalia. In loud voices they shouted over the day's fighting, wrangled about details, or waxed affectionate and made friends with the men whom they had fought. Prisoners and captors hiccoughed on one another's shoulders, and swore mighty oaths of respect and esteem. They wept over the miseries of the past, and over the miseries yet to come under the iron rule of Wolf Larsen. And all cursed him and told terrible tales of his brutality.

It was a strange and frightful spectacle—the small, bunk-lined space, the floor and walls leaping and lurching, the dim light, the swaying shadows lengthening and foreshortening monstrously, the thick air heavy with smoke and the smell of bodies and iodoform, and the inflamed faces of the men—half-men, I should call them. I noted Oofty-Oofty, holding the end of a bandage and looking upon the scene, his velvety and luminous eyes glistening in the light like those of a deer; and yet I knew the barbaric devil that lurked in his breast and belied all the softness and tenderness, almost womanly, of his face and form. And I noticed the boyish face of Harrison,—a good face once, but now a demon's,—convulsed with passion as he told the newcomers of the hell-ship they were in and shrieked curses upon the head of Wolf Larsen.

Wolf Larsen it was, always Wolf Larsen, enslaver and tormentor of men, a male Circe and these his swine, suffering brutes that groveled before him and revolted only in drunkenness and in secrecy. And was I, too, one of his swine? I thought. And Maud Brewster? No! I ground my teeth in my anger and determination till the man I was attending winced under my hand and Oofty-Oofty looked at me with curiosity. I felt endowed with a sudden strength. What with my new-found love, I was a giant. I feared nothing. I would work my will through it all, in spite of Wolf Larsen and of my own thirty-five bookish years. All would be well. I would make it well. And so, exalted, upborne by a sense of power, I turned my back on the howling inferno and climbed to the deck, where the fog drifted ghostly through the night, and the air was sweet and pure and quiet.

The steerage, where were two wounded hunters, was a repetition of the forecastle, except that Wolf Larsen was not being cursed; and it was with a great relief that I again emerged on deck and went aft to the cabin. Supper was ready, and Wolf Larsen and Maud were waiting for me.

While all his ship was getting drunk as fast as it could, Larsen remained sober. Not a drop of liquor passed his lips. He did not dare it under the circumstances, for he had only Louis and me to depend upon, and Louis was even now at the wheel. We were sailing on through the fog without a lookout and without lights. That Wolf Larsen had turned the liquor loose among his men surprised me, but he evidently knew their psychology and the best method of cementing in cordiality what had begun in bloodshed.

His victory over Death Larsen seemed to have had a remarkable effect upon him. The previous evening he had reasoned himself into the blues, and I had been waiting momentarily for one of his characteristic outbursts. Yet nothing had occurred, and he was now in splendid trim. Possibly his success in capturing so many hunters and boats had counteracted the customary reaction. At any rate, the blues were gone, and the blue devils had not put in an appearance. So I thought at the time; but, ah me! little I knew him or knew that even then, perhaps, he was meditating an outbreak more terrible than any I had seen.

As I say, he discovered himself in splendid trim when I entered the cabin. He had had no headaches for weeks, his eyes were as clear blue as the sky, his bronze skin was beautiful with perfect health; life swelled through his veins in full and magnificent flood. While waiting for me he had engaged Maud in animated discussion. Temptation was the topic they had hit upon, and from the few words I heard I made out that he was contending that temptation was temptation only when a man was seduced by it and fell.

"For look you," he was saying, "as I see it, a man does things because of desire. He has many desires. He may desire to escape pain, or to enjoy pleasure. But whatever he does, he does because he desires to do it."

"But suppose he desires to do two opposite things, neither of which will permit him to do the other?" Maud interrupted.

"The very thing I was coming to," he said.

"And between these two desires is just where the soul of the man is manifest," she went on. "If it is a good soul it will desire and do the good action, and the contrary if it is a bad soul. It is the soul that decides."

"Bosh and nonsense!" he exclaimed impatiently. "It is the desire that decides. Here is a man who wants to, say, get drunk. Also, he does n't want to get drunk. What does he do? How does he do it? He is a puppet. He is the creature of his desires, and of the two desires he obeys the stronger one, that is all. His soul has n't anything to do with it. How can he be tempted to get drunk and refuse to get drunk? If the desire to remain sober prevails, it is because it was the stronger desire. Temptation plays no part, unless—" he paused while grasping the new thought which had come into his mind—"unless he is tempted to remain sober.

"Ha! ha!" he laughed. "What do you think of that, Mr. Van Weyden?"

"That both of you are hair-splitting," I said. "The man's soul is his desires. Or, if you will, the sum of his desires is his soul. Therein you are both wrong. You lay the stress upon the desire apart from the soul, Miss Brewster lays the stress on the soul apart from the desire, and in point of fact soul and desire are the same thing.

"However," I continued, "Miss Brewster is right in contending that temptation is temptation whether the man yield or overcome. Fire is fanned by the wind until it leaps up fiercely. So is desire like fire. It is fanned, as by a wind, by sight of the thing desired, or by a new and luring description or comprehension of the thing desired. There lies the temptation. It is the wind that fans the desire until it leaps up to mastery. That 's temptation. It may not fan sufficiently to make the desire overmastering, but in so far as it fans at all, that far is it temptation. And, as you say, it may tempt for good as well as for evil."

I felt proud of myself as we sat down to the table. My words had been decisive. At least, they had put an end to the discussion.

But Wolf Larsen seemed voluble, prone to speech as I had never seen him before. It was as though he were bursting with pent energy which must find an outlet somehow. Almost immediately he launched into a discussion on love. As usual, his was the sheer materialistic side, and Maud's was the idealistic. For myself, beyond a word or so of suggestion or correction now and again, I took no part.

He was brilliant, but so was Maud; and for some time I lost the thread of the conversation through studying her face as she talked. It was a face that rarely displayed color, but to-night it was flushed and vivacious. Her wit was playing keenly, and she was enjoying the tilt as much as Wolf Larsen, and he was enjoying it hugely. For some reason, though I knew not why in the argument, so utterly had I lost it in the contemplation of one stray brown lock of Maud's hair, he quoted from "Iseult at Tintagel," where she says:

> "Blessed am I beyond women even herein,
> That beyond all born women is my sin,
> And perfect my transgression."

As he had read pessimism into Omar, so, now, he read triumph, stinging triumph and exultation, into Swinburne's lines. And he read rightly, and he read well. He had hardly ceased quoting when Louis put his head into the companionway and whispered down:

"Be easy, will ye? The fog 's lifted, an' 't is the port light iv a steamer that 's crossin' our bow this blessed minute."

Wolf Larsen sprang on deck, and so swiftly that by the time we followed him he had pulled the steerage-slide over the drunken clamor and was on his way forward to close the forecastle scuttle. The fog, though it remained, had lifted high, where it obscured the stars and made the night quite black. Directly ahead of us I could see a bright red light and a white light, and I could hear the pulsing of a steamer's engines. Beyond a doubt it was the *Macedonia.*

Wolf Larsen had returned to the poop, and we stood in a silent group, watching the lights rapidly cross our bow.

"Lucky for me he does n't carry a search-light," Wolf Larsen said.

"What if I should cry out loudly?" I queried in a whisper.

"It would be all up," he answered.

"But have you thought upon what would immediately happen?"

Before I had time to express any desire to know, he had me by the throat with his gorilla-grip, and by a faint quiver of the muscles—a hint, as it were—he suggested to me the twist that would surely have broken my neck. The next moment he had released me, and we were gazing at the *Macedonia's* lights.

"What if I should cry out?" Maud asked.

"I like you too well to hurt you," he said softly—nay, there was a tenderness and a caress in his voice that made me wince. "But don't do it just the same, for I 'd promptly break Mr. Van Weyden's neck."

"Then she has my permission to cry out," I said defiantly.

"I hardly think you 'll care to sacrifice the Dean of American Letters the Second," he sneered.

We spoke no more, though we had become too used to each other for the silence to be awkward; and when the red light and the white had disappeared we returned to the cabin to finish the interrupted supper.

Again they fell to quoting, and Maud gave Dowson's "Impenitentia Ultima." She rendered it beautifully, but I watched not her, but Wolf Larsen. I was fascinated by the fascinated look he bent upon Maud. He was quite out of himself, and I noticed the unconscious movement of his lips as he shaped word for word as fast as she uttered them. He interrupted her when she gave the lines:

"And her eyes should be my light while the sun went out behind me,
And the viols in her voice be the last sound in my ear."

"There are viols in your voice," he said bluntly, and his eyes flashed their golden light.

I could have shouted with joy at her control. She finished the concluding stanza without faltering, and then slowly guided the conversation into less perilous channels. And all the while I sat in a half-daze, the drunken riot of the steerage breaking through the bulkhead, the man I feared and the woman I loved talking on and on. The table was not cleared. The man who had taken Mugridge's place had evidently joined his comrades in the forecastle.

If ever Wolf Larsen attained the summit of living, he attained it then. From time to time I forsook my own thoughts to follow him; and I followed in amaze, mastered for the moment by his remarkable intellect, under the spell of his passion, for he was preaching the passion of revolt. It was inevitable that Milton's Lucifer should be instanced, and the keenness with which Wolf Larsen analyzed and depicted the character was a revelation of his stifled genius. It reminded me of Taine, yet I knew the man had never heard of that brilliant though dangerous thinker.

"He led a lost cause, and he was not afraid of God's thunderbolts," Wolf Larsen was saying. "Hurled into hell, he was unbeaten. A third of God's angels he had led with him, and straightway he incited man to rebel against God and gained for himself and hell the major portion of all the generations of man. Why was he beaten out of heaven? Because he was less brave than God? Less proud? Less aspiring? No! A thousand times no! God was more powerful, as he said, whom thunder hath made greater. But Lucifer was a free spirit. To serve was to suffocate. He preferred suffering in freedom to all the happiness of a comfortable servility. He did not care to serve God. He cared to serve nothing. He was no figurehead. He stood on his own legs. He was an individual."

"The first anarchist," Maud laughed, rising and preparing to withdraw to her state-room.

"Then it is good to be an anarchist," he cried. He, too, had risen, and he stood facing her, where she had paused at the door of her room, as he went on:

"'Here at least
We shall be free; the Almighty hath not built
Here for his envy; will not drive us hence:
Here we may reign secure; and in my choice
To reign is worth ambition, though in hell:
Better to reign in hell than serve in heaven.'"

It was the defiant cry of a mighty spirit. The cabin still rang with his voice, as he stood there, swaying, his bronzed face shining, his head up and dominant, and his eyes, golden and masculine, intensely masculine and insistently soft, flashing upon Maud at the door.

Again that unnamable and unmistakable

terror was in her eyes, and she said, almost in a whisper, "You are Lucifer."

The door closed, and she was gone. He stood staring after her for a minute, then returned to himself and to me.

"I 'll relieve Louis at the wheel," he said shortly, "and call upon you to relieve at midnight. Better turn in now and get some sleep."

He pulled on a pair of mittens, put on his cap, and ascended the companion-stairs, while I followed his suggestion by going to bed. For some unknown reason, prompted mysteriously, I did not undress, but lay down fully clothed. For a time I listened to the clamor in the steerage and marveled upon the love which had come to me; but my sleep on the *Ghost* had become most healthful and natural, and soon the songs and cries died away, my eyes closed, and my consciousness sank down into the half-death of slumber.

I KNEW not what had aroused me, but I found myself out of my bunk, on my feet, wide awake, my soul vibrating to the warning of danger as it might have thrilled to a trumpet call. I threw open the door. The cabin light was burning low. I saw Maud, straining and struggling and crushed in the embrace of Wolf Larsen's arms. Her face was forcibly upturned. I could see the vain beat and flutter of her as she strove, by pressing her face against his breast, to escape his lips. All this I saw on the very instant of seeing and as I sprang forward.

I struck him with my fist, on the face, as he raised his head, but it was a puny blow. He roared in a ferocious, animal-like way and gave me a shove with his hand. It was only a shove, a flirt of the wrist, yet so tremendous was his strength that I was hurled backward as from a catapult. I struck the door of the stateroom that had formerly been Mugridge's, splintering and smashing the panels with the impact of my body. I struggled to my feet, with difficulty dragging myself clear of the wrecked door, unaware of any hurt whatever. I was conscious only of an overmastering rage. I think I, too, cried aloud, as I drew the knife at my hip and sprang forward a second time.

But something had happened. They were reeling apart. I was close upon him, my knife uplifted, but I withheld the blow. I was puzzled by the strangeness of it. Maud was leaning against the wall, one hand out for support; but he was staggering, his left hand pressed against his forehead and covering his eyes, and with the right he was groping about him in a dazed sort of way. It struck against the wall, and his body seemed to express a muscular and physical relief at the contact, as though he had found his bearings, his location in space, as well as something against which to lean.

Then I saw red again. All my wrongs and humiliations flashed upon me with a dazzling brightness, all that I had suffered and others had suffered at his hands, all the enormity of the man's very existence. I sprang upon him, blindly, insanely, and drove the knife into his shoulder. I knew, then, that it was no more than a flesh-wound,—I had felt the steel grate on his shoulder-blade,—and I raised the knife to strike at a more vital part.

But Maud had seen my first blow, and she cried, "Don't! Please don't!"

I dropped my arm for a moment, and for a moment only. Again the knife was raised, and Wolf Larsen would have surely died had she not stepped between. Her arms were around me, her hair was brushing my face. My pulse rushed up in an unwonted manner, yet my rage mounted with it. She looked me bravely in the eyes.

"For my sake," she begged.

"I would kill him for your sake!" I cried, trying to free my arm without hurting her.

"Hush!" she said, and laid her fingers lightly on my lips. I could have kissed them, had I dared, even then in my rage, the touch of them was so sweet, so very sweet. "Please, please," she pleaded, and she disarmed me by the words, as I was to discover they would ever disarm me.

I stepped back, separating from her, and replaced the knife in its sheath. I looked at Wolf Larsen. He still pressed his left hand against his forehead. It covered his eyes. His head was bowed. He seemed to have grown limp. His body was sagging at the hips, his great shoulders were drooping and shrinking forward.

"Van Weyden!" he called hoarsely, and with a note of fright in his voice. "Oh, Van Weyden, where are you?"

I looked at Maud. She did not speak, but nodded her head.

"Here I am," I answered, stepping to his side. "What is the matter?"

"Help me to a seat," he said, in the same hoarse, frightened voice.

"I am a sick man, a very sick man, Hump," he said, as he left my sustaining grip and sank into a chair.

His head dropped forward on the table and was buried in his hands. From time to time it rocked back and forward as with pain. Once, when he half raised it, I saw the sweat standing in heavy drops on his forehead about the roots of his hair.

"I am a sick man, a very sick man," he repeated again, and yet once again.

"What is the matter?" I asked, resting my hand on his shoulder. "What can I do for you?"

But he shook my hand off with an irritated movement, and for a long time I stood by his side in silence. Maud was looking on, her face awed and frightened. What had happened to him we could not imagine.

"Hump," he said at last, "I must get into my bunk. Lend me a hand. I 'll be all right in a little while. It 's those d—— headaches, I believe. I was afraid of them. I had a feeling—no, I don't know what I 'm talking about. Help me into my bunk."

But when I got him into his bunk he again buried his face in his hands, covering his eyes, and as I turned to go I could hear him murmuring, "I am a sick man, a very sick man."

Maud looked at me inquiringly as I emerged. I shook my head, saying:

"Something has happened to him. What, I don't know. He is helpless, and frightened, I imagine, for the first time in his life. It must have happened before he received the knife-thrust, which made only a superficial wound. You must have seen what happened."

She shook her head. "I saw nothing. It is just as mysterious to me. He suddenly released me and staggered away. But what shall we do? What shall I do?"

"Wait until I come back," I answered.

I went on deck. Louis was at the wheel.

"You may go for'ard and turn in," I said, taking it from him.

He was quick to obey, and I found myself alone on the deck of the *Ghost*. As quietly as was possible, I clewed up the topsails, lowered the flying jib and staysail, backed the jib over, and flattened the mainsail. Then I went below to Maud. I placed my finger on my lips for silence, and entered Wolf Larsen's room. He was in the same position in which I had left him, and his head was rocking—almost writhing—from side to side.

"Anything I can do for you?" I asked.

He made no reply at first, but on my repeating the question he answered: "No, no; I 'm all right. Leave me alone till morning."

But as I turned to go I noted that his head had resumed its rocking motion. Maud was waiting patiently for me, and I took notice, with a thrill of joy, of the queenly poise of her head and her glorious calm eyes. Calm and sure they were as her spirit itself.

"Will you trust yourself to me for a journey of six hundred miles or so?" I asked.

"You mean—?" she asked, and I knew she had guessed aright.

"Yes, I mean just that," I replied. "Nothing is left for us but the open boat."

"For me, you mean," she said. "You are certainly as safe here as you have been."

"No, there is nothing left for us but the open boat," I iterated stoutly. "Dress as warmly as you can, at once, and make into a bundle whatever you wish to bring with you. And make all haste," I added, as she turned toward her state-room.

The lazaret was directly beneath the cabin, and, opening the trap-door in the floor and carrying a candle with me, I dropped down and began overhauling the ship's stores. I selected mainly from the canned goods, and by the time I was ready willing hands were extended from above to receive what I passed up.

We worked in silence. I helped myself also to blankets, mittens, oilskins, caps, and such things, from the slop-chest. It was no light adventure, this trusting ourselves in a small boat to so raw and stormy a sea, and it was imperative that we should guard ourselves against the cold and wet.

We worked feverishly at carrying our plunder on deck and depositing it amidships, so feverishly that Maud, whose strength was hardly a positive quantity, had to give over, exhausted, and sit on the steps at the break of the poop. This did not serve to recover her, and she lay on her back, on the hard deck, arms stretched out and whole body relaxed. It was a trick

I remembered of my sister, and I knew she would soon be herself again. I reëntered Wolf Larsen's state-room to get his rifle and shot-gun. I spoke to him, but he made no answer, though his head was still rocking from side to side and he was not asleep.

Next to obtain was a stock of ammunition—an easy matter, though I had to enter the steerage companionway to do it. Here the hunters stored the ammunition-boxes they carried in the boats, and here, but a few feet from their noisy revels, I took possession of two boxes.

Next, to lower a boat. Not so simple a task for one man. Having cast off the lashings, I hoisted first on the forward tackle, then on the aft, till the boat cleared the rail, when I lowered away, one tackle and then the other, for a couple of feet, till it hung snugly, above the water, against the schooner's side. I made certain that it contained the proper equipment of oars, rowlocks, and sail. Water was a consideration, and I robbed every boat aboard of its breaker. As there were nine boats all told, it meant that we should have plenty of water, and ballast as well, though there was the chance that the boat would be overloaded, with the generous supply of other things I was taking.

While Maud was passing me the provisions and I was storing them in the boat, a sailor came on deck from the forecastle. He stood by the weather rail for a time (we were lowering over the lee rail), and then sauntered slowly amidships, where he again paused and stood facing the wind, with his back toward us. I could hear my heart beating as I crouched low in the boat. Maud had sunk down upon the deck and was, I knew, lying motionless, her body in the shadow of the bulwark. But the man never turned, and after stretching his arms above his head and yawning audibly, he retraced his steps to the forecastle scuttle and disappeared.

A few minutes sufficed to finish the loading, and I lowered the boat into the water. As I helped Maud over the rail, and felt her form close to mine, it was all I could do to keep from crying out, "I love you! I love you!" Truly, Humphrey Van Weyden was at last in love, I thought, as her fingers clung to mine while I lowered her to the boat. I held on to the rail with one hand and supported her weight with the other, and I was proud at the moment of the feat. It was a strength I had not possessed a few months before, on the day I said good-by to Charley Furuseth and started for San Francisco on the ill-fated *Martinez*.

As the boat ascended on a sea, her feet touched and I released her hands. I cast off the tackles and leapt after her. I had never rowed in my life, but I put out the oars, and at the expense of much effort got the boat clear of the *Ghost*. Then I experimented with the sail. I had seen the boat-steerers and hunters set their sprit-sails many times, yet this was my first attempt. What took them possibly two minutes took me twenty, but in the end I succeeded in setting and trimming it, and with the steering-oar in my hands hauled on the wind.

"There lies Japan," I remarked, "straight before us."

"Humphrey Van Weyden," she said, "you are a brave man."

"Nay," I answered; "it is you who are a brave woman."

We turned our heads, swayed by a common impulse to see the last of the *Ghost*. Her low hull lifted and rolled to windward on a sea; her canvas loomed darkly in the night; her lashed wheel creaked as the rudder kicked; then sight and sound of her faded away, and we were alone on the dark sea.

XXVII

Day broke, gray and chill. The boat was close-hauled on a fresh breeze, and the compass indicated that it was making just the course that would bring it to Japan. Though stoutly mittened, my fingers were cold, and they pained from the grip on the steering-oar. My feet were stinging from the bite of the frost, and I hoped fervently that the sun would shine.

Before me, in the bottom of the boat, lay Maud. She, at least, was warm, for under her and over her were thick blankets. The top one I had drawn over her face to shelter it from the night, so I could see nothing but the vague shape of her, and her light-brown hair, escaped from the covering and jeweled with moisture from the air.

Long I looked at her, dwelling upon that one visible bit of her as only a man would who deemed it the most precious thing in the world. So insistent was my gaze that at last she stirred under the blankets, the top fold was thrown back, and she smiled out on me, her eyes yet heavy with sleep.

"Good morning, Mr. Van Weyden," she said. "Have you sighted land yet?"

"No," I answered, "but we are approaching it at a rate of six miles an hour."

She made a *moue* of disappointment.

"But that is equivalent to one hundred and forty-four miles in twenty-four hours," I added reassuringly.

Her face brightened. "And how far have we to go?"

"Siberia lies off there," I said, pointing to the west. "But to the southwest, some six hundred miles, is Japan. If this wind should hold, we 'll make it in five days."

"If it storms? The boat could not live?"

She had a way of looking one in the eyes and demanding the truth, and thus she looked at me as she asked the question.

"It would have to storm very hard," I temporized.

"And if it storms very hard?"

I nodded my head. "But we may be picked up any moment by a sealing-schooner. They are plentifully distributed over this part of the ocean."

"Why, you are chilled through!" she cried. "Look! You are shivering. Don't deny it; you are. And here I have been lying warm as toast."

"I don't see that it would help matters if you, too, sat up and were chilled," I laughed.

"It will, though, when I learn to steer, which I certainly shall."

She sat up and began making her simple toilet. She shook down her hair, and it fell about her in a brown cloud, hiding her face and shoulders. Dear, damp brown hair! I wanted to kiss it, to ripple it through my fingers, to bury my face in it. I gazed entranced, till the boat ran into the wind, and the flapping sail warned me I was not attending to my duties. Idealist and romanticist that I was and always had been in spite of my analytical nature, yet I had failed till now in grasping much of the physical characteristics of love. The love of man and woman, I had always held, was a sublimated something related to spirit, a spiritual bond that linked and drew their souls together. The bonds of the flesh had no part in my cosmos of love. But I was learning the sweet lesson for myself that the soul transmuted itself, expressed itself, through the flesh; that the sight and sense and touch of the loved one's hair were as much breath and voice and essence of the spirit as the light that shone from the eyes and the thoughts that fell from the lips. After all, pure spirit was unknowable, a thing to be sensed and divined only; nor could it express itself in terms of itself. Jehovah was anthropomorphic because he could address himself to the Jews only in terms of their understanding; so he was conceived as in their own image, as a cloud, a pillar of fire, a tangible, physical something which the mind of the Israelites could grasp.

And so I gazed upon Maud's light-brown hair, and loved it, and learned more of love than all the poets and singers had taught me with all their songs and sonnets. She flung it back with a sudden adroit movement, and her face emerged, smiling.

"Why don't women wear their hair down always?" I asked. "It is so much more beautiful."

"If it did n't tangle so dreadfully," she laughed. "There! I 've lost one of my precious hair-pins!"

I neglected the boat and had the sail spilling the wind again and again, such was my delight in following her every movement as she searched through the blankets for the pin. I was surprised, and joyfully, that she was so much the woman, and the display of each trait and mannerism that was characteristically feminine gave me keener joy. For I had been elevating her too highly in my concepts of her, removing her too far from the plane of the human and too far from me. I had been making of her a creature goddess-like and unapproachable. So I hailed with delight the little traits that proclaimed her only woman after all, such as the toss of the head which flung back the cloud of hair, and the search for the pin. She was woman, my kind, on my plane, and the delightful intimacy of kind, of man and woman, was possible, as well as the reverence and awe in which I knew I should always hold her.

She found the pin with an adorable little cry, and I turned my attention more fully to my steering. I proceeded to experiment, lashing and wedging the steering-oar until the boat held on fairly well by the wind without my assistance. Occasionally it came up too close, or fell off too freely;

but it always recovered itself and in the main behaved satisfactorily.

"And now we shall have breakfast," I said. "But first you must be more warmly clad."

I got out a heavy shirt, new from the slop-chest and made from blanket goods. I knew the kind, so thick and so close of texture that it could resist the rain and not be soaked through after hours of wetting. When she had slipped this on over her head, I exchanged the boy's cap she wore for a man's cap, large enough to cover her hair, and, when the flap was turned down, to cover completely her neck and ears. The effect was charming. Her face was of the sort that cannot but look well under all circumstances. Nothing could destroy its exquisite oval, its well-nigh classic lines, its delicately stenciled brows, and its large brown eyes, clear-seeing and calm, gloriously calm.

Just then a puff, slightly stronger than usual, struck us. The boat was caught as it obliquely crossed the crest of a wave. It went over suddenly, burying its gunwale level with the sea and shipping a bucketful or so of water. I was opening a can of tongue at the moment, and I sprang to the sheet and cast it off just in time. The sail flapped and fluttered, and the boat paid off. A few minutes of regulating sufficed to put it on its course again, when I returned to the preparation of breakfast.

"It does very well, it seems, though I am not versed in things nautical," she said, nodding her head with grave approval at my steering contrivance.

"But it will serve only when we are sailing by the wind," I explained. "When running more freely, with the wind astern, abeam, or on the quarter, it will be necessary for me to steer."

"I must say I don't understand your technicalities," she said; "but I do your conclusion, and I don't like it. You cannot steer night and day and forever. So I shall expect, after breakfast, to receive my first lesson. And then you shall lie down and sleep. We 'll stand watches just as they do on ships."

"I don't see how I am to teach you," I made protest. "I am just learning for myself. You little thought when you trusted yourself to me that I had had no experience whatever with small boats. This is the first time I have ever been in one."

"Then we 'll learn together, sir. And since you 've had a night's start you shall teach me what you have learned. And now, breakfast. My! this air does give one an appetite!"

"No coffee," I said regretfully, passing her buttered sea-biscuits and a slice of canned tongue. "And there will be no tea, no soups, nothing hot till we have made land somewhere, somehow."

After the simple breakfast, capped with a cup of cold water, Maud took her lesson in steering. In teaching her I learned quite a deal myself, though I was applying the knowledge already acquired by sailing the *Ghost* and by watching the boat-steerers sail the small boats. She was an apt pupil, and soon learned to keep the course, to luff in the puffs, and to cast off the sheet in an emergency.

Having grown tired, apparently, of the task, she relinquished the oar to me. I had folded up the blankets, but she now proceeded to spread them out on the bottom. When all was arranged snugly, she said:

"Now, sir, to bed. And you shall sleep until luncheon.

"Till dinner-time," she corrected, remembering the arrangement on the *Ghost*.

What could I do? She insisted and said, "Please, please"; whereupon I turned the oar over to her and obeyed. I experienced a positive sensuous delight as I crawled into the bed she had made with her hands. The calm and control which were so much a part of her seemed to have been communicated to the blankets, so that I was aware of a soft dreaminess and content, and of an oval face and brown eyes framed in a fisherman's cap and tossing against a background now of gray cloud, now of gray sea, and then I was aware that I had been asleep.

I looked at my watch. It was one o'clock. I had slept seven hours. And she had been steering seven hours! When I took the steering-oar I had first to unbend her cramped fingers. Her modicum of strength had been exhausted, and she was unable even to move from her position. I was compelled to let go the sheet while I helped her to the nest of blankets and chafed her hands and arms.

"I am so tired," she said, with a quick intake of the breath and a sigh, drooping her head wearily.

But she straightened it the next moment. "Now, don't scold, don't you dare scold," she cried, with mock defiance.

"I hope my face does not appear angry," I answered seriously; "for I assure you I am not in the least angry."

"N-no," she considered. "It looks only reproachful."

"Then it is an honest face, for it looks what I feel. You were not fair to yourself, nor to me. How can I ever trust you again?"

She looked penitent. "I 'll be good," she said, as a naughty child might say it. "I promise—"

"To obey as a sailor would obey his captain?"

"Yes," she answered. "It was stupid of me, I know."

"Then you must promise something else," I ventured.

"Readily."

"That you will not say, 'Please, please,' too often; for when you do you are sure to override my authority."

She laughed with amused appreciation. She, too, had noticed the power of the repeated "please."

"It is a good word—" I began.

"But I must not overwork it," she said.

Then she laughed weakly, and her head drooped again. I left the oar long enough to tuck the blankets about her feet and to pull a single fold across her face. Alas! she was not strong. I looked with misgiving toward the southwest and thought of the six hundred miles of hardship before us—aye, if it were no worse than hardship. On this sea a storm might blow up at any moment and destroy us. And yet I was unafraid. I was without confidence in the future, extremely doubtful, and yet I felt no underlying fear. "It must come right, it must come right," I repeated to myself over and over again.

The wind freshened in the afternoon, raising a stiffer sea and trying the boat and me severely. But the supply of food and the nine breakers of water enabled the boat to stand up to the sea and wind, and I held on as long as I dared. Then I removed the sprit, tightly hauling down the peak of the sail, and we raced along under what sailors call a leg-of-mutton.

Late in the afternoon I sighted a steamer's smoke on the horizon to leeward, and I knew it either for a Russian cruiser, or, more likely, the *Macedonia* still seeking the *Ghost*. The sun had not shone all day, and it had been bitter cold. As night drew on, the clouds darkened and the wind freshened, so that when Maud and I ate supper it was with our mittens on and with me still steering and eating morsels between puffs.

By the time it was dark, wind and sea had become too strong for the boat, and I reluctantly took in the sail and set about making a drag or sea-anchor. I had learned of the device from the talk of the hunters, and it was a simple thing to manufacture. Furling the sail and lashing it securely about the mast, boom, sprit, and two pairs of spare oars, I threw it overboard. A line connected it with the bow, and as it floated low in the water, practically unexposed to the wind, it drifted less rapidly than the boat. In consequence it held the boat bow on to the sea and wind—the safest position in which to escape being swamped when the sea is breaking into whitecaps.

"And now?" Maud asked cheerfully, when the task was accomplished and I pulled on my mittens.

"And now we are no longer traveling toward Japan," I answered. "Our drift is to the southeast, or south-southeast, at the rate of at least two miles an hour."

"That will be only twenty-four miles," she urged, "if the wind remains high all night."

"Yes, and only one hundred and forty miles if it continues for three days and nights."

"But it won't continue," she said, with easy confidence. "It will turn around and blow fair."

"The sea is the great faithless one."

"But the wind!" she retorted. "I have heard you grow eloquent over the brave trade-wind."

"I wish I had thought to bring Wolf Larsen's chronometer and sextant," I said, still gloomily. "Sailing one direction, drifting another direction, to say nothing of the set of the current in some third direction, makes a resultant which dead-reckoning can never calculate. Before long we shall not know where we are by five hundred miles."

Then I begged her pardon and promised I would not be disheartened any more. At her solicitation, I let her take the watch till midnight—it was then nine o'clock; but I wrapped her in blankets and put an oilskin about her before I lay down. I slept only cat-naps. The boat was leaping and pounding as it fell over the crests, I could hear the seas rushing past, and spray was continually being thrown aboard. And still, it was not a bad night, I mused—nothing to the nights I had been through on the *Ghost,* nothing, perhaps, to the nights we should go through in this cockle-shell. Its planking was three quarters of an inch thick. Between us and the bottom of the sea was less than an inch of wood.

And yet, I aver it, and I aver it again, I was unafraid. The death which Wolf Larsen and even Thomas Mugridge had made me fear, I no longer feared. The coming of Maud Brewster into my life seemed to have transformed me. After all, I thought, it is better and finer to love than to be loved, if it makes something in life so worth while that one is not loath to die for it. I forgot my own life in the love of another life; and yet, such is the paradox, I never wanted so much to live as right then when I placed the least value upon my own life. I never had so much reason for living, was my concluding thought; and after that, until I dozed, I contented myself with trying to pierce the darkness to where I knew Maud crouched low in the stern-sheets, watchful of the foaming sea and ready to call me on an instant's notice.

THE SEA-WOLF

BY JACK LONDON

Author of "The Call of the Wild," "The God of his Fathers," etc.

XXVIII

THERE is no need of going into an extended recital of our suffering in the small boat during the many days we were driven and drifted, here and there, willy-nilly, across the ocean. The high wind blew from the northwest for twenty-four hours, when it fell calm, and in the night sprang up from the southwest. This was dead in our teeth, but I took in the sea-anchor and set sail, hauling a course on the wind that took us in a south-southeasterly direction. It was an even choice between this and the west-northwesterly course that the wind permitted; but the warm airs of the south fanned my desire for a warmer sea and swayed my decision.

In three hours—it was midnight, I well remember, and as dark as I had ever seen it on the sea—the wind, still blowing out of the southwest, rose furiously, and once again I was compelled to set the sea-anchor.

Day broke and found me wan-eyed and the ocean lashed white, the boat pitching, almost on end, to its drag. We were in imminent danger of being swamped by the whitecaps. As it was, spray and spume came aboard in such quantities that I baled without cessation. The blankets were soaking. Everything was wet except Maud, and she, in oilskins, rubber boots, and sou'-wester, was dry, all but her face and hands and a stray wisp of hair. She relieved me at the baling-hole from time to time, and bravely she threw out the water and faced the storm. All things are relative. It was no more than a stiff blow; but to us, fighting for life in our frail craft, it was indeed a storm.

Cold and cheerless, the wind beating on our faces, the white seas roaring by, we struggled through the day. Night came, but neither of us slept. Day came, and still the wind beat on our faces and the white seas roared past. By the second night Maud was falling asleep from exhaustion. I covered her with oilskins and a tarpaulin. She was comparatively dry, but she was numb with the cold. I feared greatly that she might die in the night; but day broke, cold and cheerless, with the same clouded sky and beating wind and roaring seas.

I had had no sleep for forty-eight hours. I was wet and chilled to the marrow, till I felt more dead than alive. My body was stiff from exertion as well as from cold, and my aching muscles gave me the severest torture whenever I used them—and I used them continually. And all the time we were being driven off into the northeast, directly away from Japan and toward bleak Bering Sea.

And still we lived, and the boat lived, and the wind blew unabated. In fact, toward nightfall of the third day it increased a trifle and something more. The boat's bow plunged under a crest, and we came through quarter full of water. I baled like a madman. The liability of shipping another such sea was enormously increased by the water that weighed the boat down and robbed it of its buoyancy. And another such sea meant the end. When I had the boat empty again I was forced to take away the tarpaulin that covered Maud, in order that I might lash it down across the bow. It was well I did, for it covered the boat fully a third of the way aft, and three times in the next several hours it flung off the bulk of the down-rushing water when the bow shoved under the seas.

Maud's condition was pitiable. She sat crouched in the bottom of the boat, her lips blue, her face gray and plainly showing the pain she suffered. But ever her eyes looked bravely at me, and ever her lips uttered brave words.

The worst of the storm must have blown that night, though little I noticed it. I had succumbed and slept where I sat in the stern-sheets. The morning of the fourth day found the wind diminished to a gentle whisper, the sea dying down, and the sun shining upon us. Oh, the blessed sun! How we bathed our poor bodies in its delicious warmth, reviving like insects and crawling things after a storm! We smiled again, said amusing things, and waxed optimistic over our situation. Yet it was, if anything, worse than ever. We were farther away from Japan than the night we left the *Ghost*. Nor could I more than roughly guess our latitude and longitude. At a calculation of a two-mile drift per hour, during the seventy and odd hours of the storm we had been driven at least one hundred and fifty miles to the northeast. But was such calculated drift correct? For all I knew, it might have been four miles per hour instead of two, in which case we were another hundred and fifty miles to the bad.

Where we were I did not know, though there was quite a likelihood that we were in the vicinity of the *Ghost*. There were seals about us, and I was prepared to sight a sealing-schooner at any time. We did sight one, in the afternoon, when the northwest breeze had sprung up freshly once more; but the strange schooner lost itself on the sky-line, and we alone occupied the circle of the sea.

Came days of fog, when even Maud's spirit drooped and there were no merry words upon her lips; days of calm, when we floated on the lonely immensity of sea, oppressed by its greatness and yet marveling at the miracle of tiny life, for we still lived and struggled to live; days of sleet and wind and snow-squalls, when nothing could keep us warm; or days of drizzling rain, when we filled our water-breakers from the drip of the wet sail.

And ever I loved Maud with an increasing love. She was so many-sided, so many-mooded—"Protean-mooded" I called her. But I called her this, and other and dearer things, in my thoughts only. Though the declaration of my love urged and trembled on my tongue a thousand times, I knew that it was no time for such a declaration. If for no other reason, it was no time, when one was protecting and trying to save a woman, to ask that woman for her love. Delicate as was the situation, not alone in this but in other ways, I flattered myself that I was able to deal delicately with it; and also I flattered myself that by look or sign I gave no advertisement of the love I felt for her. We were like good comrades, and we grew better comrades as the days went by.

One thing about her that surprised me was her lack of timidity and fear. The terrible sea, the frail boat, the storms, the suffering, the strangeness and isolation of the situation,—all that should have frightened a robust woman,—seemed to make no impression upon her who had known life only in its most sheltered and consummately artificial aspects, and who was herself all fire and dew and mist, sublimated spirit—all that was soft and tender and clinging in woman. And yet I am wrong. She *was* timid and afraid, but she possessed courage. The flesh and the qualms of the flesh she was heir to, but the flesh bore heavily only on the flesh. And she was spirit, first and always spirit, etherealized essence of life, as calm as her calm eyes, and sure of permanence in the changing order of the universe.

Came days of storm, days and nights of storm, when the ocean menaced us with its roaring whiteness and the wind smote our struggling boat with a Titan's buffets. And ever we were flung off farther and farther to the northeast. It was in such a storm, and the worst that we had experienced, that I cast a weary glance to leeward, not in quest of anything, but more from the weariness of facing the elemental strife and in mute appeal, almost, to the wrathful powers to cease and let us be. What I saw I could not at first believe: days and nights of sleeplessness and anxiety had doubtless turned my head. I looked back at Maud, to identify myself, as it were, in time and space. The sight of her dear wet cheeks, her flying hair, and her brave brown eyes convinced me that my vision was still healthy. Again I turned my face to leeward, and again I saw the jutting promontory, black and high and naked, the raging surf that broke about its base and beat its front high up with spouting fountains, the black and forbidding coast-line running toward the southeast and fringed with a tremendous scarf of white.

"Maud," I said, "Maud."

She turned her head and beheld the sight.

"It cannot be Alaska!" she cried.

"No," I answered; and asked, "Can you swim?"

She shook her head.

"Neither can I," I said. "So we must get ashore without swimming, in some opening between the rocks through which we can drive the boat and clamber out. But we must be quick, very quick—and sure."

I spoke with a confidence she knew I did not feel, for she looked at me with that unfaltering gaze of hers and said:

"I have not thanked you yet for all you have done for me, but—"

She hesitated, as if in doubt how best to word her gratitude.

"Well?" I said brutally, for I was not quite pleased with her thanking me.

"You might help me," she smiled.

"To acknowledge your obligations before you die? Not at all. We are not going to die. We shall land on that island, and we shall be snug and sheltered before the day is done."

I spoke stoutly, but I did not believe a word. Nor was I prompted to lie through fear. I felt no fear, though I was sure of death in that boiling surge among the rocks which was rapidly growing nearer. It was impossible to hoist sail and claw off that shore. The wind would instantly capsize the boat; the seas would swamp it the moment it fell into the trough; and, besides, the sail, lashed to the spare oars, dragged in the sea ahead of us.

As I say, I was not afraid to meet my own death there, a few hundred yards to leeward; but I was appalled at the thought that Maud must die. My cursed imagination saw her beaten and mangled against the rocks, and it was too terrible. I strove to compel myself to think we would make the landing safely, and so I spoke not what I believed, but what I preferred to believe.

I recoiled before contemplation of that frightful death, and for a moment I entertained the wild idea of seizing Maud in my arms and leaping overboard. Then I resolved to wait, and at the last moment, when we entered on the final stretch, to take her in my arms and proclaim my love, and, with her in my embrace, to make the desperate struggle and die.

Instinctively we drew closer together in the bottom of the boat. I felt her mittened hand come out to mine; and thus, without speech, we waited the end. We were not far off the line the wind made with the western edge of the promontory, and I watched in the hope that some set of the current or send of the sea would drift us past before we reached the surf.

"We shall go clear," I said, with a confidence that I knew deceived neither of us. Five minutes later I cried: "By God! We shall go clear!"

The oath left my lips in my excitement—the first, I do believe, in my life, unless "trouble it," an expletive of my youth, be accounted an oath.

"I beg your pardon," I said.

"You have convinced me for the first time of your sincerity," she said, with a faint smile. "I do know now that we shall go clear."

I had seen a distant headland past the extreme edge of the promontory, and as we looked we could see grow the intervening coast-line of what was evidently a deep cove. At the same time there broke upon our ears a continuous and mighty bellowing. It partook of the magnitude and volume of distant thunder, and it came to us directly from leeward, rising above the crash of the surf and traveling directly in the teeth of the storm. As we passed the point, the whole cove burst upon our view, a half-moon of white sandy beach upon which broke a huge surf and which was covered with myriads of seals. It was from them that the great bellowing went up.

"A rookery!" I cried. "Now are we indeed saved. There must be men and cruisers to protect them from the seal-hunters. Possibly there is a station ashore."

But as I studied the surf that beat upon the beach, I said: "Still bad, but not so bad. And now, if the gods be truly kind, we shall drift by that next headland and come upon a perfectly sheltered beach where we may land without wetting our feet."

And the gods were kind. The first and second headlands were directly in line with the southwest wind; but once around the second,—and we went perilously close,—

we picked up the third headland, still in line with the wind and with the other two. But the cove that intervened! It penetrated deep into the land, and the tide, setting in, drifted us under the shelter of the point. Here the sea was calm, save for a heavy but smooth ground-swell, and I took in the sea-anchor and began to row. From the point the shore curved away more and more to the south and west, until, at last, it disclosed a cove within the cove, a little landlocked harbor, the water as level as a pond, broken only by tiny ripples, where vagrant breaths and wisps of the storm hurtled down from over the frowning wall of rock that backed the beach a hundred feet inshore.

Here were no seals whatever. The boat's stem touched the hard shingle. I sprang out, extending my hand to Maud. The next moment she was beside me. As my fingers released hers, she clutched for my arm hastily. At the same moment I swayed, as if about to fall to the sand. This was the startling effect of the cessation of motion. We had been so long upon the moving, rocking sea that the stable land was a shock to us. We expected the beach to lift up this way and that, and the rocky walls to swing back and forth like the sides of a ship; and when we braced ourselves automatically for these various expected movements, their non-occurrence quite overcame our equilibrium.

"I really must sit down," Maud said, with a nervous laugh and a dizzy gesture, and forthwith she sat down on the sand.

I attended to making the boat secure and joined her. Thus we landed on Endeavor Island, as we called it, land-sick from long custom of the sea.

XXIX

"FOOL!" I cried aloud in my vexation.

I had unloaded the boat and carried its contents high up on the beach, where I had set about making a camp. There was driftwood, though not much, on the beach, and the sight of a coffee-tin I had taken from the *Ghost's* larder had given me the idea of a fire.

"Blithering idiot!" I was continuing.

But Maud said, "Tut! tut!" in gentle reproval, and then asked why I was a blithering idiot.

"No matches!" I groaned. "Not a match did I bring! And now we shall have no hot coffee, soup, tea, nor anything."

"Was n't it—er—Crusoe who rubbed sticks together?" she drawled.

"But I have read the personal narratives of a score of shipwrecked men who tried, and tried in vain," I answered. "I remember Winters, a newspaper fellow with an Alaskan and Siberian reputation. Met him at the Bibelot once, and he was telling us how he attempted to make a fire with a couple of sticks. It was most amusing. He told it inimitably, but it was the story of a failure. I remember his conclusion, his black eyes flashing as he said: 'Gentlemen, the South Sea Islander may do it, the Malay may do it, but, take my word, it 's beyond the white man.'"

"Oh, well, we 've managed so far without it," she said cheerfully; "and there 's no reason why we cannot still manage without it."

"But think of the coffee!" I cried. "It 's good coffee, too. I know; I took it from Larsen's private stores. And look at that good wood."

I confess that I wanted the coffee badly, and I learned not long afterward that the berry was likewise a little weakness of Maud's. Besides, we had been so long on a cold diet that we were numb inside as well as out. Anything warm would have been most gratifying. But I complained no more, and set about making a tent of the sail for Maud.

I had looked upon it as a simple task, what with the oars, mast, boom, and sprit, to say nothing of plenty of lines. But as I was without experience, and as every detail was an experiment and every successful detail an invention, the day was well gone before her shelter was an accomplished fact. And then that night it rained, and Maud was flooded out and driven back into the boat.

The next morning I dug a shallow ditch around the tent, and, an hour later, a sudden gust of wind, whipping over the rocky wall behind us, picked up the tent and smashed it down on the sand thirty yards away.

Maud laughed at my crestfallen expression, and I said: "As soon as the wind abates I intend going in the boat to explore the island. There must be a station somewhere, and men. And ships must visit the station. Some government must protect all these seals. But I wish to have you comfortable before I start."

"I should like to go with you," was all she said.

"It would be better if you remained. You have had enough of hardship. It is a miracle that you have survived. And it won't be comfortable in the boat, rowing and sailing in this rainy weather. What you need is rest, and I should like you to remain and get it."

Something suspiciously akin to moistness dimmed her beautiful eyes before she dropped them and partly turned away her head.

"I should prefer going with you," she said in a low voice, in which there was just a hint of appeal.

"I might be able to help you a—" her voice broke—"a little. And if anything should happen to you, think of me left here alone."

"Oh, I intend being very careful," I answered. "And I shall not go so far but what I can get back before night. Yes, all said and done, I think it vastly better for you to remain and sleep and rest and do nothing."

She turned and looked me in the eyes. Her gaze was soft but unfaltering.

"Please, please!" she said very softly.

I stiffened myself to refuse, and shook my head. Still she waited and looked at me. I tried to word my refusal, but wavered. I saw the glad light spring into her eyes, and knew that I had lost. It was impossible to say no after that.

The wind died down in the afternoon, and we were prepared to start the following morning. There was no way of penetrating the island from our cove, for the walls rose perpendicularly from the beach, and on each side of the cove rose from the deep water.

Morning broke dull and gray, but calm, and I was awake early and had the boat in readiness.

"Fool! Imbecile! Yahoo!" I shouted, when I thought it was meet to arouse Maud; but this time I shouted in merriment as I danced about the beach, bareheaded, in mock despair.

Her head appeared under the flap of the sail.

"What now?" she asked sleepily and, withal, curiously.

"Coffee!" I cried. "What do you say to a cup of coffee—hot coffee, piping hot?"

"My!" she murmured, "you startled me. And you are cruel. Here I have been composing my soul to do without it, and here you are vexing me with your vain suggestions."

"Watch me," I said.

From under clefts among the rocks I gathered a few dry sticks and chips. These I whittled into shavings or split into kindling. From my note-book I tore out a page, and from the ammunition-box took a shot-gun shell. Removing the wads from the latter with my knife, I emptied the powder on a flat rock. Next I pried the primer, or cap, from the shell, and laid it on the rock in the midst of the scattered powder. All was ready. Maud still watched from the tent. Holding the paper in my left hand, I smashed down upon the cap with a rock held in my right. There was a puff of white smoke, a burst of flame, and the rough edge of the paper was alight.

Maud clapped her hands gleefully. "Prometheus!" she cried.

But I was far too busy to acknowledge her delight. The feeble flame must be cherished tenderly if it were to gather strength and live. I fed it shaving by shaving and sliver by sliver, till at last it was snapping and crackling as it laid hold of the smaller chips and sticks. To be cast away on an island had not entered into my calculations, so we were without a kettle or cooking-utensils of any sort; but I made shift with the tin used for baling the boat, and later, as we consumed our supply of canned goods, we accumulated quite an imposing array of cooking-vessels.

I boiled the water, but it was Maud who made the coffee. And how good it was! My contribution was canned beef fried with crumpled sea-biscuit and water. The breakfast was a success, and we sat about the fire much longer than enterprising explorers should have done, sipping the hot black coffee and talking over our situation.

I was confident that we would find a station in some one of the coves, for I knew that the rookeries of Bering Sea were thus guarded; but Maud advanced the theory—to prepare me for disappointment, I do believe, if disappointment were to come—that we had discovered an unknown rookery. She was in very good spirits, however, and made quite merry in accepting our plight as a grave one.

"If you are right," I said, "then we

must prepare to winter here. Our food will not last, but there are the seals. They go away in the fall, so I must soon begin to lay in a supply of meat. Then there will be huts to build, and driftwood to gather. Also, we shall try out seal fat for lighting purposes. Altogether, we 'll have our hands full if we find the island uninhabited. Which we shall not, I know."

But she was right. We sailed with a beam wind along the shore, searching the coves with our glasses, and landing occasionally, without finding a sign of human life. Yet we learned that we were not the first that had landed on Endeavor Island. High up on the beach of the second cove from ours, we discovered the splintered wreck of a boat—a sealer's boat, for the rowlocks were bound in sennit, a gun-rack was on the starboard side of the bow, and in white letters was faintly visible *Gazelle No. 2*. The boat had lain there for a long time, for it was half filled with sand, and the splintered wood had that weather-worn appearance due to long exposure to the elements. In the stern-sheets I found a rusty ten-gage shot-gun and a sailor's sheath-knife broken short across and so rusted as to be almost unrecognizable.

"They got away," I said cheerfully; but I felt a sinking at the heart and seemed to divine the presence of bleached bones somewhere on that beach.

I did not wish Maud's spirits to be dampened by such a find, so I turned seaward again with our boat and skirted the northeastern point of the island. There were no beaches on the southern shore, and by early afternoon we rounded the black promontory and completed the circumnavigation of the island. I estimated its circumference at twenty-five miles, its width as varying from two to five miles; while my most conservative calculation placed on its beaches two hundred thousand seals. The island was highest at its extreme southwestern point, the headlands and backbone diminishing regularly until the northeastern portion was only a few feet above the sea. With the exception of our little cove, the other beaches sloped gently back for a distance of half a mile or so, into what I might call rocky meadows, with here and there patches of moss and tundra grass. Here the seals hauled out, and the old bulls guarded their harems, while the young bulls hauled out by themselves.

This brief description is all that Endeavor Island merits. Damp and soggy where it was not sharp and rocky, buffeted by storm-winds and lashed by the sea, with the air continually a-tremble with the bellowing of two hundred thousand amphibians, it was a melancholy and miserable sojourning-place. Maud, who had prepared me for disappointment, and who had been sprightly and vivacious all day, broke down as we landed in our own little cove. She strove bravely to hide it from me, but while I was kindling another fire I knew she was stifling her sobs in the blankets under the sail-tent.

It was my turn to be cheerful, and I played the part to the best of my ability, and with such success that I brought the laughter back into her dear eyes and song on her lips, for she sang to me before she went to an early bed. It was the first time I had heard her sing, and I lay by the fire, listening and transported; for she was nothing if not an artist in everything she did, and her voice, though not strong, was wonderfully sweet and expressive.

I still slept in the boat, and I lay awake long that night, gazing up at the first stars I had seen in many nights and pondering the situation. Responsibility of this sort was a new thing to me. Wolf Larsen had been quite right. I had stood on my father's legs. My lawyers and agents had taken care of my money for me. I had had no responsibilities at all. Then, on the *Ghost*, I had learned to be responsible for myself. And now, for the first time in my life, I found myself responsible for some one else. And it was required of me that this should be the gravest of responsibilities, for she was the one woman in the world—the one small woman, as I loved to think of her.

XXX

No wonder we called it Endeavor Island. For two weeks we toiled at building a hut. Maud insisted on helping, and I could have wept over her bruised and bleeding hands. And still, I was proud of her because of it. There was something heroic about this gently bred woman enduring our terrible hardship and with her pittance of strength bending to the tasks of a peasant woman. She gathered many of the stones that I built into the walls of the hut; also, she turned a deaf ear to my entreaties when I begged her to desist. She compromised, however, by taking upon herself the lighter labors of cooking and of gathering drift-wood and moss for our winter's supply.

The hut's walls rose without difficulty, and everything went smoothly until the problem of the roof confronted me. Of what use the four walls without a roof? And of what could a roof be made? There were the spare oars, very true. They would serve as roof-beams; but with what was I to cover them? Moss would never do. Tundra grass was impracticable. We needed the sail for the boat, and the tarpaulin had begun to leak.

"Winters used walrus-skins on his hut," I said.

"There are the seals," she suggested.

So next day the hunting began. I did not know how to shoot, but I proceeded to learn. And when I had expended some thirty shells for three seals, I decided that the ammunition would be exhausted before I acquired the necessary knowledge. I had used eight shells for lighting fires before I hit upon the device of banking the embers with wet moss, and there remained not over a hundred shells in the box.

"We must club the seals," I announced, when convinced of my poor marksmanship. "I have heard the sealers talk about clubbing them."

"They are so pretty," she objected. "I cannot bear to think of it being done. It is so directly brutal, you know, so different from shooting them."

"That roof must go on," I answered grimly. "Winter is almost here. It is our lives against theirs. It is unfortunate we have n't plenty of ammunition, but I think, anyway, that they suffer less from being clubbed than from being all shot up. Besides, I shall do the clubbing."

"That 's just it," she began eagerly, and broke off in sudden confusion.

"Of course," I began, "if you prefer—"

"But what shall I be doing?" she interrupted, with that softness I knew full well to be insistence.

"Gathering fire-wood and cooking dinner," I answered lightly.

She shook her head. "It is too dangerous for you to attempt alone.

"I know, I know," she waived my protest. "I am only a weak woman, but just my small assistance may enable you to escape disaster."

"But the clubbing?" I suggested.

"Of course you will do that. I shall probably scream. I 'll look away when—"

"The danger is most serious," I laughed.

"I shall use my judgment when to look and when not to look," she replied, with a grand air.

The upshot of the affair was that she accompanied me next morning. I rowed into the adjoining cove and up to the edge of the beach. There were seals all about us in the water, and the bellowing thousands on the beach compelled us to shout at each other to make ourselves heard.

"I know men club them," I said, trying to reassure myself, and gazing doubtfully at a large bull, not thirty feet away, upreared on his fore flippers and regarding me intently. "But the question is, how do they club them?"

"Let us gather tundra grass and thatch the roof," Maud said.

She was as frightened as I at the prospect, and we had reason to be, gazing at close range at the gleaming teeth and dog-like mouths.

"I always thought they were afraid of men," I said. "How do I know they are not afraid?" I queried a moment later, after having rowed a few more strokes along the beach. "Perhaps if I were to step boldly ashore, they would cut for it and I could not catch up with one."

And still I hesitated.

"I heard of a man once that invaded the nesting-grounds of wild geese," Maud said. "They killed him."

"The geese?"

"Yes, the geese. My brother told me about it when I was a little girl."

"But I know men club them," I persisted.

"I think the tundra grass will make just as good a roof," she said.

Far from her intention, her words were maddening me, driving me on. I could not play the coward before her eyes.

"Here goes," I said, backing water with one oar and running the bow ashore.

I stepped out and advanced valiantly upon a long-maned bull in the midst of his wives. I was armed with the regular club with which the boat-pullers killed the wounded seals gaffed aboard by the hunters. It was only a foot and a half long, and in my superb ignorance I never dreamed that the club used ashore when raiding the rookeries measured four or five feet. The cows lumbered out of my way, and the distance between me and the bull decreased. He raised himself on his flippers with an angry movement. We were a dozen feet apart. Still I advanced steadily, looking for him to turn tail at any moment and run.

At six feet the panicky thought rushed into my mind: What if he will not run? Why, then I shall club him, came the answer. In my fear I had forgotten that I was there to get the bull instead of to make him run. And just then he gave a snort and a snarl and rushed at me. His eyes were blazing, his mouth was wide open; the teeth gleamed cruelly white. Without shame, I confess that it was I that turned tail and footed it. He ran awkwardly, but he ran well. He was but two paces behind when I tumbled into the boat, and as I shoved off with an oar his teeth crunched down upon the blade. The stout wood was crushed like an egg-shell. Maud and I were astounded. A moment later he had dived under the boat, seized the keel in his mouth, and was shaking the boat violently.

"My!" said Maud. "Let 's go back."

I shook my head. "I can do what other men have done, and I know that other men have clubbed seals. But I think I 'll leave the bulls alone next time."

"I wish you would n't," she said.

"Now don't say, 'Please, please,'" I cried, half angrily, I do believe.

She made no reply, and I knew my tone must have hurt her.

"I beg your pardon," I said, or shouted, rather, in order to make myself heard above the roar of the rookery. "If you say so, I 'll turn and go back; but honestly, I 'd rather stay."

"Now, don't say that this is what you get for bringing a woman along," she said. She smiled at me whimsically, gloriously, and I knew there was no need for forgiveness.

I rowed a couple of hundred feet along the beach so as to recover my nerves, and then stepped ashore again.

"Do be cautious!" she called after me.

I nodded my head and proceeded to make a flank attack on the nearest harem. All went well until I aimed a blow at an outlying cow's head and fell short. She snorted and tried to scramble away. I ran in close and struck another blow, hitting the shoulder instead of the head.

"Look out!" I heard Maud scream.

In my excitement I had not been taking notice of other things, and I looked up to see the lord of the harem charging down upon me. Again I fled to the boat, hotly pursued; but this time Maud made no suggestion of turning back.

"It would be better, I imagine, if you let harems alone and devoted your attention to lonely and inoffensive-looking seals," was what she said. "I think I have read something about them—Dr. Jordan's book, I believe. They are the young bulls, not old enough to have harems of their own. He called them the holluschickie, or something like that. It seems to me, if we find where they haul out—"

"It seems to me that your fighting instinct is aroused," I laughed.

She flushed quickly and prettily. "I 'll admit I don't like defeat any more than you do, nor any more than I like the idea of killing such pretty, inoffensive creatures."

"Pretty!" I sniffed. "I failed to mark anything preëminently pretty about those foamy-mouthed beasts that raced me."

"Your point of view," she laughed. "You lacked perspective. Now if you did not have to get so close to the subject—"

"The very thing!" I cried. "What I need is a longer club. And there 's that broken oar ready to hand."

"It just comes to me," she said, "that Captain Larsen was telling me how the men raided the rookeries. They drive the seals, in small herds, a short distance inland before they kill them."

"I don't care to undertake the herding of one of those harems," I objected.

"But there are the holluschickie," she said. "The holluschickie haul out by themselves, and Dr. Jordan says that paths are left between the harems, and that as long as the holluschickie keep strictly to the paths they are unmolested by the masters of the harem."

"There 's one now," I said, pointing to a young bull in the water. "Let 's watch him and follow him if he hauls out."

He swam directly to the beach and clambered out into a small opening between two harems, the masters of which made warning noises, but did not attack him. We watched him travel slowly inland, threading about among the harems along what must have been the path.

"Here goes," I said, stepping out; but I confess my heart was in my mouth as I thought of going through the heart of that monstrous herd.

"It would be wise to make the boat fast," Maud said.

She had stepped out beside me, and I regarded her with wonderment.

She nodded her head determinedly. "Yes, I 'm going with you, so you may as well secure the boat and arm me with a club."

"Let 's go back," I said dejectedly. "I think tundra grass will do, after all."

"You know it won't," was her reply. "Shall I lead?"

With a shrug of the shoulders, but with the warmest admiration and pride at heart for this woman, I equipped her with the broken oar and took another for myself. It was with nervous trepidation that we made the first few rods of the journey. Once Maud screamed in terror as a cow thrust an inquisitive nose toward her foot, and several times I quickened my pace for the same reason. But, beyond warning coughs from each side, there were no signs of hostility. It was a rookery that had never been raided by the hunters, and in consequence the seals were mild-tempered and at the same time unafraid.

In the very heart of the herd the din was terrific. It was almost dizzying in its effect. I paused and smiled reassuringly at Maud, for I had recovered my equanimity sooner than she. I could see that she was still badly frightened. She came close to me and shouted:

"I 'm dreadfully afraid!"

And I was not. Though the novelty had not yet worn off, the peaceful comportment of the seals had quieted my alarm. Maud was trembling.

"I 'm afraid, and I 'm not afraid," she chattered, with shaking jaws. "It 's my miserable body, not I."

"It 's all right; it 's all right," I reassured her, my arm passing instinctively and protectingly around her.

I shall never forget, in that moment, how instantly conscious I became of my manhood. The primitive deeps of my nature stirred. I felt myself masculine, the protector of the weak, the fighting male. And, best of all, I felt myself the protector of my loved one. She leaned against me, so light and lily-frail, and as her trembling eased away it seemed as though I became aware of prodigious strength. I felt myself a match for the most ferocious bull in the herd, and I know, had such a bull charged upon me, that I would have met him unflinchingly and coolly, and I know that I would have killed him.

"I am all right now," she said, looking up at me gratefully. "Let us go on."

And that the strength in me had quieted her and given her confidence filled me with an exultant joy. The youth of the race seemed burgeoning in me, over-civilized man that I was, and I lived for myself the old hunting days and forest nights of my remote and forgotten ancestry. I had much for which to thank Wolf Larsen, was my thought as we went along the path between the jostling harems.

A quarter of a mile inland we came upon the holluschickie—sleek young bulls, living out the loneliness of their bachelorhood and gathering strength against the day when they would fight their way into the ranks of the benedicts.

Everything now went smoothly. I seemed to know just what to do and how to do it. Shouting, making threatening gestures with my club, and even prodding the lazy ones, I quickly cut out a score of the young bachelors from their companions. Whenever one made an attempt to break back toward the water, I headed him off. Maud took an active part in the drive, and with her cries and flourishings of the broken oar was of considerable assistance. I noticed, though, that whenever one looked tired and lagged she let him slip past. But I noticed, also, whenever one, with a show of fight, tried to break past, that her eyes glinted and showed bright and she rapped him smartly with her club.

"My, it 's exciting!" she cried, pausing from sheer weakness. "I think I 'll sit down."

I drove the little herd (a dozen strong, now, what of the escapes she had permitted) a hundred yards farther on; and by the time she joined me I had finished the slaughter and was beginning to skin. An hour later we went proudly back along the path between the harems. And twice again we came down the path burdened with skins, till I thought we had enough to roof the hut. I set the sail, laid one tack out of the cove, and on the other tack made our own little inner cove.

"It 's just like home-coming," Maud said, as I ran the boat ashore.

I heard her words with a responsive thrill, it was all so dearly intimate and natural, and I said:

"It seems as though I have lived this life always. The world of books and bookish folk is very vague, more like a dream-memory than an actuality. I surely have hunted and forayed and fought all the days of my life. And you, too, seem a part of it. You are—" I was on the verge of saying, "my woman, my mate," but glibly changed it to, "standing the hardship well."

But her ear had caught the flaw. She recognized a flight that midmost broke. She gave me a quick look.

"Not that. You were saying—"

"That you are living the life of a savage and living it quite successfully," I said easily.

"Oh," was all she replied; but I could have sworn there was a note of disappointment in her voice.

But "my woman, my mate," kept ringing in my head for the rest of the day and for many days. Yet never did it ring more loudly than that night, as I watched her draw back the blanket of moss from the coals, blow up the fire, and cook the evening meal. It must have been latent savagery stirring in me for the old words, so bound up with the roots of the race, to grip me and thrill me. And grip and thrill they did, till I fell asleep, murmuring them to myself over and over again.

XXXI

"It will smell," I said, "but it will keep in the heat and keep out the rain and snow."

We were surveying the completed seal-skin roof.

"It is clumsy, but it will serve the purpose, and that is the main thing," I went on, yearning for her praise.

And she clapped her hands and declared that she was hugely pleased.

"But it is dark in here," she said the next moment, her shoulders shrinking with a little involuntary shiver.

"You might have suggested a window when the walls were going up," I said. "It was for you, and you should have seen the need of a window."

"But I never do see the obvious, you know," she laughed back. "And besides, you can knock a hole in the wall at any time."

"Quite true; I had not thought of it," I replied, wagging my head sagely. "But have you thought of ordering the window-glass? Just call up the firm,—Red 4451 I think it is,—and tell them what size and kind of glass you wish."

"That means—" she began.

"No window."

It was a dark and evil-appearing thing, that hut, not fit for aught better than swine in a civilized land; but for us who had known the misery of the open boat it was a snug little habitation. Following the housewarming, which was accomplished by means of seal-oil and a wick made from cotton calking, came the hunting for our winter's meat and the building of the second hut. It was a simple affair, now, to go forth in the morning and return by noon with a boat-load of seals. And then, while I worked at building the hut, Maud tried out the oil from the blubber and kept a slow fire under the frames of meat. I had heard of jerking beef on the plains, and our seal-meat, cut in thin strips and hung in the smoke, cured excellently.

The second hut was easier to erect, for I built it against the first and only three walls were required. But it was work, hard work, all of it. Maud and I worked from dawn till dark, to the limit of our strength, so that when night came we crawled stiffly to bed and slept the animal-like sleep of exhaustion. And yet she declared that she had never felt better nor stronger in her life. I knew this was true of myself, but hers was such a lily strength that I feared she would break down. Often and often, her last reserve force gone, I have seen her stretched flat on her back on the sand, in the way she had of resting and recuperating. And then she would be up on her feet and toiling as hard as ever. Where she obtained this strength was a marvel to me.

"Think of the long rest this winter," was her reply to my remonstrances. "Why, we 'll be clamorous for something to do."

We held a housewarming in my hut the night it was roofed. It was the end of the third day of a fierce storm that had swung around the compass from the southeast to the northwest, and that was then blowing directly in upon us. The beaches of the outer cove were thundering with the surf, and even in our landlocked inner cove a respectable

Drawn by W. J. Aylward.

BUILDING THE HUT

sea was breaking. No high backbone of island sheltered us from the wind, and it whistled and bellowed about the hut till at times I feared for the strength of the walls. The skin roof, stretched tightly as a drumhead, I had thought, sagged and bellied with every gust; and innumerable interstices in the walls, not so tightly stuffed with moss as Maud had supposed, disclosed themselves. Yet the seal-oil burned brightly, and we were warm and comfortable.

It was a pleasant evening indeed, and we voted that as a social event on Endeavor Island it had not yet been eclipsed. Our minds were at ease. Not only had we resigned ourselves to the bitter winter, but we were prepared for it. The seals could depart on their mysterious journey into the south at any time, now, for all we cared; and the storms held no terror for us. Not only were we sure of being dry and warm and sheltered from the wind, but we had the softest and most luxurious mattresses that could be made from moss. This had been Maud's idea, and she had herself jealously gathered all the moss. This was to be my first night on the mattress, and I knew I should sleep the sweeter because she had made it.

As she rose to go, she turned to me with the whimsical way she had, and said:

"Something is going to happen—is happening, for that matter. I feel it. Something is coming here, to us. It is coming now. I don't know what, but it is coming."

"Good or bad?" I asked.

She shook her head. "I don't know, but it is there, somewhere."

She pointed toward the sea and wind.

"It 's a lee shore," I laughed, "and I am sure I 'd rather be here than arriving a night like this."

"You are not frightened?" I asked, as I stepped to open the door for her.

Her eyes looked bravely into mine.

"And you feel well? Perfectly well?" I said.

"Never better," was her answer.

We talked a little longer before she went.

"Good night, Maud," I said.

"Good night, Humphrey," she said.

This use of our given names had come about quite as a matter of course, and was as unpremeditated as it was natural. In that moment I could have put my arms around her and drawn her to me. I should certainly have done so out in that world to which we belonged. As it was, the situation stopped there in the only way it could; but I was left alone in my little hut, glowing warmly through and through with a pleasant satisfaction; and I knew that a tie, or a tacit something, existed between us that had not existed before.

THE SEA-WOLF

BY JACK LONDON

Author of "The Call of the Wild," "The God of his Fathers," etc.

XXXII

I AWOKE, oppressed by a mysterious sensation. There seemed something missing in my environment. But the mystery and oppressiveness vanished after the first few seconds of waking, when I identified the missing something as the wind. I had fallen asleep in that state of nerve tension with which one meets the continuous shock of sound or movement, and I had awakened, still tense, bracing myself to meet the pressure of something which no longer bore upon me.

It was the first night I had spent under cover in several months, and I lay luxuriously for some minutes under my blankets (for once not wet with fog or spray), analyzing, first, the effect produced upon me by the cessation of the wind, and next the joy which was mine from resting on the mattress made by Maud's hands. When I had dressed and opened the door, I heard the waves still lapping on the beach, garrulously attesting the fury of the night. It was a clear day, and the sun was shining. I had slept late, and I stepped outside with sudden energy, bent upon making up lost time, as befitted a dweller on Endeavor Island.

And when outside I stopped short. I believed my eyes without question, and yet I was for the moment stunned by what they disclosed to me. There, on the beach, not fifty feet away, bow on, dismasted, was a black-hulled vessel. Masts and booms, tangled with shrouds, sheets, and rent canvas, were rubbing gently alongside. I could have rubbed my eyes as I looked. There was the home-made galley we had built, the familiar break of the poop, the low yacht-cabin scarcely rising above the rail. It was the *Ghost!*

What freak of fortune had brought it here—here of all spots? What chance of chances? I looked at the bleak, inaccessible wall at my back, and knew the profundity of despair. Escape was hopeless, out of the question. I thought of Maud, asleep there in the hut we had reared; I remembered her "Good night, Humphrey." "My woman, my mate," went ringing through my brain; but now, alas! it was a knell that sounded. Then everything went black before my eyes.

Possibly it was the fraction of a second, but I had no knowledge of how long an interval had lapsed before I was myself again. There lay the *Ghost*, bow on to the beach, her splintered bowsprit projecting over the sand, her tangled spars rubbing against her side to the lift of the crooning waves. Something must be done—must be done!

It came upon me suddenly as strange that nothing moved aboard. Wearied from the night of struggle and wreck, all hands were yet asleep, I thought. My next thought was that Maud and I might yet escape. If we could take to the boat and make around the point before any one awoke! I would call her and start. My hand was lifted at her door to knock, when I recollected the smallness of the island. We could never hide ourselves upon it. There was nothing for us but the wide, raw ocean. I thought of our snug little huts, our supplies of meat and oil and moss and fire-wood, and I knew that we could never survive the wintry sea and the great storms which were to come.

So I stood, with hesitant knuckle, without her door. It was impossible—impossible. A wild thought of rushing in and killing her as she slept rose in my mind. And then, in a flash, the better solution came to me. All hands were asleep. Why not creep aboard the *Ghost*,—well I knew the way to Wolf Larsen's bunk!—and kill him in his sleep? After that—well, we would see. But with him dead there was time and space in which to prepare to do other things; and, besides, whatever new situation arose, it could not possibly be worse than the present one.

My knife was at my hip. I returned to my hut for the shot-gun, made sure it was loaded, and went down to the *Ghost*. With some difficulty, and at the expense of a wetting to the waist, I climbed aboard. The forecastle scuttle was open. I paused to listen for the breathing of the men, but there was no breathing. I almost gasped as the thought came to me: What if the *Ghost* is deserted? I listened more closely. There was no sound. I cautiously descended the ladder. The place had the empty and musty feel and smell usual to a dwelling no longer inhabited. Everywhere was a thick litter of discarded and ragged garments, old sea-boots, leaky oilskins—all the worthless forecastle dunnage of a long voyage.

Abandoned hastily, was my conclusion as I ascended to the deck. Hope was alive again in my breast, and I looked about me with greater coolness. I noted that the boats were missing. The steerage told the same tale as the forecastle. The hunters had packed their belongings with similar haste. The *Ghost* was deserted! It was Maud's and mine. I thought of the ship's stores and the lazaret beneath the cabin, and the idea came to me of surprising Maud with something nice for breakfast.

The reaction from my fear, and the knowledge that the terrible deed I had come to do was no longer necessary, made me boyish and eager. I went up the steerage companionway two steps at a time, with nothing distinct in my mind except joy and the hope that Maud would sleep on until the surprise breakfast was quite ready for her. As I rounded the galley, a new satisfaction was mine at thought of all the splendid cooking utensils inside. I sprang up the break of the poop, and saw —Wolf Larsen! What of my impetus and the stunning surprise, I clattered three or four steps along the deck before I could stop myself. He was standing in the companionway, only his head and shoulders visible, staring straight at me. His arms were resting on the half-open slide. He made no movement whatever—simply stood there, staring at me.

I began to tremble. The old stomach-sickness clutched me. I put one hand on the edge of the house to steady myself. My lips seemed suddenly dry, and I moistened them against the need of speech. Nor did I for an instant take my eyes off him. Neither of us spoke. There was something ominous in his silence, his immobility. All my old fear of him returned and by new fear was increased an hundred-fold. And still we stood, the pair of us, staring at each other.

I was aware of the demand for action, and, my old helplessness strong upon me, I was waiting for him to take the initiative. Then, as the moments went by, it came to me that the situation was analogous to the one in which I had approached the long-maned bull, my intention of clubbing obscured by fear until it became a desire to make him run. So it was at last impressed upon me that I was there, not to have Wolf Larsen take the initiative, but to take it myself.

I cocked both barrels and leveled the shot-gun at him. Had he moved, attempted to drop down the companionway, I know I should have shot him. But he stood motionless and staring as before. And as I faced him, with leveled gun shaking in my hands, I had time to note the worn and haggard appearance of his face. It was as if some strong anxiety had wasted it. The cheeks were sunken, and there was a wearied, puckered expression on the brow; and it seemed to me that his eyes were strange, not only the expression, but the physical seeming, as though the optic nerves and supporting muscles had suffered strain and slightly twisted the eyeballs.

All this I saw, and, my brain now working rapidly, I thought a thousand thoughts; and yet I could not pull the triggers. I lowered the gun and stepped to the corner of the cabin, primarily to relieve the tension on my nerves and to make a new start, and incidentally to be closer. Again I raised the gun. He was almost at arm's length. There was no hope for him. I was resolved. There was no possible chance of missing him, no matter how poor my marksmanship. And yet I wrestled with myself and could not pull the triggers.

"Well?" he demanded impatiently.

I strove vainly to force my fingers down on the triggers, and vainly I strove to say something.

"Why don't you shoot?" he asked.

I cleared my throat of a huskiness which prevented speech.

"Hump," he said slowly, "you can't do it. You are not exactly afraid: you are impotent. Your conventional morality is stronger than you. You are the slave to the opinions which have credence among the people you have known and have read about. Their code has been drummed into your head from the time you lisped, and in spite of your philosophy, and of what I have taught you, it won't let you kill an unarmed, unresisting man."

"I know it," I said hoarsely.

"And you know that I would kill an unarmed man as readily as I would smoke a cigar," he went on. "You know me for what I am, my worth in the world by your standard. You have called me snake, tiger, shark, monster, and Caliban. And yet, you little rag puppet, you little echoing mechanism, you are unable to kill me as you would a snake or a shark, because I have hands, feet, and a body shaped somewhat like yours. Bah! I had hoped better things of you, Hump."

He stepped out of the companionway and came up to me.

"Put down that gun. I want to ask you some questions. I have n't had a chance to look around yet. What place is this? How is the *Ghost* lying? How did you get wet? Where 's Maud?—I beg your pardon—Miss Brewster; or should I say 'Mrs. Van Weyden'?"

I had backed away from him, almost weeping at my inability to shoot him, but not fool enough to put down the gun. I hoped desperately that he might commit some hostile act, attempt to strike me or choke me; for in such way only I knew I could be stirred to shoot.

"This is Endeavor Island," I said.

"Never heard of it," he broke in.

"At least, that 's our name for it," I amended.

"'Our'?" he queried. "Who 's 'our'?"

"Miss Brewster and myself. And the *Ghost* is lying, as you can see for yourself, bow on to the beach."

"There are seals here," he said. "They woke me up with their barking, or I 'd be sleeping yet. I heard them when I drove in last night. They were the first warning that I was on a lee shore. It 's a rookery, the kind of a thing I 've hunted for years. Thanks to my brother Death, I 've lighted on a fortune. It 's a mint. What 's its bearings?"

"Have n't the least idea," I said. "But you ought to know quite closely. What were your last observations?"

He smiled, but did not answer.

"Well, where are all hands?" I asked him. "How does it come that you are alone?"

I was prepared for him again to set aside my question, and was surprised at the readiness of his reply.

"My brother got me inside forty-eight hours, and through no fault of mine. Boarded me in the night, with only the watch on deck. Hunters went back on me. He gave them a bigger lay. Heard him offering it. Did it right before me. Of course the crew gave me the go-by. That was to be expected. All hands went over the side, and there I was, marooned on my own vessel. It was Death's turn, and it 's all in the family, anyway."

"But how did you lose the masts?" I asked.

"Walk over and examine those lanyards," he said, pointing to where the mizzen-rigging should have been.

"They have been cut with a knife!" I exclaimed.

"Not quite," he laughed. "It was a neater job. Look again."

I looked. The lanyards had been almost severed, with just enough left to hold the shrouds till some severe strain should be put upon them.

"Cooky did that." He laughed again. "I know, though I did n't spot him at it. Kind of evened up the score a bit."

"Good for Mugridge!" I cried.

"Yes, that 's what I thought when everything went over the side. Only I said it on the other side of my mouth."

"But what were you doing while all this was going on?" I asked.

"My best, you may be sure, which was n't much under the circumstances."

I turned to reëxamine Thomas Mugridge's work.

"I guess I 'll sit down and take the sunshine," I heard Wolf Larsen saying.

There was a hint, just a slight hint, of physical feebleness in his voice, and it was so strange that I looked quickly at him. His hand was sweeping nervously across his face, as though he were brushing away cobwebs. I was puzzled—the whole thing was so unlike the Wolf Larsen I had known.

"How are your headaches?" I asked.

"They still trouble me," was his answer. "I think I have one coming on now."

He slipped down from his sitting posture till he lay on the deck. Then he rolled over on his side, his head resting on the biceps of the under arm, the forearm shielding his eyes from the sun. I stood regarding him wonderingly.

"Now 's your chance, Hump," he said.

"I don't understand," I lied, for I thoroughly understood.

"Oh, nothing," he added softly, as if he were drowsing; "only you 've got me where you want me."

"No, I have n't," I retorted; "for I want you a few thousand miles away from here."

He chuckled, and thereafter spoke no more. He did not stir as I passed by him and went down into the cabin. I lifted the trap in the floor, but for some moments gazed dubiously into the darkness of the lazaret beneath. I hesitated to descend. What if his lying down were a ruse? Pretty indeed to be caught there like a rat! I crept softly up the companionway and peeped at him. He was lying as I had left him. Again I went below; but before I dropped into the lazaret I took the precaution of casting down the door in advance. At least there would be no lid to the trap. But it was all needless. I regained the cabin with a store of jams, sea-biscuits, canned meats, and such things,—all I could carry,—and replaced the trap-door.

A peep at Wolf Larsen showed me that he had not moved. A bright thought struck me. I stole into his state-room and possessed myself of his revolvers. There were no other weapons, though I thoroughly ransacked the three remaining state-rooms. To make sure, I returned and went through the steerage and forecastle, and in the galley gathered up all the sharp meat- and vegetable-knives. Then I bethought me of the great yachtsman's knife he always carried, and I came to him and spoke to him, first softly, then loudly. He did not move. I bent over and took it from his pocket. I breathed more freely. He had no arms with which to attack me from a distance, while I, armed, could always forestall him should he attempt to grapple me with his terrible gorilla arms.

Filling a coffee-pot and frying-pan with part of my plunder, and taking some chinaware from the cabin pantry, I left Wolf Larsen lying in the sun and went ashore.

Maud was still asleep. I blew up the embers (we had not yet arranged a winter kitchen), and quite feverishly cooked the breakfast. Toward the end I heard her moving about within the hut, making her simple toilet. Just as all was ready and the coffee poured, the door opened and she came forth.

"It 's not fair of you," was her greeting. "You are usurping one of my prerogatives. You know you agreed that the cooking should be mine, and—"

"But just this once," I pleaded.

"If you promise not to do it again," she smiled. "Unless, of course, you have grown tired of my poor efforts."

To my delight, she never once looked toward the beach, and I maintained the banter with such success that all unconsciously she sipped coffee from the china cup, ate fried evaporated potatoes, and spread marmalade on her biscuit. But it could not last. I saw the surprise that came over her. She had discovered the china plate from which she was eating. She looked over the breakfast, noting detail after detail. Then she looked at me, and her face turned slowly toward the beach.

"Humphrey!" she said.

The old unnamable terror mounted into her eyes.

"Is—he—?" she quavered.

I nodded my head.

XXXIII

We waited all day for Wolf Larsen to come ashore. It was an intolerable period of anxiety. Each moment one or the other of us cast expectant glances toward the *Ghost*. But he did not come. He did not even appear on deck.

"Perhaps it is his headache," I said. "I left him lying on the poop. He may lie there all night. I think I 'll go and see."

Maud looked entreaty at me.

"It is all right," I assured her. "I shall take the revolvers. You know, I collected every weapon on board."

"But there are his arms, his hands, his terrible, terrible hands," she objected. And then she cried, "Oh, Humphrey, I am afraid of him. Don't go! Please don't go!"

She rested her hand appealingly on mine and sent my pulse fluttering. My heart was surely in my eyes for a moment. The dear and lovely woman! And she was so much the woman, clinging and appealing, sunshine and dew to my manhood, rooting it deeper and sending through it the sap of a new strength. I was for putting my arm around her, as when in the midst of the seal-herd, but I considered and refrained.

"I shall not take any risks," I said. "I 'll merely peep over the bow and see."

She pressed my hand earnestly and let me go. But the space on deck where I had left him lying was vacant. He had evidently gone below. That night we stood alternate watches, one of us sleeping at a time; for there was no telling what Wolf Larsen might do.

The next day we waited, and the next, and still he made no sign.

"These headaches of his, these attacks—" Maud said, on the afternoon of the fourth day. "Perhaps he is ill, very ill. He may be dead."

"Or dying," was her afterthought, when she had waited some time for me to speak.

"Better so," I answered.

"But think, Humphrey—a fellow-creature in his last lonely hour!"

"Perhaps," I suggested.

"Yes, even perhaps," she acknowledged. "But we do not know. It would be terrible if he were. I could never forgive myself. We must do something."

"Perhaps," I suggested again.

I waited, smiling inwardly at the woman of her which compelled a solicitude for Wolf Larsen, of all creatures. Where was her solicitude for me? I thought—for me whom she had been afraid to have merely peep aboard?

She was too subtle not to follow the trend of my silence. And she was as direct as she was subtle.

"You must go aboard, Humphrey, and find out," she said. "And if you want to laugh at me you have my consent and forgiveness."

I arose obediently and went down the beach.

"Do be careful," she called after me.

I waved my arm from the forecastle-head and dropped down to the deck. Aft I walked to the cabin companion, where I contented myself with hailing below. Wolf Larsen answered, and as he started to ascend the stairs I cocked my revolver. I displayed it openly during our conversation, but he took no notice of it. He appeared the same, physically, as when last I saw him, but he was gloomy and silent. In fact, the few words we spoke could hardly be called a conversation. I did not inquire why he had not been ashore, nor did he ask why I had not come aboard. His head was all right again, he said; and so, without further parley, I left him.

Maud received my report with obvious relief, and the sight of smoke which later rose in the galley put her in a more cheerful mood. The next day, and the next, we saw the galley smoke rising, and sometimes we caught glimpses of him on the poop. But that was all. He made no attempt to come ashore. This we knew, for we still maintained our night watches. We were waiting for him to do something,—to show his hand, so to say,—and his inaction puzzled and worried us.

A week of this passed by. We had no other interest than Wolf Larsen, and his presence weighed us down with an apprehension which prevented us from doing any of the little things we had planned.

But at the end of the week the smoke ceased rising from the galley, and he no longer showed himself on the poop. I could see Maud's solicitude again growing, though she timidly—and even proudly, I think—forbore a repetition of her request. After all, what censure could be put upon her? Besides, I myself was aware of hurt at thought of this man whom I had tried to kill dying alone with his fellow-creatures so near. He was right. The code of my group was stronger than I. The fact that he had hands, feet, and a body shaped somewhat like mine constituted a claim that I could not ignore.

So I did not wait a second time for Maud to send me. I discovered that we stood in need of condensed milk and marmalade, and announced that I was going aboard. I could see that she wavered. She even went so far as to murmur that they were non-essentials and that my trip after them might be inexpedient. And, as she had followed the trend of my silence, she now followed the trend of my speech; and she knew that I was going aboard, not because of condensed milk and marmalade, but because of her and of her anxiety, which she knew she had failed to hide.

I took off my shoes when I gained the forecastle-head, and went noiselessly aft in my stocking-feet. Nor did I call this time from the top of the companionway. Cautiously descending, I found the cabin deserted. The door to his state-room was closed. At first I thought of knocking; then I remembered my ostensible errand and resolved to carry it out. Carefully avoiding noise, I lifted the trap-door in the floor and set it to one side. The slop-chest, as well as the provisions, was stored in the lazaret, and I took advantage of the opportunity to lay in a stock of under-clothing.

As I emerged from the lazaret I heard sounds in Wolf Larsen's state-room. I crouched and listened. The door-knob rattled. Furtively, instinctively, I slunk back behind the table, and drew and cocked my revolver. The door swung open and he came forth. Never had I seen so profound a despair as that which I saw on his face—the face of Wolf Larsen the fighter, the strong man, the indomitable one. For all the world like a woman wringing her hands, he raised his clenched fists and groaned. One fist unclosed, and the open palm swept across his eyes as though brushing away cobwebs.

"God! God!" he groaned; and the clenched fists were raised again to the infinite despair with which his throat vibrated.

It was horrible. I was trembling all over, and I could feel the shivers running up and down my spine and the sweat standing out on my forehead. Surely there can be little in this world more awful than the spectacle of a strong man in the moment when he is utterly weak and broken.

But Wolf Larsen regained control of himself by an exertion of his remarkable will. And it was exertion. His whole frame shook with the struggle. He resembled a man on the verge of a fit. His face strove to compose itself, writhing and twisting in the effort till he broke down again. Once more the clenched fists went upward and he groaned. He caught his breath once or twice and sobbed. Then he was successful. I could have thought him the old Wolf Larsen, and yet there was in his movements a vague suggestion of weakness and indecision. He started for the companionway, and stepped forward quite as I had been accustomed to see him do; and yet again, in his very walk, there seemed that suggestion of weakness and indecision.

I was now concerned with fear for myself. The open trap lay directly in his path, and his discovery of it would lead instantly to his discovery of me. I was angry with myself for being caught in so cowardly a position, crouching on the floor. There was yet time. I rose swiftly to my feet, and, I know, quite unconsciously assumed a defiant attitude. He took no notice of me. Nor did he notice the open trap. Before I could grasp the situation, or act, he had walked right into the trap. One foot was descending into the opening, while the other foot was just on the verge of beginning the uplift. But when the descending foot missed the solid flooring and felt vacancy beneath, it was the old Wolf Larsen and the tiger muscles that made the falling body spring across the opening, even as it fell, so that he struck on his chest and stomach, with arms outstretched, on the floor of the opposite side. The next instant he had drawn up his legs and rolled clear. But he rolled into my marmalade and underclothes and against the trap-door.

The expression on his face was one of complete comprehension. But before I could guess what he had comprehended, he had dropped the trap-door into place, closing the lazaret. Then I understood. He thought he had me inside. Also, he was blind—blind as a bat. I watched him, breathing carefully so that he should not hear me. He stepped quickly to his stateroom. I saw his hand miss the door-knob by an inch, quickly fumble for it, and find it. This was my chance. I tiptoed across the cabin and to the top of the stairs. He came back, dragging a heavy sea-chest, which he deposited on top of the trap. Not content with this, he fetched a second chest and placed it on top of the first. Then he gathered up the marmalade and underclothes and put them on the table. When he started up the companionway, I retreated, silently rolling over on top of the cabin.

He shoved the slide part away back and rested his arms on it, his body still in the companionway. His attitude was of one looking forward the length of the schooner, or staring, rather, for his eyes were fixed and unblinking. I was only five feet away and directly in what should have been his line of vision. It was uncanny. I felt myself a ghost, in my invisibility. I waved my hand back and forth, of course without effect; but when the moving shadow fell across his face I saw at once that he was susceptible to the impression. His face became more expectant and tense as he tried to analyze and identify the impression. He knew that he had responded to something from without, that his sensibility had been touched by a changing something in his environment; but what it was he could not discover. I ceased waving my hand, so that the shadow remained stationary. He slowly moved his head back and forth under it and turned from side to side, now in the sunshine, now in the shade, feeling the shadow, as it were, testing it by sensation.

I, too, was busy, trying to reason out how he was aware of the existence of so intangible a thing as a shadow. If it were his eyeballs only that were affected, or if his optic nerve were not wholly destroyed, the explanation was simple. If otherwise, then the only conclusion I could reach was that the sensitive skin recognized the difference of temperature between shade and sunshine. Or perhaps—and who could tell?—it was that fabled sixth sense which conveyed to him the loom and feel of an object close at hand.

Giving over his attempt to determine the shadow, he stepped out on deck and started forward, walking with a swiftness and confidence which surprised me. And still there was that hint of the feebleness of the blind in his walk. I knew it now for what it was.

To my amused chagrin, he discovered my shoes on the forecastle-head and brought them back with him into the galley. I watched him build the fire and set about cooking food for himself; then I stole into the cabin for my marmalade and underclothes, slipped back past the galley, and climbed down to the beach to deliver my barefoot report.

XXXIV

"It's too bad the *Ghost* has lost her masts. Why, we could sail away in her. Don't you think we could, Humphrey?"

I sprang excitedly to my feet.

"I wonder—I wonder," I repeated, pacing up and down.

Maud's eyes were shining with anticipation as they followed me. She had such faith in me! And the thought of it was so much added power. I remembered Michelet's: "To man, woman is as the earth was to her legendary son; he has but to fall down and kiss her breast and he is strong again." For the first time I knew the wonderful truth of his words. Why, I was living them. Maud was all this to me, an unfailing source of strength and courage. I had but to look at her, or think of her, and be strong again.

"It can be done—it can be done," I was thinking and asserting aloud. "What men have done I can do, and if they have never done this before, still I can do it."

"What, for goodness' sake?" Maud demanded. "Do be merciful. What is it you can do?"

"We can do it," I amended. "Why, nothing else than put the masts back into the *Ghost* and sail away."

"Humphrey!" she exclaimed.

And I felt as proud of my conception as if it were already a fact accomplished.

"But how is it possibly to be done?" she asked.

"I don't know," was my answer. "I know only that I am capable of doing anything these days."

I smiled proudly at her—too proudly, for she dropped her eyes and was for the moment silent.

"But there is Captain Larsen," she objected.

"Blind and helpless," I answered promptly, waving him aside as a straw.

"But those terrible hands of his! You know how he leaped across the opening of the lazaret."

"And you know also how I crept about and avoided him," I contended gaily.

"And lost your shoes."

"You 'd hardly expect them to avoid Wolf Larsen without my feet inside of them."

We both laughed, and then went seriously to work constructing the plan whereby we were to step the masts of the *Ghost* and return to the world. I remembered hazily the physics of my school-days, while the last few months had given me practical experience with mechanical purchases. I must say, though, when we walked down to the *Ghost* to inspect more closely the task before us, that the sight of the great masts lying in the water almost disheartened me. Where were we to begin? If there had been one mast standing, something high up to which to fasten blocks and tackles! But there was nothing. It reminded me of the problem of lifting oneself by one's boot-straps. I understood the mechanics of levers; but where was I to get a fulcrum?

There was the mainmast, fifteen inches in diameter at what was now the butt, still sixty-five feet in length, and weighing, I roughly calculated, at least three thousand pounds. And then came the foremast, larger in diameter and weighing surely thirty-five hundred pounds. Where was I to begin? Maud stood silently by my side while I evolved in my mind the contrivance known among sailors as "shears." But, though known to sailors, I invented it there on Endeavor Island. By crossing and lashing the ends of two spars and then elevating them in the air like an inverted V, I could get a point above the deck to which to make fast my hoisting-tackle. To this tackle I could, if necessary, attach a second tackle. And then there was the windlass!

Maud saw that I had achieved a solution, and her eyes warmed sympathetically.

"What are you going to do?" she asked.

"Clear that raffle," I answered, pointing to the tangled wreckage overside.

Ah, the decisiveness, the very sound of the words, was good in my ears. "Clear that raffle!" Imagine so salty a phrase on the lips of the Humphrey Van Weyden of a few months gone!

There must have been a touch of the melodramatic in my pose and voice, for Maud smiled. Her appreciation of the ridiculous was keen, and in all things she unerringly saw and felt, where it existed, the touch of sham, the overshading, the overtone. It was this which had given poise and penetration to her own work and made her of worth to the world. The serious critic, with the sense of humor and the power of expression, must inevitably command the world's ear. And so it was that she had commanded. Her sense of humor was really the artist's instinct for proportion.

"I 'm sure I 've heard it before, somewhere, in books," she murmured gleefully.

I had an instinct for proportion myself, and I collapsed forthwith, descending from the dominant pose of a master of matter to a state of humble confusion which was, to say the least, very miserable.

Her hand leaped out at once to mine.

"I 'm so sorry," she said.

"No need to be," I gulped. "It does me good. There 's too much of the schoolboy in me. All of which is neither here nor there. What we 've got to do is actually and literally to clear that raffle. If you 'll come with me in the boat, we 'll get to work and straighten things out."

"'When the topmen clear the raffle with their
clasp-knives in their teeth,'"

she quoted at me; and for the rest of the afternoon we made merry over our labor.

Her task was to hold the boat in position while I worked at the tangle. And such a tangle—halyards, sheets, guys, downhauls, shrouds, stays, all washed about and back and forth and through and twined and knotted by the sea. I cut no more than was necessary, and what with passing the long ropes under and around the booms and masts, of unreeving the halyards and sheets, of coiling down in the boat and uncoiling in order to pass through another knot in the bight, I was soon wet to the skin.

The sails did require some cutting, and the canvas, heavy with water, tried my strength severely; but I succeeded before nightfall in getting it all spread out on the beach to dry. We were both very tired when we knocked off for supper, and we had done good work, too, though to the eye it appeared insignificant.

Next morning, with Maud as able assistant, I went into the hold of the *Ghost* to clear the steps of the mast-butts. We had no more than begun work when the sound of my knocking and hammering brought Wolf Larsen.

"Hello, below!" he cried down the open hatch.

The sound of his voice made Maud quickly draw close to me, as for protection, and she rested one hand on my arm while we parleyed.

"Hello, on deck!" I replied. "Good morning to you."

"What are you doing down there?" he demanded. "Trying to scuttle my ship for me?"

"Quite the opposite; I 'm repairing her," was my answer.

"But what in thunder are you repairing?" There was puzzlement in his voice.

"Why, I 'm getting everything ready for restepping the masts," I replied easily, as though it were the simplest project imaginable.

"It seems as though you 're standing on your own legs at last, Hump," we heard him say; and then for some time he was silent.

"But I say, Hump," he called down, "you can't do it."

"Oh, yes, I can," I retorted. "I 'm doing it now."

"But this is my vessel, my particular property. What if I forbid you?"

"You forget," I replied. "You are no longer the biggest bit of the ferment. You were once, and able to eat me, as you were pleased to phrase it; but there has been a diminishing, and I am now able to eat you. The yeast has grown stale."

He gave a short, disagreeable laugh. "I see you 're working my philosophy back on me for all it is worth. But don't make the mistake of underestimating me. For your own good I warn you."

"Since when have you become an altruist?" I queried. "Confess, now, in warning me for my own good, that you are very inconsistent."

He ignored my sarcasm, saying, "Suppose I clap the hatch on now? You won't fool me as you did in the lazaret."

"Wolf Larsen," I said sternly, for the first time addressing him by this his most familiar name, "I am unable to shoot a helpless, unresisting man. You have proved that to my satisfaction as well as yours. But I warn you now, and not so much for your own good as for mine, that I shall shoot you the moment you attempt a hostile act. I can shoot you now, as I stand here; and if you are so minded, just go ahead and try to clap on the hatch."

"Nevertheless I forbid you; I distinctly forbid your tampering with my ship."

"But, man!" I expostulated. "You advance the fact that it is your ship as though it were a moral right. You have never considered moral rights in your dealings with others. You surely do not dream that I 'll consider them in dealing with you?"

I had stepped underneath the open hatchway so that I could see him. The lack of expression on his face, so different from when I had watched him unseen, was enhanced by the unblinking, staring eyes. It was not a pleasant face to look upon.

"And none so poor, not even Hump, to do him reverence," he sneered.

The sneer was wholly in his voice. His face remained expressionless as ever.

"How do you do, Miss Brewster?" he said suddenly, after a pause.

I started. She had made no noise whatever, had not even moved. Could it be that some glimmer of vision remained to him? Or that his vision was coming back?

"How do you do, Captain Larsen?" she answered. "Pray how did you know I was here?"

"Heard you breathing, of course. I say, Hump 's improving; don't you think so?"

"I don't know," she answered, smiling at me. "I have never seen him otherwise."

"You should have seen him before, then."

"Wolf Larsen in large doses," I murmured, "before and after taking."

"I want to tell you again, Hump," he said threateningly, "that you 'd better leave things alone."

"But don't you care to escape as well as we?" I asked incredulously.

"No," was his answer. "I intend dying here."

"Well, we don't," I concluded defiantly, beginning again my knocking and hammering.

XXXV

NEXT day, the mast-steps clear and everything in readiness, we started to get the two topmasts aboard. The maintopmast was over thirty feet in length, the foretopmast nearly thirty, and it was of these that I intended making the shears. It was puzzling work. Fastening one end of a heavy tackle to the windlass, and with the other end fast to the butt of the foretopmast, I began to heave. Maud held the turn on the windlass and coiled down the slack.

We were astonished at the ease with which the spar was lifted. It was an improved crank windlass, and the purchase it gave was enormous. Of course, what it gave us in power we paid for in distance; as many times as it doubled my strength, that many times was doubled the length of rope I heaved in. The tackle dragged heavily across the rail, increasing its drag as the spar arose more and more out of the water, and the exertion on the windlass grew severe.

But when the butt of the topmast was level with the rail everything came to a standstill.

"I might have known it," I said impatiently. "Now we have to do it all over again."

"Why not fasten the tackle part 'way down the mast?" Maud suggested.

"It's what I should have done at first," I answered, hugely disgusted with myself.

Slipping off a turn, I lowered the mast back into the water and fastened the tackle a third of the way down from the butt. In an hour, what of this and of rests between the heaving, I had hoisted it to the point where I could hoist no more. Eight feet of the butt was above the rail, and I was as far away as ever from getting the spar on board. I sat down and pondered the problem. It did not take long. I sprang jubilantly to my feet.

"Now I have it!" I cried. "I ought to make the tackle fast at the point of balance. And what we learn of this will serve us with everything else we have to hoist aboard."

Once again I undid all my work by lowering the mast into the water. But I miscalculated the point of balance, so that when I heaved, the top of the mast came up instead of the butt. Maud looked despair, but I laughed and said it would do just as well.

Instructing her how to hold the turn and be ready to slack away at command, I laid hold of the mast with my hands and tried to balance it inboard across the rail. When I thought I had it I cried to her to slack away; but the spar righted, despite my efforts, and dropped back toward the water. Again I heaved it up to its old position, for I had now another idea. I remembered the watch-tackle,—a small double- and single-block affair,—and fetched it.

While I was rigging it between the top of the spar and the opposite rail, Wolf Larsen came on the scene. We exchanged nothing more than good mornings, and though he could not see, he sat on the rail out of the way and followed by the sound all that I did.

Again instructing Maud to slack away at the windlass when I gave the word, I proceeded to heave on the watch-tackle. Slowly the mast swung in until it balanced at right angles across the rail; and then I discovered, to my amazement, that there was no need for Maud to slack away. In fact, the very opposite was necessary. Making the watch-tackle fast, I hove on the windlass and brought in the mast, inch by inch, till its top tilted down to the deck and finally its whole length lay on the deck.

I looked at my watch. It was twelve o'clock. My back was aching sorely, and I felt extremely tired and hungry. And there on the deck was a single stick of timber to show for a whole morning's work. For the first time I thoroughly realized the extent of the task before us. But I was learning, I was learning. The afternoon would show far more accomplished. And it did; for we returned at one o'clock, rested, and strengthened by a hearty dinner.

In less than an hour I had the maintopmast on deck and was constructing the shears. Lashing the two topmasts together, and making allowance for their unequal length, at the point of intersection I attached the double block of the main-throat-halyards. This, with the single block and the throat-halyards themselves, gave me a hoisting-tackle. To prevent the butts of the masts from slipping on the deck, I nailed down thick cleats. Everything in readiness, I made a line fast to the apex of the shears and carried it directly to the windlass. I was growing to have faith in that windlass, for it gave me power beyond all expectation. As usual, Maud held the turn while I heaved. The shears rose in the air.

Then I discovered I had forgotten guy-ropes. This necessitated my climbing the shears, which I did twice before I finished guying it fore and aft and to each side. Twilight had set in by the time this was accomplished. Wolf Larsen, who had sat about and listened all afternoon and never opened his mouth, had taken himself off to the galley and started his supper. I felt quite stiff across the small of the back, so much so that I straightened up with an effort and with pain. I looked proudly at my work. It was beginning to show. I was wild with desire, like a child with a new toy, to hoist something with my shears.

"I wish it were n't so late," I said. "I 'd like to see how it works."

"Don't be a glutton, Humphrey," Maud chided me. "Remember, to-morrow is coming, and you 're so tired now that you can hardly stand."

"And you?" I said, with sudden solicitude. "You must be very tired. You have worked hard and nobly. I am proud of you, Maud."

"Not half so proud as I am of you, nor with half the reason," she answered, looking me straight in the eyes for a moment with an expression in her own and a dancing, tremulous light which I had not seen before and which gave me a pang of quick delight, I knew not why, for I did not understand it. Then she dropped her eyes, to lift them again, laughing.

"If our friends could see us now!" she said. "Look at us. Have you ever paused for a moment to consider our appearance?"

"Yes, I have considered yours frequently," I answered, puzzled over what I had seen in her eyes and by her sudden change of subject.

"Mercy!" she cried. "And what do I look like, pray?"

"A scarecrow, I 'm afraid," I replied. "Just glance at your draggled skirts, for instance. Look at those three-cornered tears. And such a waist! It would not require a Sherlock Holmes to deduce that you have been cooking over a camp-fire, to say nothing of trying out seal-blubber. And, to cap it all, that cap! And all that is the woman who wrote 'A Kiss Endured.'"

She made me an elaborate and stately curtsy, and said, "As for you, sir—"

And yet, through the five minutes of banter which followed, there was a serious something underneath the fun which I could not but relate to the strange and fleeting expression I had caught in her eyes. What was it? Could it be that our eyes were speaking beyond the will of our speech? My eyes had spoken, I knew, until I had found the culprits out and silenced them. This had occurred several times. But had she seen the clamor in them and understood? And had her eyes so spoken to me? What else could that expression have meant?—that dancing, tremulous light and a something more which words could not describe. And yet it could not be. It was impossible. Besides, I was not skilled in the speech of eyes. I was only Humphrey Van Weyden, a bookish fellow who loved. And to love, and to wait and win love, that surely was glorious enough for me. And thus I thought, even as we chaffed each other, until we arrived ashore and there were other things to think about.

"It 's a shame, after working hard all day, that we cannot have an uninterrupted night's sleep," I complained, after supper.

"But there can be no danger now, from a blind man?" she queried.

"I shall never be able to trust him," I averred; "and far less now that he is blind. The liability is that his part-helplessness will make him more malignant than ever. I know what I shall do to-morrow, the first thing—run out a light anchor and kedge the schooner off the beach. And each night when we come ashore in the boat, Mr. Wolf Larsen will be left, virtually a prisoner, on board. So this will be the last night we have to stand watch, and because of that it will go the easier."

We were awake early, and just finishing breakfast as daylight came.

"Oh, Humphrey!" I heard Maud cry in dismay, and suddenly stop.

I looked at her. She was gazing at the

Ghost. I followed her gaze, but could see nothing unusual. She looked at me, and I looked inquiry back.

"The shears," she said, and her voice trembled.

I had forgotten their existence. I looked again, but could not see them.

"If he has—" I muttered savagely.

She put her hand sympathetically on mine, and said, "You will have to begin over again."

"Oh, believe me, my anger means nothing; I could not hurt a fly," I smiled back bitterly. "And the worst of it is, he knows it. You are right. If he has destroyed the shears, I shall do nothing except begin over again."

"But I 'll stand my watch on board hereafter," I blurted out a moment later. "And if he interferes—"

"But I dare not stay ashore, all night, alone," Maud was saying when I came back to myself. "It would be so much nicer if he would be friendly with us and help us. We could all live comfortably aboard."

"We will," I asserted, still savagely, for the destruction of my beloved shears had hit me hard. "That is, you and I will live aboard, friendly or not with Wolf Larsen."

"It 's childish," I laughed, later, "for him to do such things, and for me to grow angry over them, for that matter."

But my heart smote me when we climbed aboard and looked at the havoc he had done. The shears were gone altogether. The guys had been slashed right and left. The throat-halyards which I had rigged were cut across through every part—and he knew I could not splice. A thought struck me: I ran to the windlass. It would not work! He had broken it. We looked at each other in consternation. Then I ran to the side. The masts, booms, and gaffs I had cleared were gone. He had found the line which held them and cast it adrift.

Tears were in Maud's eyes, and I do believe they were for me. I could have wept myself. Where now was our project of remasting the *Ghost?* He had done his work well. I sat down on the hatch-combing and rested my chin on my hands in black despair.

"He deserves to die," I cried out; "and—God forgive me—I am not man enough to be his executioner."

But Maud was by my side, passing her hand soothingly through my hair as though I were a child, and saying, "There, there; it will all come right. We are in the right and it must come right."

I remembered Michelet, and leaned my head against her; and truly I became strong again. The blessed woman was an unfailing fount of power to me. What did it matter? Only a setback, a delay. The tide could not have carried the masts far to seaward, and there had been no wind. It meant merely more work to find them and tow them back. And, besides, it was a lesson. I knew what to expect. He might have waited and destroyed our work more effectually when we had more accomplished.

"Here he comes now," she whispered.

I glanced up. He was strolling leisurely along the poop on the port side.

"Take no notice of him," I whispered. "He 's coming to see how we take it. Don't let him know that we know. We can deny him that satisfaction. Take off your shoes—that 's right—and carry them in your hand."

And then we played hide-and-seek with the blind man. As he came up the port side we slipped past on the starboard; and from the poop we watched him turn and start aft on our track.

He must have known, somehow, that we were on board, for he said "Good morning" very confidently, and waited for the greeting to be returned. Then he strolled aft, and we slipped for'ard.

"Oh, I know you 're aboard," he called out, and I could see him listen intently after he had spoken.

It reminded me of the great hoot-owl, listening, after its booming cry, for the stir of its frightened prey. But we did not stir, and we moved only when he moved. And so we dodged about the deck, hand in hand, like a couple of children chased by a wicked ogre, till Wolf Larsen, evidently in disgust, left the deck for the cabin. There was glee in our eyes, and suppressed titters in our mouths, as we put on our shoes and clambered over the side into the boat. And as I looked into Maud's clear brown eyes I forgot the evil he had done, and I knew only that I loved her and that because of her the strength was mine to win our way back to the world.

Drawn by W. J. Aylward.

"THE OPEN PALM SWEPT ACROSS HIS EYES"

THE SEA-WOLF

BY JACK LONDON

Author of "The Call of the Wild," "The God of his Fathers," etc.

XXXVI

FOR two days Maud and I ranged the sea and explored the beaches in search of the missing masts. But it was not till the third day that we found them, all of them, the shears included, and, of all perilous places, in the pounding surf of the grim southwestern promontory. And how we worked! At the dark end of the first day we returned, exhausted, to our little cove, towing the mainmast behind us. And we had been compelled to row, in a dead calm, virtually every inch of the way.

Another day of heartbreaking and dangerous toil saw us in camp with the two topmasts to the good. The day following I was desperate, and I rafted together the fore-mast, the fore- and main-booms, and the fore- and main-gaffs. The wind was favorable, and I had thought to tow them back under sail; but the wind baffled, then died away, and our progress with the oars was a snail's pace. And it was such dispiriting effort! To throw one's whole strength and weight on the oars, and to feel the boat checked in its forward lunge by the heavy drag behind, was not exactly exhilarating.

Night began to fall, and, to make matters worse, the wind sprang up ahead. Not only did all forward motion cease, but we began to drift back and out to sea. I struggled at the oars till I was played out. Poor Maud, whom I could never prevent from working to the limit of her strength, lay weakly back in the stern-sheets. I could row no more. My bruised and swollen hands could no longer close on the oar-handles. My wrists and arms ached intolerably, and, though I had eaten heartily of a twelve-o'clock lunch, I had worked so hard that I was faint from hunger.

I pulled in the oars and bent forward to the line which held the tow. But Maud's hand leapt out restrainingly to mine.

"What are you going to do?" she asked in a strained, tense voice.

"Cast it off," I answered, slipping a turn of the rope.

But her fingers closed on mine.

"Please don't!" she begged.

"It is useless," I answered. "Here is night and the wind blowing us off the land."

"But think, Humphrey. If we cannot sail away on the *Ghost* we may remain for years on the island—for life, even. If it has never been discovered all these years, it may never be discovered."

"You forget the boat we found on the beach," I reminded her.

"It was a seal-hunting boat," she replied. "And you know perfectly well that if the men had escaped they would have been back to make their fortunes from the rookery. You know they never escaped."

I remained silent, undecided.

"Besides," she added haltingly, "it 's your idea, and I want to see you succeed."

Now I could harden my heart. As soon as she put it on a flattering personal basis, generosity compelled me to deny her.

"Better years on the island than to die to-night or to-morrow or the next day in the open boat. We are not prepared to brave the sea. We have no food, no water, no blankets, nothing. Why, you 'd not survive the night without blankets. I know how strong you are. You are shivering now."

"It is only nervousness," she answered. "I am afraid you will cast off the masts in spite of me. Oh, please, please, Humphrey, don't!" she burst out.

And so it ended, with the phrase she knew had all power over me. We shivered miserably throughout the night. Now and again I slept fitfully, but the pain of the cold always aroused me. How Maud could stand it was beyond me. I was too tired to thrash my arms about and warm myself, but I found strength time and again to chafe her hands and feet to restore the circulation. And still she pleaded with me not to cast off the masts. About three in the morning she was caught by a cold cramp, and after I had rubbed her out of that she became quite numb. I was frightened. I got out the oars and made her row, though she was so weak I thought she would faint at every stroke.

Morning broke, and we looked long in the growing light for our island. At last it showed, small and black, on the horizon, fully fifteen miles away. I scanned the sea with my glasses. Far away in the southwest I could see a dark line on the water, which grew even as I looked at it.

"Fair wind!" I cried in a husky voice I did not recognize as my own.

Maud tried to reply, but could not speak. Her lips were blue with cold, and she was hollow-eyed; but oh, how bravely her brown eyes looked at me—how piteously brave!

Again I fell to chafing her hands, and to moving her arms up and down and about until she could thrash them herself. Then I compelled her to stand up; and though she would have fallen had I not supported her, I forced her to walk back and forth the several steps between the thwart and the stern-sheets, and finally to spring up and down.

"Oh, you brave, brave woman!" I said, when I saw the life coming back into her face. "Did you know that you were brave?"

"I never used to be," she answered. "I was never brave till I knew you. It is you who have made me brave."

"Nor I until I knew you," I answered.

She gave me a quick look, and again I caught that dancing, tremulous light and something more in her eyes. But it was only for the moment. Then she smiled.

"It must have been the conditions," she said; but I knew she was wrong, and I wondered if she likewise knew.

Then the wind came, fair and fresh, and the boat was soon laboring through a heavy sea toward the island. At half-past three in the afternoon we passed the southwestern promontory. Not only were we hungry, but we were now suffering from thirst. Our lips were dry and cracked, nor could we longer moisten them with our tongues. Then the wind slowly died down. By night it was dead calm, and I was toiling once more at the oars, but weakly, most weakly. At two in the morning the boat's bow touched the beach of our own inner cove, and I staggered out to make the painter fast. Maud could not stand, nor had I strength to carry her. I fell in the sand with her, and, when I had recovered, contented myself with putting my hands under her shoulders and dragging her up the beach to the hut.

The next day we did no work. In fact, we slept till three in the afternoon—or at least I did, for I awoke to find Maud cooking dinner. Her power of recuperation was wonderful. There was something tenacious about that lily-frail body of hers, a clutch on existence which one could not reconcile with its patent weakness.

"You know I was traveling to Japan for my health," she said, as we lingered at the fire after dinner and delighted in the movelessness of loafing. "I was not very strong. I never was. The doctors recommended a sea voyage, and I chose the longest."

"You little knew what you were choosing," I laughed.

"But I shall be a different woman for the experience, as well as a stronger woman," she answered, "and, I hope, a better woman. At least I shall understand a great deal more of life."

Then, as the short day waned, we fell to discussing Wolf Larsen's blindness. It was inexplicable, and I instanced his statement that he intended to stay and die on Endeavor Island. There had been his terrific headaches, and we were agreed that it was some sort of brain breakdown, and that in his attacks he endured pain beyond our comprehension.

I noticed, as we talked over his condition, that Maud's sympathy went out to him more and more; yet I could not but love her for it, so sweetly womanly was it.

Besides, there was no false sentiment about her feeling. She was agreed that the most rigorous treatment was necessary if we were to escape, though she recoiled at the suggestion that I might sometime be compelled to take his life to save my own—"our own," she put it.

In the morning we had breakfast and were at work by daylight. I found a light kedge-anchor in the forehold, where such things were kept, and with a deal of exertion got it on deck and into the boat. With a long running-line coiled down in the stern, I rowed well out into our little cove and dropped the anchor into the water. There was no wind, the tide was high, and the schooner floated. Casting off the shore-lines, I kedged her out by main strength (the windlass being broken), till she rode nearly up and down to the small anchor—too small to hold her in any breeze. So I lowered the big starboard anchor, giving plenty of slack; and by afternoon I was at work on the windlass.

Three days I worked on that windlass. Least of all things was I a mechanic, and in that time I accomplished what an ordinary machinist would have done in as many hours. I had to learn my tools, to begin with, and every simple mechanical principle which such a man would have at his finger-ends I had likewise to learn. And at the end of three days I had a windlass which worked clumsily. It never gave the satisfaction the old windlass had given, but it worked and made my work possible.

In half a day I got the two topmasts aboard and the shears rigged and guyed as before. And that night I slept on board, and on deck beside my work. Maud, who refused to stay alone ashore, slept in the forecastle. Wolf Larsen had sat about, listening to my repairing the windlass, and talking with Maud and me upon indifferent subjects. No reference was made on either side to the destruction of the shears, nor did he say anything further about my leaving his ship alone. But still I feared him, blind and helpless and listening, always listening, and I never let his strong arms get within reach of me while I worked.

On this night, sleeping under my beloved shears, I was aroused by his footsteps on the deck. It was a starlight night, and I could see the bulk of him dimly as he moved about. I rolled out of my blankets and crept noiselessly after him in my stocking-feet. He had armed himself with a draw-knife from the tool-locker, and with this he prepared to cut across the throat-halyards I had again rigged to the shears. He felt the halyards with his hands, and discovered that I had not made them fast. This would not do for a draw-knife, so he laid hold of the running part, hove taut, and made fast. Then he prepared to saw across with the draw-knife.

"I would n't, if I were you," I said quietly.

He heard the click of my pistol and laughed.

"Hello, Hump," he said. "I knew you were here all the time. You can't fool my ears."

"That 's a lie, Wolf Larsen," I said, just as quietly as before. "However, I am aching for a chance to kill you, so go ahead and cut."

"You have the chance always," he sneered.

"Go ahead and cut," I threatened ominously.

"I 'd rather disappoint you," he laughed, and turned on his heel and went aft.

"Something must be done, Humphrey," Maud said next morning, when I had told her of the night's occurrence. "If he has liberty, he may do anything. He may sink the vessel, or set fire to it. There is no telling what he may do. We must make him a prisoner."

"But how?" I asked, with a helpless shrug. "I dare not come within reach of his arms, and he knows that so long as his resistance is passive I cannot shoot him."

"There must be some way," she contended. "Let me think."

"There is one way," I said grimly.

She waited.

I picked up a seal-club.

"It won't kill him," I said. "And before he could recover I 'd have him bound hard and fast."

She shook her head with a shudder. "No, not that. There must be some less brutal way. Let us wait."

But we did not have to wait long, and the problem solved itself. In the morning, after several trials, I found the point of balance in the foremast and attached my hoisting-tackle a few feet above it. Maud held the turn on the windlass and coiled down while I heaved. Had the windlass been in order it would not have been so difficult; as it was, I was compelled to apply all my weight and strength to every inch of the heaving. I had to rest frequently. Maud even contrived, at times when all my effort could not budge the windlass, to hold the turn with one hand and with the other to throw the weight of her slim body to my assistance.

At the end of an hour the single and double blocks came together at the top of the shears. I could hoist no more. And yet the mast was not swung entirely inboard. The butt rested against the outside of the port rail, while the top of the mast overhung the water far beyond the starboard rail. My shears were too short. All my work had been for nothing. But I no longer despaired in the old way. I was acquiring more confidence in myself and more confidence in the possibilities of windlasses, shears, and hoisting-tackles. There was a way in which it could be done, and it remained for me to find that way.

While I was considering the problem Wolf Larsen came on deck. We noticed something strange about him at once. The indecisiveness or feebleness of his movements was more pronounced. His walk was actually tottery as he came down the port side of the cabin. At the break of the poop he reeled, raised one hand to his eyes with the familiar brushing gesture, and fell down the steps, still on his feet, to the main-deck, across which he staggered, falling and flinging his arms out for support. He regained his balance by the steerage companionway, and stood there dizzily for a space, when he suddenly crumpled up and collapsed, his legs bending under him as he sank to the deck.

"One of his attacks," I whispered to Maud.

She nodded her head, and I could see sympathy warm in her eyes.

We went up to him, but he seemed unconscious, breathing heavily and spasmodically. Maud took charge of him, lifting his head to keep the blood out of it, and despatching me to the cabin for a pillow. I also brought blankets, and we made him comfortable. I took his pulse. It beat steadily and strong, was quite normal. This puzzled me; I became suspicious.

"What if he should be feigning this?" I asked, still holding his wrist.

Maud shook her head, and there was reproof in her eyes. But just then the wrist I held leapt from my hand, and the hand clasped like a steel trap about my own wrist. I cried aloud in awful fear, a wild, inarticulate cry; and I caught one glimpse of his face, malignant and triumphant, as his other hand compassed my body and I was drawn down to him in a terrible grip.

My wrist was released, but his other arm, passed around my back, held both my arms so that I could not move. His free hand went to my throat, and in that moment I knew the bitter foretaste of death earned by one's own idiocy. Why had I trusted myself within reach of those terrible arms? I could feel other hands at my throat. They were Maud's hands, striving vainly to tear loose the hand that was throttling me. She gave it up, and I heard her scream in a way that cut me to the soul; for it was the woman's scream of fear and heartbreaking despair. I had heard it before, during the sinking of the *Martinez*.

My face was against his chest, and I could not see, but I heard Maud turn and run swiftly away along the deck. Everything was happening quickly. I had not yet had a glimmering of unconsciousness, and it seemed that an interminable period of time was lapsing before I heard her feet flying back. And just then I felt the whole man sink under me. The breath was leaving his lungs, and his chest was collapsing under my weight. Whether it was merely the expelled breath, or consciousness of his growing impotence, I know not, but his throat vibrated with a deep groan. The hand at my throat relaxed. I breathed. His hand fluttered and tightened again. But even his tremendous will could not overcome the dissolution that assailed it. That will of his was breaking down. He was fainting.

Maud's footsteps were very near as his hand fluttered for the last time and my throat was released. I rolled off and over to the deck on my back, gasping and blinking in the sunshine. Maud was pale but composed,—my eyes had gone instantly to her face,—and she was looking at me with mingled alarm and relief. A heavy seal-club in her hand caught my eyes, and at that moment she followed my gaze down to it. The club dropped from her hand as if it had suddenly stung her, and at the same moment my heart surged with a great joy. Truly she was my woman—my mate-woman, fighting for me as the mate of a caveman would have fought, all the primitive in her aroused, forgetful of her culture, hard under the softening civilization of the only life she had ever known.

"Dear woman!" I cried, scrambling to my feet.

The next moment she was in my arms, weeping convulsively on my shoulder while I clasped her close. I looked down at the brown glory of her hair, glinting gems in the sunshine far more precious to me than those in the treasure-chests of kings. And I bent my head and kissed her hair softly, so softly that she did not know.

Then sober thought came to me. After all, she was only a woman, crying her relief, now that the danger was past, in the arms of her protector or of the one who had been endangered. Had I been father or brother, the situation would have been nowise different. Besides, time and place were not meet, and I wished to earn a better right to declare my love. So once again I softly kissed her hair as I felt her receding from my clasp.

"It is a real attack this time," I said; "another shock like the one that made him blind. He feigned at first, and in doing so brought it on."

Maud was already rearranging his pillow.

"No," I said; "not yet. Now that I have him helpless, helpless he shall remain. From this day we live in the cabin. Wolf Larsen shall live in the steerage."

I caught him under the shoulders and dragged him to the companionway. At my direction Maud fetched a rope. Placing this under his shoulders, I balanced him across the threshold and lowered him down the steps to the floor. I could not lift him directly into a bunk, but with Maud's help I lifted first his shoulders and head, then his body, balanced him across the edge, and rolled him into a lower bunk.

But this was not to be all. I recollected the handcuffs in his state-room, which he preferred to use on sailors instead of the ancient and clumsy ship-irons. So, when we left him, he lay handcuffed hand and foot. For the first time in many days I breathed freely. I felt strangely light as I came on deck, as though a weight had been lifted from my shoulders. I felt, also, that Maud and I had drawn more closely together; and I wondered if she, too, felt it as we walked along the deck side by side to where the stalled foremast hung in the shears.

XXXVII

At once we moved aboard the *Ghost*, occupying our old state-rooms and cooking in the galley. The imprisonment of Wolf Larsen had happened most opportunely, for what must have been the Indian summer of this high latitude was gone, and drizzling, stormy weather had set in. We were very comfortable; and the inadequate shears, with the foremast suspended from them, gave a businesslike air to the schooner and a promise of departure.

And now that we had Wolf Larsen in irons, how little did we need it! Like his first attack, his second had been accompanied by serious disablement. Maud made the discovery in the afternoon, while trying to give him nourishment. He had shown signs of consciousness, and she had spoken to him, eliciting no response. He was lying on his left side at the time, and in evident pain. With a restless movement he rolled his head around, clearing his left ear from the pillow against which it had been pressed. At once he heard and answered her, and at once she came to me.

Pressing the pillow against his left ear, I asked him if he heard me, but he gave no sign. Removing the pillow and repeating the question, I was answered promptly that he did.

"Do you know you are deaf in the right ear?" I asked.

"Yes," he answered in a low, strong voice, "and worse than that. My whole right side is affected. It seems asleep. I cannot move arm or leg."

"Feigning again?" I demanded angrily.

He shook his head, his stern mouth shaping a strange, twisted smile. It was indeed a twisted smile, for it was on the left side only, the facial muscles of the right side moving not at all.

"That was the last stroke of the Wolf," he said. "I am paralyzed; I shall never walk again. Oh, only on the right side," he added, as though divining the suspicious glance I flung at his left leg, the knee of which had just then drawn up and elevated the blankets.

"It's unfortunate," he continued. "I'd

like to have done for you first, Hump. And I thought I had that much left in me."

"But why?" I asked, partly in horror, partly out of curiosity.

Again his stern mouth framed the twisted smile, as he said:

"Oh, just to be alive, to be living and doing, to be the biggest bit of the ferment to the end—to eat you. But to die this way—"

He shrugged his shoulders, or attempted to shrug them, rather, for the left shoulder alone moved. Like the smile, the shrug was twisted.

"But how can you account for it?" I asked. "Where is the seat of trouble?"

"The brain," he said at once. "It was those cursed headaches brought it on."

"Symptoms," I said.

He nodded his head. "There is no accounting for it. I was never sick in my life. Something 's gone wrong with my brain. A cancer or tumor or something of that nature—a thing that devours and destroys. It 's attacking my nerve-centers, eating them up, bit by bit, cell by cell—from the pain."

"The motor-centers, too," I suggested.

"So it would seem. And the curse of it is that I must lie here, conscious, mentally unimpaired, knowing that the lines are going down, breaking bit by bit communication with the world. I cannot see; hearing and feeling are leaving me: at this rate I shall soon cease to speak. Yet all the time I shall be here, alive, active, and powerless."

"When you say *you* are here, I 'd suggest the likelihood of the soul," I said.

"Bosh!" was his retort. "It simply means that in the attack on my brain the higher psychical centers are untouched. I can remember, think, and reason. When that goes, I go. I am not. The soul?"

He broke out in mocking laughter, then turned his left ear to the pillow as a sign that he wished no further conversation.

Maud and I went about our work oppressed by the fearful fate which had overtaken him—how fearful we were yet fully to realize. There was the awfulness of retribution about it. Our thoughts were deep and solemn, and we spoke to each other scarcely above whispers.

"You might remove the handcuffs," he said that night, as we stood in consultation over him. "It 's dead safe. I 'm a paralytic now. The next thing to watch out for is bed-sores."

He smiled his twisted smile, and Maud, her eyes wide with horror, was compelled to turn away her head.

"Do you know that your smile is crooked?" I asked him; for I knew that she must attend him, and I wished to save her as much as possible.

"Then I shall smile no more," he said calmly. "I thought something was wrong. My right cheek has been numb all day. Yes, and I 've had warnings of this for the last three days, by spells: my right side seemed going to sleep, sometimes arm or hand, sometimes leg or foot.

"So my smile is crooked?" he queried, a short while after. "Well, consider henceforth that I smile internally with my soul, if you please—my soul. Consider that I am smiling now."

And for the space of several minutes he lay there, quiet, indulging his grotesque fancy.

The man of him was not changed. It was the old, indomitable, terrible Wolf Larsen imprisoned somewhere within that flesh which had once been so invincible and splendid. Now it bound him with insentient fetters, walling his soul in darkness and silence, blocking it from the world which to him had been a riot of action. No more would he "conjugate the verb to do in every mood and tense." "To be" was all that remained to him—to be, as he had defined death, without movement; to will, but not to execute; to think and reason, and in his spirit to be as alive as ever, but in the flesh to be dead, quite dead.

And yet, though I even removed the handcuffs, we could not adjust ourselves to his condition. Our minds revolted. To us he was full of potentiality. We knew not what to expect of him next, what fearful thing, rising above the flesh, he might break out and do. Our experience warranted this state of mind, and we went about with anxiety always upon us.

I had solved the problem which had arisen through the shortness of the shears. By means of the watch-tackle (I had made a new one) I heaved the butt of the foremast across the rail and then lowered it to the deck. Next, by means of the shears, I hoisted the main-boom on board. Its forty feet of length would supply the height necessary properly to swing the mast. By means of a secondary tackle I had attached to the shears, I swung the boom to a nearly perpendicular position, then lowered the butt to the deck, where, to prevent slipping, I spiked great cleats around it. The single block of my original shears-tackle I had attached to the end of the boom. Thus by carrying this tackle to the windlass I could raise and lower the end of the boom at will, the butt always remaining stationary, and by means of guys I could swing the boom from side to side. To the end of the boom I had likewise rigged a hoisting-tackle, and when the whole arrangement was complete I could not but be startled by the power and latitude it gave me.

Of course two days' work was required for the accomplishment of this part of my task, and it was not till the morning of the third day that I swung the foremast from the deck and proceeded to square its butt to fit the step. Here I was especially awkward. I sawed and chopped and chiseled the weathered wood till it had the appearance of having been gnawed by some gigantic mouse. But it fitted.

"It will work—I know it will work!" I cried.

Wolf Larsen had received another stroke. He had lost his voice, or was losing it. He had only intermittent use of it. As he phrased it, the wires were like the stock market, now up, now down. Occasionally the wires were up and he spoke as well as ever, though slowly and heavily. Then speech would suddenly desert him, in the middle of a sentence perhaps, and for hours, sometimes, we would wait for the connection to be reestablished. He complained of great pain in his head, and it was during this period that he arranged a system of communication against the time when speech should leave him altogether—one pressure of the hand for "yes," two for "no." It was well that it was arranged, for by evening his voice had gone from him. By hand-pressures, after that, he answered our questions, and when he wished to speak he scrawled his thoughts with his left hand, quite legibly, on a sheet of paper.

The fierce winter had now descended upon us. Gale followed gale, with snow and sleet and rain. The seals had started on their great southern migration, and the rookery was virtually deserted. I worked feverishly. In spite of the bad weather, and of the wind which especially hindered me, I was on deck from daylight till dark, and making substantial progress.

I profited by my lesson learned through raising the shears, and then climbed them to attach the guys. To the top of the foremast, which was lifted conveniently from the deck, I attached the rigging, stays, and throat- and peak-halyards. As usual, I had underrated the amount of work involved in this portion of the task, and two long days were necessary to complete it. And there was so much yet to be done: the sails, for instance, had to be made over.

While I toiled at rigging the foremast, Maud sewed on the canvas, ready always to drop everything and come to my assistance when more hands than two were required. The canvas was heavy and hard, and she sewed with the regular sailor's palm and three-cornered sail-needle. Her hands were soon sadly blistered, but she struggled bravely on, and, in addition, did the cooking and took care of the sick man.

"A fig for superstition," I said on Friday morning. "That mast goes in to-day."

Everything was ready for the attempt. Carrying the boom-tackle to the windlass, I hoisted the mast nearly clear of the deck. Making this tackle fast, I took to the windlass the shears-tackle (which was connected with the end of the boom), and with a few turns had the mast perpendicular and clear.

Maud clapped her hands the instant she was relieved from holding the turn, crying:

"It works! It works! We 'll trust our lives to it!"

Then she assumed a rueful expression.

"It 's not over the hole," she said. "Will you have to begin all over?"

I smiled in superior fashion, and, slacking off on one of the boom-guys and taking in on the other, swung the mast perfectly in the center of the deck. Still it was not over the hole. Again the rueful expression came on her face, and again I smiled in a superior way. Slacking away on the boom-tackle and hoisting an equivalent amount on the shears-tackle, I brought the butt of the mast into position directly over the hole in the deck. Then I gave Maud careful instructions for lowering away, and went into the hold to the step on the schooner's bottom.

I called to her, and the mast moved easily and accurately. Straight toward the square hole of the step the square butt descended; but as it descended it slowly twisted, so that square would not fit into square. But I had not even a moment's indecision. Calling to Maud to cease lowering, I went on deck and made the watch-tackle fast to the mast with a rolling hitch. I left Maud to pull on it while I went below. By the light of the lantern I saw the butt twist slowly around till its sides coincided with the sides of the step. Maud made fast and returned to the windlass. Slowly the butt descended the several intervening inches, at the same time slightly twisting again. Once more Maud rectified the twist with the watch-tackle, and once more she lowered away from the windlass. Square fitted into square. The mast was stepped.

I raised a shout, and she ran down to see. In the yellow lantern-light we peered at what we had accomplished. We looked at each other, and our hands felt their way and clasped. The eyes of both of us, I think, were moist with the joy of success.

"It was done so easily, after all," I remarked. "All the work was in the preparation."

"And all the wonder in the completion," Maud added. "I can scarcely bring myself to realize that that great mast is really up and in—that you have lifted it from the water, swung it through the air, and deposited it here where it belongs. It is a Titan's task."

"And they made themselves many inventions—" I began merrily, then paused to sniff the air.

I looked hastily at the lantern. It was not smoking. Again I sniffed.

"Something is burning," Maud said with sudden conviction.

We sprang together for the ladder, but I raced past her to the deck. A dense volume of smoke was pouring out of the steerage companionway.

"The Wolf is not yet dead," I muttered to myself as I sprang down through the smoke.

It was so thick in the confined space that I was compelled to feel my way; and, so potent was the spell of Wolf Larsen on my imagination, I was quite prepared for the helpless giant to grip my neck in a strangle-hold. I hesitated, the desire to race back and up the steps to the deck almost overpowering me. Then I recollected Maud. The vision of her, as I had last seen her, in the lantern-light of the schooner's hold, her brown eyes warm and moist with joy, flashed before me, and I knew that I could not go back.

I was choking and suffocating by the time I reached Wolf Larsen's bunk. I reached in my hand and felt for him. He was lying motionless, but moved slightly at the touch of my hand. I felt over and under his blankets. There was no warmth, no sign of fire. Yet that smoke which blinded me and made me cough and gasp must have a source. I lost my head temporarily, and dashed frantically about the steerage. A collision with the table partly knocked the wind from my body and brought me to myself. I reasoned that a helpless man could start a fire only near to where he lay.

I returned to Wolf Larsen's bunk. There I encountered Maud. How long she had been there in that suffocating atmosphere I could not guess.

"Go up on deck," I commanded peremptorily.

"But, Humphrey—" she began to protest in a queer, husky voice.

"Please! please!" I shouted at her, harshly.

She drew away obediently; and then I thought, What if she cannot find the steps? I started after her, to stop at the foot of the companionway. Perhaps she had gone up. As I stood there, hesitant, I heard her cry softly:

"Oh, Humphrey, I am lost!"

I found her fumbling at the wall of the after-bulkhead, and, half leading, half carrying her, I took her up the companionway. The pure air was like nectar. Maud was only faint and dizzy, and I left her lying on the deck when I took my second plunge below.

The source of the smoke must be very close to Wolf Larsen: my mind was made up to this, and I went straight to his bunk. As I felt about among his blankets, something hot fell on the back of my hand. It burned me, and I jerked my hand away. Then I understood. Through the cracks in the bottom of the upper bunk he had set fire to the mattress. He still retained sufficient use of his left arm to do this. The damp straw of the mattress, fired from beneath and denied air, had been smoldering all the while.

As I dragged the mattress out of the bunk it seemed to disintegrate in mid-air, at the same time bursting into flames. I beat out the burning remnants of straw in the bunk, then made a dash for the deck for fresh air.

Several buckets of water sufficed to put out the burning mattress in the middle of the steerage floor; and ten minutes later, when the smoke had fairly cleared, I allowed Maud to come below. Wolf Larsen was unconscious, but it was a matter of minutes for the fresh air to restore him. We were working over him, however, when he signed for paper and pencil.

"Pray do not interrupt me," he wrote. "I am smiling."

"I am still a bit of the ferment, you see," he wrote a little later.

"I am glad you are as small a bit as you are," I said.

"Thank you," he wrote. "But just think of how much smaller I shall be before I die."

"And yet I am all here, Hump," he wrote with a final flourish. "I can think more clearly than ever in my life before. Nothing to disturb me. Concentration is perfect. I am all here and more than here."

It was like a message from the night of the grave, for this man's body had become his mausoleum. And there, in so strange a sepulcher, his spirit fluttered and lived. It would flutter and live till the last line of communication was broken, and after that who was to say how much longer it might continue to flutter and live?

XXXVIII

"I THINK my left side is going," Wolf Larsen wrote, the morning after his attempt to fire the ship. "The numbness is growing. I can hardly move my hand. You will have to speak louder. The last lines are going down."

"Are you in pain?" I asked.

I was compelled to repeat my question loudly before he answered:

"Not all the time."

The left hand stumbled slowly and painfully across the paper, and it was with extreme difficulty that we deciphered the scrawl. It was like a "spirit message," such as are delivered at séances of spiritualists for a dollar admission.

"But I am still here, all here," the hand scrawled, more slowly and painfully than ever.

The pencil dropped, and we had to replace it in the hand.

"When there is no pain I have perfect peace and quiet. I have never thought so clearly. I can ponder life and death like a Hindu sage."

"And immortality?" Maud queried loudly in the ear.

Three times the hand essayed to write, but fumbled hopelessly. The pencil fell. In vain we tried to replace it. The fingers could not close on it. Then Maud pressed and held the fingers about the pencil with her own hand, and the hand wrote, in large letters, and so slowly that the minutes ticked off to each letter:

"B-O-S-H."

It was Wolf Larsen's last word,—"bosh,"—skeptical and invincible to the end. The arm and hand relaxed. The trunk of the body moved slightly. Then there was no movement. Maud released the hand. The fingers spread, falling apart of their own weight, and the pencil rolled away.

"Do you still hear?" I shouted, holding the fingers and waiting for the single pressure which would signify "yes." There was no response. The hand was dead.

"I noticed the lips slightly move," Maud said.

I repeated the question. The lips moved. She placed the tips of her fingers on them. Again I repeated the question. "Yes," Maud announced. We looked at each other expectantly.

"What good is it?" I asked. "What can we say now?"

"Oh, ask him—"

She hesitated.

"Ask him something that requires 'no' for an answer," I suggested. "Then we shall know with certainty."

"Are you hungry?" she cried.

The lips moved under her fingers, and she answered, "Yes."

"Will you have some beef?" was her next query.

"No," she announced.

"Beef-tea?"

"Yes, he will have some beef-tea," she said quietly, looking up at me. "Until his hearing goes we shall be able to communicate with him. And after that—"

She looked at me queerly. I saw her lips trembling and the tears swimming up in her eyes. She swayed toward me, and I caught her in my arms.

"Oh, Humphrey," she sobbed, "when will it all end? I am so tired, so tired!"

She buried her head on my shoulder, her frail form shaken with a storm of weeping. She was like a feather in my arms, so slender, so ethereal. "She has broken down at last," I thought. "What can I do without her help?"

But I soothed and comforted her, till she pulled herself bravely together and recuperated mentally as quickly as she was wont to do physically.

"I ought to be ashamed of myself," she said. Then added, with the whimsical smile I adored, "But I am only one small woman."

That phrase, "one small woman," startled me like an electric shock. It was my own phrase, my pet, secret phrase, my love-phrase for her.

"Where did you get that phrase?" I demanded, with an abruptness that in turn startled her.

"What phrase?" she asked.

"'One small woman.'"

"Is it yours?" she asked.

"Yes," I answered, "mine. I made it."

"Then you must have talked in your sleep," she smiled.

The dancing, tremulous light was in her eyes. Mine, I knew, were speaking beyond the will of my speech. I leaned toward her. Without volition I leaned toward her, as a tree is swayed by the wind. Ah, we were very close together in that moment. But she shook her head, as one might shake off sleep or a dream, saying:

"I have known it all my life. It was my father's name for my mother."

"It is my phrase, too," I said stubbornly.

"For your mother?"

"No," I answered; and she questioned no further, though I could have sworn her eyes retained for some time a mocking, teasing expression.

With the foremast in, the work now went on apace. Almost before I knew it, and without one serious hitch, I had the mainmast stepped. A derrick-boom rigged to the foremast had accomplished this; and several days more found all stays and shrouds in place and everything set up taut. Topsails would be a nuisance and a danger for a crew of two, so I heaved the topmasts on deck and lashed them fast.

Several more days were consumed in finishing the sails and putting them on. There were only three—the jib, foresail, and mainsail; and, patched, shortened, and distorted, they were a ridiculously ill-fitting suit for so trim a craft as the *Ghost*.

"But they 'll work," Maud cried jubilantly. "We 'll make them work, and trust our lives to them!"

Certainly, among my many new trades, I shone least as a sailmaker. I could sail them better than make them, and I had no doubt of my power to bring the schooner to some northern port of Japan. In fact, I had crammed navigation from text-books aboard; and, besides, there was Wolf Larsen's star-scale, so simple a device that a child could work it.

As for its inventor, beyond an increasing deafness and the movement of the lips growing faint and fainter, there had been little change in his condition for a week. But on the day we finished bending the schooner's sails he heard his last, and the last movement of the lips died away, but not before I had asked him, "Are you all there?" and the lips had answered, "Yes."

The last line was down. Somewhere within that tomb of the flesh still dwelt the soul of the man. Walled by the living clay, that fierce intelligence we had known burned on; but it burned on in silence and darkness. And it was disembodied. To that intelligence there could be no objective knowledge of a body. It knew no body. The very world was not. It knew only itself and the vastness and profundity of the quiet and the dark.

XXXIX

THE day came for our departure. There was no longer anything to detain us on Endeavor Island. The *Ghost's* stumpy masts were in place, her crazy sails bent. All my handiwork was strong, none of it beautiful; but I knew that it would work, and I felt myself a man of power as I looked at it.

"I did it! I did it! With my own hands I did it!" I wanted to cry aloud.

But Maud and I had a way of voicing

each other's thoughts; and she said, as we prepared to hoist the mainsail:

"To think, Humphrey, you did it all with your own hands!"

"But there were two other hands," I answered—"two small hands. And don't say that was also a phrase of your father's."

She shook her head and laughed, and held her hands up for inspection.

"I can never get them clean again," she wailed, "nor soften the weather-beat."

"Then dirt and weather-beat shall be your guerdon of honor," I said, holding them in mine; and, spite of my resolutions, I would have kissed the two dear hands had she not swiftly withdrawn them.

Our comradeship was becoming tremulous. I had mastered my love long and well, but now it was mastering me. Wilfully had it disobeyed and won my eyes to speech, and now it was winning my tongue—aye, and my lips, for they were mad this moment to kiss the two small hands which had toiled so faithfully and hard. And I, too, was mad. There was a cry in my being like bugles calling me to her. And there was a wind blowing upon me which I could not resist, swaying the very body of me till I leaned toward her, all unconscious that I leaned. And she knew it. She could not but know it as she swiftly drew away her hands, and yet could not forbear one quick, searching look before she turned away her eyes.

By means of deck-tackles I had arranged to carry the halyards forward to the windlass; and now I hoisted the mainsail, peak and throat, at the same time. It was a clumsy way, but it did not take long, and soon the foresail as well was up and fluttering.

"We can never get that anchor up in this narrow place, once it has left the bottom," I said. "We should be on the rocks first."

"What can you do?" she asked.

"Slip it," was my answer. "And when I do, you must do your first work on the windlass. I shall have to run at once to the wheel, and at the same time you must be hoisting the jib."

This manœuver of getting under way I had studied and worked out a score of times; and, with the jib-halyard to the windlass, I knew Maud was capable of hoisting that most necessary sail. A brisk wind was blowing into the cove, and, though the water was calm, rapid work was required to get us safely out.

When I knocked the shackle-bolt loose, the chain roared out through the hawse-hole and into the sea. I raced aft, putting the wheel up. The *Ghost* seemed to start into life as she heeled to the first fill of her sails. The jib was rising. As it filled, the *Ghost's* bow swung off, and I had to put the wheel down a few spokes and steady her.

I had devised an automatic jib-sheet which passed the jib across of itself, so there was no need for Maud to attend to that; but she was still hoisting the jib when I put the wheel hard down. It was a moment of anxiety, for the *Ghost* was rushing directly upon the beach, a stone's throw distant. But she swung obediently on her heel into the wind. There was a great fluttering and flapping of canvas and reef-points, most welcome to my ears, then she filled away on the other tack.

Maud had finished her task and come aft, where she stood beside me, a small cap perched on her wind-blown hair, her cheeks flushed from exertion, her eyes wide and bright with the excitement, her nostrils quivering to the rush and bite of the fresh salt air. Her brown eyes were like a startled deer's. There was a wild, keen look in them I had never seen before, and her lips parted and her breath suspended as the *Ghost*, charging upon the wall of rock at the entrance to the inner cove, swept into the wind and filled away into safe water.

My first mate's berth on the sealing-grounds stood me in good stead, and I cleared the inner cove and laid a long tack along the shore of the outer cove. Once again about, and the *Ghost* headed out to open sea. She had now caught the bosom-breathing of the ocean, and was herself abreath with the rhythm of it as she smoothly mounted and slipped down each broad-backed wave. The day had been dull and overcast, but the sun now burst through the clouds, a welcome omen, and shone upon the curving beach where together we had dared the lords of the harem and slain the holluschickie. All Endeavor Island brightened under the sun. Even the grim southwestern promontory showed less grim, and here and there, where the sea-spray wet its surface, high lights flashed and dazzled in the sun.

"I shall always think of it with pride," I said to Maud.

She threw her head back in a queenly way, but said, "Dear, dear Endeavor Island! I shall always love it."

"And I," I said quickly.

It seemed our eyes must meet in a great understanding, and yet, loath, they struggled away and did not meet.

There was a silence I might almost call awkward, till I broke it, saying:

"See those black clouds to windward. You remember, I told you last night the barometer was falling."

"And the sun is gone," she said, her eyes still fixed upon our island where we had proved our mastery over matter and attained to the truest comradeship which may fall to man and woman.

"And it 's slack off the sheets for Japan!" I cried gaily. "A fair wind and a flowing sheet, you know, or however it goes."

Lashing the wheel, I ran forward, eased the fore- and main-sheets, took in on the boom-tackles, and trimmed everything for the quartering breeze which was ours. Unfortunately, when running free it is impossible to lash the wheel, so I faced an all-night watch. Maud insisted on relieving me, but proved that she had not the strength to steer in a heavy sea, even if she could have gained the wisdom on such short notice. She appeared quite heart-broken over the discovery, but recovered her spirits by coiling down tackles and halyards and all stray ropes. Then there were meals to be cooked in the galley, beds to make, Wolf Larsen to be attended upon, and she finished the day with a grand house-cleaning attack upon the cabin and steerage.

All night I steered, without relief, the wind slowly and steadily increasing and the sea rising. At five in the morning Maud brought me hot coffee and biscuits she had baked, and at seven a substantial and piping hot breakfast put new life into me.

Throughout the day, and as slowly and steadily as ever, the wind increased. And still the *Ghost* foamed along, racing off the miles till I was certain she was making at least eleven knots. It was too good to lose, but by nightfall I was exhausted. Though in splendid physical trim, a thirty-six-hour trick at the wheel was the limit of my endurance. Besides, I knew, if the wind and sea increased at the same rate during the night, that it would soon be impossible to heave to. So, as twilight deepened, gladly, and at the same time reluctantly, I brought the *Ghost* up on the wind.

But I had not reckoned upon the colossal task the reefing of three sails meant for one man. While running away from the wind I had not appreciated its force, but when we ceased to run, I learned, to my sorrow, and well-nigh to my despair, how fiercely it was really blowing. The wind balked my every effort, ripping the canvas out of my hands and in an instant undoing what I had gained by ten minutes of severest struggle. At eight o'clock I had succeeded only in putting the second reef into the foresail. At eleven o'clock I was no further along. Blood dripped from every finger-end, while the nails were broken to the quick. From pain and sheer exhaustion, I wept in the darkness, secretly, so that Maud should not know.

Then, in desperation, I abandoned the attempt to reef the mainsail, and resolved to try the experiment of heaving to under the close-reefed foresail. Three hours more were required to gasket the mainsail and jib, and at two in the morning, nearly dead, the life almost buffeted and worked out of me, I had barely sufficient consciousness to know the experiment was a success.

I was famished, but Maud tried vainly to get me to eat. So sleepily helpless was I that she was compelled to hold me in my chair to prevent my being flung to the floor by the violent pitching of the schooner.

Of the passage from the galley to the cabin I knew nothing. In fact, I was aware of nothing till I awoke in my bunk, with my boots off. It was dark. I was stiff and lame, and cried out with pain when the bedclothes touched my poor finger-ends. Morning had evidently not come, so I closed my eyes and went to sleep again. I did not know it, but I had slept the clock around and it was night again.

Once more I awoke, troubled because I could sleep no better. I struck a match and looked at my watch. It marked midnight. And I had not left the deck until three! I should have been puzzled had I not guessed the solution. No wonder I

Drawn by W. J. Aylward.

"BEFORE I KNEW IT, MY ARMS WERE ABOUT HER"

was sleeping brokenly. I had slept twenty-one hours. I listened for a while to the behavior of the *Ghost*, to the pounding of the seas and the muffled roar of the wind on deck, and then turned over on my side and slept peacefully until morning.

When I arose at seven I saw no sign of Maud, and concluded she was in the galley preparing breakfast. On deck I found the *Ghost* doing splendidly under her patch of canvas. But in the galley, though a fire was burning and water boiling, I found no Maud.

I discovered her in the steerage, by Wolf Larsen's bunk. I looked at him—the man who had been hurled down from the topmost pitch of life to be buried alive and be worse than dead. There seemed a relaxation of his expressionless face which was new. Maud looked at me, and I understood.

"His life flickered out in the storm," I said.

"But he still lives," she answered, infinite faith in her voice.

"He had too great strength."

"Yes," she said; "but now it no longer shackles him. He is a free spirit."

"He is a free spirit surely," I answered; and, taking her hand, I led her on deck.

The storm broke that night, which is to say that it diminished as slowly as it had arisen. After breakfast next morning, when I had hoisted Wolf Larsen's body on deck ready for burial, it was still blowing heavily and a large sea was running. The deck was continually awash with the sea which came inboard over the rail and through the scuppers. The wind smote the schooner with a sudden gust, and she heeled over till her lee rail was buried, the roar in her rigging rising in pitch to a shriek. We stood in the water to our knees as I bared my head.

"I remember only one part of the service," I said, "and that is, 'And the body shall be cast into the sea.'"

Maud looked at me, surprised and shocked; but the spirit of something I had seen before was strong upon me, impelling me to give service to Wolf Larsen as Wolf Larsen had once given service to another man. I lifted the end of the hatch-cover, and the canvas-shrouded body slipped feet first into the sea. The weight of iron dragged it down. It was gone.

"Good-by, Lucifer, proud spirit!" Maud whispered so low that it was drowned by the shouting of the wind; but I saw the movement of her lips, and knew.

As we clung to the lee rail and worked our way aft, I happened to glance to leeward. The *Ghost*, at the moment, was uptossed on a sea, and I caught a clear view of a small steamship two or three miles away, rolling and pitching head on to the sea as it steamed toward us. It was painted black, and from the talk of the hunters of their poaching exploits I recognized it as a United States revenue cutter. I pointed it out to Maud, and hurriedly led her aft to the safety of the poop.

I started to rush below to the flag-locker, then remembered that in rigging the *Ghost* I had forgotten to make provision for a flag-halyard.

"We need no distress signal," Maud said. "They have only to see us."

"We are saved!" I said soberly and solemnly. And then, in an exuberance of joy, "I hardly know whether to be glad or not."

I looked at her. Our eyes were not loath to meet. We leaned toward each other, and before I knew it, my arms were about her.

"Need I?" I asked.

And she answered: "There is no need; though the telling of it would be sweet, so sweet."

Her lips met the press of mine, and, by what strange trick of the imagination I know not, the scene in the cabin of the *Ghost* flashed upon me, when she had pressed her fingers lightly on my lips and said, "Hush, hush."

"My woman, my one small woman," I said, my free hand petting her shoulder in the way all lovers know though never learn in school.

"My man," she said, looking at me for an instant with tremulous lids which fluttered down and veiled her eyes as she rested her head against my breast with a happy little sigh.

I looked toward the cutter. It was very close. A boat was being lowered.

"One kiss, dear love," I whispered. "One kiss more before they come."

"And rescue us from ourselves," she completed, with a most adorable smile, whimsical as I had never seen it, for it was whimsical with love.

THE END

17
Planchette

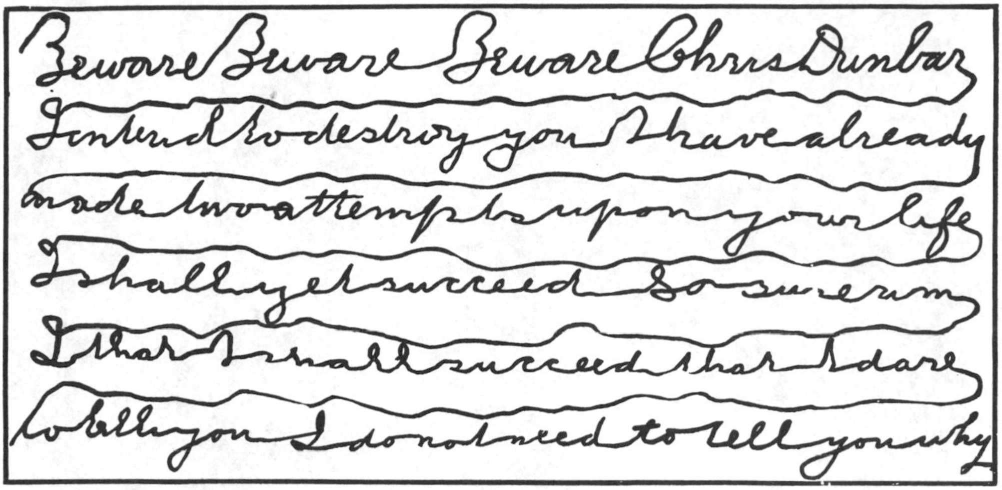
Beware Beware Beware Chris Dunbar
I intend to destroy you I have already
made two attempts upon your life
I shall yet succeed So sure am
I that I shall succeed that I dare
to kill you I do not need to tell you why

Planchette

BY JACK LONDON

Illustrated by Charles M. Relyea

I

"IT is my right to know," the girl said.

Her voice was firm. There was no hint of pleading in it, yet it was the determination that is worked up to through a long period of pleading. But in her case it had been pleading, not of speech, but of personality. Her lips had been ever mute, but her face and eyes, and the very attitude of her soul, had been for a long time eloquent with questioning. This the man had known, but he had never answered; and now she was demanding by the spoken word that he answer.

"It is my right," the girl repeated.

"I know it," he answered, desperately.

She waited, in the silence that followed, her eyes fixed upon the light that filtered down through the lofty boughs and bathed the great redwood trunks in mellow warmth. This light, subdued and colored, seemed almost a radiation from the trunks themselves, so strongly did they saturate it with their hue. The girl saw without seeing, as she heard without hearing, the deep gurgling of the stream far below on the canyon bottom.

She looked down at the man. "Well?" she asked, with the firmness that feigns belief that obedience will be forthcoming.

She was sitting upright, her back against a fallen tree, while he lay near her, on his side.

"Dear, dear Lute," he murmured.

She shivered at the sound of his voice, not from repulsion, but from struggle against the fascination of its caressing gentleness. She had come to know well the lure of the man—the wealth of easement and rest that was promised by every caressing intonation of his voice, by the mere touch of hand on hand or the faint impact of his breath on neck or cheek. The man could not express himself by word or look or touch without weaving into the expression, subtly and occultly, the feeling as of a hand that passed and that in passing stroked softly and soothingly, Nor was this all-pervading caress a something that cloyed with too great sweetness; nor was it sickly sentimental; nor was it

Drawn by Charles M. Relyea

HE WOULD NOT SPEAK—SHE KNEW IT; AND SHE KNEW, LIKEWISE, WITH THE SURENESS OF FAITH, THAT IT WAS BECAUSE HE COULD NOT

maudlin with love's madness. It was vigorous, compelling, masculine. For that matter, it was largely unconscious on the man's part; he was only dimly aware of it. It was a part of him, the breath of his soul as it were.

But now, resolved and desperate, she steeled herself against him. He tried to face her, but her gray eyes looked out at him steadily from under cool, level brows, and he dropped his head upon her knee. Her hand strayed into his hair softly, and her face melted into solicitude and tenderness. But when he looked up again, her eyes were steady, her brows cool and level.

"What more can I tell you?" the man asked. He raised his head and met her gaze. "I cannot marry you. I cannot marry any woman. I love you—you know that—better than my own life. I weigh you in the scales against all the dear things of living, and you outweigh everything. I would give everything to possess you, yet I may not. I can never marry you."

Her lips were compressed with the effort of control. His head was sinking back to her knee, when she checked him.

"You are already married, Chris?"

"No! no!" he cried, vehemently. "I have never been married. I want to marry only you, and I cannot!"

"Then——"

"Don't!" he interrupted; "don't ask me!"

"It is my right to know," she repeated.

"I know it," he again interrupted; "but I cannot tell you."

"You have not considered me, Chris," she went on gently. "You do not know what I have had to bear from my people because of you."

"I did not think they felt so very unkindly toward me," he said bitterly.

"It is true. They can scarcely tolerate you. They do not show it to you, but they almost hate you. It is I who have to bear all this. It was not always so, though. They liked you at first as—as I liked you. But that was four years ago. The time passed by—a year, two years; and then they began to turn against you. They are not to be blamed; you spoke no word. They felt that you were destroying my life. It is four years now, and you have never once mentioned marriage to them. What were they to think? Just what they have thought, that you were destroying my life."

As she talked, she continued to pass her fingers caressingly through his hair, sorrowful for the pain that she was inflicting.

"They did like you at first—who can help liking you? You seem to draw affection from all living things, as the trees draw the moisture from the ground. Aunt Mildred and Uncle Robert thought there was nobody like you. The sun rose and set in you. They thought I was the luckiest girl alive to win the love of a man like you. 'For it looks very much like it,' Uncle Robert used to say, wagging his head wickedly at me. Of course they liked you. Aunt Mildred used to sigh, and look across teasingly at uncle, and say, 'When I think of Chris it almost makes me wish I were younger myself.' And uncle would answer, 'I don't blame you, my dear, not in the least.' And then the pair of them would literally beam upon me their congratulations that I had won the love of a man like you.

"And they knew I loved you as well. How could I hide it—this great, wonderful thing that had entered into my life and swallowed up all my days? For four years, Chris, I have lived only for you. Every moment was yours. Waking I loved you; sleeping I dreamed of you. Every act I have performed was shaped by you, by the thought of you. I had no end, petty or great, that you were not there waiting for me."

"I had no idea of imposing such slavery," he muttered.

"You imposed nothing. You always let me have my own way; it was you who were the obedient slave. You did for me without offending me. You forestalled my wishes without the semblance of forestalling them, so natural and inevitable was everything you did for me. You were no dancing puppet; you made no fuss. Don't you see? You did not seem to do things at all. Somehow they were always there, just done, as a matter of course.

"The slavery was love's slavery. It was just my love for you that made you swallow up all my days. You did not force yourself into my thoughts. You crept in, always, and you were there always—how much you will never know.

"But as time went by, Aunt Mildred and uncle grew afraid. What was to become of me? You were destroying my life. My music — you know how my dream of it has dimmed away. That spring when I first met you, I was twenty, and I was about to start for Germany. I was going to study hard. That was four years ago, and I am still here in California.

"I had other lovers. You drove them away. No! no! I don't mean that. It was I that drove them away. What did I care for lovers, for anything when you were near? But as I said, Aunt Mildred and uncle grew afraid. There has been talk—friends, busybodies, and all the rest. The time went by; you did not speak. I could only wonder, wonder. I knew you loved me. Much was said against you by uncle at first, and then by Aunt Mildred. They were father and mother to me, you know. I could not defend you; yet I was loyal to you. I refused to discuss you. There was half-estrangement in my home —Uncle Robert with a face like an undertaker's, and Aunt Mildred's heart breaking. But what could I do, Chris? What could I do?"

The man, his head resting on her knee again, groaned, but made no other reply.

"Aunt Mildred was mother to me; but I went to her no more with my confidences. My childhood's book was closed. It was a sweet book, Chris. The tears come into my eyes sometimes when I think of it. But never mind that. Great happiness has been mine as well. I am glad I can talk frankly of my love for you. And the attaining of such frankness has been very sweet. I do love you, Chris. I love you—I cannot tell you how. You are everything to me, and more besides. You remember that Christmas tree of the children's, when we played blindman's buff, and you caught me by the arm, so, with such a clutching of fingers that I cried out with the hurt? I never told you, but the arm was badly bruised. And such sweet I got of it you could never guess. There, black and blue, was the imprint of your fingers—your fingers, Chris! It was the touch of you made visible. It was there a week, and I kissed the marks—oh, so often! I was loath to see them go, fain to rebruise the arm and make them linger. I was jealous of the returning white that drove the bruise away. Somehow — oh! I cannot explain, but I loved you so!"

In the silence that fell she continued her caressing of his hair, while she idly watched a great squirrel, boisterous and hilarious, as it scampered back and forth in a distant vista of the redwoods. A crimson-crested woodpecker, energetically drilling a fallen trunk, caught and transferred her gaze. The man did not lift his head. Rather, he crushed his face harder against her knee, while his heaving shoulders marked the hardness with which he breathed.

"You must tell me, Chris," the girl said gently. "This mystery—it is killing me. I must know why we cannot be married. Are we to be ever thus—merely lovers, meeting often, it is true, and yet with the long absences between the meetings? Is it all the world holds for you and me, Chris? Are we never to be more to each other? I want all our days to be together. I want all the companionship, the comradeship, which cannot be ours now, and which will be ours when we are married——" She caught her breath quickly. "But we are never to be married. I forgot. And you must tell me why."

The man raised his head and looked her in the eyes. It was a way he had with whomever he talked.

"I have considered you, Lute," he began, doggedly. "I did consider you at the very first. I should never have gone on with it; I should have gone away. I knew it. And I considered you in the light of that knowledge, and yet—I did not go away. My God! what was I to do? I loved you. I could not go away. I could not help it. I stayed. I resolved, but I broke my resolves. I was like a drunkard. I was drunk of you. I was weak, I know. I failed. I could not go away—I tried. I went away, you will remember, though you did not know why. You know now. I went away, but I could not remain away. Send me away, Lute; I have not the power to go myself."

"But why should you go away?" she asked. "Besides, I must know why before I can send you away."

"Don't ask me."

"Tell me," she said, her voice tenderly imperative.

"Don't, Lute; don't force me," the man pleaded, and there was appeal in his eyes and voice.

"But you must tell me," she insisted. "It is a justice you owe me."

The man wavered. "If I do——" he began. Then he ended with determination, "I should never be able to forgive myself. No, I cannot tell you. Don't try to compel me, Lute. You would be as sorry as I."

"If there is anything—if there are obstacles—if this mystery does really prevent——" She was speaking slowly, with long pauses, seeking the more delicate ways of speech for the framing of her thought. "Chris, I do truly love you. I love you as deeply as it is possible for any woman to love, I am sure. If you were to say to me now, 'Come,' I would arise and go with you. I would follow wherever you led me. I would be your page, as in the days of old when ladies went with their knights to far lands. You are my knight, Chris, and you can do no wrong. Your will is my wish. I was once afraid of the censure of the world; now that you have come into my life I am no longer afraid. I would laugh at the world and its censure for your sake—for my sake, too. I would laugh, for I should have you, and you are more to me than the good will and approval of the world. If you say 'Come,' I will."

"Don't! Don't!" he cried. "It is impossible! Marriage or not, I cannot even say 'Come.' I'll tell you why."

He sat up beside her, the action stamped with resolve. He took her hand in his and held it closely. His lips moved to the verge of speech. The mystery trembled for utterance; the air was palpitant with its presence. As if it were an irrevocable decree of fate, the girl steeled herself to hear. But the man paused, gazing straight out before him. She felt his hand relax in hers, and she pressed it sympathetically, encouragingly. But she felt the rigidity going out of his tense body, and she knew that spirit and flesh were relaxing together. His resolution was ebbing. He would not speak—she knew it; and she knew, likewise, with the sureness of faith, that it was because he could not.

She gazed despairingly before her, a numb feeling at her heart as though hope and happiness had died. She watched the sun flickering down through the warm-trunked redwoods. But she looked at the scene as from a long way off, without interest, herself an alien, no longer an intimate part of the earth and trees she loved so well.

So far removed did she seem that she was aware of a curiosity, strangely impersonal, in what lay around her. Through a near vista she looked at a buckeye tree in full blossom as though her eyes encountered it for the first time. Her eyes paused and dwelt upon a yellow cluster of Diogenes' lanterns that grew on the edge of an open space. It was the way of flowers always to give her quick pleasure-thrills, but no thrill was hers now. She pondered the flowers slowly and thoughtfully, as a hasheesh-eater, heavy with the drug, might ponder some whim-flower that obtruded on his vision. In her ears was the voice of the stream, a hoarse-throated, sleepy old giant muttering and mumbling his somnolent fancies. But her fancy was not in turn aroused, as was its wont; she knew the sound merely for water rushing over the rocks of the deep canyon bottom.

Her gaze wandered beyond the Diogenes' lanterns into the open space. Knee-deep in the wild oats of the hillside grazed two horses, chestnut-sorrels the pair of them, perfectly matched, warm and golden in the sunshine, their spring coats a sheen of high-lights shot through with color-flashes that glowed like fiery jewels. She recognized, almost with a shock, that one of them was hers—Dolly, the companion of her girlhood and womanhood, on whose neck she had sobbed her sorrows and sung her joys. A moisture welled into her eyes at the sight, and she came back from the remoteness of her mood, quick with passion and sorrow, to be part of the world again.

The man sank forward from the hips, relaxing entirely, and with a groan dropped his head on her knee. She leaned over him and pressed her lips softly and lingeringly to his hair.

"Come, let us go," she said softly, almost in a whisper.

She caught her breath in a half sob, then tightened her lips as she arose. His face was white to ghastliness, so shaken was he by the struggle through which he had passed. They did not look at each other, but walked directly to the horses. She leaned against Dolly's neck while he tightened the girths. Then she gathered the reins in her hand and waited. He looked at her as he bent down, an appeal for forgiveness in his eyes; and in that moment her own eyes answered. Her foot rested in his hands, and from there she vaulted into the saddle.

Without speaking, without further looking at each other, they turned the horses' heads and took the narrow trail that wound down through the somber redwood aisles and across the open glades to the pasture lands below. The trail became a cow-path, the cowpath became a wood-road, which later joined with a hay-road; and they ran down through the low-rolling, tawny California hills to where a set of bars let out on the country road that ran along the bottom of the valley. The girl sat her horse while the man dismounted and began taking down the bars.

"No! Wait!" she cried, before he had touched the two lower bars.

She urged the mare forward a couple of strides, and then the animal lifted over the bars in a clean little jump. The man's eyes sparkled, and he clapped his hands.

"You beauty! you beauty!" the girl cried, leaning forward impulsively in the saddle and pressing her cheek to the mare's neck.

"Let's trade horses for the ride in," she suggested, when he had led his horse through and finished putting up the bars. "You've never sufficiently loved Dolly!"

"No, no," he protested.

"You think she is too old, too sedate," Lute insisted. "She's only sixteen, and she can outrun nine colts out of ten. Only she never cuts up. She's too steady and you don't approve of her—no, don't deny it, sir; I know. And I know also that she can outrun your much-vaunted Washoe Ban. There! I challenge you! And furthermore, you may ride her yourself. You know what Ban can do; so you must ride Dolly and see for yourself what she can do."

They proceeded to exchange the saddles, glad of the diversion and making the most of it.

"I'm glad I was born in California," Lute remarked, as she swung astride of Ban. "It's an outrage both to horse and woman to ride in a sidesaddle."

"You look like a young amazon," the man said approvingly.

"Are you ready?" she asked.

"All ready!"

"To the old mill," she called, as the horses sprang forward. "That's less than a mile."

"This is to a finish?" he demanded.

She nodded, and the horses, feeling the urge of the reins, caught the spirit of the race. The dust rose in clouds behind them as they tore along the level road.

They rode side by side, saving the animals for the rush in at the finish, yet putting them at a pace that drew upon vitality and staying power. Curving around a clump of white oaks, the road straightened out before them for several hundred yards, at the end of which they could see the ruined mill.

"Now for it!" the girl cried.

She urged the horse by suddenly leaning forward with her body, at the same time, for an instant, letting the rein slack and touching the neck with her bridle hand. She began to draw away from the man.

"Touch her on the neck!" she cried.

With this, the mare pulled alongside and began gradually to pass the girl. Chris and Lute looked at each other for a moment, the mare still drawing ahead, so that Chris was compelled slowly to turn his head. The mill was a hundred yards away.

"Shall I give him the spurs?" Lute shouted.

The man nodded, and the girl drove the spurs in sharply and quickly, calling upon the horse for its utmost, but saw her own horse forge slowly ahead of her.

"Beaten by three lengths!" Lute beamed triumphantly, as they pulled into a walk. "Confess, sir, confess! You didn't think the old mare had it in her." Lute leaned to the side and rested her hand for a moment on Dolly's wet neck.

"Ban's a sluggard alongside of her," Chris affirmed. "Dolly's all right if she is in her Indian summer."

Lute nodded approval. "That's a sweet way of putting it—Indian summer. It just describes her. But she's not lazy; she has all the fire and none of the folly. She is very wise, what of her years."

"That accounts for it," Chris demurred. "Her folly passed with her youth. Many's the lively time she's given you."

"No," Lute answered; "I never knew her really to cut up. I think the only trouble she ever gave me was when I was training her to open gates. She was afraid when they swung back upon her—the animal's fear of the trap, perhaps. But she bravely got over it. And she never was vicious. She never bolted, nor bucked, nor cut up in all her life—never, not once."

The horses went on at a walk, still breathing heavily from their run. The road wound along the bottom of the valley, now and again crossing the stream. From either side rose the drowsy purr of mowing machines, punctuated by the occasional sharp cries of the men who were gathering the hay crop. On the western side of the valley the hills rose green and dark, but the eastern side was already burned brown and tan by the sun.

"There is summer, here is spring," Lute said. "Oh, beautiful Sonoma Valley!"

Her eyes were glistening and her face was radiant with love of the land. Her gaze wandered on across orchard patches and sweeping vineyard stretches, seeking out the purple which seemed to hang like a dim smoke in the wrinkles of the hills and in the more distant canyon gorges. Far up, among the more rugged crests, where the steep slopes were covered with manzanita and chaparral, she caught a glimpse of a clear space where the wild grass had not yet lost its green.

"Have you ever heard of the secret pasture?" she asked, her eyes still fixed on the remote green.

A snort of fear brought her eyes back to the man beside her. Dolly, upreared, with distended nostrils and wild eyes, was pawing the air madly with her fore legs. Chris threw himself forward against her neck to keep her from falling backward, and at the same time touched her with the spurs to compel her to drop her fore feet to the ground in order to obey the go-ahead impulse of the spurs.

"Why, Dolly, this is most remarkable," Lute began reprovingly.

But to her surprise the mare threw her head down, arched her back as she went up in the air and, returning, struck the ground stiff-legged and bunched.

"A genuine buck!" Chris called out, and the next moment the mare was rising under him in a second buck.

Lute looked on, astounded at the unprecedented conduct of her mare, and admiring her lover's horsemanship. He was quite cool, and was himself evidently enjoying the performance. Again and again, half a dozen times, Dolly arched herself into the air and struck, stiffly bunched. Then she threw her head straight up and rose on her hind legs, pivoting about and striking with her fore feet. Lute whirled the horse she was riding into safety, and as she did so caught a glimpse of Dolly's eyes, with the look in them of blind brute-madness, bulging until it seemed they must burst from her head. The faint pink in the whites of the eyes was gone, replaced by a white that was like dull marble and that yet flashed as from some inner fire.

A faint cry of fear, suppressed in the instant of utterance, slipped past Lute's lips. One hind leg of the mare seemed to collapse under her, and for a moment the whole quivering body, upreared and perpendicular, swayed back and forth, and there was uncertainty as to whether it would fall forward or backward. The man, half slipping sidewise from the saddle, to fall clear if the mare toppled backward, threw his weight to the front and alongside her neck. This overcame the dangerous teetering balance, and the mare struck the ground on her feet again.

But there was no let-up. Dolly straightened out so that the line of the face was almost a continuation of the line of the stretched neck; this position enabled her to master the bit, which she did by bolting straight ahead down the road.

For the first time Lute became really frightened. She spurred Washoe Ban in pursuit, but he could not hold his own with the mad mare, and dropped gradually behind. Lute saw Dolly check and rear in the air again, and caught up just as the mare made a second bolt. As Dolly dashed around a bend, she stopped suddenly, stiff-legged, and Lute saw her lover torn out of the saddle, his thigh-grip broken by the sudden jerk. Though he had lost his seat, he had not been thrown, and as the mare dashed on Lute saw him clinging to the side of the mare, a hand in her mane and a leg across the saddle. With a quick effort he regained his seat and proceeded to fight with the mare for control.

But Dolly swerved from the road and dashed down a grassy slope yellowed with innumerable Mariposa lilies. An old fence at the bottom was no obstacle; she burst through as though it were filmy spider web and disappeared in the underbrush. Lute followed unhesitatingly, putting Ban through the gap in the fence and plunging on into the thicket. She lay along his neck closely, to escape the ripping and

DOLLY, UPREARED, WITH DISTENDED NOSTRILS AND WILD EYES, WAS PAWING THE AIR MADLY WITH HER FORE LEGS

tearing of the trees and vines. She felt the horse drop down through leafy branches and into the cool gravel of a stream's bottom. From ahead came a splashing of water, and she caught a glimpse of Dolly dashing up the small bank and into a clump of scrub oaks, against the trunks of which she was trying to scrape off her rider.

Lute almost caught up among the trees, but was hopelessly outdistanced on the fallow field adjoining, across which the mare tore with a fine disregard for heavy ground and gopher holes. When she turned at a sharp angle into the thicket land beyond, Lute took the long diagonal, skirted the thicket, and reined in Ban at the other side. She had arrived first. From within the thicket she could hear a tremendous crashing of brush and branches. Then the mare burst through and into the open, falling to her knees, exhausted, on the soft earth. She arose and staggered forward, then came limply to a halt. She was in a lather-sweat of fear, and stood trembling pitiably.

Chris was still on her back. His shirt was in ribbons, the backs of his hands were bruised and lacerated, while his face was streaming with blood from a gash near the temple. Lute had controlled herself well, but now she was aware of a quick nausea and a trembling of weakness.

"Chris!" she said, so softly that it was almost a whisper; then "Thank God!"

"Oh, I'm all right," he cried to her, putting into his voice all the heartiness he could command, which was not much, for he had himself been under no mean nervous strain. He showed the reaction he was undergoing, when he swung down out of the saddle. He began with a brave muscular display as he lifted his leg over, but ended, on his feet, leaning against the limp Dolly for support. Lute flashed out of her saddle, and her arms were about him in an embrace of thankfulness.

"I know where there is a spring," she said, a moment later.

They left the horses standing untethered, and she led her lover to where crystal water bubbled from out the base of the mountain.

"What was that you said about Dolly's never cutting up?" he asked, when the blood had been stanched and his nerves and pulse beats were at normal again.

"I am stunned," Lute answered; "I cannot understand it. She never did anything like it in all her life. Why, she is a child's horse. I was only a little girl when I first rode her, and to this day——"

"Well, this day she was everything but a child's horse," Chris broke in. "She was a devil. She tried to scrape me off against the trees, and to batter my brains out against the limbs. And did you see those bucks?"

Lute nodded.

"Regular bucking-broncho proposition."

"But what should she know about bucking?" Lute demanded. "She was never known to buck—never."

He shrugged his shoulders. "Some forgotten instinct, perhaps, long-lapsed and come to life again."

The girl rose to her feet determinedly.

"I'm going to find out," she said.

They went back to the horses, where they subjected Dolly to a rigid examination that disclosed nothing. Hoofs, legs, bit, mouth, body—everything was as it should be. The saddle and saddlecloth were innocent of burr or sticker; the back was smooth and unbroken. They searched for sign of snake bite and sting of fly or insect, but found nothing.

"Whatever it was, it was subjective, that much is certain," Chris said.

"Obsession," Lute suggested.

They laughed together at the idea, for both were twentieth-century products, healthy minded and normal, with souls that delighted in the butterfly-chase of ideals, but that halted before the brink where superstition begins.

"An evil spirit," Chris laughed; "but what evil have I done that I should be so punished?"

"You think too much of yourself, sir," she rejoined. "It is more likely some evil, I don't know what, that Dolly has done. You were a mere accident. I might have been on her back at the time, or Aunt Mildred, or anybody."

As she talked she took hold of the saddle girth and started to loosen it.

"What are you doing?" Chris demanded.

"I'm going to ride Dolly in."

"No, you're not," he announced. "It would be bad discipline. After what has happened I am simply compelled to ride her in myself."

But it was a very weak and very sick mare he rode, stumbling and halting, afflicted with nervous jerks and recurring muscular spasms—the aftermath of a tremendous excitement.

"I feel like a book of verse and a hammock, after all that has happened," Lute said, as they rode into camp.

It was a summer camp of city-tired people, pitched in a grove of towering redwoods through whose lofty boughs the sunshine trickled down, broken and subdued to soft light and cool shadow. Apart from the main camp were the kitchen and the servants' tents; and midway between was the great dining-hall, walled by the living redwood columns, where fresh whispers of air were always to be found, and where no canopy was needed to keep the sun away.

"Poor Dolly, she is really sick," Lute said that evening, when they had returned from a last look at the mare. "But you weren't hurt, Chris, and that's enough for one small woman to be thankful for. I thought I knew, but I really did not know till to-day how much you mean to me."

"My thoughts were of you," Chris answered, and felt the responsive pressure of the hand that rested on his arm.

She turned her face up to his and met his lips.

"Good night," she said.

"Dear Lute, dear Lute," he caressed her with his voice as she moved away among the shadows.

"Who's going for the mail?" called a woman's voice through the trees.

Lute closed the book from which they had been reading, and sighed.

"We weren't going to ride to-day," she said.

"Let me go," Chris proposed; "you stay here. I'll be down and back in no time."

She shook her head.

"Who's going for the mail?" the voice insisted.

"Where's Martin?" Lute called, lifting her voice in answer.

"I don't know," came the voice. "I think Robert took him along somewhere—horse-buying, or fishing, or I don't know what. There's really nobody left but Chris and you. Besides, it will give you an appetite for dinner. You've been lounging in the hammock all day. And Robert *must* have his newspaper."

"All right, aunty, we're starting," Lute called back, getting out of the hammock.

A few minutes later, in riding-clothes, they were saddling the horses. They rode out onto the county road, where blazed the afternoon sun, and turned toward Glen Ellen. The little town slept in the sun, and the somnolent storekeeper and postmaster scarcely kept his eyes open long enough to make up the packet of letters and newspapers.

An hour later Lute and Chris turned aside from the road and dipped along a cowpath down the high bank to water the horses before going into camp.

"Dolly looks as though she'd forgotten all about yesterday," Chris said, as they sat their horses knee-deep in the rushing water. "Look at her."

The mare had raised her head, and cocked her ears at the rustling of a quail in the thicket. Chris leaned over and rubbed around her ears. Her enjoyment was evident, and she drooped her head over against the shoulder of his own horse.

"Like a kitten," was Lute's comment.

"Yet I shall never be able wholly to trust her again," Chris said. "Not after yesterday's mad freak."

"I have a feeling myself that you are safer on Ban," Lute laughed. "It is strange. My trust in Dolly is as implicit as ever. I feel confident so far as I am concerned, but I should never care to see you on her back again. Now with Ban, my faith is still unshaken."

"I feel the same way," Chris laughed back. "Ban could never possibly betray me."

They turned their horses out of the stream. Dolly stopped to brush a fly from her knee with her nose, and Ban urged past into the narrow way of the path. The space was too restricted to make him return, save with much trouble, and Chris allowed him to go on. Lute, riding behind, dwelt with her eyes upon her lover's back, pleasuring in the lines of the bare neck and the sweep out to the muscular shoulders.

Suddenly she reined in her horse. There was nothing else for her to do but look, so brief was the duration of the happening. Beneath and above was the almost perpendicular bank. The path itself was barely wide enough for footing; yet Washoe Ban, whirling and rearing at the same time, toppled for a moment in the air and fell backward off the path.

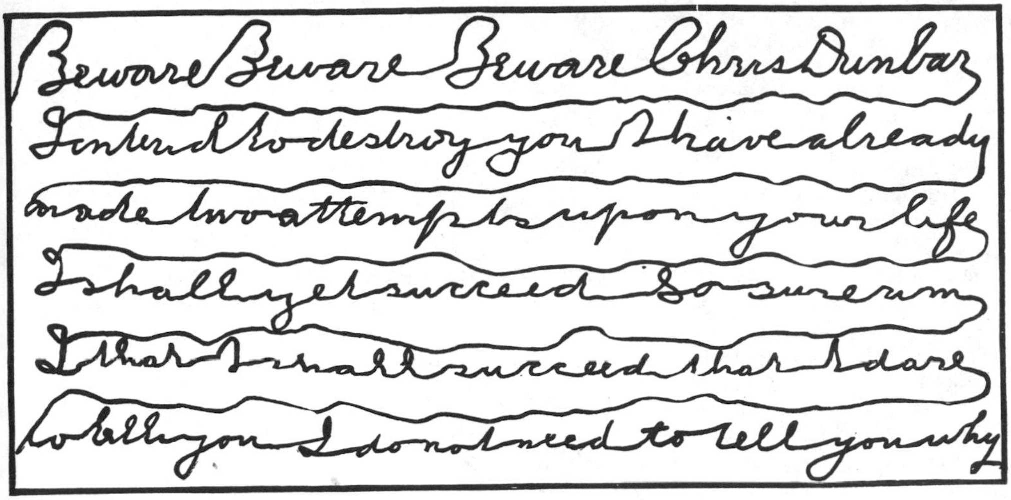
Beware Beware Beware Chris Dunbar
I intend to destroy you I have already
made two attempts upon your life
I shall yet succeed So sure am
I that I shall succeed that I dare
to tell you I do not need to tell you why

Planchette

BY JACK LONDON

Illustrated by Charles M. Relyea

SYNOPSIS: A party of city people is camping in the Sonoma Valley, California. Two of its members, Chris and Lute, ride one afternoon into the redwood forest. They are lovers, but the man tells the girl, as he has often told her before, that he cannot marry her. Lute urges that it is her right to know why; Chris simply repeats that he cannot explain the situation, and says that if he does she will be as sorry as he. It becomes time to return to camp. She mounts her gentle mare, Dolly, and he his horse, Washoe Ban. On the way they trade horses for the ride in. Suddenly, and for no apparent reason, Dolly, with Chris on her back, uprears and paws the air madly. She bolts into a thicket and tries unsuccessfully to scrape her rider off against the trees, stopping finally through exhaustion. Chris is badly shaken but not much hurt. The cause of the mare's performance is a complete mystery. They decide it must be an evil spirit come to punish Chris for something he has done. The next afternoon the young couple go for the mail. On the way back they are riding along a narrow path cut in an almost perpendicular bank. At this point Washoe Ban suddenly rears and topples backward off the path.

II

SO unexpected and so quick was it, that the man was involved in the fall. There had been no time for him to throw himself to the path. He was falling ere he knew it, and he did the only thing possible—slipped the stirrups and threw his body into the air, to the side, and at the same time down. It was twelve feet to the rocks below. He maintained an upright position, his head up and his eyes fixed on the horse above him and falling upon him.

He struck like a cat, on his feet, on the instant making a leap to the side. The next instant Ban crashed down beside him. The animal struggled little, but sounded the terrible cry that horses sometimes sound when they have received mortal hurt. He had struck almost squarely on his back, and in that position he remained, his head twisted partly under, his hind legs relaxed and motionless, his fore legs futilely striking the air.

Chris looked up reassuringly.

"I am getting used to it," Lute smiled down to him. "Of course I need not ask if you are hurt. Can I do anything?"

He smiled back and went over to the

fallen beast, letting go the girths of the saddle and getting the head straightened out.

"I thought so," he said, after a cursory examination; "I thought so at the time. Did you hear that sort of crunching snap?"

Lute shuddered.

"Well, that was the punctuation of life, the final period dropped at the end of Ban's usefulness." He started around to come up by the path. "I've been astride of Ban for the last time. Let us go home."

At the top of the bank Chris turned and looked down.

"Good-by, Washoe Ban!" he called out; "good-by, old fellow."

The animal was struggling to lift its head. There were tears in Chris's eyes as he turned abruptly away, and tears in Lute's eyes as they met his. She was silent in her sympathy, though the pressure of her hand was firm in his as he walked beside her horse down the dusty road.

"It was done deliberately," Chris burst forth suddenly. "There was no warning. He deliberately flung himself over backward."

"There was no warning," Lute concurred. "I was looking; I saw him. He whirled and threw himself at the same time, just as if you had done it yourself with a tremendous jerk and backward pull on the bit."

"It was not my hand, I swear it. I was not even thinking of him. He was going up with a fairly loose rein, as a matter of course."

"I should have seen it, had you done it," Lute said. "But it was all done before you had a chance to do anything. It was not your hand, not even your unconscious hand."

"Then it was some invisible hand, reaching out from I don't know where."

He looked up whimsically at the sky and smiled at the conceit.

Martin stepped forward to receive Dolly when they came into the stable end of the grove, but his face expressed no surprise at sight of Chris coming in on foot. Chris lingered behind Lute for a moment.

"Can you shoot a horse?" he asked.

The groom nodded, then added, "Yes, sir."

"How do you do it?"

"Draw a line from the eyes to the ears —I mean the opposite ears, sir—and where the lines cross——"

"That will do," Chris interrupted. "You know the watering-place at the second bend. You'll find Ban there with a broken back."

"Oh, here you are, sir. I have been looking for you everywhere since dinner. You are wanted immediately."

Chris tossed his cigar away, then went over and pressed his foot on its glowing fire.

"You haven't told anybody about it?—Ban?" he queried.

Lute shook her head. "They'll learn soon enough. Martin will mention it to Uncle Robert to-morrow. But don't feel too badly about it," she said, after a moment's pause, slipping her hand into his.

"He was my colt," he said; "nobody has ridden him but you. I broke him myself. I knew him from the time he was born. I knew every bit of him, every trick, every caper; and I would have staked my life that it was impossible for him to do a thing like that. There was no warning, no fighting for the bit, no previous unruliness. I have been thinking it over. He didn't fight for the bit, for that matter. He wasn't unruly, nor disobedient, there wasn't time. It was an impulse, and he acted upon it like lightning. I am astounded now at the swiftness with which it took place. Inside the first second we were over the edge and falling.

"It was suicide—deliberate suicide—and attempted murder. It was a trap; I was the victim. He had me, and he threw himself over with me. Yet he did not hate me. He loved me as much as it is possible for a horse to love. I am confounded. I cannot understand it any more than you can understand Dolly's behavior yesterday."

"But horses go insane, Chris," Lute said. "You know that. It's merely a coincidence that two horses in two days should have spells under you."

"That's the only explanation," he answered, starting off with her. "But why am I wanted so urgently?"

"Planchette."

"Oh, I remember. It will be a new experience to me."

"And to all of us," Lute replied, "except Mrs. Grantly. It is her favorite phantom, it seems."

"A weird little thing," he remarked, "a bundle of nerves and black eyes. I'll wager she doesn't weigh ninety pounds, and most of that's magnetism."

"Positively uncanny—at times." Lute shivered involuntarily. "She gives me the creeps."

"Contact of the healthy with the morbid," he explained dryly. "You will notice it is the healthy person that always has the creeps. The morbid one never has the creeps. Morbidness gives the creeps—that's its function. Where did you people pick her up anyway?"

"I don't know—yes, I do, too. Aunt Mildred met her in Boston, I think. Oh, I don't know. At any rate, Mrs. Grantly came to California, and of course had to visit Aunt Mildred. You know the open house we keep."

They halted where a passageway between two great redwood trunks gave entrance to the dining-room. Above, through lacing boughs, could be seen the stars. Candles lighted the tree-columned space. About the table, examining the Planchette contrivance, were four people. Chris's gaze roved over them and he was aware of a guilty sorrow-pang as he paused for a moment on Lute's Aunt Mildred and Uncle Robert, mellow with ripe middle age and genial with the gentle buffets life had dealt them. He passed amusedly over the black-eyed, frail-bodied Mrs. Grantly, and halted on the fourth person, a portly, massive-headed man, whose gray temples belied the youthful solidity of his face.

"Who's that?" Chris whispered.

"A Mr. Barton. The train was late; that's why you didn't see him at dinner. He's only a capitalist—water-power-long-distance-electricity-transmitter, or something like that."

"Doesn't look as though he could give an ox points on imagination."

"He can't. He inherited his money, but he knows enough to hold on to it and hire other men's brains. He is very conservative."

"That is to be expected," was Chris's comment. His gaze went back to the man and woman who had been father and mother to the girl beside him. "Do you know," he said, "it came to me with a shock yesterday when you told me that they had turned against me, that I was scarcely tolerated. I met them afterward, last evening, guiltily, in fear and trembling—and to-day, too. And yet I could see no difference from of old."

"Dear man," Lute sighed, "hospitality is as natural to them as the act of breathing. But it isn't that, after all. It is all genuine in their dear hearts. No matter how severe the censure they put upon you when you are absent, the moment they are with you they soften and are all kindness and warmth. As soon as their eyes rest on you, affection and love come bubbling up. You are so made. Every animal likes you. All people like you—they can't help it. You can't help it. You are universally lovable, and the best of it is that you don't know it. You don't know it now. Even as I tell it to you, you don't realize it, you won't realize it—and that very incapacity to realize it, is one of the reasons why you are so loved. You are incredulous now, and you shake your head; but I know, who am your slave, as all people know, for they likewise are your slaves.

"Why, in a minute we shall go in and join them. Mark the affection, almost maternal, that will well up in Aunt Mildred's eyes. Listen to the tone of Uncle Robert's voice when he says, 'Well, Chris, my boy?' Watch Mrs. Grantly melt, literally melt, like a dewdrop in the sun.

"Take Mr. Barton, there. You have never seen him before. Why, you will invite him out to smoke a cigar with you when the rest of us have gone to bed—you, a mere nobody, and he a man of many millions, a man of power, a man obtuse and stupid like the ox; and he will follow you about, smoking the cigar, like a little dog, your little dog, trotting at your back. He will not know he is doing it, but he will be doing it just the same. Don't I know, Chris? Oh, I have watched you, watched you, so often, and loved you for it, and loved you again for it, because you were so delightfully and blindly unaware of what you were doing."

"I'm almost bursting with vanity from listening to you," he laughed, passing his arm around her and drawing her against him.

"Yes," she whispered, "and in this very moment when you are laughing at all that I have said, you, the feel of you, your soul—call it what you will, it is you—is calling for all the love that is in me."

She leaned more closely against him, and sighed as with fatigue. He breathed a kiss into her hair and held her with firm tenderness.

Aunt Mildred stirred briskly and looked up from the Planchette board.

"Come, let us begin," she said; "it will soon grow chilly. Robert, where are those children?"

"Here we are," Lute called out, disengaging herself.

"Now for a bundle of creeps," Chris whispered, as they started in.

Lute's prophecy of the manner in which her lover would be received, was realized. Mrs. Grantly, unreal, unhealthy, scintillant with frigid magnetism, warmed and melted as though of truth she were dew and he sun; Mr. Barton beamed broadly upon him, and was colossally gracious; Aunt Mildred greeted him with a glow of fondness and motherly kindness; while Uncle Robert genially and heartily demanded, "Well, Chris, my boy, and what of the riding?"

But Aunt Mildred drew her shawl more closely around her and hastened them to the business in hand. On the table was a sheet of paper. On the paper, riding on three supports, was a small triangular board. Two of the supports were easily moving casters. The third support, placed at the apex of the triangle, was a lead pencil.

"Who's first?" Uncle Robert demanded.

There was a moment's hesitancy, then Aunt Mildred placed her hand on the board, and said,

"Some one always has to be the fool for the delectation of the rest."

"Brave woman," applauded her husband. "Now, Mrs. Grantly, do your worst."

"I?" that lady queried. "I do nothing. The power, or whatever you care to think it, is outside of me, as it is outside of all of you. As to what that power is, I will not dare to say. But there is such a power; I have had evidences of it. And you will undoubtedly have evidences of it. Now please be quiet, everybody. Touch the board very lightly, but firmly, Mrs. Story; but do nothing of your own volition."

Aunt Mildred nodded, and stood with her hand on Planchette, while the rest formed about her in a silent and expectant circle. But nothing happened. The minutes ticked away, and Planchette remained motionless.

"Be patient," Mrs. Grantly counseled. "Do not struggle against any influences you may feel working on you. But do not do anything yourself, the influences will take care of that. You will feel impelled to do things, and such impulses will be practically irresistible."

"I wish the influences would hurry up," Aunt Mildred protested at the end of five motionless minutes.

"Just a little longer, Mrs. Story, just a little longer," Mrs. Grantly said soothingly.

Suddenly Aunt Mildred's hand began to twitch into movement. A mild concern showed in her face as she observed the movement of her hand and heard the scratching of the pencil-point at the apex of Planchette.

For another five minutes this continued, when Aunt Mildred withdrew her hand with an effort and said, with a nervous laugh:

"I don't know whether I did it myself or not. I do know that I was growing nervous, standing there like a psychic fool with all your solemn faces turned upon me."

"Hen-scratches," was Uncle Robert's judgment, when he looked over the paper upon which she had scrawled.

"Quite illegible," was Mrs. Grantly's dictum. "It does not resemble writing at all. The influences have not got to working yet. Do you try it, Mr. Barton."

That gentleman stepped forward, ponderously willing to please, and placed his hand on the board. And for ten solid, stolid minutes he stood there, motionless as a statue, the frozen personification of the commercial age. Uncle Robert's face began to work. He blinked, stiffened his mouth, uttered suppressed, throaty sounds, deep down, finally snorted, lost his self-control, and broke out in a roar of laughter. All joined in his merriment, including Mrs. Grantly. Mr. Barton laughed with them, but he was vaguely nettled.

"You try it, Story," he said.

Uncle Robert, still laughing and urged on by Lute and his wife, took the board. Suddenly his face sobered. His hand had begun to move, and the pencil could be heard scratching across the paper.

"By George!" he muttered; "that's curious. Look at it. I'm not doing it, I know I'm not doing it. Look at that hand go! Just look at it!"

"Now, Robert, none of your ridiculousness," his wife warned him.

CHRIS LOOKED UP REASSURINGLY. "I AM GETTING USED TO IT," LUTE SMILED DOWN TO HIM

"I tell you I'm not doing it," he replied indignantly. "The force has got hold of me. Ask Mrs. Grantly. Tell her to make it stop, if you want it to stop. I can't stop it. By George! look at that flourish. I didn't do that; I never wrote a flourish in my life."

"Do try to be serious," Mrs. Grantly warned them. "An atmosphere of levity does not conduce to the best operation of Planchette."

"There, that will do, I guess," Uncle Robert said as he took his hand away. "Now let's see."

He bent over and adjusted his glasses. "It's handwriting at any rate, and that's better than the rest of you did. Here, Lute, your eyes are young."

"Oh, what flourishes!" Lute exclaimed, as she looked at the paper. "And look there, there are two different handwritings."

She began to read: "'*This is the first lecture. Concentrate on this sentence: "I am a positive spirit and not negative to any condition." Then follow with concentration on positive love. After that peace and harmony will vibrate through and around your body. Your soul——*' The other writing breaks right in. This is the way it goes: '*Bullfrog* 95, *Dixie* 16, *Golden Anchor* 65, *Gold Mountain* 13, *Jim Butler* 70, *Jumbo* 75, *North Star* 42, *Rescue* 7, *Black Butte* 75, *Brown Hope* 16, *Iron Top* 3.'"

"Iron Top's pretty low," Mr. Barton murmured.

"Robert, you've been dabbling again!" Aunt Mildred cried accusingly.

"No, I've not," he denied; "I only read the quotations. But how the devil—I beg your pardon—they got there on that piece of paper I'd like to know."

"Your subconscious mind," Chris suggested. "You read the quotations in to-day's paper."

"No, I didn't; but last week I glanced over the column."

"A day or a year is all the same in the subconscious mind," said Mrs. Grantly. "The subconscious mind never forgets. But I am not saying that this is due to the subconscious mind. I refuse to state to what I think it is due."

"But how about that other stuff?" Uncle Robert demanded. "Sounds like what I'd think Christian Science ought to sound like."

"Or theosophy," Aunt Mildred volunteered. "Some message to a neophyte."

"Go on, read the rest," her husband commanded.

"'*This puts you in touch with the mightier spirits,*'" Lute read. "'*You shall become one with us, and your name will be "Arya," and you will——Conqueror* 20, *Empire* 12, *Columbia Mountain* 18, *Midway* 140——' and that is all. Oh, no! here's a last flourish, '*Arya, from Kandor.*' That must surely be the Mahatma."

"I'd like to have you explain that theosophy stuff on the basis of the subconscious mind, Chris," Uncle Robert challenged.

Chris shrugged his shoulders. "No explanation. You must have got a message intended for some one else."

"Lines were crossed, eh?" Uncle Robert chuckled. "Multiplex spiritual wireless telegraphy, I'd call it."

"It *is* nonsense," Mrs. Grantly said. "I never knew Planchette to behave so outrageously. There are disturbing influences at work. I felt them from the first. Perhaps it is because you are all making too much fun at it. You are too hilarious."

"A certain befitting gravity should grace the occasion," Chris agreed, placing his hand on Planchette. "Let me try. And not one of you must laugh or giggle, or even think laugh or giggle. And if you dare to snort, even once, Uncle Robert, there is no telling what occult vengeance may be wreaked upon you."

"I'll be good," Uncle Robert rejoined. "But if I really must snort, may I silently slip away?"

Chris nodded. His hand had already begun to work. There had been no preliminary twitching nor tentative essays at writing. At once his hand had started off, and Planchette was moving swiftly and smoothly across the paper.

"Look at him," Lute whispered to her aunt. "See how white he is."

Chris betrayed disturbance at the sound of her voice, and thereafter silence was maintained. Only the steady scratching of the pencil could be heard. Suddenly, as though it had been stung, he jerked his hand away. With a sigh and a yawn he stepped back from the table, then glanced with the curiosity of a newly awakened man at their faces.

"I think I wrote something," he said.

"I should say you did," Mrs. Grantly

remarked with satisfaction, holding up the sheet of paper and glancing at it.

"Read it aloud," Uncle Robert said.

"Here it is, then. It begins with 'beware' written three times, in a bold hand. '*Beware! Beware! Beware! Chris Dunbar, I intend to destroy you. I have already made two attempts upon your life, and failed. I shall yet succeed. So sure am I that I shall succeed that I dare to tell you. I do not need to tell you why. In your own heart you know. The wrong you are doing——*' and here it abruptly ends."

Mrs. Grantly laid the paper down on the table and looked at Chris, who had already become the center of all eyes, and who was yawning as from an overpowering drowsiness.

"Quite a sanguinary turn, I should say," Uncle Robert remarked.

"'*I have already made two attempts upon your life,*'" Mrs. Grantly read from the paper, which she was going over a second time.

"On my life?" Chris demanded between yawns. "Why, my life hasn't been attempted even once. My! I am sleepy!"

"Ah, my boy, you are thinking of flesh-and-blood men," Uncle Robert laughed. "But this is a spirit. Your life has been attempted by unseen things. Most likely ghostly hands have tried to throttle you in your sleep."

"Oh, Chris!" Lute cried impulsively; "this afternoon! the hand you said must have seized your rein!"

"But I was joking," he objected.

"Nevertheless——" Lute left her thought unspoken.

Mrs. Grantly had become keen on the scent. "What was that about this afternoon? Was your life in danger?"

Chris's drowsiness had disappeared. "I'm becoming interested myself," he acknowledged. "We haven't said anything about it. Ban broke his back this afternoon. He threw himself off the bank, and I ran the risk of being caught underneath."

"I wonder, I wonder," Mrs. Grantly communed aloud. "There is something in this. It is a warning. Ah! You were hurt yesterday riding Miss Story's horse! That makes the two attempts!"

She looked triumphantly at them. Planchette had been vindicated.

"Nonsense," laughed Uncle Robert, but with a slight hint of irritation in his manner. "Such things do not happen these days. This is the twentieth century, my dear madam. The thing, at the very latest, smacks of mediævalism."

"I have had such wonderful tests with Planchette," Mrs. Grantly began; then broke off suddenly to go to the table and place her hand on the board.

"Who are you?" she asked. "What is your name?"

The board immediately began to write. By this time all heads, with the exception of Mr. Barton's, were bent over the table and following the pencil.

"It's Dick," Aunt Mildred cried, a note of the mildly hysterical in her voice.

Her husband straightened up, his face for the first time grave.

"It's Dick's signature," he said. "I'd know his fist in a thousand."

"'*Dick Curtis,*'" Mrs. Grantly read aloud. "Who is Dick Curtis?"

"By Jove, that's remarkable!" Mr. Barton broke in. "The handwriting in both instances is the same. Clever, I should say, really clever," he added admiringly.

"Let me see," Uncle Robert demanded, taking the paper and examining it. "Yes, it is Dick's handwriting."

"But who is Dick?" Mrs. Grantly insisted. "Who is this Dick Curtis?"

"Dick Curtis, why, he was Captain Richard Curtis," Uncle Robert answered.

"He was Lute's father," Aunt Mildred supplemented. "Lute took our name. She never saw him; he died when she was a few weeks old. He was my brother."

"Remarkable, most remarkable." Mrs. Grantly was revolving the message in her mind. "There were two attempts on Mr. Dunbar's life. The subconscious mind cannot explain that, for none of us knew of the accident to-day."

"I knew," Chris answered, "and it was I that operated Planchette. The explanation is simple."

"But the handwriting," interposed Mr. Barton. "What you wrote and what Mrs. Grantly wrote are identical."

Chris bent over and compared the handwritings.

"Besides," Mrs. Grantly cried, "Mr. Story recognizes the handwriting."

She looked at him for verification.

He nodded his head. "Yes, it is Dick's fist, I'll swear to that."

But to Lute had come a visioning. While the rest argued pro and con, and the air was filled with phrases—"psychic phenomena," "self-hypnotism," "residuum of unexplained truth," and "spiritualism"—she was reviving mentally the girlhood pictures she had conjured of this soldier-father she had never seen. She possessed his sword, there were several old-fashioned daguerreotypes, there was much that had been said of him, stories told of him—and all this had constituted the material out of which she had builded him in her childhood fancy.

"There is the possibility of one mind unconsciously suggesting to another mind," Mrs. Grantly was saying; but through Lute's mind was trooping her father on his great roan war horse. Now he was leading his men. She saw him on lonely scouts, or in the midst of the yelling Indians at Salt Meadows, when of his command he returned with one man in ten. And in the picture she had of him, in the physical semblance she had made of him, was reflected his spiritual nature—reflected by her worshipful artistry in form and feature and expression—his bravery, his quick temper, his impulsive championship, his madness of wrath in a righteous cause, his warm generosity and swift forgiveness, and his chivalry that epitomized codes and ideals primitive as the days of knighthood. And first, last, and always, dominating all, she saw in the face of him the hot passion and quickness of deed that had earned for him the name, "Fighting Dick Curtis."

"Let me put it to the test," she heard Mrs. Grantly saying. "Let Miss Story try Planchette. There may be a further message."

"No, no, I beg of you," Aunt Mildred interposed. "It is too uncanny. It surely is wrong to tamper with the dead. Besides, I am nervous. Or, better, let me go to bed, leaving you to go on with your experiments. That will be the best way, and you can tell me in the morning." Mingled with the "good nights," were half-hearted protests from Mrs. Grantly, as Aunt Mildred withdrew.

"Robert can return," she called back, "as soon as he has seen me to my tent."

"It would be a shame to give it up now," Mrs. Grantly said. "There is no telling what we are on the verge of. Won't you try it, Miss Story?"

Lute obeyed, but when she placed her hand on the board she was conscious of a vague and nameless fear at this toying with the supernatural. She was twentieth century, and the thing in essence, as her uncle had said, was mediæval. Yet she could not shake off the instinctive fear that arose in her—man's inheritance from the wild and howling ages when his hairy, ape-like prototype was afraid of the dark, and personified the elements into things of fear.

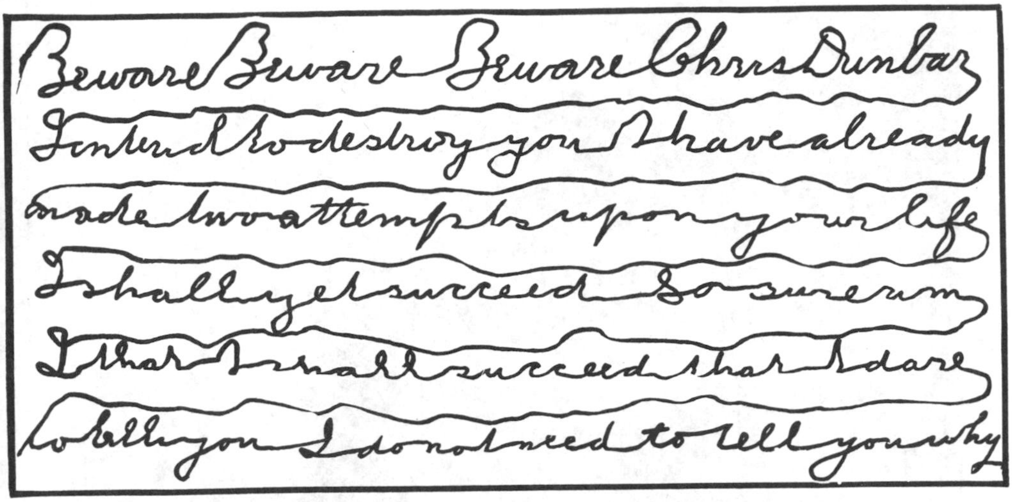

Planchette

BY JACK LONDON

Illustrated by Charles M. Relyea

SYNOPSIS: Chris Dunbar and Lute Story are members of a camping party in the Sonoma Valley, California. The man is in love with the girl, but tells her that he cannot marry her. In spite of her questionings, he refuses to say why, simply repeating that he cannot explain. Chris meets with some extraordinary adventures. One day while he is riding Lute's gentle mare she suddenly bolts, and the young man has a narrow escape from injury. The next day his own horse throws itself backward off the path, down an embankment, and breaks its back. Chris is unhurt. Mrs. Grantly, a woman interested in psychic phenomena, comes to the camp as a visitor. She brings a Planchette board, which the company is eager to try. There is little success until Chris places his hand on it. Instantly comes a message warning him that he is to be killed, and telling him that two attempts have already been made upon his life. The latter statement Chris denies. The handwriting is recognized as that of Lute's father, an army officer, long since dead. To get a further message it is proposed that Lute try the board.

III

AS the mysterious influence seized Lute's hand and sent it writing across the paper, all the unusual passed out of the situation and she was unaware of more than a feeble curiosity. For she was intent on another visioning—this time of her mother, who was also unremembered in the flesh—not sharp and vivid like that of her father, but dim and nebulous as the picture she shaped of her mother—a saint's head in an aureole of sweetness and goodness and meekness, and, withal, shot through with a hint of reposeful determination of will, stubborn and unobtrusive, that in life had expressed itself mainly in resignation.

Lute's hand had ceased moving and Mrs. Grantly was already reading the message that had been written.

"It is a different handwriting," she said, "a woman's hand. 'Martha,' it is signed. Who is Martha?"

Lute was not surprised. "It s my mother," she said simply. "What does she say?"

She had not been made sleepy, as Chris had; but the keen edge of her vitality had

LUTE WAS OFF HER HORSE, SHE KNEW NOT HOW, AND TO THE EDGE

been blunted, and she was experiencing a sweet and pleasing lassitude. And while the message was being read, in her eyes persisted the vision of her mother.

"'*Dear child,*'" Mrs. Grantly read, "'*do not mind him. He was ever quick of speech and rash. Be no niggard with your love. Love cannot hurt you. To deny love is to sin. Obey your heart and you can do no wrong. Obey worldly considerations, obey pride, obey those that prompt you against your heart's prompting, and you do sin. Do not mind your father. He is angry now, as was his way to be in the earth-life; but he will come to see the wisdom of my counsel, for this, too, was his way in the earth-life. Love, my child, and love well.—Martha.*'"

"Let me see it," Lute cried, seizing the paper and devouring the handwriting with her eyes. She was thrilling with unexpressed love for the mother she had never seen, and this written speech from the grave seemed to give more tangibility to her having ever existed than did the vision of her.

"This *is* remarkable," Mrs. Grantly was reiterating. "There was never anything like it. Think of it, my dear, both your father and mother here with us to-night."

Lute shivered. The lassitude was gone, and she was her natural self again, vibrant with the instinctive fear of the things unseen. And it was offensive to her mind that, real or illusive, the presence or the memoried existence of her father and mother should be touched by these two people who were practically strangers—Mrs. Grantly, unhealthy and morbid, and Mr. Barton, stolid and stupid with a grossness both of the flesh and the spirit. And it further seemed a trespass that these strangers should thus enter into the intimacy between her and Chris.

She could hear the steps of her uncle approaching, and the situation flashed upon her, luminous and clear. She hurriedly folded the sheet of paper and thrust it into her bosom.

"Don't say anything to him about this second message, Mrs. Grantly, please, and Mr. Barton; nor to Aunt Mildred. It will only cause them irritation and needless anxiety."

In her mind there was also the desire to protect her lover, for she knew that the strain of his present standing with her aunt and uncle would be added to, unconsciously in their minds, by the weird message of Planchette.

"And please don't let us have any more Planchette," Lute continued hastily. "Let us forget all the nonsense that has occurred."

"'Nonsense,' my dear child?" Mrs. Grantly was indignantly protesting when Uncle Robert strode into the circle.

"Hello!" he demanded; "what's being done?"

"Too late," Lute answered lightly. "No more stock quotations for you. Planchette is adjourned, and we're just winding up the discussion of the theory of it. Do you know how late it is?"

"Well, what did you do last night after we left?"

"Oh, took a stroll," Chris answered.

Lute's eyes were quizzical as she asked with a tentativeness that was palpably assumed, "With—a—with Mr. Barton?"

"Why, yes."

"And a smoke?"

"Yes; and now what's it all about?"

Lute broke into merry laughter. "Just as I told you that you would do. Am I not a prophet? But I knew before I saw you that my forecast had come true. I have just left Mr. Barton, and I knew he had walked with you last night, for he is vowing by all his fetiches and idols that you are a perfectly splendid young man. I could see it with my eyes shut. The Chris-Dunbar glamour has fallen upon him. But I have not finished the catechism, by any means. Where have you been all morning?"

"Where I am going to take you this afternoon."

"You plan well without knowing my wishes."

"I knew well what your wishes are. It is to see a horse I have found."

Her voice betrayed her delight as she cried, "Oh, good!"

"He is a beauty," Chris said.

But her face had suddenly gone grave, and apprehension brooded in her eyes.

"He's called 'Comanche,'" Chris went on. "A beauty, a regular beauty, the perfect type of the Californian cow-pony. And his lines—why, what's the matter?"

"Don't let us ride any more," Lute said, "at least for a while. Really, I think I am a tiny bit tired of it, too."

He was looking at her in astonishment, and she was bravely meeting his eyes.

"I see a hearse and flowers for you, and a funeral oration; I see the end of the world, and the stars falling out of the sky, and the heavens rolling up as a scroll; I see the living and the dead gathered together for the final judgment, the sheep and the goats, the lambs and the rams and all the rest of it, the white-robed saints, the sound of golden harps, and the lost souls howling as they fall into the pit—all this I see on the day that you, Lute Story, no longer care to ride a horse—a horse, Lute! a horse!"

"For a while, at least," she pleaded.

"Ridiculous!" he cried. "What's the matter? Aren't you well?—you who are always so abominably and adorably well?"

"No, it's not that," she answered. "I know it is ridiculous, Chris, I know it, but the doubt will arise. I cannot help it. You always say I am so sanely rooted to the earth and reality and all that, but—perhaps it's superstition, I don't know—but the whole occurrence, the messages of Planchette, the possibility of my father's hand, I know not how, reaching out to Ban's rein and hurling him and you to death, the correspondence between my father's statement that he has twice attempted your life and the fact that in the last two days your life has twice been endangered by horses—my father was a great horseman—all this, I say, causes the doubt to arise in my mind. What if there be something in it? I am not so sure. Science may be too dogmatic in its denial of the unseen. The forces of the unseen, of the spirit, may well be too subtle, too sublimated, for science to lay hold of and recognize and formulate. Don't you see, Chris, that there is rationality in the very doubt? It may be a very small doubt—oh, so small—but I love you too much to run even that slight risk. Besides, I am a woman, and that should in itself fully account for my predisposition toward superstition.

"Yes, yes, I know, call it unreality. But I've heard you paradoxing upon the reality of the unreal—the reality of delusion to the mind that is sick. And so with me, if you will, it is delusive and unreal; but to me, constituted as I am, it is very real—is real as a nightmare is real, before one awakes."

"The most logical argument for illogic I have ever heard," Chris smiled. "It is a good gaming proposition, at any rate. You manage to embrace more chances in your philosophy than I do in mine. It reminds me of Sam—the gardener you had a couple of years ago. I overheard him and Martin arguing in the stable. You know what a bigoted atheist Martin is. Well, Martin had deluged Sam with floods of logic. Sam pondered a while, and then he said, 'Foh a fack, Mis' Martin, you jis' tawk like a house afire; but you ain't got de show I has.' 'How's that?' Martin asked. 'Well, you see, Mis' Martin, you has one chance to mah two.' 'I don't see it,' Martin said. 'Mis' Martin, it's dis way. You has jis' de chance, lak you say, to become worms foh de fruitification of de cabbage garden. But I's got de chance to lif' mah voice to de glory of de Lawd as I go paddin' dem golden streets—along 'ith de chance to be jis' worms along 'ith you, Mis' Martin.' "

"You refuse to take me seriously," Lute said, when she had laughed her appreciation.

"How can I take that Planchette rigmarole seriously?" he asked.

"You don't explain it—the handwriting of my father which Uncle Robert recognized—oh, the whole thing, you don't explain it."

"I don't know all the mysteries of mind," Chris answered; "but I believe such phenomena will all yield themselves to scientific explanation in the not distant future."

"Just the same, I have a sneaking desire to find out some more from Planchette," Lute confessed. "The board is still down in the dining-room. We could try it now, you and I, and no one would know."

Chris caught her hand, crying, "Come on! It will be a lark."

Hand in hand they ran down the path to the tree-pillared room.

"The camp is deserted," Lute said, as she placed Planchette on the table. "Mrs. Grantly and Aunt Mildred are lying down, and Mr. Barton has gone off with Uncle Robert. There is nobody to disturb us." She placed her hand on the board. "Now begin."

For a few minutes nothing happened. Chris started to speak, but she hushed him to silence. The preliminary twitchings had appeared in her hand and arm. Then the pencil began to write. They read the message, word by word, as it was written:

"*There is wisdom greater than the wisdom of reason. Love proceeds not out of the dry-as-dust way of the mind. Love is of the heart, and is beyond all reason, and logic, and philosophy. Trust your own heart, my daughter. And if your heart bids you have faith in your lover, then laugh at the mind and its cold wisdom, and obey your heart, and have faith in your lover.—Martha.*"

"But that whole message is the dictate of your own heart," Chris cried. "Don't you see, Lute? The thought is your very own, and your subconscious mind has expressed it there on the paper."

"But there is one thing I don't see," she objected.

"And that?"

"Is the handwriting. Look at it; it does not resemble mine at all. It is mincing, it is old-fashioned, it is the old-fashioned feminine of a generation ago."

"But you don't mean to tell me that you really believe that this is a message from the dead?" he interrupted.

"I don't know, Chris," she wavered; "I am sure I don't know."

"It is absurd!" he cried. "These are cobwebs of fancy. When one dies he is dead; he is dust. He goes to the worms, as Martin says. The dead? I laugh at the dead. They do not exist. They are not. I defy the powers of the grave, the men dead and dust and gone!"

"And what have you to say to that?" he challenged, placing his hand on Planchette.

On the instant his hand began to write. Both were startled by the suddenness of it. The message was brief:

"*Beware! Beware! Beware!*"

He was distinctly sobered, but he laughed. "It is like a miracle play. Death we have, speaking to us from the grave. But Good Deeds, where art thou? and Kindred? and Joy? and Household Goods? and Friendship? and all the goodly company?"

But Lute did not share his bravado. Her fright showed itself in her face as she laid her trembling hand on his arm.

"Oh, Chris, let us stop. I am sorry we began it. Let us leave the quiet dead to their rest. It is wrong, it must be wrong. I confess I am affected by it. I cannot help it. As my body is trembling, so is my soul. This speech of the grave, this dead man reaching out from the mold of a generation to protect me from you—there *is* reason in it! There is the living mystery that prevents you from marrying me. Were my father alive he would protect me from you. Dead, he still strives to protect me. His hands, his ghostly hands, are against your life!"

"Do be calm," Chris said soothingly. "Listen to me. It is all a lark. We are playing with the subjective forces of our own being, with phenomena which science has not yet explained, that is all. Psychology is so young a science! The subconscious mind has just been discovered, one might say. It is all mystery as yet; the laws of it are yet to be formulated. This is simply unexplained phenomena. But that is no reason why we should immediately account for it by labeling it spiritualism. As yet we do not know, that is all. As for Planchette——"

He abruptly ceased, for at that moment, to enforce his remark, he had placed his hand on Planchette, and at that moment his hand had been seized, as by a paroxysm, and sent dashing, willy nilly, across the paper, writing as the hand of an angry person would write.

"No, I don't care for any more of it," Lute said, when the message was completed. "It is like witnessing a fight between you and my father in the flesh. There is in it the savor of struggle and blows."

She pointed out a sentence that read, "*You cannot escape me nor the just punishment that is yours.*"

"Perhaps I visualize too vividly for my own comfort, for I can see his hands at your throat. I know that he is, as you say, dead and dust. But for all that I see him as a man that is alive and walks the earth; I see the anger in his face, the anger and the vengeance, and I see it all directed against you."

She crumpled up the sheets of paper, and put Planchette away.

"We won't bother with it any more," Chris said. "I didn't think it would affect you so strongly. But it's all subjective, I'm sure, with possibly a bit of suggestion thrown in—that and nothing more. And the whole strain of our situation has made conditions unusually favorable for striking phenomena."

"And about our situation," Lute said, as they went slowly up the path they had run down; "what we are to do, I don't know. Are we to go on, as we have gone on? What is best? Have you thought of anything?"

He debated for a few steps. "I have thought of telling your uncle and aunt."

"What you couldn't tell me?" she asked quickly.

"No," he answered slowly; "but just as much as I have told you. I have no right to tell them more than I have told you."

This time it was she that debated. "No, don't tell them," she said finally; "they wouldn't understand. I don't understand, for that matter, but I have faith in you, and in the nature of things they are not capable of the same implicit faith. You raise up before me a mystery that prevents our marriage, and I believe you; but they could not believe you without doubts arising as to the wrong and ill nature of the mystery. Besides, it would but make their anxieties greater."

"I should go away, I know I should go away," he said, half under his breath. "And I can. I am no weakling. Because I have failed to remain away once is no proof that I shall fail again."

She caught her breath with a quick gasp. "It is like a bereavement to hear you speak of going away and remaining away. I should never see you again. It is too terrible. And do not reproach yourself for weakness. It is I who am to blame. It is I who prevented you from remaining away before, I know. I wanted you so, I want you so.

"There is nothing to be done, Chris, nothing to be done but to go on with it and—and let it work itself out somehow. That is one thing we are sure of: it will work out somehow."

"But it would be easier if I went away," he suggested.

"I am happier when you are here."

"The cruelty of circumstance," he muttered savagely.

"Go or stay—that will be part of the working out. But I do not want you to go, Chris; you know that. And now no more about it. Talk cannot mend it. Let us never mention it again unless—unless some time, some wonderful happy time, you can come to me and say: 'Lute, all is well with me. The mystery no longer binds me. I am free.' Until that time let us bury it, along with Planchette and all the rest, and make the most of the little that is given us.

"And now, to show you how prepared I am to make the most of that little, I am even ready to go with you this afternoon to see the horse—though I wish you wouldn't ride any more, for a few days, anyway, or for a week. What did you say is his name?"

"Comanche," he answered. "I know you will like him."

Chris lay on his back, his head propped by the bare jutting wall of stone, his gaze attentively directed across the canyon to the opposing, tree-covered slope. There was a sound of crashing through underbrush, the ringing of steel-shod hoofs on stone, and an occasional and mossy descent of a dislodged bowlder that bounded from the hill and fetched up with a final splash in the torrent that rushed over a wild chaos of rocks beneath him. Now and again he caught glimpses, framed in green foliage, of the golden-brown of Lute's corduroy riding-habit and of the bay horse which moved beneath her.

She rode out into an open space where a loose earth-slide denied lodgment to trees and grass. She halted the horse at the brink of the slide, and glanced down it with a measuring eye. Forty feet beneath, the slide terminated in a small, firm-surfaced terrace, the banked accumulation of fallen earth and gravel.

"It's a good test," she called across the canyon. "I'm going to put him down it."

The animal gingerly launched himself on the treacherous footing, irregularly losing and gaining his hind feet, keeping his fore legs stiff, and steadily and calmly, without panic or nervousness, extricating the fore feet as fast as they sank too deeply into the sliding earth that surged along in a wave before him. When the firm footing at the bottom was reached, he strode out on the little terrace with a quickness and springiness of gait and with glintings of muscular fires that gave the lie to the calm deliberation of his movements on the slide.

"Bravo!" Chris shouted across the canyon, clapping his hands.

"The wisest-footed, clearest-headed horse I ever saw," Lute called back, as she turned the animal to the side and dropped down a broken slope of rubble into the trees again.

Chris followed her by the sound of her progress, and by occasional glimpses where the foliage was more open, as she zigzagged down the steep and trailless descent. She emerged below him at the rugged rim of the torrent, dropped the horse down a three-foot wall, and halted to study the crossing.

Four feet out in the stream, a narrow ledge thrust above the surface of the water. Beyond the ledge boiled an angry pool. But to the left from the ledge, and several feet lower, was a tiny bed of gravel. A giant bowlder prevented direct access to the gravel bed. The only way to gain it was by first leaping to the ledge of rock. She studied it carefully, and the tightening of her bridle arm advertised that she had made up her mind.

Chris, in his anxiety, had sat up to observe more closely what she meditated.

"Don't tackle it," he called.

"I have faith in Comanche," she replied.

"He can't make that side jump to the gravel," Chris warned. "He'll never keep his legs; he'll topple over into the pool. Only one horse in a thousand could do that stunt."

"And Comanche is that very horse," she called back. "Watch him."

She gave the animal his own head, and he leaped cleanly and accurately to the ledge, striking with feet close together on the narrow space. On the instant he struck, Lute lightly touched his neck with the rein, impelling him to the left; and in that instant, tottering on the insecure footing, with front feet slipping over into the pool beyond, he lifted on his hind legs, with a half turn, sprang to the left, and dropped squarely down to the tiny gravel bed. An easy jump brought him across the stream, and Lute angled him up the bank and halted before her lover.

"Well?" she asked.

"I am all tense," Chris answered. "I was holding my breath."

"Buy him by all means," Lute said, dismounting. "He is a bargain. I could dare anything on him. I never in my life had such confidence in a horse's feet."

"His owner says that he has never been known to lose his feet, that it is impossible to get him down."

"Buy him, buy him at once," she counseled, "before the man changes his mind. If you don't, I shall. Oh, such feet! I feel such confidence in them that when I am on him I don't consider he has feet at all. And he's quick as a cat, and instantly obedient. Bridle-wise is no name for it! You could guide him with silken threads. Oh, I know I'm enthusiastic, but if you don't buy him, Chris, I shall. Remember, I've second refusal."

Chris smiled agreement as he changed the saddles. Meanwhile she compared the two horses.

"Of course he doesn't match Dolly the way Ban did," she concluded regretfully; "but his coat is splendid just the same. And think of the horse that is under the coat."

Chris gave her a hand into the saddle, and followed her up the slope to the county road. She reined in suddenly, saying,

"We won't go straight back to camp."

"You forget dinner," he warned.

"But I remember Comanche," she retorted. "We'll ride directly over to the ranch and buy him. Dinner will keep."

"But the cook won't," Chris laughed. "She's already threatened to leave, what of our late-comings."

"Even so," was the answer. "Aunt Mildred may have to get another cook, but at any rate we shall have got Comanche."

They turned the horses in the other direction, and took the climb of the Nun Canyon road that led over the divide and down into the Napa Valley. But the climb was hard, the going was slow. Sometimes they topped the bed of the torrent by hundreds of feet, and again they dipped down and crossed and recrossed it twenty times in twice as many rods. They rode through the deep shade of clean-trunked maples and towering redwoods, to emerge on open stretches of mountain shoulder where the earth lay dry and cracked under the sun.

On one such shoulder they emerged, where the road stretched level before them for a quarter of a mile. On one side rose the huge bulk of the mountain. On the other side the steep wall of the canyon fell away in impossible slopes and sheer drops to the torrent at the bottom. It was an abyss of green beauty and shady depths, pierced by vagrant shafts of the sun and mottled here and there by the sun's broader blazes. The sound of rushing water ascended on the windless air, and there was a hum of mountain bees.

The horses broke into an easy lope. Chris rode on the outside, looking down into the great depths and pleasuring with his eyes in what he saw. Disassociating itself from the murmur of the bees, a murmur arose of falling water. It grew louder with every stride of the horses.

"Look!" he cried.

Lute leaned well out from her horse to see. Beneath them the water slid foaming down a smooth-faced rock to the lip, whence it leaped clear—a pulsating ribbon of white, a-breath with movement, ever falling and ever remaining, changing its substance but never its form, an aërial waterway as immaterial as gauze and as permanent as the hills, that spanned space and the free air from the lip of the rock to the tops of the trees far below, into whose green screen it disappeared to fall into a secret and unseen pool.

They had flashed past. The descending water became a distant murmur that merged again into the murmur of the bees and ceased. Swayed by a common impulse, they looked at each other.

"Oh, Chris, it is good to be alive—and to have you here by my side!"

He answered her by the warm light in his eyes.

All things tended to key them to an exquisite pitch—the movement of their bodies, at one with the moving bodies of the animals beneath them; the gently stimulated blood, caressing the flesh through and through with the soft vigors of health; the warm air fanning their faces, flowing over the skin with balmy and tonic touch, permeating them and bathing them subtly, with faint, sensuous delight; and the beauty of the world, more subtly still, flowing upon them and bathing them in the delight that is of the spirit and is personal and holy, that is inexpressible, yet communicable by the flash of an eye and the dissolving of the veils of the soul.

So looked they at each other, the horses bounding beneath them, the spring of the world and the spring of their youth astir in their blood, the secret of being trembling in their eyes to the brink of disclosure, as if about to dispel, with one magic word, all the unrealities and riddles of existence.

The road curved before them, so that the upper reaches of the canyon could be seen, the distant bed of it towering high above their heads. They were rounding the curve, leaning toward the inside, gazing before them at the swift-growing picture. There was no sound of warning. Lute heard nothing, but even before the horse went down, she experienced a feeling that the unison of the two leaping animals was broken. She turned her head, and so quickly that she saw Comanche fall. It was not a stumble nor a trip. He fell as though abruptly, in mid-leap, he had died or been struck a stunning blow.

And in that moment she remembered Planchette; it seared her brain as a lightning flash of all-embracing memory. Her horse was back on its haunches, the weight of her body on the reins; but her head was turned and her eyes were on the falling Comanche. He struck the roadbed squarely, with his legs loose and lifeless beneath him.

It all occurred in one of those age-long seconds that embrace an eternity of happening. There was a slight but perceptible rebound from the impact of Comanche's body with the earth. The violence with which he struck forced the air from his great lungs in an audible groan. His momentum swept him onward and over the edge The weight of the rider on his neck turned him over head first as he pitched to the fall.

Lute was off her horse, she knew not how, and to the edge. Her lover was out of the saddle and clear of Comanche, though held to the animal by his right foot, which was caught in the stirrup. The slope was too steep for them to come to a stop. Earth and small stones, dislodged by their struggles, were rolling down with them and before them in a miniature avalanche. She stood very quietly, holding one hand against her breast and gazing down. But while she saw the real happening, in her eyes was also the vision of her father dealing the spectral blow that had smashed Comanche down in mid-leap and sent horse and rider hurtling over the edge.

Beneath horse and man the steep terminated in an up-and-down wall, from the base of which, in turn, a second slope ran down to a second wall. A third slope terminated in a final wall that based itself on the canyon bed four hundred feet beneath the point where the girl stood and watched. She could see Chris vainly kicking his leg to free the foot from the trap of the stirrup. Comanche fetched up hard against an outjetting point of rock. For a fraction of a second his fall was stopped, and in that slight interval the man managed to grip hold of a young shoot of manzanita. Lute saw him complete the grip with his other hand. Then Comanche's fall began again. She saw the stirrup strap draw taut, then her lover's body and arms. The manzanita shoot yielded its roots, and horse and man plunged over the edge and out of sight.

They came into view on the next slope, together and rolling over and over, with sometimes the man under and sometimes the horse. Chris no longer struggled, and together they dashed over to the third slope. Near the edge of the final wall, Comanche lodged on a hummock of stone. He lay quietly, and near him, still attached to him by the stirrup, face downward, lay his rider.

"If only he will lie quietly," Lute breathed aloud, her mind at work on the means of rescue.

But she saw Comanche begin to struggle again and, clear on her vision, it seemed, was the spectral arm of her father clutching the reins and dragging the animal over. Comanche floundered across the hummock, the inert body following, and together, horse and man, they plunged from sight. They did not appear again; they had fetched bottom.

Lute looked about her. She stood alone on the world—her lover was gone. There was naught to show of his existence, save the marks of Comanche's hoofs on the road and of his body where it had slid over the brink.

"Chris!" she called once, and twice; but she called hopelessly.

Out of the depths, on the windless air, arose only the murmur of bees and of running water.

"Chris!" she called yet a third time, and sank slowly down in the dust of the road.

She felt the touch of Dolly's muzzle on her arm, and she leaned her head against the mare's neck and waited. She knew not why she waited, nor for what, only there seemed nothing else but waiting left for her to do.

(The End.)

18
The League of the Old Men

THE LEAGUE OF THE OLD MEN

At the Barracks a man was being tried for his life. He was an old man, a native from the Whitefish River, which empties into the Yukon below Lake Le Barge. All Dawson was wrought up over the affair, and likewise the Yukon-dwellers for a thousand miles up and down. It has been the custom of the land-robbing and sea-robbing Anglo-Saxon to give the law to conquered peoples, and ofttimes this law is harsh. But in the case of Imber the law for once seemed inadequate and weak. In the mathematical nature of things, equity did not reside in the punishment to be accorded him. The punishment was a foregone conclusion, there could be no doubt of that; and though it was capital, Imber had but one life, while the tale against him was one of scores.

In fact, the blood of so many was upon his hands that the killings attributed to him did not permit of precise enumeration. Smoking a pipe by the trailside or lounging around the stove, men made rough estimates of the numbers that had perished at his hand. They had been whites, all of them, these poor murdered people, and they had been slain singly, in pairs, and in parties. And so purposeless and wanton had been these killings, that they had long been a mystery to the mounted police, even in the time of the captains, and later, when the creeks realized, and a governor came from the Dominion to make the land pay for its prosperity.

But more mysterious still was the coming of Imber to Dawson to give himself up. It was in the late spring, when the Yukon was growling and writhing under its ice, that the old Indian climbed painfully up the bank from the river trail and stood blinking on the main street. Men who had witnessed his advent, noted that he was weak and tottery, and that he staggered over to a heap of cabin-logs and sat down. He sat there a full day, staring straight before him at the unceasing tide of white men that flooded past. Many a head jerked curiously to the side to meet his stare, and more than one remark was dropped anent the old Siwash with so strange a look upon his face. No end of men remembered afterward that they had been struck by his extraordinary figure, and forever afterward prided themselves upon their swift discernment of the unusual.

But it remained for Dickensen, Little Dickensen, to be the hero of the occasion. Little Dickensen had come into the land with great dreams and a pocketful of cash; but with the cash the dreams vanished, and to earn his passage back to the States he had accepted a clerical position with the brokerage firm of Holbrook and Mason. Across the street from the office of Holbrook and Mason was the heap of cabin-logs upon which Imber sat. Dickensen looked out of the window at him before he went to lunch; and when he came back from lunch he looked out of the window, and the old Siwash was still there.

Dickensen continued to look out of the window, and he, too, forever afterward prided himself upon his swiftness of discernment. He was a romantic little chap, and he likened the immobile old heathen to the genius of the Siwash race, gazing calm-eyed upon the hosts of the invading Saxon. The hours swept along, but Imber did not vary his posture, did not by a hair's-breadth move a muscle; and Dickensen remembered the man who once sat upright on a sled in the main street where men passed to and fro. They thought the man was resting, but later, when they touched him, they found him stiff and cold, frozen to death in the midst of the busy street. To undouble him, that he might fit into a coffin, they had been forced to lug him to a fire and thaw him out a bit. Dickensen shivered at the recollection.

Later on, Dickensen went out on the sidewalk to smoke a cigar and cool off; and a little later Emily Travis happened along. Emily Travis was dainty and delicate and rare, and whether in London or Klondike she gowned herself as befitted the daughter of a millionnaire mining engineer. Little Dickensen deposited his cigar on an outside window ledge where he could find it again, and lifted his hat.

They chatted for ten minutes or so, when Emily Travis, glancing past Dickensen's shoulder, gave a startled little scream. Dickensen turned about to see, and was startled, too. Imber had crossed the street and was standing there, a gaunt and hungry-looking shadow, his gaze riveted upon the girl.

"What do you want?" Little Dickensen demanded, tremulously plucky.

Imber grunted and stalked up to Emily Travis. He looked her over, keenly and carefully, every square inch of her. Especially did he appear interested in her silky brown hair, and in the color of her cheek, faintly sprayed and soft, like the downy bloom of a butterfly wing. He walked around her, surveying her with the calculating eye of a man who studies the lines upon which a horse or a boat is builded. In the course of his circuit the pink shell of her ear came between his eye and the westering sun, and he stopped to contemplate its rosy transparency. Then he returned to her face and looked long and intently into her blue eyes. He grunted and laid a hand on her arm midway between the shoulder and elbow. With his other hand he lifted her forearm and doubled it back. Disgust and wonder showed in his face, and he dropped her arm with a contemptuous grunt. Then he muttered a few guttural syllables, turned his back upon her, and addressed himself to Dickensen.

Dickensen could not understand his speech, and Emily Travis laughed. Imber turned from one to the other, frowning, but both shook their heads. He was about to go away, when she called out:

"Oh, Jimmy! Come here!"

Jimmy came from the other side of the street. He was a big, hulking Indian clad in approved white-man style, with an Eldorado king's sombrero on his head. He talked with Imber, haltingly, with throaty spasms. Jimmy was a Sitkan, possessed of no more than a passing knowledge of the interior dialects.

"Him Whitefish man," he said to Emily Travis. "Me savve um talk no very much. Him want to look see chief white man."

"The Governor," suggested Dickensen.

Jimmy talked some more with the Whitefish man, and his face went grave and puzzled.

"I t'ink um want Cap'n Alexander," he explained. "Him say um kill white man, white woman, white boy, plenty kill um white people. Him want to die."

"Insane, I guess," said Dickensen.

"What you call dat?" queried Jimmy.

Dickensen thrust a finger figuratively inside his head and imparted a rotary motion thereto.

"Mebbe so, mebbe so," said Jimmy, returning to Imber, who still demanded the chief man of the white men.

A mounted policeman (unmounted for Klondike service) joined the group and heard Imber's wish repeated. He was a stalwart young fellow, broad-shouldered, deep-chested, legs cleanly built and stretched wide apart, and tall though Imber was, he towered above him by half a head. His eyes were cool, and gray, and steady, and he carried himself with the peculiar confidence of power that is bred of blood and tradition. His splendid masculinity was emphasized by his excessive boyishness, — he was a mere lad, — and his smooth cheek promised a blush as willingly as the cheek of a maid.

Imber was drawn to him at once. The fire leaped into his eyes at sight of a sabre slash that scarred his cheek. He ran a withered hand down the young fellow's leg and caressed the swelling thew. He smote the broad chest with his knuckles, and pressed and prodded the thick muscle-pads that covered the shoulders like a cuirass. The group had been added to by curious passers-by — husky miners, mountaineers, and frontiersmen, sons of the long-legged and broad-shouldered generations. Imber glanced from one to another, then he spoke aloud in the Whitefish tongue.

"What did he say?" asked Dickensen.

"Him say um all the same one man, dat p'liceman," Jimmy interpreted.

Little Dickensen was little, and what of Miss Travis, he felt sorry for having asked the question.

The policeman was sorry for him and stepped into the breach. "I fancy there may be something in his story. I'll take him up to the captain for examination. Tell him to come along with me, Jimmy."

Jimmy indulged in more throaty spasms, and Imber grunted and looked satisfied.

"But ask him what he said, Jimmy, and what he meant when he took hold of my arm."

So spoke Emily Travis, and Jimmy put the question and received the answer.

"Him say you no afraid," said Jimmy.

Emily Travis looked pleased.

"Him say you no *skookum*, no strong, all the same very soft like little baby. Him break you, in um two hands, to little pieces. Him t'ink much funny, very strange, how you can be mother of men so big, so strong, like dat p'liceman."

Emily Travers kept her eyes up and unfaltering, but her cheeks were sprayed with scarlet. Little Dickensen blushed and was quite embarrassed. The policeman's face blazed with his boy's blood.

"Come along, you," he said gruffly, setting his shoulder to the crowd and forcing a way.

Thus it was that Imber found his way to the Barracks, where he made full and voluntary confession, and from the precincts of which he never emerged.

Imber looked very tired. The fatigue of hopelessness and age was in his face. His shoulders drooped depressingly, and his eyes were lack-lustre. His mop of hair should have been white, but sun and weatherbeat had burned and bitten it so that it hung limp and lifeless and colorless. He took no interest in what went on around him. The courtroom was jammed with the men of the creeks and trails, and there was an ominous note in the rumble and grumble of their low-pitched voices, which came to his ears like the growl of the sea from deep caverns.

He sat close by a window, and his apathetic eyes rested now and again on the dreary scene without. The sky was overcast, and a gray drizzle was falling. It was flood-time on the Yukon. The ice was gone, and the river was up in the town. Back and forth on the main street, in canoes and poling-boats, passed the people that never rested. Often he saw these boats turn aside from the street and enter the flooded square that marked the Barracks' parade-ground. Sometimes they disappeared beneath him, and he heard them jar against the houselogs and their occupants scramble in through the window. After that came the slush of water against men's legs as they waded across the lower room and mounted the stairs. Then they appeared in the doorway, with doffed hats and dripping seaboots, and added themselves to the waiting crowd.

And while they centred their looks on him, and in grim anticipation enjoyed the penalty he was to pay, Imber looked at them, and mused on their ways, and on their Law that never slept, but went on unceasing, in good times and bad, in flood and famine, through trouble and terror and death, and which would go on unceasing, it seemed to him, to the end of time.

A man rapped sharply on a table, and the conversation droned away into silence. Imber looked at the man. He seemed one in authority, yet Imber divined the square-browed man who sat by a desk farther back to be the one chief over them all and over the man who had rapped. Another man by the same table uprose and began to read aloud from many fine sheets of paper. At the top of each sheet he cleared his throat, at the bottom moistened his fingers. Imber did not understand his speech, but the others did, and he knew that it made them angry. Sometimes it made them very angry, and once a man cursed him, in single syllables, stinging and tense, till a man at the table rapped him to silence.

For an interminable period the man read. His monotonous, sing-song utterance lured Imber to dreaming, and he was dreaming deeply when the man ceased. A voice spoke to him in his own Whitefish tongue, and he roused up, without surprise, to look upon the face of his sister's son, a young man who had wandered away years agone to make his dwelling with the whites.

"Thou dost not remember me," he said by way of greeting.

"Nay," Imber answered. "Thou art Howkan who went away. Thy mother be dead."

"She was an old woman," said Howkan.

But Imber did not hear, and Howkan, with hand upon his shoulder, roused him again.

"I shall speak to thee what the man has spoken, which is the tale of the troubles thou hast done and which thou hast told, O fool, to the Captain Alexander. And thou

"First, there was the man...with cunning traps made of iron, who sought the beaver of the Whitefish. Him I slew"

shalt understand and say if it be true talk or talk not true. It is so commanded."

Howkan had fallen among the mission folk and been taught by them to read and write. In his hands he held the many fine sheets from which the man had read aloud, and which had been taken down by a clerk when Imber first made confession, through the mouth of Jimmy, to Captain Alexander. Howkan began to read. Imber listened for a space, when a wonderment rose up in his face and he broke in abruptly.

"That be my talk, Howkan. Yet from thy lips it comes when thy ears have not heard."

Howkan smirked with self-appreciation. His hair was parted in the middle. "Nay, from the paper it comes, O Imber. Never have my ears heard. From the paper it comes, through my eyes, into my head, and out of my mouth to thee. Thus it comes."

"Thus it comes? It be there in the paper?" Imber's voice sank in whisperful awe as he crackled the sheets 'twixt thumb and finger and stared at the charactery scrawled thereon. "It be a great medicine, Howkan, and thou art a worker of wonders."

"It be nothing, it be nothing," the young man responded carelessly and pridefully. He read at hazard from the document: *"In that year, before the break of the ice, came an old man, and a boy who was lame of one foot. These also did I kill, and the old man made much noise —"*

"It be true," Imber interrupted breathlessly. "He made much noise and would not die for a long time. But how dost thou know, Howkan? The chief man of the white men told thee, mayhap? No one beheld me, and him alone have I told."

Howkan shook his head with impatience. "Have I not told thee it be there in the paper, O fool?"

Imber stared hard at the ink-scrawled surface. "As the hunter looks upon the snow and says, Here but yesterday there passed a rabbit; and here by the willow scrub it stood and listened, and heard, and was afraid; and here it turned upon its trail; and here it went with great swiftness, leaping wide; and here, with greater swiftness and wider leapings, came a lynx; and here, where the claws cut deep into the snow, the lynx made a very great leap; and here it struck, with the rabbit under and rolling belly up; and here leads off the trail of the lynx alone, and there is no more rabbit, — as the hunter looks upon the markings of the snow and says thus and so and here, dost thou, too, look upon the paper and say thus and so and here be the things old Imber hath done?"

"Even so," said Howkan. "And now do thou listen, and keep thy woman's tongue between thy teeth till thou art called upon for speech."

Thereafter, and for a long time, Howkan read to him the confession, and Imber remained musing and silent. At the end, he said:

"It be my talk, and true talk, but I am grown old, Howkan, and forgotten things come back to me which were well for the head man there to know. First, there was the man who came over the Ice Mountains, with cunning traps made of iron, who sought the beaver of the Whitefish. Him I slew. And there were three men seeking gold on the Whitefish long ago. Them also I slew, and left them to the wolverines. And at the Five Fingers there was a man with a raft and much meat."

At the moments when Imber paused to remember, Howkan translated and a clerk reduced to writing. The courtroom listened stolidly to each unadorned little tragedy, till Imber told of a red-haired man whose eyes were crossed and whom he had killed with a remarkably long shot.

"Hell," said a man in the forefront of the onlookers. He said it soulfully and sorrowfully. He was red-haired. "Hell," he repeated. "That was my brother Bill." And at regular intervals throughout the session, his solemn "Hell" was heard in the courtroom; nor did his comrades check him, nor did the man at the table rap him to order.

Imber's head drooped once more, and his eyes went dull, as though a film rose up and covered them from the world. And he dreamed as only age can dream upon the colossal futility of youth.

Later, Howkan roused him again, saying: "Stand up, O Imber. It be commanded that thou tellest why you did these troubles, and slew these people, and at the end journeyed here seeking the Law."

Imber rose feebly to his feet and swayed back and forth. He began to speak in a low and faintly rumbling voice, but Howkan interrupted him.

"This old man, he is damn crazy," he said in English to the square-browed man. "His talk is foolish and like that of a child."

"We will hear his talk which is like that of a child," said the square-browed man. "And we will hear it, word for word, as he speaks it. Do you understand?"

Howkan understood, and Imber's eyes flashed, for he had witnessed the play between his sister's son and the man in authority. And then began the story, the epic of a bronze patriot which might well itself be wrought into bronze for the generations unborn. The crowd fell strangely silent, and the square-browed judge leaned head on hand and pondered his soul and the soul of his race. Only was heard the deep tones of Imber, rhythmically alternating with the shrill voice of the interpreter, and now and again, like the bell of the Lord, the wondering and meditative "Hell" of the red-haired man.

"I am Imber of the Whitefish people." So ran the interpretation of Howkan, whose inherent barbarism gripped hold of him, and who lost his mission culture and veneered civilization as he caught the savage ring and rhythm of old Imber's tale. "My father was Otsbaok, a strong man. The land was warm with sunshine and gladness when I was a boy. The people did not hunger after strange things, nor hearken to new voices, and the ways of their fathers were their ways. The women found favor in the eyes of the young men, and the young men looked upon them with content. Babes hung at the breasts of the women, and they were heavy-hipped with increase of the tribe. Men were men in those days. In peace and plenty, and in war and famine, they were men.

"At that time there was more fish in the water than now, and more meat in the forest. Our dogs were wolves, warm with thick hides and hard to the frost and storm. And as with our dogs so with us, for we were likewise hard to the frost and storm. And when the Pellys came into our land we slew them and were slain. For we were men, we Whitefish, and our fathers and our fathers' fathers had fought against the Pellys and determined the bounds of the land.

"As I say, with our dogs, so with us. And one day came the first white man. He dragged himself, so, on hand and knee, in the snow. And his skin was stretched tight, and his bones were sharp beneath. Never was such a man, we thought, and we wondered of what strange tribe he was, and of its land. And he was weak, most weak, like a little child, so that we gave him a place by the fire, and warm furs to lie upon, and we gave him food as little children are given food.

"And with him was a dog, large as three of our dogs, and very weak. The hair of this dog was short, and not warm, and the tail was frozen so that the end fell off. And this strange dog we fed, and bedded by the fire, and fought from it our dogs, which else would have killed him. And what of the moose meat and the sun-dried salmon, the man and dog took strength to themselves; and what of the strength they became big and unafraid. And the man spoke loud words and laughed at the old men and young men, and looked boldly upon the maidens. And the dog fought with our dogs, and for all of his short hair and softness slew three of them in one day.

"When we asked the man concerning his people, he said, 'I have many brothers,' and laughed in a way that was not good. And when he was in his full strength he went away, and with him went Noda, daughter to the chief. First, after that, was one of our bitches brought to pup. And never was there such a breed of dogs, — big-headed, thick-jawed, and short-haired, and helpless. Well do I remember my father, Otsbaok, a strong man. His face was black with anger at such helplessness, and he took a stone, so, and so, and there was no more helplessness. And two summers after that came Noda back to us with

"And that was the beginning. Came a second white man, with short-haired dogs, which he left behind him when he went. And with him went six of our strongest dogs, for which, in trade, he had given Koo-So-Tee, my mother's brother, a wonderful pistol that fired with great swiftness six times. And Koo-So-Tee was very big, what of the pistol, and laughed at our bows and arrows. 'Woman's things,' he called them, and went forth against the bald-face grizzly, with the pistol in his hand. Now it be known that it is not good to hunt the bald-face with a pistol, but how were we to know? and how was Koo-So-Tee to know? So he went against the bald-face, very brave, and fired the pistol with great swiftness six times; and the bald-face but grunted and broke in his breast like it were an egg, and like honey from a bee's nest dripped the brains of Koo-So-Tee upon the ground. He was a good hunter, and there was no one to bring meat to his squaw and children. And we were bitter, and we said, 'That which for the white men is well, is for us not well.' And this be true. There be many white men and fat, but their ways have made us few and lean.

"Came the third white man, with great wealth of all manner of wonderful foods and things. And twenty of our strongest dogs he took from us in trade. Also, what of presents and great promises, ten of our young hunters did he take with him on a journey which fared no man knew where. It is said they died in the snow of the Ice Mountains where man has never been, or in the Hills of Silence which are beyond the edge of the earth. Be that as it may, dogs and young hunters were seen never again by the Whitefish people.

"And more white men came with the years, and ever, with pay and presents, they led the young men away with them. And sometimes the young men came back with strange tales of dangers and toils in the lands beyond the Pellys, and some times they did not come back. And we said: 'If they be unafraid of life, these white men, it is because they have many lives; but we be few by the Whitefish, and the young men shall go away no more.' But the young men did go away; and the young women went also; and we were very wroth.

"It be true, we ate flour, and salt pork, and drank tea which was a great delight; only, when we could not get tea, it was very bad and we became short of speech and quick of anger. So we grew to hunger for the things the white men brought in trade. Trade! trade! all the time was it trade! One winter we sold our meat for clocks that would not go, and watches with broken guts, and files worn smooth, and pistols without cartridges and worthless. And then came famine, and we were without meat, and two score died ere the break of spring.

"'Now are we grown weak,' we said; 'and the Pellys will fall upon us, and our bounds be overthrown.' But as it fared with us, so had it fared with the Pellys, and they were too weak to come against us.

"My father, Otsbaok, a strong man, was now old and very wise. And he spoke to the chief, saying: 'Behold, our dogs be worthless. No longer are they thick-furred and strong, and they die in the frost and harness. Let us go into the village and kill them, saving only the wolf ones, and these let us tie out in the night that they may mate with the wild wolves of the forest. Thus shall we have dogs warm and strong again.'

"And his word was harkened to, and we Whitefish became known for our dogs, which were the best in the land. But known we were not for ourselves. The best of our young men and women had gone away with the white men to wander on trail and river to far places. And the young women came back old and broken, as Noda had come, or they came not at all. And the young men came back to sit by our fires for a time, full of ill speech and rough ways, drinking evil drinks and gambling through long nights and days, with a great unrest always in their hearts, till the call of the white men came to them and they went away again to the unknown places. And they were without honor and respect, jeering the old-time customs and laughing in the faces of chief and shamans.

"As I say, we were become a weak breed, we Whitefish. We sold our warm skins and furs for tobacco and whiskey and thin cotton things that left us shivering in the cold. And the coughing sickness came upon us, and men and women coughed and sweated through the long nights, and the hunters on trail spat blood upon the snow. And now one, and now another, bled swiftly from the mouth and died. And the women bore few children, and those they bore were weak and given to sickness. And other sicknesses came to us from the white men, the like of which we had never known and could not understand. Smallpox, likewise measles, have I heard these sicknesses named, and we died of them as die the salmon in the still eddies when in the fall their eggs are spawned and there is no longer need for them to live.

"And yet, and here be the strangeness of it, the white men come as the breath of death; all their ways lead to death, their nostrils are filled with it; and yet they do not die. Theirs the whiskey, and tobacco, and short-haired dogs; theirs the many sicknesses, the smallpox and measles, the coughing and mouth-bleeding; theirs the white skin, and softness to the frost and storm; and theirs the pistols that shoot six times very swift and are worthless. And yet they grow fat on their many ills, and prosper, and lay a heavy hand over all the world and tread mightily upon its peoples. And their women, too, are soft as little babes, most breakable and never broken, the mothers of men. And out of all this softness, and sickness, and weakness, come strength, and power, and authority. They be gods, or devils, as the case may be. I do not know. What do I know, I, old Imber of the Whitefish? Only do I know that they are past understanding, these white men, far-wanderers and fighters over the earth that they be.

"As I say, the meat in the forest became less and less. It be true, the white man's gun is most excellent and kills a long way off; but of what worth the gun, when there is no meat to kill? When I was a boy on the Whitefish there was moose on every hill, and each year came the caribou uncountable. But now the hunter may take the trail ten days and not one moose gladden his eyes, while the caribou uncountable come no more at all. Small worth the gun, I say, killing a long way off, when there be nothing to kill.

"And I, Imber, pondered upon these things, watching the while the Whitefish, and the Pellys, and all the tribes of the land, perishing as perished the meat of the forest. Long I pondered. I talked with the shamans and the old men who were wise. I went apart that the sounds of the village might not disturb me, and I ate no meat so that my belly should not press upon me and make me slow of eye and ear. I sat long and sleepless in the forest, wide-eyed for the sign, my ears patient and keen for the word that was to come. And I wandered alone in the blackness of night to the river bank, where was wind-moaning and sobbing of water, and where I sought wisdom from the ghosts of old shamans in the trees and dead and gone.

"And in the end, as in a vision, came to me the short-haired and detestable dogs, and the way seemed plain. By the wisdom of Otsbaok, my father and a strong man, had the blood of our own wolf-dogs been kept clean, wherefore had they remained warm of hide and strong in the harness. So I returned to my village and made oration to the men. 'This be a tribe, these white men,' I said. 'A very large tribe, and doubtless there is no longer meat in their land, and they are come among us to make a new land for themselves. But they weaken us, and we die. They are a very hungry folk. Already has our meat gone from us, and it were well, if we would live, that we deal by them as we have dealt by their dogs.'

"And further oration I made, counselling fight. And the men of the Whitefish listened, and some said one thing, and some another, and some spoke of other and worthless things, and no man made brave talk of deeds and war. But while the young men were weak as water and afraid, I watched that the old men sat silent, and that in their eyes fires came and went. And later, when the village slept and no one knew, I drew the old men away into the forest and made more talk. And now we were agreed, and we remembered the good young days, and the free land, and the times of plenty, and the gladness and sunshine; and we called ourselves brothers, and swore great secrecy, and a mighty oath to cleanse the land of the evil breed that had come upon it. It be plain we were fools, but how were we to know, we old men of the Whitefish?

"And to hearten the others, I did the first deed. I kept guard upon the Yukon till the first canoe came down. In it were two white men, and when I stood upright upon the bank and raised my hand they changed their course and drove in to me. And as the man in the bow lifted his head, so, that he might know wherefore I wanted him, my arrow sang through the air straight to his throat, and he knew. The second man, who held paddle in the stern, had his rifle half to his shoulder when the first of my three spear-casts smote him.

" 'These be the first,' I said, when the old men had gathered to me. 'Later we will bind together all the old men of all the tribes, and after that the young men who remain strong, and the work will become easy.'

"And then the two dead white men we cast into the river. And of the canoe, which was a very good canoe, we made a fire, and a fire, also, of the things within the canoe. But first we looked at the things, and they were pouches of leather which we cut open with our knives. And inside these pouches were many papers, like that from which thou hast read, O Howkan, with markings on them which we marvelled at and could not understand. Now, I am become wise, and I know them for the speech of men as thou hast told me."

A whisper and buzz went around the courtroom when Howkan finished interpreting the affair of the canoe, and one man's voice spoke up: "That was the lost '91 mail, Peter James and Delaney bringing it in and last spoken at Le Barge by Matthews going out." The clerk scratched steadily away, and another paragraph was added to the history of the North.

"There be little more," Imber went on slowly. "It be there on the paper, the things we did. We were old men, and we did not understand. Even I, Imber, do not now understand. Secretly we slew, and continued to slay, for with our years we were crafty and we had learned the swiftness of going without haste. When white men came among us with black looks and rough words, and took away six of the young men with irons binding them helpless, we knew we must slay wider and farther. And one by one we old men departed up river and down to the unknown lands. It was a brave thing. Old we were, and unafraid, but the fear of far places is a terrible fear to men who are old.

"So we slew, without haste and craftily. On the Chilcoot and in the Delta we slew, from the passes to the sea, wherever the white men camped or broke their trails. It be true, they died, but it was without worth. Ever did they come over the mountains, ever did they grow and grow, while we, being old, became less and less. I remember, by the Caribou Crossing, the camp of a white man. He was a very little white man, and three of the old men came upon him in his sleep. And the next day I came upon the four of them. The white man alone still breathed, and there was breath in him to curse me once and well before he died.

"And so it went, now one old man, and now another. Sometimes the word reached us long after of how they died, and sometimes it did not reach us. And the old men of the other tribes were weak and afraid, and would not join us. As I say, one by one, till I alone was left. I am Imber, of the Whitefish people. My father was Otsbaok, a strong man. There are no Whitefish now. Of the old men I am the last. The young men and young women are gone away, some to live with the Pellys, some with the Salmons, and more with the white men. I am very old, and very tired, and it being vain fighting the Law, as thou sayest, Howkan, I am come seeking the Law."

"O Imber, thou art indeed a fool," said Howkan.

But Imber was dreaming. The square-browed judge likewise dreamed, and all his race rose up before him in a mighty phantasmagoria — his steel-shod, mail-clad race, the lawgiver and world-maker among the families of men. He saw it dawn red-flickering across the dark forests and sullen seas; he saw it blaze, bloody and red, to full and triumphant noon; and down the shaded slope he saw the blood-red sands dropping into night. And through it all he observed the Law, pitiless and potent, ever unswerving and ever ordaining, greater than the motes of men who fulfilled it or were crushed by it, even as it was greater than he, his heart speaking for softness.

19
A Hyperborean Brew

A HYPERBOREAN BREW

THOMAS STEVENS'S veracity may have been indeterminate as *x*, and his imagination the imagination of ordinary men increased to the *n*th power, but this, at least, must be said: never did he deliver himself of word nor deed that could be branded as a lie outright.... He may have played with probability, and verged on the extremest edge of possibility, but in his tales the machinery never creaked. That he knew the Northland like a book, not a soul can deny. That he was a great traveller, and had set foot on countless unknown trails, many evidences affirm. Outside of my own personal knowledge, I knew men that had met him everywhere, but principally on the confines of Nowhere. There was Johnson, the ex-Hudson Bay Company factor, who had housed him in a Labrador factory until his dogs rested up a bit, and he was able to strike out again. There was McMahon, agent for the Alaska Commercial Company, who had run across him in Dutch Harbor, and later on, among the outlying islands of the Aleutian group. It was indisputable that he had guided one of the earlier United States surveys, and history states positively that in a similar capacity he served the Western Union when it attempted to put through its trans-Alaskan and Siberian telegraph to Europe. Further, there was Joe Lamson, the whaling captain, who, when ice-bound off the mouth of the Mackenzie, had had him come aboard after tobacco.

This last touch proves Thomas Stevens's identity conclusively. His quest for tobacco was perennial and untiring. Ere we became fairly acquainted, I learned to greet him with one hand, and pass the pouch with the other. But the night I met him in John O'Brien's Dawson saloon, his head was wreathed in a nimbus of fifty-cent cigar smoke, and instead of my pouch he demanded my sack. We were standing by a faro table, and forthwith he tossed it upon the "high card." "Fifty," he said, and the gamekeeper nodded. The "high card" turned, and he handed back my sack, called for a "tab," and drew me over to the scales, where the weigher nonchalantly cashed him out fifty dollars in dust.

"And now we'll drink," he said; and later, at the bar, when he lowered his glass: "R-eminds me of a little brew I had up Tattarat way. No, you have no knowledge of the place, nor is it down on the charts. But it's up by the rim of the Arctic Sea, not so many hundred miles from the American line, and all of half a thousand God-forsaken souls live there, giving and taking in marriage, and starving and dying in-between-whiles. Explorers have overlooked them, and you will not find them in the census of 1890. A whale-ship was pinched there once, but the men, who had made shore over the ice, pulled out for the south and were never heard of.

"But it was a great brew we had, Moosu and I," he added a moment later, with just the slightest suspicion of a sigh.

I knew there were big deeds and wild doings behind that sigh, so I haled him into a corner, between a roulette outfit and a poker layout, and waited for his tongue to thaw.

"Had one objection to Moosu," he began, cocking his head meditatively — "one objection, and only one. He was an Indian from over on the edge of the Chippewyan country, but the trouble was, he'd picked up a smattering of the Scriptures. Been campmate a season with a renegade French Canadian who'd studied for the church. Moosu'd never seen applied Christianity, and his head was crammed with miracles, battles, and dispensations, and what not he didn't understand. Otherwise he was a good sort, and a handy man on trail or over a fire.

"We'd had a hard time together and were badly knocked out when we plumped upon Tattarat. Lost outfits and dogs crossing a divide in a fall blizzard, and our bellies clove to our backs and our clothes were in rags when we crawled into the village. They weren't much surprised at seeing us — because of the whalemen — and gave us the meanest shack in the village to live in, and the worst of their leavings to live on. What struck me at the time as strange was that they left us strictly alone. But Moosu explained it.

"'Shaman *sick tumtum,*' he said, meaning the shaman, or medicine man, was jealous, and had advised the people to have nothing to do with us. From the little he'd seen of the whalemen, he'd learned that mine was a stronger race, and a wiser; so he'd only behaved as shamans have always behaved the world over. And before I get done, you'll see how near right he was.

"'These people have a law,' said Moosu: 'Whoso eats of meat must hunt. We be awkward, you and I, O master, in the weapons of this country; nor can we string bows nor fling spears after the manner approved. Wherefore the shaman and Tummasook, who is chief, have put their heads together, and it has been decreed that we work with the women and children in dragging in the meat and tending the wants of the hunters.'

"'And this is very wrong,' I made to answer; 'for we be better men, Moosu, than these people who walk in darkness. Further, we should rest and grow strong, for the way south is long, and on that trail the weak cannot prosper.'

"'But we have nothing,' he objected, looking about him at the rotten timbers of the igloo, the stench of the ancient walrus meat that had been our supper disgusting his nostrils. 'And on this fare we cannot thrive. We have nothing save the bottle of "painkiller," which will not fill emptiness, so we must bend to the yoke of the unbeliever and become hewers of wood and drawers of water. And there be good things in this place, the which we may not have. Ah, master, never has my nose lied to me, and I have followed it to secret cachés and among the fur-bales of the igloos. Good provender did these people extort from the poor whalemen, and this provender has wandered into few hands. The woman Ipsukuk, who dwelleth in the far end of the village next the igloo of the chief, possesseth much flour and sugar, and even have my eyes told me of molasses smeared on her face. And in the igloo of Tummasook, the chief, there be tea — have I not seen the old pig guzzling? And the shaman owneth a caddy of "Star" and two buckets of prime smoking. And what have we? Nothing! Nothing! Nothing!'

"But I was stunned by the word he brought of the tobacco, and made no answer.

"And Moosu, what of his own desire, broke silence: 'And there be Tukeliketa, daughter of a big hunter and wealthy man. A likely girl. Indeed, a very nice girl.'

"I figured hard during the night while Moosu snored, for I could not bear the thought of the tobacco so near which I could not smoke. True, as he had said, we had nothing. But the way became clear to me, and in the morning I said to him: 'Go thou cunningly abroad, after thy fashion, and procure me some sort of bone, crooked like a gooseneck, and hollow. Also, walk humbly, but have eyes awake to the lay of pots and pans and cooking contrivances. And remember, mine is the white man's wisdom, and do what I have bid you, with sureness and despatch.'

"While he was away I placed the whaleoil cooking lamp in the middle of the igloo, and moved the mangy sleeping furs back that I might have room. Then I took apart his gun and put the barrel by handy, and afterward braided many wicks from the cotton that the women gather wild in the summer. When he came back, it was with the bone I had commanded, and with news that in the igloo of Tummasook there was a five-gallon kerosene can and a big copper kettle. So I said he had done well and we would tarry through the day. And when midnight was near I made harangue to him.

"'This chief, this Tummasook, hath a copper kettle, likewise a kerosene can.' I put a rock, smooth and wave-washed, in Moosu's hand. 'The camp is hushed and the stars are winking. Go thou, creep into the chief's igloo softly, and smite him thus upon the belly, and hard. And let the meat and good grub of the days to come put strength into thine arm. There will be uproar and outcry, and the village will come hot afoot. But be thou unafraid. Veil thy movements and lose thy form in the obscurity of the night and the confusion of men. And when the woman Ipsukuk is anigh thee, — she who smeareth her face with molasses, — do thou smite her likewise, and whosoever else that possesseth flour and cometh to thy hand. Then do thou lift thy voice in pain and double up with clasped hands, and make outcry in token that thou, too, hast felt the visitation of the night. And in this way shall we achieve honor and great possessions, and the caddy of "Star" and the prime smoking, and thy Tukeliketa, who is a likely maiden.'

"When he had departed on this errand, I bided patiently in the shack, and the tobacco seemed very near. Then there was a cry of affright in the night, that became an uproar and assailed the sky. I seized the 'painkiller' and ran forth. There was much noise, and a wailing among the women, and fear sat heavily on all. Tummasook and the woman Ipsukuk rolled on the ground in pain, and with them there were divers others, also Moosu. I thrust aside those that cluttered the way of my feet, and put the mouth of the bottle to Moosu's lips. And straightway he became well and ceased his howling. Whereat there was a great clamor for the bottle from the others so stricken. But I made harangue, and ere they tasted and were made well I had mulcted Tummasook of his copper kettle and kerosene can, and the woman Ipsukuk of her sugar and molasses, and the other sick ones of goodly measures of flour. The shaman glowered wickedly at the people around my knees, though he poorly concealed the wonder that lay beneath. But I held my head high, and Moosu groaned beneath the loot as he followed my heels to the shack.

"There I set to work. In Tummasook's copper kettle I mixed three quarts of wheat flour with five of molasses, and to this I added of water twenty quarts. Then I placed the kettle near the lamp, that it might sour in the warmth and grow strong. Moosu understood, and said my wisdom passed understanding and was greater than Solomon's, who he had heard was a wise man of old time. The kerosene can I set over the lamp, and to its nose I affixed a snout, and into the snout the bone that was like a gooseneck. I sent Moosu without to pound ice, while I connected the barrel of his gun with the gooseneck, and midway on the barrel I piled the ice he had pounded. And at the far end of the gun barrel, beyond the pan of ice, I placed a small iron pot. When the brew was strong enough (and it was two days ere it could stand on its own legs), I filled the kerosene can with it, and lighted the wicks I had braided.

"Now that all was ready, I spoke to Moosu. 'Go forth,' I said, 'to the chief men of the village, and give them greeting, and bid them come into my igloo and sleep the night away with me and the gods.'

"The brew was singing merrily when they began shoving aside the skin flap and crawling in, and I was heaping cracked ice on the gun barrel. Out of the priming hole at the far end, drip, drip, drip into the iron pot fell the liquor — *hooch*, you know. But they'd never seen the like, and giggled nervously when I made harangue about its virtues. As I talked I noted the jealousy in the shaman's eye, so when I had done, I placed him side by side with Tummasook and the woman Ipsukuk. Then I gave them to drink, and their eyes watered and their stomachs warmed, till from being afraid they reached greedily for more; and when I had them well started, I turned to the others. Tummasook made a brag about how he had once killed a polar bear, and in the vigor of his pantomime nearly slew his mother's brother. But nobody heeded. The woman Ipsukuk fell to weeping for a son lost long years agone in the ice, and the shaman made incantation and prophecy. So it went, and before morning they were all on the floor, sleeping soundly with the gods.

"The story tells itself, does it not? The news of the magic potion spread. It was too marvellous for utterance. Tongues could tell but a tithe of the miracles it performed. It eased pain, gave surcease to sorrow, brought back old memories, dead faces, and forgotten dreams. It was a fire that ate through all the blood, and, burning, burned not. It stoutened the heart, stiffened the back, and made men more than men. It revealed the future, and gave visions and prophecy. It brimmed with wisdom and unfolded secrets. There was no end of the things it could do, and soon there was a clamoring on all hands to sleep with the gods. They brought their warmest furs, their strongest dogs, their best meats; but I sold the *hooch* with discretion, and only those were favored that brought flour and molasses and sugar. And such stores poured in that I set Moosu to build a caché to hold them, for there was soon no space in the igloo. Ere three days had passed Tummasook had gone bankrupt. The shaman, who was never more than half drunk after the first night, watched me closely and hung on for the better part of the week. But before ten days were gone even the woman Ipsukuk exhausted her provisions, and went home weak and tottery.

"But Moosu complained. 'O master,' he said, 'we have laid by great wealth in molasses and sugar and flour, but our shack is yet mean, our clothes thin, and our sleeping furs mangy. There is a call of the belly for meat the stench of which offends not the stars, and for tea such as Tummasook guzzles, and there is a great yearning for the tobacco of Neewak, who is shaman and who plans to destroy us. I have flour until I am sick, and sugar and molasses without stint, yet is the heart of Moosu sore and his bed empty.'

"'Peace!' I answered, 'thou art weak of understanding and a fool. Walk softly and wait, and we will grasp it all. But grasp now, and we grasp little, and in the end it will be nothing. Thou art a child in the way of the white man's wisdom. Hold thy tongue and watch, and I will show you the way my brothers do overseas, and, so doing, gather to themselves the riches of the earth. It is what is called "business," and what dost thou know about business?'

"But the next day he came in breathless. 'O master, a strange thing happeneth in the igloo of Neewak, the shaman; wherefore we are lost, and we have neither worn the warm furs nor tasted the good tobacco, what of your madness for the molasses and flour. Go thou and witness whilst I watch by the brew.'

"So I went to the igloo of Neewak. And behold, he had made his own still, fashioned cunningly after mine. And as he beheld me he could ill conceal his triumph. For he was a man of parts, and his sleep with the gods when in my igloo had not been sound.

"But I was not disturbed, for I knew what I knew, and when I returned to my own igloo, I descanted to Moosu and said: 'Happily the property right obtains amongst this people, who otherwise have been blessed with but few of the institutions of men. And because of this respect for property shall you and I wax fat, and, further, we shall introduce amongst them new institutions that other peoples have worked out through great travail and suffering.'

"But Moosu understood dimly, till the shaman came forth, with eyes flashing and a threatening note in his voice, and demanded to trade with me. 'For look you,' he cried, 'there be of flour and molasses none in all the village. The like have you gathered with a shrewd hand from my people, who have slept with your gods and who now have nothing save large heads, and weak knees, and a thirst for cold water that they cannot quench. This is not good, and my voice has power among them; so it were well that we trade, you and I, even as you have traded with them, for molasses and flour.'

"And I made answer: 'This be good talk, and wisdom abideth in thy mouth. We will trade. For this much of flour and molasses givest thou me the caddy of "Star" and the two buckets of smoking.'

"And Moosu groaned, and when the trade was made and the shaman departed, he upbraided me: 'Now, because of thy madness, are we, indeed, lost! Neewak maketh *hooch* on his own account, and when the time is ripe, he will command the people to drink of no *hooch* but his *hooch*. And in this way are we undone, and our goods worthless, and our igloo mean, and the bed of Moosu cold and empty!'

"And I answered: 'By the body of the wolf, say I, thou art a fool, and thy fathers before thee, and thy children after thee, down to the last generation. Thy wisdom is worse than no wisdom and thine eyes blinded to business, of which I have spoken and whereof thou knowest nothing. Go, thou son of a thousand fools, and drink of the *hooch* that Neewak brews in his igloo, and thank thy gods that thou hast a white man's wisdom to make soft the bed thou liest in. Go! and when thou hast drunken, return with the taste still on thy lips, that I may know.'

"And two days after, Neewak sent greeting and invitation to his igloo. Moosu went, but I sat alone, with the song of the still in my ears, and the air thick with the shaman's tobacco; for trade was slack that night, and no one dropped in but Angeit, a young hunter that had faith in me. Later, Moosu came back, his speech thick with chuckling and his eyes wrinkling with laughter.

"'Thou art a great man,' he said. 'Thou

art a great man, O master, and because of thy greatness thou wilt not condemn Moosu, thy servant, who ofttimes doubts and cannot be made to understand.'

"'And wherefore now?' I demanded. 'Hast thou drunk overmuch? And are they sleeping sound in the igloo of Neewak, the shaman?'

"'Nay, they are angered and sore of body, and Chief Tummasook has thrust his thumbs in the throat of Neewak, and sworn by the bones of his ancestors to look upon his face no more. For behold! I went to the igloo, and the brew simmered and bubbled, and the steam journeyed through the gooseneck even as thy steam, and even as thine it became water where it met the ice, and dropped into the pot at the far end. And Neewak gave us to drink, and lo, it was not like thine, for there was no bite to the tongue nor tingling to the eyeballs, and of a truth it was water. So we drank, and we drank overmuch; yet did we sit with cold hearts and solemn. And Neewak was perplexed and a cloud came on his brow. And he took Tummasook and Ipsukuk alone of all the company and sat them apart, and bade them drink and drink and drink. And they drank and drank and drank, and yet sat solemn and cold, till Tummasook arose in wrath and demanded back the furs and the tea he had paid. And Ipsukuk raised her voice, thin and angry. And the company demanded back what they had given, and there was a great commotion.'

"'Does the son of a dog deem me a whale?' demanded Tummasook, shoving back the skin flap and standing erect, his face black and his brows angry.

"'Wherefore I am filled, like a fish-bladder, to bursting, till I can scarce walk, what of the weight within me? Lalah! I have drunken as never before, yet are my eyes clear, my knees strong, my hand steady.'

"'The shaman cannot send us to sleep with the gods,' the people complained, stringing in and joining us, 'and only in thy igloo may the thing be done.'

"So I laughed to myself as I passed the *hooch* around and the guests made merry. For in the flour I had traded to Neewak I had mixed much soda that I had got from the woman Ipsukuk. So how could his brew ferment when the soda kept it sweet? Or his *hooch* be *hooch* when it would not sour?

"After that our wealth flowed in without let or hindrance. Furs we had without number, and the fancy work of the women, all of the chief's tea, and no end of meat. One day Moosu retold for my benefit, and sadly mangled, the story of Joseph in Egypt, but from it I got an idea, and soon I had half the tribe at work building me great meat cachés. And of all they hunted I got the lion's share and stored it away. Nor was Moosu idle. He made himself a pack of cards from birch bark, and taught Neewak the way to play seven-up. He also inveigled the father of Tukeliketa into the game. And one day he married the maiden, and the next day he moved into the shaman's house, which was the finest in the village. The fall of Neewak was complete, for he lost all his possessions, his walrus-hide drums, his incantation tools — everything. And in the end he became a hewer of wood and drawer of water at the beck and call of Moosu. And Moosu — he set himself up as shaman, or high priest, and out of his garbled Scripture created new gods and made incantation before strange altars.

"And I was well pleased, for I thought it good that church and state go hand in hand, and I had certain plans of my own concerning the state. Events were shaping as I had foreseen. Good temper and smiling faces had vanished from the village. The people were morose and sullen. There were quarrels and fighting, and things were in an uproar night and day. Moosu's cards were duplicated and the hunters fell to gambling among themselves. Tummasook beat his wife horribly, and his mother's brother objected and smote him with a tusk of walrus till he cried aloud in the night and was shamed before the people. Also, amid such diversions no hunting was done, and famine fell upon the land. The nights were long and dark, and without meat no *hooch* could be bought; so they murmured against the chief. This I had played for, and when they were well and hungry, I summoned the whole village, made a great harangue, posed as patriarch, and fed the famishing. Moosu made harangue likewise, and because of this and the thing I had done I was made chief. Moosu, who had the ear of God and decreed his judgments, anointed me with whale blubber, and right blubberly he did it, not understanding the ceremony. And between us we interpreted to the people the new theory of the divine right of kings. There was *hooch* galore, and meat and feasting, and they took kindly to the new order.

"So you see, O man, I have sat in the high places, and worn the purple, and ruled populations. And I might yet be a king had the tobacco held out, or had Moosu been more fool and less knave. For he cast eyes upon Esanetuk, eldest daughter to Tummasook, and I objected.

"'O brother,' he explained, 'thou has seen fit to speak of introducing new institutions amongst this people, and I have listened to thy words and gained wisdom thereby. Thou rulest by the God-given right, and by the God-given right I marry.'

"I noted that he 'brothered' me, and was angry and put my foot down. But he fell back upon the people and made incantations for three days, in which all hands joined; and then, speaking with the voice of God, he decreed polygamy by divine fiat. But he was shrewd, for he limited the number of wives by a property qualification, and because of which he, above all men, was favored by his wealth. Nor could I fail to admire, though it was plain that power had turned his head, and he would not be satisfied till all the power and all the wealth rested in his own hands. So he became swollen with pride, forgot it was I that had placed him there, and made preparations to destroy me.

"But it was interesting, for the beggar was working out in his own way an evolution of primitive society. Now I, by virtue of the *hooch* monopoly, drew a revenue in which I no longer permitted him to share. So he meditated for a while and evolved a system of ecclesiastical taxation. He laid tithes upon the people, harangued about fat firstlings and such things, and twisted whatever twisted texts he had ever heard to serve his purpose. Even this I bore in silence, but when he instituted what may be likened to a graduated income tax, I rebelled, and blindly, for this was what he worked for. Thereat, he appealed to the people, and they, envious of my great wealth and well taxed themselves, upheld him. 'Why should we pay,' they asked, 'and not you? Does not the voice of God speak through the lips of Moosu, the shaman?' So I yielded. But at the same time I raised the price of *hooch*, and lo, he was not a whit behind me in raising my taxes.

"Then there was open war. I made a play for Neewak and Tummasook, because of the traditionary rights they possessed; but Moosu won out by creating a priesthood and giving them both high office. The problem of authority presented itself to him, and he worked it out as it has often been worked before. There was my mistake. I should have been made shaman, and he chief; but I saw it too late, and in the clash of spiritual and temporal power I was bound to be worsted. A great controversy waged, but it quickly became one-sided. The people remembered that he had anointed me, and it was clear to them that the source of my authority lay, not in me, but in Moosu. Only a few faithful ones clung to me, chief among whom Angeit was; while he headed the popular party and set whispers afloat that I had it in mind to overthrow him and set up my own gods, which were most unrighteous gods. And in this the clever rascal had anticipated me, for it was just what I had intended — forsake my kingship, you see, and fight spiritual with spiritual. So he frightened the people with the iniquities of my peculiar gods — especially the one he named 'Biz-e-Nass' — and nipped the scheme in the bud.

"Now, it happened that Kluktu, youngest daughter to Tummasook, had caught my fancy, and I likewise hers. So I made overtures, but the ex-chief refused bluntly — after I had paid the purchase price — and informed me that she was set aside for Moosu. This was too much, and I was half of a mind to go to his igloo and slay him with my naked hands; but I recollected that the tobacco was near gone, and went home laughing. The next day he made incantation, and distorted the miracle of the loaves and fishes till it became prophecy, and I, reading between the lines, saw that it was aimed at the wealth of meat stored in my cachés. The people also read between the lines, and, as he did not urge them to go on the hunt, they remained at home, and few caribou or bear were brought in.

"But I had plans of my own, seeing that not only the tobacco but the flour and molasses were near gone. And further, I felt it my duty to prove the white man's wisdom and bring sore distress to Moosu, who had waxed high-stomached, what of the power

I had given him. So that night I went to my meat cachés and toiled mightily, and it was noted next day that all the dogs of the village were lazy. No one suspected, and I toiled thus every night, and the dogs grew fat and fatter, and the people lean and leaner. They grumbled and demanded the fulfilment of prophecy, but Moosu restrained them, waiting for their hunger to grow yet greater. Nor did he dream, to the very last, of the trick I had been playing on the empty cachés.

"When all was ready, I sent Angeit, and the faithful ones whom I had fed privily, through the village to call assembly. And the tribe gathered on a great space of beaten snow before my door, with the meat cachés towering stilt-legged in the rear. Moosu came also, standing on the inner edge of the circle opposite me, confident that I had some scheme afoot, and prepared at the first break to down me. But I arose, giving him salutation before all men.

"'O Moosu, thou blessed of God,' I began, 'doubtless thou has wondered in that I have called this convocation together; and doubtless, because of my many foolishnesses, art thou prepared for rash sayings and rash doings. Not so. It has been said, that those the gods would destroy they first make mad. And I have been indeed mad. I have crossed thy will, and scoffed at thy authority, and done divers evil and wanton things. Wherefore, last night a vision was vouchsafed me, and I have seen the wickedness of my ways. And thou stoodst forth like a shining star, with brows aflame, and I knew in mine own heart thy greatness. I saw all things clearly. I knew that thou didst command the ear of God, and that when you spoke he listened. And I remembered that whatever of the good deeds that I had done, I had done through the grace of God, and the grace of Moosu.

"'Yes, my children,' I cried, turning to the people, 'whatever right I have done, and whatever good I have done, have been because of the counsel of Moosu. When I listened to him, affairs prospered; when I closed my ears, and acted according to my folly, things came to folly. By his advice it was that I laid my store of meat, and in time of darkness fed the famishing. By his grace it was that I was made chief. And what have I done with my chiefship? Let me tell you. I have done nothing. My head was turned with power, and I deemed myself greater than Moosu, and, behold, I have come to grief. My rule has been unwise, and the gods are angered. Lo, ye are pinched with famine, and the mothers are dry-breasted, and the little babies cry through the long nights. Nor do I, who have hardened my heart against Moosu, know what shall be done, nor in what manner of way grub shall be had.'

"At this there was nodding and laughing, and the people put their heads together and I knew they whispered of the loaves and fishes. I went on hastily. 'So I was made aware of my foolishness and of Moosu's wisdom; of my own unfitness and of Moosu's fitness. And because of this, being no longer mad, I make acknowledgment and rectify evil. I did cast unrighteous eyes upon Kluktu, and lo, she was sealed to Moosu. Yet is she mine, for did I not pay to Tummasook the goods of purchase? But I am well unworthy of her, and she shall go from the igloo of her father to the igloo of Moosu. Can the moon shine in the sunshine? And further, Tummasook shall keep the goods of purchase, and she be a free gift to Moosu, whom God hath ordained her rightful lord.

"'And further yet, because I have used my wealth unwisely, and to oppress ye, O my children, do I make gifts of the kerosene can to Moosu, and the gooseneck, and the gun barrel, and the copper kettle. Therefore, I can gather to me no more possessions, and when ye are athirst for *hooch*, he will quench ye and without robbery. For he is a great man, and God speaketh through his lips.

"'And yet further, my heart is softened, and I have repented me of my madness. I, who am a fool and a son of fools; I, who am the slave of the bad god Biz-e-Nass; I, who see thy empty bellies and know not wherewith to fill them — why shall I be chief, and sit above thee, and rule to thine own destruction? Why should I do this, which is not good? But Moosu, who is shaman, and who is wise above men, is so made that he can rule with a soft hand and justly. And because of the things I have related do I make abdication and give my chiefship to Moosu, who alone knoweth how ye may be fed in this day when there be no meat in the land.'

"At this there was a great clapping of hands, and the people cried, '*Kloshe!*

Kloshe!' which means, 'good.' I had seen the wonder-worry in Moosu's eyes; for he could not understand, and was fearful of my white man's wisdom. I had met his wishes all along the line, and even anticipated some; and standing there, selfshorn of all my power, he knew the time did not favor to stir the people against me.

"Before they could disperse I made announcement that while the still went to Moosu, whatever *hooch* I possessed went to the people. Moosu tried to protest at this, for never had we permitted more than a handful to be drunk at a time; but they cried, *'Kloshe! Kloshe!'* and made festival before my door. And while they waxed uproarious without, as the liquor went to their heads, I held council within with Angeit and the faithful ones. I set them the tasks they were to do, and put into their mouths the words they were to say. Then I slipped away to a place back in the woods where I had two sleds, well loaded, with teams of dogs that were not overfed. Spring was at hand, you see, and there was a crust to the snow; so it was the best time to take the way south. Moreover, the tobacco was gone. There I waited, for I had nothing to fear. Did they bestir themselves on my trail, their dogs were too fat, and themselves too lean, to overtake me; also, I deemed their bestirring would be of an order for which I had made due preparation.

"First came a faithful one, running, and after him another. 'O master,' the first cried breathless, 'there be great confusion in the village, and no man knoweth his own mind, and they be of many minds. Everybody hath drunken overmuch, and some be stringing bows, and some be quarrelling one with another. Never was there such a trouble.'

"And the second one: 'And I did as thou biddest, O master, whispering shrewd words in thirsty ears, and raising memories of the things that were of old time. The woman Ipsukuk waileth her poverty and the wealth that no longer is hers. And Tummasook thinketh himself once again chief, and the people are hungry and rage up and down.'

"And a third one: 'And Neewak hath overthrown the altars of Moosu, and maketh incantation before the time-honored and ancient gods. And all the people remember the wealth that ran down their throats, and which they possess no more. And first, Esanetuk, who be *sick tumtum*, fought with Kluktu, and there was much noise. And next, being daughters of the one mother, did they fight with Tukeliketa. And after that did they three fall upon Moosu, like wind-squalls, from every hand, till he ran forth from the igloo, and the people mocked him. For a man who cannot command his womankind is a fool.'

"Then came Angeit: 'Great trouble hath befallen Moosu, O master, for I have whispered to advantage, till the people came to Moosu, saying they were hungry and demanding the fulfilment of prophecy. And there was a loud shout of "Itlwillie! Itlwillie!" (Meat.) So he cried peace to his womenfolk, who were overwrought with anger and with *hooch*, and led the tribe even to thy meat cachés. And he bade the men open them and be fed. And lo, the cachés were empty. There was no meat. They stood without sound, the people being frightened, and in the silence I lifted my voice. "O Moosu, where is the meat? That there was meat we know. Did we not hunt it and drag it in from the hunt? And it were a lie to say one man hath eaten it; yet have we seen nor hide nor hair. Where is the meat, O Moosu? Thou hast the ear of God. Where is the meat?"

"'And the people cried, "Thou hast the ear of God. Where is the meat?" And they put their heads together and were afraid. Then I went among them, speaking fearsomely of the unknown things, of the dead that come and go like shadows and do evil deeds, till they cried aloud in terror and gathered all together, like little children afraid of the dark. Neewak made harangue, laying this evil that had come upon them at the door of Moosu. When he had done, there was a furious commotion, and they took spears in their hands, and tusks of walrus, and clubs, and stones from the beach. But Moosu ran away home, and because he had not drunken of *hooch* they could not catch him, and fell one over another and made haste slowly. Even now they do howl without his igloo, and his womanfolk within, and what of the noise, he cannot make himself heard.'

"'O Angeit, thou hast done well,' I commended. 'Go now, taking this empty sled and the lean dogs, and ride fast to the igloo of Moosu; and before the people, who are drunken, are aware, throw him quick upon the sled and bring him to me.'

"I waited and gave good advice to the faithful ones till Angeit returned. Moosu was on the sled, and I saw by the finger-marks on his face that his womankind had done well by him. But he tumbled off and fell in the snow at my feet, crying: 'O master, thou wilt forgive Moosu, thy servant, for the wrong things he has done! Thou art a great man! Surely wilt thou forgive!'

"'Call me "brother," Moosu — call me "brother," ' I chided, lifting him to his feet with the toe of my moccasin. 'Wilt thou evermore obey?'

"'Yea, master,' he whimpered, 'evermore.'

"'Then dispose thy body, so, across the sled.' I shifted the dogwhip to my right hand. 'And direct thy face downward, toward the snow. And make haste, for we journey south this day.' And when he was well fixed I laid the lash upon him, reciting, at every stroke, the wrongs he had done me. 'This, for thy disobedience in general — whack! And this for thy disobedience in particular — whack! whack! And this for Esanetuk! And this for thy soul's welfare! And this for the grace of thy authority! And this for Kluktu! And this for thy rights God-given! And this for thy fat firstlings! And this and this for thy income tax and thy loaves and fishes! And this for all thy disobedience! And this, finally, that thou mayest henceforth walk softly and with understanding! Now cease thy sniffling and get up! Gird on thy snowshoes and go to the fore and break trail for the dogs. *Chook! Mush-on!* Git!' "

Thomas Stevens smiled quietly to himself as he lighted his fifth cigar and sent curling smoke-rings ceilingward.

"But how about the people of Tattarat?" I asked. "Kind of rough, wasn't it, to leave them flat with famine?"

And he answered, laughing, between two smoke-rings, "Were there not the fat dogs?"

20
Nam-Bok the Unveracious

NAM-BOK THE UNVERACIOUS

"A bidarka, is it not so? Look! a bidarka, and one man who drives clumsily with a paddle!"

Old Bask-Wah-Wan rose to her knees, trembling with weakness and eagerness, and gazed out over the sea.

"Nam-Bok was ever clumsy at the paddle," she maundered reminiscently, shading the sun from her eyes and staring across the silver-spilled water. "Nam-Bok was ever clumsy. I remember ..."

But the women and children laughed loudly, and there was a gentle mockery in their laughter, and her voice dwindled till her lips moved without sound.

Koogah lifted his grizzled head from his bone-carving and followed the path of her eyes. Except when wide yaws took it off its course, a bidarka was heading in for the beach. Its occupant was paddling with more strength than dexterity, and made his approach along the zigzag line of most resistance. Koogah's head dropped to his work again, and on the ivory tusk between his knees he scratched the dorsal fin of a fish the like of which never swam in the sea.

"It is doubtless the man from the next village," he said finally, "come to consult with me about the marking of things on bone. And the man is a clumsy man. He will never know how."

"It is Nam-Bok," old Bask-Wah-Wan repeated. "Should I not know my son?" she demanded shrilly. "I say, and I say again, it is Nam-Bok."

"And so thou hast said these many summers," one of the women chided softly. "Ever when the ice passed out of the sea hast thou sat and watched through the long day, saying at each chance canoe, 'This is Nam-Bok.' Nam-Bok is dead, O Bask-Wah-Wan, and the dead do not come back. It cannot be that the dead come back."

"Nam-Bok!" the old woman cried, so loud and clear that the whole village was startled and looked at her.

She struggled to her feet and tottered down the sand. She stumbled over a baby lying in the sun, and the mother hushed its crying and hurled harsh words after the old woman, who took no notice. The children ran down the beach in advance of her, and as the man in the bidarka drew closer, nearly capsizing with one of his ill-directed strokes, the women followed. Koogah dropped his walrus tusk and went also, leaning heavily upon his staff, and after him loitered the men in twos and threes.

The bidarka turned broadside and the ripple of surf threatened to swamp it, only a naked boy ran into the water and pulled the bow high up on the sand. The man stood up and sent a questing glance along the line of villagers. A rainbow sweater, dirty and the worse for wear, clung loosely to his broad shoulders, and a red cotton handkerchief was knotted in sailor fashion about his throat. A fisherman's tam-o'-shanter on his close-clipped head, and dungaree trousers and heavy brogans, completed his outfit.

But he was none the less a striking personage to these simple fisherfolk of the great Yukon Delta, who, all their lives, had stared out on Bering Sea and in that time seen but two white men, — the census enumerator and a lost Jesuit priest. They were a poor people, with neither gold in the ground nor valuable furs in hand, so the whites had passed them afar. Also, the Yukon, through the thousands of years, had shoaled that portion of the sea with the detritus of Alaska till vessels grounded out of sight of land. So the sodden coast, with its long inside reaches and huge mud-land archipelagoes, was avoided by the ships of men, and the fisherfolk knew not that such things were.

Koogah, the Bone-Scratcher, retreated backward in sudden haste, tripping over his staff and falling to the ground. "Nam-Bok!" he cried, as he scrambled wildly for footing. "Nam-Bok, who was blown off to sea, come back!"

The men and women shrank away, and the children scuttled off between their legs. Only Opee-Kwan was brave, as befitted the head man of the village. He strode forward and gazed long and earnestly at the newcomer.

"It *is* Nam-Bok," he said at last, and at the conviction in his voice the women wailed apprehensively and drew farther away.

The lips of the stranger moved indecisively, and his brown throat writhed and wrestled with unspoken words.

"La la, it is Nam-Bok," Bask-Wah-Wan croaked, peering up into his face. "Ever did I say Nam-Bok would come back."

"Ay, it is Nam-Bok come back." This time it was Nam-Bok himself who spoke, putting a leg over the side of the bidarka and standing with one foot afloat and one ashore. Again his throat writhed and wrestled as he grappled after forgotten words. And when the words came forth they were strange of sound and a spluttering of the lips accompanied the gutturals. "Greeting, O brothers," he said, "brothers of old time before I went away with the off-shore wind."

He stepped out with both feet on the sand, and Opee-Kwan waved him back.

"Thou art dead, Nam-Bok," he said.

Nam-Bok laughed. "I am fat."

"Dead men are not fat," Opee-Kwan confessed. "Thou hast fared well, but it is strange. No man may mate with the off-shore wind and come back on the heels of the years."

"I have come back," Nam-Bok answered simply.

"Mayhap thou art a shadow, then, a passing shadow of the Nam-Bok that was. Shadows come back."

"I am hungry. Shadows do not eat."

But Opee-Kwan doubted, and brushed his hand across his brow in sore puzzlement. Nam-Bok was likewise puzzled, and as he looked up and down the line found no welcome in the eyes of the fisherfolk. The men and women whispered together. The children stole timidly back among their elders, and bristling dogs fawned up to him and sniffed suspiciously.

"I bore thee, Nam-Bok, and I gave thee suck when thou wast little," Bask-Wah-Wan whimpered, drawing closer; "and shadow though thou be, or no shadow, I will give thee to eat now."

Nam-Bok made to come to her, but a growl of fear and menace warned him back. He said something in a strange tongue which sounded like "Goddam," and added, "No shadow am I, but a man."

"Who may know concerning the things of mystery?" Opee-Kwan demanded, half of himself and half of his tribespeople. "We are, and in a breath we are not. If the man may become shadow, may not the shadow become man? Nam-Bok was, but is not. This we know, but we do not know if this be Nam-Bok or the shadow of Nam-Bok."

Nam-Bok cleared his throat and made answer. "In the old time long ago, thy father's father, Opee-Kwan, went away and came back on the heels of the years. Nor was a place by the fire denied him. It is said..." He paused significantly, and they hung on his utterance. "It is said," he repeated, driving his point home with deliberation, "that Sipsip, his *klooch,* bore him two sons after he came back."

"But he had no doings with the off-shore wind," Opee-Kwan retorted. "He went away into the heart of the land, and it is in the nature of things that a man may go on and on into the land."

"And likewise the sea. But that is neither here nor there. It is said... that thy father's father told strange tales of the things he saw."

"Ay, strange tales he told."

"I, too, have strange tales to tell," Nam-Bok stated insidiously. And, as they wavered, "And presents likewise."

He pulled from the bidarka a shawl, marvellous of texture and color, and flung it about his mother's shoulders. The women voiced a collective sigh of admiration, and old Bask-Wah-Wan ruffled the gay material and patted it and crooned in childish joy.

"He has tales to tell," Koogah muttered. "And presents," a woman seconded.

And Opee-Kwan knew that his people were eager, and further, he was aware himself of an itching curiosity concerning those untold tales. "The fishing has been good," he said judiciously, "and we have oil in plenty. So come, Nam-Bok, let us feast."

Two of the men hoisted the bidarka on their shoulders and carried it up to the fire. Nam-Bok walked by the side of Opee-Kwan, and the villagers followed after, save those of the women who lingered a moment to lay caressing fingers on the shawl.

There was little talk while the feast went on, though many and curious were the glances stolen at the son of Bask-Wah-Wan. This embarrassed him — not because he was modest of spirit, however, but for the fact that the stench of the seal-oil had robbed him of his appetite, and that he keenly desired to conceal his feelings on the subject.

"Eat; thou art hungry," Opee-Kwan commanded, and Nam-Bok shut both his eyes and shoved his fist into the big pot of putrid fish.

"La la, be not ashamed. The seal were many this year, and strong men are ever hungry." And Bask-Wah-Wan sopped a particularly offensive chunk of salmon into the oil and passed it fondly and dripping to her son.

In despair, when premonitory symptoms warned him that his stomach was not so strong as of old, he filled his pipe and struck up a smoke. The people fed on noisily and watched. Few of them could boast of intimate acquaintance with the precious weed, though now and again small quantities and abominable qualities were obtained in trade from the Eskimos to the northward. Koogah, sitting next to him, indicated that he was not averse to taking a draw, and between two mouthfuls, with the oil thick on his lips, sucked away at the amber stem. And thereupon Nam-Bok held his stomach with a shaky hand and declined the proffered return. Koogah could keep the pipe, he said, for he had intended so to honor him from the first. And the people licked their fingers and approved of his liberality.

Opee-Kwan rose to his feet. "And now, O Nam-Bok, the feast is ended, and we would listen concerning the strange things you have seen."

The fisherfolk applauded with their hands, and gathering about them their work, prepared to listen. The men were busy fashioning spears and carving on ivory, while the women scraped the fat from the hides of the hair seal and made them pliable or sewed muclucs with threads of sinew. Nam-Bok's eyes roved over the scene, but there was not the charm about it that his recollection had warranted him to expect. During the years of his wandering he had looked forward to just this scene, and now that it had come he was disappointed. It was a bare and meagre life, he deemed, and not to be compared to the one to which he had become used. Still, he would open their eyes a bit, and his own eyes sparkled at the thought.

"Brothers," he began, with the smug complacency of a man about to relate the big things he has done, "it was late summer of many summers back, with much such weather as this promises to be, when I went away. You all remember the day, when the gulls flew low, and the wind blew strong from the land, and I could not hold my bidarka against it. I tied the covering of the bidarka about me so that no water could get in, and all of the night I fought with the storm. And in the morning there was no land,—only the sea,—and the off-shore wind held me close in its arms and bore me along. Three such nights whitened into dawn and showed me no land, and the off-shore wind would not let me go.

"And when the fourth day came, I was as a madman. I could not dip my paddle for want of food; and my head went round and round, what of the thirst that was upon me. But the sea was no longer angry, and the soft south wind was blowing, and as I looked about me I saw a sight that made me think I was indeed mad."

Nam-Bok paused to pick away a sliver of salmon lodged between his teeth, and the men and women, with idle hands and heads craned forward, waited.

"It was a canoe, a big canoe. If all the canoes I have ever seen were made into one canoe, it would not be so large."

There were exclamations of doubt, and Koogah, whose years were many, shook his head.

"If each bidarka were as a grain of sand," Nam-Bok defiantly continued, "and if there were as many bidarkas as there be grains of sand in this beach, still would they not make so big a canoe as this I saw on the morning of the fourth day. It was a very big canoe, and it was called a *schooner*. I saw this thing of wonder, this great schooner, coming after me, and on it I saw men—"

"Hold, O Nam-Bok!" Opee-Kwan broke in. "What manner of men were they? — big men?"

"Nay, mere men like you and me."

"Did the big canoe come fast?"

"Ay."

"The sides were tall, the men short." Opee-Kwan stated the premises with conviction. "And did these men dip with long paddles?"

Nam-Bok grinned. "There were no paddles," he said.

Mouths remained open, and a long silence dropped down. Opee-Kwan borrowed Koogah's pipe for a couple of contemplative sucks. One of the younger women giggled nervously and drew upon herself angry eyes.

"There were no paddles?" Opee-Kwan asked softly, returning the pipe.

"The south wind was behind," Nam-Bok explained.

"But the wind-drift is slow."

"The schooner had wings—thus." He sketched a diagram of masts and sails in the sand, and the men crowded around and studied it. The wind was blowing briskly, and for more graphic elucidation he seized the corners of his mother's shawl and spread them out till it bellied like a sail. Bask-Wah-Wan scolded and struggled, but was blown down the beach for a score of feet and left breathless and stranded in a heap of driftwood. The men uttered sage grunts of comprehension, but Koogah suddenly tossed back his hoary head.

"Ho! Ho!" he laughed. "A foolish thing, this big canoe! A most foolish thing! The plaything of the wind! Wheresoever the wind goes, it goes too. No man who journeys therein may name the landing beach, for always he goes with the wind, and the wind goes everywhere, but no man knows where."

"It is so," Opee-Kwan supplemented gravely. "With the wind the going is easy, but against the wind a man striveth hard; and for that they had no paddles these men on the big canoe did not strive at all."

"Small need to strive," Nam-Bok cried angrily. "The schooner went likewise against the wind."

"And what said you made the sch—sch—schooner go?" Koogah asked, tripping craftily over the strange word.

"The wind," was the impatient response.

"Then the wind made the sch—sch—schooner go against the wind." Old Koogah dropped an open leer to Opee-Kwan, and, the laughter growing around him, continued: "The wind blows from the south and blows the schooner south. The wind blows against the wind. The wind blows one way and the other at the same time. It is very simple. We understand, Nam-Bok. We clearly understand."

"Thou art a fool!"

"Truth falls from thy lips," Koogah answered meekly. "I was over-long in understanding, and the thing was simple."

But Nam-Bok's face was dark, and he said rapid words which they had never heard before. Bone-scratching and skin-scraping were resumed, but he shut his lips tightly on the tongue that could not be believed.

"This sch—sch—schooner," Koogah imperturbably asked; "it was made of a big tree?"

"It was made of many trees," Nam-Bok snapped shortly. "It was very big."

He lapsed into sullen silence again, and Opee-Kwan nudged Koogah, who shook his head with slow amazement and murmured, "It is very strange."

Nam-Bok took the bait. "That is nothing," he said airily; "you should see the *steamer*. As the grain of sand is to the bidarka, as the bidarka is to the schooner, so the schooner is to the steamer. Further, the steamer is made of iron. It is all iron."

"Nay, nay, Nam-Bok," cried the head man; "how can that be? Always iron goes to the bottom. For behold, I received an iron knife in trade from the head man of the next village, and yesterday the iron knife slipped from my fingers and went down, down, into the sea. To all things there be law. Never was there one thing outside the law. This we know. And, moreover, we know that things of a kind have the one law, and that all iron has the one law. So unsay thy words, Nam-Bok, that we may yet honor thee."

"It is so," Nam-Bok persisted. "The steamer is all iron and does not sink."

"Nay, nay; this cannot be."

"With my own eyes I saw it."

"It is not in the nature of things."

"But tell me, Nam-Bok," Koogah interrupted, for fear the tale would go no farther, "tell me the manner of these men in finding their way across the sea when there is no land by which to steer."

"The sun points out the path."

"But how?"

"At midday the head man of the schooner takes a thing through which his eye looks at the sun, and then he makes the sun climb down out of the sky to the edge of the earth."

"Now this be evil medicine!" cried Opee-Kwan, aghast at the sacrilege. The men held up their hands in horror, and the women moaned. "This be evil medicine. It is not good to misdirect the great sun which drives away the night and gives us the seal, the salmon, and warm weather."

"What if it be evil medicine?" Nam-Bok demanded truculently. "I, too, have looked through the thing at the sun and made the sun climb down out of the sky."

Those who were nearest drew away from him hurriedly, and a woman covered the face of a child at her breast so that his eye might not fall upon it.

"But on the morning of the fourth day, O Nam-Bok," Koogah suggested; "on the morning of the fourth day when the sch—sch—schooner came after thee?"

"I had little strength left in me and could not run away. So I was taken on board and water was poured down my throat and good food given me. Twice, my brothers, you have seen a white man. These men were all white and as many as have I fingers and toes. And when I saw they were full of kindness, I took heart, and I resolved to bring away with me report of all that I saw. And they taught me the work they did, and gave me good food and a place to sleep.

"And day after day we went over the sea, and each day the head man drew the sun down out of the sky and made it tell where we were. And when the waves were kind, we hunted the fur seal and I marvelled much, for always did they fling the meat and the fat away and save only the skin."

Opee-Kwan's mouth was twitching violently, and he was about to make denunciation of such waste when Koogah kicked him to be still.

"After a weary time, when the sun was gone and the bite of the frost come into the air, the head man pointed the nose of the schooner south. South and east we travelled for days upon days, with never the land in sight, and we were near to the village from which hailed the men—"

"How did they know they were near?" Opee-Kwan, unable to contain himself longer, demanded. "There was no land to see."

Nam-Bok glowered on him wrathfully. "Did I not say the head man brought the sun down out of the sky?"

Koogah interposed, and Nam-Bok went on.

"As I say, when we were near to that village a great storm blew up, and in the night we were helpless and knew not where we were—"

"Thou hast just said the head man knew—"

"Oh, peace, Opee-Kwan! Thou art a fool and cannot understand. As I say, we were helpless in the night, when I heard, above the roar of the storm, the sound of the sea on the beach. And next we struck with a mighty crash and I was in the water, swimming. It was a rock-bound coast, with one patch of beach in many miles, and the law was that I should dig my hands into the sand and draw myself clear of the surf. The other men must have pounded against the rocks, for none of them came ashore but the head man, and him I knew only by the ring on his finger.

"When day came, there being nothing of the schooner, I turned my face to the land and journeyed into it that I might get food and look upon the faces of the people. And when I came to a house I was taken in and given to eat, for I had learned their speech, and the white men are ever kindly. And it was a house bigger than all the houses built by us and our fathers before us."

"It was a mighty house," Koogah said, masking his unbelief with wonder.

"And many trees went into the making of such a house," Opee-Kwan added, taking the cue.

"That is nothing." Nam-Bok shrugged his shoulders in belittling fashion. "As our houses are to that house, so that house was to the houses I was yet to see."

"And they are not big men?"

"Nay; mere men like you and me," Nam-Bok answered. "I had cut a stick that I might walk in comfort, and remembering that I was to bring report to you, my brothers, I cut a notch in the stick for each person who lived in that house. And I stayed there many days, and worked, for which they gave me *money*—a thing of which you know nothing, but which is very good.

"And one day I departed from that place to go farther into the land. And as I walked I met many people, and I cut smaller notches in the stick, that there might be room for all. Then I came upon a strange thing. On the ground before me was a bar of iron, as big in thickness as my arm, and a long step away was another bar of iron—"

"Then wert thou a rich man," Opee-Kwan asserted; "for iron be worth more than anything else in the world. It would have made many knives."

"Nay, it was not mine."

"It was a find, and a find be lawful."

"Not so; the white men had placed it there. And further, these bars were so long that no man could carry them away—so long that as far as I could see there was no end to them."

"Nam-Bok, that is very much iron. Opee-Kwan cautioned.

"Ay, it was hard to believe with my own eyes upon it; but I could not gainsay my eyes. And as I looked I heard ..." He turned abruptly upon the head man. "Opee-Kwan, thou hast heard the sea-lion bellow in his anger. Make it plain in thy mind of as many sea-lions as there be waves to the sea, and make it plain that all these sea-lions be made into one sea-lion, and as that one sea-lion would bellow so bellowed the thing I heard."

The fisherfolk cried aloud in astonishment, and Opee-Kwan's jaw lowered and remained lowered.

"And in the distance I saw a monster like unto a thousand whales. It was one-eyed, and vomited smoke, and it snorted with exceeding loudness. I was afraid and ran with shaking legs along the path between the bars. But it came with the speed of the wind, this monster, and I leaped the iron bars with its breath hot on my face..."

Opee-Kwan gained control of his jaw again. "And—and then, O Nam-Bok?"

"Then it came by on the bars, and harmed me not; and when my legs could hold me up again it was gone from sight. And it is a very common thing in that country. Even the women and children are not afraid. Men make them to do work, these monsters."

"As we make our dogs do work?" Koogah asked, with sceptic twinkle in his eye.

"Ay, as we make our dogs do work."

"And how do they breed these—these things?" Opee-Kwan questioned.

"They breed not at all. Men fashion them cunningly of iron, and feed them with stone, and give them water to drink. The stone becomes fire, and the water becomes steam, and the steam of the water is the breath of their nostrils, and—"

"There, there, O Nam-Bok," Opee-Kwan interrupted. "Tell us of other wonders. We grow tired of this which we may not understand."

"You do not understand?" Nam-Bok asked despairingly.

"Nay, we do not understand," the men and women wailed back. "We cannot understand."

Nam-Bok thought of a combined harvester, and of the machines wherein visions of living men were to be seen, and of the machines from which came the voices of men, and he knew his people could never understand.

"Dare I say I rode this iron monster through the land?" he asked bitterly.

Opee-Kwan threw up his hands, palms outward, in open incredulity. "Say on; say anything. We listen."

"Then did I ride the iron monster, for which I gave money—"

"Thou saidst it was fed with stone."

"And likewise, thou fool, I said money was a thing of which you know nothing. As I say, I rode the monster through the land, and through many villages, until I came to a big village on a salt arm of the sea. And the houses shoved their roofs among the stars in the sky, and the clouds drifted by them, and everywhere was much smoke. And the roar of that village was like the roar of the sea in storm, and the people were so many that I flung away my stick and no longer remembered the notches upon it."

"Hadst thou made small notches," Koogah reproved, "thou mightst have brought report."

Nam-Bok whirled upon him in anger. "Had I made small notches! Listen, Koogah, thou scratcher of bone! If I had made small notches, neither the stick, nor twenty sticks, could have borne them — nay, not all the driftwood of all the beaches between this village and the next. And if all of you, the women and children as well, were twenty times as many, and if you had twenty hands each, and in each hand a stick and a knife, still the notches could not be cut for the people I saw, so many were they and so fast did they come and go."

"There cannot be so many people in all the world," Opee-Kwan objected, for he was stunned and his mind could not grasp such magnitude of numbers.

"What dost thou know of all the world and how large it is?" Nam-Bok demanded.

"But there cannot be so many people in one place."

"Who art thou to say what can be and what can not be?"

"It stands to reason there cannot be so many people in one place. Their canoes would clutter the sea till there was no room. And they could empty the sea each day of its fish, and they would not all be fed."

"So it would seem," Nam-Bok made final answer; "yet it was so. With my own eyes I saw, and flung my stick away." He yawned heavily and rose to his feet. "I have paddled far. The day has been long, and I am tired. Now I will sleep, and to-morrow we will have further talk upon the things I have seen."

Bask-Wah-Wan, hobbling fearfully in advance, proud indeed, yet awed by her wonderful son, led him to her igloo and stowed him away among the greasy, ill-smelling furs. But the men lingered by the fire, and a council was held wherein was there much whispering and low-voiced discussion.

An hour passed, and a second, and Nam-Bok slept, and the talk went on. The evening sun dipped toward the northwest, and at eleven at night was nearly due north. Then it was that the head man and the bone-scratcher separated themselves from the council and aroused Nam-Bok. He blinked up into their faces and turned on his side to sleep again. Opee-Kwan gripped him by the arm and kindly but firmly shook his senses back into him.

"Come, Nam-Bok, arise!" he commanded. "It be time."

"Another feast?" Nam-Bok cried. "Nay, I am not hungry. Go on with the eating and let me sleep."

"Time to be gone!" Koogah thundered.

But Opee-Kwan spoke more softly. "Thou wast bidarka-mate with me when we were boys," he said. "Together we first chased the seal and drew the salmon from the traps. And thou didst drag me back to life, Nam-Bok, when the sea closed over me and I was sucked down to the black rocks. Together we hungered and bore the chill of the frost, and together we crawled beneath the one fur and lay close to each other. And because of these things, and the kindness in which I stood to thee, it grieves me sore that thou shouldst return such a remarkable liar. We cannot understand, and our heads be dizzy with the things thou hast spoken. It is not good, and there has been much talk in the council. Wherefore we send thee away, that our heads may remain clear and strong and be not troubled by the unaccountable things."

"These things thou speakest of be shadows," Koogah took up the strain. "From the shadow-world thou hast brought them, and to the shadow-world thou must return them. Thy bidarka be ready, and the tribespeople wait. They may not sleep until thou art gone."

Nam-Bok was perplexed, but hearkened to the voice of the head man.

"If thou art Nam-Bok," Opee-Kwan was saying, "thou art a fearful and most wonderful liar; if thou art the shadow of Nam-Bok, then thou speakest of shadows, concerning which it is not good that living men have knowledge. This great village thou hast spoken of we deem the village of shadows. Therein flutter the souls of the dead; for the dead be many and the living few. The dead do not come back. Never have the dead come back — save thou with thy wonder-tales. It is not meet that the dead come back, and should we permit it, great trouble may be our portion."

Nam-Bok knew his people well and was aware that the voice of the council was supreme. So he allowed himself to be led down to the water's edge, where he was put aboard his bidarka and a paddle thrust into his hand. A stray wild-fowl honked somewhere to seaward, and the surf broke limply and hollowly on the sand. A dim twilight brooded over land and water, and in the north the sun smouldered, vague and troubled, and draped about with blood-red mists. The gulls were flying low. The off-shore wind blew keen and chill, and the black-massed clouds behind it gave promise of bitter weather.

"Out of the sea thou camest," Opee-Kwan chanted oracularly, "and back into the sea thou goest. Thus is balance achieved and all things brought to law."

Bask-Wah-Wan limped to the froth-mark and cried, "I bless thee, Nam-Bok, for that thou remembered me."

But Koogah, shoving Nam-Bok clear of the beach, tore the shawl from her shoulders and flung it into the bidarka.

"It is cold in the long nights," she wailed; "and the frost is prone to nip old

A shaft of light shot across the dim-lit sea and wrapped boat and man in a splendor of red and gold

bones."

"The thing is a shadow," the bone-scratcher answered, "and shadows cannot keep thee warm."

Nam-Bok stood up that his voice might carry. "O Bask-Wah-Wan, mother that bore me!" he called. "Listen to the words of Nam-Bok, thy son. There be room in his bidarka for two, and he would that thou camest with him. For his journey is to where there are fish and oil in plenty. There the frost comes not, and life is easy, and the things of iron do the work of men. Wilt thou come, O Bask-Wah-Wan?"

She debated a moment, while the bidarka drifted swiftly from her, then raised her voice to a quavering treble. "I am old, Nam-Bok, and soon I shall pass down among the shadows. But I have no wish to go before my time. I am old, Nam-Bok, and I am afraid."

A shaft of light shot across the dim-lit sea and wrapped boat and man in a splendor of red and gold. Then a hush fell upon the fisherfolk, and only was heard the moan of the off-shore wind and the cries of the gulls flying low in the air.

21
The Death of Ligoun

THE DEATH OF LIGOUN

"Hear now the death of Ligoun —"

The speaker ceased, or rather suspended utterance, and gazed upon me with an eye of understanding. I held the bottle between our eyes and the fire, indicated with my thumb the depth of the draught, and shoved it over to him; for was he not Palitlum, the Drinker? Many tales had he told me, and long had I waited for this scriptless scribe to speak of the things concerning Ligoun; for he, of all men living, knew these things best.

He tilted back his head with a grunt that slid swiftly into a gurgle, and the shadow of man's torso, monstrous beneath a huge inverted bottle, wavered and danced on the frown of the cliff at our backs. Palitlum released his lips from the glass with a caressing suck and glanced regretfully up into the ghostly vault of the sky where played the wan white light of the summer borealis.

"It be strange," he said; "cold like water and hot like fire. To the drinker it giveth strength, and from the drinker it taketh away strength. It maketh old men young, and young men old. To the man who is weary it leadeth him to get up and go onward, and to the man unweary it burdeneth him into sleep. My brother was possessed of the heart of a rabbit, yet did he drink of it, and forthwith slay four of his enemies. My father was like a great wolf, showing his teeth to all men, yet did he drink of it and was shot through the back, running swiftly away. It be most strange."

"It is 'Three Star,' and a better than what they poison their bellies with down there," I answered, sweeping my hand, as it were, over the yawning chasm of blackness and down to where the beach fires glinted far below — tiny jets of flame which gave proportion and reality to the night.

Palitlum sighed and shook his head. "Wherefore I am here with thee."

And here he embraced the bottle and me in a look which told more eloquently than speech of his shameless thirst.

"Nay," I said, snuggling the bottle in between my knees. "Speak now of Ligoun. Of the 'Three Star' we will hold speech hereafter."

"There be plenty, and I am not wearied," he pleaded brazenly. "But the feel of it on my lips, and I will speak great words of Ligoun and his last days."

"From the drinker it taketh away strength," I mocked, "and to the man unweary it burdeneth him into sleep."

"Thou art wise," he rejoined, without anger and pridelessly. "Like all of thy brothers, thou art wise. Waking or sleeping, the 'Three Star' be with thee, yet never have I known thee to drink overlong or overmuch. And the while you gather to you the gold that hides in our mountains and the fish that swim in our seas; and Palitlum, and the brothers of Palitlum, dig the gold for thee and net the fish, and are glad to be made glad when out of thy wisdom thou deemest it fit that the 'Three Star' should wet our lips."

"I was minded to hear of Ligoun," I said impatiently. "The night grows short, and we have a sore journey to-morrow."

I yawned and made as though to rise, but Palitlum betrayed a quick anxiety, and with abruptness began:—

"It was Ligoun's desire, in his old age, that peace should be among the tribes. As a young man he had been first of the fighting men and chief over the war-chiefs of the Islands and the Passes. All his days had been full of fighting. More marks he boasted of bone and lead and iron than any other man. Three wives he had, and for each wife two sons; and the sons, eldest born and last and all, died by his side in battle. Restless as the bald-face, he ranged wide and far — north to Unalaska and the Shallow Sea; south to the Queen Charlottes, ay, even did he go with the Kakes, it is told, to far Puget Sound, and slay thy brothers in their sheltered houses.

"But, as I say, in his old age he looked for peace among the tribes. Not that he was become afraid, or overfond of the corner by the fire and the well-filled pot. For he slew with the shrewdness and blood-hunger of the fiercest, drew in his belly to famine with the youngest, and with the stoutest faced the bitter seas and stinging trail. But because of his many deeds, and in punishment, a warship carried him away, even to thy country, O Hair-Face and Boston Man; and the years were many ere he came back, and I was grown to something more than a boy and something less than a young man. And Ligoun, being childless in his old age, made much of me, and grown wise, gave me of his wisdom.

"'It be good to fight, O Palitlum,' said he. Nay, O Hair-Face, for I was unknown as Palitlum in those days, being called Olo, the Ever-Hungry. The drink was to come after. 'It be good to fight,' spake Ligoun, 'but it be foolish. In the Boston Man Country, as I saw with mine eyes, they are not given to fighting one with another, and they be strong. Wherefore, of their strength, they come against us of the Islands and Passes, and we are as camp smoke and sea mist before them. Wherefore I say it be good to fight, most good, but it be likewise foolish.'

"And because of this, though first always of the fighting men, Ligoun's voice was loudest, ever, for peace. And when he was very old, being greatest of chiefs and richest of men, he gave a potlatch. Never was there such a potlatch. Five hundred canoes were lined against the river bank, and in each canoe there came not less than ten of men and women. Eight tribes were there; from the first and oldest man to the last and youngest babe were they there. And then there were men from far-distant tribes, great travellers and seekers who had heard of the potlatch of Ligoun. And for the length of seven days they filled their bellies with his meat and drink. Eight thousand blankets did he give to them, as I well know, for who but I kept the tally and apportioned according to degree and rank? And in the end Ligoun was a poor man; but his name was on all men's lips, and other chiefs gritted their teeth in envy that he should be so great.

"And so, because there was weight to his words, he counselled peace; and he journeyed to every potlatch and feast and tribal gathering that he might counsel peace. And so it came that we journeyed together, Ligoun and I, to the great feast given by Niblack, who was chief over the river Indians of the Skoot, which is not far from the Stickeen. This was in the last days, and Ligoun was very old and very close to death. He coughed of cold weather and camp smoke, and often the red blood ran from out his mouth till we looked for him to die.

"'Nay,' he said once at such time; 'it were better that I should die when the blood leaps to the knife, and there is a clash of steel and smell of powder, and men crying aloud what of the cold iron and quick lead.' So, it be plain, O Hair-Face, that his heart was yet strong for battle.

"It is very far from the Chilcat to the Skoot, and we were many days in the canoes. And the while the men bent to the paddles, I sat at the feet of Ligoun and received the Law. Of small need for me to say the Law, O Hair-Face, for it be known to me that in this thou art well skilled. Yet do I speak of the Law of blood for blood, and rank for rank. Also did Ligoun go deeper into the matter, saying:—

"'But know this, O Olo, that there be little honor in the killing of a man less than thee. Kill always the man who is greater, and thy honor shall be according to his greatness. But if, of two men, thou killest the lesser, then is shame thine, for which the very squaws will lift their lips at thee. As I say, peace be good; but remember, O Olo, if kill thou must, that thou killest by the Law.'

"It is a way of the Thlinket-folk," Palitlum vouchsafed half apologetically.

And I remembered the gun-fighters and bad men of my own Western land, and was not perplexed at the way of the Thlinket-folk.

"In time," Palitlum continued, "we came to Chief Niblack and the Skoots. It was a feast great almost as the potlatch of Ligoun. There were we of the Chilcat, and the Sitkas, and the Stickeens who are neighbors to the Skoots, and the Wrangels and the Hoonahs. There were Sundowns and Tahkos from Port Houghton, and their neighbors the Awks from Douglass Channel; the Naass River people, and the Tongas from north of Dixon, and the Kakes who come from the island called Kupreanoff. Then there were Siwashes from Vancouver, Cassiars from the Gold Mountains,

Teslin men, and even Sticks from the Yukon Country.

"It was a mighty gathering. But first of all, there was to be a meeting of the chiefs with Niblack, and a drowning of all enmities in quass. The Russians it was who showed us the way of making quass, for so my father told me, — my father, who got it from his father before him. But to this quass had Niblack added many things, such as sugar, flour, dried apples, and hops, so that it was a man's drink, strong and good. Not so good as 'Three Star,' O Hair-Face, yet good.

"This quass-feast was for the chiefs, and the chiefs only, and there was a score of them. But Ligoun being very old and very great, it was given that I walk with him that he might lean upon my shoulder and that I might ease him down when he took his seat and raise him up when he arose. At the door of Niblack's house, which was of logs and very big, each chief, as was the custom, laid down his spear or rifle and his knife. For as thou knowest, O Hair-Face, strong drink quickens, and old hates flame up, and head and hand are swift to act. But I noted that Ligoun had brought two knives, the one he left outside the door, the other slipped under his blanket, snug to the grip. The other chiefs did likewise, and I was troubled for what was to come.

"The chiefs were ranged, sitting, in a big circle about the room. I stood at Ligoun's elbow. In the middle was the barrel of quass, and by it a slave to serve the drink. First, Niblack made oration, with much show of friendship and many fine words. Then he gave a sign, and the slave dipped a gourd full of quass and passed it to Ligoun, as was fit, for his was the highest rank.

"Ligoun drank it, to the last drop, and I gave him my strength to get on his feet so that he, too, might make oration. He had kind speech for the many tribes, noted the greatness of Niblack to give such a feast, counselled for peace as was his custom, and at the end said that the quass was very good.

"Then Niblack drank, being next of rank to Ligoun, and after him one chief and another in degree and order. And each spoke friendly words and said that the quass was good, till all had drunk. Did I say all? Nay, not all, O Hair-Face. For last of them was one, a lean and cat-like man, young of face, with a quick and daring eye, who drank darkly, and spat forth upon the ground, and spoke no word.

"To not say that the quass was good were insult; to spit forth upon the ground were worse than insult. And this very thing did he do. He was known for a chief over the Sticks of the Yukon, and further naught was known of him.

"As I say, it was an insult. But mark this, O Hair-Face: it was an insult, not to Niblack the feast-giver, but to the man chiefest of rank who sat among those of the circle. And that man was Ligoun. There was no sound. All eyes were upon him to see what he might do. He made no movement. His withered lips trembled not into speech; nor did a nostril quiver, nor an eyelid droop. But I saw that he looked wan and gray, as I have seen old men look of bitter mornings when famine pressed, and the women wailed and the children whimpered, and there was no meat nor sign of meat. And as the old men looked, so looked Ligoun.

"There was no sound. It were as a circle of the dead, but that each chief felt beneath his blanket to make sure, and that each chief glanced to his neighbor, right and left, with a measuring eye. I was a stripling; the things I had seen were few; yet I knew it to be the moment one meets but once in all a lifetime.

"The Stick rose up, with every eye upon him, and crossed the room till he stood before Ligoun.

"'I am Opitsah, the Knife,' he said.

"But Ligoun said naught, nor looked at him, but gazed unblinking at the ground.

"'You are Ligoun,' Opitsah said. 'You have killed many men. I am still alive.'

"And still Ligoun said naught, though he made the sign to me and with my strength arose and stood upright on his two feet. He was as an old pine, naked and gray, but still a-shoulder to the frost and storm. His eyes were unblinking, and as he had not heard Opitsah, so it seemed he did not see him.

"And Opitsah was mad with anger, and danced stiff-legged before him, as men do when they wish to give another shame. And Opitsah sang a song of his own greatness and the greatness of his people, filled with bad words for the Chilcats and for Ligoun. And as he danced and sang, Opitsah threw off his blanket and with his knife drew bright circles before the face of Ligoun. And the song he sang was the Song of the Knife.

"And there was no other sound, only the singing of Opitsah, and the circle of chiefs that were as dead, save that the flash of the knife seemed to draw smouldering fire from their eyes. And Ligoun, also, was very still. Yet did he know his death, and was unafraid. And the knife sang closer and yet closer to his face, but his eyes were unblinking and he swayed not to right or left, or this way or that.

"And Opitsah drove in the knife, so, twice on the forehead of Ligoun, and the red blood leaped after it. And then it was that Ligoun gave me the sign to bear up under him with my youth that he might walk. And he laughed with a great scorn, full in the face of Opitsah, the Knife. And he brushed Opitsah to the side, as one brushes to the side a low-hanging branch on the trail and passes on.

"And I knew and understood, for there was but shame in the killing of Opitsah before the faces of a score of greater chiefs. I remembered the Law, and knew Ligoun had it in mind to kill by the Law. And who, chiefest of rank but himself, was there but Niblack? And toward Niblack, leaning on my arm, he walked. And to his other arm, clinging and striking, was Opitsah, too small to soil with his blood the hands of so great a man. And though the knife of Opitsah bit in again and again, Ligoun noted it not, nor winced. And in this fashion we three went our way across the room, Niblack sitting in his blanket and fearful of our coming.

"And now old hates flamed up and forgotten grudges were remembered. Lamuk, a Kake, had had a brother drowned in the bad water of the Stickeen, and the Stickeens had not paid in blankets for their bad water, as was the custom to pay. So Lamuk drove straight with his long knife to the heart of Klok-Kutz the Stickeen. And Katchahook remembered a quarrel of the Naass River people with the Tongas of north of Dixon, and the chief of the Tongas he slew with a pistol which made much noise. And the blood-hunger gripped all the men who sat in the circle, and chief slew chief, or was slain, as chance might be. Also did they stab and shoot at Ligoun, for whoso killed him won great honor and would be unforgotten for the deed. And they were about him like wolves about a moose, only they were so many they were in their own way, and they slew one another to make room. And there was great confusion.

"But Ligoun went slowly, without haste, as though many years were yet before him. It seemed that he was certain he would make his kill, in his own way, ere they could slay him. And as I say, he went slowly, and knives bit into him, and he was red with blood. And though none sought after me, who was a mere stripling, yet did the knives find me, and the hot bullets burn me. And still Ligoun leaned his weight on my youth, and Opitsah struck at him, and we three went forward. And when we stood by Niblack, he was afraid, and covered his head with his blanket. The Skoots were ever cowards.

"And Goolzug and Kadishan, the one a fish-eater and the other a meat-killer, closed together for the honor of their tribes. And they raged madly about, and in their battling swung against the knees of Opitsah, who was overthrown and trampled upon. And a knife, singing through the air, smote Skulpin, of the Sitkas, in the throat, and he flung his arms out blindly, reeling, and dragged me down in his fall.

"And from the ground I beheld Ligoun bend over Niblack, and uncover the blanket from his head, and turn up his face to the light. And Ligoun was in no haste. Being blinded with his own blood, he swept it out of his eyes with the back of his hand, so he might see and be sure. And when he was sure that the upturned face was the face of Niblack, he drew the knife across his throat as one draws a knife across the throat of a trembling deer. And then Ligoun stood erect, singing his death-song and swaying gently to and fro. And Skulpin, who had dragged me down, shot with a pistol from where he lay, and Ligoun toppled and fell, as an old pine topples and falls in the teeth of the wind."

Palitlum ceased. His eyes, smouldering moodily, were bent upon the fire, and his cheek was dark with blood.

"And thou, Palitlum?" I demanded. "And thou?"

"I? I did remember the Law, and I slew Opitsah the Knife, which was well. And I drew Ligoun's own knife from the throat of Niblack, and slew Skulpin, who had dragged me down. For I was a stripling, and I could slay any man and it were honor. And further, Ligoun being dead, there was no

...and Ligoun toppled and fell, as an old pine topples and falls in the teeth of the wind

need for my youth, and I laid about me with his knife, choosing the chiefest of rank that yet remained."

Palitlum fumbled under his shirt and drew forth a beaded sheath, and from the sheath, a knife. It was a knife home-wrought and crudely fashioned from a whip-saw file; a knife such as one may find possessed by old men in a hundred Alaskan villages.

"The knife of Ligoun?" I said, and Palitlum nodded.

"And for the knife of Ligoun," I said, "will I give thee ten bottles of 'Three Star.'"

But Palitlum looked at me slowly. "Hair-Face, I am weak as water, and easy as a woman. I have soiled my belly with quass, and hooch, and 'Three Star.' My eyes are blunted, my ears have lost their keenness, and my strength has gone into fat. And I am without honor in these days, and am called Palitlum, the Drinker. Yet honor was mine at the potlatch of Niblack, on the Skoot, and the memory of it, and the memory of Ligoun, be dear to me. Nay, didst thou turn the sea itself into 'Three Star' and say that it were all mine for the knife, yet would I keep the knife. I am Palitlum, the Drinker, but I was once Olo, the Ever-Hungry, who bore up Ligoun with his youth!"

"Thou art a great man, Palitlum," I said, "and I honor thee."

Palitlum reached out his hand.

"The 'Three Star' between thy knees be mine for the tale I have told," he said.

And as I looked on the frown of the cliff at our backs, I saw the shadow of a man's torso, monstrous beneath a huge inverted bottle.

22
Li Wan the Fair

LI WAN, THE FAIR

"The sun sinks, Canim, and the heat of the day is gone!"

So called Li Wan to the man whose head was hidden beneath the squirrel-skin robe, but she called softly, as though divided between the duty of waking him and the fear of him awake. For she was afraid of this big husband of hers, who was like unto none of the men she had known.

The moose-meat sizzled uneasily, and she moved the frying-pan to one side of the red embers. As she did so she glanced warily at the two Hudson Bay dogs dripping eager slaver from their scarlet tongues and following her every movement. They were huge, hairy fellows, crouched to leeward in the thin smoke-wake of the fire to escape the swarming myriads of mosquitoes. As Li Wan gazed down the steep to where the Kondike flung its swollen flood between the hills, one of the dogs bellied its way forward like a worm, and with a deft, catlike stroke of the paw dipped a chunk of hot meat out of the pan to the ground. But Li Wan caught him from out the tail of her eye, and he sprang back with a snap and a snarl as she rapped him over the nose with a stick of firewood.

"Nay, Olo," she laughed, recovering the meat without removing her eye from him. "Thou art ever hungry, and for that thy nose leads thee into endless troubles."

But the mate of Olo joined him, and together they defied the woman. The hair on their backs and shoulders bristled in recurrent waves of anger, and the thin lips writhed and lifted into ugly wrinkles, exposing the flesh-tearing fangs, cruel and menacing. Their very noses serrulated and shook in brute passion, and they snarled as the wolves snarl, with all the hatred and malignity of the breed impelling them to spring upon the woman and drag her down.

"And thou, too, Bash, fierce as thy master and never at peace with the hand that feeds thee! This is not thy quarrel, so that be thine! and that!"

As she cried, she drove at them with the firewood, but they avoided the blows and refused to retreat. They separated and approached her from either side, crouching low and snarling. Li Wan had struggled with the wolf-dog for mastery from the time she toddled among the skin-bales of the teepee, and she knew a crisis was at hand. Bash had halted, his muscles stiff and tense for the spring; Olo was yet creeping into striking distance.

Grasping two blazing sticks by the charred ends, she faced the brutes. The one held back, but Bash sprang, and she met him in mid-air with the flaming weapon. There were sharp yelps of pain and swift odors of burning hair and flesh as he rolled in the dirt and the woman ground the fiery embers into his mouth. Snapping wildly, he flung himself sidewise out of her reach and in a frenzy of fear scrambled for safety. Olo, on the other side, had begun his retreat, when Li Wan reminded him of her primacy by hurling a heavy stick of wood into his ribs. Then the pair retreated under a rain of firewood, and on the edge of the camp fell to licking their wounds and whimpering by turns and snarling.

Li Wan blew the ashes off the meat and sat down again. Her heart had not gone up a beat, and the incident was already old, for this was the routine of life. Canim had not stirred during the disorder, but instead had set up a lusty snoring.

"Come, Canim!" she called. "The heat of the day is gone, and the trail waits for our feet."

The squirrel-skin robe was agitated and cast aside by a brown arm. Then the man's eyelids fluttered and drooped again.

"His pack is heavy," she thought, "and he is tired with the work of the morning."

A mosquito stung her on the neck, and she daubed the unprotected spot with wet clay from a ball she had convenient to hand. All morning, toiling up the divide and enveloped in a cloud of the pests, the man and woman had plastered themselves with the sticky mud, which, drying in the sun, covered their faces with masks of clay. These masks, broken in divers places by the movement of the facial muscles, had constantly to be renewed, so that the deposit was irregular of depth and peculiar of aspect.

Li Wan shook Canim gently but with persistence till he roused and sat up. His first glance was to the sun, and after consulting the celestial timepiece he hunched over to the fire and fell-to ravenously on the meat. He was a large Indian fully six feet in height, deep-chested and heavy-muscled, and his eyes were keener and vested with greater mental vigor than the average of his kind. The lines of will had marked his face deeply, and this, coupled with a sternness and primitiveness, advertised a native indomitability, unswerving of purpose, and prone, when thwarted, to sullen cruelty.

"To-morrow, Li Wan, we shall feast." He sucked a marrow-bone clean and threw it to the dogs. "We shall have *flapjacks* fried in *bacon grease*, and *sugar*, which is more toothsome—"

"*Flapjacks?*" she questioned, mouthing the word curiously.

"Ay," Canim answered with superiority; "and I shall teach you new ways of cookery. Of these things I speak you are ignorant, and of many more things besides. You have lived your days in a little corner of the earth and know nothing. But I," — he straightened himself and looked at her pridefully, — "I am a great traveller, and have been all places, even among the white people, and I am versed in their ways, and in the ways of many peoples. I am not a tree, born to stand in one place always and know not what there be over the next hill; for I am Canim, the Canoe, made to go here and there and to journey and quest up and down the length and breadth of the world."

She bowed her head humbly. "It is true. I have eaten fish and meat and berries all my days and lived in a little corner of the earth. Nor did I dream the world was so large until you stole me from my people and I cooked and carried for you on the endless trails." She looked up at him suddenly. "Tell me, Canim, does this trail ever end?"

"Nay," he answered. "My trail is like the world; it never ends. My trail *is* the world, and I have travelled it since the time my legs could carry me, and I shall travel it until I die. My father and my mother may be dead, but it is long since I looked upon them, and I do not care. My tribe is like your tribe. It stays in the one place — which is far from here, — but I care naught for my tribe, for I am Canim, the Canoe!"

"And must I, Li Wan, who am weary, travel always your trail until I die?"

"You, Li Wan, are my wife, and the wife travels the husband's trail wheresoever it goes. It is the law. And were it not the law, yet would it be the law of Canim, who is lawgiver unto himself and his."

She bowed her head again, for she knew no other law than that man was the master of woman.

"Be not in haste," Canim cautioned her, as she began to strap the meagre camp outfit to her pack. "The sun is yet hot, and the trail leads down and the footing is good."

She dropped her work obediently and resumed her seat.

Canim regarded her with speculative interest. "You do not squat on your hams like other women," he remarked.

"No," she answered. "It never came easy. It tires me, and I cannot take my rest that way."

"And why is it your feet point not straight before you?"

"I do not know, save that they are unlike the feet of other women."

A satisfied light crept into his eyes, but otherwise he gave no sign.

"Like other women, your hair is black; but have you ever noticed that it is soft and fine, softer and finer than the hair of other women?"

"I have noticed," she answered shortly, for she was not pleased at such cold analysis of her sex-deficiencies.

"It is a year, now, since I took you from your people," he went on, "and you are nigh as shy and afraid of me as when first I looked upon you. How does this thing be?"

Li Wan shook her head. "I am afraid of you, Canim, you are so big and strange. And further, before you looked upon me even, I was afraid of all the young men. I do not know ... I cannot say ... only it seemed, somehow, as though I should not be for them, as though ..."

"Ay," he encouraged, impatient at her faltering.

"As though they were not my kind."

"Not your kind?" he demanded slowly. "Then what is your kind?"

"I do not know, I..." She shook her head in a bewildered manner. "I cannot put into words the way I felt. It was strangeness in me. I was unlike other maidens, who sought the young men slyly. I could not care for the young men that way. It would have been a great wrong, it seemed, and an ill deed."

"What is the first thing you remember?" Canim asked with abrupt irrelevance.

"Pow-Wah-Kaan, my mother."

"And naught else before Pow-Wah-Kaan?"

"Naught else."

But Canim, holding her eyes with his, searched her secret soul and saw it waver.

"Think, and think hard, Li Wan!" he threatened.

She stammered, and her eyes were piteous and pleading, but his will dominated her and wrung from her lips the reluctant speech.

"But it was only dreams, Canim, ill dreams of childhood, shadows of things not real, visions such as the dogs, sleeping in the sun-warmth, behold and whine out against."

"Tell me," he commanded, "of the things before Pow-Wah-Kaan, your mother."

"They are forgotten memories," she protested. "As a child I dreamed awake, with my eyes open to the day, and when I spoke of the strange things I saw I was laughed at, and the other children were afraid and drew away from me. And when I spoke of the things I saw to Pow-Wah-Kaan, she chided me and said they were evil; also she beat me. It was a sickness, I believe, like the falling-sickness that comes to old men; and in time I grew better and dreamed no more. And now... I cannot remember" — she brought her hand in a confused manner to her forehead — "they are there, somewhere, but I cannot find them, only ..."

"Only," Canim repeated, holding her.

"Only one thing. But you will laugh at its foolishness, it is so unreal."

"Nay, Li Wan. Dreams are dreams. They may be memories of other lives we have lived. I was once a moose. I firmly believe I was once a moose, what of the things I have seen in dreams, and heard."

Strive as he would to hide it, a growing anxiety was manifest, but Li Wan, groping after the words with which to paint the picture, took no heed.

"I see a snow-tramped space among the trees," she began, "and across the snow the sign of a man where he has dragged himself heavily on hand and knee. And I see, too, the man in the snow, and it seems I am very close to him when I look. He is unlike real men, for he has hair on his face, much hair, and the hair of his face and head is yellow like the summer coat of the weasel. His eyes are closed, but they open and search about. They are blue like the sky, and look into mine and search no more. And his hand moves, slow, as from weakness, and I feel ..."

"Ay," Canim whispered hoarsely. "You feel — ?"

"No! no!" she cried in haste. "I feel nothing. Did I say 'feel'? I did not mean it. It could not be that I should mean it. I see, and I see only, and that is all I see — a man in the snow, with eyes like the sky, and hair like the weasel. I have seen it many times, and always it is the same — a man in the snow —"

"And do you see yourself?" he asked, leaning forward and regarding her intently. "Do you ever see yourself and the man in the snow?"

"Why should I see myself? Am I not real?"

His muscles relaxed and he sank back, an exultant satisfaction in his eyes which he turned from her so that she might not see.

"I will tell you, Li Wan," he spoke decisively; "you were a little bird in some life before, a little moose-bird, when you saw this thing, and the memory of it is with you yet. It is not strange. I was once a moose, and my father's father afterward became a bear — so said the shaman, and the shaman cannot lie. Thus, on the Trail of the Gods we pass from life to life, and the gods know only and understand. Dreams and the shadows of dreams be memories, nothing more, and the dog, whining asleep in the sun-warmth, doubtless sees and remembers things gone before. Bash, there, was a warrior once. I do firmly believe he was once a warrior."

Canim tossed a bone to the brute and got upon his feet. "Come, let us begone. The sun is yet hot, but it will get no cooler."

"And these white people, what are they like?" Li Wan made bold to ask.

"Like you and me," he answered, "only they are less dark of skin. You will be among them ere the day is dead."

Canim lashed the sleeping-robe to his one-hundred-and-fifty-pound pack, smeared his face with wet clay, and sat down to rest till Li Wan had finished loading the dogs. Olo cringed at sight of the club in her hand, and gave no trouble when the bundle of forty pounds and odd was strapped upon him. But Bash was aggrieved and truculent, and could not forbear to whimper and snarl as he was forced to receive the burden. He bristled his back and bared his teeth as she drew the straps tight, the while throwing all the malignancy of his nature into the glances shot at her sideways and backward. And Canim chuckled and said, "Did I not say he was once a very great warrior?"

"These furs will bring a price," he remarked as he adjusted his head-strap and lifted his pack clear of the ground. "A big price. The white men pay well for such goods, for they have no time to hunt and are soft to the cold. Soon shall we feast, Li Wan, as you have feasted never in all the lives you have lived before."

She grunted acknowledgment and gratitude for her lord's condescension, slipped into the harness, and bent forward to the load.

"The next time I am born, I would be born a white man," he added, and swung off down the trail which dived into the gorge at his feet.

The dogs followed close at his heels, and Li Wan brought up the rear. But her thoughts were far away, across the Ice Mountains to the east, to the little corner of the earth where her childhood had been lived. Ever as a child, she remembered, she had been looked upon as strange, as one with an affliction. Truly she had dreamed awake and been scolded and beaten for the remarkable visions she saw, till, after a time, she had outgrown them. But not utterly. Though they troubled her no more waking, they came to her in her sleep, grown woman that she was, and many a night of nightmare was hers, filled with fluttering shapes, vague and meaningless. The talk with Canim had excited her, and down all the twisted slant of the divide she harked back to the mocking fantasies of her dreams.

"Let us take breath," Canim said, when they had tapped midway the bed of the main creek.

He rested his pack on a jutting rock, slipped the head-strap, and sat down. Li Wan joined him, and the dogs sprawled panting on the ground beside them. At their feet rippled the glacial drip of the hills, but it was muddy and discolored, as if soiled by some commotion of the earth.

"Why is this?" Li Wan asked.

"Because of the white men who work in the ground. Listen!" He held up his hand, and they heard the ring of pick and shovel, and the sound of men's voices. "They are made mad by *gold*, and work without ceasing that they may find it. *Gold?* It is yellow and comes from the ground, and is considered of great value. It is also a measure of price."

But Li Wan's roving eyes had called her attention from him. A few yards below and partly screened by a clump of young spruce, the tiered logs of a cabin rose to meet its overhanging roof of dirt. A thrill ran through her, and all her dream-phantoms roused up and stirred about uneasily.

"Canim," she whispered in an agony of apprehension. "Canim, what is that?"

"The white man's teepee, in which he eats and sleeps."

She eyed it wistfully, grasping its virtues at a glance and thrilling again at the unaccountable sensations it aroused. "It must be very warm in time of frost," she said aloud, though she felt that she must make strange sounds with her lips.

She felt impelled to utter them, but did not, and the next instant Canim said, "It is called a *cabin*."

Her heart gave a great leap. The sounds! the very sounds! She looked about her in sudden awe. How should she know that strange word before ever she heard it? What could be the matter? And then with a shock, half of fear and half of delight, she realized that for the first time in her life there had been sanity and significance in the promptings of her dreams.

"*Cabin*," she repeated to herself. "*Cabin*." An incoherent flood of dream-stuff welled up and up till her head was dizzy and her heart seemed bursting. Shadows, and looming bulks of things, and unintelligible associations fluttered and whirled about, and she strove vainly with her consciousness to grasp and hold them. For she felt that there, in that welter of memories, was the key of the mystery; could she but grasp and hold it, all would be clear and plain —

O Canim! O Pow-Wah-Kaan! O shades and shadows, what was that?

She turned to Canim, speechless and trembling, the dream-stuff in mad, overwhelming riot. She was sick and fainting, and could only listen to the ravishing sounds which proceeded from the cabin in a wonderful rhythm.

"Hum, *fiddle*," Canim vouchsafed.

But she did not hear him, for in the ecstasy she was experiencing, it seemed at last that all things were coming clear. Now! now! she thought. A sudden moisture swept into her eyes, and the tears trickled down her cheeks. The mystery was unlocking, but the faintness was overpowering her. If only she could hold herself long enough! If only — but the landscape bent and crumpled up, and the hills swayed back and forth across the sky as she sprang upright and screamed, "*Daddy! Daddy!*" Then the sun reeled, and darkness smote her, and she pitched forward limp and headlong among the rocks.

Canim looked to see if her neck had been broken by the heavy pack, grunted his satisfaction, and threw water upon her from the creek. She came to slowly, with choking sobs, and sat up.

"It is not good, the hot sun on the head," he ventured.

And she answered, "No, it is not good, and the pack bore upon me hard."

"We shall camp early, so that you may sleep long and win strength," he said gently. "And if we go now, we shall be the quicker to bed."

Li Wan said nothing, but tottered to her feet in obedience and stirred up the dogs. She took the swing of his pace mechanically, and followed him past the cabin, scarce daring to breathe. But no sounds issued forth, though the door was open and smoke curling upward from the sheet-iron stovepipe.

They came upon a man in the bend of the creek, white of skin and blue of eye, and for a moment Li Wan saw the other man in the snow. But she saw dimly, for she was weak and tired from what she had undergone. Still, she looked at him curiously, and stopped with Canim to watch him at his work. He was washing gravel in a large pan, with a circular, tilting movement; and as they looked, giving a deft flirt, he flashed up the yellow gold in a broad streak across the bottom of the pan.

"Very rich, this creek," Canim told her, as they went on. "Sometime I will find such a creek, and then I shall be a big man."

Cabins and men grew more plentiful, till they came to where the main portion of the creek was spread out before them. It was the scene of a vast devastation. Everywhere the earth was torn and rent as though by a Titan's struggles. Where there were no upthrown mounds of gravel, great holes and trenches yawned, and chasms where the thick rime of the earth had been peeled to bed-rock. There was no worn channel for the creek, and its waters, dammed up, diverted, flying through the air on giddy flumes, trickling into sinks and low places, and raised by huge water-wheels, were used and used again a thousand times. The hills had been stripped of their trees, and their raw sides gored and perforated by great timber-slides and prospect holes. And over all, like a monstrous race of ants, was flung an army of men — mud-covered, dirty, dishevelled men, who crawled in and out of the holes of their digging, crept like big bugs along the flumes, and toiled and sweated at the gravel-heaps which they kept in constant unrest — men, as far as the eye could see, even to the rims of the hilltops, digging, tearing, and scouring the face of nature.

Li Wan was appalled at the tremendous upheaval. "Truly, these men are mad," she said to Canim.

"Small wonder. The gold they dig after is a great thing," he replied. "It is the greatest thing in the world."

For hours they threaded the chaos of greed, Canim eagerly intent, Li Wan weak and listless. She knew she had been on the verge of disclosure, and she felt that she was still on the verge of disclosure, but the nervous strain she had undergone had tired her, and she passively waited for the thing, she knew not what, to happen. From every hand her senses snatched up and conveyed to her innumerable impressions, each of which became a dull excitation to her jaded imagination. Somewhere within her, responsive notes were answering to the things without, forgotten and undreamed-of correspondences were being renewed; and she was aware of it in an incurious way, and her soul was troubled, but she was not equal to the mental exultation necessary to transmute and understand. So she plodded wearily on at the heels of her lord, content to wait for that which she knew, somewhere, somehow, must happen.

After undergoing the mad bondage of man, the creek finally returned to its ancient ways, all soiled and smirched from its toil, and coiled lazily among the broad flats and timbered spaces where the valley widened to its mouth. Here the "pay" ran out, and men were loth to loiter with the lure yet beyond. And here, as Li Wan paused to prod Olo with her staff, she heard the mellow silver of a woman's laughter.

Before a cabin sat a woman, fair of skin and rosy as a child, dimpling with glee at the words of another woman in the doorway. But the woman who sat shook about her great masses of dark, wet hair which yielded up its dampness to the warm caresses of the sun.

For an instant Li Wan stood transfixed. Then she was aware of a blinding flash, and a snap, as though something gave way; and the woman before the cabin vanished, and the cabin and the tall spruce timber, and the jagged sky-line, and Li Wan saw another woman, in the shine of another sun, brushing great masses of black hair, and singing as she brushed. And Li Wan heard the words of the song, and understood, and was a child again. She was smitten with a vision, wherein all the troublesome dreams merged and became one, and shapes and shadows took up their accustomed round, and all was clear and plain and real. Many pictures jostled past, strange scenes, and trees, and flowers, and people; and she saw them and knew them all.

"When you were a little bird, a little moose-bird," Canim said, his eyes upon her and burning into her.

"When I was a little moose-bird," she whispered, so faint and low he scarcely heard. And she knew she lied, as she bent her head to the strap and took the swing of the trail.

And such was the strangeness of it, the real now became unreal. The mile tramp and the pitching of camp by the edge of the stream seemed like a passage in a nightmare. She cooked the meat, fed the dogs, and unlashed the packs as in a dream, and it was not until Canim began to sketch his next wandering that she became herself again.

"The Kondike runs into the Yukon," he was saying; "a mighty river, mightier than the Mackenzie, of which you know. So we go, you and I, down to Fort o' Yukon. With dogs, in time of winter, it is twenty sleeps. Then we follow the Yukon away into the west — one hundred sleeps, two hundred — I have never heard. It is very far. And then we come to the sea. You know nothing of the sea, so let me tell you. As the lake is to the island, so the sea is to the land; all the rivers run to it, and it is without end. I have seen it at Hudson Bay; I have yet to see it in Alaska. And then we may take a great canoe upon the sea, you and I, Li Wan, or we may follow the land into the south many a hundred sleeps. And after that I do not know, save that I am Canim, the Canoe, wanderer and far-journeyer over the earth!"

She sat and listened, and fear ate into her heart as she pondered over this plunge into the illimitable wilderness. "It is a weary way," was all she said, head bowed on knee in resignation.

Then it was a splendid thought came to her, and at the wonder of it she was all aglow. She went down to the stream and washed the dried clay from her face. When the ripples died away, she stared long at her mirrored features; but sun and weather-beat had done their work, and, what of roughness and bronze, her skin was not soft and dimpled as a child's. But the thought was still splendid and the glow unabated as she crept in beside her husband under the sleeping-robe.

She lay awake, staring up at the blue of the sky and waiting for Canim to sink into the first deep sleep. When this came about, she wormed slowly and carefully away, tucked the robe around him, and stood up. At her second step, Bash growled savagely. She whispered persuasively to him and glanced at the man. Canim was snoring profoundly. Then she turned, and with swift, noiseless feet sped up the back trail.

Mrs. Evelyn Van Wyck was just preparing for bed. Bored by the duties put upon her by society, her wealth, and widowed blessedness, she had journeyed into the Northland and gone to housekeeping in a cosey cabin on the edge of the diggings. Here, aided and abetted by her friend and companion, Myrtle Giddings, she played at living close to the soil, and cultivated the primitive with refined abandon.

She strove to get away from the generations of culture and parlor selection, and sought the earth-grip her ancestors had forfeited. Likewise she induced mental states which she fondly believed to approximate those of the stone-folk, and just now, as she put up her hair for the pillow, she was indulging her fancy with a palaeolithic wooing. The details consisted principally of cave-dwellings and cracked marrow-bones, intersprinkled with fierce carnivora, hairy mammoths, and combats with rude flaked knives of flint; but the sensations were delicious. And as Evelyn Van Wyck fled through the sombre forest aisles before the too arduous advances of her slant-browed, skin-clad wooer, the door of the cabin opened, without the courtesy of a knock, and a skin-clad woman, savage and primitive, came in.

"Mercy!"

With a leap that would have done credit to a cave-woman, Miss Giddings landed in safety behind the table. But Mrs. Van Wyck held her ground. She noticed that the intruder was laboring under a strong excitement, and cast a swift glance backward to assure herself that the way was clear to the bunk, where the big Colt's revolver lay beneath a pillow.

"Greeting, O Woman of the Wondrous Hair," said Li Wan.

But she said it in her own tongue, the tongue spoken in but a little corner of the earth, and the women did not understand.

"Shall I go for help?" Miss Giddings quavered.

"The poor creature is harmless, I think," Mrs. Van Wyck replied. "And just look at her skin-clothes, ragged and trail-worn and all that. They are certainly unique. I shall buy them for my collection. Get my sack, Myrtle, please, and set up the scales."

Li Wan followed the shaping of the lips, but the words were unintelligible, and then, and for the first time, she realized, in a moment of suspense and indecision, that there was no medium of communication between them.

And at the passion of her dumbness she cried out, with arms stretched wide apart, "O Woman, thou art sister of mine!"

The tears coursed down her cheeks as she yearned toward them, and the break in her voice carried the sorrow she could not utter. But Miss Giddings was trembling, and even Mrs. Van Wyck was disturbed.

"I would live as you live. Thy ways are my ways, and our ways be one. My husband is Canim, the Canoe, and he is big and strange, and I am afraid. His trail is all the world and never ends, and I am weary. My mother was like you, and her hair was as thine, and her eyes. And life was soft to me then, and the sun warm."

She knelt humbly, and bent her head at Mrs. Van Wyck's feet. But Mrs. Van Wyck drew away, frightened at her vehemence.

Li Wan stood up, panting for speech. Her dumb lips could not articulate her overmastering consciousness of kind.

"Trade? you trade?" Mrs. Van Wyck questioned, slipping, after the fashion of the superior peoples, into pigeon tongue.

She touched Li Wan's ragged skins to indicate her choice, and poured several hundreds of gold into the blower. She stirred the dust about and trickled its yellow lustre temptingly through her fingers. But Li Wan saw only the fingers, milk-white and shapely, tapering daintily to the rosy, jewel-like nails. She placed her own hand alongside, all work-worn and calloused, and wept.

Mrs. Van Wyck misunderstood. "Gold," she encouraged. "Good gold! You trade? You changee for changee?" And she laid her hand again on Li Wan's skin garments.

"How much? You sell? How much?" she persisted, running her hand against the way of the hair so that she might make sure of the sinew-thread seam.

But Li Wan was deaf as well, and the woman's speech was without significance. Dismay at her failure sat upon her. How could she identify herself with these women? For she knew they were of the one breed, blood-sisters among men and the women of men. Her eyes roved wildly about the interior, taking in the soft draperies hanging around, the feminine garments, the oval mirror, and the dainty toilet accessories beneath. And the things haunted her, for she had seen like things before; and as she looked at them her lips involuntarily formed sounds which her throat trembled to utter. Then a thought flashed upon her, and she steadied herself. She must be calm. She must control herself, for there must be no misunderstanding this time, or else, — and she shook with a storm of suppressed tears and steadied herself again.

She put her hand on the table. "*Table,*" she clearly and distinctly enunciated. "*Table,*" she repeated.

She looked at Mrs. Van Wyck, who nodded approbation. Li Wan exulted, but brought her will to bear and held herself steady. "*Stove,*" she went on. "*Stove.*"

And at every nod of Mrs. Van Wyck, Li Wan's excitement mounted. Now stumbling and halting, and again in feverish haste, as the recrudescence of forgotten words was fast or slow, she moved about the cabin, naming article after article. And when she paused finally, it was in triumph, with body erect and head thrown back, expectant, waiting.

"Cat," Mrs. Van Wyck, laughing, spelled out in kindergarten fashion. "I—see—the—cat—catch—the—rat."

Li Wan nodded her head seriously. They were beginning to understand her at last, these women. The blood flushed darkly under her bronze at the thought, and she smiled and nodded her head still more vigorously.

Mrs. Van Wyck turned to her companion. "Received a smattering of mission education somewhere, I fancy, and has come to show it off."

"Of course," Miss Giddings tittered. "Little fool! We shall lose our sleep with her vanity."

"All the same I want that jacket. If it *is* old, the workmanship is good — a most excellent specimen." She returned to her visitor. "Changee for changee? You! Changee for changee? How much? Eh? How much, you?"

"Perhaps she'd prefer a dress or something," Miss Giddings suggested.

Mrs. Van Wyck went up to Li Wan and made signs that she would exchange her wrapper for the jacket. And to further the transaction, she took Li Wan's hand and placed it amid the lace and ribbons of the flowing bosom, and rubbed the fingers back and forth so they might feel the texture. But the jewelled butterfly which loosely held the fold in place was insecurely fastened, and the front of the gown slipped to the side, exposing a firm white breast, which had never known the lip-clasp of a child.

Mrs. Van Wyck coolly repaired the mischief; but Li Wan uttered a loud cry, and ripped and tore at her skin-shirt till her own breast showed firm and white as Evelyn Van Wyck's. Murmuring inarticulately and making swift signs, she strove to establish the kinship.

"A half-breed," Mrs. Van Wyck commented. "I thought so from her hair."

Miss Giddings made a fastidious gesture. "Proud of her father's white skin. It's beastly! Do give her something, Evelyn, and make her go."

But the other woman sighed. "Poor creature, I wish I could do something for her."

A heavy foot crunched the gravel without. Then the cabin door swung wide, and Canim stalked in. Miss Giddings saw a vision of sudden death, and screamed; but Mrs. Van Wyck faced him composedly.

"What do you want?" she demanded.

"How do?" Canim answered suavely and directly, pointing at the same time to Li Wan. "Um my wife."

He reached out for her, but she waved him back.

"Speak, Canim! Tell them that I am —"

"Daughter of Pow-Wah-Kaan? Nay, of what is it to them that they should care? Better should I tell them thou art an ill wife, given to creeping from thy husband's bed when sleep is heavy in his eyes."

Again he reached out for her, but she fled away from him to Mrs. Van Wyck, at whose feet she made frenzied appeal, and whose knees she tried to clasp. But the lady stepped back and gave permission with her eyes to Canim. He gripped Li Wan under the shoulders and raised her to her feet. She fought with him, in a madness of despair, till his hest was heaving with the exertion, and they had reeled about over half the room.

"Let me go, Canim," she sobbed.

But he twisted her wrist till she ceased to struggle. "The memories of the little moose-bird are overstrong and make trouble," he began.

"I know! I know!" she broke in. "I see the man in the snow, and as never before I see him crawl on hand and knee. And I, who am a little child, am carried on his back. And this is before Pow-Wah-Kaan and the time I came to live in a little corner of the earth."

"You know," he answered, forcing her toward the door; "but you will go with me down the Yukon and forget."

"Never shall I forget! So long as my skin is white shall I remember!" She clutched frantically at the door-post and looked a last appeal to Mrs. Evelyn Van Wyck.

"Then will I teach thee to forget, I, Canim, the Canoe!"

As he spoke he pulled her fingers clear and passed out with her upon the trail.

23
The Marriage of Lit-lit

THE MARRIAGE OF LIT-LIT

When John Fox came into a country where whiskey freezes solid and may be used as a paper-weight for a large part of the year, he came without the ideals and illusions that usually hamper the progress of more delicately nurtured adventurers. Born and reared on the frontier fringe of the United States, he took with him into Canada a primitive cast of mind, an elemental simplicity and grip on things, as it were, that insured him immediate success in his new career. From a mere servant of the Hudson's Bay Company, driving a paddle with the voyageurs and carrying goods on his back across the portages, he swiftly rose to a Factorship and took charge of a trading post at Fort Angelus.

Here, because of his elemental simplicity, he took himself a native wife, and, by reason of the connubial bliss that followed, he escaped the unrest and vain longings that curse the days of more fastidious men, spoil their work, and conquer them in the end. He lived contentedly, was at single purposes with the business he was set there to do, and achieved a brilliant record in the service of the Company. About this time his wife died, was claimed by her people, and buried with savage circumstance in a tin trunk in the top of a tree.

Two sons she had borne him, and when the Company promoted him, he journeyed with them still deeper into the vastness of the Northwest Territory to a place called Sin Rock, where he took charge of a new post in a more important fur field. Here he spent several lonely and depressing months, eminently disgusted with the unprepossessing appearance of the Indian maidens, and greatly worried by his growing sons who stood in need of a mother's care. Then his eyes chanced upon Lit-lit.

"Lit-lit — well, she is Lit-lit," was the fashion in which he despairingly described her to his chief clerk, Alexander McLean.

McLean was too fresh from his Scottish upbringing — "not dry behind the ears yet," John Fox put it — to take to the marriage customs of the country. Nevertheless he was not averse to the Factor's imperilling his own immortal soul, and, especially, feeling an ominous attraction himself for Lit-lit, he was sombrely content to clinch his own soul's safety by seeing her married to the Factor.

Nor is it to be wondered that McLean's austere Scotch soul stood in danger of being thawed in the sunshine of Lit-lit's eyes. She was pretty, and slender, and willowy, without the massive face and temperamental stolidity of the average squaw. "Lit-lit," so called from her fashion, even as a child, of being fluttery, of darting about from place to place like a butterfly, of being inconsequent and merry, and of laughing as lightly as she darted and danced about.

Lit-lit was the daughter of Snettishane, a prominent chief in the tribe, by a half-breed mother, and to him the Factor fared casually one summer day to open negotiations of marriage. He sat with the chief in the smoke of a mosquito smudge before his lodge, and together they talked about everything under the sun, or, at least, everything that in the Northland is under the sun, with the sole exception of marriage. John Fox had come particularly to talk of marriage; Snettishane knew it, and John Fox knew he knew it, wherefore the subject was religiously avoided. This is alleged to be Indian subtlety. In reality it is transparent simplicity.

The hours slipped by, and Fox and Snettishane smoked interminable pipes, looking each other in the eyes with a guilelessness superbly histrionic. In the mid-afternoon McLean and his brother clerk, McTavish, strolled past, innocently uninterested, on their way to the river. When they strolled back again an hour later, Fox and Snettishane had attained to a ceremonious discussion of the condition and quality of the gunpowder and bacon which the Company was offering in trade.

Meanwhile Lit-lit, divining the Factor's errand, had crept in under the rear wall of the lodge and through the front flap was peeping out at the two logomachists by the mosquito smudge. She was flushed and happy-eyed, proud that no less a man than the Factor (who stood next to God in the Northland hierarchy) had singled her out, femininely curious to see at close range what manner of man he was. Sunglare on the ice, camp smoke, and weather beat had burned his face to a copper-brown, so that her father was as fair as he, while she was fairer. She was remotely glad of this, and more immediately glad that he was large and strong, though his great black beard half frightened her, it was so strange.

Being very young, she was unversed in the ways of men. Seventeen times she had seen the sun travel south and lose itself beyond the sky-line, and seventeen times she had seen it travel back again and ride the sky day and night till there was no night at all. And through these years she had been cherished jealously by Snettishane, who stood between her and all suitors, listening disdainfully to the young hunters as they bid for her hand, and turning them away as though she were beyond price. Snettishane was mercenary. Lit-lit was to him an investment. She represented so much capital, from which he expected to receive, not a certain definite interest, but an incalculable interest.

And having thus been reared in a manner as near to that of the nunnery as tribal conditions would permit, it was with a great and maidenly anxiety that she peeped out at the man who had surely come for her, at the husband who was to teach her all that was yet unlearned of life, at the masterful being whose word was to be her law, and who was to mete and bound her actions and comportment for the rest of her days.

But, peeping through the front flap of the lodge, flushed and thrilling at the strange destiny reaching out for her, she grew disappointed as the day wore along, and the Factor and her father still talked pompously of matters concerning other things and not pertaining to marriage things at all. As the sun sank lower and lower toward the north and midnight approached, the Factor began making unmistakable preparations for departure. As he turned to stride away Lit-lit's heart sank; but it rose again as he halted, half turning on one heel.

"Oh, by the way, Snettishane," he said, "I want a squaw to wash for me and mend my clothes."

Snettishane grunted and suggested Wanidani, who was an old woman and toothless.

"No, no," interposed the Factor. "What I want is a wife. I've been kind of thinking about it, and the thought just struck me that you might know of some one that would suit."

Snettishane looked interested, whereupon the Factor retraced his steps, casually and carelessly to linger and discuss this new and incidental topic.

"Kattou?" suggested Snettishane.

"She has but one eye," objected the Factor.

"Laska?"

"Her knees be wide apart when she stands upright. Kips, your biggest dog, can leap between her knees when she stands upright."

"Senatee?" went on the imperturbable Snettishane.

But John Fox feigned anger, crying: "What foolishness be this? Am I old, that thou shouldst mate me with old women? Am I toothless? lame of leg? blind of eye? Or am I poor that no bright-eyed maiden may look with favor upon me? Behold! I am the Factor, both rich and great, a power in the land, whose speech makes men tremble and is obeyed!"

Snettishane was inwardly pleased, though his sphinxlike visage never relaxed. He was drawing the Factor, and making him break ground. Being a creature so elemental as to have room for but one idea at a time, Snettishane could pursue that one idea a greater distance than could John Fox. For John Fox, elemental as he was, was still complex enough to entertain several glimmering ideas at a time, which debarred him from pursuing the one as single-heartedly or as far as did the chief.

Snettishane calmly continued calling the roster of eligible maidens, which, name by name, as fast as uttered, were stamped ineligible by John Fox, with specified objections appended. Again he gave it up and started to return to the Fort. Snettishane watched him go, making no effort to stop him, but seeing him, in the end, stop himself.

"Come to think of it," the Factor remarked, "we both of us forgot Lit-lit. Now I wonder if she'll suit me?"

Snettishane met the suggestion with a mirthless face, behind the mask of which his soul grinned wide. It was a distinct victory. Had the Factor gone but one step farther, perforce Snettishane would himself have mentioned the name of Lit-lit, but — the Factor had not gone that one step farther.

The chief was non-committal concerning Lit-lit's suitability, till he drove the white man into taking the next step in order of procedure.

"Well," the Factor meditated aloud, "the only way to find out is to make a try of it." He raised his voice. "So I will give for Lit-lit ten blankets and three pounds of tobacco which is good tobacco."

Snettishane replied with a gesture which seemed to say that all the blankets and tobacco in all the world could not compensate him for the loss of Lit-lit and her manifold virtues. When pressed by the Factor to set a price, he coolly placed it at five hundred blankets, ten guns, fifty pounds of tobacco, twenty scarlet cloths, ten bottles of rum, a music-box, and lastly the good-will and best offices of the Factor, with a place by his fire.

The Factor apparently suffered a stroke of apoplexy, which stroke was successful in reducing the blankets to two hundred and in cutting out the place by the fire — an unheard-of condition in the marriages of white men with the daughters of the soil. In the end, after three hours more of chaffering, they came to an agreement. For Lit-lit Snettishane was to receive one hundred blankets, five pounds of tobacco, three guns, and a bottle of rum, good-will and best offices included, which, according to John Fox, was ten blankets and a gun more than she was worth. And as he went home through the wee sma' hours, the three o'clock sun blazing in the due northeast, he was unpleasantly aware that Snettishane had bested him over the bargain.

Snettishane, tired and victorious, sought his bed, and discovered Lit-lit before she could escape from the lodge.

He grunted knowingly: "Thou hast seen. Thou hast heard. Wherefore it be plain to thee thy father's very great wisdom and understanding. I have made for thee a great match. Heed my words and walk in the way of my words, go when I say go, come when I bid thee come, and we shall grow fat with the wealth of this big white man who is a fool according to his bigness."

The next day no trading was done at the store. The Factor opened whiskey before breakfast to the delight of McLean and McTavish, gave his dogs double rations, and wore his best moccasins. Outside the Fort preparations were under way for a *potlatch*. Potlatch means "a giving," and John Fox's intention was to signalize his marriage with Lit-lit by a potlatch as generous as she was good-looking. In the afternoon the whole tribe gathered to the feast. Men, women, children, and dogs gorged to repletion, nor was there one person, even among the chance visitors and stray hunters from other tribes, who failed to receive some token of the bridegroom's largess.

Lit-lit, tearfully shy and frightened, was bedecked by her bearded husband with a new calico dress, splendidly beaded moccasins, a gorgeous silk handkerchief over her raven hair, a purple scarf about her throat, brass earrings and finger-rings, and a whole pint of pinchbeck jewellery, including a Waterbury watch. Snettishane could scarce contain himself at the spectacle, but watching his chance drew her aside from the feast.

"Not this night, nor the next night," he began ponderously, "but in the nights to come, when I shall call live a raven by the river bank, it is for thee to rise up from thy big husband who is a fool and come to me.

"Nay, nay," he went on hastily, at sight of the dismay in her face at turning her back upon her wonderful new life. "For no sooner shall this happen than thy big husband who is a fool will come wailing to my lodge. Then it is for thee to wail likewise, claiming that this thing is not well, and that the other thing thou dost not like, and that to be the wife of the Factor is more than thou didst bargain for, only wilt thou be content with more blankets, and more tobacco, and more wealth of various sorts for thy poor old father Snettishane. Remember well, when I call in the night, like a raven, from the river bank."

Lit-lit nodded; for to disobey her father was a peril she knew well; and, furthermore, it was a little thing he asked, a short separation from the Factor, who would know only greater gladness at having her back. She returned to the feast, and, midnight being well at hand, the Factor sought her out and led her away to the Fort amid joking and outcry in which the squaws were especially conspicuous.

Lit-lit quickly found that married life with the head-man of a fort was even better than she had dreamed. No longer did she have to fetch wood and water and wait hand and foot upon cantankerous menfolk. For the first time in her life she could lie abed till breakfast was on the table. And what a bed! — clean and soft, and comfortable as no bed she had ever known. And such food! Flour, cooked into biscuits, hot-cakes and bread, three times a day and every day, and all one wanted! Such prodigality was hardly believable.

To add to her contentment, the Factor was cunningly kind. He had buried one wife, and he knew how to drive with a slack rein that went firm only on occasion, and then went very firm. "Lit-lit is boss of this place," he announced significantly at the table the morning after the wedding. "What she says goes. Understand?" And McLean and McTavish understood. Also, they knew that the Factor had a heavy hand.

But Lit-lit did not take advantage. Taking a leaf from the book of her husband, she at once assumed charge of his two growing sons, giving them added comforts and a measure of freedom like to that which he gave her. The two sons were loud in the praise of their new mother; McLean and McTavish lifted their voices; and the Factor bragged of the joys of matrimony till the story of her good behavior and her husband's satisfaction became the property of all the dwellers in the Sin Rock district.

Whereupon Snettishane, with visions of his incalculable interest keeping him awake of nights, thought it time to bestir himself. On the tenth night of her wedded life Lit-lit was awakened by the croaking of a raven, and she knew that Snettishane was waiting for her by the river bank. In her great happiness she had forgotten her pact, and now it came back to her with behind it all the childish terror of her father. For a time she lay in fear and trembling, loath to go, afraid to stay. But in the end the Factor won the silent victory, and his kindness, plus his great muscles and square jaw, nerved her to disregard Snettishane's call.

But in the morning she arose very much afraid, and went about her duties in momentary fear of her father's coming. As the day wore along, however, she began to recover her spirits. John Fox, soundly berating McLean and McTavish for some petty dereliction of duty, helped her to pluck up courage. She tried not to let him go out of her sight, and when she followed him into the huge caché and saw him twirling and tossing great bales around as though they were feather pillows, she felt strengthened in her disobedience to her father. Also (it was her first visit to the warehouse, and Sin Rock was the chief distributing point to several chains of lesser posts), she was astounded at the endlessness of the wealth there stored away.

This sight, and the picture in her mind's eye of the bare lodge of Snettishane, put all doubts at rest. Yet she capped her conviction by a brief word with one of her stepsons. "White daddy good?" was what she asked, and the boy answered that his father was the best man he had ever known. That night the raven croaked again. On the night following the croaking was more persistent. It awoke the Factor, who tossed restlessly for a while. Then he said aloud, "Damn that raven," and Lit-lit laughed quietly under the blankets.

In the morning, bright and early, Snettishane put in an ominous appearance, and was set to breakfast in the kitchen with Wanidani. He refused "squaw food," and a little later bearded his son-in-law in the store where the trading was done. Having learned, he said, that his daughter was such a jewel, he had come for more blankets, more tobacco, and more guns — especially more guns. He had certainly been cheated in her price, he held, and he had come for justice. But the Factor had neither blankets nor justice to spare. Whereupon he was informed that Snettishane had seen the missionary at Three Forks, who had notified him that such marriages were not made in heaven, and that it was his father's duty to demand his daughter back.

"I am good Christian man now," Snettishane concluded. "I want my Lit-lit to go to heaven."

The Factor's reply was short and to the point; for he directed his father-in-law to go to the heavenly antipodes, and by the scruff of the neck and the slack of the blanket propelled him on that trail as far as the door.

But Snettishane sneaked around and in by the kitchen, cornering Lit-lit in the great living-room of the Fort.

"Mayhap thou didst sleep oversound last night when I called by the river bank," he began, glowering darkly.

"Nay, I was awake and heard." Her heart was beating as though it would choke her, but she went on steadily, "And the night before I was awake and heard, and yet again the night before."

And thereat, out of her great happiness and out of the fear that it might be taken from her, she launched into an original and glowing address upon the status and rights of woman — the first new-woman lecture delivered north of Fifty-three.

But it fell on unheeding ears. Snettishane was still in the dark ages. As she paused for breath, he said threateningly, "To-night I shall call again like the raven."

At this moment the Factor entered the room and again helped Snettishane on his way to the heavenly antipodes.

That night the raven croaked more persistently than ever. Lit-lit, who was a light sleeper, heard and smiled. John Fox tossed restlessly. Then he awoke and tossed about with greater restlessness. He grumbled and snorted, swore under his breath and over his breath, and finally flung out of bed. He groped his way to the great living-room and from the rack took down a loaded shot-gun — loaded with bird shot, left therein by the careless McTavis.

The Factor crept carefully out of the Fort and down to the river. The croaking had ceased, but he stretched out in the long grass and waited. The air seemed a chilly balm, and the earth, after the heat of the day, now and again breathed soothingly against him. The Factor, gathered into the rhythm of it all, dozed off, with his head upon his arm, and slept.

Fifty yards away, head resting on knees, and with his back to John Fox, Snettishane likewise slept, gently conquered by the quietude of the night. An hour slipped by and then he awoke, and, without lifting his head, set the night vibrating with the hoarse gutturals of the raven call.

The Factor roused, not with the abrupt start of civilized man, but with the swift and comprehensive glide from sleep to waking of the savage. In the night light he made out a dark object in the midst of the grass and brought his gun to bear upon it. A second croak began to rise, and he pulled the trigger. The crickets ceased from their sing-song chant, the wild fowl from their squabbling, and the raven croak broke midmost and died away in gasping silence.

John Fox ran to the spot and reached for the thing he had killed, but his fingers closed on a coarse mop of hair and he turned Snettishane's face upward to the starlight. He knew how a shot-gun scattered at fifty yards, and he knew that he had peppered Snettishane across the shoulders and in the small of the back. And Snettishane knew that he knew, but neither referred to it.

"What dost thou here?" the Factor demanded. "It were time old bones should be in bed."

But Snettishane was stately in spite of the bird shot burning under his skin.

"Old bones will not sleep," he said solemnly. "I weep for my daughter, for my daughter Lit-lit, who liveth and who yet is dead, and who goeth without doubt to the white man's hell."

"Weep henceforth on the far bank, beyond earshot of the fort," said John Fox, turning on his heel, "for the noise of thy weeping is exceeding great and will not let one sleep of nights."

"My heart is sore," Snettishane answered, "and my days and nights be black with sorrow."

"As the raven is black," said John Fox.

"As the raven is black," Snettishane said.

Never again was the voice of the raven heard by the river bank. Lit-lit grows matronly day by day and is very happy. Also, there are sisters to the sons of John Fox's first wife who lies buried in a tree. Old Snettishane is no longer a visitor at the Fort, and spends long hours raising a thin, aged voice against the filial ingratitude of children in general and of his daughter Lit-lit in particular. His declining years are embittered by the knowledge that he was cheated, and even John Fox has withdrawn the assertion that the price for Lit-lit was too much by ten blankets and a gun.

24
The Lost Poacher

THE LOST POACHER

"But they won't take excuses. You're across the line, and that's enough. They'll take you. In you go, Siberia and the salt-mines. And as for Uncle Sam, why, what's he to know about it? Never a word will get back to the States. 'The *Mary Thomas,*' the papers will say, 'the *Mary Thomas* lost with all hands. Probably in a typhoon in the Japanese seas.' That's what the papers will say, and people too. In you go, Siberia and the salt-mines. Dead to the world and kith and kin, though you live fifty years."

In such manner John Lewis, commonly known as the "sea-lawyer," settled the matter out of hand.

It was a serious moment in the forecastle of the *Mary Thomas.* No sooner had the watch below begun to talk the trouble over, than the watch on deck came down and joined them. As there was no wind, every hand could be spared with the exception of the man at the wheel, and he remained only for the sake of discipline. Even "Bub" Russell, the cabin-boy, had crept forward to hear what was going on.

However, it was a serious moment, as the grave faces of the sailors bore witness. For the three preceding months the *Mary Thomas,* sealing schooner, had hunted the seal pack along the coast of Japan and north to Bering Sea. Here, on the Asiatic side of the sea, they were forced to give over the chase, or rather, to go no farther; for beyond, the Russian cruisers patrolled forbidden ground, where the seals might breed in peace. And here, on the very edge of the line, the *Mary Thomas* had hunted back and forth, picking up the laggards which had not gone on with the pack.

A week before she had fallen into a heavy fog accompanied by calm. Since then the fog-bank had not lifted, and the only wind had been light airs and catspaws. This in itself was not so bad, for the sealing schooners are never in a hurry so long as they are in the midst of the seals; but the trouble lay in the fact that the current at this point bore heavily to the north. Thus the *Mary Thomas* had unwittingly drifted across the line, and every hour she was penetrating, unwillingly, farther and farther into the dangerous waters where the Russian bear kept guard.

How far she had drifted no man knew. The sun had not been visible for a week, nor the stars, and the captain had been unable to take observations in order to determine his position. At any moment a cruiser might swoop down and hale the crew away to Siberia. The fate of other poaching seal-hunters was too well known to the men of the *Mary Thomas,* and there was cause for grave faces.

"Mine friends," spoke up a German boat-steerer, "it vas a pad piziness. Shust as ve make a big catch, und all honest, somedings go wrong, und der Russians nab us, dake our skins und our schooner, und send us mit der anarchists to Siberia. Ach! a pretty pad piziness!"

"Yes, that's where it hurts," the sea-lawyer went on. "Fifteen hundred skins in the salt piles, and all honest, a big pay-day coming to every man Jack of us, and then to be captured and lose it all! It'd be different if we'd been poaching, but it's all honest work in open water."

"But if we haven't done anything wrong, they can't do anything to us, can they?" Bub queried.

"It strikes me as 'ow it ain't the proper thing for a boy o' your age shovin' in when 'is elders is talkin'," protested an English sailor, from over the edge of his bunk.

"Oh, that's all right, Jack," answered the sea-lawyer. "He's a perfect right to. Ain't he just as liable to lose his wages as the rest of us?"

"Wouldn't give thruppence for them!" Jack sniffed back. He had been planning to go home and see his family in Chelsea when he was paid off, and he was now feeling rather blue over the highly possible loss, not only of his pay, but of his liberty.

"How are they to know?" the sea-lawyer asked, in answer to Bub's previous question. "Here we are in forbidden water. How do they know but what we came here of our own accord? Here we are, fifteen hundred skins in the hold. How do they know whether we got them in open water or in the closed sea? Don't you see, Bub, the evidence is all against us. If you caught a man with his pockets full of apples like those which grow on your tree, and if you caught him in your tree besides, what'd you think if he told you he couldn't help it, and had just been sort of blown there, and that anyway those apples came from some other tree — what'd you think, eh?"

Bub saw it clearly when put in that light, and shook his head despondently.

"You'd rather be dead than go to Siberia," one of the boat-pullers said. "They put you into the salt-mines and work you till you die. Never see daylight again. Why, I've heard tell of one fellow that was chained to his mate, and that mate died. And they were both chained together! And if they send you to the quicksilver-mines you get salivated. I'd rather be hung than salivated."

"Wot's salivated?" Jack asked, suddenly sitting up in his bunk at the hint of fresh misfortunes.

"Why, the quicksilver gets into your blood; I think that's the way. And your gums all swell like you had the scurvy, only worse, and your teeth get loose in your jaws. And big ulcers form, and then you die horrible. The strongest man can't last long a-mining quicksilver."

"A pad piziness," the boat-steerer reiterated, dolorously, in the silence which followed. "A pad piziness. I vish I vas In Yokohama. Eh? Vot vas dot?"

Every face lighted up. The *Mary Thomas* heeled over. The decks were aslant. A tin pannikin rolled down the inclined plane, rattling and banging. From above came the slapping of canvas and the quivering rat-tat-tat of the after-leech of the loosely stretched foresail. Then the mate's voice sang down the hatch, "All hands on deck and make sail!"

Never had such summons been answered with more enthusiasm. The calm had broken. The wind had come which was to carry them south into safety. With a wild cheer all sprang on deck. Working with mad haste, they flung out topsails, flying jibs and staysails. As they worked, the fog-bank lifted and the black vault of heaven, bespangled with the old familiar stars, rushed into view. When all was shipshape, the *Mary Thomas* was lying gallantly over on her side to a beam wind and plunging ahead due south.

"Steamer's lights ahead on the port bow, sir!" cried the lookout from his station on the forecastle-head. There was excitement in the man's voice.

The captain sent Bub below for his night-glasses. Everybody crowded to the lee-rail to gaze at the suspicious stranger, which already began to loom up vague and indistinct. In those unfrequented waters the chance was one in a thousand that it could be anything else than a Russian patrol. The captain was still anxiously gazing through the glasses, when a flash of flame left the stranger's side, followed by the loud report of a cannon. The worst fears were confirmed. It was a patrol, evidently firing across the bows of the *Mary Thomas* in order to make her heave to.

"Hard down with your helm!" the captain commanded the steersman, all the life gone out of his voice. Then to the crew, "Back over the jib and foresail! Run down the flying jib! Clew up the foretopsail! And aft here and swing on to the main-sheet!"

The *Mary Thomas* ran into the eye of the wind, lost headway, and fell to courtesying gravely to the long seas rolling up from the west.

The cruiser steamed a little nearer and lowered a boat. The sealers watched in heartbroken silence. They could see the white bulk of the boat as it was slacked away to the water, and its crew sliding aboard. They could hear the creaking of the davits and the commands of the officers. Then the boat sprang away under the impulse of the oars, and came toward them. The wind had been rising, and already the sea was too rough to permit the frail craft to lie alongside the tossing schooner; but watching their chance, and taking advantage of the boarding ropes thrown to them, an officer and a couple of men clambered aboard. The boat then sheered off into safety and lay to its oars, a young midshipman, sitting in the stern and holding the yoke-lines, in charge.

The officer, whose uniform disclosed his rank as that of second lieutenant in the Russian navy, went below with the captain of the *Mary Thomas* to look at the ship's papers. A few minutes later he emerged, and upon his sailors removing the hatch-covers, passed down into the hold with a lantern to inspect the salt piles. It was a goodly heap which confronted him — fifteen hundred fresh skins, the season's catch; and under the circumstances he could have had but one conclusion.

"I am very sorry," he said, in broken English to the sealing captain when he again came on deck, "but it is my duty, in the name of the tsar, to seize your vessel as a poacher caught with fresh skins in the closed sea. The penalty, as you may know, is confiscation and imprisonment."

The captain of the *Mary Thomas* shrugged his shoulders in seeming indifference, and turned away. Although they may restrain all outward show, strong men, under unmerited misfortune, are sometimes very close to tears. Just then the vision of his little California home, and of the wife and two yellow-haired boys, was strong upon him, and there was a strange choking sensation in his throat, which made him afraid that if he attempted to speak he would sob instead.

And also there was upon him the duty he owed his men. No weakness before them, for he must be a tower of strength to sustain them in misfortune. He had already explained to the second lieutenant, and knew the hopelessness of the situation. As the sea-lawyer had said, the evidence was all against him. So he turned aft, and fell to pacing up and down the poop of the vessel over which he was no longer commander.

The Russian officer now took temporary charge. He ordered more of his men aboard, and had all the canvas clewed up and furled snugly away. While this was being done, the boat plied back and forth between the two vessels, passing a heavy hawser, which was made fast to the great towing-bitts on the schooner's forecastle-head. During all this work the sealers stood about in sullen groups. It was madness to think of resisting, with the guns of a man-of-war not a biscuit-toss away; but they refused to lend a hand, preferring instead to maintain a gloomy silence.

Having accomplished his task, the lieutenant ordered all but four of his men back into the boat. Then the midshipman, a lad of sixteen, looking strangely mature and dignified in his uniform and sword, came aboard to take command of the captured sealer. Just as the lieutenant prepared to depart, his eyes chanced to alight upon Bub. Without a word of warning, he seized him by the arm and dropped him over the rail into the waiting boat; and then, with a parting wave of his hand, he followed him.

It was only natural that Bub should be frightened at this unexpected happening. All the terrible stories he had heard of the Russians served to make him fear them, and now returned to his mind with double force. To be captured by them was bad enough, but to be carried off by them, away from his comrades, was a fate of which he had not dreamed.

"Be a good boy, Bub," the captain called to him, as the boat drew away from the *Mary Thomas's* side, "and tell the truth!"

"Aye, aye, sir!" he answered, bravely enough by all outward appearance. He felt a certain pride of race, and was ashamed to be a coward before these strange enemies, these wild Russian bears.

"Und be politeful!" the German boat-steerer added, his rough voice lifting across the water like a fog-horn.

Bub waved his hand in farewell, and his mates clustered along the rail as they answered with a cheering shout. He found room in the sternsheets, where he fell to regarding the lieutenant. He didn't look so wild or bearish, after all — very much like other men, Bub concluded, and the sailors were much the same as all other man-of-war's men he had ever known. Nevertheless, as his feet struck the steel deck of the cruiser, he felt as if he had entered the portals of a prison.

For a few minutes he was left unheeded. The sailors hoisted the boat up, and swung it in on the davits. Then great clouds of black smoke poured out of the funnels, and they were under way — to Siberia, Bub could not help but think. He saw the *Mary Thomas* swing abruptly into line as she took the pressure from the hawser, and her side-lights, red and green, rose and fell as she was towed through the sea.

Bub's eyes dimmed at the melancholy sight, but — but just then the lieutenant came to take him down to the commander, and he straightened up and set his lips firmly, as if this were a very commonplace affair and he were used to being sent to

Into the dangerous waters where the Russian Bear kept guard

Siberia every day in the week. The cabin in which the commander sat was like a palace compared to the humble fittings of the *Mary Thomas*, and the commander himself, in gold lace and dignity, was a most august personage, quite unlike the simple man who navigated his schooner on the trail of the seal pack.

Bub now quickly learned why he had been brought aboard, and in the prolonged questioning which followed, told nothing but the plain truth. The truth was harmless; only a lie could have injured his cause. He did not know much, except that they had been sealing far to the south in open water, and that when the calm and fog came down upon them, being close to the line, they had drifted across. Again and again he insisted that they had not lowered a boat or shot a seal in the week they had been drifting about in the forbidden sea; but the commander chose to consider all that he said to be a tissue of falsehoods, and adopted a bullying tone in an effort to frighten the boy. He threatened and cajoled by turns, but failed in the slightest to shake Bub's statements, and at last ordered him out of his presence.

By some oversight, Bub was not put in anybody's charge, and wandered up on deck unobserved. Sometimes the sailors, in passing, bent curious glances upon him, but otherwise he was left strictly alone. Nor could he have attracted much attention, for he was small, the night dark, and the watch on deck intent on its own business. Stumbling over the strange decks, he made his way aft where he could look upon the side-lights of the *Mary Thomas*, following steadily in the rear.

For a long while he watched, and then lay down in the darkness close to where the hawser passed over the stern to the captured schooner. Once an officer came up and examined the straining rope to see if it were chafing, but Bub cowered away in the shadow undiscovered. This, however, gave him an idea which concerned the lives and liberties of twenty-two men, and which was to avert crushing sorrow from more than one happy home many thousand miles away.

In the first place, he reasoned, the crew were all guiltless of any crime, and yet were being carried relentlessly away to imprisonment in Siberia — a living death, he had heard, and he believed it implicitly. In the second place, he was a prisoner, hard and fast, with no chance of escape. In the third, it was possible for the twenty-two men on the *Mary Thomas* to escape. The only thing which bound them was a four-inch hawser. They dared not cut it at their end, for a watch was sure to be maintained upon it by their Russian captors; but at his end, ah! at his end —

Bub did not stop to reason further. Wriggling close to the hawser, he opened his jack-knife and went to work. The blade was not very sharp, and he sawed away, rope-yarn by rope-yarn, the awful picture of the solitary Siberian exile he must endure growing clearer and more terrible at every stroke. Such a fate was bad enough to undergo with one's comrades, but to face it alone seemed frightful. And besides, the very act he was performing was sure to bring greater punishment upon him.

In the midst of such somber thoughts, he heard footsteps approaching. He wriggled away into the shadow. An officer stopped where he had been working, half-stooped to examine the hawser, then changed his mind and straightened up. For a few minutes he stood there, gazing at the lights of the captured schooner, and then went forward again.

Now was the time! Bub crept back and went on sawing. Now two parts were severed. Now three. But one remained. The tension upon this was so great that it readily yielded. Splash! The freed end went overboard. He lay quietly, his heart in his mouth, listening. No one on the cruiser but himself had heard.

He saw the red and green lights of the *Mary Thomas* grow dimmer and dimmer. Then a faint hallo came over the water from the Russian prize crew. Still nobody heard. The smoke continued to pour out of the cruiser's funnels, and her propellers throbbed as mightily as ever.

What was happening on the *Mary Thomas?* Bub could only surmise; but of one thing he was certain: his comrades would assert themselves and overpower the four sailors and the midshipman. A few minutes later he saw a small flash, and straining his ears heard the very faint report of a pistol. Then, oh joy! both the red and green lights suddenly disappeared. The *Mary Thomas* was retaken!

Just as an officer came aft, Bub crept forward, and hid away in one of the boats.

Not an instant too soon. The alarm was given. Loud voices rose in command. The cruiser altered her course. An electric search-light began to throw its white rays across the sea, here, there, everywhere; but in its flashing path no tossing schooner was revealed.

Bub went to sleep soon after that, nor did he wake till the gray of dawn. The engines were pulsing monotonously, and the water, splashing noisily, told him the decks were being washed down. One sweeping glance, and he saw that they were alone on the expanse of ocean. The *Mary Thomas* had escaped. As he lifted his head, a roar of laughter went up from the sailors. Even the officer, who ordered him taken below and locked up, could not quite conceal the laughter in his eyes. Bub thought often in the days of confinement which followed, that they were not very angry with him for what he had done.

He was not far from right. There is a certain innate nobility deep down in the hearts of all men, which forces them to admire a brave act, even if it is performed by an enemy. The Russians were in nowise different from other men. True, a boy had outwitted them; but they could not blame him, and they were sore puzzled as to what to do with him. It would never do to take a little mite like him to represent all that remained of the lost poacher.

So, two weeks later, a United States man-of-war, steaming out of the Russian port of Vladivostok, was signaled by a Russian cruiser. A boat passed between the two ships, and a small boy dropped over the rail upon the deck of the American vessel. A week later he was put ashore at Hakodate, and after some telegraphing, his fare was paid on the railroad to Yokohama.

From the depot he hurried through the quaint Japanese streets to the harbor, and hired a *sampan* boatman to put him aboard a certain vessel whose familiar rigging had quickly caught his eye. Her gaskets were off, her sails unfurled; she was just starting back to the United States. As he came closer, a crowd of sailors sprang upon the forecastle-head, and the windlass-bars rose and fell as the anchor was torn from its muddy bottom.

"'Yankee ship come down the ribber!'" the sea-lawyer's voice rolled out as he led the anchor song.

"'Pull, my bully boys, pull!'" roared back the old familiar chorus, the men's bodies lifting and bending to the rhythm.

Bub Russell paid the boatman and stepped on deck. The anchor was forgotten. A mighty cheer went up from the men, and almost before he could catch his breath he was on the shoulders of the captain, surrounded by his mates, and endeavoring to answer twenty questions to the second.

The next day a schooner hove to off a Japanese fishing village, sent ashore four sailors and a little midshipman, and sailed away. These men did not talk English, but they had money and quickly made their way to Yokohama. From that day the Japanese village folk never heard anything more about them, and they are still a much-talked-of mystery. As the Russian government never said anything about the incident, the United States is still ignorant of the whereabouts of the lost poacher, nor has she ever heard, officially, of the way in which some of her citizens "shanghaied" five subjects of the tsar. Even nations have secrets sometimes.

25
The Sunlanders

THE SUNLANDERS

Mandell is an obscure village on the rim of the polar sea. It is not large, and the people are peaceable, more peaceable even than those of the adjacent tribes. There are few men in Mandell, and many women; wherefore a wholesome and necessary polygamy is in practice; the women bear children with ardor, and the birth of a man-child is hailed with acclamation. Then there is Aab-Waak, whose head rests always on one shoulder, as though at some time the neck had become very tired and refused forevermore its wonted duty.

The cause of all these things, — the peaceableness, and the polygamy, and the tired neck of Aab-Waak, — goes back among the years to the time when the schooner *Search* dropped anchor in Mandell Bay, and when Tyee, chief man of the tribe, conceived a scheme of sudden wealth. To this day the story of things that happened is remembered and spoken of with bated breath by the people of Mandell, who are cousins to the Hungry Folk who live in the west. Children draw closer when the tale is told, and marvel sagely to themselves at the madness of those who might have been their forebears had they not provoked the Sunlanders and come to bitter ends.

It began to happen when six men came ashore from the *Search*, with heavy outfits, as though they had come to stay, and quartered themselves in Neegah's igloo. Not but that they paid well in flour and sugar for the lodging, but Neegah was aggrieved because Mesahchie, his daughter, elected to cast her fortunes and seek food and blanket with Bill-Man, who was leader of the party of white men.

"She is worth a price," Neegah complained to the gathering by the council-fire, when the six white men were asleep. "She is worth a price, for we have more men than women, and the men be bidding high. The hunter Ounenk offered me a kayak, new-made, and a gun which he got in trade from the Hungry Folk. This was I offered, and behold, now she is gone and I have nothing!"

"I, too, did bid for Mesahchie," grumbled a voice, in tones not altogether joyless, and Peelo shoved his broad-cheeked, jovial face for a moment into the light.

"Thou, too," Neegah affirmed. "And there were others. Why is there such a restlessness upon the Sunlanders?" he demanded petulantly. "Why do they not stay at home? The Snow People do not wander to the lands of the Sunlanders."

"Better were it to ask why they come," cried a voice from the darkness, and Aab-Waak pushed his way to the front.

"Ay! Why they come!" clamored many voices, and Aab-Waak waved his hand for silence.

"Men do not dig in the ground for nothing," he began. "And I have it in mind of the Whale People, who are likewise Sunlanders, and who lost their ship in the ice. You all remember the Whale People, who came to us in their broken boats, and who went away into the south with dogs and sleds when the frost arrived and snow covered the land. And you remember, while they waited for the frost, that one man of them dug in the ground, and then two men and three, and then all men of them, with great excitement and much disturbance. What they dug out of the ground we do not know, for they drove us away so we could not see. But afterward, when they were gone, we looked and found nothing. Yet there be much ground and they did not dig it all."

"Ay, Aab-Waak! Ay!" cried the people in admiration.

"Wherefore I have it in mind," he concluded, "that one Sunlander tells another, and that these Sunlanders have been so told and are come to dig in the ground."

"But how can it be that Bill-Man speaks our tongue?" demanded a little weazened old hunter, — "Bill-Man, upon whom never before our eyes have rested?"

"Bill-Man has been other times in the Snow Lands," Aab-Waak answered, "else would he not speak the speech of the Bear People, which is like the speech of the Hungry Folk, which is very like the speech of the Mandells. For there have been many Sunlanders among the Bear People, few among the Hungry Folk, and none at all among the Mandells, save the Whale People and those who sleep now in the igloo of Neegah."

"Their sugar is very good," Neegah commented, "and their flour."

"They have great wealth," Ounenk added. "Yesterday I was to their ship, and beheld most cunning tools of iron, and knives, and guns, and flour, and sugar, and strange foods without end."

"It is so, brothers!" Tyee stood up and exulted inwardly at the respect and silence his people accorded him. "They be very rich, these Sunlanders. Also, they be fools. For behold! They come among us boldly, blindly, and without thought for all of their great wealth. Even now they snore, and we are many and unafraid."

"Mayhap they, too, are unafraid, being great fighters," the weazened little old hunter objected.

But Tyee scowled upon him. "Nay, it would not seem so. They live to the south, under the path of the sun, and are soft as their dogs are soft. You remember the dog of the Whale People? Our dogs ate him the second day, for he was soft and could not fight. The sun is warm and life easy in the Sun Lands, and the men are as women, and the women as children."

Heads nodded in approval, and the women craned their necks to listen.

"It is said they are good to their women, who do little work," tittered Likeeta, a broad-hipped, healthy young woman, daughter to Tyee himself.

"Thou wouldst follow the feet of Mesahchie, eh?" he cried angrily. Then he turned swiftly to the tribesmen. "Look you, brothers, this is the way of the Sunlanders! They have eyes for our women, and take them one by one. As Mesahchie has gone, cheating Neegah of her price, so will Likeeta go, so will they all go, and we be cheated. I have talked with a hunter from the Bear People, and I know. There be Hungry Folk among us; let them speak if my words be true."

The six hunters of the Hungry Folk attested the truth and fell each to telling his neighbor of the Sunlanders and their ways. There were mutterings from the younger men, who had wives to seek, and from the older men, who had daughters to fetch prices, and a low hum of rage rose higher and clearer.

"They are very rich, and have cunning tools of iron, and knives, and guns without end," Tyee suggested craftily, his dream of sudden wealth beginning to take shape.

"I shall take the gun of Bill-Man for myself," Aab-Waak suddenly proclaimed.

"Nay, it shall be mine!" shouted Neegah; "for there is the price of Mesahchie to be reckoned."

"Peace! O brothers!" Tyee swept the assembly with his hands. "Let the women and children go to their igloos. This is the talk of men; let it be for the ears of men."

"There be guns in plenty for all," he said when the women had unwillingly withdrawn. "I doubt not there will be two guns for each man, without thought of the flour and sugar and other things. And it is easy. The six Sunlanders in Neegah's igloo will we kill to-night while they sleep. To-morrow will we go in peace to the ship to trade, and there, when the time favors, kill all their brothers. And to-morrow night there shall be feasting and merriment and division of wealth. And the least man shall possess more than did ever the greatest before. Is it wise, that which I have spoken, brothers?"

A low growl of approval answered him, and preparation for the attack was begun. The six Hungry Folk, as became members of a wealthier tribe, were armed with rifles and plenteously supplied with ammunition. But it was only here and there that a Mandell possessed a gun, many of which were broken, and there was a general slackness of powder and shells. This poverty of war weapons, however, was relieved by myriads of bone-headed arrows and casting-spears for work at a distance, and for close quarters steel knives of Russian and Yankee make.

"Let there be no noise," Tyee finally instructed; "but be there many on every side of the igloo, and close, so that the Sunlanders may not break through. Then do you, Neegah, with six of the young men behind, crawl in to where they sleep. Take no guns, which be prone to go off at unexpected times, but put the strength of your arms into the knives."

"And be it understood that no harm befall Mesahchie, who is worth a price," Neegah whispered hoarsely.

Flat upon the ground, the small army concentred on the igloo, and behind, deliciously expectant, crouched many women and children, come out to witness the murder. The brief August night was passing, and in the gray of dawn could be dimly discerned the creeping forms of Neegah and the young men. Without pause, on hands and knees, they entered the long passageway and disappeared. Tyee rose up and rubbed his hands. All was going well. Head after head in the big circle lifted and waited. Each man pictured the scene according to his nature — the sleeping men, the plunge of the knives, and the sudden death in the dark.

A loud hail, in the voice of a Sunlander, rent the silence, and a shot rang out. Then an uproar broke loose inside the igloo. Without premeditation, the circle swept forward into the passageway. On the inside, half a dozen repeating rifles began to chatter, and the Mandells, jammed in the confined space, were powerless. Those at the front strove madly to retreat from the fire-spitting guns in their very faces, and those in the rear pressed as madly forward to the attack. The bullets from the big 45:90's drove through half a dozen men at a shot, and the passageway, gorged with surging, helpless men, became a shambles. The rifles, pumped without aim into the mass, withered it away like a machine gun, and against that steady stream of death no man could advance.

"Never was there the like!" panted one of the Hungry Folk. "I did but look in, and the dead were piled like seals on the ice after a killing!"

"Did I not say, mayhap, they were fighters?" cackled the weazened old hunter.

"It was to be expected," Aab-Waak answered stoutly. "We fought in a trap of our making."

"O ye fools!" Tyee chided. "Ye sons of fools! It was not planned, this thing ye have done. To Neegah and the six young men only was it given to go inside. My cunning is superior to the cunning of the Sunlanders, but ye take away its edge, and rob me of its strength, and make it worse than no cunning at all!"

No one made reply, and all eyes centred on the igloo, which loomed vague and monstrous against the clear northeast sky. Through a hole in the roof the smoke from the rifles curled slowly upward in the pulseless air, and now and again a wounded man crawled painfully through the gray.

"Let each ask of his neighbor for Neegah and the six young men," Tyee commanded.

And after a time the answer came back, "Neegah and the six young men are not."

"And many more are not!" wailed a woman to the rear.

"The more wealth for those who are left," Tyee grimly consoled. Then, turning to Aab-Waak, he said: "Go thou, and gather together many sealskins filled with oil. Let the hunters empty them on the outside wood of the igloo and of the passage. And let them put fire to it ere the Sunlanders make holes in the igloo for their guns."

Even as he spoke a hole appeared in the dirt plastered between the logs, a rifle muzzle protruded, and one of the Hungry Folk clapped hand to his side and leaped in the air. A second shot, through the lungs, brought him to the ground. Tyee and the rest scattered to either side, out of direct range, and Aab-Waak hastened the men forward with the skins of oil. Avoiding the loopholes, which were making on every side of the igloo, they emptied the skins on the dry drift-logs brought down by the Mandell River from the tree-lands to the south. Ounenk ran forward with a blazing brand, and the flames leaped upward. Many minutes passed, without sign, and they held their weapons ready as the fire gained headway.

Tyee rubbed his hands gleefully as the dry structure burned and crackled. "Now we have them, brothers! In the trap!"

"And no one may gainsay me the gun of Bill-Man," Aab-Waak announced.

"Save Bill-Man," squeaked the old hunter. "For behold, he cometh now!"

Covered with a singed and blackened blanket, the big white man leaped out of the blazing entrance, and on his heels, likewise shielded, came Mesahchie, and the five other Sunlanders. The Hungry Folk tried to check the rush with an ill-directed volley, while the Mandells hurled in a cloud of spears and arrows. But the Sunlanders cast their flaming blankets from them as they ran, and it was seen that each bore on his shoulders a small pack of ammunition. Of all their possessions, they had chosen to save that. Running swiftly and with purpose, they broke the circle and headed directly for the great cliff, which towered blackly in the brightening day a half-mile to the rear of the village.

But Tyee knelt on one knee and lined the sights of his rifle on the rearmost Sunlander. A great shout went up when he pulled the trigger and the man fell forward, struggled partly up, and fell again. Without regard for the rain of arrows, another Sunlander ran back, bent over him, and lifted him across his shoulders. But the Mandell spearmen were crowding up into closer range, and a strong cast transfixed the wounded man. He cried out and became swiftly limp as his comrade lowered him to the ground. In the meanwhile, Bill-Man and the three others had made a stand and were driving a leaden hail into the advancing spearmen. The fifth Sunlander bent over his stricken fellow, felt the heart, and then coolly cut the straps of the pack and stood up with the ammunition and extra gun.

"Now is he a fool!" cried Tyee, leaping high, as he ran forward, to clear the squirming body of one of the Hungry Folk.

His own rifle was clogged so that he could not use it, and he called out for some one to spear the Sunlander, who had turned and was running for safety under the protecting fire. The little old hunter poised his spear on the throwing-stick, swept his arm back as he ran, and delivered the cast.

"By the body of the Wolf, say I, it was a good throw!" Tyee praised, as the fleeing man pitched forward, the spear standing upright between his shoulders and swaying slowly forward and back.

The little weazened old man coughed and sat down. A streak of red showed on his lips and welled into a thick stream. He coughed again, and a strange whistling came and went with his breath.

"They, too, are unafraid, being great fighters," he wheezed, pawing aimlessly with his hands. "And behold! Bill-Man comes now!"

Tyee glanced up. Four Mandells and one of the Hungry Folk had rushed upon the fallen man and were spearing him from his knees back to the earth. In the twinkling of an eye, Tyee saw four of them cut down by the bullets of the Sunlanders. The fifth, as yet unhurt, seized the two rifles, but as he stood up to make off he was whirled almost completely around by the impact of a bullet in the arm, steadied by a second, and overthrown by the shock of a third. A moment later and Bill-Man was on the spot, cutting the pack-straps and picking up the guns.

This Tyee saw, and his own people falling as they straggled forward, and he was aware of a quick doubt, and resolved to lie where he was and see more. For some unaccountable reason, Mesahchie was running back to Bill-Man; but before she could reach him, Tyee saw Peelo run out and throw arms about her. He essayed to sling her across his shoulder, but she grappled with him, tearing and scratching at his face. Then she tripped him, and the pair fell heavily. When they regained their feet, Peelo had shifted his grip so that one arm was passed under her chin, the wrist pressing into her throat and strangling her. He buried his face in her breast, taking the blows of her hands on his thick mat of hair, and began slowly to force her off the field. Then it was, retreating with the weapons of his fallen comrades, that Bill-Man came upon them. As Mesahchie saw him, she twirled the victim around and held him steady. Bill-Man swung the rifle in his right hand, and hardly easing his stride, delivered the blow. Tyee saw Peelo drive to the earth as smote by a falling star, and the Sunlander and Neegah's daughter fleeing side by side.

A bunch of Mandells, led by one of the Hungry Folk, made a futile rush which melted away into the earth before the scorching fire.

Tyee caught his breath and murmured, "Like the young frost in the morning sun."

"As I say, they are great fighters," the old hunter whispered weakly, far gone in hemorrhage. "I know. I have heard. They be sea-robbers and hunters of seals; and they shoot quick and true, for it is their way of life and the work of their hands."

"Like the young frost in the morning sun," Tyee repeated, crouching for shelter behind the dying man and peering at intervals about him.

It was no longer a fight, for no Mandell man dared venture forward, and as it was, they were too close to the Sunlanders to go back. Three tried it, scattering and scurrying like rabbits; but one came down with a

Tyee saw Peelo drive to the earth as smote by a falling star, and the Sunlander and Neegah's daughter fleeing side by side

broken leg, another was shot through the body, and the third, twisting and dodging, fell on the edge of the village. So the tribesmen crouched in the hollow places and burrowed into the dirt in the open, while the Sunlanders' bullets searched the plain.

"Move not," Tyee pleaded, as Aab-Waak came worming over the ground to him. "Move not, good Aab-Waak, else you bring death upon us."

"Death sits upon many," Aab-Waak laughed; "wherefore, as you say, there will be much wealth in division. My father breathes fast and short behind the big rock yon, and beyond, twisted like in a knot, lieth my brother. But their share shall be my share, and it is well."

"As you say, good Aab-Waak, and as I have said; but before division must come that which we may divide, and the Sunlanders be not yet dead."

A bullet glanced from a rock before them, and singing shrilly, rose low over their heads on its second flight. Tyee ducked and shivered, but Aab-Waak grinned and sought vainly to follow it with his eyes.

"So swiftly they go, one may not see them," he observed.

"But many be dead of us," Tyee went on.

"And many be left," was the reply. "And they hug close to the earth, for they have become wise in the fashion of fighting. Further, they are angered. Moreover, when we have killed the Sunlanders on the ship, there will remain but four on the land. These may take long to kill, but in the end it will happen."

"How may we go down to the ship when we cannot go this way or that?" Tyee questioned.

"It is a bad place where lie Bill-Man and his brothers," Aab-Waak explained. "We may come upon them from every side, which is not good. So they aim to get their backs against the cliff and wait until their brothers of the ship come to give them aid."

"Never shall they come from the ship, their brothers! I have said it."

Tyee was gathering courage again, and when the Sunlanders verified the prediction by retreating to the cliff, he was light-hearted as ever.

"There be only three of us!" complained one of the Hungry Folk as they came together for council.

"Therefore, instead of two, shall you have four guns each," was Tyee's rejoinder.

"We did good fighting."

"Ay; and if it should happen that two of you be left, then will you have six guns each. Therefore, fight well."

"And if there be none of them left?" Aab-Waak whispered slyly.

"Then will *we* have the guns, you and I," Tyee whispered back.

However, to propitiate the Hungry Folk, he made one of them leader of the ship expedition. This party comprised fully two-thirds of the tribesmen, and departed for the coast, a dozen miles away, laden with skins and things to trade. The remaining men were disposed in a large half-circle about the breastwork which Bill-Man and his Sunlanders had begun to throw up. Tyee was quick to note the virtues of things, and at once set his men to digging shallow trenches.

"The time will go before they are aware," he explained to Aab-Waak; "and their minds being busy, they will not think overmuch of the dead that are, nor gather trouble to themselves. And in the dark of night they may creep closer, so that when the Sunlanders look forth in the morning light they will find us very near."

In the midday heat the men ceased from their work and made a meal of dried fish and seal oil which the women brought up. There was some clamor for the food of the Sunlanders in the igloo of Neegah, but Tyee refused to divide it until the return of the ship party. Speculations upon the outcome became rife, but in the midst of it a dull boom drifted up over the land from the sea. The keen-eyed ones made out a dense cloud of smoke, which quickly disappeared, and which they averred was directly over the ship of the Sunlanders. Tyee was of the opinion that it was a big gun. Aab-Waak did not know, but thought it might be a signal of some sort. Anyway, he said, it was time something happened.

Five or six hours afterward a solitary man was descried coming across the wide flat from the sea, and the women and children poured out upon him in a body. It was Ounenk, naked, winded, and wounded. The blood still trickled down his face from a gash on the forehead. His left arm, frightfully mangled, hung helpless at his side. But most significant of all, there was a wild gleam in his eyes which betokened the women knew not what.

"Where be Peshack?" an old squaw queried sharply.

"And Olitlie?" "And Polak?" "And Mah-Kook?" the voices took up the cry.

But he said nothing, brushing his way through the clamorous mass and directing his staggering steps toward Tyee. The old squaw raised the wail, and one by one the women joined her as they swung in behind. The men crawled out of their trenches and ran back to gather about Tyee, and it was noticed that the Sunlanders climbed upon their barricade to see.

Ounenk halted, swept the blood from his eyes, and looked about. He strove to speak, but his dry lips were glued together. Likeeta fetched him water, and he grunted and drank again.

"Was it a fight?" Tyee demanded finally,—"a good fight?"

"Ho! ho! ho!" So suddenly and so fiercely did Ounenk laugh that every voice hushed. "Never was there such a fight! So I say, I, Ounenk, fighter beforetime of beasts and men. And ere I forget, let me speak fat words and wise. By fighting will the Sunlanders teach us Mandell Folk how to fight. And if we fight long enough, we shall be great fighters, even as the Sunlanders, or else we shall be — dead. Ho! ho! ho! It was a fight!"

"Where be thy brothers?" Tyee shook him till he shrieked from the pain of his hurts.

Ounenk sobered. "My brothers? They are not."

"And Pome-Lee?" cried one of the two Hungry Folk; "Pome-Lee, the son of my mother?"

"Pome-Lee is not," Ounenk answered in a monotonous voice.

"And the Sunlanders?" from Aab-Waak.

"The Sunlanders are not."

"Then the ship of the Sunlanders, and the wealth and guns and things?" Tyee demanded.

"Neither the ship of the Sunlanders, nor the wealth and guns and things," was the unvarying response. "All are not. Nothing is. I only am."

"And thou art a fool."

"It may be so," Ounenk answered, unruffled. "I have seen that which would well make me a fool."

Tyee held his tongue, and all waited till it should please Ounenk to tell the story in his own way.

"We took no guns, O Tyee," he at last began; "no guns, my brothers — only knives and hunting bows and spears. And in twos and threes, in our kayaks, we came to the ship. They were glad to see us, the Sunlanders, and we spread our skins and they brought out their articles of trade, and everything was well. And Pome-Lee waited — waited till the sun was well overhead and they sat at meat, when he gave the cry and we fell upon them. Never was there such a fight, and never such fighters. Half did we kill in the quickness of surprise, but the half that was left became as devils, and they multiplied themselves, and everywhere they fought like devils. Three put their backs against the mast of the ship, and we ringed them with our dead before they died. And some got guns and shot with both eyes wide open, and very quick and sure. And one got a big gun, from which at one time he shot many small bullets. And so behold!"

Ounenk pointed to his ear, neatly pierced by a buckshot.

"But I, Ounenk, drove my spear through his back from behind. And in such fashion, one way and another, did we kill them all — all save the head man. And him we were about, many of us, and he was alone, when he made a great cry and broke through us, five or six dragging upon him, and ran down inside the ship. And then, when the wealth of the ship was ours, and only the head man down below whom we would kill presently, why then there was a sound as of all the guns in the world — a mighty sound! And like a bird I rose up in the air, and the living Mandell Folk, and the dead Sunlanders, the little kayaks, the big ship, the guns, the wealth — everything rose up in the air. So I say, I, Ounenk, who tell the tale, am the only one left."

A great silence fell upon the assemblage. Tyee looked at Aab-Waak with awe-struck eyes, but forbore to speak. Even the women were too stunned to wail the dead.

Ounenk looked about him with pride. "I, only, am left," he repeated.

But at that instant a rifle cracked from Bill-Man's barricade, and there was a sharp spat and thud on the chest of Ounenk. He swayed backward and came forward again, a look of startled surprise on his face. He gasped, and his lips writhed in a grim smile. There was a shrinking together of the shoulders and a bending of the knees. He shook himself, as might a drowsing man, and straightened up. But the shrinking and bending began again, and he sank down slowly, quite slowly, to the ground.

It was a clean mile from the pit of the Sunlanders, and death had spanned it. A great cry of rage went up, and in it there was much of blood-vengeance, much of the unreasoned ferocity of the brute. Tyee and Aab-Waak tried to hold the Mandell Folk back, were thrust aside, and could only turn and watch the mad charge. But no shots came from the Sunlanders, and ere half the distance was covered, many affrighted by the mysterious silence of the pit, halted and waited. The wilder spirits bore on and when they had cut the remaining distance in half, the pit still showed no sign of life. At two hundred yards they slowed down and bunched; at one hundred, they stopped, a score of them, suspicious, and conferred together.

Then a wreath of smoke crowned the barricade, and they scattered like a handful of pebbles thrown at random. Four went down, and four more, and they continued swiftly to fall, one and two at a time, till but one remained, and he in full flight with death singing about his ears. It was Nok, a young hunter, long-legged and tall, and he ran as never before. He skimmed across the naked open like a bird, and soared and sailed and curved from side to side. The rifles in the pit rang out in solid volley; they flut-flut-flut-flutted in ragged sequence; and still Nok rose and dipped and rose again unharmed. There was a lull in the firing, as though the Sunlanders had given over, and Nok curved less and less in his flight till he darted straight forward at every leap. And then, as he leaped cleanly and well, one lone rifle barked from the pit, and he doubled up in mid-air, struck the ground in a ball, and like a ball bounced from the impact, and came down in a broken heap.

"Who so swift as the swift-winged lead?" Aab-Waak pondered.

Tyee grunted and turned away. The incident was closed and there was more pressing matter at hand. One Hungry Man and forty fighters, some of them hurt, remained; and there were four Sunlanders yet to reckon with.

"We will keep them in their hole by the cliff," he said, "and when famine has gripped them hard we will slay them like children."

"But of what matter to fight?" queried Oloof, one of the younger men. "The wealth of the Sunlanders is not; only remains that in the igloo of Neegah, a paltry quantity—"

He broke off hastily as the air by his ear split sharply to the passage of a bullet.

Tyee laughed scornfully. "Let that be thy answer. What else may we do with this mad breed of Sunlanders which will not die?"

"What a thing is foolishness!" Oloof protested, his ears furtively alert for the coming of other bullets. "It is not right that they should fight so, these Sunlanders. Why will they not die easily? They are fools not to know that they are dead men, and they give us much trouble."

"We fought before for great wealth; we fight now that we may live," Aab-Waak summed up succinctly.

That night there was a clash in the trenches, and shots exchanged. And in the morning the igloo of Neegah was found empty of the Sunlanders' possessions. These they themselves had taken, for the signs of their trail were visible to the sun. Oloof climbed to the brow of the cliff to hurl great stones down into the pit, but the cliff overhung, and he hurled down abuse and insult instead, and promised bitter torture to them in the end. Bill-Man mocked him back in the tongue of the Bear Folk, and Tyee, lifting his head from a trench to see, had his shoulder scratched deeply by a bullet.

And in the dreary days that followed, and in the wild nights when they pushed the trenches closer, there was much discussion as to the wisdom of letting the Sunlanders go. But of this they were afraid, and the women raised a cry always at the thought. This much they had seen of the Sunlanders; they cared to see no more. All the time the whistle and blub-blub of bullets filled the air, and all the time the death-list grew. In the golden sunrise came the faint, far crack of a rifle, and a stricken woman would throw up her hands on the distant edge of the village; in the noonday heat, men in the trenches heard the shrill sing-song and knew their deaths; or in the gray afterglow of evening, the dirt kicked up in puffs by the winking fires. And through the nights the long "Wah-hoo-ha-a wah-hoo-ha-a!" of mourning women held dolorous sway.

As Tyee had promised, in the end famine gripped the Sunlanders. And once, when an early fall gale blew, one of them crawled through the darkness past the trenches and stole many dried fish. But he could not get back with them, and the sun found him vainly hiding in the village. So he fought the great fight by himself, and in a narrow ring of Mandell Folk shot four with his revolver, and ere they could lay hands on him for the torture, turned it on himself and died.

This threw a gloom upon the people. Oloof put the question, "If one man die so hard, how hard will die the three who yet are left?"

Then Mesahchie stood up on the barricade and called in by name three dogs which had wandered close, — meat and life, — which set back the day of reckoning and put despair in the hearts of the Mandell Folk. And on the head of Mesahchie were showered the curses of a generation.

The days dragged by. The sun hurried south, the nights grew long and longer, and there was a touch of frost in the air. And still the Sunlanders held the pit. Hearts were breaking under the unending strain, and Tyee thought hard and deep. Then he sent forth word that all the skins and hides of all the tribe be collected. These he had made into huge cylindrical bales, and behind each bale he placed a man.

When the word was given the brief day was almost spent, and it was slow work and tedious, rolling the big bales forward foot by foot. The bullets of the Sunlanders blub-blubbed and thudded against them, but could not go through, and the men howled their delight. But the dark was at hand, and Tyee, secure of success, called the bales back to the trenches.

In the morning, in the face of an unearthly silence from the pit, the real advance began. At first, with large intervals between, the bales slowly converged as the circle drew in. At a hundred yards they were quite close together, so that Tyee's order to halt was passed along in whispers. The pit showed no sign of life. They watched long and sharply, but nothing stirred. The advance was taken up and the manoeuvre repeated at fifty yards. Still no sign nor sound. Tyee shook his head, and even Aab-Waak was dubious. But the order was given to go on, and go on they did, till bale touched bale and a solid rampart of skin and hide bowed out from the cliff about the pit and back to the cliff again.

Tyee looked back and saw the women and children clustering blackly in the deserted trenches. He looked ahead at the silent pit. The men were wriggling nervously, and he ordered every second bale forward. This double line advanced till bale touched bale as before. Then Aab-Waak, of his own will, pushed one bale forward alone. When it touched the barricade, he waited a long while. After that he tossed unresponsive rocks over into the pit, and finally, with great care, stood up and peered in. A carpet of empty cartridges, a few white-picked dog bones, and a soggy place where water dripped from a crevice, met his eyes. That was all. The Sunlanders were gone.

There were murmurings of witchcraft, vague complaints, dark looks which foreshadowed to Tyee dread things which yet might come to pass, and he breathed easier when Aab-Waak took up the trail along the base of the cliff.

"The cave!" Tyee cried. "They foresaw my wisdom of the skin-bales and fled away into the cave!"

The cliff was honey-combed with a labyrinth of subterranean passages which found vent in an opening midway between the pit and where the trench tapped the wall. Thither, and with many exclamations, the tribesmen followed Aab-Waak, and, arrived, they saw plainly where the Sunlanders had climbed to the mouth, twenty and odd feet above.

"Now the thing is done," Tyee said, rubbing his hands. "Let word go forth that rejoicing be made, for they are in the trap now, these Sunlanders, — in the trap. The young men shall climb up, and the mouth of the cave be filled with stones, so that Bill-Man and his brothers and Mesahchie shall by famine be pinched to shadows and die cursing in the silence and dark."

Cries of delight and relief greeted this, and Howgah, the last of the Hungry Folk, swarmed up the steep slant and drew himself, crouching, upon the lip of the opening. But as he crouched, a muffled report rushed forth, and as he clung desperately to the slippery edge, a second. His grip loosed with reluctant weakness, and he pitched down at the feet of Tyee, quivered for a moment like some monstrous jelly, and was still.

"How should I know they were great fighters and unafraid?" Tyee demanded, spurred to defence by recollection of the dark looks and vague complaints.

"We were many and happy," one of the men stated baldly. Another fingered his spear with a prurient hand.

But Oloof cried them cease. "Give ear, my brothers! There be another way! As a boy I chanced upon it playing along the steep. It is hidden by the rocks, and there is no reason that a man should go there; wherefore it is secret, and no man knows. It is very small, and you crawl on your belly a long way, and then you are in the cave. To-night we will so crawl, without noise, on our bellies, and come upon the Sunlanders from behind. And to-morrow we will be at peace, and never again will we quarrel with the Sunlanders in the years to come."

"Never again!" chorussed the weary men. "Never again!" And Tyee joined with them.

That night, with the memory of their dead in their hearts, and in their hands stones and spears and knives, the horde of women and children collected about the known mouth of the cave. Down the twenty and odd precarious feet to the ground no Sunlander could hope to pass and live. In the village remained only the wounded men, while every able man — and there were thirty of them — followed Oloof to the secret opening. A hundred feet of broken ledges and insecurely heaped rocks were between it and the earth, and because of the rocks, which might be displaced by the touch of hand or foot, but one man climbed at a time. Oloof went up first, called softly for the next to come on, and disappeared inside. A man followed, a second, and a third, and so on, till only Tyee remained. He received the call of the last man, but a quick doubt assailed him and he stayed to ponder. Half an hour later he swung up to the opening and peered in. He could feel the narrowness of the passage, and the darkness before him took on solidity. The fear of the walled-in earth chilled him and he could not venture. All the men who had died, from Neegah the first of the Mandells, to Howgah the last of the Hungry Folk, came and sat with him, but he chose the terror of their company rather than face the horror which he felt to lurk in the thick blackness. He had been sitting long when something soft and cold fluttered lightly on his cheek, and he knew the first winter's snow was falling. The dim dawn came, and after that the bright day, when he heard a low guttural sobbing, which came and went at intervals along the passage and which drew closer each time and more distinct. He slipped over the edge, dropped his feet to the first ledge, and waited.

That which sobbed made slow progress, but at last, after many halts, it reached him, and he was sure no Sunlander made the noise. So he reached a hand inside, and where there should have been a head felt the shoulders of a man uplifted on bent arms. The head he found later, not erect, but hanging straight down so that the crown rested on the floor of the passage.

"Is it you, Tyee?" the head said. "For it is I, Aab-Waak, who am helpless and broken as a rough-flung spear. My head is in the dirt, and I may not climb down unaided."

Tyee clambered in, dragged him up with his back against the wall, but the head hung down on the chest and sobbed and wailed.

"Ai-oo-o, ai-oo-o!" it went. "Oloof forgot, for Mesahchie likewise knew the secret and showed the Sunlanders, else they would not have waited at the end of the narrow way. Wherefore, I am a broken man, and helpless — ai-oo-o, ai-oo-o!"

"And did they die, the cursed Sunlanders, at the end of the narrow way?" Tyee demanded.

"How should I know they waited?" Aab-Waak gurgled. "For my brothers had gone before, many of them, and there was no sound of struggle. How should I know why there should be no sound of struggle? And ere I knew, two hands were about my neck so that I could not cry out and warn my brothers yet to come. And then there were two hands more on my head, and two more on my feet. In this fashion the three Sunlanders had me. And while the hands held my head in the one place, the hands on my feet swung my body around, and as we wring the neck of a duck in the marsh, so my neck was wrung.

"But it was not given that I should die," he went on, a remnant of pride yet glimmering. "I, only, am left. Oloof and the rest lie on their backs in a row, and their faces turn this way and that, and the faces of some be underneath where the backs of their heads should be. It is not good to look upon; for when life returned to me I saw them all by the light of a torch which the Sunlanders left, and I had been laid with them in the row."

"So? So?" Tyee mused, too stunned for speech.

He started suddenly, and shivered, for the voice of Bill-Man shot out at him from the passage.

"It is well," it said. "I look for the man who crawls with the broken neck, and lo, do I find Tyee. Throw down thy gun, Tyee, so that I may hear it strike among the rocks."

Tyee obeyed passively, and Bill-Man crawled forward into the light. Tyee looked at him curiously. He was gaunt and worn and dirty, and his eyes burned like twin coals in their cavernous sockets.

"I am hungry, Tyee," he said. "Very hungry."

"And I am dirt at thy feet," Tyee responded. "Thy word is my law. Further, I commanded my people not to withstand thee. I counselled—"

But Bill-Man had turned and was calling back into the passage. "Hey! Charley! Jim! Fetch the woman along and come on!"

"We go now to eat," he said, when his comrades and Mesahchie had joined him.

Tyee rubbed his hands deprecatingly. "We have little, but it is thine."

"After that we go south on the snow," Bill-Man continued.

"May you go without hardship and the trail be easy."

"It is a long way. We will need dogs and food — much!"

"Thine the pick of our dogs and the food they may carry."

Bill-Man slipped over the edge of the opening and prepared to descend. "But we come again, Tyee. We come again, and our days shall be long in the land."

And so they departed into the trackless south, Bill-Man, his brothers, and Mesahchie. And when the next year came, the *Search Number Two* rode at anchor in Mandell Bay. The few Mandell men, who survived because their wounds had prevented their crawling into the cave, went to work at the hest of the Sunlanders and dug in the ground. They hunt and fish no more, but receive a daily wage, with which they buy flour, sugar, calico, and such things which the *Search Number Two* brings on her yearly trip from the Sunlands.

And this mine is worked in secret, as many Northland mines have been worked; and no white man outside the Company, which is Bill-Man, Jim, and Charley, knows the whereabouts of Mandell on the rim of the polar sea. Aab-Waak still carries his head on one shoulder, is become an oracle, and preaches peace to the younger generation, for which he receives a pension from the Company. Tyee is foreman of the mine. But he has achieved a new theory concerning the Sunlanders.

"They that live under the path of the sun are not soft," he says, smoking his pipe and watching the day-shift take itself off and the night-shift go on. "For the sun enters into their blood and burns them with a great fire till they are filled with lusts and passions. They burn always, so that they may not know when they are beaten. Further, there is an unrest in them, which is a devil, and they are flung out over the earth to toil and suffer and fight without end. I know. I am Tyee."

26
Where the Trail Forks

WHERE THE TRAIL FORKS

The singer, clean-faced and cheery-eyed, bent over and added water to a pot of simmering beans, and then, rising, a stick of firewood in hand, drove back the circling dogs from the grub-box and cooking-gear. He was blue of eye, and his long hair was golden, and it was a pleasure to look upon his lusty freshness. A new moon was thrusting a dim horn above the white line of close-packed snow-capped pines which ringed the camp and segregated it from all the world. Overhead, so clear it was and cold, the stars danced with quick, pulsating movements. To the southeast an evanescent greenish glow heralded the opening revels of the aurora borealis. Two men, in the immediate foreground, lay upon the bearskin which was their bed. Between the skin and naked snow was a six-inch layer of pine boughs. The blankets were rolled back. For shelter, there was a fly at their backs, — a sheet of canvas stretched between two trees and angling at forty-five degrees. This caught the radiating heat from the fire and flung it down upon the skin. Another man sat on a sled, drawn close to the blaze, mending moccasins. To the right, a heap of frozen gravel and a rude windlass denoted where they toiled each day in dismal groping for the pay-streak. To the left, four pairs of snowshoes stood erect, showing the mode of travel which obtained when the stamped snow of the camp was left behind.

That Schwabian folk-song sounded strangely pathetic under the cold northern stars, and did not do the men good who lounged about the fire after the toil of the day. It put a dull ache into their hearts, and a yearning which was akin to belly-hunger, and sent their souls questing southward across the divides to the sun-lands.

"For the love of God, Sigmund, shut up!" expostulated one of the men. His hands were clenched painfully, but he hid them from sight in the folds of the bearskin upon which he lay.

"And what for, Dave Wertz?" Sigmund demanded. "Why shall I not sing when the heart is glad?"

"Because you've got no call to, that's why. Look about you, man, and think of the grub we've been defiling our bodies with for the last twelvemonth, and the way we've lived and worked like beasts!"

Thus abjured, Sigmund, the golden-haired, surveyed it all, and the frost-rimmed wolf-dogs and the vapor breaths of the men. "And why shall not the heart be glad?" he laughed. "It is good; it is all good. As for the grub —" He doubled up his arm and caressed the swelling biceps. "And if we have lived and worked like beasts, have we not been paid like kings? Twenty dollars to the pan the streak is running, and we know it to be eight feet thick. It is another Klondike — and we know it — Jim Hawes there, by your elbow, knows it and complains not. And there's Hitchcock! He sews moccasins like an old woman, and waits against the time. Only you can't wait and work until the wash-up in the spring. Then we shall all be rich, rich as kings, only you cannot wait. You want to go back to the States. So do I, and I was born there, but I can wait, when each day the gold in the pan shows up yellow as butter in the churning. But you want your good time, and, like a child, you cry for it now. Bah! Why shall I not sing:

"In a year, in a year, when the grapes
are ripe,
I shall stay no more away.
Then if you still are true, my love,
It will be our wedding day.
In a year, in a year, when my time is
past,
Then I'll live in your love for aye.
Then if you still are true, my love,
It will be our wedding day."

The dogs, bristling and growling, drew in closer to the firelight. There was a monotonous crunch-crunch of webbed shoes, and between each crunch the dragging forward of the heel of the shoe like the sound of sifting sugar. Sigmund broke off for his song to hurl oaths and firewood at the animals. Then the light was parted by a fur-clad figure, and an Indian girl slipped out of the webs, threw back the hood of her squirrel-skin *parka,* and stood in their midst. Sigmund and the men on the bearskin greeted her as "Sipsu," with the customary "Hello," but Hitchcock made room on the sled that she might sit beside him.

"And how goes it, Sipsu?" he asked, talking, after her fashion, in broken English and bastard Chinook. "Is the hunger still mighty in the camp? and has the witch doctor yet found the cause wherefore game is scarce and no moose in the land?"

"Yes; even so. There is little game, and we prepare to eat the dogs. Also has the witch doctor found the cause of all this evil, and to-morrow will he make sacrifice and cleanse the camp."

"And what does the sacrifice chance to be? — a new-born babe or some poor devil of a squaw, old and shaky, who is a care to the tribe and better out of the way?"

"It chanced not that wise; for the need was great, and he chose none other than the chief's daughter; none other than I, Sipsu."

"Hell!" The word rose slowly to Hitchcock's lips, and brimmed over full and deep, in a way which bespoke wonder and consideration.

"Wherefore we stand by a forking of the trail, you and I," she went on calmly, "and I have come that we may look once more upon each other, and once more only."

She was born of primitive stock, and primitive had been her traditions and her days; so she regarded life stoically, and human sacrifice as part of the natural order. The powers which ruled the daylight and the dark, the flood and the frost, the bursting of the bud and the withering of the leaf, were angry and in need of propitiation. This they exacted in many ways, — death in the bad water, through the treacherous ice-crust, by the grip of the grizzly, or a wasting sickness which fell upon a man in his own lodge till he coughed, and the life of his lungs went out through his mouth and nostrils. Likewise did the powers receive sacrifice. It was all one. And the witch doctor was versed in the thoughts of the powers and chose unerringly. It was very natural. Death came by many ways, yet was it all one after all, — a manifestation of the all-powerful and inscrutable.

But Hitchcock came of a later world-breed. His traditions were less concrete and without reverence, and he said, "Not so, Sipsu. You are young, and yet in the full joy of life. The witch doctor is a fool, and his choice is evil. This thing shall not be."

She smiled and answered, "Life is not kind, and for many reasons. First, it made of us twain the one white and the other red, which is bad. Then it crossed our trails, and now it parts them again; and we can do nothing. Once before, when the gods were angry, did your brothers come to the camp. They were three, big men and white, and they said the thing shall not be. But they died quickly, and the thing was."

Hitchcock nodded that he heard, half-turned, and lifted his voice. "Look here, you fellows! There's a lot of foolery going on over to the camp, and they're getting ready to murder Sipsu. What d' ye say?"

Wertz looked at Hawes, and Hawes looked back, but neither spoke. Sigmund dropped his head, and petted the shepherd dog between his knees. He had brought Shep in with him from the outside, and thought a great deal of the animal. In fact, a certain girl, who was much in his thoughts, and whose picture in the little locket on his breast often inspired him to sing, had given him the dog and her blessing when they kissed good-by and he started on his Northland quest.

"What d' ye say?" Hitchcock repeated.

"Mebbe it's not so serious," Hawes answered with deliberation. "Most likely it's only a girl's story."

"That isn't the point!" Hitchcock felt a hot flush of anger sweep over him at their evident reluctance. "The question is, if it is so, are we going to stand it? What are we going to do?"

"I don't see any call to interfere," spoke up Wertz. "If it is so, it is so, and that's all there is about it. It's a way these people have of doing. It's their religion, and it's no concern of ours. Our concern is to get the dust and then get out of this God-forsaken land. 'T isn't fit for naught else but beasts? And what are these black devils but beasts? Besides, it'd be damn poor policy."

"That's what I say," chimed in Hawes.

"Here we are, four of us, three hundred miles from the Yukon or a white face. And what can we do against half-a-hundred Indians? If we quarrel with them, we have to vamose; if we fight, we are wiped out. Further, we've struck pay, and, by God! I, for one, am going to stick by it!"

"Ditto here," supplemented Wertz.

Hitchcock turned impatiently to Sigmund, who was softly singing, —

"In a year, in a year, when the grapes are ripe,
I shall stay no more away."

"Well, it's this way, Hitchcock," he finally said, "I'm in the same boat with the rest. If three-score bucks have made up their mind to kill the girl, why, we can't help it. One rush, and we'd be wiped off the landscape. And what good'd that be? They'd still have the girl. There's no use in going against the customs of a people except you're in force."

"But we are in force!" Hitchcock broke in.

"Four whites are a match for a hundred times as many reds. And think of the girl!"

Sigmund stroked the dog meditatively. "But I do think of the girl. And her eyes are blue like summer skies, and laughing like summer seas, and her hair is yellow, like mine, and braided in ropes the size of a big man's arms. She's waiting for me, out there, in a better land. And she's waited long, and now my pile's in sight I'm not going to throw it away."

"And shamed I would be to look into the girl's blue eyes and remember the black ones of the girl whose blood was on my hands," Hitchcock sneered; for he was born to honor and championship, and to do the thing for the thing's sake, nor stop to weigh or measure.

Sigmund shook his head. "You can't make me mad, Hitchcock, nor do mad things because of your madness. It's a cold business proposition and a question of facts. I did n't come to this country for my health, and, further, it's impossible for us to raise a hand. If it is so, it is too bad for the girl, that's all. It's a way of her people, and it just happens we're on the spot this one time. They've done the same for a thousand-thousand years, and they're going to do it now, and they'll go on doing it for all time to come. Besides, they're not our kind. Nor's the girl. No, I take my stand with Wertz and Hawes, and —"

But the dogs snarled and drew in, and he broke off, listening to the crunch-crunch of many snowshoes. Indian after Indian stalked into the firelight, tall and grim, fur-clad and silent, their shadows dancing grotesquely on the snow. One, the witch doctor, spoke gutturally to Sipsu. His face was daubed with savage paint blotches, and over his shoulders was drawn a wolfskin, the gleaming teeth and cruel snout surmounting his head. No other word was spoken. The prospectors held the peace. Sipsu arose and slipped into her snowshoes.

"Good-by, O my man," she said to Hitchcock. But the man who had sat beside her on the sled gave no sign, nor lifted his head as they filed away into the white forest.

Unlike many men, his faculty of adaptation, while large, had never suggested the expediency of an alliance with the women of the Northland. His broad cosmopolitanism had never impelled toward covenanting in marriage with the daughters of the soil. If it had, his philosophy of life would not have stood between. But it simply had not. Sipsu? He had pleasured in camp-fire chats with her, not as a man who knew himself to be man and she woman, but as a man might with a child, and as a man of his make certainly would if for no other reason than to vary the tedium of a bleak existence. That was all. But there was a certain chivalric thrill of warm blood in him, despite his Yankee ancestry and New England upbringing, and he was so made that the commercial aspect of life often seemed meaningless and bore contradiction to his deeper impulses.

So he sat silent, with head bowed forward, an organic force, greater than himself, as great as his race, at work within him. Wertz and Hawes looked askance at him from time to time, a faint but perceptible trepidation in their manner. Sigmund also felt this. Hitchcock was strong, and his strength had been impressed upon them in the course of many an event in their precarious life. So they stood in a certain definite awe and curiosity as to what his conduct would be when he moved to action.

But his silence was long, and the fire nigh out, when Wertz stretched his arms and yawned, and thought he'd go to bed. Then Hitchcock stood up his full height.

"May God damn your souls to the deepest hells, you chicken-hearted cowards! I'm done with you!" He said it calmly enough, but his strength spoke in every syllable, and every intonation was advertisement of intention. "Come on," he continued, "whack up, and in whatever way suits you best. I own a quarter-interest in the claims; our contracts show that. There're twenty-five or thirty ounces in the sack from the test pans. Fetch out the scales. We'll divide that now. And you, Sigmund, measure me my quarter-share of the grub and set it apart. Four of the dogs are mine, and I want four more. I'll trade you my share in the camp outfit and mining-gear for the dogs. And I'll throw in my six or seven ounces and the spare 45-90 with the ammunition. What d' ye say?"

The three men drew apart and conferred. When they returned, Sigmund acted as spokesman. "We'll whack up fair with you, Hitchcock. In everything you'll get your quarter-share, neither more nor less; and you can take it or leave it. But we want the dogs as bad as you do, so you get four, and that's all. If you don't want to take your share of the outfit and gear, why, that's your lookout. If you want it, you can have it; if you don't, leave it."

"The letter of the law," Hitchcock sneered. "But go ahead. I'm willing. And hurry up. I can't get out of this camp and away from its vermin any too quick."

The division was effected without further comment. He lashed his meagre belongings upon one of the sleds, rounded in his four dogs, and harnessed up. His portion of outfit and gear he did not touch, though he threw onto the sled half a dozen dog harnesses, and challenged them with his eyes to interfere. But they shrugged their shoulders and watched him disappear in the forest.

A man crawled upon his belly through the snow. On every hand loomed the moose-hide lodges of the camp. Here and there a miserable dog howled or snarled abuse upon his neighbor. Once, one of them approached the creeping man, but the man became motionless. The dog came closer and sniffed, and came yet closer, till its nose touched the strange object which had not been there when darkness fell. Then Hitchcock, for it was Hitchcock, upreared suddenly, shooting an unmittened hand out to the brute's shaggy throat. And the dog knew its death in that clutch, and when the man moved on, was left broken-necked under the stars. In this manner Hitchcock made the chief's lodge. For long he lay in the snow without, listening to the voices of the occupants and striving to locate Sipsu. Evidently there were many in the tent, and from the sounds they were in high excitement.

At last he heard the girl's voice, and crawled around so that only the moose-hide divided them. Then burrowing in the snow, he slowly wormed his head and shoulders underneath. When the warm inner air smote his face, he stopped and waited, his legs and the greater part of his body still on the outside. He could see nothing, nor did he dare lift his head. On one side of him was a skin bale. He could smell it, though he carefully felt to be certain. On the other side his face barely touched a furry garment which he knew clothed a body. This must be Sipsu. Though he wished she would speak again, he resolved to risk it.

He could hear the chief and the witch doctor talking high, and in a far corner some hungry child whimpering to sleep. Squirming over on his side, he carefully raised his head, still just touching the furry garment. He listened to the breathing. It was a woman's breathing; he would chance it.

He pressed against her side softly but firmly, and felt her start at the contact. Again he waited, till a questioning hand slipped down upon his head and paused among the curls. The next instant the hand turned his face gently upward, and he was gazing into Sipsu's eyes.

She was quite collected. Changing her position casually, she threw an elbow well over on the skin bale, rested her body upon it, and arranged her *parka*. In this way he was completely concealed. Then, and still most casually, she reclined across him, so that he could breathe between her arm and breast, and when she lowered her head her ear pressed lightly against his lips.

"When the time suits, go thou," he whispered, "out of the lodge and across the snow, down the wind to the bunch of jackpine in the curve of the creek. There wilt thou find my dogs and my sled, packed for the trail. This night we go down to the Yukon; and since we go fast, lay thou hands upon what dogs come nigh thee, by the scruff of the neck, and drag them to the sled in the curve of the creek."

Sipsu shook her head in dissent; but her eyes glistened with gladness, and she was proud that this man had shown toward her such favor. But she, like the women of all her race, was born to obey the will masculine, and when Hitchcock repeated "Go!" he did it with authority, and though she made no answer he knew that his will was law.

"And never mind harness for the dogs," he added, preparing to go. "I shall wait. But waste no time. The day chaseth the night alway, nor does it linger for man's pleasure."

Half an hour later, stamping his feet and swinging his arms by the sled, he saw her coming, a surly dog in either hand. At the approach of these his own animals waxed truculent, and he favored them with the butt of his whip till they quieted. He had approached the camp up the wind, and sound was the thing to be most feared in making his presence known.

"Put them into the sled," he ordered when she had got the harness on the two dogs. "I want my leaders to the fore."

But when she had done this, the displaced animals pitched upon the aliens. Though Hitchcock plunged among them with clubbed rifle, a riot of sound went up and across the sleeping camp.

"Now we shall have dogs, and in plenty," he remarked grimly, slipping an axe from the sled lashings. "Do thou harness whichever I fling thee, and betweenwhiles protect the team."

He stepped a space in advance and waited between two pines. The dogs of the camp were disturbing the night with their jangle, and he watched for their coming. A dark spot, growing rapidly, took form upon the dim white expanse of snow. It was a forerunner of the pack, leaping cleanly, and, after the wolf fashion, singing direction to its brothers. Hitchcock stood in the shadow. As it sprang past, he reached out, gripped its forelegs in mid-career, and sent it whirling earthward. Then he struck it a well-judged blow beneath the ear, and flung it to Sipsu. And while she clapped on the harness, he, with his axe, held the passage between the trees, till a shaggy flood of white teeth and glistening eyes surged and crested just beyond reach. Sipsu worked rapidly. When she had finished, he leaped forward, seized and stunned a second, and flung it to her. This he repeated thrice again, and when the sled team stood snarling in a string of ten, he called, "Enough!"

But at this instant a young buck, the forerunner of the tribe, and swift of limb, wading through the dogs and cuffing right and left, attempted the passage. The butt of Hitchcock's rifle drove him to his knees, whence he toppled over sideways. The witch doctor, running lustily, saw the blow fall.

Hitchcock called to Sipsu to pull out. At her shrill "Chook!" the maddened brutes shot straight ahead, and the sled, bounding mightily, just missed unseating her. The powers were evidently angry with the witch doctor, for at this moment they plunged him upon the trail. The lead-dog fouled his snowshoes and tripped him up, and the nine succeeding dogs trod him under foot and the sled bumped over him. But he was quick to his feet, and the night might have turned out differently had not Sipsu struck backward with the long dog-whip and smitten him a blinding blow across the eyes. Hitchcock, hurrying to overtake her, collided against him as he swayed with pain in the middle of the trail. Thus it was, when this primitive theologian got back to the chief's lodge, that his wisdom had been increased in so far as concerns the efficacy of the white man's fist. So, when he orated then and there in the council, he was wroth against all white men.

"Tumble out, you loafers! Tumble out! Grub'll be ready before you get into your footgear!"

Dave Wertz threw off the bearskin, sat up, and yawned.

Hawes stretched, discovered a lame muscle in his arm, and rubbed it sleepily. "Wonder where Hitchcock bunked last night?" he queried, reaching for his moccasins. They were stiff, and he walked gingerly in his socks to the fire to thaw them out. "It's a blessing he's gone," he added, "though he was a mighty good worker."

"Yep. Too masterful. That was his trouble. Too bad for Sipsu. Think he cared for her much?"

"Don't think so. Just principle. That's all. He thought it wasn't right — and, of course, it wasn't, — but that was no reason for us to interfere and get hustled over the divide before our time."

"Principle is principle, and it's good in its place, but it's best left to home when you go to Alaska. Eh?" Wertz had joined his mate, and both were working pliability into their frozen moccasins. "Think we ought to have taken a hand?"

Sigmund shook his head. He was very busy. A scud of chocolate-colored foam was rising in the coffee-pot, and the bacon needed turning. Also, he was thinking about the girl with laughing eyes like summer seas, and he was humming softly.

His mates chuckled to each other and ceased talking. Though it was past seven, daybreak was still three hours distant. The aurora borealis had passed out of the sky, and the camp was an oasis of light in the midst of deep darkness. And in this light the forms of the three men were sharply defined. Emboldened by the silence, Sigmund raised his voice and opened the last stanza of the old song: —

"In a year, in a year, when the
grapes are ripe —"

Then the night was split with a rattling volley of rifle-shots. Hawes sighed, made an effort to straighten himself, and collapsed. Wertz went over on an elbow with drooping head. He choked a little, and a dark stream flowed from his mouth. And Sigmund, the Golden-Haired, his throat a-gurgle with the song, threw up his arms and pitched across the fire.

The witch doctor's eyes were well blackened, and his temper none of the best; for he quarrelled with the chief over the possession of Wertz's rifle, and took more than his share of the part-sack of beans. Also he appropriated the bearskin, and caused grumbling among the tribesmen. And finally, he tried to kill Sigmund's dog, which the girl had given him, but the dog ran away, while he fell into the shaft and dislocated his shoulder on the bucket. When the camp was well looted they went back to their own lodges, and there was a great rejoicing among the women. Further, a band of moose strayed over the south divide and fell before the hunters, so the witch doctor attained yet greater honor, and the people whispered among themselves that he spoke in council with the gods.

But later, when all were gone, the shepherd dog crept back to the deserted camp, and all the night long and a day it wailed the dead. After that it disappeared, though the years were not many before the Indian hunters noted a change in the breed of timber wolves, and there were dashes of bright color and variegated markings such as no wolf bore before.

27
To Build a Fire

TO BUILD A FIRE

BY JACK LONDON

Author of "The Call of the Wild," "The Sea-Wolf," etc.

He travels fastest who travels alone . . . but not after the frost has dropped below zero fifty degrees or more.—*Yukon Code.*

DAY had broken cold and gray, exceedingly cold and gray, when the man turned aside from the main Yukon trail and climbed the high earth-bank, where a dim and little-traveled trail led eastward through the fat spruce timberland. It was a steep bank, and he paused for breath at the top, excusing the act to himself by looking at his watch. It was nine o'clock. There was no sun or hint of sun, though there was not a cloud in the sky. It was a clear day, and yet there seemed an intangible pall over the face of things, a subtle gloom that made the day dark, and that was due to the absence of sun. This fact did not worry the man. He was used to the lack of sun. It had been days since he had seen the sun, and he knew that a few more days must pass before that cheerful orb, due south, would just peep above the sky-line and dip immediately from view.

The man flung a look back along the way he had come. The Yukon lay a mile wide and hidden under three feet of ice. On top of this ice were as many feet of snow. It was all pure white, rolling in gentle, snow-covered undulations where the ice-jams of the freeze-up had formed. North and south, as far as his eye could see, it was unbroken white, save for a dark hair-line that curved and twisted from around the spruce-covered island to the south, and that curved and twisted away into the north, where it disappeared behind another spruce-covered island. This dark hair-line was the trail—the main trail—that led south five hundred miles to the Chilcoot Pass, Dyea, and salt water; and that led north seventy miles to Dawson, and still on to the north a thousand miles to Nulato, and finally to St. Michael on Bering Sea, a thousand miles and half a thousand more.

But all this—the mysterious, far-reaching hair-line trail, the absence of sun from the sky, the tremendous cold, and the strangeness and weirdness of it all—made no impression on the man. It was not because he was long used to it. He was a new-comer in the land, a *chechaquo,* and this was his first winter. The trouble with him was that he was without imagination. He was quick and alert in the things of life, but only in the things, and not in the significances. Fifty degrees below zero meant eighty-odd degrees of frost. Such fact impressed him as being cold and uncomfortable, and that was all. It did not lead him to meditate upon his frailty as a creature of temperature, and upon man's frailty in general, able only to live within certain narrow limits of temperature; and from there on it did not lead him to the conjectural field of immortality and man's place in the universe. Fifty degrees below zero stood for a bite of frost that hurt and that must be guarded against by the use of mittens, ear-flaps, warm moccasins, and thick socks. Fifty degrees below zero was to him just precisely fifty degrees below zero. That there should be anything more to it than that was a thought that never entered his head.

As he turned to go on, he spat speculatively. There was a sharp, explosive crackle that startled him. He spat again. And again, in the air, before it could fall to the snow, the spittle crackled. He knew that at fifty below spittle crackled on the snow, but this spittle had crackled in the air. Undoubtedly it was colder than fifty below—how much colder he did not know. But the temperature did not matter. He was bound for the old claim on the left fork of Henderson Creek, where the boys were already. They had come over across the divide from the Indian Creek country while he had come the round-about way to take a look at the possibilities of getting out logs in the spring from the islands in the Yukon. He would be in to camp by six o'clock; a bit after dark, it was true, but the boys would be there, a fire would be going, and a hot supper would be ready. As for lunch, he pressed his hand against the protruding bundle under his jacket. It was also under his shirt, wrapped up in a handkerchief, and lying against the naked skin. It was the only way to keep the biscuits from freezing. He smiled agreeably to himself as he thought of those biscuits, each cut open and sopped in bacon grease, and each inclosing a generous slice of fried bacon.

He plunged in among the big spruce-trees. The trail was faint. A foot of snow had fallen since the last sled had passed over, and he was glad he was without a sled, traveling light. In fact, he carried nothing but the lunch wrapped in the handkerchief. He was surprised, however, at the cold. It certainly was cold, he concluded, as he rubbed his numb nose and cheek-bones with his mittened hand. He was a warm-whiskered man, but the hair on his face did not protect the high cheek-bones and the eager nose that thrust itself aggressively into the frosty air.

At the man's heels trotted a dog, a big native husky, the proper wolf-dog, gray-coated and without any visible or temperamental difference from its brother, the wild wolf. The animal was depressed by the tremendous cold. It knew that it was no time for traveling. Its instinct told it a truer tale than was told to the man by the man's judgment. In reality, it was not merely colder than fifty below zero; it was colder than sixty below, than seventy below. It was seventy-five below zero. Since the freezing-point is thirty-two above zero, it meant that one hundred and seven degrees of frost obtained. The dog did not know anything about thermometers. Possibly in its brain there was no sharp consciousness of a condition of very cold such as was in the man's brain. But the brute had its instinct. It experienced a vague but menacing apprehension that subdued it and made it shrink along at the man's heels, and that made it question eagerly every unwonted movement of the man as if expecting him to go into camp or to seek shelter somewhere and build a fire. The dog had learned fire, and it wanted fire, or else to burrow under the snow and cuddle its warmth in the confined space.

The frozen moisture of its breathing had settled on its fur in a fine powder of frost, and especially were its jowls, muzzle, and eyelashes whitened by its crystalled breath. The man's red beard and mustache were likewise frosted, but more solidly, the deposit taking the form of ice, and increasing with every warm, moist breath he exhaled. Also, the man was chewing tobacco, and the muzzle of ice held his lips so rigidly that he was unable to clear his chin when he expelled the juice. The result was that a crystal beard of the color and solidity of amber was increasing its length on his chin. If he fell down it would shatter itself, like glass, into brittle fragments. But he did not mind the appendage. It was the penalty all tobacco-chewers paid in that country, and he had been out before in two cold snaps. They had not been so cold as this, he knew, but by the spirit thermometer at Sixty Mile he knew they had been registered at fifty below and at fifty-five.

He held on through the level stretch of woods for several miles, crossed a wide flat of nigger-heads, and dropped down a bank to the frozen bed of a small stream. This was Henderson Creek, and he knew he was ten miles from the forks. He looked at his watch. It was ten o'clock. He was making four miles an hour, and he calculated that he would arrive at the forks at half-past twelve. He decided to celebrate that event by eating his lunch there.

The dog dropped in again at his heels with a tail drooping discouragement as the man swung along the creek-bed. The furrow of the old sled-trail was plainly visible, but a dozen inches of snow covered the marks of the last runners. In a month no man had come up or down that silent creek. The man held steadily on. He was not much given to thinking, and just then particularly he had nothing to think about save that he would eat lunch at the forks and that at six o'clock he would be in camp with the boys. There was nobody to talk to; and, had there been, speech would have been impossible because of the ice-muzzle on his mouth. So he continued monotonously to chew tobacco and to increase the length of his amber beard.

Once in a while the thought reiterated itself that it was very cold and that he had never experienced such cold. As he walked along he rubbed his cheek-bones and nose with the back of his mittened hand. He did this automatically, now and again changing hands. But rub as he would, the instant he stopped, his cheek-bones went numb, and the following instant the end of his nose went numb. He was sure to frost his cheeks; he knew that, and experienced a pang of regret that he had not devised a nose-strap of the sort Bud wore in cold snaps. Such a strap passed across the cheeks, as well, and saved them. But it did n't matter much, after all. What were frosted cheeks? A bit painful, that was all; they were never serious.

Empty as the man's mind was of thoughts, he was keenly observant, and he noticed the changes in the creek, the curves and bends and timber-jams, and always he sharply noted where he placed his feet. Once, coming around a bend, he shied abruptly, like a startled horse, curved away from the place where he had been walking, and retreated several paces back along the trail. The creek he knew was frozen clear to the bottom,—no creek could contain water in that arctic winter,—but he knew also that there were springs that bubbled out from the hillsides and ran along under the snow and on top the ice of the creek. He knew that the coldest snaps never froze these springs, and he knew likewise their danger. They were traps. They hid pools of water under the snow that might be three inches deep, or three feet. Sometimes a skin of ice half an inch thick covered them, and in turn was covered by the snow. Sometimes there were alternate layers of water and ice-skin, so that when one broke through he kept on breaking through for a while, sometimes wetting himself to the waist.

That was why he had shied in such panic. He had felt the give under his feet and heard the crackle of a snow-hidden ice-skin. And to get his feet wet in such a temperature meant trouble and danger. At the very least it meant delay, for he would be forced to stop and build a fire, and under its protection to bare his feet while he dried his socks and moccasins. He stood and studied the creek-bed and its banks, and decided that the flow of water came from the right. He reflected awhile, rubbing his nose and cheeks, then skirted to the left, stepping gingerly and testing the footing for each step. Once clear of the danger, he took a fresh chew of tobacco, and swung along at his four-mile gait.

In the course of the next two hours he came upon several similar traps. Usually the snow above the hidden pools had a sunken, candied appearance that advertised the danger. Once again, however, he had a close call; and once, suspecting danger, he compelled the dog to go on in front. The dog did not want to go. It hung back until the man shoved it forward, and then it went quickly across the white, unbroken surface. Suddenly it broke through, floundered to one side, and got away to firmer footing. It had wet its forefeet and legs, and almost immediately the water that clung to it turned to ice. It made quick efforts to lick the ice off its legs, then dropped down in the snow, and began to bite out the ice that had formed between the toes. This was a matter of instinct. To permit the ice to remain would mean sore feet. It did not know this. It merely obeyed the mysterious prompting that arose from the deep crypts of its being. But the man knew, having achieved a judgment on the subject, and he removed the mitten from his right hand and helped tear out the ice-particles. He did not expose his fingers more than a minute, and was astonished at the swift numbness that smote them. It certainly was cold. He pulled on the mitten hastily, and beat the hand savagely across his chest.

At twelve o'clock the day was at its brightest. Yet the sun was too far south on its winter journey to clear the horizon. The bulge of the earth intervened between it and Henderson Creek, where the man walked under a clear sky at noon and cast no shadow. At half past twelve to the minute he arrived at the forks of the creek. He was pleased at the speed he had made. If he kept it up, he would certainly be with the boys by six. He unbuttoned his jacket and shirt and drew forth his lunch. The action consumed no more than a quarter of a minute, yet in that brief moment the numbness laid hold of the exposed fingers. He did not put the mitten on, but, instead, struck the fingers a dozen sharp smashes against his leg. Then he sat down on a snow-covered log to eat. The sting that followed upon the striking of his fingers against his leg ceased so quickly that he was startled. He had had no chance to take a bite of biscuit. He struck the fingers repeatedly and returned them to the mitten, baring the other hand for the purpose of eating. He tried to take a mouthful, but the ice-muzzle prevented. He had forgotten to build a fire and thaw out. He chuckled at his foolishness, and as he chuckled he noted the numbness creeping into the exposed fingers. Also, he noted that the stinging which had first come to his toes when he sat down was already passing away. He wondered whether the toes were warm or numb. He moved them inside the moccasins and decided that they were numb.

He pulled the mitten on hurriedly and stood up. He was a bit frightened. He stamped up and down until the stinging returned into the feet. It certainly was cold, was his thought. That man from Sulphur Creek had spoken the truth when telling how cold it sometimes got in the country. And he had laughed at him at the time! That showed one must not be too sure of things. There was no mistake about it, it *was* cold. He strode up and down, stamping his feet and threshing his arms, until reassured by the returning warmth. Then he got out matches and proceeded to make a fire. From the undergrowth, where high water of the previous spring had lodged a supply of seasoned twigs, he got his fire-wood. Working carefully from a small beginning, he soon had a roaring fire, over which he thawed the ice from his face, and in the protection of which he ate his biscuits. For the moment the cold of space was outwitted. The dog took satisfaction in the fire, stretching out close enough for warmth and far enough away to escape being singed.

When the man had finished, he filled his pipe and took his comfortable time over a smoke. Then he pulled on his mittens, settled the ear-flaps of his cap firmly about his ears, and took the creek trail up the left fork. The dog was disappointed and yearned back toward the fire. This man did not know cold. Possibly all the generations of his ancestry had been ignorant of cold, of real cold, of cold one hundred and seven degrees below freezing-point. But the dog knew; all its ancestry knew, and it had inherited the knowledge. And it knew that it was not good to walk abroad in such fearful cold. It was the time to lie snug in a hole in the snow and wait for a curtain of cloud to be drawn across the face of outer space whence this cold came. On the other hand, there was no keen intimacy between the dog and the man. The one was the toil-slave of the other, and the only caresses it had ever received were the caresses of the whip-lash and of harsh and menacing throat-sounds that threatened the whip-lash. So the dog made no effort to communicate its apprehension to the man. It was not concerned in the welfare of the man; it was for its own sake that it yearned back toward the fire. But the man whistled, and spoke to it with the sound of whip-lashes, and the dog swung in at the man's heels and followed after.

The man took a chew of tobacco, and proceeded to start a new amber beard. Also, his moist breath quickly powdered with white his mustache, eyebrows, and lashes. There did not seem to be so many springs on the left fork of the Henderson, and for half an hour the man saw no signs of any. And then it happened. At a place where there were no signs, where the soft, unbroken snow seemed to advertise solidity beneath, the man broke through. It was not deep. He wet himself half-way to the knees before he floundered out to the firm crust.

He was angry, and cursed his luck aloud. He had hoped to get into camp with the boys at six o'clock, and this would delay him an hour; for he would have to build a fire and dry out his foot-gear. This was imperative at that low temperature—he knew that much; and he turned aside to the bank, which he climbed. On top, tangled in the underbrush about the trunks of several small spruce-trees, was a high-water deposit of dry fire-wood—sticks and twigs, principally, but also larger portions of seasoned branches and fine, dry, last-year's grasses. He threw down several large pieces on top of the snow. This served for a foundation, and prevented the young flame from drowning itself in the snow it otherwise would melt. The flame he got by touching a match to a small shred of birch-bark that he took from his pocket. This burned even more readily than paper. Placing it on the foundation, he fed the young flame with wisps of dry grass and with the tiniest dry twigs.

He worked slowly and carefully, keenly aware of his danger. Gradually, as the flame grew stronger, he increased the size of the twigs with which he fed it. He squatted in the snow, pulling the twigs out from their entanglement in the brush, and feeding directly to the flame. He knew there must be no failure. When it is seventy-five below zero a man must not fail in his first attempt to build a fire—that is, if his feet arc wet. If his feet are dry, and he fails, he can run along the trail for half a mile and restore his circulation. But the circulation of wet and freezing feet cannot be restored by running when it is seventy-five below. No matter how fast he runs, the wet feet will freeze the harder.

All this the man knew. The old-timer on Sulphur Creek had told him about it the previous fall, and now he was appreciating the advice. Already all sensation had gone out of his feet. To build the fire he had been forced to remove his mittens, and the fingers had quickly gone numb. His pace of four miles an hour had kept his heart pumping blood to the surface of his body and to all the extremities. But the instant he stopped, the action of the pump eased down. The cold of space smote the unprotected tip of the planet, and he, being on that unprotected tip, received the full force of the blow. The blood of his body recoiled before it. The blood was alive, like the dog, and like the dog it wanted to hide away and cover itself up from the fearful cold. So long as he walked four miles an hour, he pumped that blood, willy-nilly, to the surface; but now it ebbed away and sank down into the recesses of his body. The extremities were the first to feel its absence. His wet feet froze the faster, and his exposed fingers numbed the faster, though they had not yet begun to freeze. Nose and cheeks were already freezing, while the skin of all his body chilled as it lost its blood.

But he was safe. Toes and nose and cheeks would be only touched by the frost, for the fire was beginning to burn with strength. He was feeding it with twigs the size of his finger. In another minute he would be able to feed it with branches the size of his wrist, and then he could remove his wet foot-gear, and while it dried, he could keep his naked feet warm by the fire, rubbing them at first, of course, with snow. The fire was a success. He was safe. He remembered the advice of the old-timer on Sulphur Creek and smiled. The old-timer had been very serious in laying down the law that no man must travel alone in the Klondike after fifty below. Well, here he was; he had had the accident; he was alone; and he had saved himself. Those old-timers were rather womanish, some of them, he thought. All a man had to do was to keep his head, and he was all right. Any man who was a man could travel alone. But it was surprising, the rapidity with which his cheeks and nose were freezing. And he had not thought his fingers could go lifeless in so short a time. Lifeless they were, for he could scarcely make them move together to grip a twig, and they seemed remote from his body and from him. When he touched a twig he had to look and see whether or not he had hold of it. The wires were pretty well down between him and his finger-ends.

All of which counted for little. There was the fire, snapping and crackling and promising life with every dancing flame. He started to untie his moccasins. They were coated with ice; the thick German socks were like sheaths of iron half-way to the knees; and the moccasin-strings were like rods of steel all twisted and knotted as by some conflagration. For a moment he tugged with his numb fingers, then, realizing the folly of it, he drew his sheath-knife.

But before he could cut the strings, it happened. It was his own fault, or, rather, his mistake. He should not have built the fire under the spruce-tree. He should have built it in the open. But it had been easier to pull the twigs from the brush and drop them directly on the fire. Now the tree under which he had done this carried a weight of snow on its boughs. No wind had blown for weeks, and each bough was fully freighted. Each time he had pulled a twig he had communicated a slight agitation to the tree—an imperceptible agitation, so far as he was concerned, but an agitation sufficient to bring about the disaster. High up in the tree one bough capsized its load of snow. This fell on the boughs beneath, capsizing them. This process continued, spreading out and involving the whole tree. It grew like an avalanche, and it descended without warning upon the man and the fire, and the fire was blotted out! Where it had burned was a mantle of fresh and disordered snow.

The man was shocked. It was as though he had just heard his own sentence of death. For a moment he sat and stared at the spot where the fire had been. Then he grew very calm. Perhaps the old-timer on Sulphur Creek was right. If he had only had a trail-mate he would have been in no danger now. The trail-mate could have built the fire. Well, it was up to him to build the fire over again, and this second time there must be no failure. Even if he succeeded, he would most likely lose some toes. His feet must be badly frozen by now, and there would be some time before the second fire was ready.

Such were his thoughts, but he did not sit and think them. He was busy all the time they were passing through his mind. He made a new foundation for a fire, this time in the open, where no treacherous tree could blot it out. Next, he gathered dry grasses and tiny twigs from the high-water flotsam. He could not bring his fingers together to pull them out, but he was able to gather them by the handful. In this way he got many rotten twigs and bits of green moss that were undesirable, but it was the best he could do. He worked methodically, even collecting an armful of the larger branches to be used later when the fire gathered strength. And all the while the dog sat and watched him, a certain yearning wistfulness in its eyes, for it looked upon him as the fire-provider, and the fire was slow in coming.

When all was ready, the man reached in his pocket for a second piece of birch-bark. He knew the bark was there, and, though he could not feel it with his fingers, he could hear its crisp rustling as he fumbled for it. Try as he would, he could not clutch hold of it. And all the time, in his consciousness, was the knowledge that each instant his feet were freezing. This thought tended to put him in a panic, but he fought against it and kept calm. He pulled on his mittens with his teeth, and threshed his arms back and forth, beating his hands with all his might against his sides. He did this sitting down, and he stood up to do it; and all the while the dog sat in the snow, its wolf-brush of a tail curled around warmly over its forefeet, its sharp wolf-ears pricked forward intently as it watched the man. And the man, as he beat and threshed with his arms and hands, felt a great surge of envy as he regarded the creature that was warm and secure in its natural covering.

After a time he was aware of the first far-away signals of sensation in his beaten fingers. The faint tingling grew stronger till it evolved into a stinging ache that was excruciating, but which the man hailed with satisfaction. He stripped the mitten from his right hand and fetched forth the birch-bark. The exposed fingers were quickly going numb again. Next he brought out his bunch of sulphur matches. But the tremendous cold had already driven the life out of his fingers. In his effort to separate one match from the others, the whole bunch fell in the snow. He tried to pick it out of the snow, but failed. The dead fingers could neither touch nor clutch. He was very careful. He drove the thought of his freezing feet, and nose, and cheeks, out of his mind, devoting his whole soul to the matches. He watched, using the sense of vision in place of that of touch, and when he saw his fingers on each side the bunch, he closed them—that is, he willed to close them, for the wires were down, and the fingers did not obey. He pulled the mitten on the right hand and beat it fiercely against his knee. Then, with both mittened hands, he scooped the bunch of matches, along with much snow, into his lap. Yet he was no better off.

After some manipulation he managed

Drawn by F. E. Schoonover. Half-tone plate engraved by H. C. Merrill

"AS HE LOOKED APATHETICALLY ABOUT HIM, HIS EYES CHANCED ON THE DOG"

to get the bunch between the heels of his mittened hands. In this fashion he carried it to his mouth. The ice crackled and snapped when by a violent effort he opened his mouth. He drew the lower jaw in, curled the upper lip out of the way, and scraped the bunch with his upper teeth in order to separate a match. He succeeded in getting one, which he dropped on his lap. He was no better off. He could not pick it up. Then he devised a way. He picked it up in his teeth and scratched it on his leg. Twenty times he scratched before he succeeded in lighting it. As it flamed he held it with his teeth to the birch-bark. But the burning brimstone went up his nostrils and into his lungs, causing him to cough spasmodically. The match fell into the snow and went out.

The old-timer on Sulphur Creek was right, he thought in the moment of controlled despair that ensued: after fifty below a man should travel with a partner. He beat his hands, but failed in exciting any sensation. Suddenly he bared both hands, removing the mittens with his teeth. He caught the whole bunch between the heels of his hands. His arm-muscles not being frozen enabled him to press the hand-heels tightly against the matches. Then he scratched the bunch along his leg. It flared into flame, seventy sulphur matches at once! There was no wind to blow them out. He kept his head to one side to escape the strangling fumes, and held the blazing bunch to the birch-bark. As he so held it, he became aware of sensation in his hand. His flesh was burning. He could smell it. Deep down below the surface he could feel it. The sensation developed into pain that grew acute. And still he endured it, holding the flame of the matches clumsily to the bark that would not light readily because his own burning hands were in the way, absorbing most of the flame.

At last, when he could endure no more, he jerked his hands apart. The blazing matches fell sizzling into the snow, but the birch-bark was alight. He began laying dry grasses and the tiniest twigs on the flame. He could not pick and choose, for he had to lift the fuel between the heels of his hands. Small pieces of rotten wood and green moss clung to the twigs, and he bit them off as well as he could with his teeth. He cherished the flame carefully and awkwardly. It meant life, and it must not perish. The withdrawal of blood from the surface of his body now made him begin to shiver, and he grew more awkward. A large piece of green moss fell squarely on the little fire. He tried to poke it out with his fingers, but his shivering frame made him poke too far, and he disrupted the nucleus of the little fire, the burning grasses and tiny twigs separating and scattering. He tried to poke them together again, but in spite of the tenseness of the effort, his shivering got away with him, and the twigs were hopelessly scattered. Each twig gushed a puff of smoke and went out. The fire-provider had failed. As he looked apathetically about him, his eyes chanced on the dog, sitting across the ruins of the fire from him, in the snow, making restless, hunching movements, slightly lifting one forefoot and then the other, shifting its weight back and forth on them with wistful eagerness.

The sight of the dog put a wild idea into his head. He remembered the tale of the man, caught in a blizzard, who killed a steer and crawled inside the carcase, and so was saved. He would kill the dog and bury his hands in the warm body until the numbness went out of them. Then he could build another fire. He spoke to the dog, calling it to him; but in his voice was a strange note of fear that frightened the animal, who had never known the man to speak in such way before. Something was the matter, and its suspicious nature sensed danger—it knew not what danger, but somewhere, somehow, in its brain arose an apprehension of the man. It flattened its ears down at the sound of the man's voice, and its restless, hunching movements and the liftings and shiftings of its forefeet became more pronounced; but it would not come to the man. He got on his hands and knees and crawled toward the dog. This unusual posture again excited suspicion, and the animal sidled mincingly away.

The man sat up in the snow for a moment and struggled for calmness. Then he pulled on his mittens, by means of his teeth, and got upon his feet. He glanced down at first in order to assure himself that he was really standing up, for the absence of sensation in his feet left him unrelated to the earth. His erect position in itself started to drive the webs of suspicion from the dog's mind; and when he spoke peremptorily, with the sound of whip-lashes in his voice, the dog rendered its customary allegiance and came to him. As it came within reaching distance the man lost his control. His arms flashed out to the dog, and he experienced genuine surprise when he discovered that his hands could not clutch, that there was neither bend nor feeling in the fingers. He had forgotten for the moment that they were frozen and that they were freezing more and more. All this happened quickly, and before the animal could get away he encircled its body with his arms. He sat down in the snow, and in this fashion held the dog, while it snarled and whined and struggled.

But it was all he could do, hold its body encircled in his arms and sit there. He realized that he could not kill the dog. There was no way to do it. With his helpless hands he could neither draw nor hold his sheath-knife nor throttle the animal. He released it, and it plunged wildly away, with tail between its legs, and still snarling. It halted forty feet away and surveyed him curiously, with ears sharply pricked forward. The man looked down at his hands in order to locate them, and found them hanging on the ends of his arms. It struck him as curious that one should have to use his eyes in order to find out where his hands were. He began threshing his arms back and forth, beating the mittened hands against his sides. He did this for five minutes, violently, and his heart pumped enough blood up to the surface to put a stop to his shivering. But no sensation was aroused in the hands. He had an impression that they hung like weights on the ends of his arms, but when he tried to run the impression down, he could not find it.

A certain fear of death, dull and oppressive, came to him. This fear quickly became poignant as he realized that it was no longer a mere matter of freezing his fingers and toes, or of losing his hands and feet, but that it was a matter of life and death with the chances against him. This threw him into a panic, and he turned and ran up the creek-bed along the old, dim trail. The dog joined in behind and kept up with him. He ran blindly, without intention, in fear such as he had never known in his life. Slowly, as he plowed and floundered through the snow, he began to see things again,—the banks of the creek, the old timber-jams, the leafless aspens, and the sky. The running made him feel better. He did not shiver. Maybe, if he ran on, his feet would thaw out; and, anyway, if he ran far enough he would reach camp and the boys. Without doubt he would lose some fingers and toes and some of his face; but the boys would take care of him, and save the rest of him when he got there. And at the same time there was another thought in his mind that said he would never get to the camp and the boys; that it was too many miles away, that the freezing had too great a start on him, and that he would soon be stiff and dead. This thought he kept in the background, and refused to consider. Sometimes it pushed itself forward and demanded to be heard, but he thrust it back and strove to think of other things.

It struck him as curious that he could run at all on feet so frozen that he could not feel them when they struck the earth and took the weight of his body. He seemed to himself to skim along above the surface, and to have no connection with the earth. Somewhere he had once seen a winged Mercury, and he wondered if Mercury felt as he felt when skimming over the earth.

His theory of running until he reached camp and the boys had one flaw in it: he lacked the endurance. Several times he stumbled, and finally he tottered, crumpled up, and fell. When he tried to rise, he failed. He must sit and rest, he decided, and next time he would merely walk and keep on going. As he sat and regained his breath, he noted that he was feeling quite warm and comfortable. He was not shivering, and it even seemed that a warm glow had come to his chest and trunk. And yet, when he touched his nose or cheeks, there was no sensation. Running would not thaw them out. Nor would it thaw out his hands and feet. Then the thought came to him that the frozen portions of his body must be extending. He tried to keep this thought down, to forget it, to think of something else; he was aware of the panicky feeling that it caused, and he was afraid of the panic. But the thought asserted itself, and persisted, until it produced a vision of his body totally frozen. This was too much, and he made another wild run along the trail. Once he slowed down to a walk, but the thought of the freezing extending itself made him run again.

And all the time the dog ran with him, at his heels. When he fell down a second time, it curled its tail over its forefeet and sat in front of him, facing him, curiously eager and intent. The warmth and security of the animal angered him, and he cursed it till it flattened down its ears appeasingly. This time the shivering came more quickly upon the man. He was losing in his battle with the frost. It was creeping into his body from all sides. The thought of it drove him on, but he ran no more than a hundred feet, when he staggered and pitched headlong. It was his last panic. When he had recovered his breath and control, he sat up and entertained in his mind the conception of meeting death with dignity. However, the conception did not come to him in such terms. His idea of it was that he had been making a fool of himself, running around like a chicken with its head cut off—such was the simile that occurred to him. Well, he was bound to freeze anyway, and he might as well take it decently. With this new-found peace of mind came the first glimmerings of drowsiness. A good idea, he thought, to sleep off to death. It was like taking an anesthetic. Freezing was not so bad as people thought. There were lots worse ways to die.

He pictured the boys finding his body next day. Suddenly he found himself with them, coming along the trail and looking for himself. And, still with them, he came around a turn in the trail and found himself lying in the snow. He did not belong with himself any more, for even then he was out of himself, standing with the boys and looking at himself in the snow. It certainly was cold, was his thought. When he got back to the States he could tell the folks what real cold was. He drifted on from this to a vision of the old-timer on Sulphur Creek. He could see him quite clearly, warm, and comfortable, and smoking a pipe.

"You were right, old hoss; you were right," the man mumbled to the old-timer of Sulphur Creek.

Then the man drowsed off into what seemed to him the most comfortable and satisfying sleep he had ever known. The dog sat facing him and waiting. The brief day drew to a close in a long, slow twilight. There were no signs of a fire to be made, and, besides, never in the dog's experience had it known a man to sit like that in the snow and make no fire. As the twilight drew on, its eager yearning for the fire mastered it, and with a great lifting and shifting of forefeet, it whined softly, then flattened its ears down in anticipation of being chidden by the man. But the man remained silent. Later, the dog whined loudly. And still later it crept close to the man and caught the scent of death. This made the animal bristle and back away. A little longer it delayed, howling under the stars that leaped and danced and shone brightly in the cold sky. Then it turned and trotted up the trail in the direction of the camp it knew, where were the other food-providers and the fire-providers.

28
All Gold Cañon

ALL GOLD CAÑON

BY JACK LONDON

IT was the green heart of the cañon, where the walls swerved back from the rigid plan and relieved their harshness of line by making a little sheltered nook and filling it to the brim with sweetness and roundness and softness. Here all things rested. Even the narrow stream ceased its turbulent down-rush long enough to form a quiet pool. Knee-deep in the water, with drooping head and half-shut eyes, drowsed a red-coated, many-antlered buck.

On one side, beginning at the very lip of the pool, was a tiny meadow, a cool, resilient surface of green that extended to the base of the frowning wall. Across the pool a gentle slope of earth ran up and up to meet the opposing wall. Fine grass covered the slope — grass that was spangled with flowers, with here and there patches of color, orange and purple and golden. Below, the cañon was shut in. There was no view. The walls leaned together abruptly and the cañon ended in a chaos of rocks, moss-covered and hidden by a green screen of vines and creepers and boughs of trees. Up the cañon rose far hills and peaks, the big foothills, pine-covered and remote. And far beyond, like clouds upon the border of the sky, towered minarets of white, where the Sierra's eternal snows flashed austerely the blazes of the sun.

There was no dust in the cañon. The leaves and flowers were clean and virginal. The grass was young velvet. Over the pool three cottonwoods sent their snowy fluffs fluttering down the quiet air. On the slope the blossoms of the wine-wooded manzanita filled the air with springtime odors, while the leaves, wise with experience, were already beginning their vertical twist against the coming aridity of summer. In the open spaces on the slope, beyond the farthest shadow-reach of the manzanita, poised the mariposa lilies, like so many flights of jeweled moths suddenly arrested and on the verge of trembling into flight again. Here and there that woods harlequin, the madrone, permitting itself to be caught in the act of changing its pea-green trunk to madder-red, breathed its fragrance into the air from great clusters of waxen bells. Creamy white were these bells, shaped like lilies-of-the-valley, with the sweetness of perfume that is of the springtime.

There was not a sigh of wind. The air was drowsy with its weight of perfume. It was a sweetness that would have been cloying had the air been heavy and humid. But the air was sharp and thin. It was as starlight transmuted into atmosphere, shot through and warmed by sunshine, and flower-drenched with sweetness.

An occasional butterfly drifted in and out through the patches of light and shade. And from over all rose the low and sleepy hum of mountain bees — feasting Sybarites that jostled one another good-naturedly at the board, nor found time for rough discourtesy. So quietly did the little stream drip and ripple its way through the cañon that it spoke only in faint and occasional gurgles. The voice of the stream was as a drowsy whisper, ever interrupted by dozings and silences, ever lifted again in the awakenings.

The motion of all things was a drifting in the heart of the cañon. Sunshine and butterflies drifted in and out among the trees. The hum of the bees and the whisper of the stream were a drifting of sound. And the drifting sound and drifting color seemed to weave together in the making of a delicate and intangible fabric which was the spirit of the place. It was a spirit of peace that was not of death, but of smooth-pulsing life, of quietude that was not silence, of movement that was not action, of repose that was quick with existence without being violent with struggle and travail. The spirit of the place was the spirit of the peace of the living, somnolent with the easement and content of prosperity, and undisturbed by rumors of far wars.

The red-coated, many-antlered buck acknowledged the lordship of the spirit of the place and dozed knee-deep in the cool, shaded pool. There seemed no flies to vex him and he was languid with rest. Sometimes his ears moved when the stream awoke and whispered; but they moved lazily, with foreknowledge that it was merely the stream grown garrulous at discovery that it had slept.

But there came a time when the buck's ears lifted and tensed with swift eagerness for sound. His head was turned down the cañon. His sensitive, quivering nostrils scented the air. His eyes could not pierce the green screen through which the stream rippled away, but to his ears came the voice of a man. It was a steady, monotonous, singsong voice. Once the buck heard the harsh clash of metal upon rock. At the sound he snorted with a sudden start that jerked him through the air from water to meadow, and his feet sank into the young velvet, while he pricked his ears and again scented the air. Then he stole across the tiny meadow, pausing once and again to listen, and faded away out of the cañon like a wraith, soft-footed and without sound.

The clash of steel-shod soles against the rocks began to be heard, and the man's voice grew louder. It was raised in a sort of chant and became distinct with nearness, so that the words could be heard:

"Tu'n around an' tu'n yo' face
Untoe them sweet hills of grace
(D' pow'rs of sin yo' am scornin'!).
Look about an' look aroun',
Fling yo' sin-pack on d' groun'
(Yo' will meet wid d' Lord in d' mornin'!)."

A sound of scrambling accompanied the song, and the spirit of the place fled away on the heels of the red-coated buck. The green screen was burst asunder and a man peered out at the meadow and the pool and the sloping side-hill. He was a deliberate sort of man. He took in the scene with one embracing glance, then ran his eyes over the details to verify the general impression. Then, and not until then, did he open his mouth in vivid and solemn approval:

"Smoke of life an' snakes of purgatory! Will you just look at that! Wood an' water an' grass an' a side-hill! A pocket-hunter's delight an' a cayuse's paradise! Cool green for tired eyes! Pink pills for pale people ain't in it. A secret pasture for prospectors and a resting-place for tired burros, by damn!"

He was a sandy-complexioned man in whose face geniality and humor seemed the salient characteristics. It was a mobile face, quick-changing to inward mood and thought. Thinking was in him a visible process. Ideas chased across his face like wind-flaws across the surface of a lake. His hair, sparse and unkempt of growth, was as indeterminate and colorless as his complexion. It would seem that all the color of his frame had gone into his eyes, for they were blue eyes—startlingly blue. Also, they were laughing and merry eyes, within them much of the naiveté and wonder of the child; and yet, in an unassertive way, they contained much of calm self-reliance and strength of purpose founded upon self-experience and experience of the world.

From out of the screen of vines and creepers he flung ahead of him a miner's pick and shovel and gold-pan. Then he crawled out himself into the open. He was clad in faded overalls and black cotton shirt, with hobnailed brogans on his feet, and on his head a hat whose shapelessness and stains advertised the rough usage of wind and rain and sun and camp-smoke. He stood erect, seeing wide-eyed the secrecy of the scene and sensuously inhaling the warm, sweet breath of the cañon-garden through nostrils that dilated and quivered with delight. His eyes narrowed to laughing slits of blue, his face wreathed itself in joy, and his mouth curled in a smile as he cried aloud:

"Jumping dandelions and happy hollyhocks, but that smells good to me! Talk about your attar o' roses an' cologne factories! They ain't in it!"

He had the habit of soliloquy. His quick-changing facial expressions might tell every thought and mood, but the tongue, perforce, ran hard after, like a second Boswell, repeating it all over again.

The man lay down on the lip of the pool and drank long and deep of its water. "Tastes good to me," he murmured, lifting his head and gazing across the pool at the side-hill, while he wiped his mouth with the back of his hand. The side-hill attracted his attention. Still lying on his stomach, he studied the hill formation long and carefully. It was a practised eye that traveled up the slope to the crumbling cañon-wall and back and down again to the edge of the pool. He scrambled to his feet and favored the side-hill with a second survey.

"Looks good to me," he concluded, picking up his pick and shovel and gold-pan.

He crossed the stream below the pool, stepping agilely from stone to stone. Where the side-hill touched the water he dug up a shovelful of dirt and put it into the gold-pan. He squatted down, holding the pan in his two hands and partly immersing it in the stream. Then he imparted to the pan a deft circular motion that sent the water sluicing in and out through the dirt and gravel. The larger and lighter particles worked to the surface, and these, by a skilful dipping movement of the pan, he spilled out and over the edge. Occasionally, to expedite matters, he rested the pan and with his fingers raked out the large pebbles and rocks.

The contents of the pan diminished rapidly until only fine dirt and the smallest bits of gravel remained. At this stage he began to work very deliberately and carefully. It was fine washing, and he washed fine and finer, with a keen scrutiny and delicate and fastidious touch. At last the pan seemed empty of everything but water; but with a quick semicircular flirt that sent the water flying over the shallow rim into the stream, he disclosed a layer of black sand on the bottom of the pan. So thin was this layer that it was like a streak of paint. He examined it closely. In the midst of it was a tiny golden speck. He dribbled a little water in over the depressed edge of the pan. With a quick flirt he sent the water sluicing across the bottom, turning the grains of black sand over and over. A second tiny golden speck rewarded his effort.

The washing had now become very fine—fine beyond all need of ordinary placer-mining. He worked the black sand, a small portion at a time, up the shallow rim of the pan. Each small portion he examined sharply, so that his eyes saw every grain of it before he allowed it to slide over the edge and away. Jealously, bit by bit, he let the black sand slip away. A golden speck, no larger than a pin-point, appeared on the rim, and by his manipulation of the water it returned to the bottom of the pan. And in such fashion another speck was disclosed, and another. Great was his care of them. Like a shepherd he herded his flock of golden specks so that not one should be lost. At last, of the pan of dirt nothing remained but his golden herd. He counted it, and then, after all his labor, sent it flying out of the pan with one final swirl of water.

But his blue eyes were shining with desire as he rose to his feet. "Seven," he muttered aloud, enumerating the specks for which he had toiled so hard and which he had so wantonly thrown away. "Seven," he repeated, with the emphasis of one trying to impress a number on his memory.

He stood still a long while, surveying the side-hill. In his eyes there was a curiosity, new-aroused and burning. There was an exultance about his bearing and a keenness like that of a hunting animal catching the fresh scent of game.

He moved down the stream a few steps and took a second panful of dirt.

Again came the careful washing, the jealous herding of the golden specks, and the wantonness with which he sent them flying into the stream when he had counted their number.

"Five," he muttered, and repeated, "five."

He could not forbear another survey of the hill before filling the pan farther down the stream. His golden herds diminished. "Four, three, two, two, one," were his memory-tabulations as he moved down the stream. When but one speck of gold rewarded his washing, he stopped and built a fire of dry twigs. Into this he thrust the gold-pan and burned it till it was blue-black. He held up the pan and examined it critically. Then he nodded approbation. Against such a color-background he could defy the tiniest yellow speck to elude him.

Still moving down the stream, he panned again. A single speck was his reward. A third pan contained no gold at all. Not satisfied with this, he panned three times again, taking his shovels of dirt within a foot of one another. Each pan proved empty of gold, and the fact, instead of discouraging him, seemed to give him satisfaction. His elation increased with each barren washing, until he arose, exclaiming jubilantly:

"If it ain't the real thing may God knock off my head with sour apples!"

Returning to where he had started operations, he began to pan up the stream. At first his golden herds increased—increased prodigiously. "Fourteen, eighteen, twenty-one, twenty-six," ran his memory-tabulations. Just above the pool he struck his richest pan—thirty-five colors.

"Almost enough to save," he remarked regretfully as he allowed the water to sweep them away.

The sun climbed to the top of the sky. The man worked on. Pan by pan, he went up the stream, the tally of results steadily decreasing.

"It 's just booful, the way it peters out," he exulted when a shovelful of dirt contained no more than a single speck of gold.

And when no specks at all were found in several pans he straightened up and favored the side-hill with a confident glance.

"Ah, ha! Mr. Pocket!" he cried out, as though to an auditor hidden somewhere above him beneath the surface of the slope. "Ah, ha! Mr. Pocket! I 'm a-comin', I 'm a-comin', an' I 'm shorely gwine to get yer! You heah me, Mr. Pocket? I 'm gwine to get yer as shore as punkins ain't cauliflowers!"

He turned and flung a measuring glance at the sun poised above him in the azure of the cloudless sky. Then he went down the cañon, following the line of shovel-holes he had made in filling the pans. He crossed the stream below the pool and disappeared through the green screen. There was little opportunity for the spirit of the place to return with its quietude and repose, for the man's voice, raised in rag-time song, still dominated the cañon with possession.

After a time, with a greater clashing of steel-shod feet on rock, he returned. The green screen was tremendously agitated. It surged back and forth in the throes of a struggle. There was a loud grating and clanging of metal. The man's voice leaped to a higher pitch and was sharp with imperativeness. A large body plunged and panted. There was a snapping and ripping and rending, and amid a shower of falling leaves a horse burst through the screen. On its back was a pack, and from this trailed broken vines and torn creepers. The animal gazed with astonished eyes at the scene into which it had been precipitated, then dropped its head to the grass and began contentedly to graze. A second horse scrambled into view, slipping once on the mossy rocks and regaining equilibrium when its hoofs sank into the yielding surface of the meadow. It was riderless, though on its back was a high-horned Mexican saddle scarred and discolored by long usage.

The man brought up the rear. He threw off pack and saddle, with an eye to camp location, and gave the animals their freedom to graze. He unpacked his food and got out frying-pan and coffee-pot. He gathered an armful of dry wood, and with a few stones made a place for his fire.

"My!" he said, "but I 've got an appetite. I could scoff iron-filings an' horseshoe nails an' thank you kindly, ma'am, for a second helpin'."

He straightened up, and, while he reached for matches in the pocket of his overalls, his eyes traveled across the pool to the side-hill. His fingers had clutched the match-box, but they relaxed their hold and the hand came out empty. The man wavered perceptibly. He looked at his preparations for cooking and he looked at the hill.

"Guess I 'll take another whack at her," he concluded, starting to cross the stream.

"They ain't no sense in it, I know," he mumbled apologetically. "But keepin' grub back half an hour ain't goin' to hurt none, I reckon."

A few feet back from his first line of

test-pans he started a second line. The sun dropped down the western sky, the shadows lengthened, but the man worked on. He began a third line of test-pans. He was crosscutting the hillside, line by line, as he ascended. The center of each line produced the richest pans, while the ends came where no colors showed in the pan. And as he ascended the side-hill the lines grew perceptibly shorter. The regularity with which their length diminished served to indicate that somewhere up the slope the last line would be so short as to have scarcely length at all, and that beyond could come only a point. The design was growing into an inverted "V." The converging sides of this "V" marked the boundaries of the gold-bearing dirt.

The apex of the "V" was evidently the man's goal. Often he ran his eye along the converging sides and on up the hill, trying to divine the apex, the point where the gold-bearing dirt must cease. Here resided "Mr. Pocket"—for so the man familiarly addressed the imaginary point above him on the slope, crying out:

"Come down out o' that, Mr. Pocket! Be right smart an' agreeable, an' come down!"

"All right," he would add later, in a voice resigned to determination. "All right, Mr. Pocket. It 's plain to me I got to come right up an' snatch you out bald-headed. An' I 'll do it! I 'll do it!" he would threaten still later.

Each pan he carried down to the water to wash, and as he went higher up the hill the pans grew richer, until he began to save the gold in an empty baking-powder can which he carried carelessly in his hip-pocket. So engrossed was he in his toil that he did not notice the long twilight of oncoming night. It was not until he tried vainly to see the gold colors in the bottom of the pan that he realized the passage of time. He straightened up abruptly. An expression of whimsical wonderment and awe overspread his face as he drawled:

"Gosh darn my buttons! if I did n't plumb forget dinner!"

He stumbled across the stream in the darkness and lighted his long-delayed fire. Flapjacks and bacon and warmed-over beans constituted his supper. Then he smoked a pipe by the smoldering coals, listening to the night noises and watching the moonlight stream through the cañon. After that he unrolled his bed, took off his heavy shoes, and pulled the blankets up to his chin. His face showed white in the moonlight, like the face of a corpse. But it was a corpse that knew its resurrection; for the man rose suddenly on one elbow and gazed across at his hillside.

"Good night, Mr. Pocket," he called sleepily. "Good night."

He slept through the early gray of morning until the direct rays of the sun smote his closed eyelids, when he awoke with a start and looked about him until he had established the continuity of his existence and identified his present self with all the days previously lived.

To dress, he had merely to buckle on his shoes. He glanced at his fireplace and at his hillside, wavered, but fought down the temptation and started the fire.

"Keep yer shirt on, Bill; keep yer shirt on," he admonished himself. "What 's the good of rushin'? No use in gettin' all het up an' sweaty. Mr. Pocket 'll wait for you. He ain't a-runnin' away before you can get yer breakfast. Now, what you want, Bill, is something fresh in yer bill o' fare. So it 's up to you to go an' get it."

He cut a short pole at the water's edge and drew from one of his pockets a bit of line and a draggled fly that had once been a royal coachman.

"Mebbe they 'll bite in the early morning," he muttered, as he made his first cast into the pool. And a moment later he was gleefully crying: "What 'd I tell you, eh? What 'd I tell you?"

He had no reel, nor any inclination to waste time, and by main strength, and swiftly, he drew out of the water a flashing ten-inch trout. Three more, caught in rapid succession, furnished his breakfast. When he came to the stepping-stones on his way to his hillside, he was struck by a sudden thought, and paused.

"I 'd just better take a hike down-stream a ways," he said. "There 's no tellin' what cuss may be snoopin' around."

But he crossed over on the stones, and with a "I really oughter take that hike," the need of the precaution passed out of his mind and he fell to work.

At nightfall he straightened up. The small of his back was stiff from stooping toil, and as he put his hand behind him to soothe the protesting muscles he said:

"Now what d' ye think of that, by

damn! I clean forgot my dinner again! If I don't watch out I 'll sure be degeneratin' into a two-meal-a-day crank."

"Pockets is the damnedest things I ever see for makin' a man absent-minded," he communed that night as he crawled into his blankets. Nor did he forget to call up the hillside, "Good night, Mr. Pocket! Good night!"

Rising with the sun, and snatching a hasty breakfast, he was early at work. A fever seemed to be growing in him, nor did the increasing richness of the test-pans allay this fever. There was a flush in his cheek other than that made by the heat of the sun, and he was oblivious to fatigue and the passage of time. When he filled a pan with dirt he ran down the hill to wash it; nor could he forbear running up the hill again, panting and stumbling profanely, to refill the pan.

He was now a hundred yards from the water, and the inverted "V" was assuming definite proportions. The width of the pay-dirt steadily decreased, and the man extended in his mind's eye the sides of the "V" to their meeting-place far up the hill. This was his goal, the apex of the "V," and he panned many times to locate it.

"Just about two yards above that manzanita bush an' a yard to the right," he finally concluded.

Then the temptation seized him. "As plain as the nose on your face," he said, as he abandoned his laborious crosscutting and climbed to the indicated apex. He filled a pan and carried it down the hill to wash. It contained no trace of gold. He dug deep, and he dug shallow, filling and washing a dozen pans, and was unrewarded even by the tiniest golden speck. He was enraged for having yielded to the temptation, and cursed himself blasphemously and pridelessly. Then he went down the hill and took up the crosscutting.

"Slow an' certain, Bill; slow an' certain," he crooned. "Short-cuts to fortune ain't in your line, an' it 's about time you know it. Get wise, Bill; get wise. Slow an' certain 's the only hand you can play; so go to it, an' keep to it, too."

As the cross-cuts decreased, showing that the sides of the "V" were converging, the depth of the "V" increased. The gold-trace was dipping into the hill. It was only at thirty inches beneath the surface that he could get colors in his pan. The dirt he found at twenty-five inches from the surface, and at thirty-five inches, yielded barren pans. At the base of the "V," by the water's edge, he had found the gold colors at the grass roots. The higher he went up the hill, the deeper the gold dipped. To dig a hole three feet deep in order to get one test-pan was a task of no mean magnitude; while between the man and the apex intervened an untold number of such holes to be dug. "An' there 's no tellin' how much deeper it 'll pitch," he sighed, in a moment's pause, while his fingers soothed his aching back.

Feverish with desire, with aching back and stiffening muscles, with pick and shovel gouging and mauling the soft, browned earth, the man toiled up the hill. Before him was the smooth slope, spangled with flowers and made sweet with their breath. Behind him was devastation. It looked like some terrible eruption breaking out on the smooth skin of the hill. His slow progress was like that of a snail, befouling beauty with a monstrous trail.

Though the dipping gold-trace increased the man's work, he found consolation in the increasing richness of the pans. Twenty cents, thirty cents, fifty cents, sixty cents, were the values of the gold found in the pans, and at nightfall he washed his banner pan, which gave him a dollar's worth of gold-dust from a shovelful of dirt.

"I 'll just bet it 's my luck to have some inquisitive cuss come buttin' in here on my pasture," he mumbled sleepily that night as he pulled the blankets up to his chin.

Suddenly he sat upright. "Bill!" he called sharply. "Now, listen to me, Bill; d' ye hear! It 's up to you, to-morrow mornin', to mosey round an' see what you can see. Understand? To-morrow mornin', an' don't you forget it!"

He yawned and glanced across at his side-hill. "Good night, Mr. Pocket," he called.

In the morning he stole a march on the sun, for he had finished breakfast when its first rays caught him, and he was climbing the wall of the cañon where it crumbled away and gave footing. From the outlook at the top he found himself in the midst of loneliness. As far as he could see, chain after chain of mountains heaved themselves into his vision. To the east his eyes, leaping the miles between range and range and between many ranges, brought up at last against the white-peaked Sierras—the main crest, where the backbone of the Western world reared itself against the sky. To the north and south he could see more distinctly the cross-systems that broke through the main trend of the sea of mountains. To the west the ranges fell away, one behind the other, diminishing and fading into the gentler foothills that, in turn, descended into the great valley which he could not see.

And in all that mighty sweep of earth he saw no sign of man or of the handiwork of man—save only the torn bosom of the side-hill at his feet. The man looked long and carefully. Once, far down his own cañon, he thought he saw in the air a faint hint of smoke. He looked again and decided that it was the purple haze of the hills made dark by a convolution of the cañon wall at its back.

"Hey, you, Mr. Pocket!" he called down into the cañon. "Stand out from under! I 'm a-comin', Mr. Pocket! I 'm a-comin'!"

The heavy brogans on the man's feet made him appear clumsy-footed, but he swung down from the giddy height as lightly and airily as a mountain goat. A rock, turning under his foot on the edge of the precipice, did not disconcert him. He seemed to know the precise time required for the turn to culminate in disaster, and in the meantime he utilized the false footing itself for the momentary earth-contact necessary to carry him on into safety. Where the earth sloped so steeply that it was impossible to stand for a second upright, the man did not hesitate. His foot pressed the impossible surface for but a fraction of the fatal second and gave him the bound that carried him onward. Again, where even the fraction of a second's footing was out of the question, he would swing his body past by a moment's hand-grip on a jutting knob of rock, a crevice, or a precariously rooted shrub. At last, with a wild leap and yell, he exchanged the face of the wall for an earth-slide and finished the descent in the midst of several tons of sliding earth and gravel.

His first pan of the morning washed out over two dollars in coarse gold. It was from the center of the "V." To either side the diminution in the values of the pans was swift. His lines of crosscutting holes were growing very short. The converging sides of the inverted "V" were only a few yards apart. Their meeting-point was only a few yards above him. But the pay-streak was dipping deeper and deeper into the earth. By early afternoon he was sinking the test-holes five feet before the pans could show the gold-trace.

For that matter, the gold-trace had become something more than a trace; it was a placer-mine in itself, and the man resolved to come back after he had found the pocket and work over the ground. But the increasing richness of the pans began to worry him. By late afternoon the worth of the pans had grown to three and four dollars. The man scratched his head perplexedly and looked a few feet up the hill at the manzanita bush that marked approximately the apex of the "V." He nodded his head and said oracularly:

"It 's one o' two things, Bill; one o' two things. Either Mr. Pocket 's spilled himself all out an' down the hill, or else Mr. Pocket's that damned rich you, maybe, won't be able to carry him all away with you. And that 'd be hell, would n't it, now?" He chuckled at contemplation of so pleasant a dilemma.

Nightfall found him by the edge of the stream, his eyesight wrestling with the gathering darkness over the washing of a five-dollar pan.

"Wisht I had an electric light to go on working," he said.

He found sleep difficult that night. Many times he composed himself and closed his eyes for slumber to overtake him; but his blood pounded with too strong desire, and as many times his eyes opened and he murmured wearily, "Wisht it was sun-up."

Sleep came to him in the end, but his eyes were open with the first paling of the stars, and the gray of dawn caught him with breakfast finished and climbing the hillside in the direction of the secret abiding-place of Mr. Pocket.

The first cross-cut the man made, there was space for only three holes, so narrow had become the pay-streak and so close was he to the fountainhead of the golden stream he had been following for four days.

"Be ca'm, Bill; be ca'm," he admonished himself, as he broke ground for the final hole where the sides of the "V" had at last come together in a point.

"I 've got the almighty cinch on you, Mr. Pocket, an' you can't lose me," he said many times as he sank the hole deeper and deeper.

Four feet, five feet, six feet, he dug his way down into the earth. The digging grew harder. His pick grated on broken rock. He examined the rock. "Rotten quartz," was his conclusion as, with the shovel, he cleared the bottom of the hole of loose dirt. He attacked the crumbling quartz with the pick, bursting the disintegrating rock asunder with every stroke.

He thrust his shovel into the loose mass. His eye caught a gleam of yellow. He dropped the shovel and squatted suddenly on his heels. As a farmer rubs the clinging earth from fresh-dug potatoes, so the man, a piece of rotten quartz held in both hands, rubbed the dirt away.

"Sufferin' Sardanapolis!" he cried. "Lumps an' chunks of it! Lumps an' chunks of it!"

It was only half rock he held in his hand. The other half was virgin gold. He dropped it into his pan and examined another piece. Little yellow was to be seen, but with his strong fingers he crumbled the rotten quartz away till both hands were filled with glowing yellow. He rubbed the dirt away from fragment after fragment, tossing them into the gold-pan. It was a treasure-hole. So much had the quartz rotted away that there was less of it than there was of gold. Now and again he found a piece to which no rock clung—a piece that was all gold. A chunk, where the pick had laid open the heart of the gold, glittered like a handful of yellow jewels, and he cocked his head at it and slowly turned it around and over to observe the rich play of the light upon it.

"Talk about yer Too Much Gold diggin's!" the man snorted contemptuously. "Why, this diggin' 'd make it look like thirty cents. This diggin' is All Gold. An' right here an' now I name this yere cañon 'All Gold Cañon,' b' gosh!"

Still squatting on his heels, he continued examining the fragments and tossing them into the pan. Suddenly there came to him a premonition of danger. It seemed a shadow had fallen upon him. But there was no shadow. His heart had given a great jump up into his throat and was choking him. Then his blood slowly chilled and he felt the sweat of his shirt cold against his flesh.

He did not spring up nor look around. He did not move. He was considering the nature of the premonition he had received, trying to locate the impact of the mysterious force that had warned him, striving to sense the imperative presence of the unseen thing that threatened him. There is an aura of things hostile, made manifest by messengers too refined for the senses to know; and this aura he felt, but knew not how he felt it. His was the feeling as when a cloud passes over the sun. It seemed that between him and life had passed something dark and smothering and menacing; a gloom, as it were, that swallowed up life and made for death—his death.

Every force of his being impelled him to spring up and confront the unseen danger, but his soul dominated the panic, and he remained squatting on his heels, in his hands a chunk of gold. He did not dare to look around, but he knew by now that there was something behind him and above him. He made believe to be interested in the gold in his hand. He examined it critically, turned it over and over, and rubbed the dirt from it. And all the time he knew that something behind him was looking at the gold over his shoulder.

Still feigning interest in the chunk of gold in his hand, he listened intently and he heard the breathing of the thing behind him. His eyes searched the ground in front of him for a weapon, but they saw only the uprooted gold, worthless to him now in his extremity. There was his pick, a handy weapon on occasion; but this was not such an occasion. The man realized his predicament. He was in a narrow hole that was seven feet deep. His head did not come to the surface of the ground. He was in a trap.

He remained squatting on his heels. He was quite cool and collected; but his mind, considering every factor, showed him only his helplessness. He continued rubbing the dirt from the quartz fragments and throwing the gold into the pan. There was nothing else for him to do. Yet he knew that he would have to rise up, sooner or later, and face the danger that breathed at his back. The minutes passed, and with the passage of each minute he knew that by that much he was nearer the time when

Drawn by Jay Hambidge.

"HIS BODY CRUMPLED IN LIKE A LEAF"

he must stand up, or else—and his wet shirt went cold against his flesh again at the thought—or else he might receive death as he stooped there over his treasure.

Still he squatted on his heels, rubbing dirt from gold and debating in just what manner he should rise up. He might rise up with a rush and claw his way out of the hole to meet whatever threatened on the even footing above ground. Or he might rise up slowly and carelessly, and feign casually to discover the thing that breathed at his back. There was much to be said for either method. His instinct and every fighting fiber of his body favored the mad, clawing rush to the surface. His intellect, and the craft thereof, favored the slow and cautious meeting with the thing that menaced and which he could not see. And while he debated, a loud, crashing noise burst on his ear. At the same instant he received a stunning blow on the left side of the back, and from the point of impact felt a rush of flame through his flesh. He sprang up in the air, but half-way to his feet collapsed. His body crumpled in like a leaf withered in sudden heat, and he came down, his chest across his pan of gold, his face in the dirt and rock, his legs tangled and twisted because of the restricted space at the bottom of the hole. His legs twitched convulsively several times. His body was shaken as with a mighty ague. There was a slow expansion of the lungs, accompanied by a deep sigh. Then the air was slowly, very slowly exhaled, and his body as slowly flattened itself down into inertness.

Above, revolver in hand, a man was peering down over the edge of the hole. He peered for a long time at the prone and motionless body beneath him. After a while the stranger sat down on the edge of the hole so that he could see into it, and rested the revolver on his knee. Reaching his hand into a pocket, he drew out a wisp of brown paper. Into this he dropped a few crumbs of tobacco. The combination was a cigarette, brown and squat, with the ends turned in. Not once did he take his eyes from the body at the bottom of the hole. He lighted the cigarette and drew its smoke into his lungs with a caressing intake of the breath. He smoked slowly. Once the cigarette went out and he relighted it. And all the while he studied the body beneath him.

In the end he tossed the cigarette stub away and rose to his feet. He walked to the edge of the hole. Spanning it, a hand resting on each edge, and with the revolver still in the right hand, he muscled his body down into the hole. While his feet were yet a yard from the bottom he released his hands and dropped down.

At the instant his feet struck bottom he saw the pocket-miner's arm leap out and his own legs knew a swift, jerking grip that overthrew him. In the nature of the jump his revolver-hand was above his head. Swiftly as the grip had flashed about his legs, just as swiftly he brought the revolver down. He was still in the air, his fall in process of completion, when he pulled the trigger. The explosion was deafening in the confined space. The smoke filled the hole so that he could see nothing. He struck the bottom on his back, and like a cat's the pocket-miner's body was on top of him. Even as the miner's body passed on top, the stranger crooked in his right arm to fire; and even in that instant the miner, with a quick thrust of elbow, struck his wrist. The muzzle was thrown up and the bullet thudded into the dirt of the side of the hole.

The next instant the stranger felt the miner's hand grip his wrist. The struggle was now for the revolver. Each man strove to turn it against the other's body. The smoke in the hole was clearing. The stranger, lying on his back, was beginning to see dimly. But suddenly he was blinded by a handful of dirt deliberately flung into his eyes by his antagonist. In that moment of shock his grip on the revolver was broken. In the next moment he felt a smashing darkness descend upon his brain, and in the midst of the darkness even the darkness ceased.

But the pocket-miner fired again and again, until the revolver was empty. Then he tossed it from him and, breathing heavily, sat down on the dead man's legs.

The miner was sobbing and struggling for breath. "Measly skunk!" he panted; "a-campin' on my trail an' lettin' me do the work, an' then shootin' me in the back!"

He was half crying from anger and exhaustion. He peered at the face of the dead man. It was sprinkled with loose dirt and gravel, and it was difficult to distinguish the features.

"Never laid eyes on him before," the miner concluded his scrutiny. "Just a common an' ordinary thief, damn him! An' he shot me in the back! He shot me in the back!"

He opened his shirt and felt himself, front and back, on his left side.

"Went clean through, and no harm done!" he cried jubilantly. "I 'll bet he aimed all right, all right; but he drew the gun over when he pulled the trigger—the cuss! But I fixed 'm! Oh, I fixed 'm!"

His fingers were investigating the bullet-hole in his side, and a shade of regret passed over his face. "It 's goin' to be stiffer 'n hell," he said. "An' it 's up to me to get mended an' get out o' here."

He crawled out of the hole and went down the hill to his camp. Half an hour later he returned, leading his pack-horse. His open shirt disclosed the rude bandages with which he had dressed his wound. He was slow and awkward with his left-hand movements, but that did not prevent him using the arm.

The bight of the pack-rope under the dead man's shoulders enabled him to heave the body out of the hole. Then he set to work gathering up his gold. He worked steadily for several hours, pausing often to rest his stiffening shoulder and to exclaim:

"He shot me in the back, the measly skunk! He shot me in the back!"

When his treasure was quite cleaned up and wrapped securely into a number of blanket-covered parcels, he made an estimate of its value.

"Four hundred pounds, or I 'm a Hottentot," he concluded. "Say two hundred in quartz an' dirt—that leaves two hundred pounds of gold. Bill! Wake up! Two hundred pounds of gold! Forty thousand dollars! An' it 's yourn—all yourn!"

He scratched his head delightedly and his fingers blundered into an unfamiliar groove. They quested along it for several inches. It was a crease through his scalp where the second bullet had plowed.

He walked angrily over to the dead man.

"You would, would you?" he bullied. "You would, eh? Well, I fixed you good an' plenty, an' I 'll give you decent burial, too. That 's more 'n you 'd have done for me."

He dragged the body to the edge of the hole and toppled it in. It struck the bottom with a dull crash, on its side. the face twisted up to the light. The miner peered down at it.

"An' you shot me in the back!" he said accusingly.

With pick and shovel he filled the hole. Then he loaded the gold on his horse. It was too great a load for the animal, and when he had gained his camp he transferred part of it to his saddle-horse. Even so, he was compelled to abandon a portion of his outfit—pick and shovel and gold-pan, extra food and cooking-utensils, and divers odds and ends.

The sun was at the zenith when the man forced the horses at the screen of vines and creepers. To climb the huge boulders the animals were compelled to uprear and struggle blindly through the tangled mass of vegetation. Once the saddle-horse fell heavily and the man removed the pack to get the animal on its feet. After it started on its way again the man thrust his head out from among the leaves and peered up at the side-hill.

"The measly skunk!" he said, and disappeared.

There was a ripping and tearing of vines and boughs. The trees surged back and forth, marking the passage of the animals through the midst of them. There was a clashing of steel-shod hoofs on stone, and now and again an oath or a sharp cry of command. Then the voice of the man was raised in song:

"Tu'n around an' tu'n yo' face
Untoe them sweet hills of grace
(D' pow'rs of sin yo' am scornin'!).
Look about an' look aroun',
Fling yo' sin-pack on d' groun'
(Yo' will meet widd' Lord in d' mornin'!)."

The song grew faint and fainter, and through the silence crept back the spirit of the place. The stream once more drowsed and whispered; the hum of the mountain bees rose sleepily. Down through the perfume-weighted air fluttered the snowy fluffs of the cottonwoods. The butterflies drifted in and out among the trees, and over all blazed the quiet sunshine. Only remained the hoof-marks in the meadow and the torn hillside to mark the boisterous trail of the life that had broken the peace of the place and passed on.

29
Dutch Courage

DUTCH COURAGE

"Just our luck!"

Gus Lafee finished wiping his hands and sullenly threw the towel upon the rocks. His attitude was one of deep dejection. The light seemed gone out of the day and the glory from the golden sun. Even the keen mountain air was devoid of relish, and the early morning no longer yielded its customary zest.

"Just our luck!" Gus repeated, this time avowedly for the edification of another young fellow who was busily engaged in sousing his head in the water of the lake.

"What are you grumbling about, anyway?" Hazard Van Dorn lifted a soap-rimed face questioningly. His eyes were shut. "What's our luck?"

"Look there!" Gus threw a moody glance skyward. "Some duffer's got ahead of us. We've been scooped, that's all!"

Hazard opened his eyes, and caught a fleeting glimpse of a white flag waving arrogantly on the edge of a wall of rock nearly a mile above his head. Then his eyes closed with a snap, and his face wrinkled spasmodically. Gus threw him the towel, and uncommiseratingly watched him wipe out the offending soap. He felt too blue himself to take stock in trivialities.

Hazard groaned.

"Does it hurt — much?" Gus queried, coldly, without interest, as if it were no more than his duty to ask after the welfare of his comrade.

"I guess it does," responded the suffering one.

"Soap's pretty strong, eh? Noticed it myself."

"'Tisn't the soap. It's — it's *that!*" He opened his reddened eyes and pointed toward the innocent little white flag. "That's what hurts."

Gus Lafee did not reply, but turned away to start the fire and begin cooking breakfast. His disappointment and grief were too deep for anything but silence, and Hazard, who felt likewise, never opened his mouth as he fed the horses, nor once laid his head against their arching necks or passed caressing fingers through their manes. The two boys were blind, also, to the manifold glories of Mirror Lake which reposed at their very feet. Nine times, had they chosen to move along its margin the short distance of a hundred yards, could they have seen the sunrise repeated; nine times, from behind as many successive peaks, could they have seen the great orb rear his blazing rim; and nine times, had they but looked into the waters of the lake, could they have seen the phenomena reflected faithfully and vividly. But all the Titanic grandeur of the scene was lost to them. They had been robbed of the chief pleasure of their trip to Yosemite Valley. They had been frustrated in their long-cherished design upon Half Dome, and hence were rendered disconsolate and blind to the beauties and the wonders of the place.

Half Dome rears its ice-scarred head fully five thousand feet above the level floor of Yosemite Valley. In the name itself of this great rock lies an accurate and complete description. Nothing more nor less is it than a cyclopean, rounded dome, split in half as cleanly as an apple that is divided by a knife. It is, perhaps, quite needless to state that but one-half remains, hence its name, the other half having been carried away by the great ice-river in the stormy time of the Glacial Period. In that dim day one of those frigid rivers gouged a mighty channel from out the solid rock. This channel to-day is Yosemite Valley. But to return to the Half Dome. On its northeastern side, by circuitous trails and stiff climbing, one may gain the Saddle. Against the slope of the Dome the Saddle leans like a gigantic slab, and from the top of this slab, one thousand feet in length, curves the great circle to the summit of the Dome. A few degrees too steep for unaided climbing, these one thousand feet defied for years the ad-

He made a last supreme effort and gripped the coveted peg

venturous spirits who fixed yearning eyes upon the crest above.

One day, a couple of clear-headed mountaineers proceeded to insert iron eye-bolts into holes which they drilled into the rock every few feet apart. But when they found themselves three hundred feet above the Saddle, clinging like flies to the precarious wall with on either hand a yawning abyss, their nerves failed them and they abandoned the enterprise. So it remained for an indomitable Scotchman, one George Anderson, finally to achieve the feat. Beginning where they had left off, drilling and climbing for a week, he at last set foot upon that awful summit and gazed down into the depths where Mirror Lake reposed, nearly a mile beneath.

In the years which followed, many bold men took advantage of the huge rope ladder which he had put in place; but one winter ladder, cables and all were carried away by the snow and ice. True, most of the eyebolts, twisted and bent, remained. But few men essayed the hazardous undertaking, and of those few more than one gave up his life on the treacherous heights, and not one succeeded.

But Gus Lafee and Hazard Van Dorn had left the smiling valley-land of California and journeyed into the high Sierras, intent on the great adventure. And thus it was that their disappointment was deep and grievous when they awoke on this morning to receive the forestalling message of the little white flag.

"Camped at the foot of the Saddle last night and went up at the first peep of day," Hazard ventured, long after the silent breakfast had been tucked away and the dishes washed.

Gus nodded. It was not in the nature of things that a youth's spirits should long remain at low ebb, and his tongue was beginning to loosen.

"Guess he's down by now, lying in camp and feeling as big as Alexander," the other went on. "And I don't blame him, either, only I wish it were we."

"You can be sure he's down," Gus spoke up at last. "It's mighty warm on that naked rock with the sun beating down on it at this time of year. That was our plan, you know, to go up early and come down early. And any man, sensible enough to get to the top, is bound to have sense enough to do it before the rock gets hot and his hands sweaty."

"And you can be sure he didn't take his shoes with him." Hazard rolled over on his back and lazily regarded the speck of flag fluttering briskly on the sheer edge of the precipice. "Say!" He sat up with a start. "What's that?"

A metallic ray of light flashed out from the summit of Half Dome, then a second and a third. The heads of both boys were craned backward on the instant, agog with excitement.

"What a duffer!" Gus cried. "Why didn't he come down when it was cool?"

Hazard shook his head slowly, as if the question were too deep for immediate answer and they had better defer judgment.

The flashes continued, and as the boys soon noted, at irregular intervals of duration and disappearance. Now they were long, now short; and again they came and went with great rapidity, or ceased altogether for several moments at a time.

"I have it!" Hazard's face lighted up with the coming of understanding. "I have it! That fellow up there is trying to talk to us. He's flashing the sunlight down to us on a pocket-mirror — dot, dash; dot, dash; don't you see?"

The light also began to break in Gus's face. "Ah, I know! It's what they do in wartime — signaling. They call it heliographing, don't they? Same thing as telegraphing, only it's done without wires. And they use the same dots and dashes, too."

"Yes, the Morse alphabet. Wish I knew it."

"Same here. He surely must have something to say to us, or he wouldn't be kicking up all that rumpus."

Still the flashes came and went persistently, till Gus exclaimed: "That chap's in trouble, that's what's the matter with him! Most likely he's hurt himself or something or other."

"Go on!" Hazard scouted.

Gus got out the shotgun and fired both barrels three times in rapid succession. A perfect flutter of flashes came back before the echoes had ceased their antics. So unmistakable was the message that even doubting Hazard was convinced that the man who had forestalled them stood in some grave danger.

"Quick, Gus," he cried, "and pack! I'll see to the horses. Our trip hasn't come to nothing, after all. We've got to go right up

Half Dome and rescue him. Where's the map? How do we get to the Saddle?"

"'Taking the horse-trail below the Vernal Falls,'" Gus read from the guide-book, "'one mile of brisk travelling brings the tourist to the world-famed Nevada Fall. Close by, rising up in all its pomp and glory, the Cap of Liberty stands guard —'"

"Skip all that!" Hazard impatiently interrupted. "The trail's what we want."

"Oh, here it is! 'Following the trail up the side of the fall will bring you to the forks. The left one leads to Little Yosemite Valley, Cloud's Rest and other points.'"

"Hold on; that'll do! I've got it on the map now," again interrupted Hazard. "From the Cloud's Rest trail a dotted line leads off to Half Dome. That shows the trail's abandoned. We'll have to look sharp to find it. It's a day's journey."

"And to think of all that travelling, when right here we're at the bottom of the Dome!" Gus complained, staring up wistfully at the goal.

"That's because this is Yosemite, and all the more reason for us to hurry. Come on! Be lively, now!"

Well used as they were to trail life, but few minutes sufficed to see the camp equipage on the backs of the packhorses and the boys in the saddle. In the late twilight of that evening they hobbled their animals in a tiny mountain meadow, and cooked coffee and bacon for themselves at the very base of the Saddle. Here, also, before they turned into their blankets, they found the camp of the unlucky stranger who was destined to spend the night on the naked roof of the Dome.

"What's that for?" Gus asked, pointing to a leather-shielded flask which Hazard was securely fastening in his shirt pocket.

"Dutch courage, of course," was the reply. "We'll need all our nerve in this undertaking, and a little bit more, and," he tapped the flask significantly, "here's the little bit more."

"Good idea," Gus commented.

How they had ever come possessed of this erroneous idea, it would be hard to discover; but they were young yet, and there remained for them many uncut pages of life. Believers, also, in the efficacy of whisky as a remedy for snakebite, they had brought with them a fair supply of medicine-chest liquor. As yet they had not touched it.

"Have some before we start?" Hazard asked.

Gus looked into the gulf and shook his head. "Better wait till we get up higher and the climbing is more ticklish."

Some seventy feet above them projected the first eye-bolt. The winter accumulations of ice had twisted and bent it down till it did not stand more than a bare inch and a half above the rock — a most difficult object to lasso at such a distance. Time and again Hazard coiled his lariat in true cowboy fashion and made the cast, and time and again was he baffled by the elusive peg. Nor could Gus do better. Taking advantage of inequalities in the surface, they scrambled twenty feet up the Dome and found they could rest in a shallow crevice. The cleft side of the Dome was so near that they could look over its edge from the crevice and gaze down the smooth, absolutely vertical wall for nearly two thousand feet. It was yet too dark down below for them to see farther.

The peg was now fifty feet away, but the path they must cover to get to it was quite smooth, and ran at an inclination of nearly fifty degrees. It seemed impossible, in that intervening space, to find a resting-place. Either the climber must keep going up, or he must slide down; he could not stop. But just here rose the danger. The Dome was sphere-shaped, and if he should begin to slide, his course would be, not to the point from which he had started and where the Saddle would catch him, but off to the south toward Little Yosemite. This meant a plunge of half a mile.

"I'll try it," Gus said, simply.

They knotted the two lariats together, so that they had over a hundred feet of rope between them; and then each boy tied an end to his waist.

"If I slide," Gus cautioned, "come in on the slack and brace yourself. If you don't, you'll follow me, that's all!"

"Ay, ay!" was the confident response. "Better take a nip before you start?"

Gus glanced at the proffered bottle. He knew himself and of what he was capable. "Wait till I make the peg and you join me. All ready?"

"Ay."

He struck out like a cat, on all fours, clawing energetically as he urged his upward progress, his comrade paying out the rope carefully. At first his speed was good, but gradually it dwindled. Now he was fifteen feet from the peg, now ten, now eight — but going, oh, so slowly! Hazard, looking up from his crevice, felt a contempt for him and disappointment in him. It did look easy. Now Gus was five feet away, and after a painful effort, four feet. But when only a yard intervened, he came to a standstill — not exactly a standstill, for, like a squirrel in a wheel, he maintained his position on the face of the Dome by the most desperate clawing.

He had failed, that was evident. The question now was, how to save himself. With a sudden, catlike movement he whirled over on his back, caught his heel in a tiny, saucer-shaped depression and sat up. Then his courage failed him. Day had at last penetrated to the floor of the valley, and he was appalled at the frightful distance.

"Go ahead and make it!" Hazard ordered; but Gus merely shook his head.

"Then come down!"

Again he shook his head. This was his ordeal, to sit, nerveless and insecure, on the brink of the precipice. But Hazard, lying safely in his crevice, now had to face his own ordeal, but one of a different nature. When Gus began to slide, — as he soon must, — would he, Hazard, be able to take in the slack and then meet the shock as the other tautened the rope and darted toward the plunge? It seemed doubtful. And there he lay, apparently safe, but in reality harnessed to death. Then rose the temptation. Why not cast off the rope about his waist? He would be safe at all events. It was a simple way out of the difficulty. There was no need that two should perish. But it was impossible for such temptation to overcome his pride of race, and his own pride in himself and in his honor. So the rope remained about him.

"Come down!" he ordered; but Gus seemed to have become petrified.

"Come down," he threatened, "or I'll drag you down!" He pulled on the rope to show he was in earnest.

"Don't you dare!" Gus articulated through his chattering teeth.

"Sure, I will, if you don't come!" Again he jerked the rope.

With a despairing gurgle Gus started, doing his best to work sideways from the plunge. Hazard, every sense on the alert, almost exulting in his perfect coolness, took in the slack with deft rapidity. Then, as the rope began to tighten, he braced himself. The shock drew him half out of the crevice; but he held firm and served as the center of the circle, while Gus, with the rope as a radius, described the circumference and ended up on the extreme southern edge of the Saddle. A few moments later Hazard was offering him the flask.

"Take some yourself," Gus said.

"No; you. I don't need it."

"And I'm past needing it." Evidently Gus was dubious of the bottle and its contents.

Hazard put it away in his pocket. "Are you game," he asked, "or are you going to give it up?"

"Never!" Gus protested. "I *am* game. No Lafee ever showed the white feather yet. And if I did lose my grit up there, it was only for the moment — sort of like seasickness. I'm all right now, and I'm going to the top."

"Good!" encouraged Hazard. "You lie in the crevice this time, and I'll show you how easy it is."

But Gus refused. He held that it was easier and safer for him to try again, arguing that it was less difficult for his one hundred and sixteen pounds to cling to the smooth rock than for Hazard's one hundred and sixty-five; also, that it was easier for one hundred and sixty-five pounds to bring a sliding one hundred and sixteen to a stop than *vice versa*. And further, that he had the benefit of his previous experience. Hazard saw the justice of this, although it was with great reluctance that he gave in.

Success vindicated Gus's contention. The second time, just as it seemed as if his slide would be repeated, he made a last supreme effort and gripped the coveted peg. By means of the rope, Hazard quickly joined him. The next peg was nearly sixty feet away; but for nearly half that distance the base of some glacier in the forgotten past had ground a shallow furrow. Taking advantage of this, it was easy for Gus to lasso the eye-bolt. And it seemed, as was really the case, that the hardest part of the task was over. True, the curve steepened to nearly sixty degrees above them, but a comparatively unbroken line of eye-bolts, six feet apart, awaited the lads. They no longer had even to use the lasso. Standing on one peg it was child's play to throw the bight of the rope over the next and to draw themselves up to it.

A bronzed and bearded man met them at the top and gripped their hands in hearty fellowship.

"Talk about your Mont Blancs!" he exclaimed, pausing in the midst of greeting them to survey the mighty panorama. "But there's nothing on all the earth, nor over it, nor under it, to compare with this!" Then he recollected himself and thanked them for coming to his aid. No, he was not hurt or injured in any way. Simply because of his own carelessness, just as he had arrived at the top the previous day, he had dropped his climbing rope. Of course it was impossible to descend without it. Did they understand heliographing? No? That was strange! How did they —

"Oh, we knew something was the matter," Gus interrupted, "from the way you flashed when we fired off the shotgun."

"Find it pretty cold last night without blankets?" Hazard queried.

"I should say so. I've hardly thawed out yet."

"Have some of this." Hazard shoved the flask over to him.

The stranger regarded him quite seriously for a moment, then said, "My dear fellow, do you see that row of pegs? Since it is my honest intention to climb down them very shortly, I am forced to decline. No, I don't think I'll have any, though I thank you just the same."

Hazard glanced at Gus and then put the flask back in his pocket. But when they pulled the doubled rope through the last eye-bolt and set foot on the Saddle, he again drew out the bottle.

"Now that we're down, we don't need it," he remarked, pithily. "And I've about come to the conclusion that there isn't very much in Dutch courage, after all." He gazed up the great curve of the Dome. "Look at what we've done without it!"

Several seconds thereafter a party of tourists, gathered at the margin of Mirror Lake, were astounded at the unwonted phenomenon of a whisky flask descending upon them like a comet out of a clear sky; and all the way back to the hotel they marveled greatly at the wonders of nature, especially meteorites.

30
Martin Eden

JACK LONDON.

From his most recent Portrait by Arnold Genthe.

Jack London's

Great Novel, "Martin Eden"

Editorial Announcement

IT may not be customary to review a novel before it is published either serially or in book form,—yet what objection may be justly offered? Doubtless half the readers of books are persuaded to the reading by the critical reviews, or by more or less curiosity-stimulating discussion. However, let us be in fashion, and call this a "foreword." One of London's most intimate friends who has read the manuscript of *Martin Eden,* which will begin serially in this magazine next month, says that London has put into its pages a vivid picture of his own wonderful struggle for success in authorship. Perhaps this accounts for the peculiar effectiveness of the story. There is no taking up of one set of characters for a chapter or two and then returning to the main one, but it is all Martin Eden. Had it been put in narrative form it might have been called "The Confessions of a Conqueror."

A somewhat captious critic of one of London's books once said that he lacked restraint, and Mr. Porter Garnett has said of him in *The Pacific Monthly*: "He has more of the brass band in his idiom than of the string quartet. London sometimes plays the 'cello of passion, and often the viola of sentiment," but in *Martin Eden* he also plays, we believe, "the violin of the supernal sense."

It has more than once been noted by reviewers and critical essayists, that where an author puts his own story into a book, if he be a great author, it is apt to be his masterpiece. Jack London, still but a youth of thirty-two, has already done a prodigious amount of work. Think of his record! Seventeen complete volumes of novels and short stories, besides this latest,—and every one of them a hit with the reading public. Not every one a hit with all literary critics, but most of them the recipients of unstinted praise by the most famous and authoritative reviewers.

Now comes *Martin Eden,* and those who remember his expression in the essay, "What Life Means To Me," which appeared in *The Cosmopolitan* two years ago: "I resolved to sell no more muscle, and to become a vendor of brains. Then began a frantic pursuit of knowledge," are able to see no other than Jack London himself in *Martin Eden.* Dickens, in the opinion of many, did his best in *David Copperfield.* Two characters and two life stories, reputed to be pictures from the experiences of the writers, could scarcely be more opposite than those of Martin Eden and David Copperfield. London's understanding is clear of how to achieve the great end of the finest art in literary creation (just as it is in painting), viz: to stir the emotions; and he has written nothing that stirs them so profoundly as does *Martin Eden.* "Through everything that London has written, Force stalks with indomitable stride," and Force stalks through the pages of *Martin Eden.*

The novel is an epic,—an epic that may appall the whining underling in the struggle for success; the lazy dilettante who complains that the Fates are against him; but to the rugged, militant soul it is an extraordinary inspiration. To the heroic struggler in any field of high endeavor, *Martin Eden* beats the war drum of power. London has been accused of "padding" because of the "ten cents a word," but it is impossible to blue pencil the manuscript of *Martin Eden* without injury to the work. Everything extraneous has been eliminated; every word is a brick in a mighty structure.

If one were asked to select its most striking passage the effort would be found impossible. Turning the leaves at random one encounters vivid passage after vivid passage, like the following:

He walked at the other's heels with a swing to his shoulders, and his legs spread unwittingly, as if the level floors were tilting up and sinking down to the heave and lunge of the sea. The wide rooms seemed too narrow for his rolling gait, and to himself he was in terror lest his broad shoulders should collide with the doorways or sweep the bric-a-brac from the low mantel.

* * * *

Then they fell upon each other, like young bulls, in all the glory of youth, with naked fists, with hatred, with desire to hurt, to maim, to destroy. All the painful thousand-years' gains of man in his upward climb through creation, were lost. Only the electric light remained, a milestone on the path of the great human adventure. Martin and Cheese-Face were two savages, of the stone-age, of the squatting place and the tree refuge. * * * They were twin whirlwinds of hatred, revolving about each other monstrously. The time passed, and the two hostile gangs became very quiet. They had never witnessed such intensity of ferocity, and they were awed by it. The two fighters were greater brutes than they. The first splendid velvet edge of youth and condition wore off, and they fought more cautiously and deliberately. There had been no advantage gained either way. "It 's anybody's fight," Martin heard someone saying. Then he followed up a feint, right and left, was fiercely countered, and felt his cheek laid open to the bone. No bare knuckles had done that. He heard mutters of amazement at the ghastly damage wrought, and was drenched with his own blood. But he gave no sign. He became immensely wary, for he was wise with knowledge of the low cunning and foul vileness of his kind. He watched and waited, until he feigned a wild rush, which he stopped midway, for he had seen the glint of metal.

* * * *

He saw her hand coming out to his, and she looked him straight in the eyes as she shook hands, frankly, like a man. The women he had known did not shake hands that way. For that matter, most of them did not shake hands at all. A flood of associations, visions of various ways he had made the acquaintance of women, rushed into his mind and threatened to swamp it. But he shook them aside and looked at her. Never had he seen such a woman. The women he had known! Immediately, beside her, on the other hand, ranged the women he had known. For an eternal second he stood in the midst of a portrait gallery, wherein she occupied the central place, while about her were limned many women, all to be weighed and measured by a fleeting glance, herself the unit of weight and measure. He saw the weak and sickly faces of the girls of the factories, and the simpering, boisterous girls from the south of Market. There were women of the cattle camps, and swarthy cigarette-smoking women of Old Mexico. These, in turn, were crowded out by Japanese women, doll-like, stepping mincingly on wooden clogs; Eurasians, delicate-featured, stamped with degeneracy; by full-bodied South-Sea-Island women, flower-crowned and brown-skinned.

* * * *

In his eyes was a rich vision of that hot, starry night at Salina Cruz, the white strip of beach, the lights of the sugar steamers in the harbor, the voices of the drunken sailors in the distance, the jostling stevedores, the flaming passion in the Mexican's face, the glint of the beast-eyes in the starlight, the sting of the steel in his neck and the rush of blood, the crowd and the cries, the two bodies, his and the Mexican's locked together, rolling over and over and tearing up the sand, and from away off somewhere the mellow tinkling of a guitar.

* * * *

There was no life beyond, he had contended; it was here and now, then darkness everlasting. But what he had seen in her eyes was soul—immortal soul that could never die. No man he had known, nor any woman, had given him the message of immortality. But she had. She had whispered it to him the first moment she looked at him. Her face shimmered before his face as he walked alone, pale and serious, sweet and sensitive, smiling with pity and tenderness as only a spirit could smile, and pure as he had never dreamed purity could be. Her purity smote him like a blow.

* * * *

And he felt the stir in him, like a throe of yearning pain, of the desire to paint these visions that flashed unsummoned on the mirror of his mind. Ah, that was it! He caught at the hem of the secret. It was the very thing that the great writers and master-poets did. That was why they were giants. They knew how to express what they thought, and felt, and saw. Dogs asleep in the sun often whined and barked, but they were unable to tell what they saw that made them whine and bark. He had often wondered what it was. And that was all he was, a dog asleep in the sun. He saw noble and beautiful visions, but he could only whine and bark at Ruth. But he would cease sleeping in the sun. He would stand up, with open eyes, and he would struggle and toil and learn until, with eyes unblinded and tongue united, he could share with her his visioned wealth. Other men had discovered the trick of expression, of making words obedient servitors, and of making combinations of words mean more than the sum of their separate meanings. He was stirred profoundly by the passing glimpse of the secret, and he was again caught up in the vision of sun-lit spaces and starry voids.

* * * *

He was amazed at the immense amount of printed stuff that was dead. No life, no light, no color, was shot through it. There was no breath of life in it, and yet it sold, at two cents a word, twenty dollars a thousand—the newspaper clippings had said so. He was puzzled by countless short stories, written lightly and cleverly he confessed, but without vitality or reality. Life was so strange and wonderful, filled with an immensity of problems, of dreams, and of heroic toils, and yet these stories dealt only with the commonplaces of life. He felt the stress and strain of life, its fevers and sweats and wild insurgences—surely this was the stuff to write about! He wanted to glorify the leaders of forlorn hopes, the mad lovers, the giants that fought under stress and strain, amid terror and tragedy, making life crackle with the strength of their endeavor. And yet the magazine short stories seemed intent on glorifying the Mr. Butlers, the sordid dollar-chasers, and the commonplace little love affairs of commonplace little men and women. Was it because the editors of the magazines were commonplace? he demanded. Or were they afraid of life?—these writers and editors and readers?

The foregoing passages might convey an idea of a nature too intense, too vital, too potential, to admit of hearty good fellowship, or to embody the saving grace of humor that is the mark of mental balance and physical health.

Plenty of excerpts could be given to throw an interesting side light on these wholesome elements in the character of Martin Eden. The following passage introduces a remarkably interesting character, in the person of Brissenden, whose friendship for Eden makes an impress on his work, and, probably, on his destiny:

"On the contrary, hack-work is above you, so far above that you can never hope to rise to it. Why, man, I could insult you by asking you to have something to eat."

Martin felt the heat in his face of the involuntary blood, and Brissenden laughed triumphantly.

"A full man is not insulted by such an invitation," he concluded.

"You are a devil," Martin cried irritably.

"Anyway, I did n't ask you."

"You did n't dare."

"Oh, I dont know about that. I invite you now."

Brissenden half rose from his chair as he spoke, as if with the intention of departing to the restaurant forthwith.

Martin's fists were tight,—clenched and his blood was drumming in his temples.

"Bosco! He eats 'em alive! Eats 'em alive!" Brissenden exclaimed, imitating the spieler of a locally famous snake eater.

"I could certainly eat you alive," Martin said, in turn running insolent eyes over the other's disease-ravaged frame.

"Only I 'm not worthy of it?"

"On the contrary," Martin considered, "because the incident is not worthy." He broke into a laugh, hearty and wholesome. "I confess you made a fool of me, Brissenden. That I am hungry and you are aware of it, are only ordinary phenomena, and there 's no disgrace. You see, I laugh at the conventional little moralities of the herd; then you drift by, say a sharp, true word, and immediately I am the slave of the same little moralities."

"You were insulted," Brissenden affirmed.

"I certainly was, a moment ago.—The prejudice of early youth, you know. I learned such things then, and they cheapen what I have since learned. They are the skeletons in my particular closet."

"But you 've got the door shut on them now?"

"I certainly have."

"Sure?"

"Sure."

"Then let 's go and get something to eat."

Martin Eden is a character study—the story of a fighter—a fighter as a newsboy in the alleys of San Francisco; a fighter as a rowdy in slums; and, finally, a fighter for education and culture, struggling against the odds of common birth and vulgar environment, with a desperation of courage that presents a powerful blending of brutality of strength with sublimity of purpose. His inspiration is a woman of the higher sphere of life, but his motive is the mighty impulse that animates a soul and brain born to expand until fettering ignorance is sundered and ignoble influence trampled under foot.

It is not too much to say of *Martin*

Eden that it possesses more of fascination and virility, grips the imagination and the sympathies more keenly, and imparts more of courage, than any book produced in years.

The keynote of the novel is sounded in the four quoted lines with which the author begins the first chapter:

Let me live my years in heat of blood;
Let me lie drunken with the dreamer's wine!
Let me not see this soul-house built of mud
Go toppling to the dust of a vacant shrine!

The personality of few latter-day writers is so interesting as that of London. His career has been exceptional,—seemingly a sudden leap from obscurity to the foremost rank of writers, and maintaining that position not through a first one successful novel or book of short stories, but by a series of works of sustained strength.

Mrs. Ninetta Eames, formerly of the old *Overland Monthly* staff, (and whom Mr. London affectionately calls "Mother Mine") wrote for that magazine a very interesting account of London, in which she says in part:

"To the *Overland* is due the introduction of Jack London to the reading public, and not long afterwards his stories, which dealt mainly with Alaskan fact and fiction, began to appear in various standard publications throughout the East and West.

" 'Jack London,' proves to be no adroitly chosen pseudonym, but the name a fortuitous fate bestowed upon the subject of this sketch at birth. His father, John London, a nomadic trapper, scout and frontiersman, in 1873 came to San Francisco, where Jack, the youngest of ten half-brothers and sisters was born January 12, 1876. * * * * There is a mingled strain of English, Welsh, Dutch, Swiss and German in London.

"To use London's own simple hyperbole at the beginning of his success, 'I have just been sort of hammering round in the dark till I knocked holes through, here and there, and caught glimpses of the daylight.' "

"These heralding day-gleams were the lad's compensation in a life cramped and embittered by omnipresent poverty. The spring of a higher, ampler living was at the root of his consciousness, and he turned instinctively and inevitably toward literature, his imagination and feeling drawing out the romance of surroundings which to others appeared mean and commonplace. * * * * Up to his ninth year he spent a somewhat joyous childhood on California ranches, his chief pleasure the books that fell into his hands—*Trowbridge's Works For Boys, Captain Cook's Voyages, Paul du Chaillu's Travels, Rip Van Winkle* and occasionally a Seaside Library book borrowed from some farm hand. Then followed the moving of the family into Oakland, where the boy first had access to a free library—an inestimable privilege to one with his insatiate love of reading.

"After school hours he sold newspapers on the streets, and not infrequently did battle to establish his right of route. An instance of this kind, told by an old neighbor of the Londons, is illustrative not only of Jack's grit and courage at thirteen, but of a certain phlegm and philosophic justice in his father. Jack had borne innumerable petty affronts from a sixteen-year-old boy until patience was exhausted, and he resolved to fight it out. Accordingly, at their next encounter the two fell to blows, Jack cool and determined as one predestined to conquer, and his antagonist swelling with the surface pride and arrogance of the bully. For more than two hours they stuck to it manfully, neither winning a serious advantage over the other. The neighbor watcher thought it time to put a stop to the pommeling, and ran to the London cottage, where she found the old man sunning himself on the doorstep.

" 'O, Mr. London,' she cried, 'Jack's been fighting for hours! Do come and stop it!'

"He composedly returned, 'Is my boy fighting fair?'

" 'Yes, sir; he is.'

"He nodded, his pleased eyes twinkling:

" 'An' tother one—is *he* fighting fair?'

" 'Yes,—leastwise it looks so.'

" 'Well, let 'em alone. There dont seem no call to interfere.'

"That this placidity did not argue indifference was seen by the father's appearance a few minutes later on the field of action. He did nothing, however; only pulled steadily at his pipe and looked on, one of a motley crowd of spectators. Jack's opponent was getting winded and bethought him of a subterfuge. He gave a blow and then threw himself on the ground, knowing that Jack would not hit him when he was down. The latter saw his little game, and when it was thrice repeated, struck his falling adversary. There was a yell of 'Foul blow!' from the two younger brothers of the vanquished pugilist, and the elder, an overgrown boy of fifteen sprang red-hot into the circle and demanded satisfaction. Jack panting and holding to his swollen wrist (that last blow of his had strained the tendons), pranced into position and fired back the answer. 'Come on! I 'll lick you, too!'

"It was observed that his father forgot to smoke during the spirited tussle that ensued, though he said never a word, even when Jack, dripping gore and sweat, drew off victorious from his prostrate foe only to face the third brother, a lad of his own age. Him he downed with a single thrust of his fist, for his blood was up and he felt cordial to himself and invincibly confident in his strength to overcome a host of irate brothers.

"Then it was that John London, bright of eye and smiling, took a gentle grip of his son's arm and marched him in triumph from the field.

"Between school hours and work Jack found time to pore over books of history, poetry and fiction, and to nurse the secret wish to become a writer. He was graduated from the Oakland grammar school at fourteen and a few months after drifted into an adventurous life longshore. Here he shared the industries and pastimes of the marine population huddled along the water-front, taking his chances at salmon-fishing, oyster pirating, schooner-sailing and other bayfaring ventures, never holding himself aloof when comrades were awake, but when they slept turning to his book with the avidity of a mind athirst for knowledge.

"About this period of his life his sympathies and emotions were deeply stirred by the wrongs inflicted upon the laboring classes, and with youthful fervor he took up their defense, haranguing the crowds nightly in the plaza and urging upon them the necessity of social and political reconstruction. He became known in Bay whereabouts as the 'Boy Socialist,' and more than one of his street-hearers looked upon him as a kind of secular evangelist.

"When he was seventeen, Young London shipped before the mast on a sealing schooner which cruised to Japan and up the north coast to the Russian side of Bering Sea." * * * * Nevertheless Jack did not take specially to a seafaring life, and not long afterward we find him again in Oakland, plunging with characteristic ardor into the study of sociology and economics. Not satisfied with a theoretical understanding of the problems involved in socialistic reforms, like Josiah Flynt, he took to the road, living for months the life of a tramp, and learning by hard knocks the true import of the survival of the fittest under existing economic conditions. Speaking of the outcome of this practical test Mr. London says:

" 'The months I spent on the road bred in me a permanent interest in the institutions of man, both from an economic and an ethical standpoint. Among other things I learned that society is an organism, the inertia of the masses profound, and the evolution of institutions a slow and painful process. Like every normal man who has thought along these lines, I learned to temper my radicalism, and was helped in this by a deeper inquiry into the science of evolution as taught by a host of writers; Herbert Spencer in the lead. I am still a socialist but an evolved product, possessing a faith in humanity equalled only by a conception of its frailities and faults."

"Though his tramp life mellowed and broadened his views, it in no wise lessened his zeal to better the conditions of the masses. He joined the Oakland section of the Socialist Labor Party, and was the first of their number to be arrested for violating the ordinance regulating public speaking on the streets. When the case came to trial he defended himself with dignity and logic, and was forthwith acquitted. About this time he returned to study entering the Oakland High School and completing the first year's course. Then to save time and money he took up lessons at home, cramming a two years' curriculum into three months, when he passed the examination to enter the State University at Berkeley.

"Unfortunately his college course was limited to his freshman year, finances obliging him to turn-to at the familiar grind. This was in '97, and impelled by the promise of gold and adventure Jack London was among the first to join the fall rush to the Klondike. He was among the few doughty Argonauts who at this season made it over the Chilcoot Pass, the great majority waiting for spring. * * * * Thus it would seem that his actual development as a writer began on the trail, though at the time he set no word to paper, not even jottings by the way in a note-book. A tireless brooding on the wish to write shaped his impulse to definite purpose, but outwardly he continued to share the interests and labors of his companion prospectors.

"After a year spent in that weirdly picturesque but hazardous life, he succumbed to scurvy, and impatient of the delay of homeward bound steamers, he and two companions decided to embark in an open boat for the Bering Sea. The three accordingly made the start midway in June, and the voyage turned out to be a memorably novel and perilous one—nineteen hundred miles of river travel in nineteen days!

* * * * "When London reached California he learned of the death of his father, and thenceforth devolved upon him the care of his widowed mother and a six-year-old nephew. There were debts also to meet,—doctors' and undertakers' bills,—which the son resolutely faced, his mind bent determinedly upon winning a livelihood by his pen. His brain seethed with stories founded upon the wonderful life of the past year. Could he transcribe these simply and dramatically so as to appeal to the reader? If this were possible then success was assured. He began at once, and the result excited highest hopes; before the year was out Eastern publishers were making him flattering offers for stories and articles, urging upon the young writer the advisability of bringing out a book.

* * * * "Aside from native talent, Jack London has assuredly the genius for hard work. He devotes himself to his labors with care and precision, coining his time with miserly stint and observing a method of collection and classification as amusing as it is effective. Across an angle of his study he stretched what he calls his 'clothes-line,' a wire on which are strung batches of excerpts and notes fastened on by clothes-pins, the kind with a wire spring. A hastily scribbled thought and an extract bearing upon the same theme are duly clamped in their proper place, and the 'clothes-line' usually dangles a dozen or more of these bunched tatters of literature.

"His plan of reading has also a like simplicity, with a hazard at the economy of vital force. He does not read books consecutively but collectively. A dozen volumes are selected on divers subjects—science, philosophy, fiction—and arranged with regard to their relative profundity. Then he begins with the weightiest matter, reads it until his brain is a trifle wearied when he lays the work aside for one requiring less effort, and so on until at one sitting he has delved into each, always bringing up finally with the novel or poetry as the wine and walnuts of his literary feast."

VOL. XX SEPTEMBER, 1908 No. 3

Martin Eden

By Jack London

Author of "The Call of the Wild," "Sea Wolf," "The God of His Fathers," "White Fang," Etc.

"Let me live out my years in heat of blood!
Let me lie drunken with the dreamer's wine!
Let me not see this soul-house built of mud
Go toppling to the dust a vacant shrine!"

CHAPTER I.

THE one opened the door with a latch key and went in, followed by a young fellow who awkwardly removed his cap. He wore rough clothes that smacked of the sea, and he was manifestly out of place in the spacious hall in which he found himself. He did not know what to do with his cap, and was stuffing it into his coat pocket when the other took it from him. The act was done quietly and naturally, and the awkward young fellow appreciated it. "He understands," was his thought. "He 'll see me through all right."

He walked at the other's heels with a swing to his shoulders, and his legs spread unwittingly, as if the level floors were tilting up and sinking down to the heave and lunge of the sea. The wide rooms seemed too narrow for his rolling gait, and to himself he was in terror lest his broad shoulders should collide with the doorways or sweep the bric-a-brac from the low mantel. He recoiled from side to side between the various objects and multiplied the hazards that in reality lodged only in his mind. Between a grand piano and a center table piled high with books was space for half a dozen to walk abreast, yet he essayed it with trepidation. His heavy arms hung loosely at his sides. He did not know what to do with those arms and hands, and when, to his excited vision, one arm seemed liable to brush against the books on the table, he lurched away like a frightened horse, barely missing the piano stool. He watched the easy walk of the other in front of him, and for the first time realized that his walk was different from that of other men. He experienced a momentary pang of shame that he should walk so uncouthly. The sweat burst through the skin of his forehead in tiny beads, and he paused and mopped his bronzed face with his handkerchief.

"Hold on, Arthur, my boy," he said, attempting to mask his anxiety with facetious utterance. "This is too much all at once for yours truly. Give me a chance to get my nerve. You know I did n't want to come, an' I guess your fam'ly aint hankerin' to see me neither."

"That 's all right," was the reassuring answer. "You must n't be frightened at us. We 're just homely people—hello, there 's a letter for me."

He stepped back to the table, tore open the envelope, and began to read, giving the stranger an opportunity to recover himself. And the stranger understood and appreciated. His was the gift of sympathy, understanding; and beneath his alarmed exterior that sympathetic process went on. He mopped his forehead dry and glanced about him with a controlled face, though in the eyes there was an expression such as wild animals betray when they fear the trap. He was surrounded by the unknown, apprehensive of what might happen, ignorant of what he should do, aware that he walked and bore himself awkwardly, fearful that every attribute and power of him was similarly afflicted. He was keenly sensitive, hopelessly self-conscious, and the amused glance that the other stole privily at him over the top of the letter burned into him like a dagger-thrust He saw the glance, but he gave no sign, for among the things he had learned was discipline. Also, that dagger-thrust went to his pride. He cursed himself for having come, and at the same time resolved that, happen what would, having come, he would carry it through. The lines of his face hardened, and into his eyes came a fighting light. He looked about more unconcernedly, sharply observant, every detail of the pretty interior registering itself on his brain. His eyes were wide apart; nothing in their field of vision escaped; and as they drank in the beauty before them the fighting light died out and a warm glow took its place. He was responsive to beauty, and here was cause to respond.

An oil painting caught and held him. A heavy surf thundered and burst over an outjutting rock; lowering storm-clouds covered the sky; and, outside the line of surf, a pilot-schooner, close-hauled, heeled over till every detail of her deck was visible, was surging along against a stormy sunset sky. There was beauty, and it drew him irresistibly. He forgot his awkward walk and came closer to the painting, very close. The beauty faded out of the canvas. His face expressed his bepuzzlement. He stared at what seemed a careless daub of paint, then stepped away. Immediately all the beauty flashed back into the canvas. "A trick picture," was his thought, as he dismissed it, though in the midst of the multitudinous impressions he was receiving he found time to feel a prod of indignation that so much beauty should be sacrificed to make a trick. He did not know painting. He had been brought up on chromos and lithographs that were always definite and sharp, near or far. He had seen oil paintings, it was true, in the show windows of shops, but the glass of the windows had prevented his eager eyes from approaching too near.

He glanced around at his friend reading the letter and saw the books on the table. Into his eyes leaped a wistfulness and a yearning as promptly as the yearning leaps into the eyes of a starving man at sight of food. An impulsive stride, with one lurch to right and left of the shoulders, brought him to the table, where he began affectionately handling the books. He glanced at the titles and the authors' names, read fragments of text, caressing the volumes with his eyes and hands, and, once, recognized a book he had read. For the rest, they were strange books and strange authors. He chanced upon a volume of Swinburne and began reading steadily, forgetful of where he was, his face glowing. Twice he closed the book on his forefinger to look at the name of the author. Swinburne!—he would remember that name.

"SWINBURNE! THAT FELLOW HAD EYES AND HE HAD CERTAINLY SEEN COLOR AND FLASHING LIGHT, BUT WHO WAS SWINBURNE?"

That fellow had eyes, and he had certainly seen color and flashing light. But who was Swinburne? Was he dead a hundred years or so like most of the poets? Or was he alive still, and writing? He turned to the title-page—yes, he had written other books; well, he would go to the free library the first thing in the morning and try to get hold of some of Swinburne's stuff. He went back to the text and lost himself. He did not notice that a young woman had entered the room. The first he knew was when he heard Arthur's voice saying:

"Ruth, this is Mr. Eden."

The book was closed on his forefinger, and before he turned he was thrilling to the first new impression, which was not of the girl, but of her brother's words. Under that muscled body of his he was a mass of quivering sensibilities. At the slightest impact of the outside world upon his consciousness, his thoughts, sympathies, and emotions leapt and played like lambent flame. He was extraordinarily receptive and responsive, while his imagination, pitched high, was ever at work establishing relations of likeness and difference. "Mr. Eden," was what he had thrilled to—he who had been called "Eden," or "Martin Eden," or just "Martin," all his life. And "*Mister!*" It was certainly going some, was his internal comment. His mind seemed to turn, on the instant, into a vast *camera obscura,* and he saw arrayed around his consciousness endless pictures from his life, of stoke-holes and forecastles, camps and beaches, jails and boozing-kens, fever-hospitals and slum streets, wherein the thread of association was the fashion in which he had been addressed in those various situations.

And then he turned and saw the girl. The phantasmagoria of his brain vanished at sight of her. She was a pale ethereal creature, with wide, spiritual blue eyes and a wealth of golden hair. He did not know how she was dressed, except that the dress was as wonderful as she. He likened her to a pale gold flower upon a slender stem. No, she was a spirit, a divinity, a goddess; such sublimated beauty was not of the earth. Or perhaps the books were right, and there were many such as she in the upper walks of life. She might well be sung by that chap Swinburne. Perhaps he had had somebody like her in mind when he painted that girl, Iseult, in the book there on the table. All this plethora of sight, and feeling, and thought, occurred on the instant. There was no pause of the realities wherein he moved. He saw her hand coming out to his, and she looked him straight in the eyes as she shook hands, frankly, like a man. The women he had known did not shake hands that way. For that matter, most of them did not shake hands at all. A flood of associations, visions of various ways he had made the acquaintance of women, rushed into his mind and threatened to swamp it. But he shook them aside and looked at her. Never had he seen such a woman. The women he had known! Immediately, beside her, on either hand, ranged the women he had known. For an eternal second he stood in the midst of a portrait gallery, wherein she occupied the central place, while about her were limned many women, all to be weighed and measured by a fleeting glance, herself the unit of weight and measure. He saw the weak and sickly faces of the girls of the factories, and the simpering, boisterous girls from the south of Market. There were women of the cattle camps, and swarthy cigarette-smoking women of Old Mexico. These, in turn, were crowded out by Japanese women, doll-like, stepping mincingly on wooden clogs; by Eurasians, delicate-featured, stamped with degeneracy; by full-bodied South-Sea-Island women, flower-crowned and brown-skinned. All these were blotted out by a grotesque and terrible nightmare brood—frowsy, shuffling creatures from the pavements of Whitechapel, gin-bloated hags of the stews, and all the vast hell's following of harpies, vile-mouthed and filthy, that under the guise of monstrous female form prey upon sailors, the scrapings of the ports, the scum and slime of the human pit.

"Wont you sit down, Mr. Eden?" the girl was saying. "I have been looking forward to meeting you ever since Ar-

"SHE SHOOK HANDS, FRANKLY, LIKE A MAN. * * * NEVER HAD HE SEEN SUCH A WOMAN."

thur told us. It was brave of you——"

He waved his hand deprecatingly and muttered that it was nothing at all, what he had done, and that any fellow would have done it. She noticed that the hand he waved was covered with fresh abrasions, in the process of healing, and a glance at the other loose-hanging hand showed it to be in the same condition. Also, with quick, critical eye, she noted a scar on his cheek, another that peeped out from under the hair of the forehead, and a third that ran down and disappeared under the starched collar. She repressed a smile at sight of the red line that marked the chafe of the collar against the bronzed neck. He was evidently unused to stiff collars. Likewise her feminine eye took in the clothes he wore, the cheap and unesthetic cut, the wrinkling of the coat across the shoulders, and the series of wrinkles in the sleeves that advertised bulging biceps muscles.

While he waved his hand and muttered that he had done nothing at all, he was obeying her behest by trying to get into a chair. He found time to admire the ease with which she sat down, then lurched toward a chair facing her, overwhelmed with consciousness of the awkward figure he was cutting. This was a new experience for him. All his life, up to then, he had been unaware of being either graceful or awkward. Such thoughts of self had never entered his mind. He sat down gingerly on the edge of the chair, greatly worried by his hands. They were in the way wherever he put them. Arthur was leaving the room, and Martin Eden followed his exit with longing eyes. He felt lost, alone there in the room with that pale spirit of a woman. There was no barkeeper upon whom to call for drinks, no small boy to send around the corner for a can of beer and by means of that social fluid start the amenities of friendship flowing.

"You have such a scar on your neck, Mr. Eden," the girl was saying. "How did it happen? I am sure it must have been some adventure."

"A Mexican with a knife, Miss," he answered, moistening his parched lips and clearing his throat. "It was just a fight. After I got the knife away, he tried to bite off my nose."

Badly as he had stated it, in his eyes was a rich vision of that hot, starry night at Salina Cruz, the white strip of beach, the lights of the sugar steamers in the harbor, the voices of the drunken sailors in the distance, the jostling stevedores, the flaming passion in the Mexican's face, the glint of the beast-eyes in the starlight, the sting of the steel in his neck and the rush of blood, the crowd and the cries, the two bodies, his and the Mexican's, locked together, rolling over and over and tearing up the sand, and from away off somewhere the mellow tinkling of a guitar. Such was the picture, and he thrilled to the memory of it, wondering if the man could paint it who had painted the pilot-schooner on the wall. The white beach, the stars, and the lights of the sugar steamers would look great, he thought, and midway on the sand the dark group of figures that surrounded the fighters. The knife occupied a place in the picture, he decided, and would show well, with a sort of gleam, in the light of the stars. But of all this no hint had crept into his speech. "..he tried to bite off my nose," he concluded.

"Oh," said the girl in a faint, far voice, and he noticed the shock in her sensitive face.

He felt a shock himself, and a blush of embarrassment shone faintly on his sunburned cheeks, though to him it burned as hotly as when his cheeks had been exposed to the open furnace-door in the fire-room. Such sordid things as stabbing affrays were evidently not fit subjects for conversation with a lady. People in the books, in her walk of life, did not talk about such things—perhaps they did not know about them, either.

There was a brief pause in the conversation they were trying to get started. Then she asked tentatively about the scar on his cheek. Even as she asked, he realized that she was making an effort to talk his talk, and he resolved to get away from it and talk hers.

"It was just an accident," he said, putting his hand to his cheek. "One night,

" 'BUT I 'M GOIN' TO MAKE IT MY CLASS' * * * HIS VOICE WAS DETERMINED, HIS EYES FLASHING, THE LINES OF HIS FACE HAD GROWN HARSH."

"THAT BUNCH OF HOODLUMS WAS LOOKIN' FOR TROUBLE, AN' ARTHUR WAS N'T BOTHERIN' 'EM NONE. THEY BUTTED IN ON 'M AN' THEN I BUTTED IN ON THEM AN' POKED A FEW!"

in a calm, with a heavy sea running, the main-boom-lift carried away, an' next the tackle. The lift was wire, an' it was threshin' around like a snake. The whole watch was tryin' to grab it. an' I rushed in an' got swatted."

"Oh," she said, this time with an accent of comprehension, though secretly his speech had been so much Greek to her and she was wondering what a *lift* was and what *swatted* meant.

"This man Swineburne," he began, attempting to put his plan into execution and pronouncing the *i* long.

"Who?"

"Swineburne," he repeated, with the same mispronunciation. "The poet."

"Swinburne," she corrected.

"Yes, that 's the chap," he stammered, his cheeks hot again. "How long since he died?"

"Why I have n't heard that he was dead." She looked at him curiously. "Where did you make his acquaintance?"

"I never clapped eyes on him," was the reply. "But I read some of his poetry out of that book there on the table just before you came in. How do you like his poetry?"

And thereat she began to talk quickly and easily upon the subject he had suggested. He felt better, and settled back slightly from the edge of the chair, holding tightly to its arms with his hands, as if it might get away from him and buck him to the floor. He had succeeded in making her talk her talk, and while she rattled on he strove to follow her, marveling at all the knowledge that was stowed away in that pretty head of hers, and drinking in the pale beauty of her face. Follow her he did, though bothered by unfamiliar words that fell glibly from her lips, and by critical phrases and thought-processes that were foreign to his mind but that nevertheless stimulated his mind and set it tingling. Here was intellectual life, he thought, and here was beauty, warm and wonderful as he had never dreamed it could be. He forgot himself and stared at her with hungry eyes. Here was something to live for, to win to, to fight for—ay, and die for. The books were true. There were such women in the world. She was one of them. She lent wings to his imagination, and great, luminous canvases spread themselves before him, whereon loomed vague, gigantic figures of love and romance, and of heroic deeds for woman's sake—for a pale woman, a flower of gold. And through the swaying, palpitant vision, as through a fairy mirage, he stared at the real woman, sitting there and talking of literature and art. He listened as well, but he stared, unconscious of the fixity of his gaze or of the fact that all that was essentially masculine in his nature was shining in his eyes. But she, who knew little of the world of men, being a woman, was keenly aware of his burning eyes. She had never had men look at her in such fashion, and it embarrassed her. She stumbled and halted in her utterance. The thread of argument slipped from her. He frightened her, and at the same time it was strangely pleasant to be so looked upon. Her training warned her of peril and of wrong, subtle, mysterious, luring; while her instincts rang clarion-voiced through her being, impelling her to hurdle caste and place and gain to this traveler from another world, to this uncouth young fellow with lacerated hands and a line of raw red caused by the unaccustomed linen at his throat, who, all too evidently, was soiled and tainted by ungracious existence. She was clean, and her cleanness revolted; but she was a woman, and she was just beginning to learn the paradox of woman.

"As I was saying—what was I saying?" She broke off abruptly and laughed merrily at her predicament.

"You was saying that this man Swinburne failed bein' a great poet because—an' that was as far as you got, Miss," he prompted, while to himself he seemed suddenly hungry, and delicious little thrills crawled up and down his spine at the sound of her laughter. Like silver, he thought to himself, like tinkling silver bells; and on the instant, and for an instant, he was transported to a far land, where, under pink cherry blossoms, he smoked a cigarette and listened to the bells of the peaked *pagoda* calling straw-sandled devotees to worship.

"Yes, thank you," she said. "Swinburne fails, when all is said, because he is, well, indelicate. There are many of his poems that should never be read. Every line of the really great poets is filled with beautiful truth, and calls to all that is high and noble in the human. Not a line of the great poets can be spared without impoverishing the world by that much."

"I thought it was great," he said hesitatingly, "the little I read. I had no idea he was such a—a scoundrel. I guess that crops out in his other books."

"There are many lines that could be spared from the book you were reading," she said, her voice primly firm and dogmatic.

"I must a-missed 'em," he announced. "What I read was the real goods. It was all lighted up an' shining, an' it shun right into me an' lighted me up inside, like the sun or a searchlight. That 's the way it landed on me, but I guess I aint up much on poetry, Miss."

He broke off lamely. He was confused, painfully conscious of his inarticulateness. He had felt the bigness and glow of life in what he had read, but his speech was inadequate. He could not express what he felt, and to himself he likened himself to a sailor, in a strange ship, on a dark night, groping about in the unfamiliar running rigging. Well, he decided, it was up to him to get acquainted in this new world. He had never seen anything that he could n't get the hang of when he wanted to, and it was about time for him to want to learn to talk the things that were inside of him so that she could understand. *She* was bulking large on his horizon.

"Now Longfellow—" she was saying.

"Yes, I 've read 'm," he broke in impulsively, spurred on to exhibit and make the most of his little store of book-knowledge, desirous of showing her that he was not wholly a stupid clod. *The Psalm of Life, Excelsior,* an'—I guess that 's all."

She nodded her head and smiled, and he felt, somehow, that her smile was tolerant,—pitifully tolerant. He was a fool to attempt to make a pretense that way. That Longfellow chap most likely had written countless books of poetry.

"Excuse me, Miss, for buttin' in that way. I guess the real facts is that I dont know nothin' much about such things. It aint in my class. But I 'm goin' to make it in my class."

It sounded like a threat. His voice was determined, his eyes were flashing, the lines of his face had grown harsh. And to her it seemed that the angle of his jaw had changed; its pitch had become unpleasantly aggressive. At the same time a wave of intense virility seemed to surge out from him and impinge upon her.

"I think you could make it in—in your class," she finished, with a laugh. "You are very strong."

Her gaze rested for a moment on the muscular neck, heavy-corded, almost bull-like, bronzed by the sun, spilling over with rugged health and strength. And though he sat there, blushing and humble, again she felt drawn to him. She was surprised by a wanton thought that rushed into her mind. It seemed to her that if she could lay her two hands upon that neck that all its strength and vigor would flow out to her. She was shocked by this thought. It seemed to reveal to her an undreamed depravity in her nature. Besides, strength, to her, was a gross and brutish thing. Her ideal of masculine beauty had always been slender gracefulness. Yet the thought still persisted. It bewildered her that she should desire to place her hands on that sunburned neck. In truth, she was far from robust, and the need of her body and mind was for strength. But she did not know it. She knew only that no man had ever affected her before as this one had, who shocked her from moment to moment with his awful grammar.

"Yes, I aint no invalid," he said. "When it comes down to hard pan I can digest scrap-iron. But just now I 've got dyspepsia. Most of what you was sayin' I cant digest. Never trained that way, you see. I like books and poetry, and what time I 've had I 've read 'em, but I 've never thought about 'em the way you have. That 's why I cant talk about 'em. I 'm like a navigator adrift on a strange sea without chart or compass. Now I want to get my bearin's. Mebbe you can put me right. How did you learn all this you 've been talkin'?"

"By going to school, I fancy, and by studying," she answered.

"I went to school, when I was a kid," he began to object.

"Yes, but I mean high school, and lectures, and the university."

"You 've gone to the university?" he demanded in frank amazement. He felt that she had become remoter from him by at least a million miles.

"I 'm going there now. I 'm taking special courses in English."

He did not know what "English" meant, but he made a mental note of that item of ignorance and passed on.

"How long would I have to study before I could go to the university?" he asked.

She beamed encouragement upon his desire for knowledge, and said, "That depends upon how much studying you have already done. You have never attended high school? Of course not. But did you finish grammar school?"

"I had two years to run, when I left," he answered. "But I was always honorably promoted at school."

The next moment, angry with himself for the boast, he had gripped the arms of the chair so savagely that every finger-end was stinging. At the same moment he became aware that a woman was entering the room. He saw the girl leave her chair and trip swiftly across the floor to the newcomer. They kissed each other, and, with arms around each other's waists, they advanced toward him. That must be her mother, he thought. She was a tall, blond woman, slender, and stately, and beautiful. Her gown was what he might expect in such a house. His eyes delighted in the graceful lines of it. She and her dress together reminded him of women on the stage. Then he remembered seeing similar grand ladies and gowns entering the London theatres while he stood and watched and the policemen shoved him back into the drizzle beyond the awning. Next his mind leaped to the Grand Hotel at Yokohama, where, too, from the sidewalk, he had seen grand ladies. Then the city and the harbor of Yokohama, in a thousand pictures, began flashing before his eyes. But he swiftly dismissed the kaleidoscope of memory, oppressed by the urgent need of the present. He knew that he must stand up to be introduced, and he struggled painfully to his feet, where he stood with trousers bagging at the knees, his arms loose-hanging and ludicrous, his face set hard for the impending ordeal.

CHAPTER II.

THE process of getting into the dining-room was a nightmare to him. Between halts and stumbles, jerks and lurches, locomotion had at times seemed impossible. But at last he had made it, and was seated alongside of Her. The array of knives and forks frightened him. They bristled with unknown perils, and he gazed at them, fascinated, till their dazzle became a background across which moved a succession of forecastle pictures, wherein he and his mates sat eating salt beef with sheath-knives and fingers, or scooping thick pea-soup out of pannikins by means of battered iron spoons. The stench of bad beef was in his nostrils, while in his ears, to the accompaniment of creaking timbers and groaning bulkheads, echoed the loud mouth-noises of the eaters. He watched them eating, and decided that they ate like pigs. Well, he would be careful here. He would make no noise. He would keep his mind upon it all the time.

He glanced around the table. Opposite him was Arthur, and Arthur's brother, Norman. They were her brothers, he reminded himself, and his heart warmed toward them. How they loved each other, the members of this family! There flashed into his mind the picture of her mother, of the kiss of greeting, and of the pair of them walking toward him with arms entwined. Not in his world were such displays of affection between parents and children made. It was a revelation of the heights of existence that were attained in the world above. It was the finest thing yet that he had seen in this small glimpse of that world. He was moved deeply by appreciation of it, and his heart was melting with sympathetic tenderness. He had starved for love all his life. His nature craved love. It was an organic demand of his being. Yet he had gone without, and hardened himself in the process. He had not known that he needed love. Nor did he know it now. He merely saw it in operation, and thrilled to it, and thought it fine, and high, and splendid.

He was glad that Mr. Morse was not there. It was difficult enough getting acquainted with her, and her mother, and her brother, Norman. Arthur he already knew somewhat. The father would have been too much for him, he felt sure. It seemed to him that he had never worked so hard in his life The severest toil was child's-play compared with this. Tiny nodules of moisture stood out on his forehead, and his shirt was wet with sweat from the exertion of doing so many unaccustomed things at once. He had to eat as he had never eaten before, to handle strange tools, to glance surreptitiously about and learn how to accomplish each new thing, to receive the flood of impressions that was pouring in upon him and being mentally annotated and classified; to be conscious of a yearning for her that perturbed him in the form of a dull, aching restlessness; to feel the prod of desire to win to the walk in life whereon she trod, and to have his mind ever and again straying off in speculation and vague plans of how to reach to her. Also, when his secret glance went across to Norman opposite him, or to anyone else, to ascertain just what knife or fork was to be used in any particular occasion, that person's features were seized upon by his mind, which automatically strove to appraise them and to divine what they were—all in relation to her. Then he had to talk, to hear what was said to him and what was said back and forth, and to answer, when it was necessary, with a tongue prone to looseness of speech that required a constant curb. And to add confusion to confusion, there was the servant, an unceasing menace that appeared noiselessly at his shoulder, a dire Sphinx that propounded puzzles and conundrums demanding instantaneous solution. He was oppressed throughout the meal by the thought of finger bowls. Irrelevantly, insistently, scores of times, he wondered when they would come on and what they looked like. He had heard of such things, and now, sooner or later, somewhere in the next few mintues, he would see them, sit at table with exalted beings who used them—ay, and he would use them himself. And most important of all, far down and yet always at the surface of his thought, was the problem of how he should comport himself toward these persons. What should his attitude be? He wrestled continually and anxiously with the problem. There were cowardly suggestions that he should make believe, assume a part; and there were still more cowardly suggestions that warned him that he would fail in such a course, that his nature was not fitted to live up to it, and that he would make a fool of himself.

It was during the first part of the dinner, struggling to decide upon his attitude, that he was very quiet. He did not know that his quietness was giving the lie to Arthur's words of the day before, when that brother of hers had announced that he was going to bring a wild man home to dinner and for them not to be alarmed, because they would find him an interesting wild man. Martin Eden could not have found it in him, just then, to believe that her brother could be guilty of such treachery—especially when he had been the means of getting this particular brother out of an unpleasant row. So he sat at table, perturbed by his own unfitness and at the same time charmed by all that went on about him. For the first time he realized that eating was something more than a utilitarian function. He was unaware of what he ate. It was merely food. He was feasting his love of beauty at this table where eating was an aesthetic function. It was an intellectual function too. His mind was stirred. He heard words spoken that were meaningless to him, and other words that he had seen only in books and that no man or woman he had known was of large enough mental caliber to pronounce. When he heard such words dropping carelessly from the lips of the members of this marvelous family, her family, he thrilled with delight. The romance, and beauty, and high vigor of the books were coming true. He was in that rare and blissful state wherein a man sees his dreams stalk out from the crannies of fantasy and become fact.

Never had he been at such an altitude of living, and he kept himself in the background, listening, observing, and pleasuring, replying in reticent monosyllables, saying "Yes, Miss," and "No, Miss," to her, and "Yes, Ma'am," and "No, Ma'am," to her mother. He curbed the impulse, arising out of his sea-training, to say "Yes, sir," and "No, sir," to her brothers. He felt that it would be inappropriate and a confession of inferiority on his part—which would never do if he was to win her. Also, it was a dictate of his pride. "By God!" he cried to himself, once, "I 'm just as good as them, and if they do know lots that I dont, I could learn 'm a few myself, all the same!" And the next moment, when she or her mother addressed him as "Mr. Eden," his aggressive pride was forgotten, and he was glowing and warm with delight. He was a civilized man, that was what he was, shoulder to shoulder, at dinner, with people he had read about in books. He was in the books himself, adventuring through the printed pages of bound volumes.

But while he belied Arthur's description, and appeared a gentle lamb rather than a wild man, he was racking his brains for a course of action. He was no gentle lamb, and the part of second fiddle would never do for the high-pitched dominance of his nature. He talked only when he had to, and then his speech was like his walk to the table, filled with jerks and halts as he groped in his polyglot vocabulary for words, debating over words he knew were fit but which he feared he could not pronounce, rejecting other words he knew would not be understood or would be raw and harsh. But all the time he was oppressed by the consciousness that this carefulness of diction was making a booby of him, preventing him from expressing what he had in him. Also, his love of freedom chafed against the restriction in much the same way his neck chafed against the starched fetter of a collar. Besides, he was confident that he could not keep it up. He was by nature powerful of thought and sensibility, and the creative spirit was restive and urgent. He was swiftly mastered by the concept or sensation in him that struggled in birth-throes to receive expression and form, and then he forgot himself and where he was, and the old words—the tools of speech he knew—slipped out.

Once, he declined something from the servant who interrupted and pestered at his shoulder, and he said shortly and emphatically, "Pow!"

On the instant those at the table were keyed up and expectant, the servant was smugly pleased, and he was wallowing in mortification. But he recovered himself quickly.

"It's the *Kanaka* for 'finish,'" he explained, "and it just come out naturally. It 's spelt p-a-u."

He caught her curious and speculative eyes fixed on his hands, and, being in an explanatory mood, he said:

"I just come down the Coast on one of the Pacific mail steamers. She was behind time, an' around the Puget Sound ports we worked like niggers, storing cargo—mixed freight, if you know what that means. That 's how the skin got knocked off."

"Oh, it was n't that," she hastened to explain, in turn. "Your hands seemed too small for your body."

His cheeks were hot. He took it as an exposure of another of his deficiencies.

"Yes," he said deprecatingly. "They aint big enough to stand the strain. I can hit like a mule with my arms and shoulders. They are too strong, an' when I smash a man on the jaw the hands get smashed, too."

He was not happy at what he had said. He was filled with disgust at himself. He had loosed the guard upon his tongue and talked things that were not nice.

"It was brave of you to help Arthur the way you did—and you a stranger," she said tactfully, aware of his discomfiture, though not of the reason for it.

He, in turn, realized what she had done, and, in the consequent warm surge of gratefulness that overwhelmed him, forgot his loose-worded tongue.

"It was n't nothin' at all," he said. "Any guy 'ud do it for another. That bunch of hoodlums was lookin' for trouble, an' Arthur was n't botherin' 'em none. They butted in on 'm, an' then I butted in on them an' poked a few. That 's where some of the skin off my hands went, along with some of the teeth of the gang. I would n't a-missed it for anything. When I seen——"

He paused, open-mouthed, on the verge of the pit of his own depravity and utter worthlessness to breathe the same air she did. And, while Arthur took up the tale, for the twentieth time, of his adventure with the drunken hoodlums on the ferry-boat and of how Martin Eden had rushed in and rescued him, that individual, with frowning brows, meditated upon the fool he had made of himself and wrestled more determinedly with the problem of how he should conduct himself toward these people He certainly had not succeeded so far. He was n't of their tribe, and he could n't talk their lingo, was the way he put it to himself. He could n't fake being their kind. The masquerade would fail, and besides, masquerade was foreign to his nature. There was no room in him for sham or artifice. Whatever happened, he must be real. He could n't talk their talk just yet, though in time he would. Upon that he was resolved. But in the meantime, talk he must, and it must be his own talk, toned down, of course, so as to be comprehensible to them and so as not to shock them too much. And furthermore, he would n't claim, not even by tacit acceptance, to be familiar with anything that was unfamiliar. In pursuance of this decision, when the two brothers, talking university shop, had used "trig" several times, Martin Eden demanded:

"What is *trig?*"

"Trigonometry," Norman said; "a higher form of math."

"And what is *math?*" was the next question, which, somehow, brought the laugh on Norman.

"Mathematics, arithmetic," was the answer.

Martin Eden nodded. He had caught a glimpse of the apparently illimitable vistas of knowledge. What he saw took on tangibility. His abnormal power of vision made abstractions take on concrete form. In the alchemy of his brain, trigonometry and mathematics and the whole field of knowledge which they betokened were transmuted into so much landscape. The vistas he saw were vistas of green foliage and forest glades, all softly luminous or shot through with flashing lights. In the distance, detail was veiled and blurred by a purple haze, but behind this purple haze, he knew, was the glamor of the unknown, the lure of romance. It was like wine to him. Here was adventure, something to do with head and hand, a world to conquer—and straightway from the back of his consciousness rushed the thought, *conquering to win to her, that lily-pale spirit sitting beside him.*

The glimmering vision was rent asunder and dissipated by Arthur, who, all evening, had been trying to draw his wild man out. Martin Eden remembered his decision. For the first time he became himself, consciously and deliberately at first, but soon lost in the joy of creating, in making life as he knew it appear before his listeners' eyes. He had been a member of the crew of the smuggling schooner *Halcyon* when she was captured by a revenue cutter. He saw with wide eyes, and he could tell what he saw. He brought the pulsing sea before them, and the men and the ships upon the sea. He communicated his power of vision, till they saw with his eyes what he had seen. He selected from the vast mass of detail with an artist's touch, drawing pictures of life that glowed and burned with light and color, injecting movement so that his listeners surged along with him on the flood of rough eloquence, enthusiasm, and power. At times he shocked them with the vividness of the narrative and his terms of speech, but beauty always followed fast upon the heels of violence, and tragedy was relieved by humor, by interpretations of the twists and quirks of sailors' minds.

And while he talked the girl looked at him with startled eyes. His fire warmed her. She wondered if she had been cold all her days. She wanted to lean toward this burning, blazing man that was like a volcano spouting forth strength, robustness, and health. She felt that she must lean toward him, and resisted by an effort. Then, too, there was the counter impulse to shrink away from him. She was repelled by those lacerated hands, grimed by toil so that the very dirt of life was ingrained in the flesh itself, by that red chafe of the collar and those bulging muscles. His roughness frightened her; each roughness of speech was an insult to her ear, each rough phase of his life an insult to her soul. And ever and again would come the draw of him, till she thought he must be evil to have such power over her: All that was most firmly established in her mind was rocking. His romance and adventure were battering at the conventions. Before his facile perils and ready laugh, life was no longer an affair of serious effort and restraint, but a toy, to be played with and turned topsy-turvy, carelessly to be lived and pleasured in, and carelessly to be flung aside. "Therefore, play!" was the cry that rang through her. "Lean toward him, if so you will, and place your two hands upon his neck!" She wanted to cry out at the recklessness of the thought, and in vain she appraised her own cleanness and culture and balanced all that she was against what he was not. She glanced about her and saw the others gazing at him with rapt attention; and she would have despaired had not she seen horror in her mother's eyes—fascinated horror, it was true, but none-the-less horror. This man from outer darkness was evil. Her mother saw it, and her mother was right. She would trust her mother's judgment in this as she had always trusted it in all things. The fire of him was no longer warm, and the fear of him was no longer poignant.

Later, at the piano, she played for him, and at him, aggressively, with the vague intent of emphasizing the impassableness of the gulf that separated them. Her music was a club that she swung brutally upon his head; and though it stunned him and crushed him down, it incited him. He gazed upon her in awe. In his mind, as in her own, the gulf widened; but faster than it widened, towered his ambition to win across it. But he was too complicated a plexus of sensibilities to sit staring at a gulf a whole evening, especially when there was music. He was remarkably susceptible to music. It was like strong drink, firing him to audacities of feeling; a drug that laid hold of his imagination and went cloud-soaring through the sky. It banished sordid fact, flooded his mind with beauty, loosed romance and to its heels added wings. He did not understand the music she played. It was different from the dance-hall piano-banging and blatant brass bands he had heard. But he had caught hints of such music from the books, and he accepted her playing largely on faith, patiently waiting, at first, for the lilting measures of pronounced and simple rhythm, puzzled because those measures were not long-continued. Just as he caught the swing of them and started his imagination attuned in flight, always they vanished away in a chaotic scramble of sounds that was meaningless to him and that dropped his imagination, an inert weight, back to earth.

Once, it entered his mind that there was a deliberate rebuff in all this. He caught her spirit of antagonism and strove to divine the message that her hands pronounced upon the keys. Then he dismissed the thought as unworthy and impossible, and yielded himself more freely to the music. The old delightful condition began to be induced. His feet were no longer clay, and his flesh became spirit; before his eyes and behind his eyes shone a great glory; and then the scene before him vanished and he was away, rocking over the world that was to him a very dear world. The known and the unknown were commingled in the dream-pageant that thronged his vision. He entered strange ports of sun-washed lands, and trod market-places among barbaric peoples that no man had ever seen. The scent of the spice islands was in his nostrils as he had known it on warm breathless nights at sea, or he beat up against the southeast trades through long tropic days, sinking palm-tufted coral islets in the turquoise sea behind and lifting palm-tufted coral islets in the turquoise sea ahead. Swift as thought the pictures came and went. One instant he was astride a broncho and flying through the fairy-colored Painted Desert country; the next instant he was gazing down through shimmering heat into the whited sepulchre of Death Valley, or pulling an oar on a freezing ocean where great ice islands towered and glistened in the sun. He lay on a coral beach where the cocoanuts grew down to the mellow-sounding surf. The hulk of an ancient wreck burned with blue fires, in the light of which danced the *hula* dancers to the barbaric love-calls of the singers, who chanted to tinkling *ukuleles* and rumbling *tom-toms.* It was a sensuous, tropic night. In the background a volcano crater was silhouetted against the stars. Overhead drifted a pale crescent moon, and the Southern Cross burned low in the sky.

He was as a harp; all life that he had known and that was his consciousness, was the strings; and the flood of music was a wind that poured against these strings and set them vibrating with memories and dreams. He did not merely feel. Sensation invested itself in form and color and radiance, and what his imagination dared, it objectified in some sublimated and magic way. Past, present, and future mingled; and he went on oscillating across the broad, warm world, through high adventure and noble deeds to Her—ay, and with her, winning her, his arms about her, and carrying her on in flight through the empery of his mind.

And she, glancing at him across her shoulder, saw something of all this in his face. It was a transfigured face, with great shining eyes that gazed beyond the veil of sound and saw behind it the leap and pulse of life and the gigantic phantoms of the spirit. She was startled. The raw, stumbling lout was gone. The ill-fitting clothes, battered hands, and sunburned face remained; but these seemed the prison bars through which she saw a great soul looking forth, inarticulate and dumb because of those feeble lips that would not give it speech. Only for a flashing moment did she see this, then she saw the lout returned, and she laughed at the whim of her fancy. But the impression of that fleeting glimpse lingered, and when the time came for him to beat a stumbling retreat and go, she lent him the volume of Swinburne, and another of Browning—she was studying Browning in one of her English courses. He seemed such a boy, as he stood blushing and stammering his thanks, that a wave of pity, maternal in its prompting, welled up in her. She did not remember the lout, nor the imprisoned soul, nor the man who had stared at her in all masculineness and delighted and frightened her. She saw before her only a boy, who was shaking her hand with a hand so calloused that it felt like a nutmeg-grater and rasped her skin, and who was saying jerkily:

"The greatest time of my life. You see, I aint used to things"—he looked about him helplessly "To people and houses like this. It's all new to me, and I like it."

"I hope you 'll call again," she said, as he was saying goodnight to her brothers.

He pulled on his cap, lurched desperately through the doorway, and was gone.

"Well, what do you think of him?" Arthur demanded.

"He is most interesting; a whiff of ozone," she answered. "How old is he?"

"Twenty—almost twenty-one. I asked him this afternoon. I did n't think he was that young."

And I am three years older, was the thought in her mind as she kissed her brothers goodnight.

CHAPTER III.

AS Martin Eden went down the steps, his hand dropped into his coat pocket. It came out with a brown rice paper and a pinch of Mexican tobacco, which were deftly rolled together into a cigarette.

He drew the first whiff of smoke deep into his lungs and expelled it in a long and lingering exhalation. "By God!" he said aloud in a voice of awe and wonder. "By God!" he repeated. And yet again he murmured, "By God!" Then his hand went to his collar, which he ripped out of the shirt and stuffed into his pocket. A cold drizzle was falling, but he bared his head to it and unbuttoned his vest, swinging along in splendid unconcern. He was only dimly aware that it was raining. He was in an ecstacy, dreaming dreams and reconstructing the scenes just past.

He had met the woman at last—the woman that he had thought little about, not being given to thinking about women, but whom he had expected, in a remote way, he would some time meet. He had sat next to her at table. He had felt her hand in his, he had looked into her eyes and caught a vision of a beautiful spirit—but no more beautiful than the eyes through which it shone, nor than the flesh that gave it expression and form. He did not think of her flesh as flesh; which was new to him, for of the women he had known that was the only way he thought. Her flesh was somehow different. He did not conceive of her body as a body, subject to the ills and frailties of bodies. Her body was more than the garb of her spirit. It was an emanation of her spirit, a pure and gracious crystallization of her divine escence. This feeling of the divine startled him. It shocked him from his dreams to sober thought. No word, no clew nor hint, of the divine had ever reached him before. He had never believed in the divine. He had always been irreligious, scoffing good-naturedly at the sky-pilots and their immortality of the soul. There was no life beyond, he had contended; it was here and now, then darkness everlasting. But what he had seen in her eyes was soul—immortal soul that could never die. No man he had known, nor any woman, had given him the message of immortality. But she had. She had whispered it to him the first moment she looked at him. Her face shimmered before his eyes as he walked along, pale and serious, sweet and sensitive, smiling with pity and tenderness, as only a spirit could smile, and pure as he had never dreamed purity could be. Her purity smote him like a blow. It startled him. He had known good and bad; but purity, as an attribute of existence, had never entered his mind. And now, in her, he conceived purity to be the superlative of goodness and of cleanness, the sum of which constituted eternal life.

And promptly urged his ambition to grasp at eternal life. He was not fit to carry water for her—he knew that; it was a miracle of luck and a fantastic stroke that had enabled him to see her and be with her and talk with her that night. It was accidental. There was no merit in it. He did not deserve such fortune. His mood was essentially religious. He was humble and meek, filled with self-disparagement and abasement. In such frame of mind sinners come to the penitent form. He was convicted of sin. But as the meek and lowly at the penitent form catch splendid glimpses of their future lordly existence, so did he catch similar glimpses of the state he would gain to by possessing her. But this possession of her was dim and nebulous and totally different from possession as he had known it. Ambition soared on mad wings, and he saw himself climbing the heights with her, sharing thoughts with her, pleasuring in beautiful and noble things with her. It was a soul-possession he dreamed, refined beyond any grossness, a free comradeship of spirit that he could not put into definite thought. He did not think it. For that matter, he did not think at all. Sensation usurped reason, and he was palpitant with emotions he had never known, drifting deliciously on a sea of sensibility where feeling itself was exalted and spiritualized and carried beyond the summits of life.

He staggered along like a drunken man, murmuring fervently aloud, "By God! By God!"

A policeman on a street corner eyed him suspiciously, then noted his sailor roll.

"Where did you get it?" the policeman demanded.

Martin Eden came back to earth. His was a fluid organism, swiftly adjustable, capable of flowing into and filling all sorts of nooks and crannies With the policeman's hail he was immediately his ordinary self, grasping the situation clearly.

"It 's a beaut, aint it?" he laughed back. "I did n't know I was talkin' out loud."

"You 'll be singing next," was the policeman's diagnosis.

"No I wont. Gimme a match an' I 'll catch the next car home."

He lighted his cigarette, said good night, and went on. "Now would n't that rattle you?" he ejaculated under his breath. "That copper thought I was drunk." He smiled to himself and meditated. "I guess I was," he added; "but I did n't think a woman's face 'd do it."

He caught a Telegraph Avenue car that was going to Berkeley. It was crowded with youths and young men who were singing songs and ever and again barking out college yells. He studied them curiously. They were university boys. They went to the same university that she did, were in her class socially, could know her, could see her every day if they wanted to. He wondered that they did not want to, that they had been out having a good time instead of being with her that evening, talking with her, sitting around her in a worshipful and adoring circle. His thoughts wandered on. He noticed one with narrow-slitted eyes and a loose-lipped mouth. That fellow was vicious, he decided. On shipboard he would be a sneak, a whiner, a tattler. He, Martin Eden, was a better man than that fellow. The thought cheered him. It seemed to draw him nearer to Her. He began comparing himself with the students. He grew conscious of the muscled mechanism of his body and felt confident that he was physically their master. But their heads were filled with knowledge that enabled them to talk her talk—the thought depressed him. But what was a brain for? he demanded passionately. What they had done, he could do. They had been studying about life from the books while he had been busy living life. His brain was just as full of knowledge as theirs, though it was a different kind of knowledge. How many of them could tie a lanyard knot, or take a wheel or a lookout? His life spread out before him in a series of pictures of danger and daring, hardship and toil. He remembered his failures and scrapes in the process of learning. He was that much to the good, anyway. Later on they would have to begin living life and going through the mill as he had gone. Very well. While they were busy with that, he could be learning the other side of life from the books.

As the car crossed the zone of scattered dwellings that separated Oakland from Berkeley, he kept a lookout for a familiar, two-story building along the front of which ran the proud sign: HIGGINBOTHAM'S CASH STORE. Martin Eden got off at this corner. He stared up for a moment at the sign. It carried a message to him beyond its mere wording. A personality of smallness and egotism and petty underhandedness seemed to emanate from the letters themselves. Bernard Higginbotham had married his sister, and he knew him well. He let himself in with a latch-key and climbed the stairs to the second floor. Here lived his brother-in-law. The grocery was below. There was a smell of stale vegetables in the air. As he groped his way across the hall he stumbled over a toy-cart, left there by one of his numerous nephews and nieces, and brought up against a door with a resounding bang. "The pincher," was his thought; "too miserly to burn two cents' worth of gas and save his boarders' necks."

He fumbled for the knob and entered a lighted room, where sat his sister and Bernard Higginbotham. She was patching a pair of his trousers, while his lean body was distributed over two chairs, his feet dangling in dilapidated carpet-slippers over the edge of the second chair. He glanced across the top of the paper he was reading, showing a pair of dark, insincere, sharp-staring eyes. Martin Eden never looked at him without experiencing a sense of repulsion. What his sister had seen in the man was beyond him. The other affected him as so much vermin, and always aroused in him an impulse to crush under his foot. "Some day I 'll beat the face off of him," was the way he often consoled himself for enduring the man's existence. The eyes, weasel-like and cruel, were looking at him complainingly.

"Well?" Martin demanded. "Out with it."

"I had that door painted only last week," Mr. Higginbotham half-whined, half-bullied; "and you know what union wages are. You should be more careful."

Martin had intended to reply, but he was struck by the hopelessness of it. He gazed across the monstrous sordidness of soul to a chromo on the wall. It surprised him. He had always liked it, but it seemed that now he was seeing it for the first time. It was cheap, that was what it was, like everything else in this house. His mind went back to the house he had just left, and he saw, first, the paintings, and next, Her, looking at him with melting sweetness as she shook his hand at leaving. He forgot where he was and Bernard Higginbotham's existence, till that gentleman demanded:

"Seen a ghost?"

Martin came back and looked at the beady eyes, sneering, truculent, cowardly, and there leaped into his vision, as on a screen, the same eyes when their owner was making a sale in the store below—subservient eyes, smug, and oily, and flattering.

"Yes," Martin answered. "I seen a ghost. Goodnight. Goodnight, Gertrude."

He started to leave the room, tripping over a loose seam in the slatternly carpet.

"Dont bang the door," Mr. Higginbotham cautioned him.

He felt the blood crawl in his veins, but controlled himself and closed the door softly behind him.

Mr. Higginbotham looked at his wife exultantly.

"He's been drinkin'," he proclaimed in a hoarse whisper. "I told you he would."

She nodded her head resignedly.

"His eyes were pretty shiny," she confessed; "and he did n't have no collar, though he went away with one. But mebbe he did n't have more 'n a couple of glasses."

"He could n't stand up straight," asserted her husband. "I watched him. He could n't walk across the floor without stumblin'. You heard 'm yourself almost fall down in the hall."

"I think it was over Alice's cart," she said. "He could n't see it in the dark."

Mr. Higginbotham's voice and wrath began to rise. All day he effaced himself in the store, reserving for the evening, with his family, the privilege of being himself.

"I tell you that precious brother of yours was drunk."

His voice was cold, sharp, and final, his lips stamping the enunciation of each word like the die of a machine. His wife sighed and remained silent. She was a large, stout woman, always dressed slatternly and always tired from the burden of her flesh, her work, and her husband.

"He 's got it in him, I tell you, from his father," Mr. Higginbotham went on accusingly. "An' he 'll croak in the gutter the same way. You know that."

She nodded, sighed, and went on stitching. They were agreed that Martin had come home drunk. They did not have it in their souls to know beauty, or they would have known that those shining eyes and that glowing face betokened youth's first vision of love.

"Settin' a fine example to the children," Mr. Higginbotham snorted, suddenly, in the silence for which his wife was responsible and which he resented. Sometimes he almost wished she would oppose him more. "If he does it again, he 's got to get out. Understand! I wont put up with his shinanigan—debotchin' innocent children with his boozing." Mr. Higginbotham liked the word, which was a new one in his vocabulary, recently gleaned from a newspaper column. "That 's what it is, debotchin'—there aint no other name for it."

Still his wife sighed, shook her head sorrowfully, and stitched on. Mr. Higginbotham resumed the newspaper.

"Has he paid last week's board?" he shot across the top of the newspaper.

She nodded, then added, "He still has some money."

"When is he goin' to sea again?"

"When his pay-day 's spent, I guess," she answered. "He was over to San Francisco yesterday looking for a ship. But he 's got money, yet, an' he 's particular about the kind of ship he signs for."

"It 's not for a deck-swab like him to put on airs," Mr. Higginbotham snorted. "Particular! Him!"

"He said something about a schooner that 's gettin' ready to go off to some outlandish place to look for buried treasure, that he 'd sail on her if his money held out."

"If he only wanted to steady down, I 'd give him a job drivin' the wagon," her husband said, but with no trace of benevolence in his voice. "Tom 's quit."

His wife looked alarm and interrogation.

"Quit tonight. Is goin' to work for Carruthers. They paid 'm more 'n I could afford."

"I told you you 'd lose 'm," she cried out. "He was worth more 'n you was giving him."

"Now look here, old woman," Higginbotham bullied. "For the thousandth time I 've told you to keep your nose out of the business. I wont tell you again."

"I dont care," she sniffled. "Tom was a good boy."

Her husband glared at her. This was unqualified defiance.

"If that brother of yours was worth his salt, he could take the wagon," he snorted.

"He pays his board, just the same," was the retort. "An' he 's my brother, an' so long as he dont owe you money you 've got no right to be jumping on him all the time. I 've got some feelings, if I have been married to you for seven years."

"Did you tell 'm you 'd charge him for gas if he goes on readin' in bed?" he demanded.

Mrs. Higginbotham made no reply. Her revolt faded away, her spirit wilting down into her tired flesh. Her husband was triumphant. He had her. His eyes snapped vindictively, while his ears joyed in the sniffles she emitted. He extracted great happiness from squelching her, and she squelched easily these days, though it had been different in the first years of their married life, before the brood of children and his incessant nagging had sapped her energy.

"Well, you tell 'm tomorrow, that 's all," he said. "An' I just want to tell you, before I forget it, that you 'd better send for Marian tomorrow to take care of the children. With Tom quit, I 'll have to be out on the wagon, an' you can make up your mind to it to be down below waitin' on the counter."

"But tomorrow 's wash day," she objected weakly.

"Get up early, then, an' do it first. I wont start out till ten o'clock."

He crinkled the paper viciously and resumed his reading.

Martin Eden

By Jack London

Author of "The Call of the Wild," "Sea Wolf," "The God of His Fathers," "White Fang," etc.

CHAPTER IV.

MARTIN EDEN, with flesh still crawling from contact with his brother-in-law, felt his way along the unlighted back hall and entered his room, a tiny cubby hole with a space for a bed, a washstand, and one chair. Mr. Higginbotham was too thrifty to keep a servant when his wife could do the work. Besides, the servant's room enabled them to take in two boarders instead of one. Martin placed the *Swinburne* and *Browning* on the chair, took off his coat, and sat down on the bed. A screeching of asthmatic springs greeted the weight of his body, but he did not notice them. He started to take off his shoes, but fell to staring at the white plaster wall opposite him, broken by long streaks of dirty brown where rain had leaked through the roof. On this befouled background visions began to flow and burn. He forgot his shoes and stared long, till his lips began to move and he murmured, "Ruth."

"Ruth." He had not thought a simple sound could be so beautiful. It delighted his ear, and he grew intoxicated with the repetition of it. "Ruth." It was a talisman, a magic word to conjure with. Each time he murmured it, her face shimmered before him, suffusing the foul wall with a golden radiance. This radiance did not stop at the wall. It extended on into infinity, and through its golden depths his soul went questing after hers. The best that was in him was pouring out in splendid flood. The very thought of her ennobled and purified him, made him better, and made him want to be better. This was new to him. He had never known women who had made him better. They had always had the counter effect of making him beastly. He did not know that many of them had done their best, bad as it was. Never having been conscious of himself, he did not know that he had that in his being that drew love from women and which had been the cause of their reaching out for his youth. Though they had often bothered him, he had never bothered about them; and he would never have dreamed that there were women who had been better because of him. Always in sublime carelessness had he lived, till now, and now it seemed to him that they had always reached out and dragged at him with vile hands. This was not just to them, nor to himself. But he, who for the first time was becoming conscious of himself, was in no condition to judge, and he burned with shame as he stared at the vision of his infamy.

He got up abruptly and tried to see himself in the dirty looking-glass over the washstand. He passed a towel over it and looked again, long and carefully. It was the first time he had ever really seen himself. His eyes were made for seeing, but up to that moment they had been filled with the ever-changing panorama of the world, at which he had been too busy gazing ever to gaze at himself. He saw the head and face of a young fellow of twenty, but, being unused to such appraisement, he did not know how to value it. Above a square-domed forehead he saw a mop of brown hair, nut-brown, with a wave to it and hints of curls that were a delight to any woman, making hands tingle to stroke it and fingers tingle to pass caresses through it. But he passed it by as without merit, in Her eyes, and dwelt long and thoughtfully on the high, square forehead, striving to penetrate it and learn the quality of its contents. What kind of a brain lay behind there? was his insistent interrogation. What was it capable of? How far would it take him? Would it take him to her?

He wondered if there was soul in those steel-grey eyes that were often quite blue of color and that were strong with the briny airs of the sun-washed deep. He wondered, also, how his eyes looked to her. He tried to imagine himself her, gazing into those eyes of his, but failed in the jugglery. He could successfully put himself inside other men's minds, but they had to be men whose ways of life he knew. He did not know her way of life. She was wonder and mystery, and how could he guess one thought of hers? Well, they were honest eyes, he concluded, and in them was neither smallness nor meanness. The brown sunburn of his face surprised him. He had not dreamed he was so black. He rolled up his shirt-sleeve and compared the white under-side of the arm with his face. Yes, he was a white man after all. But the arms were sunburned, too. He twisted his arm, rolled the biceps over with his other hand, and gazed underneath where he was least touched by the sun. It was very white. He laughed at his bronzed face in the glass, at the thought that it was once as white as the under-side of his arm; nor did he dream that in the world there were few pale spirits of women who could boast fairer or smoother skins than he—fairer than where he had escaped the ravages of the sun.

His might have been a cherub's mouth, had not the full, sensuous lips a trick, under stress, of drawing firmly across the teeth. At times, so tightly did they draw, the mouth became stern and harsh, even ascetic. They were the lips of a fighter and of a lover. They could taste the sweetness of life with relish, and they could put the sweetness aside and command life. The chin and jaw, strong and just hinting of square aggressiveness, helped the lips to command life. Strength balanced sensuousness and had upon it a tonic effect, compelling him to love beauty that was healthy and making him vibrate to sensations that were wholesome. And between the lips were teeth that had never known nor needed the dentist's care. They were white and strong and regular, he decided, as he looked at them. But as he looked, he began to be troubled. Somewhere, stored away in the recesses of his mind and vaguely remembered was the impression that there were people who washed their teeth every day. They were the people from up above—people in her class. She must wash her teeth every day, too. What would she think if she learned that he had never washed his teeth in all the days of his life? He resolved to get a tooth-brush and form the habit. He would begin at once, to-morrow. It was not by mere achievement that he could hope to win her. He must make a personal reform in all things, even to tooth-washing and neck-gear, though a starched collar affected him as a renunciation of freedom.

He held up his hand, rubbing the ball of the thumb over the calloused palm and gazing at the dirt that was ingrained in the flesh itself and which no brush could scrub away. How different was her palm! He thrilled deliciously at the remembrance. Like a rose-petal, he thought; cool and soft as a snowflake. He had never thought that a mere woman's hand could be so sweetly soft. He caught himself imagining the wonder of a caress from such a hand, and flushed guiltily. It was too gross a thought for her. In ways it seemed to impugn her high spirituality. She was a pale slender spirit, exalted far beyond the flesh; but nevertheless the softness of her palm persisted in his thoughts. He was used to the harsh callousness of factory girls and working women. Well he knew why their hands were rough; but this hand of hers. * * * It was soft because she had never used it to work with. The gulf yawned between her and him at the awesome thought of a person who did not have to work for a living. He suddenly saw the aristocracy of the people who did not labor. It towered before him on the wall, a figure in brass, arrogant and powerful. He had worked himself; his first memories seemed connected with work, and all his family had worked. There was Gertrude. When her hands were not hard from the endless housework they were swollen and red like boiled beef, what of the washing. And there was his sister Marian. She had worked in the cannery the preceding summer, and her slim, pretty hands were all scarred with the tomato-knives. Besides, the tips of two of her fingers had been left in the cutting machine at the paper-box factory the preceding winter. He remembered the hard palms of his mother as she lay in her coffin. And his father had worked to the last fading gasp; the horned growth of his hands must have been half an inch thick when he died. But Her hands were soft, and her mother's hands, and her brothers'. This last came to him as a surprise; it was tremendously indicative of the highness of their caste, of the enormous distance that stretched between her and him.

He sat back on the bed with a bitter laugh, and finished taking off his shoes. He was a fool; he had been made drunken by a woman's face and by a woman's soft, white hands. And then, suddenly, before his eyes, on the foul plaster-wall, appeared a vision. He stood in front of a gloomy tenement house. It was nighttime, in the East End of London, and before him stood Margey, a little factory girl of fifteen. He had seen her home after the bean-feast. She lived in that gloomy tenement, a place not fit for swine. His hand was going out to hers as he said good-night. She had put her lips up to be kissed, but he was n't going to kiss her. Somehow he was afraid of her. And then her hand closed on his and pressed feverishly. He felt her callouses grind and grate on his, and a great wave of pity welled over him. He saw her yearning, hungry eyes, and her ill-fed female form rushed from childhood into a frightened and ferocious maturity; then he put his arms about her in large tolerance and stooped and kissed her on the lips. Her glad little cry rang in his ears, and he felt her clinging to him like a cat. Poor little starveling! He continued to stare at the vision of what had happened in the long ago. His flesh was crawling as it had crawled that night when she clung to him, and his heart was warm with pity. It was a gray scene, greasy-gray, and the rain drizzled greasily on the pavement stones. And then a radiant glory shone on the wall, and up through the other vision, displacing it, glimmered Her pale face under its crown of golden hair, remote and inaccessible as a star.

He took the *Browning* and the *Swinburne* from the chair and kissed them. Just the same, she told me to call again, he thought. He took another look at himself in the glass, and said aloud, with great solemnity:

''Martin Eden, the first thing to-morrow you go to the free library an' read up on etiquette. Understand?''

He turned off the gas, and the springs shrieked under his body.

''But you 've got to quit cussin', Martin, old boy; you've got to quit cussin','' he said aloud.

Then he dozed off to sleep and to dream dreams that for madness and audacity rivaled those of poppy-eaters.

CHAPTER V.

HE awoke next morning from rosy scenes of dream to a steamy atmosphere that smelled of soapsuds and dirty clothes, and that was vibrant with the jar and jangle of tormented life. As he came out of his room he heard the slosh of water, a sharp exclamation, and a resounding smack as his sister visited her irritation upon one of her numerous progeny. The squall of the child went through him like a knife. He was aware that the whole thing, the very air he breathed, was repulsive and mean. How different, he thought, from the atmosphere of beauty and repose of the house wherein Ruth dwelt. There it was all spiritual. Here it was all material, and meanly material.

''Come here, Alfred,'' he called to the crying child, at the same time thrusting his hand into his trousers pocket where he carried his money loose in the same large way that he lived life in general. He put a quarter in the youngster's hand and held him in his arms a moment, soothing his sobs. ''Now run along and get some candy, and dont forget to give some to your brothers and sisters. Be sure and get the kind that lasts longest.''

His sister lifted her flushed face from the wash-tub and looked at him.

''A nickel 'd ha' ben enough,'' she said. ''It's just like you, no idea of the value of money. The child 'll eat himself sick.''

"That's all right, Sis," he answered jovially. "My money 'll take care of itself. If you were n't so busy I'd kiss you good morning."

He wanted to be affectionate to his sister who was good, and who, in her way, he knew, loved him. But, somehow, she grew less herself as the years went by, and more and more baffling. It was the hard work, the many children, and the nagging of her husband, he decided, that had changed her. It came to him, in a flash of fancy, that her nature seemed taking on the attributes of stale vegetables, smelly soapsuds, and of the greasy dimes, nickels, and quarters she took in over the counter of the store.

"Go along an' get your breakfast," she said roughly, though secretly pleased. Of all her wandering brood of brothers he had always been her favorite. "I declare I *will* kiss you," she said, with a sudden stir at her heart.

With thumb and forefinger she swept the dripping suds first from one arm and then from the other. He put his arms around her massive waist and kissed her wet steamy lips. The tears welled into her eyes—not so much from strength of feeling as from the weakness of chronic overwork. She shoved him away from her, but not before he caught a glimpse of her moist eyes.

"You 'll find breakfast in the oven," she said hurriedly. "Jim ought to be up now. I had to get up early for the washing. Now get along with you, and get out of the house early. It wont be nice to-day, what of Tom quittin' an' nobody but Bernard to drive the wagon."

Martin went into the kitchen with a sinking heart, the image of her red face and slatternly form eating its way like acid into his brain. She might love him if she only had some time, he concluded. But she was worked to death. Bernard Higginbotham was a brute to work her so hard. But he could not help but feel, on the other hand, that there had not been anything beautiful in that kiss. It was true, it was an unusual kiss. For years she had kissed him only when he returned from voyages or departed on voyages. But this kiss had tasted of soapsuds, and the lips, he had noticed, were flabby. There had been no quick, vigorous lip-pressure such as should accompany any kiss. Hers was the kiss of a tired woman who had been tired so long that she had forgotten how to kiss. He remembered her as a girl, before her marriage, when she would dance with the best, all night, after a hard day's work at the laundry, and think nothing of leaving the dance to go to another day's hard work. And then he thought of Ruth and the cool sweetness that must reside in her lips as it resided in all about her. Her kiss would be like her handshake or the way she looked at one, firm and frank. In imagination he dared to think of her lips on his, and so vividly did he imagine that he went dizzy at the thought and seemed to drift through clouds of rose-petals, filling his brain with their perfume.

In the kitchen he found Jim, the other boarder, eating mush very languidly, with a sick, far-away look in his eyes. Jim was a plumber's apprentice whose weak chin and hedonistic temperament, coupled with certain nervous stupidity, promised to take him nowhere in the race for bread and butter.

"Why dont you eat?" he demanded, as Martin dipped dolefully into the cold, half-cooked oatmeal mush. "Was you drunk again last night?"

Martin shook his head. He was oppressed by the utter squalidness of it all. Ruth Morse seemed farther removed than ever.

"I was," Jim went on with a boastful, nervous giggle. "I was loaded right to the neck. Oh, she was a daisy. Billy brought me home."

Martin nodded that he heard—it was a habit of nature with him to pay heed to whomever talked to him—and poured a cup of lukewarm coffee.

"Goin' to the Lotus Club dance to-night?" Jim demanded. "They're goin' to have beer an' if that Temescal bunch comes there 'll be a rough house. I dont care, though. I'm takin' my lady friend just the same. Cripes, but I 've got a taste in my mouth."

He made a wry face and attempted to wash the taste away with coffee.

"D 'ye know Julia?"

Martin shook his head.

"She 's my lady friend," Jim explained, "and she 's a peach. I 'd introduce you to her, only you 'd win her. I dont see what the girls see in you, honest, I dont, but the way you win them away from the fellers is sickenin'."

"I never got any away from you," Martin answered uninterestedly. The breakfast had to be got through somehow.

"Yes you did, too," the other asserted warmly. "There was Maggie."

"Never had anything to do with her. Never danced with her except that one night."

"Yes, an' that 's just what did it," Jim cried out. "You just danced with her an' looked at her, an' it was all off. Of course, you did n't mean nothing by it, but it settled me for keeps. Would n't look at me again. Always askin' about you. She 'd have made dates fast enough with you if you 'd wanted to."

"But I did n't want to."

"Was n't necessary. I was left at the pole." Jim looked at him admiringly. "How d 'ye do it, anyway, Mart?"

"By not carin' about 'em," was the answer.

"You mean making' b'lieve you dont care about them?" Jim queried eagerly.

Martin considered for a moment, then answered, "Perhaps that will do, but with me I guess it 's different. I never have cared * * * much. If you can put it on, it 's all right most likely."

"You should 'a' ben up at Riley's barn last night," Jim announced inconsequentially. "A lot of the fellers put on the gloves. There was a peach from West Oakland. They called 'm 'The Rat.' Slick as silk. No one could touch 'm. We was all wishin' you was there. Where was you anyway?"

"Down in Oakland," Martin replied.

"To the show?"

Martin shoved his plate away and got up.

"Comin' to the dance tonight?" the other called after him.

"No, I think not," he answered.

He went downstairs and out into the street, breathing great breaths of air. He had been suffocating in that atmosphere, while the apprentice's chatter had driven him frantic. There had been times when it was all he could do to refrain from reaching over and mopping Jim's face in the mush-plate. The more he had chattered the more remote had Ruth seemed to him. How could he, herding with such cattle, ever become worthy of her? He was appalled at the problem confronting him, weighted down by the incubus of his working-class station. Everything reached out to hold him down—his sister, his sister's house and family, Jim the apprentice, everybody he knew, every tie of life. Existence did not taste good in his mouth. Up to then he had accepted existence, as he had lived it with all about him, as a good thing. He had never questioned it, except when he read books; but then, they were only books, fairy stories of a fairer and impossible world. But now he had seen that world, possible and real, with a flower of a woman called Ruth in the midmost center of it; and thenceforth he must know bitter tastes, and longings sharp as pain, and hopelessness that tantalized because it fed on hope.

He had debated between the Berkeley Free Library and the Oakland Free Library, and decided upon the latter because Ruth lived in Oakland. Who could tell?—a library was a most likely place for her, and he might see her there. He did not know the way of libraries, and he wandered through endless rows of fiction, till the delicate-featured French-looking girl who seemed in charge, told him that the reference department was upstairs. He did not know enough to ask the man at the desk, and began his adventures in the philosophy alcove. He had heard of book philosophy, but had not imagined there had been so much written about it. The high bulging shelves of heavy tomes humbled him and at the same time stimulated him. Here was work for the vigor of his brain. He found books on trigonometry in the mathematics section, and ran the pages, and stared at the meaningless formulas and figures. He could read English, but he saw there an alien speech. Norman and Arthur knew that speech. He had heard them talking it. And they were her brothers. He left the alcove in despair. From every side the books seemed to press upon him and crush him. He had never dreamed that the fund of human knowledge bulked so big. He was frightened.

How could his brain ever master it all? Later, he remembered that there were other men, many men, who had mastered it; and he breathed a great oath, passionately, under his breath, swearing that his brain could do what theirs had done.

And so he wandered on, alternating between depression and elation as he stared at the shelves packed with wisdom. In one miscellaneous section he came upon a *Norrie's Epitome*. He turned the pages reverently. In a way, it spoke a kindred speech. Both he and it were of the sea. Then he found a *Bowditch* and books by Leckey and Marshall. There it was, he would teach himself navigation. He would quit drinking, work up, and become a captain. Ruth seemed very near to him in that moment. As a captain, he would marry her (if she would have him). And if she would n't, well, he would live a good life among men, because of Her, and he would quit drinking anyway. Then he remembered the underwriters and the owners, the two masters a captain must serve, either of which could and would break him and whose interests were diametrically opposed. He cast his eyes about the room and closed the lids down on a vision of ten thousand books. No; no more of the sea for him. There was power in all that wealth of books, and if he would do great things he must do them on the land. Besides, captains were not allowed to take their wives to sea with them.

Noon came, and afternoon. He forgot to eat, and sought on for the books on etiquette; for, in addition to career, his mind was vexed by a simply and very concrete problem. *When you meet a young lady and she asks you to call, how soon can you call?* was the way he worded it to himself. But when he found the right shelf, he sought vainly for the answer. He was appalled at the vast edifice of ettiquette, and lost himself in the mazes of visiting-card conduct between persons in polite society. He abandoned his search. He had not found what he wanted, though he found that it would take all of a man's time to be polite, and that he would have to live a preliminary life in which to learn how to be polite.

"Did you find what you wanted?" the man at the desk asked him as he was leaving.

"Yes, sir," he answered. "You have a fine library here."

The man nodded. "We should be glad to see you here often. Are you a sailor?"

"Yes, sir," he answered. "And I 'll come again."

Now how did he know that? he asked himself as he went down the stairs.

And for the first block along the street he walked very stiff and straight and awkwardly, until he forgot himself in his thoughts, whereupon his rolling gait gracefully returned to him.

CHAPTER VI.

A TERRIBLE restlessness that was akin to hunger afflicted Martin Eden. He was famished for a sight of the girl whose slender hands had gripped his life with a giant's grasp. He could not steel himself to call upon her. He was afraid that he might call too soon, and, so, be guilty of an awful breach of that awful thing called etiquette. He spent long hours in the Oakland and Berkeley libraries, and made out application blanks for membership for himself, his sisters Gertrude and Marian, and Jim, the latter's consent being obtained at the expense of several glasses of beer. With four cards permitting him to draw books, he burned the gas late in the servant's room and was charged fifty cents a week for it by Mr. Higginbotham.

The many books he read but served to whet his unrest. Every page of every book was a peep-hole into the realm of knowledge. His hunger fed upon what he read and increased. Also, he did not know where to begin, and continually suffered from lack of preparation. The commonest references, that he could see plainly every reader was expected to know, he did not know. And the same was true of the poetry he read which maddened him with delight. He read more of *Swinburne* than was contained in the volume Ruth had lent him; and *Dolores* he understood thoroughly. But surely Ruth did not understand it, he concluded. How could she, living the refined life she did? Then he chanced upon Kipling's poems, and was swept away by the lilt and swing and glamor with which familiar things had been invested. He was amazed at the man's sympathy with life and at his incisive psychology. *Psychology* was a new word in Martin's vocabulary. He had bought a dictionary, which deed had decreased his supply of money and brought nearer the day on which he must sail in search of more. Also, it incensed Mr. Higginbotham, who would have preferred the money taking the form of board.

He dared not go near Ruth's neighborhood in the daytime, but night found him lurking like a thief around the Morse home, stealing glimpses at the windows and loving the very walls that sheltered her. Several times he barely escaped being caught by her brothers, and once he trailed Mr. Morse down town and studied his face in the lighted streets, longing all the while for some quick danger of death to threaten so that he might spring in and save her father. On another night, his vigil was rewarded by a glimpse of Ruth through a second-story window. He saw only her head and shoulders, and her arms raised as she fixed her hair before a mirror. It was only a moment, but it was a long moment to him, during which his blood turned to wine and sang through his veins.Then she pulled down the shade. But it was her room—he had learned that; and thereafter he strayed there often, hiding under a dark tree on the opposite side of the street and smoking countless cigarettes. One afternoon he saw her mother coming out of a bank, and received another proof of the enormous distance that separated Ruth from him. She was of the class that dealt with banks. He had never been inside a bank in his life, and he had an idea that such institutions were frequented only by the very rich and the very powerful.

In one way, he had undergone a moral revolution. Her cleanness and purity had reacted upon him, and he felt in his being a crying need to be clean. He must be that if he were ever to be worthy of breathing the same air with her. He washed his teeth, and scrubbed his hands with a kitchen scrub-brush till he saw a nail-brush in a drugstore window and divined its use. While purchasing it, the clerk, glancing at his nails, suggested a nail-file, and so he became possessed of an additional toilet-tool. He ran across a book in the library on the care of the body, and promptly developed a penchant for a cold-water bath every morning, much to the amazement of Jim, and to the bewilderment of Mr. Higginbotham, who was not in sympathy with such high-fangled notions and who seriously debated whether or not he would charge Martin extra for the water. Another stride was in the direction of creased trousers. Now that Martin was aroused in such matters, he swiftly noted the difference between the baggy knees of the trousers worn by the working class and the straight line from knee to foot of those worn by the men above the working class. Also, he learned the reason why, and invaded his sister's kitchen in search of irons and ironing-board. He had misadventure at first, hopelessly burning one pair and buying another, which expenditure again brought nearer the day on which he must put to sea.

But the reform went deeper than mere outward appearance. He still smoked, but he drank no more. Up to that time, drinking had seemed to him the proper thing for men to do and he had prided himself on his strong head which enabled him to drink most men to the floor. Whenever he encountered a chance shipmate, and there were many in San Francisco, he treated them and was treated in turn, as of old, but he ordered for himself root-beer or ginger ale and good-naturedly endured their chaffing. And as they waxed maudlin he studied them, watching the beast rise and master them, and thanking God that he was no longer as they. They had their limitations to forget, and when they were drunk their dim, stupid spirits were even as gods and each ruled in his haven of intoxicated desire. With Martin the need for strong drink had vanished. He was drunken in new and more profound ways—with Ruth, who had fired him with love and with a glimpse of higher and eternal life; with books, that had set a myriad maggots of desire gnawing in his brain; and with the sense of personal cleanliness he was achieving, that gave him even superber health than what he had enjoyed and that made his whole body sing with physical well-being.

One night he went to the theatre, on the blind chance that he might see her there, and from the second balcony he did see her. He saw her come down the aisle, with Arthur and a strange young man with a football mop of hair and eye-glasses, the sight of whom spurred him to instant apprehension and jealousy. He saw her take her seat in the orchestra circle, and little else than her did he see that night—a pair of slender white shoulders and a mass of pale-gold hair, dim with distance. But there were others who saw, and now and again, glancing at those about him, he noted two young girls who looked back from the row in front, a dozen seats along, and who smiled at him with bold eyes. He had always been easy-going. It was not in his nature to give rebuff. In the old days he would have smiled back, and gone further and encouraged smiling. But now it was different. He did smile back, then looked away, and looked no more deliberately. But several times, forgetting the existence of the two girls, his eyes caught their smiles. He could not re-thumb himself in a day, nor could he violate the intrinsic kindliness of his nature; so, at such moments, he smiled at the girls in warm human friendliness. It was nothing new to him. He knew they were reaching out their woman's hands to him. But it was different now. Far down there in the orchestra circle was the one woman in all the world, so different, so terrifically different, from these two girls of his class, that he could feel for them only pity and sorrow. He had it in his heart to wish that they could possess in some small measure her goodness and glory. And not for the world could he hurt them because of their outreaching. He was not flattered by it; he even felt a slight shame at his lowliness that permitted it. He knew, did he belong in Ruth's class, that there would be no overtures from these girls; and with each glance of theirs he felt the fingers of his own class clutching at him to hold him down.

He left his seat before the curtain went down on the last act, intent on seeing Her as she passed out. There were always numbers of men who stood on the sidewalk outside, and he could pull his cap down over his eyes and screen himself behind some one's shoulder so that she should not see him. He emerged from the theatre with the first of the crowd; but scarcely had he taken his position on the edge of the sidewalk when the two girls appeared. They were looking for him, he knew; and for the moment he could have cursed that in him which drew women. Their casual edging across the sidewalk to the curb, as they drew near, apprised him of discovery. They slowed down and were in the thick of the crowd as they come up with him. One of them brushed against him and apparently for the first time noticed him. She was a slender, dark girl, with black, defiant eyes. But they smiled at him, and he smiled back.

"Hello," he said.

It was automatic; he had said it so often before under similar circumstances of first meetings. Besides, he could do no less. There was that large tolerance and sympathy in his nature that would permit him to do no less. The black-eyed girl smiled gratification and greeting, and showed signs of stopping, while her companion, arm linked in arm, giggled and likewise showed signs of halting. He thought quickly. It would never do for Her to come out and see him talking there with them. Quite naturally, as a matter of course, he swung in alongside the dark-eyed one and walked with her. There was no awkwardness on his part, no numb tongue. He was at home here, and he held his own royally in the badinage, bristling with slang and sharpness, that was always the preliminary to getting acquainted in these swift-moving affairs. At the corner, where the main stream of people flowed onward, he started to edge out into the cross street. But the girl with the black eyes caught his arm, following him and dragging her companion after her, as she cried:

"Hold on, Bill! What 's yer rush? You 're not goin' to shake us so sudden as all that?"

He halted with a laugh, and turned, facing them. Across the shoulders he could see the moving throng passing under the street lamps. Where he stood it was not so light, and, unseen, he would be able to see Her as she passed by. She would certainly pass by, for that way led home.

"What's her name?" he asked of the giggling girl, nodding at the dark-eyed one.

"You ask her," was the convulsed response.

"Well, what is it?" he demanded, turning squarely on the girl in question.

"You aint told me yours, yet," she retorted.

"You never asked it," he smiled. "Besides, you guessed the first rattle. It's Bill, all right all right."

"Aw, go 'long with you." She looked him in the eyes, her own sharply passionate and inviting. "What is it, honest?"

Again she looked. All the centuries of woman since sex began were eloquent in her eyes. And he measured her in a careless way, and knew, bold now, that she would begin to retreat, coyly and delicately, as he pursued, ever ready to reverse the game should he turn faint-hearted. And, too, he was human, and could feel the draw of her, while his ego could not but appreciate the flattery of her kindness. Oh, he knew it all, and knew them well, from A to Z. Good, as goodness might be measured in their particular class, hard-working for meagre wages and scorning the sale of self for easier ways, nervously desirous for some small pinch of happiness in the desert of existence, and facing a future that was a gamble between the ugliness of unending toil and the black pit of more terrible wretchedness, the way whereto being briefer though better paid.

"Bill," he answered, nodding his head. "Sure Pete, Bill an' no other."

"No joshin'?" she queried.

"It aint Bill at all," the other broke in.

"How do you know?" he demanded. "You never laid eyes on me before."

"No need to, to know you 're lyin'," was the retort.

"Straight, Bill, what is it?" the first girl asked.

"Bill 'll do," he confessed.

She reached out to his arm and shook him playfully. "I knew you was lyin', but you look good to me just the same."

He captured the hand that invited, and felt on the palm familiar markings and distortions.

"When 'd you chuck the cannery?" he asked.

"How 'd yeh know?" and "My, aint cheh a mind-reader!" the girls chorused.

And while he exchanged the stupidities of stupid minds with them, before his inner sight towered the book-shelves of the library, filled with the wisdom of ages. He smiled bitterly at the incongruity of it, and was assailed by doubts. But between inner vision and outward pleasantry he found time to watch the theatre crowd streaming by. And then he saw Her, under the lights, between her brother and the strange young man with glasses, and his heart seemed to stand still. He had waited long for this moment. He had time to note the light, fluffy something that hid her queenly head, the tasteful lines of her wrapped figure, the gracefulness of her carriage and of the hand that caught up her skirts; and then she was gone and he was left staring at the two girls of the cannery, at their tawdry attempts at prettiness of dress, their tragic efforts to be clean and trim, the cheap cloth, the cheap ribbons, and the cheap rings on the fingers. He felt a tug at his arm, and heard a voice saying:

"Wake up, Bill! What's the matter with you?"

"What was you sayin'?" he asked.

"Oh, nothin'," the dark girl answered, with a toss of her head. "I was only remarkin'——"

"What?"

"Well, I was whisperin', it 'd be a good idea if you could dig up a gentleman friend—for her," (indicating her companion), "and then, we could go off an' have ice-cream soda somewhere, or coffee, or anything."

He was afflicted by a sudden spiritual nausea. The transition from Ruth to this had been too abrupt. Ranged side by side with the bold, defiant eyes of the girl before him, he saw Ruth's clear, luminous eyes, like a saint's, gazing at him out of unplumbed depths of purity. And, somehow, he felt within him a stir of power. He was better than this. Life meant more to him than it meant to these girls whose thoughts did not go beyond ice-cream and a gentleman friend. He remembered that he had led always a secret life in his thoughts. These thoughts he had tried to share, but never had he found a woman capable of understanding—nor a man. He had tried, at times, but had only puzzled his listeners. And as his thoughts had been beyond them, so he argued now, he must be beyond them. He felt power move in him, and clenched his fists. If life meant more to him, then it was for him to demand more from life, but he could not demand it from such companionship as this. Those bold black eyes had nothing to offer. He knew the thoughts behind them—of ice-cream and of something else. But those saint's eyes alongside—they offered all he knew and more than he could guess. They offered books and painting, beauty and repose and all the fine elegance of higher existence. Behind those black eyes he knew every thought process. It was like clockwork. He could watch every wheel go around. Their bid was low pleasure, narrow as the grave, that palled, and the grave was at the end of it. But the bid of the saint's eyes was mystery, and wonder unthinkable, and eternal life. He had caught glimpses of the soul in them, and glimpses of his own soul, too.

"There's only one thing wrong with the program," he said aloud. "I 've got a date already."

The girl's eyes blazed her disappointment.

"To sit up with a sick friend, I suppose?" she sneered.

"No, a real, honest date with—" he faltered. "With a girl."

"You 're not stringin' me?" she asked earnestly.

He looked her in the eyes and answered, "It 's straight, all right. But why cant we meet some other time? You aint told me your name yet. An' where d 'ye live?"

"Lizzie," she replied, softening toward him, her hand pressing his arm while her body leaned against his. "Lizzie Connolly. And I live at Fifth and Market."

He talked on a few minutes before saying good-night. He did not go home immediately; and under the tree where he kept his vigils he looked up at a window, and murmured: "That date was with you, Ruth. I kept it for you."

CHAPTER VII.

A WEEK of heavy reading had passed since the evening he first met Ruth Morse, and still he dared not call. Time and again he nerved himself to call, but under the doubts that assailed him his determination died away. He did not know the proper time to call, nor was there anyone to tell him, and he was afraid of committing himself to an irretrievable blunder. Having shaken himself free from his old companions and old ways of life, and having no new companions, nothing remained for him but to read, and the long hours he devoted to it would have ruined a dozen pairs of ordinary eyes. But his eyes were strong, and they were backed by a body superbly strong. Furthermore, his mind was fallow. It had lain fallow all his life so far as the abstract thought of the books was concerned, and it was ripe for the sowing. It had never been jaded by study, and it bit hold of the knowledge in the books with sharp teeth that would not let go.

It seemed to him by the end of the week, that he had lived centuries, so far behind were the old life and outlook. But he was baffled by lack of preparation. He attempted to read books that required years of preliminary specialization. One day he would read a book of antiquated philosophy, and the next day one that was ultra-modern, so that his head would be whirling with the conflict and contradiction of ideas. It was the same with the economists. On the one shelf at the library he found *Karl Marx, Ricardo, Adam Smith,* and *Mill*, and the abstruse formulas of the one gave no clew that the ideas of another were obsolete. He was bewildered, and yet he wanted to know. He had become interested, in a day, in economics, industry, and politics. Passing through the City Hall Park, he had noticed a group of men, in the center of which were half a dozen, with flushed faces and raised voices, earnestly carrying on a discussion. He joined the listeners, and heard a new alien tongue in the mouths of the philosophers of the people. One was a tramp, another was a labor agitator, a third was a law school student and the remainder was composed of wordy workingmen. For the first time he heard of socialism, anarchism, and single tax, and learned that there were warring social philosophies. He heard hundreds of technical words that were new to him, belonging to fields of thought that his meagre reading had never touched upon. Because of this he could not follow the arguments closely, and he could only guess at and surmise the ideas wrapped up in such strange expressions. Then there was a black-eyed restaurant waiter who was a theosophist, a union baker who was an agnostic, an old man who baffled all of them with the strange philosophy that *what is is right*, and another old man who discoursed interminably about the cosmos and the father-atom and the mother-atom.

Martin Eden's head was in a state of addlement when he went away after several hours, and he hurried to the library to look up the definitions of a dozen unusual words. And when he left the library he carried under his arm four volumes: Madame Blavatsky's *Secret Doctrine, Progress and Poverty, The Quintessence of Socialism,* and *Warfare of Religion and Science*. Unfortunately, he began on the *Secret Doctrine*. Every line bristled with many-syllabled words he did not understand. He sat up in bed, and the dictionary was in front of him more often than the book. He looked up so many new words that when they recurred he had forgotten their meaning and had to look them up again. He devised the plan of writing the definitions in a note-book, and filled page after page with them. And still he could not understand. He read until three in the morning, and his brain was in a turmoil, but not one essential thought in the text had he grasped. He looked up, and it seemed that the room was lifting, heeling, and plunging like a ship upon the sea. Then he hurled the *Secret Doctrine* and many curses across the room, turned off the gas, and composed himself to sleep. Nor did he have much better luck with the other three books. It was not that his brain was weak or incapable; it could think these thoughts were it not for lack of training in thinking and lack of the thought-tools with which to think. He guessed this, and for a while entertained the idea of reading nothing but the dictionary until he had mastered every word in it.

Poetry, however, was his solace, and he read much of it, finding his greatest joy in the simpler poets, who were more understandable. He loved beauty, and there he found beauty. Poetry, like music, stirred him profoundly, and, though he did not know it, he was preparing his mind for the heavier work that was to come. The pages of his mind were blank, and without effort, much he read and liked, stanza by stanza, was impressed upon those pages, so that he was soon able to extract great joy from chanting aloud or under his breath the music and the beauty of the printed words he had read. Then he stumbled upon Gayley's *Classic Myths* and Bullfinch's *Age of Fable*, side by side on a library shelf. It was illumination, a great light in the darkness of his ignorance, and he read poetry more avidly than ever.

The man at the desk in the library had seen Martin there so often that he had become quite pleasant, always greeting him with a smile and a nod when he entered. It was because of this that Martin did a daring thing. Drawing some books at the desk, and while the man was stamping the cards, Martin blurted out:

"Say, there's something I 'd like to ask you."

The man smiled and paid attention.

"When you meet a young lady an' she asks you to call, how soon can you call?"

Martin felt his shirt press and cling to his shoulders, what of the sweat of the effort.

"Why, I 'd say any time," the man answered.

"Yes, but this is different," Martin objected. "She—I—well, you see, it's this way: maybe she wont be there. She goes to the University."

"Then call again."

"What I said aint what I meant," Martin confessed falteringly, while he made up his mind to throw himself wholly upon the man's mercy. "I 'm just a rough sort of a fellow, an' I aint never seen anything of society. This girl is all that I aint, an' I aint anything that she is. You dont think I'm playing the fool, do you?" he demanded abruptly.

"No, no; not at all, I assure you," the other protested. "Your request is not exactly in the scope of the reference department, but I shall be only too pleased to assist you."

Martin looked at him admiringly.

"If I could tear it off that way I 'd be all right," he said.

"I beg pardon?"

"I mean if I could talk easy that way, an' polite, an' all the rest."

''Oh,'' said the other, with comprehension.

''What 's the best time to call? The afternoon?—not too close to meal-time? Or the evening? Or Sunday?''

''I 'll tell you,'' the librarian said with a brightening face. ''You call her up on the telephone and find out.''

''I 'll do it,'' he said, picking up his books and starting away.

He turned back and asked:

''When you 're speaking to a young lady—say for instance, Miss Lizzie Smith—do you say 'Miss Lizzie?' or 'Miss Smith?'''

''Say 'Miss Smith,''' the librarian stated authoritatively. ''Say 'Miss Smith' always—until you come to know her better.''

So it was that Martin Eden solved the problem.

''Come down any time; I 'll be at home all afternoon,'' was Ruth's reply over the telephone to his stammered request as to when he could return the borrowed books.

She met him at the door herself, and her woman's eyes took in immediately the creased trousers and the certain slight but indefinable change in him for the better. Also, she was struck by his face. It was almost violent, this health of his, and it seemed to rush out of him and at her in waves of force. She felt the urge again of the desire to lean toward him for warmth, and marveled again at the effect his presence produced upon her. And he, in turn, knew again the swimming sensation of bliss when he felt the contact of her hand in greeting. The difference between them lay in that she was cool and self-possessed while his face flushed to the roots of the hair. He stumbled with his old awkwardness after her, and his shoulders swung and lurched perilously.

Once they were seated in the living-room, he began to get on easily—more easily by far than he had expected. She made it easy for him; and it made him love her more madly than ever. They talked first of the borrowed books, of the *Swinburne* he was devoted to, and of the *Browning* he did not understand; and she led the conversation on from subject to subject, while she pondered the problem of how she could be of help to him. She had thought of this often since their first meeting. She wanted to help him. He made a call upon her pity and tenderness that no one had ever made before, and the pity was not so much derogatory of him as maternal in her. Her pity could not be of the common sort, when the man who drew it was so much man as to shock her with maidenly fears and set her mind and pulse thrilling with strange thoughts and feelings. The old fascination of his neck was there, and there was sweetness in the thought of laying her hands upon it. It seemed still a wanton impulse, but she had grown more used to it. She did not dream that in such guise new-born love would epitomize itself. Nor did she dream that the feeling he excited in her was love. She thought she was merely interested in him as an unusual type possessing various potential excellencies, and she even felt philanthropic about it.

She did not know she desired him; but with him it was different. He knew that he loved her, and he desired her as he had never before desired anything in his life. He had loved poetry for beauty's sake; but since he met her the gates to the vast field of love-poetry had been opened wide. She had given him understanding even more than Bullfinch and Gayley. There was a line that a week before he would not have favored with a second thought—''God's own mad lover dying on a kiss;'' but now it was ever insistent in his mind. He marveled at the wonder of it and the truth; and as he gazed upon her he knew that he could die gladly upon a kiss. He felt himself God's own mad lover, and no accolade of knighthood could have given him greater pride. And at last he knew the meaning of life and why he had been born.

As he gazed at her and listened, his thoughts grew daring. He reviewed all the wild delight of the pressure of her hand in his at the door, and longed for it again. His gaze wandered often toward her lips, and he yearned for them hungrily. But there was nothing gross or earthly about this yearning. It gave him exquisite delight to watch every movement and play of those lips as they enunciated the words she spoke; yet they were not ordinary lips such as all men and women had. Their substance was not mere human clay. They were lips of pure spirit, and his desire for them seemed absolutely different from the desire that had led him to other women's lips. He could kiss her lips, rest his own physical lips upon them, but it would be with the lofty and awful fervor with which one would kiss the robe of God. He was not conscious of this transvaluation of values that had taken place in him, and was unaware that the light that shone in his eyes when he looked at her was quite the same light that shines in all men's eyes when the desire of love is upon them. He did not dream how ardent and masculine his gaze was, nor that the warm flame of it was affecting the alchemy of her spirit. Her penetrative virginity exalted and disguised his own emotions, elevating his thoughts to a star-cool chastity, and he would have been startled to learn that there was that shining out of his eyes, like warm waves, that flowed through her and kindled a kindred warmth. She was subtly perturbed by it, and more than once, though she knew not why, it disrupted her train of thought with its delicious intrusion and compelled her to grope for the remainder of ideas partly uttered. Speech was always easy with her, and these interruptions would have puzzled her had she not decided that it was because he was a remarkable type. She was very sensitive to impressions, and it was not strange, after all, that this aura of a traveler from another world should so affect her.

The problem in the background of her consciousness was how to help him, and she directed the conversation in that direction; but it was Martin who came to the point first.

"I wonder if I can get some advice from you," he began, and received an acquiesence of willingness that made his heart bound. "You remember the other time I was here I said I could n't talk about books an' things because I did n't know how? Well, I 've ben doin' a lot of thinkin' ever since. I 've ben to the library a whole lot, but most of the books I 've tackled have ben over my head. Mebee I'd better begin at the beginnin'. I aint never had no advantages. I 've worked pretty hard ever since I was a kid, an' since I 've ben to the library, lookin' with new eyes at books—an' lookin' at new books, too—I 've just about concluded that I aint ben reading the right kind. You know the books you find in cattle-camps an' fo'c's'ls aint the same you 've got in this house, for instance. Well, that 's the sort of readin' matter I 've ben accustomed to. And yet—an' I aint just makin' a brag of it—I 've ben different from the people I 've herded with. Not that I 'm any better than the sailors an' cow-punchers I traveled with—I was cow-punchin' for a short time, you know—but I always liked books, read everything I could lay hands on, an'—well, I guess I think differently from most of 'em."

"Now, to come to what I 'm drivin' at. I was never inside a house like this. When I come a week ago, an' saw all this, an' you, an' your mother, an' brothers, an' everything—well, I liked it. I 'd heard about such things, an' read about such things in some of the books, an' when I looked around at your house, why, the books come true. But the thing I 'm after is I liked it. I wanted it. I want it now. I want to breathe air like you get in this house—air that is filled with books, and pictures, and beautiful things, where people talk in low voices, an' are clean, an' their thoughts are clean. The air I always breathed was mixed up with grub, an' house-rent an' scrappin', and booze, an' that 's all they talked about, too. Why, when you was crossin' the room to kiss your mother I thought it was the most beautiful thing I ever seen. I 've seen a whole lot of life, an' somehow I 've seen a whole lot more of it than most of them that was with me. I like to see, an' I want to see more, an' I want to see it different.

"But I aint got to the point yet. Here it is. I want to make my way to the kind of life you have in this house. There 's more in life than booze, an' hard work, knockin' about. Now, how am I goin' to get it? Where do I take hold an' begin? I 'm willin' to work my passage, you know, an' I can make most men sick when it comes to hard work. Once I get started, I 'll work night an' day. Mebbe you think it 's funny, me askin' you about all this. I know you 're the last person in the world I ought to ask, but I dont know anybody else I could ask—unless it 's Arthur.

Mebbe I ought to ask him. If I was——''

His voice died away. His firmly planned intention had come to a halt on the verge of the horrible probability that he should have asked Arthur and that he had made a fool of himself. Ruth did not speak immediately. She was too absorbed in striving to reconcile the stumbling uncouth speech and its simplicity of thought with what she saw in his face. She had never looked in eyes that expressed greater power. Here was a man who could do anything, was the message she read there, and it accorded ill with the weakness of his spoken thought. And for that matter, so complex and quick was her own mind that she did not have a just appreciation of simplicity. And yet she had caught an impression of power in the very groping of this mind. It had seemed to her like a giant writhing and straining at the bonds that held him down. Her face was all sympathy when she did speak.

''What you need, you realize yourself, and it is education. You should go back and finish grammer school, and then go through the high school and university.''

''But that takes money,'' he interrupted.

''Oh,'' she cried. ''I had not thought of that. But then you have relatives, somebody who could assist you?''

He shook his head.

''My father and mother are dead. I 've two sisters, one married, an' the other 'll get married soon, I suppose. Then I 've a string of brothers—I 'm the youngest—but they never helped nobody. They 've just knocked around over the world, lookin' out for number one. The oldest died in India. Two are in South Africa now, an' another 's on a whaling voyage, an' one 's travelin' with a circus—he does trapeze work. An' I guess I 'm just like them. I 've taken care of myself since I was eleven—that 's when my mother died. I 've got to study by myself, I guess, an' what I want to know is where to begin.''

''I should say the first thing of all would be to get a grammar. Your grammar is—'' She had intended saying ''awful,'' but she amended it to, ''is not particularly good.''

He flushed and sweated.

''I know I must talk a lot of slang an' words you dont understand. But then they 're the only words I know—how to speak. I 've got other words in my mind, picked 'em up from books, but I cant pronounce 'em, so I dont use 'em.''

''It is n't what you say, so much as how you say it. You dont mind my being frank, do you? I dont want to hurt you.''

''No, no,'' he cried, while he secretly blessed her for her kindness. ''Fire away. I've got to know, an' I 'd sooner know from you than anybody else.''

''Well, then you say, 'You was'; it should be 'You were.' You say 'I seen' for 'I saw.' You use the double negative——''

''What 's the double negative?'' he demanded, then added humbly, ''You see, I dont even understand your explanations.''

''I 'm afraid I did n't explain that,'' she smiled. ''A double negative is * * let me see * * * well, you say, 'never helped nobody.' 'Never' is a negative. 'Nobody' is another negative. It is a rule that two negatives make a positive. 'Never helped nobody' means that, not helping nobody, they must have helped somebody.''

''That's pretty clear,'' he said. ''I never thought of it before. But it dont mean they *must* have helped somebody, does it? Seems to me that 'never helped nobody' just naturally fails to say whether or not they helped somebody. I never thought of it before, and I 'll never say it again.''

She was pleased and surprised with the quickness and surety of his mind. As soon as he had got the clew he not only understood but corrected her error.

''You 'll find it all in the grammar,'' she went on. ''There 's something else I noticed in your speech. You say 'dont' when you should n't. 'Dont' is a contraction and stands for two words. Do you know them?''

He thought a moment, then answered, '''Do not.'''

She nodded her head, and said, ''And you use 'dont' when you mean 'does not.''

He was puzzled over this, and did not get it so quickly.

''Give me an illustration,'' he asked.

''Well——.'' She puckered her brows and pursed up her mouth as she thought, while he looked on and decided that her expression was most adorable. "'It dont do to be hasty.' Change 'dont' to 'do not,' and it reads, 'It do not do to be hasty,' which is perfectly absurd."

He turned it over in his mind and considered.

"Does n't it jar on your ear?" she suggested.

"Can 't say that it does," he replied judicially.

"Why did n't you say, 'can 't say that it do?'" she queried.

"That sounds wrong," he said slowly. "As for the other I can 't make up my mind. I guess my ear aint had the trainin' yours has."

"There is no such word as 'aint,'" she said, prettily emphatic.

Martin flushed again.

"And you say 'ben' for 'been,'" she continued; "'I come' for 'I came'; and the way you chop your endings is something dreadful."

"How do you mean?" He leaned forward, feeling that he ought to get down on his knees before so marvelous a mind. "How do I chop?"

"You dont complete the endings. 'A-n-d' spells 'and.' You pronounce it 'an.' 'I-n-g' spells 'ing.' Sometimes you pronounce it 'ing' and sometimes you leave off the 'g.' And then you slur by dropping initial letters and dipthongs. 'T-h-e-m' spells 'them.' You pronounce it——oh, well, it is not necessary to go over all of them. What you need is the grammar. I 'll get one and show you how to begin."

As she arose, there shot through his mind something that he had read in the etiquette books, and he stood up awkwardly, worrying as to whether he was doing the right thing, and fearing that she might take it as a sign that he was about to go.

"By the way, Mr. Eden," she called back, as she was leaving the room. "What is *booze?* You used it several times, you know."

"Oh, booze," he laughed. "It 's slang. It means whiskey an' beer—anything that will make you drunk."

"And another thing," she laughed back. "Dont use 'you' when you are impersonal. 'You' is very personal, and your use of it just now was not precisely what you meant."

"I dont just see that."

"Why, you said just now, to me, 'whiskey and beer—anything that will make you drunk'—make *me* drunk, dont you see?"

"Well, it would, would n't it?"

"Yes, of course," she smiled. "But it would be nicer not to bring me into it. Substitute 'one' for 'you' and see how much better it sounds."

When she returned with the grammar she drew a chair near his—he wondered if he should have helped her with the chair—and sat down beside him. She turned the pages of the grammar, and their heads were inclined toward each other. He could hardly follow her outlining of the work he must do, so amazed was he by her delightful propinquity. But when she began to lay down the importance of conjugation, he forgot all about her. He had never heard of conjugation, and was fascinated by the glimpse he was catching into the tie-ribs of language. He leaned closer to the page, and her hair touched his cheek. He had fainted but once in his life, and he thought he was going to faint then. He could scarcely breathe, and his heart was pounding the blood up into his throat and suffocating him. Never had she seemed so accessible as now. For the moment the great gulf that separated them was bridged. But there was no diminution in the loftiness of his feeling for her. She had not descended to him. It was he who had been caught up into the clouds and carried to her. His reverence for her, in that moment, was of the same order as religious awe and fervor. It seemed to him that he had intruded upon the holy of holies, and slowly and carefully he moved his head aside from the contact which thrilled him like an electric shock and of which she had not been aware.

CHAPTER VIII.

SEVERAL weeks went by, during which Martin Eden studied his grammar, reviewed the books on etiquette, and read voraciously the books that caught his fancy. Of his own class he saw nothing. The girls of the Lotus Club wondered what had become of him and worried Jim with questions, and some of the fellows who put on the gloves at Riley's were glad that Martin came no more. He made another discovery of treasure-trove in the library. As the grammar had shown him the tie-ribs of language, so this book showed him the tie-ribs of poetry, and he began to learn meter and construction of form, beneath the beauty he loved finding the why and wherefore of that beauty. Another book he found treated poetry as a representative art, treated it exhaustively, with copious illustrations from the best in literature. Never had he read fiction with such keen zest as he studied these books. And his fresh mind, untaxed for twenty years and impelled by maturity of desire, gripped with a virility unusual to the student mind.

When he looked back now from his vantage-ground, the old world he had known, the world of land and sea and ships, of sailor-men and harpy-women, seemed a very small world; and yet it blended in with this new world and expanded. His mind made for unity, and he was surprised when at first he began to see points of contact between the two worlds. And he was ennobled, as well, by the loftiness of thought and beauty he found in the books. This led him to believe more firmly than ever that up above him in society, like Ruth and her family, all men and women thought these thoughts and lived them. Down below where he lived was the ignoble, and he wanted to purge himself of the ignoble that had soiled all his days, and to rise to that sublimated realm where dwelt the upper classes. All his childhood and youth had been troubled by a vague unrest; he had never known what he wanted, but he had wanted something that he had hunted vainly for until he met Ruth. And now his unrest had become sharp and painful, and he knew at last, clearly and definitely, that it was beauty, and intellect, and love that he must have.

During those several weeks he saw Ruth half a dozen times, and each time was an added inspiration. She helped him with his English, corrected his pronunciation, and started him on arithmetic. But their intercourse was not all devoted to elementary study. He had seen too much of life, and his mind was too matured to be wholly content with fractions, cube root, parsing, and analysis; and there were times when their conversation turned on other themes—the last poetry he had read, the latest poet she had studied. And when she read aloud to him her favorite passages, he ascended to the topmost heaven of delight. Never, in all the women he had heard speak, had he heard a voice like hers. The least sound of it was stimulus to his love, and he thrilled and throbbed with every word she uttered. It was the quality of it, the repose, and the musical modulation—the soft, rich, indefinable product of culture and a gentle soul. As he listened to her, there rang in the ears of his memory the harsh cries of barbarian women and of hags, and, in lesser degrees of harshness, the strident voices of workingwomen and of the girls of his own class. Then the chemistry of vision would begin to work, and they would troop in review across his mind, each, by contrast, multiplying Ruth's glories. Then, too, his bliss was heightened by the knowledge that her mind was comprehending what she read and was quivering with appreciation of the beauty of the written thought. She read to him much from "The Princess," and often he saw her eyes swimming with tears, so finely was her aesthetic nature strung. At such moments her own emotions elevated him till he was as a god, and, as he gazed at her and listened, he seemed gazing on the face of life and reading its deepest secrets. And then, becoming aware of the heights of exquisite sensibility he attained, he decided that this was love and that love was the greatest thing in the world. And in review would pass along the corridors of memory all previous thrills and burnings he had known—the drunkenness of wine, the caresses of women, the rough play and give and take of physical contests—and they seemed trivial and mean compared with this sublime ardor he now enjoyed.

The situation was obscured to Ruth. She had never had any experiences of the heart. Her only experiences in such matters were of the books, where the facts of ordinary day were translated by fancy into a fairy realm of unreality; and she little knew that this rough sailor was creeping into her heart and storing there pent forces that would some day burst forth and surge through her in waves of fire. She did not know the actual fire of love. Her knowledge of love was purely theoretical, and she conceived of it as lambent flame, gentle as the fall of dew or the ripple of quiet water, and cool as the velvet-dark of summer nights. Her idea of love was more that of placid affection, serving the loved one softly in an atmosphere, flower-scented and dim-lighted, of ethereal calm. She did not dream of the volcanic convulsions of love, its scorching heat and sterile wastes of parched ashes. She knew neither her own potencies, nor the potencies of the world; and the deeps of life were to her seas of illusion. The conjugal affection of her father and mother constituted her ideal of love-affinity, and she looked forward some day to emerging, without shock or friction, into that same quiet sweetness of existence with a loved one.

So it was that she looked upon Martin Eden as a novelty, a strange individual, and she identified with novelty and strangeness the effects he produced upon her. It was only natural. In similar ways she had experienced unusual feelings when she looked at wild animals in the menagerie, or when she witnessed a storm of wind, or shuddered at the bright-ribbed lightning. There was something cosmic in such things, and there was something cosmic in him. He came to her breathing of large airs and great spaces. The blaze of tropic suns was in his face, and in his swelling, resilient muscles was the primordial vigor of life. He was marred and scarred by that mysterious world of rough men and rougher deeds, the outposts of which began beyond her horizon. He was untamed, wild, and in secret ways her vanity was touched by the fact that he came so mildly to her hand. Likewise she was stirred by the common impulse to tame the wild thing. It was an unconscious impulse, and farthest from her thoughts that her desire was to re-thumb the clay of him into a likeness of her father's image, which image she believed to be the finest in the world. Nor was there any way, out of her inexperience, for her to know that the cosmic feel she caught of him was that most cosmic of things, love, which with equal power drew men and women together across the world, compelled stags to kill each other in the rutting season, and drove even the elements irresistibly to unite.

His swift development was a source of surprise and interest. She detected unguessed finenesses in him, that seemed to bud, day by day, like flowers in congenial soil. She read Browning aloud to him, and was often puzzled by the strange interpretations he gave to mooted passages. It was beyond her to realize that, out of his experience of men and women and life, his interpretations were far more frequently correct than hers. His conceptions seemed *naive* to her, though she was often fired by his daring flights of comprehension, whose orbit-path was so wide among the stars that she could not follow and could only sit and thrill to the impact of unguessed power. Then she played to him—no longer at him—and probed him with music that sank to depths beyond her plumb-line. His nature opened to music as a flower to the sun, and the transition was quick from his working-class rag-time and jingles to her classical display pieces that she knew nearly by heart. Yet he betrayed a democratic fondness for Wagner, and the "Tannhauser" overture, when she had given him the clew to it, claimed him as nothing else she played. In an immediate way it personified his life. All his past was the *Venusburg* motif, while her he identified somehow with the *Pilgrim's Chorus* motif; and from the exalted state this elevated him to, he swept onward and upward into that vast shadow-realm of spirit-groping where good and evil war eternally.

Sometimes he questioned, and induced in her mind temporary doubts as to the correctness of her own definitions and conceptions of music. But her singing he did not question. It was too wholly her, and he sat always amazed at the divine melody of her pure soprano voice. And he could not help but contrast it with the weak pipings and shrill quaverings of factory girls, ill-nourished and untrained, and with the raucous shriekings from gin-cracked throats of the women of the sea-port towns. She enjoyed singing and playing to him. In truth, it was the first time she had ever had a human soul to play with, and the plastic clay of him was a delight to mould; for she thought she was moulding it, and her intentions were good. Besides, it was pleasant to be with him. He did not repel her. That first repulsion had been really a fear of her undiscovered self, and the fear had gone to sleep. Though she did not know it, she had a feeling in him of proprietary right. Also, he had a tonic effect upon her. She was studying hard at the university, and it seemed to strengthen her to emerge from the dusty books and have the fresh sea-breeze of his personality blow upon her. Strength! Strength was what she needed, and he gave it to her in generous measure. To come into the same room with him, or to meet him at the door, was to take heart of life. And when he had gone, she would return to her books with a keener zest and fresh store of energy.

She knew her Browning, but it had never sunk into her that it was an awkward thing to play with souls. As her interest in Martin increased, the remodeling of his life became a passion with her.

"There is Mr. Butler," she said one afternoon, when grammar and arithmetic and poetry had been put aside. "He had comparatively no advantages at first. His father had been a bank cashier, but he lingered for years, dying of consumption in Arizona, so that when he was dead, Mr. Butler—Charles Butler he was called—found himself alone in the world. His father had come from Australia, you know, and so he had no relatives in California. He went to work in a printing office—I have heard him tell of it many times—and he got three dollars a week, at first. His income today is at least thirty thousand a year. How did he do it? He was honest, and faithful, and industrious, and economical. He denied himself the enjoyments that most boys indulge in. He made it a point to save so much every week, no matter what he had to do without in order to save it. Of course, he was soon earning more than three dollars a week, and as his wages increased he saved more and more.

"He worked in the day-time, and at night he went to night-school. He had his eyes fixed always on the future. Later on he went to night high school. When he was only seventeen he was earning excellent wages at setting type, but he was ambitious. He wanted a career, not a livelihood, and he was content to make immediate sacrifices for his ultimate gain. He decided upon the law, and he entered father's office as an office-boy—think of that—and got only four dollars a week. But he had learned how to be economical, and out of that four dollars he went on saving money."

She paused for breath, and to note how Martin was receiving it. His face was lighted up with interest in the youthful struggles of Mr. Butler; but there was a frown upon his face as well.

"I 'd say they was pretty hard lines

for a young fellow," he remarked. "Four dollars a week. How could he live on it? You can bet he did n't have any frills. Why, I pay five dollars a week for board now, an' there 's nothin' excitin' about it, you can lay to that. He must have lived like a dog. The food he ate——"

"He cooked for himself," she interrupted, "on a little kerosene stove."

"The food he ate must have been worse than what a sailor gets on the worst-feedin' deep-water ships, than which there aint much that can be possibly worse."

"But think of him now!" she cried enthusiastically. "Think of what his income affords him. His early denials are paid for a thousand-fold."

Martin looked at her sharply.

"There 's one thing I 'll bet you," he said, "and it is that Mr. Butler is nothin' gay-hearted now in his fat days. He fed himself like that for years an' years, on a boy's stomach, an' I bet his stomach 's none too good now for it."

Her eyes dropped before his searching gaze.

"I 'll bet he 's got dyspepsia right now!" Martin challenged.

"Yes, he has," she confessed; "but ——"

"An' I bet," Martin dashed on, "that he 's solemn an' serious as an old owl, an' does n't care a rap for a good time for all his thirty thousand a year. An' I 'll bet he 's not particularly joyful at seein' others have a good time. Aint I right?"

She nodded her head in agreement, and hastened to explain.

"But he 's not that type of man. By nature he is sober and serious. He always was that."

"You can bet he was," Martin proclaimed. "Three dollars a week, an' four dollars a week, an' a young boy cookin' for himself on an oil-burner an' layin' up money, workin' all day an' studyin' all night, just workin' an' never playin', never havin' a good time, an' never learnin' how to have a good time—of course his thirty thousand came along too late."

His sympathetic imagination was flashing upon his inner sight all the thousands of details of the boy's existence and of his narrow spiritual development into a thirty-thousand-dollar-a year man. With the swiftness and wide-reaching of multitudinous thought Charles Butler's whole life was telescoped upon his vision.

"Do you know," he added, "I feel sorry for Mr. Butler. He was too young to know better, but he robbed himself of life for the sake of thirty thousand a year that 's clean wasted upon him. Why, thirty thousand, lump sum, would n't buy for him right now what ten cents he was layin' up would have bought him, when he was a kid, in the way of candy an' peanuts or a seat in 'nigger heaven.' "

It was just such uniqueness of points of view that startled Ruth. Not only were they new to her, and contrary to her own beliefs, but she always felt in them germs of truth that threatened to unseat or modify her own convictions. Had she been fourteen instead of twenty-four, she might have been changed by them; but she was twenty-four, conservative by nature and upbringing, and already crystallized into the cranny of life where she had been born and formed. It was true, his *bizarre* judgments troubled her in the moments they were uttered, but she ascribed them to his novelty of type and strangeness of living, and they were soon forgotten. Nevertheless, while she disapproved of them, the strength of their utterance, and the flashing of eyes and earnestness of face that accompanied them, always thrilled her and drew her toward him. She would never have guessed that this man who had come from beyond her horizon, was, in such moments, flashing on beyond her horizon with wider and deeper concepts. Her own limits were the limits of her horizon; but limited minds can recognize limitations only in others. And so she felt that her outlook was very wide indeed, and that where his conflicted with hers marked his limitations, and she dreamed of helping him to see as she saw, of widening his horizon until it was identified with hers.

"But I have not finished my story," she said. "He worked, so father says, as no other office-boy he ever had. Mr. Butler was always eager to work. He never was late, and he was usually at the office a few minutes before his regular time. Yet he saved his time. Every spare moment was devoted to study. He studied book-keeping and typewriting, and he paid for lessons in shorthand by dictating at night to a court reporter who needed practice. He quickly became a clerk, and he made himself invaluable. Father appreciated him and saw that he was bound to rise. It was on father's suggestion that he went to law college. He became a lawyer, and hardly was he back in the office when father took him in as a junior partner. He is a great man. He refused the United States Senate several times, and father says he could become justice of the Supreme Court any time a vacancy occurs, if he wants to. Such a life is an inspiration to all of us. It shows us that a man with will may rise superior to his environment."

"He is a great man," Martin said sincerely.

But it seemed to him there was something in the recital that jarred upon his sense of beauty and life. He could not find an adequate motive in Mr. Butler's life of pinching and privation. Had he done it for love of a woman, or for attainment of beauty, Martin would have understood. God's own mad lover should do anything for the kiss, but not for thirty thousand dollars a year. He was dissatisfied with Mr. Butler's career. There was something paltry about it after all. Thirty thousand a year was all right, but dyspepsia and inability to be humanly happy robbed such princely income of all its value.

Much of this he strove to express to Ruth, and shocked her and made it clear that more remodeling was necessary. Hers was that common insularity of mind that makes human creatures believe that their color, creed, and politics are best and right, and that other human creatures scattered over the world are less fortunately placed than they. It was the same insularity of mind that made the ancient Jew thank God he was not born a woman, and sent the modern missionary god-substituting to the ends of the earth; and it made Ruth desire to shape this man from other crannies of life into the likeness of the man who lived in her particular cranny.

CHAPTER IX.

BACK from the sea Martin Eden came, homing for California with a lover's desire. His store of money exhausted, he had shipped before the mast on the treasure-hunting schooner; and Solomon Islands, after eight months of failure to find treasure, had witnessed the breaking-up of the expedition. The men had been paid off in Australia, and Martin had immediately shipped on a deep-water vessel for San Francisco. Not alone had those eight months earned him enough money to stay on land for many weeks, but they had enabled him to do a great deal of studying and reading.

His was the student's mind, and behind his ability to learn was the indomitability of his nature and his love for Ruth. The grammar he had taken along he went through again and again until his unjaded brain had mastered it. He noticed the bad grammar used by his shipmates, and made a point of mentally correcting and reconstructing their crudities of speech. To his great joy he discovered that his ear was becoming sensitive and that he was developing grammatical nerves. A double-negative jarred him like a discord, and often, from lack of practice, it was from his own lips that the jar came. His tongue refused to learn new tricks in a day.

After he had been through the grammar repeatedly, he took up the dictionary and added twenty words a day to his vocabulary. He found that this was no light task, and at wheel or lookout he steadily went over and over his lengthening list of pronunciations and definitions, while he invariably memorized himself to sleep. "Never did anything," "if I were," and "those things," were phrases, with many variations, that he repeated under his breath in order to accustom his tongue to the language spoken by Ruth. "And" and "ing," with the "d" and "g" pronounced emphatically, he went over thousands of times;

and to his surprise he noticed that he was beginning to speak cleaner and correcter English than the officers themselves and the gentleman-adventurers in the cabin who had financed the expedition.

The captain was a fishy-eyed Norwegian, who somehow had fallen into possession of a complete *Shakespeare,* which he never read, and Martin had washed his clothes for him and in return been permitted access to the precious volumes. For a time, so steeped was he in the plays and in the many favorite passages that impressed themselves almost without effort on his brain, that all the world seemed to shape itself into forms of Elizabethan tragedy or comedy and his very thoughts were in blank verse. It trained his ear and gave him a fine appreciation for noble English, withal it introduced into his mind much that was archaic and obsolete.

The eight months had been well spent, and, in addition to what he had learned of right speaking and high thinking, he had learned much of himself. Along with his humbleness because he knew so little, there arose a conviction of power. He felt a sharp gradation between himself and his shipmates, and was wise enough to realize that the difference lay in potentiality rather than achievement. What he could do, they could do; but within him he felt a confused ferment working that told him there was more in him than he had done. He was tortured by the exquisite beauty of the world, and wished that Ruth were there to share it with him. He decided that he would describe to her many of the bits of South Sea beauty. The creative spirit in him flamed up at the thought and urged that he recreate this beauty for a wider audience than Ruth. And then, in splendor and glory, came the great idea. He would write. He would be one of the eyes through which the world saw, one of the ears through which it heard, one of the hearts through which it felt. He would write—everything—poetry and prose, fiction and description, and plays like Shakespeare. There was career and the way to win to Ruth. The men of literature were the world's giants, and he conceived them to be far finer than the Mr. Butlers who earned thirty thousand a year and could be Supreme Court justices if they wanted.

Once the idea had germinated, it mastered him, and the return voyage to San Francisco was like a dream. He was drunken with unguessed power and felt that he could do anything. In the midst of the great and lonely sea he gained perspective. Clearly, and for the first time, he saw Ruth and her world. It was all visualized in his mind as a concrete thing which he could take up in his two hands and turn around and about and examine. There was much that was dim and nebulous in that world, but he saw it as a whole and not in detail, and he saw, also, the way to master it. To write! The thought was fire in him. He would begin as soon as he got back. The first thing he would do would be to describe the voyage of the treasure-hunters. He would sell it to some San Francisco newspaper. He would not tell Ruth anything about it, and she would be surprised and pleased when she saw his name in print. While he wrote he could go on studying. There were twenty-four hours in each day. He was invincible. He knew how to work, and the citadels would go down before him. He would not have to go to sea again—as a sailor; and for the instant he caught a vision of a steam yacht. There were other writers who possessed steam yachts. Of course, he cautioned himself, it would be slow succeeding at first, and for a time he would be content to earn enough money by his writing to enable him to go on studying. And then, after some time—a very indeterminate time—when he had learned and prepared himself, he would write the great things and his name would be on all men's lips. But greater than that, infinitely greater and greatest of all, he would have proved himself worthy of Ruth. Fame was all very well, but it was for Ruth that his splendid dream arose. He was not a fame-monger, but merely one of God's mad lovers.

Arrived in Oakland, with his snug pay-day in his pocket, he took up his old room at Bernard Higginbotham's and set to work. He did not even let Ruth know he was back. He would go and see her when he finished the article on the treasure-hunters. It was not so difficult to abstain from seeing her, because of the violent heat of creative fever that burned in him. Besides, the very article he was writing would bring her nearer to him. He did not know how long an article he should write, but he counted the words in a double-page article in the Sunday supplement of the *San Francisco Examiner* and guided himself by that. Three days, at white heat, completed his narrative; but when he had copied it carefully, in a large scrawl that was easy to read, he learned from a rhetoric he picked up in the library that there were such things as paragraphs and quotation marks. He had never thought of such things before; and he promptly set to work writing the article over, referring continually to the pages of the rhetoric and learning more in a day about composition than the average school-boy in a year. When he had copied the article a second time and rolled it up carefully, he read in a newspaper an item on hints to beginners, and discovered the iron law that manuscripts should never be rolled and that they should be written on one side of the paper. He had violated the law on both counts. Also, he learned from the item that first-class papers paid a minimum of ten dollars a column. So, while he copied the manuscript a third time, he consoled himself by multiplying ten columns by ten dollars. The product was always the same, one hundred dollars, and he decided that that was better than seafaring. If it had n't been for his blunders, he would have finished the article in three days. One hundred dollars in three days! It would have taken him three months and longer on the sea to earn a similar amount. A man was a fool to go to sea when he could write, he concluded, though the money in itself meant nothing to him. Its value was in the liberty it would get him, the presentable garments it would buy him, all of which would bring him nearer, swiftly nearer, to the slender pale girl who had turned his life back upon itself and given him inspiration.

He mailed the manuscript in a flat envelope, and addressed it to the editor of the *San Francisco Examiner.* He had an idea that anything accepted by a paper was published immediately, and as he had sent the manuscript in on Friday he expected it to come out on the following Sunday. He conceived that it would be fine to let that event appraise Ruth of his return. Then, Sunday afternoon, he would call and see her. In the meantime he was occupied by another idea, which he prided himself upon as being a particularly sane, careful, and modest idea. He would write an adventure story for boys and sell it to the *Youth's Companion.* He went to the free reading-room and looked through the files of the *Youth's Companion.* Serial stories, he found, were usually published in that weekly in five instalments of about three thousand words each. He discovered several serials that ran to seven instalments and decided to write one of that length.

He had been on a whaling voyage in the Arctic, once—a voyage that was to have been for three years and which had terminated in shipwreck at the end of six months. While his imagination was fanciful, even fantastic at times, he had a basic love of reality that compelled him to write about the things he knew. He knew whaling, and out of the real materials of his knowledge he proceeded to manufacture the fictitious adventures of the two boys he intended to use as joint-heroes. It was easy work, he decided, on Saturday evening. He had completed on that day the first instalment of three thousand words—much to the amusement of Jim, and to the open derision of Mr. Higginbotham, who sneered throughout meal-time at the "litery" person they had discovered in the family.

Martin contented himself by picturing his brother-in-law's surprise on Sunday morning when he opened his *Examiner* and saw the article on the treasure-hunters. Early that morning he was out himself to the front door, nervously racing through the many-sheeted newspaper. He went through it a second time, very carefully, then folded it up and left it where he had found it. He was glad he had not told any one about his article. On second thought he concluded that he had been wrong about the speed with which things found their way into newspaper columns. Besides, there had not been any news value in his article, and most likely the editor would write to him about it first.

After breakfast he went on with his serial. The words flowed from his pen, though he broke off from the writing frequently to look up definitions in the dictionary or to refer to the rhetoric. He often read or re-read a chapter at a time, during such pauses; and he consoled himself that while he was not writing the great things he felt to be in him, he was learning composition, at any rate, and training himself to shape up and express his thoughts. He toiled on till dark, when he went out to the reading-room and explored magazines and weeklies until the place closed at ten o'clock. This was his program for a week. Each day he did three thousand words, and each evening he puzzled his way through the magazines, taking note of the stories, articles, and poems that editors saw fit to publish. One thing was certain: What these multitudinous writers did he could do, and only give him time and he would do what they could not do. He was cheered to read in *Book News,* in a paragraph on the payment of magazine writers, not that Rudyard Kipling received a dollar per word, but that the minimum rate paid by first-class magazines was two cents a word. The *Youth's Companion* was certainly first-class, and at that rate the three thousand words he had written that day would bring him sixty dollars—two months' wages on the sea!

On Friday night he finished the serial, twenty-one thousand words long. At two cents a word, he calculated, that would bring him four hundred and twenty dollars. Not a bad week's work. It was more money than he had ever possessed at one time. He did not know how he could spend it all. He had tapped a gold mine. Where this came from he could always get more. He planned to buy some more clothes, to subscribe to many magazines, and to buy dozens of reference books that at present he was compelled to go to the library to consult. And still there was a large portion of the four hundred and twenty dollars unspent. This worried him until the thought came to him of hiring a servant for Gertrude and of buying a bicycle for Marion.

He mailed the bulky manuscript to the *Youth's Companion,* and on Saturday afternoon, after having planned an article on pearl-diving, he went to see Ruth. He had telephoned, and she went herself to greet him at the door. The old familiar blaze of health rushed out from him and struck her like a blow. It seemed to enter into her body and course through her veins in a liquid glow, and to set her quivering with its imparted strength. He flushed warmly as he took her hand and looked into her blue eyes, but the fresh bronze of eight months of sun hid the flush, though it did not protect the neck from the gnawing chafe of the stiff collar. She noted the red line of it with amusement which quickly vanished as she glanced at his clothes. They really fitted him—it was his first made-to-order suit—and he seemed slimmer and better modeled. In addition, his cloth cap had been replaced by a soft hat, which she commanded him to put on and then complimented him on his appearance. She did not remember when she had felt so happy. This change in him was her handiwork, and she was proud of it and fired with ambition further to help him.

But the most radical change of all, and the one that pleased her most, was the change in his speech. Not only did he speak more correctly, but he spoke more easily, and there were many new words in his vocabulary. When he grew excited or enthusiastic, however, he dropped back into the old slurring and the dropping of final consonants. Also, there was an awkward hesitancy, at times, as he essayed the new words he had learned. On the other hand, along with his ease of expression, he displayed a lightness and facetiousness of thought that delighted her. It was his old spirit of humor and badinage that had made him a favorite in his own class, but which he had hitherto been unable to use in her presence through lack of words and training. He was just beginning to orientate himself and to feel that he was not wholly an intruder. But he was very tentative, fastidiously so, letting Ruth set the pace of sprightliness and fancy, keeping up with her but never daring to go beyond her.

He told her of what he had been doing, and of his plan to write for a livelihood and of going on with his studies. But he was disappointed at her lack of approval. She did not think much of his plan.

"You see," she said frankly, "writing must be a trade, like anything else. Not that I know anything about it, of course. I only bring common judgment to bear. You could n't hope to be a blacksmith without spending three years at learning the trade—or is it five years? Now writers are so much better paid than blacksmiths that there must be ever so many more men who would like to write, who—try to write."

"But then, may not I be peculiarly constituted to write?" he queried, secretly exulting at the language he had used, his swift imagination throwing the whole scene and atmosphere upon a vast screen along with a thousand other scenes from his life—scenes that were rough and raw, gross and bestial.

The whole composite vision was achieved with the speed of light, producing no pause in the conversation, nor interrupting his calm train of thought. On the screen of his imagination he saw himself and this sweet and beautiful girl, facing each other and conversing in good English, in a room of books and paintings and tone and culture, and all illuminated by a bright light of steadfast brilliance; while ranged about and fading away to the remote edges of the screen were antithetical scenes, each scene a picture, and he the onlooker, free to look at will upon what he wished. He saw these other scenes through drifting vapors and swirls of sullen fog dissolving before shafts of red and garish light. He saw cowboys at the bar, drinking fierce whiskey, the air filled with obscenity and ribald language, and he saw himself with them, drinking and cursing with the wildest, or sitting at table with them, under smoking kerosene lamps, while the chips clicked and clattered and the cards were dealt around. He saw himself, stripped to the waist, with naked fists, fighting his great fight with Liverpool Red in the forecastle of the *Susquehanna;* and he saw the bloody deck of the *John Rogers* that gray morning of attempted mutiny, the mate kicking in death-throes on the main-hatch, the revolver in the old man's hand spitting fire and smoke, the men with passion-wrenched faces of brutes screaming vile blasphemies and falling about him—and then he returned to the central scene, calm and clean in the steadfast light, where Ruth sat and talked with him amid books and paintings; and he saw the grand piano upon which she would later play to him; and he heard the echoes of his own selected and correct words, "But then, may I not be peculiarly constituted to write?"

"But no matter how peculiarly constituted a man may be for blacksmithing," she was laughing, "I never heard of one becoming a blacksmith without first serving his apprenticeship."

"What would you advise?" he asked. "And dont forget that I feel in me this capacity to write—I can 't explain it; I just know that it is in me."

"You must get a thorough education," was the answer, "whether or not you ultimately become a writer. This education is indispensable for whatever career you select, and it must not be slipshod or sketchy. You should go to high school."

"Yes——" he began; but she interrupted with an afterthought:

"Of course, you could go on with your writing, too."

"I would have to," he said grimly.

"Why?" She looked at him, prettily puzzled, for she did not quite like the persistence with which he clung to his notion.

"Because, without writing there would n't be any high school. I must live and buy books and clothes, you know."

"I 'd forgotten that," she laughed. "Why were n't you born with an income?"

"I 'd rather have good health and imagination," he answered. "I can make good on the income, but the other things have to be made good for——" He almost said "you," then amended his sentence to "have to be made good for one."

"Dont say 'make good,'" she cried, sweetly petulant. "It 's slang, and it 's horrid."

He flushed, and stammered, "That 's right, and I only wish you 'd correct me every time."

"I—I 'd like to," she said haltingly. "You have so much in you that is good that I want to see you perfect."

He was clay in her hands immediately, as passionately desirous of being moulded by her as she was desirous of shaping him into the image of her ideal of man. And when she pointed out the opportuneness of the time, that the entrance examinations to high school began on the following Monday, he promptly volunteered that he would take them.

Then she played and sang to him, while he gazed with hungry yearning at her, drinking in her loveliness and marveling that there should not be a hundred suitors listening there and longing for her as he listened and longed.

CHAPTER X.

HE stopped to dinner that evening, and, much to Ruth's satisfaction, made a favorable impression on her father. They talked about the sea as a career, a subject which Martin had at his finger-ends, and Mr. Morse remarked afterwards that he seemed a very clear-headed young man. In his avoidance of slang and his search after right words, Martin was compelled to talk slowly, which enabled him to find the best thoughts that were in him. He was more at ease than that first night at dinner nearly a year before, and his shyness and modesty even commended him to Mrs. Morse, who was pleased at his manifest improvement.

"He is the first man that ever drew passing notice from Ruth," she told her husband. "She has been so singularly backward where men are concerned that I have been worried greatly."

Mr. Morse looked at his wife curiously.

"You mean to use this young sailor to wake her up?" he questioned.

"I mean that she is not to die an old maid if I can help it," was the answer. "If this young Eden can arouse her interest in mankind in general, it will be a good thing."

"A very good thing," he commented. "But suppose, and we must suppose sometimes, my dear, suppose he arouses her interest too particularly in him?"

"Impossible," Mrs. Morse laughed. "She is three years older than he, and, besides, it is impossible. Nothing will ever come of it. Trust that to me."

And so Martin's role was arranged for him, while he, led on by Arthur and Norman, was meditating an extravagance. They were going out for a ride into the hills Sunday morning on their wheels, which did not interest Martin until he learned that Ruth, too, rode a wheel and was going along. He did not ride, nor own a wheel, but if Ruth rode it was up to him to begin, was his decision; and when he said good-night he stopped in at a cyclery on his way home and spent forty dollars for a wheel. It was more than a month's hard-earned wages, and it reduced his stock of money amazingly; but when he added the hundred dollars he was to receive from *The Examiner* to the four hundred and twenty dollars that was the least the *Youth's Companion* could pay him, he felt that he had reduced the perplexity the unwonted amount of money had caused him. Nor did he mind, in the course of learning to ride the wheel home, the fact that he ruined his suit of clothes. He caught the tailor by telephone that night from Mr. Higginbotham's store and ordered another suit. Then he carried the wheel up the narrow stairway that clung like a fire-escape to the rear wall of the building, and, when he had moved his bed out from the wall, found there was just space enough in the small room for himself and the wheel.

Sunday he had intended to devote to

studying for the high school examination, but the pearl-diving article lured him away, and he spent the day in the white-hot fever of re-creating beauty and romance that burned in him. The fact that *The Examiner* of that morning had failed to publish his treasure-hunting article did not dash his spirits. He was at too great a height for that, and, having been deaf to a twice repeated summons, he went without the heavy Sunday dinner with which Mr. Higginbotham invariably graced his table. To Mr. Higginbotham such a dinner was advertisement of his worldly achievement and prosperity, and he honored it by delivering platitudinous sermonettes upon American institutions and the opportunities said institutions gave to any hard-workingman to rise—the rise, in his case, which he pointed out unfailingly, being from a grocer's clerk to the ownership of Higginbotham's Cash Store.

Martin Eden looked with a sigh at his unfinished "Pearl-Diving" on Monday morning, and took the car down to Oakland to the High School. And when, days later, he applied for the results of his examinations, he learned that he had failed in everything save grammar.

"Your grammar is excellent," Professor Hilton informed him, staring at him through heavy spectacles; "but you know nothing, positively nothing, in the other branches, and your United States history is abominable—there is no other word for it—abominable. I should advise you——"

Professor Hilton paused and glared at him, unsympathetic and unimaginative as one of his own test tubes. He was professor of physics in the High School, possessor of a large family, a meager salary, and a select fund of parrot-learned knowledge.

"Yes, sir," Martin said humbly, wishing somehow that the man at the desk in the library was in Professor Hilton's place just then.

"And I should advise you to go back to the grammar school for at least two years. Good-day."

Martin was not deeply affected by his failure, though he was surprised at Ruth's shocked expression when he told her Professor Hilton's advice. Her disappointment was so evident that he was sorry he had failed, but chiefly so for her sake.

"You see, I was right," she said "You know far more than any of the students entering high school, and yet you cant pass the examinations. It is because what education you have is fragmentary, sketchy. You need the discipline of study, such as only skilled teachers can give you. You must be thoroughly grounded. Professor Hilton is right, and if I were you I 'd go to night school. A year and a half of it might enable you to catch up that additional six months. Besides, that would leave you your days in which to write, or, if you could not make your living by your pen, you would have your days in which to work in some position."

But if my days are taken up with work and my nights with school, when am I going to see you?—was Martin's first thought, though he refrained from uttering it. Instead, he said:

"It seems so babyish for me to be going to night school. But I would n't mind that, if I thought it would pay. But I dont think it will pay. I can do the work quicker than they can teach me. It would be a loss of time——" He thought of her and his desire to have her—"And I cant afford the time. I have n't the time to spare, in fact."

"There is so much that is necessary." She looked at him gently, and he felt that he was a brute to oppose her. "Physics and chemistry—you can 't do them without laboratory study; and you 'll find algebra and geometry almost hopeless without instruction. You need the skilled teachers, the specialists in the art of imparting knowledge."

He was silent for a minute, casting about for the least vainglorious way in which to express himself.

"Please dont think I 'm bragging," he began. "I dont intend it that way at all. But I have a feeling that I am what I may call a natural student. I can study by myself. I take to it kindly, like a duck to water. You see yourself what I did with grammar. And I 've learned much of other things—you would never dream how much. And I 'm only getting started. Wait till I get——" He hesitated and assured himself of the pronunciation before he said "momentum. I'm getting my first real feel of things now. I 'm beginning to size up the situation——"

"Please dont say 'size up'" she interrupted.

"To get a line on things," he hastily amended.

"That does n't mean anything, in correct English," she objected.

He floundered for a fresh start.

"What I 'm driving at is that I 'm beginning to get the lay of the land."

Out of pity she forebore, and he went on:

"Knowledge seems to me like a chart-room. Whenever I go into the library I am impressed that way. The part played by teachers is to teach the student the contents of the chart-room in a systematic way. The teachers are guides to the chart-room, that 's all. It 's not something that they have in their own heads. They dont make it up, dont create it. It 's all in the chart-room and they know their way about in it, and it 's their business to show the place to strangers who might else get lost. Now I dont get lost easily. I have the bump of location. I usually know where I 'm at—what 's wrong now?"

"Dont say 'where I 'm at.'"

"That 's right," he said gratefully. "where I am. But where am I at—I mean, where am I? Oh, yes, in the chart-room. Well, some people——"

"Persons," she corrected.

"Some persons need guides; most persons do, but I think I can get along without them. I 've spent a lot of time in the chart-room now, and I'm on the edge of knowing my way about, what charts I want to refer to, what coasts I want to explore. And from the way I line it up, I 'll explore a whole lot more quickly by myself. The speed of a fleet, you know, is the speed of the slowest ship, and the speed of the teachers is affected in the same way. They cant go any faster than the ruck of their scholars, and I can set a faster pace for myself than they can set for a whole schoolroom."

"'He travels the fastest who travels alone,'" she quoted at him.

But I 'd travel faster with you just the same, was what he wanted to blurt out, as he caught a vision of a world without end of sun-lit spaces and starry voids through which he drifted with her, his arm around her, her pale-gold hair blowing about his face. In the same instant he was aware of the pitiful inadequacy of speech. God! If he could so frame words that she could see what he then saw! And he felt the stir in him, like a throe of yearning pain, of the desire to paint these visions that flashed unsummoned on the mirror of his mind. Ah, that was it! He caught at the hem of the secret. It was the very thing that the great writers and master-poets did. That was why they were giants. They knew how to express what they thought, and felt, and saw. Dogs asleep in the sun often whined and barked, but they were unable to tell what they saw that made them whine and bark. He had often wondered what it was. And that was all he was, a dog asleep in the sun. He saw noble and beautiful visions, but he could only whine and bark at Ruth. But he would cease sleeping in the sun. He would stand up, with open eyes, and he would struggle and toil and learn until, with eyes unblinded and tongue untied, he could share with her his visoned wealth. Other men had discovered the trick of expression, of making words obedient servitors, and of making combinations of words mean more than the sum of their separate meanings. He was stirred profoundly by the passing glimpse of the secret, and he was again caught up in the vision of sun-lit spaces and starry voids—until it came to him that it was very quiet, and he saw Ruth regarding him with an amused expression and a smile in her eyes.

"I have had a great visioning," he said, and at the sound of his words in his own ears his heart gave a leap. Where had those words come from? They had adequately expressed the pause his vision had put in the conversation. It was a miracle. Never had he so loftily framed a lofty thought. But never had he attempted to frame lofty thoughts in words. That was it. That explained it. He had never tried. But Swinburne had, and Tennyson, and Kipling, and all the other poets. His mind flashed on to his "Pearl-Diving." He had never dared the big things, the spirit of the beauty that was a fire in him. That article would be a different thing when he was done with it. He was appalled by the vastness of the beauty that rightfully belonged in it, and again his mind flashed and dared, and he demanded of himself why he could not chant that beauty in noble verse as the great poets did. And there was all the mysterious delight and spiritual wonder of his love for Ruth. Why could he not chant that, too, as the poets did? They had sung of love. So would he. By God!——

And in his frightened ears he heard his exclamation echoing. Carried away, he had breathed it aloud. The blood surged into his face, wave upon wave, mastering the bronze of it till the blush of shame flaunted itself from the collar-rim to the roots of his hair.

"I—I—beg your pardon," he stammered. "I was thinking."

"It sounded as if you were praying," she said bravely, but she felt herself inside to be withering and shrinking. It was the first time she had heard an oath from the lips of a man she knew, and she was shocked, not merely as a matter of principle and training, but shocked in spirit by this rough blast of life in the garden of her sheltered maidenhood.

But she forgave, and with surprise at the ease of her forgiveness. Somehow, it was not so difficult to forgive him anything. He had not had a chance to be as other men, and he was trying so hard, and succeeding, too. It never entered her head that there could be any other reason for her being kindly disposed toward him. She was tenderly disposed toward him, but she did not know it. She had no way of knowing it. The placid poise of twenty-four years without a single love affair did not fit her with a keen perception of her own feelings, and she, who had never warmed to actual love, was unaware that she was warming now.

CHAPTER XI.

MARTIN went back to his pearl-diving article, which would have been finished sooner if it had not been broken in upon so frequently by his attempts to write poetry. His poems were love poems, inspired by Ruth, but they were never completed. Not in a day could he learn to chant in noble verse. Rhyme and metre and structure were serious enough in themselves, but there was, over and beyond them, an intangible and evasive something that he caught in all great poetry, but which he could not catch and imprison in his own. It was the elusive spirit of poetry itself that he sensed and sought after but could not capture. It seem a glow to him, a warm and trailing vapor, ever beyond his reaching, though sometimes he was rewarded by catching at shreds of it and weaving them into phrases that echoed in his brain with haunting notes or drifted across his vision in misty wafture of unseen beauty. It was baffling. He ached with desire to express and could but gibber prosaically as everybody gibbered. He read his fragments aloud. The meter marched along on perfect feet, and the rhyme pounded a longer and equally faultless rhythm, but the glow and high exaltation that he felt within were lacking. He could not understand, and time and again, in despair, defeated and depressed, he returned to his article. Prose was certainly an easier medium.

Following the "Pearl-Diving," he wrote an article on the sea as a career, another on turtle-catching, and a third on the northeast trades. Then he tried, as an experiment, a short story, and before he broke his stride he had finished six short stories and dispatched them to various magazines. He wrote prolifically, intensely, from morning till night and late at night, except when he broke off to go to the reading-room, draw books from the library, or to call on Ruth. He was profoundly happy. Life was pitched high. He was in a fever that never broke. The joy of creation that is supposed to belong to the gods, was his. All the life about him, the odors of stale vegetables and soapsuds, the slatternly form of his sister and the jeering face of Mr. Higginbotham, was a dream. The real world was in his mind, and the stories he wrote were so many pieces of reality out of his mind.

The days were too short. There was so much he wanted to study. He cut his sleep down to five hours and found that he could get along upon it. He tried four hours and a half, and regretfully came back to five. He could joyfully have spent all his waking hours upon any one of his pursuits. It was with regret that he ceased from writing to study, that he ceased from study to go to the library, that he tore himself away from that chart-room of knowledge or from the magazines in the reading-room that were filled with the secrets of writers who succeeded in selling their wares. It was like severing heart-strings, when he was with Ruth, to stand up and go; and he scorched through the dark streets so as to get home to his books at the least possible expense of time. And hardest of all was it to shut up the algebra or physics, put note-book and pencil aside, and close his tired eyes in sleep. He hated the thought of ceasing to live, even for so short a time, and his sole consolation was that the alarm clock was set five hours ahead. He would lose only five hours anyway, and then the jangling bell would jerk him out of unconsciousness and he would have before him another glorious day of nineteen hours.

In the meantime the weeks were passing, his money was ebbing low, and there was no money coming in. A month after he had mailed it, the adventure serial for boys was returned to him by the *Youth's Companion*. The rejection slip was so tactfully worded that he felt kindly toward the editor. But he did not feel so kindly toward the editor of the *San Francisco Examiner*. After waiting two whole weeks, Martin had written to him. A week later he wrote again. At the end of the month, he went over to San Francisco and personally called upon the editor. But he did not meet that exalted personage, thanks to a Cerberus of an office-boy, of tender years and red hair, who guarded the portals. At the end of the fifth week the manuscript came back to him, by mail, without comment. There was no rejection slip, no explanation, nothing. In the same way his other articles were tied up with the other leading San Francisco papers. When he recovered them he sent them to the magazines in the East, from which they were returned more promptly, accompanied always by the printed rejection slips.

The short stories were returned in similar fashion. He read them over and over, and liked them so much that he could not puzzle out the cause of their rejection, until, one day, he read in a newspaper that manuscripts should always be typewritten. That explained it. Of course, editors were so busy that they could not afford the time and strain of reading handwriting. Martin rented a typewriter and spent a day mastering the machine. Each day he typed what he composed, and he typed his earlier manuscripts as fast as they were returned to him. He was surprised when the typed ones began to come back. His jaw seemed to become squarer, his chin more aggressive, and he bundled the manuscripts off to new editors.

The thought came to him that he was not a good judge of his own work. He tried it out on his sister. He read his stories aloud to her. Gertrude's eyes glistened, and she looked at him proudly as she said:

"Aint it grand, you writin' those sort of things."

"Yes, yes," he demanded impatiently. "But the story—how did you like it?"

"Just grand," was the reply. "Just grand, an' thrilling, too. I was all worked up."

He could see that her mind was not clear. The perplexity was strong in her good-natured face. So he waited.

"But, say, Mart," after a long pause, "how did it end? Did that young man who spoke so highfalutin' get her?"

And, after he had explained the end, which he thought he had made artistically obvious, she would say:

"That's what I wanted to know.

Why did n't you write that way in the story?"

One thing he learned, after he had read her a number of stories, namely, that she liked happy endings.

"That story was perfectly grand," she announced, straightening up from the wash-tub with a tired sigh and wiping the sweat from her forehead with a red, steamy hand; "but it makes me sad. I want to cry. There is too many sad things in the world anyway. It makes me happy to think about happy things. Now if he 'd married her, and * * * You dont mind, Mart?" she queried apprehensively. "I just happen to feel that way, because I 'm tired, I guess. But the story was grand just the same, perfectly grand. Where are you goin' to sell it?"

"That 's a horse of another color," he laughed.

"But if you *did* sell it, what do you think you 'd get for it?"

"Oh, a hundred dollars. That would be the least, the way prices go."

"My! I do hope you 'll sell it!"

"Easy money, eh?" Then he added proudly, "I wrote it in two days. That 's fifty dollars a day."

He longed to read his stories to Ruth, but did not dare. He would wait till some were published, he decided, then she would understand what he had been working for. In the meantime he toiled on. Never had the spirit of adventure lured him more strongly than on this amazing exploration of the realm of mind. He bought the text-books on physics and chemistry, and, along with his algebra, worked out problems and demonstrations. He took the laboratory proofs on faith, and his intense power of vision enabled him to see the reactions of chemicals more understandingly than the average student saw them in the laboratory. Martin wandered on through the heavy pages, overwhelmed by the clews he was getting to the nature of things. He had accepted the world as the world, but now he was comprehending the organization of it, the play and interplay of force and matter. Spontaneous explanations of old matters were continually arising in his mind. Levers and purchases fascinated him, and his mind roved backward to hand-spikes and blocks-and-tackles at sea. The theory of navigation, which enabled the ships to travel unerringly their courses over the pathless ocean, was made clear to him The mysteries of storm, and rain, and tide were revealed, and the reason for the existence of trade-winds made him wonder whether he had written his article on the northeast trade too soon. At any rate he knew he could write it better now. One afternoon he went out with Arthur to the University of California, and, with bated breath and a feeling of religious awe, went through the laboratories, saw demonstrations, and listened to a physics professor lecturing to his classes.

But he did not neglect his writing. A stream of short stories flowed from his pen, and he branched out into the easier forms of verse—the kind he saw printed in the magazines; though he lost his head and wasted two weeks on a tragedy in blank verse, the swift rejection of which, by half-a-dozen magazines dumbfounded him. Then he discovered Henley and wrote a series of sea-poems on the model of *Hospital Sketches.* They were simple poems, of light and color, and romance and adventure. "Sea Lyrics," he called them, and he judged them to be the best work he had yet done. There were thirty, and he completed them in a month, doing one a day after having done his regular day's work on fiction, which day's work was the equivalent to a week's work of the average successful writer. The toil meant nothing to him. It was not toil. He was finding speech, and all the beauty and wonder that had been pent for years behind his inarticulate lips was now pouring forth in a wild and virile flood.

He showed the "Sea Lyrics" to no one, not even to the editors. He had become distrustful of editors. But it was not distrust that prevented him from submitting the "Lyrics." They were so beautiful to him that he was impelled to save them to share with Ruth in some glorious, far-off time when he would dare to read to her what he had written. Against that time he kept them with him, reading them aloud, going over them until he knew them by heart.

He lived every moment of his waking hours, and he lived in his sleep, his subjective mind rioting through his five hours of surcease and combining the thoughts and events of the day into grotesque and impossible marvels. In reality, he never rested, and a weaker body or a less firmly poised brain would have been prostrated in a general break-down. His late afternoon calls on Ruth were rarer now, for June was approaching, when she would take her degree and finish with the University. Bachelor of Arts!—when he thought of her degree it seemed she fled beyond him faster than he could pursue.

One afternoon a week she gave to him, and, arriving late, he usually stayed for dinner and for music afterward. Those were his red-letter days. The atmosphere of the house, in such contrast with that in which he lived, and the mere nearness to her, sent him forth each time with a firmer grip on his resolve to climb the heights. In spite of the beauty in him, and the aching desire to create, it was for her that he struggled. He was a lover first and always. All other things he subordinated to love. Greater than his adventure in the world of thought was his love-adventure. The world itself was not so amazing because of the atoms and molecules that composed it according to the propulsions of irresistible force; what made it amazing was the fact that Ruth lived in it. She was the most amazing thing he had ever known, or dreamed, or guessed.

But he was oppressed always by her remoteness. She was so far from him, and he did not know how to approach her. He had been a success with girls and women in his own class; but he had never loved any of them, while he did love her, and, besides, she was not merely of another class. His very love elevated her above all classes. She was a being apart, so far apart that he did not know how to draw near to her as a lover should draw near. It was true, as he acquired knowledge and language, that he was drawing nearer, talking her speech, discovering ideas and delights in common; but this did not satisfy his lover's yearning. His lover's imagination had made her holy, too holy, too spiritualized to have any kinship with him in the flesh. It was his own love that thrust her from him and made her seem impossible for him. Love itself denied him the one thing that it desired.

And then, one day, without warning, the gulf between them was bridged for a moment, and thereafter, though the gulf remained, it was ever narrower. They had been eating cherries—great, luscious black cherries with a juice of the color of dark wine. And later, as she read aloud to him from "The Princess," he chanced to notice the stain of cherries on her lips. For the moment her divinity was shattered. She was clay, after all, mere clay, subject to the common law of clay as his clay was subject, or anybody's clay. Her lips were flesh like his, and cherries dyed them as cherries dyed his. And if so with her lips, then was it so with all of her. She was woman, all woman, just like any woman. It came upon him abruptly. It was a revelation that stunned him. It was as if he had seen the sun fall out of the sky, or had seen worshiped purity polluted.

Then he realized the significance of it, and his heart began pounding and challenging him to play the lover with this woman who was not a spirit from other worlds, but a mere woman with lips a cherry could stain. He trembled at the audacity of his thought; but all his soul was singing, and reason, in a triumphant paean, assured him he was right. Something of this change in him must have reached her, for she paused from her reading, looked up at him, and smiled. His eyes dropped from her blue eyes to her lips, and the sight of the stain maddened him. His arms all but flashed out to her and around her, in the way of his old careless life. She seemed to lean toward him, to wait, and all his will fought to hold him back.

"You were not following a word," she pouted.

Then she laughed at him, delighting in his confusion, and as he looked into her frank eyes and knew that she had divined nothing of what he felt, he became abashed. He had indeed in thought dared too far. Of all the women he had known there was no woman who would not have guessed—save her. And she had not guessed. There was the difference. She *was* different. He was appalled by his own grossness, awed by her clear innocence, and he gazed again at her across the gulf. The bridge had broken down.

But still the incident had brought him nearer. The memory of it persisted, and in the moments when he was most cast down he dwelt upon it eagerly. The gulf was never again so wide. He had accomplished a distance vastly greater than a bachelorship of arts, or a dozen bachelorships. She was pure, it was true, as he had never dreamed of purity; but cherries stained her lips. She was subject to the laws of the universe just as inexorably as he was. She had to eat to live, and when she got her feet wet she caught cold. But that was not the point. If she could feel hunger and thirst, and heat and cold, then could she feel love—and love for a man. Well, he was a man. And why could he not be *the* man. "It 's up to me to make good," he would murmur fervently. "I will be *the* man. I will make myself *the* man. I will make good."

CHAPTER XII.

EARLY one evening, struggling with a sonnet that twisted all awry the beauty and thought that trailed in glow and vapor through his brain, Martin was called to the telephone.

"It 's a lady's voice, a fine lady's," Mr. Higginbotham, who had called him, jeered.

Martin went to the telephone in the corner of the room, and felt a wave of warmth rush through him as he heard Ruth's voice. In his battle with the sonnet he had forgotten her existence, and at the sound of her voice his love for her smote him like a sudden blow. And such a voice!—delicate and sweet, like a strain of music heard far off and faint, or better, like a bell of silver, a perfect tone, crystal-pure. No mere woman had a voice like that. There was something celestial about it, and it came from other worlds. He could scarcely hear what it said, so ravished was he, though he controlled his face, for he knew that Mr. Higginbotham's ferret-eyes were fixed upon him.

It was not much that Ruth wanted to say—merely that Norman had been going to take her to a lecture that night, but that he had a headache, and she was so disappointed, and she had the tickets, and that if he had no other engagement would he be good enough to take her?

——Would he! He fought to suppress the eagerness in his voice. It was amazing. He had always seen her in her own house. And he had never dared to ask her to go anywhere with him. Quite irrelevantly, still at the telephone and talking with her, he felt an overpowering desire to die for her, and visions of heroic sacrifice shaped and dissolved in his whirling brain. He loved her so much, so terribly, so hopelessly. In that moment of mad happiness that she should go out with him, go to a lecture with him—with him, Martin Eden—she soared so far above him that there seemed nothing else for him to do than die for her. It was the only fit way in which he could express the tremendous and lofty emotion he felt for her. It was the sublime abnegation of true love that comes to all lovers, and it came to him there, at the telephone, in a whirlwind of fire and glory; and to die for her, he felt, was to have lived and loved well. And he was only twenty-one, and he had never been in love before.

His hand trembled as he hung up the receiver, and he was weak from the orgasm which had stirred him. His eyes were shining like an angel's, and his face was transfigured, purged of all earthly dross and pure and holy.

"Makin' dates outside, eh?" his brother-in-law sneered. "You know what that means. You 'll be in the police-court yet."

But Martin could not come down from the height. Not even the bestiality of the allusion could bring him back to earth. Anger and hurt were beneath him. He had seen a great vision and was as a god, and he could feel only profound and awful pity for this maggot of a man. He did not look at him, and, though his eyes passed over him, he did not see him; and as in a dream he passed out of the room to dress. It was not until he had reached his own room and was tying his necktie that he became aware of a sound that lingered unpleasantly in his ears. On investigating this sound he identified it as the final snort of Bernard Higginbotham which somehow had not penetrated to his brain before.

As Ruth's front door closed behind them and he came down the steps with her, he found himself greatly perturbed. It was not unalloyed bliss, taking her to the lecture. He did not know what he ought to do. He had seen on the streets, with persons of her class, that the women took the men's arms. But then, again, he had seen them when they did n't; and he wondered if it was only in the evening that arms were taken, or only between husbands and wives and relatives.

Just before he reached the sidewalk, he remembered Minnie. Minnie had always been a stickler. She had called him down, the second time she walked out with him, because he had gone along on the inside, and she had laid the law down to him that a gentleman always walked on the outside—when he was with a lady. And Minnie had made a practice of kicking his heels, whenever they crossed from one side the street to the other, to remind him to get over on the outside. He wondered where she had got that item of etiquette, and whether it had filtered down from above and was all right.

It would n't do any harm to try it, he decided, by the time they had reached the sidewalk; and he swung behind Ruth and took up his station on the outside. Then the other problem presented itself. Should he offer her his arm? He had never offered anybody his arm in his life. The girls he had known never took the fellows' arms. For the first several times they walked freely, side by side, and after that it was arms around the waists, and heads against the fellows' shoulders where the streets were unlighted. But this was different. She was n't that kind of a girl. He must do something.

He crooked the arm next to her—crooked it very slightly and with secret tentativeness, not invitingly, but just casually, as though he was accustomed to walk that way. And then the wonderful thing happened. He felt her hand upon his arm. Delicious thrills ran through him at the contact, and for a few sweet moments it seemed that he had left the solid earth and was flying with her through the air. But he was soon back again, perturbed by a new complication. They were crossing the street. This would put him on the inside. He should be on the outside. Should he therefore drop her arm and change over? And if he did so, would he have to repeat the maneuver the next time? And the next? There was something wrong about it, and he resolved not to caper about and play the fool. Yet he was not satisfied with his conclusion, and when he found himself on the inside he talked quickly and earnestly, making a show of being carried away by what he was saying, so that, in case he was wrong in not changing sides, his enthusiasm would seem the cause for his carelessness.

As they crossed Broadway, he came face to face with a new problem. In the blaze of the electric lights, he saw Lizzie Connolly and her giggly friend. Only for an instant he hesitated, then his hand went up and his hat came off. He could not be disloyal to his kind, and it was to more than Lizzie Connolly that his hat was lifted. She nodded and looked at him boldly, not with soft and gentle eyes like Ruth's, but with eyes that were handsome and hard and that swept on past him to Ruth and itemized her face and dress and station. And he was aware that Ruth looked, too, with quick eyes that were timid and mild as a dove's, but which saw, in a look that was a flutter on and past, the working-class girl in her cheap finery and under the strange hat that all working-class girls were wearing just then.

"What a pretty girl," Ruth said, a moment later.

Martin could have blessed her, though he said:

"I dont know. I guess it 's all a matter of personal taste, but she does n't strike me as being particularly pretty."

"Why, there is n't one woman in ten thousand with features as regular as hers. They are splendid. Her face is as clear-cut as a cameo. And her eyes are beautiful."

"Do you think so?" Martin queried absently, for to him there was only one beautiful woman in the world, and she was beside him, her hand upon his arm.

"Do I think so? If that girl had proper opportunity to dress, Mr. Eden, and if she were taught how to carry herself, you would be fairly dazzled by her, and so would all men."

"She would have to be taught how to speak," he commented, "or else most of the men would n't understand her. I 'm sure you could n't understand a quarter of what she said, if she just spoke naturally."

"Nonsense! You are as bad as Arthur when you try to make your point."

"You forget how I talked when you first met me. I have learned a new language since then. Before that time I talked as that girl talks. Now I can manage to make myself understood sufficiently in your language to explain that you do not know that other girl's language. And do you know why she carries herself the way she does? I think about such things now, though I never used to think about them, and I am beginning to understand—much."

"But why does she?"

"She has worked long hours for years at machines. When one's body is young it is very pliable, and hard work will mould it like putty according to the nature of the work. I can tell at a glance the trades of many workingmen I meet on the street. Look at me. Why am I rolling all about the shop? Because of the years I put in on the sea. If I 'd put in the same years cow-punching, with my body young and pliable, I would n't be rolling now, but I 'd be bow-legged. And so with that girl. You noticed that her eyes were what I might call hard. She has never been sheltered. She has had to take care of herself, and a young girl cant take care of herself and keep her eyes soft and gentle like—like yours, for example."

"I think you are right," Ruth said in a low voice. "And it is too bad. She is such a pretty girl."

He looked at her and saw her eyes luminous with pity. And then he remembered that he loved her and was lost in amazement at his fortune that permitted him to love her and to take her on his arm to a lecture.

Who are you, Martin Eden? he demanded of himself in the looking-glass, that night, when he got back to his room. He gazed at himself long and curiously. Who are you? What are you? Where do you belong? You belong by rights to girls like Lizzie Connolly. You belong with the legions of toil, with all that is low, and vulgar, and unbeautiful. You belong with the oxen and the drudges, in dirty surroundings among smells and stenches. There are the stale vegetables now. Those potatoes are rotting. Smell them, damn you, smell them. And yet you dare to open the books, to listen to beautiful music, to learn to love beautiful paintings, to speak good English, to think thoughts that none of your own kind thinks, to tear yourself away from the oxen and the Lizzie Connollys and to love a pale spirit of a woman who is a million miles beyond you and who lives in the stars. Who are you? and what are you? damn you! And are you going to make good?

He shook his fist at himself in the glass, and sat down on the edge of the bed to dream for a space with wide eyes. Then he got out notebook and algebra and lost himself in quadratic equations while the hours slipped by, and the stars dimmed, and the gray of dawn flooded against his window.

Martin Eden

By Jack London

Author of "The Call of the Wild," "Sea Wolf," "The God of His Fathers," "White Fang," etc.

CHAPTER XIII.

IT WAS the knot of wordy socialists and working-class philosophers that held forth in the City Hall Park on warm afternoons that was responsible for the great discovery. Once or twice in the month, while riding through the park on his way to the library, Martin dismounted from his wheel and listened to the arguments, and each time he tore himself away reluctantly. The tone of discussion was much lower than at Mr. Morse's table. The men were not grave and dignified. They lost their tempers easily and called one another names, while oaths and obscene allusions were frequent on their lips. Once or twice he had seen them come to blows. And yet, he knew not why, there seemed something vital about the stuff of these men's thoughts. Their logomachy was far more stimulating to his intellect than the reserved and quiet dogmatism of Mr. Morse. These men, who slaughtered English, gesticulated like lunatics, and fought one another's ideas with primitive anger, seemed somehow to be more alive than Mr. Morse and his crony, Mr. Butler.

Martin had heard Herbert Spencer quoted several times in the park, but one afternoon a disciple of Spencer's appeared, a seedy tramp with a dirty coat buttoned tightly at the throat to conceal the absence of a shirt. Battle royal was waged, amid the smoking of many cigarettes and the expectoration of much tobacco juice, wherein the tramp successfully held his own, even when a socialist workman sneered: "There is no god but the Unknowable, and Herbert Spencer is his prophet." Martin was puzzled as to what the discussion was about, but when he rode on to the library he carried with him a new-born interest in Herbert Spencer, and because of the frequency with which the tramp had mentioned *First Principles* Martin drew out that volume.

So the great discovery began. Once before he had tried Spencer, and, choosing the *Principles of Psychology* to begin with, he had failed as abjectly as he had failed with Madame Blavatsky. There had been no understanding the book, and he had returned it unread. But this night, after algebra and physics, and an attempt at a sonnet, he got into bed and opened *First Principles*. Morning found him still reading. It was impossible for him to sleep. Nor did he write that day. He lay on the bed till his body grew tired, when he tried the hard floor, reading on his back, the book held in the air above him, or changing from side to side. He slept that night, and did his writing next morning, and then the book tempted him and he fell, reading all afternoon, oblivious to everything and oblivious to the fact that that was the afternoon Ruth gave to him. His first consciousness of the immediate world about him was when Bernard Higginbotham jerked open the door and demanded to know if he thought they were running a restaurant.

Martin Eden had been mastered by curiosity all his days. He wanted to know, and it was this desire that had sent him adventuring over the world. But he was now learning from Spencer that he never had known, and that he never could have known had he continued his sailing and wandering forever. He had merely skimmed over the surface of things, observing detached phenomena, accumulating fragments of facts, making superficial little generalizations—and all and everything quite unrelated in a capricious and disorderly world of whim and chance. The mechanism of the flight of birds he had watched and reasoned about with understanding; but it had never entered his head to try to explain the process whereby birds, as organic flying mechanisms, had been developed. He had never dreamed there was such a process. That birds should have come to be, was unguessed. They always had been. They just happened.

And as it was with birds, so it had been with everything. His ignorant and unprepared attempts at philosophy had been fruitless. The medieval metaphysics of Kant had given him the key to nothing, and had served the sole purpose of making him doubt his own intellectual powers. In similar manner, his attempt to study evolution had been confined to a hopelessly technical volume by Romanes. He had understood nothing, and the only idea he had gathered was that evolution was a dry-as-dust theory of a lot of little men possessed of huge and unintelligible vocabularies. And now he learned that evolution was no mere theory but an accepted process of development; that scientists no longer disagreed about it; their only differences being over the method of evolution.

And here was the man Spencer, organizing all knowledge for him, reducing everything to unity, elaborating ultimate realities, and presenting to his startled gaze a universe so concrete of realization that it was like the model of a ship such as sailors make and put into glass bottles. There was no caprice, no chance. All was law. It was in obedience to law that the bird flew, and it was in obedience to the same law that fermenting slime had writhed and squirmed and put out legs and wings and become a bird.

Martin had ascended from pitch to pitch of intellectual living, and here he was at a higher pitch than ever. All the hidden things were laying their secrets bare. He was drunken with comprehension. At night, asleep, he lived with the gods in colossal nightmare; and awake, in the day, he went around like a somnambulist, with absent stare, gazing upon the world he had just discovered. At table he failed to hear the conversation about petty and ignoble things, his eager mind seeking out and following cause and effect in everything before him. In the meat on the platter he saw the shining sun and traced its energy back through all its transformations to its source a hundred million miles away, or traced its energy ahead to the moving muscles in his arms that enabled him to cut the meat, and to the brain wherewith he willed the muscles to move to cut the meat, until, with inward gaze, he saw the same sun shining in his brain. He was entranced by illumination, and did not hear the "bughouse," whispered by Jim, nor see the anxiety on his sister's face, nor notice the rotary motion of Bernard Higginbotham's finger whereby he imparted the suggestion of wheels revolving in his brother-in-law's head.

What, in a way, most profoundly impressed Martin, was the correlation of knowledge—of all knowledge. He had been curious to know things, and whatever he acquired he had filed away in separate memory compartments in his brain. Thus, on the subject of sailing he had an immense store. On the subject of woman he had a fairly large store. But these two subjects had been unrelated. Between the two memory compartments there had been no connection. That, in the fabric of knowledge, there should be any connection whatever between a woman with hysterics and a schooner carrying a weather-helm or heaving to in a gale, would have struck him as ridiculous and impossible. But Herbert Spencer had shown him not only that it was not ridiculous, but that it was impossible for there to be no connection. All things were related to all other things, from the farthermost star in the wastes of space to the myriads of atoms in the grain of sand under one's foot. This new concept was a perpetual amazement to Martin, and he found himself engaged continually in tracing the relationship between all things under the sun and on the other side of the sun. He drew up lists of the most incongruous things and was unhappy until he succeeded in establishing kinship between them all—kinship between love, poetry, earthquake, fire, rattlesnakes, rainbows, precious gems, monstrosities, sunsets, the roaring of lions, illuminating gas, cannibalism, beauty, murder, levers and fulcrums, and tobacco. Thus, he unified the universe and held it up and looked at it, or wandered through its byways and alleys and jungles, not as a terrified traveler in the thick of mysteries seeking an unknown goal, but observing and charting and becoming familiar with all there was to know. And the more he knew, the more passionately he admired the universe, and life, and his own life in the midst of it all.

"You fool!" he cried at his image in the looking-glass. "You wanted to write, and you tried to write, and you had nothing in you to write about. What did you have in you?—some childish notions, a few half-baked sentiments, a lot of undigested beauty, a great black mass of ignorance, a heart filled to bursting with love, and an ambition as big as your love and as futile as your ignorance. And you wanted to write! Why, you're just on the edge of beginning to get something in you to write about. You wanted to create beauty, but how could you when you knew nothing about the nature of beauty? You wanted to write about life when you knew nothing of the essential characteristics of life. You wanted to write about the world and the scheme of existence when the world was a Chinese puzzle to you, and all that you could have written would have been about what you did not know of the scheme of existence. But cheer up, Martin, my boy. You'll write yet. You know a little, a very little, and you're on the right road now to know more. Some day, if you're lucky, you may come pretty close to knowing all that may be known. Then you will write."

He brought his great discovery to Ruth, sharing with her all his joy and wonder in it. But she did not seem to be so enthusiastic over it. She tacitly accepted it, and, in a way, seemed aware of it from her own studies. It did not stir her deeply, as it did him, and he would have been surprised had he not reasoned it out that it was not new and fresh to her as it was to him. Arthur and Norman, he found, believed in evolution and had read Spencer, though it did not seem to have made any vital impression upon them, while the young fellow with the glasses and the mop of hair, Will Olney, sneered disagreeably at Spencer and repeated the epigram: "There is no God but the Unknowable, and Herbert Spencer is his prophet."

But Martin forgave him the sneer, for he had begun to discover that Olney was not in love with Ruth. Later, he was dumbfounded to learn from various little happenings not only that Olney did not care for Ruth, but that he had a positive dislike for her. Martin could not understand this. It was a bit of phenomena that he could not correlate with all the rest of the phenomena in the universe. But nevertheless he felt sorry for the young fellow because of the great lack in his nature that prevented him from a proper appreciation of Ruth's fineness and beauty. They rode out into the hills several Sundays on their wheels, and Martin had ample opportunity to observe the armed truce that existed between Ruth and Olney. The latter chummed with Norman, throwing Arthur and Martin into company with Ruth, for which Martin was duly grateful.

Those Sundays were great days for Martin, greatest because he was with Ruth, and great, also, because they were putting him more on a par with the young men of her class. In spite of their long years of disciplined education, he was finding himself their intellectual equal, and the hours spent with them in conversation was so much practice for him in the use of the grammar he had studied so hard. He had abondoned the etiquette books, falling back upon observation to show him the right things to do. Except when carried away by his enthusiasm, he was always on guard, keenly watchful of their actions and learning their little courtesies and refinements of conduct.

The fact that Spencer was very little read was for some time a source of surprise to Martin. "Herbert Spencer—" said the man at the desk in the library. "Oh, yes, a great mind." But the man did not seem to know anything of the content of that great mind. One evening, at dinner, when Mr. Butler was there, Martin turned the conversation upon Spencer. Mr. Morse bitterly arraigned the English philosopher's agnosticism, but confessed that he had not read *First Principles;* while Mr. Butler stated that he had no patience with Spencer, had never read a line of him, and had managed to get along quite well without him. Doubts arose in Martin's mind, and had he been less strongly individual, he would have accepted the general opinion and given Herbert Spencer up. As it was, he found Spencer's explanation of things convincing; and, as he phrased it to himself, to give up Spencer would be equivalent to a navigator throwing the compass and chronometer overboard. So Martin went on into a thorough study of evolution, mastering more and more the subject himself, and being convinced by the corroborative testimony of a thousand independent writers. The more he studied the more vistas he caught of fields of knowledge yet unexplored, and the regret that days were only twenty-four hours long became a chronic complaint with him.

One day, because the days were so short, he decided to give up algebra and geometry. Trigonometry he had not even attempted. Then he cut chemistry from his study list, retaining only physics.

"I am not a specialist," he said, in defense, to Ruth. "Nor am I going to try to be a specialist. There are too many special fields for any one man, in a whole lifetime, to master a tithe of them. I must pursue general knowledge. When I need the work of specialists I shall refer to their books."

"But that is not like having the knowledge yourself," she protested.

"But it is unnecessary to have it. We profit from the work of the specialists. That's what they are for. When I came in I noticed the chimney-sweeps at work. They're specialists, and when they get done you will enjoy clean chimneys without knowing anything about the construction of chimneys."

"That's far-fetched, I am afraid."

She looked at him curiously, and he felt a reproach in her gaze and manner. But he was convinced of the rightness of his position.

"All thinkers on general subjects, the greatest minds in the world, in fact, rely on the specialists. Herbert Spencer did that. He generalized upon the findings of thousands of investigators. He would have had to live a thousand lives in order to do it all himself. And so with Darwin. He took advantage of all that had been learned by the florists and cattlebreeders."

"You're right, Martin," Olney said. "You know what you're after, and Ruth does n't. She does n't know what she is after for herself even."

"——Oh, yes," Olney rushed on, heading off her objection, "I know you call it general culture. But it does n't matter what you study if you want general culture. You can study French, or you can study German, or cut them both out and study Esperanto, you'll get the culture tone just the same. You can study Greek or Latin, too, for the same purpose, though it will never by any use to you. It will be culture, though. Why, Ruth studied Saxon, became clever in it—that was two years ago, and all that she remembers of it now is, 'Whan that sweet Aprile with his schowers soote'—is n't that the way it goes?

"But it's given you the culture tone just the same," he laughed, again heading her off. "I know. We were in the same classes."

"But you speak of culture as if it should be a means to something," Ruth cried out. Her eyes were flashing, and in her cheeks were two spots of color. "Culture is the end in itself."

"But that is not what Martin wants."

"How do you know?"

"What do you want, Martin?" Olney demanded, turning squarely upon him.

Martin felt very uncomfortable, and looked entreaty at Ruth.

"Yes, what do you want?" Ruth asked. "That will settle it."

"Yes, of course, I want culture," Martin faltered. "I love beauty, and culture will give me a finer and keener appreciation of beauty."

She nodded her head and looked triumph.

"Rot, and you know it," was Olney's comment. "Martin's after career, not culture. It just happens that culture, in his case, is incidental to career. If he wanted to be a chemist, culture would be unnecessary. Martin wants to write, but he's afraid to say so because it will put you in the wrong.

"And why does Martin want to write?" he went on. "Because he is n't rolling in wealth. Why do you fill your head with Saxon and general culture? Because you dont have to make your way in the world. Your father sees to that. He buys your clothes for you, and all the rest. What rotten good is our education, yours and mine, and Arthur's and Norman's? We're soaked in general culture, and if our daddies went broke today, we'd be falling down tomorrow on teachers' examinations. The best job you could get, Ruth, would be a country school or music teacher in a girls' boarding school."

"And pray what would you do?" she asked.

"Not a blessed thing. I could earn a dollar and a half a day, common labor, and I might get in as instructor in Hanley's cramming joint—I say might, mind you, and I might be chucked out at the end of the week for sheer inability."

Martin followed the discussion closely, and while he was convinced that Olney was right, he resented the rather cavalier treatment he accorded Ruth. A new conception of love formed in his mind as he listened. Reason had nothing to do with love. It mattered not whether the woman he loved reasoned correctly or incorrectly. Love was above reason. If it just happened that she did not fully appreciate his necessity for a career, that did not make her a bit less lovable. She was all lovable, and what she thought had nothing to do with her lovableness.

"What's that?" he replied to a question from Olney that broke in upon his train of thought.

"I was saying that I hoped you would'nt be fool enough to tackle Latin."

"But Latin is more than culture," Ruth broke in. "It is equipment."

"Well, are you going to tackle it?" Olney persisted.

Martin was sore beset. He could see that Ruth was hanging eagerly upon his answer.

"I am afraid I won't have time," he said finally. "I'd like to, but I won't have time."

"You see, Martin's not soaking culture," Olney exulted. "He's trying to get somewhere, to do something."

"Oh, but it's mental training. It's mind discipline. It's what makes disciplined minds." Ruth looked expectantly at Martin, as if waiting for him to change his judgment. "You know, the football players have to train before the big game. And that is what Latin does for the thinker. It trains."

"Rot and bosh! That's what they told us when we were kids. But there is one thing they did n't tell us then. They let us find it out for ourselves afterwards." Olney paused for effect, then added, "and what they did n't tell us was that every gentleman should have studied Latin but that no gentleman should know Latin."

"Now, that's unfair," Ruth cried. "I knew you were turning the conversation just in order to get off something."

"It's clever all right," was the retort, "but it's fair, too. The only men who know their Latin are the apothecaries, the lawyers, and the Latin professors. And if Martin wants to be one of them, I miss my guess. But what's all that got to do with Herbert Spencer, anyway? Martin's just discovered Spencer, and he's wild over him. Why? Because Spencer is taking him somewhere. Spencer could n't take me anywhere, nor you. We have n't got anywhere to go. You'll get married some day, and I'll have nothing to do but keep track of the lawyers and business agents who will take care of the money my father's going to leave me."

Olney got up to go, but turned at the door and delivered this parting shot:

"You leave Martin alone, Ruth. He knows what's best for himself. Look at what he's done already. He makes me sick sometimes, sick and ashamed of myself. He knows more now about the world, and life, and man's place, and all the rest, than Arthur, or Norman, or I, or you, too, for that matter, and in spite of all our Latin, and French, and Saxon, and culture."

"But Ruth is my teacher," Martin answered chivalrously. "She is responsible for what little I have learned."

"Rats." Olney looked at Ruth, and his expression was malicious. "I suppose you'll be telling me next that you read Spencer on her recommendation—only you did n't. And she does n't know anything more about Darwin and evolution than I do about King Solomon's mines.

What's that jawbreaker definition about something or other of Spencer's, that you sprang on us the other day?—that indefinite, incoherent homogeneity thing. Spring it on her, and see if she understands a word of it. That is n't culture, you see. Well, tra la, and if you tackle Latin, Martin, I wont have any respect for you."

And all the while, interested in the discussion, Martin had been aware of an irk in it as well. It was about studies and lessons, dealing with the rudiments of knowledge, and the schoolboyish tone of it conflicted with the big things that were stirring in him—with the grip upon life that was even then crooking his fingers like eagle's talons, with the cosmic thrills that made him ache, and with the inchoate consciousness of mastery of it all. He likened himself to a poet, wrecked on the shores of a strange land, filled with power of beauty, stumbling and stammering and vainly trying to sing in the rough barbaric tongue of his brethren in the new land. And so with him. He was alive, painfully alive, to the great universal things, and yet he was compelled to potter and grope among schoolboy topics and debate whether or not he should study Latin.

"What in hell has Latin to do with it?" he demanded before his mirror that night. "I wish dead people would stay dead. Why should I and the beauty in me be ruled by the dead? Beauty is alive and everlasting. Languages come and go. They are the dust of the dead."

And his next thought was that he had been phrasing her ideas very well, and he went to bed wondering why he could not talk in similar fashion when he was with Ruth. He was only a schoolboy, with a schoolboy's tongue, when he was in her presence.

"Give me time," he said aloud. "Only give me time."

Time! Time! Time! was his unending plaint.

CHAPTER XIV.

IT WAS not because of Olney, but in spite of Ruth, and his love for Ruth, that he finally decided not to take up Latin. His money meant time. There was so much that was more important than Latin, so many studies that clamored with imperious voices. And he must write. He must earn money. He had had no acceptances. Two score of manuscripts were traveling the endless round of the magazines. How did the others do it? He spent long hours in the free reading-room, going over what others had written, studying their work eagerly and critically, comparing it with his own, and wondering, wondering, about the secret trick they had discovered which enabled them to sell their work.

He was amazed at the immense amount of printed stuff that was dead. No light, no life, no color, was shot through it. There was no breath of life in it, and yet it sold, at two cents a word, twenty dollars a thousand—the newspaper clipping had said so. He was puzzled by countless short stories, written lightly and cleverly, he confessed, but without vitality or reality. Life was so strange and wonderful, filled with an immensity of problems, of dreams, and of heroic toils, and yet these stories dealt only with the commonplaces of life. He felt the stress and strain of life, its fevers and sweats and wild insurgences—surely this was the stuff to write about! He wanted to glorify the leaders of forlorn hopes, the mad lovers, the giants that fought under stress and strain, amid terror and tragedy, making life crackle with the strength of their endeavor. And yet the magazine short stories seemed intent on glorifying the Mr. Butlers, the sordid dollar-chasers, and the commonplace little love affairs of commonplace little men and women. Was it because the editors of the magazines were commonplace? he demanded. Or were they afraid of life?—these writers and editors and readers?

But his chief trouble was that he did not know any editors or writers. And not merely did he not know any writers, but he did not know anybody who had ever attempted to write. There was nobody to tell him, to hint to him, to give him the least word of advice. He began to doubt that editors were real men. They seemed cogs in a machine. That was what it was, a machine. He poured his soul into stories, articles and poems, and entrusted them to the machine. He folded them just so, put the proper stamps inside the long envelope along with the manuscript, sealed the envelope, put more stamps outside, and dropped it into the mail-box. It traveled across the continent, and after a certain lapse of time the postman returned him the manuscript in another long envelope, on the outside of which were the stamps he had inclosed. There was no human editor at the other end, but a mere cunning arrangement of cogs that changed the manuscript from one envelope to another and stuck on the stamps. It was like the slot machines wherein one dropped pennies, and, with a metallic whirl of machinery, had delivered to him a stick of chewing-gum or a tablet of chocolate. It depended upon which slot one dropped the penny in, whether he got chocolate or gum. And so with the editorial machine. One slot brought checks and the other brought rejection slips. So far he had found only the latter slot.

It was the rejection slips that completed the horrible machine-likeness of the process. These slips were printed, in stereotyped forms, and he had received hundreds of them—as many as a dozen or more on each of his earlier manuscripts. If he had received one line, one personal line, along with one rejection of all his rejections, he would have been cheered. But not one editor had given that proof of existence. And he could conclude only that there were no warm human men at the other end, only mere cogs, well-oiled and running beautifully in the machine.

He was a good fighter, whole-souled and stubborn, and he would have been content to continue feeding the machine for years; but he was bleeding to death, and not years but weeks would determine the fight. Each week his board bill brought him nearer destruction, while the postage on forty manuscripts bled him almost as severely. He no longer bought books, and he economized in petty ways and sought to delay the inevitable end; though he did not know how to economize, and brought the end nearer by a week when he gave his sister Marian five dollars for a dress.

He struggled in the dark, without advice, without encouragement, and in the teeth of discouragement. Even Gertrude was beginning to look askance. At first she had tolerated with sisterly fondness what she conceived to be his foolishness; but now, out of sisterly solicitude, she grew anxious. To her it seemed that his foolishness was becoming a madness. Martin knew this and suffered more keenly from it than from the open and nagging contempt of Bernard Higginbotham. Martin had faith in himself, but he was alone in this faith. Not even Ruth had faith. She wanted him to devote himself to study, and, though she had not openly disapproved of his writing, she had never approved.

He had never offered to show her his work. A fastidious delicacy had prevented him. Besides, she had been studying heavily at the University, and he felt averse to robbing her of her time. But when she had taken her degree she asked him herself to let her see something of what he had been doing. Martin was elated and diffident. Here was a judge. She was a bachelor of arts. She had studied literature under skilled instructors. Perhaps the editors were capable judges, too. But she would be different from them. She would not hand him a stereotyped rejection slip, nor would she inform him that lack of preference for his work did not necessarily imply lack of merit in his work. She would talk, a warm human being, in her quick, bright way, and, most important of all, she would catch glimpses of the real Martin Eden. In his work she would discern what his heart and soul were like, and she would come to understand something, a little something, of the stuff of his dreams and the strength of his power.

Martin gathered together a number of carbon copies of his short stories, hesitated a moment, then added his "Sea Lyrics." They mounted their wheels on a late June afternoon and rode for the hills. It was the second time he had been out with her alone, and as they rode along through the balmy warmth, just chilled by the sea breeze to refreshing coolness, he was profoundly impressed by the fact that it was a very beautiful and well-ordered world and that it was good to be alive and to love. They left their wheels by the roadside and climbed to the brown top of an open knoll where the sunburnt grass breathed a harvest breath of dry sweetness and content.

"It's work is done," Martin said, as they seated themselves, she upon his coat, and he sprawling close to the warm earth. He sniffed the sweetness of the tawny grass, which entered his brain and set his thoughts whirling on from the particular to the universal. "It has achieved its reason for existence," he went on, patting the dry grass affectionately. "It quickened with ambition under the dreary downpour of last winter, fought the violent early spring, flowered and lured the insects and the bees, scattered its seeds, squared itself with its duty and the world, and—"

"Why do you always look at things with such dreadfully practical eyes?" she interrupted.

"Because I've been studying evolution, I guess. It's only recently that I got my eyesight, if the truth were told."

"But it seems to me you lose sight of beauty by being so practical, that you destroy beauty like the boys who catch butterflies and rub the down off their beautiful wings."

He shook his head.

"Beauty has significance, but I never knew its significance before. I just accepted beauty as something meaningless, as something that was just beautiful without rhyme or reason. I did not know anything about beauty. But now I know, or, rather, am just beginning to know. This grass is more beautiful to me now that I know why it is grass and all the hidden chemistry of sun and rain and earth that makes it become grass. Why, there is romance in the life-history of any grass, yes, and adventure, too. The very thought of it stirs me. When I think of the play of force and matter and all the tremendous struggle of it, I feel as if I could write an epic on the grass."

"How well you talk," she said absently, and he noted that she was looking at him in a searching way.

He was all confusion and embarrassment on the instant, the blood flushing red on his neck and brow.

"I hope I am learning to talk," he stammered. "There seems to me to be so much in me I want to say. But it is all so big. I can't find ways to say what is really in me. Sometimes it seems to me that all the world, all life, everything, had taken up residence inside of me and was clamoring for me to be the spokesman. I feel—oh, I can't describe it—I feel the bigness of it, but when I speak I babble like a little child. It is a great task to transmute feeling and sensation into speech, written or spoken, that will, in turn, in him who reads or listens, transmute itself back into the self-same feeling and sensation. It is a lordly task. See, I bury my face in the grass, and the breath I draw in through my nostrils sets me quivering with a thousand thoughts and fancies. It is a breath of the universe I have breathed. I know song and laughter, and success and pain, and struggle and death; and I see visions that arise in my brain somehow out of the scent of the grass, and I would like to tell them to you, to the world. But how can I? My tongue is tied. I have tried, by the spoken word, just now, to describe to you the effect on me of the scent of the grass. But I have not succeeded. I have no more than hinted in awkward speech. My words seem gibberish to me. And yet I am stifled with desire to tell. Oh!—" He threw up his hands with a despairing gesture— "It is impossible. It is not understandable! It is incommunicable!"

"But you do talk well," she insisted. "Just think how you have improved in the short time I have known you. Mr. Butler is a noted public speaker. He is always asked by the state committee to go out on stump during campaign. Yet you talked just as well as he the other night at dinner. Only he was more controlled. You get too excited; but you will get over that with practice. Why, you would make a good public speaker. You can go far . . . if you want to. You are masterly. You can lead men, I am sure, and there is no reason why you should not succeed at anything you set your hand to, just as you have succeeded with grammar. You would make a good lawyer. You would shine in politics. There is nothing to prevent you from making as great a success as Mr. Butler has made. And minus the dyspepsia," she added with a smile.

They talked on, she in her gently persistent way, returning always to the need of thorough grounding in education and to the advantages of Latin as part of the foundation for any career. She drew her ideal of the successful man, and it was largely in her father's image, with a few unmistakable lines and touches of color from the image of Mr. Butler. He listened eagerly, with receptive ears, lying on his back and looking up and joying in each movement of her lips as she talked. But his brain was not receptive. There was nothing alluring in the pictures she drew, and he was aware of a dull pain of disappointment and of a sharper ache of love for her. In all she said there was no mention of his writing, and the manuscripts he had brought to read lay neglected on the ground.

At last, in a pause, he glanced at the sun, measured its height above the horizon, and suggested his manuscripts by picking them up.

"I had forgotten," she said quickly. "And I am so anxious to hear."

He read to her a story, one that he flattered himself was among his very best. He called it "The Wine of Life," and the wine of it, that had stolen into his brain when he wrote it, stole into his brain now as he read it. There was a certain magic in the original conception, and he had adorned it with more magic of phrase and touch. All the old fire and passion with which he had written it were reborn in him, and he was swayed and swept away so that he was blind and deaf to the faults of it. But it was not so with Ruth. Her trained ear detected the weaknesses and exaggerations, the over-emphasis of the tyro, and she was instantly aware each time the sentence-rhythm tripped and faltered. She scarcely noted the rhythm otherwise, except when it became too pompous, at which moments she was disagreeably impressed with its amateurishness. That was her final judgment on the story as a whole—amateurish, though she did not tell him so. Instead, when he had done, she pointed out the minor flaws and said that she liked the story.

But he was disappointed. Her criticism was just. He acknowledged that, but he had a feeling that he was not sharing his work with her for the purpose of schoolroom correction. The details did not matter. They could take care of themselves. He could mend them, he could learn to mend them. Out of life he had captured something big and attempted to imprison it in the story. It was the big thing out of life he had read to her, not sentence structure and semicolons. He wanted her to feel with him this big thing that was his, that he had seen with his own eyes, grappled with his own brain, and placed there on the page with his own hands in printed words. Well, he had failed, was his secret decision. Perhaps the editors were right. He had felt the big thing, but he had failed to transmute it. He concealed his disappointment, and joined so easily with her in her criticism that she did not realize that deep down in him was running a strong undercurrent of disagreement.

This next thing I've called 'The Pot,''' he said, unfolding the manuscript. "It has been refused by four or five magazines now, but still I think it is good. In fact I dont know what to think of it, except that I've caught something there. Maybe it wont affect you as it does me. It's a short thing—only two thousand words."

"How dreadful!" she cried, when he had finished. "It is horrible, unutterably horrible!"

He noted her pale face, her eyes wide and tense, and her clenched hands, with secret satisfaction. He had succeeded. He had communicated the stuff of fancy and feeling from out of his brain. It had struck home. No matter whether she liked it or not, it had gripped her and mastered her, made her sit there and listen and forget details.

"It is life," he said, "and life is not always beautiful. And yet, perhaps because I am strangely made, I find something beautiful there. It seems to me that the beauty is tenfold enhanced because it is there—"

"But why could n't the poor woman —" she broke in disconnectedly. Then she felt the revolt of her thought unexpressed to cry out, "Oh! It is degrading! It is not nice! It is nasty!"

For the moment it seemed to him that his heart stood still. *Nasty!* He had never dreamed it. He had not meant it. The whole sketch stood before him in letters of fire, and in such blaze of illumination he sought vainly for nastiness. Then his heart began to beat again. He was not guilty.

"Why did n't you select a nice subject?" she was saying. "We know there are nasty things in the world, but that is no reason—"

She talked on in her indignant strain, but he was not following her. He was smiling to himself as he looked up into her virginal face, so innocent, so penetratingly innocent, that its purity seemed always to enter into him, driving out of him all dross and bathing him in some ethereal effulgence that was as cool and soft and velvety as starshine. *We know there are nasty things in the world!* He cuddled to him the notion of her knowing, and chuckled over it as a love-joke. The next moment, in a flashing vision of multitudinous detail, he sighted the whole sea of life's nastiness that he had known and voyaged over and through, and he forgave her for not understanding the story. It was through no fault of hers that she could not understand. He thanked God that she had been born and sheltered to such innocence. But he knew life, its foulness as well as its fairness, its greatness in spite of the slime that infested it, and by God he was going to have his say on it to the world. Saints in heaven—how could they be anything but fair and pure? No praise to them. But saints in slime—ah, that was the everlasting wonder! That was what made life worth while. To see moral grandeur rising out of cesspools of iniquity; to rise himself and first glimpse beauty, faint and far, through mud-dripping eyes; to see, out of weakness, and frailty, and viciousness, and all abyssmal brutishness, arising strength, and truth, and high spiritual endowment—

He caught a stray sequence of sentences she was uttering.

"The tone of it all is low. And there is so much that is high. Take 'In Memoriam.'"

He was impelled to suggest "Locksley Hall" and would have done so, had not his vision gripped him again and left him staring at her, the female of his kind, who, out of the primordial ferment, creeping and crawling up the vast ladder of life for a thousand thousand centuries, had emerged on the topmost rung, having become one, Ruth, pure, and fair and divine, and with power to make him know love, and to aspire toward purity, and to desire to taste divinity—him, Martin Eden, who, too, had come up in some amazing fashion from out of the ruck and the mire and the countless mistakes and abortions of unending creation. There was the romance, and the wonder, and the glory. There was the stuff to write, if he could only find speech. Saints in heaven!—They were only saints and could not help themselves. But he was a man.

"You have strength," he could hear her saying, "but it is untutored strength."

"Like a bull in a china shop," he suggested, and won a smile.

"And you must develop discrimination. You must consult taste, and fineness, and tone."

"I dare too much," he muttered.

She smiled approbation, and settled herself to listen to another story.

"I don't know what you'll make of this," he said, apologetically. "It's a funny thing. I'm afraid I got beyond my depth in it, but my intentions were good. Dont bother about the little features of it. Just see if you catch the feel of the big thing in it. It is big, and it is true, though the chance is large that I have failed to make it intelligible."

He read, and as he read he watched her. At last he had reached her, he thought. She sat without movement, her eyes steadfast upon him, scarcely breathing, caught up and out of herself, he thought, by the witchery of the thing he had created. He had entitled the story, "Adventure," and it was the apotheosis of adventure—not of the adventure of the story-books, but of real adventure, the savage taskmaster, awful of punishment and awful of reward, faithless and whimsical, demanding terrible patience and heartbreaking days and nights of toil, offering the blazing sunlight glory or dark death at the end of thirst and famine or of the long drag and monstrous delirium of rotting fever, through blood and sweat and stinging insects leading up by long chains of petty and ignoble contacts to royal culminations and lordly achievements.

It was this, all of it, and more, that he had put into his story, and it was this, he believed, that warmed her as she sat and listened. Her eyes were wide, color was in her pale cheeks, and before he finished it seemed to him that she was almost panting. Truly she was warmed; but she was warmed, not by the story, but by him. She did not think much of the story; it was Martin's intensity of power, the old excess of strength that seemed to pour from his body and on and over her. The paradox of it was that it was the story itself that was freighted with his power, that was the channel, for the time being, through which his strength poured out to her. She was aware only of the strength, and not of the medium, and when she seemed most carried away by what he had written, in reality she had been carried away by something quite foreign to it—by a thought, terrible and perilous, that had formed itself unsummoned in her brain. She had caught herself wondering what marriage was like, and the becoming conscious of the waywardness and ardor of the thought had terrified her. It was unmaidenly. It was not like her. She had never been tormented by womanhood, and she had lived in a dreamland of Tennysonian poesy, dense even to the full significance of that delicate master's delicate allusions to the grossnesses that intrude upon the relations of queens and knights. She had been asleep, always, and now life was thundering imperatively at all her doors. Mentally she was in a panic to shoot the bolts and drop the bars into place, while wanton instincts urged her to throw wide her portals and bid the deliciously strange visitor to enter in.

Martin waited with satisfaction for her verdict. He had no doubt of what it would be, and he was astounded when he heard her say:

"It is beautiful."

"It *is* beautiful," she repeated, with emphasis, after a pause.

Of course it was beautiful; but there was something more than mere beauty in it, something more stingingly splendid which had made beauty its handmaiden. He sprawled silently on the ground, watching the grisly form of a great doubt rising before him. He had failed. He was inarticulate. He had seen one of the greatest things in the world, and he had not expressed it.

"What did you think of the—" He hesitated, abashed at his first attempt to use a strange word. "Of the *motif?*" he asked.

"It was confused," she answered. "That is my only criticism in the large way. I followed the story, but there seemed so much else. It is too wordy. You clog the action by introducing so much extraneous material."

"That was the major *motif,*" he hurriedly explained, "the big under-running *motif,* the cosmic and universal thing. I tried to make it keep time with the story itself, which was only superficial after all. I was on the right scent, but I guess I did it badly. I did not succeed in suggesting what I was driving at. But I'll learn in time."

She did not follow him. She was a bachelor of arts, but he had gone beyond her limitations. This she did not comprehend, attributing her incomprehension to his incoherence.

"You were too voluble," she said. "But it was beautiful, in places."

He heard her voice as from afar off, for he was debating whether he would read her the "Sea Lyrics." He lay in dull despair, while she watched him searchingly, pondering again upon unsummoned and wayward thoughts of marriage.

"You want to be famous?" she asked abruptly.

"Yes, a little bit," he confessed. "That is part of the adventure. It is not the being famous, but the process of becoming so that counts. And after all, to be famous would be, for me, only a means to something else. I want to be famous very much, for that matter, and for that reason."

"For your sake," he wanted to add, and might have added had she proved enthusiastic over what he had read to her.

But she was too busy in her mind, carving out a career for him that would at least be possible, to ask what the ultimate something was which he had hinted at. There was no career for him in literature. Of that she was convinced. He had proved it today, with his amateurish and sophomoric productions. He could talk well, but he was incapable of expressing himself in a literary way. She compared Tennyson, and Browning, and her favorite prose masters with him, and to his hopeless discredit. Yet she did not tell him her whole mind. Her strange interest in him led her to temporize. His desire to write was, after all, a little weakness which he would grow out of in time. Then he would devote himself to the more serious affairs of life. And he would succeed, too. She knew that. He was so strong that he could not fail—if only he would drop writing.

"I wish you would show me all you write, Mr. Eden," she said.

He flushed with pleasure. She was interested, that much was sure. And at least she had not given him a rejection slip. She had called certain portions of his work beautiful, and that was the first encouragement he had ever received from any one.

"I will," he said, passionately. "And I promise you, Miss Morse, that I will make good. I have come far, I know that; and I have far to go, and I will cover it if I have to do it on my hands and knees." He held up a bunch of manuscript. "Here are the 'Sea Lyrics.' When you get home I'll turn them over to you to read at your leisure. And you must be sure to tell me just what you think of them. What I need, you know, above all things, is criticism. And do please be frank with me."

"I will be perfectly frank," she promised, with an uneasy conviction that she had not been frank with him and with a doubt if she could be quite frank with him the next time.

CHAPTER XV.

"THE first battle fought and finished," Martin said to the looking-glass ten days later. "But there will be a second battle, and a third battle, and battles to the end of time, unless—"

He did not finish the sentence, but looked about the lean little room and let his eyes dwell sadly upon a heap of returned manuscripts, still in their long envelopes, which lay in a corner on the floor. He had no stamps with which to continue them on their travels, and for a week they had been piling up. More of them would come in on the morrow, and on the next day, and the next, till they were all in. And he would be unable to start them out again. He was a month's rent behind on the typewriter, which he could not pay, having barely enough for the week's board which was due and for the employment office fees.

He sat down and regarded the table thoughtfully. There were ink stains upon it, and he suddenly discovered that he was fond of it.

"Dear old table," he said, "I've spent some happy hours with you, and you've been a pretty good friend when all is said and done. You never turned me down, never passed me out a reward-of-unmerit rejection-slip, never complained about working overtime."

He dropped his arms upon the table and buried his face in them. His throat was aching, and he wanted to cry. It reminded him of his first fight, when he was six years old, when he punched away with the tears running down his cheeks, while the other boy, two years his elder, had beaten and pounded him into exhaustion. He saw the ring of boys, howling like barbarians as he went down at last, writhing in the throes of nausea, the blood streaming from his nose and the tears from his bruised eyes.

"Poor little shaver," he murmured. "And you're just as badly licked now. You're beaten to a pulp. You're down and out."

But the vision of that first fight still lingered under his eyelids, and as he watched he saw it dissolve and reshape into the series of fights which had followed. Six months later Cheese-Face (that was the boy) had whipped him again. But he had blacked Cheese-Face's eye that time. That was going some. He saw them all, fight after fight, himself always whipped and Cheese-Face exulting over him. But he had never run away. He felt strengthened by the memory of that. He had always stayed and taken his medicine. Cheese-Face had been a little fiend at fighting, and had never once shown mercy to him. But he had stayed! He had stayed with it!

Next, he saw a narrow alley, between ramshackle frame buildings. The end of the alley was blocked by a one-story brick building, out of which issued the rhythmic thunder of the presses, running off the first edition of the *Enquirer*. He was eleven, and Cheese-Face was thirteen, and they both carried the *Enquirer*. That was why they were there, waiting for their papers. And of course Cheese-Face had picked on him again, and there was another fight that was indeterminate, because at quarter to four the door of the pressroom was thrown open and the gang of boys crowded in to fold their papers.

"I 'll lick you tomorrow," he heard Cheese-Face promise; and he heard his own voice, piping and trembling with unshed tears, agreeing to be there on the morrow.

And he had come there the next day, hurrying from school to be there first, and beating Cheese-Face by two minutes. The other boys said he was all right, and gave him advice, pointing out his faults as a scrapper and promising him victory if he carried out their instructions. The same boys gave Cheese-Face advice, too. How they had enjoyed the fight! He paused in his recollections long enough to envy them the spectacle he and Cheese-Face had put up. Then the fight was on, and it went on, without rounds, for thirty minutes, until the press-room door was opened.

He watched the youthful apparition of himself day after day, hurrying from school to the *Enquirer* alley. He could not walk very fast. He was stiff and lame from the incessant fighting. His forearms were black and blue from wrist to elbow, what of the countless blows he had warded off, and here and there the tortured flesh was beginning to fester. His head and arms and shoulders ached, the small of his back ached; he ached all over, and his brain was heavy and dazed. He did not play at school. Nor did he study. Even to sit still all day at his desk, as he did, was a torment. It seemed centuries since he had begun the round of daily fights, and time stretched away into a nightmare and infinite future of daily fights. Why could n't Cheese-Face be licked? he often thought; that would put him, Martin, out of his misery. It never entered his head to cease fighting, to allow Cheese-Face to whip him.

And so he dragged himself to the *Enquirer* alley, sick in body and soul but learning the long patience, to confront his eternal enemy, Cheese-Face, who was just as sick as he, and just a bit willing to quit if it were not for the gang of newsboys that looked on and made pride painful and necessary. One afternoon, after twenty minutes of desperate efforts to annihilate each other according to set rules that did not permit kicking, striking below the belt, nor hitting when one was down, Cheese-Face, panting for breath and reeling, offered to call it quits. And Martin, head on arms, thrilled at the picture he caught of himself, at that moment in the afternoon of long ago, when he reeled and panted and choked with the blood that ran into his mouth and down his throat from his cut lips; when he tottered toward Cheese-Face, spitting out a mouthful of blood so that he could speak, crying out that he never would quit, though Cheese-Face could give in if he wanted to. And Cheese-Face did not give in, and the fight went on.

The next day and the next, days without end, witnessed the afternoon fight. When he put up his arms, each day, to begin, they pained exquisitely, and the first few blows, struck and received, racked his soul; after that things grew numb, and he fought on blindly, seeing as in a dream, dancing and wavering, the large features and burning, animal-like eyes of Cheese-Face. He concentrated upon that face. All else about him was a whirling void. There was nothing else in the world but that face, and he would never know rest, blessed rest, until he had beaten that face into a pulp with his bleeding knuckles, or until the bleeding knuckles that somehow belonged to that face had beaten him into a pulp. And then, one way or the other, he would have rest. But to quit, for him, Martin, to quit, that was impossible.

Came the day when he dragged himself into the *Enquirer* alley, and there was no Cheese-Face. Nor did Cheese-Face come. The boys congratulated him and told him that he had licked Cheese-Face. But Martin was not satisfied. He had not licked Cheese-Face, nor had Cheese-Face licked him. The problem had not been solved. It was not until afterward that they learned that Cheese-Face's father had died suddenly that very day.

Martin skipped on through the years to the night in the "nigger heaven" at the Auditorium. He was seventeen, and just back from sea. A row started. Somebody was bullying somebody, and Martin interfered, to be confronted by Cheese-Face's blazing eyes.

"I'll fix you after de show," his ancient enemy hissed.

Martin nodded. The "nigger heaven" bouncer was making his way toward the disturbance.

"I'll meet you outside after the last act," Martin whispered, the while his face showed undivided interest in the buck-and-wing dancing on the stage.

The bouncer glared and went away.

"Got a gang?" he asked Cheese-Face, at the end of the act.

"Sure."

"Then I got to get one," Martin announced.

Between the acts he mustered his following—three fellows he knew from the nail works, a railroad fireman, and half a dozen of the Boo Gang, along with as many more from the dread Eighteenth-and-Market Gang.

When the theatre let out, the two gangs strung along inconspicuously on opposite sides of the street. When they came to a quiet corner they united and held a council of war.

"Eight Street bridge is the place," said a red-headed fellow belonging to Cheese-Face's gang. "You kin fight in the middle, under the electric light, an' whichever way the bulls come, we can sneak the other way."

"That's agreeable to me," Martin said, after consulting with the leaders of his own gang.

The Eighth Street Bridge, crossing an arm of San Antonio Estuary, was the length of three city blocks. In the middle of the bridge, and at each end, were electric lights. No policeman could pass those end-lights unseen. It was the safe place for the battle that revived itself under Martin's eyelids. He saw the two gangs, aggressive and sullen, rigidly keeping apart from each other and backing their respective champions; and he saw himself and Cheese-Face stripping. A short distance away lookouts were set, their task being to watch the lighted ends of the bridge. A member of the Boo Gang held Martin's coat, and shirt, and cap, ready to race with them into safety in case the police interfered. Martin watched himself go into the center, facing Cheese-Face, and he heard himself say, as he held up his hand warningly:

"They aint no hand-shaking in this. Understand? They aint nothing but scrap. No throwin' up the sponge. This is a grudge-fight an' it 's to a finish. Understand? Somebody's going to get licked."

Cheese-Face wanted to demur—Martin could see that—but Cheese-Face's old perilous pride was touched before the two gangs.

"Aw, come on," he replied. "Wot's the good of chewin' de rag about it. I 'm wit' cheh to de finish."

Then they fell upon each other, like young bulls, in all the glory of youth, with naked fists, with hatred, with desire to hurt, to maim, to destroy. All the painful, thousand years' gains of man in his upward climb through creation, were lost. Only the electric light remained, a milestone on the path of the great human adventure. Martin and Cheese-Face were two savages, of the stone-age, of the squatting place and the tree refuge. They sank lower and lower into the muddy abyss, back into the dregs of the raw beginnings of life, striving blindly and chemically, as the atoms strive, as the star-dust of the heavens strives, colliding, recoiling, and colliding again and eternally again.

"God! We were animals! Brute beasts!" Martin muttered aloud, as he watched the progress of the fight. It was to him, with his splendid power of vision, like gazing into a kinetoscope. He was both onlooker and participant. His long months of culture and refinement shuddered at the sight; then the present was blotted out of his consciousness and the ghosts of the past possessed him, and he was Martin Eden, just returned from sea and fighting Cheese-Face on the Eighth Street Bridge. He suffered, and toiled, and sweated and bled, and exulted when his naked knuckles smashed home.

They were twin whirlwinds of hatred, revolving about each other monstrously. The time passed, and the two hostile gangs became very quiet. They had never witnessed such intensity of ferocity, and they were awed by it. The two fighters were greater brutes than they. The first splendid velvet edge of youth and condition wore off, and they fought more cautiously and deliberately. There had been no advantage gained either way. "It 's anybody's fight," Martin heard some one saying. Then he followed up a feint, right and left, was fiercely countered, and felt his cheek laid open to the bone. No bare knuckle had done that. He heard mutters of amazement at the ghastly damage wrought, and was drenched with his own blood. But he gave no sign. He became immensely wary, for he was wise with knowledge of the low cunning and foul vileness of his kind. He watched and waited, until he feigned a wild rush, which he stopped midway, for he had seen the glint of metal.

"Hold up yer hand!" he screamed. "Them's brass knuckles, an' you hit me with 'em!"

Both gangs surged forward, growling and snarling. In a second there would be a free-for-all fight, and he would be robbed of his vengeance. He was beside himself.

"You guys keep out!" he screamed hoarsely. "Understand! Say, d' ye understand!"

They shrank away from him. They were brutes, but he was the arch-brute, a thing of terror that towered over them and dominated them.

"This is my scrap, an' they ain't goin' to be no buttin' in. Gimme them knuckles."

Cheese-Face, sobered and a bit frightened, surrendered the foul weapon.

"You passed 'em to him, you Red-Head sneakin' in behind the push there," Martin went on, as he tossed the knuckles into the water. "I seen you, an' I was wonderin' what you was up to. If you try anything like that again I 'll beat cheh to death. Understand!"

They fought on, through exhaustion and beyond, to exhaustion immeasurable and inconceivable, until the crowd of brutes, its blood-lust sated, terrified by what it saw, begged them impartially to cease. And Cheese-Face, ready to drop and die, or to stay on his legs and die, a grisly monster out of whose features all likeness to Cheese-Face had been beaten, wavered and hesitated; but Martin sprang in and smashed him again and again.

Next, after a seeming century or so, with Cheese-Face weakening fast, in a mix-up of blows there was a loud snap, and Martin's right arm dropped to his side. It was a broken bone. Everybody heard it and knew; and Cheese-Face knew, rushing like a tiger in the other's extremity and raining blow on blow. Martin's gang surged forward to interfere. Dazed by the rapid succession of blows, Martin warned them back with vile and earnest curses sobbed out and groaned in ultimate desolation and despair.

He punched on, with his left hand only, and as he punched, doggedly, only half-conscious, as from a remote distance he heard murmurs of fear in the gangs, and one who said with shaking voice: "This ain't a scrap, fellows. It 's murder, an' we ought to stop it."

But no one stopped it, and he was glad, punching on wearily and endlessly with his one arm, battering away at a bloody something before him that was not a face, but a horror, an oscillating, hideous, gibbering, nameless thing that persisted before his wavering vision and would not go away. And he punched on and on, slower and slower as the last shreds of vitality oozed from him, through centuries and aeons and enormous lapses of time, until, in a dim way, he became aware that the nameless thing was sinking, slowly sinking down to the rough board planking of the bridge. And the next moment he was standing over it, staggering and swaying on shaky legs, clutching at the air for support, and saying in a voice he did not recognize:

"D' ye want any more? Say, d' ye want any more?"

He was still saying it, over and over—demanding, entreating, threatening, to know if it wanted any more—when he felt the fellows of his gang laying hands on him, patting him on the back, and trying to put his coat on him. And then came a sudden rush of blackness and oblivion.

The tin alarm clock on the table ticked on, but Martin Eden, his face buried on his arm, did not hear it. He heard nothing. He did not think. So absolutely had he relived life that he had fainted, just as he fainted years before on the Eighth Street Bridge. For a full minute the blackness and the blankness endured. Then, like one from the dead, he sprang upright, eyes flaming, sweat pouring down his face, shouting:

"I licked you, Cheese-Face! It took me eleven years, but I licked you!"

His knees were trembling under him, he felt faint, and he staggered back to the bed, sinking down and sitting on the edge of it. He was still in the clutch of the past. He looked about the room, perplexed, alarmed, wondering where he was, until he caught sight of the pile of manuscripts in the corner. Then the wheels of memory slipped ahead through four years of time, and he was aware of the present, of the books he had opened and the universe he had won from their pages, of his dreams and ambitions, and of his love for a pale wraith of a girl, sensitive and sheltered and ethereal, who would die of horror did she witness but one moment of what he had just lived through—one moment of all the muck of life through which he had waded.

He arose to his feet and confronted himself in the looking glass.

"And so you arise from the mud, Martin Eden," he said solemnly. "And you cleanse your eyes in a great brightness, and thrust your shoulders among the stars, doing what all life has done, letting the 'ape and tiger die' and wresting highest heritage from all powers that be."

He looked more closely at himself and laughed.

"A bit of hysteria and melodrama, eh?" he queried. "Well, never mind. You licked Cheese-Face, and you 'll lick the editors if it takes twice eleven years to do it in. You can't stop here. You 've got to go on. It 's to a finish, you know."

CHAPTER XVI.

THE alarm clock went off, jerking Martin out of sleep with a suddenness that would have given headache to one with less splendid constitution. Though he slept soundly, he awoke instantly, like a cat, and he awoke eagerly, glad that the five hours of unconsciousness were gone. He hated the oblivion of sleep. There was too much to do, too much of life to live. He grudged every moment of life sleep robbed him of, and before the clock had ceased its clattering he was head and ears in the wash basin and thrilling to the cold bite of the water.

But he did not follow his regular program. There was no unfinished story waiting his hand, no new story demanding articulation. He had studied late, and it was nearly time for breakfast. He tried to read a chapter in *Fiske,* but his brain was restless and he closed the book. Today, witnessed the beginning of the new battle, wherein for some time there would be no writing. He was aware of a sadness akin to that with which one leaves home and family. He looked at the manuscripts in the corner. That was it. He was going away from them, his pitiful, dishonored children that were welcome nowhere. He went over and began to rummage among them, reading snatches here and there, his favorite portions. "The Pot" he honored with reading aloud, as he did "Adventure." "Joy," his latest-born, completed the day before and tossed into the corner for lack of stamps, won his keenest approbation.

"I can't understand," he murmured. "Or maybe it 's the editors who can 't understand. There's nothing wrong with that. They publish worse every month. Everything they publish is worse—nearly everything, anyway."

After breakfast he put the typewriter in its case and carried it down into Oakland.

"I owe a month on it," he told the clerk in the store. "But you tell the manager I 'm going to work and that I 'll be in in a month or so and straighten up."

He crossed on the ferry to San Francisco and made his way to an employment office. "Any kind of work, no trade," he told the agent; and was interrupted by a newcomer, dressed rather foppishly, as some workingmen dress who have instincts for finer things. The agent shook his head despondently.

"Nothin' doin', eh?" said the other. "Well, I got to get somebody today."

He turned and stared at Martin, and Martin, staring back, noted the puffed and discolored face, handsome and weak, and knew that he had been making a night of it.

''Lookin' for a job?'' the other queried. ''What can you do?''

''Hard labor, sailorizing, run a typewriter, no shorthand, can sit on a horse, willing to do anything and tackle anything,'' was the answer.

The other nodded.

''Sounds good to me. My name's Dawson, Joe Dawson, an' I 'm tryin' to scare up a laundryman.''

''Too much for me.'' Martin caught an amusing glimpse of himself ironing fluffy white things that women wear. But he had taken a liking to the other, and he added, ''I might do the plain washing. I learned that much at sea.''

Joe Dawson thought visibly for a moment.

''Look here, let 's get together an' frame it up. Willin' to listen?''

Martin nodded.

''This is a small laundry, up country, belongs to Shelly Hot Springs—hotel, you know. Two men do the work, boss and assistant. I 'm the boss. You don't work for me, but you work under me. Think you 'd be willing to learn?''

Martin paused to think. The prospect was alluring. A few months of it, and he would have time to himself for study. He could work hard and study hard.

''Good grub and a room to yourself,'' Joe said.

That settled it. A room to himself where he could burn the midnight oil unmolested.

''But work like hell,'' the other added.

Martin caressed his swelling shoulder-muscles significantly. ''That came from hard work.''

''Then let 's get to it.'' Joe held his hand to his head for a moment. ''Gee, but it 's a stem-winder. Can hardly see. I went down the line last night—everything—everything. Here 's the frame-up. The wages for two is a hundred and board. I 've been drawin' down sixty, the second man forty. But he knew the biz. You 're green. If I break you in, I 'll be doing plenty of your work at first. Suppose you begin at thirty, an' work up to the forty. I 'll play fair. Just as soon as you can do your share you get the forty.''

''I 'll go you,'' Martin announced, stretching out his hand, which the other shook. ''Any advance?—for railroad ticket and extras?''

''I blew it in,'' was Joe's sad answer, with another reach at his aching head. ''All I got is a return ticket.''

''And I 'm broke—when I pay my board.''

''Jump it,'' Joe advised.

''Can't. Owe it to my sister.''

Joe whistled a long, perplexed whistle, and racked his brains to little purpose.

''I 've got the price of the drinks,'' he said desperately. ''Come on, an' mebbe we 'll cook up something.''

Martin declined.

''Water-wagon?''

This time Martin nodded, and Joe lamented, ''Wish I was.''

''But I somehow just can't,'' he said in extenuation. ''After I 've ben workin' like hell all week I just got to booze up. If I did n't I 'd cut my throat or burn up the premises. But I 'm glad you 're on the wagon. Stay with it.''

Martin knew of the enormous gulf between him and this man—the gulf the books had made; but he found no difficulty in crossing back over that gulf. He had lived all his life in the working-class world, and the *camaraderie* of labor was second nature with him. He solved the difficulty of transportation that was too much for the other's aching head. He would send his trunk up to Shelly Hot Springs on Joe's ticket. As for himself, there was his wheel. It was seventy miles, and he could ride it on Sunday and be ready for work Monday morning. In the meantime he would go home and pack up. There was no one to say good-bye to. Ruth, and her whole family, were spending the long summer in the Sierras, at Lake Tahoe.

He arrived at Shelly Hot Springs, tired and dusty, on Sunday night. Joe greeted him exuberantly. With a wet towel bound about his aching brow, he had been at work all day.

''Part of last week's washin' mounted up, me bein' away to get you,'' he explained. ''Your box arrived all right. It 's in your room. But it 's a hell of a thing to call a trunk. An' what 's in it? Gold-bricks?''

Joe sat on the bed while Martin unpacked. The box was a packing-case for breakfast food, and Mr. Higginbotham had charged him half a dollar for it. Two rope handles, nailed on by Martin, had technically transformed it into a trunk eligible for the baggage car. Joe watched, with bulging eyes, a few shirts and several changes of underclothes come out of the box, followed by books, and more books.

"Books clean to the bottom?" he asked.

Martin nodded, and went on arranging the books on a kitchen table which served in the room in place of a wash-stand.

"Gee!" Joe exploded, then waited in silence for the deduction to arise in his brain. At last it came.

"Say, you dont care for the girls—much?" he queried.

"No,' was the answer. "I used to chase a lot before I tackled the books. But since then there 's no time."

"And there won't be any time here. All you can do is work an' sleep."

Martin thought of his five hours' sleep a night, and smiled. The room was situated over the laundry and was in the same building with the engine that pumped water, made electricity, and ran the laundry machinery. The engineer, who occupied the adjoining room, dropped in to meet the new hand, and helped Martin rig up an electric bulb, on an extension wire, so that it traveled along a stretched cord from over the table to the bed.

The next morning, at quarter past six, Martin was routed out for a quarter-to-seven breakfast. There happened to be a bath-tub for the servants in the laundry building, and he electrified Joe by taking a cold bath.

"Gee, but you 're a hummer," Joe announced, as they sat down to breakfast in a corner of the hotel kitchen.

With them was the engineer, the gardener and the assistant gardener, and two or three men from the stable. They ate hurriedly and gloomily, with but little conversation, and as Martin ate and listened he realized how far he had traveled from their status. Their small mental caliber was depressing to him, and he was anxious to get away from them. So he bolted his breakfast, a sickly, sloppy affair, as rapidly as they, and heaved a sigh of relief when he passed out through the kitchen door.

It was a perfectly appointed, small steam laundry, wherein the most modern machinery did everything that was possible for machinery to do. Martin, after a few instructions, sorted the great heaps of soiled clothes, while Joe started the washer and made up fresh supplies of soft soap, compounded of biting chemicals that compelled him to swathe his mouth and nostrils and eyes in bathtowels till he resembled a mummy. Finished the sorting, Martin lent a hand in wringing the clothes. This was done by dumping them into a spinning receptacle that went at a rate of a few thousand revolutions a minute, tearing the water from the clothes by centrifugal force. Then Martin began to alternate between the dryer and the wringer, between times "shaking out" socks and stockings. By the afternoon, one feeding and one stacking up, they were running socks and stockings through the mangle while the irons were heating. Then it was hot irons and underclothes till six o'clock, at which time Joe shook his head dubiously.

"'Way behind," he said. "Got to work after supper."

And after supper they worked until ten o'clock, under the blazing electric lights, until the last piece of underclothing was ironed and folded away in the distributing room. It was a hot California night, and though the windows were thrown wide, the room, with its red-hot ironing-stove, was a furnace. Martin and Joe, down to undershirts, barearmed, sweated and panted for air.

"Like trimming cargo in the tropics," Martin said, when they went upstairs.

"You 'll do," Joe answered. "You take hold like a good fellow. If you keep up the pace, you 'll be on thirty dollars only one month. The second month you 'll be gettin' your forty. But dont tell me you never ironed before. I know better."

"Never ironed a rag in my life, honestly, until today," Martin protested.

He was surprised at his weariness when he got into his room, forgetful of the fact that he had been on his feet and working without let up for fourteen hours. He set the alarm at six, and measured back five hours to one o'clock. He could read until then. Slipping off his shoes, to ease his swollen feet, he sat down at the table with his books. He opened *Fiske,* where he had left off two days before, and began to read. But he found trouble with the first paragraph and began to read it through a second time. Then he awoke, in pain from his stiffened muscles and chilled by the mountain wind that had begun to blow in through the window. He looked at the clock. It marked two. He had been asleep four hours. He pulled off his clothes and crawled into bed, where he was asleep the moment after his head touched the pillow.

Tuesday was a day of similar unremitting toil. The speed with which Joe worked won Martin's admiration. Joe was a demon for work. He was keyed up to concert pitch, and there was never a moment in the long day when he was not fighting for moments. He concentrated himself upon his work and upon how to save time, pointing out to Martin where he did in five motions what could be done in three, or in three motions what could be done in two. ''Elimination of waste motion,'' Martin phrased it as he watched and patterned after. He was a good workman himself, quick and deft, and it had always been a point of pride with him that no man should do any of his work for him or outwork him. As a result, he concentrated with a similar singleness of purpose, greedily snapping up the hints and suggestions thrown out by his working mate. He ''rubbed out'' collars and cuffs, rubbing the starch out from between the double thicknesses of linen so that there would be no blisters when it came to the ironing, and doing it at a pace that elicited Joe's praise.

There was never an interval when something was not at hand to be done. Joe waited for nothing, waited on nothing, and went on the jump from task to task. They starched two hundred white shirts, with a single gathering movement seizing a shirt so that the wristbands, neckband, yoke and bosom protruded beyond the circling right hand. At the same moment the left hand held up the body of the shirt so that it would not enter the starch, and at the same moment the right hand dipped into the starch—starch so hot that, in order to wring it out, their hands had to be thrust, and thrust continually, into a bucket of cold water. And that night they worked till half past ten, dipping ''fancy starch''—all the frilled and airy delicate wear of ladies.

''Me for the tropics and no clothes,'' Martin laughed.

''And me out of a job,'' Joe answered seriously. ''I dont know nothin' but laundrying.''

''And you know it well.''

''I ought to. Began in the Contra Costa in Oakland when I was eleven, shakin' out for the mangle. That was eighteen years ago an' I 've never done a tap of anything else. But this job is the fiercest I ever had. Ought to be one more man on it at least. We work tomorrow night. Always run the mangle Wednesday nights—collars an' cuffs.''

Martin set his arm, drew up to the table, and opened *Fiske*. He did not finish the first paragraph. The lines blurred and ran together and his head nodded. He walked up and down, batting his head savagely with his fists, but he could not conquer the numbness of sleep. He propped the book before him, and propped his eyelids with his fingers, and fell asleep with his eyes wide open. Then he surrendered, and, scarcely conscious of what he did, got off his clothes and into bed. He slept seven hours of heavy, animal-like sleep, and awoke by the alarm, feeling that he had not had enough.

''Doin' much readin?'' Joe asked.

Martin shook his head.

''Never mind. We got to run the mangle tonight, but Thursday we 'll knock off at six. That 'll give you a chance.''

Martin washed woolens that day, by hand, in a large barrel, with strong soft soap, by means of a hub from a wagon wheel, mounted on a plunger-pole that was attached to a spring-pole overhead.

''My invention,'' Joe said proudly. ''Beats a washboard an' your knuckles, and, besides, it saves at least fifteen minutes in the week, an' fifteen minutes aint to be sneezed at in this shebang.''

Running the collars and cuffs through the mangle was also Joe's idea. That night, while they toiled on under the electric lights, he explained it.

''Something no laundry ever does, except this one. An' I got to do it if I 'm goin' to get done Saturday afternoon at three o'clock. But I know how, an' that 's the difference. Got to have right heat, right pressure, and run 'em through three times. Look at that!'' He held a cuff aloft. ''Could n't do it better by hand or on a tiler.''

Thursday, Joe was in a rage. A bundle of extra ''fancy starch'' had come in.

''I 'm goin' to quit,'' he announced. ''I wont stand for it. I 'm goin' to quit it cold. What 's the good of me workin' like a slave all week, a-savin' minutes, an' them a-comin' an' ringin' in fancy starch extras on me? This is a free country, an' I 'm goin' to tell that fat Dutchman what I think of him. An' I wont tell 'm in French. Plain United States is good enough for me. Him a-ringin' in fancy starch extras!''

''We got to work tonight,'' he said the next moment, reversing his judgment and surrendering to fate.

Martin Eden

By Jack London

Author of "The Call of the Wild," "Sea Wolf," "The God of His Fathers," "White Fang," etc.

CHAPTER XVII.

AND Martin did no reading that night. he had seen no daily paper all week, and, strangely to him, felt no desire to see one. He was not interested in the news. He was too tired and jaded to be interested in anything, though he planned to leave Saturday afternoon, if they finished at three, and ride on his wheel to Oakland. It was seventy miles, and the same distance back on Sunday afternoon would leave him anything but rested for the second week's work. It would have been easier to go on the train, but the round trip was two dollars and a half, and he was intent on saving money.

Martin learned to do many things. In the course of the first week, in one afternoon, he and Joe accounted for the two hundred white shirts. Joe ran the tiler, a machine wherein a hot iron was hooked on a steel spring which furnished the pressure. By this means he ironed the yoke, wristbands and neckband, setting the latter at right angles to the shirt, and put the glossy finish on the bosom. As fast as he finished them, he flung the shirts on a rack between him and Martin, who caught them up and "backed" them. This task consisted of ironing all the unstarched portions of the shirts.

It was exhausting work, carried on, hour after hour, at top speed. Out on the broad verandas of the hotel, men and women, in cool white, sipped iced drinks and kept their circulation down. But in the laundry the air was sizzling. The huge stove roared red hot and white hot, while the irons, moving over the damp cloth, sent up clouds of steam. The heat of these irons was different from that used by housewives. An iron that stood the ordinary test of a wet finger was too cold for Joe and Martin, and such test was useless. They went wholly by holding the irons close to their cheeks, gauging the heat by some secret mental process that Martin admired but could not understand. When the fresh irons proved too hot, they hooked them on iron rods and dipped them into cold water. This again required a precise and subtle judgment. A fraction of a second too long in the water, and the fine and silken edge of the proper heat was lost, and Martin found time to marvel at the accuracy he developed—an automatic accuracy, founded upon criteria that were machine-like and unerring.

But there was little time in which to marvel. All Martin's consciousness was concentrated in the work. Ceaselessly active, head and hand, an intelligent machine, all that constituted him a man was devoted to furnishing that intelligence. There was no room in his brain for the universe and its mighty problems. All the broad and spacious corridors of his mind were closed and hermetically sealed. The echoing chamber of his soul was a narrow room, a conning tower, whence was directed his arm and shoulder muscles, his ten nimble fingers, and the swift-moving iron along its steaming path in broad, sweeping strokes, just so many strokes and no more, just so far with each stroke and not a fraction of an inch farther, rushing along interminable sleeves, sides, backs and tails, and tossing the finished shirts, without rumpling, upon the receiving frame. And even as his hurrying soul tossed, it was reaching for another shirt. This went on, hour after hour, while outside all the world swooned under the overhead California sun. But there was no swooning in that superheated room. The cool guests on the verandas needed clean linen.

The sweat poured from Martin. He drank enormous quantities of water, but so great was the heat of the day and of his exertions, that the water sluiced through the interstices of his flesh and out at all his pores. Always, at sea, except at rare intervals, the work he performed had given him ample opportunity to commune with himself. The master of the ship had been lord of Martin's time; but here, the manager of the hotel was lord of Martin's thoughts as well. He had no thoughts save for the nerve-racking, body-destroying toil. Outside of that, it was impossible to think. He did not know that he loved Ruth. She did not even exist, for his driven soul had no time to remember her. It was only when he crawled to bed at night, or to breakfast in the morning, that she asserted herself to him in fleeting memories.

''This is hell, ain't it?'' Joe remarked once.

Martin nodded, but felt a rasp of irritation. The statement had been obvious and unnecessary. They did not talk while they worked. Conversation threw them out of their stride, as it did this time, compelling Martin to miss a stroke of his iron and to make two extra motions before he caught his stride again.

On Friday morning the washer ran. Twice a week they had to put through hotel linen, the sheets, pillow-slips, spreads, table-cloths and napkins. This finished, they buckled down to ''fancy starch.''It was slow work, fastidious and delicate, and Martin did not learn it so readily. Besides, he could not take chances. Mistakes were disastrous.

''See that,'' Joe said, holding up a filmy corset cover that he could have crumpled from view in one hand. ''Scorch that an' it 's twenty dollars out of your wages.''

So Martin did not scorch that, and eased down on his muscular tension, though nervous tension rose higher than ever, and he listened sympathetically to the other's blasphemies as he toiled and suffered over the beautiful things that women wear when they do not have to do their own laundrying. ''Fancy starch'' was Martin's nightmare, and it was Joe's, too. It was ''fancy starch'' that robbed them of their hard-won minutes. They toiled at it all day. At seven in the evening they broke off to run the hotel linen through the mangle. At ten o'clock, while the hotel guests slept, the two laundrymen sweated on at ''fancy starch'' till midnight, till one, till two. At half-past two they knocked off.

Saturday morning it was ''fancy starch,'' and odds and ends, and at three in the afternoon the week's work was done.

''You ain't a-goin' to ride them seventy miles into Oakland on top of this?'' Joe demanded, as they sat on the stairs and took a triumphant smoke.

''Got to,'' was the answer.

''What are you goin' for?—a girl?''

''No; to save two and a half on the railroad ticket. I want to renew some books at the library.''

''Why dont you send 'em down an' up by express? That 'll cost only a quarter each way.''

Martin considered it.

''An' take a rest tomorrow,'' the other urged. ''You need it. I know I do. I 'm plum tuckered out.''

He looked it. Indomitable, never resting, fighting for seconds and minutes all week, circumventing delays and crushing down obstacles, a fount of resistless energy, a high-driven human motor, a demon for work, now that he had accomplished the week's task he was in a state of collapse. He was worn and haggard, and his handsome face drooped in lean exhaustion. He puffed his cigarette spiritlessly, and his voice was peculiarly dead and monotonous. All the snap and fire had gone out of him. His triumph seemed a sorry one.

''An' next week we got to do it all over again,'' he said, sadly. ''An' what 's the good of it all, hey? Sometimes I wish I was a hobo. They dont work, an' they get their livin'. Gee! I wish I had a glass of beer; but I can't get up the gumption to go down to the village an' get it. You 'll stay over, an' send your books down by express, or else you 're a damn fool.''

''But what can I do here all day Sunday?'' Martin asked.

''Rest. You dont know how tired you are. Why, I 'm that tired Sunday I can't even read the papers. I was sick once—typhoid. In the hospital two months an' a half. Did n't do a tap of work all that time. It was beautiful.

"It was beautiful," he repeated dreamily, a minute later.

Martin took a bath, after which he found that the head laundryman had disappeared. Most likely he had gone for the glass of beer, Martin decided, but the half-mile walk down to the village to find out seemed a long journey to him. He lay on his bed with his shoes off, trying to make up his mind. He did not reach out for a book. He was too tired to feel sleepy, and he lay, scarcely thinking, in a semi-stupor of weariness, until it was time for supper. Joe did not appear for that function, and when Martin heard the gardener remark that most likely he was ripping the slats off the bar, Martin understood. He went to bed immediately afterward, and in the morning decided that he was greatly rested. Joe being still absent, Martin procured a Sunday paper and lay down in a shady nook under the trees. The morning passed, he knew not how. He did not sleep, nobody disturbed him, and he did not finish the paper. He came back to it in the afternoon, after dinner, and fell asleep over it.

So passed Sunday, and Monday morning he was hard at work, sorting clothes, while Joe, a towel bound tightly around his head, with groans and blasphemies, was running the washer and mixing soft-soap.

"I simply can't help it," he explained. "I got to drink when Saturday night comes around."

Another week passed, a great battle that continued under the electric lights each night and that culminated on Saturday afternoon at three o'clock, when Joe tasted his moment of wilted triumph and then drifted down to the village to forget. Martin's Sunday was the same as before. He slept in the shade of the trees, toiled aimlessly through the newspaper, and spent long hours lying on his back, doing nothing, thinking nothing. He was too dazed to think, though he was aware that he did not like himself. He was self-repelled, as though he had undergone some degradation or was intrinsically foul. All that was god-like in him was blotted out. The spur of ambition was blunted; he had no vitality with which to feel the prod of it. He was dead. His soul seemed dead. He was a beast, a work-beast. He saw no beauty in the sunshine sifting down through the green leaves, nor did the azure vault of the sky whisper as of old and hint of cosmic vastness and secrets trembling to disclosure. Life was intolerably dull and stupid, and its taste was bad in his mouth. A black screen was drawn across his mirror of inner vision, and fancy lay in a darkened sickroom where entered no ray of light. He envied Joe, down in the village, rampant, tearing the slats off the bar, his brain gnawing with maggots, exulting in maudlin ways over maudlin things, fantastically and gloriously drunk and forgetful of Monday morning and the week of deadening toil to come.

A third week went by, and Martin loathed himself, loathed life. He was oppressed by a sense of failure. There was reason for the editors refusing his stuff. He could see that clearly now, and laugh at himself and the dreams he had dreamed. Ruth returned his "Sea Lyrics" by mail. He read her letter apathetically. She did her best to say how much she liked them and that they were beautiful. But she could not lie, and she could not disguise the truth from herself. She knew they were failures, and he read her disapproval in every perfunctory and unenthusiastic line of her letter. And she was right. He was firmly convinced of it as he read the poems over. Beauty and wonder had departed from him, and as he read the poems he caught himself puzzling as to what he had had in mind when he wrote them. His audacities of phrase struck him as grotesque, his felicities of expression were monstrosities, and everything was absurd, unreal and impossible. He would have burned the "Sea Lyrics" on the spot, had his will been strong enough to set them aflame. There was the engine-room, but the exertion of carrying them to the furnace was not worth while. All his exertion was used in washing other persons' clothes. He did not have any left for private affairs.

He resolved that when Sunday came he would pull himself together and answer

Ruth's letter. But Saturday afternoon, after work was finished and he had taken a bath, the desire to forget overpowered him. "I guess I 'll go down and see how Joe's getting on," was the way he put it to himself; and in the same moment he knew that he lied. But he did not have the energy to consider the lie. If he had the energy he would have refused to consider the lie, because he wanted to forget. He started for the village slowly and casually, increasing his pace in spite of himself as he neared the saloon.

"I thought you was on the waterwagon," was Joe's greeting.

Martin did not deign to offer excuses, but called for whiskey, filling his own glass brimming before he passed the bottle.

"Don't take all night about it," he said, roughly.

The other was dawdling with the bottle, and Martin refused to wait for him, tossing the glass off in a gulp and refilling it.

"Now I can wait for you," he said, grimly; "but hurry up."

Joe hurried, and they drank together.

"The work did it, eh?" Joe queried.

Martin refused to discuss the matter.

"It 's fair hell, I know," the other went on, "but I kind of hate to see you come off the wagon, Mart. Well, here 's how!"

Martin drank on silently, biting out his orders and invitations and awing the barkeeper, an effiminate country youngster with watery blue eyes and hair parted in the middle.

"It 's something scandalous the way they work us poor devils," Joe was remarking. "If I did n't bowl up I'd break loose an' burn down the shebang. My bowlin' up is all that saves 'em, I can tell you that."

But Martin made no answer. A few more drinks, and in his brain he felt the maggots of intoxication beginning to crawl. Ah, it was living, the first breath of life he had breathed in three weeks. His dreams came back to him. Fancy came out of the darkened room and lured him on, a thing of flaming brightness. His mirror of vision was silver-clear, a flashing, dazzling palimpsest of imagery. Wonder and beauty walked with him hand in hand, and all power was his. He tried to tell it to Joe, but Joe had visions of his own, infallible schemes whereby he would escape the slavery of laundry-work and become himself the owner of a great steam laundry.

"I tell yeh, Mart, they won't be no kids workin' in my laundry—not on yer life. An' they won't be no workin' a livin' soul after six P. M. You hear me talk? They 'll be machienry enough an' hands enough to do it all in decent workin' hours, an' Mart, s' help me, I 'll make yeh superintendent of the shebang—the whole of it, all of it. Now, here 's the scheme. I get on the water-wagon an' save my money for two years—savve, an' then—"

But Martin turned away, leaving him to tell it to the barkeeper, until that worthy was called away to furnish drinks to two farmers who, coming in, accepted Martin's invitation. Martin dispensed royal largess, inviting everybody up, farm-hands, a stableman and the gardener's assistant from the hotel, the barkeeper, and the furtive hobo who slid in like a shadow and like a shadow hovered at the end of the bar.

CHAPTER XVIII.

MONDAY morning, Joe groaned over the first truck-load of clothes to the washer.

"I say," he began.

"Don't talk to me," Martin snarled.

"I 'm sorry, Joe," he said at noon, when they knocked off for dinner.

Tears came into the other's eyes.

"That 's all right, old man," he said. "We're in hell, an' we can't help ourselves. An' you know, I kind of like you a whole lot. That 's what made it hurt. I cottoned to you from the first."

Martin shook his head.

"Let 's quit," Joe suggested. "Let 's chuck it, an' go hoboin'. I ain't never tried it, but it must be dead easy. An' nothin' to do. Just think of it, nothin' to do. I was sick once, typhoid, in the hospital, an' it was beautiful. I wish I 'd get sick again."

The week dragged on. The hotel was full, and extra "fancy starch" poured in upon them. They performed prodigies of valor. They fought late each night under the electric lights, bolted their meals, and even got in a half hour's work before breakfast. Martin no longer took his cold baths. Every moment was drive, drive, drive, and Joe was the masterful shepherd of moments, herding them carefully, never losing one, counting them over like a miser counting gold, working on in a frenzy, toil-mad, a feverish machine, aided ably by that other machine that thought of itself as once having been one Martin Eden, a man.

But it was only at rare moments that Martin was able to think. The house of thought was closed, its windows boarded up, and he was its shadowy caretaker. He was a shadow. Joe was right. They were both shadows, and this was the unending limbo of toil. Or was it a dream? Sometimes, in the steaming, sizzling heat, as he swung the heavy irons back and forth over the white garments, it came to him that it was a dream. In a short while, or maybe, after a thousand years or so, he would awake, in his little room with the ink-stained table, and take up his writing where he had left off the day before. Or maybe that was a dream, too, and the awakening would be the changing of the watches, when he would drop down out of his bunk in the lurching forecastle and go up on deck, under the tropic stars, and take the wheel and feel the cool trade-wind blowing through his flesh.

Came Saturday and its hollow victory at three o'clock.

"Guess I 'll go down an' get a glass of beer," Joe said, in the queer, monotonous tones that marked his week-end collapse.

Martin seemed suddenly to wake up. He opened the kit bag and oiled his wheel, putting graphite on the chain and adjusting the bearings. Joe was halfway down to the saloon when Martin passed by, bending low over the handlebars, his legs driving the ninety-six gear with rhythmic strength, his face set for seventy miles of road and grade and dust. He slept in Oakland that night, and on Sunday covered the seventy miles back. And on Monday morning, weary, he began the new week's work, but he had kept sober.

A fifth week passed, and a sixth, during which he lived and toiled as a machine, with just a spark of something more in him, just a glimmering bit of soul, that compelled him, at each weekend, to scorch off the hundred and forty miles. But this was not rest. It was super-machinelike, and it helped to crush out the glimmering bit of soul that was all that was left him from former life. At the end of the seventh week, without intending it, too weak to resist, he drifted down to the village with Joe and drowned life and found life until Monday morning.

Again, at the week-ends, he ground out the one hundred and forty miles, obliterating the numbness of too-great exertion by the numbness of still greater exertion. At the end of three months he went down a third time to the village with Joe. He forgot and lived again, and, living, he saw, in clear illumination, the beast he was making of himself—not by the drink, but by the work. The drink was an effect, nor a cause. It followed inevitably upon the work, as the night follows upon the day. Not by becoming a toil-beast could he win to the heights, was the message the whiskey whispered to him, and he nodded approbation. The whiskey was wise. It told secrets on itself.

He called for paper and pencil, and for drinks all around, and while they drank his very good health, he clung to the bar and scribbled.

"A telegram, Joe," he said. "Read it."

Joe read it with a drunken, quizzical leer. But what he read seemed to sober him. He looked at the other reproachfully, tears oozing into his eyes and down his cheeks.

"You ain't goin' back on me, Mart?" he queried hopelessly.

Martin nodded, and called one of the loungers to him to take the message to the telegraph office.

"Hold on," Joe muttered, thickly. "Lemme think."

He held on to the bar, his legs wobbling under him, Martin's arm around him and supporting him, while he thought.

"Make that two laundrymen," he said, abruptly. "Here, lemme fix it."

"What are you quitting for?" Martin demanded.

"Same reason as you."

"But I 'm going to sea. You can't do that."

"Nope," was the answer, "but I can hobo all right, all right."

Martin looked at him searchingly for a moment, then cried:

"By God, I think you 're right! Better a hobo than a beast of toil. Why, man, you 'll live. And that 's more than you ever did before."

"I was in hospital, once," Joe corrected. "It was beautiful. Typhoid—did I tell you?"

While Martin changed the telegram to "two laundrymen," Joe went on:

"I never wanted to drink when I was in hospital. Funny, ain't it? But when I 've ben workin' like a slave all week, I just got to bowl up. Ever noticed that cooks drink like hell?—an' bakers, too? It 's the work. They 've sure got to. Here, lemme pay half of that telegram."

"I 'll shake you for it," Martin offered.

"Come on, everybody drink," Joe called, as they rattled the dice and rolled them on the damp bar.

Monday morning Joe was wild with anticipation. He did not mind his aching head, nor did he take interest in his work. Whole herds of moments stole away and were lost while their careless shepherd gazed out of the window at the sunshine and the trees.

"Just look at it!" he cried. "An' it 's all mine! It 's free. I can lie down under them trees an' sleep for a thousan' years if I want to. Aw, come on, Mart, let 's chuck it. What 's the good of waitin' another moment. That 's the land of Nothin'-to-do out there, an' I got a ticket for it—an' it aint no return ticket, b-gosh!"

A few moments later, filling the truck with soiled clothes for the washer, Joe spied the hotel manager's shirt. He knew its mark, and with a sudden glorious consciousness of freedom he threw it on the floor and stamped on it.

"I wish you was in it, you pig-headed Dutchman!" he shouted. "In it, an' right there where I 've got you. Take that! an that! an' that! damn you! Hold me back, somebody! Hold me back!"

Martin laughed and held him to his work. On Tuesday night the new laundrymen arrived, and the rest of the week was spent breaking them into the routine. Joe sat around and explained his system, but he did no more work.

"Not a tap," he announced. "Not a tap. They can fire me if they want to, but if they do I 'll quit. No more work in mine, thank you kindly. Me for the freight cars an' the shade under the trees. Go to it, you slaves! That 's right. Slave an' sweat! Slave an' sweat! An' when you 're dead you 'll rot the same as me, an' what 's it matter how you live?—eh? Tell me that, what 's it matter in the long run?"

On Saturday they drew their pay and came to the parting of the ways.

"They aint no use in me askin' you to change your mind an' hit the road with me?" Joe asked hopelessly.

Martin shook his head. He was standing by his wheel, ready to start. They shook hands, and Joe held on to his for a moment, as he said :

"I'm goin' to see you again, Mart, before you an' me die. That 's straight dope. I feel it in my bones. Goodbye, Mart, an' be good. I like you like hell, you know."

He stood, a forlorn figure, in the middle of the road, watching until Martin turned a bend and was gone from sight.

"He 's a good Indian, that boy," he muttered. "A good Indian."

Then he plodded down the road himself, to the water-tank, where half a dozen empties lay on a side-track waiting for the up freight.

CHAPTER XIX.

RUTH and her family were home again, and Martin, returned to Oakland, saw much of her. Having gained her degree, she was doing no more studying; and he, having worked all vitality out of his mind and body, was doing no writing. This gave them time for each other that they had never had before, and their intimacy ripened fast.

At first, Martin had done nothing but rest. He had slept a great deal, and spent long hours musing and thinking and doing nothing. He was like one recovering from some terrible bout of hardship. The first signs of reawakening came when he discovered more than languid interest in the daily paper. Then he began to read again—light novels, and poetry; and after several days more he was head over heels in his long-neglected *Fiske*. His splendid body and health made new vitality, and he possessed all the resiliency and rebound of youth.

Ruth showed her disappointment plainly when he announced that he was going to sea for another voyage as soon as he was well rested.

''Why do you want to do that?'' she asked.

''Money,'' was the answer. ''I 'll have to lay in a supply for my next attack on the editors. Money is the sinews of war, in my case—money and patience.''

''But if all you wanted was money, why did n't you stay in the laundry?''

''Because the laundry was making a beast of me. Too much work of that sort drives to drink.''

She stared at him with horror in her eyes.

''Do you mean—?'' she quavered.

It would have been easy for him to get out of it; but his natural impulse was for frankness, and he remembered his old resolve to be frank no matter what happened.

''Yes,'' he answered. ''Just that. Several times.''

She shivered, and drew away from him.

''No man that I have ever known did that,—ever did that.''

''Then they never worked in the laundry at Shelley Hot Springs,'' he laughed, bitterly. ''Toil is a good thing. It is necessary for human health, so all the preachers say, and heaven knows I 've never been afraid of it. But there is such a thing as too much of a good thing, and the laundry up there is one of them. And that 's why I 'm going to sea one more voyage. It will be my last, I think, for when I come back I shall break into the magazines. I am certain of it.''

She was silent, unsympathetic, and he watched her moodily, realizing how impossible it was for her to understand what he had been through.

''Some day I shall write it up—'The Degradation of Toil,' or the 'Psychology of Drink in the Working Class,' or something like that for a title.''

Never, since the first meeting, had they seemed so far apart as that day. His confession, told in frankness, with the spirit of revolt behind, had repelled her. But she was more shocked by the repulsion itself than by the cause of it. It pointed out to her how near she had drawn to him, and, once accepted, it paved the way for greater intimacy. Pity, too, was aroused, and innocent, idealistic thoughts of reform. She would save this raw young man who had come so far. She would save him from the curse of his early environment, and she would save him from himself in spite of himself. And all this affected her as a very noble state of consciousness; nor did she dream that behind it and underlying it were the jealousy and desire of love.

They rode on their wheels much in the delightful fall weather, and out in the hills they read poetry aloud, now one and now the other, noble uplifting poetry that turned one's thoughts to higher things. Renunciation, sacrifice, patience, industry and high endeavor were the principles she thus indirectly preached—such abstractions being objectified in her mind by her father, and Mr. Butler, and by Andrew Carnegie, who, from a poor immigrant boy had arisen to be the bookgiver of the world.

All of which was appreciated and enjoyed by Martin. He followed her mental processes more clearly now, and her soul was no longer the sealed wonder it had been. He was on terms of intellectual equality with her. But the points of disagreement did not affect his love. His love was more ardent than ever, for he loved her for what she was, and even her physical frailty was an added charm in his eyes. He read of sickly Elizabeth Barrett, who for years had not placed her feet upon the ground, until that day of flame when she eloped with Browning and stood upright, upon the earth, under the open sky; and what Browning had done for her, Martin decided he could do for Ruth. But first, she must love him. The rest would be easy. He would give her strength and health. And he caught glimpses of their life, in the years to come, wherein, against a background of work and comfort and general well-being, he saw himself and Ruth reading and discussing poetry, she propped amid a multitude of cushions on the ground while she read aloud to him. This was the key to the life they would live. And always he saw that particular picture. Sometimes it was she who leaned against him while he read, one arm about her, her head upon his shoulder. Sometimes they pored together over the printed pages of beauty. Then, too, she loved nature, and with generous imagination he changed the scene of their reading—sometimes they read in closed-in valleys with precipitous walls, or in high mountain meadows, and again, down by the gray sand-dunes with a wreath of billows at their feet, or afar on some volcanic tropic isle where waterfalls descended and became mist, reaching the sea in vapor veils that swayed and shivered to every vagrant wisp of wind. But always, in the foreground, lords of beauty and eternally reading and sharing, lay he and Ruth, and always in the background that was beyond the background of nature, dim and hazy, were work and success and money earned that made them free of the world and all its treasures.

"I should recommend my little girl to be careful," her mother warned her one day.

"I know what you mean. But it is impossible. He is not—"

Ruth was blushing, but it was the blush of maidenhood called upon for the first time to discuss the sacred things of life with a mother held equally sacred.

"Your kind," her mother finished the sentence for her.

Ruth nodded.

"I did not want to say it, but he is not. He is rough, brutal, strong—too strong. He has not—"

She hesitated and could not go on. It was a new experience talking over such matters with her mother. And again her mother completed her thought for her.

"He has not lived a clean life, is what you wanted to say."

Again Ruth nodded, and again a blush mantled her face.

"It is just that," she said. "It has not been his fault, but he has played much with—"

"With pitch?"

"Yes, with pitch. And he frightens me. Sometimes I am positively in terror of him, when he talks in that free and easy way of the things he has done—as if they did not matter. They do matter, don't they?"

They sat with their arms twined around each other, and in the pause her mother patted her hand and waited for her to go on.

"But I am interested in him dreadfully," she continued. "In a way he is my protege. Then, too, he is my first boy friend—but not exactly friend; rather protege and friend combined. Sometimes, too, when he frightens me, it seems that he is a bulldog I have taken for a plaything, like some of the 'frat' girls, and he is tugging hard, and showing his teeth, and threatening to break loose."

Again her mother waited.

"He interests me, I suppose, like the bulldog. And there is much good in him, too; but there is much in him that I would not like in—in the other way. You see, I have been thinking. He swears, he smokes, he drinks, he has fought with his fists (he has told me so, and he likes it, he says so). He is all that a man should not be—a man I would want for my"—her voice sank very low—"husband. Then he is too strong. My prince must be tall, and slender, and dark—a graceful, bewitching prince. No, there is no danger of my falling in love with Martin Eden. It would be the worst fate that could befall me."

"But it is not that that I spoke about," her mother equivocated. "Have you thought about him? He is so ineligible in every way, you know, and suppose he should come to love you?"

"But he does—already," she cried.

"It was to be expected," Mrs. Morse said, gently. "How could it be otherwise with any one who knew you?"

"Olney hates me!" she exclaimed passionately. "And I hate Olney. I feel always like a cat when he is around. I feel that I must be nasty to him, and even when I dont happen to feel that way, why, he 's nasty to me anyway. But I am happy with Martin Eden. No one ever loved me before—no man, I mean, in that way. And it is sweet to be loved—that way. You know what I mean, mother, dear. It is sweet to feel that you are really and truly a woman." She buried her face in her mother's lap, sobbing. "You think I am dreadful, I know, but I am honest, and I tell you just how I feel."

Mrs. Morse was strangely sad and happy. Her child-daughter who was a bachelor of arts was gone; but in her place was a woman-daughter. The experiment had succeeded. The strange void in Ruth's nature had been filled, and filled without danger or penalty. This rough sailor-fellow had been the instrument, and, though Ruth did not love him, he had made her conscious of her womanhood.

"His hand trembles," Ruth was confessing, her face for shame's sake still buried. "It is most amusing and ridiculous; but I feel sorry for him, too. And when his hands are too trembly, and his eyes too shiny, why, I lecture him about his life and the wrong way he is going about it to mend it. But he worships me, I know. His eyes and his hands do not lie. And it makes me feel grown-up, the thought of it, the very thought of it; and I feel that I am possessed of something that is by rights my own—that makes me like the other girls—and—and young women. And then, too, I knew that I was not like them before, and I knew that it worried you. You thought you did not let me know that dear worry of yours, but I did, and I wanted to—'to make good,' as Martin Eden says."

It was a holy hour for mother and daughter, and their eyes were wet as they talked on in the twilight, Ruth all white innocence and frankness, her mother sympathetic, receptive, yet calmly explaining and guiding.

"He is four years younger than you," she said. "He has no place in the world. He has neither position nor salary. He is impractical. Loving you, he should, in the name of common sense, be doing something that would give him the right to marry, instead of paltering around with those stories of his and with childish dreams. Martin Eden, I am afraid, will never grow up. He does not take to responsibility and a man's work in the world like your father did, or like all our friends, Mr. Butler for one. Martin Eden, I am afraid will never be a money-earner. And this world is so ordered that money is necessary to happiness—oh, no, not these swollen fortunes, but enough of money to permit of common comfort and decency. He—he has never spoken?"

"He has not breathed a word. He has not attempted to, but if he did I would not let him, because, you see, I do not love him."

"I am glad of that. I should not care to see my daughter, my one daughter, who is so clean and pure, love a man like him. There are noble men in the world who are clean and true and manly. Wait for them. You will find one some day, and you will love him and be loved by him, and you will be happy with him as your father and I have been happy with each other. And there is one thing you must always carry in mind—"

"Yes, mother."

Mrs. Morse's voice was low and sweet as she said, "And that is the children."

"I—I have thought about them," Ruth confessed, remembering the wanton thoughts that had vexed her in the past, her face again red with maiden shame that she should be telling such things.

"And it is that, the children, that makes Mr. Eden impossible," Mrs. Morse went on incisively. "Their heritage must be clean, and he is, I am afraid, not clean. Your father has told me of sailors' lives, and—and you understand."

Ruth pressed her mother's hand in assent, feeling that she really did understand, though her conception was of something vague, remote and terrible that was beyond the scope of imagination.

"You know I do nothing without telling you," she began, "—only, sometimes you must ask me, like this time. I wanted to tell you, but I did not know how. It is false modesty, I know it is that, but you can make it easy for me. Sometimes, like this time, you must ask me, you must give me a chance.

"Why, mother, you are a woman, too!" she cried exultantly, as they stood up, catching her mother's hands and standing erect, facing her in the twilight, conscious of a stangely sweet equality between them. "I should never have thought of you in that way if we had not had this talk. I had to learn that I was a woman to know that you were one, too."

"We are women together," her mother said, drawing her to her and kissing her. "We are women together," she repeated, as they went out of the room, their arms around each other's waists, their hearts swelling with a new sense of companionship.

"Our little girl has become a woman," Mrs. Morse said proudly to her husband an hour later.

"That means," he said, after a long look at his wife, "that means she is in love."

"No, but that she is loved," was the smiling rejoinder. "The experiment has succeeded. She is awakened at last."

"Then we 'll have to get rid of him." Mr. Morse spoke briskly, in matter-of-fact, business-like tones.

But his wife shook her head. "It will not be necessary. Ruth says he is going to sea in a few days. When he comes back she will not be here. We will send her to Aunt Clara's. And, besides, a year in the East, with the change in climate, people, ideas, and everything, is just the thing she needs."

CHAPTER XX.

THE desire to write was stirring in Martin once more. Stories and poems were springing into spontaneous creation in his brain, and he made notes of them against the future time when he would give them expression. But he did not write. This was his little vacation; he had resolved to devote it to rest and love, and in both matters he prospered. He was soon spilling over with vitality, and each day he saw Ruth, at the moment of meeting, she experienced the old shock of his strength and health.

"Be careful," her mother warned her once again. "I am afraid you are seeing too much of Martin Eden."

But Ruth laughed from security. She was sure of herself, and in a few days he would be off to sea. Then, by the time he returned, she would be away on her visit East. There was a magic, however, in the strength and health of Martin. He, too, had been told of her contemplated Eastern trip, and he felt the need for haste. Yet he did not know how to make love to a girl like Ruth. Then, too, he was handicapped by the possession of a great fund of experience with girls and women who had been absolutely different from her. They had known about love and life and flirtation, while she knew nothing about such things. Her prodigious innocence appalled him, freezing on his lips all ardours of speech and convincing him, in spite of himself, of his own unworthiness. Also, he was handicapped in another way. He had himself never been in love before. He had liked women in that turgid past of his, and had been fascinated by some of them, but he had not known what it was to love them. He had whistled in a masterful, careless way, and they had come to him. They had been diversions, incidents, part of the game men play, but a small part at most. And now, and for the first time, he was a suppliant, tender, and timid and doubting. He did not know the way of love, nor its speech, while he was frightened at his loved one's clear innocence.

In the course of getting acquainted with a varied world, whirling on through the ever-changing phases of it, he had learned a rule of conduct which was to the effect that when one played a strange game he should let the other fellow play first. This had stood him in good stead a thousand times and trained him as an observer as well. He knew how to watch the thing that was strange, and to wait for a weakness, for a place of entrance, to divulge itself. It was like sparring for an opening in fist-fighting. And when such an opening came, he knew by long experience to play for it and to play hard.

So he waited with Ruth and watched, desiring to speak his love, but not daring. He was afraid of shocking her, and he was not sure of himself. Had he but known it, he was following the right course with her. Love came into the world before articulate speech, and in its own early youth it had learned ways and means that it had never forgotten. It was in this old, primitive way that Martin wooed Ruth. He did not know he was doing it at first, though later he divined it. The touch of his hand on hers was vastly more potent than any word he could utter, the impact of his strength on her imagination was more alluring than the printed poems and spoken passions of a thousand generations of lovers. Whatever his tongue could express would have appealed in part, to her judgment; but the touch of hand, the fleeting contact, made its way directly to her instinct. Her judgment was as young as she, but her instincts were as old as the race and older. They had been young when love was young, and they were wiser than convention and opinion and all the newborn things. So her judgment did not act. There was no call upon it, and she did not realize the strength of the appeal Martin made from moment to moment to her love-nature. That he loved her, on the other hand, was as clear as day, and she consciously delighted in beholding his love-manifestations—the glowing eyes with their tender lights, the trembling hands, and the never-failing swarthy flush that flooded darkly under his sunburn. She even went farther, in a timid way inciting him, but doing it so delicately, that he never suspected, and doing it half-consciously so that she scarcely suspected herself. She thrilled with these proofs of her power that proclaimed her a woman, and she took an Eve-like delight in tormenting him and playing upon him.

Tongue-tied by inexperience and by excess of ardor, wooing unwittingly and awkwardly, Martin continued his approach by contact. The touch of his hand was pleasant to her, and something deliciously more than pleasant. Martin did not know it, but he did know that it was not distasteful to her. Not that they touched hands often, save at meeting and parting; but that in handling the bicycles, in strapping on the books of verse they carried into the hills, and in conning the pages of books side by side, there were opportunities for hand to stray against hand. And there were opportunities, too, for her hair to brush his cheek, and for shoulder to touch shoulder, as they leaned together over the beauty of the books. She smiled to herself at vagrant impulses which arose from nowhere and suggested that she rumple his hair; while he desired greatly, when they tired of reading, to rest his head in her lap and dream with closed eyes about the future that was to be theirs. On Sunday picnics at Shellmound Park and Schuetzen Park, in the past, he had rested his head on many laps, and, usually, he had slept soundly and selfishly while the girls shaded his face from the sun and looked down and loved him and wondered at his lordly carelessness of their love. To rest his head in a girl's lap had been the easiest thing in the world until now, and now he found Ruth's lap inaccessible and impossible. Yet it was right here, in his reticence, that the strength of his wooing lay. It was because of this reticence that he never alarmed her. Herself fastidious and timid, she never awakened to the perilous trend of their intercourse. Subtly and unaware she grew toward him and closer to him, while he, sensing the growing closeness, longed to dare, but was afraid.

Once he dared, one afternoon, when he found her in the darkened living-room with a blinding headache.

''Nothing can do it any good,'' she had answered his inquiries. ''And besides, I dont take headache powders. Doctor Hall wont permit me.''

''I can cure it, I think, and without drugs,'' was Martin's answer. ''I am not sure, of course, but I 'd like to try. It 's simple massage. I learned the trick first from the Japanese. They are a race of masseurs, you know. Then I learned it all over again with variations from the Hawaiians. They call it *lomi-lomi*. It can accomplish most of the things drugs accomplish and a few things that drugs can 't.

Scarcely had his hands touched her head, when she sighed deeply.

''That is so good,'' she said.

She spoke once again, half an hour later, when she asked, ''Are n't you tired?''

The question was perfunctory, and she knew what the answer would be. Then she lost herself in drowsy contemplation of the soothing balm of his strength. Life poured from the ends of his fingers, driving the pain before it, or so it seemed to her, until with the easement of pain, she fell asleep and he stole away.

She called him up by telephone that evening to thank him.

''I slept until dinner,'' she said. ''You cured me completely, Mr. Eden, and I dont know how to thank you.''

He was warm, and bungling of speech,

and very happy, as he replied to her, and there was dancing in his mind, throughout the telephone conversation, the memory of Browning and of sickly Elizabeth Barrett. What had been done could be done again, and he, Martin Eden, could do it and would do it for Ruth Morse. He went back to his room and to the volume of Spencer's *Sociology* lying open on the bed. But he could not read. Love tormented him and overrode his will, so that, despite all determination, he found himself at the little ink-stained table. The sonnet he composed that night was the first of a love-cycle of fifty sonnets which he completed within two months. He had the "Love-Sonnets from the Portuguese" in mind as he wrote, and he wrote under the best conditions for great work, at a climacteric of living, in the throes of his own sweet love-madness.

The many hours he was not with Ruth he devoted to the "Love-Cycle," to reading at home, or to the public reading rooms where he got more closely in touch with the magazines of the day, and the nature of their policy and content. The hours he spent with Ruth were maddening alike in promise and inconclusiveness. It was a week after he cured her headache, that a moonlight sail on Lake Merritt was proposed by Norman and seconded by Arthur and Olney. Martin was the only one capable of handling a boat, and he was pressed into service. Ruth sat near him in the stern, while the three young fellows lounged amidships, deep in a wordy wrangle over "frat" affairs.

The moon had not yet risen, and Ruth, gazing into the starry vault of the sky and exchanging no speech with Martin, experienced a sudden feeling of loneliness. She glanced at him. A puff of wind was heeling the boat over till the deck was awash, and he, one hand on tiller and the other on the main-sheet, was luffing slightly, at the same time peering ahead to make out the near-lying north shore. He was unaware of her gaze, and she watched him intently, speculating fancifully about the strange warp of soul that led him, a young man with signal powers, to fritter away his time on the writing of stories and poems foredoomed to mediocrity and failure.

Her eyes wandered along the strong throat, dimly seen in the starlight, and over the firm-poised head, and the old desire to lay her hands upon his neck came back to her. The strength she abhored attracted her. Her feeling of loneliness became more pronounced, and she felt tired. Her position on the heeling boat irked her, and she remembered the headache he had cured and the soothing rest that resided in him. He was sitting beside her, quite beside her, and the boat seemed to tilt her toward him. Then arose in her the impulse to lean against him, to rest herself against his strength—a vague, half-formed impulse, which, even as she considered it, mastered her and made her lean toward him. Or was it the heeling of the boat? She did not know. She never knew. She knew only that she was leaning against him and that the easement and soothing rest were very good. Perhaps it had been the boat's fault, but she made no effort to retrieve it. She leaned lightly against his shoulder, but she leaned, and she continued to lean when he shifted his position to make it more comfortable for her.

It was a madness, but she refused to consider the madness. She was no longer herself, but a woman, with a woman's clinging need; and, though she leaned ever so lightly, the need seemed satisfied. She was no longer tired. Martin did not speak. Had he, the spell would have been broken. But his reticence of love prolonged it. He was dazed and dizzy. He could not understand what was happening. It was too wonderful to be anything but a delirium. He conquered a mad desire to let go sheet and tiller and to clasp her in his arms. His intuition told him it was the wrong thing to do, and he was glad that sheet and tiller kept his hands occupied and fended off temptation. But he luffed the boat less delicately, spilling the wind shamelessly from the sail so as to prolong the tack to the north shore. The shore would compel him to go about, and the contact would be broken. He sailed with skill, stopping way on the boat without exciting the notice of the wranglers, and mentally forgiving his hardest voyages in that they had made this marvelous night possible, giving him mastery over sea and boat and wind so that he could sail with her beside him, her dear weight against him on his shoulder.

When the first light of the rising moon touched the sail, illuminating the boat with pearly radiance, Ruth moved away from him. And, even as she moved, she felt him move away. The impulse to avoid detection was mutual. The episode was tacitly and secretly intimate. She sat apart from him with burning cheeks, while the full force of it came home to her. She had been guilty of something she would never have her brothers see, nor Olney see. Why had she done it? She had never done anything like it in her life, and yet she had been moonlight-sailing with young men before. She had never desired to do anything like it. She was overcome with shame and with the mystery of her own burgeoning womanhood. She stole a glance at Martin, who was busy putting the boat about on the other tack, and she could have hated him for having made her do an immodest and shameful thing. And he, of all men! Perhaps her mother was right, and she was seeing too much of him. It would never happen again, she resolved, and she would see less of him in the future. She entertained a wild idea of explaining to him the first time they were alone together, of lying to him, of mentioning casually the attack of faintness that had overpowered her just before the moon came up. Then she remembered how they had drawn mutually away before the revealing moon, and she knew he would know it for a lie.

In the days that swiftly followed she was no longer herself but a strange, puzzling creature, wilful over judgment and scornful of self-analysis, refusing to peer into the future or to think about herself and whither she was drifting. She was in a fever of tingling mystery, alternately frightened and charmed, and in constant bewilderment. She had one idea firmly fixed, however, which insured her security. She would not let Martin speak his love. As long as she did this, all would be well. In a few days he would be off to sea. And even if he did speak, all would be well. It could not be otherwise, for she did not love him. Of course, it would be a painful half hour for him, and an embarrassing half hour for her, because it would be her first proposal. She thrilled deliciously at the thought. She was really a woman, with a man ripe to ask for her in marriage. It was a lure to all that was fundamental in her sex. The fabric of her life, of all that constituted her, quivered and grew tremulous. The thought fluttered in her mind like a flame-attracted moth. She went so far as to imagine Martin proposing, herself putting the words into his mouth; and she rehearsed her refusal tempering it with kindness and exhorting him to true and noble manhood. And especially he must stop smoking cigarettes. She would make a point of that. But no, she must not let him speak at all. She could stop him, and she had told her mother that she would.

All flushed and burning, she regretfully dismissed the conjured situation. Her first proposal would have to be deferred to a more propitious time and a more eligible suitor.

Martin Eden

By Jack London

Author of 'The Call of the Wild,' 'Sea Wolf,' 'The God of His Fathers,' 'White Fang,' etc.

CHAPTER XXI.

CAME a beautiful fall day, warm and languid, palpitant with the hush of the changing season, a California Indian Summer day, with hazy sun and wandering wisps of breeze that did not stir the slumber of the air. Filmy purple mists, that were not vapors but fabrics woven of color, hid in the recesses of the hills. San Francisco lay like a blur of smoke upon her heights. The intervening bay was a dull sheen of molten metal, whereon sailing craft lay motionless or drifted with the lazy tide. Far Tamalpais, barely seen in the silver haze, bulked hugely by the Golden Gate, the latter a pale-gold pathway under the westering sun. Beyond, the Pacific, dim and vast, was raising on its sky-line tumbled cloud-masses that swept landward, giving warning of the first blustering breath of winter.

The erasure of summer was at hand. Yet summer lingered, fading and fainting among her hills, deepening the purple of her valleys, spinning a shroud of haze from waning powers and sated raptures, dying with the calm content of having lived and lived well. And among the hills, on their favorite knoll, Martin and Ruth sat side by side, their heads bent over the same pages, he reading aloud from the love-sonnets of the woman who had loved Browning as it is given to few men to be loved.

But the reading languished. The spell of passing beauty all about them was too strong. The golden year was dying as it had lived, a beautiful and unrepentant voluptuary, and reminiscent rapture and content freighted heavily the air. It entered into them, dreamy and languorous, weakening the fibers of resolution, suffusing the face of morality, or of judgment, with haze and purple mist. Martin felt tender and melting, and from time to time warm glows passed over him. His head was very near to hers, and when wandering phantoms of breeze stirred her hair so that it touched his face, the printed pages swam before his eyes.

"I dont believe you know a word of what you are reading," she said, once, when he had lost his place.

He looked at her with burning eyes, and was on the verge of becoming awkward, when a retort came to his lips.

"I dont believe you know either. What was the last sonnet about?"

"I dont know," she laughed frankly. "I 've already forgotten. Dont let us read any more. The day is too beautiful."

"It will be our last in the hills for some time," he announced gravely. "There 's a storm gathering out there on the sea-rim."

The book slipped from his hands to the ground, and they sat idly and silently, gazing out over the dreamy bay with eyes that dreamed and did not see. Ruth glanced sidewise at his neck. She did not lean toward him. She was drawn by some force outside of herself and stronger than gravitation, strong as destiny. It was only an inch to lean, and it was accomplished without volition on her part. Her shoulder touched his as lightly as a butterfly touches a flower, and just as lightly was the counter-pressure. She felt his shoulder press hers, and a tremor run through him. Then was the time for her to draw back. But she had become an automaton. Her actions had passed beyond the control of her will—she never thought of control or will in the delicious madness that was upon her.

His arm began to steal behind her and around her. She waited its slow progress in a torment of delight. She waited, she knew not for what, panting, with dry, burning lips, a leaping pulse, and a fever of expectancy in all her blood. The girdling arm lifted higher and drew her toward him, drew her slowly and caressingly. She could wait no longer. With a tired sigh, and with an impulsive movement all her own, unpremeditated, spasmodic, she rested her head upon his breast. His head bent over swiftly, and, as his lips approached, hers flew to meet them.

This must be love, she thought, in the one rational moment that was vouchsafed her. If it was not love, it was too shameful. It could be nothing else than love. She loved the man whose arms were around her and whose lips were pressed to hers. She pressed more tightly to him, with a snuggling movement of her body. And a moment later, tearing herself half out of his embrace, suddenly and exultantly she reached up and placed both hands upon Martin Eden's sunburnt neck. So exquisite was the pang of love and desire fulfilled that she uttered a low moan, relaxed her hands, and lay half-swooning in his arms.

Not a word had been spoken, and not a word was spoken for a long time. Twice he bent and kissed her, and each time her lips met his shyly and her body made its happy, nestling movement. She clung to him, unable to release herself, and he sat, half-supporting her in his arms, as he gazed with unseeing eyes at the blur of the great city across the bay. For once there were no visions in his brain. Only colors and lights and glows pulsed there, warm as the day and warm as his love. He bent over her. She was speaking.

"When did you love me?" she whispered.

"From the first, the very first, the first moment I laid eyes on you. I was mad for love of you then, and in all the time that has passed since then I have grown only the madder. I am maddest, now, dear. I am almost a lunatic, my head is so turned with joy."

"I am glad I am a woman Martin—dear," she said, after a long sigh.

He crushed her in his arms again and again, and then asked:

"And you? When did you first know?"

"Oh, I knew it all the time, almost from the first."

"And I have been as blind as a bat!" he cried, a ring of vexation in his voice. "I never dreamed it until just now, when I—when I kissed you."

"I did n't mean that." She drew herself partly away and looked at him. "I meant I knew you loved me almost from the first."

"And you?" he demanded.

"It came to me suddenly." She was speaking very slowly, her eyes warm and fluttery and melting, a soft flush on her cheeks that did not go away. "I never knew until just now when—you put your arms around me. And I never expected to marry you, Martin, not until just now. How did you make me love you?"

"I dont know," he laughed, "unless just by loving you, for I loved you hard enough to melt the heart of a stone, much less the heart of the living, breathing woman you are."

"This is so different from what I thought love would be," she announced irrelevantly.

"What did you think it would be like?"

"I did n't think it would be like this." She was looking into his eyes at the moment, but her own dropped as she continued. "You see, I did n't know what this was like."

He offered to draw her toward him again, but it was no more than a tentative muscular movement of the girdling arm, for he feared that he might be greedy. Then he felt her body yielding, and once again she was close in his arms and lips were pressed on lips.

"What will my people say?" she

queried, with sudden apprehension, in one of the pauses.

"I dont know. We may find out very easily any time we are so minded."

"But if mamma objects? I am sure I am afraid to tell her."

"Let me tell her," he volunteered valiantly. "I think your mother does not like me, but I can win her around. A fellow who can win you can win anything. And if we dont—"

"Yes?"

"Why, we 'll have each other. But there 's no danger of not winning your mother to our marriage. She loves you too well."

"I should not like to break her heart," Ruth said pensively.

He felt like assuring her that mothers' hearts were not so easily broken, but instead he said: "And love is the greatest thing in the world."

"Do you know, Martin, you sometimes frighten me. I am frightened now, when I think of you and of what you have been. You must be very, very good to me. Remember, after all, that I am only a child. I never loved before."

"Nor I. We are both children together. And we are fortunate above most, for we have found our first love in each other."

"But that is impossible!" she cried, withdrawing herself from his arms with a swift, passionate movement. "Impossible for you. You have been a sailor, and sailors, I have heard, are—are—"

Her voice faltered and died away.

"Are addicted to having a wife in every port?" he suggested. "Is that what you mean?"

"Yes," she answered in a low voice.

"But that is not love." He spoke authoritatively. "I have been in many ports, but I never knew a passing touch of love until I saw you that first night. Do you know, when I said good night and went away I was almost arrested."

"Arrested?"

"Yes. The policeman thought I was drunk; and I was, too—with love for you."

"But you said we were children, and I said it was impossible, for you, and we have strayed away from the point."

"I said that I had never loved anybody but you," he replied. "You are my first, my very first."

"And yet you have been a sailor," she objected.

"But it does n't prevent me from loving you the first."

"And there have been women—other women—oh!"

And to Martin Eden's supreme surprise, she burst into a storm of tears that took more kisses than one and many caresses to drive away. And all the while there was running through his head Kipling's line: *"And the Colonel's lady and Judy O'Grady are sisters under their skins."* It was true, he decided: though the novels he had read had led him to believe otherwise. His idea, for which the novels were responsible, had been that only formal proposals obtained in the upper classes. It was all right enough, down whence he had come, for youths and maidens to win to each other by contact; but for the exalted personages up above on the heights to make love in similar fashion had seemed unthinkable. Yet the novels were wrong. Here was a proof of it. The same pressures and caresses, unaccompanied by speech, that were efficacious with the girls of the working class, were equally efficacious with the girls above the working class. They were all of the same flesh, after all, sisters under their skins; and he might have known as much himself had he remembered his *Spencer*. As he held Ruth in his arms and soothed her, he took great consolation in the thought that the Colonel's lady and Judy O'Grady were pretty much alike under their skin. It brought Ruth closer to him, made her possible. Her dear flesh was as anybody's flesh, as his flesh. There was no bar to their marriage. Class difference was the only difference, and class was extrinsic. It could be shaken off. A slave, he had read, had risen to the Roman purple. That being so, then he could rise to Ruth. Under her purity, and saintliness, and culture, and ethereal beauty of soul, she was, in things fundamentally human, just like Lizzie Connolly and all Lizzie Connollys. All that was possible of them was possible of her. She could love, and hate, maybe have hysteria; and she could certainly be jealous, as she was jealous now, uttering her last sobs in his arms.

"Besides, I am older than you," she remarked suddenly, opening her eyes and looking up at him. "Three years older."

"Hush, you are only a child, and I am forty years older than you, in experience," was his answer.

In truth, they were children together, so far as love was concerned, and they were as naive and immature in the expression of their love as a pair of children, and this, despite the fact that she was crammed with a university education and that his head was full of scientific philosophy and the hard facts of life.

They sat on through the passing glory of the day, talking as lovers are prone to talk, marveling at the wonder of love and at destiny that had flung them so strangely together, and dogmatically believing that they loved to a degree never attained by lovers before. And they returned insistently, again and again, to a rehearsal of their first impressions of each other and to hopeless attempts to analyze just precisely what they felt for each other and how much there was of it.

The cloud-masses on the western horizon received the descending sun, and the circle of the sky turned to rose, while the zenith glowed with the same warm color. The rosy light was all about them, flooding over them, as she sang, "Goodbye Sweet Day." She sang softly, leaning in the cradle of his arm, her hands in his, their hearts in each other's hands.

CHAPTER XXII.

MRS. MORSE did not require a mother's intuition to read the advertisement in Ruth's face when she returned home. The flush that would not leave the cheeks told the simple story, and more eloquently did the eyes, large and bright, reflecting an unmistakable inward glory.

"What has happened?" Mrs. Morse asked, having bided her time till Ruth had gone to bed.

"You know?" Ruth queried, with trembling lips.

For reply, her mother's arm went around her, and a hand was softly caressing her hair.

"He did not speak," she blurted out. "I did not intend that it should happen, and I would never have let him speak—only he did n't speak."

"But if he did not speak, then nothing could have happened, could it?"

"But it did, just the same."

"In the name of goodness, child, what are you babbling about?" Mrs. Morse was bewildered. "I dont think I know what happened after all. What did happen?"

Ruth looked at her mother in surprise.

"I thought you knew. Why, we 're engaged, Martin and I."

Mrs. Morse laughed with incredulous vexation.

"No, he did n't speak," Ruth explained. "He just loved me, that was all. I was as surprised as you are. He did n't say a word. He just put his arm around me. And—and I was not myself. And he kissed me, and I kissed him. I could n't help it. I just had to. And then I knew I loved him."

She paused, waiting with expectancy the benediction of her mother's kiss, but Mrs. Morse was coldly silent.

"It is a dreadful accident, I know," Ruth recommenced, with a sinking voice. "And I dont know how you will ever forgive me. But I could n't help it. I did not dream that I loved him until that moment. And you must tell father for me."

"Would it not be better not to tell your father? Let me see Martin Eden, and talk with him, and explain. He will understand, and release you."

"No! no!" Ruth cried, starting up. "I do not want to be released. I love him, and love is very sweet. I am going to marry him—of course, if you will let me."

"We have other plans for you, Ruth, dear, your father and I—oh, no, no; no man picked out for you, or anything like that. Our plans go no farther than your marrying some man in your own station in life, a good and honorable gentleman, whom you will select yourself, when you love him."

"But I love Martin already," was the plaintive protest.

"We would not influence your choice in any way; but you are our daughter, and we could not bear to see you make a marriage such as this. He has nothing but roughness and coarseness to offer you in exchange for all that is refined and delicate in you. He is no match for you in any way. He could not support you. We have no foolish ideas about wealth, but comfort is another matter, and our daughter should at least marry a man who can give her that—and not a penniless adventurer, a sailor, a cowboy, a smuggler, and heaven knows what else, who, in addition to everything, is hare-brained and irresponsible."

Ruth was silent. Every word she recognized as true.

"He wastes his time over his writing, trying to accomplish what geniuses and rare men with college educations sometimes accomplish. A man, thinking of marriage, should be preparing for marriage. But not he. As I have said, and I know you agree with me, he is irresponsible. And why should he not be? It is the way of sailors. He has never learned to be economical or temperate. The spendthrift years have marked him. It is not his fault, of course, but that does not alter his nature. And have you thought of the years of licentiousness he inevitably has lived? Have you thought of that, daughter? You know what marriage means."

Ruth shuddered and clung close to her mother.

"I have thought." Ruth waited a long time for the thought to frame itself. "And it is terrible. It sickens me to think of it. I told you it was a dreadful accident, my loving him; but I can't help myself. Could you help loving father? Then it is the same with me. There is something in me, in him—I never knew it was there until today—but it is there, and it makes me love him. I never thought to love him, but, you see, I do," she concluded, a certain faint triumph in her voice.

They talked long, and to little purpose, in conclusion agreeing to wait an indeterminate time without doing anything.

The same conclusion was reached, a little later that night, between Mrs. Morse and her husband, after she had made due confession of the miscarriage of her plans.

"It could hardly have come otherwise," was Mr. Morse's judgment. "This sailor-fellow has been the only man she was in touch with. Sooner or later she was going to awaken anyway; and she did awaken, and lo! here was this sailor-fellow, the only accessible man at the moment, and of course she promptly loved him, or thought she did, which amounts to the same thing."

Mrs. Morse took it upon herself to work slowly and indirectly upon Ruth, rather than to combat her. There would be plenty of time for this, for Martin was not in position to marry.

"Let her see all she wants of him," was Mr. Morse's advice. "The more she knows him the less she'll love him, I wager. And give her plenty of contrast. Make a point of having young people at the house; young women and young men, all sorts of young men, clever men, men who have done something or who are doing things, men of her own class, gentlemen. She can guage him by them. They will show him up for what he is. And after all, he is a mere boy of twenty-one. Ruth is no more than a child. It is calf love with the pair of them, and they will grow out of it."

So the matter rested. Within the family it was accepted that Ruth and Martin were engaged, but no announcement was made. The family did not think it would ever be necessary. Also, it was tacitly understood that it was to be a long engagement. They did not ask Martin to go to work, nor to cease writing. They did not intend to encourage him to mend himself. And he aided and abetted them in their unfriendly designs, for going to work was farthest from his thoughts.

"I wonder if you 'll like what I have done?" he said to Ruth several days later. "I 've decided that boarding with my sister is too expensive, and I am going to board myself. I 've rented a little room out in North Oakland, retired neighborhood and all the rest, you know, and I 've bought an oil-burner on which to cook."

Ruth was overjoyed. The oil-burner especially pleased her.

"That was the way Mr. Butler began his start,' she said.

Martin frowned inwardly at the citation of that worthy gentleman, and went on:

"I put stamps on all my manuscripts and started them off to the editors again Then today I moved in, and tomorrow I start to work."

"A position!" she cried, betraying the gladness of her surprise in all her body, nestling closer to him, pressing his hand, smiling. "And you never told me! What is it?"

He shook his head.

"I meant that I was going to work at my writing." Her face fell, and he went on hastily. "Dont misjudge me. I am not going in this time with any iridescent ideas. It is to be a cold, prosaic, matter-of-fact, business proposition. It is better than going to sea again, and I shall earn more money than any position in Oakland can bring an unskilled man.

"You see, this vacation I have taken has given me perspective. I have n't been working the life out of my body, and I have n't been writing, at least not for publication. All I 've done has been to love you and to think. I 've read some, too, but it has been part of my thinking, and I have read principally magazines. I have generalized about myself, and the world, my place in it, and my chance to win to a place that will be fit for you. Also, I 've been reading Spencer's *Philosophy of Style*, and found out a lot of what was the matter with me—or my writing, rather; and for that matter, with most of the writing that is published every month in the magazines.

"But the upshot of it all—of my thinking and reading and loving—is that I am going to move to Grub street. I shall leave masterpieces alone and do hack-work—jokes, paragraphs, feature articles, humorous verse, and society verse—all the rot for which there seems so much demand. Then there are the newspaper syndicates, and the newspaper short-story syndicates, and the syndicates for the Sunday supplements. I can go ahead and hammer out the stuff they want, and earn the equivalent of a good salary by it. There are free-lances, you know, who earn as much as four or five hundred a month. I dont care to become as they; but I 'll earn a good living, and have plenty of time to myself, which I would n't have in any position.

"Then, I 'll have my spare time for study and for real work. In between the grind I 'll try my hand at masterpieces, and I 'll study and prepare myself for the writing of masterpieces. Why, I am amazed at the distance I have come already. When I first tried to write, I had nothing to write about except a few paltry experiences which I neither understood nor appreciated. But I had no thoughts. I really did n't. I did n't even have the words with which to think. My experiences were so many meaningless pictures. But as I began to add to my knowledge, and to my vocabulary, I saw something more in my experiences than mere pictures. I retained the pictures and I found their interpretation. That was when I began to do good work, when I wrote 'Adventure,' 'Joy,' 'The Pot,' 'The Wine of Life,' 'The Jostling Street,' the 'Love-Cycle,' and the 'Sea Lyrics.' I shall write more like them, and better; but I shall do it in my spare time. My feet are on the solid earth, now. Hack-work and income first, masterpieces afterward. Just to show you, I wrote half a dozen jokes last night for the comic weeklies; and just as I was going to bed, the thought struck me to try my hand at a triolet—a humorous one; and inside an hour I had written four. They ought to be worth a dollar apiece. Four dollars right there for a few after-thoughts on the way to bed.

"Of course; it 's all valueless, just so much dull and sordid plodding; but it is no more dull and sordid than keeping books at sixty dollars a month, adding up endless columns of meaningless figures until one dies. And furthermore, the hack-work keeps me in touch with things literary and gives me time to try bigger things."

"But what good are these bigger things, these masterpieces?" Ruth demanded. "You can 't sell them."

"Oh, yes I can," he began; but she interrupted.

"All those you named, and which you say yourself are good—you have not sold any of them. We can 't get married on masterpieces that wont sell."

"Then we 'll get married on triolets that will sell," he asserted stoutly, putting his arm around her and drawing a very unresponsive sweetheart toward him.

"Listen to this," he went on, in attempted gaiety. "It 's not art, but it 's a dollar:

He came in
  When I was out,
To borrow some tin
Was why he came in,
  And he went without;
So I was in
  And he was out.

The merry lilt with which he had invested the jingle was at variance with the dejection that came into his face as he finished. He had drawn no smile from Ruth. She was looking at him in an earnest and troubled way.

"It may be a dollar," she said, "but it is a jester's dollar, the fee of a clown. Dont you see, Martin, the whole thing is lowering. I want the man I love and honor to be something finer and higher than a perpetrator of jokes and doggerel."

"You want him to be like—say Mr. Butler?" he suggested.

"I know you dont like Mr. Butler," she began.

"Mr. Butler 's all right," he interrupted. "It 's only his indigestion I find fault with. But to save me I can 't see any difference between writing jokes or comic verse and running a typewriter, taking dictation, or keeping sets of books. It is all a means to an end. Your theory is for me to begin with keeping books in order to become a successful lawyer or man of business. Mine is to begin with hack-work and develop into an able author."

"There is a difference," she insisted.

"What is it?"

"Why, your good work, what you yourself call good, you can 't sell. You have tried—you know that—but the editors wont buy it."

"Give me time, dear," he pleaded. "The hack-work is only makeshift, and I dont take it seriously. Give me two years. I shall succeed in that time, and the editors will be glad to buy my good work. I know what I am saying; I have faith in myself. I know what I have in me; I know what literature is, now; I know the average rot that is poured out by a lot of little men; and I know that at the end of two years I shall be on the high-road to success. As for business, I shall never succeed at it. I am not in sympathy with it. It strikes me as dull, and stupid, and mercenary, and tricky. Anyway, I am not adapted for it. I 'd never get beyond a clerkship, and how could you and I be happy on the paltry earnings of a clerk? I want the best of everything in the world for you, and the only time when I wont want it will be when there is something better. And I 'm going to get it, going to get all of it. The income of a successful author makes Mr. Butler look cheap. A 'best-seller' will earn anywhere between fifty and a hundred thousand dollars—sometimes more and sometimes less; but, as a rule, pretty close to those figures."

She remained silent; her disappointment was apparent.

"Well?" he asked.

"I had hoped and planned otherwise. I had thought, and I still think that the best thing for you would be to study shorthand—you already know typewriting—and go into father's office. You have a good mind, and I am confident you would succeed as a lawyer."

CHAPTER XXIII.

THAT Ruth had little faith in his power as a writer, did not alter her nor diminish her in Martin's eyes. In the breathing spell of the vacation he had taken, he had spent many hours in self-analysis, and thereby learned much of himself. He had discovered that he loved beauty more than fame, and that what desire he had for fame was largely for Ruth's sake. It was for this reason that his desire for fame was strong. He wanted to be great in the world's eyes, "to make good" as he expressed it, in order that the woman he loved should be proud of him and deem him worthy.

As for himself, he loved beauty passionately, and the joy of serving her was to him sufficient wage. And more than beauty, he loved Ruth. He considered love the finest thing in the world. It was love that had worked the revolution in him, changing him from an uncouth sailor to a student and an artist; therefore, to him, the finest and greatest of the three, greater than learning and artistry, was love. Already he had discovered that his brain went beyond Ruth's, just as it went beyond the brains of her brothers, or the brain of her father. In spite of every advantage of university training, and in the face of her bachelorship of arts, his power of intellect overshadowed hers, and his year or so of self-study and equipment gave him a mastery of the affairs of the world and art and life that she could never hope to possess.

All this he realized, but it did not affect his love for her, nor her love for him. Love was too fine and noble, and he was too loyal a lover for him to besmirch love with criticism. What did love have to do with Ruth's divergent views on art, right conduct, the French Revolution, or equal suffrage? They were mental processes, but love was beyond reason; it was superrational. He could not belittle love. He worshipped it. Love lay on the mountain-tops beyond the valley-land of reason. It was a sublimated condition of existence, the topmost peak of living, and it came rarely. Thanks to the school of scientific philosophers he favored, he knew the biological significance of love; but by a refined process of the same scientific reasoning he reached the conclusion that the human organism achieved its highest purpose in love, that love must not be questioned but must be accepted as the highest guerdon of life. Thus, he considered the lover blessed over all creatures, and it was a delight to him to think of "God's own mad lover," rising above the things of earth, above wealth and judgment, public opinion and applause, rising above life itself and "dying on a kiss."

Much of this Martin had already reasoned out, and some of it he reasoned out later. In the meantime he worked, taking no recreation except when he went to see Ruth, and living like a Spartan. He paid two dollars and a half a month rent for the small room he got from his Portuguese landlady, Maria Silva, a virago and a widow, hard-working and harsher-tempered, rearing her large brood of children somehow, and drowning her sorrow and fatigue at irregular intervals in a gallon of the thin, sour wine that she bought from the corner grocery and saloon for fifteen cents. From detesting her and her foul tongue at first, Martin grew to admire her as he observed the brave fight she made. There were but four rooms in the little house, three, when Martin's was subtracted. One of these, the parlor, gay with an ingrain carpet and dolorous with a funeral card and a death-picture of one of her numerous departed babes, was kept strictly for company. The blinds were always down, and her barefooted tribe was never permitted to enter the sacred precinct save on state occasions. She cooked, and all ate, in the kitchen, where she likewise washed, starched, and ironed clothes on all days of the week except Sunday; for her income came largely from taking in washing from her more prosperous neighbors. Remained the bed-room, small as the one occupied by Martin, into which she and her seven little ones crowded and slept. It was an everlasting miracle to Martin, how it was accomplished, and from her side of the thin partition he heard nightly every detail of the going to bed, the squalls and squabbles, the soft chattering, and the sleepy, twittering noises as of birds. Another source of income to Maria was her cows, two of them, which she milked night and morning and which gained a surreptitious livelihood from vacant lots and the grass that grew on either side the public sidewalks, attended always by one or more of her ragged boys, whose watchful guardianship consisted chiefly in keeping their eyes out for the poundmen.

In his own small room Martin lived, slept, studied, wrote and kept house. Before the one window, looking out on the tiny front porch, was the kitchen table that served as desk, library, and typewriting stand. The bed against the rear wall, occupied two-thirds of the total space of the room. The table was flanked on one side by a gaudy bureau, manufactured for profit and not for service, the thin veneer of which was shed day by day. This bureau stood in the corner, and in the opposite corner, on the table's other flank, was the kitchen—the oil-stove on a drygoods box, inside of which were dishes and cooking utensils, a shelf on the wall for provisions, and a bucket of water on the floor. Martin had to carry his water from the kitchen sink, there being no tap in his room. On days when there was much steam to his cooking, the harvest of veneer from the bureau was unusually generous. Over the bed, hoisted by a tackle to the ceiling, was his bicycle. At first he had tried to keep it in the basement; but the tribe of Silva, loosening the bearings and puncturing the tires, had driven him out. Next he attempted the tiny front porch, until a howling southeaster drenched the wheel a night long. Then he had retreated with it to his room and slung it aloft.

A small closet contained his clothes and the books he had accumulated and for which there was no room on the table or under the table. Hand in hand with reading, he had developed the habit of making notes, and so copiously did he make them that there would have been no existence for him in the confined quarters had he not rigged several clotheslines across the room on which the notes were hung. Even so, he was crowded until navigating the room was a difficult task. He could not open the door without first closing the closet door, and vice versa. It was impossible for him anywhere to traverse the room in a straight line. To go from the door to the head of the bed was a zigzag course that he was never quite able to accomplish in the dark without collisions. Having settled the difficulty of the conflicting doors, he had to steer sharply to the right to avoid the kitchen. Next, he sheered to the left, to escape the foot of the bed; but this sheer, if too generous, brought him against the corner of the table. With a sudden twitch and lurch, he terminated the sheer and bore off to the right along a sort of canal, one bank of which was the bed, the other the table. When the one chair in the room was at its usual place before the table, the canal was unnavigable. When the chair was not in use, it reposed on top of the bed, though sometimes he sat on the chair when cooking, reading a book while water boiled, and even becoming skillful enough to manage a paragraph or two while steak was frying. Also, so small was the little corner that constituted the kitchen, he was able, sitting down, to reach anything he needed. In fact, it was expedient to cook sitting down; standing up he was too often in his own way.

In conjunction with a perfect stomach that could digest anything, he possessed knowledge of the various foods that were at the same time nutritious and cheap. Pea soup was a common article in his diet, as well as potatoes and beans, the latter large and brown and cooked in Mexican style. Rice, cooked as American housewives never cook it and can never learn to cook it, appeared on Martin's table at least once a day. Dried fruits were less expensive than fresh, and he had usually a pot of them, cooked and ready at hand, for they took the place of butter on his bread. Occasionally he graced his table with a piece of round-steak, or with a soup-bone. Coffee, without cream or milk, he had twice a day, in the evening substituting tea; but both coffee and tea were excellently cooked.

There was need for him to be economical. His vacation had consumed nearly all he had earned in the laundry, and he was so far from his market that weeks must elapse before he could hope for the first returns from his hack-work. Except at such times he saw Ruth, or dropped in to see his sister Gertrude, he lived a recluse, in each day accomplishing at least three days' labor of ordinary men. He slept a scant five hours, and only one with a constitution of iron could have held himself down, as Martin did, day after day, to nineteen consecutive hours of toil. He never lost a moment. On the looking glass were lists of definitions and pronunciations; when shaving, or dressing, or combing his hair, he conned these lists over. Similar lists were on the wall over the oil stove, and they were similarly conned while he was engaged in cooking or in washing the dishes. New lists continually displaced the old ones. Every strange or partly familiar word encountered in his reading was immediately jotted down, and later, when a sufficient number had been accumulated, were typed and pinned to the wall or looking glass. He even carried them in his pockets, and reviewed them at odd moments on the street, or while waiting in butcher shop or grocery to be served.

He went farther in the matter. Reading the works of men who had arrived, he noted every result achieved by them, and worked out the tricks by which they had been achieved—the tricks of narrative, of exposition, of style, the points of view, the contrasts, the epigrams; and of all these he made lists for study. He did not ape. He sought principles. He drew up lists of effective and fetching mannerisms, till out of many such, culled from many writers, he was able to induce the general principle of mannerism, and, thus equipped, to cast about for new and original ones of his own, and to weigh and measure and appraise them properly. In similar manner he collected lists of strong phrases, the phrases of living language, phrases that bit like acid and scorched like flame, or that glowed and were mellow and luscious in the midst of the arid desert of common speech. He sought always for the principle that lay behind and beneath. He wanted to know how the thing was done; after that he could do it for himself. He was not content with the fair face of beauty. He dissected beauty in his crowded little bedroom laboratory, where cooking smells alternated with the outer Bedlam of the Silva tribe; and, having dissected and learned the anatomy of beauty, he was nearer being able to create beauty himself.

He was so made that he could work only with understanding. He could not work blindly, in the dark, ignorant of what he was producing and trusting to chance and the star of his genius that the effect produced should be right and fine. He had no patience with chance effects. He wanted to know why and how. His was deliberate creative genius, and, before he began a story or poem, the thing itself was already alive in his brain, with the end in sight and the means of realizing that end in his conscious possession. Otherwise the effort was doomed to failure. On the other hand, he appreciated the chance effects in words and phrases that came lightly and easily into his brain and that later stood all tests of beauty and power and developed tremendous and incommunicable connotations. Before such be bowed down and marveled, knowing that they were beyond the deliberate creation of any man. And no matter how much he dissected beauty in search of the principles that underlie beauty and make beauty possible, he was aware, always, of the innermost mystery of beauty to which he did not penetrate and to which no man had ever penetrated. He knew full well, from his *Spencer,* that man can never attain ultimate knowledge of anything, and that the mystery of beauty was no less than that of life—nay, more—that the fibers of beauty and life were intertwisted, and that he himself was but a bit of the same nonunderstandable fabric, twisted of sunshine and star-dust and wonder.

In fact, it was when filled with these thoughts that he wrote his essay entitled "Star-Dust," in which he had his fling, not at the principles of criticism, but at the principal critics. It was brilliant, deep, philosophical, and deliciously touched with laughter. Also it was promptly rejected by the magazines as often as it was submitted. But having cleared his mind of it, he went serenely on his way. It was a habit he developed, of incubating and maturing his thought upon a subject, and of then rushing to the typewriter with it. That it did not see print was a matter of small moment with him. The writing of it was the culminating act of a long mental process the drawing together of scattered threads of thought and the final generalizing upon all the data with which his mind was burdened. To write such an article was the conscious effort by which he freed his mind and made it ready for fresh material and problems. It was in a way akin to that common habit of men and women, troubled by real or fancied grievances, who periodically and volubly break their long-suffering silence and "have their say" till the last word is said.

Martin Eden

By Jack London

Author of "The Call of the Wild," "Sea Wolf," "The God of His Fathers," "White Fang," etc.

CHAPTER XXIV.

THE weeks passed, Martin ran out of money, and publishers' checks were far away as ever. All his important manuscripts had come back and been started out again, and his hack-work fared no better. His little kitchen was no longer graced with a variety of foods. Caught in the pinch with a part-sack of rice and a few pounds of dried apricots, rice and apricots was his menu three times a day for five days handrunning. Then he started to realize on his credit. The Portuguese grocer, to whom he had hitherto paid cash, called a halt when Martin's bill reached the magnificent total of three dollars and eighty-five cents.

"For you see," said the grocer, "you no catcha da work, I losa da mon'."

And Martin could reply nothing. There was no way of explaining. It was not true business principle to allow credit to a strong-bodied young fellow of the working class who was too lazy to work.

"You catcha da job, I let you have mora da grub," the grocer assured Martin. "No job, no grub. Thata da business." And then, to show that it was purely business foresight and not prejudice, "Hava da drink on da house—good friends justa da same."

So Martin drank, in his easy way, to show that he was good friends with the house, and then went supperless to bed.

The fruit store, where Martin had bought his vegetables, was run by an American whose business principles were so weak that he let Martin run a bill of five dollars before stopping his credit. The baker stopped at two dollars, and the butcher at four dollars. Martin added his debts and found that he was possessed of a total credit in all the world of fourteen dollars and eighty-five cents. He was up with his typewriter rent, but he estimated that he could get two months' credit on that, which would be eight dollars. When that occurred, he would have exhausted all possible credit.

The last purchase from the fruit store had been a sack of potatoes and for a week he had potatoes, and nothing but potatoes, three times a day. An occasional dinner at Ruth's helped to keep strength in his body, though he found it tantalizing enough to refuse further helping when his appetite was raging at sight of so much food spread before it. Now and again, though afflicted with secret shame, he dropped in at his sister's at meal-time and ate as much as he dared—more than he dared at the Morse table.

Day by day he worked on, and day by day the postman delivered to him rejected manuscripts. He had no money for stamps, so the manuscripts accumulated in a heap under the table. Came a day when for forty hours he had not tasted food. He could not hope for a meal at Ruth's, for she was away to San Rafael on a two weeks' visit; and for very shame's sake he could not go to his sister's. To cap misfortune, the postman, in his afternoon round, brought him five returned manuscripts. Then it was that Martin wore his overcoat down into Oakland and came back without it, but with five dollars tinkling in his pocket. He paid a dollar each on account to the four tradesmen, and in his kitchen fried steak and onions, made coffee, and stewed a large pot of prunes. And having dined, he sat down at his table-desk and completed before midnight an essay which he entitled "The Dignity of Usury." Having typed it out, he flung it under the table, for there had been nothing left from the five dollars with which to buy stamps.

Later on he pawned his watch, and still later his wheel, reducing the amount available for food by putting stamps on all his manuscripts and sending them out. He was disappointed with his hackwork. Nobody cared to buy. He compared it with what he found in the newspapers, weeklies, and cheap magazines, and decided that his was better, far better, than the average; yet it would not sell. Then he discovered that most of the newspapers printed a great deal of what was called "plate" stuff, and he got the address of the association that furnished it. His own work that he sent in was returned along with a stereotyped slip informing him that the staff supplied all the copy that was needed.

In one of the great juvenile periodicals he noted whole columns of incident and anecdote. Here was a chance. His paragraphs were returned, and though he tried repeatedly he never succeeded in placing one. Later on, when it no longer mattered, he learned that the associate editors and sub-editors augmented their salaries by supplying those paragraphs themselves. The comic weeklies returned his jokes and humorous verse, and the light society verse he wrote for the large magazines found no abiding place. Then there was the newspaper storiette. He knew that he could write better ones than were published. Managing to obtain the addresses of two newspaper syndicates, he deluged them with storiettes. When he had written twenty and failed to place one of them, he ceased. And yet, from day to day, he read storiettes in the dailies and weeklies, scores and scores of storiettes, not one of which would compare with his. In his despondency, he concluded that he had no judgment whatever, that he was hypnotized by what he wrote, and that he was a self-deluded pretender.

The inhuman editorial machine ran smoothly as ever. He folded the stamps in with his manuscript, dropped it into the letter box, and from three weeks to a month afterward the postman came up the steps and handed him the manuscript. Surely there were no live, warm editors at the other end. It was all wheels and cogs and oil-cups—a clever mechanism operated by automatons. He reached stages of despair wherein he doubted if editors existed at all. He had never received a sign of the existence of one, and from absence of judgment in rejecting all he wrote it seemed plausible that editors were myths, manufactured and maintained by office boys, typesetters and pressmen.

The hours he spent with Ruth were the only happy ones he had, and they were not all happy. He was afflicted always with a gnawing restlessness, more tantalizing than in the old days before he possessed her love; for now that he did possess her love, the possession of her was far away as ever. He had asked for two years, time was flying, and he was achieving nothing. Again, he was always conscious of the fact that she did not approve what he was doing. She did not say so directly. Yet indirectly she let him understand it as clearly and definitely as could she have spoken it. It was not resentment with her, but disapproval; though less sweet-natured women might have resented where she was no more than disappointed. Her disappointment lay in that this man she had taken to mould, refused to be moulded. To a certain extent she had found his clay plastic, then it had developed stubbornness, declining to be shaped in the image of her father or of Mr. Butler.

What was great and strong in him, she missed, or, worse, yet, misunderstood. This man, whose clay was so plastic that he could live in any number of pigeonholes of human existence, she thought wilful and most obstinate because she could not shape him to live in her pigeonhole, which was the only one she knew. She could not follow the flights of his mind, and when his brain got beyond her she deemed him erratic. Nobody else's brain ever got beyond her. She could always follow her father and mother, her brothers and Olney; wherefore, when she could not follow Martin, she believed the fault lay with him. It was the old tragedy of insularity trying to serve as mentor to the universal.

"You worship at the shrine of the established," he told her once, in a discussion they had over Praps and Vanderwater. "I grant that as authorities to quote they are most excellent—the two foremost literary critics in the United States. Every school teacher in the land looks up to Vanderwater as the Dean of American criticism. Yet I read his stuff, and it seems to me the perfection of the felicitous expression of the inane. Why, he is no more than a ponderous bromide, thanks to Gelett Burgess. And Praps is no better. His *Hemlock Mosses* for instance, is beautifully written. Not a comma is out of place; and the tone—ah!—is lofty, so lofty. He is the best paid critic in the United States. Though, heaven forbid, he 's not a critic at all. They do criticism better in England.

"But the point is, they sound the popular note, and they sound it so beautifully and morally and contentedly. Their reviews remind me of a British Sunday. They are the popular mouthpieces. They back up your professors of English, and your professors of English back them up. And there is n't an original idea in any of their skulls. They know only the established—in fact, they are the established. They are weak minded, and the established impresses itself upon them as easily as the name of the brewery is impressed on a beer bottle. And their function is to catch all the young fellows attending the university, to drive out of their minds any glimmering originality that may chance to be there, and to put upon them the stamp of the established."

"I think I am nearer the truth," she replied, "when I stand by the established, then you are, raging around like an iconoclastic South Sea Islander."

"It was the missionary who did the image breaking," he laughed. "And unfortunately, all the missionaries are off among the heathen, so there are none left at home to break those old images, Mr. Vanderwater and Mr. Praps."

"And the college professors, as well," she added.

He shook his head emphatically. "No; the science professors should live. They 're really great. But it would be a good deed to break the heads of nine-tenths of the English professors—little, microscopic-minded parrots!"

Which was rather severe on the professors, but which to Ruth was blasphemy. She could not help but measure the professors, neat, scholarly, in fitting clothes, speaking in well-modulated voices, breathing of culture and refinement, with this almost indescribable young fellow whom somehow she loved, whose clothes never would fit him, whose heavy muscles told of damning toil, who grew excited when he talked, substituting abuse for calm statement and passionate utterance for cool self-possession. They at least earned good salaries and were—yes, she compelled herself to face it—were gentlemen; while he could not earn a penny, and he was not as they.

She did not weigh Martin's words nor judge his argument by them. Her conclusion that his argument was wrong was reached—unconsciously, it is true—by a comparison of externals. They, the professors, were right in their literary judgments because they were successes. Martin's literary judgments were wrong because he could not sell his wares. To use his own phrase, they made good, and he did not make good. And besides, it did not seem reasonable that he should be right—he who had stood, so short a time before, in that same living room, blushing and awkward, acknowledging his introduction, looking fearfully about him at the bric-a-brac his swinging shoulders threatened to break, asking how long since Swinburne died, and boastfully announcing that he had read "Excelsior" and the "Psalm of Life."

Unwittingly, Ruth herself proved his point that she worshiped the established. Martin followed the processes of her thoughts, but forebore to go further. He did not love her for what she thought of Praps and Vanderwater and English professors, and he was coming to realize, with increasing conviction, that he possessed brain-areas and stretches of knowledge which she could never comprehend nor know existed.

In music, she thought him unreasonable, and in the matter of opera not only unreasonable but wilfully perverse.

"How did you like it?" she asked him one night, on the way home from the opera.

It was a night when he had taken her at the expense of a month's rigid economizing on food. After vainly waiting for him to speak about it, herself still tremulous and stirred by what she had just seen and heard, she had asked the question.

''I liked the overture,'' was his answer. ''It was splendid.''

''Yes, but the opera itself?''

''That was splendid too, that is the orchestra was, though I 'd have enjoyed it more if those jumping-jacks had kept quiet or gone off the stage.''

Ruth was aghast.

''You dont mean Tetralani or Barillo?'' she queried.

''All of them—the whole kit and crew.''

''But they are great artists,'' she protested.

''They spoiled the music just the same with their antics and unrealities.''

''But dont you like Barillo's voice?'' Ruth asked. ''He is next to Caruso, they say.''

''Of course I liked him, and I liked Tetralani even better. Her voice is exquisite—or at least I think so.''

''But, but—'' Ruth stammered. ''I dont know what you mean, then. You admire their voices, yet say they spoiled the music.''

''Precisely that. I 'd give anything to hear them in concert, and I 'd give even a bit more not to hear them when the orchestra is playing. I 'm afraid I am a hopeless realist. Great singers are not great actors. To hear Barillo sing a love passage with the voice of an angel, and to hear Tetralani reply like another angel, and to hear it all accompanied by a perfect orgy of glowing and colorful music—is ravishing, most ravishing. I do not admit it. I assert it. But the whole effect is spoiled when I look at them—at Tetralani, five feet ten in her stocking feet and weighing a hundred and ninety pounds, and at Barillo, a scant five feet four, greasy-featured, with the chest of a squat, undersized blacksmith, and at the pair of them, attitudinizing, clasping their breasts, flinging their arms in the air like demented creatures in an asylum; and when I am expected to accept all this as the faithful illusion of a love-scene between a slender and beautiful princess and a handsome, romantic young prince—why, I can 't accept it, that 's all. It 's rot; it 's absurd; it 's unreal. That 's what 's the matter with it. It 's not real. Dont tell me that anybody in this world ever made love that way. Why, if I 'd made love to you in that fashion, you 'd have boxed my ears.''

''But you misunderstand,'' Ruth protested. ''Every form of art has its limitations.'' (She was busy recalling a lecture she had heard at the university on the conventions of the arts). ''In painting, there are only two dimensions to the canvas, yet you accept the illusion of three dimensions which the art of the painter enables him to throw into the canvas. In writing, again, the author must be omnipotent. You accept as perfectly legitimate the author's account of the secret thoughts of the heroine, and yet all the time you know that the heroine was alone when thinking these thoughts, and that neither the author nor any one else was capable of hearing them. And so with the stage, with sculpture, with opera, with every art-form. Certain irreconcilable things must be accepted.''

''Yes, I understand that,'' Martin answered. ''All the arts have their conventions.'' (Ruth was surprised at his use of the word. It was as if he had studied at the university himself, instead of being ill-equipped from browsing at haphazard through the books in the library). ''But even the conventions must be real. Trees, painted on flat cardboard and stuck up on each side of the stage, we accept as a forest. It is a real enough convention. But, on the other hand, we would not accept a sea scene as a forest. We can 't do it. It violates our senses. Nor would you, or, rather, should you, accept the ravings and writhings and agonized contortions of those two lunatics tonight as a convincing portrayal of love.''

''But you dont hold yourself superior to all the judges of music?'' she protested.

''No, no, not for a moment. I merely maintain my right as an individual. I have just been telling you what I think, in order to explain why the elephantine gambols of Madame Tetralani spoil the orchestra for me. The world's judges of music may all be right. But I am I, and I wont subordinate my taste to the unanimous judgment of mankind. If I dont like a thing, I dont like it, that 's all; and there is no reason under the sun why I should ape a liking for it just because the majority of my fellow creatures like it, or make believe they like it. I can 't follow the fashions in the things I like or dislike."

"But music, you know, is a matter of training," Ruth argued; "and opera is even more a matter of training. May it not be—"

"That I am not trained in opera?" he dashed in.

She nodded.

"The very thing," he agreed. "And I consider I am fortunate in not having been caught when I was young. If I had, I could have wept sentimental tears tonight, and the clownish antics of that precious pair would have but enhanced the beauty of their voices and the beauty of the accompanying orchestra. You are right. It 's mostly a matter of training. And I am too old, now. I must have the real or nothing. An illusion that wont convince is a palpable lie, and that 's what grand opera is to me when little Barillo throws a fit, clutches mighty Tetralani in his arms (also in a fit), and tells her how passionately he adores her." Again Ruth measured his thoughts by comparison of externals and in accordance with her belief in the established. Who was he that he should be right and all the cultured world wrong? His words and thoughts made no impression upon her. She was too firmly entrenched in the established to have any sympathy with revolutionary ideas. She had always been used to music, and she had enjoyed opera ever since she was a child, and all her world had enjoyed it, too. Then by what right did Martin Eden emerge, as he had so recently emerged, from his ragtime and working-class songs, and pass judgment on the world's music? She was vexed with him, and as she walked beside him she had a vague feeling of outrage. At the best, in her most charitable frame of mind, she considered the statement of his views to be a caprice, an erratic and uncalled for prank. But when he took her in his arms at the door and kissed her good night in tender lover-fashion, she forgot everything in the outrush of her own love to him. And later, on a sleepless pillow, she puzzled, as she had often puzzled of late, as to how it was that she loved so strange a man, and loved him despite the disapproval of her people.

And next day Martin Eden cast hackwork aside, and at white heat hammered out an essay to which he gave the title, "The Philosophy of Illusion." A stamp started it on its travels, but it was destined to receive many stamps and to be started on many travels in the months that followed.

CHAPTER XXV.

MARIA SILVA was poor, and all the ways of poverty were clear to her. Poverty, to Ruth, was a word, signifying a not-nice condition of existence. That was her total knowledge on the subject. She knew Martin was poor, and his condition she associated in her mind with the boyhood of Abraham Lincoln, of Mr. Butler, and of other men who had become successes. Also, while aware that poverty was anything but delectable, she had a comfortable middle-class feeling that poverty was salutary, that it was a sharp spur that urged on to success all men who were not degraded and hopeless drudges. So that her knowledge that Martin was so poor that he had pawned his watch and overcoat did not disturb her. She even considered it the hopeful side of the situation, believing that sooner or later it would arouse him and compel him to abandon his writing.

Ruth never read hunger in Martin's face, which had grown lean and had enlarged the slight hollows in the cheeks. In fact, she marked the change in his face with satisfaction. It seemed to refine him, to remove from him much of the dross of flesh and the too-animal-like vigor that lured her while she detested it. Sometimes, when with her, she noted an unusual brightness in his eyes, and she admired it, for it made him appear more the poet and the scholar—the things he would have liked to be and which she would have liked him to be. But Maria Silva read a different tale in the hollow cheeks and the burning eyes, and she noted the changes in them from day to day, by them following the ebb and flow of his fortunes. She saw him leave the house with his overcoat and return without it though the day was chill and raw, and promptly she saw his cheeks fill out slightly and the fire of hunger leave his eyes. In the same way she had seen his wheel and watch go, and after each event she had seen his vigor bloom again.

Likewise she watched his toils, and knew the measure of the midnight oil he burned. Work! She knew that he outdid her, though his work was of a different order. And she was surprised to behold that the less food he had the harder he worked. On occasion, in a casual sort of way, when she thought hunger pinched hardest, she would send him in a loaf of new baking, awkwardly covering the act with banter to the effect that it was better than he could bake. And again, she would send one of her toddlers in to him with a great pitcher of hot soup, debating inwardly the while whether she was justified in taking it from the mouths of her own flesh and blood. Nor was Martin ungrateful, knowing as he did the lives of the poor and that if ever in the world there was charity this was it.

On a day when she had filled her brood with what was left in the house, Maria invested her last fifteen cents in a gallon of cheap wine. Martin, coming into her kitchen to fetch water, was invited to sit down and drink. He drank her very good health, and in return she drank his. Then she drank to prosperity in his undertakings, and he drank to the hope that James Grant would show up and pay her for his washing. James Grant was a journeyman carpenter who did not always pay his bills and who owed Maria three dollars.

Both Maria and Martin drank the sour, new wine on empty stomachs, and it went swiftly to their heads. Utterly differentiated creatures that they were, they were lonely in their misery, and, though the misery was tacitly ignored, it was the bond that drew them together. Maria was amazed to learn that he had been in the Azores, where she had lived until she was eleven. She was doubly amazed that he had been in the Hawaiian Islands, whither she had migrated from the Azores with her people. But her amazement passed all bounds when he told her he had been on Maui, the particular island whereon she had attained womanhood and married. Kahului, where she had first met her husband—he, Martin, had been there twice! Yes, she remembered the sugar steamers, and he had been on them—well, well, it was a small world. And Wailuku! That place, too! Did he know the head-luna of the plantation? Yes, and had had a couple of drinks with him.

And so they reminiscenced and drowned their hunger in the raw, sour wine. To Martin the future did not seem so dim. Success trembled just before him. He was on the verge of clasping it. Then he studied the deep-lined face of the toil-worn woman before him, remembered her soups and loaves of new baking, and felt spring up in him the warmest gratitude and philanthropy.

"Maria," he exclaimed suddenly. "What would you like to have?"

She looked at him bepuzzled.

"What would you like to have now, right now, if you could get it?"

"Shoe alla da roun' for da childs—seven pairs da shoe."

"You shall have them," he announced, while she nodded her head gravely. "But I mean a big wish, something big that you want."

Her eyes sparkled good-naturedly. He was choosing to make fun with her, Maria, with whom few made fun these days.

"Think hard," he cautioned, just as she was opening her mouth to speak.

"Alla right," she answered. "I thinka da hard. I lika da house, dis house—all mine, no paya da rent, seven dollar da month."

"You shall have it," he granted, "and in a short time. Now wish the great wish. Make believe I am God, and I say to you anything you want you can have. Then you wish that thing, and I listen."

Maria considered solemnly for a space.

"You no 'fraid?" she asked warningly.

"No, no," he laughed, "I 'm not afraid. Go ahead."

"Most verra big," she warned again.

"All right. Fire away."

"Well, den—" she drew a big breath like a child, as she voiced to the uttermost all she cared to demand of life. "I lika da have one milka ranch—good milka ranch. Plenty cow, plenty land, plenty grass. I lika da have near San Le-an'; my sister liva dere. I sella da milk in Oakland. I maka da plentee mon'. Joe an' Nick no runna da cow. Dey go-a to school. Bimeby maka da good engineer, worka da railroad. Yes, I like da milka ranch."

She paused and regarded Martin with twinkling eyes.

"You shall have it," he answered promptly.

She nodded her head and touched her lips courteously to the wine-glass and to the giver of the gift she knew would never be given. His heart was right, and in her own heart she appreciated his intention as much as if the gift had gone with it.

"No, Maria," he went on; "Nick and Joe wont have to peddle milk, and all the kids can go to school and wear shoes the whole year around. It will be a first-class milk ranch—everything complete. There will be a house to live in and a stable for the horses, and cow-barns of course. There will be chickens, pigs, vegetables, fruit trees and everything like that; and there will be enough cows to pay for a hired man or two. Then you wont have anything to do but take care of the children. For that matter, if you find a good man, you can marry and take it easy while he runs the ranch."

And from such largess, dispensed from his future, Martin turned and took his one good suit of clothes to the pawnshop. His plight was desperate for him to do this, for it cut him off from Ruth. He had no second-best suit that was presentable, and though he could go to the butcher and the baker, and even on occasion to his sister's, it was beyond all daring to dream of entering the Morse home so disreputably appareled.

He toiled on, miserable and well-nigh hopeless. It began to appear to him that the second battle was lost and that he would have to go to work. In doing this he would satisfy everbody—the grocer, his sister, Ruth, and even Maria, to whom he owed a month's room-rent. He was two months behind with his typewriter, and the agency was clamoring for payment or for the return of the machine. In desperation, all but ready to surrender, to make a truce with fate until he could get a fresh start, he took the civil service examinations for the Railway Mail. To his surprise, he passed first. The job was assured, though when the call should come to enter upon his duties nobody knew.

It was at this time, at the lowest ebb, that the smooth-running editorial machine broke down. A cog must have slipped or an oil-cup run dry, for the postman brought him one morning a short thin envelope. Martin glanced at the upper left-hand corner and read the name and address of the *Occidental Magazine*. His heart gave a great leap, and he suddenly felt faint, the sinking feeling accompanied by a strange trembling of the knees. He staggered into his room and sat down on the bed, the envelope still unopened, and in that moment came understanding to him how people suddenly fall dead upon receipt of extraordinary good news.

Of course this was good news. There was no manuscript in that thin envelope, therefore it was an acceptance. He knew the story in the hands of the *Occidental*. It was "The Ring of Bells," one of his horror stories, and it was an even five thousand words. And, since first-class magazines always paid on acceptance, there was a check inside. Two cents a word—twenty dollars a thousand; the check must be a hundred dollars. One hundred dollars! As he tore the envelope open, every item of all his debts surged in his brain—$3.85 to the grocer, butcher $4.00 flat, baker $2.00, fruit store $5.00; total, $14.85. Then there was room-rent $2.50, another month in advance $2.50; two months' typewriter $8.00; a month in advance $4.00; total $31.85. And finally to be added, his pledges, plus interest, with the pawnbroker—watch $5.50, overcoat $5.50, wheel $7.75, suit of clothes $5.50 (sixty per cent interest but what did it matter?)—grand total $56.10. He saw, as if visible in the air before him, in illuminate figures, the whole sum, and the subtraction that followed and that gave a remainder of $43.90. When he had squared every debt, redeemed every pledge, he would still have jingling in his pockets a princely $43.90. And on top of that he would have a month's rent paid in advance on the typewriter and on the room.

By this time he had drawn the single sheet of typewritten letter out and spread it open. There was no check. He peered into the envelope, held it to the light, but could not trust his eyes, and in trembling haste tore the envelope apart. There was no check. He read the letter, skimming it line by line, dashing through the editor's praise of his story to the meat of the letter, the statement why the check had not been sent. He found no such statement, but he did find that which made him suddenly wilt. The letter slid from his hand. His eyes went lack-luster, and he lay back on the pillow, pulling the blanket about him and up to his chin.

Five dollars, for "The Ring of Bells"—five dollars for five thousand words—instead of two cents a word, ten words for a cent. And the editor had praised it, too. And he would receive the check when the story was published. Then it was all poppycock, two cents a word for minimum rate and payment upon acceptance. It was a lie, and it had led him astray. He would never have attempted to write, had he known that. He would have gone to work—to work for Ruth. He went back to the day he first attempted to write, and was appalled at the enormous waste of time—and all for ten words for a cent. And the other high rewards of writers, that he had read about, must be lies, too. His second-hand ideas of authorship were wrong, for here was the proof of it.

Well, he had taken the bait, the newspaper lies about writers and their pay, and he had wasted two years over it. But he would disgorge the bait now. Not another line would he ever write. He would do what Ruth wanted him to do, what everybody wanted him to do—get a job. The thought of going to work reminded him of Joe—Joe, tramping through the land of Nothing-to-do. Martin heaved a great sigh of envy. The reaction of nineteen hours a day for many days was strong upon him. But then, Joe was not in love, had none of the responsibilites of love, and he could afford to loaf through the land of Nothing-to-do. He, Martin, had something to work for, and go to work he would. He would start out early next morning to hunt a job. And he would let Ruth know, too, that he had mended his ways and was willing to go into her father's office.

Five dollars for five thousand words, ten words for a cent the market price for art. The disappointment of it, the lie of it, the infamy of it, were uppermost in his thoughts; and under his closed eyelids, in fiery figures, burned the "$3.85" he owed the grocer. He shivered, and was aware of an aching in his bones. The small of his back ached especially. His head ached, the top of it ached, the back of it ached, the brains inside of it ached and seemed to be swelling, while the ache over his brows was intolerable. And beneath the brows, planted under his lids, was the merciless "$3.85." He opened his eyes to escape it, but the white light of the room seemed to sear the balls and forced him to close his eyes, when the "$3.85" confronted him again.

Five dollars for five thousand words, ten words for a cent—that particular thought took up its residence in his brain, and he could no more escape it than he could the "$3.85" under his eyelids. A change seemed to come over the latter, and he watched curiously, till "$2.00" burned in its stead. Ah, he thought, that was the baker. The next sum that appeared was "$2.50." It puzzled him, and he pondered it as if life and death hung on the solution. He owed somebody two dollars and a half, that was certain, but who was it? To find it was the task set him by an imperious and malignant universe, and he wandered through the endless corridors of his mind, opening all manner of lumber rooms and chambers stored with odds and ends of memories and knowledge as he vainly sought the answer. After several centuries it came to him, easily, without effort, that it was Maria. With a great relief he turned his soul to the screen of torment under his lids. He had solved the problem; now he could rest. But no, the "$2.50" faded away, and in its place burned "$8.00." Who was that? He must go the dreary round of his mind again and find out.

How long he was gone on this quest he did not know, but after what seemed an enormous lapse of time, he was called back to himself by a knock at the door, and by Maria's asking if he was sick. He replied in a muffled voice he did not recognize, saying that he was merely taking a nap. He was surprised when he noted the darkness of night in the room. He had received the letter at two in the afternoon, and he realized that he was sick.

Then the "$8.00" began to smoulder under his lids again, and he returned himself to servitude. But he grew cunning. There was no need for him to wander through his mind. He had been a fool. He pulled a lever and made his mind revolve about him, a monstrous wheel of fortune, a merry-go-round of memory, a revolving sphere of wisdom. Faster and faster it revolved, until its vortex sucked him in and he was flung whirling through black chaos.

Quite naturally he found himself at a mangle, feeding starched cuffs. But as he fed he noticed figures printed on the cuffs. It was a new way of marking linen, he thought, until, looking closer, he saw "$3.85" on one of the cuffs. Then it came to him that it was the grocer's bill, and that these were his bills flying around on the drum of the mangle. A crafty idea came to him. He would throw the bills on the floor and so escape paying them. No sooner thought than done, and he crumpled the cuffs spitefully as he flung them upon an unusually dirty floor. Ever the heap grew, and though each bill was duplicated a thousand times, he found only one for two dollars and a half, which was what he owed Maria. That meant that Maria would not press for payment, and he resolved generously that it would be the only one he would pay; so he began searching through the cast-out heap for hers. He sought it desperately, for ages, and was still searching when the manager of the hotel entered, the fat Dutchman. His face blazed with wrath, and he shouted in stentorian tones that echoed down the universe: "I shall deduct the cost of those cuffs from your wages!" The pile of cuffs grew into a mountain and Martin knew that he was doomed to toil for a thousand years to pay for them. Well, there was nothing left to do but kill the manager and burn down the laundry. But the big Dutchman frustrated him, seizing him by the nape of the neck and dancing him up and down. He danced him over the ironing tables, the stove, and the mangles, and out into the wash-room and over the wringer and washer. Martin was danced until his teeth rattled and his head ached, and he marveled that the Dutchman was so strong.

And then he found himself before the mangle, this time receiving the cuffs an editor of a magazine was feeding from the other side. Each cuff was a check, and Martin went over them anxiously, in a fever of expectation, but they were all blanks. He stood there and received the blanks for a million years or so, never letting one go by for fear it might be filled out. At last he found it. With trembling fingers he had held it to the light. It was for five dollars. "Ha! Ha!" laughed the editor across the mangle. "Well, then I shall kill you," Martin said. He went out into the wash-room to get the axe, and found Joe starching manuscripts. He tried to make him desist, then swung the axe for him. But the weapon remained poised in mid-air, for Martin found himself back in the ironing-room in the midst of a snow storm. No, it was not snow that was falling, but checks of large denomination, the smallest not less than a thousand dollars. He began to collect them and sort them out, in packages of a hundred, tying each package securely with twine.

He looked up from his task and saw Joe standing before him, juggling flatirons, starched shirts, and manuscripts. Now and again he reached out and added a bundle of checks to the flying miscellany that soared through the roof and out of sight in a tremendous circle. Martin struck at him, but he seized the axe and added it to the flying circle. Then he plucked Martin and added him. Martin went up through the roof, clutching at manuscripts, so that by the time he came down he had a large armful. But no sooner down than up again, and a second and a third time and countless times he flew around the circle. From far off he could hear a childish treble singing: "Waltz me around again, Willie, around, around, around."

He recovered the axe in the midst of the Milky Way of checks, starched shirts and manuscripts, and prepared, when he came down, to kill Joe. But he did not come down. Instead, at two in the morning, Maria, having heard his groans through the thin partition, came into his room, to put hot flat-irons against his body and damp cloths upon his aching eyes.

CHAPTER XXVI.

MARTIN EDEN did not go out to hunt for a job in the morning. It was late afternoon before he came out of his delirium and gazed with aching eyes about the room. Mary, one of the tribe of Silva, eight years old, keeping watch, raised a screech at sight of his returning consciousness. Maria hurried into the room from the kitchen. She put her work-calloused hand upon his hot forehead and felt his pulse.

"You lika da eat?" she asked.

He shook his head. Eating was farthest from his desire, and he wondered that he should ever have been hungry in his life.

"I 'm sick, Maria," he said weakly. "What is it? Do you know?"

"Grip," she answered. "Two or three days you alla da right. Better you no eat now. Bimeby plenty can eat, tomorrow can eat maybe."

Martin was not used to sickness, and when Maria and her little girl left him, he essayed to get up and dress. By a supreme exertion of will, with reeling brain and eyes that ached so that he could not keep them open, he managed to get out of bed, only to be left stranded by his senses upon the table. Half an hour later he managed to regain the bed, where he was content to lie with closed eyes and analyze his various pains and weaknesses. Maria came in several times to change the cold cloths on his forehead. Otherwise she left him in peace, too wise to vex him with chatter. This moved him to gratitude, and he murmured to himself, "Maria, you getta da malka ranch, all righta, all right."

Then he remembered his long-buried past of yesterday. It seemed a life-time since he had received that letter from the *Occidental,* a life-time since it was all over and done with and a new page turned. He had shot his bolt, and shot it hard, and now he was down on his back. If he had n't starved himself he would n't have been caught by LaGrippe. He had been run down, and he had not had the strength to throw off the germ of disease which had invaded his system. This was what resulted.

"What does it profit a man to write a whole library and lose his own life!" he demanded aloud. "This is no place for me. No more literature in mine. Me for the counting-house and ledger, the monthly salary, and the little home with Ruth."

Two days later, having eaten an egg and two slices of toast and drunk a cup of tea, he asked for his mail, but found his eyes still hurt too much to permit him to read.

"You read for me, Maria," he said. "Never mind the big, long letters. Throw them under the table. Read me the small letters."

"No can," was the answer, "Teresa, she go to school, she can."

So Teresa Silva, aged nine, opened his letters and read them to him. He listened absently to a long dun from the typewriter people, his mind busy with ways and means of finding a job. Suddenly he was shocked back to himself.

"'We offer you forty dollars for all serial rights in your story,'" Teresa slowly spelled out, "'provided you allow us to make the alterations suggested.'"

"What magazine is that?" Martin shouted. "Here, give it to me."

He could see to read, now, and he was unaware of the pain of the action. It was the *White Mouse* that was offering him forty dollars, and the story was "The Whirlpool," another of his early horror stories. He read the letter through again and again. The editor told him plainly that he had not handled the idea properly, but that it was the idea they were buying because it was original. If they could cut the story down one-third, they would take it and send him forty dollars on receipt of his answer.

He called for pen and ink, and told the editor he could cut the story down three-thirds if he wanted to, and to send the forty dollars right along.

The letter dispatched to the letter-box by Teresa, Martin lay back and thought. It was n't a lie after all. The *White Mouse* paid on acceptance. There were three thousand words in "The Whirlpool." Cut down a third, there would be two thousand. At forty dollars that would be two cents a word. Pay on acceptance and two cents a word—the newspapers had told the truth. And he had thought the *White Mouse* a third-rater! It was evident that he did not know the magazines. He had deemed the *Occidental* a first-rater, and it paid a cent for ten words. He had classed the *White Mouse* as of no account, and it paid twenty times as much as the *Occidental,* and, also, it paid on acceptance.

Well, there was one thing certain: when he got well he would not go out looking for a job. There were more stories in his head as good as "The Whirlpool," and at forty dollars apiece he could earn far more than in any job or position. Just when he thought the battle lost, it was won. He had proved for his career. The way was clear. Beginning with the *White Mouse,* he would add magazine after magazine to his growing list of patrons. Hack-work could be put aside. For that matter, it had been wasted time, for it had not brought him a dollar. He would devote himself to work, good work, and he would pour out the best that was in him. He wished Ruth was there to share in his joy, and when he went over the letters left lying on his bed he found one from her. It was sweetly reproachful, wondering what had kept him away for so dreadful a length of time. He re-read the letter adoringly, dwelling over her handwriting, loving each stroke of her pen, and in the end kissing her signature.

And when he answered, he told her recklessly that he had not been to see her because his best clothes were in pawn. He told her that he had been sick but was once more nearly well, and that inside ten days or two weeks, (as soon as a letter could travel to New York City and return), he would redeem his clothes and be with her.

But Ruth did not care to wait ten days or two weeks. Besides, her lover was sick. The next afternoon, accompanied by Arthur, she arrived in the Morse carriage, to the unqualified delight of the Silva tribe and of all the urchins on the street, and to the consternation of Maria. She boxed the ears of the Silvas who crowded about the visitors on the tiny front porch, and in more than usual atrocious English tried to apologize for her appearance. Sleeves rolled up from soap-flecked arms and a wet gunny-sack around her waist told of the task at which she had been caught. So flustered was she by two such grand young people asking for her lodger, that she forgot to invite them to sit down in the little parlor. To enter Martin's room, they passed through the kitchen, warm and moist and steamy from the big washing in progress. Maria, in her excitement, jammed the bedroom and bedroom-closet doors together, and for five minutes, through the partly open door, clouds of steam, smelling of soapsuds and dirt, poured into the sick chamber.

Ruth succeeded in veering right and left and right again, and in running the narrow passage between table and bed to Martin's side; but Arthur veered too wide and fetched up with clatter and bang of pots and pans in the corner where Martin did his cooking. Arthur did not linger long. Ruth occupied the only chair, and having done his duty he went outside and stood by the gate, the center of seven marveling Silvas, who watched him as they would have watched a curiosity in a side-show. All about the carriage were gathered the children from a dozen blocks, waiting and eager for some tragic and terrible denouement. Carriages were seen on their street only for weddings and funerals; here was neither marriage nor death, therefore, it was something transcending experience and well worth waiting for.

Martin had been wild to see Ruth. His was essentially a love-nature, and he possessed more than the average man's need for sympathy. He was starving for sympathy, which, with him, meant intelligent understanding; and he had yet to learn that Ruth's sympathy was largely sentimental and tactful, and that it proceeded from gentleness of nature rather than from understanding of the objects of her sympathy. So it was while Martin held her hand and gladly talked, that her love for him prompted her to press his hand in return, and that her eyes were moist and luminous at sight of his helplessness and of the marks suffering had stamped upon his face.

But while he told her of his two acceptances, of his despair when he received the one from the *Occidental* and of the corresponding delight with which he received the one from the *White Mouse,* she did not follow him. She heard the words he uttered and understood their literal import, but she was not with him in his despair and his delight. She could not get out of herself. She was not interested in selling stories to magazines. What was important to her was matrimony. She was not aware of it, however, any more than she was aware that her desire that Martin take a position was the instinctive and preparative impulse of motherhood. She would have blushed had she been told as much in plain, set terms, and, next, she might have grown indignant and asserted that her sole interest lay in the man she loved and her desire for him to make the best of himself. So, while Martin poured out his heart to her, elated with the first success his chosen work in the world had received, she paid heed to his bare words only, gazing now and again about the room, shocked by what she saw.

For the first time Ruth gazed upon the sordid face of poverty. Starving lovers had always seemed romantic to her, but she had had no idea how starving lovers lived. She had never dreamed it could be like this. Ever her gaze shifted from the room to him and back again. The steamy smell of dirty clothes, which had entered with her from the kitchen, was sickening. Martin must be soaked with it, Ruth concluded, if that awful woman washed frequently. Such was the contagiousness of degradation. When she looked at Martin, she seemed to see the smirch left upon him by his surroundings. She had never seen him unshaven, and the three days' growth of beard on his face was repulsive to her. Not alone did it give him the same dark and murky aspect of the Silva house, inside and out, but it seemed to emphasize that animal-like strength of his which she detested. And here he was, being confirmed in his madness by the two acceptances he took such pride in telling her about. A little longer and he would have surrendered and gone to work. Now he would continue on in this horrible house, writing and starving for a few more months.

"What is that smell?" she asked suddenly.

"Some of Maria's washing-smells, I imagine," was the answer.

"No, no; not that. It is something else. A stale, sickish smell."

Martin sampled the air before replying.

"I can 't smell anything else, except stale tobacco smoke," he announced.

"That 's it. It is terrible. Why do you smoke so much, Martin?"

"I dont know, except that I smoke more than usual when I am lonely. And then, too, it 's such a long-standing habit. I learned when I was only a youngster."

"It is not a nice habit, you know," she reproved. "It smells to heaven."

"That 's the fault of the tabacco. I can afford only the cheapest. But wait until I get that forty-dollar check. I 'll use a brand that it not offensive even to the angels. But that was n't so bad, was it, two acceptances in three days! That forty-five dollars will pay about all my debts."

"For two years' work?" she queried.

"No, for less than a week's work. Please pass me that book over on the far corner of the table, the account book with the gray cover." He opened it and began turning over the pages rapidly. "Yes, I was right. Four days for 'The Ring of Bells,' two days for 'The Whirlpool.' That 's forty-five dollars for a week's work, one hundred and eighty dollars a month. That beats any salary I can command. And, besides, I 'm just beginning. A thousand dollars a month is not too much to buy for you all I want you to have. A salary of five hundred a month would be too small. That forty-five dollars is just a starter. Wait till I get my stride. Then watch my smoke."

Ruth misunderstood his slang, and reverted to cigarettes.

"You smoke more than enough as it is, and the brand of tobacco will make no difference. It is the smoking itself that is not nice, no matter what the brand may be. You are a chimney, a living volcano, a perambulating smokestack, and you are a perfect disgrace, Martin dear, you know you are."

She leaned toward him, entreaty in her eyes, and as he looked at her delicate face and into her pure, limpid eyes, as of old he was struck with his own unworthiness.

"I wish you would n't smoke any more," she whispered. "Please, for—my sake!"

"All right, I wont," he cried. "I 'll do

anything you ask, dear love, anything, you know that."

A great temptation assailed her. In an insistent way she had caught glimpses of the large, easy-going side of his nature, and she felt sure, if she asked him to cease attempting to write, that he would grant her wish. In the swift instant that elapsed, the words trembled on her lips. But she did not utter them. She was not quite brave enough, she did not quite dare. Instead, she leaned toward him to meet him, and in his arms murmured:

"You know, it is really not for my sake, Martin, but for your own. I am sure smoking hurts you; and besides, it is not good to be a slave to anything, to a drug least of all."

"I shall always be your slave," he smiled.

"In which case, I shall begin issuing my commands."

She looked at him mischievously, though deep down she was already regretting that she had not preferred her largest request.

"I live but to obey, your majesty."

"Well, then, my first commandment is: Thou shalt not omit to shave every day. Look how you have scratched my cheek."

And so it ended in caresses and love-laughter. But she had made one point and she could not expect to make more than one at a time. She felt a woman's pride in that she had made him stop smoking. Another time she would persuade him to take a position, for had he not said he would do anything she asked?

She left his side to explore the room, examining the clothes-lines of notes overhead, learning the mystery of the tackle used for suspending his wheel under the ceiling, and being saddened by the heap of manuscripts under the table which represented to her just so much wasted time. The oil-stove won her admiration, but on investigating the food-shelves she found them empty.

"Why, you have n't anything to eat, you poor dear," she said with tender compassion. "You must be starving."

"I store my food in Maria's safe and in her pantry," he lied. "It keeps better there. No danger of my starving. Look at that."

She had come back to his side, and she saw him double his arm at the elbow, the biceps crawling under his shirt-sleeve and swelling into a knot of muscle, heavy and hard. The sight repelled her. Sentimentally, she disliked it. But her pulse, her blood, every fiber of her, loved it and yearned for it, and, in the old inexplicable way, she leaned toward him, not away from him. And in the moment that followed, when he crushed her in his arms, the brain of her, concerned with the superficial aspects of life, was in revolt, while the heart of her, the woman of her, concerned with life itself, exulted triumphantly. It was in moments like this that she felt to the uttermost the greatness of her love for Martin, for it was almost a swoon of delight to her to feel his strong arms about her, holding her tightly, hurting her with the grip of their fervor. At such moments she found justification for her treason to her standards, for he violation of her own high ideals, and, most of all, for her tacit disobedience to her mother and father. They did not want her to marry this man. It shocked them that she should love him. It shocked her, too, sometimes, when she was apart from him, a cool and reasoning creature. With him, she loved him—in truth, at times a vexed and worried love; but love it was, a love that was stronger than she.

"This LaGrippe is nothing," he was saying. "It hurts a bit, and gives one a nasty headache, but it does n't compare with break-bone fever."

"Have you had that, too?" she queried absently, intent on the heaven-sent justification she was finding in his arms.

And so, with absent queries, she led him on, till suddenly his words startled her.

He had had the fever in a secret colony of thirty lepers on one of the Hawaiian Islands.

"But why did you go there!" she demanded.

Such royal carelessness of body seemed criminal.

"Because I did n't know," he answered. "I never dreamed of lepers. When I deserted the schooner and landed on the beach, I headed inland for some place of hiding. For three days I lived off guavas, *chia*-apples and bananas, all of which grew wild in the jungle. On the fourth day I found the trail—a mere foot-trail. It led inland, and it led up. It was the way I wanted to go, and it showed signs of recent travel. At one place it ran along the crest of a ridge that was no more than a knife-edge. The trail was n't three feet wide on the crest; and on either side the ridge fell away in precipices hundreds of feet deep. One man, with plenty of ammunition could have held it against a hundred thousand.

It was the only way in to the hiding place. Three hours after I found the trail I was there, in a little mountain valley, a pocket in the midst of lava peaks. The whole place was terraced for taro-patches, fruit trees grew there, and there were eight or ten grass huts. But as soon as I saw the inhabitants I knew what I 'd struck. One sight of them was enough.''

''What did you do?'' Ruth demanded breathlessly, listening, like any Desdemona, appalled and fascinated.

''Nothing for me to do. Their leader was a kind old fellow, pretty far gone, but he ruled like a king. He had discovered the little valley and founded the settlement—all of which was against the law. But he had guns, plenty of ammunition, and those Kanakas, trained to the shooting of wild cattle and wild pig, were dead shots. No, there was n't any running away for Martin Eden. He stayed—for three months.''

''But how did you escape?''

''He 'd have been there yet, if it had n't been for a girl there, a half-Chinese, quarter-white, and quarter-Hawaiian. She was a beauty, poor thing, and well educated. Her mother, in Honolulu, was worth a million or so. Well, this girl got me away at last. Her mother financed the settlement, you see, so the girl was n't afraid of being punished for letting me go. But she made me swear, first, never to reveal the hiding-place; and I never have. This is the first time I have even mentioned it. The girl just had the first signs of leprosy. The fingers of her right hand were slightly twisted, and there was a small spot on her arm. That was all. I guess she is dead, now.''

''But were n't you frightened? And were n't you glad to get away without catching that dreadful disease?''

''Well,'' he confessed, ''I was a bit shivery at first; but I got used to it. I used to feel sorry for that poor girl, though. That made me forget to be afraid. She was such a beauty, in spirit as well as in appearance, and she was only slightly touched; yet she was doomed to lie there, living the life of a primitive savage and rotting slowly away. Leprosy is far more terrible than you can imagine it.''

''Poor thing,'' Ruth murmured softly. ''It 's a wonder she let you get away.''

''How do you mean?'' Martin asked unwittingly.

''Because she must have loved you,'' Ruth said, still softly. ''Candidly, now, did n't she?''

Martin's sunburn had been bleached by his work in the laundry and by the indoor life he was living, while the hunger and the sickness had made his face even pale; and across this pallor flowed the slow wave of a blush. He was opening his mouth to speak, but Ruth shut him off.

''Never mind, dont answer, it 's not necessary,'' she laughed.

But it seemed to him there was something metallic in her laughter, and that the light in her eyes was cold. On the spur of the moment it reminded him of a gale he had once experienced in the North Pacific. And for the moment the apparition of the gale rose before his eyes—a gale at night, with a clear sky and under a full moon, the huge seas glinting coldly in the moonlight. Next, he saw the girl in the leper refuge and remembered it was for love for him that she had let him go.

''She was noble,'' he said simply. ''She gave me life.''

That was all of the incident, but he heard Ruth muffle a dry sob in her throat, and noticed that she turned her face away to gaze out of the window. When she turned it back to him it was composed and there was no hint of the gale in her eyes.

''I 'm such a silly,'' she said plaintively. ''But I can 't help it. I do so love you, Martin, I do, I do. I shall grow more catholic in time, but at present I can 't help being jealous of those ghosts of the past, and you know your past is full of ghosts.

''It must be,'' she silenced his protest. ''It could not be otherwise. And there 's poor Arthur motioning me to come. He 's tired waiting. And now good bye, dear.

"There 's some kind of a mixture, put up by the druggists, that helps men to stop the use of tobacco," she called back from the door, "and I am going to send you some."

The door closed, but opened again.

"I do, I do," she whispered to him; and this time she was really gone.

Maria, with worshipful eyes that none the less were keen to note the texture of Ruth's garments and the cut of them (a cut unknown that produced an effect mysteriously beautiful), saw her to the carriage. The crowd of disappointed urchins stared till the carriage disappeared from view, then transferred their stare to Maria, who had abruptly become the most important person on the street. But it was one of her progeny who blasted Maria's reputation by announcing that the grand visitors had been for her lodger. After that Maria dropped back into her old obscurity and Martin began to notice the respectful manner in which he was regarded by the small fry of the neighborhood. As for Maria, Martin rose in her estimation a full hundred percent, and had the Portuguese grocer witnessed that afternoon carriage-call he would have allowed Martin an additional three-dollars-and-eighty-five-cents' worth of credit.

Martin Eden

By Jack London

Author of "The Call of the Wild," "Sea Wolf," "The God of His Fathers," "White Fang," etc.

CHAPTER XXVII.

THE sun of Martin's good fortune rose. The day after Ruth's visit he received a check for three dollars from a New York scandal weekly in payment for three of his triolets. Two days later a newspaper published in Chicago accepted his "Treasure Hunters," promising to pay ten dollars for it on publication. The price was small, but it was the first article he had written, his very first attempt to express his thought on the printed page. To cap everything, the adventure serial for boys, his second attempt, was accepted before the end of the week by a juvenile monthly calling itself *Youth and Age*. It was true, the serial was twenty-one thousand words, and they offered to pay him sixteen dollars on publication, which was something like seventy-five cents a thousand words; but it was equally true that it was the second thing he had attempted to write and that he was himself thoroughly aware of its clumsy worthlessness.

But even his earliest efforts were not marked with the clumsiness of mediocrity. What characterized them was the clumsiness of too-great strength—the clumsiness which the tyro betrays when he crushes butterflies with battering rams and hammers out vignettes with a war-club. So it was that Martin was glad to sell his early efforts for songs He knew them for what they were, and it had not taken him long to acquire this knowledge. What he pinned his faith to was his later work. He had striven to be something more than a mere writer of magazine fiction. He had sought to equip himself with the tools of artistry. On the other hand, he had not sacrificed strength. His conscious aim had been to increase his strength by avoiding excess of strength. Nor had he departed from his love of reality. His work was realism, though he had endeavored to fuse with it the fancies and beauties of imagination. What he sought was an impassioned realism, shot through with human aspiration and faith. What he wanted was life as it was, with all its spirit-groping and soul-reaching left in.

He had discovered, in the course of his reading, two schools of fiction. One treated of man as a god, ignoring his earthly origin; the other treated of him as a clod, ignoring his heaven-sent dreams and divine possibilities. Both the god and the clod schools erred, in Martin's estimation, and erred through too-great singleness of sight and purpose. There was a compromise that approximated the truth, though it flattered not the school of god, while it challenged the brute-savageness of the school of clod. It was his story, "Adventure," which had dragged with Ruth, that Martin believed had achieved his ideal of the true in fiction; and it was in an essay, "God and Clod," that he had expressed his views on the whole general subject.

But "Adventure," and all that he deemed his best work, still went begging among the editors. His early work counted for nothing in his eyes except for the money it brought, and his horror stories, two of which he had sold, he did not consider high work nor his best work. To him they were frankly imaginative and fantastic, though invested with all the glamor of the real, wherein lay their power. This investiture of the grotesque and impossible with reality, he looked upon as a trick, a skillful trick at best. Great literature could not reside in such a field. Their artistry was high, but he denied the worthwhileness of artistry when divorced from humanness. The trick had been to fling over the face of his artistry a mask of humanness, and this he had done in the half-dozen or so stories of the horror brand he had written before he emerged upon the high peaks of "Adventure," "Joy," "The Pot," and "Wine of Life."

The three dollars he received for the triolets he used to eke out a precarious existence against the arrival of the *White Mouse* check. He cashed the first check with the suspicious Portuguese grocer, paying a dollar on account and dividing the remaining two dollars between the baker and the fruit-store. Martin was not yet rich enough to afford meat, and he was on slim allowance when the *White Mouse* check arrived. He was divided on the cashing of it. He had never been in a bank in his life, much less been in one on business, and he had a naive and childlike desire to walk into one of the big banks down in Oakland and fling down his endorsed check for forty dollars. On the other hand, practical common sense ruled that he should cash it with his grocer and thereby make an impression that would later result in an increase of credit. Reluctantly Martin yielded to the claims of the grocer, paying his bill with him in full, and receiving in change a pocketful of jingling coin. Also, he paid the other tradesmen in full, redeemed his suit and his bicycle, paid one month's rent on the typewriter. and paid Maria the overdue month for his room and a month in advance. This left him in his pocket, for emergencies, a balance of nearly three dollars.

In itself, this small sum seemed a fortune. Immediately on recovering his clothes he had gone to see Ruth, and on the way he could not refrain from jingling the little handful of silver in his pocket. He had been so long without money, that, like a rescued starving man who cannot let the unconsumed food out of his sight, Martin could not keep his hand off the silver. He was not mean, nor avaricious, but the money meant more than so many dollars and cents. It stood for success, and the eagles stamped upon the coins were to him so many winged victories.

It came to him insensibly that it was a very good world. It certainly appeared more beautiful to him. For weeks it had been a very dull and somber world; but now, with nearly all debts paid, three dollars jingling in his pocket, and in his mind the consciousness of success, the sun shone bright and warm, and even a rain-squall that soaked unprepared pedestrians seemed a merry happening to him. When he starved, his thoughts had dwelt often upon the thousands he knew were starving the world over; but now that he was feasted full, the fact of the thousands starving was no longer pregnant in his brain. He forgot about them, and, being in love, remembered the countless lovers in the world. Without deliberately thinking about it, *motifs* for love-lyrics began to agitate his brain. Swept away by the creative impulse, he got off the electric car, without vexation, two blocks beyond his crossing.

He found a number of persons in the Morse home. Ruth's two girl-cousins were visiting her from San Rafael, and Mrs. Morse, under pretext of entertaining them, was pursuing her plan of surrounding Ruth with young people. The campaign had begun during Martin's enforced absence, and was already in full swing. She was making a point of having at the house men who were doing things. Thus, in addition to the cousins Dorothy and Florence, Martin encountered two university professors, one of Latin, the other of English; a young army officer just back from the Philippines, one-time schoolmate of Ruth; a young fellow named Melville, private secretary to Joseph Perkins, head of the San Francisco Trust Company; and finally, of the men, a live bank cashier, Charles Hapgood, a youngish man of thirty-five, graduate of Stanford University, member of the Nile Club and the Unity Club, and a conservative speaker for the Republican Party during campaigns—in short, a rising young man in every way. Among the women was one who painted portraits, another who was a professional musician, and still another who possessed the degree of Doctor of Sociology and who was locally famous for her social settlement work in the slums of San Francisco. But the women did not count for much in Mrs. Morse's plan. At the best, they were necessary accessories. The men who did things must be drawn to the house somehow.

"Don't get excited when you talk," Ruth admonished Martin, before the ordeal of introduction began.

He bore himself a bit stiffly at first, oppressed by a sense of his own awkwardness, especially of his shoulders, which were up to their old trick of threatening destruction to furniture and ornaments. Also, he was rendered self-conscious by the company. He had never before been in contact with such exalted beings nor with so many of them. Melville, the bank cashier, fascinated him, and he resolved to investigate him at the first opportunity. For underneath Martin's awe, lurked his own assertive ego, and he felt the urge to measure himself with these men and women and to find out what they had learned from the books and life which he had not learned.

Ruth's eyes roved to him frequently to see how he was getting on, and she was surprised and gladdened by the ease with which he got acquainted with her cousins. He certainly did not grow excited, while being seated removed from him the worry of his shoulders. Ruth knew them for clever girls, superficially brilliant, and she could scarcely understand their praise of Martin later that night at going to bed. But he, on the other hand, a wit in his own class, a gay quizzer and laughter-maker at dances and Sunday picnics, had found the making of fun and the breaking of good-natured lances simple enough in this environment. And on this evening success stood at his back, patting him on the shoulder and telling him that he was making good, so that he could afford to laugh and make laughter and remain unabashed.

Later, Ruth's anxiety found justification. Martin and Professor Caldwell had got together in a conspicuous corner, and though Martin no longer wove the air with his hands, to Ruth's critical eye he permitted his own eyes to flash and glitter too frequently, talked too rapidly and warmly, grew too intense, and allowed his aroused blood to redden his cheeks too much. He lacked decorum and control, and was in decided contrast to the young professor of English with whom he talked.

But Martin was not concerned with appearances. He had been swift to note the other's trained mind and to appreciate his command of knowledge. Furthermore, Professor Caldwell did not realize Martin's concept of the average English professor. Martin wanted him to talk shop, and, though he seemed averse at first, succeeded in making him do it. For Martin did not see why a man should not talk shop.

"It 's absurd and unfair," he had told Ruth weeks before, "this objection to talking shop. For what reason under the sun do men and women come together if not for the exchange of the best that is in them! And the best that is in them is what they are interested in, the thing by which they make their living, the thing they 've specialized on and sat up days and nights over, and even dreamed about. Imagine Mr. Butler living up to social etiquette and enunciating his views on Paul Verlaine or the German drama, or the novels of D'Annunzio. We 'd be bored to death. I, for one, if I must listen to Mr. Butler, prefer to hear him talk about his law. It 's the best that is in him, and life is so short that I want the best of every man and woman I meet."

"But," Ruth had objected, "there are the topics of general interest to all."

"There, you mistake," he had rushed on. "All persons in society, all cliques in society—or, rather, nearly all persons and cliques—ape their betters. Now, who are the best betters? The idlers, the wealthy idlers. They do not know, as a rule, the things known by the persons who are doing something in the world. To listen to conversation about such things would mean to be bored, wherefore the idlers decree that such things are shop and must not be talked about. Likewise they decree the things that are not shop and which may be talked about, and those things are the latest operas, latest novels, cards, billiards, cocktails, automobiles, horse shows, trout-fishing, tuna-fishing, big game shooting, yacht-sailing, and so forth—and mark you, these are the things the idlers know. In all truth, they constitute the shop-talk of the idlers. And the funniest part of it is that many of the clever people, and all the would-be clever people, allow the idlers so to impose upon them. As for me, I want the best a man 's got in him, call it shop, vulgarity, or anything you please."

And Ruth had not understood. This attack of his on the established had seemed to her just so much wilfulness of opinion.

So Martin contaminated Professor Caldwell with his own earnestness, challenging him to speak his mind. As Ruth paused beside them she heard Martin saying:

"You surely dont pronounce such heresies in the University of California?"

Professor Caldwell shrugged his shoulders. "The honest taxpayer and the politician, you know. Sacramento gives us our appropriations, and therefore we kowtow to Sacramento, and to the Board of Regents, and to the party press, or to the press of both parties."

"Yes, that 's clear, but how about you?" Martin urged. "You must be a fish out of water."

"Few like me, I imagine, in the University pond. Sometimes I am fairly sure I am out of water, and that I should belong in Paris, in Grub Street, in a hermit's cave, or in some sadly wild Bohemian crowd, drinking claret—dago-red they call it in San Francisco—dining in cheap restaurants in the Latin Quarter, and expressing vociferously radical views upon all creation. Really, I am frequently almost sure that I was cut out to be a radical. But then, there are so many questions on which I am not sure. I grow timid when I am face to face with my human frailty which ever prevents me from grasping all the factors in any problem—human, vital problems, you know."

And as he talked on, Martin became aware that to his own lips had come the "Song of the Trade Wind":

I am strongest at noon,
But under the moon
I stiffen the bunt of the sail.

He was almost humming the words, and it dawned upon him that the other reminded him of the trade wind, of the Northeast Trade, steady, and cool, and strong. He was equable, he was to be relied upon, and withal there was a certain bafflement about him. Martin had the feeling that he never spoke his full mind, just as he had often had the feeling that the trades never blew their strongest, but always held reserves of strength that were never used. Martin's trick of visioning was active as ever. His brain was a most accessible storehouse of remembered fact and fancy, and its contents seemed ever ordered and spread for his inspection. Whatever occurred in the instant present, Martin's mind immediately presented associated antithesis or similitude which ordinarily expressed themselves to him in vision. It was sheerly automatic, and his visioning was an unfailing accompaniment to the living present. Just as Ruth's face, in a momentary jealousy, had called before his eyes a forgotten moonlight gale, and as Professor Caldwell made him see again the Northeast Trade herding the white billows across the purple sea, so, from moment to moment, not disconcerting, but rather identifying and classifying, new memory-visions rose before him, or spread under his eyelids; or were thrown upon the screen of his consciousness. These visions came out of the actions and sensations of the past, out of things and events and books of yesterday and last week—a countless host of apparitions that, waking or sleeping, forever thronged his mind.

So it was, as he listened to Professor Caldwell's easy flow of speech—the conversation of a clever, cultured man—that Martin kept seeing himself down all his past. He saw himself when he had been quite the hoodlum, wearing a "stiff-rim" Stetson hat and a square-cut, double-breasted coat, with a certain swagger to the shoulders and possessing the ideal of being as tough as the police permitted. He did not disguise it to himself, nor attempt to palliate it. At one time in his life he had been just a common hoodlum, the leader of a gang that worried the police and terrorized honest, working-class householders. But his ideals had changed. He glanced about him at the well-bred, well-dressed men and women, and breathed into his lungs the atmosphere of culture and refinement, and at the same moment, the ghost of his early youth, in stiff-rim and square-cut, with swagger and toughness, stalked across the room. This figure of the corner hoodlum he saw merge into himself, sitting and talking with an actual university professor.

For, after all, he had never found his permanent abiding place. He had fitted in wherever he found himself, been a favorite always and everywhere by virtue of holding his own at work and at play and by his willingness and ability to fight for his rights and command respect. But he had never taken root. He had fitted in sufficiently to satisfy his fellows, but not to satisfy himself. He had been perturbed always by a feeling of unrest, had heard always the call of something from beyond, and had wandered on through life seeking it until he found books, and art, and love. And here he was, in the midst of all this, the only one of all the comrades he had adventured with who could have made themselves eligible for the inside of the Morse home.

But such thoughts and visions did not prevent him from following Professor Caldwell closely. And as he followed, comprehendingly and critically, he noted the unbroken field of the other's knowledge. As for himself, from moment to moment the conversation showed him gaps and open stretches, whole subjects with which he was unfamiliar. Nevertheless, thanks to his *Spencer,* he saw that he possessed the outlines of the field of knowledge. It was a matter only of time, when he would fill in the outline. Then watch out, he thought—'ware shoal everybody! He felt like sitting at the feet of the professor, worshipful and absorbent; but, as he listened, he began to discern a weakness in the other's judgments—a weakness so stray and elusive that he might not have caught it had it not been ever present. And when he did catch it, he leaped to equality at once.

Ruth came up to them a second time, just as Martin began to speak.

"I 'll tell you where you are wrong, or, rather, what weakens your judgments," he said. "You lack biology. It has no place in your scheme of things—Oh, I mean the real interpretive biology, from the ground up, from the laboratory and the test tube and the vitalized inorganic right on up to the widest esthetic and sociological generalizations."

Ruth was appalled. She had sat two lecture courses under Professor Caldwell and looked up to him as the living repository of all knowledge.

"I scarcely follow you," he said dubiously.

Martin was not so sure but that he had followed him.

"Then I 'll try to explain," he said. "I remember reading in Egyptian history something to the effect that understanding could not be had of Egyptian art without first studying the land question."

"Quite right," the professor nodded.

"And it seems to me," Martin continued, "that knowledge of the land question, in turn, of all questions, for that matter, cannot be had without previous knowledge of the stuff and the constitution of life. How can we understand laws and institutions, religions and customs, without understanding, not merely the nature of the creatures that made them, but the nature of the stuff out of which the creatures are made? Is literature less human than the architecture and sculpture of Egypt? Is there one thing in the known universe that is not subject to the law of evolution?—Oh, I know there is an elaborate evolution of the various arts laid down, but it seems to me to be too mechanical. The human himself is left out. The evolution of the tool, of the harp, of music and song and dance are all beautifully elaborated; but how about the evolution of the human himself, the development of the basic and intrinsic parts that were in him before he made his first tool or gibbered his first chant? It is that which you do not consider, and which I call biology. It is biology in its largest aspects.

"I know I express myself incoherently, but I 've tried to hammer out the idea. It came to me as you were talking, so I was not primed and ready to deliver it. You spoke yourself of the human frailty that prevented one from taking all the factors into consideration. And you, in turn—or so it seems to me—leave out the biological factor, the very stuff out of which has been spun the fabric of all the arts, the warp and the woof of all human actions and achievements."

To Ruth's amazement, Martin was not immediately crushed, and that the professor replied in the way he did struck her as forbearance for Martin's youth. Professor Caldwell sat for a full minute, silent and fingering his watch chain.

"Do you know," he said at last, "I 've had that same criticism passed on me once before—by a very great man, a scientist and an evolutionist, Joseph Le Conte. But he is dead, and I thought to remain undetected; and now you come along and expose me. Seriously, though—and this is a confession—I think there is something in your contention—a great deal, in fact. I am too classical, not enough up to date in the interpretive branches of science, and I can only plead the disadvantages of my education and a temperamental slothfulness that prevents me from doing the work. I wonder if you 'll believe that I 've never been inside a physics or chemistry laboratory? It is true, nevertheless. Le Conte was right, and so are you, Mr. Eden, at least to an extent—how much I do not know."

Ruth drew Martin away with her on a pretext, when she had got him aside, whispering:

"You should n't have monopolized Professor Caldwell that way. There may be others who want to talk with him."

"My mistake," Martin admitted contritely. "But I 'd got him stirred up, and he was so interesting that I did not think. Do you know, he is the brightest, the most intellectual man I have ever talked with. And I 'll tell you something else. I once thought that everybody who went to universities, or who sat in the high places in society, was just as brilliant and intelligent as he."

"He 's an exception," she answered.

"I should say so. Whom do you want me to talk to now?—Oh, say, bring me up against that cashier-fellow."

Martin talked for fifteen minutes with him, nor could Ruth have wished better behavior on her lover's part. Not once did his eyes flash nor his cheeks flush, while the calmness and poise with which he talked surprised her. But in Martin's estimation the whole tribe of bank cashiers fell a few hundred per cent, and for the rest of the evening he labored under the impression that bank cashiers and talkers of platitudes were synonymous phrases. The army officer he found good-natured and simple, a healthy, wholesome young fellow, content to occupy the place in life into which birth and luck had flung him. On learning that he had completed two years in the university, Martin was puzzled to know where he had stored it away. Nevertheless Martin liked him better than the platitudinous bank cashier.

"I really dont object to platitudes," he told Ruth later; "but what worries me into nervousness is the pompous, smugly complacent, superior certitude with which they are uttered and the time taken to do it. Why, I could give that man the whole history of the Reformation in the time he took to tell me that the Union-Labor Party had fused with the Democrats. Do you know, he skins his words as a professional poker-player skins the cards that are dealt out to him. Some day I'll show you what I mean."

"I 'm sorry you dont like him," was her reply. "He 's a favorite of Mr. Butler's. Mr. Butler says he is safe and honest—calls him the Rock, Peter, and says that upon him any banking institution can well be built."

"I dont doubt it—from the little I saw of him and the less I heard from him; but I dont think so much of banks as I did. You dont mind my speaking my mind this way, dear?"

"No, no; it is most interesting."

"Yes," Martin went on heartily, "I 'm

no more than a barbarian getting my first impressions of civilization. Such impressions must be entertainingly novel to the civilized person."

"What did you think of my cousins?" Ruth queried.

"I liked them better than the other women. There's plenty of fun in them along with paucity of pretense."

"Then you did not like the other women?"

He shook his head.

"That social-settlement woman is no more than a sociological poll-parrot. I swear, if you winnowed her out between the stars, like Tomlinson, there would be found in her not one original thought. As for the portrait-painter, she was a positive bore. She 'd make a good wife for the cashier. And the musician woman! I dont care how nimble her fingers are, how perfect her technique, how wonderful her expression—the fact is, she knows nothing about music."

"She plays beautifully," Ruth protested.

"Yes, she 's undoubtedly gymnastic in the externals of music, but the intrinsic spirit of music is unguessed by her. I asked her what music meant to her—you know I 'm always curious to know that particular thing; and she did not know what it meant to her, except that she adored it, that it was the greatest of the arts, and that it meant more than life to her."

"You were making them talk shop," Ruth charged him.

"I confess it. And if they were failures on shop, imagine my sufferings if they had discoursed on other subjects. Why, I used to think that up here, where all the advantages of culture were enjoyed——" He paused for a moment, and watched the youthful shade of himself, in stiff-rim and square-cut, enter the door and swagger across the room. "As I was saying, up here I thought all men and women were brilliant and radiant. But now, from what little I 've seen of them, they strike me as a pack of ninnies, most of them, and ninety per cent of the remainder as bores. Now, there 's Professor Caldwell—he 's different. He 's a man, every inch of him and every atom of his gray matter."

Ruth 's face brightened.

"Tell me about him," she urged. "Not what is large and brilliant—I know those qualities; but whatever you feel is adverse. I am most curious to know."

"Perhaps I 'll get myself in a pickle." Martin debated humorously for a moment. "Suppose you tell me first? Or maybe you find in him nothing less than the best."

"I attended two lecture courses under him, and I have known him for two years, that is why I am anxious for your first impression."

"Bad impression, you mean? Well, here goes. He is all the fine things you think about him, I guess. At least, he is the finest specimen of intellectual man I have met; but he is a man with a secret shame.

"Oh, no, no," he hastened to cry. "Nothing paltry nor vulgar. What I mean is that he strikes me as a man who has gone to the bottom of things, and is so afraid of what he saw that he makes believe to himself that he never saw it. Perhaps that 's not the clearest way to express it. Here 's another way. A man who has found the path to the hidden temple but has not followed it; who has, perhaps, caught glimpses of the temple and striven afterward to convince himself that it was only a mirage of foliage. Yet another way. A man who could have done things but who placed no value on the doing, and who, all the time, in his innermost heart, is regretting that he has not done them; who has secretly laughed at the rewards for doing, and yet, still more secretly, has yearned for the rewards and for the joy of doing."

"I dont read him that way," she said. "And for that matter, I dont see just what you mean."

"It is only a vague feeling on my part," Martin temporized. "I have no reason for it. It is only a feeling, and most likely it is wrong. You certainly should know him better than I."

From the evening at Ruth's Martin brought away with him strange confusions and conflicting feelings. He was disappointed in his goal, in the persons he had climbed to be with. On the other hand, he was encouraged with his success. The climb had been easier than he expected. He was superior to the climb, and (he did not, with false modesty, hide it from himself), he was superior to the beings among whom he had climbed—with the exception, of course, of Professor Caldwell. About life and the books he knew more than they, and he wondered into what nooks and crannies they had cast aside their educations. He did not know that he was himself possessed of unusual brain vigor; nor did he know that the persons who were given to probing the depths and to thinking ultimate thoughts were not to be found in the drawing rooms of the world's Morses; nor did he dream that such persons were as lonely eagles sailing solitary in the azure sky far above the earth and its swarming freight of gregarious life.

CHAPTER XXVIII.

BUT success had lost Martin's address, and her messengers no longer came to his door. For twenty-five days, working Sundays and holidays, he toiled on "The Shame of the Sun," a long essay of some thirty thousand words. It was a deliberate attack on the mysticism of the Maeterlinck school—an attack from the citadel of positive science upon the wonder-dreamers, but an attack nevertheless that retained much of beauty and wonder of the sort compatible with ascertained fact. It was a little later that he followed up the attack with two short essays, "The Wonder-Dreamers," and "The Yard-stick of the Ego." And on essays, long and short, he began to pay the traveling expenses from magazine to magazine.

During the twenty-five days spent on "The Shame of the Sun," he sold hack-work to the extent of six dollars and fifty cents. A joke had brought in fifty cents, and a second one, sold to a high-grade comic weekly, had fetched a dollar. Then two humorous poems had earned two dollars and three dollars respectively. As a result, having exhausted his credit with the tradesmen (though he had increased his credit with the grocer to five dollars), his wheel and suit of clothes went back to the pawnbroker. The typewriter people were again clamoring for money, insistently pointing out that according to the agreement rent was to be paid strictly in advance.

Encouraged by his several small sales, Martin went back to hack-work. Perhaps there was a living in it after all. Stored away under his table were the twenty storiettes which had been rejected by the newspaper short-story syndicate. He read them over in order to find out how not to write newspaper storiettes, and, so doing, reasoned out the perfect formula. He found that the newspaper storiette should never be tragic, should never end unhappily, and should never contain beauty of language, subtlety of thought, nor real delicacy of sentiment. Sentiment it must contain, plenty of it, pure and noble, of the sort that in his own early youth had brought his applause from "nigger heaven"—the "For-God-my-country-and-the-Czar" and "I-may-be-poor-but-I-am-honest" brand of sentiment.

Having learned such precautions, Martin consulted The Duchess for tone, and proceeded to mix according to formula. The formula consisted of three parts: (1) a pair of lovers are jarred apart; (2) by some deed or event they are reunited; (3) marriage bells. The third part was an unvarying quantity, but the first and second parts could be varied an infinite number of times. Thus, the pair of lovers could be jarred apart by misunderstood motives, by accidents of fate, by jealous rivals, by irate parents, by crafty guardians, by scheming relatives, and so forth and so forth; they could be reunited by brave deed of the man lover, by similar deed of woman lover, by change of heart in one lover or the other, by forced confession of crafty guardian, scheming relative, or jealous rival, by voluntary confession of same, by discovery of some unguessed secret, by lover storming girl's heart, by lover making long and noble self-sacrifice, and so on, endlessly. It was very fetching to make the girl propose in the course of being reunited, and Martin discovered, bit by bit, other decidedly piquant and fetching ruses. But marriage bells at the end was the one thing he could take no liberties with; though the heavens rolled up as a scroll and the stars fell, the wedding bells must go on ringing just the same. In quantity, the formula prescribed twelve hundred words minimum dose, fifteen hundred words maximum dose.

Before he got very far along in the art of the storiette, Martin worked out half a dozen stock forms, which he always consulted when constructing storiettes. These forms were like the cunning tables used by mathematicians, which may be entered from top, bottom, right and left, which entrances consist of scores of lines and dozens of columns, and from which may be drawn, without reasoning or thinking, thousands of different conclusions, all unchallengably precise and true. Thus, in the course of half an hour with his forms, Martin could frame up a dozen or so storiettes, which he put aside and filled in at his convenience. He found that he could fill one in, after a day of serious work, in the hour before going to bed. As he later confessed to Ruth, he could almost do it in his sleep. The real work was in constructing the frames, and that was merely mechanical.

He had no doubt whatever of the efficacy of his formula, and for once he knew the editorial mind when he said positively to himself that the first two he sent off would bring checks. And checks they brought, for four dollars each, at the end of twelve days.

In the meantime he was making fresh and alarming discoveries concerning the magazines. Though the *Occidental* had published "The Ring of Bells," no check was forthcoming. Martin needed it, and he wrote for it. An evasive answer and a request for more of his work was all he received. He had gone hungry two days waiting for the reply, and it was then that he put his wheel back in pawn. He wrote regularly, twice a week, to the *Occidental* for his five dollars, though it was only semi-occasionally that he elicited a reply.

The ten dollars, for which Martin had sold "Treasure Hunters" to the Chicago newspaper, did not come to hand. The article had been published, as he had ascertained at the file in the Central Reading Room, but no word could he get from the editor. His letters were ignored. To satisfy himself that they had been received, he registered several of them. It was nothing less than robbery, he concluded—a cold-blooded steal; while he starved he was pilfered of his merchandise, of his goods the sale of which was the sole way of getting bread to eat.

Youth and Age was a weekly, and it had published two-thirds of his twenty-one-thousand-word serial when it went out of business. With it went all hopes of getting his sixteen dollars.

To cap the situation, "The Pot," which he looked upon as one of the best things he had written, was lost to him. In despair, casting about frantically among the magazines, he had sent it to *The Billow,* a society weekly in San Francisco. His chief reason for submitting it to that publication was that, having only to travel across the bay from Oakland, a quick decision could be reached. Two weeks later he was overjoyed to see, in the latest number on the news stand, his story printed in full, illustrated, and in the place of honor. He went home with leaping pulse, wondering how much they would pay him for one of the best things he had done. Also, the celerity with which it had been accepted and published was a pleasant thought to him. That the editor had not informed him of the acceptance made the surprise more complete. After waiting a week, two weeks, and half a week longer, desperation conquered diffidence, and he wrote to the editor of *The Billow* suggesting that possibly through some negligence of the business manager his little account had been overlooked.

Even if it is n't more than five dollars, Martin thought to himself, it will buy enough beans and peasoup to enable me to write half a dozen like it and possibly as good.

Back came a cool letter from the editor that at least elicited Martin's admiration.

We thank you for your excellent contribution. All of us in the office enjoyed it immensely, and, as you see, it was given the place of honor and immediate publication. We earnestly hope that you liked the illustrations.

On re-reading your letter it seems to us that you are laboring under the misapprehension that we pay for unsolicited manuscripts. This is not our custom, and of course yours was unsolicited. We assumed, naturally, when we received your story, that you understood the situation. We can only deeply regret this unfortunate misunderstanding, and assure you of our unfailing regard. Again thanking you for your kind contribution, and hoping to receive more from you in the near future, we remain, etc.

There was also a postscript to the effect that though *The Billow* carried no free list, it took great pleasure in sending him a complimentary subscription for the ensuing year.

After that experience, Martin typed at the top of the first sheet of all his manuscripts: "Submitted at your usual rate."

Some day, he consoled himself. they will be submitted at my usual rate.

He discovered in himself, at this period, a passion for perfection, under the sway of which he rewrote and polished "The Jostling Street," "The Wine of Life," "Joy," the "Sea Lyrics," and others of his earlier work. As of old, nineteen hours of labor a day was all too little to suit him. He wrote prodigiously, and he read prodigiously, forgetting in his toil the pangs caused by giving up his tobacco. Ruth's promised cure for the habit, flamboyantly labeled, he stowed away in the most inaccessible corner of his bureau. Especially during his stretches of famine he suffered from lack of the weed; but no matter how often he mastered the craving, it remained with him as strong as ever. He regarded it as the biggest thing he had ever achieved. Ruth's point of view was that he was doing no more than was right. She brought him the anti-tobacco remedy, purchased out of her glove money, and in a few days forgot all about it.

His machine-made storiettes, though he hated them and derided them, were successful. By means of them he redeemed all his pledges, paid most of his bills, and bought a new set of tires for his wheel. The storiettes at least kept the pot a-boiling and gave him time for ambitious work; while the one thing that upheld him was the forty dollars he had received from *The White Mouse*. He anchored his faith to that, and was confident that the really first-class magazines would pay an unknown writer at least an equal rate if not a better one. But the thing was, how to get into the first-class magazines. His best stories, essays, and poems went begging among them, and yet, each month, he read reams of dull, prosy, inartistic stuff between all their various covers. If only one editor, he sometimes thought, would descend from his high seat of pride to write me one cheering line! No matter if my work is unusual, no matter if it is unfit, for prudential reasons, for their pages, surely there must be some sparks in it, somewhere, a few, to warm them to some sort of appreciation. And thereupon he would get out one or another of his manuscripts, such as "Adventure," and read it over and over in vain attempt to vindicate the editorial silence.

As the sweet California spring came on, his period of plenty came to an end. For several weeks he had been worried by a strange silence on the part of the newspaper storiette syndicate. Then, one day, came back to him through the mail, ten of his immaculate machine-made storiettes. They were accompanied by a brief letter to the effect that the syndicate was overstocked and that some months would elapse before it would be in the market again for manuscripts. Martin had even been extravagant on the strength of those ten storiettes. Toward the last the syndicate had been paying him five dollars each for them and accepting every one he sent. So he had looked upon the ten as good as sold, and he had lived accordingly, on a basis of fifty dollars in the bank. So it was that he entered abruptly upon a lean period, wherein he continued selling his earlier efforts to publications that would not pay and submitting his later work to magazines that would not buy. Also, he resumed his trips to the pawnbroker down in Oakland. A few jokes and snatches of humorous verse, sold to the New York weeklies, made existence barely possible for him. It was at this time that he wrote letters of inquiry to the several great monthly and quarterly reviews, and learned in reply that they rarely considered unsolicited articles, and that most of their contents were written upon order by well-known specialists who were authorities in their fields

Martin Eden

By Jack London

Author of "The Call of the Wild," "Sea Wolf," "The God of His Fathers," "White Fang," etc.

CHAPTER XXIX.

IT was a hard summer for Martin. Manuscript readers and editors were away on vacation, and publications that ordinarily returned a decision in three weeks now retained his manuscripts for three months or more. The consolation he drew from it was that a saving in postage was effected by the deadlock. Only the robber-publications seemed to remain actively in business, and to them Martin disposed of all his early efforts, such as "Pearl Diving," "The Sea as a Career," "Turtle-Catching," and "The Northeast Trades." For these manuscripts he never received a penny. It is true, after six months' correspondence, he effected a compromise, whereby he received a safety razor for "Turtle-Catching," and that the *Acropolis* having agreed to give him five dollars cash and five yearly subscriptions for "The Northeast Trades," fulfilled the second part of the agreement.

For a sonnet on Stevenson he managed to wring two dollars out of a Boston editor who was running a magazine with a Matthew Arnold taste and a penny-dreadful purse. "The Peri and the Pearl," a clever skit of a poem of two hundred lines, just finished, white-hot from his brain, won the heart of the editor of a San Francisco magazine published in the interest of a great railroad. When the editor wrote, offering him payment in transportation, Martin wrote back to inquire if the transportation was transferable. It was not, and so, being prevented from peddling it, he asked for the return of the poem. Back it came, with the editor's regrets, and Martin sent it to San Francisco again, this time to *The Hornet,* a pretentious monthly that had been fanned into a constellation of the first magnitude by the brilliant journalist who founded it. But *The Hornet's* light had begun to dim long before Martin was born. The editor promised Martin fifteen dollars for the poem, but when it was published seemed to forget about it. Several of his letters being ignored, Martin indited an angry one which drew a reply. It was written by a new editor, who coolly informed Martin that he declined to be held responsible for the old editor's mistakes, and that he did not think much of "The Peri and the Pearl" anyway.

But *The Globe,* a Chicago magazine, gave Martin the cruelest treatment of all. He had refrained from offering his "Sea Lyrics" for publication, until driven to it by starvation. After having been rejected by a dozen magazines, they had come to rest in *The Globe* office. There were thirty poems in the collection, and he was to receive a dollar apiece for them. The first month four were published, and he promptly received a check for four dollars; but when he looked over the magazine he was appalled at the slaughter. In some cases the titles had been altered, "Finis," for instance, being changed to "The Finish," and "The Song of the Outer Reef," to "The Song of the Coral Reef." In one case, an absolutely different title, a misappropriate title, was substituted. In place of his own, "Medusa Lights," the editor had printed "The Backward Track." But the slaughter in the body of the poems was terrifying. Martin groaned and sweated and thrust has hands through his hair. Phrases, lines, and stanzas were cut out, interchanged, or juggled about in most incomprehensible manner. Sometimes lines and stanzas not his own were substituted for his. He could not believe that a sane editor could be guilty of such maltreatment, and his favorite hypothesis was that his poems must have been doctored by the office boy or the stenographer. Martin wrote immediately, begging the editor to cease publishing the lyrics and to return them to him. He wrote again and again, begging, entreating, threatening, but his letters were ignored, month by month the slaughter went on till the thirty poems were published, and month by month he received a check for those which had appeared in the current number.

Despite these various misadventures, the memory of *The White Mouse* forty-dollar check sustained him, though he was driven more and more to hack-work. He discovered a bread-and-butter field in the agricultural weeklies and trade journals, though among the religious weeklies he found he could easily starve. At his lowest ebb, when his black suit was in pawn, he made a ten-strike—or so it seemed to him—in a prize contest arranged by the County Committee of the Republican Party. There were three branches of the contest, and he entered them all, laughing at himself bitterly the while in that he was driven to such straits to live. His poem won the first prize of ten dollars, his campaign song the second prize of five dollars, his essay on the principles of the Republican Party the first prize of twenty-five dollars. Which was very gratifying to him until he tried to collect. Something had gone wrong in the County Committee, and, though a rich banker and a state senator were members of it, the money was not forthcoming. While this affair was hanging fire, he proved that he understood the principles of the Democratic Party by winning the first prize for his essay in a similar contest. And, moreover, he received the money, twenty-five dollars. But the forty dollars won in the first contest he never received.

Driven to shifts in order to see Ruth, and deciding that the long walk from North Oakland to her house and back again consumed too much time, he kept his black suit in pawn in place of his bicycle. The latter gave him exercise, saved him hours of time for work, and enabled him to see Ruth just the same. A pair of knee duck-trousers and an old sweater made him a presentable wheel costume so that he could go with Ruth on afternoon rides. Besides, he no longer had opportunity to see much of her in her own home, where Mrs. Morse was thoroughly prosecuting her campaign of entertainment. The exalted beings he met there and to whom he had looked up but a short time before, now bored him. They were no longer exalted. He was nervous and irritable, what of his hard times, disappointments, and close application to work, and the conversation of such people was maddening. He was not unduly egotistic. He measured the narrowness of their minds by the minds of the thinkers in the books he read. At Ruth's home he never met a large mind, with the exception of Professor Caldwell, and Caldwell he had met there only once. As for the rest, they were numb skulls, ninnies, superficial, dogmatic, and ignorant. It was their ignorance that astounded him. What was the matter with them? What had they done with their educations? They had had access to the same books he had. How did it happen that they had drawn nothing from them?

He knew that the great minds, the deep and rational thinkers, existed. He had his proofs from the books, the books that had educated him beyond the Morse standard. And he knew that higher intellects than those of the Morse circle were to be found in the world. He read English society novels, wherein he caught glimpses of men and women talking politics and philosophy. And he read of salons in great cities, even in the United States, where art and intellect congregated. Foolishly, in the past, he had conceived that all well-groomed persons above the working class were persons with power of intellect and vigor of beauty. Culture and collars had gone together, to him, and he had been deceived into believing that college educations and mastery were the same things.

Well, he would fight his way on and

up higher. And he would take Ruth with him. Her he dearly loved, and he was confident that she would shine anywhere. As it was clear to him that he had been handicapped by his early environment, so now he perceived that she was similarly handicapped. She had not had a chance to expand. The books on her father's shelves, the paintings on the walls, the music on the piano—all was just so much meretricious display. To real literature, real painting, real music, the Morses and their kind were dead. And bigger than such things was life, of which they were densely, hopelessly ignorant. In spite of their Unitarian proclivities and their masks of conservative broadmindedness, they were two generations behind interpretive science; their mental processes were medieval, while their thinking on the ultimate data of existence and of the universe struck him as the same meta-physical method that was as young as the youngest race, as old as the caveman, and older—the same that moved the first Pleiestocene ape-man to fear the dark; that moved the first hasty Hebrew savage to incarnate Eve from Adam's rib; that moved Descarte to build an idealistic system of the universe out of the projections of his own puny ego; and that moved the famous British ecclesiastic to denounce evolution in satire so scathing as to win immediate applause and leave his name a notorious scrawl on the page of history.

So Martin thought, and he thought further, till it dawned upon him that the difference between these lawyers, officers, business men, and bank-cashiers he had met and the members of the working class he had known was on a par with the difference in the food they ate, clothes they wore, neighborhoods in which they lived. Certainly in all of them was lacking the something more which he found in himself and in the books. The Morses had shown him the best their social position could produce, and he was not infatuated by it. A pauper himself, a slave to the money-lender, he knew himself the superior of those he met at the Morses'; and, when his one decent suit of clothes was out of pawn, he moved among them a lord of life, quivering with a sense of outrage akin to what a prince would suffer if condemned to live with goat-herds.

"You hate and fear the socialists," he remarked to Mr. Morse, one evening at dinner; "but why? You neither know them nor their doctrines."

The conversation had been swung in that direction by Mrs. Morse, who had been invidiously singing the praises of Mr. Hapgood. The cashier was Martin's black beast, and his temper was a trifle short where the talker of platitudes was concerned.

"Yes," he had said, "Charley Hapgood is what they call a rising young man—somebody told me as much. And it is true. He 'll make the Governor's chair before he dies, and who knows? maybe the United States Senate."

"What makes you think so?" Mrs. Morse had inquired.

"I 've heard him make a campaign speech. It was so cleverly stupid and unoriginal, and also so convincing, that the leaders cannot help but regard him as safe and sure, while his platitudes are so much like the platitudes of the average voter that—oh, well, you know you flatter any man by dressing up his own thoughts for him and presenting them to him."

"I actually think you are jealous of Mr. Hapgood," Ruth had chimed in.

"Heaven forbid!"

The look of horror on Martin's face stirred Mrs. Morse to belligerence.

"You surely dont mean to say that Mr. Hapgood is stupid?" she demanded icily.

"No more than the average republican," was the retort, "or average democrat, either. They are all stupid when they are not crafty, and very few of them are crafty. The only wise republicans are the millionaires and their conscious henchmen. They know which side their bread is buttered on, and they know why."

"I am a republican," Mr. Morse put in lightly. "Pray how do you classify me?"

"Oh, you are an unconscious henchman."

"Henchman?"

"Why, yes. You do corporation work. You have no working-class nor criminal practice. You dont depend upon wife-beaters and pickpockets for your income. You get your livelihood from the masters of society, and whoever feeds a man is that man's master. Yes, you are a henchman. You are interested in advancing the interests of the aggregations of capital you serve."

Mr. Morse's face was a trifle red.

"I confess, sir," he said, "that you talk like a scoundrelly socialist."

Then it was that Martin remarked;

"You hate and fear the socialists; but why? You neither know them nor their doctrines."

"Your doctrine certainly sounds like socialism," Mr. Morse replied, while Ruth gazed anxiously from one to the other, and Mrs. Morse beamed happily at the opportunity afforded of rousing her liege lord's antagonism.

"Because I say republicans are stupid, and hold that liberty, equality, and fraternity are exploded bubbles, does not make me a socialist," Martin said with a smile. "Because I question Jefferson and the unscientific Frenchmen who informed his mind, does not make me a socialist. Believe me, Mr. Morse, you are far nearer socialism than I who am its avowed enemy."

"Now you please to be facetious," was all the other could say.

"Not at all. I speak in all seriousness. You still believe in equality, and yet you do the work of the corporations, and the corporations, from day to day, are busily engaged in burying equality. And you call me a socialist because I deny equality, because I affirm just what you live up to. The republicans are foes to equality, though most of them fight the battle against equality with the very word itself the slogan on their lips. In the name of equality they destroy equality. That was why I called them stupid. As for myself, I am an individualist. I believe the race is to the swift, the battle to the strong. Such is the lesson I have learned from biology, or at least think I have learned. As I said, I am an individualist, and individualism is the hereditary and eternal foe of socialism."

"But you frequent socialist meetings," Mr. Morse challenged.

"Certainly, just as spies frequent hostile camps. How else are you to learn about the enemy? Besides, I enjoy myself at their meetings. They are good fighters, and, right or wrong, they have read the books. Any one of them knows far more about sociology and all the other ologies than the average captain of industry. Yes, I have been to half a dozen of their meetings, but that does n't make me a socialist any more than hearing Charley Hapgood orate made me a republican."

"I can 't help it," Mr. Morse said feebly, "but I still believe you incline that way."

Bless me, Martin thought to himself; he does n't know what I was talking about. He has n't understood a word of it. What did he do with his education anyway?

Thus, in his development, Martin found himself face to face with economic morality or the morality of class; and soon it became to him a grisly monster. Personally, he was an intellectual moralist, and more offending to him than platitudinous pomposity was the morality of those about him, which was a curious hotch-potch of the economic, the metaphysical, the sentimental, and the imitative.

A sample of this curious, messy mixture he encountered nearer home. His sister, Marian, had been keeping company with an industrious young mechanic, of German extraction, who, after thoroughly learning the trade, had set up for himself in a bicycle-repair shop. Also, having got the agency for a low-grade make of wheel, he was prosperous. Marian had called on Martin in his room a short time before to announce her engagement, during which visit she had playfully inspected Martin's palm and told his fortune. On her next visit she brought Hermann von Schmidt along with her. Martin did the honors and congratulated both of them in language so easy and graceful as to affect disagreeably the peasant-mind of his sister's lover. This bad impression was further heightened by Martin's reading aloud the half-dozen stanzas of verse with which he had commemorated Marion's previous visit. It was a bit of society verse, airy and delicate, which he had named "The Palmist." He was surprised, when he finished reading it, to note no enjoyment in his sister's face. Instead, her eyes were fixed anxiously upon her betrothed, and Martin, following her gaze, saw spread on that worthy's assymetrical features nothing but black and sullen disapproval. The incident passed over, they made an early departure, and Martin forgot all about it, though for the moment he had been puzzled that any woman, even of the working class, should not have been flattered and delighted by having poetry written about her.

Several evenings later, Marian again visited him, this time alone. Nor did she waste time in coming to the point, upbraiding him sorrowfully for what he had done.

"Why, Marian," he chided, "you talk as though you were ashamed of your relatives, or of your brother at any rate."

"And I am, too," she blurted out.

Martin was bewildered by the tears of mortification he saw in her eyes. The mood, whatever it was, was genuine.

"But, Marian, why should your Hermann be jealous of my writing poetry about my own sister."

"He aint jealous," she sobbed. "He says it was indecent, ob—obscene."

Martin emitted a long, low whistle of incredulity, then proceeded to resurrect and read a carbon copy of "The Palmist."

"I can 't see it," he said finally, proffering the manuscript to her. "Read it yourself and show me whatever strikes you as obscene—that was the word, was n't it?"

"He says so, and he ought to know," was the answer, with a wave aside of the manuscript, accompanied by a look of loathing. "And he says you 've got to tear it up. He says he wont have no wife of his with such things written about her which anybody can read. He says it 's a disgrace, an' he wont stand for it."

"Now, look here, Marian, this is nothing but nonsense," Martin began, then abruptly changed his mind.

He saw before him an unhappy girl, knew the futility of attempting to convince her husband or her, and, though the whole situation was absurd and preposterous, he resolved to surrender.

"All right," he announced, tearing the manuscript into half a dozen pieces and throwing it into the waste-basket.

He contented himself with the knowledge that even then the original typewritten manuscript was reposing in the office of a New York magazine. Marian and her husband would never know, and neither himself nor they nor the world would lose if the pretty harmless poem ever were published.

Marian, starting to reach into the waste-basket, refrained.

"Can I?" she pleaded.

He nodded his head, regarding her thoughtfully as she gathered the torn pieces of manuscript and tucked them into the pocket of her jacket—ocular evidence of the success of her mission. She reminded him of Lizzie Connolly, though there was less of fire and gorgeous flaunting life in her than in that other girl of the working class whom he had seen twice. But they were on a par, the pair of them, in dress and carriage, and he smiled with inward amusement at the caprice of his fancy which suggested the appearance of either of them in Mrs. Morse's drawing room. The amusement faded, and he was aware of a great loneliness. This sister of his and the Morse drawing room were milestones of the road he had traveled. And he had left them behind. He glanced affectionately about him at his few books. They were all the comrades left to him.

"Hello, what 's that?" he demanded in startled surprise.

Marian repeated her question.

"Why dont I go to work?" He broke into a laugh that was only half-hearted. "That Hermann of yours has been talking to you."

She shook her head.

"Dont lie," he commanded, and the nod of her head affirmed his charge.

"Well, you tell that Hermann of yours to mind his own business. That when I write poetry about the girl he 's keeping company with it 's his business, but that outside of that he 's got no say so. Understand?

"So you dont think I 'll succeed as a writer, eh?" he went on. "You think I 'm no good?—that I 've fallen down and am a disgrace to the family?"

"I think it would be better if you got a job," she said firmly, and he saw she was sincere. "Hermann says—"

"Damn Hermann!" he broke out good-naturedly. "What I want to know is when you 're going to get married. Also, you find out from your Hermann if he will deign to permit you to accept a wedding present from me."

He mused over the incident after she had gone, and once or twice broke out into laughter that was bitter as he saw his sister and her betrothed, all the members of his own class and the members of Ruth's class, directing their narrow little lives by narrow little formulas—herd-creatures, flocking together and patterning their lives by one another's opinions, failing of being individuals and of really living life because of the childlike formulas by which they were enslaved. He summoned them before him in apparitional procession, Bernard Higginbotham arm in arm with Mr. Butler, Hermann von Schmidt cheek by jowl with Charley Hapgood, and one by one and in pairs he judged them and dismissed them—judged them by the standards of intellect and morality he had learned from the books. Vainly he asked: Where are the great souls, the great men and women? He found them not among the careless, gross, and stupid intelligences that answered the call of vision to his narrow room. He felt a loathing for them such, as Circe must have felt for her swine. When he had dismissed the last one and thought himself alone, a late-comer entered, unexpected and unsummoned. Martin watched him and saw the stiff-rim, the square-cut, double-breasted coat, and the swaggering shoulders of the youthful hoodlum who had once been he.

"You were like all the rest, young fellow," Martin sneered. "Your morality and your knowledge were just the same as theirs. You did not think and act for yourself. Your opinions, like your clothes, were ready-made; your acts were shaped by popular approval. You were cock of your gang because others acclaimed you the real thing. You fought and ruled the gang, not because you liked to—you know you really despised it—but because the other fellows patted you on the shoulder. You licked Cheeseface because you would n't give in, and you would n't give in, partly because you were abysmal brute, and for the rest, because you believed what every one about you believed: that the measure of manhood was the carniverous ferocity displayed in injuring and marring fellow-creatures' anatomies. Why, you whelp, you even won other fellows' girls away from them, not because you wanted the girls, but because, in the marrow of those about you, those who set your moral pace, was the instinct of the wild stallion and the bull-seal. Well, the years have passed, and what do you think about it now?"

As if in reply, the vision underwent a swift metamorphosis. The stiff-rim and the square-cut vanished, being replaced by milder garments; the toughness went out of the face, the hardness out of the eyes; and the face, chastened and refined, was irradiated from an inner life of communion with beauty and knowledge. The apparition was very like his present self, and, as he regarded it, he noted the student-lamp by which it was illuminated, and the book over which it pored. He glanced at the title and read: *The Science of Aesthetics.* Next, he entered into the apparition, trimmed the student-lamp, and himself went on reading *The Science of Aesthetics.*

CHAPTER XXX.

ON a beautiful fall day, a day of similar Indian Summer to that which had seen their love declared the year before, Martin read his "Love-Cycle" to Ruth. It was in the afternoon, and, as before, they had ridden out to their favorite knoll in the hills. Now and again she had interrupted his reading with exclamations of pleasure, and now, as he laid the last sheet of manuscript with its fellows, he waited her judgment.

She delayed to speak, and at last she spoke haltingly, hesitating to frame in words the harshness of her thought.

"I think they are beautiful, very beautiful," she said "but you can 't sell them, can you? You see what I mean," she said, almost pleaded. "This writing of yours is not practical. Something is the matter—maybe it is with the market—that prevents you from earning a living by it. And please, dear, dont misunderstand me. I am flattered, and made proud, and all that—I could not be a true woman were it otherwise—that you should write these poems to me. But they do not make our marriage possible. Dont you see, Martin? Dont think me mercenary. It is love, the thought of our future, with which I am burdened. A whole year has gone by since we learned we loved each other, and our wedding day is no nearer. Dont think me immodest in thus talking about our wedding, for really I have my heart, all that I am, at stake. Why dont you try to get work on a newspaper, if you are so bound up in your writing? Why not become a reporter?—for a while, at least?"

"It would spoil my style," was his answer, in a low, monotonous voice. "You have no idea how I 've worked for style."

"But those storiettes," she argued. "You called them hack-work. You wrote many of them. Did n't they spoil your style?"

"No, the cases are different. The storiettes were ground out, jaded, at the end of a long day of application to style. But a reporter's work is all hack from morning till night, is the one paramount thing of life. And it is a whirlwind life, the life of the moment, with neither past nor future, and certainly without thought of any style but reportorial style, and that certainly is not literature. To become a reporter now, just as my style is taking form, crystalizing, would be to commit literary suicide. As it is, every storiette, every word of every storiette, was a violation of myself, of my self-respect, of my respect for beauty. I tell you it was sickening. I was guilty of sin. And I was secretly glad when the market failed, even if my clothes did go into pawn. But the joy of writing the 'Love Cycle!' The creative joy in its noblest form! That was compensation for everything."

Martin did not know that Ruth was unsympathetic concerning the creative joy. She used the phrase—it was on her lips he had first heard it. She had read about it, studied about it, in the university in the course of earning her Bachelorship of Arts; but she was not original, not creative, and all manifestations of culture on her part were but harpings of the harpings of others.

"May not the editor have been right in his revision of your 'Sea Lyrics?' " she questioned. "Remember, an editor must have proved qualifications or else he would not be an editor."

"That 's in line with the persistence of the established," he rejoined, his heat against the editor-folk getting the better of him. "What is is not only right but is the best possible. The existence of anything is sufficient vindication of its fitness to exist—to exist, mark you, as the average person unconsciously believes, not merely in present conditions, but in all conditions. It is their ignorance, of course, that makes them believe such rot—their ignorance, which is nothing more nor less than the mental process described by Weininger. They think they think, and such thinkless creatures are the arbiters of the lives of the few who really think."

He paused, overcome by the consciousness that he had been talking over Ruth's head.

"I 'm sure I dont know who this Weininger is," she retorted, "and you are so dreadfully general that I fail to follow you. What I was speaking of was the qualification of editors—"

"And I 'll tell you," he interrupted. "The chief qualification of ninety-nine per cent of all editors is failure. They have failed as writers. Dont think they prefer the drudgery of the desk and the slavery to their circulation and to the business manager to the joy of writing. They have tried to write, and they have failed. And right there is the cursed paradox of it. Every portal to success in literature is guarded by those watch-dogs, the failures in literature. The editors, sub-editors, associate editors, most of them, and the manuscript-readers for the magazines and book-publishers, most of them, nearly all of them, are men who wanted to write and who have failed. And yet they, of all creatures under the sun the most unfit, are the very creatures who decide what shall and what shall not find its way into print—they, who have proved themselves not original, who have demonstrated that they lack the divine fire, sit in judgment upon originality and genius. And after them come the reviewers, just so many more failures. Dont tell me that they have not dreamed the dream and attempted to write poetry or fiction; for they have and they have failed. Why, the average review is more nauseating than cod-liver oil. But you know my opinion on the reviewers and the alleged critics. There are great critics, but they are as rare as comets. If I fail as a writer I shall have proved for the career of editorship. There 's bread and butter and jam at any rate."

Ruth's mind was quick, and her disapproval of her lover's views was buttressed by the contradiction she found in his contention.

"But, Martin, if that be so, if all the doors are closed as you have shown so conclusively, how is it possible that any of the great writers ever arrived?"

"They arrived by achieving the impossible," he answered. "They did such blazing, glorious work as to burn to ashes those that opposed them. They arrived by course of miracle, by winning a thousand-to-one wager against them. They arrived because they were Carlyle's battle-scarred giants who will not be kept down. And that is what I must do; I must achieve the impossible."

"But if you fail? You must consider me as well, Martin."

"If I fail?" He regarded her for a moment as though the thought she had uttered was unthinkable. Then intelligence illumined his eyes. "If I fail, I shall become an editor, and you will be an editor's wife."

She frowned at his facetiousness—a pretty, adorable frown that made him put his arms around her and kiss it away.

"There, that 's enough," she urged, by an effort of will withdrawing herself from the fascination of his strength. "I have talked with father and mother. I never before asserted myself so against them. I demanded to be heard. I was very undutiful. They are against you, you know; but I assured them over and over of my abiding love for you, and at last father agreed, that if you wanted to, you could begin right away in his office. And then, of his own accord, he said he would pay you enough at the start so that we could get married and have a little cottage somewhere. Which I think was very fine of him—dont you?"

Martin, with the dull pain of despair at his heart, mechanically reaching for the tobacco and paper (which he no longer carried) to roll a cigarette, muttered something inarticulate, and Ruth went on:

"Frankly, though, and dont let it hurt you—I tell you to show you precisely how you stand with him—he does n't like your radical views, and he thinks you are lazy. Of course I know you are not. I know you work hard."

How hard, even she did not know, was the thought in Martin's mind.

"Well, then," he said, "how about my views? Do you think they are so radical?"

He held her eyes and waited the answer.

"I think them, well, very disconcerting," she replied.

The question was answered for him, and so oppressed was he by the grayness of life that he forgot the tentative proposition she had made for him to go to work. And she, having gone as far as she dared, was willing to wait the answer till she should bring the question up again.

She had not long to wait. Martin had a question of his own to propound to her. He wanted to ascertain the measure of her faith in him, and within the week each was answered. Martin precipitated it by reading to her his "The Shame of the Sun."

"Why dont you become a reporter?" she asked when he had finished. "You love writing so, and I am sure you would succeed. You could rise in journalism and make a name for yourself. There are a number of great special correspondents. Their salaries are large, and their field is the world. They are sent everywhere, to the heart of Africa, like Stanley, or to interview the Pope, or to explore unknown Thibet."

"Then you dont like my essay?" he rejoined. "You believe that I have some show in journalism but none in literature?"

"No, no; I do like it. It reads well. But I am afraid it 's over the heads of your readers. At least it is over mine. It sounds beautiful, but I dont understand it. Your scientific slang is beyond me. You are an extremist, you know, dear, and what may be intelligible to you may not be intelligible to the rest of us."

"I imagine it 's the philosophic slang that bothers you," was all he could say.

He was flaming from the fresh reading of the ripest thought he had expressed, and her verdict stunned him.

"No matter how poorly it is done," he persisted, "dont you see anything in it? —in the thought of it, I mean?"

She shook her head.

"No, it is so different from anything I have read. I read Materlinck and understand him——"

"His mysticism, you understand that?" Martin flashed out.

"Yes, but this of yours, which is supposed to be an attack upon him, I dont understand. Of course, if originality counts——"

He stopped her with an impatient gesture that was not followed by speech. He became suddenly aware that she was speaking and that she had been speaking for some time.

"After all, your writing has been a toy to you," she was saying. "Surely you have played with it long enough. It is time to take up life seriously—*our* life, Martin. Hitherto you have lived solely your own."

"You want me to go to work?" he asked.

"Yes. Father has offered—"

"I understand all that," he broke in; "but what I want to know is whether or not you have lost faith in me?"

She pressed his hand mutely, her eyes dim.

"In your writing, dear," she admitted in a half-whisper.

"You 've read lots of my stuff," he went on brutally. "What do you think of it? Is it utterly hopeless? How does it compare with other men's work?"

"But they sell theirs, and you—dont."

"That does n't answer my question. Do you think that literature is not at all my vocation?"

"Then I will answer." She steeled herself to do it. "I dont think you were made to write. Forgive me, dear. You compel me to say it; and you know I know more about literature than you do."

"Yes, you are a Bachelor of Arts," he said meditatively; "and you ought to know.

"But there is more to be said," he continued, after a pause painful to both. "I know what I have in me. No one knows that so well as I. I know I shall succeed. I will not be kept down. I am afire with what I have to say in verse, and fiction, and essay. I do not ask you to have faith in that, though. I do not ask you to have faith in me, nor in my writing. What I do ask of you is to love me and have faith in love.

"A year ago I begged for two years. One of those years is yet to run. And I do believe, upon my honor and my soul, that before that year is run I shall have succeeded. You remember what you told me long ago, that I must serve my apprenticeship to writing. Well, I have served it. I have crammed it and telescoped it. With you at the end awaiting me, I have never shirked. Do you know, I have forgotten what it is to fall peacefully asleep. A few million years ago I knew what it was to sleep my fill and to wake naturally from very glut of sleep. I am awakened always now by an alarm clock. If I fall asleep early or late, I set the alarm accordingly; and this, and the putting out of the lamp, are my last conscious actions.

"When I begin to feel drowsy, I

change the heavy book I am reading for a lighter one. And when I doze over that I beat my head with my knuckles in order to drive sleep away. Somewhere I read of a man who was afraid to sleep. Kipling wrote the story. This man arranged a spur so that when unconsciousness came his naked body pressed against the iron teeth. Well, I 've done the same. I look at the time, and I resolve that not until midnight, or not until one o'clock, or two o'clock, or three o'clock, shall the spur be removed. And so it rowells me awake until the appointed time. That spur has been my bed-mate for months. I have grown so desperate that five and a half hours of sleep is an extravagance. I sleep four hours, now. I am starved for sleep. There are times when I am light-headed from want of sleep; times when death, with its rest and sleep, is a positive lure to me; times when I am haunted by Longfellow's lines:

" 'The sea is still and deep;
All things within its bosom sleep;
A single step and all is o'er,
A plunge, a bubble, and no more.'

"Of course, this is sheer nonsense. It comes from nervousness, from an overwrought mind. But the point is: Why have I done this? For you. To shorten my apprenticeship. To compel Success to hasten. And my apprenticeship is now served. I know my equipment. I swear that I learn more each month than the average college man learns in a year. I know it, I tell you. But were my need for you to understand not so desperate I should not tell you. It is not boasting. I measure the results by the books. Your brothers, today, are ignorant barbarians compared with me and the knowledge I have wrung from the books in the hours they were sleeping. Long ago I wanted to be famous. I care very little for fame now. What I want is you; I am more hungry for you than for food, or clothing, or recognition. I have a dream of laying my head on your breast and sleeping an aeon or so, and the dream will come true ere another year is gone."

His power beat against her, wave upon wave; and in the moment his will opposed hers most she felt herself most strongly drawn toward him. The strength that had always poured out from him to her was now flowering in his impassioned voice, his flashing eyes, and the vigor of life and intellect surging in him. And in that moment, and for the moment, she was aware of a rift that showed in her certitude—a rift through which she caught sight of the real Martin Eden, splendid and invincible; and as animal-trainers have their moments of doubt, so she, for the instant, seemed to doubt her power to tame this wild spirit of a man.

"And another thing," he swept on. "You love me. But why do you love me? The thing in me that compels me to write is the very thing that draws your love. You love me because I am somehow different from the men you have known and might have loved. I was not made for the desk and counting-house, for petty business squabbling and legal jangling. Make me do such things, make me like those other men, doing the work they do, breathing the air they breathe, developing the point of view they have developed, and you have destroyed the difference, destroyed me, destroyed the thing you love. My desire to write is the most vital thing in me. Had I been a mere clod, neither would I have desired to write, nor would you have desired me for a husband."

"But you forget," she interrupted, the quick surface of her mind glimpsing a parallel. "There have been eccentric inventors, starving their families while they sought such chimeras as perpetual motion. Doubtless their wives loved them, and suffered with them and for them, not because of, but in spite of, their infatuation for perpetual motion."

"True," was the reply. "But there have been inventors who were not eccentric and who starved while they sought to invent practical things; and sometimes, it is recorded, they succeeded. Certainly I do not seek impossibilities—"

"You have called it 'achieving the impossible,' " she interpolated.

"I spoke figuratively. I seek to do what men have done before me—to write and to live by my writing."

Her silence spurred him on.

"To you, then, my goal is as much a chimera as perpetual motion?" he demanded.

He read her answer in the pressure of her hand on his—the pitying mother-hand for the hurt child. And to her, just then, he was the hurt child, the infatuated man striving to achieve the impossible.

Toward the close of their talk she warned him again of the antagonism of her father and mother.

"But you love me?" he asked.

"I do! I do!" she cried.

"And I love you, not them, and nothing they do can hurt me." Triumph sounded in his voice. "For I have faith in your love, not fear of their enmity. All things may go astray in this world, but not love. Love cannot go wrong unless it be a weakling that faints and stumbles by the way."

CHAPTER XXXI.

MARTIN had encountered his sister Gertrude by chance on Broadway—as it proved, a most propitious yet disconcerting chance. Waiting on the corner for a car, she had seen him first, and noted the eager, hungry lines of his face and the desperate, worried look of his eyes. In truth, he was desperate and worried. He had just come from a fruitless interview with the pawnbroker, from whom he had tried to wring an additional loan on his wheel. The muddy fall weather having come on, Martin had pledged his wheel some time since and retained his black suit.

"There 's the black suit," the pawnbroker, who knew his every asset, had answered. "You need n't tell me you 've gone and pledged it with that Jew, Lipka. Because if you have—"

The man looked the threat, and Martin hastened to cry:

"No, no; I 've got it. But I want to wear it on a matter of business."

"All right," the mollified usurer had replied. "And I want it on a matter of business before I can let you have any more money. You dont think I 'm in it for my health?"

"But it 's a forty-dollar wheel, in good condition," Martin had argued. "And you 've only let me have seven dollars on it. No, not even seven. Six and a quarter; you took the interest in advance."

"If you want some more, bring the suit," had been the reply that sent Martin out of the stuffy little den, so desperate at heart as to reflect it in his face and touch his sister to pity.

Scarcely had they met when the Telegraph Avenue car came along and stopped to take on a crowd of afternoon shoppers. Mrs. Higginbotham divined from the grip on her arm as he helped her on, that he was not going to follow her. She turned on the step and looked down upon him. His haggard face smote her to the heart again.

"Ain't you comin'?" she asked.

The next moment she had descended to his side.

"I 'm walking—exercise, you know," he explained.

"Then I 'll go along for a few blocks," she announced. "Mebbe it 'll do me good. I ain't ben feelin' any too spry these last few days."

Martin glanced at her and verified her statement in her general slovenly appearance, in the unhealthy fat, in the drooping shoulders, the tired face with the sagging lines, and in the heavy fall of her feet, without elasticity—a very caricature of the walk that belongs to a free and happy body.

"You 'd better stop here," he said, though she had already come to a halt at the first corner; "and take the next car."

"My goodness!—if I ain't all tired a'ready!" she panted. "But I 'm just as able to walk as you in them soles. They 're that thin they 'll bust long before you git out to North Oakland."

"I 've a better pair at home," was the answer.

"Come out to dinner tomorrow!" she invited irrelevantly. "Mr. Higginbotham wont be there. He 's goin' to San Leandro on business."

Martin shook his head, but he had failed to keep back the wolfish, hungry look that leapt into his eyes at the suggestion of dinner.

"You haven 't a penny, Mart, and that 's why you 're walkin'. Exercise!" she tried to sniff contemptuously, but succeeded in producing only a sniffle. "Here, lemme see."

And, fumbling in her satchel, she pressed a five-dollar piece into his hand. "I guess I forgot your last birthday, Mart," she mumbled lamely.

Martin's hand instinctively closed on the piece of gold. In the same instant he knew he ought not to accept, and found himself struggling in the throes of indecision. That bit of gold meant food, life and light in his body and brain, power to go on writing, and—who was to say?—maybe to write something that would bring in many pieces of gold. Clear on his vision burned the manuscripts of two essays he had just completed. He saw them under the table on top the heap of returned manuscripts for which he had no stamps, and he saw their titles, just as he had typed them—"The High Priests of Mystery," and "The Cradle of Beauty." He had never submitted them anywhere. They were as good as anything he had done in that line. If only he had stamps for them! Then the certitude of his ultimate success rose up in him, an able ally of hunger, and with a quick movement he slipped the coin into his pocket.

"I 'll pay you back, Gertrude, a hundred times over," he gulped out, his throat painfully contracted and in his eyes a swift hint of moisture.

"Mark my words!" he cried with abrupt positiveness. "Before the year is out I 'll put an even hundred of those little yellow-boys into your hand. I dont ask you to believe me. All you have to do is to wait and see."

Nor did she believe. Her incredulity made her uncomfortable, and, failing of other expedient, she said:

"I know you 're hungry, Mart. It 's stickin' out all over you. Come in to meals any time. I 'll send one of the children to tell you when Mr. Higginbotham aint to be there. An' Mart—"

He waited, though he knew in his secret heart what she was about to say, so visible was her thought process to him.

"Dont you think it 's about time you got a job?"

"You dont think I 'll win out?" he asked.

She shook her head.

"Nobody has faith in me, Gertrude, except myself." His voice was passionately rebellious. "I 've done good work already, plenty of it, and sooner or later it will sell."

"How do you know it is good?"

"Because—" He faltered as the whole vast field of literature and the history of literature stirred in his brain and pointed the futility of his attempting to convey to her the reasons for his steadfast faith.

"Well, because it 's better than ninety-nine per cent of what is published in the magazines."

"I wisht you 'd listen to reason," she answered feebly, but with unwavering belief in the correctness of her diagnosis of what was ailing him. "I wisht you'd listen to reason," she repeated, "an' come to dinner tomorrow."

After Martin had helped her on the car, he hurried to the post office and invested three of the five dollars in stamps; and when, later in the day, on the way to the Morse home, he stopped in at the post office to weigh a large number of long, bulky envelopes, he affixed to them all the stamps save three of the two-cent denomination.

It proved a momentous night for Martin, for after dinner he met Russ Brissenden. How he chanced to come there, whose friend he was or what acquaintance brought him, Martin did not know. Nor had he the curiosity to inquire about him of Ruth. In short, Brissenden struck Martin as anaemic and feather-brained, and was promptly dismissed from his mind. An hour later he decided that Brissenden was a boor as well, what of the way he prowled about from one room to another, staring at the pictures or poking his nose into books and magazines he picked up from the table or drew from the shelves. Though a stranger in the house, he finally isolated himself in the midst of the company, huddling into a capacious Morris chair and reading steadily from a thin volume he had drawn from his pocket. As he read, he abstractedly ran his fingers, with a caressing movement, through his hair. Martin noticed him no more that evening, except once when he observed him chaffing with great apparent success with several of the young women.

It chanced that when Martin was leaving, he overtook Brissenden already half down the walk to the street.

"Hello, is that you?" Martin said.

The other replied with an ungracious grunt, but swung alongside. Martin made no further attempt at conversation, and for several blocks unbroken silence lay upon them.

"Pompous old ass!"

The suddenness and the virulence of the exclamation startled Martin. He felt amused, and at the same time was aware of a growing dislike for the other.

"What do you go to such a place for?" was abruptly flung at him after another block of silence.

"Why do you?" Martin countered.

"Bless me, I dont know," came back. "At least this is my first indiscretion. There are twenty-four hours in each day, and I must spend them somehow. Come and have a drink."

"All right," Martin answered.

The next moment he was nonplussed by the readiness of his acceptance. At home was several hours' hack-work waiting for him before he went to bed and after he went to bed there was a volume of *Weismann* waiting for him, to say nothing of *Herbert Spencer's Autobiography,* which was as replete for him with romance as any thrilling novel. Why should he waste any time with this man he did not like? was his thought. And yet, it was not so much the man nor the drink as was it what was associated with the drink—the bright lights, the mirrors and dazzling array of glasses, the warm and glowing faces, and the resonant hum of the voices of men. That was it, it was the voices of men, optimistic men, men who breathed success and spent their money for drinks like men. He was lonely, that was what was the matter with him; that was why he had snapped at the invitation as a bonita strikes at a white rag on a hook. Not since with Joe, at Shelley Hot Springs, with the one exception of the wine he took with the Portuguese grocer, had Martin had a drink at a public bar. Mental exhaustion did not produce a craving for liquor such as physical exhaustion did, and he had felt no need for it. But just now he felt desire for the drink, or rather, for the atmosphere wherein drinks were dispensed and disposed of. Such a place was the Grotto, where Brissenden and he lounged in capacious leather chairs and drank Scotch and soda.

They talked. They talked about many things, and now Brissenden and now Martin took turn in ordering Scotch and soda. Martin, who was extremely strong-headed, marveled at the other's capacity for liquor, and ever and anon broke off to marvel at the other's conversation. He was not long in assuming that Brissenden knew everything, and in deciding that here was the second intellectual man he had met. But he noted that Brissenden had what Professor Caldwell lacked—namely, fire, the flashing insight and perception, the flaming uncontrol of genius. Living language flowed from him. His thin lips, like the dies of a machine, stamped out phrases that cut and stung; or again, pursing caressingly about the inchoate sound they articulated, the thin lips shaped soft and velvety things, mellow phrases of glow and glory, of haunting beauty, reverberant of the mystery and inscrutableness of life; and yet again the thin lips were like a bugle, from which rang the crash and tumult of cosmic strife, phrases that sounded clear as silver, that were luminous as starry spaces, that epitomized the final word of science and yet said something more—the poet's word, the transcendental truth, elusive and without words which could express, and which none the less found expression in the subtle and all but ungraspable connotations of common words. He, by some wonder of vision, saw beyond the farthest outpost of empiricism, where was no language for narration, and yet, by some golden miracle of speech, investing known words with unknown significance, he conveyed to Martin's consciousness messages that were incommunicable to ordinary souls.

Martin forgot his first impression of

dislike. Here was the best the books had to offer coming true. Here was an intelligence, a living man for him to look up to. "I am down in the dirt at your feet," Martin repeated to himself again and again.

"You 've studied biology," he said aloud, in significant allusion.

To his surprise Brissenden shook his head.

"But you are stating truths that are substantiated only by biology," Martin insisted, and was rewarded by a blank stare. "Your conclusions are in line with the books which you must have read."

"I am glad to hear it," was the answer. "That my smattering of knowledge should enable me to short-cut my way to truth is most reassuring. As for myself, I never bother to find out if I am right or not. It is all valueless anyway. Man can never know the ultimate verities."

"You are a disciple of Spencer!" Martin cried triumphantly.

"I have n't read him since adolescence, and all I read then was his *Education*."

"I wish I could gather knowledge as carelessly," Martin broke out half an hour later. He had been closely analyzing Brissenden's mental equipment. "You are a sheer dogmatist, and that 's what makes it so marvelous. You state dogmatically the latest facts which science has been able to establish only by *a posteriori* reasoning. You jump at correct conclusions. You certainly short-cut with a vengeance. You feel your way with the speed of light, by some hyperrational process, to truth."

"Yes, that was what used to bother Father Joseph, and Brother Dutton," Brissenden replied. "Oh, no," he added; "I am not anything. It was a lucky trick of fate that sent me to a Catholic college for my education. Where did you pick up what you know?"

And while Martin told him, he was busy studying Brissenden, ranging from his long, lean, aristocratic face and his drooping shoulders to the overcoat on a neighboring chair, its pockets sagged and bulged by the freightage of many books. Brissenden's face and long, slender hands were browned by the sun—excessively browned, Martin thought. This sunburn bothered Martin. It was patent that Brissenden was no out-door man. Then how had he been ravaged by the sun? Something morbid and significant attached to that sunburn, was Martin's thought as he returned to study of the face, narrow, with high cheek-bones and cavernous hollows, and graced with as delicate and fine an aquiline nose as Martin had ever seen. There was nothing remarkable about the size of the eyes. They were neither large nor small, while their color was a nondescript brown; but in them smouldered a fire, or, rather, lurked an expression dual and strangely contradictory. Defiant, indomitable, even harsh to excess, they at the same time aroused pity. Martin found himself pitying him, he knew not why, though he was soon to learn.

"Oh, I 'm a lunger," Brissenden announced off-hand a little later, having already stated that he came from Arizona. "I 've been down there a couple of years living on the climate."

"Are n't you afraid to venture it up in this climate?"

"Afraid?"

There was no special emphasis of his repetition of Martin's word. But Martin saw in that ascetic face the advertisement that there was nothing of which it was afraid. The eyes had narrowed till they were eagle-like, and Martin almost caught his breath as he noted the eagle beak with its dilated nostrils, defiant, assertive, aggressive. Magnificent, was what he commented to himself, his blood thrilling at the sight. Aloud, he quoted:

"'Under the bludgeoning of Chance
My head is bloody but unbowed.'"

"You like Henley," Brissenden said, his expression changing swiftly to large graciousness and tenderness. "Of course, I could n't have expected anything else of you. Ah, Henley! A brave soul. He stands out among contemporary rhymesters—magazine rhymesters—as a gladiator stands out in the midst of a band of eunuchs."

"You dont like the magazines," Martin softly impeached.

"Do you?" was snarled back at him so savagely as to startle him.

"I——I write, or rather, try to write, for the magazines," Martin faltered.

"That 's better," was the mollified rejoinder. "You try to write, but you dont succeed. I respect and admire your failure. I know what you write. I can see it with half an eye, and there 's one ingredient in it that shuts it out of the magazines. It 's red meat, and magazines have no use for that particular commodity. What they want is wish-wash and slush, and God knows they get it, but not from you."

"I 'm not above hack-work," Martin contended.

"On the contrary—" Brissenden paused and ran an insolent eye over Martin's objective poverty, passing from the well-worn tie and the saw-edged collar to the shiny sleeves of the coat and on to the slight fray of one cuff, winding up and dwelling upon Martin's sunken cheeks. "On the contrary, hack-work is above you, so far above that you can never hope to rise to it. Why, man, I could insult you by asking you to have something to eat."

Martin felt the heat in his face of the involuntary blood, and Brissenden laughed triumphantly.

"A full man is not insulted by such an invitation," he concluded.

"You are a devil," Martin cried irritably.

"Anyway, I did n't ask you."

"You did n't dare."

"Oh, I dont know about that. I invite you now."

Brissenden half rose from his chair as he spoke, as if with the intention of departing to the restaurant forthwith. He paused.

Martin's fists were tight-clenched, and his blood was drumming in his temples.

"Bosco! He eats 'em alive! Eats 'em alive!" Brissenden exclaimed, imitating the *spieler* of a locally famous snake-eater.

"I could certainly eat you alive," Martin said, in turn running insolent eyes over the other's disease-ravaged frame.

"Only I 'm not worthy of it?"

"On the contrary," Martin considered, "because the incident is not worthy." He broke into a laugh, hearty and wholesome. "I confess you made a fool of me, Brissenden. That I am hungry and you are aware of it, are only ordinary phenomena, and there 's no disgrace. You see, I laugh at the conventional little moralities of the herd; then you drift by, say a sharp, true word, and immediately I am the slave of the same little moralities."

"You were insulted," Brissenden affirmed.

"I certainly was, a moment ago. The prejudice of early youth, you know. I learned such things then, and they cheapen what I have since learned. They are the skeletons in my particular closet."

"But you 've got the door shut on them now?"

"I certainly have."

"Sure?"

"Sure."

"Then let 's go and get something to eat."

"I 'll go you," Martin answered, attempting to pay for the current Scotch and soda with the last change from his two dollars and seeing the waiter bullied by Brissenden into putting that change back on the table.

Martin pocketed it with a grimace, and felt for a moment the kindly weight of Brissenden's hand upon his shoulder.

Martin Eden

By Jack London

Author of "The Call of the Wild," "Sea Wolf," "The God of His Fathers," "White Fang," etc.

CHAPTER XXXII.

PROMPTLY, the next afternoon, Maria was excited by Martin's second visitor. But she did not lose her head this time, for she seated Brissenden in her parlor's grandeur of respectability.

"Hope you dont mind my coming?" Brissenden began.

"No, no, not at all," Martin answered, shaking hands and waving him to the solitary chair, himself taking to the bed. "But how did you know where I lived?"

"Called up the Morses. Miss Morse answered the 'phone. And here I am." He tugged at his coat pocket and flung a thin volume on the table. "There 's a book, by a poet. Read it and keep it." And then, in reply to Martin's protest. "What have I to do with books? I had another hemorrhage this morning. Got any whisky? No, of course not. Wait a minute."

He was off and away. Martin watched his long figure go down the outside steps, and, on turning to close the gate, noted with a pang the shoulders, which had once been broad, drawn in now over the collapsed ruin of the chest. Martin got two tumblers, and fell to reading the book of verse, Henry Vaughn Marlow's latest collection.

"No Scotch," Brissenden announced on his return. "The beggar sells nothing but American whisky. But here 's a quart of it."

"I 'll send one of the youngsters for lemons, and we 'll make a toddy," Martin offered.

"I wonder what a book like that will earn Marlow?" he went on, holding up the volume in question.

"Possibly fifty dollars," came the answer. "Though he 's lucky if he pulls even on it, or if he can inveigle a publisher to risk bringing it out."

"Then one cant make a living out of poetry?"

Martin's tone and face alike showed his dejection.

"Certainly not. What fool expects to? Out of rhyming, yes. There 's Bruce, and Virginia Spring, and Sedgwick. They do very nicely. But poetry—do you know how Vaughn Marlow makes his living?—teaching in a boys' cramming-joint down in Pennsylvania, and of all private little hells such a billet is the limit. I would n't trade places with him if he had fifty years of life before him. And yet his work stands out from the ruck of the contemporary versifiers as a balus ruby among carrots. And the reviews he gets! Damn them, all of them, the little manikins!"

"Too much is written by the men who cant write about the men who do write," Martin concurred. "Why, I was appalled at the quantities of rubbish written about Stevenson and his work."

"Ghouls and harpies!" Brissenden snapped out with clicking teeth. "Yes, I know the spawn—complacently pecking at him for his Father Damien letter, analyzing him, weighing him—"

"Measuring him by the yardstick of their own miserable egos," Martin broke in.

"Yes, that 's it; a good phrase; mouthing and besliming the True, and Beautiful, and Good, and finally patting him on the back and saying, 'Good dog, Fido.' Faugh! 'The little chattering daws of men,' Richard Realfe called them the night he died."

"Pecking at star-dust," Martin took up the strain warmly; "at the meteoric flight of the master men. I once wrote a squib on them—the critics, or the reviewers, rather."

"Let 's see it," Brissenden begged eagerly.

So Martin unearthed a copy of "Star-Dust," and during the reading of it Brissenden chuckled, rubbed his hands, and forgot to sip his toddy.

"Strikes me you 're a bit of star-dust yourself, flung into a world of cowled gnomes who cannot see," was his comment at the end of it. "Of course it was snapped up by the first magazine?"

Martin ran over the pages of his manuscript book.

"It has been refused by twenty-seven of them."

Brissenden essayed a long and hearty laugh, but broke down in a fit of coughing.

"Say, you need n't tell me you have n't tackled poetry," he gasped. "Let me see some of it."

"Dont read it now," Martin pleaded. "I want to talk with you. I 'll make up a bundle and you can take it home."

Brissenden departed with the "Love Cycle," and "The Peri and the Pearl," returning next day to greet Martin with:

"I want more."

Not only did he assure Martin that he was a poet, but Martin learned that Brissenden also was one. He was swept off his feet by the other's work, and astounded that no attempt had been made to publish it.

"A plague on all their houses!" was Brissenden's answer to Martin's volunteering to market his work for him. "Love beauty for its own sake," was his counsel, "and leave the magazines alone. Back to your ships and your sea—that 's my advice to you, Martin Eden. What do you want in these sick and rotten cities of men. You are cutting your throat every day you waste in them trying to prostitute beauty to the needs of magazinedom. What was it you quoted me the other day? Oh, yes, 'Man, the latest of the ephemera.' Well, what do you, the latest of the ephemera, want with fame? If you got it, it would be poison to you. You are too simple, too elemental, and too rational, by my faith, to prosper on such pap. I hope you never do sell a line to the magazines. Beauty is the only master to serve. Serve her and damn the multitude. Success! What in hell 's success if it is n't right there in your Stevenson sonnet, which outranks Henley's 'Apparition,' in that 'Love-Cycle,' in those sea-poems?

"It is not in what you succeed in doing that you get your joy, but in the doing of it. I know it. You know it. Beauty hurts you. It is an everlasting pain in you, a wound that does not heal, a knife of flame. Why should you palter with magazines? Let beauty be your end. Why should you mint beauty into gold? Anyway, you cant; so there 's no use in my getting excited over it. You can read the magazines for a thousand years and you wont find the value of one line of *Keats*. Leave fame and coin alone, sign away on a ship tomorrow, and go back to your sea."

"Not for fame, but for love," Martin laughed. "Love seems to have no place in your Cosmos; in mine, Beauty is the handmaiden of Love."

Brissenden looked at him pityingly and admiringly. "You are so young, Martin boy, so young. You will flutter high, but your wings are of the finest gauze, dusted with the fairest pigments. Do not scorch them. But of course you have scorched them already. It required some glorified petticoat to account for that 'Love Cycle,' and that 's the shame of it."

"It glorifies love as well as the petticoat," Martin laughed.

"The philosophy of madness," was the retort. "So have I assured myself when wandering in hasheesh dreams. But beware. These bourgeois cities will kill you. Look at that den of traders where I met you. Dry rot is no name for it. One cant keep his sanity in such an atmosphere. It 's degrading. There 's not one of them who is not degrading, man and woman, all of them animated stomachs guided by the high intellectual and art impulses of clams—"

He broke off suddenly and regarded Martin. Then, with a flash of divination, he saw the situation. The expression on his face turned to wondering horror.

"And you wrote that tremendous 'Love-Cycle' to her—that pale, shriveled, female thing!"

The next instant Martin's right hand had shot to a throttling clutch on his throat, and he was being shaken till his teeth rattled. But Martin, looking into his eyes, saw no fear there, naught but a curious and mocking devil. Martin remembered himself, and flung Brissenden, by the neck, side-long upon the bed, at the same moment releasing his hold.

Brissenden panted and gasped painfully for a minute, then began to chuckle.

"You had made me eternally your debtor had you shaken out the flame," he said.

"My nerves are on a hair-trigger these days," Martin apologized. "Hope I did n't hurt you. Here, let me mix a fresh toddy."

"Ah, you young Greek!" Brissenden went on. "I wonder if you take just pride in that body of yours. You are devilish strong. You are a young panther, a lion cub. Well, well, it is you who must pay for that strength."

"What do you mean?" Martin asked curiously, passing him a glass. "Here, down this and be good."

"Because—." Brissenden sipped his toddy and smiled appreciation of it. "Because of the women. They will worry you until you die, as they have already worried you, or else I was born yesterday. Now, there 's no use in your choking me; I 'm going to have my say. This is undoubtedly your calf love; but for Beauty's sake show better taste next time. What under heaven do you want with a daughter of the bourgeoisie? Leave them alone. Pick out some great, wanton flame of a woman, who laughs at life and jeers at death and loves one while she may. There are such women, and they will love you just as readily as any pusillanimous product of bourgeois sheltered life."

"Pusillanimous!" Martin protested.

"Just so, pusillanimous, prattling out little moralities that have been prattled into them, and afraid to live life. They will love you, Martin, but they will love their little moralities more. What you want is the magnificent abandon of life, the great free souls, the blazing butterflies and not the little gray moths. Oh, you will grow tired of them, too, of all the female things, if you are unlucky enough to live. But you wont live. You wont go back to your ships and sea, therefore you 'll hang around these pest-holes of cities until your bones are rotten, and then you 'll die."

"You can lecture me, but you cant make me talk back," Martin said. "After all, you have but the wisdom of your temperament, and the wisdom of my temperament is just as unimpeachable as yours."

They disagreed about love, and the magazines, and many things, but they liked each other, and on Martin's part it was no less than a profound liking. Day after day they were together, if for no more than the hour Brissenden spent in Martin's stuffy room. Brissenden never arrived without his quart of whiskey, and when they dined together down town he drank Scotch and soda throughout the meal. He invariably paid the way for both, and it was through him that Martin learned the refinements of food, drank his first champagne, and made acquaintance with Rhine wine.

But Brissenden was always an enigma. With the face of an ascetic, he was, in all the failing blood of him, a frank voluptuary. He was unafraid to die, bitter and cynical of all the ways of living, and yet, dying, he loved life, to the last atom of it. He was possessed by a madness to live, to thrill, "to squirm my little space in the cosmic dust whence I came," as he phrased it once himself. He had tampered with drugs and done many strange things in quest of new thrills, new sensations. As he told Martin, he had once gone three days without water, had done so voluntarily, in order to experience the exquisite delight of such a thirst assauged. Who or what he was, Martin never learned. He was a man without a past, whose future was the imminent grave, and whose present was a bitter fever of living.

CHAPTER XXXIII.

MARTIN was steadily losing his battle. Economize as he would, the earnings from hack-work did not balance expenses. Thanksgiving found him with his black suit in pawn and unable to accept the Morse's invitation to dinner. Ruth was not made happy by his reason for not coming, and the corresponding effect on him was one of desperation. He told her that he would come after all, that he would go over to San Francisco to the *Occidental* office, collect the five dollars due him, and with it redeem his suit of clothes.

In the morning he borrowed ten cents from Maria. He would have borrowed it, by preference, from Brissenden, but that erratic individual had disappeared. Two weeks had passed since Martin had seen him, and he vainly cudgeled his brains for some cause of offense. The ten cents carried Martin across the ferry to San Francisco, and as he walked up Market Street he speculated upon his predicament in case he failed to collect the money. There would then be no way for him to return to Oakland, and he knew no one in San Francisco from whom to borrow another ten cents.

The door to the *Occidental* office was ajar, and Martin, in the act of opening it, was brought to a sudden pause by a loud voice from within, which exclaimed:

"But that is not the question, Mr. Adams." (Adams, Martin knew, from his correspondence, to be the editor's name.) "The question is, are you prepared to pay?—cash, and cash down, I mean. I am not interested in the prospects of the *Occidental*, and what you expect to make it next year. What I want is to be paid for what I do. And I tell you, right now, the Christmas *Occidental* dont go to press till I have the money in my hand. Good day. When you get the money come and see me."

The door jerked open and the man flung past Martin with an angry countenance and went down the corridor muttering curses and clenching his fists. Martin decided not to enter immediately, and lingered in the hallways for a quarter of an hour. Then he shoved the door open and walked in. It was a new experience, the first time he had been inside an editorial office. Cards evidently were not necessary in that office, for the boy carried word to an inner room that there was a man who wanted to see Mr. Adams. Returning, the boy beckoned him from half way across the room and led him to the private office, the editorial sanctum. Martin's first impression was of the disorder and cluttered confusion of the room. Next he noticed a youthful-looking man, sitting at a roll-top desk, who regarded him curiously. Martin marveled at the calm repose of his face. It was evident that the squable with the printer had not affected his equanimity.

"I—I am Martin Eden," Martin began the conversation. ("And I want my five dollars," was what he would have liked to say.)

But this was his first editor, and under the circumstances, he did not desire to scare him too abruptly. To his surprise, Mr. Adams leaped into the air with a "You dont say so," and the next moment, with both hands, was shaking Martin's hand effusively.

"Cant say how glad I am to see you, Mr. Eden. Often wondered what you were like."

Here he held Martin off at arm's length and ran his beaming eyes over Martin's second-best suit, which was also his worst suit, and which was ragged and past repair, though the trousers showed the careful crease Martin had put in with Maria's flat-irons.

"I confess, though, I conceived you to be a much older man than you are. Your story, you know, showed such breadth, and vigor, such maturity and depth of thought. A masterpiece, that story—I knew it when I had read the first half-dozen lines. Let me tell you how I first read it. But no; first let me introduce you to the staff."

Still talking, Mr. Adams led him into the general office, where he introduced him to the associate editor, Mr. Jones, a slender, frail little man whose hand seemed strangely cold, as if he were suffering from a chill.

"And Mr. Pierce, Mr. Eden. Mr. Pierce is our business manager, you know."

Martin found himself shaking hands with a stout, round-headed man, whose face looked youthful enough.

The three men surrounded Martin, all talking admiringly and at once, until it seemed to him that they were talking against time for a wager.

"We often wondered why you did n't call," Mr. Jones was saying.

"I did n't have the car fare,and I live across the Bay," Martin answered bluntly, with the idea of showing them his imperative need for the money.

Surely, he thought to himself, my glad rags in themselves are eloquent advertisement of my need. Time and again, whenever opportunity offered, he hinted about the purpose of his visit. But his admirers' ears were deaf. They sang his praises, told him what they had thought of his story at first sight, what they subsequently thought, what their wives and families thought; but not one hint did they breathe of intention to pay him for it.

"Did I tell you how I first read your story?" Mr. Adams said. "Of course I did n't. I was coming West from New York, and when the train stopped at Ogden the train-boy on the new run brought aboard the current number of the *Occidental*."

My God! Martin thought; you can travel in a Pullman while I starve for the paltry five dollars you owe me. A wave of anger rushed over him. The wrong done him by the *Occidental* loomed colossal, for strong upon him were all the dreary months of vain yearning, of hunger and privation, and his present hunger awoke and gnawed at him, reminding him that he had eaten nothing since the day before and little enough then. For the moment he saw red. These creatures were not even robbers. They were sneak thieves. By lies and broken promises they had tricked him out of his story. Well, he would show them. And a great resolve surged into his will to the effect that he would not leave the office until he got his money. He remembered, if he did not get it, that there was no way for him to go back to Oakland. He controlled himself with an effort, but not before the wolfish expression of his face had awed and perturbed them.

They became more voluble than ever. Mr. Adams started anew to tell him how he had first read "The Ring of Bells," and Mr. Pierce at the same time was striving to repeat his niece's appreciation of "The Ring of Bells," said niece being a school-teacher in Alameda.

"I 'll tell you what I came for," Martin said finally. "To be paid for that story all of you like so well. Five dollars, I believe, is what you promised me would be paid on publication."

Mr. Adams, with an expression on his mobile features of immediate and happy acquiescence, started to reach for his pocket, then turned suddenly to Mr. Pierce, and said that he had left his money home. That Mr. Pierce resented this was patent; and Martin saw the twitch of his arm as if to protect his trousers pocket. Martin knew that the money was there.

"I am sorry," said Mr. Pierce, "but I paid the printer not an hour ago, and he took my ready change. It was careless of me to be so short; but the bill was not yet due, and the printer's request, as a favor, to make an immediate advance, was quite unexpected."

Both men looked expectantly at Mr. Jones, but that gentleman laughed and shrugged his shoulders. His conscience was clean at any rate. He had come into the *Occidental* to learn magazine-literature, instead of which he had principally learned finance. The *Occidental* owed him four months' salary, and he knew that the printer must be appeased before the associate editor.

"It 's rather absurd, Mr. Eden, to have caught us in this shape," Mr. Adams preambled airily. "All carelessness, I assure you. But I 'll tell you what we 'll do. We 'll mail you a check the first thing in the morning. You have Mr. Eden's address, have n't you, Mr. Pierce?"

Yes, Mr. Pierce had the address, and the check would be mailed the first thing in the morning. Martin's knowledge of banks and checks was hazy, but he could see no reason why they should not give him the check on this day as well as on the next.

"Then it is understood, Mr. Eden, that we 'll mail you the check tomorrow," Mr. Adams said.

"I need the money today," Martin answered stolidly.

"The unfortunate circumstances—if you had chanced here any other day," Mr. Adams began suavely, only to be interrupted by Mr. Pierce.

"Mr. Adams has already explained the situation," he said with asperity. "And so have I. The check will be mailed—"

"I also have explained," Martin broke in, "and I have explained that I want the money today."

He had felt his pulse quicken a trifle at the business manager's brusqueness, and upon him he kept an alert eye, for it was in that gentleman's trousers pocket that he divined the *Occidental's* ready cash was reposing.

"It is too bad—" Mr. Adams began.

But at that moment, with an impatient movement, Mr. Pierce turned as if about to leave the room. At the same instant Martin sprang for him, clutching him by the throat with one hand in such fashion that Mr. Pierce's fat chin pointed ceilingward at an angle of forty-five degrees. To the horror of Mr. Jones and Mr. Adams, they saw their business manager shaken like an Astrakhan rug.

"Dig up, you swindler!" Martin exhorted. "Dig up or I 'll shake it out of you even if it 's all in nickels." Then, to the two affrighted onlookers: "Keep away. If you interfere somebody 's liable to get hurt."

Mr. Pierce was choking, and it was not until the grip on his throat was eased that he was able to signify his acquiescence in the digging-up program. Altogether, after repeated digs, his trousers' pocket yielded four dollars and fifteen cents.

"Inside out with it," Martin commanded.

An additional ten cents fell out. Martin counted the result of his raid a second time to make sure.

"You next!" he shouted at Mr. Adams. "I want seventy-five cents more."

Mr. Adams did not wait, but ransacked his pockets with the result of sixty cents.

"Sure that is all?" Martin demanded menacingly, possessing himself of it. "What have you got in your vest-pockets?"

In token of his good faith, Mr. Adams turned two of his pockets inside out. A strip of cardboard fell to the floor from one of them. He recovered it and was in the act of returning it, when Martin cried:

"What 's that? A ferry ticket. Here, give it to me. It 's worth ten cents. I 'll credit you with it. I 've now got four dollars and ninety-five cents, including the ticket. Five cents is still due me."

He looked fiercely at Mr. Jones, and found that fragile creature in the act of handing him a nickel.

"Thank you," Martin said, addressing them collectively. "I wish you a good day."

"Robber!" Mr. Pierce snarled after him.

"Sneak thief," Martin retorted, slamming the door as he passed out.

Martin was elated—so elated that when he recollected the *Hornet* owed him fifteen dollars for "The Peri and the Pearl," he decided forthwith to go and collect it. But the *Hornet* was run by a set of clean-shaven, strapping young men, frank buccaneers who robbed everything and everybody, not excepting one another. After some breakage of the office furniture, the editor (an ex-college athlete), ably assisted by the business manager, an advertising agent, and the porter, succeeded in removing Martin from the office and in accelerating, by initial impulse, his descent of the first flight of stairs.

"Come again, Mr. Eden; glad to see you any time," they laughed down at him from the landing above.

Martin grinned as he picked himself up.

"Phew!" he murmured back. "The *Occidental* crowd were nanny-goats, but you fellows are a lot of prize-fighters."

More laughter greeted this.

"I must say, Mr. Eden," the editor of the *Hornet* called down, "that for a poet you can go some yourself. Where did you learn that right cross—if I may ask."

"Where you learned that half-Nelson," Martin answered. "Anyway, you 're going to have a black eye."

"I hope your neck does n't stiffen up," the editor wished solicitously. "What do you say we all go out and have a drink on it?—not the neck, of course, but the little rough house."

"I 'll go you if I lose," Martin accepted.

And robbers and robbed drank together, amicably agreeing that the battle was to the strong, and that the fifteen dollars for "The Peri and the Pearl" belonged by right to the *Hornet's* editorial staff.

CHAPTER XXXIV.

ARTHUR remained at the gate while Ruth climbed Maria's front steps. She heard the rapid click of the typewriter, and, when Martin let her in, found him on the last page of a manuscript. She had come to make certain whether or not he would be at their table for Thanksgiving dinner; but before she could broach the subject Martin plunged into the one with which he was full.

"Here, let me read you this," he cried, separating the carbon copies and running the pages of manuscript into shape. "It 's my latest, and different from anything I' ve done. It is so altogether different that I am almost afraid of it, and yet I 've a sneaking idea it is good. You be judge. It's an Hawaiian story. I 've called it 'Wiki-Wiki.' "

His face was bright with the creative glow, though she shivered in the cold room and had been struck by the coldness of his hands at greeting. She listened closely while he read, and though he from time to time had seen only disapprobation in her face, at the close he asked:

"Frankly, what do you think of it?"

"I—I dont know," she answered. "Will it—do you think it will sell?"

"I 'm afraid not," was the confession. "It 's too strong for the magazines. But is 's true, on my word it 's true."

"But why do you persist in writing such things when you know they wont sell?" she went on inexorably. "The reason for your writing is to make a living, is n't it?"

"Yes, that 's right; but the miserable story got away with me. I could n't help writing it. It demanded to be written."

"But that character, that Wiki-Wiki, why do you make him talk so roughly? Surely it will offend your readers, and surely that is why the editors are justified in refusing your work."

"Because the real Wiki-Wiki would have talked that way."

"But it is not good taste."

"It is life," he replied bluntly. "It is real. It is true. And I must write life as I see it."

She made no answer, and for an awkward moment they sat silent. It was because he loved her that he did not quite understand her, and she could not understand him because he was so large that he bulked beyond her horizon.

"Well, I 've collected from the *Occidental,*" he said, in an effort to shift the conversation to a more comfortable subject. The picture of the bewildered trio, as he had last seen them, mulcted of four dollars and ninety cents and a ferry ticket, made him chuckle.

"Then you 'll come!" she cried, joyously. "That was what I came to find out."

"Come?" he muttered absently—"Where?"

"Why, to dinner tomorrow. You know you said you 'd recover your suit if you got that money."

"I forgot all about it," he said, humbly. "You see, this morning the poundman got Maria's two cows and the baby calf, and—well, it happened that Maria did n't have any money, and so

I had to recover her cows for her. That 's where the *Occidental* fiver went —'The Ring of Bells' went into the poundman's pocket."

"Then you wont come?"

He looked down at his clothing.

"I cant."

Tears of disappointment and reproach glistened in her blue eyes, but she said nothing.

"Next Thanksgiving you 'll have dinner with me in Delmonico's," he said cheerily; "or in London, or Paris, or anywhere you wish. I know it."

"I saw in the paper a few days ago," she announced abruptly, "that there had been several local appointments to the Railway Mail. You passed first, did n't you?"

He was compelled to admit that the call had come for him, but that he had declined it. "I was so sure—I am so sure—of myself," he concluded. "A year from now I 'll be earning more than a dozen men in the Railway Mail. You wait and see."

"Oh," was all she said, when he finished. She stood up, pulling at her gloves. "I must go, Martin. Arthur is waiting for me."

He took her in his arms and kissed her, but she proved a passive sweetheart. There was no tenseness in her body, her arms did not go around him, and her lips met his without their wonted pressure. She was angry with him, he concluded, as he returned from the gate. But why? It was unfortunate that the poundman had gobbled Maria's cows. But it was only a stroke of fate. Nobody could be blamed for it. Nor did it enter his head that he could have done aught otherwise than what he had done. Well, yes, he was to blame a little, was his next thought, for having refused the call to the Railway Mail. And she had not liked "Wiki-Wiki."

He turned at the head of the steps to meet the letter carrier on his afternoon round. The ever-recurrent fever of expectancy assailed Martin as he took the bundle of long envelopes. One was not long. It was short and thin, and outside was printed the address of the *New York Outview*. He paused in the act of tearing the envelope open. It could not be an acceptance. He had no manuscripts with that publication. Perhaps—his heart almost stood still at the wild thought—perhaps they were ordering an article from him; but the next instant he dismissed the surmise as hopelessly impossible.

It was a short, formal letter, signed by the office editor, merely informing him that an anonymous letter which they had received was enclosed, and that he could rest assured the *Outview's* staff never under any circumstances gave consideration to anonymous correspondence.

The enclosed letter Martin found to be crudely printed by hand. It was a hotch-potch of illiterate abuse of Martin, and of assertion that the "so-called Martin Eden," who was selling stories to magazines, was no writer at all, and that in reality he was stealing stories from old magazines, typing them, and sending them out as his own. The envelope was postmarked "San Leandro." Martin did not require a second thought to discover the author. Higginbotham's grammar, Higginbotham's colloquialisms, Higginbotham's mental quirks and processes, were apparent throughout. Martin saw in every line, not the fine Italian hand, but the coarse grocer's fist, of his brother-in-law.

But why? he vainly questioned. What injury had he done Bernard Higginbotham? The thing was so unreasonable, so wanton. There was no explaining it. In the course of the week a dozen similar letters were forwarded to Martin by the editors of various Eastern magazines. The editors were behaving handsomely, Martin concluded. He was wholly unknown to them, yet some of them had even been sympathetic. It was evident that they detested anonymity. He saw that the malicious attempt to hurt him had failed. In fact, if anything came of it, it was bound to be good, for at least his name had been called to the attention of a number of editors. Some time, perhaps, reading a submitted manuscript of his, they might remember him as the fellow about whom they had received an anonymous letter. And who was to say that such a remembrance might not sway the balance of their judgment just a trifle in his favor?

It was about this time that Martin took a great slump in Maria's estimation. He found her in the kitchen one morning, groaning with pain, tears of weakness running down her cheeks, vainly endeavoring to put through a large ironing. He promptly diagnosed her affliction as La Grippe, dosed her with hot whisky (the remnants in the bottles for which Brissenden was responsible), and ordered her to bed. But Maria was refractory. The ironing had to be done, she protested, and delivered that night, or else there would be no food on the morrow for the seven small and hungry Silvas.

To her astonishment (and it was something that she never ceased from relating to her dying day), she saw Martin Eden seize an iron from the stove and throw a fancy shirt-waist on the ironing-board. It was Kate Flannagan's best Sunday waist, than whom there was no more exacting and fastidiously dressed woman in Maria's world. Also, Miss Flannagan had sent special instruction that said waist must be delivered by that night. As every one knew, she was keeping company with John Collins, the blacksmith, and, as Maria knew privily, Miss Flannagan and Mr. Collins were going next day to Golden Gate Park. Vain was Maria's attempt to rescue the garment. Martin guided her tottering footsteps to a chair, from where she watched him with bulging eyes. In a quarter of the time it would have taken her she saw the shirt-waist safely ironed, and ironed as well as she could have done it, as Martin made her grant.

"I could work faster," he explained, "if your irons were only hotter."

To her, the irons he swung were much hotter than she ever dared to use.

"Your sprinkling is all wrong," he complained next. "Here, let me teach you how to sprinkle. Pressure is what 's wanted. Sprinkle under pressure if you want to iron fast."

He procured a packing case from the wood-pile in the cellar, fitted a cover to it, and raided the scrap-iron the Silva tribe was collecting for the junkman. With fresh-sprinkled garments in the box, covered with the board and pressed by the iron, the device was complete and in operation.

"Now you watch me, Maria," he said, stripping off to his undershirt and gripping an iron that was what he called "really hot."

"An' when he feenish da iron, he washa da wools," as she described it afterward. "He say, 'Maria, you are da greata fool. I showa you how to washa da wools,' an' he showa me, too. Ten minutes he maka da machine—one barrel, one wheel-hub, two poles, justa like dat."

Martin had learned the contrivance from Joe at the Shelley Hot Springs. The old wheel-hub, fixed on the end of the upright pole, constituted the plunger. Making this, in turn, fast to the spring-pole attached to the kitchen rafters, so that the hub played upon the woolens in the barrel, he was able, with one hand thoroughly to pound them.

"No more Maria washa da wools," her story always ended. "I maka da kids worka da pole an' da hub, an' da barrel. Him da smarta man, Mister Eden."

Nevertheless, by his masterly operation and improvement of her kitchen-laundry, he fell an immense distance in her regard. The glamor of romance with which her imagination had invested him, faded away in the cold light of fact that he was an ex-laundryman. All his books, and his grand friends who visited him in carriages or with countless bottles of whiskey, went for naught. He was, after all, a mere working-man, a member of her own class and caste. He was more human and approachable, but he was no longer a mystery.

Martin's alienation from his family continued. Following upon Mr. Higginbotham's unprovoked attack, Mr. Hermann von Schmidt showed his hand. The fortunate sale of several storiettes, some humorous verse, and a few jokes, gave Martin a temporary splurge of prosperity. Not only did he partially pay up his bills, but he had sufficient balance left to redeem his black suit and wheel. The latter, by virtue of a twisted crank-hanger, required repairing, and, as a matter of friendliness with his future brother-in-law, he sent it to Von Schmidt's shop.

The afternoon of the same day Martin was pleased by the wheel being delivered by a small boy. Von Schmidt was also inclined to be friendly, was Martin's conclusion from this unusual favor. Repaired wheels usually had to be called for. But when he examined the wheel he discovered no repairs had been made. A little later in the day he telephoned his sister's betrothed and learned that that person did n't want anything to do with him in "any shape, manner, or form."

"Hermann von Schmidt," Martin answered cheerfully, "I 've a good mind to come over and punch that Dutch nose of yours."

"You come to my shop," came the reply, "an' I 'll send for the police. An' I 'll put you through, too. Oh, I know you, but you cant make no rough house with me. I dont want nothin' to do with the likes of you. You 're a loafer, that 's what, an' I ain't asleep. You ain't goin' to do no spongin' off me just because I 'm marrying your sister. Why dont you go to work an' earn an honest livin', eh? Answer me that."

Martin's philosophy asserted itself, dissipating his anger, and he hung up the receiver with a long whistle of incredulous amusement. But after the amusement, came the reaction, and he was oppressed by his loneliness. Nobody understood him, nobody seemed to have any use for him, except Brissenden, and Brissenden had disappeared, God alone knew where.

Twilight was falling as Martin left the fruit-store and turned homeward, his marketing on his arm. At the corner an electric car had stopped, and at sight of a lean, familiar figure alighting, his heart leaped with joy. It was Brissenden, and in the fleeting glimpse, ere the car started up, Martin noted the overcoat pockets, one bulging with books, the other bulging with a quart bottle of whiskey.

CHAPTER XXXV.

BRISSENDEN gave no explanation of his long absence, nor did Martin pry into it. He was content to see his friend's cadaverous face opposite him through the steam rising from a tumbler of toddy.

"I, too, have not been idle," Brissenden proclaimed, after hearing Martin's account of the work he had accomplished.

He pulled a manuscript from his inside coat pocket and passed it to Martin, who looked at the title and glanced up curiously.

"Yes, that 's it," Brissenden laughed. "Pretty good title, eh? 'Ephemera'—it is the one word. And you 're responsible for it, what of your *man,* who is always the erected, the vitalized inorganic, the latest of the ephemera, the creature of temperature strutting his little space on the thermometer. It got into my head and I had to write it to get rid of it. Tell me what you think of it."

Martin's face, flushed at first, paled as he read on. It was perfect art. Form triumphed over substance, if triumph it could be called where the last conceivable atom of substance had found expression in so perfect construction as to make Martin's head swim with delight, to put passionate tears into his eyes, and to send chill creeping up and down his back. It was a long poem of six or seven hundred lines, and it was a fantastic, amazing, unearthly thing. It was was terrific, impossible, and yet it was scrawled in black ink across the sheets of paper. It dealt with man and his soul-gropings in their ultimate terms, plumbing the abysses of space for the testimony of remotest suns and rainbow spectrums. It was a mad orgy of imagination, wassailing in the skull of a dying man who half-sobbed under his breath and was quick with the wild flutter of fading heart-beats. The poem swung in majestic rhythm to the cool tumult of interstellar conflict, to the onset of starry hosts, to the impact of cold suns and the flaming up of nebulas in the darkened void; and through it all, unceasing and faint, like a silver shuttle, ran the frail, piping voice of man, a querulous chirp amid the screaming of planets and the crash of systems.

"There is nothing like it in literature," Martin said, when at last he was able to speak. "It 's wonderful!—wonderful! It has gone to my head. I am drunken with it. That great, infinitessimal question—I cant shake it out of my thoughts. That questing, eternal, ever-recurring, thin little wailing voice of man is still ringing in my ears. It is like the dead march of a gnat amid the trumpeting of elephants and the roaring of lions. It is insatiable with microscopic desire. I know I 'm making a fool of myself, but the thing has obsessed me. You are—I dont know what you are—you are wonderful, that 's all. But how do you do it? How do you do it?"

Martin paused from his rhapsody, only to break out afresh.

"I shall never write again. I am a dauber in clay. You have shown me the work of the real artificer-artisan. Genius! This is something more than genius. It transcends genius. It is truth gone mad. It is true, man, every line of it. I wonder if you realize that, you dogmatist. Science cannot give you the lie. It is the truth of the seer, stamped out from the black iron of the Cosmos and interwoven with mighty rhythms of sound into a fabric of splendor and beauty. And now I wont say another word. I am overwhelmed, crushed. Yes I will, too. Let me market it for you."

Brissenden grinned. "There 's not a magazine in Christendom that would dare to publish it—you know that."

"I know nothing of the sort. I know there 's not a magazine in Christendom that would n't jump at it. They dont get things like that every day. That 's no mere poem of the year. It 's the poem of the century."

"I 'd like to take you up on the proposition."

"Now dont get cynical," Martin exhorted. "The magazine editors are not wholly fatuous. I know that. And I 'll close with you on the bet. I 'll wager anything you want that 'Ephemera' is accepted either on the first or second offering."

"There 's just one thing that prevents me from taking you." Brissenden waited a moment. "The thing is big—the biggest thing I 've ever done. I know that. It 's my swan song. I am almighty proud of it. I worship it. It 's better than whiskey. It is what I dreamed of—the great and perfect thing—when I was a simple young man, with sweet illusions and clean ideals. And I 've got it, now, in my last gasp, and I 'll not have it pawed over and soiled by a lot of swine. No, I wont take the bet. It 's mine, I made it, and I 've shared it with you."

"But think of the rest of the world," Martin protested. "The function of beauty is joy-making."

"It 's my beauty."

"Dont be selfish."

"I 'm not selfish." Brissenden grinned soberly in the way he had when pleased by the thing his thin lips were about to shape. "I 'm as unselfish as a famished hog."

In vain Martin strove to shake him from his decision. Martin told him that his hatred of the magazines was rabid, fanatical, and that his conduct was a thousand times more despicable than that of the youth who burned the temple of Diana at Ephesus. Under the storm of denunciation Brissenden complacently sipped his toddy and affirmed that everything the other said was quite true, with the exception of the magazine editors. His hatred of them knew no bounds, and he excelled Martin in denunciation when he turned upon them.

"I wish you 'd type it for me," he said. "You know how a thousand times better than any stenographer. And now I want to give you some advice." He drew a bulky manuscript from his outside coat-pocket. "Here 's your 'Shame of the Sun.' I 've read it not once, but twice and three times—the highest compliment I can pay you. After what you 've said about 'Ephemera' I must be silent. But this I will say: when 'The Shame of the Sun' is published it will make a hit. It will start a controversy that will be worth thousands to you just in advertising."

Martin laughed. "I suppose your next advice will be to submit it to the magazines."

"By all means no—that is, if you want to see it in print. Offer it to the first-class houses. Some publisher's reader may be mad enough or drunk enough to report favorably on it. You 've read the books. The meat of them has been transmuted in the alembic of Martin Eden's mind and poured into 'The Shame of the Sun,' and one day Martin Eden will be famous, and not the least of his fame will rest upon that work. So you must get a publisher for it—the sooner the better."

Brissenden went home late that night; and, just as he mounted the first step of the car, he swung suddenly back on Martin and thrust into his hand a small, tightly crumpled wad of paper.

"Here, take this," he said. "I was out to the races today, and I had the right dope."

The bell clanged and the car pulled out, leaving Martin wondering as to the nature of the crinkly, greasy wad he clutched in his hand. Back in his room he unrolled it and found a hundred-dollar bill.

He did not scruple to use it. He knew his friend had always plenty of money, and he knew also, with profound certitude, that his success would enable him to repay it. In the morning he paid every bill, gave Maria three months' advance on the room, and redeemed every pledge at the pawnshop. Next he bought Marian's wedding present, and simpler presents, suitable to Christmas, for Ruth and Gertrude. And finally, on the balance remaining to him, he herded the whole Silva tribe down into Oakland. He was a winter late in redeeming his promise, but redeemed it was, for the last, least Silva got a pair of shoes, as well as Maria herself. Also, there were horns, and dolls, and toys of various sorts, and parcels and bundles of candies and nuts that filled the arms of all the Silvas to overflowing.

It was with this extraordinary procession trooping at his and Maria's heels into a confectioner's in quest of the biggest candy-cane ever made, that he encountered Ruth and her mother. Mrs. Morse was shocked. Even Ruth was hurt, for she had some regard for appearences, and her lover, cheek by jowl with Maria at the head of that army of Portuguese ragamuffins, was not a pretty sight. But it was not that which hurt so much, as what she took to be his lack of pride and self-respect. Further, and keenest of all, she read into the incident the impossibility of his living down his working-class origin. There was stigma enough in the fact of it, but shamelessly to flaunt it in the face of the world—her world—was going too far. Though her engagement to Martin had been kept secret, their long intimacy had not been unproductive of gossip; and in the shop, glancing covertly at her lover and his following, had been several of her acquaintances. She lacked the easy largeness of Martin and could not rise suprior to her environment. She had been hurt to the quick, and her sensitive nature was quivering with the shame of it. So it was, when Martin arrived later in the day, that he kept her present in his breast-pocket, deferring the giving of it to a more propitious occasion. Ruth in tears—passionate, angry tears—was a revelation to him. The spectacle of her suffering convinced him that he had been a brute, yet in the soul of him he could not see how nor why. It never entered his mind to be ashamed of those he knew, and to take the Silvas out to a Christmas treat, could in no way, so it seemed to him, show lack of consideration for Ruth. On the other hand, he did see Ruth's point of view, after she had explained it; and he looked upon it as a feminine weakness, such as afflicted all women and the best of women.

CHAPTER XXXVI.

"COME on—I 'll show you the real dirt," Brissenden said to him, one evening in January.

They had dined together in San Francisco, and were at the Ferry Building, returning to Oakland, when the whim came to him to show Martin the "real dirt." He turned and fled across the water-front, a meager shadow in a flapping overcoat, with Martin straining to keep up with him. At a wholesale liquor store he bought two gallon-demijohns of old port, and with one in each hand boarded a Mission street car, Martin at his heels burdened with several quart-bottles of whiskey.

If Ruth could see me now, was his thought, while he wondered as to what constituted the real dirt.

"Maybe nobody will be there," Brissenden said, when they dismounted and plunged off to the right into the heart of the working-class ghetto, south of Market street. "In which case you 'll miss what you 've been looking for so long."

"And what the deuce is that?" Martin asked.

"Men, intelligent men, and not the gibbering nonentities I found you consorting with in that trader's den. You read the books and you found yourself all alone. Well, I 'm going to show you tonight some other men who 've read the books, so that you wont be lonely any more.

"Not that I bother my head about their everlasting discussions," he said at the end of a block. "I 'm not interested in book philosophy. But you 'll find these fellows intelligent and not bourgeoise swine. But watch out, they 'll talk an arm off you on any subject under the sun.

"Hope Norton 's there," he panted a little later, resisting Martin's effort to relieve him of the two demijohns. "Norton 's an idealist—a Harvard man. Prodigious memory. Idealism led him to philosophic anarchy, and his family threw him off. Father 's a railroad president and many times millionaire, but the son 's starving in 'Frisco, editing an anarchist sheet for twenty-five a month."

Martin was little acquainted in San Francisco, and not at all south of Market; so he had no idea of where he was being led.

"Go ahead," he said, "tell me about them beforehand. What do they do for a living? How do they happen to be here?"

"Hope Hamilton 's there." Brissenden paused and rested his hands. "Strawn-Hamilton 's his name—hyphenated, you know—comes of old Southern stock. He 's a tramp—laziest man I ever knew, though he 's clerking, or trying to, in a socialist co-operative store for six dollars a week. But he 's a confirmed hobo. Tramped into town. I 've seen him sit all day on a bench and never a bite pass his lips, and in the evening, when I invited him to dinner—restaurant two blocks away—have him say, 'Too much trouble, old man. Buy me a package of cigarettes instead.' He was a Spencerian like you till Kreis turned him to materialistic monism. I 'll start him on monism if I can. Norton 's another monist—only he affirms naught but spirit. He can give Kreis and Hamilton all they want to."

"Who is Kreis?" Martin asked.

"His rooms we 're going to. One time professor—fired from university—usual story. A mind like a steel trap. Makes his living any old way. I know he 's been a street fakir when he was down. Unscrupulous. Rob a corpse of a shroud—anything. Difference between him and the bourgeoisie is that he robs without illusion. He 'll talk Nietzsche, or Schopenhauer, or Kant, or anything, but the only thing in this world, not excepting Mary, that he really cares for, is his monism. Haeckel is his little tin god. The only way to insult him is to take a slap at Haeckel—

"Here 's the hang-out." Brissenden rested his demijohn at the upstairs entrance, preliminary to the climb. It was the usual two-story corner building, with a saloon and grocery underneath. "The gang lives here—got the whole upstairs to themselves. But Kreis is the only one who has two rooms. Come on."

No lights burned in the upper hall, but Brissenden threaded the utter blackness like a familiar ghost. He stopped to speak to Martin.

"There 's one fellow—Stevens. A theosophist. Makes a pretty tangle when he gets going. Just now he 's a dish-washer in a restaurant. Likes a good cigar. I 've seen him eat in a ten-cent hash house and pay fifty cents for the cigar he smoked afterward. I 've got a couple in my pocket for him, if he shows up.

"And there 's another fellow—Parry, an Australian, a statistician and a sporting encyclopedia. Ask him the grain output of Paraguay for 1903, or the English importation of sheetings into China for 1890, or at what weight Jimmy Britt fought Battling Nelson, or who was welter-weight champion of the United States in '68, and you 'll get the correct answer with the automatic celerity of a slot-machine. And there 's Andy, a stone-mason, has ideas on everything, a good chess-player; and another fellow, Harry, a baker, red-hot socialist and strong union man. By the way, you remember the Cooks' and Waiters' strike —Hamilton was the chap who organized that union and precipitated the strike—planned it all out in advance, right here in Kreis' rooms. Did it just for the fun of it, but was too lazy to stay by the union. Yet he could have risen high if he wanted to. There 's no end to the possibilities in that man—if he were n't so superbly lazy."

Brissenden advanced through the darkness till a thread of light marked the threshold of a door. A knock and answer opened it, and Martin found himself shaking hands with Kreis, a handsome brunette man, with dazzling white teeth, a drooping black mustache, and large, flashing black eyes. Mary, a matronly young blond, was washing dishes in the little back room that served for kitchen and dining room. The front room served as bed-chamber and living room. Overhead was the week's washing, hanging in festoons so low that Martin did not see at first the two men talking in a corner. They hailed Brissenden and his demijohns with acclamation, and, on being introduced, Martin learned they were Andy and Parry. He joined them and listened attentively to the description of a prize-fight Parry had seen the night before; while Brissenden, in his glory, plunged into the manufacture of a toddy and the serving of wine and whiskey-and-sodas. At his command, "Bring in the clan," Andy departed to go the round of the rooms for the lodgers.

"We 're lucky that most of them are here," Brissenden whispered to Martin. "There 's Norton and Hamilton; come on and meet them. Stevens is n't around, I hear. I 'm going to get them started on monism if I can. Wait till they get a few jolts in them and they 'll warm up."

At first the conversation was desultory. Nevertheless Martin could not fail to appreciate the keen play of their minds. They were men with opinions, though the opinions often clashed, and, though they were witty and clever, they were not superficial. He swiftly saw, no matter upon what they talked, that each man applied the correlation of knowledge and had also a deep-seated and unified conception of society and the Cosmos. Nobody manufactured their opinions for them, they were all rebels of one variety or another, and their lips were strangers to platitudes. Never had Martin, at the Morses, heard so amazing a range of topics discussed. There seemed no limit save time to the things they were alive to. The talk wandered from Mrs. Humphrey Ward's new book to Shaw's latest play, through the future of the drama to reminiscences of Nat Goodwin. They appreciated or sneered at the morning editorials, jumped from labor conditions in New Zealand to Henry James and Brander Matthews, passed on to the German designs in the Far East and the economic aspect of the Yellow Peril, wrangled over the German elections and Bebel's last speech, and settled down to local politics, the latest plans and scandals in the union labor party administration, and the wires that were pulled to bring about the Coast Seamen's strike. Martin was struck by the inside knowledge they possessed. They knew what was never printed in the newspapers—the wires and strings and the hidden hands that made the puppets dance. To Martin's surprise, the girl, Mary, joined in the conversation, displaying an intelligence he had never encountered in the few women he had met. They talked together on Swinburne and Rosetti, after which she led him beyond his depth into the by-paths of French literature. His revenge came when she defended Maeterlinck and he brought into action the carefully thought-out thesis of "The Shame of the Sun."

Several other men had dropped in, and the air was thick with tobacco smoke, when Brissenden waved the red flag.

"Here 's fresh meat for your axe, Kreis," he said; "—a rose-white youth with the ardor of a lover for Herbert Spencer. Make a Haeckelite of him —if you can."

Kreis seemed to wake up and flash like some metallic magnetic thing, while Norton looked at Martin sympathetically, with a sweet, girlish smile, as much as to say that he would be amply protected.

Kreis began directly on Martin, but step by step Norton interfered, until he and Kreis were off and away in a personal battle. Martin listened and fain would have rubbed his eyes. It was impossible that this should be, much less in the labor ghetto south of Market. The books were alive in these men. They talked with fire and enthusiasm, the intellectual stimulant stirring them as he had seen drink and anger stir other men. What he heard was no longer the philosophy of the dry, printed word, written by half-mythical demi-gods like Kant and Spencer. It was living philosophy, with warm, red blood, incarnated in these two men till its very features worked with excitement. Now and again other men joined in, and all followed the discussion with cigarettes going out in their hands and with alert, intent faces.

Idealism had never attracted Martin, but the exposition it now received at the hands of Norton was a revelation. The logical plausibility of it that made an appeal to his intellect, seemed missed by Kreis and Hamilton, who sneered at Norton as a metaphysician, and who, in turn, sneered back at them as metaphysicians. *Phenomenon* and *noumenon* were bandied back and forth. They charged him with attempting to explain consciousness by itself. He charged them with word-jugglery, with reasoning from words to theory instead of from facts to theory. At this they were aghast. It was the cardinal tenet of their mode of reasoning to start with facts and to give names to the facts.

When Norton wandered into the intricacies of Kant, Kreis reminded him that all good little German philosophies when they died went to Oxford. A little later Norton reminded them of Hamilton's Law of Parsimony, the application of which they immediately claimed for every reasoning process of theirs. And Martin hugged his knees and exulted in it all. But Norton was no Spencerian, and he, too, strove for Martin's philosophic soul, talking as much at him as to his two opponents.

"You know Berkeley has never been answered," he said, looking directly at Martin. "Herbert Spencer came the nearest, which was not very near. Even the staunchest of Spencer's followers will not go farther. I was reading an essay of Saleeby's the other day, and the best Saleeby could say was that Herbert Spencer *nearly* succeeded in answering Berkeley."

"You know what Hume said?" Hamilton asked. Norton nodded, but Hamilton gave it for the benefit of the rest. "He said that Berkeley's arguments admit of no answer and produce no conviction."

"In his, Hume's, mind," was the reply. "And Hume's mind was the same as yours, with this difference: he was wise enough to admit that there was no answering Berkeley."

Norton was sensitive and excitable, though he never lost his head, while Kreis and Hamilton were like a pair of cold-blooded savages, seeking out tender places to prod and poke. As the evening grew late, Norton, smarting under the repeated charges of being a metaphysician, clutching his chair to keep from jumping to his feet, his gray eyes snapping and his girlish face grown harsh and sure, made a grand attack upon their position.

"All right, you Haeckelites, I may reason like a medicine man, but pray how do you reason? You have nothing to stand on, you unscientific dogmatists with your positive science which you are always lugging about into places it has no right to be. Long before the school of materialistic monism arose, the ground was removed so that there could be no foundation. Locke was the man, John Locke. Two hundred years ago—more than that, even—in his 'Essay Concerning the Human Understanding,' he proved the non-existence of innate ideas. The best of it is that that is precisely what you claim. Tonight, again and again, you have asserted the non-existence of innate ideas.

"And what does that mean? It means that you can never know ultimate reality. Your brains are empty when you are born. Appearances, or phenomena, are all the content your minds can receive from your five senses. Then noumena, which are not in your minds when you are born, have no way of getting in—"

"I deny—" Kreis interrupted.

"You wait till I 'm done," Norton shouted. You can know only that much of the play and interplay of force and matter as impinges in one way or another on your senses. You see, I am willing to admit, for the sake of the argument, that matter exists; and what I am about to do is to efface you by your own argument. I cant do it any other way, for you both are congenitally unable to understand a philosophic abstraction.

"And now, what do you know of matter, according to your own positive science? You know it only by its phenomena, its appearances. You are aware only of its changes, or of such changes in it that cause changes in your consciousness. Positive science deals only with phenomena, yet you are foolish enough to strive to be ontologists and to deal with noumena. Yet, by the very definition of positive science, science is concerned only with appearances. As somebody has said, phenomenal knowledge cannot transcend phenomena.

"You cannot answer Berkeley, even if you have annihilated Kant, and yet, perforce, you assume that Berkeley is wrong when you affirm that science proves the non-existence of God, or, as much to the point, the existence of matter. You know I granted the reality of matter only in order to make myself intelligible to your understanding. Be positive scientists if you please; but ontology has no place in positive science, so leave it alone. Spencer is right in his agnosticism, but if Spencer—"

But it was time to catch the last ferry boat for Oakland, and Brissenden and Martin slipped out, leaving Norton still talking and Kreis and Hamilton waiting to pounce on him like a pair of hounds as soon as he finished.

"You have given me a glimpse of fairyland," Martin said, on the ferry boat. "It makes life worth while to meet people like that. My mind is all worked up. I never appreciated idealism before. Yet I cant accept it. I know that I shall always be a realist. I am so made, I guess. But I 'd like to have made a reply to Kreis and Hamilton, and I think I 'd have had a word or two for Norton. I did n't see that Spencer was damaged any. I 'm as excited as a child on its first visit to the circus. I see I must read up some more. I am going to get hold of Saleeby, I will think Spencer is unassailable, and next time I'm going to take a hand myself."

But Brissenden, breathing painfully, had dropped off to sleep, his chin buried in a scarf and resting on his sunken chest, his body wrapped in the long overcoat and shaking to the vibration of the propellers.

Martin Eden

By Jack London

Author of "The Call of the Wild," "Sea Wolf," "The God of His Fathers," "White Fang," etc.

CHAPTER XXXVII.

THE first thing Martin did next morning was to go counter both to Brissenden's advice and command. "The Shame of the Sun" he wrapped and mailed to the *Acropolis*. He believed he could find magazine publication for it, and he felt that recognition by the magazines would commend him to the book publishing houses. "Ephemera," he likewise wrapped and mailed to a magazine. Despite Brissenden's prejudice against the magazines, which was a pronounced mania with him, Martin decided that the great poem should see print. He did not intend, however, to publish it without the other's permission. His plan was to get it accepted by one of the high-class magazines, and, thus armed, again to wrestle with Brissenden for consent.

Martin began, that morning, a story which he had sketched out a number of weeks before and which ever since had been worrying him with its insistent clamor to be created. Apparently it was to be a rattling sea story, a tale of twentieth-century adventure and romance, handling real characters, in a real world, under real conditions. But beneath the swing and go of the story was to be something else—something that the superficial reader would never discern and which, on the other hand, would not diminish in any way the interest and enjoyment for such a reader. It was this, and not the mere story, that impelled Martin to write it. For that matter, it was always the great, universal motif that suggested plots to him. After having found such a motif, he cast about for the particular persons and particular location in time and space wherewith and wherein to utter the universal thing. "Overdue" was the title he had decided for it, and its length he believed would not be more than sixty thousand words—a bagatelle for him with his splendid vigor of production. On this first day he took hold of it with conscious delight in the mastery of his tools. He no longer worried for fear that the sharp, cutting edges should slip and mar his work. The long months of intense application and study had brought their reward. He could now devote himself, with sure hand, to the larger phases of the thing he shaped; and as he worked, hour after hour, he felt, as never before, the sure and cosmic grasp with which he held life and the affairs of life. "Overdue" would tell a story that would be true of its particular characters and its particular events; but it would tell, too, he was confident, great vital things that would be true of all time, and all sea, and all life—thanks to Herbert Spencer, he thought, leaning back for a moment from the table. Ay, thanks to Herbert Spencer and to the master key of life, evolution, which Spencer had placed in his hands.

He was conscious that it was great stuff he was writing. "It will go! It will go!" was the refrain that kept sounding in his ears. Of course it would go. At last he was turning out the thing at which the magazines would jump. The whole story worked out before him in lightning flashes. He broke off from it long enough to write a paragraph in his note book. This would be the last paragraph in "Overdue"; but so thoroughly was the whole book already composed in his brain that he could write, weeks before he had arrived at the end, the end itself. He compared the tale, as yet unwritten, with the tales of the sea-writers, and he felt it to be immeasurably superior. "There's only one man who could touch it," he murmured aloud, "and that's Conrad. And it ought to make even him sit up and shake hands with me, and say, 'Well done, Martin, my boy.' "

He toiled on all day, recollecting, at the last moment, that he was to have dinner at the Morses. Thanks to Brissenden, his black suit was out of pawn and he was again eligible for dinner parties. Down town he stopped off long enough to run into the library and search for Saleeby's books. He drew out *The Cycle of Life,* and on the car turned to the essay Norton had mentioned on Spencer. As Martin read, he grew angry. His face flushed, his jaw set, and, unconsciously, his hand clenched, unclenched, and clenched again as if he were taking fresh grips upon some hateful thing out of which he was squeezing the life. When he left the car he strode along the sidewalk as a wrathful man will stride, and he rang the Morse bell with such viciousness that it roused him to consciousness of his condition, so that he entered in good nature, smiling with amusement at himself. No sooner, however, was he inside, than a great depression descended upon him. He fell from the height where he had been upborne all day on the wings of inspiration. "Bourgeois," "trader's den" — Brissenden's epithets repeated themselves in his mind. But what of that? he demanded angrily. He was marrying Ruth, not her family.

It seemed to him that he had never seen Ruth more beautiful, more spiritual and ethereal and at the same time more healthy. There was color in her cheeks, and her eyes drew him again and again —the eyes in which he had first read immortality. He had forgotten immortality of late, and the trend of his scientific reading had been away from it; but here, in Ruth's eyes, he read an argument without words that transcended all worded arguments. He saw that in her eyes before which all discussion fled away, for he saw love there. And in his own eyes was love; and love was unanswerable. Such was his passionate doctrine.

The half hour he had with her, before they went in to dinner, left him supremely happy and supremely satisfied with life. Nevertheless, at table, the inevitable reaction and exhaustion consequent upon the hard day seized hold of him. He was aware that his eyes were tired and that he was irritable. He remembered it was at this table, at which he now sneered and was so often bored, that he had first eaten with civilized beings in what he had imagined was an atmosphere of high culture and refinement. He caught a glimpse of that pathetic figure of him, so long ago, a self-conscious savage, sprouting sweat at every pore in an agony of apprehension, puzzled by the bewildering minutia of eating-implements, tortured by the ogre of a servant, striving at a leap to live at such dizzy social altitude, and deciding in the end to be frankly himself, pretending no knowledge and no polish he did not possess.

He glanced at Ruth for reassurance, much in the same manner that a passenger, with sudden panic thought of possible shipwreck, will strive to locate the life-preservers. Well, that much had come out of it—love and Ruth. All the rest had failed to stand the test of the books. But Ruth and love had stood the test; for them he found a biological sanction. Love was the most exalted expression of life. Nature had been busy designing him, as she had been busy with all normal men, for the purpose of loving. She had spent ten thousand centuries—ay, a hundred thousand and a million centuries—upon the task, and he was the best she could do. She had made love the strongest thing in him, increased its power a myriad per cent with her gift of imagination, and sent him forth into the ephemera to thrill and melt and mate. His hand sought Ruth's hand beside him hidden by the table, and a warm pressure was given and received. She looked at him a swift instant, and her eyes were radiant and melting. So were his in the thrill that pervaded him; nor did he realize how much that was radiant and melting in her eyes had been aroused by what she had seen in his.

Across the table from him, cater-cornered, at Mr. Morse's right, sat Judge Blount, a local superior court judge. Martin had met him a number of times and had failed to like him. He and Ruth's father were discussing labor union politics, the local situation, and socialism, and Mr. Morse was endeavoring to twit Martin on the latter topic. At last Judge Blount looked across the table with benignant and fatherly pity. Martin smiled to himself.

"You 'll grow out of it, young man," he said soothingly. "Time is the best cure for such youthful distempers." He turned to Mr. Morse. "I do not believe discussion is good in such cases. It makes the patient obstinate."

"That is true," the other assented gravely. "But it is well to warn the patient ocassionally of his condition."

Martin laughed merrily, but it was with an effort. The day had been too long, the day's effort too intense, and he was deep in the throes of the reaction.

"Undoubtedly you are both excellent doctors," he said; "but, if you care a whit for the opinion of the patient, let him tell you that you are poor diagnosticians. In fact, you are both suffering from the disease you think you find in me. As for me, I am immune. The socialist philosophy that riots half-baked in your veins has passed me by."

"Clever, clever," murmured the judge. "An excellent ruse in controversy, to reverse positions."

"Out of your mouth." Martin's eyes were sparkling, but he kept control of himself. "You see, Judge, I 've heard your campaign speeches. By some henidical process—henidical, by the way, is a favorite word of mine which nobody understands—by some henidical process you persuade yourself that you believe in the competitive system and the survival of the strong, and at the same time you indorse with might and main all sorts of measures to shear the strength from the strong."

"My young man—"

"Remember, I 've heard your campaign speeches," Martin warned. "It 's on record, your position on interstate commerce regulation, on regulation of the railway trust and Standard Oil, on the conservation of the forests, on a thousand and one restrictive measures that are nothing else than socialistic."

"Do you mean to tell me that you do not believe in regulating these various outrageous exercises of power—?"

"That 's not the point. I mean to tell you that you are a poor diagnostician. I mean to tell you that I am not suffering from the microbe of socialism. I mean to tell you that it is you who are suffering from the emasculating ravages of that same microbe. As for me, I am an inveterate opponent of socialism, just as I am an inveterate opponent of your own mongrel democracy that is nothing else than pseudo-socialism masquerading under a garb of words that will not stand the test of the dictionary.

"I am a reactionary—so complete a reactionary that my position is incomprehensible to you who live in a veiled lie of social organization and whose sight is not keen enough to pierce the veil. You make believe that you believe in the survival of the strong, and the rule of the strong. I believe. That is the difference. When I was a trifle younger—a few months younger—I believed the same thing. You see, the ideas of you and yours had impressed me. But merchants and traders are cowardly rulers at best, they grunt and grub all their days in the trough of money-getting, and I have swung back to aristocracy, if you please. I am the only individualist in this room. I look to the state for nothing. I look only to the strong man, the man on horseback, to save the state from its own rotten futility.

"Nietzsche was right—I wont take the time to tell you who Nietzsche was. But he was right. The world belongs to the strong—to the strong who are noble as well and who do not wallow in the swine-trough of trade and exchange. The world belongs to the true noblemen, to the great blond beasts, to the noncompromisers, to the 'yes-sayers.' And they will eat you up, you socialists who are afraid of socialism and who think yourselves individualists. Your slave-morality of the meek and lowly will never save you.—Oh, it 's all Greek, I know, and I wont bother you any more with it. But remember one thing. There are n't half a dozen individualists in Oakland, but Martin Eden is one of them."

He signified that he was done with the discussion, and turned to Ruth.

"I 'm wrought up today," he said in an undertone. "All I want to do is to love, not talk."

He ignored Mr. Morse, who said:

"I am unconvinced. All socialists are Jesuits. That is the way to tell them."

"We 'll make a good Republican out of you yet," said Judge Blount.

"The man on horseback will arrive before that time," Martin retorted with good humor, and returned to Ruth.

But Mr. Morse was not content. He did not like the laziness and the disinclination for sober, legitimate work of this prospective son-in-law of his for whose ideas he had no respect and for whose nature he had no understanding. So Mr. Morse turned the conversation to Herbert Spencer. Judge Blount ably seconded him, and Martin, whose ears had pricked at the first mention of the philosopher's name, listened to the judge enunciate a grave and complacent diatribe against Spencer. From time to time Mr. Morse glanced at Martin as much as to say, "There, my boy, you see."

"Chattering daws," Martin muttered under his breath and went on talking with Ruth and Arthur.

But the long day and the "real dirt" of the night before were telling upon him; and, besides, still burning in his mind was what had made him angry when he read it on the car.

"What is the matter?" Ruth asked suddenly, alarmed by the effort he was making to contain himself.

"There is no God but the Unknowable, and Herbert Spencer is its prophet," Judge Blount was saying at that moment.

Martin turned upon him.

"A cheap judgment," he remarked quietly. "I heard it first in the City Hall Park, on the lips of a workingman who ought to have known better. I have heard it often since, and each time the clap-trap of it nauseates me. You ought to be ashamed of yourself. To hear that great and noble man's name upon your lips is like finding a dew-drop in a cess-pool. You are disgusting."

It was like a thunderbolt. Judge Blount glared at him with apoplectic countenance, and silence reigned. Mr. Morse was secretly pleased. He could see that his daughter was shocked. It was what he wanted to do—to bring out the innate ruffianism of this man he did not like.

Ruth's hand sought Martin's beseechingly under the table, but his blood was up. He was inflamed by the intellectual pretence and fraud of those who sat in the high places. A Superior Court Judge! It was only several years before that he had looked up from the mire at such glorious entities and deemed them gods.

Judge Blount recovered himself and attempted to go on, addressing himself to Martin with an assumption of politeness that the latter understood was for the benefit of the ladies. Even this added to his anger. Was there no honesty in the world?

"You can 't discuss Spencer with me," he cried. "You do not know any more about Spencer than do his own countrymen. But it is no fault of yours, I grant. It is just a phase of the contemptible ignorance of the times. I ran across a sample of it on my way here this evening. I was reading an essay by Saleeby on Spencer. You should read it. It is accessible to all men. You can buy it in any book-store or draw it from the public library. You would feel ashamed of your paucity of abuse and ignorance of that noble man compared with what Saleeby has collected on the subject. It is a record of shame that would shame your shame.

"'The philosopher of the half-educated,' he was called by an academic philosopher who was not worthy to pollute the atmosphere he breathed. I dont think you have read ten pages of Spencer, but there have been critics assumably more intelligent than you, who have read no more than you of Spencer, who publicly challenged his followers to adduce one single idea from all his writings—from Herbert Spencer's writings, the man who has impressed the stamp of his genius over the whole field of scientific research and modern thought; the father of psychology; the man who revolutionized pedagogy, so that today the child of the French peasant is taught the three r's according to principles laid down by him. And the little gnats of men sting his memory when they get their very bread and butter from the technical application of his ideas. What little of worth resides in their brains is largely due to him. It is certain that had he never lived most of what is correct in their parrot-learned knowledge would be absent.

"And yet a man like Principal Fairbanks of Oxford—a man who sits in an even higher place than you, Judge Blount —has said that Spencer will be dismissed by posterity as a poet and a dreamer rather than a thinker. Yappers and blatherskites, the whole brood of them. '*First Principles* is not wholly destitute of a certain literary power,' said one of them. And others of them have said that he was an industrious plodder rather than an original thinker. Yappers and blatherskites! Yappers and blatherskites!"

Martin ceased abruptly, in a dead silence. Everybody in Ruth's family looked up to Judge Blount as a man of power and achievement, and they were horrified at Martin's outbreak. The remainder of the dinner passed like a funeral, the Judge and Mr. Morse confining their talk to each other, and the rest of the conversation being extremely desultory. Then afterwards, when Ruth and Martin were alone, there was a scene.

"You are unbearable," she wept.

But his anger still smouldered, and he kept muttering, "The beasts! The beasts!"

When she averred he had insulted the judge, he retorted:

"By telling the truth about him!"

"I dont care whether it was true or not," she insisted. "There are certain bounds of decency, and you had no license to insult anybody."

"Then where did Judge Blount get the license to assault truth?" Martin demanded. "Surely to assault truth is a more serious misdemeanor than to insult a pigmy personality such as the Judge's. He did worse than that. He blackened the name of a great, noble man who is dead. Oh, the beasts! the beasts!"

His complex anger flamed afresh, and Ruth was in terror of him. Never had she seen him so angry, and it was all mystified and unreasonable to her comprehension. And yet, through her very terror ran the fibers of fascination that had drawn and that still drew her to him —that had compelled her to lean toward him, and, in that mad culminating moment, lay her hands upon his neck. She was hurt and outraged by what had taken place, and yet she lay in his arms and quivered while he went on muttering. "The beasts! the beasts!" And she still lay there when he said: "I 'll not bother your table again, dear. They do not like me, and it is wrong of me to thrust my objectionable presence upon them. Besides, they are just as objectionable to me. Faugh! They are sickening. And to think of it, I dreamed in my innocence that the persons who sat in the high places, who lived in fine houses and had educations and bank accounts, were worth while!"

CHAPTER XXXVIII.

"COME on, let 's go down to the Local."

So spoke Brissenden, faint from a hemorrhage of half an hour before—the second hemorrhage in three days. The perennial whiskey glass was in his hands and he drained it with shaking fingers.

"What do I want with socialism?" Martin demanded.

"Outsiders are allowed five-minute speeches," the sick man urged. "Get up and spout. Tell them why you dont want socialism. Tell them what you think about them and their ghetto ethics. Slam Nietzsche into them and get walloped for your pains. Make a scrap of it. It will do them good. Discussion is what they want, and what you want, too. You see, I 'd like to see you a socialist before I 'm gone. It will give you a sanction for your existence. It is the one thing that will save you in the time of disappointment that is coming to you."

"I never can puzzle out why you, of all men, are a socialist," Martin pondered. "You detest the crowd so. Surely there is nothing in the *canaille* to recommend it to your aesthetic soul." He pointed an accusing finger at the whiskey glass which the other was refilling. "Socialism doesn't seem to save you."

"I 'm very sick," was the answer. "With you it is different. You have health and much to live for. And you must be handcuffed to life somehow. As for me, you wonder why I am a socialist. I 'll tell you. It is because socialism is inevitable; because the present rotten and irrational system cannot endure; because the day is past for your man on horseback. The slaves wont stand for it. They are too many, and willy-nilly they 'll drag down the would-be equestrian before ever he gets astride. You can 't get away from them, and you 'll have to swallow the whole slave-morality. It 's not a nice mess, I 'll allow. But it 's been a-brewing and swallow it you must. You are antediluvian anyway, with your Nietzsche ideas. The past is past, and the man who says history repeats itself is a liar. Of course I dont like the crowd, but what 's a poor chap to do? We can 't have the man on horseback, and anything is preferable to the timid swine that now rule. But come on any way. I 'm loaded to the guards now, and if I sit here any longer I 'll get drunk. And you know the doctor says—damn the doctor! I 'll fool him yet."

It was Sunday night, and they found the small hall packed by the Oakland socialists, chiefly members of the working class. The speaker, a clever Jew, won Martin's admiration at the same time that he aroused his antagonism. The man's stooped and narrow shoulders and weazened chest proclaimed him the true child of the crowded ghetto, and strong on Martin was the age-long struggle of the feeble wretched slaves against the lordly handful of men who had ruled over them and would rule over them to the end of time. To Martin this withered wisp of a creature was a symbol. He was the figure that stood forth representative of the whole miserable mass of weaklings and inefficients who perished according to biological law on the ragged confines of life. They were the unfit. In spite of their cunning philosophy and of their ant-like proclivities for co-operation, Nature rejected them for the exceptional man. Out of the plentiful spawn of life she flung from her prolific hand she selected only the best. It was by the same method that men, aping her, bred race-horses and cucumbers. Doubtless, a creator of a Cosmos could have devised a better method; but creatures of this particular Cosmos must put up with its particular method. Of course, they could squirm as they perished, as the socialists squirmed, as the speaker on the platform and the perspiring crowd were squirming even now as they counseled together for some new device with which to minimize the penalties of living and outwit the Cosmos.

So Martin thought, and so he spoke when Brissenden urged him to give them hell. He obeyed the mandate, walking up to the platform, as was the custom, and addressing the chairman. He began in a low voice, haltingly, forming into order the ideas which had surged in his brain while the Jew was speaking. In such meetings five minutes was the time allotted to each speaker; but when Martin's five minutes were up he was in full stride, his attack upon their doctrines but half completed. He had caught their interest, and the audience urged the chairman by acclamation to extend Martin's time. They appreciated him as a foeman worthy of their intellect, and they listened intently, following every word. He spoke with fire and conviction, mincing no words in his attack upon the slaves and their morality and tactics, and frankly alluding to his hearers as the slaves in question. He quoted Spencer and Malthus, and enunciated the biological law of development.

"And so," he concluded, in a swift resume, "no state composed of the slave-types can endure. The old law of development still holds. In the struggle for existence, as I have shown, the strong and the progeny of the strong tend to survive, while the weak and the progeny of the weak are crushed and tend to perish. The result is that the strong and the progeny of the strong survive, and, so long as the struggle obtains, the strength of each generation increases. That is development. But you slaves—it is too bad to be slaves, I grant—but you slaves dream of a society where the law of development will be annulled, where no weaklings and inefficients will perish, where every inefficient will have as much as he wants to eat as many times a day as he desires, and where all will marry and have progeny—the weak as well as the strong. What will be the result? No longer will the strength and life-value of each generation increase. On the contrary, it will diminish. There is the Nemesis of your slave philosophy. Your society of slaves—of, by, and for slaves—must inevitably weaken and go to pieces as the life which composes it weakens and goes to pieces.

"Remember, I am enunciating biology and not sentimental ethics. No state of slaves can stand—"

"How about the United States?" a man yelled from the audience.

"And how about it?" Martin retorted. "The thirteen colonies threw off their rulers and formed the Republic so-called. The slaves were their own masters. There were no more masters of the sword. But you could n't get along without masters of some sort, and arose a new set of masters—not the great, virile, noble men, but the shrewd and spidery traders and money-lenders. And they enslaved you over again—but not frankly as the true noble men would do with weight of their own right arms, but secretly, by spidery machinations and by wheedling and cajolery and lies. They have purchased your slave-judges, they have debauched your slave-legislatures, and they have forced to worse horrors than chattel slavery your slave-boys and girls. Two million of your children are toiling today in this trader-oligarchy of the United States. Ten millions of you slaves are not properly sheltered nor properly fed.

"But to return. I have shown that no society of slaves can endure, because, in its very nature, such society must annul the law of development. No sooner can a slave society be organized than deterioration sets in. It is easy for you to talk of annulling the law of development but where is the new law of development that will maintain your strength? Formulate it. Is it already formulated? Then state it."

Martin took his seat amidst an uproar of voices. A score of men were on their feet clamoring for recognition from the chair. And one by one, encouraged by vociferous applause, speaking with fire and enthusiasm and excited gestures, they replied to the attack. It was a wild night—but it was wild intellectually, a battle of ideas. Some strayed from the point, but most of the speakers replied directly to Martin. They shocked him with lines of thought that were new to him; and gave him insights, not into new biological laws, but into new applications of the old laws. They were too earnest to be always polite, and more than once the chairman rapped and pounded for order.

It chanced that a cub reporter sat in the audience, detailed there on a day dull of news and impressed by the urgent need of journalism for sensation. He was not a bright cub reporter. He was merely facile and glib. He was too dense to follow the discussion. In fact, he had a comfortable feeling that he was vastly superior to these wordy maniacs of the working class. Also, he had a great respect for those who sat in the high places and dictated the policies of nations and newspapers. Further, he had an ideal, namely of achieving that excellence of the perfect reporter who is able to make something—even a great deal—out of nothing.

He did not know what all the talk was about. It was not necessary. Words like *revolution* gave him his cue. Like a paleontologist, able to reconstruct an entire skeleton from one fossil bone, he was able to reconstruct a whole speech from the one word, *revolution*. He did it that night, and he did it well; and since Martin had made the biggest stir, he put it all into his mouth and made him the arch-anarch of the show, transforming his reactionary individualism into the most lurid, red-shirt socialist utterance. The cub reporter was an artist, and it was a large brush with which he laid on the local color—wild-eyed, long-haired men, neurasthenic and degenerate types of men, voices shaken with passion, clenched fists raised on high, and all projected against a background of oaths, yells and the throaty rumbling of angry men.

CHAPTER XXXIX.

OVER the coffee, in his little room, Martin read next morning's paper. It was a novel experience to find himself head-lined, on the first page at that; and he was surprised to learn that he was the most notorious leader of the Oakland socialists. He ran over the violent speech the cub reporter had constructed for him, and, though at first he was angered by the fabrication in the end he tossed the paper aside with a laugh.

"Either the man was drunk or criminally malicious," he said that afternoon, from his perch on the bed, when Brissenden had arrived and dropped limply into the one chair.

"But what do you care?" Brissenden asked. "Surely you dont desire the approval of the bourgeois swine that read the newspapers?"

Martin thought for a while, then said:

"No, I really dont care for their approval, not a whit. On the other hand, it 's very liable to make my relations with Ruth's family a trifle awkward. Her father always contended I was a socialist, and this miserable stuff will clinch his belief. Not that I care for his opinion—but what 's the odds? I want to read you what I 've been doing today. It 's 'Overdue,' of course, and I 'm just about half way through.

He was reading aloud when Maria thrust open the door and ushered in a young man in a natty suit who glanced briskly about him, noting the oil-burner and the kitchen in the corner before his gaze wandered on to Martin.

"Sit down," Brissenden said.

Martin made room for the young man on the bed and waited for him to broach his business.

"I heard you speak last night, Mr. Eden, and I 've come to interview you," he began.

Brissenden burst out in a hearty laugh.

"A brother socialist?" the reporter asked, with a quick glance at Brissenden that appraised the color-value of that cadaverous and dying man.

"And he wrote that report," Martin said softly. "Why, he is only a boy."

"Why dont you poke him?" Brissenden asked. "I 'd give a thousand dollars to have my lungs back for five minutes."

The cub reporter was a trifle perplexed by this talking over him and around him and at him. But he had been commended for his brilliant description of the socialist meeting and had further been detailed to get a personal interview with Martin Eden, the leader of the organized menace to society.

"You do not object to having your picture taken, Mr. Eden?" he said. "I 've a staff photographer outside, you see, and he says it will be better to take you right away before the sun gets lower. Then we can have the interview afterward."

"A photographer," Brissenden said meditatively. "Poke him, Martin. Poke him."

"I guess I 'm getting old," was the answer. "I know I ought, but I really have n't the heart. It does n't seem to matter."

"For his mother's sake," Brissenden urged.

"It 's worth considering," Martin replied; "but it does n't seem worth while enough, to rouse sufficient energy in me. You see, it does take energy to give a fellow a poking. Besides, what does it matter?"

"That 's right—that 's the way to take it," the cub announced airily, though he had already begun to glance anxiously at the door.

"But it was n't true, not a word of what he wrote," Martin went on, confining his attention to Brissenden.

"It was just in a general way a description, you understand," the cub ventured, "and besides, it 's good advertising. That 's what counts. It was a favor to you."

"It 's good advertising, Martin, old boy." Brissenden repeated solemnly.

"And it was a favor to me—think of that!" was Martin's contribution.

"Let me see—where were you born, Mr. Eden?" the cub asked, assuming an air of expectant attention.

"He does n't take notes," said Brissenden. "He remembers it all."

"That is sufficient for me." The cub was trying not to look worried. "No decent reporter needs to bother with notes."

"That was sufficient—for last night." But Brissenden was not a disciple of quietism, and he changed his attitude abruptly. "Martin, if you dont poke him I 'll do it myself, if I fall dead on the floor the next moment."

"How will a spanking do?" Martin asked.

Brissenden considered judicially, and nodded his head.

The next instant Martin was seated on the edge of the bed with the cub face downward across his knees.

"Now dont bite," Martin warned, "or else I 'll have to punch your face. It would be a pity, for it is such a pretty face."

His uplifted hand descended, and thereafter rose and fell in a swift and steady rhythm. The cub struggled and cursed and squirmed, but did not offer to bite. Brissenden looked on gravely, though once he grew excited and gripped the whisky bottle, pleading, "Here, just let me swat him once."

"Sorry my hand played out," Martin said when at last he desisted. "It is quite numb."

He uprighted the cub and perched him on the bed.

"I 'll have you arrested for this," he snarled, tears of boyish indignation running down his flushed cheeks. "I 'll make you sweat for this. You 'll see."

"The pretty thing," Martin remarked. "He does n't realize that he has entered upon the downward path. It is not honest, it is not square, it is not manly, to tell lies about one's fellow creatures the way he has done, and he does n't know it."

"He has to come to us to be told," Brissenden filled in a pause.

"Yes, to me whom he has maligned and injured. My grocer will undoubtedly refuse me credit now. The worst of it is that the poor boy will keep on this way until he deteriorates into a first-class newspaper man."

"But there is yet time," quoth Brissenden. "Who knows but that you may prove the humble instrument to save him. Why did n't you let me swat him just once? I 'd like to have had a hand in it."

"I 'll have you arrested, the pair of you, you b-b-big brutes," sobbed the erring soul.

"No, his mouth is too pretty and too weak." Martin shook his head lugubriously. "I 'm afraid I 've numbed my hand in vain. The young man cannot reform. He will become eventually a very great and successful newspaperman. He has no conscience. That alone will make him great."

With that the cub passed out the door, in trepidation to the last for fear that Brissenden would hit him in the back with the bottle he still clutched.

In the next morning's paper Martin learned a great deal more about himself that was new to him. "We are the sworn enemies of society," he found himself quoted as saying in a column interview. "No, we are not anarchists but socialists." When the reporter pointed out to him that there seemed little difference between the two schools, Martin had shrugged his shoulders in silent affirmation. His face was described as bi-laterally asymetrical, and various other signs of degeneration were described. Especially notable were his thug-like hands and the fiery gleams in his blood-shot eyes.

He learned, also, that he spoke nightly to the workmen in the city hall park, and that among the anarchists and agitators that there inflamed the minds of the people he drew the largest audiences and made the most revolutionary speeches. The cub painted a high-light picture of his poor little room, its oil-stove and the one chair, and of the death's head tramp who kept him company and who looked as if he had just emerged from twenty years of solitary confinement in some fortress dungeon.

The cub had been industrious. He had scurried around and nosed out Martin's family history, and procured a photograph of Higginbotham's Cash Store with Bernard Higginbotham himself standing out in front. That gentleman was depicted as an intelligent, dignified business man who had no patience with his brother-in-law's socialistic views, and no patience with the brother-in-law, either, whom he was quoted as characterizing as a lazy good-for-nothing who would n't take a job when it was offered to him, and who would go to jail yet. Herrmann Von Schmidt, Marion's husband, had likewise been interviewed. He had called Martin the black sheep of the family and repudiated him. "He tried to sponge off of me, but I put a stop to that good and quick," Von Schmidt had said to the reporter. "He knows better than to come bumming around here. A man who wont work is no good, take that from me."

This time Martin was genuinely angry. Brissenden looked upon the affair as a good joke, but he could not console Martin, who knew that it would be no easy task to explain to Ruth. As for her father, he knew that he must be overjoyed with what had happened and that he would make the most of it to break off the engagement. How much he would make of it he was soon to realize. The afternoon mail brought a letter from Ruth. Martin opened it with a premonition of disaster, and read it standing at the open door when he had received it from the postman. As he read, mechanically his hand sought his pocket for the tobacco and brown paper of his old cigarette days. He was not aware that the pocket was empty or that he had even reached for the materials with which to roll a cigarette.

It was not a passionate letter. There were no touches of anger in it. But all the way through, from the first sentence to the last, was sounded the note of hurt and disappointment. She had expected better of him. She had thought he had got over his youthful wildness, that her love for him had been sufficiently worth while to enable him to live seriously and decently. And now her father and mother had taken a firm stand and commanded that the engagement be broken. That they were justified in this she could not but admit. Their relation could never be a happy one. It had been unfortunate from the first. But one regret she voiced in the whole letter, and it was a bitter one to Martin. "If only you had settled down to some position and attempted to make something of yourself," she wrote. "But it was not to be. Your past life had been too wild and irregular. I can understand that you are not to be blamed. You could act only according to your nature and your early training. So I do not blame you, Martin. Please remember that. It was simply a mistake. As father and mother have contended, we were not made for each other, and we should both be happy because it was discovered not too late."—"There is no use trying to see me," she said toward the last. "It would be an unhappy meeting for both of us, as well as for my mother. I feel, as it is, that I have caused her great pain and worry. I shall have to do much living to atone for it."

He read it through to the end, carefully, a second time, then sat down and replied. He outlined the remarks he had uttered at the socialist meeting, pointing out that they were in all ways the converse of what the newspaper had put in his mouth. Toward the end of the letter he was God's own lover pleading passionately for love. "Please answer," he said, "and in your answer you have to tell me but one thing. Do you love me? That is all—the answer to that one question."

But no answer came the next day, nor the next. "Overdue" lay untouched upon the table, and each day the heap of returned manuscripts under the table grew larger. For the first time Martin's glorious sleep was interrupted by insomnia, and he tossed through long restless nights. Three times he called at the Morse home, but was turned away by the servant who answered the bell. Brissenden lay sick in his hotel, too feeble to stir out, and, though Martin was with him often, he did not worry him with his troubles.

For Martin's troubles were many. The

aftermath of the cub reporter's deed was even wider than Martin had anticipated. The Portuguese grocer refused him further credit, while the greengrocer, who was an American and proud of it, had called him a traitor to his country and refused further dealings with him—carrying his patriotism to such a degree that he canceled Martin's account and forbade him ever to attempt to pay it. The talk in the neighborhood reflected the same feeling, and indignation against Martin ran high. No one would have anything to do with a socialist traitor. Poor Maria was dubious and frightened, but she remained loyal. The children of the neighborhood recovered from the awe of the grand carriage which had once visited Martin, and from safe distances they called him "hobo" and "bum." The Silva tribe, however, staunchly defended him, fighting more than one pitched battle for his honor, and black eyes and bloody noses became quite the order of the day and added to Maria's perplexities and troubles.

Once, Martin met Gertrude on the street, down in Oakland, and learned what he knew could not be otherwise—that Bernard Higginbotham was furious with him for having dragged the family into public disgrace, and that he had forbidden him the house.

"Why dont you go away, Martin?" Gertrude had begged. "Go away and get a job somewhere and steady down. Afterwards, when this all blows over, you can come back."

Martin shook his head, but gave no explanations. How could he explain? He was appalled at the awful intellectual chasm that yawned between him and his people. He could never cross it and explain to them his position, the Nietzschean position, in regard to socialism. There were not words enough in the English language, nor in any language, to make his attitude and conduct intelligible to them. Their highest concept of right conduct, in his case, was to get a job. That was their first word and their last. It constituted their whole lexicon of ideas. Get a job! Go to work! Poor, stupid slaves, he thought, while his sister talked. Small wonder the world belonged to the strong. The slaves were obsessed by their own slavery. A job was to them a golden fetich before which they fell down and worshiped.

He shook his head again, when Gertrude offered him money, though he knew that within the day he would have to make a trip to the pawnbroker.

"Dont come near Bernard now," she admonished him. "After a few months, when he 's cooled down, if you want to you can get the job of drivin' delivery-wagon for him. Any time you want me, just send for me an' I 'll come. Dont forget."

She went away weeping audibly, and he felt a pang of sorrow shoot through him at sight of her heavy body and uncouth gait. As he watched her go, the Nietzschean edifice seemed to shake and totter. The slave-class in the abstract was all very well, but it was not wholly satisfactory when it was brought home to his own family. And yet, if there was ever a slave trampled by the strong, that slave was his sister Gertrude. He grinned savagely at the paradox. A fine Nietzsche-man he was, to allow his intellectual concepts to be shaken by the first sentiment or emotion that strayed along—ay, to be shaken by the slave-morality itself, for that was what his pity for his sister really was. The true noble men were above pity and compassion. Pity and compassion had been generated in the subterranean barracoons of the slaves and were no more than the agony and sweat of the crowded miserables and weaklings.

Martin Eden

By Jack London

Author of "The Call of the Wild," "Sea Wolf," "The God of His Fathers," "White Fang," etc.

CHAPTER XL.

"OVERDUE" still continued to lie forgotten on the table. Every manuscript that he had had out now lay under the table. Only one manuscript he kept going, and that was Brissenden's "Ephemera." His bicycle and black suit were again in pawn, and the typewriter people were once more worrying about the rent. But such things no longer bothered him. He was seeking a new orientation, and until that was found his life must stand still.

After several weeks, what he had been waiting for, happened. He met Ruth on the street. It was true, she was accompanied by her brother, Norman, and it was true that they tried to ignore him and that Norman attempted to wave him aside.

"If you interfere with my sister I 'll call an officer," Norman threatened. "She does not wish to speak with you, and your insistence is insult."

"If you persist, you 'll have to call that officer, and then you 'll get your name in the papers," Martin answered grimly. "And now, get out of my way and get the officer if you want to. I 'm going to talk with Ruth.

"I want to have it from your own lips," he said to her.

She was pale and trembling, but she held up and looked inquiringly.

"The question I asked in my letter," he prompted.

Norman made an impatient movement, but Martin checked him with a swift look.

She shook her head.

"Is all this of your own free will?" he demanded.

"It is." She spoke in a low, firm voice and with deliberation. "It is of my own free will. You have disgraced me so that I am ashamed to meet my friends. They are all talking about me, I know. That is all I can tell you. You have made me very unhappy, and I never wish to see you again."

"Friends! Gossip! Newspaper mis-reports! Surely such things are not stronger than love? I can only believe that you never loved me."

A blush drove the pallor from her face.

"After what has passed?" she said faintly. "Martin, you do not know what you are saying. I am not common."

"You see, she does n't want to have anything to do with you," Norman blurted out, starting on with her.

Martin stood aside and let them pass, fumbling unconsciously in his coat-pocket for the tobacco and brown papers that were not there.

It was a long walk to North Oakland, but it was not until he went up the steps and entered his room that he knew he had walked it. He found himself sitting on the edge of the bed and staring about him like an awakened somnambulist. He noticed "Overdue" lying on the table, and drew up his chair and reached for his pen. There was in his nature a logical compulsion toward completeness. Here was something undone. It had been deferred against the completion of something else. Now that something else had been finished and he would apply himself to this task until it was finished. What he would do next he did not know. All that he did know was that a climacteric in his life had been attained. A period had been reached, and he was rounding it off in workmanlike fashion. He was not curious about the future. He would soon enough find out what it held in store for him. Whatever it was, it did not matter. Nothing seemed to matter.

For five days he toiled on at "Overdue," going nowhere, seeing nobody, and eating meagerly. On the morning of the sixth day the postman brought him a thin letter from the editor of the *Parthenon*. A glance told him that "Ephemera" was accepted. "We have submitted the poem to Mr. Cartwright Bruce," the editor went on to say, "and he has reported so favorably upon it that we cannot let it go. As an earnest of our pleasure in publishing the poem, let me tell you that we have set it for the August number, our July number being already made up. Kindly extend our pleasure and our thanks to Mr. Brissenden. Please send by return mail his photograph and biographical data. If our honorarium is unsatisfactory, kindly telegraph us at once and state what you consider a fair price."

Since the honorarium they had offered was three hundred and fifty dollars, Martin thought it not worth while to telegraph. Then, too, there was Brissenden's consent to be gained. Well, he had been right after all. Here was one magazine editor who knew real poetry when he saw it. And the price was splendid, even though it was for the poem of a century. As for Cartwright Bruce, Martin knew that he was the one critic for whose opinions Brissenden had any respect.

Martin rode down town on an electric car, and as he watched the houses and cross-streets slipping by he was aware of a regret that he was not more elated over his friend's success and over his own signal victory. The one critic in the United States had pronounced favorably on the poem, while his own contention that good stuff could find its way into the magazines had proved correct. But enthusiasm had lost its spring in him, and he found that he was more anxious to see Brissenden than he was to carry the good news. The acceptance of the *Parthenon* had recalled to him that during his five days' devotion to "Overdue" he had not heard from Brissenden nor even thought about him. For the first time Martin realized the daze he had been in, and he felt shame for having forgotten his friend. But even the shame did not burn very sharply. He was numb to emotions of any sort save the artistic ones concerned in the writing of "Overdue." So far as other affairs were concerned, he had been in a trance. For that matter, he was still in a trance. All this life through which the electric car whirred seemed remote and unreal, and he would have experienced little interest and less shock if the great stone steeple of the church he passed had suddenly crumbled to mortar-dust upon his head.

At the hotel he hurried up to Brissenden's room, and hurried down again. The room was empty. All luggage was gone.

"Did Mr. Brissenden leave any address?" he asked the clerk, who looked at him curiously for a moment.

"Have n't you heard?" he asked.

Martin shook his head.

"Why, the papers were full of it. He was found dead in bed. Suicide. Shot himself through the head."

"Is he buried yet?" Martin seemed to hear his voice, like some one else's voice, from a long way off, asking the question.

"No. The body was shipped East after the inquest. Lawyers engaged by his people saw to the arrangements."

"They were quick about it, I must say," Martin commented.

"Oh," I don 't know. It happened five days ago."

"Five days ago?"

"Yes, five days ago."

"Oh," Martin said, as he turned and went out.

At the corner he stepped into the Western Union and sent a telegram to the *Parthenon*, advising them to proceed with the publication of the poem. He had in his pocket but five cents with which to pay his carfare home, so he sent the message collect.

Once in his room, he resumed his writing. The days and nights came and went, and he sat at his table and wrote on. He went nowhere, save to the pawnbroker, took no exercise, and ate methodically when he was hungry and had something to cook, and just as methodically went without when he had nothing to cook. Composed as the story was, in advance, chapter by chapter, he nevertheless saw and developed an opening that increased the power of it, though it necessitated twenty thousand additional words. It was not that there was any vital need that the thing should be well done, but that his artistic canons compelled him to do it well. He worked on in the daze, strangely detached from the world around him, feeling like a familiar ghost among these literary trappings of his former life. He remembered that some one had said that a ghost was the spirit of a man who was dead and who did not have sense enough to know it; and he paused for the moment to wonder if he were really dead and unaware of it.

Came the day when "Overdue" was finished. The agent of the typewriter firm had come for the machine, and he sat on the bed while Martin, on the one chair, typed the last pages of the final chapter. "Finis," he wrote, in capitals, at the end, and to him it was indeed finis. He watched the typewriter carried out the door with a feeling of relief, then went over and lay down on the bed. He was faint from hunger. Food had not passed his lips in thirty-six hours, but he did not think about it. He lay on his back, with closed eyes, and did not think at all, while the daze or stupor slowly welled up, saturating his consciousness. Half in delirium, he began muttering aloud the lines of an anonymous poem Brissenden had been fond of quoting to him. Maria, listening anxiously outside his door, was perturbed by his monotonous utterance. The words in themselves were not significant to her, but the fact that he was saying them was. "I have done," was the burden of the poem.

I have done——
Put by the lute.
Song and singing soon are over
As the airy shades that hover
In among the purple clover.
I have done——
Put by the lute.
Once I sang as early thrushes
Sing among the dewy bushes;
Now I 'm mute.
I am like a weary linnet,
For my throat has no song in it;
I have had my singing minute.
I have done.
Put by the lute.

Maria could stand it no longer, and hurried away to the stove, where she filled a quart-bowl with soup, putting into it the lion's share of chopped meat and vegetables which her ladle scraped from the bottom of the pot. Martin roused himself and sat up and began to eat, between spoonfuls reassuring Maria that he had not been talking in his sleep and that he did not have any fever.

After she left him he sat drearily, with drooping shoulders, on the edge of the bed, gazing about him with lack-luster eyes that saw nothing until the torn wrapper of a magazine, which had come in the morning's mail and which lay unopened, shot a gleam of light into his darkened brain. It is the *Parthenon*, he thought, the August *Parthenon,* and it must contain "Ephemera." If only Brissenden were here to see.

He was turning the pages of the magazine, when suddenly he stopped. "Ephemera" had been featured, with gorgeous head-piece and Beardsley-like margin decorations. On one side of the headpiece was Brissenden's photograph, on the other side was the photograph of Sir John Value, the British Embassador. A preliminary editorial note, quoted Sir John Value as saying that there were no poets in America, and the publication of "Ephemera" was the *Parthenon's* "There, take that, Sir John Value!" Cartwright Bruce was described as the greatest critic in America, and he was quoted as saying that "Ephemera" was the greatest poem ever written in America. And, finally, the editor's foreword ended with: "We have not yet made up our minds entirely as to the merits of 'Ephemera;' perhaps we shall never be able to do so. But we have read it often, wondering at the words and their arrangement, wondering where Mr. Brissenden got them, and how he could fasten them together." Then followed the poem.

"Pretty good thing you died, Briss, old man," Martin murmured, letting the magazine slip between his knees to the floor.

The cheapness and vulgarity of it was nauseating, and Martin noted apathetically that he was not nauseated very much. He wished he could get angry, but did not have energy enough to try. He was too numb. His blood was too congealed to accelerate to the swift tidal-flow of indignation. After all, what did it matter? It was on a par with all the rest that Brissenden had condemned in bourgeois society.

"Poor Briss," Martin communed; "he would never have forgiven me."

Rousing himself with an effort, he possessed himself of a box which had once contained typewriter paper. Going through its contents, he drew forth eleven poems which his friend had written. These he tore lengthwise and crosswise and dropped into the waste basket. He did it languidly, and, when he had finished, sat on the edge of the bed staring blankly before him.

How long he sat there he did not know, until, suddenly, across his sightless vision, he saw form a long horizontal line of white. It was curious. But as he watched it grow in definiteness he saw that it was a coral reef smoking in the White Pacific surges. Next, in the line of breakers, he made out a small canoe, an outrigger canoe. In the stern he saw a young bronzed god in scarlet hip-cloth, dipping a flashing paddle. He recognized him. He was Moti, the youngest son of Tati, the chief, and this was Tahiti, and beyond that smoking reef lay the sweet land of Papara and the chief's grass house by the river's mouth. It was the end of the day, and Moti was coming home from the fishing. He was waiting for the rush of a big breaker whereon to jump the reef. Then he saw himself, sitting forward in the canoe as he had often sat in the past, dipping a paddle that waited Moti's word to dig in like mad when the turquoise wall of the great breaker rose behind them. Next he was no longer an onlooker, but was himself in the canoe, Moti was crying out, they were both thrusting hard with their paddles, racing on the steep face of the flying turquoise. Under the bow the water was hissing as from a steam jet, the air was filled with driven spray, there was a rush and rumble and long-echoing roar, and the canoe floated on the placid water of the lagoon. Moti laughed and shook the salt water from his eyes, and together they paddled in to the pounded-coral beach where Tati's grass walls through the cocoanut-palms showed golden in the setting sun.

The picture faded, and before his eyes stretched the disorder of his squalid room. He strove in vain to see Tahiti again. He knew there was singing among the trees and that the maidens were dancing in the moonlight, but he could not see them. He could see only the littered writing table, the empty space where the typewriter had stood, and the unwashed window-pane. He closed his eyes with a groan, and slept.

CHAPTER XLI.

HE slept heavily all night, and did not stir until aroused by the postman on his morning round. Martin felt tired and passive, and went through his letters aimlessly. One thin envelope, from a robber magazine, contained a check for twenty-two dollars. He had been dunning for it for a year and a half. He noted its amount apathetically. The old-time thrill at receiving a publisher's check was gone. Unlike his earlier checks, this one was not pregnant with promise of great things to come. To him it was a check for twenty-two dollars, that was all, and it would buy him something to eat.

Another check was in the same mail, sent from a New York weekly, in payment for some humorous verse which had been accepted months before. It was for ten dollars. An idea came to him, which he calmly considered. He did not know what he was going to do, and he felt in no hurry to do anything. In the meantime he must live. Also he owed numerous debts. Would it not be a paying investment to put stamps on the huge pile of manuscripts under the table and start them on their travels again? One or two of them might be accepted. That would help him to live. He decided on the investment, and, after he had cashed the checks at the bank down in Oakland, he bought ten dollars' worth of postage stamps. The thought of going home to cook breakfast in his stuffy little room was repulsive to him. For the first time he refused to consider his debts. He knew that in his room he could manufacture a substantial breakfast at a cost of from fifteen to twenty cents. But, instead, he went into the Forum Cafe and ordered a breakfast that cost two dollars. He tipped the waiter a quarter, and spent fifty cents for a package of Egyptian cigarettes. It was the first time he had smoked since Ruth had asked him to stop. But he could see now no reason why he should not, and, besides, he wanted to smoke. And what did the money matter? For five cents he could have bought a package of Durham and brown papers and rolled forty cigarettes—but what of it? Money had no meaning to him now except what it would immediately buy. He was chartless and rudderless, and he had no port to make, while drifting involved the least living, and it was living that hurt.

The days slipped along, and he slept eight hours regularly every night. Though now, while waiting for more checks, he ate in the Japanese restaurants where meals were served for ten cents, his wasted body filled out, as did the hollows in his cheeks. He no longer abused himself with short sleep, overwork and over-study. He wrote nothing, and the books were closed. He walked much, out in the hills, and loafed long hours in quiet parks. He had no friends nor acquaintances, nor did he make any. He had no inclination. He was waiting for some impulse, from he knew not where, to put his stopped life into motion again. In the meantime his life remained run down, planless and empty and idle.

Once he made a trip to San Francisco to look up the "real dirt." But at the last moment, as he stepped into the upstairs entrance, he recoiled and turned and fled through the swarming ghetto. He was frightened at the thought of hearing philosophy discussed, and he fled furtively, for fear that some one of the "real dirt" might chance along and recognize him.

Sometimes he glanced over the magazines and newspapers to see how "Ephemera" was being maltreated. It had made a hit. But what a hit! Everybody had read it, and everybody was discussing whether or not it was really poetry. The local papers had taken it up, and daily appeared columns of learned criticisms, facetious editorials, and serious letters from subscribers. Helen Della Delmar (proclaimed with a flourish of trumpets and rolling of tomtoms to be the greatest woman poet in the United States) denied Brissenden a seat beside her on Pegasus and wrote voluminous letters to the public, proving that he was no poet.

The *Parthenon* came out in its next number patting itself on the back for the stir it had made, sneering at Sir John Value, and exploiting Brissenden's death with ruthless commercialism. A newspaper with a sworn circulation of half a million published an original and spontaneous poem by Helen Della Delmar, in which she gibed and sneered at Brissenden. Also, she was guilty of a second poem, in which she parodied him.

Martin had many times to be glad that Brissenden was dead. He had hated the crowd so, and here all that was finest and most sacred of him had been thrown to the crowd. Daily the vivisection of Beauty went on. Every nincompoop in the land rushed into free print, floating their weazened little egos into the public eye on the surge of Brissenden's greatness. Quoth one paper: "We have received a letter from a gentleman who wrote a poem just like it, only better, some time ago." Another paper, in deadly seriousness, reproving Helen Della Delmar for her parody, said: "But unquestionably Miss Delmar wrote it in a moment of badinage and not quite with the respect that one great poet should show to another and perhaps to the greatest. However, whether Miss Delmar be jealous or not of the man who invented 'Ephemera,' it is certain that she, like thousands of others, is fascinated by his work, and that the day may come when she will try to write lines like his."

Ministers began to preach sermons against "Ephemera," and one, who too stoutly stood for much of its content, was expelled for heresy. The great poem contributed to the gayety of the world. The comic verse-writers and the cartoonists took hold of it with screaming laughter, and in the personal columns of society weeklies jokes were perpetrated on it to the effect that Charley Frensham told Archie Jennings, in confidence, that five lines of "Ephemera" would drive a man to beat a cripple, and that ten lines would send him to the bottom of the river.

Martin did not laugh; nor did he grit his teeth in anger. The effect produced upon him was one of great sadness. In the crash of his whole world, with love on the pinnacle, the crash of magazinedom and the dear public was a small crash indeed. Brissenden had been wholly right in his judgment of the magazines, and he, Martin, had spent arduous and futile years in order to find it out for himself. The magazines were all Brissenden had said they were, and more. Well, he was done, he solaced himself. He had hitched his wagon to a star and been landed in a pestiferous marsh. The visions of Tahiti—clean, sweet Tahiti—were coming to him more frequently. And there were the low Paumotus, and the high Marquesas; he saw himself often, now, on board trading schooners or frail little cutters, slipping out at dawn through the reef at Papeete and beginning the long beat through the pearl-atolls to Nuka-hiva and the Bay of Taichae, where Tamari, he knew, would kill a pig in honor of his coming, and where Tamari's flower-garlanded daughters would seize his hands and with song and laughter garland him with flowers. The South Seas were calling, and he knew that sooner or later he would answer the call.

In the meantime he drifted, resting and recuperating after a long traverse he had made through the realm of knowledge. When the *Parthenon* check of three hundred and fifty dollars was forwarded to him, he turned it over to the local lawyer who had attended to Brissenden's affairs for his family. Martin took a receipt for the check, and at the same time gave a note for the hundred dollars Brissenden had let him have.

The time was not long when Martin ceased patronizing the Japanese restaurants. At the very moment when he had abandoned the fight, the tide turned. But it had turned too late. Without a thrill he opened a thin envelope from the *Millennium,* scanned the face of a check that represented three hundred dollars, and noted that it was the payment on acceptance for "Adventure." Every debt he owed in the world, including the pawnshop with its usurious interest, amounted to less than a hundred dollars. And when he had paid everything, and lifted the hundred-dollar note with Brissenden's lawyer, he still had over a hundred dollars in pocket. He ordered a suit of clothes from the tailor and ate his meals in the best cafes in town. He still slept in his little room at Maria's, but the sight of his new clothes caused the neighborhood children to cease from calling him "hobo" and "tramp" from the roofs of wood-sheds and over back fences.

"Wiki-Wiki," his Hawaiian short story, was bought by *Warren's Monthly* for two hundred and fifty dollars. The *Northern Review* took his essay, "The Cradle of Beauty," and *Mackintosh's Magazine* took "The Palmist"—the poem he had written to Marian. The editors and readers were back from their summer vacations, and manuscripts were being handled quickly. But Martin could not puzzle out what strange whim animated them to this general acceptance of the things they had persistently rejected for two years. Nothing of his had been published. He was not known anywhere outside of Oakland, and in Oakland, with the few who thought they knew him, he was notorious as a red-shirt and a socialist. So there was no explaining this sudden acceptability of his wares. It was sheer jugglery of fate.

After it had been refused by a number of magazines, he had taken Brissenden's rejected advice and started "The Shame of the Sun" on the round of publishers. After several refusals, Singletree, Darnley & Co. accepted it, promising fall publication. When Martin asked for an advance on royalties, they wrote that such was not their custom, that books of that nature rarely paid for themselves, and that they doubted if his book would sell a thousand copies. Martin figured what the book would earn him on such a sale. Retailed at a dollar, on a royalty of fifteen per cent, it would bring him one hundred and fifty dollars. He decided that if he had to do over again he would confine himself to fiction. "Adventure," one-fourth as long, had brought him twice as much from the *Millennium.* That newspaper paragraph he had read so long ago had been true after all. The first-class magazines did pay on acceptance, and they paid well. Not two cents a word, but four cents a word, had the *Millennium* paid him. And furthermore, they bought good stuff, too, for were they not buying his?—this last thought he accompanied with a grin.

He wrote to Singletree, Darnley & Co., offering to sell out his rights in "The Shame of the Sun" for a hundred dollars, but they did not care to take the risk. In the meantime he was not in need of money, for several of his later stories had been accepted and paid for. He actually opened a bank account, where, without a debt in the world, he had several hundred dollars to his credit. "Overdue," after having been declined by a number of magazines, came to rest at the Meredith-Lowell Company. Martin remembered the five dollars Gertrude had given him, and his resolve to return it to her a hundred times over; so he wrote for an advance on royalties of five hundred dollars. To his surprise a check for that amount, accompanied by a contract, came by return mail. He cashed the check into five-dollar gold pieces and telephoned Gertrude that he wanted to see her.

She arrived at the house, panting and short of breath from the haste she had made. Apprehensive of trouble, she had stuffed the few dollars she possessed into her hand-satchel; and so sure was she that disaster had overtaken her brother, that she stumbled forward, sobbing, into his arms, at the same time thrusting the satchel mutely at him.

"I 'd have come myself," he said. "But I did n't want a row with Mr. Higginbotham, and that is what would have surely happened."

"He 'll be all right after a time," she assured him, while she wondered what the trouble was that Martin was in. "But you 'd best get a job first an' steady down. Bernard does like to see a man at honest work. That stuff in the newspapers broke 'm all up. I never saw'm so mad before."

"I'm not going to get a job," Martin said with a smile. "And you can tell him so from me. I dont need a job, and there 's the proof of it."

He emptied the hundred gold pieces into her lap in a glinting, tinkling stream.

"You remember that fiver you gave me the time I did n't have carfare? Well, there it is, with ninety-nine brothers of different ages but all of the same size."

If Gertrude had been frightened when she arrived, she was now in a panic of fear. Her fear was such that it was certitude. She was not suspicious. She was convinced. She looked at Martin in horror, and her heavy limbs shrank under the golden stream as though it were burning her.

"It 's yours," he laughed.

She burst into tears, and began to moan, "My poor boy, my poor boy."

He was puzzled for a moment. Then he divined the cause of her agitation and handed her the Meredith-Lowell letter which had accompanied the check. She stumbled through it, pausing now and again to wipe her eyes, and when she had finished, said:

"An' does it mean that you come by the money honestly?"

"More honestly than if I'd won it in a lottery. I earned it."

Slowly faith came back to her, and she re-read the letter carefully. It took him long to explain to her the nature of the transaction which had put the money into his possession, and longer still to get her to understand that the money was really hers and that he did not need it.

"I 'll put it in the bank for you," she said finally.

"You 'll do nothing of the sort. It 's yours, to do with as you please, and if you wont take it I 'll give it to Maria. She 'll know what to do with it. I 'd suggest, though, that you hire a servant and take a good long rest."

"I 'm going to tell Bernard all about it," she announced, when she was leaving.

Martin winced, then grinned.

"Yes, do," he said."And then, maybe, he 'll invite me to dinner again."

"Yes, he will—I 'm sure he will!" she exclaimed fervently, as she drew him to her and kissed and hugged him.

CHAPTER XLII.

ONE day Martin became aware that he was lonely. He was healthy and strong, and had nothing to do. The cessation from writing and studying, the death of Brissenden, and the estrangement from Ruth, had made a big hole in his life; and his life refused to be pinned down to good living in cafés and the smoking of Egyptian cigarettes. It was true, the South Seas were calling to him, but he had a feeling that the game was not yet played out in the United States. Two books were soon to be published, and he had more books that might find publication. Money could be made out of them, and he would wait and take a sackful of it into the South Seas. He knew a valley and a bay in the Marquesas that he could buy for a thousand Chili dollars. The valley ran from the horse-shoe, land-locked bay to the tops of the dizzy, cloud-capped peaks and contained perhaps ten thousand acres. It was filled with tropical fruits, wild chickens and wild pigs, with an occasional herd of wild cattle, while high up among the peaks were herds of wild goats harried by packs of wild dogs. The whole place was wild. Not a human lived in it. And he could buy it and the bay for a thousand Chili dollars.

The bay, as he remembered it, was magnificent, with water deep enough to accommodate the largest vessel afloat, and so safe that the South Pacific Directory recommended it as the best careening place for ships for hundreds of miles around. He would buy a schooner—one of those yacht-like, coppered crafts that sailed like witches—and go trading copra and pearling among the islands. He would make the valley and the bay his headquarters. He would build a patriarchial grass house like Tati's, and have it and the valley and the schooner filled with dark-skinned servitors. He would entertain there the factor of Taicohae, captains of wandering traders, and all the best of the South Pacific riff-raff. He would keep open house and entertain like a prince. And he would forget the books he had opened and the world that had proved an illusion.

To do all this he must wait in California to fill his sack with money. Already it was beginning to flow in. If one of the books made a strike, it might enable him to sell the whole heap of manuscripts. Also he could collect the stories and the poems into books, and make sure of the valley and the bay and the schooner. He would never write again. Upon that he was resolved. But in the meantime, awaiting the publication of the books, he must do something more than live dazed and stupid in the sort of uncaring trance into which he had fallen.

He noted, one Sunday morning, that the Bricklayers' Picnic took place that day at Shell Mound Park, and to Shell Mound Park he went. He had been to the working-class picnics too often in his earlier life not to know what they were like, and as he entered the park he experienced a recrudescence of all the old sensations. After all, they were his kind, those working people. He had been born among them, he had lived among them, and, though he had strayed for a time, it was well to come back among them.

"It it ain't Mart," he heard some one say, and the next moment a hearty hand was on his shoulder. "Where you ben all the time? Off to sea? Come on an' have a drink."

It was the old crowd in which he found himself—the old crowd, with here and there a gap, and here and there a new face. The fellows were not bricklayers, but, as in the old days, they attended all Sunday picnics for the dancing, and the fighting, and the fun. Martin drank with them, and began to feel really human once more. He was a fool to have ever left them, he thought; and he was very certain that his sum of happiness would have been greater had he remained with them and let alone the books and the people who sat in the high places. Yet the beer seemed not so good as of yore. It did n't taste as it used to taste. Brissenden had spoiled him for steam beer, he concluded, and wondered if, after all, the books had spoiled him for companionship with these friends of his youth. He resolved that he would not be so spoiled, and he went on to the dancing pavilion. Jimmy, the plumber, he met there, in the company of a tall, blond girl who promptly forsook him for Martin.

"Gee, it 's like old times," Jimmy explained to the gang that gave him the laugh as Martin and the blond whirled away in a waltz. "An' I dont give a rap. I 'm too damned glad to see 'm back. Watch 'm waltz, eh? It 's like silk. Who 'd blame any girl?"

But Martin restored the blond to Jimmy, and the three of them, with half a dozen friends, watched the revolving couples and laughed and joked with one another. Everybody was glad to see Martin back. No book of his had been published; he carried no fictitious value in their eyes. They liked him for himself. He felt like a prince returned from exile, and his lonely heart burgeoned in the geniality in which it bathed. He made a mad day of it, and was at his best. Also, he had money in his pockets, and, as in the old days when he returned from sea with a pay-day, he made the money fly.

Once, on the dancing-floor, he saw Lizzie Connolly go by in the arms of a young workingman; and, later, when he made the round of the pavilion, he came upon her sitting by a refreshment table. Surprise and greetings over, he led her away into the grounds where they could talk without shouting down the music. From the instant he spoke to her, she was his. He knew it. She showed it in the proud humility of her eyes, in every caressing movement of her proudly carried body, and in the way she hung upon his speech. She was not the young girl as he had known her. She was a woman, now, and Martin noted that her wild, defiant beauty had improved, losing none of its wildness, while the defiance and the fire seemed more in control. ''A beauty, a perfect beauty,'' he murmured admiringly under his breath. And he knew she was his, that all he had to do was to say, ''Come,'' and she would go with him over the world wherever he led.

Even as the thought flashed through his brain he received a heavy blow on the side of his head that nearly knocked him down. It was a man's fist, directed by a man so angry and in such haste that the fist had missed the jaw for which it was aimed. Martin turned as he staggered, and saw the fist coming at him in a wild swing. Quite as a matter of course he ducked, and the fist flew harmlessly past, pivoting the man who had driven it. Martin hooked with his left, landing on the pivoting man with the weight of his body behind the blow. The man went to the ground sidewise, leaped to his feet, and made a mad rush. Martin saw his passion-distorted face and wondered what could be the cause of the fellow's anger. But while he wondered he shot in a straight left, the weight of his body behind the blow. The man went over backward and fell in a crumpled heap. Jimmy and others of the gang were running toward them.

Martin was thrilling all over. This was the old days with a vengeance, with their dancing, and their fighting, and their fun. While he kept a wary eye on his antagonist, he glanced at Lizzie. Usually the girls screamed when the fellows got to scrapping, but she had not screamed. She was looking on with bated breath, leaning slightly forward, so keen was her interest, one hand pressed to her breast, her cheek flushed, and in her eyes a great and amazed admiration.

The man had gained his feet and was struggling to escape the restraining arms that were laid on him.

''She was waitin' for me to come back'' he was proclaiming to all and sundry. ''She was waitin' for me to come back, an' then that fresh guy comes buttin' in. Let go o' me, I tell yeh. I 'm goin' to fix 'm.''

''What 's eatin' yer?'' Jimmy was demanding, as he helped hold the young fellow back. ''That guy 's Mart Eden. He 's nifty with his mits, lemme tell you that, an' he 'll eat you alive if you monkey with 'm.''

''He can't steal her on me that way,'' theother interjected.

''He licked the Flyin' Dutchman, an' you know *him,''* Jimmy went on expostulating. ''An' he did it in five rounds. You could n't last a minute against him, see!''

This information seemed to have a mollifying effect, and the irate young man favored Martin with a measuring stare.

''He dont look it,'' he sneered ; but the sneer was without passion.

''That 's what the Flyin' Dutchman thought,'' Jimmy assured him. ''Come on, now, let 's get outa this. There 's lots of other girls. Come on.''

The young fellow allowed himself to be led away toward the pavilion, and the gang followed after him.

''Who is he?'' Martin asked Lizzie. ''And what 's it all about anyway?''

Already the zest of combat, which of old had been so keen and lasting, had died down, and he discovered that he was self-analytical, too much so to live, single heart and single hand, so primitive an existence.

Lizzie tossed her head.

''Oh, he 's nobody,'' she said. ''He 's just ben keepin' company with me.

''I had to, you see,'' she explained after a pause. ''I was gettin' pretty lonesome. But I never forgot.'' Her voice sank lower, and she looked straight before her. ''I 'd throw 'm down for you any time.''

Martin looking at her averted face, knowing that all he had to do was to reach out his hand and pluck her, fell to pondering whether, after all, there was any real worth in refined, grammatical English, and, so, forget to reply to her.

''You put it all over him,'' she said tentatively, with a laugh.

''He 's a husky young fellow, though,'' he admitted generously. ''If they had n't taken him away he might have given me my hands full.''

''Who was that lady friend I seen you with that night?'' she asked abruptly.

''Oh, just a lady friend,'' was his answer.

''It was a long time ago,'' she murmured contemplatively. ''It seems like a thousand years.''

But Martin went no further into the matter. He led the conversation off into other channels. They had lunch in the restaurant, where he ordered wine and expensive delicacies, and afterwards he danced with her and with no one but her, till she was tired. He was a good dancer, and she whirled around and around with him in a heaven of delight, her head against his shoulder, wishing that it could last forever. Later in the afternoon they strayed off among the trees, where, in the good old fashion, she sat down while he sprawled on his back, his head in her lap. He lay and dozed, while she fondled his hair, looked down on his closed eyes, and loved him without reserve. Looking up suddenly, he read the tender advertisement in her face. Her eyes fluttered down, then they opened and looked into his with soft defiance.

'I 've kept straight all these years,'' she said, her voice so low that it was almost a whisper.

In his heart Martin knew that it was the miraculous truth. And at his heart pleaded a great temptation. It was in his power to make her happy. Denied happiness himself, why should he deny happiness to her? He could marry her and take her down with him to dwell in the grass-walled castle in the Marquesas. The desire to do it was strong, but stronger still was the imperative command of his nature not to do it. In spite of himself he as still faithful to Love. The old days of license and easy living were gone. He could not bring them back, nor could he go back to them. He was changed—how changed he had not realized until now.

''I am not a marrying man, Lizzie,'' he said lightly.

The hand caressing his hair paused perceptibly, then went on with the same gentle stroke. He noticed her face harden, but it was with the hardness of resolution, for still the soft color was in her cheeks and she was all glowing and melting.

''I did not mean that—'' she began, then faltered. ''Or anyway I dont care.

''I dont care,'' she repeated. ''I 'm proud to be your friend. I' do anything for you. I 'm made that way, I guess.''

Martin sat up. He took her hand in his. He did it deliberately, with warmth but without passion; and such warmth chilled her.

''Dont let 's talk about it,'' she said.

''You are a great and noble woman,'' he said. ''And it is I who should be proud to know you. And I am, I am. You are a ray of light to me in a very dark world, and I 've got to be straight with you, just as you have been.''

''I dont care whether you 're straight with me or not. You could do anything with me. You could throw me in the dirt an' walk on me. An' you 're the only man in the world that can,'' she added, with a defiant flash. ''I ain't taken care of myself ever since I was a kid for nothin'.''

''And it 's just because of that that I 'm not going to,'' he said gently. ''You are so big and generous that you challenge me to equal generousness. I 'm not marrying, and I 'm not—well, loving without marrying, though I 've done my share in the past. I 'm sorry I came here today and met you. But it can 't be helped now, and I never expected it would turn out this way.

''But look here, Lizzie. I can't begin to tell you how much I like you. I do more than like you. I admire and respect you. You are magnificent, and you are magnificently good. But what 's the use of words? Yet there 's something I 'd like to do. You 've had a hard life; let me make it easy for you." (A joyous light welled into her eyes, then faded out again). "I 'm pretty sure of getting hold of some money soon—lots of it."

In that moment he abandoned the idea of the valley and the bay, the grass-walled castle and the trim, white schooner. After all, what did it matter? He could go away, as he had done so often, before the mast, on any ship bound anywhere.

"I 'd like to turn it over to you. There must be something you want—to go to school or business college. You might like to study and be a stenographer. I could fix it for you. Or maybe your father and mother are living—I could set them up in a grocery store or something. Anything you want, just name it, and I can fix it for you."

She made no reply, but sat, gazing straight before her, dry-eyed and motionless, but with an ache in the throat which Martin divined so strongly that it made his own throat ache. He regretted that he had spoken. It seemed so tawdry what he had offered her—mere money—compared with what she offered him. He offered her an extraneous thing with which he could part without a pang, while she offered him herself, along with disgrace and shame, and sin, and all her hopes of heaven.

"Don't let 's talk about it," she said, with a catch in her voice that she changed to a cough. She stood up. "Come on, let 's go home. I 'm all tired out."

The day was done, and the merry-makers had nearly all departed. But as Martin and Lizzie emerged from the trees they found the gang waiting for them. Martin knew immediately the meaning of it. Trouble was brewing. The gang was his bodyguard. They passed out through the gates of the park with straggling in the rear a second gang, the friends that Lizzie's young man had collected to avenge the loss of his lady. Several constables and special police officers, anticipating trouble, trailed along to prevent it, and herded the two gangs separately aboard the train for San Francisco. Martin told Jimmy that he would get off at Sixteenth Street Station and catch the electric car into Oakland. Lizzie was very quiet and without interest in what was impending. The train pulled in to Sixteenth Street Station, and the waiting electric car could be seen, the conductor of which was impatiently clanging the gong.

"There she is," Jimmy counseled. "Make a run for it, an' we 'll hold 'em back. Now you go! Hit her up!"

The hostile gang was temporarily disconcerted by the maneuver, then it dashed from the train in pursuit. The staid and sober Oakland folk who sat upon the car scarcely noted the young fellow and the girl who ran for it and found a seat in front on the outside. They did not connect the couple with Jimmy, who sprang on the steps, crying to the motorman:

"Slam on the juice, old man, an' beat it outa here!"

The next moment Jimmy whirled about, and the passengers saw him land his fist on the face of a running man who was trying to board the car. But fists were landing on faces the whole length of the car. Thus, Jimmy and his gang, strung out on the long, lower steps, met the attacking gang. The car started with a great clanging of its gong, and, as Jimmy's gang drove off the last of the assailants, it, too, jumped off to finish up the job. The car dashed on, leaving the flurry of combat far behind, and its dumfounded passengers never dreamed that the quiet young man and the pretty working-girl sitting in the corner on the outside seat, had been the cause of the row.

Martin had enjoyed the fight, with a recrudescence of the old fighting thrills. But they quickly died away, and he was oppressed by a great sadness. He felt very old—centuries older than those careless, care-free young companions of his other days. He had traveled far, too far to go back. Their mode of life, which had once been his, was now distasteful to him. He was disappointed in it all. He had developed into an alien. As the steam beer had tasted raw, so their companionship seemed raw to him. He was too far removed. Too many thousands of opened books yawned between them and him. He had exiled himself. He had traveled in the vast realms of intellect until he could no longer return home. On the other hand, he was human, and his gregarious need for companionship remained unsatisfied. He had found no new home. As the gang could not understand him, as his own family could not understand him, as the bourgeoisie could not understand him, so this girl beside him, whom he honored high, could not understand him nor the honor he paid her. His sadness was not untouched with bitterness as he thought it over.

"Make it up with him," he advised Lizzie, at parting, as they stood in front of the workingman's shack in which she lived near Sixth and Market. He referred to the young fellow whose place he had usurped that day.

"I can't—now," she said.

"Oh, go on," he said jovially. "All you have to do is whistle and he 'll come running."

"I did n't mean that," she said simply.

And he knew what she had meant.

She leaned toward him as he was about to say good night. But she leaned, not imperatively, not seductively, but wistfully and humbly. He was touched to the heart. His large tolerance rose up in him. He put his arms around her and kissed her, and knew that upon his own lips rested as true a kiss as man ever received.

"My God," she sobbed. "I could die for you. I could die for you."

She tore herself from him suddenly and ran up the steps. He felt a quick moisture in his eyes.

"Martin Eden," he communed. "You 're not a brute, and you 're a damn poor Nietzscheman. You 'd marry her if you could and fill her quivering heart full with happiness. But you can't, you can't. And it 's a damn shame.

"The poor old tramp explains his poor old ulcers'," he muttered, remembering his Henley. "'Life is, I think, a blunder and a shame.' It is—a blunder and a shame."

CHAPTER XLIII.

THE Shame of the Sun" was published in October. As Martin cut the cords of the express package and the half-dozen complimentary copies from the publishers spilled out on the table, a heavy sadness fell upon him. He thought of the wild delight that would have been his had this happened a few short months before, and he contrasted that delight that should have been with his present uncaring coldness. His book, his first book, and his pulse had not gone up a fraction of a beat, and he was only sad. It meant little to him now. The most it meant was that it might bring some money, and little enough did he care for money.

He carried a copy out in the kitchen and presented it to Maria.

"I did it," he explained, in order to clear up her bewilderment. "I wrote it in the room there, and I guess some few quarts of your vegetable soup went into the making of it. Keep it. It 's yours. Just to remember me by, you know."

He was not bragging, not showing off. His sole motive was to make her happy, to make her proud of him, to justify her long faith in him. She put the book in the front room on top the family Bible. A sacred thing was this book her lodger had made, a fetich of friendship. It softened the blow of his having been a laundryman, and though she could not understand a line of it, she knew that every line of it was great. She was a simple, practical, hard-working woman, but she possessed faith in large endowment.

Just as emotionlessly as he had received "The Shame of the Sun" did he read the reviews of it that came in weekly from the clipping bureau. The book was making a hit, that was evident. It meant more gold in the money sack. He could fix up Lizzie, redeem all his promises, and still have enough left to build his grass-walled castle.

Singletree, Darnly & Co. had cautiously brought out an edition of fifteen hundred copies, but the first reviews had started a second edition of twice the size through the presses; and ere this was delivered a third edition of five thousand had been ordered. A London firm made arrangements by cable for an English edition, and hot-footed upon this came the news of French, German, and Scandinavian translations in progress. The attack upon the Maeterlinck School could not have been made at a more opportune moment. A fierce controversy was precipitated. Saleeby and Haeckel indorsed and defended "The Shame of the Sun," for once finding themselves on the same side of a question. Crookes and Wallace ranged up on the opposing side, while Sir Oliver Lodge attempted to formulate a compromise that would jibe with his particular cosmic theories. Maeterlinck's followers rallied around the standard of mysticism. Chesterton set the whole world laughing with a series of alleged non-partisan essays on the subject; and the whole affair, controversy and controversialists, was well-nigh swept into the pit by a thundering broadside from George Bernard Shaw. Needless to say the arena was crowded with hosts of lesser lights, and the dust and swear and din became terrific.

"It is a most marvelous happening," Singletree, Darnley & Co. wrote Martin, "a critical, philosophical essay selling like a novel. You could not have chosen your subject better, and all contributory factors have been unwarrantedly propitious. We need scarcely to assure you that we are making hay while the sun shines. Over 40,000 copies have already been sold in the United States and Canada, and a new edition of 20,000 is on the presses. We are overworked trying to supply the demand. Nevertheless we have helped to create that demand. We have already spent five thousand dollars in advertising. The book is bound to be a record-breaker.

"Please find herewith a contract in duplicate for your next book which we have taken the liberty of forwarding to you. You will please note that we have increased your royalties to twenty per cent, which is about as high as a conservative publishing house dares go. If our offer is agreeable to you, please fill in the proper blank space with the title of your book. We make no stipulations concerning its nature. Any book on any subject. If you have one already written, so much the better. Now is the time to strike. The iron could not be hotter.

"On receipt of signed contract we shall be pleased to make you an advance on royalties of five thousand dollars. You see, we have faith in you, and we are going in on this thing big. We should like, also, to discuss with you the drawing up of a contract for a term of years, say ten, during which we shall have the exclusive right of publishing in book-form all that you produce. But more of this anon."

Martin laid down the letter and worked a problem in mental arithmetic, finding the product of fifteen cents times 60,000 to be nine thousand dollars. He signed the new contract, inserting "The Smoke of Joy" in the blank space, and mailed it back to the publishers along with the twenty storiettes he had written in the days before he discovered the formula for the newspaper storiette. And promptly as the United States mail could deliver and return, came Singletree, Darnley & Co.'s check for five thousand dollars.

"I want you to come down town with me, Maria, this afternoon about two o'clock," Martin said, the morning the check arrived. "Or, better, meet me at Fourteenth and Broadway at two o'clock. I 'll be looking out for you."

At the appointed time she was there; but *shoes* was the only clew to the mystery her mind had been capable of evolving, and she suffered a distinct shock of disappointment when Martin walked her right by a shoe-store and dived into a real-estate office. What happened thereupon resided forever after in her memory as a dream. Fine gentlemen smiled at her benevolently as they talked with Martin and one another; a typewriter clicked; signatures were affixed to an imposing document; her own landlord was there, too, and affixed his signature; and when all was over and she was outside on the sidewalk, her landlord spoke to her, saying: "Well, Maria, you wont have to pay me no seven dollars and a half this month."

Maria was too stunned for speech.

"Or next month, or the next, or the next," her landlord said.

She thanked him incoherently, as if for a favor. And it was not until she had returned home to North Oakland and conferred with her own kind, and had the Portuguese grocer investigate, that she really knew that she was the owner of the little house in which she had lived and for which she had paid rent so long.

"Why dont you trade with me no more?" the Portuguese grocer asked Martin that evening, stepping out to hail him when he got off the car; and Martin explained that he was n't doing his own cooking any more, and then went in and had a drink of wine on the house. He noted it was the best wine the grocer had in stock.

"Maria," Martin announced that night, "I 'm going to leave you. And you 're going to leave here yourself soon. Then you can rent the house and be a landlord yourself. You 've a brother in San Leandro or Haywards, and he 's in the milk business. I want you to send all your washing back unwashed—understand?—unwashed, and to go out to San Leandro tomorrow, or Haywards, or wherever it is, and see that brother of yours. Tell him to come to see me. I 'll be stopping at the Metropole down in Oakland. He 'll know a good milk ranch when he sees one."

And so it was that Maria became a landlord and the sole owner of a dairy, with two hired men to do the work for her and a bank account that steadily increased despite the fact that her whole brood wore shoes and went to school. Few persons ever meet the fairy princes they dream about; but Maria, who worked hard and whose head was hard, had never dreamed about fairy princes, entertained hers in the guise of an ex-laundryman.

In the meantime the world had begun to ask: "Who is this Martin Eden?" He had declined to give any biographical data to his publishers, but the newspapers were not to be denied. Oakland was his own town, and the reporters nosed out scores of individuals who could supply information. All that he was and was not, all that he had done and most of what he had not done, was spread out for the delectation of the public, accompanied by snapshots and photographs—the latter procured from the local photographer who had once taken Martin's picture and who promptly copyrighted it and put it on the market. At first, so great was his disgust with the magazines and all bourgeois society, Martin fought against publicity, but in the end, because it was easier than not to, he surrendered. He found that he could not refuse himself to the special writers who traveled long distances to see him. Then again, each day was so many hours long, and, since he no longer was occupied with writing and studying, those hours had to be occupied somehow; so he yielded to what was to him a whim, permitted interviews, gave his opinions on literature and philosophy, and even accepted invitations of the bourgeoisie. He had settled down into a strange and comfortable state of mind. He no longer cared. He forgave everybody, even the cub reporter who had painted him red and to whom he now granted a full page with specially posed photographs.

He saw Lizzie occasionally, and it was patent that she regretted the greatness that had come to him. It widened the space between them. Perhaps it was with the hope of narrowing it that she yielded to his persuasions to go to night school and business college and to have herself gowned by a wonderful dressmaker who charged outrageous prices. She improved visibly from day to day, until Martin wondered if he was doing right, for he knew that all her compliance and endeavor was for his sake. She was trying to make herself of worth in his eyes—of the sort of worth he seemed to value. Yet he gave her no hope, treating her in a brotherly fashion and rarely seeing her.

"Overdue" was rushed upon the market by the Meredith-Lowell Company in the height of his popularity, and being fiction, in point of sales it made even a bigger strike than "The Shame of the Sun." Week after week his was the credit of the unprecedented performance of having two books at the head of the list of best-sellers. Not only did the story take with the fiction-readers, for those who read "The Shame of the Sun" with avidity were likewise attracted to the sea-story by the cosmic grasp of mastery with which he had handled it. First, he had attacked the literature of mysticism, and done it exceeding well; and, next, he had successfully supplied the very literature he had exposited, thus proving himself to be that rare genius, a critic and a creator in one.

Money poured in on him, fame poured in on him, he flashed comet-like through the world of literature, and he was more amused than interested by the stir he was making. One thing was puzzling him, a little thing that would have puzzled the world had it known. But the world would have puzzled over his bepuzzlement, rather than over the little thing that to him loomed gigantic. Judge Blount invited him to dinner. That was the little thing or the beginning of the little thing, that was soon to become the big thing. He had insisted Judge Blount, treated him abominably, and Judge Blount, meeting him on the street, invited him to dinner. Martin bethought himself of the numerous occasions on which he had met Judge Blount at the Morse's and when Judge Blount had not invited him to dinner. Why had he not invited him to dinner then? he asked himself. He had not changed. He was the same Martin Eden. What made the difference? The fact that the stuff he had written had appeared inside the covers of books? But it was work performed. It was not something he had done since. It was achievement accomplished at the very time Judge Blount was sharing this general view and sneering at his Spencer and his intellect. Therefore it was not for any real value, but for a purely fictitious value that Judge Blount invited him to dinner.

Martin grinned and accepted the invitation, marveling the while at his complacence. And at the dinner, where, with their women-kind, were half a dozen of those that sat in high places, and where Martin found himself quite the lion, Judge Blount, warmly seconded by Judge Hanwell, urged privately that Martin should permit his name to be put up for the Styx—the ultra-select club to which belonged, not the mere men of wealth, but the men of attainment. And Martin declined, and was more puzzled than ever.

He was kept busy disposing of his heap of manuscripts. He was overwhelmed by requests from editors. It had been discovered that he was a stylist, with meat under his style. The *Northern Review*, after publishing "The Cradle of Beauty," had written him for half a dozen similar essays, which would have been supplied out of the heap had not *Burton's Magazine*, in a speculative mood, offered him five hundred dollars each for five essay. He remembered that all these manuscripts had been refused by the very magazines that were now clamoring for them. And their refusals had been cold-blooded, automatic, stereotyped. They had made him sweat, and now he intended to make them sweat. *Burton's Magazine* paid his price for five essays, and the remaining four, at the same rate, were snapped up by *Mackintosh's Monthly,* the *Northern Review* being too poor to stand the pace. Thus went out to the world "The High Priests of Mystery," "The Wonder-Dreamers," "The Yard-stick of the Ego," "Philosophy of Illusion," "God and Clod," "Art and Biology," "Critics and Test Tubes," "Star-Dust," and "The Dignity of Usury"—to raise storms and rumblings and mutterings that were many a day in dying down.

Editors wrote to him, telling him to name his own terms, which he did, but it was always for work performed. He refused resolutely to pledge himself to any new thing. The thought of again setting pen to paper maddened him. He had seen Brissenden torn to pieces by the crowd, and despite the fact that him the crowd acclaimed, he could not get over the shock nor gather any respect for the crowd. His very popularity seemed a disgrace and a treason to Brissenden. It made him wince, but he made up his mind to go on and fill the money-bag.

He received letters from editors like the following : "About a year ago we were unfortunate enough to refuse your collection of love poems. We were greatly impressed by them at the time, but certain arrangements already entered into prevented our taking them. If you still have them, and if you will be kind enough to forward them, we shall be glad to publish the entire collection on your own terms. We are also prepared to make a most advantageous offer for bringing them out in book-form."

Martin recollected his blank-verse tragedy, and sent it instead. He read it over before mailing, and was particularly impressed by its sophomoric amateurishness and general rottenness. But he sent it; and it was published, to the everlasting regret of the editor. The public was indignant and incredulous. It was too far a cry from Martin Eden's high standard to that serious bosh. It was asserted that he had never written it, that the magazine faked it very clumsily, or that Martin Eden was emulating the elder Dumas and at the height of success was hiring his writing done for him. But when he explained that the tragedy was an early effort of his literary childhood, and that the magazine had refused to be happy unless it got it, a great laugh went up at the magazine's expense and a change in the editorship followed. The tragedy was never brought out in book-form, though Martin pocketed the advance royalties that had been paid.

Coleman's Weekly sent Martin a lengthy telegram, costing nearly three hundred dollars, offering him a thousand dollars an article for twenty articles. He was to travel over the United States, with all expenses paid, and select whatever topics interested him. The body of the telegram was devoted to hypothetical topics in order to show him the freedom of range that was to be his. The only restriction placed upon him was that he must confine himself to the United States. Martin sent his inability to accept and his regrets by wire "collect."

"Wiki-Wiki," published in *Warren's Monthly,* was an instantaneous success. It was brought out afterward in a wide-margined, beautifully decorated volume that struck the holiday trade and sold like wildfire. The critics were unanimous in the belief that it would take its place with those two classics by two great writers, "The Bottle Imp" and "The Magic Skin."

The public, however, received the "Smoke of Joy" collection rather dubiously and coldly. The audacity and unconventionality of the storiettes was a shock to bourgeois morality and prejudice; but when Paris went mad over the immediate translation that was made, the American and English reading public followed suit and bought so many copies that Martin compelled the conservative house of Singletree, Darnley & Co. to pay a flat royalty of twenty-five per cent for a third book, and thirty per cent flat for a fourth. These two volumes comprised all the short stories he had written and which had received, or were receiving, serial publication. "The Ring of Bells" and his horror stories constituted one collection; the other collection was composed of "Adventure," "The Pot," "Wine of Life," "The Whirlpool," "The Jostling Street," and four other stories. The Lowell-Meredith Company captured the collection of all his essays, and the Maxmillian Company got his "Sea Lyrics" and the "Love-Cycle," the latter receiving serial publication in the *Ladies' Home Companion* after the payment of an extortionate price.

Martin heaved a sigh of relief when he had disposed of the last manuscript. The grass-walled castle and the white, coppered schooner were very near to him. Well, at any rate he had disproved Brissenden's contention that nothing of merit found its way into the magazines. His own success demonstrated that Brissenden had been wrong. And yet, somehow, he had a feeling that Brissenden had been right after all. "The Shame of the Sun" had been the cause of his success more than the stuff he had written. That stuff had been merely incidental. It had been rejected right and left by the magazines. The publication of "The Shame of the Sun" had started a controversy and precipitated the landslide, in his favor. Had there been no "Shame of the Sun," there would have been no landslide, and had there been no miracle in the go of "The Shame of the Sun" there would have been no landslide. Singletree, Darnley & Company attested that miracle. They had brought out a first edition of fifteen hundred copies and been dubious of selling it. They were experienced publishers and no one had been more astounded than they at the success which had followed. To them it had been in truth a miracle. They never got over it, and every letter they wrote him reflected their reverent awe of that first mysterious happening. They did not attempt to explain it. There was no explaining it. It had happened. In the face of all experience to the contrary, it had happened.

So it was, reasoning thus, that Martin questioned the validity of his popularity. It was the bourgeoisie that bought his books and poured its gold into his money sack, and from what little he knew of how it could possibly appreciate or comprehend what he had written. His intrinsic beauty and power meant nothing to the hundreds of thousands who were acclaiming him and buying his books. He was the fad of the hour, the adventurer who had stormed Parnassus while the gods nodded. The hundreds of thousands read him and acclaimed him with the same brute non-understanding with which they had flung themselves on Brissenden's "Ephemera" and torn it to pieces—a wolf-rabble that fawned on him instead of fanging him. Fawn or fang, it was all a matter of chance. One thing he knew with absolute certitude. "Ephemera" was infinitely greater than anything he had done. It was infinitely greater than anything he had in him. It was a poem of centuries. Then the tribute the mob paid him was a sorry tribute indeed, for that same mob had wallowed "Ephemera" into the mire. He sighed heavily and with satisfaction. He was glad the last manuscript was sold; that he would soon be done with it all.

Martin Eden

By Jack London

Author of "The Call of the Wild," "Sea Wolf," "The God of His Fathers," "White Fang," etc.

CHAPTER XLIV.

MR. MORSE met Martin in the office of the Hotel Metropole. Whether he had happened there just casually, intent on other affairs, or whether he had come there for the direct purpose of inviting him to dinner, Martin never could quite make up his mind, though he inclined toward the second hypothesis. At any rate, invited to dinner he was by Mr. Morse—Ruth's father—who had forbidden him the house and broken off the engagement.

Martin was not angry. He was not even on his dignity. He tolerated Mr. Morse, wondering the while how it felt to eat such humble pie. He did not decline the invitation. Instead, he put it off with vagueness and indefiniteness and inquired after the family, particularly after Mrs. Morse and Ruth. He spoke her name without hesitancy, naturally, though secretly surprised that he had had no inward quiver, no old, familiar increase of pulse and warm surge of blood.

He had many invitations to dinner, some of which he accepted. Persons got themselves introduced to him in order to invite him to dinner. And he went on puzzling over the little thing that was becoming a great thing. Bernard Higginbotham invited him to dinner. He puzzled the harder. He remembered the days of his desperate starvation, when no one invited him to dinner. That was the time he needed dinners, and went weak and faint for lack of them and lost weight from sheer famine. That was the paradox of it. When he wanted dinners no one gave them to him, and now that he could buy a hundred thousand dinners and was losing his appetite dinners were thrust upon him right and left. But why? There was no justice in it, no merit on his part. He was no different. All the work he had done was even at that time work performed. Mr. and Mrs. Morse had condemned him for an idler and a shirk, and through Ruth had urged that he take a clerk's position in an office. Furthermore, they had been aware of his work performed. Manuscript after manuscript of his had been turned over to them by Ruth. They had read them. It was the very same work that had put his name in all the papers, and his name being in all the papers led them to invite him.

One thing was certain: the Morses had not cared to have him for himself or for his work. Therefore they could not want him now for himself or for his work, but for the fame that was his, because he was somebody amongst men, and—why not?—because he had a hundred thousand dollars or so. That was the way bourgeois society valued a man, and who was he to expect it otherwise? But he was proud. He disdained such valuation. He desired to be valued for himself, or for his work, which, after all, was an expression of himself. That was the way Lizzie valued him. The work, with her, did not even count. She valued him, himself. That was the way Jimmy, the plumber, and all the old gang valued him. That had been proved often enough in the days when he ran with them; it had been proved that Sunday at Shell Mound Park. His work could go hang. What they liked, and were willing to scrap for, was just Mart Eden—one of the bunch, a pretty good guy.

Then there was Ruth. She had liked him for himself; that was indisputable. And yet, much as she had liked him, she had liked the bourgeois standard of valuation more. She had opposed his writing, and, principally, it seemed to him, because it did not earn money. That had been her criticism of his Love Cycle. She, too, had urged him to get a job. It was true she refined it to "position," but it meant the same thing, and in his own mind the old nomenclature stuck. He had read her all that he wrote—poems, stories, essays—"Wiki-Wiki," "The Shame of the Sun," everything. And she had always and consistently urged him to get a job, to go to work—Good God! as if he had n't been working, robbing sleep, exhausting life, in order to be worthy of her.

So the little thing grew bigger. He was healthy and normal, ate regularly, slept long hours, and yet the growing little thing was becoming an obsession. *Work performed.* The phrase haunted his brain. He sat opposite Bernard Higginbotham at a heavy Sunday dinner over Higginbotham's Cash Store, and it was all he could do to restrain himself from shouting out:

"It was work performed! And now you feed me, when then you let me starve, forbade me your house, and damned me because I would'nt get a job. And the work was already done, all done. And now, when I speak, you check the thought unuttered on your lips and hang on my lips and pay respectful attention to whatever I choose to say. I tell you your party is rotten and filled with grafters, and instead of flying into a rage you hum and haw and admit there is a great deal in what I say. And why? Because I'm famous; because I've a lot of money. Not because I'm Martin Eden, a pretty good fellow and not particularly a fool. I could tell you the moon is made of green cheese and you would subscribe to the notion; at least you would not repudiate it, because I've got dollars, mountains of them. And it was all done long ago; it was work performed, I tell you, when you spat upon me as the dirt under your feet."

But Martin did not shout out. The thought gnawed in his brain, an unceasing torment, while he smiled and succeeded in being tolerant. As he grew silent Bernard Higginbotham got the reins and did the talking. He was a success himself, and proud of it. He was self-made. No one had helped him. He owed no man. He was fulfilling his duty as a citizen and bringing up a large family. And there was Higginbotham's Cash Store, that monument of his own industry and ability. He loved Higginbotham's Cash Store as some men loved their wives. He opened up his heart to Martin, showed with what keenness and with what enormous planning he had made the store. And he had plans for it, ambitious plans. The neighborhood was growing up fast. The store was really too small. If he had more room he would be able to put in a score of labor-saving and money-saving improvements. And he would do it yet. He was straining every effort for the day when he could buy the adjoining lot and put up another two-story frame building. The upstairs he could rent, and the whole ground floor of both buildings would be Higginbotham's Cash Store. His eyes glistened when the spoke of the new sign that would stretch clear across both buildings.

Martin forgot to listen. The refrain of "Work performed" in his own brain was drowning the other's clatter. The refrain maddened him, and he tried to escape from it.

"How much did you say it would cost?" he asked suddenly.

His brother-in-law paused in the middle of an expatiation on the business opportunities of the neighborhood. He had n't said how much it would cost. But he knew. He had figured it out a score of times.

"At the way lumber is now," he said, "four thousand could do it."

"Including the sign?"

"I did n't count on that. It'd just have to come, onc't the buildin' was there."

"And the ground?"

"Three thousand more."

He leaned forward, licking his lips, nervously spreading and closing his fingers, while he watched Martin write a check. When it was passed over to him he glanced at the amount—seven thousand dollars.

"I—I cant afford to pay more than six per cent," he said huskily.

Martin wanted to laugh, but, instead, demanded:

"How much would that be?"

"Lemme see. Six per cent—six times seven—four hundred an' twenty."

"That would be thirty-five dollars a

month, would n't it?''

Higginbotham nodded.

''Then, if you've no objection, we'll arrange it this way.'' Martin glanced at Gertrude. ''You can have the principal to keep for yourself, if you'll use the thirty-five dollars a month for cooking and washing and scrubbing. The seven thousand is yours if you'll guarantee that Gertrude does no more drudgery. Is it a go?''

Mr. Higginbotham swallowed hard.

That his wife should do no more housework was an affront to his thrifty soul. The magnificent present was the coating of a pill, a bitter pill. That his wife should not work! It gagged him.

''All right, then,'' Martin said. ''I'll pay the thirty-five a month, and——''

He reached across the table for the check. But Bernard Higginbotham got his hand on it first, crying:

''I accept! I accept!''

When Martin got on the electric car he was very sick and tired. He looked up at the assertive sign.

''The swine,'' he groaned. ''The swine, the swine.''

When *Mackintosh's Magazine* published ''The Palmist,'' featuring it with decorations by Berthier and with two pictures by Wenn, Herrmann von Schmidt forgot that he had called the verses obscene. He announced that his wife had inspired the poem, saw to it that the news reached the ears of a reporter, and submitted to an interview by a staff writer who was accompanied by a staff photographer and a staff artist. The result was a full page in a Sunday supplement; filled with photographs and idealized drawings of Marian, with many intimate details of Martin Eden and his family, and with the full text of ''The Palmist'' in large type and republished by special permission of *Mackintosh's Magazine*. It caused quite a stir in the neighborhood, and good housewives were proud to have the acquaintance of the great writer's sister, while those who had not made haste to cultivate it. Herrmann von Schmidt chuckled in his little repair shop and decided to order a new lathe. ''Better than advertising,'' he told Marian, ''and it costs nothing.''

''We'd better have him to dinner,'' she suggested.

And to dinner Martin came, making himself agreeable with the fat wholesale butcher and his fatter wife—important folk, they, likely to be of use to a rising young man like Herrmann von Schmidt. No less a bait, however, had been required to draw them to his house than his great brother-in-law. Another man at table, who had swallowed the same bait, was the superintendent of the Pacific Coast agencies for the Asa Bicycle Company. Him von Schmidt desired to please and propitiate because from him could be obtained the Oakland agency for the bicycle. So Herrmann von Schmidt found it a goodly asset to have Martin for a brother-in-law, but in his heart of hearts he could n't understand where it all came in. In the silent watches of the night, while his wife slept, he had floundered through Martin's books and poems and decided that the world was a fool to buy them.

And in his heart of hearts Martin understood the situation only too well, as he leaned back and gloated at von Schmidt's head, in fancy punching it well nigh off of him, sending blow after blow home just right—the chuckle-headed Dutchman! One thing he did like about him, however. Poor as he was, and determined to rise as he was, he nevertheless hired one servant to take the heavy work off of Marian's hands. Martin talked with the superintendent of the Asa agencies, and after dinner he drew him aside with Herrmann, whom he backed financially for the best bicycle store with fittings in Oakland. He went further and in a private talk with Herrmann told him to keep his eyes open for an automobile agency and garage, for there was no reason that he should not be able to run both establishments successfully.

With tears in her eyes and her arms around his neck Marian, at parting, told Martin how much she loved him and always had loved him. It was true there was a perceptible halt midway in her assertion, which she glossed over with more tears and kisses and incoherent stammerings, and which Martin inferred to be her appeal for forgiveness for the time when she had lacked faith in him and insisted on his getting a job.

''He cant never keep his money, that 's sure,'' Herrmann von Schmidt confided to his wife. "He got mad when I spoke of interest, an' he said 'damn the principal,' and if I mentioned it again he'd punch my Dutch head off. That's what he said—my Dutch head. But he 's all right, even if he aint no business man. He 's given me my chance, an' he 's all right."

Invitations to dinner poured in on Martin; and the more they poured the more he puzzled. He sat, the guest of honor, at an Alsatian Club banquet, with men of note whom he had heard about and read about all his life; and they told him how, when they had read "The Ring of Bells" in the *Occidental,* and "The Peri and the Pearl" in the *Hornet,* they had immediately picked him for a winner. My God! And I was hungry and in rags, he thought to himself. Why did n't you give me a dinner then? Then was the time. It was work performed. If you are feeding me now for work performed, why did you not feed me then when I needed it? Not one word in "The Ring of Bells," nor in "The Peri and the Pearl," has been changed. No; you're not feeding me now for work performed. You are feeding me because everybody else is feeding me and because it is an honor to feed me. You are feeding me now because you are herd animals, because you are a part of the mob; because the one blind, automatic thought in the mob-mind just now is to feed me. And where does Martin Eden and the work Martin Eden performed come in in all this? he asked himself plaintively; then arose to respond cleverly and wittily to a clever and witty toast.

So it went. Wherever he happened to be—at the Press Club, at the Redwood Club, at pink teas and literary gatherings; always was remembered "The Ring of Bells" and "The Peri and the Pearl" when they were first published. And always was Martin's maddening and unuttered demand: Why did n't you feed me then? It was work performed. "The Ring of Bells" and "The Peri and the Pearl" are not changed one iota. They were just as artistic, just as worth while then as now. But you are not feeding me for their sake, or for the sake of anything else I have written. You're feeding me because it is the style of feeding just now, because the whole mob is crazy with the idea of feeding Martin Eden.

And often, at such times, he would abruptly see slouch in among the company a young hoodlum in square-cut coat and under a stiff-rim Stetson hat. It happened to him at the Gallina Society in Oakland one afternoon. As he rose from his chair and stepped forward across the platform he saw stalk through the wide door at the rear of the great room the young hoodlum with the square-cut coat and stiff-rim hat. Five hundred fashionably-gowned women turned their heads, so intent and steadfast was Martin's gaze, to see what he was seeing. But they saw only the empty center aisle. He saw the young tough lurching down the aisle, and wondered if he would remove the stiff-rim which never yet had he seen him without. Straight down the aisle he came, and up the platform. Martin could have wept over that youthful shade of himself when he thought of all that lay before him. Across the platform he swaggered, right up to Martin, and into the foreground of Martin's consciousness disappeared. The five hundred women applauded softly with gloved hands, seeking to encourage the bashful great man who was their guest. And Martin shook the vision from his brain, smiled, and began to speak.

The superintendent of schools, good old man, stopped Martin on the street and remembered him, recalling seances in his office when Martin was expelled from school for fighting.

"I read your 'Ring of Bells' in one of the magazines quite a time ago," he said. "It was as good as Poe. Splendid, I said at the time, splendid."

Yes, and twice in the months that followed, you passed me on the street and did not know me, Martin almost said aloud. Each time I was hungry and heading for the pawnbroker. Yet it was work performed. You did not know me then. Why do you know me now?

"I was remarking to my wife only the other day," the other was saying, "would n't it be a good idea to have you out to dinner some time. And she quite agreed with me. Yes, she quite agreed with me."

"Dinner?" Martin said so sharply that it was almost a snarl.

"Why, yes, yes, dinner, you know—just pot luck with us, with your old superintendent, you rascal," he uttered nervously, nervously poking Martin in an attempt at jocular fellowship.

Martin went down the street in a daze. He stopped at the corner and looked about him vacantly.

"Well, I'll be damned!" he murmured at last. "The old fellow was afraid of me."

CHAPTER XLV.

KREISS came to Martin one day— Kreiss of the "real dirt," and Martin turned to him with relief, to receive the glowing details of a scheme sufficiently wild-catty to interest Martin as a fictionist rather than an investor. Kreiss paused long enough in the midst of his exposition to tell him that in most of his "Shame of the Sun" he had been a chump.

"But I did n't come here to spout philosophy," Kreiss went on. "What I want to know is whether or not you will put a thousand dollars in on this deal?"

"No, I'm not chump enough for that, at any rate," Martin answered. "But I'll tell you what I will do. You gave me the greatest night of my life. You gave me what money cannot buy. Now I've got money, and it means nothing to me. I'd like to turn over to you a thousand dollars of what I dont value for what you gave me that night and which was beyond price. You need the money. I've got more than I need. You want it. You came for it. There 's no use scheming it out of me. Take it."

Kreiss betrayed no surprise. He folded the check away in his pocket.

"At that rate, I'd like the contract of providing you with many such nights," he said.

"Too late." Martin shook his head. "That night was the one night for me. I was in paradise. It 's commonplace with you, I know. But it was n't to me. I shall never live at such a pitch again. I'm done with philosophy. I want never to hear another word of it."

"The first dollar I ever made in my life out of my philosophy," Kreiss remarked, as he paused in the doorway. "And then the market broke."

Mrs Morse drove by Martin on the street one day, and smiled and nodded. He smiled back and lifted his hat. The episode did not affect him. A month before it might have disgusted him, or made him curious and set him to speculating about her state of consciousness at that moment. But now it was not provocative of a second thought. He forgot about it the next moment. He forgot about it as he would have forgotten the Central Bank Building or the City Hall after having walked past them. Yet his mind was preternaturally active. His thoughts went ever around and around a circle. The center of that circle was "Work performed." It ate at his brain like a deathless maggot. He awoke to it in the morning. It tormented his dreams at night. Every affair of life around him that penetrated through his senses immediately related itself to "work performed." He drove along the path of relentless logic to the conclusion that he was nobody, nothing. Mart Eden, the hoodlum, and Mart Eden, the sailor, had been real, had been he; but Martin Eden, the famous writer, did not exist. Martin Eden, the famous writer, was a vapor that had arisen in the mob-mind and by the mob-mind had been thrust into the corporeal being of Mart Eden, the hoodlum and sailor. But it could n't fool him. He was not that sun-myth that the mob was worshiping and sacrificing dinners to. He knew better.

He read the magazines about himself and pored over portraits of himself published therein until he was unable to associate his identity with those portraits. He was the fellow who had lived and thrilled and loved; who had been easy-going and tolerant of the frailties of life; who had served in the forecastle, wandered in strange lands, and led his gang in the old fighting days. He was the fellow who had been stunned at first by the thousands of books in the free library, and who had afterwards learned his way among them and mastered them; he was the fellow who had burned the midnight oil and bedded with a spur and written books himself. But the one thing he was not was that colossal appetite that all the mob was bent upon feeding.

There were things, however, in the magazines that amused him. All the magazines were claiming him. *Warren's Monthly* advertised to its subscribers that it was always on the quest after new writers, and that, among others, it had introduced Martin Eden to the reading public. The *White Mouse* claimed him; so did the *Northern Review* and *Mackintosh's Magazine,* until silenced by *The Globe,* which pointed triumphantly to its files, where the mangled "Sea Lyrics" lay buried. *Youth and Age,* which had come to life again after having escaped paying its bills, put in a prior claim, which nobody but farmers' children ever read. The *Occidental* made a dignified and convincing statement of how it first discovered Martin Eden, which was warmly disputed by the *Hornet* with the exhibit of "The Peri and the Pearl." The modest claim of Singletree, Darnley & Co. was lost in the din. Besides, that publishing firm did not own a magazine wherewith to make its claim less modest.

The newspapers calculated Martin's royalties. In some way the magnificent offers certain magazines had made him leaked out, and Oakland ministers called upon him in a friendly way, while professional begging letters began to clutter his mail. But worse than all this were the women. His photographs were published broadcast and special writers exploited his strong, bronzed face, his scars, his heavy shoulders, his clear, quiet eyes, and the slight hollows in his cheeks like an ascetic's. At this last he remembered his wild youth, and smiled. Often, among the women he met, he would see now one, now another, looking at him, appraising him, selecting him. He laughed to himself. He remembered Brissenden's warning and laughed again. The women would never destroy him, that much was certain. He had gone past that stage.

Once, walking with Lizzie toward night school, she caught a glance directed toward him by a well-gowned, handsome woman of the bourgeoise. The glance was a trifle too long, a shade too considerative. Lizzie knew it for what it was, and her body tensed angrily. Martin noticed, noticed the cause of it; told her how used he was becoming to it, and that he did not care anyway.

"You ought to care," she answered with blazing eyes. "You're sick. That's what's the matter."

"Never healthier in my life. I weigh five pounds more than I ever did."

"It aint your body. It 's your head. Something 's wrong with your think-machine. Even I can see that, an' I aint nobody."

He walked on beside her, reflecting.

"I'd give anything to see you get over it," she broke out impulsively. "You ought to care when women look at you that way, a man like you. It 's not natural. It's all right enough for sissyboys. But you aint made that way. So help me, I'd be willing an' glad if the right woman came along an' made you care."

When he left Lizzie at night school he returned to the Metropole.

Once in his rooms he dropped into a chair and sat staring straight before him. He did not doze. Nor did he think. His mind was a blank, save for the intervals when unsummoned memory pictures took form and color and radiance just under his eyelids. He saw these pictures, but he was scarcely conscious of them—no more so than if they had been dreams. Yet he was not asleep. Once he roused himself and glanced at his watch. It was just eight o'clock. He had nothing to do, and it was too early for bed. Then his mind went blank again, and the pictures began to form and vanish under his eyelids. There was nothing distinctive about the pictures. They were always masses of leaves and shrub-like branches shot through and through with hot sunshine.

A knock at the door aroused him. He was not asleep, and his mind immediately connected the knock with a telegram, or letter, or perhaps one of the servants bringing back clean clothes from the laundry. He was thinking about Joe and wondering where he was, as he said: "Come in."

He was still thinking about Joe, and did not turn toward the door. He heard it close softly. There was a long silence. He forgot that there had been a knock at the door, and was still staring blankly before him when he heard a woman's sob. It was involuntary, spasmodic, checked and stifled—he noted that as he turned about. The next instant he was on his feet.

"Ruth!" he said, amazed and bewildered.

Her face was white and strained. She stood just inside the door, one hand against it for support, the other pressed to her side. She extended both hands toward him piteously, and started forward to meet him. As he caught her hands and led her to a chair he noticed how cold they were. He drew up another chair and sat down on the broad arm of it. He was too confused to speak. In his own mind his affair with Ruth was closed and sealed. He felt much in the same way that he would have felt had the Shelley Hot Springs Laundry suddenly invaded the Hotel Metropole with a whole week's washing ready for him to pitch into. Several times he was about to speak, and each time he hesitated.

"No one knows I am here," Ruth said in a faint voice, with an appealing smile.

"What did you say?" he asked.

He was surprised at the sound of his own voice.

She repeated her words.

"Oh," he said; then wondered what more he could possibly say.

"I saw you come in, and I waited a few minutes."

"Oh," he said again.

He had never been so tongue-tied in his life. Positively he did not have an idea in his head. He felt stupid and awkward, but for the life of him he could think of nothing to say. It would have been easier had the intrusion been the Shelley Hot Springs Laundry. He could have rolled up his sleeves and gone to work.

"And then you came in?" he said finally.

She nodded, with a slightly arch expression, and loosened the scarf at her throat.

"I saw you first from across the street when you were with that girl."

"Oh, yes," he said simply. "I took her down to night school."

"Well, are n't you glad to see me?" she said, at the end of another silence.

"Yes, yes." He spoke hastily. "But was n't it rash of you to come here?"

"I slipped in. Nobody knows I am here. I wanted to see you. I came to tell you I have been very foolish. I came because I could no longer stay away, because my heart compelled me to come, because—because I wanted to come."

She came forward, out of her chair and over to him. She rested her hand on his shoulder a moment, breathing quickly, and then slipped into his arms. And in his large, easy way, desirous of not inflicting hurt, knowing that to repulse this proffer of herself was to inflict the most grievous hurt a woman could receive, he folded his arms around her and held her close. But there was no warmth in the embrace, no caress in the contact. She had come into his arms, and he held her; that was all. She nestled against him, and then, with a change of position, her hands crept up and rested upon his neck. But his flesh was not fire beneath those hands, and he felt awkward and uncomfortable.

"What makes you tremble so?" he asked. "Is it a chill? Shall I light the grate?"

He made a movement to disengage himself, but she clung more closely to him, shivering violently.

"It is merely nervousness," she said, with chattering teeth. "I'll control myself in a minute. There, I am better already."

Slowly her shivering died away. He continued to hold her, but he was no longer puzzled. He knew now for what she had come.

"My mother wanted me to marry Charley Hapgood," she announced.

"Charley Hapgood, that fellow who speaks always in platitudes," Martin groaned. Then he added, "And now, I suppose, your mother wants you to marry me."

He did not put it in the form of a question. He stated it as a certitude, and before his eyes began to dance the rows of figures of his royalties.

"She will not object, I know that much," Ruth said.

"She considers me quite eligible?"

Ruth nodded.

"And yet I am not a bit more eligible now than I was when she broke our engagement," he meditated. "I have n't changed any. I'm the same Martin Eden, though for that matter I'm a bit worse—I smoke now. Dont you smell my breath?"

In reply she pressed her open fingers against his lips, placed them graciously and playfully, and in expectancy of the kiss that of old had always been a consequence. But there was no caressing answer of Martin's lips. He waited until the fingers were removed, and then went on.

"I am not changed. I have n't got a

job. I'm not looking for a job. Furthermore, I am not going to look for a job. And I still believe that Herbert Spencer is a great and noble man, and that Judge Blount is an unmitigated ass. I had dinner with him the other night, so I ought to know."

"But you did n't accept father's invitation," she chided.

"So you know about that? Who sent him? Your mother?"

She remained silent.

"Then she did send him. I thought so. And now I suppose she has sent you?"

"No one knows that I am here," she protested. "Do you think my mother would permit this?"

"She'd permit you to marry me, that 's certain."

She gave a sharp cry. "Oh, Martin, dont be cruel. You have not kissed me once. You are as unresponsive as a stone. And think what I have dared to do." She looked about her with a shiver, though half the look was curiosity. "Just think of where I am."

"*I could die for you! I could die for you!*"—Lizzie's words were ringing in his ears.

"Why did n't you dare it before?" he asked harshly. "When I had n't a job? When I was starving? When I was just as I am now, as a man, as an artist, the same Martin Eden? That's the question I've been propounding to myself for many a day—not concerning you merely, but concerning everybody. You see I have not changed, though my sudden apparent appreciation in value compels me constantly to reassure myself on that point. I've got the same flesh on my bones, the same ten fingers and toes. I am the same. I have not developed any new strength or virtue. My brain is the same old brain. I have n't made even one new generalization on literature or philosophy. I am personally of the same value that I was when nobody wanted me. And what is puzzling me is why they want me now. Surely they dont want me for myself, for myself is the same old self they did not want. Then they must want me for something else, for something that is outside of me, for something that is not I. Shall I tell you what that something is? It is for the recognition I have received. That recognition is not I. It resides in the minds of others. Then, again, for the money I have earned and am earning. But that money is not I. It resides in banks and in the pockets of Tom, Dick and Harry. And is it for that, for the recognition and the money, that you now want me?"

"You are breaking my heart," she sobbed. "You know I love you, that I am here because I love you."

"I am afraid you dont see my point," he said gently. "What I mean is, if you love me, how does it happen that you love me now so much more than you did when your love was weak enough to deny me?"

"Forget and forgive," she cried passionately. "I loved you all the time, remember that, and I am here now in your arms."

"I'm afraid I am a shrewd merchant, peering into the scales, trying to weigh your love and find out what manner of thing it is."

She withdrew herself from his arms, sat upright, and looked at him long and searchingly. She was about to speak, then faltered and changed her mind.

"You see, it appears this way to me," he went on. "When I was all that I am now nobody out of my own class seemed to care for me. When my books were all written no one who had read the manuscripts seemed to care for them. In point of fact, because of the stuff I had written, they seemed to care even less for me. In writing the stuff it seemed that I had committed acts that were, to say the least, derogatory. 'Get a job,' everybody said."

She made a movement of dissent.

"Yes, yes," he said, "except in your case you told me to get a position. The homely word *job,* like much that I have written, offends you. It is brutal. But I assure you it was no less brutal to me when everybody I knew recommended it to me as they would recommend right conduct to an immoral creature. But to return. The publication of what I had written, and the public notice I received, wrought a change in the fiber of your love. Martin Eden, with his work all performed, you would not marry. Your love for him was not strong enough to enable you to marry him. But your love is now strong enough, and I cannot avoid the conclusion that its strength arises from the publication and the public notice. In your case I do not mention royalties, though I am certain that they apply to the change wrought in your mother and father. Of course, all this is not flattering to me. But, worst of all, it makes me question Love, sacred Love. Is Love so gross a thing that it must feed upon publication and public notice? It would seem so. I have sat and thought upon it till my head went around.''

''Poor, dear head.'' She reached up a hand and passed the fingers soothingly through his hair. ''Let it go around no more. Let us begin anew, now. I loved you all the time. I know that I was weak in yielding to my mother's will. I should not have done so. Yet I have heard you speak so often with broad charity of the fallibility and frailty of humankind. Extend that charity to me. I acted mistakenly. Forgive me.''

''Oh, I do forgive,'' he said impatiently. ''It is easy to forgive where there is really nothing to forgive. Nothing that you have done requires forgiveness. One acts according to one's lights, and more than that one cannot do. As well might I ask you to forgive me for my not getting a job.''

''I meant well,'' she protested. ''You know that. I could not have loved you and not meant well.''

''True; but you would have destroyed me out of your well-meaning.

''Yes, yes,'' he shut off her attempted objection. ''You would have destroyed my writing and my success. Realism is imperative to my nature, and the bourgeoise spirit hates realism. The bourgeoise is cowardly. It is afraid of life. And all your effort was to make me afraid of life. You would have formalized me. You would have compressed me into a two-by-four pigeonhole of life, where all life's values are unreal, and false, and vulgar.'' He felt her stir protestingly. ''Vulgarity—a hearty vulgarity, I'll admit—is the basis of bourgeois refinement and culture. As I say, you wanted to formalize me, to make me over into one of your own class, with your class-ideals, class-values and class-prejudices.'' He shook his head sadly. ''And you do not understand, even now, what I am saying. My words do not mean to you what I endeavor to make them mean. What I say is so much fantasy to you. Yet to me it is vital reality. At the best you are a trifle puzzled and amused that this raw boy, crawling up out of the mire of the abyss, should pass judgment upon your class and call it vulgar.''

She leaned her head wearily against his shoulder, and her body shivered with recurrent nervousness. He waited for a time for her to speak, and then went on.

''And now you want to renew our love. You want us to be married. You want me. And yet, listen—if my books had not been noticed I'd nevertheless have been just what I am now. And you would have stayed away. It is all those damned books——''

''Dont swear,'' she interrupted.

Her reproof startled him. He broke into a harsh laugh.

''That's it,'' he said, ''at a high moment, when what seems your life's happiness is at stake, you are afraid of life in the same old way—afraid of life and a healthy oath.''

She was stung by his words into realization of the puerility of her act, and yet she felt that he had magnified it unduly and was consequently resentful. They sat in silence for a long time, she thinking desperately and he pondering upon his love which had departed. He knew now that he had not really loved her. It was an idealized Ruth he had loved, an ethereal creature of his own creating, the bright and luminous spirit of his love poems. The real bourgeois Ruth, with all the bourgeois failings and with the hopeless cramp of the bourgeois psychology in her mind, he had never loved.

She suddenly began to speak.

''I know that much you have said is so. I have been afraid of life. I did not love you well enough. I have learned to love better. I love you for what you are, for what you were, for the ways even by which you have become. I love you for the ways wherein you differ from what you call my class, for your beliefs which I do not understand, but which I know I can come to understand. I shall devote myself to understanding them. And even your smoking and your swearing—they are part of you, and I will love you for them, too. I can still learn. In the last ten minutes I have learned much. That I have dared to come here is a token of what I have already learned. Oh, Martin!——''

She was sobbing and nestling close against him.

For the first time his arms folded her gently and with sympathy, and she acknowledged it with a happy movement and a brightening face.

''It is too late,'' he said. He remembered Lizzie's words. ''I am a sick man——oh, not my body. It is my soul, my brain, I seem to have lost all values. I care for nothing. If you had been this way a few months ago it would have been different. It is too late now.''

''It is not too late!'' she cried. ''I will show you. I will prove to you that my love has grown, that it is greater to me than my class and all that is dearest to me. All that is dearest to the bourgeoise I will flout. I am no longer afraid of life. I will leave my father and mother, and let my name become a by-word with my friends. I will come to you here and now, in free love if you will, and I will be proud and glad to be with you. If I have been a traitor to love I will now, for love's sake, be a traitor to all that made that eariler treason.''

She stood before him with shining eyes.

''I am waiting, Martin,'' she whispered, ''waiting for you to accept me. Look at me.''

It was splendid, he thought, looking at her. She had redeemed herself for all that she had lacked, rising up at last, true woman, superior to the iron rule of bourgeois convention. It was splendid, magnificent, desperate. And yet, what was the matter with him? He was not thrilled nor stirred by what she had done. It was splendid and magnificent only intellectually. In what should have been a moment of fire he coldly appraised her. His heart was untouched. He was unaware of any desire for her. Again he remembered Lizzie's words.

''I am sick, very sick,'' he said, with a despairing gesture. ''How sick I did not know till now. Something has gone out of me. I have always been unafraid of life, but I never dreamed of being sated with life. Life has so filled me that I am empty of any desire for anything. If there was room I should want you, now. You see how sick I am.''

He leaned his head back and closed his eyes, and like a child, crying, that forgets its grief in watching the sunlight percolate through the tear-dimmed films over the pupils, so Martin forgot his sickness, the presence of Ruth—everything—in watching the masses of vegetation, shot through hotly with sunshine, that took form and blazed against the background of his eyelids. It was not restful, that green foliage. The sunlight was too raw and glaring. It hurt him to look at it, and yet he looked, he knew not why.

He was brought back to himself by the rattle of the door-knob. Ruth was at the door.

''How shall I get out?'' she questioned tearfully. ''I am afraid.''

''Oh, forgive me,'' he cried, springing to his feet. ''I'm not myself, you know. I forgot you were here.'' He put his hand to his head. ''You see, I'm not just right. I'll take you home. We can go out by the servants' entrance. No one will see us. Pull down that veil and everything will be all right.''

She clung to his arm through the dim-lighted passages and down the narrow stairs.

''I am safe now,'' she said, when they emerged on the sidewalk, at the same time starting to take her hand from his arm.

''No, no, I'll see you home,'' he answered.

''No, please dont,'' she objected. ''It is unnecessary.''

Again she started to remove her hand. He felt a momentary curiosity. Now that she was out of danger she was afraid. She was in almost a panic to be quit of him. He could see no reason for it, and attributed it to her nervousness. So he restrained her withdrawing hand and started to walk on with her. Half-way down the block he saw a man in a long overcoat shrink back into a doorway. He shot a glance in as he passed by, and, despite the high turned-up collar, he was certain that he recognized Ruth's brother, Norman.

During the walk Ruth and Martin held little conversation. She was stunned. He was apathetic. Once he mentioned that he was going away, back to the South Seas, and, once, she aksed him to forgive her having come to him. And that was all. The parting at her door was conventional. They shook hands, said good-night, and he lifted his hat. The door swung shut, and he lighted a cigarette and turned back for his hotel. When he came to the doorway into which he had seen Norman shrink he stopped and looked in in a speculative humor.

"She lied," he said aloud. "She made believe to me that she had dared greatly, and all the while she knew the brother that brought her was waiting to take her back." He burst into laughter. "Oh, these bourgeois! When I was broke I was not fit to be seen with his sister. When I have a bank account he brings her to me."

As he swung on his heel to go on, a tramp, going in the same direction, begged him over his shoulder.

"Say, mister, can you give me a quarter to get a bed?" were the words.

But it was the voice that made Martin turn around. The next instant he had Joe by the hand.

"D'ye remember that time we parted at the Hot Springs?" the other was saying. "I said then we'd meet again. I felt it in my bones. An' here we are."

"You're looking good," Martin said admiringly, "and you've put on weight."

"I sure have." Joe's face was beaming. "I never knew what it was to live till I hit hoboin'. I'm thirty pounds heavier an' feel tiptop all the time. Why, I was worked to skin an' bones in them old days. Hoboin' sure agrees with me."

"But you're looking for a bed just the same," Martin chided "and it 's a cold night."

"Huh? Lookin' for a bed?" Joe shot a hand into his hip pocket and brought it out filled with small change. "That beats hard graft," he exulted. "You just looked good, that 's why I battered you."

Martin laughed and gave in.

"You've several full-sized drunks right there," he insinuated.

Joe slid the money back into his pocket.

"Not in mine," he announced. "No gettin' oryide for me, though there aint nothin' to stop me except I dont want to. I've been drunk once since I seen you last, an' then it was unexpected, bein' on an empty stomach. When I work like a beast I drink like a beast. When I live like a man I drink like a man—a jolt now an' again when I feel like it, an' that 's all."

Martin arranged to meet him next day, and went on to the hotel. He paused in the office to look up steamer sailings. The *Mariposa* sailed for Tahiti in five days.

"Telephone over tomorrow and reserve a stateroom for me," he told the clerk. "No deck stateroom, but down below, on the weather side—the port side, remember that, the port side. You'd better write it down."

Once in his room he got into bed and slipped off to sleep as gently as a child. The occurrences of the evening had made no impression on him. His mind was dead to impressions. The glow of warmth with which he met Joe had been most fleeting. The succeeding minute he had been bothered by the ex-laundry-man's presence and by the compulsion of conversation. That in five more days he sailed for his loved South Seas meant nothing to him. So he closed his eyes and slept normally and comfortably for eight uninterrupted hours. He was not restless. He did not change his position, nor did he dream. Sleep had become to him oblivion, and each day that he awoke he awoke with regret. Life worried and bored him, and time was a vexation.

CHAPTER XLVI.

"SAY, Joe," was his greeting to his gold-time working mate next morning; "there 's a Frenchman out on Twenty-eighth street. He 's made a pot of money and he 's going back to France. It 's a dandy, well-appointed, small steam laundry. There 's a start for you if you want to settle down. Here, take this; buy some clothes with it and be at this man's office by ten o'clock. He looked up the laundry for me, and he'll take you out and show you around. If you like it, and think it is worth the price—twelve thousand—let me know, and it is yours. Now, run along. I'm busy. I'll see you later."

"Now, look here, Mart," the other said slowly, with kindling anger, "I come here this mornin' to see you. Savve? I did n't come here to get no laundry. I come here for a talk for old friends' sake, an' you shove a laundry at me. I tell you what you can do. You can take that laundry an' go to hell.''

He was starting to fling out of the room when Martin caught him by the shoulder and whirled him around.

''Now, look here, Joe,'' he said, ''if you act that way I'll punch your head. And for old friends' sake I'll punch it hard. Savve?—you will, will you?''

Joe had clinched and attempted to throw him, and he was twisting and writhing out of the advantage of the other's hold. They reeled about the room, locked in each other's arms, and came down with a crash across the splintered wreckage of a wicker chair. Joe was underneath, with arms spread out, and held, and with Martin's knee in his chest. He was panting and gasping for breath when Martin released him.

''Now we'll talk a moment,'' Martin said. ''You cant get fresh with me. I want that laundry business finished first of all. Then you can come back and we'll talk for old sake's sake. I told you I was busy. Look at that.''

A servant had just come in with the morning mail, a great mass of letters and magazines.

''How can I wade through that and talk with you? You go and fix up that laundry, and then we'll get together.''

''All right,'' Joe admitted reluctantly. ''I thought you was turnin' me down, but I guess I was mistaken. But you cant lick me, Mart, in a stand-up fight. I've got the reach on you.''

''We'll put on the gloves some time and see,'' Martin said with a smile.

''Sure; as soon as I get that laundry going.'' Joe extended his arm. ''You see that reach? It'll make you go a few.''

Martin heaved a sigh of relief when the door closed behind the laundryman. He was becoming anti-social. Daily he found it a severer strain to be decent with people. Their presence perturbed him, and the effort of conversation irritated him. They made him restless, and no sooner was he in contact with them than he was casting about for excuses to get rid of them.

He did not proceed to attack his mail, and for a half-hour he lolled in his chair, doing nothing, while no more than vague, half-formed thoughts occasionally filtered through his intelligence, or rather, at wide intervals, themselves constituted the flickering of his intelligence.

He roused himself and began glancing through his mail. There were a dozen requests for autographs—he knew them at sight; there were professional begging letters; and there were letters from cranks, ranging from the man with a working model of perpetual motion, and the man who demonstrated that the surface of the earth was the inside of a hollow sphere, to the man seeking financial aid to purchase the Peninsula of Lower California for the purpose of communist colonization. There were letters from women seeking to know him, and over one such he smiled, for enclosed was her receipt for pew rent, sent as evidence of her good faith and as proof of her respectability.

Editors and publishers contributed to the daily heap of letters; the former on their knees for his manuscripts, the latter on their knees for his books—his poor, disdained manuscripts that had kept all he possessed in pawn for so many dreary months in order to find them in postage. There were unexpected checks for English serial rights, and for advance payments on foreign translations. His English agent announced the sale of German translation rights in three of his books, and informed him that Swedish editions, from which he could expect nothing because Sweden was not a party to the Berne Convention, were already on the market. Then there was a nominal request for his permission for a Russian translation, that country being likewise outside the Berne Convention.

He turned to the huge bundle of clippings which had come in from the press bureau, and read about himself and his vogue, which had become a furore. All his creative output had been flung to the public in one magnificent sweep. That seemed to account for it. He had taken the public off his feet, the way Kipling had, that time when he lay near to death and all the mob, animated by a mob-mind thought, began suddenly to read him. Martin remembered how that same world-mob, having read him and acclaimed him and not understood him in the least, had, abruptly, a few months later, flung itself upon him and torn him to pieces. Martin grinned at the thought. Who was he that he should not be similarly treated in a few more months? Well, he would fool the mob. He would be away, in the South Seas, building his grass house, trading for pearls and copra, jumping reefs in frail outriggers, catching sharks and bonitas, hunting wild goats among the cliffs of the valley that lay next to the Valley of Taichae.

In the moment of that thought the desperateness of his situation dawned upon him. He saw, clear-eyed, that he was in the Valley of the Shadow. All the life that was in him was fading, fainting, making toward death. He realized how much he slept, and how much he desired to sleep. Of old he had hated sleep. It had robbed him of precious moments of living. Four hours of sleep in the twenty-four had meant being robbed of four hours of life. How he had grudged sleep! Now it was life he grudged. Life was not good. Its taste in his mouth was without tang and bitter. This was his peril. Life that did not yearn toward life was in fair way toward ceasing. Some remote instinct for preservation stirred in him, and he knew he must get away. He glanced about the room, and the thought of packing was burdensome. Perhaps it would be better to leave that to the last. In the meantime he might be getting an outfit.

He put on his hat and went out, stopping in at a gunstore, where he spent the remainder of the morning buying automatic rifles, ammunition and fishing tackle. Fashions changed in trading, and he knew he would have to wait till he reached Tahiti before ordering his trade goods. They could come up from Australia, anyway. This solution was a source of pleasure. He had avoided doing something, and the doing of anything just now was unpleasant. He went back to the hotel gladly, with a feeling of satisfaction in that the comfortable Morris chair was waiting for him; and he groaned inwardly, on entering his room at sight of Joe in the Morris chair.

Joe was delighted with the laundry. Everything was settled, and he would enter into possession next day. Martin lay on the bed, with closed eyes, while the other talked on. Martin's thoughts were far away—so far away that he was rarely aware that he was thinking. It was only by an effort that he occasionally responded. And yet this was Joe, whom he had always liked. But Joe was too keen with life. The boisterous impact of it on Martin's jaded mind was a hurt. It was an aching probe to his tired sensitiveness. When Joe reminded him that some time in the future they were going to put on the gloves together he could almost have screamed.

"Remember, Joe, you're to run the laundry according to those old rules you used to lay down at Shelly Hot Springs," he said. "No overworking. No working at night. And no children at the mangles. No children anywhere. And a fair wage."

Joe nodded and pulled out a notebook.

"Look at here. I was workin' out them rules before breakfast this A.M. What d'ye think of them?"

He read them aloud, and Martin approved, worrying at the same time as to when Joe would take himself off.

It was late afternoon when he awoke. Slowly the fact of life came back to him. He glanced about the room. Joe had evidently stolen away after he had dozed off. That was considerate of Joe, he thought. Then he closed his eyes and slept again.

In the days that followed Joe was too busy organizing and taking hold of the laundry to bother him much, and it was not until the day before sailing that the newspapers made the announcement that he had taken passage on the *Mariposa*. Once, when the instinct of preservation fluttered, he went to a doctor and underwent a searching physical examination. Nothing could be found the matter with him. His heart and lungs were pronounced magnificent. Every organ, so far as the doctor could know, was normal and was working normally.

"There is nothing the matter with you, Mr. Eden," he said, "positively nothing the matter with you. You are in the pink of condition. Candidly, I envy you your health. It is superb. Look at that chest. There, and in your stomach, lies the secret of your remarkable constitution. Physically, you are a man in a thousand—in ten thousand. Barring accidents, you should live to be a hundred.''

And Martin knew that Lizzie's diagnosis had been correct. Physically he was all right. It was his ''think-machine'' that had gone wrong, and there was no cure for that except to get away to the South Seas. The trouble was that now, on the verge of departure, he had no desire to go. The South Seas charmed him no more than did bourgeois civilization. There was no zest in the thought of departure, while the act of departure appalled him as a weariness of the flesh. He would have felt better if he were already on board and gone.

The last day was a sore trial. Having read of his sailing in the morning papers, Bernard Higginbotham, Gertrude and all the family came to say goodbye, as did Herrmann von Schmidt and Marian. Then there was business to be transacted, bills to be paid, and everlasting reporters to be endured. He said goodbye to Lizzie Connolly abruptly at the entrance to night school, and hurried away. At the hotel he found Joe, too busy all day with the laundry to have come to him earlier. It was the last straw, but Martin gripped the arms of his chair and talked and listened for half an hour.

''You know, Joe,'' he said, ''that you are not tied down to that laundry. There are no strings on it. You can sell it any time and blow the money. Any time you get sick of it and want to hit the road, just pull out. Do what will make you the happiest.''

Joe shook his head.

''No more road in mine, thank you kindly. Hoboin' 's all right, exceptin' for one thing—the girls. I cant help it, but I'm a ladies' man. I cant get along without 'em, and you've got to get along without 'em when you're hoboin'. The times I've passed by houses where dances an' parties was goin' on, an' heard the women laugh, an' saw their white dresses and smiling faces through the windows—Gee! I tell you them moments was plain hell. I like dancin' an' picnics, an' walking in the moonlight, an' all the rest too well. Me for the laundry, and a good front, with big iron dollars clinkin' in my jeans. I seen a girl already, just yesterday, an' d'ye know, I'm feelin' already I'd just as soon marry her as not. I've been whistlin' all day at the thought of it. She's a beaut, with the kindest eyes and softest voice you ever heard. Me for her, you can stack on that. Say, why dont you get married with all this money to burn? You could get the finest girl in the land.''

Martin shook his head with a smile, but in his secret heart he was wondering why any man wanted to marry. It seemed an amazing and incomprehensible thing.

From the deck of the *Mariposa* at the sailing hour he saw Lizzie Connolly hiding on the skirts of the crowd on the wharf. Take her with you, came the thought. It is easy to be kind. She will be supremely happy. It was almost a temptation one moment, and the succeeding moment it became a terror. He was in a panic at the thought of it. His tired soul cried out in protest. He turned away from the rail with a groan, muttering, ''Man, you are too sick, you are too sick.''

He fled to his stateroom, where he lurked until the steamer was clear of the dock. In the dining saloon, at luncheon, he found himself in the place of honor, at the Captain's right, and he was not long in discovering that he was the great man on board. But no more unsatisfactory great man ever sailed on a ship. He spent the afternoon in a deck chair, with closed eyes, dozing brokenly most of the time, and in the evening went early to bed.

After the second day, recovered from seasickness, the full passenger list was in evidence, and the more he saw of the passengers the more he disliked them. Yet he knew that he did them injustice. They were good and kindly people, he forced himself to acknowledge, and in the moment of acknowledgment he qualified—good and kindly, like all the bourgeoisie, with all the psychological cramp and intellectual futility of their kind. They bored him when they talked with him, their little superficial minds were so filled with emptiness; while the boisterous high spirits and the excessive energy of the younger people shocked him. They were never quiet, ceaselessly playing deck-quoits, tossing rings, promenading or rushing to the rail with loud cries to watch the leaping porpoises and the first schools of flying fish.

He slept much. After breakfast he sought his deck chair with a magazine he never finished. The printed pages tired him. He puzzled that men found so much to write about, and, puzzling, dozed in his chair. When the gong awoke him for luncheon he was irritated that he must awaken. There was no satisfaction in being awake.

Once, he tried to arouse himself from his lethargy, and went forward into the forecastle with the sailors. But the breed of sailors seemed to have changed since the days he had lived in the forecastle. He could find no kinship with these stolid-faced, ox-minded, bestial creatures. He was in despair. Up above nobody had wanted Martin Eden for his own sake, and he could not go back to those of his own class who had wanted him in the past. He did not want them. He could not stand them any more than he could stand the stupid first-cabin passengers and the riotous young people.

Life was to him like strong white light that hurts the tired eyes of a sick person. During every conscious moment life blazed in a raw glare around him and upon him. It hurt. It hurt intolerably. It was the first time in his life that Martin had traveled first-class. On ships at sea he had always been in the forecastle, the steerage or in the black depths of the coal-hold passing coal. In those days, climbing up the iron ladders from out the pit of stifling heat, he had often caught glimpses of the passengers, in cool white, doing nothing but enjoy themselves, under awnings spread to keep the sun and wind away from them, with subservient stewards taking care of their every want and whim, and it had seemed to him that the realm in which they moved and had their being was nothing else than paradise. Well, here he was, the great man on board, in the midmost center of it, sitting at the Captain's right hand, and yet vainly harking back to forecastle and stoke-hole in quest of the paradise he had lost. He had found no new one, and now he could not find the old one.

He strove to stir himself and find something to interest him. He ventured the petty officers' mess, and was glad to get away. He talked with a quartermaster off duty, an intelligent man, who promptly prodded him with the socialist propaganda and forced into his hands a bunch of leaflets and pamphlets. He listened to the man expounding the slave-morality, and as he listened he thought languidly of his own Nietzsche philosophy. But what was it worth after all? He remembered one of Nietzsche's mad utterances wherein that madman had doubted truth. And who was to say? Perhaps Nietzsche had been right. Perhaps there was no truth in anything, no truth in truth—no such thing as truth. But his mind wearied quickly, and he was content to go back to his chair and doze.

Miserable as he was on the steamer, a new misery came upon him. What when the steamer reached Tahiti? He would have to go ashore. He would have to order his trade-goods, to find a passage on a schooner to the Marquesas, to do a thousand and one things that were awful to contemplate. Whenever he steeled himself deliberately to think he could see the desperate peril in which he stood. In all truth he was in the Valley of the Shadow, and his danger lay in that he was not afraid. If he were only afraid he would make toward life. Being unafraid, he was drifting deeper into the shadow. He found no delight in the old familiar things of life. The *Mariposa* was now in the northeast trades, and this wine of wind, surging against him, irritated him. He had his chair moved to escape the embrace of this lusty comrade of old days and nights.

The day the *Mariposa* entered the doldrums Martin was more miserable than ever. He could no longer sleep. He was soaked with sleep, and perforce he must now stay awake and endure the white glare of life. He moved about restlessly. The air was sticky and humid, and the rain squalls were unrefreshing. He ached with life. He walked around the deck until that hurt too much, then sat in his chair until he was compelled to walk again. He forced himself at last to finish the magazine, and from the steamer library he culled several volumes of poetry. But they could not hold him, and once more he took to walking.

He stayed late on deck after dinner, but that did not help him, for when he went below he could not sleep. This surcease from life had failed him. It was too much. He turned on the electric light and tried to read. One of the volumes was a *Swinburne*. He lay in bed, glancing through its pages, until suddenly he became aware that he was reading with interest. He finished the stanza, attempted to read on, then came back to it. He rested the book face downward on his breast and fell to thinking. That was it. The very thing. Strange that it had never come to him before. That was the meaning of it all; he had been drifting that way all the time, and now Swinburne showed him that it was the happy way out. He wanted rest, and here was rest awaiting him. He glanced at the open porthole. Yes, it was large enough. For the first time in weeks he felt happy. At last he had discovered the cure of his ill. He picked up the book and read the stanza slowly aloud:

"'From too much hope of living,
  From hope and fear set free,
We thank with brief thanksgiving
  Whatever gods may be,
That no life lives forever,
That dead men rise up never,
  That even the weariest river
  Winds somewhere safe to sea.'"

He looked again at the open port. Swinburne had furnished the key. Life was ill, or, rather, it had become ill—an unbearable thing. "That dead men rise up never!" That line stirred him with a profound feeling of gratitude. It was the one beneficent thing in the universe. When life became an aching weariness death was ready to soothe away to everlasting sleep. But what was he waiting for? It was already time to go.

He arose and thrust his head out the porthole, looking down into the milky wash. The *Mariposa* was deeply loaded, and, hanging by his hands, his feet would be in the water. He could slip in noiselessly. No one would hear. A smother of spray dashed up, wetting his face. It tasted salt on his lips, and the taste was good. He wondered if he ought to write a swan song, but laughed the thought away. There was no time. He was too impatient to be gone.

Turning off the light in his room so that it might not betray him, he went out the porthole feet first. His shoulders stuck, and he forced himself back so as to try it with one arm down by his side. A roll of the steamer aided him, and he was through, hanging by his hands. When his feet touched the sea he let go. He was in a milky froth of water. The side of the *Mariposa* rushed past him like a dark wall, broken here and there by lighted ports. She was certainly making time. Almost before he knew it he was astern, swimming gently on the foam-crackling surface.

A bonita struck at his white body, and he laughed aloud. It had taken a piece out, and the sting of it reminded him of why he was there. In the work to do he had forgotten the purpose of it. The lights of the *Mariposa* were growing dim in the distance, and there he was, swimming confidently, as though it were his intention to make for the nearest land a thousand miles or so away.

It was the automatic instinct to live. He ceased swimming, but the moment he felt the water rising above his mouth the hands struck out sharply with a lifting movement. The will to live was his thought, and the thought was accompanied by a sneer. Well, he had will—ay, will strong enough that with one last exertion it could destroy itself and cease to be.

He changed his position to a vertical one. He glanced up at the quiet stars, at the same time emptying his lungs of air. With swift, vigorous propulsion of hands and feet he lifted his shoulders and half his chest out of water. This was to gain impetus for the descent. Then he let himself go and sank without movement, a white statue, into the sea. He breathed in the water deeply, deliberately, after the manner of a man taking an anaesthetic. When he strangled, quite involuntarily his arms and legs clawed the water and drove him up to the surface and into the clear sight of the stars.

The will to live, he thought disdainfully, vainly endeavoring not to breathe the air into his bursting lungs. Well, he would have to try a new way. He filled his lungs with air, filled them full. This supply would take him far down. He turned over and went down head first, swimming with all his strength and all his will. Deeper and deeper he went. His eyes were open, and he watched the ghostly, prosphorescent trails of the darting bonita. As he swam he hoped that they would not strike at him, for it might snap the tension of his will. But they did not strike, and he found time to be grateful for this last kindness of life.

Down, down, he swam till his arms and legs grew tired and hardly moved. He knew that he was deep. The pressure on his ear-drums was a pain, and there was a buzzing in his head. His endurance was faltering, but he compelled his arms and legs to drive him deeper until his will snapped and the air drove from his lungs in a great explosive rush. The bubbles rubbed and bounded like tiny balloons against his cheeks and eyes as they took their upward flight. Then came pain and strangulation. This hurt was not death, was the thought that oscillated through his reeling consciousness. Death did not hurt. It was life, the pangs of life, this awful, suffocating feeling; it was the last blow life could deal him.

His wilful hands and feet began to beat and churn about spasmodically and feebly. But he had fooled them and the will to live that made them beat and churn. He was too deep down. They could never bring him to the surface. He seemed floating languidly in a sea of dreamy vision. Colors and radiances surrounded him and bathed him and pervaded him. What was that? It seemed a lighthouse, but it was inside his brain—a flashing, bright white light. If flashed swifter and swifter. There was a long rumble of sound, and it seemed to him that he was falling down a vast and interminable stairway. And somewhere at the bottom he fell into darkness. That much he knew. He had fallen into darkness. And at the instant he knew, he ceased to know.